I0763278

The Three Cities Trilogy
Lourdes, Rome, Paris

By

Émile Zola

Cover Artwork: Igor

ISBN: 978-1-78139-432-8

Contents

LOURDES

ROME

PARIS

BOOK IV.

BOOK V.

LOURDES

Of the Three Cities

Translated By Ernest A. Vizetelly

PREFACE

BEFORE perusing this work, it is as well that the reader should understand M. Zola's aim in writing it, and his views—as distinct from those of his characters—upon Lourdes, its Grotto, and its cures. A short time before the book appeared M. Zola was interviewed upon the subject by his friend and biographer, Mr. Robert H. Sherard, to whom he spoke as follows:

"'Lourdes' came to be written by mere accident. In 1891 I happened to be travelling for my pleasure, with my wife, in the Basque country and by the Pyrenees, and being in the neighbourhood of Lourdes, included it in my tour. I spent fifteen days there, and was greatly struck by what I saw, and it then occurred to me that there was material here for just the sort of novel that I like to write—a novel in which great masses of men can be shown in motion—*un grand mouvement de foule*—a novel the subject of which stirred up my philosophical ideas.

"It was too late then to study the question, for I had visited Lourdes late in September, and so had missed seeing the best pilgrimage, which takes place in August, under the direction of the Peres de la Misericorde, of the Rue de l'Assomption in Paris—the National Pilgrimage, as it is called. These Fathers are very active, enterprising men, and have made a great success of this annual national pilgrimage. Under their direction thirty thousand pilgrims are transported to Lourdes, including over a thousand sick persons.

"So in the following year I went in August, and saw a national pilgrimage, and followed it during the three days which it lasts, in addition to the two days given to travelling. After its departure, I stayed on ten or twelve days, working up the subject in every detail. My book is the story of such a national pilgrimage, and is, accordingly, the story of five days. It is divided into five parts, each of which parts is limited to one day.

"There are from ninety to one hundred characters in the story: sick persons, pilgrims, priests, nuns, hospitallers, nurses, and peasants; and the book shows Lourdes under every aspect. There are the piscinas, the processions, the Grotto, the churches at night, the people in the streets. It is, in one word, Lourdes in its entirety. In this canvas is worked out a very delicate central intrigue, as in 'Dr. Pascal,' and around this are many little stories or subsidiary plots. There is the story of the sick person who gets well, of the sick person who is not cured, and so on. The philosophical idea which pervades the whole book is the idea of human suffering, the exhibition of the desperate and despairing sufferers who, abandoned by science and by man, address themselves to a higher Power in the hope of relief; as where parents have a dearly loved daughter dying of consumption, who has been given up, and for whom nothing remains but death. A sudden hope, however, breaks in upon them: 'supposing that after all there should be a Power greater than that of man, higher than that of science.' They will haste to try this last chance of safety. It is the instinctive hankering after the lie which creates human credulity.

"I will admit that I came across some instances of real cure. Many cases of nervous disorders have undoubtedly been cured, and there have also been other cures which may, perhaps be attributed to errors of diagnosis on the part of doctors who attended the patients so cured. Often a patient is described by his doctor as suffering from consumption. He goes to Lourdes, and is cured. However, the probability is that the doctor made a mistake. In my own case I was at one time suffering from a violent pain in my chest, which presented all the symptoms of *angina pectoris*, a mortal malady. It was nothing of the sort. Indigestion, doubtless, and, as such, curable. Remember that most of the sick persons who go to Lourdes come from the country, and that the country doctors are not usually men of either great skill or great experience. But all doctors mistake symptoms. Put three doctors together to discuss a case, and in nine cases out of ten they will disagree in their diagnosis. Look at the quantities of tumours, swellings, and sores, which cannot be properly classified. These cures are based on the ignorance of the medical profession. The sick pretend, believe, that they suffer from such and such a desperate malady, whereas it is from some other malady that they are suffering. And so the legend forms itself. And, of course, there must be cures out of so large a number of cases. Nature often cures without medical aid. Certainly, many of the workings of Nature are wonderful, but they are not supernatural. The Lourdes miracles can neither be proved nor denied. The miracle is based on human ignorance. And so the doctor who lives at Lourdes, and who is commissioned to register the cures and to tabulate the miracles, has a very careless time of it. A person comes, and gets cured. He has but to get three doctors together to examine the case. They will disagree as to what was the disease from which the patient suffered, and the only explanation left which will be acceptable to the public, with its hankering after the lie, is that a miracle has been vouchsafed.

"I interviewed a number of people at Lourdes, and could not find one who would declare that he had witnessed a miracle. All the cases which I describe in my book are real cases, in which I have only changed the names of the persons concerned. In none of these instances was I able to discover any real proof for or against the miraculous nature of the cure. Thus, in the case of Clementine Trouve, who figures in my story as Sophie—the patient who, after suffering for a long time from a horrid open sore on her foot, was suddenly cured, according to current report, by bathing her foot in the piscina, where the bandages fell off, and her foot was entirely restored to a healthy condition—I investigated that case thoroughly. I was told that there were three or four ladies living in Lourdes who could guarantee the facts as stated by little Clementine. I looked up those ladies. The first said No, she could not vouch for anything. She had seen nothing. I had better consult somebody else. The next answered in the same way, and nowhere was I able to find any corroboration of the girl's story. Yet the little girl did not look like a liar, and I believe that she was fully convinced of the miraculous nature of her cure. It is the facts themselves which lie.

PREFACE

"Lourdes, the Grotto, the cures, the miracles, are, indeed, the creation of that need of the Lie, that necessity for credulity, which is a characteristic of human nature. At first, when little Bernadette came with her strange story of what she had witnessed, everybody was against her. The Prefect of the Department, the Bishop, the clergy, objected to her story. But Lourdes grew up in spite of all opposition, just as the Christian religion did, because suffering humanity in its despair must cling to something, must have some hope; and, on the other hand, because humanity thirsts after illusions. In a word, it is the story of the foundation of all religions."

To the foregoing account of "Lourdes" as supplied by its author, it may be added that the present translation, first made from early proofs of the French original whilst the latter was being completed, has for the purposes of this new American edition been carefully and extensively revised by Mr. E. A. Vizetelly,—M. Zola's representative for all English-speaking countries. "Lourdes" forms the first volume of the "Trilogy of the Three Cities," the second being "Rome," and the third "Paris."

THE FIRST DAY

I. PILGRIMS AND PATIENTS

THE pilgrims and patients, closely packed on the hard seats of a third-class carriage, were just finishing the "Ave maris Stella," which they had begun to chant on leaving the terminus of the Orleans line, when Marie, slightly raised on her couch of misery and restless with feverish impatience, caught sight of the Paris fortifications through the window of the moving train.

"Ah, the fortifications!" she exclaimed, in a tone which was joyous despite her suffering. "Here we are, out of Paris; we are off at last!"

Her delight drew a smile from her father, M. de Guersaint, who sat in front of her, whilst Abbe Pierre Froment, who was looking at her with fraternal affection, was so carried away by his compassionate anxiety as to say aloud: "And now we are in for it till to-morrow morning. We shall only reach Lourdes at three-forty. We have more than two-and-twenty hours' journey before us."

It was half-past five, the sun had risen, radiant in the pure sky of a delightful morning. It was a Friday, the 19th of August. On the horizon, however, some small, heavy clouds already presaged a terrible day of stormy heat. And the oblique sunrays were enfilading the compartments of the railway carriage, filling them with dancing, golden dust.

"Yes, two-and-twenty hours," murmured Marie, relapsing into a state of anguish. "*Mon Dieu*! what a long time we must still wait!"

Then her father helped her to lie down again in the narrow box, a kind of wooden gutter, in which she had been living for seven years past. Making an exception in her favour, the railway officials had consented to take as luggage the two pairs of wheels which could be removed from the box, or fitted to it whenever it became necessary to transport her from place to place. Packed between the sides of this movable coffin, she occupied the room of three passengers on the carriage seat; and for a moment she lay there with eyes closed. Although she was three-and-twenty; her ashen, emaciated face was still delicately infantile, charming despite everything, in the midst of her marvellous fair hair, the hair of a queen, which illness had respected. Clad with the utmost simplicity in a gown of thin woollen stuff, she wore, hanging from her neck, the card bearing her name and number, which entitled her to *hospitalisation*, or free treatment. She herself had insisted on making the journey in this humble fashion, not wishing to be a source of expense to her relatives, who little by little had fallen into very straitened circumstances. And thus it was that she found herself in a third-class carriage of the "white train," the train which carried the greatest sufferers, the most woeful of the fourteen trains going to Lourdes that day, the one in which, in addition to five hundred healthy pilgrims, nearly three hundred unfortunate wretches, weak to the point of exhaustion, racked by suffering, were heaped together, and borne at express speed from one to the other end of France.

Sorry that he had saddened her, Pierre continued to gaze at her with the air of a compassionate elder brother. He had just completed his thirtieth year, and was pale and slight, with a broad forehead. After busying himself with all the arrangements for the journey, he had been desirous of accompanying her, and, having obtained admission among the Hospitallers of Our Lady of Salvation as an auxiliary member, wore on his cassock the red, orange-tipped cross of a bearer. M. de Guersaint on his side had simply pinned the little scarlet cross of the pilgrimage on his grey cloth jacket. The idea of travelling appeared to delight him; although he was over fifty he still looked young, and, with his eyes ever wandering over the landscape, he seemed unable to keep his head still—a bird-like head it was, with an expression of good nature and absent-mindedness.

However, in spite of the violent shaking of the train, which constantly drew sighs from Marie, Sister Hyacinthe had risen to her feet in the adjoining compartment. She noticed that the sun's rays were streaming in the girl's face.

"Pull down the blind, Monsieur l'Abbe," she said to Pierre. "Come, come, we must install ourselves properly, and set our little household in order."

Clad in the black robe of a Sister of the Assumption, enlivened by a white coif, a white wimple, and a large white apron, Sister Hyacinthe smiled, the picture of courageous activity. Her youth bloomed upon her small, fresh lips, and in the depths of her beautiful blue eyes, whose expression was ever gentle. She was not pretty, perhaps, still she was charming, slender, and tall, the bib of her apron covering her flat chest like that of a young man; one of good heart, displaying a snowy complexion, and overflowing with health, gaiety, and innocence.

"But this sun is already roasting us," said she; "pray pull down your blind as well, madame."

Seated in the corner, near the Sister, was Madame de Jonquiere, who had kept her little bag on her lap. She slowly pulled down the blind. Dark, and well built, she was still nice-looking, although she had a daughter, Raymonde, who was four-and-twenty, and whom for motives of propriety she had placed in the charge of two lady-hospitallers, Madame Desagneaux and Madame Volmar, in a first-class carriage. For her part, directress as she was of a ward of the Hospital of Our Lady of Dolours at Lourdes, she did not quit her patients; and outside, swinging against the door of her compartment, was the regulation placard bearing under her own name those of the two Sisters of the Assumption who accompanied her. The widow of a ruined man, she lived with her daughter on the scanty income of four or five thousand francs a year, at the rear of a courtyard in the Rue Vanneau. But her charity was inexhaustible, and she gave all her time to the work of the Hospitality of Our Lady of Salvation, an institution whose red cross she wore on her gown of carmelite poplin, and whose aims she furthered with the most active zeal. Of a somewhat proud disposition, fond of being flattered and loved, she took great delight in this annual journey, from which both her heart and her passion derived contentment.

"You are right, Sister," she said, "we will organise matters. I really don't know why I am encumbering myself with this bag."

And thereupon she placed it under the seat, near her.

"Wait a moment," resumed Sister Hyacinthe; "you have the water-can between your legs—it is in your way."

"No, no, it isn't, I assure you. Let it be. It must always be somewhere."

Then they both set their house in order as they expressed it, so that for a day and a night they might live with their patients as comfortably as possible. The worry was that they had not been able to take Marie into their compartment, as she wished to have Pierre and her father near her; however neighbourly intercourse was easy enough over the low partition. Moreover the whole carriage, with its five compartments of ten seats each, formed but one moving chamber, a common room as it were which the eye took in at a glance from end to end. Between its wooden walls, bare and yellow, under its white-painted panelled roof, it showed like a hospital ward, with all the disorder and promiscuous jumbling together of an improvised ambulance. Basins, brooms, and sponges lay about, half-hidden by the seats. Then, as the train only carried such luggage as the pilgrims could take with them, there were valises, deal boxes, bonnet boxes, and bags, a wretched pile of poor worn-out things mended with bits of string, heaped up a little bit everywhere; and overhead the litter began again, what with articles of clothing, parcels, and baskets hanging from brass pegs and swinging to and fro without a pause.

Amidst all this frippery the more afflicted patients, stretched on their narrow mattresses, which took up the room of several passengers, were shaken, carried along by the rumbling gyrations of the wheels; whilst those who were able to remain seated, leaned against the partitions, their faces pale, their heads resting upon pillows. According to the regulations there should have been one lady-hospitaller to each compartment. However, at the other end of the carriage there was but a second Sister of the Assumption, Sister Claire des Anges. Some of the pilgrims who were in good health were already getting up, eating and drinking. One compartment was entirely occupied by women, ten pilgrims closely pressed together, young ones and old ones, all sadly, pitifully ugly. And as nobody dared to open the windows on account of the consumptives in the carriage, the heat was soon felt and an unbearable odour arose, set free as it were by the jolting of the train as it went its way at express speed.

They had said their chaplets at Juvisy; and six o'clock was striking, and they were rushing like a hurricane past the station of Bretigny, when Sister Hyacinthe stood up. It was she who directed the pious exercises, which most of the pilgrims followed from small, blue-covered books.

"The Angelus, my children," said she with a pleasant smile, a maternal air which her great youth rendered very charming and sweet.

Then the "Aves" again followed one another, and were drawing to an end when Pierre and Marie began to feel interested in two women who occupied the other corner seats of their compartment. One of them, she who sat at Marie's feet, was a blonde of slender build and *bourgeoise* appearance, some thirty and odd years of age, and faded before she had grown old. She shrank back, scarcely occupying any room, wearing a dark dress, and showing colourless hair, and a long grief-stricken face which expressed unlimited self-abandonment, infinite sadness. The woman in front of her, she who sat on the same seat as Pierre, was of the same age, but belonged to the working classes. She wore a black cap and displayed a face ravaged by wretchedness and anxiety, whilst on her lap she held a little girl of seven, who was so pale, so wasted by illness, that she scarcely seemed four. With her nose contracted, her eyelids lowered and showing blue in her waxen face, the child was unable to speak, unable to give utterance to more than a low plaint, a gentle moan, which rent the heart of her mother, leaning over her, each time that she heard it.

"Would she eat a few grapes?" timidly asked the lady, who had hitherto preserved silence. "I have some in my basket."

"Thank you, madame," replied the woman, "she only takes milk, and sometimes not even that willingly. I took care to bring a bottleful with me."

Then, giving way to the desire which possesses the wretched to confide their woes to others, she began to relate her story. Her name was Vincent, and her husband, a gilder by trade, had been carried off by consumption. Left alone with her little Rose, who was the passion of her heart, she had worked by day and night at her calling as a dressmaker in order to bring the child up. But disease had come, and for fourteen months now she had had her in her arms like that, growing more and more woeful and wasted until reduced almost to nothingness. She, the mother, who never went to mass, entered a church, impelled by despair to pray for her daughter's cure; and there she had heard a voice which had told her to take the little one to Lourdes, where the Blessed Virgin would have pity on her. Acquainted with nobody, not knowing even how the pilgrimages were organised, she had had but one idea—to work, save up the money necessary for the journey, take a ticket, and start off with the thirty sous remaining to her, destitute of all supplies save a bottle of milk for the child, not having even thought of purchasing a crust of bread for herself.

"What is the poor little thing suffering from?" resumed the lady.

"Oh, it must be consumption of the bowels, madame! But the doctors have names they give it. At first she only had slight pains in the stomach. Then her stomach began to swell and she suffered, oh, so dreadfully! it made one cry to see her. Her stomach has gone down now, only she's worn out; she has got so thin that she has no legs left her, and she's wasting away with continual sweating."

Then, as Rose, raising her eyelids, began to moan, her mother leant over her, distracted and turning pale. "What is the matter, my jewel, my treasure?" she asked. "Are you thirsty?"

But the little girl was already closing her dim eyes of a hazy sky-blue hue, and did not even answer, but relapsed into her torpor, quite white in the white frock she wore—a last coquetry on the part of her mother, who had gone to this useless expense in the hope that the Virgin would be more compassionate and gentle to a little sufferer who was well dressed, so immaculately white.

There was an interval of silence, and then Madame Vincent inquired: "And you, madame, it's for yourself no doubt that you are going to Lourdes? One can see very well that you are ill."

But the lady, with a frightened look, shrank woefully into her corner, murmuring: "No, no, I am not ill. Would to God that I were! I should suffer less."

Her name was Madame Maze, and her heart was full of an incurable grief. After a love marriage to a big, gay fellow with ripe, red lips, she had found herself deserted at the end of a twelvemonth's honeymoon. Ever travelling, following the profession of a jeweller's bagman, her husband, who earned a deal of money, would disappear for six months at a stretch, deceive her from one frontier to the other of France, at times even carrying creatures about with him. And she worshipped him; she suffered so frightfully from it all that she had sought a remedy in religion, and had at last made up her mind to repair to Lourdes, in order to pray the Virgin to restore her husband to her and make him amend his ways.

Although Madame Vincent did not understand the other's words, she realised that she was a prey to great mental affliction, and they continued looking at one another, the mother, whom the sight of her dying daughter was killing, and the abandoned wife, whom her passion cast into throes of death-like agony.

However, Pierre, who, like Marie, had been listening to the conversation, now intervened. He was astonished that the dressmaker had not sought free treatment for her little patient. The Association of Our Lady of Salvation had been founded by the Augustine Fathers of the Assumption after the Franco-German war, with the object of contributing to the salvation of France and the defence of the Church by prayer in common and the practice of charity; and it was this association which had promoted the great pilgrimage movement, in particular initiating and unremittingly extending the national pilgrimage which every year, towards the close of August, set out for Lourdes. An elaborate organisation had been gradually perfected, donations of considerable amounts were collected in all parts of the world, sufferers were enrolled in every parish, and agreements were signed with the railway companies, to say nothing of the active help of the Little Sisters of the Assumption and the establishment of the Hospitality of Our Lady of Salvation, a widespread brotherhood of the benevolent, in which one beheld men and women, mostly belonging to society, who, under the orders of the pilgrimage managers, nursed the sick, helped to transport them, and watched over the observance of good discipline. A written request was needed for the sufferers to obtain hospitalisation, which dispensed them from making the smallest payment in respect either of their journey or their sojourn; they were fetched from their homes and conveyed back thither; and they simply had to provide a few provisions for the road. By far the greater number were recommended by priests or benevolent persons, who superintended the inquiries concerning them and obtained the needful papers, such as doctors' certificates and certificates of birth. And, these matters being settled, the sick ones had nothing further to trouble about, they became but so much suffering flesh, food for miracles, in the hands of the hospitallers of either sex.

"But you need only have applied to your parish priest, madame," Pierre explained. "This poor child is deserving of all sympathy. She would have been immediately admitted."

"I did not know it, monsieur l'Abbe."

"Then how did you manage?"

"Why, Monsieur l'Abbe, I went to take a ticket at a place which one of my neighbours, who reads the newspapers, told me about."

She was referring to the tickets, at greatly reduced rates, which were issued to the pilgrims possessed of means. And Marie, listening to her, felt great pity for her, and also some shame; for she who was not entirely destitute of resources had succeeded in obtaining *hospitalisation*, thanks to Pierre, whereas that mother and her sorry child, after exhausting their scanty savings, remained without a copper.

However, a more violent jolt of the carriage drew a cry of pain from the girl. "Oh, father," she said, "pray raise me a little! I can't stay on my back any longer."

When M. de Guersaint had helped her into a sitting posture, she gave a deep sigh of relief. They were now at Etampes, after a run of an hour and a half from Paris, and what with the increased warmth of the sun, the dust, and the noise, weariness was becoming apparent already. Madame de Jonquiere had got up to speak a few words of kindly encouragement to Marie over the partition; and Sister Hyacinthe moreover again rose, and gaily clapped her hands that she might be heard and obeyed from one to the other end of the carriage.

"Come, come!" said she, "we mustn't think of our little troubles. Let us pray and sing, and the Blessed Virgin will be with us."

She herself then began the rosary according to the rite of Our Lady of Lourdes, and all the patients and pilgrims followed her. This was the first chaplet—the five joyful mysteries, the Annunciation, the Visitation, the Nativity, the Purification, and Jesus found in the Temple. Then they all began to chant the canticle: "Let us contemplate the heavenly Archangel!" Their voices were lost amid the loud rumbling of the wheels; you heard but the muffled surging of that human wave, stifling within the closed carriage which rolled on and on without a pause.

Although M. de Guersaint was a worshipper, he could never follow a hymn to the end. He got up, sat down again, and finished by resting his elbow on the partition and conversing in an undertone with a patient who sat against this same partition in the next compartment. The patient in question was a thick-set man of fifty, with a good-natured face and a large head, completely bald. His name was Sabathier, and for fifteen years he had been stricken with ataxia. He only suffered pain by fits and starts, but he had quite lost the use of his legs, which his wife, who accompanied him, moved for him as though they had been dead legs, whenever they became too heavy, weighty like bars of lead.

"Yes, monsieur," he said, "such as you see me, I was formerly fifth-class professor at the Lycee Charlemagne. At first I thought that it was mere sciatica, but afterwards I was seized with sharp, lightning-like pains, red-hot sword thrusts, you know, in the muscles. For nearly ten years the disease kept on mastering me more and more. I consulted all the doctors, tried every imaginable mineral spring, and now I suffer less, but I can no longer move from my seat. And then, after long living without a thought of religion, I was led back to God by the idea that I was too wretched, and that Our Lady of Lourdes could not do otherwise than take pity on me."

Feeling interested, Pierre in his turn had leant over the partition and was listening.

"Is it not so, Monsieur l'Abbe?" continued M. Sabathier. "Is not suffering the best awakener of souls? This is the seventh year that I am going to Lourdes without despairing of cure. This year the Blessed Virgin will cure me, I feel sure of it. Yes, I expect to be able to walk about again; I now live solely in that hope."

M. Sabathier paused, he wished his wife to push his legs a little more to the left; and Pierre looked at him, astonished to find such obstinate faith in a man of intellect, in one of those university professors who, as a rule, are such Voltairians. How could the belief in miracles have germinated and taken root in this man's brain? As he himself said, great suffering alone explained this need of illusion, this blossoming of eternal and consolatory hope.

"And my wife and I," resumed the ex-professor, "are dressed, you see, as poor folks, for I wished to go as a mere pauper this year, and applied for *hospitalisation* in a spirit of humility in order that the Blessed Virgin might include me among the wretched, her children—only, as I did not wish to take the place of a real pauper, I gave fifty francs to the Hospitalite, and this, as you are aware, gives one the right to have a patient of one's own in the pilgrimage. I even know my patient. He was introduced to me at the railway station. He is suffering from tuberculosis, it appears, and seemed to me very low, very low."

A fresh interval of silence ensued. "Well," said M. Sabathier at last, "may the Blessed Virgin save him also, she who can do everything. I shall be so happy; she will have loaded me with favours."

Then the three men, isolating themselves from the others, went on conversing together, at first on medical subjects, and at last diverging into a discussion on romanesque architecture, *a propos* of a steeple which they had perceived on a hillside, and which every pilgrim had saluted with a sign of the cross. Swayed once more by the habits of cultivated intellect, the young priest and his two companions forgot themselves together in the midst of their fellow-passengers, all those poor, suffering, simple-minded folk, whom wretchedness stupefied. Another hour went by, two more canticles had just been sung, and the stations of Toury and Les Aubrais had been left behind, when, at Beaugency, they at last ceased their chat, on hearing Sister Hyacinthe clap her hands and intonate in her fresh, sonorous voice:

"*Parce, Domine, parce populo tuo.*"

And then the chant went on; all voices became mingled in that ever-surging wave of prayer which stilled pain, excited hope, and little by little penetrated the entire being, harassed by the haunting thought of the grace and cure which one and all were going to seek so far away.

However, as Pierre sat down again, he saw that Marie was very pale, and had her eyes closed. By the painful contraction of her features he could tell that she was not asleep. "Are you in great suffering?" he asked.

"Yes, yes, I suffer dreadfully. I shall never last to the end. It is this incessant jolting."

She moaned, raised her eyelids, and, half-fainting, remained in a sitting posture, her eyes turned on the other sufferers. In the adjoining compartment, La Grivotte, hitherto stretched out, scarce breathing, like a corpse, had just raised herself up in front of M. Sabathier. She was a tall, slip-shod, singular-looking creature of over thirty, with a round, ravaged face, which her frizzy hair and flaming eyes rendered almost pretty. She had reached the third stage of phthisis.

"Eh, mademoiselle," she said, addressing herself in a hoarse, indistinct voice to Marie, "how nice it would be if we could only doze off a little. But it can't be managed; all these wheels keep on whirling round and round in one's head."

Then, although it fatigued her to speak, she obstinately went on talking, volunteering particulars about herself. She was a mattress-maker, and with one of her aunts had long gone from yard to yard at Bercy to comb and sew up mattresses. And, indeed, it was to the pestilential wool which she had combed in her youth that she ascribed her malady. For five years she had been making the round of the hospitals of Paris, and she spoke familiarly of all the great doctors. It was the Sisters of Charity, at the Lariboisiere hospital, who, finding that she had a passion for religious ceremonies, had completed her conversion, and convinced her that the Virgin awaited her at Lourdes to cure her.

"I certainly need it," said she. "The doctors say that I have one lung done for, and that the other one is scarcely any better. There are great big holes you know. At first I only felt bad between the shoulders and spat up some froth. But then I got thin, and became a dreadful sight. And now I'm always in a sweat, and cough till I think I'm going to bring my heart up. And I can no longer spit. And I haven't the strength to stand, you see. I can't eat."

A stifling sensation made her pause, and she became livid.

"All the same I prefer being in my skin instead of in that of the Brother in the compartment behind you. He has the same complaint as I have, but he is in a worse state that I am."

She was mistaken. In the farther compartment, beyond Marie, there was indeed a young missionary, Brother Isidore, who was lying on a mattress and could not be seen, since he was unable to raise even a finger. But he was not suffering from phthisis. He was dying of inflammation of the liver, contracted in Senegal. Very long and lank, he had a yellow face, with skin as dry and lifeless as parchment. The abscess which had formed in his liver had ended by breaking out externally, and amidst the continuous shivering of fever, vomiting, and delirium, suppuration was exhausting him. His eyes alone were still alive, eyes full of unextinguishable love, whose flame lighted up his expiring face, a peasant face such as painters have given to the crucified Christ, common, but rendered sublime at moments by its expression of faith and passion. He was a Breton, the last puny child of an over-numerous family, and had left his little share of land to his elder brothers. One of his sisters, Marthe, older than himself by a couple of years, accompanied him. She had been in service in Paris, an insignificant maid-of-all-work, but withal so devoted to her brother that she had left her situation to follow him, subsisting scantily on her petty savings.

"I was lying on the platform," resumed La Grivotte, "when he was put in the carriage. There were four men carrying him—"

But she was unable to speak any further, for just then an attack of coughing shook her and threw her back upon the seat. She was suffocating, and the red flush on her cheek-bones turned blue. Sister Hyacinthe, however, immediately raised her head and wiped her lips with a linen cloth, which became spotted with blood. At the same time Madame de Jonquiere gave her attention to a patient in front of her, who had just fainted. She was called Madame Vetu, and was the wife of a petty clockmaker of the Mouffetard district, who had not been able to shut up his shop in order to accompany her to Lourdes. And to make sure that she would be cared for she had sought and obtained *hospitalisation*. The fear of death was bringing her back to religion, although she had not set foot in church since her first communion. She knew that she was lost, that a cancer in the chest was eating into her; and she already had the haggard, orange-hued mark of the cancerous patient. Since the beginning of the journey she had not spoken a word, but, suffering terribly, had remained with her lips tightly closed. Then all at once, she had swooned away after an attack of vomiting.

"It is unbearable!" murmured Madame de Jonquiere, who herself felt faint; "we must let in a little fresh air."

Sister Hyacinthe was just then laying La Grivotte to rest on her pillows, "Certainly," said she, "we will open the window for a few moments. But not on this side, for I am afraid we might have a fresh fit of coughing. Open the window on your side, madame."

The heat was still increasing, and the occupants of the carriage were stifling in that heavy evil-smelling atmosphere. The pure air which came in when the window was opened brought relief however. For a moment there were other duties to be attended to, a clearance and cleansing. The Sister emptied the basins out of the window, whilst the lady-hospitaller wiped the shaking floor with a sponge. Next, things had to be set in order; and then came a fresh anxiety, for the fourth patient, a slender girl whose face was entirely covered by a black fichu, and who had not yet moved, was saying that she felt hungry.

With quiet devotion Madame de Jonquiere immediately tendered her services. "Don't you trouble, Sister," she said, "I will cut her bread into little bits for her."

Marie, with the need she felt of diverting her mind from her own sufferings, had already begun to take an interest in that motionless sufferer whose countenance was so thickly veiled, for she not unnaturally suspected that it was a case of some distressing facial sore. She had merely been told that the patient was a servant, which was true, but it happened that the poor creature, a native of Picardy, named Elise Rouquet, had been obliged to leave her situation, and seek a home with a sister who ill-treated her, for no hospital would take her in. Extremely devout, she had for many months been possessed by an ardent desire to go to Lourdes.

While Marie, with dread in her heart, waited for the fichu to be moved aside, Madame de Jonquiere, having cut some bread into small pieces, inquired maternally: "Are they small enough? Can you put them into your mouth?"

Thereupon a hoarse voice growled confused words under the black fichu: "Yes, yes, madame." And at last the veil fell and Marie shuddered with horror.

It was a case of lupus which had preyed upon the unhappy woman's nose and mouth. Ulceration had spread, and was hourly spreading—in short, all the hideous peculiarities of this terrible disease were in full process of development, almost obliterating the traces of what once were pleasing womanly lineaments.

"Oh, look, Pierre!" Marie murmured, trembling. The priest in his turn shuddered as he beheld Elise Rouquet cautiously slipping the tiny pieces of bread into her poor shapeless mouth. Everyone in the carriage had turned pale at sight of the awful apparition. And the same thought ascended from all those hope-inflated souls. Ah! Blessed Virgin, Powerful Virgin, what a miracle indeed if such an ill were cured!

"We must not think of ourselves, my children, if we wish to get well," resumed Sister Hyacinthe, who still retained her encouraging smile.

And then she made them say the second chaplet, the five sorrowful mysteries: Jesus in the Garden of Olives, Jesus scourged, Jesus crowned with thorns, Jesus carrying the cross, and Jesus crucified. Afterwards came the canticle: "In thy help, Virgin, do I put my trust."

They had just passed through Blois; for three long hours they had been rolling onward; and Marie, who had averted her eyes from Elise Rouquet, now turned them upon a man who occupied a corner seat in the compartment on her left, that in which Brother Isidore was lying. She had noticed this man several times already. Poorly clad in an old black frock-coat, he looked still young, although his sparse beard was already turning grey; and, short and emaciated, he seemed to experience great suffering, his fleshless, livid face being covered with sweat. However, he remained motionless, ensconced in his corner, speaking to nobody, but staring straight before him with dilated eyes. And all at once Marie noticed that his eyelids were falling, and that he was fainting away.

She thereupon drew Sister's Hyacinthe's attention to him: "Look, Sister! One would think that that gentleman is dangerously ill."

"Which one, my dear child?"

"That one, over there, with his head thrown back."

General excitement followed, all the healthy pilgrims rose up to look, and it occurred to Madame de Jonquiere to call to Marthe, Brother Isidore's sister, and tell her to tap the man's hands.

"Question him," she added; "ask what ails him."

Marthe drew near, shook the man, and questioned him.

But instead of an answer only a rattle came from his throat, and his eyes remained closed.

Then a frightened voice was heard saying, "I think he is going to die."

The dread increased, words flew about, advice was tendered from one to the other end of the carriage. Nobody knew the man. He had certainly not obtained *hospitalisation*, for no white card was hanging from his neck. Somebody related, however, that he had seen him arrive, dragging himself along, but three minutes or so before the train started; and that he had remained quite motionless, scarce breathing, ever since he had flung himself with an air of intense weariness into that corner, where he was now apparently dying. His ticket was at last seen protruding from under the band of an old silk hat which was hung from a peg near him.

"Ah, he is breathing again now!" Sister Hyacinthe suddenly exclaimed. "Ask him his name."

However, on being again questioned by Marthe, the man merely gave vent to a low plaint, an exclamation scarcely articulated, "Oh, how I suffer!"

And thenceforward that was the only answer that could be obtained from him. With reference to everything that they wished to know, who he was, whence he came, what his illness was, what could be done for him, he gave no information, but still and ever continued moaning, "Oh, how I suffer—how I suffer!"

Sister Hyacinthe grew restless with impatience. Ah, if she had only been in the same compartment with him! And she resolved that she would change her seat at the first station they should stop at. Only there would be no stoppage for a long time. The position was becoming terrible, the more so as the man's head again fell back.

"He is dying, he is dying!" repeated the frightened voice.

What was to be done, *mon Dieu*? The Sister was aware that one of the Fathers of the Assumption, Father Massias, was in the train with the Holy Oils, ready to administer extreme unction to the dying; for every year some of the patients passed away during the journey. But she did not dare to have recourse to the alarm signal. Moreover, in the *cantine* van where Sister Saint Francois officiated, there was a doctor with a little medicine chest. If the sufferer should survive until they reached Poitiers, where there would be half an hour's stoppage, all possible help might be given to him.

But on the other hand he might suddenly expire. However, they ended by becoming somewhat calmer. The man, though still unconscious, began to breathe in a more regular manner, and seemed to fall asleep.

I. PILGRIMS AND PATIENTS

"To think of it, to die before getting there," murmured Marie with a shudder, "to die in sight of the promised land!" And as her father sought to reassure her she added: "I am suffering—I am suffering dreadfully myself."

"Have confidence," said Pierre; "the Blessed Virgin is watching over you."

She could no longer remain seated, and it became necessary to replace her in a recumbent position in her narrow coffin. Her father and the priest had to take every precaution in doing so, for the slightest hurt drew a moan from her. And she lay there breathless, like one dead, her face contracted by suffering, and surrounded by her regal fair hair. They had now been rolling on, ever rolling on for nearly four hours. And if the carriage was so greatly shaken, with an unbearable spreading tendency, it was from its position at the rear part of the train. The coupling irons shrieked, the wheels growled furiously; and as it was necessary to leave the windows partially open, the dust came in, acrid and burning; but it was especially the heat which grew terrible, a devouring, stormy heat falling from a tawny sky which large hanging clouds had slowly covered. The hot carriages, those rolling boxes where the pilgrims ate and drank, where the sick lay in a vitiated atmosphere, amid dizzying moans, prayers, and hymns, became like so many furnaces.

And Marie was not the only one whose condition had been aggravated; others also were suffering from the journey. Resting in the lap of her despairing mother, who gazed at her with large, tear-blurred eyes, little Rose had ceased to stir, and had grown so pale that Madame Maze had twice leant forward to feel her hands, fearful lest she should find them cold. At each moment also Madame Sabathier had to move her husband's legs, for their weight was so great, said he, that it seemed as if his hips were being torn from him. Brother Isidore too had just begun to cry out, emerging from his wonted torpor; and his sister had only been able to assuage his sufferings by raising him, and clasping him in her arms. La Grivotte seemed to be asleep, but a continuous hiccoughing shook her, and a tiny streamlet of blood dribbled from her mouth. Madame Vetu had again vomited, Elise Rouquet no longer thought of hiding the frightful sore open on her face. And from the man yonder, breathing hard, there still came a lugubrious rattle, as though he were at every moment on the point of expiring. In vain did Madame de Jonquiere and Sister Hyacinthe lavish their attentions on the patients, they could but slightly assuage so much suffering. At times it all seemed like an evil dream—that carriage of wretchedness and pain, hurried along at express speed, with a continuous shaking and jolting which made everything hanging from the pegs—the old clothes, the worn-out baskets mended with bits of string—swing to and fro incessantly. And in the compartment at the far end, the ten female pilgrims, some old, some young, and all pitifully ugly, sang on without a pause in cracked voices, shrill and dreary.

Then Pierre began to think of the other carriages of the train, that white train which conveyed most, if not all, of the more seriously afflicted patients; these carriages were rolling along, all displaying similar scenes of suffering among the three hundred sick and five hundred healthy pilgrims crowded within them. And afterwards he thought of the other trains which were leaving Paris that day, the grey train and the blue train[1] which had preceded the white one, the green train, the yellow train, the pink train, the orange train which were following it. From hour to hour trains set out from one to the other end of France. And he thought, too, of those which that same morning had started from Orleans, Le Mans, Poitiers, Bordeaux, Marseilles, and Carcassonne. Coming from all parts, trains were rushing across that land of France at the same hour, all directing their course yonder towards the holy Grotto, bringing thirty thousand patients and pilgrims to the Virgin's feet. And he reflected that other days of the year witnessed a like rush of human beings, that not a week went by without Lourdes beholding the arrival of some pilgrimage; that it was not merely France which set out on the march, but all Europe, the whole world; that in certain years of great religious fervour there had been three hundred thousand, and even five hundred thousand, pilgrims and patients streaming to the spot.

Pierre fancied that he could hear those flying trains, those trains from everywhere, all converging towards the same rocky cavity where the tapers were blazing. They all rumbled loudly amid the cries of pain and snatches of hymns wafted from their carriages. They were the rolling hospitals of disease at its last stage, of human suffering rushing to the hope of cure, furiously seeking consolation between attacks of increased severity, with the ever-present threat of death—death hastened, supervening under awful conditions, amidst the mob-like scramble. They rolled on, they rolled on again and again, they rolled on without a pause, carrying the wretchedness of the world on its way to the divine illusion, the health of the infirm, the consolation of the afflicted.

And immense pity overflowed from Pierre's heart, human compassion for all the suffering and all the tears that consumed weak and naked men. He was sad unto death and ardent charity burnt within him, the unextinguishable flame as it were of his fraternal feelings towards all things and beings.

When they left the station of Saint Pierre des Corps at half-past ten, Sister Hyacinthe gave the signal, and they recited the third chaplet, the five glorious mysteries, the Resurrection of Our Lord, the Ascension of Our Lord, the Mission of the Holy Ghost, the Assumption of the Most Blessed Virgin, the Crowning of the Most Blessed Virgin. And afterwards they sang the canticle of Bernadette, that long, long chant, composed of six times ten couplets, to which the ever recurring Angelic Salutation serves as a refrain—a prolonged lullaby slowly besetting one until it ends by penetrating one's entire being, transporting one into ecstatic sleep, in delicious expectancy of a miracle.

---

[1] Different-coloured tickets are issued for these trains; it is for this reason that they are called the white, blue, and grey trains, etc.—Trans.

II. PIERRE AND MARIE

THE green landscapes of Poitou were now defiling before them, and Abbe Pierre Froment, gazing out of the window, watched the trees fly away till, little by little, he ceased to distinguish them. A steeple appeared and then vanished, and all the pilgrims crossed themselves. They would not reach Poitiers until twelve-thirty-five, and the train was still rolling on amid the growing weariness of that oppressive, stormy day. Falling into a deep reverie, the young priest no longer heard the words of the canticle, which sounded in his ears merely like a slow, wavy lullaby.

Forgetfulness of the present had come upon him, an awakening of the past filled his whole being. He was reascending the stream of memory, reascending it to its source. He again beheld the house at Neuilly, where he had been born and where he still lived, that home of peace and toil, with its garden planted with a few fine trees, and parted by a quickset hedge and palisade from the garden of the neighbouring house, which was similar to his own. He was again three, perhaps four, years old, and round a table, shaded by the big horse-chestnut tree he once more beheld his father, his mother, and his elder brother at *dejeuner*. To his father, Michel Froment, he could give no distinct lineaments; he pictured him but faintly, vaguely, renowned as an illustrious chemist, bearing the title of Member of the Institute, and leading a cloistered life in the laboratory which he had installed in that secluded, deserted suburb. However he could plainly see his first brother Guillaume, then fourteen years of age, whom some holiday had brought from college that morning, and then and even more vividly his mother, so gentle and so quiet, with eyes so full of active kindliness. Later on he learnt what anguish had racked that religious soul, that believing woman who, from esteem and gratitude, had resignedly accepted marriage with an unbeliever, her senior by fifteen years, to whom her relatives were indebted for great services. He, Pierre, the tardy offspring of this union, born when his father was already near his fiftieth year, had only known his mother as a respectful, conquered woman in the presence of her husband, whom she had learnt to love passionately, with the frightful torment of knowing, however, that he was doomed to perdition. And, all at once, another memory flashed upon the young priest, the terrible memory of the day when his father had died, killed in his laboratory by an accident, the explosion of a retort. He, Pierre, had then been five years old, and he remembered the slightest incidents—his mother's cry when she had found the shattered body among the remnants of the chemical appliances, then her terror, her sobs, her prayers at the idea that God had slain the unbeliever, damned him for evermore. Not daring to burn his books and papers, she had contented herself with locking up the laboratory, which henceforth nobody entered. And from that moment, haunted by a vision of hell, she had had but one idea, to possess herself of her second son, who was still so young, to give him a strictly religious training, and through him to ransom her husband—secure his forgiveness from God. Guillaume, her elder boy, had already ceased to belong to her, having grown up at college, where he had been won over by the ideas of the century; but she resolved that the other, the younger one, should not leave the house, but should have a priest as tutor; and her secret dream, her consuming hope, was that she might some day see him a priest himself, saying his first mass and solacing souls whom the thought of eternity tortured.

Then between green, leafy boughs, flecked with sunlight, another figure rose vividly before Pierre's eyes. He suddenly beheld Marie de Guersaint as he had seen her one morning through a gap in the hedge dividing the two gardens. M. de Guersaint, who belonged to the petty Norman *noblesse*, was a combination of architect and inventor; and he was at that time busy with a scheme of model dwellings for the poor, to which churches and schools were to be attached; an affair of considerable magnitude, planned none too well, however, and in which, with his customary impetuosity, the lack of foresight of an imperfect artist, he was risking the three hundred thousand francs that he possessed. A similarity of religious faith had drawn Madame de Guersaint and Madame Froment together; but the former was altogether a superior woman, perspicuous and rigid, with an iron hand which alone prevented her household from gliding to a catastrophe; and she was bringing up her two daughters, Blanche and Marie, in principles of narrow piety, the elder one already being as grave as herself, whilst the younger, albeit very devout, was still fond of play, with an intensity of life within her which found vent in gay peals of sonorous laughter. From their early childhood Pierre and Marie played together, the hedge was ever being crossed, the two families constantly mingled. And on that clear sunshiny morning, when he pictured her parting the leafy branches she was already ten years old. He, who was sixteen, was to enter the seminary on the following Tuesday. Never had she seemed to him so pretty. Her hair, of a pure golden hue, was so long that when it was let down it sufficed to clothe her. Well did he remember her face as it had been, with round cheeks, blue eyes, red mouth, and skin of dazzling, snowy whiteness. She was indeed as gay and brilliant as the sun itself, a transplendency. Yet there were tears at the corners of her eyes, for she was aware of his coming departure. They sat down together at the far end of the garden, in the shadow cast by the hedge. Their hands mingled, and their hearts were very heavy. They had, however, never exchanged any vows amid their pastimes, for their innocence was absolute. But now, on the eve of separation, their mutual tenderness rose to their lips, and they spoke without knowing, swore that they would ever think of one another, and find one another again, some day, even as one meets in heaven to be very, very happy. Then, without understanding how it happened, they clasped each other tightly, to the point of suffocation, and kissed each other's face, weeping, the while, hot tears. And it was that delightful memory which Pierre had ever carried with him, which he felt alive within him still, after so many years, and after so many painful renunciations.

Just then a more violent shock roused him from his reverie. He turned his eyes upon the carriage and vaguely espied the suffering beings it contained—Madame Maze motionless, overwhelmed with grief; little Rose gently moaning in her mother's lap;

La Grivotte, whom a hoarse cough was choking. For a moment Sister Hyacinthe's gay face shone out amidst the whiteness of her coif and wimple, dominating all the others. The painful journey was continuing, with a ray of divine hope still and ever shining yonder. Then everything slowly vanished from Pierre's eyes as a fresh wave of memory brought the past back from afar; and nothing of the present remained save the lulling hymn, the indistinct voices of dreamland, emerging from the invisible.

Henceforth he was at the seminary. The classrooms, the recreation ground with its trees, rose up clearly before him. But all at once he only beheld, as in a mirror, the youthful face which had then been his, and he contemplated it and scrutinised it, as though it had been the face of a stranger. Tall and slender, he had an elongated visage, with an unusually developed forehead, lofty and straight like a tower; whilst his jaws tapered, ending in a small refined chin. He seemed, in fact, to be all brains; his mouth, rather large, alone retained an expression of tenderness. Indeed, when his usually serious face relaxed, his mouth and eyes acquired an exceedingly soft expression, betokening an unsatisfied, hungry desire to love, devote oneself, and live. But immediately afterwards, the look of intellectual passion would come back again, that intellectuality which had ever consumed him with an anxiety to understand and know. And it was with surprise that he now recalled those years of seminary life. How was it that he had so long been able to accept the rude discipline of blind faith, of obedient belief in everything without the slightest examination? It had been required of him that he should absolutely surrender his reasoning faculties, and he had striven to do so, had succeeded indeed in stifling his torturing need of truth. Doubtless he had been softened, weakened by his mother's tears, had been possessed by the sole desire to afford her the great happiness she dreamt of. Yet now he remembered certain quiverings of revolt; he found in the depths of his mind the memory of nights which he had spent in weeping without knowing why, nights peopled with vague images, nights through which galloped the free, virile life of the world, when Marie's face incessantly returned to him, such as he had seen it one morning, dazzling and bathed in tears, while she embraced him with her whole soul. And that alone now remained; his years of religious study with their monotonous lessons, their ever similar exercises and ceremonies, had flown away into the same haze, into a vague half-light, full of mortal silence.

Then, just as the train had passed through a station at full speed, with the sudden uproar of its rush there arose within him a succession of confused visions. He had noticed a large deserted enclosure, and fancied that he could see himself within it at twenty years of age. His reverie was wandering. An indisposition of rather long duration had, however, at one time interrupted his studies, and led to his being sent into the country. He had remained for a long time without seeing Marie; during his vacations spent at Neuilly he had twice failed to meet her, for she was almost always travelling. He knew that she was very ill, in consequence of a fall from a horse when she was thirteen, a critical moment in a girl's life; and her despairing mother, perplexed by the contradictory advice of medical men, was taking her each year to a different watering-place. Then he learnt the startling news of the sudden tragical death of that mother, who was so severe and yet so useful to her kin. She had been carried off in five days by inflammation of the lungs, which she had contracted one evening whilst she was out walking at La Bourboule, through having taken off her mantle to place it round the shoulders of Marie, who had been conveyed thither for treatment. It had been necessary that the father should at once start off to fetch his daughter, who was mad with grief, and the corpse of his wife, who had been so suddenly torn from him. And unhappily, after losing her, the affairs of the family went from bad to worse in the hands of this architect, who, without counting, flung his fortune into the yawning gulf of his unsuccessful enterprises. Marie no longer stirred from her couch; only Blanche remained to manage the household, and she had matters of her own to attend to, being busy with the last examinations which she had to pass, the diplomas which she was obstinately intent on securing, foreseeing as she did that she would someday have to earn her bread.

All at once, from amidst this mass of confused, half-forgotten incidents, Pierre was conscious of the rise of a vivid vision. Ill-health, he remembered, had again compelled him to take a holiday. He had just completed his twenty-fourth year, he was greatly behindhand, having so far only secured the four minor orders; but on his return a sub-deaconship would be conferred on him, and an inviolable vow would bind him for evermore. And the Guersaints' little garden at Neuilly, whither he had formerly so often gone to play, again distinctly appeared before him. Marie's couch had been rolled under the tall trees at the far end of the garden near the hedge, they were alone together in the sad peacefulness of an autumnal afternoon, and he saw Marie, clad in deep mourning for her mother and reclining there with legs inert; whilst he, also clad in black, in a cassock already, sat near her on an iron garden chair. For five years she had been suffering. She was now eighteen, paler and thinner than formerly, but still adorable with her regal golden hair, which illness respected. He believed from what he had heard that she was destined to remain infirm, condemned never to become a woman, stricken even in her sex. The doctors, who failed to agree respecting her case, had abandoned her. Doubtless it was she who told him these things that dreary afternoon, whilst the yellow withered leaves rained upon them. However, he could not remember the words that they had spoken; her pale smile, her young face, still so charming though already dimmed by regretfulness for life, alone remained present with him. But he realised that she had evoked the far-off day of their parting, on that same spot, behind the hedge flecked with sunlight; and all that was already as though dead—their tears, their embrace, their promise to find one another some day with a certainty of happiness. For although they had found one another again, what availed it, since she was but a corpse, and he was about to bid farewell to the life of the world? As the doctors condemned her, as she would never be woman, nor wife, nor mother, he, on his side, might well renounce manhood, and annihilate himself, dedicate himself to God, to whom his mother gave him. And he still felt within him the soft bitterness of that last interview: Marie smiling painfully at memory of their childish play and prattle, and speaking to him of the happiness which he would assuredly find in the service of God; so penetrated indeed with emotion at this thought, that she had made him promise that he would let her hear him say his first mass.

But the train was passing the station of Sainte-Maure, and just then a sudden uproar momentarily brought Pierre's attention back to the carriage and its occupants. He fancied that there had been some fresh seizure or swooning, but the suffering faces that he beheld were still the same, ever contracted by the same expression of anxious waiting for the divine succour which was so slow in coming. M. Sabathier was vainly striving to get his legs into a comfortable position, whilst Brother Isidore raised a feeble continuous moan like a dying child, and Madame Vetu, a prey to terrible agony, devoured by her disease, sat motionless, and kept her lips tightly closed, her face distorted, haggard, and almost black. The noise which Pierre had heard had been occa-occasioned by Madame de Jonquiere, who whilst cleansing a basin had dropped the large zinc water-can. And, despite their torment, this had made the patients laugh, like the simple souls they were, rendered puerile by suffering. However, Sister Hyacinthe, who rightly called them her children, children whom she governed with a word, at once set them saying the chaplet again, pending the Angelus, which would only be said at Chatellerault, in accordance with the predetermined programme. And thereupon the "Aves" followed one after the other, spreading into a confused murmuring and mumbling amidst the rattling of the coupling irons and noisy growling of the wheels.

Pierre had meantime relapsed into his reverie, and beheld himself as he had been at six-and-twenty, when ordained a priest. Tardy scruples had come to him a few days before his ordination, a semi-consciousness that he was binding himself without having clearly questioned his heart and mind. But he had avoided doing so, living in the dizzy bewilderment of his decision, fancying that he had lopped off all human ties and feelings with a voluntary hatchet-stroke. His flesh had surely died with his childhood's innocent romance, that white-skinned girl with golden hair, whom now he never beheld otherwise than stretched upon her couch of suffering, her flesh as lifeless as his own. And he had afterwards made the sacrifice of his mind, which he then fancied even an easier one, hoping as he did that determination would suffice to prevent him from thinking. Besides, it was too late, he could not recoil at the last moment, and if when he pronounced the last solemn vow he felt a secret terror, an indeterminate but immense regret agitating him, he forgot everything, saving a divine reward for his efforts on the day when he afforded his mother the great and long-expected joy of hearing him say his first mass.

He could still see the poor woman in the little church of Neuilly, which she herself had selected, the church where the funeral service for his father had been celebrated; he saw her on that cold November morning, kneeling almost alone in the dark little chapel, her hands hiding her face as she continued weeping whilst he raised the Host. It was there that she had tasted her last happiness, for she led a sad and lonely life, no longer seeing her elder son, who had gone away, swayed by other ideas than her own, bent on breaking off all family intercourse since his brother intended to enter the Church. It was said that Guillaume, a chemist of great talent, like his father, but at the same time a Bohemian, addicted to revolutionary dreams, was living in a little house in the suburbs, where he devoted himself to the dangerous study of explosive substances; and folks added that he was living with a woman who had come no one knew whence. This it was which had severed the last tie between himself and his mother, all piety and propriety. For three years Pierre had not once seen Guillaume, whom in his childhood he had worshipped as a kind, merry, and fatherly big brother.

But there came an awful pang to his heart—he once more beheld his mother lying dead. This again was a thunderbolt, an illness of scarce three days' duration, a sudden passing away, as in the case of Madame de Guersaint. One evening, after a wild hunt for the doctor, he had found her motionless and quite white. She had died during his absence; and his lips had ever retained the icy thrill of the last kiss that he had given her. Of everything else—the vigil, the preparations, the funeral—he remembered nothing. All that had become lost in the black night of his stupor and grief, grief so extreme that he had almost died of it—seized with shivering on his return from the cemetery, struck down by a fever which during three weeks had kept him delirious, hovering between life and death. His brother had come and nursed him and had then attended to pecuniary matters, dividing the little inheritance, leaving him the house and a modest income and taking his own share in money. And as soon as Guillaume had found him out of danger he had gone off again, once more vanishing into the unknown. But then through what a long convalescence he, Pierre, had passed, buried as it were in that deserted house. He had done nothing to detain Guillaume, for he realised that there was an abyss between them. At first the solitude had brought him suffering, but afterwards it had grown very pleasant, whether in the deep silence of the rooms which the rare noises of the street did not disturb, or under the screening, shady foliage of the little garden, where he could spend whole days without seeing a soul. His favourite place of refuge, however, was the old laboratory, his father's cabinet, which his mother for twenty years had kept carefully locked up, as though to immure within it all the incredulity and damnation of the past. And despite the gentleness, the respectful submissiveness which she had shown in former times, she would perhaps have some day ended by destroying all her husband's books and papers, had not death so suddenly surprised her. Pierre, however, had once more had the windows opened, the writing-table and the bookcase dusted; and, installed in the large leather arm-chair, he now spent delicious hours there, regenerated as it were by his illness, brought back to his youthful days again, deriving a wondrous intellectual delight from the perusal of the books which he came upon.

The only person whom he remembered having received during those two months of slow recovery was Doctor Chassaigne, an old friend of his father, a medical man of real merit, who, with the one ambition of curing disease, modestly confined himself to the *role* of the practitioner. It was in vain that the doctor had sought to save Madame Froment, but he flattered himself that he had extricated the young priest from grievous danger; and he came to see him from time to time, to chat with him and cheer him, talking with him of his father, the great chemist, of whom he recounted many a charming anecdote, many a particular, still glowing with the flame of ardent friendship. Little by little, amidst the weak languor of convalescence, the son had thus beheld an embodiment of charming simplicity, affection, and good nature rising up before him. It was his father such as he had really been, not the man of stern science whom he had pictured whilst listening to his mother. Certainly she had never taught him aught but respect for that dear memory; but had not her husband been the unbeliever, the man who denied, and made the angels weep, the artisan of impiety who sought to change the world that God had made? And so he had long remained a gloomy vision, a spectre of damnation prowling about the house, whereas now he became the house's very light, clear and gay, a worker consumed by a longing for truth, who had never desired anything but the love and happiness of all. For his part, Doctor Chassaigne, a Pyrenean by birth, born in a far-off secluded village where folks still believed in sorceresses, inclined rather towards religion, although he had not set his foot inside a church during the forty years he had been living in Paris. However, his conviction was absolute: if there were a heaven somewhere, Michel Froment was assuredly there, and not merely there, but seated upon a throne on the Divinity's right hand.

II. PIERRE AND MARIE

Then Pierre, in a few minutes, again lived through the frightful torment which, during two long months, had ravaged him. It was not that he had found controversial works of an anti-religious character in the bookcase, or that his father, whose papers he sorted, had ever gone beyond his technical studies as a *savant*. But little by little, despite himself, the light of science dawned upon him, an *ensemble* of proven phenomena, which demolished dogmas and left within him nothing of the things which as a priest he should have believed. It seemed, in fact, as though illness had renewed him, as though he were again beginning to live and learn amidst the physical pleasantness of convalescence, that still subsisting weakness which lent penetrating lucidity to his brain. At the seminary, by the advice of his masters, he had always kept the spirit of inquiry, his thirst for knowledge, in check. Much of that which was taught him there had surprised him; however, he had succeeded in making the sacrifice of his mind required of his piety. But now, all the laboriously raised scaffolding of dogmas was swept away in a revolt of that sovereign mind which clamoured for its rights, and which he could no longer silence. Truth was bubbling up and overflowing in such an irresistible stream that he realised he would never succeed in lodging error in his brain again. It was indeed the total and irreparable ruin of faith. Although he had been able to kill his flesh by renouncing the romance of his youth, although he felt that he had altogether mastered carnal passion, he now knew that it would be impossible for him to make the sacrifice of his intelligence. And he was not mistaken; it was indeed his father again springing to life in the depths of his being, and at last obtaining the mastery in that dual heredity in which, during so many years, his mother had dominated. The upper part of his face, his straight, towering brow, seemed to have risen yet higher, whilst the lower part, the small chin, the affectionate mouth, were becoming less distinct. However, he suffered; at certain twilight hours when his kindliness, his need of love awoke, he felt distracted with grief at no longer believing, distracted with desire to believe again; and it was necessary that the lighted lamp should be brought in, that he should see clearly around him and within him, before he could recover the energy and calmness of reason, the strength of martyrdom, the determination to sacrifice everything to the peace of his conscience.

Then came the crisis. He was a priest and he no longer believed. This had suddenly dawned before him like a bottomless abyss. It was the end of his life, the collapse of everything. What should he do? Did not simple rectitude require that he should throw off the cassock and return to the world? But he had seen some renegade priests and had despised them. A married priest with whom he was acquainted filled him with disgust. All this, no doubt, was but a survival of his long religious training. He retained the notion that a priest cannot, must not, weaken; the idea that when one has dedicated oneself to God one cannot take possession of oneself again. Possibly, also, he felt that he was too plainly branded, too different from other men already, to prove otherwise than awkward and unwelcome among them. Since he had been cut off from them he would remain apart in his grievous pride; And, after days of anguish, days of struggle incessantly renewed, in which his thirst for happiness warred with the energies of his returning health, he took the heroic resolution to remain a priest, and an honest one. He would find the strength necessary for such abnegation. Since he had conquered the flesh, albeit unable to conquer the brain, he felt sure of keeping his vow of chastity, and that would be unshakable; therein lay the pure, upright life which he was absolutely certain of living. What mattered the rest if he alone suffered, if nobody in the world suspected that his heart was reduced to ashes, that nothing remained of his faith, that he was agonising amidst fearful falsehood? His rectitude would prove a firm prop; he would follow his priestly calling like an honest man, without breaking any of the vows he had taken; he would, in due accordance with the rites, discharge his duties as a minister of the Divinity, whom he would praise and glorify at the altar, and distribute as the Bread of Life to the faithful. Who, then, would dare to impute his loss of faith to him as a crime, even if this great misfortune should some day become known? And what more could be asked of him than lifelong devotion to his vow, regard for his ministry, and the practice of every charity without the hope of any future reward? In this wise he ended by calming himself, still upright, still bearing his head erect, with the desolate grandeur of the priest who himself no longer believes, but continues watching over the faith of others. And he certainly was not alone; he felt that he had many brothers, priests with ravaged minds, who had sunk into incredulity, and who yet, like soldiers without a fatherland, remained at the altar, and, despite, everything, found the courage to make the divine illusion shine forth above the kneeling crowds.

On recovering his health Pierre had immediately resumed his service at the little church of Neuilly. He said his mass there every morning. But he had resolved to refuse any appointment, any preferment. Months and years went by, and he obstinately insisted on remaining the least known and the most humble of those priests who are tolerated in a parish, who appear and disappear after discharging their duty. The acceptance of any appointment would have seemed to him an aggravation of his falsehood, a theft from those who were more deserving than himself. And he had to resist frequent offers, for it was impossible for his merits to remain unnoticed. Indeed, his obstinate modesty provoked astonishment at the archbishop's palace, where there was a desire to utilise the power which could be divined in him. Now and again, it is true, he bitterly regretted that he was not useful, that he did not co-operate in some great work, in furthering the purification of the world, the salvation and happiness of all, in accordance with his own ardent, torturing desire. Fortunately his time was nearly all his own, and to console himself he gave rein to his passion for work by devouring every volume in his father's bookcase, and then again resuming and considering his studies, feverishly preoccupied with regard to the history of nations, full of a desire to explore the depths of the social and religious crisis so that he might ascertain whether it were really beyond remedy.

It was at this time, whilst rummaging one morning in one of the large drawers in the lower part of the bookcase, that he discovered quite a collection of papers respecting the apparitions of Lourdes. It was a very complete set of documents, comprising detailed notes of the interrogatories to which Bernadette had been subjected, copies of numerous official documents, and police and medical reports, in addition to many private and confidential letters of the greatest interest. This discovery had surprised Pierre, and he had questioned, Doctor Chassaigne concerning it. The latter thereupon remembered that his friend, Michel Froment, had at one time passionately devoted himself to the study of Bernadette's case; and he himself, a native of the village near Lourdes, had procured for the chemist a portion of the documents in the collection. Pierre, in his turn, then became impassioned, and for a whole month continued studying the affair, powerfully attracted by the visionary's pure, upright nature, but indignant with all that had subsequently sprouted up—the barbarous fetishism, the painful superstitions, and the triumphant simony. In the access of unbelief which had come upon him, this story of Lourdes was certainly of a nature to complete the collapse of his faith. However, it had also excited his curiosity, and he would have liked to investigate it, to establish beyond dispute what scientific truth might be in it, and render pure Christianity the service of ridding it of this scoria, this fairy tale, all touching and childish as it was. But he had been obliged to relinquish his studies, shrinking from the necessity of making a journey to the Grotto, and finding that it would be extremely difficult to obtain the information which he still needed; and of it all there at last only remained within him a tender feeling for Bernadette, of whom he could not think without a sensation of delightful charm and infinite pity.

The days went by, and Pierre led a more and more lonely life. Doctor Chassaigne had just left for the Pyrenees in a state of mortal anxiety. Abandoning his patients, he had set out for Cauterets with his ailing wife, who was sinking more and more each day, to the infinite distress of both his charming daughter and himself. From that moment the little house at Neuilly fell into deathlike silence and emptiness. Pierre had no other distraction than that of occasionally going to see the Guersaints, who had long since left the neighbouring house, but whom he had found again in a small lodging in a wretched tenement of the district. And the memory of his first visit to them there was yet so fresh within him, that he felt a pang at his heart as he recalled his emotion at sight of the hapless Marie.

That pang roused him from his reverie, and on looking round he perceived Marie stretched on the seat, even as he had found her on the day which he recalled, already imprisoned in that gutter-like box, that coffin to which wheels were adapted when she was taken out-of-doors for an airing. She, formerly so brimful of life, ever astir and laughing, was dying of inaction and immobility in that box. Of her old-time beauty she had retained nothing save her hair, which clad her as with a royal mantle, and she was so emaciated that she seemed to have grown smaller again, to have become once more a child. And what was most distressing was the expression on her pale face, the blank, frigid stare of her eyes which did not see, the ever haunting absent look, as of one whom suffering overwhelmed. However, she noticed that Pierre was gazing at her, and at once desired to smile at him; but irresistible moans escaped her, and when she did at last smile, it was like a poor smitten creature who is convinced that she will expire before the miracle takes place. He was overcome by it, and, amidst all the sufferings with which the carriage abounded, hers were now the only ones that he beheld and heard, as though one and all were summed up in her, in the long and terrible agony of her beauty, gaiety, and youth.

Then by degrees, without taking his eyes from Marie, he again reverted to former days, again lived those hours, fraught with a mournful and bitter charm, which he had often spent beside her, when he called at the sorry lodging to keep her company. M. de Guersaint had finally ruined himself by trying to improve the artistic quality of the religious prints so widely sold in France, the faulty execution of which quite irritated him. His last resources had been swallowed up in the failure of a colour-printing firm; and, heedless as he was, deficient in foresight, ever trusting in Providence, his childish mind continually swayed by illusions, he did not notice the awful pecuniary embarrassment of the household; but applied himself to the study of aerial navigation, without even realising what prodigious activity his elder daughter, Blanche, was forced to display, in order to earn the living of her two children, as she was wont to call her father and her sister. It was Blanche who, by running about Paris in the dust or the mud from morning to evening in order to give French or music lessons, contrived to provide the money necessary for the unremitting attentions which Marie required. And Marie often experienced attacks of despair—bursting into tears and accusing herself of being the primary cause of their ruin, as for years and years now it had been necessary to pay for medical attendance and for taking her to almost every imaginable spring—La Bourboule, Aix, Lamalou, Amelie-les-Bains, and others. And the outcome of ten years of varied diagnosis and treatment was that the doctors had now abandoned her. Some thought her illness to be due to the rupture of certain ligaments, others believed in the presence of a tumour, others again to paralysis due to injury to the spinal cord, and as she, with maidenly revolt, refused to undergo any examination, and they did not even dare to address precise questions to her, they each contented themselves with their several opinions and declared that she was beyond cure. Moreover, she now solely relied upon the divine help, having grown rigidly pious since she had been suffering, and finding her only relief in her ardent faith. Every morning she herself read the holy offices, for to her great sorrow she was unable to go to church. Her inert limbs indeed seemed quite lifeless, and she had sunk into a condition of extreme weakness, to such a point, in fact, that on certain days it became necessary for her sister to place her food in her mouth.

Pierre was thinking of this when all at once he recalled an evening he had spent with her. The lamp had not yet been lighted, he was seated beside her in the growing obscurity, and she suddenly told him that she wished to go to Lourdes, feeling certain that she would return cured. He had experienced an uncomfortable sensation on hearing her speak in this fashion, and quite forgetting himself had exclaimed that it was folly to believe in such childishness. He had hitherto made it a rule never to converse with her on religious matters, having not only refused to be her confessor, but even to advise her with regard to the petty uncertainties of her pietism. In this respect he was influenced by feelings of mingled shame and compassion; to lie to her of all people would have made him suffer, and, moreover, he would have deemed himself a criminal had he even by a breath sullied that fervent pure faith which lent her such strength against pain. And so, regretting that he had not been able to restrain his exclamation, he remained sorely embarrassed, when all at once he felt the girl's cold hand take hold of his own. And then, emboldened by the darkness, she ventured in a gentle, faltering voice, to tell him that she already knew his secret, his misfortune, that wretchedness, so fearful for a priest, of being unable to believe.

Despite himself he had revealed everything during their chats together, and she, with the delicate intuition of a friend, had been able to read his conscience. She felt terribly distressed on his account; she deemed him, with that mortal moral malady, to be more deserving of pity than herself. And then as he, thunderstruck, was still unable to find an answer, acknowledging the truth of her words by his very silence, she again began to speak to him of Lourdes, adding in a low whisper that she wished to confide him as well as herself to the protection of the Blessed Virgin, whom she entreated to restore him to faith. And from that evening forward she did not cease speaking on the subject, repeating again and again, that if she went to Lourdes she would be surely cured. But she was prevented from making the journey by lack of means and she did not even dare to speak to her sister of the pecuniary question. So two months went by, and day by day she grew weaker, exhausted by her longing dreams, her eyes ever turned towards the flashing light of the miraculous Grotto far away. Pierre then experienced many painful days. He had at first told Marie that he would not accompany her. But his decision was somewhat shaken by the thought that if he made up his mind to go, he might profit by the journey to continue his inquiries with regard to Bernadette, whose charming image lingered in his heart. And at last he even felt penetrated by a delightful feeling, an unacknowledged hope, the hope that Marie was perhaps right, that the Virgin might take pity on him and restore to him his former blind faith, the faith of the child who loves and does not question. Oh! to believe, to believe with his whole soul, to plunge into faith for ever! Doubtless there was no other possible happiness. He longed for faith with all the joyousness of his youth, with all the love that he had felt for his mother, with all his burning desire to escape from the torment of understanding and knowing, and to slumber forever in the depths of divine ignorance. It was cowardly, and yet so delightful; to exist no more, to become a mere thing in the hands of the Divinity. And thus he was at last possessed by a desire to make the supreme experiment.

A week later the journey to Lourdes was decided upon. Pierre, however, had insisted on a final consultation of medical men in order to ascertain if it were really possible for Marie to travel; and this again was a scene which rose up before him, with certain incidents which he ever beheld whilst others were already fading from his mind. Two of the doctors who had formerly attended the patient, and one of whom believed in the rupture of certain ligaments, whilst the other asserted the case to be one of medullary paralysis, had ended by agreeing that this paralysis existed, and that there was also, possibly, some ligamentary injury. In their opinion all the symptoms pointed to this diagnosis, and the nature of the case seemed to them so evident that they did not hesitate to give certificates, each his own, agreeing almost word for word with one another, and so positive in character as to leave no room for doubt. Moreover, they thought that the journey was practicable, though it would certainly prove an exceedingly painful one. Pierre thereupon resolved to risk it, for he had found the doctors very prudent, and very desirous to arrive at the truth; and he retained but a confused recollection of the third medical man who had been called in, a distant cousin of his named De Beauclair, who was young, extremely intelligent, but little known as yet, and said by some to be rather strange in his theories. This doctor, after looking at Marie for a long time, had asked somewhat anxiously about her parents, and had seemed greatly interested by what was told him of M. de Guersaint, this architect and inventor with a weak and exuberant mind. Then he had desired to measure the sufferer's visual field, and by a slight discreet touch had ascertained the locality of the pain, which, under certain pressure, seemed to ascend like a heavy shifting mass towards the breast. He did not appear to attach importance to the paralysis of the legs; but on a direct question being put to him he exclaimed that the girl ought to be taken to Lourdes and that she would assuredly be cured there, if she herself were convinced of it. Faith sufficed, said he, with a smile; two pious lady patients of his, whom he had sent thither during the preceding year, had returned in radiant health. He even predicted how the miracle would come about; it would be like a lightning stroke, an awakening, an exaltation of the entire being, whilst the evil, that horrid, diabolical weight which stifled the poor girl would once more ascend and fly away as though emerging by her mouth. But at the same time he flatly declined to give a certificate. He had failed to agree with his two *confreres*, who treated him coldly, as though they considered him a wild, adventurous young fellow. Pierre confusedly remembered some shreds of the discussion which had begun again in his presence, some little part of the diagnosis framed by Beauclair. First, a dislocation of the organ, with a slight laceration of the ligaments, resulting from the patient's fall from her horse; then a slow healing, everything returning to its place, followed by consecutive nervous symptoms, so that the sufferer was now simply beset by her original fright, her attention fixed on the injured part, arrested there amidst increasing pain, incapable of acquiring fresh notions unless it were under the lash of some violent emotion. Moreover, he also admitted the probability of accidents due to nutrition, as yet unexplained, and on the course and importance of which he himself would not venture to give an opinion. However, the idea that Marie *dreamt* her disease, that the fearful sufferings torturing her came from an injury long since healed, appeared such a paradox to Pierre when he gazed at her and saw her in such agony, her limbs already stretched out lifeless on her bed of misery, that he did not even pause to consider it; but at that moment felt simply happy in the thought that all three doctors agreed in authorising the journey to Lourdes. To him it was sufficient that she *might* be cured, and to attain that result he would have followed her to the end of the world.

Ah! those last days of Paris, amid what a scramble they were spent! The national pilgrimage was about to start, and in order to avoid heavy expenses, it had occurred to him to obtain *hospitalisation* for Marie. Then he had been obliged to run about in order to obtain his own admission, as a helper, into the Hospitality of Our Lady of Salvation. M. de Guersaint was delighted with the prospect of the journey, for he was fond of nature, and ardently desired to become acquainted with the Pyrenees. Moreover, he did not allow anything to worry him, but was perfectly willing that the young priest should pay his railway fare, and provide for him at the hotel yonder as for a child; and his daughter Blanche, having slipped a twenty-franc piece into his hand at the last moment, he had even thought himself rich again. That poor brave Blanche had a little hidden store of her own, savings to the amount of fifty francs, which it had been absolutely necessary to accept, for she became quite angry in her determination to contribute towards her sister's cure, unable as she was to form one of the party, owing to the lessons which she had to give in Paris, whose hard pavements she must continue pacing, whilst her dear ones were kneeling yonder, amidst the enchantments of the Grotto. And so the others had started on, and were now rolling, ever rolling along.

As they passed the station of Chatellerault a sudden burst of voices made Pierre start, and drove away the torpor into which his reverie had plunged him. What was the matter? Were they reaching Poitiers? But it was only half-past twelve o'clock, and it was simply Sister Hyacinthe who had roused him, by making her patients and pilgrims say the Angelus, the three "Aves" thrice repeated. Then the voices burst forth, and the sound of a fresh canticle arose, and continued like a lamentation. Fully five and twenty minutes must elapse before they would reach Poitiers, where it seemed as if the half-hour's stoppage would bring relief to every suffering! They were all so uncomfortable, so roughly shaken in that malodorous, burning carriage! Such wretchedness was beyond endurance. Big tears coursed down the cheeks of Madame Vincent, a muttered oath escaped M. Sabathier usually so resigned, and Brother Isidore, La Grivotte, and Madame Vetu seemed to have become inanimate, mere waifs carried along by a torrent. Moreover, Marie no longer answered, but had closed her eyes and would not open them, pursued as she was by the horrible vision of Elise Rouquet's face, that face with its gaping cavities which seemed to her to be the image of death. And whilst the train increased its speed, bearing all this human despair onward, under the heavy sky, athwart the burning plains, there was yet another scare in the carriage. The strange man had apparently ceased to breathe, and a voice cried out that he was expiring.

III. POITIERS

AS soon as the train arrived at Poitiers, Sister Hyacinthe alighted in all haste, amidst the crowd of porters opening the carriage doors, and of pilgrims darting forward to reach the platform. "Wait a moment, wait a moment," she repeated, "let me pass first. I wish to see if all is over."

Then, having entered the other compartment, she raised the strange man's head, and seeing him so pale, with such blank eyes, she did at first think him already dead. At last, however, she detected a faint breathing. "No, no," she then exclaimed, "he still breathes. Quick! there is no time to be lost." And, perceiving the other Sister, she added: "Sister Claire des Anges, will you go and fetch Father Massias, who must be in the third or fourth carriage of the train? Tell him that we have a patient in very great danger here, and ask him to bring the Holy Oils at once."

Without answering, the other Sister at once plunged into the midst of the scramble. She was small, slender, and gentle, with a meditative air and mysterious eyes, but withal extremely active.

Pierre, who was standing in the other compartment watching the scene, now ventured to make a suggestion: "And would it not be as well to fetch the doctor?" said he.

"Yes, I was thinking of it," replied Sister Hyacinthe, "and, Monsieur l'Abbe, it would be very kind of you to go for him yourself."

It so happened that Pierre intended going to the cantine carriage to fetch some broth for Marie. Now that she was no longer being jolted she felt somewhat relieved, and had opened her eyes, and caused her father to raise her to a sitting posture. Keenly thirsting for fresh air, she would have much liked them to carry her out on to the platform for a moment, but she felt that it would be asking too much, that it would be too troublesome a task to place her inside the carriage again. So M. de Guersaint remained by himself on the platform, near the open door, smoking a cigarette, whilst Pierre hastened to the cantine van, where he knew he would find the doctor on duty, with his travelling pharmacy.

Some other patients, whom one could not think of removing, also remained in the carriage. Amongst them was La Grivotte, who was stifling and almost delirious, in such a state indeed as to detain Madame de Jonquiere, who had arranged to meet her daughter Raymonde, with Madame Volmar and Madame Desagneaux, in the refreshment-room, in order that they might all four lunch together. But that unfortunate creature seemed on the point of expiring, so how could she leave her all alone, on the hard seat of that carriage? On his side, M. Sabathier, likewise riveted to his seat, was waiting for his wife, who had gone to fetch a bunch of grapes for him; whilst Marthe had remained with her brother the missionary, whose faint moan never ceased. The others, those who were able to walk, had hustled one another in their haste to alight, all eager as they were to escape for a moment from that cage of wretchedness where their limbs had been quite numbed by the seven hours' journey which they had so far gone. Madame Maze had at once drawn apart, straying with melancholy face to the far end of the platform, where she found herself all alone; Madame Vetu, stupefied by her sufferings, had found sufficient strength to take a few steps, and sit down on a bench, in the full sunlight, where she did not even feel the burning heat; whilst Elise Rouquet, who had had the decency to cover her face with a black wrap, and was consumed by a desire for fresh water, went hither and thither in search of a drinking fountain. And meantime Madame Vincent, walking slowly, carried her little Rose about in her arms, trying to smile at her, and to cheer her by showing her some gaudily coloured picture bills, which the child gravely gazed at, but did not see.

Pierre had the greatest possible difficulty in making his way through the crowd inundating the platform. No effort of imagination could enable one to picture the living torrent of ailing and healthy beings which the train had here set down—a mob of more than a thousand persons just emerging from suffocation, and bustling, hurrying hither and thither. Each carriage had contributed its share of wretchedness, like some hospital ward suddenly evacuated; and it was now possible to form an idea of the frightful amount of suffering which this terrible white train carried along with it, this train which disseminated a legend of horror wheresoever it passed. Some infirm sufferers were dragging themselves about, others were being carried, and many remained in a heap on the platform. There were sudden pushes, violent calls, innumerable displays of distracted eagerness to reach the refreshment-room and the *buvette*. Each and all made haste, going wheresoever their wants called them. This stoppage of half an hour's duration, the only stoppage there would be before reaching Lourdes, was, after all, such a short one. And the only gay note, amidst all the black cassocks and the threadbare garments of the poor, never of any precise shade of colour, was supplied by the smiling whiteness of the Little Sisters of the Assumption, all bright and active in their snowy coifs, wimples, and aprons.

When Pierre at last reached the cantine van near the middle of the train, he found it already besieged. There was here a petroleum stove, with a small supply of cooking utensils. The broth prepared from concentrated meat-extract was being warmed in wrought-iron pans, whilst the preserved milk in tins was diluted and supplied as occasion required. There were some other provisions, such as biscuits, fruit, and chocolate, on a few shelves. But Sister Saint-Francois, to whom the service was entrusted, a short, stout woman of five-and-forty, with a good-natured fresh-coloured face, was somewhat losing her head in the presence of all the hands so eagerly stretched towards her. Whilst continuing her distribution, she lent ear to Pierre, as he called the doctor, who with his travelling pharmacy occupied another corner of the van. Then, when the young priest began to explain matters, speaking of the poor unknown man who was dying, a sudden desire came to her to go and see him, and she summoned another Sister to take her place.

"Oh! I wished to ask you, Sister, for some broth for a passenger who is ill," said Pierre, at that moment turning towards her.

"Very well, Monsieur l'Abbe, I will bring some. Go on in front."

The doctor and the abbe went off in all haste, rapidly questioning and answering one another, whilst behind them followed Sister Saint-Francois, carrying the bowl of broth with all possible caution amidst the jostling of the crowd. The doctor was a dark-complexioned man of eight-and-twenty, robust and extremely handsome, with the head of a young Roman emperor, such as may still be occasionally met with in the sunburnt land of Provence. As soon as Sister Hyacinthe caught sight of him, she raised an exclamation of surprise: "What! Monsieur Ferrand, is it you?" Indeed, they both seemed amazed at meeting in this manner.

It is, however, the courageous mission of the Sisters of the Assumption to tend the ailing poor, those who lie in agony in their humble garrets, and cannot pay for nursing; and thus these good women spend their lives among the wretched, installing themselves beside the sufferer's pallet in his tiny lodging, and ministering to every want, attending alike to cooking and cleaning, and living there as servants and relatives, until either cure or death supervenes. And it was in this wise that Sister Hyacinthe, young as she was, with her milky face, and her blue eyes which ever laughed, had installed herself one day in the abode of this young fellow, Ferrand, then a medical student, prostrated by typhoid fever, and so desperately poor that he lived in a kind of loft reached by a ladder, in the Rue du Four. And from that moment she had not stirred from his side, but had remained with him until she cured him, with the passion of one who lived only for others, one who when an infant had been found in a church porch, and who had no other family than that of those who suffered, to whom she devoted herself with all her ardently affectionate nature. And what a delightful month, what exquisite comradeship, fraught with the pure fraternity of suffering, had followed! When he called her "Sister," it was really to a sister that he was speaking. And she was a mother also, a mother who helped him to rise, and who put him to bed as though he were her child, without aught springing up between them save supreme pity, the divine, gentle compassion of charity. She ever showed herself gay, sexless, devoid of any instinct excepting that which prompted her to assuage and to console. And he worshipped her, venerated her, and had retained of her the most chaste and passionate of recollections.

"O Sister Hyacinthe!" he murmured in delight.

Chance alone had brought them face to face again, for Ferrand was not a believer, and if he found himself in that train it was simply because he had at the last moment consented to take the place of a friend who was suddenly prevented from coming. For nearly a twelvemonth he had been a house-surgeon at the Hospital of La Pitie. However, this journey to Lourdes, in such peculiar circumstances, greatly interested him.

The joy of the meeting was making them forget the ailing stranger. And so the Sister resumed: "You see, Monsieur Ferrand, it is for this man that we want you. At one moment we thought him dead. Ever since we passed Amboise he has been filling us with fear, and I have just sent for the Holy Oils. Do you find him so very low? Could you not revive him a little?"

The doctor was already examining the man, and thereupon the sufferers who had remained in the carriage became greatly interested and began to look. Marie, to whom Sister Saint-Francois had given the bowl of broth, was holding it with such an unsteady hand that Pierre had to take it from her, and endeavour to make her drink; but she could not swallow, and she left the broth scarce tasted, fixing her eyes upon the man waiting to see what would happen like one whose own existence is at stake.

"Tell me," again asked Sister Hyacinthe, "how do you find him? What is his illness?"

"What is his illness!" muttered Ferrand; "he has every illness."

Then, drawing a little phial from his pocket, he endeavoured to introduce a few drops of the contents between the sufferer's clenched teeth. The man heaved a sigh, raised his eyelids and let them fall again; that was all, he gave no other sign of life.

Sister Hyacinthe, usually so calm and composed, so little accustomed to despair, became impatient.

"But it is terrible," said she, "and Sister Claire des Anges does not come back! Yet I told her plainly enough where she would find Father Massias's carriage. *Mon Dieu!* what will become of us?"

Sister Saint-Francois, seeing that she could render no help, was now about to return to the cantine van. Before doing so, however, she inquired if the man were not simply dying of hunger; for such cases presented themselves, and indeed she had only come to the compartment with the view of offering some of her provisions. At last, as she went off, she promised that she would make Sister Claire des Anges hasten her return should she happen to meet her; and she had not gone twenty yards when she turned round and waved her arm to call attention to her colleague, who with discreet short steps was coming back alone.

Leaning out of the window, Sister Hyacinthe kept on calling to her, "Make haste, make haste! Well, and where is Father Massias?"

"He isn't there."

"What! not there?"

"No. I went as fast as I could, but with all these people about it was not possible to get there quickly. When I reached the carriage Father Massias had already alighted, and gone out of the station, no doubt."

She thereupon explained, that according to what she had heard, Father Massias and the priest of Sainte-Radegonde had some appointment together. In other years the national pilgrimage halted at Poitiers for four-and-twenty hours, and after those who were ill had been placed in the town hospital the others went in procession to Sainte-Radegonde.[1] That year, however, there was some obstacle to this course being followed, so the train was going straight on to Lourdes; and Father Massias was certainly with his friend the priest, talking with him on some matter of importance.

"They promised to tell him and send him here with the Holy Oils as soon as they found him," added Sister Claire.

---

[1] The church of Sainte-Radegonde, built by the saint of that name in the sixth century, is famous throughout Poitou. In the crypt between the tombs of Ste. Agnes and St. Disciole is that of Ste. Radegonde herself, but it now only contains some particles of her remains, as the greater portion was burnt by the Huguenots in 1562. On a previous occasion (1412) the tomb had been violated by Jean, Duc de Berry, who wished to remove both the saint's head and her two rings. Whilst he was making the attempt, however, the skeleton is said to have withdrawn its hand so that he might not possess himself of the rings. A greater curiosity which the church contains is a footprint on a stone slab, said to have been left by Christ when He appeared to Ste. Radegonde in her cell. This attracts pilgrims from many parts.—Trans.

However, this was quite a disaster for Sister Hyacinthe. Since Science was powerless, perhaps the Holy Oils would have brought the sufferer some relief. She had often seen that happen.

"O Sister, Sister, how worried I am!" she said to her companion. "Do you know, I wish you would go back and watch for Father Massias and bring him to me as soon as you see him. It would be so kind of you to do so!"

"Yes, Sister," compliantly answered Sister Claire des Anges, and off she went again with that grave, mysterious air of hers, wending her way through the crowd like a gliding shadow.

Ferrand, meantime, was still looking at the man, sorely distressed at his inability to please Sister Hyacinthe by reviving him. And as he made a gesture expressive of his powerlessness she again raised her voice entreatingly: "Stay with me, Monsieur Ferrand, pray stay," she said. "Wait till Father Massias comes—I shall be a little more at ease with you here."

He remained and helped her to raise the man, who was slipping down upon the seat. Then, taking a linen cloth, she wiped the poor fellow's face which a dense perspiration was continually covering. And the spell of waiting continued amid the uneasiness of the patients who had remained in the carriage, and the curiosity of the folks who had begun to assemble on the platform in front of the compartment.

All at once however a girl hastily pushed the crowd aside, and, mounting on the footboard, addressed herself to Madame de Jonquiere: "What is the matter, mamma?" she said. "They are waiting for you in the refreshment-room."

It was Raymonde de Jonquiere, who, already somewhat ripe for her four-and-twenty years, was remarkably like her mother, being very dark, with a pronounced nose, large mouth, and full, pleasant-looking face.

"But, my dear, you can see for yourself. I can't leave this poor woman," replied the lady-hospitaller; and thereupon she pointed to La Grivotte, who had been attacked by a fit of coughing which shook her frightfully.

"Oh, how annoying, mamma!" retorted Raymonde, "Madame Desagneaux and Madame Volmar were looking forward with so much pleasure to this little lunch together."

"Well, it can't be helped, my dear. At all events, you can begin without waiting for me. Tell the ladies that I will come and join them as soon as I can." Then, an idea occurring to her, Madame de Jonquiere added: "Wait a moment, the doctor is here. I will try to get him to take charge of my patient. Go back, I will follow you. As you can guess, I am dying of hunger."

Raymonde briskly returned to the refreshment-room whilst her mother begged Ferrand to come into her compartment to see if he could do something to relieve La Grivotte. At Marthe's request he had already examined Brother Isidore, whose moaning never ceased; and with a sorrowful gesture he had again confessed his powerlessness. However, he hastened to comply with Madame de Jonquiere's appeal, and raised the consumptive woman to a sitting posture in the hope of thus stopping her cough, which indeed gradually ceased. And then he helped the lady-hospitaller to make her swallow a spoonful of some soothing draught. The doctor's presence in the carriage was still causing a stir among the ailing ones. M. Sabathier, who was slowly eating the grapes which his wife had been to fetch him, did not, however, question Ferrand, for he knew full well what his answer would be, and was weary, as he expressed it, of consulting all the princes of science; nevertheless he felt comforted as it were at seeing him set that poor consumptive woman on her feet again. And even Marie watched all that the doctor did with increasing interest, though not daring to call him herself, certain as she also was that he could do nothing for her.

Meantime, the crush on the platform was increasing. Only a quarter of an hour now remained to the pilgrims. Madame Vetu, whose eyes were open but who saw nothing, sat like an insensible being in the broad sunlight, in the hope possibly that the scorching heat would deaden her pains; whilst up and down, in front of her, went Madame Vincent ever with the same sleep-inducing step and ever carrying her little Rose, her poor ailing birdie, whose weight was so trifling that she scarcely felt her in her arms. Many people meantime were hastening to the water tap in order to fill their pitchers, cans, and bottles. Madame Maze, who was of refined tastes and careful of her person, thought of going to wash her hands there; but just as she arrived she found Elise Rouquet drinking, and she recoiled at sight of that disease-smitten face, so terribly disfigured and robbed of nearly all semblance of humanity. And all the others likewise shuddered, likewise hesitated to fill their bottles, pitchers, and cans at the tap from which she had drunk.

A large number of pilgrims had now begun to eat whilst pacing the platform. You could hear the rhythmical taps of the crutches carried by a woman who incessantly wended her way through the groups. On the ground, a legless cripple was painfully dragging herself about in search of nobody knew what. Others, seated there in heaps, no longer stirred. All these sufferers, momentarily unpacked as it were, these patients of a travelling hospital emptied for a brief half-hour, were taking the air amidst the bewilderment and agitation of the healthy passengers; and the whole throng had a frightfully woeful, poverty-stricken appearance in the broad noontide light.

Pierre no longer stirred from the side of Marie, for M. de Guersaint had disappeared, attracted by a verdant patch of landscape which could be seen at the far end of the station. And, feeling anxious about her, since she had not been able to finish her broth, the young priest with a smiling air tried to tempt her palate by offering to go and buy her a peach; but she refused it; she was suffering too much, she cared for nothing. She was gazing at him with her large, woeful eyes, on the one hand impatient at this stoppage which delayed her chance of cure, and on the other terrified at the thought of again being jolted along that hard and endless railroad.

Just then a stout gentleman whose full beard was turning grey, and who had a broad, fatherly kind of face, drew near and touched Pierre's arm: "Excuse me, Monsieur l'Abbe," said he, "but is it not in this carriage that there is a poor man dying?"

And on the priest returning an affirmative answer, the gentleman became quite affable and familiar.

"My name is Vigneron," he said; "I am the head clerk at the Ministry of Finances, and applied for leave in order that I might help my wife to take our son Gustave to Lourdes. The dear lad places all his hope in the Blessed Virgin, to whom we pray morning and evening on his behalf. We are in a second-class compartment of the carriage just in front of yours."

Then, turning round, he summoned his party with a wave of the hand. "Come, come!" said he, "it is here. The unfortunate man is indeed in the last throes."

Madame Vigneron was a little woman with the correct bearing of a respectable *bourgeoise*, but her long, livid face denoted impoverished blood, terrible evidence of which was furnished by her son Gustave. The latter, who was fifteen years of age, looked scarcely ten. Twisted out of shape, he was a mere skeleton, with his right leg so wasted, so reduced, that he had to walk with a crutch. He had a small, thin face, somewhat awry, in which one saw little excepting his eyes, clear eyes, sparkling with intelligence, sharpened as it were by suffering, and doubtless well able to dive into the human soul.

An old puffy-faced lady followed the others, dragging her legs along with difficulty; and M. Vigneron, remembering that he had forgotten her, stepped back towards Pierre so that he might complete the introduction. "That lady," said he, "is Madame Chaise, my wife's eldest sister. She also wished to accompany Gustave, whom she is very fond of." And then, leaning forward, he added in a whisper, with a confidential air: "She is the widow of Chaise, the silk merchant, you know, who left such an immense fortune. She is suffering from a heart complaint which causes her much anxiety."

The whole family, grouped together, then gazed with lively curiosity at what was taking place in the railway carriage. People were incessantly flocking to the spot; and so that the lad might be the better able to see, his father took him up in his arms for a moment whilst his aunt held the crutch, and his mother on her side raised herself on tip-toe.

The scene in the carriage was still the same; the strange man was still stiffly seated in his corner, his head resting against the hard wood. He was livid, his eyes were closed, and his mouth was twisted by suffering; and every now and then Sister Hyacinthe with her linen cloth wiped away the cold sweat which was constantly covering his face. She no longer spoke, no longer evinced any impatience, but had recovered her serenity and relied on Heaven. From time to time she would simply glance towards the platform to see if Father Massias were coming.

"Look at him, Gustave," said M. Vigneron to his son; "he must be consumptive."

The lad, whom scrofula was eating away, whose hip was attacked by an abscess, and in whom there were already signs of necrosis of the vertebrae, seemed to take a passionate interest in the agony he thus beheld. It did not frighten him, he smiled at it with a smile of infinite sadness.

"Oh! how dreadful!" muttered Madame Chaise, who, living in continual terror of a sudden attack which would carry her off, turned pale with the fear of death.

"Ah! well," replied M. Vigneron, philosophically, "it will come to each of us in turn. We are all mortal."

Thereupon, a painful, mocking expression came over Gustave's smile, as though he had heard other words than those—perchance an unconscious wish, the hope that the old aunt might die before he himself did, that he would inherit the promised half-million of francs, and then not long encumber his family.

"Put the boy down now," said Madame Vigneron to her husband. "You are tiring him, holding him by the legs like that."

Then both she and Madame Chaise bestirred themselves in order that the lad might not be shaken. The poor darling was so much in need of care and attention. At each moment they feared that they might lose him. Even his father was of opinion that they had better put him in the train again at once. And as the two women went off with the child, the old gentleman once more turned towards Pierre, and with evident emotion exclaimed: "Ah! Monsieur l'Abbe, if God should take him from us, the light of our life would be extinguished—I don't speak of his aunt's fortune, which would go to other nephews. But it would be unnatural, would it not, that he should go off before her, especially as she is so ill? However, we are all in the hands of Providence, and place our reliance in the Blessed Virgin, who will assuredly perform a miracle."

Just then Madame de Jonquiere, having been reassured by Doctor Ferrand, was able to leave La Grivotte. Before going off, however, she took care to say to Pierre: "I am dying of hunger and am going to the refreshment-room for a moment. But if my patient should begin coughing again, pray come and fetch me."

When, after great difficulty, she had managed to cross the platform and reach the refreshment-room, she found herself in the midst of another scramble. The better-circumstanced pilgrims had taken the tables by assault, and a great many priests were to be seen hastily lunching amidst all the clatter of knives, forks, and crockery. The three or four waiters were not able to attend to all the requirements, especially as they were hampered in their movements by the crowd purchasing fruit, bread, and cold meat at the counter. It was at a little table at the far end of the room that Raymonde was lunching with Madame Desagneaux and Madame Volmar.

"Ah! here you are at last, mamma!" the girl exclaimed, as Madame de Jonquiere approached. "I was just going back to fetch you. You certainly ought to be allowed time to eat!"

She was laughing, with a very animated expression on her face, quite delighted as she was with the adventures of the journey and this indifferent scrambling meal. "There," said she, "I have kept you some trout with green sauce, and there's a cutlet also waiting for you. We have already got to the artichokes."

Then everything became charming. The gaiety prevailing in that little corner rejoiced the sight.

Young Madame Desagneaux was particularly adorable. A delicate blonde, with wild, wavy, yellow hair, a round, dimpled, milky face, a gay, laughing disposition, and a remarkably good heart, she had made a rich marriage, and for three years past had been wont to leave her husband at Trouville in the fine August weather, in order to accompany the national pilgrimage as a lady-hospitaller. This was her great passion, an access of quivering pity, a longing desire to place herself unreservedly at the disposal of the sick for five days, a real debauch of devotion from which she returned tired to death but full of intense delight. Her only regret was that she as yet had no children, and with comical passion, she occasionally expressed a regret that she had missed her true vocation, that of a sister of charity.

"Ah! my dear," she hastily said to Raymonde, "don't pity your mother for being so much taken up with her patients. She, at all events, has something to occupy her." And addressing herself to Madame de Jonquiere, she added: "If you only knew how long we find the time in our fine first-class carriage. We cannot even occupy ourselves with a little needlework, as it is forbidden. I asked for a place with the patients, but all were already distributed, so that my only resource will be to try to sleep to-night."

She began to laugh, and then resumed: "Yes, Madame Volmar, we will try to sleep, won't we, since talking seems to tire you?" Madame Volmar, who looked over thirty, was very dark, with a long face and delicate but drawn features. Her magnificent eyes shone out like brasiers, though every now and then a cloud seemed to veil and extinguish them. At the first glance she did not appear beautiful, but as you gazed at her she became more and more perturbing, till she conquered you and inspired you with passionate admiration. It should be said though that she shrank from all self-assertion, comporting herself with much modesty, ever keeping in the background, striving to hide her lustre, invariably clad in black and unadorned by a single jewel, although she was the wife of a Parisian diamond-merchant.

"Oh! for my part," she murmured, "as long as I am not hustled too much I am well pleased."

She had been to Lourdes as an auxiliary lady-helper already on two occasions, though but little had been seen of her there—at the hospital of Our Lady of Dolours—as, on arriving, she had been overcome by such great fatigue that she had been forced, she said, to keep her room.

However, Madame de Jonquiere, who managed the ward, treated her with good-natured tolerance. "Ah! my poor friends," said she, "there will be plenty of time for you to exert yourselves. Get to sleep if you can, and your turn will come when I can no longer keep up." Then addressing her daughter, she resumed: "And you would do well, darling, not to excite yourself too much if you wish to keep your head clear."

Raymonde smiled and gave her mother a reproachful glance: "Mamma, mamma, why do you say that? Am I not sensible?" she asked.

Doubtless she was not boasting, for, despite her youthful, thoughtless air, the air of one who simply feels happy in living, there appeared in her grey eyes an expression of firm resolution, a resolution to shape her life for herself.

"It is true," the mother confessed with a little confusion, "this little girl is at times more sensible than I am myself. Come, pass me the cutlet—it is welcome, I assure you. Lord! how hungry I was!"

The meal continued, enlivened by the constant laughter of Madame Desagneaux and Raymonde. The latter was very animated, and her face, which was already growing somewhat yellow through long pining for a suitor, again assumed the rosy bloom of twenty. They had to eat very fast, for only ten minutes now remained to them. On all sides one heard the growing tumult of customers who feared that they would not have time to take their coffee.

All at once, however, Pierre made his appearance; a fit of stifling had again come over La Grivotte; and Madame de Jonquiere hastily finished her artichoke and returned to her compartment, after kissing her daughter, who wished her "good-night" in a facetious way. The priest, however, had made a movement of surprise on perceiving Madame Volmar with the red cross of the lady-hospitallers on her black bodice. He knew her, for he still called at long intervals on old Madame Volmar, the diamond-merchant's mother, who had been one of his own mother's friends. She was the most terrible woman in the world, religious beyond all reason, so harsh and stern, moreover, as to close the very window shutters in order to prevent her daughter-in-law from looking into the street. And he knew the young woman's story, how she had been imprisoned on the very morrow of her marriage, shut up between her mother-in-law, who tyrannised over her, and her husband, a repulsively ugly monster who went so far as to beat her, mad as he was with jealousy, although he himself kept mistresses. The unhappy woman was not allowed out of the house excepting it were to go to mass. And one day, at La Trinite, Pierre had surprised her secret, on seeing her behind the church exchanging a few hasty words with a well-groomed, distinguished-looking man.

III. POITIERS

The priest's sudden appearance in the refreshment-room had somewhat disconcerted Madame Volmar.

"What an unexpected meeting, Monsieur l'Abbe!" she said, offering him her long, warm hand. "What a long time it is since I last saw you!" And thereupon she explained that this was the third year she had gone to Lourdes, her mother-in-law having required her to join the Association of Our Lady of Salvation. "It is surprising that you did not see her at the station when we started," she added. "She sees me into the train and comes to meet me on my return."

This was said in an apparently simple way, but with such a subtle touch of irony that Pierre fancied he could guess the truth. He knew that she really had no religious principles at all, and that she merely followed the rites and ceremonies of the Church in order that she might now and again obtain an hour's freedom; and all at once he intuitively realised that someone must be waiting for her yonder, that it was for the purpose of meeting him that she was thus hastening to Lourdes with her shrinking yet ardent air and flaming eyes, which she so prudently shrouded with a veil of lifeless indifference.

"For my part," he answered, "I am accompanying a friend of my childhood, a poor girl who is very ill indeed. I must ask your help for her; you shall nurse her."

Thereupon she faintly blushed, and he no longer doubted the truth of his surmise. However, Raymonde was just then settling the bill with the easy assurance of a girl who is expert in figures; and immediately afterwards Madame Desagneaux led Madame Volmar away. The waiters were now growing more distracted and the tables were fast being vacated; for, on hearing a bell ring, everybody had begun to rush towards the door.

Pierre, on his side, was hastening back to his carriage, when he was stopped by an old priest. "Ah! Monsieur le Cure," he said, "I saw you just before we started, but I was unable to get near enough to shake hands with you."

Thereupon he offered his hand to his brother ecclesiastic, who was looking and smiling at him in a kindly way. The Abbe Judaine was the parish priest of Saligny, a little village in the department of the Oise. Tall and sturdy, he had a broad pink face, around which clustered a mass of white, curly hair, and it could be divined by his appearance that he was a worthy man whom neither the flesh nor the spirit had ever tormented. He believed indeed firmly and absolutely, with a tranquil godliness, never having known a struggle, endowed as he was with the ready faith of a child who is unacquainted with human passions. And ever since the Virgin at Lourdes had cured him of a disease of the eyes, by a famous miracle which folks still talked about, his belief had become yet more absolute and tender, as though impregnated with divine gratitude.

"I am pleased that you are with us, my friend," he gently said; "for there is much in these pilgrimages for young priests to profit by. I am told that some of them at times experience a feeling of rebellion. Well, you will see all these poor people praying,—it is a sight which will make you weep. How can one do otherwise than place oneself in God's hands, on seeing so much suffering cured or consoled?"

The old priest himself was accompanying a patient; and he pointed to a first-class compartment, at the door of which hung a placard bearing the inscription: "M. l'Abbe Judaine, Reserved." Then lowering his voice, he said: "It is Madame Dieulafay, you know, the great banker's wife. Their chateau, a royal domain, is in my parish, and when they learned that the Blessed Virgin had vouchsafed me such an undeserved favour, they begged me to intercede for their poor sufferer. I have already said several masses, and most sincerely pray for her. There, you see her yonder on the ground. She insisted on being taken out of the carriage, in spite of all the trouble which one will have to place her in it again."

On a shady part of the platform, in a kind of long box, there was, as the old priest said, a woman whose beautiful, perfectly oval face, lighted up by splendid eyes, denoted no greater age than six-and-twenty. She was suffering from a frightful disease. The disappearance from her system of the calcareous salts had led to a softening of the osseous framework, the slow destruction of her bones. Three years previously, after the advent of a stillborn child, she had felt vague pains in the spinal column. And then, little by little, her bones had rarefied and lost shape, the vertebrae had sunk, the bones of the pelvis had flattened, and those of the arms and legs had contracted. Thus shrunken, melting away as it were, she had become a mere human remnant, a nameless, fluid thing, which could not be set erect, but had to be carried hither and thither with infinite care, for fear lest she should vanish between one's fingers. Her face, a motionless face, on which sat a stupefied imbecile expression, still retained its beauty of outline, and yet it was impossible to gaze at this wretched shred of a woman without feeling a heart-pang, the keener on account of all the luxury surrounding her; for not only was the box in which she lay lined with blue quilted silk, but she was covered with valuable lace, and a cap of rare valenciennes was set upon her head, her wealth thus being proclaimed, displayed, in the midst of her awful agony.

"Ah! how pitiable it is," resumed the Abbe Judaine in an undertone. "To think that she is so young, so pretty, possessed of millions of money! And if you knew how dearly loved she was, with what adoration she is still surrounded. That tall gentleman near her is her husband, that elegantly dressed lady is her sister, Madame Jousseur."

Pierre remembered having often noticed in the newspapers the name of Madame Jousseur, wife of a diplomatist, and a conspicuous member of the higher spheres of Catholic society in Paris. People had even circulated a story of some great passion which she had fought against and vanquished. She also was very prettily dressed, with marvellously tasteful simplicity, and she ministered to the wants of her sorry sister with an air of perfect devotion. As for the unhappy woman's husband, who at the age of five-and-thirty had inherited his father's colossal business, he was a clear-complexioned, well-groomed, handsome man, clad in a closely buttoned frock-coat. His eyes, however, were full of tears, for he adored his wife, and had left his business in order to take her to Lourdes, placing his last hope in this appeal to the mercy of Heaven.

Ever since the morning, Pierre had beheld many frightful sufferings in that woeful white train. But none had so distressed his soul as did that wretched female skeleton, slowly liquefying in the midst of its lace and its millions. "The unhappy woman!" he murmured with a shudder.

The Abbe Judaine, however, made a gesture of serene hope. "The Blessed Virgin will cure her," said he; "I have prayed to her so much."

Just then a bell again pealed, and this time it was really the signal for starting. Only two minutes remained. There was a last rush, and folks hurried back towards the train carrying eatables wrapped in paper, and bottles and cans which they had filled with water. Several of them quite lost their heads, and in their inability to find their carriages, ran distractedly from one to the other end of the train; whilst some of the infirm ones dragged themselves about amidst the precipitate tapping of crutches, and others, only able to walk with difficulty, strove to hasten their steps whilst leaning on the arms of some of the lady-hospitallers. It was only with infinite difficulty that four men managed to replace Madame Dieulafay in her first-class compartment. The Vignerons, who were content with second-class accommodation, had already reinstalled themselves in their quarters amidst an extraordinary heap of baskets, boxes, and valises which scarcely allowed little Gustave enough room to stretch his poor puny limbs—the limbs as it were of a deformed insect. And then all the women appeared again: Madame Maze gliding along in silence; Madame Vincent raising her dear little girl in her outstretched arms and dreading lest she should hear her cry out; Madame Vetu, whom it had been necessary to push into the train, after rousing her from her stupefying torment; and Elise Rouquet, who was quite drenched through her obstinacy in endeavouring to drink from the tap, and was still wiping her monstrous face. Whilst each returned to her place and the carriage filled once more, Marie listened to her father, who had come back delighted with his stroll to a pointsman's little house beyond the station, whence a really pleasant stretch of landscape could be discerned.

"Shall we lay you down again at once?" asked Pierre, sorely distressed by the pained expression on Marie's face.

"Oh no, no, by-and-by!" she replied. "I shall have plenty of time to hear those wheels roaring in my head as though they were grinding my bones."

Then, as Ferrand seemed on the point of returning to the cantine van, Sister Hyacinthe begged him to take another look at the strange man before he went off. She was still waiting for Father Massias, astonished at the inexplicable delay in his arrival, but not yet without hope, as Sister Claire des Anges had not returned.

"Pray, Monsieur Ferrand," said she, "tell me if this unfortunate man is in any immediate danger."

The young doctor again looked at the sufferer, felt him, and listened to his breathing. Then with a gesture of discouragement he answered in a low voice, "I feel convinced that you will not get him to Lourdes alive."

Every head was still anxiously stretched forward. If they had only known the man's name, the place he had come from, who he was! But it was impossible to extract a word from this unhappy stranger, who was about to die there, in that carriage, without anybody being able to give his face a name!

It suddenly occurred to Sister Hyacinthe to have him searched. Under the circumstances there could certainly be no harm in such a course. "Feel in his pockets, Monsieur Ferrand," she said.

The doctor thereupon searched the man in a gentle, cautious way, but the only things that he found in his pockets were a chaplet, a knife, and three sous. And nothing more was ever learnt of the man.

At that moment, however, a voice announced that Sister Claire des Anges was at last coming back with Father Massias. All this while the latter had simply been chatting with the priest of Sainte-Radegonde in one of the waiting-rooms. Keen emotion attended his arrival; for a moment all seemed saved. But the train was about to start, the porters were already closing the carriage doors, and it was necessary that extreme unction should be administered in all haste in order to avoid too long a delay.

"This way, reverend Father!" exclaimed Sister Hyacinthe; "yes, yes, pray come in; our unfortunate patient is here."

Father Massias, who was five years older than Pierre, whose fellow-student however he had been at the seminary, had a tall, spare figure with an ascetic countenance, framed round with a light-coloured beard and vividly lighted up by burning eyes, He was neither the priest harassed by doubt, nor the priest with childlike faith, but an apostle carried away by his passion, ever ready to fight and vanquish for the pure glory of the Blessed Virgin. In his black cloak with its large hood, and his broad-brimmed flossy hat, he shone resplendently with the perpetual ardour of battle.

He immediately took from his pocket the silver case containing the Holy Oils, and the ceremony began whilst the last carriage doors were being slammed and belated pilgrims were rushing back to the train; the station-master, meantime, anxiously glancing at the clock, and realising that it would be necessary for him to grant a few minutes' grace.

"*Credo in unum Deum*," hastily murmured the Father.

"*Amen*," replied Sister Hyacinthe and the other occupants of the carriage.

Those who had been able to do so, had knelt upon the seats, whilst the others joined their hands, or repeatedly made the sign of the cross; and when the murmured prayers were followed by the Litanies of the ritual, every voice rose, an ardent desire for the remission of the man's sins and for his physical and spiritual cure winging its flight heavenward with each successive *Kyrie eleison*. Might his whole life, of which they knew nought, be forgiven him; might he enter, stranger though he was, in triumph into the Kingdom of God!

"*Christe, exaudi nos*."

"*Ora pro nobis, sancta Dei Genitrix*."

Father Massias had pulled out the silver needle from which hung a drop of Holy Oil. In the midst of such a scramble, with the whole train waiting—many people now thrusting their heads out of the carriage windows in surprise at the delay in starting—he could not think of following the usual practice, of anointing in turn all the organs of the senses, those portals of the soul which give admittance to evil.

He must content himself, as the rules authorised him to do in pressing cases, with one anointment; and this he made upon the man's lips, those livid parted lips from between which only a faint breath escaped, whilst the rest of his face, with its lowered eyelids, already seemed indistinct, again merged into the dust of the earth.

"*Per istam sanctam unctionem*," said the Father, "*et suam piissimam misericordiam indulgeat tibi Dominus quidquid per visum, auditum, odoratum, gustum, tactum, deliquisti*."[1]

The remainder of the ceremony was lost amid the hurry and scramble of the departure. Father Massias scarcely had time to wipe off the oil with the little piece of cotton-wool which Sister Hyacinthe held in readiness, before he had to leave the compartment and get into his own as fast as possible, setting the case containing the Holy Oils in order as he did so, whilst the pilgrims finished repeating the final prayer.

---

[1] Through this holy unction and His most tender mercy may the Lord pardon thee whatever sins thou hast committed by thy sight, hearing, etc.

III. POITIERS

"We cannot wait any longer! It is impossible!" repeated the station-master as he bustled about. "Come, come, make haste everybody!"

At last then they were about to resume their journey. Everybody sat down, returned to his or her corner again. Madame de Jonquiere, however, had changed her place, in order to be nearer La Grivotte, whose condition still worried her, and she was now seated in front of M. Sabathier, who remained waiting with silent resignation. Moreover, Sister Hyacinthe had not returned to her compartment, having decid-decided to remain near the unknown man so that she might watch over him and help him. By following this course, too, she was able to minister to Brother Isidore, whose sufferings his sister Marthe was at a loss to assuage. And Marie, turning pale, felt the jolting of the train in her ailing flesh, even before it had resumed its journey under the heavy sun, rolling onward once more with its load of sufferers stifling in the pestilential atmosphere of the over-heated carriages.

At last a loud whistle resounded, the engine puffed, and Sister Hyacinthe rose up to say: The *Magnificat*, my children!

IV. MIRACLES

JUST as the train was beginning to move, the door of the compartment in which Pierre and Marie found themselves was opened and a porter pushed a girl of fourteen inside, saying: "There's a seat here—make haste!"

The others were already pulling long faces and were about to protest, when Sister Hyacinthe exclaimed: "What, is it you, Sophie? So you are going back to see the Blessed Virgin who cured you last year!"

And at the same time Madame de Jonquiere remarked: "Ah! Sophie, my little friend, I am very pleased to see that you are grateful."

"Why, yes, Sister; why, yes, madame," answered the girl, in a pretty way.

The carriage door had already been closed again, so that it was necessary that they should accept the presence of this new pilgrim who had fallen from heaven as it were at the very moment when the train, which she had almost missed, was starting off again. She was a slender damsel and would not take up much room. Moreover these ladies knew her, and all the patients had turned their eyes upon her on hearing that the Blessed Virgin had been pleased to cure her. They had now got beyond the station, the engine was still puffing, whilst the wheels increased their speed, and Sister Hyacinthe, clapping her hands, repeated: "Come, come, my children, the *Magnificat*."

Whilst the joyful chant arose amidst the jolting of the train, Pierre gazed at Sophie. She was evidently a young peasant girl, the daughter of some poor husbandman of the vicinity of Poitiers, petted by her parents, treated in fact like a young lady since she had become the subject of a miracle, one of the elect, whom the priests of the district flocked to see. She wore a straw hat with pink ribbons, and a grey woollen dress trimmed with a flounce. Her round face although not pretty was a very pleasant one, with a beautifully fresh complexion and clear, intelligent eyes which lent her a smiling, modest air.

When the *Magnificat* had been sung, Pierre was unable to resist his desire to question Sophie. A child of her age, with so candid an air, so utterly unlike a liar, greatly interested him.

"And so you nearly missed the train, my child?" he said.

"I should have been much ashamed if I had, Monsieur l'Abbe," she replied. "I had been at the station since twelve o'clock. And all at once I saw his reverence, the priest of Sainte-Radegonde, who knows me well and who called me to him, to kiss me and tell me that it was very good of me to go back to Lourdes. But it seems the train was starting and I only just had time to run on to the platform. Oh! I ran so fast!"

She paused, laughing, still slightly out of breath, but already repenting that she had been so giddy.

"And what is your name, my child?" asked Pierre.

"Sophie Couteau, Monsieur l'Abbe."

"You do not belong to the town of Poitiers?"

"Oh no! certainly not. We belong to Vivonne, which is seven kilometres away. My father and mother have a little land there, and things would not be so bad if there were not eight children at home—I am the fifth,—fortunately the four older ones are beginning to work."

"And you, my child, what do you do?"

"I, Monsieur l'Abbe! Oh! I am no great help. Since last year, when I came home cured, I have not been left quiet a single day, for, as you can understand, so many people have come to see me, and then too I have been taken to Monseigneur's,[1] and to the convents and all manner of other places. And before all that I was a long time ill. I could not walk without a stick, and each step I took made me cry out, so dreadfully did my foot hurt me."

"So it was of some injury to the foot that the Blessed Virgin cured you?"

Sophie did not have time to reply, for Sister Hyacinthe, who was listening, intervened: "Of caries of the bones of the left heel, which had been going on for three years," said she. "The foot was swollen and quite deformed, and there were fistulas giving egress to continual suppuration."

On hearing this, all the sufferers in the carriage became intensely interested. They no longer took their eyes off this little girl on whom a miracle had been performed, but scanned her from head to foot as though seeking for some sign of the prodigy. Those who were able to stand rose up in order that they might the better see her, and the others, the infirm ones, stretched on their mattresses, strove to raise themselves and turn their heads. Amidst the suffering which had again come upon them on leaving Poitiers, the terror which filled them at the thought that they must continue rolling onward for another fifteen hours, the sudden advent of this child, favoured by Heaven, was like a divine relief, a ray of hope whence they would derive sufficient strength to accomplish the remainder of their terrible journey. The moaning had abated somewhat already, and every face was turned towards the girl with an ardent desire to believe.

This was especially the case with Marie, who, already reviving, joined her trembling hands, and in a gentle supplicating voice said to Pierre, "Question her, pray question her, ask her to tell us everything—cured, O God! cured of such a terrible complaint!"

Madame de Jonquiere, who was quite affected, had leant over the partition to kiss the girl. "Certainly," said she, "our little friend will tell you all about it. Won't you, my darling? You will tell us what the Blessed Virgin did for you?"

"Oh, certainly! madame-as much as you like," answered Sophie with her smiling, modest air, her eyes gleaming with intelligence. Indeed, she wished to begin at once, and raised her right hand with a pretty gesture, as a sign to everybody to be attentive. Plainly enough, she had already acquired the habit of speaking in public.

---

[1] The Bishop's residence.

She could not be seen, however, from some parts of the carriage, and an idea came to Sister Hyacinthe, who said: "Get up on the seat, Sophie, and speak loudly, on account of the noise which the train makes."

This amused the girl, and before beginning she needed time to become serious again. "Well, it was like this," said she; "my foot was past cure, I couldn't even go to church any more, and it had to be kept bandaged, because there was always a lot of nasty matter coming from it. Monsieur Rivoire, the doctor, who had made a cut in it, so as to see inside it, said that he should be obliged to take out a piece of the bone; and that, sure enough, would have made me lame for life. But when I got to Lourdes and had prayed a great deal to the Blessed Virgin, I went to dip my foot in the water, wishing so much that I might be cured that I did not even take the time to pull the bandage off. And everything remained in the water, there was no longer anything the matter with my foot when I took it out."

A murmur of mingled surprise, wonder, and desire arose and spread among those who heard this marvellous tale, so sweet and soothing to all who were in despair. But the little one had not yet finished. She had simply paused. And now, making a fresh gesture, holding her arms somewhat apart, she concluded: "When I got back to Vivonne and Monsieur Rivoire saw my foot again, he said: 'Whether it be God or the Devil who has cured this child, it is all the same to me; but in all truth she *is* cured.'"

This time a burst of laughter rang out. The girl spoke in too recitative a way, having repeated her story so many times already that she knew it by heart. The doctor's remark was sure to produce an effect, and she herself laughed at it in advance, certain as she was that the others would laugh also. However, she still retained her candid, touching air.

But she had evidently forgotten some particular, for Sister Hyacinthe, a glance from whom had foreshadowed the doctor's jest, now softly prompted her "And what was it you said to Madame la Comtesse, the superintendent of your ward, Sophie?"

"Ah! yes. I hadn't brought many bandages for my foot with me, and I said to her, 'It was very kind of the Blessed Virgin to cure me the first day, as I should have run out of linen on the morrow.'"

This provoked a fresh outburst of delight. They all thought her so nice, to have been cured like that! And in reply to a question from Madame de Jonquiere, she also had to tell the story of her boots, a pair of beautiful new boots which Madame la Comtesse had given her, and in which she had run, jumped, and danced about, full of childish delight. Boots! think of it, she who for three years had not even been able to wear a slipper.

Pierre, who had become grave, waxing pale with the secret uneasiness which was penetrating him, continued to look at her. And he also asked her other questions. She was certainly not lying, and he merely suspected a slow distortion of the actual truth, an easily explained embellishment of the real facts amidst all the joy she felt at being cured and becoming an important little personage. Who now knew if the cicatrisation of her injuries, effected, so it was asserted, completely, instantaneously, in a few seconds, had not in reality been the work of days? Where were the witnesses?

Just then Madame de Jonquiere began to relate that she had been at the hospital at the time referred to. "Sophie was not in my ward," said she, "but I had met her walking lame that very morning—"

Pierre hastily interrupted the lady-hospitaller. "Ah! you saw her foot before and after the immersion?"

"No, no! I don't think that anybody was able to see it, for it was bound round with bandages. She told you that the bandages had fallen into the piscina." And, turning towards the child, Madame de Jonquiere added, "But she will show you her foot—won't you, Sophie? Undo your shoe."

The girl took off her shoe, and pulled down her stocking, with a promptness and ease of manner which showed how thoroughly accustomed she had become to it all. And she not only stretched out her foot, which was very clean and very white, carefully tended indeed, with well-cut, pink nails, but complacently turned it so that the young priest might examine it at his ease. Just below the ankle there was a long scar, whose whity seam, plainly defined, testified to the gravity of the complaint from which the girl had suffered.

"Oh! take hold of the heel, Monsieur l'Abbe," said she. "Press it as hard as you like. I no longer feel any pain at all."

Pierre made a gesture from which it might have been thought that he was delighted with the power exercised by the Blessed Virgin. But he was still tortured by doubt. What unknown force had acted in this case? Or rather what faulty medical diagnosis, what assemblage of errors and exaggerations, had ended in this fine tale?

All the patients, however, wished to see the miraculous foot, that outward and visible sign of the divine cure which each of them was going in search of. And it was Marie, sitting up in her box, and already feeling less pain, who touched it first. Then Madame Maze, quite roused from her melancholy, passed it on to Madame Vincent, who would have kissed it for the hope which it restored to her. M. Sabathier had listened to all the explanations with a beatific air; Madame Vetu, La Grivotte, and even Brother Isidore opened their eyes, and evinced signs of interest; whilst the face of Elise Rouquet had assumed an extraordinary expression, transfigured by faith, almost beatified. If a sore had thus disappeared, might not her own sore close and disappear, her face retaining no trace of it save a slight scar, and again becoming such a face as other people had? Sophie, who was still standing, had to hold on to one of the iron rails, and place her foot on the partition, now on the right, now on the left. And she did not weary of it all, but felt exceedingly happy and proud at the many exclamations which were raised, the quivering admiration and religious respect which were bestowed on that little piece of her person, that little foot which had now, so to say, become sacred.

"One must possess great faith, no doubt," said Marie, thinking aloud. "One must have a pure unspotted soul." And, addressing herself to M. de Guersaint, she added: "Father, I feel that I should get well if I were ten years old, if I had the unspotted soul of a little girl."

"But you are ten years old, my darling! Is it not so, Pierre? A little girl of ten years old could not have a more spotless soul."

Possessed of a mind prone to chimeras, M. de Guersaint was fond of hearing tales of miracles. As for the young priest, profoundly affected by the ardent purity which the young girl evinced, he no longer sought to discuss the question, but let her surrender herself to the consoling illusions which Sophie's tale had wafted through the carriage.

The temperature had become yet more oppressive since their departure from Poitiers, a storm was rising in the coppery sky, and it seemed as though the train were rushing through a furnace. The villages passed, mournful and solitary under the burning sun. At Couhe-Verac they had again said their chaplets, and sung another canticle. At present, however, there was some slight abatement of the religious exercises. Sister Hyacinthe, who had not yet been able to lunch, ventured to eat a roll and some fruit in all haste, whilst still ministering to the strange man whose faint, painful breathing seemed to have become more regular. And it was only on passing Ruffec at three o'clock that they said the vespers of the Blessed Virgin.

"*Ora pro nobis, sancta Dei Genitrix.*"

"*Ut digni efficiamur promissionibus Christi.*"[1]

As they were finishing, M. Sabathier, who had watched little Sophie while she put on her shoe and stocking, turned towards M. de Guersaint.

"This child's case is interesting, no doubt," he remarked. "But it is a mere nothing, monsieur, for there have been far more marvellous cures than that. Do you know the story of Pierre de Rudder, a Belgian working-man?"

Everybody had again begun to listen.

"This man," continued M. Sabathier, "had his leg broken by the fall of a tree. Eight years afterwards the two fragments of the bone had not yet joined together again—the two ends could be seen in the depths of a sore which was continually suppurating; and the leg hung down quite limp, swaying in all directions. Well, it was sufficient for this man to drink a glassful of the miraculous water, and his leg was made whole again. He was able to walk without crutches, and the doctor said to him: 'Your leg is like that of a new-born child.' Yes, indeed, a perfectly new leg."

Nobody spoke, but the listeners exchanged glances of ecstasy.

"And, by the way," resumed M. Sabathier, "it is like the story of Louis Bouriette, a quarryman, one of the first of the Lourdes miracles. Do you know it? Bouriette had been injured by an explosion during some blasting operations. The sight of his right eye was altogether destroyed, and he was even threatened with the loss of the left one. Well, one day he sent his daughter to fetch a bottleful of the muddy water of the source, which then scarcely bubbled up to the surface. He washed his eye with this muddy liquid, and prayed fervently. And, all at once, he raised a cry, for he could see, monsieur, see as well as you and I. The doctor who was attending him drew up a detailed narrative of the case, and there cannot be the slightest doubt about its truth."

"It is marvellous," murmured M. de Guersaint in his delight.

"Would you like another example, monsieur? I can give you a famous one, that of Francois Macary, the carpenter of Lavaur. During eighteen years he had suffered from a deep varicose ulcer, with considerable enlargement of the tissues in the mesial part of the left leg. He had reached such a point that he could no longer move, and science decreed that he would forever remain infirm. Well, one evening he shuts himself up with a bottle of Lourdes water. He takes off his bandages, washes both his legs, and drinks what little water then remains in the bottle. Then he goes to bed and falls asleep; and when he awakes, he feels his legs and looks at them. There is nothing left;

[1] "Pray for us, O holy Mother of God, That we may be made worthy of the promises of Christ."

the varicose enlargement, the ulcers, have all disappeared. The skin of his knee, monsieur, had become as smooth, as fresh as it had been when he was twenty."

This time there was an explosion of surprise and admiration. The patients and the pilgrims were entering into the enchanted land of miracles, where impossibilities are accomplished at each bend of the pathways, where one marches on at ease from prodigy to prodigy. And each had his or her story to tell, burning with a desire to contrib-contribute a fresh proof, to fortify faith and hope by yet another example.

That silent creature, Madame Maze, was so transported that she spoke the first. "I have a friend," said she, "who knew the Widow Rizan, that lady whose cure also created so great a stir. For four-and-twenty years her left side had been entirely paralysed. Her stomach was unable to retain any solid food, and she had become an inert bag of bones which had to be turned over in bed, The friction of the sheets, too, had ended by rubbing her skin away in parts. Well, she was so low one evening that the doctor announced that she would die during the night. An hour later, however, she emerged from her torpor and asked her daughter in a faint voice to go and fetch her a glass of Lourdes water from a neighbour's. But she was only able to obtain this glass of water on the following morning; and she cried out to her daughter: 'Oh! it is life that I am drinking—rub my face with it, rub my arm and my leg, rub my whole body with it!' And when her daughter obeyed her, she gradually saw the huge swelling subside, and the paralysed, tumefied limbs recover their natural suppleness and appearance. Nor was that all, for Madame Rizan cried out that she was cured and felt hungry, and wanted bread and meat—she who had eaten none for four-and-twenty years! And she got out of bed and dressed herself, whilst her daughter, who was so overpowered that the neighbours thought she had become an orphan, replied to them: 'No, no, mamma isn't dead, she has come to life again!'"

This narrative had brought tears to Madame Vincent's eyes. Ah! if she had only been able to see her little Rose recover like that, eat with a good appetite, and run about again! At the same time, another case, which she had been told of in Paris and which had greatly influenced her in deciding to take her ailing child to Lourdes, returned to her memory.

"And I, too," said she, "know the story of a girl who was paralysed. Her name was Lucie Druon, and she was an inmate of an orphan asylum. She was quite young and could not even kneel down. Her limbs were bent like hoops. Her right leg, the shorter of the two, had ended by becoming twisted round the left one; and when any of the other girls carried her about you saw her feet hanging down quite limp, like dead ones. Please notice that she did not even go to Lourdes. She simply performed a novena; but she fasted during the nine days, and her desire to be cured was so great that she spent her nights in prayer. At last, on the ninth day, whilst she was drinking a little Lourdes water, she felt a violent commotion in her legs. She picked herself up, fell down, picked herself up again and walked. All her little companions, who were astonished, almost frightened at the sight, began to cry out 'Lucie can walk! Lucie can walk!' It was quite true. In a few seconds her legs had become straight and strong and healthy. She crossed the courtyard and was able to climb up the steps of the chapel, where the whole sisterhood, transported with gratitude, chanted the *Magnificat*. Ah! the dear child, how happy, how happy she must have been!"

As Madame Vincent finished, two tears fell from her cheeks on to the pale face of her little girl, whom she kissed distractedly.

The general interest was still increasing, becoming quite impassioned. The rapturous joy born of these beautiful stories, in which Heaven invariably triumphed over human reality, transported these childlike souls to such a point that those who were suffering the most grievously sat up in their turn, and recovered the power of speech. And with the narratives of one and all was blended a thought of the sufferer's own ailment, a belief that he or she would also be cured, since a malady of the same description had vanished like an evil dream beneath the breath of the Divinity.

"Ah!" stammered Madame Vetu, her articulation hindered by her sufferings, "there was another one, Antoinette Thardivail, whose stomach was being eaten away like mine. You would have said that dogs were devouring it, and sometimes there was a swelling in it as big as a child's head. Tumours indeed were ever forming in it, like fowl's eggs, so that for eight months she brought up blood. And she also was at the point of death, with nothing but her skin left on her bones, and dying of hunger, when she drank some water of Lourdes and had the pit of her stomach washed with it. Three minutes afterwards, her doctor, who on the previous day had left her almost in the last throes, scarce breathing, found her up and sitting by the fireside, eating a tender chicken's wing with a good appetite. She had no more tumours, she laughed as she had laughed when she was twenty, and her face had regained the brilliancy of youth. Ah! to be able to eat what one likes, to become young again, to cease suffering!"

"And the cure of Sister Julienne!" then exclaimed La Grivotte, raising herself on one of her elbows, her eyes glittering with fever. "In her case it commenced with a bad cold as it did with me, and then she began to spit blood. And every six months she fell ill again and had to take to her bed. The last time everybody said that she wouldn't leave it alive. The doctors had vainly tried every remedy, iodine, blistering, and cauterising. In fact, hers was a real case of phthisis, certified by half a dozen medical men. Well, she comes to Lourdes, and Heaven alone knows amidst what awful suffering—she was so bad, indeed, that at Toulouse they thought for a moment that she was about to die! The Sisters had to carry her in their arms, and on reaching the piscina the lady-hospitallers wouldn't bathe her. She was dead, they said. No matter! she was undressed at last, and plunged into the water, quite unconscious and covered with perspiration. And when they took her out she was so pale that they laid her on the ground, thinking that it was certainly all over with her at last. But, all at once, colour came back to her cheeks, her eyes opened, and she drew a long breath. She was cured; she dressed herself without any help and made a good meal after she had been to the Grotto to thank the Blessed Virgin. There! there's no gainsaying it, that was a real case of phthisis, completely cured as though by medicine!"

Thereupon Brother Isidore in his turn wished to speak; but he was unable to do so at any length, and could only with difficulty manage to say to his sister: "Marthe, tell them the story of Sister Dorothee which the priest of Saint-Sauveur related to us."

"Sister Dorothee," began the peasant girl in an awkward way, "felt her leg quite numbed when she got up one morning, and from that time she lost the use of it, for it got as cold and as heavy as a stone. Besides which she felt a great pain in the back. The doctors couldn't understand it. She saw half a dozen of them, who pricked her with pins and burnt her skin with a lot of drugs. But it was just as if they had sung to her. Sister Dorothee had well understood that only the Blessed Virgin could find the right remedy for her, and so she went off to Lourdes, and had herself dipped in the piscina. She thought at first that the water was going to kill her, for it was so bitterly cold. But by-and-by it became so soft that she fancied it was warm, as nice as milk. She had never felt so nice before, it seemed to her as if her veins were opening and the water were flowing into them. As you will understand, life was returning into her body since the Blessed Virgin was concerning herself in the case. She no longer had anything the matter with her when she came out, but walked about, ate the whole of a pigeon for her dinner, and slept all night long like the happy woman she was. Glory to the Blessed Virgin, eternal gratitude to the most Powerful Mother and her Divine Son!"

Elise Rouquet would also have liked to bring forward a miracle which she was acquainted with. Only she spoke with so much difficulty owing to the deformity of her mouth, that she had not yet been able to secure a turn. Just then, however, there was a pause, and drawing the wrap, which concealed the horror of her sore, slightly on one side, she profited by the opportunity to begin.

"For my part, I wasn't told anything about a great illness, but it was a very funny case at all events," she said. "It was about a woman, Celestine Dubois, as she was called, who had run a needle right into her hand while she was washing. It stopped there for seven years, for no doctor was able to take it out. Her hand shrivelled up, and she could no longer open it. Well, she got to Lourdes, and dipped her hand into the piscina. But as soon as she did so she began to shriek, and took it out again. Then they caught hold of her and put her hand into the water by force, and kept it there while she continued sobbing, with her face covered with sweat. Three times did they plunge her hand into the piscina, and each time they saw the needle moving along, till it came out by the tip of the thumb. She shrieked, of course, because the needle was moving though her flesh just as though somebody had been pushing it to drive it out. And after that Celestine never suffered again, and only a little scar could be seen on her hand as a mark of what the Blessed Virgin had done."

This anecdote produced a greater effect than even the miraculous cures of the most fearful illnesses. A needle which moved as though somebody were pushing it! This peopled the Invisible, showed each sufferer his Guardian Angel standing behind him, only awaiting the orders of Heaven in order to render him assistance. And besides, how pretty and childlike the story was—this needle which came out in the miraculous water after obstinately refusing to stir during seven long years. Exclamations of delight resounded from all the pleased listeners; they smiled and laughed with satisfaction, radiant at finding that nothing was beyond the power of Heaven, and that if it were Heaven's pleasure they themselves would all become healthy, young, and superb. It was sufficient that one should fervently believe and pray in order that nature might be confounded and that the Incredible might come to pass. Apart from that there was merely a question of good luck, since Heaven seemed to make a selection of those sufferers who should be cured.

"Oh! how beautiful it is, father," murmured Marie, who, revived by the passionate interest which she took in the momentous subject, had so far contented herself with listening, dumb with amazement as it were. "Do you remember," she continued, "what you yourself told me of that poor woman, Joachine Dehaut, who came from Belgium and made her way right across France with her twisted leg eaten away by an ulcer, the awful smell of which drove everybody away from her? First of all the ulcer was healed; you could press her knee and she felt nothing, only a slight redness remained to mark where it had been. And then came the turn of the dislocation. She shrieked while she was in the water, it seemed to her as if somebody were breaking her bones, pulling her leg away from her; and, at the same time, she and the woman who was bathing her, saw her deformed foot rise and extend into its natural shape with the regular movement of a clock hand. Her leg also straightened itself, the muscles extended, the knee replaced itself in its proper position, all amidst such acute pain that Joachine ended by fainting. But as soon as she recovered consciousness, she darted off, erect and agile, to carry her crutches to the Grotto."

M. de Guersaint in his turn was laughing with wonderment, waving his hand to confirm this story, which had been told him by a Father of the Assumption. He could have related a score of similar instances, said he, each more touching, more extraordinary than the other. He even invoked Pierre's testimony, and the young priest, who was unable to believe, contented himself with nodding his head. At first, unwilling as he was to afflict Marie, he had striven to divert his thoughts by gazing though the carriage window at the fields, trees, and houses which defiled before his eyes. They had just passed Angouleme, and meadows stretched out, and lines of poplar trees fled away amidst the continuous fanning of the air, which the velocity of the train occasioned.

They were late, no doubt, for they were hastening onward at full speed, thundering along under the stormy sky, through the fiery atmosphere, devouring kilometre after kilometre in swift succession. However, despite himself, Pierre heard snatches of the various narratives, and grew interested in these extravagant stories, which the rough jolting of the wheels accompanied like a lullaby, as though the engine had been turned loose and were wildly bearing them away to the divine land of dreams, They were rolling, still rolling along, and Pierre at last ceased to gaze at the landscape, and surrendered himself to the heavy, sleep-inviting atmosphere of the carriage, where ecstasy was growing and spreading, carrying everyone far from the world of reality across which they were so rapidly rushing, The sight of Marie's face with its brightened look filled the young priest with sincere joy, and he let her retain his hand, which she had taken in order to acquaint him, by the pressure of her fingers, with all the confidence which was reviving in her soul. And why should he have saddened her by his doubts, since he was so desirous of her cure? So he continued clasping her small, moist hand, feeling infinite affection for her, a dolorous brotherly love which distracted him, and made him anxious to believe in the pity of the spheres, in a superior kindness which tempered suffering to those who were plunged in despair, "Oh!" she repeated, "how beautiful it is, Pierre! How beautiful it is! And what glory it will be if the Blessed Virgin deigns to disturb herself for me! Do you really think me worthy of such a favour?"

"Assuredly I do," he exclaimed; "you are the best and the purest, with a spotless soul as your father said; there are not enough good angels in Paradise to form your escort."

But the narratives were not yet finished. Sister Hyacinthe and Madame de Jonquiere were now enumerating all the miracles with which they were acquainted, the long, long series of miracles which for more than thirty years had been flowering at Lourdes, like the uninterrupted budding of the roses on the Mystical Rose-tree. They could be counted by thousands, they put forth fresh shoots every year with prodigious verdancy of sap, becoming brighter and brighter each successive season. And the sufferers who listened to these marvellous stories with increasing feverishness were like little children who, after hearing one fine fairy tale, ask for another, and another, and yet another. Oh! that they might have more and more of those stories in which evil reality was flouted, in which unjust nature was cuffed and slapped, in which the Divinity intervened as the supreme healer, He who laughs at science and distributes happiness according to His own good pleasure.

First of all there were the deaf and the dumb who suddenly heard and spoke; such as Aurelie Bruneau, who was incurably deaf, with the drums of both ears broken, and yet was suddenly enraptured by the celestial music of a harmonium; such also as Louise Pourchet, who on her side had been dumb for five-and-twenty years, and yet, whilst praying in the Grotto, suddenly exclaimed, "Hail, Mary, full of grace!" And there were others and yet others who were completely cured by merely letting a few drops of water fall into their ears or upon their tongues. Then came the procession of the blind: Father Hermann, who felt the Blessed Virgin's gentle hand removing the veil which covered his eyes; Mademoiselle de Pontbriant, who was threatened with a total loss of sight, but after a simple prayer was enabled to see better than she had ever seen before; then a child twelve years old whose corneas resembled marbles, but who, in three seconds, became possessed of clear, deep eyes, bright with an angelic smile. However, there was especially an abundance of paralytics, of lame people suddenly enabled to walk upright, of sufferers for long years powerless to stir from their beds of misery and to whom the voice said: "Arise and walk!" Delannoy,[1] afflicted with ataxia, vainly cauterised and burnt, fifteen times an inmate of the Paris hospitals,

---

[1] This was one of the most notorious of the recorded cases and had a very strange sequel subsequent to the first publication of this work. Pierre Delannoy had been employed as a ward-assistant in one of the large Paris hospitals from 1877 to 1881, when he came to the conclusion that the life of an in-patient was far preferable to the one he was leading. He, therefore, resolved to pass the rest of his days inside different hospitals in the capacity of invalid. He started by feigning locomotor ataxia, and for six years deceived the highest medical experts in Paris, so curiously did he appear to suffer. He stayed in turn in all the hospitals in the city, being treated with every care and consideration, until at last he met with a doctor who insisted on cauterisation and other disagreeable remedies. Delannoy thereupon opined that the time to be cured had arrived, and cured he became, and was discharged. He next appeared at Lourdes, supported by crutches, and presenting every symptom of being hopelessly crippled. With other infirm and decrepid people he was dipped in the piscina and so efficacious did this treatment prove that he came out another man, threw his crutches to the ground and walked, as an onlooker expressed it, "like a rural postman." All Lourdes rang with the fame of the miracle, and the Church, after starring Delannoy round the country as a specimen of what could be done at the holy spring, placed him in charge of a home for invalids. But this was too much like hard work, and he soon decamped with all the money he could lay his hands on. Returning to Paris he was admitted to the Hospital of Ste. Anne as suffering from mental debility, but this did not prevent him from running off one night with about $300 belonging to a dispenser. The police were put on his track and arrested him in May, 1895, when he tried to pass himself off as a lunatic; but he had become by this time too well known, and was indicted in due course. At his trial he energetically denied that he had ever shammed, but the Court would not believe him, and sentenced him to four years' imprisonment with hard labour. — Trans.

whence he had emerged with the concurring diagnosis of twelve doctors, feels a strange force raising him up as the Blessed Sacrament goes by, and he begins to follow it, his legs strong and healthy once more. Marie Louise Delpon, a girl of fourteen, suffering from paralysis which had stiffened her legs, drawn back her hands, and twisted her mouth on one side, sees her limbs loosen and the distortion of her mouth disappear as though an invisible hand were severing the fearful bonds which had deformed her. Marie Vachier, riveted to her arm-chair during seventeen years by paraplegia, not only runs and flies on emerging from the piscina, but finds no trace even of the sores with which her long-enforced immobility had covered her body. And Georges Hanquet, attacked by softening of the spinal marrow, passes without transition from agony to perfect health; while Leonie Charton, likewise afflicted with softening of the medulla, and whose vertebrae bulge out to a considerable extent, feels her hump melting away as though by enchantment, and her legs rise and straighten, renovated and vigorous.

Then came all sorts of ailments. First those brought about by scrofula—a great many more legs long incapable of service and made anew. There was Margaret Gehier, who had suffered from coxalgia for seven-and-twenty years, whose hip was devoured by the disease, whose left knee was anchylosed, and who yet was suddenly able to fall upon her knees to thank the Blessed Virgin for healing her. There was also Philomene Simonneau, the young Vendeenne, whose left leg was perforated by three horrible sores in the depths of which her carious bones were visible, and whose bones, whose flesh, and whose skin were all formed afresh.

Next came the dropsical ones: Madame Ancelin, the swelling of whose feet, hands, and entire body subsided without anyone being able to tell whither all the water had gone; Mademoiselle Montagnon, from whom, on various occasions, nearly twenty quarts of water had been drawn, and who, on again swelling, was entirely rid of the fluid by the application of a bandage which had been dipped in the miraculous source. And, in her case also, none of the water could be found, either in her bed or on the floor. In the same way, not a complaint of the stomach resisted, all disappeared with the first glass of water. There was Marie Souchet, who vomited black blood, who had wasted to a skeleton, and who devoured her food and recovered her flesh in two days' time! There was Marie Jarlaud, who had burnt herself internally through drinking a glass of a metallic solution used for cleansing and brightening kitchen utensils, and who felt the tumour which had resulted from her injuries melt rapidly away. Moreover, every tumour disappeared in this fashion, in the piscina, without leaving the slightest trace behind. But that which caused yet greater wonderment was the manner in which ulcers, cancers, all sorts of horrible, visible sores were cicatrised as by a breath from on high. A Jew, an actor, whose hand was devoured by an ulcer, merely had to dip it in the water and he was cured. A very wealthy young foreigner, who had a wen as large as a hen's egg, on his right wrist, *beheld* it dissolve. Rose Duval, who, as a result of a white tumour, had a hole in her left elbow, large enough to accommodate a walnut, was able to watch and follow the prompt action of the new flesh in filling up this cavity! The Widow Fromond, with a lip half decoyed by a cancerous formation, merely had to apply the miraculous water to it as a lotion, and not even a red mark remained. Marie Moreau, who experienced fearful sufferings from a cancer in the breast, fell asleep, after laying on it a linen cloth soaked in some water of Lourdes, and when she awoke, two hours later, the pain had disappeared, and her flesh was once more smooth and pink and fresh.

At last Sister Hyacinthe began to speak of the immediate and complete cures of phthisis, and this was the triumph, the healing of that terrible disease which ravages humanity, which unbelievers defied the Blessed Virgin to cure, but which she did cure, it was said, by merely raising her little finger. A hundred instances, more extraordinary one than the other, pressed forward for citation.

Marguerite Coupel, who had suffered from phthisis for three years, and the upper part of whose lungs is destroyed by tuberculosis, rises up and goes off, radiant with health. Madame de la Riviere, who spits blood, who is ever covered with a cold perspiration, whose nails have already acquired a violet tinge, who is indeed on the point of drawing her last breath, requires but a spoonful of the water to be administered to her between her teeth, and lo! the rattles cease, she sits up, makes the responses to the litanies, and asks for some broth. Julie Jadot requires four spoonfuls; but then she could no longer hold up her head, she was of such a delicate constitution that disease had reduced her to nothing; and yet, in a few days, she becomes quite fat. Anna Catry, who is in the most advanced stage of the malady, with her left lung half destroyed by a cavity, is plunged five times into the cold water, contrary to all the dictates of prudence, and she is cured, her lung is healthy once more. Another consumptive girl, condemned by fifteen doctors, has asked nothing, has simply fallen on her knees in the Grotto, by chance as it were, and is afterwards quite surprised at having been cured *au passage*, through the lucky circumstance of having been there, no doubt, at the hour when the Blessed Virgin, moved to pity, allows miracles to fall from her invisible hands.

Miracles and yet more miracles! They rained down like the flowers of dreams from a clear and balmy sky. Some of them were touching, some of them were childish. An old woman, who, having her hand anchylosed, had been incapable of moving it for thirty years, washes it in the water and is at once able to make the sign of the Cross. Sister Sophie, who barked like a dog, plunges into the piscina and emerges from it with a clear, pure voice, chanting a canticle. Mustapha, a Turk, invokes the White Lady and recovers the use of his right eye by applying a compress to it. An officer of Turcos was protected at Sedan; a cuirassier of Reichsoffen would have died, pierced in the heart by a bullet, if this bullet after passing though his pocket-book had not stayed its flight on reaching a little picture of Our Lady of Lourdes! And, as with the men and women, so did the children, the poor, suffering little ones, find mercy; a paralytic boy of five rose and walked after being held for five minutes under the icy jet of the spring; another one, fifteen years of age, who, lying in bed, could only raise an inarticulate cry, sprang out of the piscina, shouting that he was cured; another one, but two years old, a poor tiny fellow who had never been able to walk, remained for a quarter of an hour in the cold water and then, invigorated and smiling, took his first steps like a little man! And for all of them, the little ones as well as the adults, the pain was acute whilst the miracle was being accomplished; for the work of repair could not be effected without causing an extraordinary shock to the whole human organism; the bones grew again, new flesh was formed, and the disease, driven away, made its escape in a final convulsion. But how great was the feeling of comfort which followed! The doctors could not believe their eyes, their astonishment burst forth at each fresh cure, when they saw the patients whom they had despaired of run and jump and eat with ravenous appetites. All these chosen ones, these women cured of their ailments, walked a couple of miles, sat down to roast fowl, and slept the soundest of sleeps for a dozen hours. Moreover, there was no convalescence, it was a sudden leap from the death throes to complete health. Limbs were renovated, sores were filled up, organs were reformed in their entirety, plumpness returned to the emaciated, all with the velocity of a lightning flash! Science was completely baffled. Not even the most simple precautions were taken, women were bathed at all times and seasons, perspiring consumptives were plunged into the icy water, sores were left to their putrefaction without any thought of employing antiseptics. And then what canticles of joy, what shouts of gratitude and love arose at each fresh miracle! The favoured one falls upon her knees, all who are present weep, conversions are effected, Protestants and Jews alike embrace Catholicism—other miracles these, miracles of faith, at which Heaven triumphs. And when the favoured one, chosen for the miracle, returns to her village, all the inhabitants crowd to meet her, whilst the bells peal merrily; and when she is seen springing lightly from the vehicle which has brought her home, shouts and sobs of joy burst forth and all intonate the *Magnificat*: Glory to the Blessed Virgin! Gratitude and love for ever!

Indeed, that which was more particularly evolved from the realisation of all these hopes, from the celebration of all these ardent thanksgivings, was gratitude—gratitude to the Mother most pure and most admirable. She was the great passion of every soul, she, the Virgin most powerful, the Virgin most merciful, the Mirror of Justice, the Seat of Wisdom.[1] All hands were stretched towards her, Mystical Rose in the dim light of the chapels, Tower of Ivory on the horizon of dreamland, Gate of Heaven leading into the Infinite. Each day at early dawn she shone forth, bright Morning Star, gay with juvenescent hope. And was she not also the Health of the weak, the Refuge of sinners, the Comforter of the afflicted? France had ever been her well-loved country, she was adored there with an ardent worship, the worship of her womanhood and her motherhood, the soaring of a divine affection; and it was particularly in France that it pleased her to show herself to little shepherdesses. She was so good to the little and the humble; she continually occupied herself with them; and if she was appealed to so willingly it was because she was known to be the intermediary of love betwixt Earth and Heaven. Every evening she wept tears of gold at the feet of her divine Son to obtain favours from Him, and these favours were the miracles which He permitted her to work,—these beautiful, flower-like miracles, as sweet-scented as the roses of Paradise, so prodigiously splendid and fragrant.

But the train was still rolling, rolling onward. They had just passed Contras, it was six o'clock, and Sister Hyacinthe, rising to her, feet, clapped her hands together and once again repeated: "The Angelus, my children!"

Never had "Aves" impregnated with greater faith, inflamed with a more fervent desire to be heard by Heaven, winged their flight on high. And Pierre suddenly understood everything, clearly realised the meaning of all these pilgrimages, of all these trains rolling along through every country of the civilised world, of all these eager

---

[1] For the information of Protestant and other non-Catholic readers it may be mentioned that all the titles enumerated in this passage are taken from the Litany of the Blessed Virgin.—Trans.

crowds, hastening towards Lourdes, which blazed over yonder like the abode of salvation for body and for mind. Ah! the poor wretches whom, ever since morning, he had heard groaning with pain, the poor wretches who exposed their sorry carcasses to the fatigues of such a journey! They were all condemned, abandoned by science, weary of consulting doctors, of having tried the torturing effects of futile remedies. And how well one could understand that, burning with a desire to preserve their lives, unable to resign themselves to the injustice and indifference of Nature, they should dream of a superhuman power, of an almighty Divinity who, in their favour, would perchance annul the established laws, alter the course of the planets, and reconsider His creation! For if the world failed them, did not the Divinity remain to them? In their cases reality was too abominable, and an immense need of illusion and falsehood sprang up within them. Oh! to believe that there is a supreme Justiciar somewhere, one who rights the apparent wrongs of things and beings; to believe that there is a Redeemer, a consoler who is the real master, who can carry the torrents back to their source, who can restore youth to the aged, and life to the dead! And when you are covered with sores, when your limbs are twisted, when your stomach is swollen by tumours, when your lungs are destroyed by disease, to be able to say that all this is of no consequence, that everything may disappear and be renewed at a sign from the Blessed Virgin, that it is sufficient that you should pray to her, touch her heart, and obtain the favour of being chosen by her. And then what a heavenly fount of hope appeared with the prodigious flow of those beautiful stories of cure, those adorable fairy tales which lulled and intoxicated the feverish imaginations of the sick and the infirm. Since little Sophie Couteau, with her white, sound foot, had climbed into that carriage, opening to the gaze of those within it the limitless heavens of the Divine and the Supernatural, how well one could understand the breath of resurrection that was passing over the world, slowly raising those who despaired the most from their beds of misery, and making their eyes shine since life was itself a possibility for them, and they were, perhaps, about to begin it afresh.

Yes, 't was indeed that. If that woeful train was rolling, rolling on, if that carriage was full, if the other carriages were full also, if France and the world, from the uttermost limits of the earth, were crossed by similar trains, if crowds of three hundred thousand believers, bringing thousands of sick along with them, were ever setting out, from one end of the year to the other, it was because the Grotto yonder was shining forth in its glory like a beacon of hope and illusion, like a sign of the revolt and triumph of the Impossible over inexorable materiality. Never had a more impassionating romance been devised to exalt the souls of men above the stern laws of life. To dream that dream, this was the great, the ineffable happiness. If the Fathers of the Assumption had seen the success of their pilgrimages increase and spread from year to year, it was because they sold to all the flocking peoples the bread of consolation and illusion, the delicious bread of hope, for which suffering humanity ever hungers with a hunger that nothing will ever appease. And it was not merely the physical sores which cried aloud for cure, the whole of man's moral and intellectual being likewise shrieked forth its wretchedness, with an insatiable yearning for happiness. To be happy, to place the certainty of life in faith, to lean till death should come upon that one strong staff of travel—such was the desire exhaled by every breast, the desire which made every moral grief bend the knee, imploring a continuance of grace, the conversion of dear ones, the spiritual salvation of self and those one loved. The mighty cry spread from pole to pole, ascended and filled all the regions of space: To be happy, happy for evermore, both in life and in death!

And Pierre saw the suffering beings around him lose all perception of the jolting and recover their strength as league by league they drew nearer to the miracle. Even Madame Maze grew talkative, certain as she felt that the Blessed Virgin would restore her husband to her. With a smile on her face Madame Vincent gently rocked her little Rose in her arms, thinking that she was not nearly so ill as those all but lifeless children who, after being plunged in the icy water, sprang out and played. M. Sabathier jested with M. de Guersaint, and explained to him that, next October, when he had recovered the use of his legs, he should go on a trip to Rome—a journey which he had been postponing for fifteen years and more. Madame Vetu, quite calmed, feeling nothing but a slight twinge in the stomach, imagined that she was hungry, and asked Madame de Jonquiere to let her dip some strips of bread in a glass of milk; whilst Elise Rouquet, forgetting her sores, ate some grapes, with face uncovered. And in La Grivotte who was sitting up and Brother Isidore who had ceased moaning, all those fine stories had left a pleasant fever, to such a point that, impatient to be cured, they grew anxious to know the time. For a minute also the man, the strange man, resuscitated. Whilst Sister Hyacinthe was again wiping the cold sweat from his brow, he raised his eyelids, and a smile momentarily brightened his pallid countenance. Yet once again he, also, had hoped.

Marie was still holding Pierre's fingers in her own small, warm hand. It was seven o'clock, they were not due at Bordeaux till half-past seven; and the belated train was quickening its pace yet more and more, rushing along with wild speed in order to make up for the minutes it had lost. The storm had ended by coming down, and now a gentle light of infinite purity fell from the vast clear heavens.

"Oh! how beautiful it is, Pierre—how beautiful it is!" Marie again repeated, pressing his hand with tender affection. And leaning towards him, she added in an undertone: "I beheld the Blessed Virgin a little while ago, Pierre, and it was your cure that I implored and shall obtain."

The priest, who understood her meaning, was thrown into confusion by the divine light which gleamed in her eyes as she fixed them on his own. She had forgotten her own sufferings; that which she had asked for was his conversion; and that prayer of faith, emanating, pure and candid, from that dear, suffering creature, upset his soul. Yet why should he not believe some day? He himself had been distracted by all those extraordinary narratives. The stifling heat of the carriage had made him dizzy, the sight of all the woe heaped up there caused his heart to bleed with pity. And contagion was doing its work; he no longer knew where the real and the possible ceased, he lacked the power to disentangle such a mass of stupefying facts, to explain such as admitted of explanation and reject the others. At one moment, indeed, as a hymn once more resounded and carried him off with its stubborn importunate rhythm, he ceased to be master of himself, and imagined that he was at last beginning to believe amidst the hallucinatory vertigo which reigned in that travelling hospital, rolling, ever rolling onward at full speed.

V. BERNADETTE

THE train left Bordeaux after a stoppage of a few minutes, during which those who had not dined hastened to purchase some provisions. Moreover, the ailing ones were constantly drinking milk, and asking for biscuits, like little children. And, as soon as they were off again, Sister Hyacinthe clapped her hands, and exclaimed: "Come, let us make haste; the evening prayer."

Thereupon, during a quarter of an hour came a confused murmuring, made up of "Paters" and "Aves," self-examinations, acts of contrition, and vows of trustful reliance in God, the Blessed Virgin, and the Saints, with thanksgiving for protection and preservation that day, and, at last, a prayer for the living and for the faithful departed.

"In the name of the Father, the Son, and the Holy Ghost. Amen."

It was ten minutes past eight o'clock, the shades of night were already bedimming the landscape—a vast plain which the evening mist seemed to prolong into the infinite, and where, far away, bright dots of light shone out from the windows of lonely, scattered houses. In the carriage, the lights of the lamps were flickering, casting a subdued yellow glow on the luggage and the pilgrims, who were sorely shaken by the spreading tendency of the train's motion.

"You know, my children," resumed Sister Hyacinthe, who had remained standing, "I shall order silence when we get to Lamothe, in about an hour's time. So you have an hour to amuse yourselves, but you must be reasonable and not excite yourselves too much. And when we have passed Lamothe, you hear me, there must not be another word, another sound, you must all go to sleep."

This made them laugh.

"Oh! but it is the rule, you know," added the Sister, "and surely you have too much sense not to obey me."

Since the morning they had punctually fulfilled the programme of religious exercises specified for each successive hour. And now that all the prayers had been said, the beads told, the hymns chanted, the day's duties were over, and a brief interval for recreation was allowed before sleeping. They were, however, at a loss as to what they should do.

"Sister," suddenly said Marie, "if you would allow Monsieur l'Abbe to read to us—he reads extremely well,—and as it happens I have a little book with me—a history of Bernadette which is so interesting—"

The others did not let her finish, but with the suddenly awakened desire of children to whom a beautiful story has been promised, loudly exclaimed: "Oh! yes, Sister. Oh! yes, Sister—"

"Of course I will allow it," replied Sister Hyacinthe, "since it is a question of reading something instructive and edifying."

Pierre was obliged to consent. But to be able to read the book he wished to be under the lamp, and it was necessary that he should change seats with M. de Guersaint, whom the promise of a story had delighted as much as it did the ailing ones. And when the young priest, after changing seats and declaring that he would be able to see well enough, at last opened the little book, a quiver of curiosity sped from one end of the carriage to the other, and every head was stretched out, lending ear with rapt attention. Fortunately, Pierre had a clear, powerful voice and made himself distinctly heard above the wheels, which, now that the train travelled across a vast level plain, gave out but a subdued, rumbling sound.

Before beginning, however, the young priest had examined the book. It was one of those little works of propaganda issued from the Catholic printing-presses and circulated in profusion throughout all Christendom. Badly printed, on wretched paper, it was adorned on its blue cover with a little wood-cut of Our Lady of Lourdes, a naive design alike stiff and awkward. The book itself was short, and half an hour would certainly suffice to read it from cover to cover without hurrying.

Accordingly, in his fine, clear voice, with its penetrating, musical tones, he began his perusal as follows:—

"It happened at Lourdes, a little town near the Pyrenees, on a Thursday, February 11, 1858. The weather was cold, and somewhat cloudy, and in the humble home of a poor but honest miller named Francois Soubirous there was no wood to cook the dinner. The miller's wife, Louise, said to her younger daughter Marie, 'Go and gather some wood on the bank of the Gave or on the common-land.' The Gave is a torrent which passes through Lourdes.

"Marie had an elder sister, named Bernadette, who had lately arrived from the country, where some worthy villagers had employed her as a shepherdess. She was a slender, delicate, extremely innocent child, and knew nothing except her rosary. Louise Soubirous hesitated to send her out with her sister, on account of the cold, but at last, yielding to the entreaties of Marie and a young girl of the neighbourhood called Jeanne Abadie, she consented to let her go.

"Following the bank of the torrent and gathering stray fragments of dead wood, the three maidens at last found themselves in front of the Grotto, hollowed out in a huge mass of rock which the people of the district called Massabielle."

Pierre had reached this point and was turning the page when he suddenly paused and let the little book fall on his knees. The childish character of the narrative, its ready-made, empty phraseology, filled him with impatience. He himself possessed quite a collection of documents concerning this extraordinary story, had passionately studied even its most trifling details, and in the depths of his heart retained a feeling of tender affection and infinite pity for Bernadette. He had just reflected, too, that on the very next day he would be able to begin that decisive inquiry which he had formerly dreamt of making at Lourdes. In fact, this was one of the reasons which had induced him to accompany Marie on her journey. And he was now conscious of an awakening of all his curiosity respecting the Visionary, whom he loved because he felt that she had been a girl of candid soul, truthful and ill-fated, though at the same time he would much have liked to analyse and explain her case. Assuredly, she had not lied, she had indeed beheld a vision and heard voices, like Joan of Arc; and like Joan of Arc also, she was now, in the opinion of the devout, accomplishing the deliverance of France—from sin if not from invaders. Pierre wondered what force could have produced her—her and her work. How was it that the visionary faculty had become developed in that lowly girl, so distracting believing souls as to bring about a renewal of the miracles of primitive times, as to found almost a new religion in the midst of a Holy City, built at an outlay of millions, and ever invaded by crowds of worshippers more numerous and more exalted in mind than had ever been known since the days of the Crusades?

And so, ceasing to read the book, Pierre began to tell his companions all that he knew, all that he had divined and reconstructed of that story which is yet so obscure despite the vast rivers of ink which it has already caused to flow. He knew the country and its manners and customs, through his long conversations with his friend Doctor Chassaigne. And he was endowed with charming fluency of language, an emotional power of exquisite purity, many remarkable gifts well fitting him to be a pulpit orator, which he never made use of, although he had known them to be within him ever since his seminary days. When the occupants of the carriage perceived that he knew the story, far better and in far greater detail than it appeared in Marie's little book, and that he related it also in such a gentle yet passionate way, there came an increase of attention, and all those afflicted souls hungering for happiness went forth towards him. First came the story of Bernadette's childhood at Bartres, where she had grown up in the abode of her foster-mother, Madame Lagues, who, having lost an infant of her own, had rendered those poor folks, the Soubirouses, the service of suckling and keeping their child for them. Bartres, a village of four hundred souls, at a league or so from Lourdes, lay as it were in a desert oasis, sequestered amidst greenery, and far from any frequented highway. The road dips down, the few houses are scattered over grassland, divided by hedges and planted with walnut and chestnut trees, whilst the clear rivulets, which are never silent, follow the sloping banks beside the pathways, and nothing rises on high save the small ancient romanesque church, which is perched on a hillock, covered with graves. Wooded slopes undulate upon all sides. Bartres lies in a hollow amidst grass of delicious freshness, grass of intense greenness, which is ever moist at the roots, thanks to the eternal subterraneous expanse of water which is fed by the mountain torrents. And Bernadette, who, since becoming a big girl, had paid for her keep by tending lambs, was wont to take them with her, season after season, through all the greenery where she never met a soul. It was only now and then, from the summit of some slope, that she saw the far-away mountains, the Pic du Midi, the Pic de Viscos, those masses which rose up, bright or gloomy, according to the weather, and which stretched away to other peaks, lightly and faintly coloured, vaguely and confusedly outlined, like apparitions seen in dreams.

Then came the home of the Lagueses, where her cradle was still preserved, a solitary, silent house, the last of the village. A meadow planted with pear and apple trees, and only separated from the open country by a narrow stream which one could jump across, stretched out in front of the house. Inside the latter, a low and damp abode, there were, on either side of the wooden stairway leading to the loft, but two spacious rooms, flagged with stones, and each containing four or five beds. The girls, who slept together, fell asleep at even, gazing at the fine pictures affixed to the walls, whilst the big clock in its pinewood case gravely struck the hours in the midst of the deep silence.

Ah! those years at Bartres; in what sweet peacefulness did Bernadette live them! Yet she grew up very thin, always in bad health, suffering from a nervous asthma which stifled her in the least veering of the wind; and on attaining her twelfth year she could neither read nor write, nor speak otherwise than in dialect, having remained quite infantile, behindhand in mind as in body. She was a very good little girl, very gentle and well behaved, and but little different from other children, except that instead of talking she preferred to listen. Limited as was her intelligence, she often evinced much natural common-sense, and at times was prompt in her *reparties*, with a kind of simple gaiety which made one smile. It was only with infinite trouble that she was taught her rosary, and when she knew it she seemed bent on carrying her knowledge no further, but repeated it all day long, so that whenever you met her with her lambs, she invariably had her chaplet between her fingers, diligently telling each successive "Pater" and "Ave." For long, long hours she lived like this on the grassy slopes of the hills, hidden away and haunted as it were amidst the mysteries of the foliage, seeing nought of the world save the crests of the distant mountains, which, for an instant, every now and then, would soar aloft in the radiant light, as ethereal as the peaks of dreamland.

Days followed days, and Bernadette roamed, dreaming her one narrow dream, repeating the sole prayer she knew, which gave her amidst her solitude, so fresh and naively infantile, no other companion and friend than the Blessed Virgin. But what pleasant evenings she spent in the winter-time in the room on the left, where a fire was kept burning! Her foster-mother had a brother, a priest, who occasionally read some marvellous stories to them—stories of saints, prodigious adventures of a kind to make one tremble with mingled fear and joy, in which Paradise appeared upon earth, whilst the heavens opened and a glimpse was caught of the splendour of the angels. The books he brought with him were often full of pictures—God the Father enthroned amidst His glory; Jesus, so gentle and so handsome with His beaming face; the Blessed Virgin, who recurred again and again, radiant with splendour, clad now in white, now in azure, now in gold, and ever so amiable that Bernadette would see her again in her dreams. But the book which was read more than all others was the Bible, an old Bible which had been in the family for more than a hundred years, and which time and usage had turned yellow. Each winter evening Bernadette's foster-father, the only member of the household who had learnt to read, would take a pin, pass it at random between the leaves of the book, open the latter, and then start reading from the top of the right-hand page, amidst the deep attention of both the women and the children, who ended by knowing the book by heart, and could have continued reciting it without a single mistake.

However, Bernadette, for her part, preferred the religious works in which the Blessed Virgin constantly appeared with her engaging smile. True, one reading of a different character amused her, that of the marvellous story of the Four Brothers Aymon. On the yellow paper cover of the little book, which had doubtless fallen from the bale of some peddler who had lost his way in that remote region, there was a naive cut showing the four doughty knights, Renaud and his brothers, all mounted on Bayard, their famous battle charger, that princely present made to them by the fairy

Orlanda. And inside were narratives of bloody fights, of the building and besieging of fortresses, of the terrible swordthrusts exchanged by Roland and Renaud, who was at last about to free the Holy Land, without mentioning the tales of Maugis the Magician and his marvellous enchantments, and the Princess Clarisse, the King of Aquitaine's sister, who was more lovely than sunlight. Her imagination fired by such stories as these, Bernadette often found it difficult to get to sleep; and this was especially the case on the evenings when the books were left aside, and some person of the company related a tale of witchcraft. The girl was very superstitious, and after sundown could never be prevailed upon to pass near a tower in the vicinity, which was said to be haunted by the fiend. For that matter, all the folks of the region were superstitious, devout, and simple-minded, the whole countryside being peopled, so to say, with mysteries—trees which sang, stones from which blood flowed, cross-roads where it was necessary to say three "Paters" and three "Aves," if you did not wish to meet the seven-horned beast who carried maidens off to perdition. And what a wealth of terrifying stories there was! Hundreds of stories, so that there was no finishing on the evenings when somebody started them. First came the wehrwolf adventures, the tales of the unhappy men whom the demon forced to enter into the bodies of dogs, the great white dogs of the mountains. If you fire a gun at the dog and a single shot should strike him, the man will be delivered; but if the shot should fall on the dog's shadow, the man will immediately die. Then came the endless procession of sorcerers and sorceresses. In one of these tales Bernadette evinced a passionate interest; it was the story of a clerk of the tribunal of Lourdes who, wishing to see the devil, was conducted by a witch into an untilled field at midnight on Good Friday. The devil arrived clad in magnificent scarlet garments, and at once proposed to the clerk that he should buy his soul, an offer which the clerk pretended to accept. It so happened that the devil was carrying under his arm a register in which different persons of the town, who had already sold themselves, had signed their names. However, the clerk, who was a cunning fellow, pulled out of his pocket a pretended bottle of ink, which in reality contained holy water, and with this he sprinkled the devil, who raised frightful shrieks, whilst the clerk took to flight, carrying the register off with him. Then began a wild, mad race, which might last throughout the night, over the mountains, through the valleys, across the forests and the torrents. "Give me back my register!" shouted the fiend. "No, you sha'n't have it!" replied the clerk. And again and again it began afresh: "Give me back my register!"—"No, you sha'n't have it'!" And at last, finding himself out of breath, near the point of succumbing, the clerk, who had his plan, threw himself into the cemetery, which was consecrated ground, and was there able to deride the devil at his ease, waving the register which he had purloined so as to save the souls of all the unhappy people who had signed their names in it. On the evening when this story was told, Bernadette, before surrendering herself to sleep, would mentally repeat her rosary, delighted with the thought that hell should have been baffled, though she trembled at the idea that it would surely return to prowl around her, as soon as the lamp should have been put out.

Throughout one winter, the long evenings were spent in the church. Abbe Ader, the village priest, had authorised it, and many families came, in order to economise oil and candles. Moreover, they felt less cold when gathered together in this fashion. The Bible was read, and prayers were repeated, whilst the children ended by falling asleep. Bernadette alone struggled on to the finish, so pleased she was at being there, in that narrow nave whose slender nervures were coloured blue and red. At the farther end was the altar, also painted and gilded, with its twisted columns and its screens on which appeared the Virgin and Ste. Anne, and the beheading of St. John the Baptist—the whole of a gaudy and somewhat barbaric splendour. And as sleepiness grew upon her, the child must have often seen a mystical vision as it were of those crudely coloured designs rising before her—have seen the blood flowing from St. John's severed head, have seen the aureolas shining, the Virgin ever returning and gazing at her with her blue, living eyes, and looking as though she were on the point of opening her vermilion lips in order to speak to her. For some months Bernadette spent her evenings in this wise, half asleep in front of that sumptuous, vaguely defined altar, in the incipiency of a divine dream which she carried away with her, and finished in bed, slumbering peacefully under the watchful care of her guardian angel.

And it was also in that old church, so humble yet so impregnated with ardent faith, that Bernadette began to learn her catechism. She would soon be fourteen now, and must think of her first communion. Her foster-mother, who had the reputation of being avaricious, did not send her to school, but employed her in or about the house from morning till evening. M. Barbet, the schoolmaster, never saw her at his classes, though one day, when he gave the catechism lesson, in the place of Abbe Ader who was indisposed, he remarked her on account of her piety and modesty. The village priest was very fond of Bernadette and often spoke of her to the schoolmaster, saying that he could never look at her without thinking of the children of La Salette, since they must have been good, candid, and pious as she was, for the Blessed Virgin to have appeared to them.[1] On another occasion whilst the two men were walking one morning near the village, and saw Bernadette disappear with her little flock under some spreading trees in the distance, the Abbe repeatedly turned round to look for her, and again remarked "I cannot account for it, but every time I meet that child it seems to me as if I saw Melanie, the young shepherdess, little Maximin's companion." He was certainly beset by this singular idea, which became, so to say, a prediction. Moreover, had he not one day after catechism, or one evening, when the villagers were gathered in the church, related that marvellous story which was already twelve years old, that story of the Lady in the dazzling robes who walked upon the grass without even making it bend, the Blessed Virgin who showed herself to Melanie and Maximin on the banks of a stream in the mountains, and confided to them a great secret and announced the anger of her Son? Ever since that day a source had sprung up from the tears which she had shed, a source which cured all ailments, whilst the secret, inscribed on parchment fastened with three seals, slumbered at Rome! And

[1] It was on September 19, 1846, that the Virgin is said to have appeared in the ravine of La Sezia, adjacent to the valley of La Salette, between Corps and Eutraigues, in the department of the Isere. The visionaries were Melanie Mathieu, a girl of fourteen, and Maximin Giraud, a boy of twelve. The local clergy speedily endorsed the story of the miracle, and thousands of people still go every year in pilgrimage to a church overlooking the valley, and bathe and drink at a so-called miraculous source. Two priests of Grenoble, however, Abbe Deleon and Abbe Cartellier, accused a Mlle. de Lamerliere of having concocted the miracle, and when she took proceedings against them for libel she lost her case.—Trans.

Bernadette, no doubt, with her dreamy, silent air, had listened passionately to that wonderful tale and carried it off with her into the desert of foliage where she spent her days, so that she might live it over again as she walked along behind her lambs with her rosary, slipping bead by bead between her slender fingers.

Thus her childhood ran its course at Bartres. That which delighted one in this Bernadette, so poor-blooded, so slight of build, was her ecstatic eyes, beautiful visionary eyes, from which dreams soared aloft like birds winging their flight in a pure limpid sky. Her mouth was large, with lips somewhat thick, expressive of kindliness; her square-shaped head had a straight brow, and was covered with thick black hair, whilst her face would have seemed rather common but for its charming expression of gentle obstinacy. Those who did not gaze into her eyes, however, gave her no thought. To them she was but an ordinary child, a poor thing of the roads, a girl of reluctant growth, timidly humble in her ways. Assuredly it was in her glance that Abbe Ader had with agitation detected the stifling ailment which filled her puny, girlish form with suffering—that ailment born of the greeny solitude in which she had grown up, the gentleness of her bleating lambs, the Angelic Salutation which she had carried with her, hither and thither, under the sky, repeating and repeating it to the point of hallucination, the prodigious stories, too, which she had heard folks tell at her foster-mother's, the long evenings spent before the living altar-screens in the church, and all the atmosphere of primitive faith which she had breathed in that far-away rural region, hemmed in by mountains.

At last, on one seventh of January, Bernadette had just reached her fourteenth birthday, when her parents, finding that she learnt nothing at Bartres, resolved to bring her back to Lourdes for good, in order that she might diligently study her catechism, and in this wise seriously prepare herself for her first communion. And so it happened that she had already been at Lourdes some fifteen or twenty days, when on February 11, a Thursday, cold and somewhat cloudy—

But Pierre could carry his narrative no further, for Sister Hyacinthe had risen to her feet and was vigorously clapping her hands. "My children," she exclaimed, "it is past nine o'clock. Silence! silence!"

The train had indeed just passed Lamothe, and was rolling with a dull rumble across a sea of darkness—the endless plains of the Landes which the night submerged. For ten minutes already not a sound ought to have been heard in the carriage, one and all ought to have been sleeping or suffering uncomplainingly. However, a mutiny broke out.

"Oh! Sister!" exclaimed Marie, whose eyes were sparkling, "allow us just another short quarter of an hour! We have got to the most interesting part."

Ten, twenty voices took up the cry: "Oh yes, Sister, please do let us have another short quarter of an hour!"

They all wished to hear the continuation, burning with as much curiosity as though they had not known the story, so captivated were they by the touches of compassionate human feeling which Pierre introduced into his narrative. Their glances never left him, all their heads were stretched towards him, fantastically illumined by the flickering light of the lamps. And it was not only the sick who displayed this interest; the ten women occupying the compartment at the far end of the carriage had also become impassioned, and, happy at not missing a single word, turned their poor ugly faces now beautified by naive faith.

"No, I cannot!" Sister Hyacinthe at first declared; "the rules are very strict—you must be silent."

However, she weakened, she herself feeling so interested in the tale that she could detect her heart beating under her stomacher. Then Marie again repeated her request in an entreating tone; whilst her father, M. de Guersaint, who had listened like one hugely amused, declared that they would all fall ill if the story were not continued. And thereupon, seeing Madame de Jonquiere smile with an indulgent air, Sister Hyacinthe ended by consenting.

"Well, then," said she, "I will allow you another short quarter of an hour; but only a short quarter of an hour, mind. That is understood, is it not? For I should otherwise be in fault."

Pierre had waited quietly without attempting to intervene. And he resumed his narrative in the same penetrating voice as before, a voice in which his own doubts were softened by pity for those who suffer and who hope.

The scene of the story was now transferred to Lourdes, to the Rue des Petits Fosses, a narrow, tortuous, mournful street taking a downward course between humble houses and roughly plastered dead walls. The Soubirous family occupied a single room on the ground floor of one of these sorry habitations, a room at the end of a dark passage, in which seven persons were huddled together, the father, the mother, and five children. You could scarcely see in the chamber; from the tiny, damp inner courtyard of the house there came but a greenish light. And in that room they slept, all of a heap; and there also they ate, when they had bread. For some time past, the father, a miller by trade, could only with difficulty obtain work as a journeyman. And it was from that dark hole, that lowly wretchedness, that Bernadette, the elder girl, with Marie, her sister, and Jeanne, a little friend of the neighbourhood, went out to pick up dead wood, on the cold February Thursday already spoken of.

Then the beautiful tale was unfolded at length; how the three girls followed the bank of the Gave from the other side of the castle, and how they ended by finding themselves on the Ile du Chalet in front of the rock of Massabielle, from which they were only separated by the narrow stream diverted from the Gave, and used for working the mill of Savy. It was a wild spot, whither the common herdsman often brought the pigs of the neighbourhood, which, when showers suddenly came on, would take shelter under this rock of Massabielle, at whose base there was a kind of grotto of no great depth, blocked at the entrance by eglantine and brambles. The girls found dead wood very scarce that day, but at last on seeing on the other side of the stream quite a gleaning of branches deposited there by the torrent, Marie and Jeanne crossed over through the water; whilst Bernadette, more delicate than they were, a trifle young-ladyfied, perhaps, remained on the bank lamenting, and not daring to wet her feet. She was suffering slightly from humour in the head, and her mother had expressly bidden her to wrap herself in her *capulet*,[1] a large white *capulet* which contrasted vividly with her old black woollen dress. When she found that her companions would not help her, she resignedly made up her mind to take off her *sabots*, and pull down her stockings. It was then about noon, the three strokes of the Angelus rang out from the

---

[1] This is a kind of hood, more generally known among the Bearnese peasantry as a sarot. Whilst forming a coif it also completely covers the back and shoulders.—Trans.

parish church, rising into the broad calm winter sky, which was somewhat veiled by fine fleecy clouds. And it was then that a great agitation arose within her, resounding in her ears with such a tempestuous roar that she fancied a hurricane had descended from the mountains, and was passing over her. But she looked at the trees and was stupefied, for not a leaf was stirring. Then she thought that she had been mistaken, and was about to pick up her *sabots*, when again the great gust swept through her; but, this time, the disturbance in her ears reached her eyes, she no longer saw the trees, but was dazzled by a whiteness, a kind of bright light which seemed to her to settle itself against the rock, in a narrow, lofty slit above the Grotto, not unlike an ogival window of a cathedral. In her fright she fell upon her knees. What could it be, *mon Dieu*? Sometimes, during bad weather, when her asthma oppressed her more than usual, she spent very bad nights, incessantly dreaming dreams which were often painful, and whose stifling effect she retained on awaking, even when she had ceased to remember anything. Flames would surround her, the sun would flash before her face. Had she dreamt in that fashion during the previous night? Was this the continuation of some forgotten dream? However, little by little a form became outlined, she believed that she could distinguish a figure which the vivid light rendered intensely white. In her fear lest it should be the devil, for her mind was haunted by tales of witchcraft, she began to tell her beads. And when the light had slowly faded away, and she had crossed the canal and joined Marie and Jeanne, she was surprised to find that neither of them had seen anything whilst they were picking up the wood in front of the Grotto. On their way back to Lourdes the three girls talked together. So she, Bernadette, had seen something then? What was it? At first, feeling uneasy, and somewhat ashamed, she would not answer; but at last she said that she had seen something white.

From this the rumours started and grew. The Soubirouses, on being made acquainted with the circumstance, evinced much displeasure at such childish nonsense, and told their daughter that she was not to return to the rock of Massabielle. All the children of the neighbourhood, however, were already repeating the tale, and when Sunday came the parents had to give way, and allow Bernadette to betake herself to the Grotto with a bottle of holy water to ascertain if it were really the devil whom one had to deal with. She then again beheld the light, the figure became more clearly defined, and smiled upon her, evincing no fear whatever of the holy water. And, on the ensuing Thursday, she once more returned to the spot accompanied by several persons, and then for the first time the radiant lady assumed sufficient corporality to speak, and say to her: "Do me the kindness to come here for fifteen days."

Thus, little by little, the lady had assumed a precise appearance. The something clad in white had become indeed a lady more beautiful than a queen, of a kind such as is only seen in pictures. At first, in presence of the questions with which all the neighbours plied her from morning till evening, Bernadette had hesitated, disturbed, perhaps, by scruples of conscience. But then, as though prompted by the very interrogatories to which she was subjected, she seemed to perceive the figure which she had beheld, more plainly, so that it definitely assumed life, with lines and hues from which the child, in her after-descriptions, never departed. The lady's eyes were blue and very mild, her mouth was rosy and smiling, the oval of her face expressed both the grace of youth and of maternity. Below the veil covering her head and falling to her heels, only a glimpse was caught of her admirable fair hair, which was slightly curled. Her robe, which was of dazzling whiteness, must have been of some material unknown on earth, some material woven of the sun's rays. Her sash, of the same hue as the heavens, was fastened loosely about her, its long ends streaming downwards, with the light airiness of morning. Her chaplet, wound about her right arm, had beads of a milky whiteness, whilst the links and the cross were of gold. And on her bare feet, on her adorable feet of virgin snow, flowered two golden roses, the mystic roses of this divine mother's immaculate flesh.

Where was it that Bernadette had seen this Blessed Virgin, of such traditionally simple composition, unadorned by a single jewel, having but the primitive grace imagined by the painters of a people in its childhood? In which illustrated book belonging to her foster-mother's brother, the good priest, who read such attractive stories, had she beheld this Virgin? Or in what picture, or what statuette, or what stained-glass window of the painted and gilded church where she had spent so many evenings whilst growing up? And whence, above all things, had come those golden roses poised on the Virgin's feet, that piously imagined florescence of woman's flesh—from what romance of chivalry, from what story told after catechism by the Abbe Ader, from what unconscious dream indulged in under the shady foliage of Bartres, whilst ever and ever repeating that haunting Angelic Salutation?

Pierre's voice had acquired a yet more feeling tone, for if he did not say all these things to the simple-minded folks who were listening to him, still the human explanation of all these prodigies which the feeling of doubt in the depths of his being strove to supply, imparted to his narrative a quiver of sympathetic, fraternal love. He loved Bernadette the better for the great charm of her hallucination—that lady of such gracious access, such perfect amiability, such politeness in appearing and disappearing so appropriately. At first the great light would show itself, then the vision took form, came and went, leant forward, moved about, floating imperceptibly, with ethereal lightness; and when it vanished the glow lingered for yet another moment, and then disappeared like a star fading away. No lady in this world could have such a white and rosy face, with a beauty so akin to that of the Virgins on the picture-cards given to children at their first communions. And it was strange that the eglantine of the Grotto did not even hurt her adorable bare feet blooming with golden flowers.

Pierre, however, at once proceeded to recount the other apparitions. The fourth and fifth occurred on the Friday and the Saturday; but the Lady, who shone so brightly and who had not yet told her name, contented herself on these occasions with smiling and saluting without pronouncing a word. On the Sunday, however, she wept, and said to Bernadette, "Pray for sinners." On the Monday, to the child's great grief, she did not appear, wishing, no doubt, to try her. But on the Tuesday she confided to her a secret which concerned her (the girl) alone, a secret which she was never to divulge[1]; and then she at last told her what mission it was that she entrusted to her: "Go and tell the priests," she said, "that they must build a chapel here." On the Wednesday she frequently murmured the word "Penitence! penitence! penitence!" which the child repeated, afterwards kissing the earth. On the Thursday the Lady said to her: "Go, and

---

[1] In a like way, it will be remembered, the apparition at La Salette confided a secret to Melanie and Maximin (see ante, note). There can be little doubt that Bernadette was acquainted with the story of the miracle of La Salette.—Trans.

drink, and wash at the spring, and eat of the grass that is beside it," words which the Visionary ended by understanding, when in the depths of the Grotto a source suddenly sprang up beneath her fingers. And this was the miracle of the enchanted fountain.

Then the second week ran its course. The lady did not appear on the Friday, but was punctual on the five following days, repeating her commands and gazing with a smile at the humble girl whom she had chosen to do her bidding, and who, on her side, duly told her beads at each apparition, kissed the earth, and repaired on her knees to the source, there to drink and wash. At last, on Thursday, March 4, the last day of these mystical assignations, the Lady requested more pressingly than before that a chapel might be erected in order that the nations might come thither in procession from all parts of the earth. So far, however, in reply to all Bernadette's appeals, she had refused to say who she was; and it was only three weeks later, on Thursday, March 25, that, joining her hands together, and raising her eyes to Heaven, she said: "I am the Immaculate Conception." On two other occasions, at somewhat long intervals, April 7 and July 16, she again appeared: the first time to perform the miracle of the lighted taper, that taper above which the child, plunged in ecstasy, for a long time unconsciously left her hand, without burning it; and the second time to bid Bernadette farewell, to favour her with a last smile, and a last inclination of the head full of charming politeness. This made eighteen apparitions all told; and never again did the Lady show herself.

Whilst Pierre went on with his beautiful, marvellous story, so soothing to the wretched, he evoked for himself a vision of that pitiable, lovable Bernadette, whose sufferings had flowered so wonderfully. As a doctor had roughly expressed it, this girl of fourteen, at a critical period of her life, already ravaged, too, by asthma, was, after all, simply an exceptional victim of hysteria, afflicted with a degenerate heredity and lapsing into infancy. If there were no violent crises in her case, if there were no stiffening of the muscles during her attacks, if she retained a precise recollection of her dreams, the reason was that her case was peculiar to herself, and she added, so to say, a new and very curious form to all the forms of hysteria known at the time. Miracles only begin when things cannot be explained; and science, so far, knows and can explain so little, so infinitely do the phenomena of disease vary according to the nature of the patient! But how many shepherdesses there had been before Bernadette who had seen the Virgin in a similar way, amidst all the same childish nonsense! Was it not always the same story, the Lady clad in light, the secret confided, the spring bursting forth, the mission which had to be fulfilled, the miracles whose enchantments would convert the masses? And was not the personal appearance of the Virgin always in accordance with a poor child's dreams—akin to some coloured figure in a missal, an ideal compounded of traditional beauty, gentleness, and politeness. And the same dreams showed themselves in the naivete of the means which were to be employed and of the object which was to be attained—the deliverance of nations, the building of churches, the processional pilgrimages of the faithful! Then, too, all the words which fell from Heaven resembled one another, calls for penitence, promises of help; and in this respect, in Bernadette's case the only new feature was that most extraordinary declaration: "I am the Immaculate Conception," which burst forth—very usefully—as the recognition by the Blessed Virgin herself of the dogma promulgated by the Court of Rome but three years previously! It was not the Immaculate Virgin who appeared: no, it was the Immaculate Conception, the abstraction itself, the thing, the dogma, so that one might well ask oneself if really the Virgin had spoken in such a fashion. As for the other words, it was possible that Bernadette had heard them somewhere and stored them up in some unconscious nook of her memory. But these—"I am the Immaculate Conception"—whence had they come as though expressly to fortify a dogma—still bitterly discussed—with such prodigious support as the direct testimony of the Mother conceived without sin? At this thought, Pierre, who was convinced of Bernadette's absolute good faith, who refused to believe that she had been the instrument of a fraud, began to waver, deeply agitated, feeling his belief in truth totter within him.

The apparitions, however, had caused intense emotion at Lourdes; crowds flocked to the spot, miracles began, and those inevitable persecutions broke out which ensure the triumph of new religions. Abbe Peyramale, the parish priest of Lourdes, an extremely honest man, with an upright, vigorous mind, was able in all truth to declare that he did not know this child, that she had not yet been seen at catechism. Where was the pressure, then, where the lesson learnt by heart? There was nothing but those years of childhood spent at Bartres, the first teachings of Abbe Ader, conversations possibly, religious ceremonies in honour of the recently proclaimed dogma, or simply the gift of one of those commemorative medals which had been scattered in profusion. Never did Abbe Ader reappear upon the scene, he who had predicted the mission of the future Visionary. He was destined to remain apart from Bernadette and her future career, he who, the first, had seen her little soul blossom in his pious hands. And yet all the unknown forces that had sprung from that sequestered village, from that nook of greenery where superstition and poverty of intelligence prevailed, were still making themselves felt, disturbing the brains of men, disseminating the contagion of the mysterious. It was remembered that a shepherd of Argeles, speaking of the rock of Massabielle, had prophesied that great things would take place there. Other children, moreover, now fell in ecstasy with their eyes dilated and their limbs quivering with convulsions, but these only saw the devil. A whirlwind of madness seemed to be passing over the region. An old lady of Lourdes declared that Bernadette was simply a witch and that she had herself seen the toad's foot in her eye. But for the others, for the thousands of pilgrims who hastened to the spot, she was a saint, and they kissed her garments. Sobs burst forth and frenzy seemed to seize upon the souls of the beholders, when she fell upon her knees before the Grotto, a lighted taper in her right hand, whilst with the left she told the beads of her rosary. She became very pale and quite beautiful, transfigured, so to say. Her features gently ascended in her face, lengthened into an expression of extraordinary beatitude, whilst her eyes filled with light, and her lips parted as though she were speaking words which could not be heard. And it was quite certain that she had no will of her own left her, penetrated as she was by a dream, possessed by it to such a point in the confined, exclusive sphere in which she lived, that she continued dreaming it even when awake, and thus accepted it as the only indisputable reality, prepared to testify to it even at the cost of her blood, repeating it over and over again, obstinately, stubbornly clinging to it, and never varying in the details she gave. She did not lie, for she did not know, could not and would not desire anything apart from it.

Forgetful of the flight of time, Pierre was now sketching a charming picture of old Lourdes, that pious little town, slumbering at the foot of the Pyrenees. The castle, perched on a rock at the point of intersection of the seven valleys of Lavedan, had formerly been the key of the mountain districts. But, in Bernadette's time, it had become a mere dismantled, ruined pile, at the entrance of a road leading nowhere. Mod-Modern life found its march stayed by a formidable rampart of lofty, snow-capped peaks, and only the trans-Pyrenean railway—had it been constructed—could have established an active circulation of social life in that sequestered nook where human existence stagnated like dead water. Forgotten, therefore, Lourdes remained slumbering, happy and sluggish amidst its old-time peacefulness, with its narrow, pebble-paved streets and its bleak houses with dressings of marble. The old roofs were still all massed on the eastern side of the castle; the Rue de la Grotte, then called the Rue du Bois, was but a deserted and often impassable road; no houses stretched down to the Gave as now, and the scum-laden waters rolled through a perfect solitude of pollard willows and tall grass. On week-days but few people passed across the Place du Marcadal, such as housewives hastening on errands, and petty cits airing their leisure hours; and you had to wait till Sundays or fair days to find the inhabitants rigged out in their best clothes and assembled on the Champ Commun, in company with the crowd of graziers who had come down from the distant tablelands with their cattle. During the season when people resort to the Pyrenean-waters, the passage of the visitors to Cauterets and Bagneres also brought some animation; *diligences* passed through the town twice a day, but they came from Pau by a wretched road, and had to ford the Lapaca, which often overflowed its banks. Then climbing the steep ascent of the Rue Basse, they skirted the terrace of the church, which was shaded by large elms. And what soft peacefulness prevailed in and around that old semi-Spanish church, full of ancient carvings, columns, screens, and statues, peopled with visionary patches of gilding and painted flesh, which time had mellowed and which you faintly discerned as by the light of mystical lamps! The whole population came there to worship, to fill their eyes with the dream of the mysterious. There were no unbelievers, the inhabitants of Lourdes were a people of primitive faith; each corporation marched behind the banner of its saint, brotherhoods of all kinds united the entire town, on festival mornings, in one large Christian family. And, as with some exquisite flower that has grown in the soil of its choice, great purity of life reigned there. There was not even a resort of debauchery for young men to wreck their lives, and the girls, one and all, grew up with the perfume and beauty of innocence, under the eyes of the Blessed Virgin, Tower of Ivory and Seat of Wisdom.

And how well one could understand that Bernadette, born in that holy soil, should flower in it, like one of nature's roses budding in the wayside bushes! She was indeed the very florescence of that region of ancient belief and rectitude; she would certainly not have sprouted elsewhere; she could only appear and develop there, amidst that belated race, amidst the slumberous peacefulness of a childlike people, under the moral discipline of religion. And what intense love at once burst forth all around her! What blind confidence was displayed in her mission, what immense consolation and hope came to human hearts on the very morrow of the first miracles! A long cry of relief had greeted the cure of old Bourriette recovering his sight, and of little Justin Bouhohorts coming to life again in the icy water of the spring. At last, then, the Blessed Virgin was intervening in favour of those who despaired, forcing that unkind mother, Nature, to be just and charitable. This was divine omnipotence returning to reign on earth, sweeping the laws of the world aside in order to work the happiness of the suffering and the poor. The miracles multiplied, blazed forth, from day to day more and more extraordinary, like unimpeachable proof of Bernadette's veracity. And she was, indeed, the rose of the divine garden, whose deeds shed perfume, the rose who beholds all the other flowers of grace and salvation spring into being around her.

Pierre had reached this point of his story, and was again enumerating the miracles, on the point of recounting the prodigious triumph of the Grotto, when Sister Hyacinthe, awaking with a start from the ecstasy into which the narrative had plunged her, hastily rose to her feet. "Really, really," said she, "there is no sense in it. It will soon be eleven o'clock."

This was true. They had left Morceux behind them, and would now soon be at Mont de Marsan. So Sister Hyacinthe clapped her hands once more, and added: "Silence, my children, silence!"

This time they did not dare to rebel, for they felt she was in the right; they were unreasonable. But how greatly they regretted not hearing the continuation, how vexed they were that the story should cease when only half told! The ten women in the farther compartment even let a murmur of disappointment escape them; whilst the sick, their faces still outstretched, their dilated eyes gazing upon the light of hope, seemed to be yet listening. Those miracles which ever and ever returned to their minds and filled them with unlimited, haunting, supernatural joy.

"And don't let me hear anyone breathe, even," added Sister Hyacinthe gaily, "or otherwise I shall impose penance on you."

Madame de Jonquiere laughed good-naturedly. "You must obey, my children," she said; "be good and get to sleep, so that you may have strength to pray at the Grotto tomorrow with all your hearts."

Then silence fell, nobody spoke any further; and the only sounds were those of the rumbling of the wheels and the jolting of the train as it was carried along at full speed through the black night.

Pierre, however, was unable to sleep. Beside him, M. de Guersaint was already snoring lightly, looking very happy despite the hardness of his seat. For a time the young priest saw Marie's eyes wide open, still full of all the radiance of the marvels that he had related. For a long while she kept them ardently fixed upon his own, but at last closed them, and then he knew not whether she was sleeping, or with eyelids simply closed was living the everlasting miracle over again. Some of the sufferers were dreaming aloud, giving vent to bursts of laughter which unconscious moans interrupted. Perhaps they beheld the Archangels opening their flesh to wrest their diseases from them. Others, restless with insomnia, turned over and over, stifling their sobs and gazing fixedly into the darkness. And, with a shudder born of all the mystery he had evoked, Pierre, distracted, no longer master of himself in that delirious sphere of fraternal suffering, ended by hating his very mind, and, drawn into close communion with all those humble folks, sought to believe like them. What could be the use of that physiological inquiry into Bernadette's case, so full of gaps and intricacies? Why should he not accept her as a messenger from the spheres beyond, as one of the elect chosen for the divine mystery? Doctors were but ignorant men with rough and brutal hands, and it would be so delightful to fall asleep in childlike faith, in the enchanted gardens of the impossible. And for a moment indeed he surrendered himself, experiencing a delightful feeling of comfort, no longer seeking to explain anything, but accepting the Visionary with her sumptuous *cortege* of miracles, and relying on God to think and determine for him. Then he looked out through the window, which they did not dare to open on account of the consumptive patients, and beheld the immeasurable night which enwrapped the country across which the train was fleeing. The storm must have burst forth there; the sky was now of an admirable nocturnal purity, as though cleansed by the masses of fallen water. Large stars shone out in the dark velvet, alone illumining, with their mysterious gleams, the silent, refreshed fields, which incessantly displayed only the black solitude of slumber. And across the Landes, through the valleys, between the hills, that carriage of wretchedness and suffering rolled on and on, over-heated, pestilential, rueful, and wailing, amidst the serenity of the august night, so lovely and so mild.

They had passed Riscle at one in the morning. Between the jolting, the painful, the hallucinatory silence still continued. At two o'clock, as they reached Vic-de-Bigorre, low moans were heard; the bad state of the line, with the unbearable spreading tendency of the train's motion, was sorely shaking the patients. It was only at Tarbes, at half-past two, that silence was at length broken, and that morning prayers were said, though black night still reigned around them. There came first the "Pater," and then the "Ave," the "Credo," and the supplication to God to grant them the happiness of a glorious day.

"O God, vouchsafe me sufficient strength that I may avoid all that is evil, do all that is good, and suffer uncomplainingly every pain."

And now there was to be no further stoppage until they reached Lourdes. Barely three more quarters of an hour, and Lourdes, with all its vast hopes, would blaze forth in the midst of that night, so long and cruel. Their painful awakening was enfevered by the thought; a final agitation arose amidst the morning discomfort, as the abominable sufferings began afresh.

Sister Hyacinthe, however, was especially anxious about the strange man, whose sweat-covered face she had been continually wiping. He had so far managed to keep alive, she watching him without a pause, never having once closed her eyes, but unremittingly listening to his faint breathing with the stubborn desire to take him to the holy Grotto before he died.

All at once, however, she felt frightened; and addressing Madame de Jonquiere, she hastily exclaimed, "Pray pass me the vinegar bottle at once—I can no longer hear him breathe."

For an instant, indeed, the man's faint breathing had ceased. His eyes were still closed, his lips parted; he could not have been paler, he had an ashen hue, and was cold. And the carriage was rolling along with its ceaseless rattle of coupling-irons; the speed of the train seemed even to have increased.

"I will rub his temples," resumed Sister Hyacinthe. "Help me, do!"

But, at a more violent jolt of the train, the man suddenly fell from the seat, face downward.

"Ah! *mon Dieu*, help me, pick him up!"

They picked him up, and found him dead. And they had to seat him in his corner again, with his back resting against the woodwork. He remained there erect, his torso stiffened, and his head wagging slightly at each successive jolt. Thus the train continued carrying him along, with the same thundering noise of wheels, while the engine, well pleased, no doubt, to be reaching its destination, began whistling shrilly, giving vent to quite a flourish of delirious joy as it sped through the calm night.

And then came the last and seemingly endless half-hour of the journey, in company with that wretched corpse. Two big tears had rolled down Sister Hyacinthe's cheeks, and with her hands joined she had begun to pray. The whole carriage shuddered with terror at sight of that terrible companion who was being taken, too late alas! to the Blessed Virgin.

Hope, however, proved stronger than sorrow or pain, and although all the sufferings there assembled awoke and grew again, irritated by overwhelming weariness, a song of joy nevertheless proclaimed the sufferers' triumphal entry into the Land of Miracles. Amidst the tears which their pains drew from them, the exasperated and howling sick began to chant the "Ave maris Stella" with a growing clamour in which lamentation finally turned into cries of hope.

Marie had again taken Pierre's hand between her little feverish fingers. "Oh, *mon Dieu!*" said she, "to think that poor man is dead, and I feared so much that it was I who would die before arriving. And we are there—there at last!"

The priest was trembling with intense emotion. "It means that you are to be cured, Marie," he replied, "and that I myself shall be cured if you pray for me—"

The engine was now whistling in a yet louder key in the depths of the bluish darkness. They were nearing their destination. The lights of Lourdes already shone out on the horizon. Then the whole train again sang a canticle—the rhymed story of Bernadette, that endless ballad of six times ten couplets, in which the Angelic Salutation ever returns as a refrain, all besetting and distracting, opening to the human mind the portals of the heaven of ecstasy:—

"It was the hour for ev'ning pray'r;
Soft bells chimed on the chilly air.
Ave, ave, ave Maria!

"The maid stood on the torrent's bank,
A breeze arose, then swiftly sank.
Ave, ave, ave Maria!

"And she beheld, e'en as it fell,
The Virgin on Massabielle.
Ave, ave, ave Maria!

"All white appeared the Lady chaste,
A zone of Heaven round her waist.
Ave, ave, ave Maria!

"Two golden roses, pure and sweet,
Bloomed brightly on her naked feet.
Ave, ave, ave Maria!

"Upon her arm, so white and round,
Her chaplet's milky pearls were wound.
Ave, ave, ave Maria!

V. BERNADETTE

"The maiden prayed till, from her eyes,
The vision sped to Paradise.
Ave, ave, ave Maria!"

THE SECOND DAY

I. THE TRAIN ARRIVES

IT was twenty minutes past three by the clock of the Lourdes railway station, the dial of which was illumined by a reflector. Under the slanting roof sheltering the platform, a hundred yards or so in length, some shadowy forms went to and fro, resignedly waiting. Only a red signal light peeped out of the black countryside, far away.

Two of the promenaders suddenly halted. The taller of them, a Father of the Assumption, none other indeed than the Reverend Father Fourcade, director of the national pilgrimage, who had reached Lourdes on the previous day, was a man of sixty, looking superb in his black cloak with its large hood. His fine head, with its clear, domineering eyes and thick grizzly beard, was the head of a general whom an intelligent determination to conquer inflames. In consequence, however, of a sudden attack of gout he slightly dragged one of his legs, and was leaning on the shoulder of his companion, Dr. Bonamy, the practitioner attached to the Miracle Verification Office, a short, thick-set man, with a square-shaped, clean-shaven face, which had dull, blurred eyes and a tranquil cast of features.

Father Fourcade had stopped to question the station-master whom he perceived running out of his office. "Will the white train be very late, monsieur?" he asked.

"No, your reverence. It hasn't lost more than ten minutes; it will be here at the half-hour. It's the Bayonne train which worries me; it ought to have passed through already."

So saying, he ran off to give an order; but soon came back again, his slim, nervous figure displaying marked signs of agitation. He lived, indeed, in a state of high fever throughout the period of the great pilgrimages. Apart from the usual service, he that day expected eighteen trains, containing more than fifteen thousand passengers. The grey and the blue trains which had started from Paris the first had already arrived at the regulation hour. But the delay in the arrival of the white train was very troublesome, the more so as the Bayonne express—which passed over the same rails—had not yet been signalled. It was easy to understand, therefore, what incessant watchfulness was necessary, not a second passing without the entire staff of the station being called upon to exercise its vigilance.

"In ten minutes, then?" repeated Father Fourcade.

"Yes, in ten minutes, unless I'm obliged to close the line!" cried the station-master as he hastened into the telegraph office.

Father Fourcade and the doctor slowly resumed their promenade. The thing which astonished them was that no serious accident had ever happened in the midst of such a fearful scramble. In past times, especially, the most terrible disorder had prevailed. Father Fourcade complacently recalled the first pilgrimage which he had organised and led, in 1875; the terrible endless journey without pillows or mattresses, the patients exhausted, half dead, with no means of reviving them at hand; and then the arrival at Lourdes, the train evacuated in confusion, no *materiel* in readiness, no straps, nor stretchers, nor carts. But now there was a powerful organisation; a hospital awaited the sick, who were no longer reduced to lying upon straw in sheds. What a shock for those unhappy ones! What force of will in the man of faith who led them to the scene of miracles! The reverend Father smiled gently at the thought of the work which he had accomplished.

Then, still leaning on the doctor's shoulder, he began to question him: "How many pilgrims did you have last year?" he asked.

"About two hundred thousand. That is still the average. In the year of the Coronation of the Virgin the figure rose to five hundred thousand. But to bring that about an exceptional occasion was needed with a great effort of propaganda. Such vast masses cannot be collected together every day."

A pause followed, and then Father Fourcade murmured: "No doubt. Still the blessing of Heaven attends our endeavours; our work thrives more and more. We have collected more than two hundred thousand francs in donations for this journey, and God will be with us, there will be many cures for you to proclaim to-morrow, I am sure of it." Then, breaking off, he inquired: "Has not Father Dargeles come here?"

Dr. Bonamy waved his hand as though to say that he did not know. Father Dargeles was the editor of the "Journal de la Grotte." He belonged to the Order of the Fathers of the Immaculate Conception whom the Bishop had installed at Lourdes and who were the absolute masters there; though, when the Fathers of the Assumption came to the town with the national pilgrimage from Paris, which crowds of faithful Catholics from Cambrai, Arras, Chartres, Troyes, Rheims, Sens, Orleans, Blois, and Poitiers joined, they evinced a kind of affectation in disappearing from the scene. Their omnipotence was no longer felt either at the Grotto or at the Basilica; they seemed to surrender every key together with every responsibility. Their superior, Father Capdebarthe, a tall, peasant-like man, with a knotty frame, a big head which looked as if it had been fashioned with a bill-hook, and a worn face which retained a ruddy mournful reflection of the soil, did not even show himself. Of the whole community you only saw little, insinuating Father Dargeles; but he was met everywhere, incessantly on the look-out for paragraphs for his newspaper. At the same time, however, although the Fathers of the Immaculate Conception disappeared in this fashion, it could be divined that they were behind the vast stage, like a hidden sovereign power, coining money and toiling without a pause to increase the triumphant prosperity of their business. Indeed, they turned even their humility to account.

"It's true that we have had to get up early—two in the morning," resumed Father Fourcade gaily. "But I wished to be here. What would my poor children have said, indeed, if I had not come?"

He was alluding to the sick pilgrims, those who were so much flesh for miracle-working; and it was a fact that he had never missed coming to the station, no matter what the hour, to meet that woeful white train, that train which brought such grievous suffering with it.

"Five-and-twenty minutes past three—only another five minutes now," exclaimed Dr. Bonamy repressing a yawn as he glanced at the clock; for, despite his obsequious air, he was at bottom very much annoyed at having had to get out of bed so early. However, he continued his slow promenade with Father Fourcade along that platform which resembled a covered walk, pacing up and down in the dense night which the gas jets here and there illumined with patches of yellow light. Little parties, dimly outlined, composed of priests and gentlemen in frock-coats, with a solitary officer of dragoons, went to and fro incessantly, talking together the while in discreet murmuring tones. Other people, seated on benches, ranged along the station wall, were also chatting or putting their patience to proof with their glances wandering away into the black stretch of country before them. The doorways of the offices and waiting-rooms, which were brilliantly lighted, looked like great holes in the darkness, and all was flaring in the refreshment-room, where you could see the marble tables and the counter laden with bottles and glasses and baskets of bread and fruit.

On the right hand, beyond the roofing of the platform, there was a confused swarming of people. There was here a goods gate, by which the sick were taken out of the station, and a mass of stretchers, litters, and hand-carts, with piles of pillows and mattresses, obstructed the broad walk. Three parties of bearers were also assembled here, persons of well-nigh every class, but more particularly young men of good society, all wearing red, orange-tipped crosses and straps of yellow leather. Many of them, too, had adopted the Bearnese cap, the convenient head-gear of the region; and a few, clad as though they were bound on some distant expedition, displayed wonderful gaiters reaching to their knees. Some were smoking, whilst others, installed in their little vehicles, slept or read newspapers by the light of the neighbouring gas jets. One group, standing apart, were discussing some service question.

Suddenly, however, one and all began to salute. A paternal-looking man, with a heavy but good-natured face, lighted by large blue eyes, like those of a credulous child, was approaching. It was Baron Suire, the President of the Hospitality of Our Lady of Salvation. He possessed a great fortune and occupied a high position at Toulouse.

"Where is Berthaud?" he inquired of one bearer after another, with a busy air. "Where is Berthaud? I must speak to him."

The others answered, volunteering contradictory information. Berthaud was their superintendent, and whilst some said that they had seen him with the Reverend Father Fourcade, others affirmed that he must be in the courtyard of the station inspecting the ambulance vehicles. And they thereupon offered to go and fetch him.

"No, no, thank you," replied the Baron. "I shall manage to find him myself."

Whilst this was happening, Berthaud, who had just seated himself on a bench at the other end of the station, was talking with his young friend, Gerard de Peyrelongue, by way of occupation pending the arrival of the train. The superintendent of the bearers was a man of forty, with a broad, regular-featured, handsome face and carefully trimmed whiskers of a lawyer-like pattern. Belonging to a militant Legitimist family and holding extremely reactionary opinions, he had been Procureur de la

Republique (public prosecutor) in a town of the south of France from the time of the parliamentary revolution of the twenty-fourth of May[1] until that of the decree of the Religious Communities,[2] when he had resigned his post in a blusterous fashion, by addressing an insulting letter to the Minister of Justice. And he had never since laid down his arms, but had joined the Hospitality of Our Lady of Salvation as a sort of protest, repairing year after year to Lourdes in order to "demonstrate"; convinced as he was that the pilgrimages were both disagreeable and hurtful to the Republic, and that God alone could re-establish the Monarchy by one of those miracles which He worked so lavishly at the Grotto. Despite all this, however, Berthaud possessed no small amount of good sense, and being of a gay disposition, displayed a kind of jovial charity towards the poor sufferers whose transport he had to provide for during the three days that the national pilgrimage remained at Lourdes.

"And so, my dear Gerard," he said to the young man seated beside him, "your marriage is really to come off this year?"

"Why yes, if I can find such a wife as I want," replied the other. "Come, cousin, give me some good advice."

Gerard de Peyrelongue, a short, thin, carroty young man, with a pronounced nose and prominent cheek-bones, belonged to Tarbes, where his father and mother had lately died, leaving him at the utmost some seven or eight thousand francs a year. Extremely ambitious, he had been unable to find such a wife as he desired in his native province—a well-connected young woman capable of helping him to push both forward and upward in the world; and so he had joined the Hospitality, and betook himself every summer to Lourdes, in the vague hope that amidst the mass of believers, the torrent of devout mammas and daughters which flowed thither, he might find the family whose help he needed to enable him to make his way in this terrestrial sphere. However, he remained in perplexity, for if, on the one hand, he already had several young ladies in view, on the other, none of them completely satisfied him.

"Eh, cousin? You will advise me, won't you?" he said to Berthaud. "You are a man of experience. There is Mademoiselle Lemercier who comes here with her aunt. She is very rich; according to what is said she has over a million francs. But she doesn't belong to our set, and besides I think her a bit of a madcap."

Berthaud nodded. "I told you so; if I were you I should choose little Raymonde, Mademoiselle de Jonquiere."

"But she hasn't a copper!"

"That's true—she has barely enough to pay for her board. But she is fairly good-looking, she has been well brought up, and she has no extravagant tastes. That is the really important point, for what is the use of marrying a rich girl if she squanders the dowry she brings you? Besides, I know Madame and Mademoiselle de Jonquiere very well, I meet them all through the winter in the most influential drawing-rooms of Paris. And, finally, don't forget the girl's uncle, the diplomatist, who has had the painful

---

[1] The parliamentary revolution of May, 1873, by which M. Thiers was overthrown and Marshal MacMahon installed in his place with the object of restoring the Monarchy in France.—Trans.

[2] M. Grevy's decree by which the Jesuits were expelled.—Trans.

courage to remain in the service of the Republic. He will be able to do whatever he pleases for his niece's husband."

For a moment Gerard seemed shaken, and then he relapsed into perplexity. "But she hasn't a copper," he said, "no, not a copper. It's too stiff. I am quite willing to think it over, but it really frightens me too much."

This time Berthaud burst into a frank laugh. "Come, you are ambitious, so you must be daring. I tell you that it means the secretaryship of an embassy before two years are over. By the way, Madame and Mademoiselle de Jonquiere are in the white train which we are waiting for. Make up your mind and pay your court at once."

"No, no! Later on. I want to think it over."

At this moment they were interrupted, for Baron Suire, who had already once gone by without perceiving them, so completely did the darkness enshroud them in that retired corner, had just recognised the ex-public prosecutor's good-natured laugh. And, thereupon, with the volubility of a man whose head is easily unhinged, he gave him several orders respecting the vehicles and the transport service, deploring the circumstance that it would be impossible to conduct the patients to the Grotto immediately on their arrival, as it was yet so extremely early. It had therefore been decided that they should in the first instance be taken to the Hospital of Our Lady of Dolours, where they would be able to rest awhile after their trying journey.

Whilst the Baron and the superintendent were thus settling what measures should be adopted, Gerard shook hands with a priest who had sat down beside him. This was the Abbe des Hermoises, who was barely eight-and-thirty years of age and had a superb head—such a head as one might expect to find on the shoulders of a worldly priest. With his hair well combed, and his person perfumed, he was not unnaturally a great favourite among women. Very amiable and distinguished in his manners, he did not come to Lourdes in any official capacity, but simply for his pleasure, as so many other people did; and the bright, sparkling smile of a sceptic above all idolatry gleamed in the depths of his fine eyes. He certainly believed, and bowed to superior decisions; but the Church—the Holy See—had not pronounced itself with regard to the miracles; and he seemed quite ready to dispute their authenticity. Having lived at Tarbes he was already acquainted with Gerard.

"Ah!" he said to him, "how impressive it is—isn't it?—this waiting for the trains in the middle of the night! I have come to meet a lady—one of my former Paris penitents—but I don't know what train she will come by. Still, as you see, I stop on, for it all interests me so much."

Then another priest, an old country priest, having come to sit down on the same bench, the Abbe considerately began talking to him, speaking of the beauty of the Lourdes district and of the theatrical effect which would take place by-and-by when the sun rose and the mountains appeared.

However, there was again a sudden alert, and the station-master ran along shouting orders. Removing his hand from Dr. Bonamy's shoulder, Father Fourcade, despite his gouty leg, hastily drew near.

"Oh! it's that Bayonne express which is so late," answered the station-master in reply to the questions addressed to him. "I should like some information about it; I'm not at ease."

At this moment the telegraph bells rang out and a porter rushed away into the darkness swinging a lantern, whilst a distant signal began to work. Thereupon the station-master resumed: "Ah! this time it's the white train. Let us hope we shall have time to get the sick people out before the express passes."

He started off once more and disappeared. Berthaud meanwhile called to Gerard, who was at the head of a squad of bearers, and they both made haste to join their men, into whom Baron Suire was already instilling activity. The bearers flocked to the spot from all sides, and setting themselves in motion began dragging their little vehicles across the lines to the platform at which the white train would come in—an unroofed platform plunged in darkness. A mass of pillows, mattresses, stretchers, and litters was soon waiting there, whilst Father Fourcade, Dr. Bonamy, the priests, the gentlemen, and the officer of dragoons in their turn crossed over in order to witness the removal of the ailing pilgrims. All that they could as yet see, far away in the depths of the black country, was the lantern in front of the engine, looking like a red star which grew larger and larger. Strident whistles pierced the night, then suddenly ceased, and you only heard the panting of the steam and the dull roar of the wheels gradually slackening their speed. Then the canticle became distinctly audible, the song of Bernadette with the ever-recurring "Aves" of its refrain, which the whole train was chanting in chorus. And at last this train of suffering and faith, this moaning, singing train, thus making its entry into Lourdes, drew up in the station.

The carriage doors were at once opened, the whole throng of healthy pilgrims, and of ailing ones able to walk, alighted, and streamed over the platform. The few gas lamps cast but a feeble light on the crowd of poverty-stricken beings clad in faded garments, and encumbered with all sorts of parcels, baskets, valises, and boxes. And amidst all the jostling of this scared flock, which did not know in which direction to turn to find its way out of the station, loud exclamations were heard, the shouts of people calling relatives whom they had lost, mingled with the embraces of others whom relatives or friends had come to meet. One woman declared with beatifical satisfaction, "I have slept well." A priest went off carrying his travelling-bag, after wishing a crippled lady "good luck!" Most of them had the bewildered, weary, yet joyous appearance of people whom an excursion train sets down at some unknown station. And such became the scramble and the confusion in the darkness, that they did not hear the railway *employes* who grew quite hoarse through shouting, "This way! this way!" in their eagerness to clear the platform as soon as possible.

Sister Hyacinthe had nimbly alighted from her compartment, leaving the dead man in the charge of Sister Claire des Anges; and, losing her head somewhat, she ran off to the cantine van in the idea that Ferrand would be able to help her. Fortunately she found Father Fourcade in front of the van and acquainted him with the fatality in a low voice. Repressing a gesture of annoyance, he thereupon called Baron Suire, who was passing, and began whispering in his ear. The muttering lasted for a few seconds, and then the Baron rushed off, and clove his way through the crowd with two bearers carrying a covered litter. In this the man was removed from the carriage as though he were a patient who had simply fainted, the mob of pilgrims paying no further attention to him amidst all the emotion of their arrival. Preceded by the Baron, the bearers carried the corpse into a goods office, where they provisionally lodged it behind some barrels; one of them, a fair-haired little fellow, a general's son, remaining to watch over it.

Meanwhile, after begging Ferrand and Sister Saint-Francois to go and wait for her in the courtyard of the station, near the reserved vehicle which was to take them to the

Hospital of Our Lady of Dolours, Sister Hyacinthe returned to the railway carriage and talked of helping her patients to alight before going away. But Marie would not let her touch her. "No, no!" said the girl, "do not trouble about me, Sister. I shall remain here the last. My father and Abbe Froment have gone to the van to fetch the wheels; I am waiting for their return; they know how to fix them, and they will take me away all right, you may be sure of it."

In the same way M. Sabathier and Brother Isidore did not desire to be moved until the crowd had decreased. Madame de Jonquiere, who had taken charge of La Grivotte, also promised to see to Madame Vetu's removal in an ambulance vehicle. And thereupon Sister Hyacinthe decided that she would go off at once so as to get everything ready at the hospital. Moreover, she took with her both little Sophie Couteau and Elise Rouquet, whose face she very carefully wrapped up. Madame Maze preceded them, while Madame Vincent, carrying her little girl, who was unconscious and quite white, struggled through the crowd, possessed by the fixed idea of running off as soon as possible and depositing the child in the Grotto at the feet of the Blessed Virgin.

The mob was now pressing towards the doorway by which passengers left the station, and to facilitate the egress of all these people it at last became necessary to open the luggage gates. The *employes*, at a loss how to take the tickets, held out their caps, which a downpour of the little cards speedily filled. And in the courtyard, a large square courtyard, skirted on three sides by the low buildings of the station, the most extraordinary uproar prevailed amongst all the vehicles of divers kinds which were there jumbled together. The hotel omnibuses, backed against the curb of the footway, displayed the most sacred names on their large boards—Jesus and Mary, St. Michel, the Rosary, and the Sacred Heart. Then there were ambulance vehicles, landaus, cabriolets, brakes, and little donkey carts, all entangled together, with their drivers shouting, swearing, and cracking their whips—the tumult being apparently increased by the obscurity in which the lanterns set brilliant patches of light.

Rain had fallen heavily a few hours previously. Liquid mud splashed up under the hoofs of the horses; the foot passengers sank into it to their ankles. M. Vigneron, whom Madame Vigneron and Madame Chaise were following in a state of distraction, raised Gustave, in order to place him in the omnibus from the Hotel of the Apparitions, after which he himself and the ladies climbed into the vehicle. Madame Maze, shuddering slightly, like a delicate tabby who fears to dirty the tips of her paws, made a sign to the driver of an old brougham, got into it, and quickly drove away, after giving as address the Convent of the Blue Sisters. And at last Sister Hyacinthe was able to install herself with Elise Rouquet and Sophie Couteau in a large *char-a-bancs*, in which Ferrand and Sisters Saint-Francois and Claire des Anges were already seated. The drivers whipped up their spirited little horses, and the vehicles went off at a breakneck pace, amidst the shouts of those left behind, and the splashing of the mire.

In presence of that rushing torrent, Madame Vincent, with her dear little burden in her arms, hesitated to cross over. Bursts of laughter rang out around her every now and then. Oh! what a filthy mess! And at sight of all the mud, the women caught up their skirts before attempting to pass through it. At last, when the courtyard had somewhat emptied, Madame Vincent herself ventured on her way, all terror lest the mire should make her fall in that black darkness. Then, on reaching a downhill road, she noticed there a number of women of the locality who were on the watch, offering furnished rooms, bed and board, according to the state of the pilgrim's purse.

"Which is the way to the Grotto, madame, if you please?" asked Madame Vincent, addressing one old woman of the party.

Instead of answering the question, however, the other offered her a cheap room. "You won't find anything in the hotels," said she, "for they are all full. Perhaps you will be able to eat there, but you certainly won't find a closet even to sleep in."

Eat, sleep, indeed! Had Madame Vincent any thought of such things; she who had left Paris with thirty sous in her pocket, all that remained to her after the expenses she had been put to!

"The way to the Grotto, if you please, madame?" she repeated.

Among the women who were thus touting for lodgers, there was a tall, well-built girl, dressed like a superior servant, and looking very clean, with carefully tended hands. She glanced at Madame Vincent and slightly shrugged her shoulders. And then, seeing a broad-chested priest with a red face go by, she rushed after him, offered him a furnished room, and continued following him, whispering in his ear.

Another girl, however, at last took pity on Madame Vincent and said to her: "Here, go down this road, and when you get to the bottom, turn to the right and you will reach the Grotto."

Meanwhile, the confusion inside the station continued. The healthy pilgrims, and those of the sick who retained the use of their legs could go off, thus, in some measure, clearing the platform; but the others, the more grievously stricken sufferers whom it was difficult to get out of the carriages and remove to the hospital, remained waiting. The bearers seemed to become quite bewildered, rushing madly hither and thither with their litters and vehicles, not knowing at what end to set about the profusion of work which lay before them.

As Berthaud, followed by Gerard, went along the platform, gesticulating, he noticed two ladies and a girl who were standing under a gas jet and to all appearance waiting. In the girl he recognised Raymonde, and with a sign of the hand he at once stopped his companion. "Ah! mademoiselle," said he, "how pleased I am to see you! Is Madame de Jonquiere quite well? You have made a good journey, I hope?" Then, without a pause, he added: "This is my friend, Monsieur Gerard de Peyrelongue."

Raymonde gazed fixedly at the young man with her clear, smiling eyes. "Oh! I already have the pleasure of being slightly acquainted with this gentleman," she said. "We have previously met one another at Lourdes."

Thereupon Gerard, who thought that his cousin Berthaud was conducting matters too quickly, and was quite resolved that he would not enter into any hasty engagement, contented himself with bowing in a ceremonious way.

"We are waiting for mamma," resumed Raymonde. "She is extremely busy; she has to see after some pilgrims who are very ill."

At this, little Madame Desagneaux, with her pretty, light wavy-haired head, began to say that it served Madame de Jonquiere right for refusing her services. She herself was stamping with impatience, eager to join in the work and make herself useful, whilst Madame Volmar, silent, shrinking back as though taking no interest in it at all, seemed simply desirous of penetrating the darkness, as though, indeed, she were seeking somebody with those magnificent eyes of hers, usually bedimmed, but now shining out like brasiers.

Just then, however, they were all pushed back. Madame Dieulafay was being removed from her first-class compartment, and Madame Desagneaux could not restrain an exclamation of pity. "Ah! the poor woman!"

There could in fact be no more distressing sight than this young woman, encompassed by luxury, covered with lace in her species of coffin, so wasted that she seemed to be a mere human shred, deposited on that platform till it could be taken away. Her husband and her sister, both very elegant and very sad, remained standing near her, whilst a man-servant and maid ran off with the valises to ascertain if the carriage which had been ordered by telegram was in the courtyard. Abbe Judaine also helped the sufferer; and when two men at last took her up he bent over her and wished her *au revoir*, adding some kind words which she did not seem to hear. Then as he watched her removal, he resumed, addressing himself to Berthaud, whom he knew: "Ah! the poor people, if they could only purchase their dear sufferer's cure. I told them that prayer was the most precious thing in the Blessed Virgin's eyes, and I hope that I have myself prayed fervently enough to obtain the compassion of Heaven. Nevertheless, they have brought a magnificent gift, a golden lantern for the Basilica, a perfect marvel, adorned with precious stones. May the Immaculate Virgin deign to smile upon it!"

In this way a great many offerings were brought by the pilgrims. Some huge bouquets of flowers had just gone by, together with a kind of triple crown of roses, mounted on a wooden stand. And the old priest explained that before leaving the station he wished to secure a banner, the gift of the beautiful Madame Jousseur, Madame Dieulafay's sister.

Madame de Jonquiere was at last approaching, however, and on perceiving Berthaud and Gerard she exclaimed: "Pray do go to that carriage, gentlemen—that one, there! We want some men very badly. There are three or four sick persons to be taken out. I am in despair; I can do nothing myself."

Gerard ran off after bowing to Raymonde, whilst Berthaud advised Madame de Jonquiere to leave the station with her daughter and those ladies instead of remaining on the platform. Her presence was in nowise necessary, he said; he would undertake everything, and within three quarters of an hour she would find her patients in her ward at the hospital. She ended by giving way, and took a conveyance in company with Raymonde and Madame Desagneaux. As for Madame Volmar, she had at the last moment disappeared, as though seized with a sudden fit of impatience. The others fancied that they had seen her approach a strange gentleman, with the object no doubt of making some inquiry of him. However, they would of course find her at the hospital.

Berthaud joined Gerard again just as the young man, assisted by two fellow-bearers, was endeavouring to remove M. Sabathier from the carriage. It was a difficult task, for he was very stout and very heavy, and they began to think that he would never pass through the doorway of the compartment. However, as he had been got in they ought to be able to get him out; and indeed when two other bearers had entered the carriage from the other side, they were at last able to deposit him on the platform.

The dawn was now appearing, a faint pale dawn; and the platform presented the woeful appearance of an improvised hospital. La Grivotte, who had lost consciousness, lay there on a mattress pending her removal in a litter; whilst Madame Vetu had been seated against a lamp-post, suffering so severely from another attack of her ailment that they scarcely dared to touch her. Some hospitallers, whose hands were gloved, were with difficulty wheeling their little vehicles in which were poor, sordid-looking women with old baskets at their feet. Others, with stretchers on which lay the stiffened, woeful bodies of silent sufferers, whose eyes gleamed with anguish, found themselves unable to pass; but some of the infirm pilgrims, some unfortunate cripples, contrived to slip through the ranks, among them a young priest who was lame, and a little humpbacked boy, one of whose legs had been amputated, and who, looking like a gnome, managed to drag himself with his crutches from group to group. Then there was quite a block around a man who was bent in half, twisted by paralysis to such a point that he had to be carried on a chair with his head and feet hanging downward. It seemed as though hours would be required to clear the platform.

The dismay therefore reached a climax when the station-master suddenly rushed up shouting: "The Bayonne express is signalled. Make haste! make haste! You have only three minutes left!"

Father Fourcade, who had remained in the midst of the throng, leaning on Doctor Bonamy's arm, and gaily encouraging the more stricken of the sufferers, beckoned to Berthaud and said to him: "Finish taking them out of the train; you will be able to clear the platform afterwards!"

The advice was very sensible, and in accordance with it they finished placing the sufferers on the platform. In Madame de Jonquiere's carriage Marie now alone remained, waiting patiently. M. de Guersaint and Pierre had at last returned to her, bringing the two pairs of wheels by means of which the box in which she lay was rolled about. And with Gerard's assistance Pierre in all haste removed the girl from the train. She was as light as a poor shivering bird, and it was only the box that gave them any trouble. However, they soon placed it on the wheels and made the latter fast, and then Pierre might have rolled Marie away had it not been for the crowd which hampered him.

"Make haste! make haste!" furiously repeated the station-master.

He himself lent a hand, taking hold of a sick man by the feet in order to remove him from the compartment more speedily. And he also pushed the little hand-carts back, so as to clear the edge of the platform. In a second-class carriage, however, there still remained one woman who had just been overpowered by a terrible nervous attack. She was howling and struggling, and it was impossible to think of touching her at that moment. But on the other hand the express, signalled by the incessant tinkling of the electric bells, was now fast approaching, and they had to close the door and in all haste shunt the train to the siding where it would remain for three days, until in fact it was required to convey its load of sick and healthy passengers back to Paris. As it went off to the siding the crowd still heard the cries of the suffering woman, whom it had been necessary to leave in it, in charge of a Sister, cries which grew weaker and weaker, like those of a strengthless child whom one at last succeeds in consoling.

"Good Lord!" muttered the station-master; "it was high time!"

In fact the Bayonne express was now coming along at full speed, and the next moment it rushed like a crash of thunder past that woeful platform littered with all the grievous wretchedness of a hospital hastily evacuated. The litters and little handcarts were shaken, but there was no accident, for the porters were on the watch, and pushed back the bewildered flock which was still jostling and struggling in its eagerness to get away. As soon as the express had passed, however, circulation was re-established, and the bearers were at last able to complete the removal of the sick with prudent deliberation.

Little by little the daylight was increasing—a clear dawn it was, whitening the heavens whose reflection illumined the earth, which was still black. One began to distinguish things and people clearly.

"Oh, by-and-by!" Marie repeated to Pierre, as he endeavoured to roll her away. "Let us wait till some part of the crowd has gone."

Then, looking around, she began to feel interested in a man of military bearing, apparently some sixty years of age, who was walking about among the sick pilgrims. With a square-shaped head and white bushy hair, he would still have looked sturdy if he had not dragged his left foot, throwing it inward at each step he took. With the left hand, too, he leant heavily on a thick walking-stick. When M. Sabathier, who had visited Lourdes for six years past, perceived him, he became quite gay. "Ah!" said he, "it is you, Commander!"

Commander was perhaps the old man's name. But as he was decorated with a broad red riband, he was possibly called Commander on account of his decoration, albeit the latter was that of a mere chevalier. Nobody exactly knew his story. No doubt he had relatives and children of his own somewhere, but these matters remained vague and mysterious. For the last three years he had been employed at the railway station as a superintendent in the goods department, a simple occupation, a little berth which had been given him by favour and which enabled him to live in perfect happiness. A first stroke of apoplexy at fifty-five years of age had been followed by a second one three years later, which had left him slightly paralysed in the left side. And now he was awaiting the third stroke with an air of perfect tranquillity. As he himself put it, he was at the disposal of death, which might come for him that night, the next day, or possibly that very moment. All Lourdes knew him on account of the habit, the mania he had, at pilgrimage time, of coming to witness the arrival of the trains, dragging his foot along and leaning upon his stick, whilst expressing his astonishment and reproaching the ailing ones for their intense desire to be made whole and sound again.

This was the third year that he had seen M. Sabathier arrive, and all his anger fell upon him. "What! you have come back *again*!" he exclaimed. "Well, you *must* be desirous of living this hateful life! But *sacrebleu*! go and die quietly in your bed at home. Isn't that the best thing that can happen to anyone?"

M. Sabathier evinced no anger, but laughed, exhausted though he was by the handling to which he had been subjected during his removal from the carriage. "No, no," said he, "I prefer to be cured."

"To be cured, to be cured! That's what they all ask for. They travel hundreds of leagues and arrive in fragments, howling with pain, and all this to be cured—to go through every worry and every suffering again. Come, monsieur, you would be nicely caught if, at your age and with your dilapidated old body, your Blessed Virgin should be pleased to restore the use of your legs to you. What would you do with them, *mon Dieu?* What pleasure would you find in prolonging the abomination of old age for a few years more? It's much better to die at once, while you are like that! Death is happiness!"

He spoke in this fashion, not as a believer who aspires to the delicious reward of eternal life, but as a weary man who expects to fall into nihility, to enjoy the great everlasting peace of being no more.

Whilst M. Sabathier was gaily shrugging his shoulders as though he had a child to deal with, Abbe Judaine, who had at last secured his banner, came by and stopped for a moment in order that he might gently scold the Commander, with whom he also was well acquainted.

"Don't blaspheme, my dear friend," he said. "It is an offence against God to refuse life and to treat health with contempt. If you yourself had listened to me, you would have asked the Blessed Virgin to cure your leg before now."

At this the Commander became angry. "My leg! The Virgin can do nothing to it! I'm quite at my ease. May death come and may it all be over forever! When the time comes to die you turn your face to the wall and you die—it's simple enough."

The old priest interrupted him, however. Pointing to Marie, who was lying on her box listening to them, he exclaimed: "You tell all our sick to go home and die—even mademoiselle, eh? She who is full of youth and wishes to live."

Marie's eyes were wide open, burning with the ardent desire which she felt to *be*, to enjoy her share of the vast world; and the Commander, who had drawn near, gazed upon her, suddenly seized with deep emotion which made his voice tremble. "If mademoiselle gets well," he said, "I will wish her another miracle, that she be happy."

Then he went off, dragging his foot and tapping the flagstones with the ferrule of his stout stick as he continued wending his way, like an angry philosopher among the suffering pilgrims.

Little by little, the platform was at last cleared. Madame Vetu and La Grivotte were carried away, and Gerard removed M. Sabathier in a little cart, whilst Baron Suire and Berthaud already began giving orders for the green train, which would be the next one to arrive. Of all the ailing pilgrims the only one now remaining at the station was Marie, of whom Pierre jealously took charge. He had already dragged her into the courtyard when he noticed that M. de Guersaint had disappeared; but a moment later he perceived him conversing with the Abbe des Hermoises, whose acquaintance he had just made. Their admiration of the beauties of nature had brought them together. The daylight had now appeared, and the surrounding mountains displayed themselves in all their majesty.

"What a lovely country, monsieur!" exclaimed M. de Guersaint. "I have been wishing to see the Cirque de Gavarnie for thirty years past. But it is some distance away and the trip must be an expensive one, so that I fear I shall not be able to make it."

"You are mistaken, monsieur," said the Abbe; "nothing is more easily managed. By making up a party the expense becomes very slight. And as it happens, I wish to return there this year, so that if you would like to join us—"

"Oh, certainly, monsieur. We will speak of it again. A thousand thanks," replied M. de Guersaint.

His daughter was now calling him, however, and he joined her after taking leave of the Abbe in a very cordial manner. Pierre had decided that he would drag Marie to the hospital so as to spare her the pain of transference to another vehicle. But as the omnibuses, landaus, and other conveyances were already coming back, again filling the courtyard in readiness for the arrival of the next train, the young priest had some difficulty in reaching the road with the little chariot whose low wheels sank deeply in the mud. Some police agents charged with maintaining order were cursing that fearful mire which splashed their boots; and indeed it was only the touts, the young and old women who had rooms to let, who laughed at the puddles, which they crossed and crossed again in every direction, pursuing the last pilgrims that emerged from the station.

When the little car had begun to roll more easily over the sloping road Marie suddenly inquired of M. de Guersaint, who was walking near her: "What day of the week is it, father?"

"Saturday, my darling."

"Ah! yes, Saturday, the day of the Blessed Virgin. Is it to-day that she will cure me?"

Then she began thinking again; while, at some distance behind her, two bearers came furtively down the road, with a covered stretcher in which lay the corpse of the man who had died in the train. They had gone to take it from behind the barrels in the goods office, and were now conveying it to a secret spot of which Father Fourcade had told them.

II. HOSPITAL AND GROTTO

BUILT, so far as it extends, by a charitable Canon, and left unfinished through lack of money, the Hospital of Our Lady of Dolours is a vast pile, four storeys high, and consequently far too lofty, since it is difficult to carry the sufferers to the topmost wards. As a rule the building is occupied by a hundred infirm and aged paupers; but at the season of the national pilgrimage these old folks are for three days sheltered elsewhere, and the hospital is let to the Fathers of the Assumption, who at times lodge in it as many as five and six hundred patients. Still, however closely packed they may be, the accommodation never suffices, so that the three or four hundred remaining sufferers have to be distributed between the Hospital of Salvation and the town hospital, the men being sent to the former and the women to the latter institution.

That morning at sunrise great confusion prevailed in the sand-covered courtyard of Our Lady of Dolours, at the door of which a couple of priests were mounting guard. The temporary staff, with its formidable supply of registers, cards, and printed formulas, had installed itself in one of the ground-floor rooms on the previous day. The managers were desirous of greatly improving upon the organisation of the preceding year. The lower wards were this time to be reserved to the most helpless sufferers; and in order to prevent a repetition of the cases of mistaken identity which had occurred in the past, very great care was to be taken in filling in and distributing the admission cards, each of which bore the name of a ward and the number of a bed. It became difficult, however, to act in accordance with these good intentions in presence of the torrent of ailing beings which the white train had brought to Lourdes, and the new formalities so complicated matters that the patients had to be deposited in the courtyard as they arrived, to wait there until it became possible to admit them in something like an orderly manner. It was the scene witnessed at the railway station all over again, the same woeful camping in the open, whilst the bearers and the young seminarists who acted as the secretary's assistants ran hither and thither in bewilderment.

"We have been over-ambitious, we wanted to do things too well!" exclaimed Baron Suire in despair.

There was much truth in his remark, for never had a greater number of useless precautions been taken, and they now discovered that, by some inexplicable error, they had allotted not the lower—but the higher-placed wards to the patients whom it was most difficult to move. It was impossible to begin the classification afresh, however, and so as in former years things must be allowed to take their course, in a haphazard way. The distribution of the cards began, a young priest at the same time entering each patient's name and address in a register. Moreover, all the *hospitalisation* cards bearing the patients' names and numbers had to be produced, so that the names of the wards and the numbers of the beds might be added to them; and all these formalities greatly protracted the *defile*.

Then there was an endless coming and going from the top to the bottom of the building, and from one to the other end of each of its four floors. M. Sabathier was one of the first to secure admittance, being placed in a ground-floor room which was known as the Family Ward. Sick men were there allowed to have their wives with them; but to the other wards of the hospital only women were admitted. Brother Isidore, it is true, was accompanied by his sister; however, by a special favour it was agreed that they should be considered as conjoints, and the missionary was accordingly placed in the bed next to that allotted to M. Sabathier. The chapel, still littered with plaster and with its unfinished windows boarded up, was close at hand. There were also various wards in an unfinished state; still these were filled with mattresses, on which sufferers were rapidly placed. All those who could walk, however, were already besieging the refectory, a long gallery whose broad windows looked into an inner courtyard; and the Saint-Frai Sisters, who managed the hospital at other times, and had remained to attend to the cooking, began to distribute bowls of coffee and chocolate among the poor women whom the terrible journey had exhausted.

"Rest yourselves and try to gain a little strength," repeated Baron Suire, who was ever on the move, showing himself here, there, and everywhere in rapid succession. "You have three good hours before you, it is not yet five, and their reverences have given orders that you are not to be taken to the Grotto until eight o'clock, so as to avoid any excessive fatigue."

Meanwhile, up above on the second floor, Madame de Jonquiere had been one of the first to take possession of the Sainte-Honorine Ward of which she was the superintendent. She had been obliged to leave her daughter Raymonde downstairs, for the regulations did not allow young girls to enter the wards, where they might have witnessed sights that were scarcely proper or else too horrible for such eyes as theirs. Raymonde had therefore remained in the refectory as a helper; however, little Madame Desagneaux, being a lady-hospitaller, had not left the superintendent, and was already asking her for orders, in her delight that she should at last be able to render some assistance.

"Are all these beds properly made, madame?" she inquired; "perhaps I had better make them afresh with Sister Hyacinthe."

The ward, whose walls were painted a light yellow, and whose few windows admitted but little light from an inner yard, contained fifteen beds, standing in two rows against the walls.

"We will see by-and-by," replied Madame de Jonquiere with an absorbed air. She was busy counting the beds and examining the long narrow apartment. And this accomplished she added in an undertone: "I shall never have room enough. They say that I must accommodate twenty-three patients. We shall have to put some mattresses down."

Sister Hyacinthe, who had followed the ladies after leaving Sister Saint-Francois and Sister Claire des Anges in a small adjoining apartment which was being transformed into a linen-room, then began to lift up the coverlets and examine the bedding.

And she promptly reassured Madame Desagneaux with regard to her surmises. "Oh! the beds are properly made," she said; "everything is very clean too. One can see that the Saint-Frai Sisters have attended to things themselves. The reserve mattresses are in the next room, however, and if madame will lend me a hand we can place some of them between the beds at once.

"Oh, certainly!" exclaimed young Madame Desagneaux, quite excited by the idea of carrying mattresses about with her weak slender arms.

It became necessary for Madame de Jonquiere to calm her. "By-and-by," said the lady-superintendent; "there is no hurry. Let us wait till our patients arrive. I don't much like this ward, it is so difficult to air. Last year I had the Sainte-Rosalie Ward on the first floor. However, we will organise matters, all the same."

Some other lady-hospitallers were now arriving, quite a hiveful of busy bees, all eager to start on their work. The confusion which so often arose was, in fact, increased by the excessive number of nurses, women of the aristocracy and upper-middle class, with whose fervent zeal some little vanity was blended. There were more than two hundred of them, and as each had to make a donation on joining the Hospitality of Our Lady of Salvation, the managers did not dare to refuse any applicants, for fear lest they might check the flow of alms-giving. Thus the number of lady-hospitallers increased year by year. Fortunately there were among them some who cared for nothing beyond the privilege of wearing the red cloth cross, and who started off on excursions as soon as they reached Lourdes. Still it must be acknowledged that those who devoted themselves were really deserving, for they underwent five days of awful fatigue, sleeping scarcely a couple of hours each night, and living in the midst of the most terrible and repulsive spectacles. They witnessed the death agonies, dressed the pestilential sores, cleaned up, changed linen, turned the sufferers over in their beds, went through a sickening and overwhelming labour to which they were in no wise accustomed. And thus they emerged from it aching all over, tired to death, with feverish eyes flaming with the joy of the charity which so excited them.

"And Madame Volmar?" suddenly asked Madame Desagneaux. "I thought we should find her here."

This was apparently a subject which Madame de Jonquiere did not care to have discussed; for, as though she were aware of the truth and wished to bury it in silence, with the indulgence of a woman who compassionates human wretchedness, she promptly retorted: "Madame Volmar isn't strong, she must have gone to the hotel to rest. We must let her sleep."

Then she apportioned the beds among the ladies present, allotting two to each of them; and this done they all finished taking possession of the place, hastening up and down and backwards and forwards in order to ascertain where the offices, the linen-room, and the kitchens were situated.

"And the dispensary?" then asked one of the ladies.

But there was no dispensary. There was no medical staff even. What would have been the use of any?—since the patients were those whom science had given up, despairing creatures who had come to beg of God the cure which powerless men were unable to promise them. Logically enough, all treatment was suspended during the pilgrimage. If a patient seemed likely to die, extreme unction was administered. The only medical man about the place was the young doctor who had come by the white train with his little medicine chest; and his intervention was limited to an endeavour to assuage the sufferings of those patients who chanced to ask for him during an attack.

As it happened, Sister Hyacinthe was just bringing Ferrand, whom Sister Saint-Francois had kept with her in a closet near the linen-room which he proposed to make his quarters. "Madame," said he to Madame de Jonquiere, "I am entirely at your disposal. In case of need you will only have to ring for me."

She barely listened to him, however, engaged as she was in a quarrel with a young priest belonging to the management with reference to a deficiency of certain utensils. "Certainly, monsieur, if we should need a soothing draught," she answered, and then, reverting to her discussion, she went on: "Well, Monsieur l'Abbe, you must certainly get me four or five more. How can we possibly manage with so few? Things are bad enough as it is."

Ferrand looked and listened, quite bewildered by the extraordinary behaviour of the people amongst whom he had been thrown by chance since the previous day. He who did not believe, who was only present out of friendship and charity, was amazed at this extraordinary scramble of wretchedness and suffering rushing towards the hope of happiness. And, as a medical man of the new school, he was altogether upset by the careless neglect of precautions, the contempt which was shown for the most simple teachings of science, in the certainty which was apparently felt that, if Heaven should so will it, cure would supervene, sudden and resounding, like a lie given to the very laws of nature. But if this were the case, what was the use of that last concession to human prejudices—why engage a doctor for the journey if none were wanted? At this thought the young man returned to his little room, experiencing a vague feeling of shame as he realised that his presence was useless, and even a trifle ridiculous.

"Get some opium pills ready all the same," said Sister Hyacinthe, as she went back with him as far as the linen-room. "You will be asked for some, for I feel anxious about some of the patients."

While speaking she looked at him with her large blue eyes, so gentle and so kind, and ever lighted by a divine smile. The constant exercise which she gave herself brought the rosy flush of her quick blood to her skin all dazzling with youthfulness. And like a good friend who was willing that he should share the work to which she gave her heart, she added: "Besides, if I should need somebody to get a patient in or out of bed, you will help me, won't you?"

Thereupon, at the idea that he might be of use to her, he was pleased that he had come and was there. In his mind's eye, he again beheld her at his bedside, at the time when he had so narrowly escaped death, nursing him with fraternal hands, with the smiling, compassionate grace of a sexless angel, in whom there was something more than a comrade, something of a woman left. However, the thought never occurred to him that there was religion, belief, behind her.

"Oh! I will help you as much as you like, Sister," he replied. "I belong to you, I shall be so happy to serve you. You know very well what a debt of gratitude I have to pay you."

In a pretty way she raised her finger to her lips so as to silence him. Nobody owed her anything. She was merely the servant of the ailing and the poor.

At this moment a first patient was making her entry into the Sainte-Honorine Ward. It was Marie, lying in her wooden box, which Pierre, with Gerard's assistance, had just brought up-stairs. The last to start from the railway station, she had secured admission before the others, thanks to the endless complications which, after keeping them all in suspense, now freed them according to the chance distribution of the admission cards. M. de Guersaint had quitted his daughter at the hospital door by her own desire; for, fearing the hotels would be very full, she had wished him to secure two rooms for himself and Pierre at once. Then, on reaching the ward, she felt so weary that, after venting her chagrin at not being immediately taken to the Grotto, she consented to be laid on a bed for a short time.

"Come, my child," repeated Madame de Jonquiere, "you have three hours before you. We will put you to bed. It will ease you to take you out of that case."

Thereupon the lady-superintendent raised her by the shoulders, whilst Sister Hyacinthe held her feet. The bed was in the central part of the ward, near a window. For a moment the poor girl remained on it with her eyes closed, as though exhausted by being moved about so much. Then it became necessary that Pierre should be readmitted, for she grew very fidgety, saying that there were things which she must explain to him.

"Pray don't go away, my friend," she exclaimed when he approached her. "Take the case out on to the landing, but stay there, because I want to be taken down as soon as I can get permission."

"Do you feel more comfortable now?" asked the young priest.

"Yes, no doubt—but I really don't know. I so much want to be taken yonder to the Blessed Virgin's feet."

However, when Pierre had removed the case, the successive arrivals of the other patients supplied her with some little diversion. Madame Vetu, whom two bearers had brought up-stairs, holding her under the arms, was laid, fully dressed, on the next bed, where she remained motionless, scarce breathing, with her heavy, yellow, cancerous mask. None of the patients, it should be mentioned, were divested of their clothes, they were simply stretched out on the beds, and advised to go to sleep if they could manage to do so. Those whose complaints were less grievous contented themselves with sitting down on their mattresses, chatting together, and putting the things they had brought with them in order. For instance, Elise Rouquet, who was also near Marie, on the other side of the latter's bed, opened her basket to take a clean fichu out of it, and seemed sorely annoyed at having no hand-glass with her. In less than ten minutes all the beds were occupied, so that when La Grivotte appeared, half carried by Sister Hyacinthe and Sister Claire des Anges, it became necessary to place some mattresses on the floor.

"Here! here is one," exclaimed Madame Desagneaux; "she will be very well here, out of the draught from the door."

Seven other mattresses were soon added in a line, occupying the space between the rows of beds, so that it became difficult to move about. One had to be very careful, and follow narrow pathways which had been left between the beds and the mattresses. Each of the patients had retained possession of her parcel, or box, or bag, and round about the improvised shakedowns were piles of poor old things, sorry remnants of garments, straying among the sheets and the coverlets. You might have thought yourself in some woeful infirmary, hastily organised after some great catastrophe, some conflagration or earthquake which had thrown hundreds of wounded and penniless beings into the streets.

II. HOSPITAL AND GROTTO

Madame de Jonquiere made her way from one to the other end of the ward, ever and ever repeating, "Come, my children, don't excite yourselves; try to sleep a little."

However, she did not succeed in calming them, and indeed, she herself, like the other lady-hospitallers under her orders, increased the general fever by her own bewilderment. The linen of several patients had to be changed, and there were other needs to be attended to. One woman, suffering from an ulcer in the leg, began moaning so dreadfully that Madame Desagneaux undertook to dress her sore afresh; but she was not skilful, and despite all her passionate courage she almost fainted, so greatly was she distressed by the unbearable odour. Those patients who were in better health asked for broth, bowlfuls of which began to circulate amidst the calls, the answers, and the contradictory orders which nobody executed. And meanwhile, let loose amidst this frightful scramble, little Sophie Couteau, who remained with the Sisters, and was very gay, imagined that it was playtime, and ran, and jumped, and hopped in turn, called and petted first by one and then by another, dear as she was to all alike for the miraculous hope which she brought them.

However, amidst this agitation, the hours went by. Seven o'clock had just struck when Abbe Judaine came in. He was the chaplain of the Sainte-Honorine Ward, and only the difficulty of finding an unoccupied altar at which he might say his mass had delayed his arrival. As soon as he appeared, a cry of impatience arose from every bed.

"Oh! Monsieur le Cure, let us start, let us start at once!"

An ardent desire, which each passing minute heightened and irritated, was upbuoying them, like a more and more devouring thirst, which only the waters of the miraculous fountain could appease. And more fervently than any of the others, La Grivotte, sitting up on her mattress, and joining her hands, begged and begged that she might be taken to the Grotto. Was there not a beginning of the miracle in this—in this awakening of her will power, this feverish desire for cure which enabled her to set herself erect? Inert and fainting on her arrival, she was now seated, turning her dark glances in all directions, waiting and watching for the happy moment when she would be removed. And colour also was returning to her livid face. She was already resuscitating.

"Oh! Monsieur le Cure, pray do tell them to take me—I feel that I shall be cured," she exclaimed.

With a loving, fatherly smile on his good-natured face, Abbe Judaine listened to them all, and allayed their impatience with kind words. They would soon set out; but they must be reasonable, and allow sufficient time for things to be organised; and besides, the Blessed Virgin did not like to have violence done her; she bided her time, and distributed her divine favours among those who behaved themselves the best.

As he paused before Marie's bed and beheld her, stammering entreaties with joined hands, he again paused. "And you, too, my daughter, you are in a hurry?" he said. "Be easy, there is grace enough in heaven for you all."

"I am dying of love, Father," she murmured in reply. "My heart is so swollen with prayers, it stifles me—"

He was greatly touched by the passion of this poor emaciated child, so harshly stricken in her youth and beauty, and wishing to appease her, he called her attention to Madame Vetu, who did not move, though with her eyes wide open she stared at all who passed.

"Look at madame, how quiet she is!" he said. "She is meditating, and she does right to place herself in God's hands, like a little child."

However, in a scarcely audible voice, a mere breath, Madame Vetu stammered: "Oh! I am suffering, I am suffering."

At last, at a quarter to eight o'clock, Madame de Jonquiere warned her charges that they would do well to prepare themselves. She herself, assisted by Sister Hyacinthe and Madame Desagneaux, buttoned several dresses, and put shoes on impotent feet. It was a real toilette, for they all desired to appear to the greatest advantage before the Blessed Virgin. A large number had sufficient sense of delicacy to wash their hands. Others unpacked their parcels, and put on clean linen. On her side, Elise Rouquet had ended by discovering a little pocket-glass in the hands of a woman near her, a huge, dropsical creature, who was very coquettish; and having borrowed it, she leant it against the bolster, and then, with infinite care, began to fasten her fichu as elegantly as possible about her head, in order to hide her distorted features. Meanwhile, erect in front of her, little Sophie watched her with an air of profound interest.

It was Abbe Judaine who gave the signal for starting on the journey to the Grotto. He wished, he said, to accompany his dear suffering daughters thither, whilst the lady-hospitallers and the Sisters remained in the ward, so as to put things in some little order again. Then the ward was at once emptied, the patients being carried downstairs amidst renewed tumult. And Pierre, having replaced Marie's box upon its wheels, took the first place in the *cortege*, which was formed of a score of little hand-carts, bath-chairs, and litters. The other wards, however, were also emptying, the courtyard became crowded, and the *defile* was organised in haphazard fashion. There was soon an interminable train descending the rather steep slope of the Avenue de la Grotte, so that Pierre was already reaching the Plateau de la Merlasse when the last stretchers were barely leaving the precincts of the hospital.

It was eight o'clock, and the sun, already high, a triumphant August sun, was flaming in the great sky, which was beautifully clear. It seemed as if the blue of the atmosphere, cleansed by the storm of the previous night, were quite new, fresh with youth. And the frightful *defile*, a perfect "Cour des Miracles" of human woe, rolled along the sloping pavement amid all the brilliancy of that radiant morning. There was no end to the train of abominations; it appeared to grow longer and longer. No order was observed, ailments of all kinds were jumbled together; it seemed like the clearing of some inferno where the most monstrous maladies, the rare and awful cases which provoke a shudder, had been gathered together. Eczema, roseola, elephantiasis, presented a long array of doleful victims. Well-nigh vanished diseases reappeared; one old woman was affected with leprosy, another was, covered with impetiginous lichen like a tree which has rotted in the shade. Then came the dropsical ones, inflated like wine-skins; and beside some stretchers there dangled hands twisted by rheumatism, while from others protruded feet swollen by oedema beyond all recognition, looking, in fact, like bags full of rags. One woman, suffering from hydrocephalus, sat in a little cart, the dolorous motions of her head bespeaking her grievous malady. A tall girl afflicted with chorea—St. Vitus's dance—was dancing with every limb, without a pause, the left side of her face being continually distorted by sudden, convulsive grimaces. A younger one, who followed, gave vent to a bark, a kind of plaintive animal cry, each time that the tic douloureux which was torturing her twisted her mouth and her right cheek, which she seemed to throw forward. Next came the consumptives, trembling with fever, exhausted by dysentery, wasted to skeletons, with livid skins, recalling the colour of that earth in which they would soon be laid to rest; and there was one among them who was quite white, with flaming eyes, who looked indeed like a death's head in which a torch had been lighted. Then every deformity of the contractions followed in succession—twisted trunks, twisted arms, necks askew, all the distortions of poor creatures whom nature had warped and broken; and among these was one whose right hand was thrust back behind her ribs whilst her head fell to the left resting fixedly upon her shoulder. Afterwards came poor rachitic girls displaying waxen complexions and slender necks eaten away by sores, and yellow-faced women in the painful stupor which falls on those whose bosoms are devoured by cancers; whilst others, lying down with their mournful eyes gazing heavenwards, seemed to be listening to the throbs of the tumours which obstructed their organs. And still more and more went by; there was always something more frightful to come; this woman following that other one increased the general shudder of horror. From the neck of a girl of twenty who had a crushed, flattened head like a toad's, there hung so large a goitre that it fell even to her waist like the bib of an apron. A blind woman walked along, her head erect, her face pale like marble, displaying the acute inflammation of her poor, ulcerated eyes. An aged woman stricken with imbecility, afflicted with dreadful facial disfigurements, laughed aloud with a terrifying laugh. And all at once an epileptic was seized with convulsions, and began foaming on her stretcher, without, however, causing any stoppage of the procession, which never slackened its march, lashed onward as it was by the blizzard of feverish passion which impelled it towards the Grotto.

The bearers, the priests, and the ailing ones themselves had just intonated a canticle, the song of Bernadette, and all rolled along amid the besetting "Aves," so that the little carts, the litters, and the pedestrians descended the sloping road like a swollen and overflowing torrent of roaring water. At the corner of the Rue Saint-Joseph, near the Plateau de la Merlasse, a family of excursionists, who had come from Cauterets or Bagneres, stood at the edge of the footway, overcome with profound astonishment. These people were evidently well-to-do *bourgeois*, the father and mother very correct in appearance and demeanour, while their two big girls, attired in light-coloured dresses, had the smiling faces of happy creatures who are amusing themselves. But their first feeling of surprise was soon followed by terror, a growing terror, as if they beheld the opening of some pesthouse of ancient times, some hospital of the legendary ages, evacuated after a great epidemic. The two girls became quite pale, while the father and the mother felt icy cold in presence of that endless *defile* of so many horrors, the pestilential emanations of which were blown full in their faces. O God! to think that such hideousness, such filth, such suffering, should exist! Was it possible—under that magnificently radiant sun, under those broad heavens so full of light and joy whither the freshness of the Gave's waters ascended, and the breeze of morning wafted the pure perfumes of the mountains!

When Pierre, at the head of the *cortege*, reached the Plateau de la Merlasse, he found himself immersed in that clear sunlight, that fresh and balmy air. He turned round and smiled affectionately at Marie; and as they came out on the Place du Rosaire in the morning splendour, they were both enchanted with the lovely panorama which spread around them.

In front, on the east, was Old Lourdes, lying in a broad fold of the ground beyond a rock. The sun was rising behind the distant mountains, and its oblique rays clearly outlined the dark lilac mass of that solitary rock, which was crowned by the tower and crumbling walls of the ancient castle, once the redoubtable key of the seven valleys. Through the dancing, golden dust you discerned little of the ruined pile except some stately outlines, some huge blocks of building which looked as though reared by Cyclopean hands; and beyond the rock you but vaguely distinguished the discoloured, intermingled house-roofs of the old town. Nearer in than the castle, however, the new town—the rich and noisy city which had sprung up in a few years as though by miracle—spread out on either hand, displaying its hotels, its stylish shops, its lodging-houses all with white fronts smiling amidst patches of greenery. Then there was the Gave flowing along at the base of the rock, rolling clamorous, clear waters, now blue and now green, now deep as they passed under the old bridge, and now leaping as they careered under the new one, which the Fathers of the Immaculate Conception had built in order to connect the Grotto with the railway station and the recently opened Boulevard. And as a background to this delightful picture, this fresh water, this greenery, this gay, scattered, rejuvenated town, the little and the big Gers arose, two huge ridges of bare rock and low herbage, which, in the projected shade that bathed them, assumed delicate tints of pale mauve and green, fading softly into pink.

Then, upon the north, on the right bank of the Gave, beyond the hills followed by the railway line, the heights of La Buala ascended, their wooded slopes radiant in the morning light. On that side lay Bartres. More to the left arose the Serre de Julos, dominated by the Miramont. Other crests, far off, faded away into the ether. And in the foreground, rising in tiers among the grassy valleys beyond the Gave, a number of convents, which seemed to have sprung up in this region of prodigies like early vegetation, imparted some measure of life to the landscape. First, there was an Orphan Asylum founded by the Sisters of Nevers, whose vast buildings shone brightly in the sunlight. Next came the Carmelite convent, on the highway to Pau, just in front of the Grotto; and then that of the Assumptionists higher up, skirting the road to Poueyferre; whilst the Dominicans showed but a corner of their roofs, sequestered in the far-away solitude. And at last appeared the establishment of the Sisters of the Immaculate Conception, those who were called the Blue Sisters, and who had founded at the far end of the valley a home where they received well-to-do lady pilgrims, desirous of solitude, as boarders.

At that early hour all the bells of these convents were pealing joyfully in the crystalline atmosphere, whilst the bells of other convents, on the other, the southern horizon, answered them with the same silvery strains of joy. The bell of the nunnery of Sainte Clarissa, near the old bridge, rang a scale of gay, clear notes, which one might have fancied to be the chirruping of a bird. And on this side of the town, also, there were valleys that dipped down between the ridges, and mountains that upreared their bare sides, a commingling of smiling and of agitated nature, an endless surging of heights amongst which you noticed those of Visens, whose slopes the sunlight tinged ornately with soft blue and carmine of a rippling, moire-like effect.

However, when Marie and Pierre turned their eyes to the west, they were quite dazzled. The sun rays were here streaming on the large and the little Beout with their cupolas of unequal height. And on this side the background was one of gold and purple, a dazzling mountain on whose sides one could only discern the road which snaked between the trees on its way to the Calvary above. And here, too, against the sunlit background, radiant like an aureola, stood out the three superposed churches which at the voice of Bernadette had sprung from the rock to the glory of the Blessed Virgin. First of all, down below, came the church of the Rosary, squat, circular, and half cut out of the rock, at the farther end of an esplanade on either side of which, like two huge arms, were colossal gradient ways ascending gently to the Crypt church. Vast labour had been expended here, a quarryful of stones had been cut and set in position, there were arches as lofty as naves supporting the gigantic terraced avenues which had been constructed so that the processions might roll along in all their pomp, and the little conveyances containing sick children might ascend without hindrance to the divine presence. Then came the Crypt, the subterranean church within the rock, with only its low door visible above the church of the Rosary, whose paved roof, with its vast promenade, formed a continuation of the terraced inclines. And at last, from the summit sprang the Basilica, somewhat slender and frail, recalling some finely chased jewel of the Renascence, and looking very new and very white—like a prayer, a spotless dove, soaring aloft from the rocks of Massabielle. The spire, which appeared the more delicate and slight when compared with the gigantic inclines below, seemed like the little vertical flame of a taper set in the midst of the vast landscape, those endless waves of valleys and mountains. By the side, too, of the dense greenery of the Calvary hill, it looked fragile and candid, like childish faith; and at sight of it you instinctively thought of the little white arm, the little thin hand of the puny girl, who had here pointed to Heaven in the crisis of her human sufferings. You could not see the Grotto, the entrance of which was on the left, at the base of the rock. Beyond the Basilica, the only buildings which caught the eye were the heavy square pile where the Fathers of the Immaculate Conception had their abode, and the episcopal palace, standing much farther away, in a spreading, wooded valley. And the three churches were flaming in the morning glow, and the rain of gold scattered by the sun rays was sweeping the whole countryside, whilst the flying peals of the bells seemed to be the very vibration of the light, the musical awakening of the lovely day that was now beginning.

Whilst crossing the Place du Rosaire, Pierre and Marie glanced at the Esplanade, the public walk with its long central lawn skirted by broad parallel paths and extending as far as the new bridge. Here, with face turned towards the Basilica, was the great crowned statue of the Virgin. All the sufferers crossed themselves as they went by. And still passionately chanting its canticle, the fearful *cortege* rolled on, through nature in festive array. Under the dazzling sky, past the mountains of gold and purple, amidst the centenarian trees, symbolical of health, the running waters whose freshness was eternal, that *cortege* still and ever marched on with its sufferers, whom nature, if not God, had condemned, those who were afflicted with skin diseases, those whose flesh was eaten away, those who were dropsical and inflated like wine-skins, and those whom rheumatism and paralysis had twisted into postures of agony. And the victims of hydrocephalus followed, with the dancers of St. Vitus, the consumptives, the rickety, the epileptic, the cancerous, the goitrous, the blind, the mad, and the idiotic. "Ave, ave, ave, Maria!" they sang; and the stubborn plaint acquired increased volume, as nearer and nearer to the Grotto it bore that abominable torrent of human wretchedness and pain, amidst all the fright and horror of the passers-by, who stopped short, unable to stir, their hearts frozen as this nightmare swept before their eyes.

Pierre and Marie were the first to pass under the lofty arcade of one of the terraced inclines. And then, as they followed the quay of the Gave, they all at once came upon the Grotto. And Marie, whom Pierre wheeled as near to the railing as possible, was only able to raise herself in her little conveyance, and murmur: "O most Blessed Virgin, Virgin most loved!"

She had seen neither the entrances to the piscinas nor the twelve-piped fountain, which she had just passed; nor did she distinguish any better the shop on her left hand where crucifixes, chaplets, statuettes, pictures, and other religious articles were sold, or the stone pulpit on her right which Father Massias already occupied. Her eyes were dazzled by the splendour of the Grotto; it seemed to her as if a hundred thousand tapers were burning there behind the railing, filling the low entrance with the glow of a furnace and illuminating, as with star rays, the statue of the Virgin, which stood, higher up, at the edge of a narrow ogive-like cavity. And for her, apart from that glorious apparition, nothing existed there, neither the crutches with which a part of the vault had been covered, nor the piles of bouquets fading away amidst the ivy and the eglantine, nor even the altar placed in the centre near a little portable organ over which a cover had been thrown. However, as she raised her eyes above the rock, she once more beheld the slender white Basilica profiled against the sky, its slight, tapering spire soaring into the azure of the Infinite like a prayer.

"O Virgin most powerful—Queen of the Virgins—Holy Virgin of Virgins!"

Pierre had now succeeded in wheeling Marie's box to the front rank, beyond the numerous oak benches which were set out here in the open air as in the nave of a church. Nearly all these benches were already occupied by those sufferers who could sit down, while the vacant spaces were soon filled with litters and little vehicles whose wheels became entangled together, and on whose close-packed mattresses and pillows all sorts of diseases were gathered pell-mell. Immediately on arriving, the young priest had recognised the Vignerons seated with their sorry child Gustave in the middle of a bench, and now, on the flagstones, he caught sight of the lace-trimmed bed of Madame Dieulafay, beside whom her husband and sister knelt in prayer. Moreover, all the patients of Madame de Jonquiere's carriage took up position here—M. Sabathier and Brother Isidore side by side, Madame Vetu reclining hopelessly in a conveyance, Elise Rouquet seated, La Grivotte excited and raising herself on her clenched hands. Pierre also again perceived Madame Maze, standing somewhat apart from the others, and humbling herself in prayer; whilst Madame Vincent, who had fallen on her knees, still holding her little Rose in her arms, presented the child to the Virgin with ardent entreaty, the distracted gesture of a mother soliciting compassion from the mother of divine grace. And around this reserved space was the ever-growing throng of pilgrims, the pressing, jostling mob which gradually stretched to the parapet overlooking the Gave.

"O Virgin most merciful," continued Marie in an undertone, "Virgin most faithful, Virgin conceived without sin!"

Then, almost fainting, she spoke no more, but with her lips still moving, as though in silent prayer, gazed distractedly at Pierre. He thought that she wished to speak to him and leant forward: "Shall I remain here at your disposal to take you to the piscina by-and-by?" he asked.

But as soon as she understood him she shook her head. And then in a feverish way she said: "No, no, I don't want to be bathed this morning. It seems to me that one must be truly worthy, truly pure, truly holy before seeking the miracle! I want to spend the whole morning in imploring it with joined hands; I want to pray, to pray with all my strength and all my soul—" She was stifling, and paused. Then she added: "Don't come to take me back to the hospital till eleven o'clock. I will not let them take me from here till then."

However, Pierre did not go away, but remained near her. For a moment, he even fell upon his knees; he also would have liked to pray with the same burning faith, to beg of God the cure of that poor sick child, whom he loved with such fraternal affection. But since he had reached the Grotto he had felt a singular sensation invading him, a covert revolt, as it were, which hampered the pious flight of his prayer. He wished to believe; he had spent the whole night hoping that belief would once more blossom in his soul, like some lovely flower of innocence and candour, as soon as he should have knelt upon the soil of that land of miracle. And yet he only experienced discomfort and anxiety in presence of the theatrical scene before him, that pale stiff statue in the false light of the tapers, with the chaplet shop full of jostling customers on the one hand, and the large stone pulpit whence a Father of the Assumption was shouting "Aves" on the other. Had his soul become utterly withered then? Could no divine dew again impregnate it with innocence, render it like the souls of little children, who at the slightest caressing touch of the sacred legend give themselves to it entirely?

Then, while his thoughts were still wandering, he recognised Father Massias in the ecclesiastic who occupied the pulpit. He had formerly known him, and was quite stirred by his sombre ardour, by the sight of his thin face and sparkling eyes, by the eloquence which poured from his large mouth as he offered violence to Heaven to compel it to descend upon earth. And whilst he thus examined Father Massias, astonished at feeling himself so unlike the preacher, he caught sight of Father Fourcade, who, at the foot of the pulpit, was deep in conference with Baron Suire. The latter seemed much perplexed by something which Father Fourcade said to him; however he ended by approving it with a complaisant nod. Then, as Abbe Judaine was also standing there, Father Fourcade likewise spoke to him for a moment, and a scared expression came over the Abbe's broad, fatherly face while he listened; nevertheless, like the Baron, he at last bowed assent.

Then, all at once, Father Fourcade appeared in the pulpit, erect, drawing up his lofty figure which his attack of gout had slightly bent; and he had not wished that Father Massias, his well-loved brother, whom he preferred above all others, should altogether go down the narrow stairway, for he had kept him upon one of the steps, and was leaning on his shoulder. And in a full, grave voice, with an air of sovereign authority which caused perfect silence to reign around, he spoke as follows:

"My dear brethren, my dear sisters, I ask your forgiveness for interrupting your prayers, but I have a communication to make to you, and I have to ask the help of all your faithful souls. We had a very sad accident to deplore this morning, one of our brethren died in one of the trains by which you came to Lourdes, died just as he was about to set foot in the promised land."

A brief pause followed and Father Fourcade seemed to become yet taller, his handsome face beaming with fervour, amidst his long, streaming, royal beard.

"Well, my dear brethren, my dear sisters," he resumed, "in spite of everything, the idea has come to me that we ought not to despair. Who knows if God Almighty did not will that death in order that He might prove His Omnipotence to the world? It is as though a voice were speaking to me, urging me to ascend this pulpit and ask your prayers for this man, this man who is no more, but whose life is nevertheless in the hands of the most Blessed Virgin who can still implore her Divine Son in his favour. Yes, the man is here, I have caused his body to be brought hither, and it depends on you, perhaps, whether a brilliant miracle shall dazzle the universe, if you pray with sufficient ardour to touch the compassion of Heaven. We will plunge the man's body into the piscina and we will entreat the Lord, the master of the world, to resuscitate him, to give unto us this extraordinary sign of His sovereign beneficence!"

An icy thrill, wafted from the Invisible, passed through the listeners. They had all become pale, and though the lips of none of them had opened, it seemed as if a murmur sped through their ranks amidst a shudder.

"But with what ardour must we not pray!" violently resumed Father Fourcade, exalted by genuine faith. "It is your souls, your whole souls, that I ask of you, my dear brothers, my dear sisters, it is a prayer in which you must put your hearts, your blood, your very life with whatever may be most noble and loving in it! Pray with all your strength, pray till you no longer know who you are, or where you are; pray as one loves, pray as one dies, for that which we are about to ask is so precious, so rare, so astounding a grace that only the energy of our worship can induce God to answer us. And in order that our prayers may be the more efficacious, in order that they may have time to spread and ascend to the feet of the Eternal Father, we will not lower the body into the piscina until four o'clock this afternoon. And now my dear brethren, now my dear sisters, pray, pray to the most Blessed Virgin, the Queen of the Angels, the Comforter of the Afflicted!"

Then he himself, distracted by emotion, resumed the recital of the rosary, whilst near him Father Massias burst into sobs. And thereupon the great anxious silence was broken, contagion seized upon the throng, it was transported and gave vent to shouts, tears, and confused stammered entreaties. It was as though a breath of delirium were sweeping by, reducing men's wills to naught, and turning all these beings into one being, exasperated with love and seized with a mad desire for the impossible prodigy.

And for a moment Pierre had thought that the ground was giving way beneath him, that he was about to fall and faint. But with difficulty he managed to rise from his knees and slowly walked away.

III. FOUNTAIN AND PISCINA

As Pierre went off, ill at ease, mastered by invincible repugnance, unwilling to remain there any longer, he caught sight of M. de Guersaint, kneeling near the Grotto, with the absorbed air of one who is praying with his whole soul. The young priest had not seen him since the morning, and did not know whether he had managed to secure a couple of rooms in one or other of the hotels, so that his first impulse was to go and join him. Then, however, he hesitated, unwilling to disturb his meditations, for he was doubtless praying for his daughter, whom he fondly loved, in spite of the constant absent-mindedness of his volatile brain. Accordingly, the young priest passed on, and took his way under the trees. Nine o'clock was now striking, he had a couple of hours before him.

By dint of money, the wild bank where swine had formerly pastured had been transformed into a superb avenue skirting the Gave. It had been necessary to put back the river's bed in order to gain ground, and lay out a monumental quay bordered by a broad footway, and protected by a parapet. Some two or three hundred yards farther on, a hill brought the avenue to an end, and it thus resembled an enclosed promenade, provided with benches, and shaded by magnificent trees. Nobody passed along, however; merely the overflow of the crowd had settled there, and solitary spots still abounded between the grassy wall limiting the promenade on the south, and the extensive fields spreading out northward beyond the Gave, as far as the wooded slopes which the white-walled convents brightened. Under the foliage, on the margin of the running water, one could enjoy delightful freshness, even during the burning days of August.

Thus Pierre, like a man at last awakening from a painful dream, soon found rest of mind again. He had questioned himself in the acute anxiety which he felt with regard to his sensations. Had he not reached Lourdes that morning possessed by a genuine desire to believe, an idea that he was indeed again beginning to believe even as he had done in the docile days of childhood when his mother had made him join his hands, and taught him to fear God? Yet as soon as he had found himself at the Grotto, the idolatry of the worship, the violence of the display of faith, the onslaught upon human reason which he witnessed, had so disturbed him that he had almost fainted. What would become of him then? Could he not even try to contend against his doubts by examining things and convincing himself of their truth, thus turning his journey to profit? At all events, he had made a bad beginning, which left him sorely agitated, and he indeed needed the environment of those fine trees, that limpid, rushing water, that calm, cool avenue, to recover from the shock.

Still pondering, he was approaching the end of the pathway, when he most unexpectedly met a forgotten friend. He had, for a few seconds, been looking at a tall old gentleman who was coming towards him, dressed in a tightly buttoned frock-coat and broad-brimmed hat; and he had tried to remember where it was that he had previously beheld that pale face, with eagle nose, and black and penetrating eyes. These he had seen before, he felt sure of it; but the promenader's long white beard and long curly white hair perplexed him. However, the other halted, also looking extremely astonished, though he promptly exclaimed, "What, Pierre? Is it you, at Lourdes?"

Then all at once the young priest recognised Doctor Chassaigne, his father's old friend, his own friend, the man who had cured and consoled him in the terrible physical and mental crisis which had come upon him after his mother's death.

"Ah! my dear doctor, how pleased I am to see you!" he replied.

They embraced with deep emotion. And now, in presence of that snowy hair and snowy beard, that slow walk, that sorrowful demeanour, Pierre remembered with what unrelenting ferocity misfortune had fallen on that unhappy man and aged him. But a few years had gone by, and now, when they met again, he was bowed down by destiny.

"You did not know, I suppose, that I had remained at Lourdes?" said the doctor. "It's true that I no longer write to anybody; in fact, I am no longer among the living. I live in the land of the dead." Tears were gathering in his eyes, and emotion made his voice falter as he resumed: "There! come and sit down on that bench yonder; it will please me to live the old days afresh with you, just for a moment."

In his turn the young priest felt his sobs choking him. He could only murmur: "Ah! my dear doctor, my old friend, I can truly tell you that I pitied you with my whole heart, my whole soul."

Doctor Chassaigne's story was one of disaster, the shipwreck of a life. He and his daughter Marguerite, a tall and lovable girl of twenty, had gone to Cauterets with Madame Chassaigne, the model wife and mother, whose state of health had made them somewhat anxious. A fortnight had elapsed and she seemed much better, and was already planning several pleasure trips, when one morning she was found dead in her bed. Her husband and daughter were overwhelmed, stupefied by this sudden blow, this cruel treachery of death. The doctor, who belonged to Bartres, had a family vault in the Lourdes cemetery, a vault constructed at his own expense, and in which his father and mother already rested. He desired, therefore, that his wife should be interred there, in a compartment adjoining that in which he expected soon to lie himself. And after the burial he had lingered for a week at Lourdes, when Marguerite, who was with him, was seized with a great shivering, and, taking to her bed one evening, died two days afterwards without her distracted father being able to form any exact notion of the illness which had carried her off. And thus it was not himself, but his daughter, lately radiant with beauty and health, in the very flower of her youth, who was laid in the vacant compartment by the mother's side. The man who had been so happy, so worshipped by his two helpmates, whose heart had been kept so warm by the love of two dear creatures all his own, was now nothing more than an old, miserable, stammering, lost being, who shivered in his icy solitude. All the joy of his life had departed; he envied the men who broke stones upon the highways when he saw their barefooted wives and daughters bring them their dinners at noontide. And he had refused to leave Lourdes, he had relinquished everything, his studies, his practice in Paris, in order that he might live near the tomb in which his wife and his daughter slept the eternal sleep.

"Ah, my old friend," repeated Pierre, "how I pitied you! How frightful must have been your grief! But why did you not rely a little on those who love you? Why did you shut yourself up here with your sorrow?"

The doctor made a gesture which embraced the horizon. "I could not go away, they are here and keep me with them. It is all over, I am merely waiting till my time comes to join them again."

Then silence fell. Birds were fluttering among the shrubs on the bank behind them, and in front they heard the loud murmur of the Gave. The sun rays were falling more heavily in a slow, golden dust, upon the hillsides; but on that retired bench under the beautiful trees, the coolness was still delightful. And although the crowd was but a couple of hundred yards distant, they were, so to say, in a desert, for nobody tore himself away from the Grotto to stray as far as the spot which they had chosen.

They talked together for a long time, and Pierre related under what circumstances he had reached Lourdes that morning with M. de Guersaint and his daughter, all three forming part of the national pilgrimage. Then all at once he gave a start of astonishment and exclaimed: "What! doctor, so you now believe that miracles are possible? You, good heavens! whom I knew as an unbeliever, or at least as one altogether indifferent to these matters?"

He was gazing at M. Chassaigne quite stupefied by something which he had just heard him say of the Grotto and Bernadette. It was amazing, coming from a man with so strong a mind, a *savant* of such intelligence, whose powerful analytical faculties he had formerly so much admired! How was it that a lofty, clear mind, nourished by experience and method, had become so changed as to acknowledge the miraculous cures effected by that divine fountain which the Blessed Virgin had caused to spurt forth under the pressure of a child's fingers?

"But just think a little, my dear doctor," he resumed. "It was you yourself who supplied my father with memoranda about Bernadette, your little fellow-villager as you used to call her; and it was you, too, who spoke to me at such length about her, when, later on, I took a momentary interest in her story. In your eyes she was simply an ailing child, prone to hallucinations, infantile, but self-conscious of her acts, deficient of will-power. Recollect our chats together, my doubts, and the healthy reason which you again enabled me, to acquire!"

Pierre was feeling very moved, for was not this the strangest of adventures? He a priest, who in a spirit of resignation had formerly endeavoured to believe, had ended by completely losing all faith through intercourse with this same doctor, who was then an unbeliever, but whom he now found converted, conquered by the supernatural, whilst he himself was racked by the torture of no longer believing.

"You who would only rely on accurate facts," he said, "you who based everything on observation! Do you renounce science then?"

Chassaigne, hitherto quiet, with a sorrowful smile playing on his lips, now made a violent gesture expressive of sovereign contempt. "Science indeed!" he exclaimed. "Do I know anything? Can I accomplish anything? You asked me just now what malady it was that killed my poor Marguerite. But I do not know! I, whom people think so learned, so well armed against death, I understood nothing of it, and I could do nothing—not even prolong my daughter's life for a single hour! And my wife, whom I found in bed already cold, when on the previous evening she had lain down in much better health and quite gay—was I even capable of foreseeing what ought to have been done in her case? No, no! for me at all events, science has become bankrupt. I wish to know nothing; I am but a fool and a poor old man!"

He spoke like this in a furious revolt against all his past life of pride and happiness. Then, having become calm again, he added: "And now I only feel a frightful remorse. Yes, a remorse which haunts me, which ever brings me here, prowling around the people who are praying. It is remorse for not having in the first instance come and humbled myself at that Grotto, bringing my two dear ones with me. They would have knelt there like those women whom you see, I should have knelt beside them, and perhaps the Blessed Virgin would have cured and preserved them. But, fool that I was, I only knew how to lose them! It is my fault."

Tears were now streaming from his eyes. "I remember," he continued, "that in my childhood at Bartres, my mother, a peasant woman, made me join my hands and implore God's help each morning. The prayer she taught me came back to my mind, word for word, when I again found myself alone, as weak, as lost, as a little child. What would you have, my friend? I joined my hands as in my younger days, I felt too wretched, too forsaken, I had too keen a need of a superhuman help, of a divine power which should think and determine for me, which should lull me and carry me on with its eternal prescience. How great at first was the confusion, the aberration of my poor brain, under the frightful, heavy blow which fell upon it! I spent a score of nights without being able to sleep, thinking that I should surely go mad. All sorts of ideas warred within me; I passed through periods of revolt when I shook my fist at Heaven, and then I lapsed into humility, entreating God to take me in my turn. And it was at last a conviction that there must be justice, a conviction that there must be love, which calmed me by restoring me my faith. You knew my daughter, so tall and strong, so beautiful, so brimful of life. Would it not be the most monstrous injustice if for her, who did not know life, there should be nothing beyond the tomb? She will live again, I am absolutely convinced of it, for I still hear her at times, she tells me that we shall meet, that we shall see one another again. Oh! the dear beings whom one has lost, my dear daughter, my dear wife, to see them once more, to live with them elsewhere, that is the one hope, the one consolation for all the sorrows of this world! I have given myself to God, since God alone can restore them to me!"

He was shaking with a slight tremor, like the weak old man he had become; and Pierre was at last able to understand and explain the conversion of this *savant*, this man of intellect who, growing old, had reverted to belief under the influence of sentiment. First of all, and this he had previously suspected, he discovered a kind of atavism of faith in this Pyrenean, this son of peasant mountaineers, who had been brought up in belief of the legend, and whom the legend had again mastered even when fifty years, of positive study had rolled over it. Then, too, there was human weariness; this man, to whom science had not brought happiness, revolted against science on the day when it seemed to him shallow, powerless to prevent him from shedding tears. And finally there was discouragement, a doubt of all things, ending in a need of certainty on the part of one whom age had softened, and who felt happy at being able to fall asleep in credulity.

Pierre did not protest, however; he did not jeer, for his heart was rent at sight of this tall, stricken old man, with his woeful senility. Is it not indeed pitiful to see the strongest, the clearest-minded become mere children again under such blows of fate? "Ah!" he faintly sighed, "if I could only suffer enough to be able to silence my reason, and kneel yonder and believe in all those fine stories."

The pale smile, which at times still passed over Doctor Chassaigne's lips, reappeared on them. "You mean the miracles?" said he. "You are a priest, my child, and I know what your misfortune is. The miracles seem impossible to you. But what do you know of them? Admit that you know nothing, and that what to our senses seems impossible is every minute taking place. And now we have been talking together for a long time, and eleven o'clock will soon strike, so that you must return to the Grotto. However, I shall expect you, at half-past three, when I will take you to the Medical Verification Office, where I hope I shall be able to show you some surprising things. Don't forget, at half-past three."

Thereupon he sent him off, and remained on the bench alone. The heat had yet increased, and the distant hills were burning in the furnace-like glow of the sun. However, he lingered there forgetfully, dreaming in the greeny half-light amidst the foliage, and listening to the continuous murmur of the Gave, as if a voice, a dear voice from the realms beyond, were speaking to him.

Pierre meantime hastened back to Marie. He was able to join her without much difficulty, for the crowd was thinning, a good many people having already gone off to *dejeuner*. And on arriving he perceived the girl's father, who was quietly seated beside her, and who at once wished to explain to him the reason of his long absence. For more than a couple of hours that morning he had scoured Lourdes in all directions, applying at twenty hotels in turn without being able to find the smallest closet where they might sleep. Even the servants' rooms were let and you could not have even secured a mattress on which to stretch yourself in some passage. However, all at once, just as he was despairing, he had discovered two rooms, small ones, it is true, and just under the roof, but in a very good hotel, that of the Apparitions, one of the best patronised in the town. The persons who had retained these rooms had just telegraphed that the patient whom they had meant to bring with them was dead. Briefly, it was a piece of rare good luck, and seemed to make M. de Guersaint quite gay.

Eleven o'clock was now striking and the woeful procession of sufferers started off again through the sunlit streets and squares. When it reached the hospital Marie begged her father and Pierre to go to the hotel, lunch and rest there awhile, and return to fetch her at two o'clock, when the patients would again be conducted to the Grotto. But when, after lunching, the two men went up to the rooms which they were to occupy at the Hotel of the Apparitions, M. de Guersaint, overcome by fatigue, fell so soundly asleep that Pierre had not the heart to awaken him. What would have been the use of it? His presence was not indispensable. And so the young priest returned to the hospital alone. Then the *cortege* again descended the Avenue de la Grotte, again wended its way over the Plateau de la Merlasse, again crossed the Place du Rosaire, past an ever-growing crowd which shuddered and crossed itself amid all the joyousness of that splendid August day. It was now the most glorious hour of a lovely afternoon.

When Marie was again installed in front of the Grotto she inquired if her father were coming. "Yes," answered Pierre; "he is only taking a little rest."

She waved her hand as though to say that he was acting rightly, and then in a sorely troubled voice she added: "Listen, Pierre; don't take me to the piscina for another hour. I am not yet in a state to find favour from Heaven, I wish to pray, to keep on praying."

After evincing such an ardent desire to come to Lourdes, terror was agitating her now that the moment for attempting the miracle was at hand. In fact, she began to relate that she had been unable to eat anything, and a girl who overheard her at once approached saying: "If you feel too weak, my dear young lady, remember we have some broth here."

Marie looked at her and recognised Raymonde. Several young girls were in this wise employed at the Grotto to distribute cups of broth and milk among the sufferers. Some of them, indeed, in previous years had displayed so much coquetry in the matter of silk, aprons trimmed with lace, that a uniform apron, of modest linen, with a small check pattern, blue and white, had been imposed on them. Nevertheless, in spite of this enforced simplicity, Raymonde, thanks to her freshness and her active, good-natured, housewifely air, had succeeded in making herself look quite charming.

"You will remember, won't you?" she added; "you have only to make me a sign and I will serve you."

Marie thanked her, saying, however, that she felt sure she would not be able to take anything; and then, turning towards the young priest, she resumed: "One hour—you must allow me one more hour, my friend."

Pierre wished at any rate to remain near her, but the entire space was reserved to the sufferers, the bearers not being allowed there. So he had to retire, and, caught in the rolling waves of the crowd, he found himself carried towards the piscinas, where he came upon an extraordinary spectacle which stayed his steps. In front of the low buildings where the baths were, three by three, six for the women and three for the men, he perceived under the trees a long stretch of ground enclosed by a rope fastened to the tree-trunks; and here, various sufferers, some sitting in their bath-chairs and others lying on the mattresses of their litters, were drawn up in line, waiting to be bathed, whilst outside the rope, a huge, excited throng was ever pressing and surging. A Capuchin, erect in the centre of the reserved space, was at that moment conducting the prayers. "Aves" followed one after the other, repeated by the crowd in a loud confused murmur. Then, all at once, as Madame Vincent, who, pale with agony, had long been waiting, was admitted to the baths, carrying her dear burden, her little girl who looked like a waxen image of the child Christ, the Capuchin let himself fall upon his knees with his arms extended, and cried aloud: "Lord, heal our sick!" He raised this cry a dozen, twenty times, with a growing fury, and each time the crowd repeated it, growing more and more excited at each shout, till it sobbed and kissed the ground in a state of frenzy. It was like a hurricane of delirium rushing by and laying every head in the dust. Pierre was utterly distracted by the sob of suffering which arose from the very bowels of these poor folks—at first a prayer, growing louder and louder, then bursting forth like a demand in impatient, angry, deafening, obstinate accents, as though to compel the help of Heaven. "Lord, heal our sick!"—"Lord, heal our sick!" The shout soared on high incessantly.

An incident occurred, however; La Grivotte was weeping hot tears because they would not bathe her. "They say that I'm a consumptive," she plaintively exclaimed, "and that they can't dip consumptives in cold water. Yet they dipped one this morning; I saw her. So why won't they dip me? I've been wearing myself out for the last half-hour in telling them that they are only grieving the Blessed Virgin, for I am going to be cured, I feel it, I am going to be cured!"

As she was beginning to cause a scandal, one of the chaplains of the piscinas approached and endeavoured to calm her. They would see what they could do for her, by-and-by, said he; they would consult the reverend Fathers, and, if she were very good, perhaps they would bathe her all the same.

Meantime the cry continued: "Lord, heal our sick! Lord, heal our sick!" And Pierre, who had just perceived Madame Vetu, also waiting at the piscina entry, could no longer turn his eyes away from her hope-tortured face, whose eyes were fixed upon the doorway by which the happy ones, the elect, emerged from the divine presence, cured of all their ailments. However, a sudden increase of the crowd's frenzy, a perfect rage of entreaties, gave him such a shock as to draw tears from his eyes. Madame Vincent was now coming out again, still carrying her little girl in her arms, her wretched, her fondly loved little girl, who had been dipped in a fainting state in the icy water, and whose little face, but imperfectly wiped, was as pale as ever, and indeed even more woeful and lifeless. The mother was sobbing, crucified by this long agony, reduced to despair by the refusal of the Blessed Virgin, who had remained insensible to her child's sufferings. And yet when Madame Vetu in her turn entered, with the eager passion of a dying woman about to drink the water of life, the haunting, obstinate cry burst out again, without sign of discouragement or lassitude: "Lord, heal our sick! Lord, heal our sick!" The Capuchin had now fallen with his face to the ground, and the howling crowd, with arms outstretched, devoured the soil with its kisses.

Pierre wished to join Madame Vincent to soothe her with a few kind, encouraging words; however, a fresh string of pilgrims not only prevented him from passing, but threw him towards the fountain which another throng besieged. There was here quite a range of low buildings, a long stone wall with carved coping, and it had been necessary for the people to form in procession, although there were twelve taps from which the water fell into a narrow basin. Many came hither to fill bottles, metal cans, and stoneware pitchers. To prevent too great a waste of water, the tap only acted when a knob was pressed with the hand. And thus many weak-handed women lingered there a long time, the water dripping on their feet. Those who had no cans to fill at least came to drink and wash their faces. Pierre noticed one young man who drank seven small glassfuls of water, and washed his eyes seven times without wiping them. Others were drinking out of shells, tin goblets, and leather cups. And he was particularly interested by the sight of Elise Rouquet, who, thinking it useless to go to the piscinas to bathe the frightful sore which was eating away her face, had contented herself with employing the water of the fountain as a lotion, every two hours since her arrival that morning. She knelt down, threw back her fichu, and for a long time applied a handkerchief to her face—a handkerchief which she had soaked with the miraculous fluid like a sponge; and the crowd around rushed upon the fountain in such fury that folks no longer noticed her diseased face, but washed themselves and drank from the same pipe at which she constantly moistened her handkerchief.

Just then, however, Gerard, who passed by dragging M. Sabathier to the piscinas, called to Pierre, whom he saw unoccupied, and asked him to come and help him, for it would not be an easy task to move and bathe this helpless victim of ataxia. And thus

Pierre lingered with the sufferer in the men's piscina for nearly half an hour, whilst Gerard returned to the Grotto to fetch another patient. These piscinas seemed to the young priest to be very well arranged. They were divided into three compartments, three baths separated by partitions, with steps leading into them. In order that one might isolate the patient, a linen curtain hug before each entry, which was reached through a kind of waiting-room having a paved floor, and furnished with a bench and a couple of chairs. Here the patients undressed and dressed themselves with an awkward haste, a nervous kind of shame. One man, whom Pierre found there when he entered, was still naked, and wrapped himself in the curtain before putting on a bandage with trembling hands. Another one, a consumptive who was frightfully emaciated, sat shivering and groaning, his livid skin mottled with violet marks. However, Pierre became more interested in Brother Isidore, who was just being removed from one of the baths. He had fainted away, and for a moment, indeed, it was thought that he was dead. But at last he began moaning again, and one's heart filled with pity at sight of his long, lank frame, which suffering had withered, and which, with his diseased hip, looked a human remnant on exhibition. The two hospitallers who had been bathing him had the greatest difficulty to put on his shirt, fearful as they were that if he were suddenly shaken he might expire in their arms.

"You will help me, Monsieur l'Abbe, won't you?" asked another hospitaller as he began to undress M. Sabathier.

Pierre hastened to give his services, and found that the attendant, discharging such humble duties, was none other than the Marquis de Salmon-Roquebert whom M. de Guersaint had pointed out to him on the way from the station to the hospital that morning. A man of forty, with a large, aquiline, knightly nose set in a long face, the Marquis was the last representative of one of the most ancient and illustrious families of France. Possessing a large fortune, a regal mansion in the Rue de Lille at Paris, and vast estates in Normandy, he came to Lourdes each year, for the three days of the national pilgrimage, influenced solely by his benevolent feelings, for he had no religious zeal and simply observed the rites of the Church because it was customary for noblemen to do so. And he obstinately declined any high functions. Resolved to remain a hospitaller, he had that year assumed the duty of bathing the patients, exhausting the strength of his arms, employing his fingers from morning till night in handling rags and re-applying dressings to sores.

"Be careful," he said to Pierre; "take off the stockings very slowly. Just now, some flesh came away when they were taking off the things of that poor fellow who is being dressed again, over yonder."

Then, leaving M. Sabathier for a moment in order to put on the shoes of the unhappy sufferer whom he alluded to, the Marquis found the left shoe wet inside. Some matter had flowed into the fore part of it, and he had to take the usual medical precautions before putting it on the patient's foot, a task which he performed with extreme care; and so as not to touch the man's leg, into which an ulcer was eating.

"And now," he said to Pierre, as he returned to M. Sabathier, "pull down the drawers at the same time I do, so that we may get them off at one pull."

In addition to the patients and the hospitallers selected for duty at the piscinas, the only person in the little dressing-room was a chaplain who kept on repeating "Paters" and "Aves," for not even a momentary pause was allowed in the prayers. Merely a loose curtain hung before the doorway leading to the open space which the rope enclosed; and the ardent clamorous entreaties of the throng were incessantly wafted into the room, with the piercing shouts of the Capuchin, who ever repeated "Lord, heal our sick! Lord, heal our sick!" A cold light fell from the high windows of the building and constant dampness reigned there, with the mouldy smell like that of a cellar dripping with water.

At last M. Sabathier was stripped, divested of all garments save a little apron which had been fastened about his loins for decency's sake.

"Pray don't plunge me," said he; "let me down into the water by degrees."

In point of fact that cold water quite terrified him. He was still wont to relate that he had experienced such a frightful chilling sensation on the first occasion that he had sworn never to go in again. According to his account, there could be no worse torture than that icy cold. And then too, as he put it, the water was scarcely inviting; for, through fear lest the output of the source should not suffice, the Fathers of the Grotto only allowed the water of the baths to be changed twice a day. And nearly a hundred patients being dipped in the same water, it can be imagined what a terrible soup the latter at last became. All manner of things were found in it, so that it was like a frightful *consomme* of all ailments, a field of cultivation for every kind of poisonous germ, a quintessence of the most dreaded contagious diseases; the miraculous feature of it all being that men should emerge alive from their immersion in such filth.

"Gently, gently," repeated M. Sabathier to Pierre and the Marquis, who had taken hold of him under the hips in order to carry him to the bath. And he gazed with childlike terror at that thick, livid water on which floated so many greasy, nauseating patches of scum. However, his dread of the cold was so great that he preferred the polluted baths of the afternoon, since all the bodies that were dipped in the water during the early part of the day ended by slightly warming it.

"We will let you slide down the steps," exclaimed the Marquis in an undertone; and then he instructed Pierre to hold the patient with all his strength under the armpits.

"Have no fear," replied the priest; "I will not let go."

M. Sabathier was then slowly lowered. You could now only see his back, his poor painful back which swayed and swelled, mottled by the rippling of a shiver. And when they dipped him his head fell back in a spasm, a sound like the cracking of bones was heard, and breathing hard, he almost stifled.

The chaplain, standing beside the bath, had begun calling with renewed fervour: "Lord, heal our sick! Lord, heal our sick!"

M. de Salmon-Roquebert repeated the cry, which the regulations required the hospitallers to raise at each fresh immersion. Pierre, therefore, had to imitate his companion, and his pitiful feelings at the sight of so much suffering were so intense that he regained some little of his faith. It was long indeed since he had prayed like this, devoutly wishing that there might be a God in heaven, whose omnipotence could assuage the wretchedness of humanity. At the end of three or four minutes, however, when with great difficulty they drew M. Sabathier, livid and shivering, out of the bath, the young priest fell into deeper, more despairing sorrow than ever at beholding how downcast, how overwhelmed the sufferer was at having experienced no relief. Again had he made a futile attempt; for the seventh time the Blessed Virgin had not deigned to listen to his prayers. He closed his eyes, from between the lids of which big tears began to roll while they were dressing him again.

Then Pierre recognised little Gustave Vigneron coming in, on his crutch, to take his first bath. His relatives, his father, his mother, and his aunt, Madame Chaise, all three of substantial appearance and exemplary piety, had just fallen on their knees at the door. Whispers ran through the crowd; it was said that the gentleman was a functionary of the Ministry of Finances. However, while the child was beginning to undress, a tumult arose, and Father Fourcade and Father Massias, suddenly arriving, gave orders to suspend the immersions. The great miracle was about to be attempted, the extraordinary favour which had been so ardently prayed for since the morning—the restoration of the dead man to life.

The prayers were continuing outside, rising in a furious appeal which died away in the sky of that warm summer afternoon. Two bearers came in with a covered stretcher, which they deposited in the middle of the dressing-room. Baron Suire, President of the Association, followed, accompanied by Berthaud, one of its principal officers, for the affair was causing a great stir among the whole staff, and before anything was done a few words were exchanged in low voices between the gentlemen and the two Fathers of the Assumption. Then the latter fell upon their knees, with arms extended, and began to pray, their faces illumined, transfigured by their burning desire to see God's omnipotence displayed.

"Lord, hear us! Lord, grant our prayer!"

M. Sabathier had just been taken away, and the only patient now present was little Gustave, who had remained on a chair, half-undressed and forgotten. The curtains of the stretcher were raised, and the man's corpse appeared, already stiff, and seemingly reduced and shrunken, with large eyes which had obstinately remained wide open. It was necessary, however, to undress the body, which was still fully clad, and this terrible duty made the bearers momentarily hesitate. Pierre noticed that the Marquis de Salmon-Roquebert, who showed such devotion to the living, such freedom from all repugnance whenever they were in question, had now drawn aside and fallen on his knees, as though to avoid the necessity of touching that lifeless corpse. And the young priest thereupon followed his example, and knelt near him in order to keep countenance.

Father Massias meanwhile was gradually becoming excited, praying in so loud a voice that it drowned that of his superior, Father Fourcade: "Lord, restore our brother to us!" he cried. "Lord, do it for Thy glory!"

One of the hospitallers had already begun to pull at the man's trousers, but his legs were so stiff that the garment would not come off. In fact the corpse ought to have been raised up; and the other hospitaller, who was unbuttoning the dead man's old frock coat, remarked in an undertone that it would be best to cut everything away with a pair of scissors. Otherwise there would be no end of the job.

Berthaud, however, rushed up to them, after rapidly consulting Baron Suire. As a politician he secretly disapproved of Father Fourcade's action in making such an attempt, only they could not now do otherwise than carry matters to an issue; for the crowd was waiting and had been entreating God on the dead man's behalf ever since the morning. The wisest course, therefore, was to finish with the affair at once, showing as much respect as possible for the remains of the deceased. In lieu, therefore, of pulling the corpse about in order to strip it bare, Berthaud was of opinion that it would be better to dip it in the piscina clad as it was. Should the man resuscitate, it would be easy to procure fresh clothes for him; and in the contrary event, no harm would have been done. This is what he hastily said to the bearers; and forthwith he helped them to pass some straps under the man's hips and arms.

Father Fourcade had nodded his approval of this course, whilst Father Massias prayed with increased fervour: "Breathe upon him, O Lord, and he shall be born anew! Restore his soul to him, O, Lord, that he may glorify Thee!"

Making an effort, the two hospitallers now raised the man by means of the straps, carried him to the bath, and slowly lowered him into the water, at each moment fearing that he would slip away from their hold. Pierre, although overcome by horror, could not do otherwise than look at them, and thus he distinctly beheld the immersion of this corpse in its sorry garments, which on being wetted clung to the bones, outlining the skeleton-like figure of the deceased, who floated like a man who has been drowned. But the repulsive part of it all was, that in spite of the *rigor mortis*, the head fell backward into the water, and was submerged by it. In vain did the hospitallers try to raise it by pulling the shoulder straps; as they made the attempt, the man almost sank to the bottom of the bath. And how could he have recovered his breath when his mouth was full of water, his staring eyes seemingly dying afresh, beneath that watery veil?

Then, during the three long minutes allowed for the immersion, the two Fathers of the Assumption and the chaplain, in a paroxysm of desire and faith, strove to compel the intervention of Heaven, praying in such loud voices that they seemed to choke.

"Do Thou but look on him, O Lord, and he will live again! Lord! may he rise at Thy voice to convert the earth! Lord! Thou hast but one word to say and all Thy people will acclaim Thee!"

At last, as though some vessel had broken in his throat, Father Massias fell groaning and choking on his elbows, with only enough strength left him to kiss the flagstones. And from without came the clamour of the crowd, the ever-repeated cry, which the Capuchin was still leading: "Lord, heal our sick! Lord, heal our sick!" This appeal seemed so singular at that moment, that Pierre's sufferings were increased. He could feel, too, that the Marquis was shuddering beside him. And so the relief was general when Berthaud, thoroughly annoyed with the whole business, curtly shouted to the hospitallers: "Take him out! Take him out at once!"

The body was removed from the bath and laid on the stretcher, looking like the corpse of a drowned man with its sorry garments clinging to its limbs. The water was trickling from the hair, and rivulets began falling on either side, spreading out in pools on the floor. And naturally, dead as the man had been, dead he remained.

The others had all risen and stood looking at him amidst a distressing silence. Then, as he was covered up and carried away, Father Fourcade followed the bier leaning on the shoulder of Father Massias and dragging his gouty leg, the painful weight of which he had momentarily forgotten. But he was already recovering his strong serenity, and as a hush fell upon the crowd outside, he could be heard saying: "My dear brothers, my dear sisters, God has not been willing to restore him to us, doubtless because in His infinite goodness He has desired to retain him among His elect."

And that was all; there was no further question of the dead man. Patients were again being brought into the dressing-room, the two other baths were already occupied. And now little Gustave, who had watched that terrible scene with his keen inquisitive eyes, evincing no sign of terror, finished undressing himself. His wretched body, the body of a scrofulous child, appeared with its prominent ribs and projecting spine, its limbs so thin that they looked like mere walking-sticks. Especially was this the case as regards the left one, which was withered, wasted to the bone; and he also had two sores, one on the hip, and the other in the loins, the last a terrible one, the skin being eaten away so that you distinctly saw the raw flesh. Yet he smiled, rendered so precocious by his sufferings that, although but fifteen years old and looking no more than ten, he seemed to be endowed with the reason and philosophy of a grown man.

The Marquis de Salmon-Roquebert, who had taken him gently in his arms, refused Pierre's offer of service: "Thanks, but he weighs no more than a bird. And don't be frightened, my dear little fellow. I will do it gently."

"Oh, I am not afraid of cold water, monsieur," replied the boy; "you may duck me."

Then he was lowered into the bath in which the dead man had been dipped. Madame Vigneron and Madame Chaise, who were not allowed to enter, had remained at the door on their knees, whilst the father, M. Vigneron, who was admitted into the dressing-room, went on making the sign of the cross.

Finding that his services were no longer required, Pierre now departed. The sudden idea that three o'clock must have long since struck and that Marie must be waiting for him made him hasten his steps. However, whilst he was endeavouring to pierce the crowd, he saw the girl arrive in her little conveyance, dragged along by Gerard, who had not ceased transporting sufferers to the piscina. She had become impatient, suddenly filled with a conviction that she was at last in a frame of mind to find grace. And at sight of Pierre she reproached him, saying, "What, my friend, did you forget me?"

He could find no answer, but watched her as she was taken into the piscina reserved for women, and then, in mortal sorrow, fell upon his knees. It was there that he would wait for her, humbly kneeling, in order that he might take her back to the Grotto, cured without doubt and singing a hymn of praise. Since she was certain of it, would she not assuredly be cured? However, it was in vain that he sought for words of prayer in the depths of his distracted being. He was still under the blow of all the terrible things that he had beheld, worn out with physical fatigue, his brain depressed, no longer knowing what he saw or what he believed. His desperate affection for Marie alone remained, making him long to humble himself and supplicate, in the thought that when little ones really love and entreat the powerful they end by obtaining favours. And at last he caught himself repeating the prayers of the crowd, in a distressful voice that came from the depths of his being "Lord, heal our sick! Lord, heal our sick!"

Ten minutes, a quarter of an hour perhaps, went by. Then Marie reappeared in her little conveyance. Her face was very pale and wore an expression of despair. Her beautiful hair was fastened above her head in a heavy golden coil which the water had not touched. And she was not cured. The stupor of infinite discouragement hollowed and lengthened her face, and she averted her eyes as though to avoid meeting those of the priest who thunderstruck, chilled to the heart, at last made up his mind to grasp the handle of the little vehicle, so as to take the girl back to the Grotto.

And meantime the cry of the faithful, who with open arms were kneeling there and kissing the earth, again rose with a growing fury, excited by the Capuchin's shrill voice: "Lord, heal our sick! Heal our sick, O Lord!"

III. FOUNTAIN AND PISCINA

As Pierre was placing Marie in position again in front of the Grotto, an attack of weakness came over her and she almost fainted. Gerard, who was there, saw Raymonde quickly hurry to the spot with a cup of broth, and at once they began zealously rivalling each other in their attentions to the ailing girl. Raymonde, holding out the cup in a pretty way, and assuming the coaxing airs of an expert nurse, especially insisted that Marie should accept the bouillon; and Gerard, glancing at this portionless girl, could not help finding her charming, already expert in the business of life, and quite ready to manage a household with a firm hand without ceasing to be amiable. Berthaud was no doubt right, this was the wife that he, Gerard, needed.

"Mademoiselle," said he to Raymonde, "shall I raise the young lady a little?"

"Thank you, monsieur, I am quite strong enough. And besides I will give it to her in spoonfuls; that will be the better way."

Marie, however, obstinately preserving her fierce silence as she recovered consciousness, refused the broth with a gesture. She wished to be left in quietness, she did not want anybody to question her. And it was only when the others had gone off smiling at one another, that she said to Pierre in a husky voice: "Has not my father come then?"

After hesitating for a moment the priest was obliged to confess the truth. "I left him sleeping and he cannot have woke up."

Then Marie relapsed into her state of languid stupor and dismissed him in his turn, with the gesture with which she declined all succour. She no longer prayed, but remained quite motionless, gazing fixedly with her large eyes at the marble Virgin, the white statue amidst the radiance of the Grotto. And as four o'clock was now striking, Pierre with his heart sore went off to the Verification Office, having suddenly remembered the appointment given him by Doctor Chassaigne.

IV. VERIFICATION

THE doctor was waiting for the young priest outside the Verification Office, in front of which a compact and feverish crowd of pilgrims was assembled, waylaying and questioning the patients who went in, and acclaiming them as they came out whenever the news spread of any miracle, such as the restoration of some blind man's sight, some deaf woman's hearing, or some paralytic's power of motion.

Pierre had no little difficulty in making his way through the throng, but at last he reached his friend. "Well," he asked, "are we going to have a miracle—a real, incontestable one I mean?"

The doctor smiled, indulgent despite his new faith. "Ah, well," said he, "a miracle is not worked to order. God intervenes when He pleases."

Some hospitallers were mounting guard at the door, but they all knew M. Chassaigne, and respectfully drew aside to let him enter with his companion. The office where the cures were verified was very badly installed in a wretched wooden shanty divided into two apartments, first a narrow ante-chamber, and then a general meeting room which was by no means so large as it should have been. However, there was a question of providing the department with better accommodation the following year; with which view some large premises, under one of the inclined ways of the Rosary, were already being fitted up.

The only article of furniture in the antechamber was a wooden bench on which Pierre perceived two female patients awaiting their turn in the charge of a young hospitaller. But on entering the meeting room the number of persons packed inside it quite surprised him, whilst the suffocating heat within those wooden walls on which the sun was so fiercely playing, almost scorched his face. It was a square bare room, painted a light yellow, with the panes of its single window covered with whitening, so that the pressing throng outside might see nothing of what went on within. One dared not even open this window to admit a little fresh air, for it was no sooner set ajar than a crowd of inquisitive heads peeped in. The furniture was of a very rudimentary kind, consisting simply of two deal tables of unequal height placed end to end and not even covered with a cloth; together with a kind of big "canterbury" littered with untidy papers, sets of documents, registers and pamphlets, and finally some thirty rush-seated chairs placed here and there over the floor and a couple of ragged arm-chairs usually reserved for the patients.

Doctor Bonamy at once hastened forward to greet Doctor Chassaigne, who was one of the latest and most glorious conquests of the Grotto. He found a chair for him and, bowing to Pierre's cassock, also made the young priest sit down. Then, in the tone of extreme politeness which was customary with him, he exclaimed: "*Mon cher confrere*, you will kindly allow me to continue. We were just examining mademoiselle."

He referred to a deaf peasant girl of twenty, who was seated in one of the arm-chairs. Instead of listening, however, Pierre, who was very weary, still with a buzzing in his head, contented himself with gazing at the scene, endeavouring to form some notion of the people assembled in the room. There were some fifty altogether, many of them standing and leaning against the walls. Half a dozen, however, were seated at the two tables, a central position being occupied by the superintendent of the piscinas, who was constantly consulting a thick register; whilst around him were a Father of the Assumption and three young seminarists who acted as secretaries, writing, searching for documents, passing them and classifying them again after each examination. Pierre, however, took most interest in a Father of the Immaculate Conception, Father Dargeles, who had been pointed out to him that morning as being the editor of the "Journal de la Grotte." This ecclesiastic, whose thin little face, with its blinking eyes, pointed nose, and delicate mouth was ever smiling, had modestly seated himself at the end of the lower table where he occasionally took notes for his newspaper. He alone, of the community to which he belonged, showed himself during the three days of the national pilgrimage. Behind him, however, one could divine the presence of all the others, the slowly developed hidden power which organised everything and raked in all the proceeds.

The onlookers consisted almost entirely of inquisitive people and witnesses, including a score of doctors and a few priests. The medical men, who had come from all parts, mostly preserved silence, only a few of them occasionally venturing to ask a question; and every now and then they would exchange oblique glances, more occupied apparently in watching one another than in verifying the facts submitted to their examination. Who could they be? Some names were mentioned, but they were quite unknown. Only one had caused any stir, that of a celebrated doctor, professor at a Catholic university.

That afternoon, however, Doctor Bonamy, who never sat down, busy as he was conducting the proceedings and questioning the patients, reserved most of his attentions for a short, fair-haired man, a writer of some talent who contributed to one of the most widely read Paris newspapers, and who, in the course of a holiday tour, had by chance reached Lourdes that morning. Was not this an unbeliever whom it might be possible to convert, whose influence it would be desirable to gain for advertisement's sake? Such at all events appeared to be M. Bonamy's opinion, for he had compelled the journalist to take the second arm-chair, and with an affectation of smiling good-nature was treating him to a full performance, again and again repeating that he and his patrons had nothing to hide, and that everything took place in the most open manner.

"We only desire light," he exclaimed. "We never cease to call for the investigations of all willing men."

Then, as the alleged cure of the deaf girl did not seem at all a promising case, he addressed her somewhat roughly: "Come, come, my girl, this is only a beginning. You must come back when there are more distinct signs of improvement." And turning to the journalist he added in an undertone: "If we were to believe them they would all be healed. But the only cures we accept are those which are thoroughly proven, which are as apparent as the sun itself. Pray notice moreover that I say cures and not miracles; for we doctors do not take upon ourselves to interpret and explain. We are simply here to see if the patients, who submit themselves to our examination, have really lost all symptoms of their ailments."

Thereupon he struck an attitude. Doubtless he spoke like this in order that his rectitude might not be called in question. Believing without believing, he knew that science was yet so obscure, so full of surprises, that what seemed impossible might always come to pass; and thus, in the declining years of his life, he had contrived to secure an exceptional position at the Grotto, a position which had both its inconveniences and its advantages, but which, taken for all in all, was very comfortable and pleasant.

And now, in reply to a question from the Paris journalist, he began to explain his mode of proceeding. Each patient who accompanied the pilgrimage arrived provided with papers, amongst which there was almost always a certificate of the doctor who had been attending the case. At times even there were certificates given by several doctors, hospital bulletins and so forth—quite a record of the illness in its various stages. And thus if a cure took place and the cured person came forward, it was only necessary to consult his or her set of documents in order to ascertain the nature of the ailment, and then examination would show if that ailment had really disappeared.

Pierre was now listening. Since he had been there, seated and resting himself, he had grown calmer, and his mind was clear once more. It was only the heat which at present caused him any inconvenience. And thus, interested as he was by Doctor Bonamy's explanations, and desirous of forming an opinion, he would have spoken out and questioned, had it not been for his cloth which condemned him to remain in the background. He was delighted, therefore, when the little fair-haired gentleman, the influential writer, began to bring forward the objections which at once occurred to him.[1] Was it not most unfortunate that one doctor should diagnose the illness and that another one should verify the cure? In this mode of proceeding there was certainly a source of frequent error. The better plan would have been for a medical commission to examine all the patients as soon as they arrived at Lourdes and draw up reports on every case, to which reports the same commission would have referred whenever an alleged cure was brought before it. Doctor Bonamy, however, did not fall in with this suggestion. He replied, with some reason, that a commission would never suffice for such gigantic labour. Just think of it! A thousand patients to examine in a single morning! And how many different theories there would be, how many contrary diagnoses, how many endless discussions, all of a nature to increase the general uncertainty! The preliminary examination of the patients, which was almost always impossible, would, even if attempted, leave the door open for as many errors as the present system. In practice, it was necessary to remain content with the certificates delivered by the medical men who had been in attendance on the patients, and these certificates accordingly acquired capital, decisive importance. Doctor Bonamy ran through the documents lying on one of the tables and gave the Paris journalist some

[1] The reader will doubtless have understood that the Parisian journalist is none other than M. Zola himself—Trans.

of these certificates to read. A great many of them unfortunately were very brief. Others, more skilfully drawn up, clearly specified the nature of the complaint; and some of the doctors' signatures were even certified by the mayors of the localities where they resided. Nevertheless doubts remained, innumerable and not to be surmounted. Who were these doctors? Who could tell if they possessed sufficient scientific authority to write as they did? With all respect to the medical profession, were there not in-innumerable doctors whose attainments were very limited? And, besides, might not these have been influenced by circumstances that one knew nothing of, in some cases by considerations of a personal character? One was tempted to ask for an inquiry respecting each of these medical men. Since everything was based on the documents supplied by the patients, these documents ought to have been most carefully controlled; for there could be no proof of any miracle if the absolute certainty of the alleged ailments had not been demonstrated by stringent examination.

Very red and covered with perspiration, Doctor Bonamy waved his arms. "But that is the course we follow, that is the course we follow!" said he. "As soon as it seems to us that a case of cure cannot be explained by natural means, we institute a minute inquiry, we request the person who has been cured to return here for further examination. And as you can see, we surround ourselves with all means of enlightenment. These gentlemen here, who are listening to us, are nearly every one of them doctors who have come from all parts of France. We always entreat them to express their doubts if they feel any, to discuss the cases with us, and a very detailed report of each discussion is drawn up. You hear me, gentlemen; by all means protest if anything occurs here of a nature to offend your sense of truth."

Not one of the onlookers spoke. Most of the doctors present were undoubtedly Catholics, and naturally enough they merely bowed. As for the others, the unbelievers, the *savants* pure and simple, they looked on and evinced some interest in certain phenomena, but considerations of courtesy deterred them from entering into discussions which they knew would have been useless. When as men of sense their discomfort became too great, and they felt themselves growing angry, they simply left the room.

As nobody breathed a word, Doctor Bonamy became quite triumphant, and on the journalist asking him if he were all alone to accomplish so much work, he replied: "Yes, all alone; but my functions as doctor of the Grotto are not so complicated as you may think, for, I repeat it, they simply consist in verifying cures whenever any take place." However, he corrected himself, and added with a smile: "All! I was forgetting, I am not quite alone, I have Raboin, who helps me to keep things a little bit in order here."

So saying, he pointed to a stout, grey-haired man of forty, with a heavy face and bull-dog jaw. Raboin was an ardent believer, one of those excited beings who did not allow the miracles to be called in question. And thus he often suffered from his duties at the Verification Office, where he was ever ready to growl with anger when anybody disputed a prodigy. The appeal to the doctors had made him quite lose his temper, and his superior had to calm him.

"Come, Raboin, my friend, be quiet!" said Doctor Bonamy. "All sincere opinions are entitled to a hearing."

However, the *defile* of patients was resumed. A man was now brought in whose trunk was so covered with eczema that when he took off his shirt a kind of grey flour fell from his skin. He was not cured, but simply declared that he came to Lourdes every year, and always went away feeling relieved. Then came a lady, a countess, who was fearfully emaciated, and whose story was an extraordinary one. Cured of tuberculosis by the Blessed Virgin, a first time, seven years previously, she had subsequently given birth to four children, and had then again fallen into consumption. At present she was a morphinomaniac, but her first bath had already relieved her so much, that she proposed taking part in the torchlight procession that same evening with the twenty-seven members of her family whom she had brought with her to Lourdes. Then there was a woman afflicted with nervous aphonia, who after months of absolute dumbness had just recovered her voice at the moment when the Blessed Sacrament went by at the head of the four o'clock procession.

"Gentlemen," declared Doctor Bonamy, affecting the graciousness of a *savant* of extremely liberal views, "as you are aware, we do not draw any conclusions when a nervous affection is in question. Still you will kindly observe that this woman was treated at the Salpetriere for six months, and that she had to come here to find her tongue suddenly loosened."

Despite all these fine words he displayed some little impatience, for he would have greatly liked to show the gentleman from Paris one of those remarkable instances of cure which occasionally presented themselves during the four o'clock procession—that being the moment of grace and exaltation when the Blessed Virgin interceded for those whom she had chosen. But on this particular afternoon there had apparently been none. The cures which had so far passed before them were doubtful ones, deficient in interest. Meanwhile, out-of-doors, you could hear the stamping and roaring of the crowd, goaded into a frenzy by repeated hymns, enfevered by its earnest desire for the Divine interposition, and growing more and more enervated by the delay.

All at once, however, a smiling, modest-looking young girl, whose clear eyes sparkled with intelligence, entered the office. "Ah!" exclaimed Doctor Bonamy joyously, "here is our little friend Sophie. A remarkable cure, gentlemen, which took place at the same season last year, and the results of which I will ask permission to show you."

Pierre had immediately recognized Sophie Couteau, the *miraculee* who had got into the train at Poitiers. And he now witnessed a repetition of the scene which had already been enacted in his presence. Doctor Bonamy began giving detailed explanations to the little fair-haired gentleman, who displayed great attention. The case, said the doctor, had been one of caries of the bones of the left heel, with a commencement of necrosis necessitating excision; and yet the frightful, suppurating sore had been healed in a minute at the first immersion in the piscina.

"Tell the gentlemen how it happened, Sophie," he added.

The little girl made her usual pretty gesture as a sign to everybody to be attentive. And then she began: "Well, it was like this; my foot was past cure, I couldn't even go to church any more, and it had to be kept bandaged because there was always a lot of matter coming from it. Monsieur Rivoire, the doctor, who had made a cut in it so as to see inside it, said that he should be obliged to take out a piece of the bone; and that, sure enough, would have made me lame for life. But when I got to Lourdes, and had prayed a great deal to the Blessed Virgin, I went to dip my foot in the water, wishing so much that I might be cured, that I did not even take the time to pull the bandages off. And everything remained in the water; there was no longer anything the matter with my foot when I took it out."

Doctor Bonamy listened, and punctuated each word with an approving nod. "And what did your doctor say, Sophie?" he asked.

"When I got back to Vivonne, and Monsieur Rivoire saw my foot again, he said: 'Whether it be God or the Devil who has cured this child, it is all the same to me; but in all truth, she is cured.'"

A burst of laughter rang out. The doctor's remark was sure to produce an effect.

"And what was it, Sophie, that you said to Madame la Comtesse, the superintendent of your ward?"

"Ah, yes! I hadn't brought many bandages for my foot with me, and I said to her, 'It was very kind of the Blessed Virgin to cure me the first day, as I should have run out of linen on the morrow.'"

Then there was fresh laughter, a general display of satisfaction at seeing her look so pretty, telling her story, which she now knew by heart, in too recitative a manner, but, nevertheless, remaining very touching and truthful in appearance.

"Take off your shoe, Sophie," now said Doctor Bonamy; "show your foot to these gentlemen. Let them feel it. Nobody must retain any doubt."

The little foot promptly appeared, very white, very clean, carefully tended indeed, with its scar just below the ankle, a long scar, whose whity seam testified to the gravity of the complaint. Some of the medical men had drawn near, and looked on in silence. Others, whose opinions, no doubt, were already formed, did not disturb themselves, though one of them, with an air of extreme politeness, inquired why the Blessed Virgin had not made a new foot while she was about it, for this would assuredly have given her no more trouble. Doctor Bonamy, however, quickly replied, that if the Blessed Virgin had left a scar, it was certainly in order that a trace, a proof of the miracle, might remain. Then he entered into technical particulars, demonstrating that a fragment of bone and flesh must have been instantly formed, and this, of course, could not be explained in any natural way.

"*Mon Dieu*!" interrupted the little fair-haired gentleman, "there is no need of any such complicated affair. Let me merely see a finger cut with a penknife, let me see it dipped in the water, and let it come out with the cut cicatrised. The miracle will be quite as great, and I shall bow to it respectfully." Then he added: "If I possessed a source which could thus close up sores and wounds, I would turn the world topsy-turvy. I do not know exactly how I should manage it, but at all events I would summon the nations, and the nations would come. I should cause the miracles to be verified in such an indisputable manner, that I should be the master of the earth. Just think what an extraordinary power it would be—a divine power. But it would be necessary that not a doubt should remain, the truth would have to be as patent, as apparent as the sun itself. The whole world would behold it and believe!"

Then he began discussing various methods of control with the doctor. He had admitted that, owing to the great number of patients, it would be difficult, if not impossible, to examine them all on their arrival. Only, why didn't they organise a special ward at the hospital, a ward which would be reserved for cases of visible sores? They would have thirty such cases all told, which might be subjected to the preliminary examination of a committee. Authentic reports would be drawn up, and the sores might even be photographed. Then, if a case of cure should present itself, the commission would merely have to authenticate it by a fresh report. And in all this there would be no question of any internal complaint, the diagnostication of which is difficult, and liable to be controverted. There would be visible evidence of the ailment, and cure could be proved.

Somewhat embarrassed, Doctor Bonamy replied: "No doubt, no doubt; all we ask for is enlightenment. The difficulty would be in forming the committee you speak of. If you only knew how little medical men agree! However, there is certainly an idea in what you say."

Fortunately a fresh patient now came to his assistance. Whilst little Sophie Couteau, already forgotten, was putting on, her shoes again, Elise Rouquet appeared, and, removing her wrap, displayed her diseased face to view. She related that she had been bathing it with her handkerchief ever since the morning, and it seemed to her that her sore, previously so fresh and raw, was already beginning to dry and grow paler in colour. This was true; Pierre noticed, with great surprise, that the aspect of the sore was now less horrible. This supplied fresh food for the discussion on visible sores, for the little fair-haired gentleman clung obstinately to his idea of organising a special ward. Indeed, said he, if the condition of this girl had been verified that morning, and she should be cured, what a triumph it would have been for the Grotto, which could have claimed to have healed a lupus! It would then have no longer been possible to deny that miracles were worked.

Doctor Chassaigne had so far kept in the background, motionless and silent, as though he desired that the facts alone should exercise their influence on Pierre. But he now leant forward and said to him in an undertone: "Visible sores, visible sores indeed! That gentleman can have no idea that our most learned medical men suspect many of these sores to be of nervous origin. Yes, we are discovering that complaints of this kind are often simply due to bad nutrition of the skin. These questions of nutrition are still so imperfectly studied and understood! And some medical men are also beginning to prove that the faith which heals can even cure sores, certain forms of lupus among others. And so I would ask what certainty that gentleman would obtain with his ward for visible sores? There would simply be a little more confusion and passion in arguing the eternal question. No, no! Science is vain, it is a sea of uncertainty."

He smiled sorrowfully whilst Doctor Bonamy, after advising Elise Rouquet to continue using the water as lotion and to return each day for further examination, repeated with his prudent, affable air: "At all events, gentlemen, there are signs of improvement in this case—that is beyond doubt."

But all at once the office was fairly turned topsy-turvy by the arrival of La Grivotte, who swept in like a whirlwind, almost dancing with delight and shouting in a full voice: "I am cured! I am cured!"

And forthwith she began to relate that they had first of all refused to bathe her, and that she had been obliged to insist and beg and sob in order to prevail upon them to do so, after receiving Father Fourcade's express permission. And then it had all happened as she had previously said it would. She had not been immersed in the icy water for three minutes—all perspiring as she was with her consumptive rattle—before she had felt strength returning to her like a whipstroke lashing her whole body. And now a flaming excitement possessed her; radiant, stamping her feet, she was unable to keep still.

"I am cured, my good gentlemen, I am cured!"

Pierre looked at her, this time quite stupefied. Was this the same girl whom, on the previous night, he had seen lying on the carriage seat, annihilated, coughing and spitting blood, with her face of ashen hue? He could not recognise her as she now stood there, erect and slender, her cheeks rosy, her eyes sparkling, upbuoyed by a determination to live, a joy in living already.

"Gentlemen," declared Doctor Bonamy, "the case appears to me to be a very interesting one. We will see."

Then he asked for the documents concerning La Grivotte. But they could not be found among all the papers heaped together on the tables. The young seminarists who acted as secretaries began turning everything over; and the superintendent of the piscinas who sat in their midst himself had to get up to see if these documents were in the "canterbury." At last, when he had sat down again, he found them under the register which lay open before him. Among them were three medical certificates which he read aloud. All three of them agreed in stating that the case was one of advanced phthisis, complicated by nervous incidents which invested it with a peculiar character.

Doctor Bonamy wagged his head as though to say that such an *ensemble* of testimony could leave no room for doubt. Forthwith, he subjected the patient to a prolonged auscultation. And he murmured: "I hear nothing—I hear nothing." Then, correcting himself, he added: "At least I hear scarcely anything."

Finally he turned towards the five-and-twenty or thirty doctors who were assembled there in silence. "Will some of you gentlemen," he asked, "kindly lend me the help of your science? We are here to study and discuss these questions."

At first nobody stirred. Then there was one who ventured to come forward and, in his turn subject the patient to auscultation. But instead of declaring himself, he continued reflecting, shaking his head anxiously. At last he stammered that in his opinion one must await further developments. Another doctor, however, at once took his place, and this one expressed a decided opinion. He could hear nothing at all, that woman could never have suffered from phthisis. Then others followed him; in fact, with the exception of five or six whose smiling faces remained impenetrable, they all joined the *defile*. And the confusion now attained its apogee; for each gave an opinion sensibly differing from that of his colleagues, so that a general uproar arose and one could no longer hear oneself speak. Father Dargeles alone retained the calmness of perfect serenity, for he had scented one of those cases which impassion people and redound to the glory of Our Lady of Lourdes. He was already taking notes on a corner of the table.

Thanks to all the noise of the discussion, Pierre and Doctor Chassaigne, seated at some distance from the others, were now able to talk together without being heard. "Oh! those piscinas!" said the young priest, "I have just seen them. To think that the water should be so seldom changed! What filth it is, what a soup of microbes! What a terrible blow for the present-day mania, that rage for antiseptic precautions! How is it that some pestilence does not carry off all these poor people? The opponents of the microbe theory must be having a good laugh—"

M. Chassaigne stopped him. "No, no, my child," said he. "The baths may be scarcely clean, but they offer no danger. Please notice that the temperature of the water never rises above fifty degrees, and that seventy-seven are necessary for the cultivation of germs.[1] Besides, scarcely any contagious diseases come to Lourdes, neither cholera, nor typhus, nor variola, nor measles, nor scarlatina. We only see certain organic affections here, paralysis, scrofula, tumours, ulcers and abscesses, cancers and phthisis; and the latter cannot be transmitted by the water of the baths. The old sores which are bathed have nothing to fear, and offer no risk of contagion. I can assure you that on this point there is even no necessity for the Blessed Virgin to intervene."

"Then, in that case, doctor," rejoined Pierre, "when you were practising, you would have dipped all your patients in icy water—women at no matter what season, rheumatic patients, people suffering from diseases of the heart, consumptives, and so on? For instance, that unhappy girl, half dead, and covered with sweat—would you have bathed her?"

"Certainly not! There are heroic methods of treatment to which, in practice, one does not dare to have recourse. An icy bath may undoubtedly kill a consumptive; but do we know, whether, in certain circumstances, it might not save her? I, who have ended by admitting that a supernatural power is at work here, I willingly admit that some cures must take place under natural conditions, thanks to that immersion in cold water which seems to us idiotic and barbarous. Ah! the things we don't know, the things we don't know!"

He was relapsing into his anger, his hatred of science, which he scorned since it had left him scared and powerless beside the deathbed of his wife and his daughter. "You ask for certainties," he resumed, "but assuredly it is not medicine which will give you them. Listen for a moment to those gentlemen and you will be edified. Is it not beautiful, all that confusion in which so many opinions clash together? Certainly there are ailments with which one is thoroughly acquainted, even to the most minute details of their evolution; there are remedies also, the effects of which have been studied with the most scrupulous care; but the thing that one does not know, that one cannot know, is the relation of the remedy to the ailment, for there are as many cases as there may be patients, each liable to variation, so that experimentation begins afresh every time. This is why the practice of medicine remains an art, for there can be no experimental finality in it. Cure always depends on chance, on some fortunate circumstance, on some bright idea of the doctor's. And so you will understand that all the people who come and discuss here make me laugh when they talk about the absolute laws of science. Where are those laws in medicine? I should like to have them shown to me."

He did not wish to say any more, but his passion carried him away, so he went on: "I told you that I had become a believer—nevertheless, to speak the truth, I understand very well why this worthy Doctor Bonamy is so little affected, and why he continues calling upon doctors in all parts of the world to come and study his miracles. The more doctors that might come, the less likelihood there would be of the truth being established in the inevitable battle between contradictory diagnoses and methods of treatment. If men cannot agree about a visible sore, they surely cannot do so about an internal lesion the existence of which will be admitted by some, and denied by others. And why then should not everything become a miracle? For, after all,

---

[1] The above are Fahrenheit degrees.—Trans.

whether the action comes from nature or from some unknown power, medical men are, as a rule, none the less astonished when an illness terminates in a manner which they have not foreseen. No doubt, too, things are very badly organised here. Those certificates from doctors whom nobody knows have no real value. All documents ought to be stringently inquired into. But even admitting any absolute scientific strictness, you must be very simple, my dear child, if you imagine that a positive conviction would be arrived at, absolute for one and all. Error is implanted in man, and there is no more difficult task than that of demonstrating to universal satisfaction the most insignificant truth."

Pierre had now begun to understand what was taking place at Lourdes, the extraordinary spectacle which the world had been witnessing for years, amidst the reverent admiration of some and the insulting laughter of others. Forces as yet but imperfectly studied, of which one was even ignorant, were certainly at work—auto-suggestion, long prepared disturbance of the nerves; inspiriting influence of the journey, the prayers, and the hymns; and especially the healing breath, the unknown force which was evolved from the multitude, in the acute crisis of faith. Thus it seemed to him anything but intelligent to believe in trickery. The facts were both of a much more lofty and much more simple nature. There was no occasion for the Fathers of the Grotto to descend to falsehood; it was sufficient that they should help in creating confusion, that they should utilise the universal ignorance. It might even be admitted that everybody acted in good faith—the doctors void of genius who delivered the certificates, the consoled patients who believed themselves cured, and the impassioned witnesses who swore that they had beheld what they described. And from all this was evolved the obvious impossibility of proving whether there was a miracle or not. And such being the case, did not the miracle naturally become a reality for the greater number, for all those who suffered and who had need of hope?

Then, as Doctor Bonamy, who had noticed that they were chatting apart, came up to them, Pierre ventured to inquire: "What is about the proportion of the cures to the number of cases?"

"About ten per cent.," answered the doctor; and reading in the young priest's eyes the words that he could not utter, he added in a very cordial way: "Oh! there would be many more, they would all be cured if we chose to listen to them. But it is as well to say it, I am only here to keep an eye on the miracles, like a policeman as it were. My only functions are to check excessive zeal, and to prevent holy things from being made ridiculous. In one word, this office is simply an office where a *visa* is given when the cures have been verified and seem real ones."

He was interrupted, however, by a low growl. Raboin was growing angry: "The cures verified, the cures verified," he muttered. "What is the use of that? There is no pause in the working of the miracles. What is the use of verifying them so far as believers are concerned? *They* merely have to bow down and believe. And what is the use, too, as regards the unbelievers? *They* will never be convinced. The work we do here is so much foolishness."

Doctor Bonamy severely ordered him to hold his tongue. "You are a rebel, Raboin," said he; "I shall tell Father Capdebarthe that I won't have you here any longer since you pass your time in sowing disobedience."

Nevertheless, there was truth in what had just been said by this man, who so promptly showed his teeth, eager to bite whenever his faith was assailed; and Pierre looked at him with sympathy. All the work of the Verification Office—work anything but well performed—was indeed useless, for it wounded the feelings of the pious, and failed to satisfy the incredulous. Besides, can a miracle be proved? No, you must believe in it! When God is pleased to intervene, it is not for man to try to understand. In the ages of real belief, Science did not make any meddlesome attempt to explain the nature of the Divinity. And why should it come and interfere here? By doing so, it simply hampered faith and diminished its own prestige. No, no, there must be no Science, you must throw yourself upon the ground, kiss it, and believe. Or else you must take yourself off. No compromise was possible. If examination once began it must go on, and must, fatally, conduct to doubt.

Pierre's greatest sufferings, however, came from the extraordinary conversations which he heard around him. There were some believers present who spoke of the miracles with the most amazing ease and tranquillity. The most stupefying stories left their serenity entire. Another miracle, and yet another! And with smiles on their faces, their reason never protesting, they went on relating such imaginings as could only have come from diseased brains. They were evidently living in such a state of visionary fever that nothing henceforth could astonish them. And not only did Pierre notice this among folks of simple, childish minds, illiterate, hallucinated creatures like Raboin, but also among the men of intellect, the men with cultivated brains, the *savants* like Doctor Bonamy and others. It was incredible. And thus Pierre felt a growing discomfort arising within him, a covert anger which would doubtless end by bursting forth. His reason was struggling, like that of some poor wretch who after being flung into a river, feels the waters seize him from all sides and stifle him; and he reflected that the minds which, like Doctor Chassaigne's, sink at last into blind belief, must pass though this same discomfort and struggle before the final shipwreck.

He glanced at his old friend and saw how sorrowful he looked, struck down by destiny, as weak as a crying child, and henceforth quite alone in life. Nevertheless, he was unable to check the cry of protest which rose to his lips: "No, no, if we do not know everything, even if we shall never know everything, there is no reason why we should leave off learning. It is wrong that the Unknown should profit by man's debility and ignorance. On the contrary, the eternal hope should be that the things which now seem inexplicable will some day be explained; and we cannot, under healthy conditions, have any other ideal than this march towards the discovery of the Unknown, this victory slowly achieved by reason amidst all the miseries both of the flesh and of the mind. Ah! reason—it is my reason which makes me suffer, and it is from my reason too that I await all my strength. When reason dies, the whole being perishes. And I feel but an ardent thirst to satisfy my reason more and more, even though I may lose all happiness in doing so."

Tears were appearing in Doctor Chassaigne's eyes; doubtless the memory of his dear dead ones had again flashed upon him. And, in his turn, he murmured: "Reason, reason, yes, certainly it is a thing to be very proud of; it embodies the very dignity of life. But there is love, which is life's omnipotence, the one blessing to be won again when you have lost it."

His voice sank in a stifled sob; and as in a mechanical way he began to finger the sets of documents lying on the table, he espied among them one whose cover bore the name of Marie de Guersaint in large letters. He opened it and read the certificates of the two doctors who had inferred that the case was one of paralysis of the marrow.

"Come, my child," he then resumed, "I know that you feel warm affection for Mademoiselle de Guersaint. What should you say if she were cured here? There are here some certificates, bearing honourable names, and you know that paralysis of this nature is virtually incurable. Well, if this young person should all at once run and jump about as I have seen so many others do, would you not feel very happy, would you not at last acknowledge the intervention of a supernatural power?"

Pierre was about to reply, when he suddenly remembered his cousin Beauclair's expression of opinion, the prediction that the miracle would come about like a lightning stroke, an awakening, an exaltation of the whole being; and he felt his discomfort increase and contented himself with replying: "Yes, indeed, I should be very happy. And you are right; there is doubtless only a determination to secure happiness in all the agitation one beholds here."

However, he could remain in that office no longer. The heat was becoming so great that perspiration streamed down the faces of those present. Doctor Bonamy had begun to dictate a report of the examination of La Grivotte to one of the seminarists, while Father Dargeles, watchful with regard to the phraseology employed, occasionally rose and whispered some verbal alteration in the writer's ear. Meantime, the tumult around them was continuing; the discussion among the medical men had taken another turn and now bore on certain technical points of no significance with regard to the case in question. You could no longer breathe within those wooden walls, nausea was upsetting every heart and every head. The little fair-haired gentleman, the influential writer from Paris, had already gone away, quite vexed at not having seen a real miracle.

Pierre thereupon said to Doctor Chassaigne, "Let us go; I shall be taken ill if I stay here any longer."

They left the office at the same time as La Grivotte, who was at last being dismissed. And as soon as they reached the door they found themselves caught in a torrential, surging, jostling crowd, which was eager to behold the girl so miraculously healed; for the report of the miracle must have already spread, and one and all were struggling to see the chosen one, question her, and touch her. And she, with her empurpled cheeks, her flaming eyes, her dancing gait, could do nothing but repeat, "I am cured, I am cured!"

Shouts drowned her voice, she herself was submerged, carried off amidst the eddies of the throng. For a moment one lost sight of her as though she had sunk in those tumultuous waters; then she suddenly reappeared close to Pierre and the doctor, who endeavoured to extricate her from the crush. They had just perceived the Commander, one of whose manias was to come down to the piscinas and the Grotto in order to vent his anger there. With his frock-coat tightly girding him in military fashion, he was, as usual, leaning on his silver-knobbed walking-stick, slightly dragging his left leg, which his second attack of paralysis had stiffened. And his face reddened and his eyes flashed with anger when La Grivotte, pushing him aside in order that she might pass, repeated amidst the wild enthusiasm of the crowd, "I am cured, I am cured!"

"Well!" he cried, seized with sudden fury, "so much the worse for you, my girl!"

Exclamations arose, folks began to laugh, for he was well known, and his maniacal passion for death was forgiven him. However, when he began stammering confused words, saying that it was pitiful to desire life when one was possessed of neither beauty nor fortune, and that this girl ought to have preferred to die at once rather than suffer again, people began to growl around him, and Abbe Judaine, who was passing, had to extricate him from his trouble. The priest drew him away. "Be quiet, my friend, be quiet," he said. "It is scandalous. Why do you rebel like this against the goodness of God who occasionally shows His compassion for our sufferings by alleviating them? I tell you again that you yourself ought to fall on your knees and beg Him to restore to you the use of your leg and let you live another ten years."

The Commander almost choked with anger. "What!" he replied, "ask to live for another ten years, when my finest day will be the day I die! Show myself as spiritless, as cowardly as the thousands of patients whom I see pass along here, full of a base terror of death, shrieking aloud their weakness, their passion to remain alive! Ah! no, I should feel too much contempt for myself. I want to die!—to die at once! It will be so delightful to be no more."

He was at last out of the scramble of the pilgrims, and again found himself near Doctor Chassaigne and Pierre on the bank of the Gave. And he addressed himself to the doctor, whom he often met: "Didn't they try to restore a dead man to life just now?" he asked; "I was told of it—it almost suffocated me. Eh, doctor? You understand? That man was happy enough to be dead, and they dared to dip him in their water in the criminal hope to make him alive again! But suppose they had succeeded, suppose their water had animated that poor devil once more—for one never knows what may happen in this funny world—don't you think that the man would have had a perfect right to spit his anger in the face of those corpse-menders? Had he asked them to awaken him? How did they know if he were not well pleased at being dead? Folks ought to be consulted at any rate. Just picture them playing the same vile trick on me when I at last fall into the great deep sleep. Ah! I would give them a nice reception. 'Meddle with what concerns you,' I should say, and you may be sure I should make all haste to die again!"

He looked so singular in the fit of rage which had come over him that Abbe Judaine and the doctor could not help smiling. Pierre, however, remained grave, chilled by the great quiver which swept by. Were not those words he had just heard the despairing imprecations of Lazarus? He had often imagined Lazarus emerging from the tomb and crying aloud: "Why hast Thou again awakened me to this abominable life, O Lord? I was sleeping the eternal, dreamless sleep so deeply; I was at last enjoying such sweet repose amidst the delights of nihility! I had known every wretchedness and every dolour, treachery, vain hope, defeat, sickness; as one of the living I had paid my frightful debt to suffering, for I was born without knowing why, and I lived without knowing how; and now, behold, O Lord, Thou requirest me to pay my debt yet again; Thou condemnest me to serve my term of punishment afresh! Have I then been guilty of some inexpiable transgression that thou shouldst inflict such cruel chastisement upon me? Alas! to live again, to feel oneself die a little in one's flesh each day, to have no intelligence save such as is required in order to doubt; no will, save such as one must have to be unable; no tenderness, save such as is needed to weep over one's own sorrows. Yet it was passed, I had crossed the terrifying threshold of death, I had known that second which is so horrible that it sufficeth to poison the whole of life. I had felt the sweat of agony cover me with moisture, the blood flow back from my limbs, my breath forsake me, flee away in a last gasp. And Thou ordainest that I should know this distress a second time, that I should die twice, that my human misery should exceed that of all mankind. Then may it be even now, O Lord!

Yes, I entreat Thee, do also this great miracle; may I once more lay myself down in this grave, and again fall asleep without suffering from the interruption of my eternal slumber. Have mercy upon me, and forbear from inflicting on me the torture of living yet again; that torture which is so frightful that Thou hast never inflicted it on any being. I have always loved Thee and served Thee; and I beseech Thee do not make of me the greatest example of Thy wrath, a cause of terror unto all generations. But show unto me Thy gentleness and loving kindness, O Lord! restore unto me the slumber I have earned, and let me sleep once more amid the delights of Thy nihility."

While Pierre was pondering in this wise, Abbe Judaine had led the Commander away, at last managing to calm him; and now the young priest shook hands with Doctor Chassaigne, recollecting that it was past five o'clock, and that Marie must be waiting for him. On his way back to the Grotto, however, he encountered the Abbe des Hermoises deep in conversation with M. de Guersaint, who had only just left his room at the hotel, and was quite enlivened by his good nap. He and his companion were admiring the extraordinary beauty which the fervour of faith imparted to some women's countenances, and they also spoke of their projected trip to the Cirque de Gavarnie.

On learning, however, that Marie had taken a first bath with no effect, M. de Guersaint at once followed Pierre. They found the poor girl still in the same painful stupor, with her eyes still fixed on the Blessed Virgin who had not deigned to hear her. She did not answer the loving words which her father addressed to her, but simply glanced at him with her large distressful eyes, and then again turned them upon the marble statue which looked so white amid the radiance of the tapers. And whilst Pierre stood waiting to take her back to the hospital, M. de Guersaint devoutly fell upon his knees. At first he prayed with passionate ardour for his daughter's cure, and then he solicited, on his own behalf, the favour of finding some wealthy person who would provide him with the million francs that he needed for his studies on aerial navigation.

V. BERNADETTE'S TRIALS

ABOUT eleven o'clock that night, leaving M. de Guersaint in his room at the Hotel of the Apparitions, it occurred to Pierre to return for a moment to the Hospital of Our Lady of Dolours before going to bed himself. He had left Marie in such a despairing state, so fiercely silent, that he was full of anxiety about her. And when he had asked for Madame de Jonquiere at the door of the Sainte-Honorine Ward he became yet more anxious, for the news was by no means good. The young girl, said the superintendent, had not even opened her mouth. She would answer nobody, and had even refused to eat. Madame de Jonquiere, insisted therefore that Pierre should come in. True, the presence of men was forbidden in the women's wards at night-time, but then a priest is not a man.

"She only cares for you and will only listen to you," said the worthy lady. "Pray come in and sit down near her till Abbe Judaine arrives. He will come at about one in the morning to administer the communion to our more afflicted sufferers, those who cannot move and who have to eat at daybreak. You will be able to assist him."

Pierre thereupon followed Madame de Jonquiere, who installed him at the head of Marie's bed. "My dear child," she said to the girl, "I have brought you somebody who is very fond of you. You will be able to chat with him, and you will be reasonable now, won't you?"

Marie, however, on recognising Pierre, gazed at him with an air of exasperated suffering, a black, stern expression of revolt.

"Would you like him to read something to you," resumed Madame de Jonquiere, "something that would ease and console you as he did in the train? No? It wouldn't interest you, you don't care for it? Well, we will see by-and-by. I will leave him with you, and I am sure you will be quite reasonable again in a few minutes."

Pierre then began speaking to her in a low voice, saying all the kind consoling things that his heart could think of, and entreating her not to allow herself to sink into such despair. If the Blessed Virgin had not cured her on the first day, it was because she reserved her for some conspicuous miracle. But he spoke in vain. Marie had turned her head away, and did not even seem to listen as she lay there with a bitter expression on her mouth and a gleam of irritation in her eyes, which wandered away into space. Accordingly he ceased speaking and began to gaze at the ward around him.

The spectacle was a frightful one. Never before had such a nausea of pity and terror affected his heart. They had long since dined, nevertheless plates of food which had been brought up from the kitchens still lay about the beds; and all through the night there were some who ate whilst others continued restlessly moaning, asking to be turned over or helped out of bed. As the hours went by a kind of vague delirium seemed to come upon almost all of them. Very few were able to sleep quietly. Some had been undressed and were lying between the sheets, but the greater number were simply stretched out on the beds, it being so difficult to get their clothes off that they did not even change their linen during the five days of the pilgrimage. In the semi-obscurity, moreover, the obstruction of the ward seemed to have increased. To the fifteen beds ranged along the walls and the seven mattresses filling the central space, some fresh pallets had been added, and on all sides there was a confused litter of ragged garments, old baskets, boxes, and valises. Indeed, you no longer knew where to step. Two smoky lanterns shed but a dim light upon this encampment of dying women, in which a sickly smell prevailed; for, instead of any freshness, merely the heavy heat of the August night came in through the two windows which had been left ajar. Nightmare-like shadows and cries sped to and fro, peopling the inferno, amidst the nocturnal agony of so much accumulated suffering.

However, Pierre recognised Raymonde, who, her duties over, had come to kiss her mother, before going to sleep in one of the garrets reserved to the Sisters of the hospital. For her own part, Madame de Jonquiere, taking her functions to heart, did not close her eyes during the three nights spent at Lourdes.

She certainly had an arm-chair in which to rest herself, but she never sat down in it for a moment with out being disturbed. It must be admitted that she was bravely seconded by little Madame Desagneaux, who displayed such enthusiastic zeal that Sister Hyacinthe asked her, with a smile: "Why don't you take the vows?" whereupon she responded, with an air of scared surprise: "Oh! I can't, I'm married, you know, and I'm very fond of my husband." As for Madame Volmar, she had not even shown herself; but it was alleged that Madame de Jonquiere had sent her to bed on hearing her complain of a frightful headache. And this had put Madame Desagneaux in quite a temper; for, as she sensibly enough remarked, a person had no business to offer to nurse the sick when the slightest exertion exhausted her. She herself, however, at last began to feel her legs and arms aching, though she would not admit it, but hastened to every patient whom she heard calling, ever ready as she was to lend a helping hand. In Paris she would have rung for a servant rather than have moved a candlestick herself; but here she was ever coming and going, bringing and emptying basins, and passing her arms around patients to hold them up, whilst Madame de Jonquiere slipped pillows behind them. However, shortly after eleven o'clock, she was all at once overpowered. Having imprudently stretched herself in the armchair for a moment's rest, she there fell soundly asleep, her pretty head sinking on one of her shoulders amidst her lovely, wavy fair hair, which was all in disorder. And from that moment neither moan nor call, indeed no sound whatever, could waken her.

Madame de Jonquiere, however, had softly approached the young priest again. "I had an idea," said she in a low voice, "of sending for Monsieur Ferrand, the house-surgeon, you know, who accompanies us. He would have given the poor girl something to calm her. Only he is busy downstairs trying to relieve Brother Isidore, in the Family Ward. Besides, as you know, we are not supposed to give medical attendance here; our work consists in placing our dear sick ones in the hands of the Blessed Virgin."

Sister Hyacinthe, who had made up her mind to spend the night with the superintendent, now drew, near. "I have just come from the Family Ward," she said; "I went to take Monsieur Sabathier some oranges which I had promised him, and I saw Monsieur Ferrand, who had just succeeded in reviving Brother Isidore. Would you like me to go down and fetch him?"

But Pierre declined the offer. "No, no," he replied, "Marie will be sensible. I will read her a few consoling pages by-and-by, and then she will rest."

For the moment, however, the girl still remained obstinately silent. One of the two lanterns was hanging from the wall close by, and Pierre could distinctly see her thin face, rigid and motionless like stone. Then, farther away, in the adjoining bed, he perceived Elise Rouquet, who was sound asleep and no longer wore her fichu, but openly displayed her face, the ulcerations of which still continued to grow paler. And on the young priest's left hand was Madame Vetu, now greatly weakened, in a hopeless state, unable to doze off for a moment, shaken as she was by a continuous rattle. He said a few kind words to her, for which she thanked him with a nod; and, gathering her remaining strength together, she was at last able to say: "There were several cures to-day; I was very pleased to hear of them."

On a mattress at the foot of her bed was La Grivotte, who in a fever of extraordinary activity kept on sitting up to repeat her favourite phrase: "I am cured, I am cured!" And she went on to relate that she had eaten half a fowl for dinner, she who had been unable to eat for long months past. Then, too, she had followed the torchlight procession on foot during nearly a couple of hours, and she would certainly have danced till daybreak had the Blessed Virgin only been pleased to give a ball. And once more she repeated: "I am cured, yes, cured, quite cured!"

Thereupon Madame Vetu found enough strength to say with childlike serenity and perfect, gladsome abnegation: "The Blessed Virgin did well to cure her since she is poor. I am better pleased than if it had been myself, for I have my little shop to depend upon and can wait. We each have our turn, each our turn."

One and all displayed a like charity, a like pleasure that others should have been cured. Seldom, indeed, was any jealousy shown; they surrendered themselves to a kind of epidemical beatitude, to a contagious hope that they would all be cured whenever it should so please the Blessed Virgin. And it was necessary that she should not be offended by any undue impatience; for assuredly she had her reasons and knew right well why she began by healing some rather than others. Thus with the fraternity born of common suffering and hope, the most grievously afflicted patients prayed for the cure of their neighbours. None of them ever despaired, each fresh miracle was the promise of another one, of the one which would be worked on themselves. Their faith remained unshakable. A story was told of a paralytic woman, some farm servant, who with extraordinary strength of will had contrived to take a few steps at the Grotto, and who while being conveyed back to the hospital had asked to be set down that she might return to the Grotto on foot. But she had gone only half the distance when she had staggered, panting and livid; and on being brought to the hospital on a stretcher, she had died there, cured, however, said her neighbours in the ward. Each, indeed, had her turn; the Blessed Virgin forgot none of her dear daughters unless it were her design to grant some chosen one immediate admission into Paradise.

All at once, at the moment when Pierre was leaning towards her, again offering to read to her, Marie burst into furious sobs. Letting her head fall upon her friend's shoulder, she vented all her rebellion in a low, terrible voice, amidst the vague shadows of that awful room. She had experienced what seldom happened to her, a collapse of faith, a sudden loss of courage, all the rage of the suffering being who can no longer wait. Such was her despair, indeed, that she even became sacrilegious.

"No, no," she stammered, "the Virgin is cruel; she is unjust, for she did not cure me just now. Yet I felt so certain that she would grant my prayer, I had prayed to her so fervently. I shall never be cured, now that the first day is past. It was a Saturday, and I was convinced that I should be cured on a Saturday. I did not want to speak—and oh! prevent me, for my heart is too full, and I might say more than I ought to do."

With fraternal hands he had quickly taken hold of her head, and he was endeavouring to stifle the cry of her rebellion. "Be quiet, Marie, I entreat you! It would never do for anyone to hear you—you so pious! Do you want to scandalise every soul?"

But in spite of her efforts she was unable to keep silence. "I should stifle, I must speak out," she said. "I no longer love her, no longer believe in her. The tales which are related here are all falsehoods; there is *nothing*, she does not even exist, since she does not hear when one speaks to her, and sobs. If you only knew all that I said to her! Oh! I want to go away at once. Take me away, carry me away in your arms, so that I may go and die in the street, where the passers-by, at least, will take pity on my sufferings!"

She was growing weak again, and had once more fallen on her back, stammering, talking childishly. "Besides, nobody loves me," she said. "My father was not even there. And you, my friend, forsook me. When I saw that it was another who was taking me to the piscinas, I began to feel a chill. Yes, that chill of doubt which I often felt in Paris. And that is at least certain, I doubted—perhaps, indeed, that is why she did not cure me. I cannot have prayed well enough, I am not pious enough, no doubt."

She was no longer blaspheming, but seeking for excuses to explain the non-intervention of Heaven. However, her face retained an angry expression amidst this struggle which she was waging with the Supreme Power, that Power which she had loved so well and entreated so fervently, but which had not obeyed her. When, on rare occasions, a fit of rage of this description broke out in the ward, and the sufferers, lying on their beds, rebelled against their fate, sobbing and lamenting, and at times even swearing, the lady-hospitallers and the Sisters, somewhat shocked, would content themselves with simply closing the bed-curtains. Grace had departed, one must await its return. And at last, sometimes after long hours, the rebellious complaints would die away, and peace would reign again amidst the deep, woeful silence.

"Calm yourself, calm yourself, I implore you," Pierre gently repeated to Marie, seeing that a fresh attack was coming upon her, an attack of doubt in herself, of fear that she was unworthy of the divine assistance.

Sister Hyacinthe, moreover, had again drawn near. "You will not be able to take the sacrament by-and-by, my dear child," said she, "if you continue in such a state. Come, since we have given Monsieur l'Abbe permission to read to you, why don't you let him do so?"

Marie made a feeble gesture as though to say that she consented, and Pierre at once took out of the valise at the foot of her bed, the little blue-covered book in which the story of Bernadette was so naively related. As on the previous night, however, when the train was rolling on, he did not confine himself to the bald phraseology of the book, but began improvising, relating all manner of details in his own fashion, in order to charm the simple folks who listened to him. Nevertheless, with his reasoning, analytical proclivities, he could not prevent himself from secretly re-establishing the real facts, imparting, for himself alone, a human character to this legend, whose wealth of prodigies contributed so greatly to the cure of those that suffered. Women were soon sitting up on all the surrounding beds. They wished to hear the continuation of the story, for the thought of the sacrament which they were passionately awaiting had prevented almost all of them from getting to sleep. And seated there, in the pale light of the lantern hanging from the wall above him, Pierre little by little raised his voice, so that he might be heard by the whole ward.

"The persecutions began with the very first miracles. Called a liar and a lunatic, Bernadette was threatened with imprisonment. Abbe Peyramale, the parish priest of Lourdes, and Monseigneur Laurence, Bishop of Tarbes, like the rest of the clergy, refrained from all intervention, waiting the course of events with the greatest prudence; whilst the civil authorities, the Prefect, the Public Prosecutor, the Mayor, and the Commissary of Police, indulged in excessive anti-religious zeal."

Continuing his perusal in this fashion, Pierre saw the real story rise up before him with invincible force. His mind travelled a short distance backward and he beheld Bernadette at the time of the first apparitions, so candid, so charming in her ignorance and good faith, amidst all her sufferings. And she was truly the visionary, the saint, her face assuming an expression of superhuman beauty during her crises of ecstasy. Her brow beamed, her features seemed to ascend, her eyes were bathed with light, whilst her parted lips burnt with divine love. And then her whole person became majestic; it was in a slow, stately way that she made the sign of the cross, with gestures which seemed to embrace the whole horizon. The neighbouring valleys, the villages, the towns, spoke of Bernadette alone. Although the Lady had not yet told her name, she was recognised, and people said, "It is she, the Blessed Virgin." On the first market-day, so many people flocked into Lourdes that the town quite overflowed. All wished to see the blessed child whom the Queen of the Angels had chosen, and who became so beautiful when the heavens opened to her enraptured gaze. The crowd on the banks of the Gave grew larger each morning, and thousands of people ended by installing themselves there, jostling one another that they might lose nothing of the spectacle! As soon as Bernadette appeared, a murmur of fervour spread: "Here is the saint, the saint, the saint!" Folks rushed forward to kiss her garments. She was a Messiah, the eternal Messiah whom the nations await, and the need of whom is ever arising from generation to generation. And, moreover, it was ever the same adventure beginning afresh: an apparition of the Virgin to a shepherdess; a voice exhorting the world to penitence; a spring gushing forth; and miracles astonishing and enrapturing the crowds that hastened to the spot in larger and larger numbers.

Ah! those first miracles of Lourdes, what a spring-tide flowering of consolation and hope they brought to the hearts of the wretched, upon whom poverty and sickness were preying! Old Bourriette's restored eyesight, little Bouhohort's resuscitation in the icy water, the deaf recovering their hearing, the lame suddenly enabled to walk, and so many other cases, Blaise Maumus, Bernade Soubies,[1] Auguste Bordes, Blaisette Soupenne, Benoite Cazeaux, in turn cured of the most dreadful ailments, became the subject of endless conversations, and fanned the illusions of all those who suffered either in their hearts or their flesh. On Thursday, March 4th, the last day of the fifteen visits solicited by the Virgin, there were more than twenty thousand persons assembled before the Grotto. Everybody, indeed, had come down from the mountains. And this immense throng found at the Grotto the divine food that it hungered for, a feast of the Marvellous, a sufficient meed of the Impossible to content its belief in a superior Power, which deigned to bestow some attention upon poor folks, and to intervene in the wretched affairs of this lower world, in order to re-establish some measure of justice and kindness. It was indeed the cry of heavenly charity bursting forth, the invisible helping hand stretched out at last to dress the eternal sores of humanity. Ah! that dream in which each successive generation sought refuge, with what indestructible energy did it not arise among the disinherited ones of this world as soon as it found a favourable spot, prepared by circumstances! And for centuries, perhaps, circumstances had never so combined to kindle the mystical fire of faith as they did at Lourdes.

A new religion was about to be founded, and persecutions at once began, for religions only spring up amidst vexations and rebellions. And even as it was long ago at Jerusalem, when the tidings of miracles spread, the civil authorities—the Public Prosecutor, the Justice of the Peace, the Mayor, and particularly the Prefect of Tarbes—were all roused and began to bestir themselves. The Prefect was a sincere Catholic, a worshipper, a man of perfect honour, but he also had the firm mind of a public functionary, was a passionate defender of order, and a declared adversary of fanaticism which gives birth to disorder and religious perversion. Under his orders at Lourdes there was a Commissary of Police, a man of great intelligence and shrewdness, who had hitherto discharged his functions in a very proper way, and who, legitimately enough, beheld in this affair of the apparitions an opportunity to put his gift of sagacious skill to the proof. So the struggle began, and it was this Commissary who, on the first Sunday in Lent, at the time of the first apparitions, summoned Bernadette to his office in order that he might question her. He showed himself affectionate, then angry, then threatening, but all in vain; the answers which the girl gave him were ever the same. The story which she related, with its slowly accumulated details, had little by little irrevocably implanted itself in her infantile mind. And it was no lie on the part of this poor suffering creature, this exceptional victim of hysteria, but an unconscious haunting, a radical lack of will-power to free herself from her original hallucination. She knew not how to exert any such will, she could not, she would not exert it. Ah! the poor child, the dear child, so amiable and so gentle, so incapable of any evil thought, from that time forward lost to life, crucified by her fixed idea, whence one could only have extricated her by changing her environment, by restoring her to the open air, in some land of daylight and human affection. But she was the

---

[1] I give this name as written by M. Zola; but in other works on Lourdes I find it given as "Bernarde Loubie—a bed-ridden old woman, cured of a paralytic affection by drinking the water of the Grotto."—Trans.

chosen one, she had beheld the Virgin, she would suffer from it her whole life long and die from it at last!

Pierre, who knew Bernadette so well, and who felt a fraternal pity for her memory, the fervent compassion with which one regards a human saint, a simple, upright, charming creature tortured by her faith, allowed his emotion to appear in his moist eyes and trembling voice. And a pause in his narrative ensued. Marie, who had hitherto been lying there quite stiff, with a hard expression of revolt still upon her face, opened her clenched hands and made a vague gesture of pity. "Ah," she murmured, "the poor child, all alone to contend against those magistrates, and so innocent, so proud, so unshakable in her championship of the truth!"

The same compassionate sympathy was arising from all the beds in the ward. That hospital inferno with its nocturnal wretchedness, its pestilential atmosphere, its pallets of anguish heaped together, its weary lady-hospitallers and Sisters flitting phantom-like hither and thither, now seemed to be illumined by a ray of divine charity. Was not the eternal illusion of happiness rising once more amidst tears and unconscious falsehoods? Poor, poor Bernadette! All waxed indignant at the thought of the persecutions which she had endured in defence of her faith.

Then Pierre, resuming his story, related all that the child had had to suffer. After being questioned by the Commissary she had to appear before the judges of the local tribunal. The entire magistracy pursued her, and endeavoured to wring a retractation from her. But the obstinacy of her dream was stronger than the common sense of all the civil authorities put together. Two doctors who were sent by the Prefect to make a careful examination of the girl came, as all doctors would have done, to the honest opinion that it was a case of nervous trouble, of which the asthma was a sure sign, and which, in certain circumstances, might have induced visions. This nearly led to her removal and confinement in a hospital at Tarbes. But public exasperation was feared. A bishop had fallen on his knees before her. Some ladies had sought to buy favours from her for gold. Moreover she had found a refuge with the Sisters of Nevers, who tended the aged in the town asylum, and there she made her first communion, and was with difficulty taught to read and write. As the Blessed Virgin seemed to have chosen her solely to work the happiness of others, and she herself had not been cured, it was very sensibly decided to take her to the baths of Cauterets, which were so near at hand. However, they did her no good. And no sooner had she returned to Lourdes than the torture of being questioned and adored by a whole people began afresh, became aggravated, and filled her more and more with horror of the world. Her life was over already; she would be a playful child no more; she could never be a young girl dreaming of a husband, a young wife kissing the cheeks of sturdy children. She had beheld the Virgin, she was the chosen one, the martyr. If the Virgin, said believers, had confided three secrets to her, investing her with a triple armour as it were, it was simply in order to sustain her in her appointed course.

The clergy had for a long time remained aloof, on its own side full of doubt and anxiety. Abby Peyramale, the parish priest of Lourdes, was a man of somewhat blunt ways, but full of infinite kindness, rectitude, and energy whenever he found himself in what he thought the right path. On the first occasion when Bernadette visited him, he received this child who had been brought up at Bartres and had not yet been seen at Catechism, almost as sternly as the Commissary of Police had done; in fact, he refused to believe her story, and with some irony told her to entreat the Lady to begin by making the briars blossom beneath her feet, which, by the way, the Lady never did. And if the Abbe ended by taking the child under his protection like a good pastor who defends his flock, it was simply through the advent of persecution and the talk of imprisoning this puny child, whose clear eyes shone so frankly, and who clung with such modest, gentle stubbornness to her original tale. Besides, why should he have continued denying the miracle after merely doubting it like a prudent priest who had no desire to see religion mixed up in any suspicious affair? Holy Writ is full of prodigies, all dogma is based on the mysterious; and that being so, there was nothing to prevent him, a priest, from believing that the Virgin had really entrusted Bernadette with a pious message for him, an injunction to build a church whither the faithful would repair in procession. Thus it was that he began loving and defending Bernadette for her charm's sake, whilst still refraining from active interference, awaiting as he did the decision of his Bishop.

This Bishop, Monseigneur Laurence, seemed to have shut himself up in his episcopal residence at Tarbes, locking himself within it and preserving absolute silence as though there were nothing occurring at Lourdes of a nature to interest him. He had given strict instructions to his clergy, and so far not a priest had appeared among the vast crowds of people who spent their days before the Grotto. He waited, and even allowed the Prefect to state in his administrative circulars that the civil and the religious authorities were acting in concert. In reality, he cannot have believed in the apparitions of the Grotto of Massabielle, which he doubtless considered to be the mere hallucinations of a sick child. This affair, which was revolutionising the region, was of sufficient importance for him to have studied it day by day, and the manner in which he disregarded it for so long a time shows how little inclined he was to admit the truth of the alleged miracles, and how greatly he desired to avoid compromising the Church in a matter which seemed destined to end badly. With all his piety, Monseigneur Laurence had a cool, practical intellect, which enabled him to govern his diocese with great good sense. Impatient and ardent people nicknamed him Saint Thomas at the time, on account of the manner in which his doubts persisted until events at last forced his hand. Indeed, he turned a deaf ear to all the stories that were being related, firmly resolved as he was that he would only listen to them if it should appear certain that religion had nothing to lose.

However, the persecutions were about to become more pronounced. The Minister of Worship in Paris, who had been informed of what was going on, required that a stop should be put to all disorders, and so the Prefect caused the approaches to the Grotto to be occupied by the military. The Grotto had already been decorated with vases of flowers offered by the zeal of the faithful and the gratitude of sufferers who had been healed. Money, moreover, was thrown into it; gifts to the Blessed Virgin abounded. Rudimentary improvements, too, were carried out in a spontaneous way; some quarrymen cut a kind of reservoir to receive the miraculous water, and others removed the large blocks of stone, and traced a path in the hillside. However, in presence of the swelling torrents of people, the Prefect, after renouncing his idea of arresting Bernadette, took the serious resolution of preventing all access to the Grotto by placing a strong palisade in front of it. Some regrettable incidents had lately occurred; various children pretended that they had seen the devil, some of them being guilty of simulation in this respect, whilst others had given way to real attacks of hysteria, in the contagious nervous unhinging which was so prevalent. But what a terrible business did the removal of the offerings from the Grotto prove! It was only towards evening that the Commissary was able to find a girl willing to let him have a cart on hire, and two hours later this girl fell from a loft and broke one of her ribs. Likewise, a man who had lent an axe had one of his feet crushed on the morrow by the fall of a block of stone.[1] It was in the midst of jeers and hisses that the Commissary carried off the pots of flowers, the tapers which he found burning, the coppers and the silver hearts which lay upon the sand. People clenched their fists, and covertly called him "thief" and "murderer." Then the posts for the palisades were planted in the ground, and the rails were nailed to the crossbars, no little labour being performed to shut off the Mystery, in order to bar access to the Unknown, and put the miracles in prison. And the civil authorities were simple enough to imagine that it was all over, that those few bits of boarding would suffice to stay the poor people who hungered for illusion and hope.

But as soon as the new religion was proscribed, forbidden by the law as an offence, it began to burn with an inextinguishable flame in the depths of every soul. Believers came to the river bank in far greater numbers, fell upon their knees at a short distance from the Grotto, and sobbed aloud as they gazed at the forbidden heaven. And the sick, the poor ailing folks, who were forbidden to seek cure, rushed on the Grotto despite all prohibitions, slipped in whenever they could find an aperture or climbed over the palings when their strength enabled them to do so, in the one ardent desire to steal a little of the water. What! there was a prodigious water in that Grotto, which restored the sight to the blind, which set the infirm erect upon their legs again, which instantaneously healed all ailments; and there were officials cruel enough to put that water under lock and key so that it might not cure any more poor people! Why, it was monstrous! And a cry of hatred arose from all the humble ones, all the disinherited ones who had as much need of the Marvellous as of bread to live! In accordance with a municipal decree, the names of all delinquents were to be taken by the police, and thus one soon beheld a woeful *defile* of old women and lame men summoned before the Justice of the Peace for the sole offence of taking a little water from the fount of life! They stammered and entreated, at their wit's end when a fine was imposed upon them. And, outside, the crowd was growling; rageful unpopularity was gathering around those magistrates who treated human wretchedness so harshly, those pitiless masters who after taking all the wealth of the world, would not even leave to the poor their dream of the realms beyond, their belief that a beneficent superior power took a maternal interest in them, and was ready to endow them with peace of soul and health of body. One day a whole band of poverty-stricken and ailing folks went to the Mayor, knelt down in his courtyard, and implored him with sobs to allow the Grotto to be reopened; and the words they spoke were so pitiful that all who heard them wept. A mother showed her child who was half-dead; would they let the little one die like that in her arms when there was a source yonder which had saved the children of other mothers? A blind man called attention to his dim eyes; a pale, scrofulous youth displayed the sores on his legs; a paralytic woman sought to join her woeful twisted hands: did the authorities wish to see them all perish, did they refuse them the last divine chance of life, condemned and abandoned as they were by the

[1] Both of these accidents were interpreted as miracles.—Trans.

science of man? And equally great was the distress of the believers, of those who were convinced that a corner of heaven had opened amidst the night of their mournful existences, and who were indignant that they should be deprived of the chimerical delight, the supreme relief for their human and social sufferings, which they found in the belief that the Blessed Virgin had indeed come down from heaven to bring them the priceless balm of her intervention. However, the Mayor was unable to promise anything, and the crowd withdrew weeping, ready for rebellion, as though under the blow of some great act of injustice, an act of idiotic cruelty towards the humble and the simple for which Heaven would assuredly take vengeance.

The struggle went on for several months; and it was an extraordinary spectacle which those sensible men—the Minister, the Prefect, and the Commissary of Police—presented, all animated with the best intentions and contending against the ever-swelling crowd of despairing ones, who would not allow the doors of dreamland to be closed upon them, who would not be shut off from the mystic glimpse of future happiness in which they found consolation for their present wretchedness. The authorities required order, the respect of a discreet religion, the triumph of reason; whereas the need of happiness carried the people off into an enthusiastic desire for cure both in this world and in the next. Oh! to cease suffering, to secure equality in the comforts of life; to march on under the protection of a just and beneficent Mother, to die only to awaken in heaven! And necessarily the burning desire of the multitude, the holy madness of the universal joy, was destined to sweep aside the rigid, morose conceptions of a well-regulated society in which the ever-recurring epidemical attacks of religious hallucination are condemned as prejudicial to good order and healthiness of mind.

The Sainte-Honorine Ward, on hearing the story, likewise revolted. Pierre again had to pause, for many were the stifled exclamations in which the Commissary of Police was likened to Satan and Herod. La Grivotte had sat up on her mattress, stammering: "Ah! the monsters! To behave like that to the Blessed Virgin who has cured me!"

And even Madame Vetu—once more penetrated by a ray of hope amidst the covert certainty she felt that she was going to die—grew angry at the idea that the Grotto would not have existed had the Prefect won the day. "There would have been no pilgrimages," she said, "we should not be here, hundreds of us would not be cured every year."

A fit of stifling came over her, however, and Sister Hyacinthe had to raise her to a sitting posture. Madame de Jonquiere was profiting by the interruption to attend to a young woman afflicted with a spinal complaint, whilst two other women, unable to remain on their beds, so unbearable was the heat, prowled about with short, silent steps, looking quite white in the misty darkness. And from the far end of the ward, where all was black, there resounded a noise of painful breathing, which had been going on without a pause, accompanying Pierre's narrative like a rattle. Elise Rouquet alone was sleeping peacefully, still stretched upon her back, and displaying her disfigured countenance, which was slowly drying.

Midnight had struck a quarter of an hour previously, and Abbe Judaine might arrive at any moment for the communion. Grace was now again descending into Marie's heart, and she was convinced that if the Blessed Virgin had refused to cure her it was, indeed, her own fault in having doubted when she entered the piscina. And she, therefore, repented of her rebellion as of a crime. Could she ever be forgiven? Her pale face sank down among her beautiful fair hair, her eyes filled with tears, and she looked at Pierre with an expression of anguish. "Oh! how wicked I was, my friend," she said. "It was through hearing you relate how that Prefect and those magistrates sinned through pride, that I understood my transgression. One must believe, my friend; there is no happiness outside faith and love."

Then, as Pierre wished to break off at the point which he had reached, they all began protesting and calling for the continuation of his narrative, so that he had to promise to go on to the triumph of the Grotto.

Its entrance remained barred by the palisade, and you had to come secretly at night if you wished to pray and carry off a stolen bottle of water. Still, the fear of rioting increased, for it was rumoured that whole villages intended to come down from the hills in order to deliver God, as they naively expressed it. It was a *levee en masse* of the humble, a rush of those who hungered for the miraculous, so irresistible in its impetuosity that mere common sense, mere considerations of public order were to be swept away like chaff. And it was Monseigneur Laurence, in his episcopal residence at Tarbes, who was first forced to surrender. All his prudence, all his doubts were outflanked by the popular outburst. For five long months he had been able to remain aloof, preventing his clergy from following the faithful to the Grotto, and defending the Church against the tornado of superstition which had been let loose. But what was the use of struggling any longer? He felt the wretchedness of the suffering people committed to his care to be so great that he resigned himself to granting them the idolatrous religion for which he realised them to be eager. Some prudence remaining to him, however, he contented himself in the first instance with drawing up an *ordonnance*, appointing a commission of inquiry, which was to investigate the question; this implied the acceptance of the miracles after a period of longer or shorter duration. If Monseigneur Laurence was the man of healthy culture and cool reason that he is pictured to have been, how great must have been his anguish on the morning when he signed that *ordonnance*! He must have knelt in his oratory, and have begged the Sovereign Master of the world to dictate his conduct to him. He did not believe in the apparitions; he had a loftier, more intellectual idea of the manifestations of the Divinity. Only would he not be showing true pity and mercy in silencing the scruples of his reason, the noble prejudices of his faith, in presence of the necessity of granting that bread of falsehood which poor humanity requires in order to be happy? Doubtless, he begged the pardon of Heaven for allowing it to be mixed up in what he regarded as childish pastime, for exposing it to ridicule in connection with an affair in which there was only sickliness and dementia. But his flock suffered so much, hungered so ravenously for the marvellous, for fairy stories with which to lull the pains of life. And thus, in tears, the Bishop at last sacrificed his respect for the dignity of Providence to his sensitive pastoral charity for the woeful human flock.

Then the Emperor in his turn gave way. He was at Biarritz at the time, and was kept regularly informed of everything connected with this affair of the apparitions, with which the entire Parisian press was also occupying itself, for the persecutions would not have been complete if the pens of Voltairean newspaper-men had not meddled in them. And whilst his Minister, his Prefect, and his Commissary of Police were fighting for common sense and public order, the Emperor preserved his wonted silence—the deep silence of a day-dreamer which nobody ever penetrated. Petitions arrived day by day, yet he held his tongue. Bishops came, great personages, great ladies of his circle watched and drew him on one side, and still he held his tongue. A truceless warfare was being waged around him: on one side the believers and the men of fanciful minds whom the Mysterious strongly interested; on the other the unbelievers and the statesmen who distrusted the disturbances of the imagination;—and still and ever he held his tongue. Then, all at once, with the sudden decision of a naturally timid man, he spoke out. The rumour spread that he had yielded to the entreaties of his wife Eugenie. No doubt she did intervene, but the Emperor was more deeply influenced by a revival of his old humanitarian dreams, his genuine compassion for the disinherited.[1] Like the Bishop, he did not wish to close the portals of illusion to the wretched by upholding the unpopular decree which forbade despairing sufferers to go and drink life at the holy source. So he sent a telegram, a curt order to remove the palisade, so as to allow everybody free access to the Grotto.

Then came a shout of joy and triumph. The decree annulling the previous one was read at Lourdes to the sound of drum and trumpet. The Commissary of Police had to come in person to superintend the removal of the palisade. He was afterwards transferred elsewhere like the Prefect.[2] People flocked to Lourdes from all parts, the new *cultus* was organised at the Grotto, and a cry of joy ascended: God had won the victory! God?—alas, no! It was human wretchedness which had won the battle, human wretchedness with its eternal need of falsehood, its hunger for the marvellous, its everlasting hope akin to that of some condemned man who, for salvation's sake, surrenders himself into the hands of an invisible Omnipotence, mightier than nature, and alone capable, should it be willing, of annulling nature's laws. And that which had also conquered was the sovereign compassion of those pastors, the merciful Bishop and merciful Emperor who allowed those big sick children to retain the fetich which consoled some of them and at times even cured others.

In the middle of November the episcopal commission came to Lourdes to prosecute the inquiry which had been entrusted to it. It questioned Bernadette yet once again, and studied a large number of miracles. However, in order that the evidence might be absolute, it only registered some thirty cases of cure. And Monseigneur Laurence declared himself convinced. Nevertheless, he gave a final proof of his prudence, by continuing to wait another three years before declaring in a pastoral letter that the Blessed Virgin had in truth appeared at the Grotto of Massabielle and that numerous miracles had subsequently taken place there. Meantime, he had purchased the Grotto itself, with all the land around it, from the municipality of Lourdes, on behalf of his see. Work was then begun, modestly at first, but soon on a larger and larger scale as money began to flow in from all parts of Christendom. The Grotto was cleared and

---

[1] I think this view of the matter the right one, for, as all who know the history of the Second Empire are aware, it was about this time that the Emperor began taking great interest in the erection of model dwellings for the working classes, and the plantation and transformation of the sandy wastes of the Landes.—Trans.

[2] The Prefect was transferred to Grenoble, and curiously enough his new jurisdiction extended over the hills and valleys of La Salette, whither pilgrims likewise flocked to drink, pray, and wash themselves at a miraculous fountain. Warned by experience, however, Baron Massy (such was the Prefect's name) was careful to avoid any further interference in religious matters.—Trans.

enclosed with an iron railing. The Gave was thrown back into a new bed, so as to allow of spacious approaches to the shrine, with lawns, paths, and walks. At last, too, the church which the Virgin had asked for, the Basilica, began to rise on the summit of the rock itself. From the very first stroke of the pick, Abbe Peyramale, the parish priest of Lourdes, went on directing everything with even excessive zeal, for the struggle had made him the most ardent and most sincere of all believers in the work that was to be accomplished. With his somewhat rough but truly fatherly nature, he had begun to adore Bernadette, making her mission his own, and devoting himself, soul and body, to realising the orders which he had received from Heaven through her innocent mouth. And he exhausted himself in mighty efforts; he wished everything to be very beautiful and very grand, worthy of the Queen of the Angels who had deigned to visit this mountain nook. The first religious ceremony did not take place till six years after the apparitions. A marble statue of the Virgin was installed with great pomp on the very spot where she had appeared. It was a magnificent day, all Lourdes was gay with flags, and every bell rang joyously. Five years later, in 1869, the first mass was celebrated in the crypt of the Basilica, whose spire was not yet finished. Meantime, gifts flowed in without a pause, a river of gold was streaming towards the Grotto, a whole town was about to spring up from the soil. It was the new religion completing its foundations. The desire to be healed did heal; the thirst for a miracle worked the miracle. A Deity of pity and hope was evolved from man's sufferings, from that longing for falsehood and relief which, in every age of humanity, has created the marvellous palaces of the realms beyond, where an almighty Power renders justice and distributes eternal happiness.

And thus the ailing ones of the Sainte-Honorine Ward only beheld in the victory of the Grotto the triumph of their hopes of cure. Along the rows of beds there was a quiver of joy when, with his heart stirred by all those poor faces turned towards him, eager for certainty, Pierre repeated: "God had conquered. Since that day the miracles have never ceased, and it is the most humble who are the most frequently relieved."

Then he laid down the little book. Abbe Judaine was coming in, and the Sacrament was about to be administered. Marie, however, again penetrated by the fever of faith, her hands burning, leant towards Pierre. "Oh, my friend!" said she, "I pray you hear me confess my fault and absolve me. I have blasphemed, and have been guilty of mortal sin. If you do not succour me, I shall be unable to receive the Blessed Sacrament, and yet I so greatly need to be consoled and strengthened."

The young priest refused her request with a wave of the hand. He had never been willing to act as confessor to this friend, the only woman he had loved in the healthy, smiling days of youth. However, she insisted. "I beg you to do so," said she; "you will help to work the miracle of my cure."

Then he gave way and received the avowal of her fault, that impious rebellion induced by suffering, that rebellion against the Virgin who had remained deaf to her prayers. And afterwards he granted her absolution in the sacramental form.

Meanwhile Abbe Judaine had already deposited the ciborium on a little table, between two lighted tapers, which looked like woeful stars in the semi-obscurity of the ward. Madame de Jonquiere had just decided to open one of the windows quite wide, for the odour emanating from all the suffering bodies and heaped-up rags had become unbearable. But no air came in from the narrow courtyard into which the window opened; though black with night, it seemed like a well of fire. Having offered to act as server, Pierre repeated the "Confiteor." Then, after responding with the "Misereatur" and the "Indulgentiam," the chaplain, who wore his alb, raised the pyx, saying, "Behold the Lamb of God, who taketh away the sins of the world." All the women who, writhing in agony, were impatiently awaiting the communion, like dying creatures who await life from some fresh medicine which is a long time coming, thereupon thrice repeated, in all humility, and with lips almost closed: "Lord, I am not worthy that Thou shouldst enter under my roof; but only say the word and my soul shall be healed."

Abbe Judaine had begun to make the round of those woeful beds, accompanied by Pierre, and followed by Madame de Jonquiere and Sister Hyacinthe, each of whom carried one of the lighted tapers. The Sister designated those who were to communicate; and, murmuring the customary Latin words, the priest leant forward and placed the Host somewhat at random on the sufferer's tongue. Almost all were waiting for him with widely opened, glittering eyes, amidst the disorder of that hastily pitched camp. Two were found to be sound asleep, however, and had to be awakened. Several were moaning without being conscious of it, and continued moaning even after they had received the sacrament. At the far end of the ward, the rattle of the poor creature who could not be seen still resounded. And nothing could have been more mournful than the appearance of that little *cortege* in the semi-darkness, amidst which the yellow flames of the tapers gleamed like stars.

But Marie's face, to which an expression of ecstasy had returned, was like a divine apparition. Although La Grivotte was hungering for the bread of life, they had refused her the sacrament on this occasion, as it was to be administered to her in the morning at the Rosary; Madame Vetu, however, had received the Host on her black tongue in a hiccough. And now Marie was lying there under the pale light of the tapers, looking so beautiful amidst her fair hair, with her eyes dilated and her features transfigured by faith, that everyone admired her. She received the sacrament with rapture; Heaven visibly descended into her poor, youthful frame, reduced to such physical wretchedness. And, clasping Pierre's hand, she detained him for a moment, saying: "Oh! she will heal me, my friend, she has just promised me that she will do so. Go and take some rest. I shall sleep so soundly now!"

As he withdrew in company with Abbe Judaine, Pierre caught sight of little Madame Desagneaux stretched out in the arm-chair in which weariness had overpowered her. Nothing could awaken her. It was now half-past one in the morning; and Madame de Jonquiere and her assistant, Sister Hyacinthe, were still going backwards and forwards, turning the patients over, cleansing them, and dressing their sores. However, the ward was becoming more peaceful, its heavy darkness had grown less oppressive since Bernadette with her charm had passed through it. The visionary's little shadow was now flitting in triumph from bed to bed, completing its work, bringing a little of heaven to each of the despairing ones, each of the disinherited ones of this world; and as they all at last sank to sleep they could see the little shepherdess, so young, so ill herself, leaning over them and kissing them with a kindly smile.

THE THIRD DAY

I. BED AND BOARD

AT seven o'clock on the morning of that fine, bright, warm August Sunday, M. de Guersaint was already up and dressed in one of the two little rooms which he had fortunately been able to secure on the third floor of the Hotel of the Apparitions. He had gone to bed at eleven o'clock the night before and had awoke feeling quite fresh and gay. As soon as he was dressed he entered the adjoining room which Pierre occupied; but the young priest, who had not returned to the hotel until past one in the morning, with his blood heated by insomnia, had been unable to doze off until daybreak and was now still slumbering. His cassock flung across a chair, his other garments scattered here and there, testified to his great weariness and agitation of mind.

"Come, come, you lazybones!" cried M. de Guersaint gaily; "can't you hear the bells ringing?"

Pierre awoke with a start, quite surprised to find himself in that little hotel room into which the sunlight was streaming. All the joyous peals of the bells, the music of the chiming, happy town, moreover, came in through the window which he had left open.

"We shall never have time to get to the hospital before eight o'clock to fetch Marie," resumed M. de Guersaint, "for we must have some breakfast, eh?"

"Of course, make haste and order two cups of chocolate. I will get up at once, I sha'n't be long," replied Pierre.

In spite of the fatigue which had already stiffened his joints, he sprang out of bed as soon as he was alone, and made all haste with his toilet. However, he still had his head in the washing basin, ducking it in the fresh, cool water, when M. de Guersaint, who was unable to remain alone, came back again. "I've given the order," said he; "they will bring it up. Ah! what a curious place this hotel is! You have of course seen the landlord, Master Majeste, clad in white from head to foot and looking so dignified in his office. The place is crammed, it appears; they have never had so many people before. So it is no wonder that there should be such a fearful noise. I was wakened up three times during the night. People kept on talking in the room next to mine. And you, did you sleep well?"

"No, indeed," answered Pierre; "I was tired to death, but I couldn't close my eyes. No doubt it was the uproar you speak of that prevented me."

In his turn he then began to talk of the thin partitions, and the manner in which the house had been crammed with people until it seemed as though the floors and the walls would collapse with the strain. The place had been shaking all night long; every now and then people suddenly rushed along the passages, heavy footfalls resounded, gruff voices ascended nobody knew whence; without speaking of all the moaning and coughing, the frightful coughing which seemed to re-echo from every wall. Throughout the night people evidently came in and went out, got up and lay down again, paying no attention to time in the disorder in which they lived, amid shocks of passion which made them hurry to their devotional exercises as to pleasure parties.

"And Marie, how was she when you left her last night?" M. de Guersaint suddenly inquired.

"A great deal better," replied Pierre; "she had an attack of extreme discouragement, but all her courage and faith returned to her at last."

A pause followed; and then the girl's father resumed with his tranquil optimism: "Oh! I am not anxious. Things will go on all right, you'll see. For my own part, I am delighted. I had asked the Virgin to grant me her protection in my affairs—you know, my great invention of navigable balloons. Well, suppose I told you that she has already shown me her favour? Yes, indeed yesterday evening while I was talking with Abbe des Hermoises, he told me that at Toulouse he would no doubt be able to find a person to finance me—one of his friends, in fact, who is extremely wealthy and takes great interest in mechanics! And in this I at once saw the hand of God!" M. de Guersaint began laughing with his childish laugh, and then he added: "That Abbe des Hermoises is a charming man. I shall see this afternoon if there is any means of my accompanying him on an excursion to the Cirque de Gavarnie at small cost."

Pierre, who wished to pay everything, the hotel bill and all the rest, at once encouraged him in this idea. "Of course," said he, "you ought not to miss this opportunity to visit the mountains, since you have so great a wish to do so. Your daughter will be very happy to know that you are pleased."

Their talk, however, was now interrupted by a servant girl bringing the two cups of chocolate with a couple of rolls on a metal tray covered with a napkin. She left the door open as she entered the room, so that a glimpse was obtained of some portion of the passage. "Ah! they are already doing my neighbour's room!" exclaimed M. de Guersaint. "He is a married man, isn't he? His wife is with him?"

The servant looked astonished. "Oh, no," she replied, "he is quite alone!"

"Quite alone? Why, I heard people talking in his room this morning."

"You must be mistaken, monsieur," said the servant; "he has just gone out after giving orders that his room was to be tidied up at once." And then, while taking the cups of chocolate off the tray and placing them on the table, she continued: "Oh! he is a very respectable gentleman. Last year he was able to have one of the pavilions which Monsieur Majeste lets out to visitors, in the lane by the side of the hotel; but this year he applied too late and had to content himself with that room, which greatly worried him, for it isn't a large one, though there is a big cupboard in it. As he doesn't care to eat with everybody, he takes his meals there, and he orders good wine and the best of everything, I can tell you."

"That explains it all!" replied M. de Guersaint gaily; "he dined too well last night, and I must have heard him talking in his sleep."

Pierre had been listening somewhat inquisitively to all this chatter. "And on this side, my side," said he, "isn't there a gentleman with two ladies, and a little boy who walks about with a crutch?"

"Yes, Monsieur l'Abbe, I know them. The aunt, Madame Chaise, took one of the two rooms for herself; and Monsieur and Madame Vigneron with their son Gustave have had to content themselves with the other one. This is the second year they have come to Lourdes. They are very respectable people too."

Pierre nodded. During the night he had fancied he could recognise the voice of M. Vigneron, whom the heat doubtless had incommoded. However, the servant was now thoroughly started, and she began to enumerate the other persons whose rooms were reached by the same passage; on the left hand there was a priest, then a mother with three daughters, and then an old married couple; whilst on the right lodged another gentleman who was all alone, a young lady, too, who was unaccompanied, and then a family party which included five young children. The hotel was crowded to its garrets. The servants had had to give up their rooms the previous evening and lie in a heap in the washhouse. During the night, also, some camp bedsteads had even been set up on the landings; and one honourable ecclesiastic, for lack of other accommodation, had been obliged to sleep on a billiard-table.

When the girl had retired and the two men had drunk their chocolate, M. de Guersaint went back into his own room to wash his hands again, for he was very careful of his person; and Pierre, who remained alone, felt attracted by the gay sunlight, and stepped for a moment on to the narrow balcony outside his window. Each of the third-floor rooms on this side of the hotel was provided with a similar balcony, having a carved-wood balustrade. However, the young priest's surprise was very great, for he had scarcely stepped outside when he suddenly saw a woman protrude her head over the balcony next to him—that of the room occupied by the gentleman whom M. de Guersaint and the servant had been speaking of.

And this woman he had recognised: it was Madame Volmar. There was no mistaking her long face with its delicate drawn features, its magnificent large eyes, those brasiers over which a veil, a dimming *moire*, seemed to pass at times. She gave a start of terror on perceiving him. And he, extremely ill at ease, grieved that he should have frightened her, made all haste to withdraw into his apartment. A sudden light had dawned upon him, and he now understood and could picture everything. So this was why she had not been seen at the hospital, where little Madame Desagneaux was always asking for her. Standing motionless, his heart upset, Pierre fell into a deep reverie, reflecting on the life led by this woman whom he knew, that torturing conjugal life in Paris between a fierce mother-in-law and an unworthy husband, and then those three days of complete liberty spent at Lourdes, that brief bonfire of passion to which she had hastened under the sacrilegious pretext of serving the divinity. Tears whose cause he could not even explain, tears that ascended from the very depths of his being, from his own voluntary chastity, welled into his eyes amidst the feeling of intense sorrow which came over him.

"Well, are you ready?" joyously called M. de Guersaint as he came back, with his grey jacket buttoned up and his hands gloved.

"Yes, yes, let us go," replied Pierre, turning aside and pretending to look for his hat so that he might wipe his eyes.

Then they went out, and on crossing the threshold heard on their left hand an unctuous voice which they recognised; it was that of M. Vigneron, who was loudly repeating the morning prayers. A moment afterwards came a meeting which interested them. They were walking down the passage when they were passed by a middle-aged, thick-set, sturdy-looking gentleman, wearing carefully trimmed whiskers. He bent his back and passed so rapidly that they were unable to distinguish his features, but they noticed that he was carrying a carefully made parcel. And immediately afterwards he slipped a key into the lock of the room adjoining M. de Guersaint's, and opening the door disappeared noiselessly, like a shadow.

M. de Guersaint had glanced round: "Ah! my neighbour," said he; "he has been to market and has brought back some delicacies, no doubt!"

Pierre pretended not to hear, for his companion was so light-minded that he did not care to trust him with a secret which was not his own. Besides, a feeling of uneasiness was returning to him, a kind of chaste terror at the thought that the world and the flesh were there taking their revenge, amidst all the mystical enthusiasm which he could feel around him.

They reached the hospital just as the patients were being brought out to be carried to the Grotto; and they found that Marie had slept well and was very gay. She kissed her father and scolded him when she learnt that he had not yet decided on his trip to Gavarnie. She should really be displeased with him, she said, if he did not go. Still with the same restful, smiling expression, she added that she did not expect to be cured that day; and then, assuming an air of mystery, she begged Pierre to obtain permission for her to spend the following night before the Grotto. This was a favour which all the sufferers ardently coveted, but which only a few favoured ones with difficulty secured. After protesting, anxious as he felt with regard to the effect which a night spent in the open air might have upon her health, the young priest, seeing how unhappy she had suddenly become, at last promised that he would make the application. Doubtless she imagined that she would only obtain a hearing from the Virgin when they were alone together in the slumbering peacefulness of the night. That morning, indeed, she felt so lost among the innumerable patients who were heaped together in front of the Grotto, that already at ten o'clock she asked to be taken back to the hospital, complaining that the bright light tired her eyes. And when her father and the priest had again installed her in the Sainte-Honorine Ward, she gave them their liberty for the remainder of the day. "No, don't come to fetch me," she said, "I shall not go back to the Grotto this afternoon—it would be useless. But you will come for me this evening at nine o'clock, won't you, Pierre? It is agreed, you have given me your word."

He repeated that he would endeavour to secure the requisite permission, and that, if necessary, he would apply to Father Fourcade in person.

"Then, till this evening, darling," said M. de Guersaint, kissing his daughter. And he and Pierre went off together, leaving her lying on her bed, with an absorbed expression on her features, as her large, smiling eyes wandered away into space.

It was barely half-past ten when they got back to the Hotel of the Apparitions; but M. de Guersaint, whom the fine weather delighted, talked of having *dejeuner* at once, so that he might the sooner start upon a ramble through Lourdes. First of all, however, he wished to go up to his room, and Pierre following him, they encountered quite a drama on their way. The door of the room occupied by the Vignerons was wide open, and little Gustave could be seen lying on the sofa which served as his bed. He was livid; a moment previously he had suddenly fainted, and this had made the father and mother imagine that the end had come. Madame Vigneron was crouching on a chair, still stupefied by her fright, whilst M. Vigneron rushed about the room, thrusting everything aside in order that he might prepare a glass of sugared-water, to which he added a few drops of some elixir. This draught, he exclaimed, would set the lad right again. But all the same, it was incomprehensible. The boy was still strong, and to think that he should have fainted like that, and have turned as white as a chicken! Speaking in this wise, M. Vigneron glanced at Madame Chaise, the aunt, who was standing in front of the sofa, looking in good health that morning; and his hands shook yet more violently at the covert idea that if that stupid attack had carried off his son, they would no longer have inherited the aunt's fortune. He was quite beside himself at this thought, and eagerly opening the boy's mouth he compelled him to swallow the entire contents of the glass. Then, however, when he heard Gustave sigh, and saw him open his eyes again, his fatherly good-nature reappeared, and he shed tears, and called the lad his dear little fellow. But on Madame Chaise drawing near to offer some assistance, Gustave repulsed her with a sudden gesture of hatred, as though he understood how this woman's money unconsciously perverted his parents, who, after all, were worthy folks. Greatly offended, the old lady turned on her heel, and seated herself in a corner, whilst the father and mother, at last freed from their anxiety, returned thanks to the Blessed Virgin for having preserved their darling, who smiled at them with his intelligent and infinitely sorrowful smile, knowing and understanding everything as he did, and no longer having any taste for life, although he was not fifteen.

"Can we be of any help to you?" asked Pierre in an obliging way.

"No, no, I thank you, gentlemen," replied M. Vigneron, coming for a moment into the passage. "But oh! we did have a fright! Think of it, an only son, who is so dear to us too."

All around them the approach of the *dejeuner* hour was now throwing the house into commotion. Every door was banging, and the passages and the staircase resounded with the constant pitter-patter of feet. Three big girls passed by, raising a current of air with the sweep of their skirts. Some little children were crying in a neighbouring room. Then there were old people who seemed quite scared, and distracted priests who, forgetting their calling, caught up their cassocks with both hands, so that they might run the faster to the dining-room. From the top to the bottom of the house one could feel the floors shaking under the excessive weight of all the people who were packed inside the hotel.

"Oh, I hope that it is all over now, and that the Blessed Virgin will cure him," repeated M. Vigneron, before allowing his neighbours to retire. "We are going downstairs, for I must confess that all this has made me feel faint. I need something to eat, I am terribly hungry."

When Pierre and M. de Guersaint at last left their rooms, and went down-stairs, they found to their annoyance that there was not the smallest table-corner vacant in the large dining-room. A most extraordinary mob had assembled there, and the few seats that were still unoccupied were reserved. A waiter informed them that the room never emptied between ten and one o'clock, such was the rush of appetite, sharpened by the keen mountain air. So they had to resign themselves to wait, requesting the waiter to warn them as soon as there should be a couple of vacant places. Then, scarcely knowing what to do with themselves, they went to walk about the hotel porch, whence there was a view of the street, along which the townsfolk, in their Sunday best, streamed without a pause.

All at once, however, the landlord of the Hotel of the Apparitions, Master Majeste in person, appeared before them, clad in white from head to foot; and with a great show of politeness he inquired if the gentlemen would like to wait in the drawing-room. He was a stout man of five-and-forty, and strove to bear the burden of his name in a right royal fashion. Bald and clean-shaven, with round blue eyes in a waxy face, displaying three superposed chins, he always deported himself with much dignity. He had come from Nevers with the Sisters who managed the orphan asylum, and was married to a dusky little woman, a native of Lourdes. In less than fifteen years they had made their hotel one of the most substantial and best patronised establishments in the town. Of recent times, moreover, they had started a business in religious articles, installed in a large shop on the left of the hotel porch and managed by a young niece under Madame Majeste's Supervision.

"You can wait in the drawing-room, gentlemen," again suggested the hotel-keeper whom Pierre's cassock rendered very attentive.

They replied, however, that they preferred to walk about and wait in the open air. And thereupon Majeste would not leave them, but deigned to chat with them for a moment as he was wont to do with those of his customers whom he desired to honour. The conversation turned at first on the procession which would take place that night and which promised to be a superb spectacle as the weather was so fine. There were more than fifty thousand strangers gathered together in Lourdes that day, for visitors had come in from all the neighbouring bathing stations. This explained the crush at the *table d'hote*. Possibly the town would run short of bread as had been the case the previous year.

"You saw what a scramble there is," concluded Majeste, "we really don't know how to manage. It isn't my fault, I assure you, if you are kept waiting for a short time."

At this moment, however, a postman arrived with a large batch of newspapers and letters which he deposited on a table in the office. He had kept one letter in his hand and inquired of the landlord, "Have you a Madame Maze here?"

"Madame Maze, Madame Maze," repeated the hotel-keeper. "No, no, certainly not."

Pierre had heard both question and answer, and drawing near he exclaimed, "I know of a Madame Maze who must be lodging with the Sisters of the Immaculate Conception, the Blue Sisters as people call them here, I think."

The postman thanked him for the information and went off, but a somewhat bitter smile had risen to Majeste's lips. "The Blue Sisters," he muttered, "ah! the Blue Sisters." Then, darting a side glance at Pierre's cassock, he stopped short, as though he feared that he might say too much. Yet his heart was overflowing; he would have greatly liked to ease his feelings, and this young priest from Paris, who looked so liberal-minded, could not be one of the "band" as he called all those who discharged functions at the Grotto and coined money out of Our Lady of Lourdes. Accordingly, little by little, he ventured to speak out.

"I am a good Christian, I assure you, Monsieur l'Abbe," said he. "In fact we are all good Christians here. And I am a regular worshipper and take the sacrament every Easter. But, really, I must say that members of a religious community ought not to keep hotels. No, no, it isn't right!"

And thereupon he vented all the spite of a tradesman in presence of what he considered to be disloyal competition. Ought not those Blue Sisters, those Sisters of the Immaculate Conception, to have confined themselves to their real functions, the manufacture of wafers for sacramental purposes, and the repairing and washing of church linen? Instead of that, however, they had transformed their convent into a vast hostelry, where ladies who came to Lourdes unaccompanied found separate rooms, and were able to take their meals either in privacy or in a general dining-room. Everything was certainly very clean, very well organised and very inexpensive, thanks to the thousand advantages which the Sisters enjoyed; in fact, no hotel at Lourdes did so much business. "But all the same," continued Majeste, "I ask you if it is proper. To think of nuns selling victuals! Besides, I must tell you that the lady superior is really a clever woman, and as soon as she saw the stream of fortune rolling in, she wanted to keep it all for her own community and resolutely parted with the Fathers of the Grotto who wanted to lay their hands on it. Yes, Monsieur l'Abbe, she even went to Rome and gained her cause there, so that now she pockets all the money that her bills bring in. Think of it, nuns, yes nuns, *mon Dieu*! letting furnished rooms and keeping a *table d'hote*!"

He raised his arms to heaven, he was stifling with envy and vexation.

"But as your house is crammed," Pierre gently objected, "as you no longer have either a bed or a plate at anybody's disposal, where would you put any additional visitors who might arrive here?"

Majeste at once began protesting. "Ah! Monsieur l'Abbe!" said he, "one can see very well that you don't know the place. It's quite true that there is work for all of us, and that nobody has reason to complain during the national pilgrimage. But that only lasts four or five days, and in ordinary times the custom we secure isn't nearly so great. For myself, thank Heaven, I am always satisfied. My house is well known, it occupies the same rank as the Hotel of the Grotto, where two landlords have already made their fortunes. But no matter, it is vexing to see those Blue Sisters taking all the cream of the custom, for instance the ladies of the *bourgeoisie* who spend a fortnight and three weeks here at a stretch; and that, too, just in the quiet season, when there are not many people here. You understand, don't you? There are people of position who dislike uproar; they go by themselves to the Grotto, and pray there all day long, for days together, and pay good prices for their accommodation without any higgling."

Madame Majeste, whom Pierre and M. de Guersaint had not noticed leaning over an account-book in which she was adding up some figures, thereupon intervened in a shrill voice: "We had a customer like that, gentlemen, who stayed here for two months last year. She went to the Grotto, came back, went there again, took her meals, and went to bed. And never did we have a word of complaint from her; she was always smiling, as though to say that she found everything very nice. She paid her bill, too, without even looking at it. Ah! one regrets people of that kind."

Short, thin, very dark, and dressed in black, with a little white collar, Madame Majeste had risen to her feet; and she now began to solicit custom: "If you would like to buy a few little souvenirs of Lourdes before you leave, gentlemen, I hope that you will not forget us. We have a shop close by, where you will find an assortment of all the articles that are most in request. As a rule, the persons who stay here are kind enough not to deal elsewhere."

However, Majeste was again wagging his head, with the air of a good Christian saddened by the scandals of the time. "Certainly," said he, "I don't want to show any disrespect to the reverend Fathers, but it must in all truth be admitted that they are too greedy. You must have seen the shop which they have set up near the Grotto, that shop which is always crowded, and where tapers and articles of piety are sold. A bishop declared that it was shameful, and that the buyers and sellers ought to be driven out of the temple afresh. It is said, too, that the Fathers run that big shop yonder, just across the street, which supplies all the petty dealers in the town. And, according to the reports which circulate, they have a finger in all the trade in religious articles, and levy a percentage on the millions of chaplets, statuettes, and medals which are sold every year at Lourdes."

Majeste had now lowered his voice, for his accusations were becoming precise, and he ended by trembling somewhat at his imprudence in talking so confidentially to strangers. However, the expression of Pierre's gentle, attentive face reassured him; and so he continued with the passion of a wounded rival, resolved to go on to the very end: "I am willing to admit that there is some exaggeration in all this. But all the same, it does religion no good for people to see the reverend Fathers keeping shops like us tradesmen. For my part, of course, I don't go and ask for a share of the money which they make by their masses, or a percentage on the presents which they receive, so why should they start selling what I sell? Our business was a poor one last year owing to them. There are already too many of us; nowadays everyone at Lourdes sells 'religious articles,' to such an extent, in fact, that there will soon be no butchers or wine merchants left—nothing but bread to eat and water to drink. Ah! Monsieur l'Abbe, it is no doubt nice to have the Blessed Virgin with us, but things are none the less very bad at times."

A person staying at the hotel at that moment disturbed him, but he returned just as a young girl came in search of Madame Majeste. The damsel, who evidently belonged to Lourdes, was very pretty, small but plump, with beautiful black hair, and a round face full of bright gaiety.

"That is our niece Apolline," resumed Majeste. "She has been keeping our shop for two years past. She is the daughter of one of my wife's brothers, who is in poor circumstances. She was keeping sheep at Ossun, in the neighbourhood of Bartres, when we were struck by her intelligence and nice looks and decided to bring her here; and we don't repent having done so, for she has a great deal of merit, and has become a very good saleswoman."

A point to which he omitted to refer, was that there were rumours current of somewhat flighty conduct on Mademoiselle Apolline's part. But she undoubtedly had her value: she attracted customers by the power, possibly, of her large black eyes, which smiled so readily. During his sojourn at Lourdes the previous year, Gerard de Peyrelongue had scarcely stirred from the shop she managed, and doubtless it was only the matrimonial ideas now flitting through his head that prevented him from returning thither. It seemed as though the Abbe des Hermoises had taken his place, for this gallant ecclesiastic brought a great many ladies to make purchases at the repository.

"Ah! you are speaking of Apolline," said Madame Majeste, at that moment coming back from the shop. "Have you noticed one thing about her, gentlemen—her extraordinary likeness to Bernadette? There, on the wall yonder, is a photograph of Bernadette when she was eighteen years old."

Pierre and M. de Guersaint drew near to examine the portrait, whilst Majeste exclaimed: "Bernadette, yes, certainly—she was rather like Apolline, but not nearly so nice; she looked so sad and poor."

He would doubtless have gone on chattering, but just then the waiter appeared and announced that there was at last a little table vacant. M. de Guersaint had twice gone to glance inside the dining-room, for he was eager to have his *dejeuner* and spend the remainder of that fine Sunday out-of-doors. So he now hastened away, without paying any further attention to Majeste, who remarked, with an amiable smile, that the gentlemen had not had so very long to wait after all.

To reach the table mentioned by the waiter, the architect and Pierre had to cross the dining-room from end to end. It was a long apartment, painted a light oak colour, an oily yellow, which was already peeling away in places and soiled with stains in others. You realised that rapid wear and tear went on here amidst the continual scramble of the big eaters who sat down at table. The only ornaments were a gilt zinc clock and a couple of meagre candelabra on the mantelpiece. Guipure curtains, moreover, hung at the five large windows looking on to the street, which was flooded with sunshine; some of the fierce arrow-like rays penetrating into the room although the blinds had been lowered. And, in the middle of the apartment, some forty persons were packed together at the *table d'hote*, which was scarcely eleven yards in length and did not supply proper accommodation for more than thirty people; whilst at the little tables standing against the walls upon either side another forty persons sat close together, hustled by the three waiters each time that they went by. You had scarcely reached the threshold before you were deafened by the extraordinary uproar, the noise of voices and the clatter of forks and plates; and it seemed, too, as if you were entering a damp oven, for a warm, steamy mist, laden with a suffocating smell of victuals, assailed the face.

Pierre at first failed to distinguish anything, but, when he was installed at the little table—a garden-table which had been brought indoors for the occasion, and on which there was scarcely room for two covers—he felt quite upset, almost sick, in fact, at the sight presented by the *table d'hote*, which his glance now enfiladed from end to end. People had been eating at it for an hour already, two sets of customers had followed one upon the other, and the covers were strewn about in higgledy-piggledy fashion. On the cloth were numerous stains of wine and sauce, while there was no symmetry even in the arrangement of the glass fruit-stands, which formed the only decorations of the table. And one's astonishment increased at sight of the motley mob which was collected there—huge priests, scraggy girls, mothers overflowing with superfluous fat, gentlemen with red faces, and families ranged in rows and displaying all the pitiable, increasing ugliness of successive generations. All these people were perspiring, greedily swallowing, seated slantwise, lacking room to move their arms, and unable even to use their hands deftly. And amidst this display of appetite, increased tenfold by fatigue, and of eager haste to fill one's stomach in order to return to the Grotto more quickly, there was a corpulent ecclesiastic who in no wise hurried, but ate of every dish with prudent slowness, crunching his food with a ceaseless, dignified movement of the jaws.

"*Fichtre*!" exclaimed M. de Guersaint, "it is by no means cool in here. All the same, I shall be glad of something to eat, for I've felt a sinking in the stomach ever since I have been at Lourdes. And you—are you hungry?"

"Yes, yes, I shall eat," replied Pierre, though, truth to tell, he felt quite upset.

The *menu* was a copious one. There was salmon, an omelet, mutton cutlets with mashed potatoes, stewed kidneys, cauliflowers, cold meats, and apricot tarts—everything cooked too much, and swimming in sauce which, but for its grittiness, would have been flavourless. However, there was some fairly fine fruit on the glass stands, particularly some peaches. And, besides, the people did not seem at all difficult to please; they apparently had no palates, for there was no sign of nausea. Hemmed in between an old priest and a dirty, full-bearded man, a girl of delicate build, who looked very pretty with her soft eyes and silken skin, was eating some kidneys with an expression of absolute beatitude, although the so-called "sauce" in which they swam was simply greyish water.

"Hum!" resumed even M. de Guersaint, "this salmon is not so bad. Add a little salt to it and you will find it all right."

Pierre made up his mind to eat, for after all he must take sustenance for strength's sake. At a little table close by, however, he had just caught sight of Madame Vigneron and Madame Chaise, who sat face to face, apparently waiting. And indeed, M. Vigneron and his son Gustave soon appeared, the latter still pale, and leaning more heavily than usual on his crutch. "Sit down next to your aunt," said his father; "I will take the chair beside your mother." But just then he perceived his two neighbours, and stepping up to them, he added: "Oh! he is now all right again. I have been rubbing him with some eau-de-Cologne, and by-and-by he will be able to take his bath at the piscina."

Thereupon M. Vigneron sat down and began to devour. But what an awful fright he had had! He again began talking of it aloud, despite himself, so intense had been his terror at the thought that the lad might go off before his aunt. The latter related that whilst she was kneeling at the Grotto the day before, she had experienced a sudden feeling of relief; in fact, she flattered herself that she was cured of her heart complaint, and began giving precise particulars, to which her brother-in-law listened with dilated eyes, full of involuntary anxiety. Most certainly he was a good-natured man, he had never desired anybody's death; only he felt indignant at the idea that the Virgin might cure this old woman, and forget his son, who was so young. Talking and eating, he had got to the cutlets, and was swallowing the mashed potatoes by the forkful, when he fancied he could detect that Madame Chaise was sulking with her nephew. "Gustave," he suddenly inquired, "have you asked your aunt's forgiveness?" The lad, quite astonished, began staring at his father with his large clear eyes. "Yes," added M. Vigneron, "you behaved very badly, you pushed her back just now when she wanted to help you to sit up."

Madame Chaise said nothing, but waited with a dignified air, whilst Gustave, who, without any show of appetite, was finishing the *noix* of his cutlet, which had been cut into small pieces, remained with his eyes lowered on his plate, this time obstinately refusing to make the sorry show of affection which was demanded of him.

"Come, Gustave," resumed his father, "be a good boy. You know how kind your aunt is, and all that she intends to do for you."

But no, he would not yield. At that moment, indeed, he really hated that woman, who did not die quickly enough, who polluted the affection of his parents, to such a point that when he saw them surround him with attentions he no longer knew whether it were himself or the inheritance which his life represented that they wished to save. However, Madame Vigneron, so dignified in her demeanour, came to her husband's help. "You really grieve me, Gustave," said she; "ask your aunt's forgiveness, or you will make me quite angry with you."

Thereupon he gave way. What was the use of resisting? Was it not better that his parents should obtain that money? Would he not himself die later on, so as to suit the family convenience? He was aware of all that; he understood everything, even when not a word was spoken. So keen was the sense of hearing with which suffering had endowed him, that he even heard the others' thoughts.

"I beg your pardon, aunt," he said, "for not having behaved well to you just now."

Then two big tears rolled from his eyes, whilst he smiled with the air of a tender-hearted man who has seen too much of life and can no longer be deceived by anything. Madame Chaise at once kissed him and told him that she was not at all angry. And the Vignerons' delight in living was displayed in all candour.

"If the kidneys are not up to much," M. de Guersaint now said to Pierre, "here at all events are some cauliflowers with a good flavour."

The formidable mastication was still going on around them. Pierre had never seen such an amount of eating, amidst such perspiration, in an atmosphere as stifling as that of a washhouse full of hot steam. The odour of the victuals seemed to thicken into a kind of smoke. You had to shout to make yourself heard, for everybody was talking in loud tones, and the scared waiters raised a fearful clatter in changing the plates and forks; not to mention the noise of all the jaw-crunching, a mill-like grinding which was distinctly audible. What most hurt the feelings of the young priest, however, was the extraordinary promiscuity of the *table d'hote*, at which men and women, young girls and ecclesiastics, were packed together in chance order, and satisfied their hunger like a pack of hounds snapping at offal in all haste. Baskets of bread went round and were promptly emptied. And there was a perfect massacre of cold meats, all the remnants of the victuals of the day before, leg of mutton, veal, and ham, encompassed by a fallen mass of transparent jelly which quivered like soft glue. They had all eaten too much already, but these viands seemed to whet their appetites afresh, as though the idea had come to them that nothing whatever ought to be left. The fat priest in the middle of the table, who had shown himself such a capital knife-and-fork, was now lingering over the fruit, having just got to his third peach, a huge one, which he slowly peeled and swallowed in slices with an air of compunction.

All at once, however, the whole room was thrown into agitation. A waiter had come in and begun distributing the letters which Madame Majeste had finished sorting. "Hallo!" exclaimed M. Vigneron; "a letter for me! This is surprising—I did not give my address to anybody." Then, at a sudden recollection, he added, "Yes I did, though; this must have come from Sauvageot, who is filling my place at the Ministry." He opened the letter, his hands began to tremble, and suddenly he raised a cry: "The chief clerk is dead!"

Deeply agitated, Madame Vigneron was also unable to bridle her tongue: "Then you will have the appointment!"

This was the secret dream in which they had so long and so fondly indulged: the chief clerk's death, in order that he, Vigneron, assistant chief clerk for ten years past, might at last rise to the supreme post, the bureaucratic marshalship. And so great was his delight that he cast aside all restraint. "Ah! the Blessed Virgin is certainly protecting me, my dear. Only this morning I again prayed to her for a rise, and, you see, she grants my prayer!"

However, finding Madame Chaise's eyes fixed upon his own, and seeing Gustave smile, he realised that he ought not to exult in this fashion. Each member of the family no doubt thought of his or her interests and prayed to the Blessed Virgin for such personal favours as might be desired. And so, again putting on his good-natured air, he resumed: "I mean that the Blessed Virgin takes an interest in every one of us and will send us all home well satisfied. Ah! the poor chief, I'm sorry for him. I shall have to send my card to his widow."

In spite of all his efforts he could not restrain his exultation, and no longer doubted that his most secret desires, those which he did not even confess to himself, would soon be gratified. And so all honour was done to the apricot tarts, even Gustave being allowed to eat a portion of one.

"It is surprising," now remarked M. de Guersaint, who had just ordered a cup of coffee; "it is surprising that one doesn't see more sick people here. All these folks seem to me to have first-rate appetites."

After a close inspection, however, in addition to Gustave, who ate no more than a little chicken, he ended by finding a man with a goitre seated at the *table d'hote* between two women, one of whom certainly suffered from cancer. Farther on, too, there was a girl so thin and pale that she must surely be a consumptive. And still farther away there was a female idiot who had made her entry leaning on two relatives, and with expressionless eyes and lifeless features was now carrying her food to her mouth with a spoon, and slobbering over her napkin. Perhaps there were yet other ailing ones present who could not be distinguished among all those noisy appetites, ailing ones whom the journey had braced, and who were eating as they had not eaten for a long time past. The apricot tarts, the cheese, the fruits were all engulfed amidst the increasing disorder of the table, where at last there only remained the stains of all the wine and sauce which had been spilt upon the cloth.

It was nearly noon. "We will go back to the Grotto at once, eh?" said M. Vigneron.

Indeed, "To the Grotto! To the Grotto!" were well-nigh the only words you now heard. The full mouths were eagerly masticating and swallowing, in order that they might repeat prayers and hymns again with all speed. "Well, as we have the whole afternoon before us," declared M. de Guersaint, "I suggest that we should visit the town a little. I want to see also if I can get a conveyance for my excursion, as my daughter so particularly wishes me to make it."

Pierre, who was stifling, was glad indeed to leave the dining-room. In the porch he was able to breathe again, though even there he found a torrent of customers, new arrivals who were waiting for places. No sooner did one of the little tables become vacant than its possession was eagerly contested, whilst the smallest gap at the *table d'hote* was instantly filled up. In this wise the assault would continue for more than another hour, and again would the different courses of the *menu* appear in procession, to be engulfed amidst the crunching of jaws, the stifling heat, and the growing nausea.

II. THE "ORDINARY."

WHEN Pierre and M. de Guersaint got outside they began walking slowly amidst the ever-growing stream of the Sundayfied crowd. The sky was a bright blue, the sun warmed the whole town, and there was a festive gaiety in the atmosphere, the keen delight that attends those great fairs which bring entire communities into the open air. When they had descended the crowded footway of the Avenue de la Grotte, and had reached the corner of the Plateau de la Merlasse, they found their way barred by a throng which was flowing backward amidst a block of vehicles and stamping of horses. "There is no hurry, however," remarked M. de Guersaint. "My idea is to go as far as the Place du Marcadal in the old town; for the servant girl at the hotel told me of a hairdresser there whose brother lets out conveyances cheaply. Do you mind going so far?"

"I?" replied Pierre. "Go wherever you like, I'll follow you."

"All right—and I'll profit by the opportunity to have a shave."

They were nearing the Place du Rosaire, and found themselves in front of the lawns stretching to the Gave, when an encounter again stopped them. Mesdames Desagneaux and Raymonde de Jonquiere were here, chatting gaily with Gerard de Peyrelongue. Both women wore light-coloured gowns, seaside dresses as it were, and their white silk parasols shone in the bright sunlight. They imparted, so to say, a pretty note to the scene—a touch of society chatter blended with the fresh laughter of youth.

"No, no," Madame Desagneaux was saying, "we certainly can't go and visit your 'ordinary' like that—at the very moment when all your comrades are eating."

Gerard, however, with a very gallant air, insisted on their accompanying him, turning more particularly towards Raymonde, whose somewhat massive face was that day brightened by the radiant charm of health.

"But it is a very curious sight, I assure you," said the young man, "and you would be very respectfully received. Trust yourself to me, mademoiselle. Besides, we should certainly find M. Berthaud there, and he would be delighted to do you the honours."

Raymonde smiled, her clear eyes plainly saying that she was quite agreeable. And just then, as Pierre and M. de Guersaint drew near in order to present their respects to the ladies, they were made acquainted with the question under discussion. The "ordinary" was a kind of restaurant or *table d'hote* which the members of the Hospitality of Our Lady of Salvation—the bearers, the hospitallers of the Grotto, the piscinas, and the hospitals—had established among themselves with the view of taking their meals together at small cost. Many of them were not rich, for they were recruited among all classes; however, they had contrived to secure three good meals for the daily payment of three francs apiece. And in fact they soon had provisions to spare and distributed them among the poor. Everything was in their own management; they purchased their own supplies, recruited a cook and a few waiters, and did not disdain to lend a hand themselves, in order that everything might be comfortable and orderly.

"It must be very interesting," said M, de Guersaint, when these explanations had been given him. "Let us go and see it, if we are not in the way."

Little Madame Desagneaux thereupon gave her consent. "Well, if we are going in a party," said she, "I am quite willing. But when this gentleman first proposed to take Raymonde and me, I was afraid that it might not be quite proper."

Then, as she began to laugh, the others followed her example. She had accepted M. de Guersaint's arm, and Pierre walked beside her on the other hand, experiencing a sudden feeling of sympathy for this gay little woman, who was so full of life and so charming with her fair frizzy hair and creamy complexion.

Behind them came Raymonde, leaning upon Gerard's arm and talking to him in the calm, staid voice of a young lady who holds the best principles despite her air of heedless youth. And since here was the husband whom she had so often dreamt of, she resolved that she would this time secure him, make him beyond all question her own. She intoxicated him with the perfume of health and youth which she diffused, and at the same time astonished him by her knowledge of housewifely duties and of the manner in which money may be economised even in the most trifling matters; for having questioned him with regard to the purchases which he and his comrades made for their "ordinary," she proceeded to show him that they might have reduced their expenditure still further.

Meantime M. de Guersaint and Madame Desagneaux were also chatting together: "You must be fearfully tired, madame," said the architect.

But with a gesture of revolt, and an exclamation of genuine anger, she replied: "Oh no, indeed! Last night, it is true, fatigue quite overcame me at the hospital; I sat down and dozed off, and Madame de Jonquiere and the other ladies were good enough to let me sleep on." At this the others again began to laugh; but still with the same angry air she continued: "And so I slept like a log until this morning. It was disgraceful, especially as I had sworn that I would remain up all night." Then, merriment gaining upon her in her turn, she suddenly burst into a sonorous laugh, displaying her beautiful white teeth. "Ah! a pretty nurse I am, and no mistake! It was poor Madame de Jonquiere who had to remain on her legs all the time. I tried to coax her to come out with us just now. But she preferred to take a little rest."

Raymonde, who overheard these words, thereupon raised her voice to say: "Yes, indeed, my poor mamma could no longer keep on her feet. It was I who compelled her to lie down, telling her that she could go to sleep without any uneasiness, for we should get on all right without her—"

So saying, the girl gave Gerard a laughing glance. He even fancied that he could detect a faint squeeze of the fresh round arm which was resting on his own, as though, indeed, she had wished to express her happiness at being alone with him so that they might settle their own affairs without any interference. This quite delighted him; and he began to explain that if he had not had *dejeuner* with his comrades that day, it was because some friends had invited him to join them at the railway-station refreshment-room at ten o'clock, and had not given him his liberty until after the departure of the eleven-thirty train.

"Ah! the rascals!" he suddenly resumed. "Do you hear them, mademoiselle?"

The little party was now nearing its destination, and the uproarious laughter and chatter of youth rang out from a clump of trees which concealed the old zinc and plaster building in which the "ordinary" was installed. Gerard began by taking the visitors into the kitchen, a very spacious apartment, well fitted up, and containing a huge range and an immense table, to say nothing of numerous gigantic cauldrons. Here, moreover, the young man called the attention of his companions to the circumstance that the cook, a fat, jovial-looking man, had the red cross pinned on his white jacket, being himself a member of the pilgrimage. Then, pushing open a door, Gerard invited his friends to enter the common room.

It was a long apartment containing two rows of plain deal tables; and the only other articles of furniture were numerous rush-seated tavern chairs, with an additional table which served as a sideboard. The whitewashed walls and the flooring of shiny, red tiles looked, however, extremely clean amidst this intentional bareness, which was similar to that of a monkish refectory. But, the feature of the place which more particularly struck you, as you crossed the threshold, was the childish gaiety which reigned there; for, packed together at the tables, were a hundred and fifty hospitallers of all ages, eating with splendid appetites, laughing, applauding, and singing, with their mouths full. A wondrous fraternity united these men, who had flocked to Lourdes from every province of France, and who belonged to all classes, and represented every degree of fortune. Many of them knew nothing of one another, save that they met here and elbowed one another during three days every year, living together like brothers, and then going off and remaining in absolute ignorance of each other during the rest of the twelvemonth. Nothing could be more charming, however, than to meet again at the next pilgrimage, united in the same charitable work, and to spend a few days of hard labour and boyish delight in common once more; for it all became, as it were, an "outing" of a number of big fellows, let loose under a lovely sky, and well pleased to be able to enjoy themselves and laugh together. And even the frugality of the table, with the pride of managing things themselves, of eating the provisions which they had purchased and cooked, added to the general good humour.

"You see," explained Gerard, "we are not at all inclined to be sad, although we have so much hard work to get through. The Hospitality numbers more than three hundred members, but there are only about one hundred and fifty here at a time, for we have had to organise two successive services, so that there may always be some of us on duty at the Grotto and the hospitals."

The sight of the little party of visitors assembled on the threshold of the room seemed to have increased the general delight; and Berthaud, the superintendent of the bearers, who was lunching at the head of one of the tables, gallantly rose up to receive the ladies.

"But it smells very nice," exclaimed Madame Desagneaux in her giddy way. "Won't you invite us to come and taste your cookery to-morrow?"

"Oh! we can't ask ladies," replied Berthaud, laughing. "But if you gentlemen would like to join us to-morrow we should be extremely pleased to entertain you."

He had at once noticed the good understanding which prevailed between Gerard and Raymonde, and seemed delighted at it, for he greatly wished his cousin to make this match. He laughed pleasantly, at the enthusiastic gaiety which the young girl displayed as she began to question him. "Is not that the Marquis de Salmon-Roquebert," she asked, "who is sitting over yonder between those two young men who look like shop assistants?"

"They are, in fact, the sons of a small stationer at Tarbes," replied Berthaud; "and that is really the Marquis, your neighbour of the Rue de Lille, the owner of that magnificent mansion, one of the richest and most noble men of title in France. You see how he is enjoying our mutton stew!"

It was true, the millionaire Marquis seemed delighted to be able to board himself for his three francs a day, and to sit down at table in genuine democratic fashion by the side of petty *bourgeois* and workmen who would not have dared to accost him in the street. Was not that chance table symbolical of social communion, effected by the joint practice of charity? For his part, the Marquis was the more hungry that day, as he had bathed over sixty patients, sufferers from all the most abominable diseases of unhappy humanity, at the piscinas that morning. And the scene around him seemed like a realisation of the evangelical commonalty; but doubtless it was so charming and so gay simply because its duration was limited to three days.

Although M. de Guersaint had but lately risen from table, his curiosity prompted him to taste the mutton stew, and he pronounced it perfect. Meantime, Pierre caught sight of Baron Suire, the director of the Hospitality, walking about between the rows of tables with an air of some importance, as though he had allotted himself the task of keeping an eye on everything, even on the manner in which his staff fed itself. The young priest thereupon remembered the ardent desire which Marie had expressed to spend the night in front of the Grotto, and it occurred to him that the Baron might be willing to give the necessary authorisation.

"Certainly," replied the director, who had become quite grave whilst listening to Pierre, "we do sometimes allow it; but it is always a very delicate matter! You assure me at all events that this young person is not consumptive? Well, well, since you say that she so much desires it I will mention the matter to Father Fourcade and warn Madame de Jonquiere, so that she may let you take the young lady away."

He was in reality a very good-natured fellow, albeit so fond of assuming the air of an indispensable man weighed down by the heaviest responsibilities. In his turn he now detained the visitors, and gave them full particulars concerning the organisation of the Hospitality. Its members said prayers together every morning. Two board meetings were held each day, and were attended by all the heads of departments, as well as by the reverend Fathers and some of the chaplains. All the hospitallers took the Sacrament as frequently as possible. And, moreover, there were many complicated tasks to be attended to, a prodigious rotation of duties, quite a little world to be governed with a firm hand. The Baron spoke like a general who each year gains a great victory over the spirit of the age; and, sending Berthaud back to finish his *dejeuner*, he insisted on escorting the ladies into the little sanded courtyard, which was shaded by some fine trees.

"It is very interesting, very interesting," repeated Madame Desagneaux. "We are greatly obliged to you for your kindness, monsieur."

"Don't mention it, don't mention it, madame," answered the Baron. "It is I who am pleased at having had an opportunity to show you my little army."

II. THE "ORDINARY."

So far Gerard had not quitted Raymonde's side; but M. de Guersaint and Pierre were already exchanging glances suggestive of leave-taking, in order that they might repair by themselves to the Place du Marcadal, when Madame Desagneaux suddenly remembered that a friend had requested her to send her a bottle of Lourdes water. And she thereupon asked Gerard how she was to execute this commission. The young man began to laugh. "Will you again accept me as a guide?" said he. "And by the way, if these gentlemen like to come as well, I will show you the place where the bottles are filled, corked, packed in cases, and then sent off. It is a curious sight."

M. de Guersaint immediately consented; and all five of them set out again, Madame Desagneaux still between the architect and the priest, whilst Raymonde and Gerard brought up the rear. The crowd in the burning sunlight was increasing; the Place du Rosaire was now overflowing with an idle sauntering mob resembling some concourse of sight-seers on a day of public rejoicing.

The bottling and packing shops were situated under one of the arches on the left-hand side of the Place. They formed a suite of three apartments of very simple aspect. In the first one the bottles were filled in the most ordinary of fashions. A little green-painted zinc barrel, not unlike a watering-cask, was dragged by a man from the Grotto, and the light-coloured bottles were then simply filled at its tap, one by one; the blouse-clad workman entrusted with the duty exercising no particular watchfulness to prevent the water from overflowing. In fact there was quite a puddle of it upon the ground. There were no labels on the bottles; the little leaden capsules placed over the corks alone bore an inscription, and they were coated with a kind of ceruse, doubtless to ensure preservation. Then came two other rooms which formed regular packing shops, with carpenters' benches, tools, and heaps of shavings. The boxes, most frequently made for one bottle or for two, were put together with great care, and the bottles were deposited inside them, on beds of fine wood parings. The scene reminded one in some degree of the packing halls for flowers at Nice and for preserved fruits at Grasse.

Gerard went on giving explanations with a quiet, satisfied air. "The water," he said, "really comes from the Grotto, as you can yourselves see, so that all the foolish jokes which one hears really have no basis. And everything is perfectly simple, natural, and goes on in the broad daylight. I would also point out to you that the Fathers don't sell the water as they are accused of doing. For instance, a bottle of water here costs twenty centimes,[1] which is only the price of the bottle itself. If you wish to have it sent to anybody you naturally have to pay for the packing and the carriage, and then it costs you one franc and seventy centimes.[2] However, you are perfectly at liberty to go to the source and fill the flasks and cans and other receptacles that you may choose to bring with you."

Pierre reflected that the profits of the reverend Fathers in this respect could not be very large ones, for their gains were limited to what they made by manufacturing the boxes and supplying the bottles, which latter, purchased by the thousand, certainly did not cost them so much as twenty centimes apiece. However, Raymonde and Madame Desagneaux, as well as M. de Guersaint, who had such a lively imagination, experi-

---

[1] Four cents, U.S.A.

[2] About 32 cents, U.S.A.

enced deep disappointment at sight of the little green barrel, the capsules, sticky with ceruse, and the piles of shavings lying around the benches. They had doubtless imagined all sorts of ceremonies, the observance of certain rites in bottling the miraculous water, priests in vestments pronouncing blessings, and choir-boys singing hymns of praise in pure crystalline voices. For his part, Pierre, in presence of all this vulgar bottling and packing, ended by thinking of the active power of faith. When one of those bottles reaches some far-away sick-room, and is unpacked there, and the sufferer falls upon his knees, and so excites himself by contemplating and drinking the pure water that he actually brings about the cure of his ailment, there must truly be a most extraordinary plunge into all-powerful illusion.

"Ah!" exclaimed Gerard as they came out, "would you like to see the storehouse where the tapers are kept, before going to the offices? It is only a couple of steps away."

And then, not even waiting for their answer, he led them to the opposite side of the Place du Rosaire. His one desire was to amuse Raymonde, but, in point of fact, the aspect of the place where the tapers were stored was even less entertaining than that of the packing-rooms which they had just left. This storehouse, a kind of deep vault under one of the right-hand arches of the Place, was divided by timber into a number of spacious compartments, in which lay an extraordinary collection of tapers, classified according to size. The overplus of all the tapers offered to the Grotto was deposited here; and such was the number of these superfluous candles that the little conveyances stationed near the Grotto railing, ready to receive the pilgrims' offerings, had to be brought to the storehouse several times a day in order to be emptied there, after which they were returned to the Grotto, and were promptly filled again. In theory, each taper that was offered ought to have been burnt at the feet of the Virgin's statue; but so great was the number of these offerings, that, although a couple of hundred tapers of all sizes were kept burning by day and night, it was impossible to exhaust the supply, which went on increasing and increasing. There was a rumour that the Fathers could not even find room to store all this wax, but had to sell it over and over again; and, indeed, certain friends of the Grotto confessed, with a touch of pride, that the profit on the tapers alone would have sufficed to defray all the expenses of the business.

The quantity of these votive candles quite stupefied Raymonde and Madame Desagneaux. How many, how many there were! The smaller ones, costing from fifty centimes to a franc apiece, were piled up in fabulous numbers. M. de Guersaint, desirous of getting at the exact figures, quite lost himself in the puzzling calculation he attempted. As for Pierre, it was in silence that he gazed upon this mass of wax, destined to be burnt in open daylight to the glory of God; and although he was by no means a rigid utilitarian, and could well understand that some apparent acts of extravagance yield an illusive enjoyment and satisfaction which provide humanity with as much sustenance as bread, he could not, on the other hand, refrain from reflecting on the many benefits which might have been conferred on the poor and the ailing with the money represented by all that wax, which would fly away in smoke.

"But come, what about that bottle which I am to send off?" abruptly asked Madame Desagneaux.

"We will go to the office," replied Gerard. "In five minutes everything will be settled."

II. THE "ORDINARY."

They had to cross the Place du Rosaire once more and ascend the stone stairway leading to the Basilica. The office was up above, on the left hand, at the corner of the path leading to the Calvary. The building was a paltry one, a hut of lath and plaster which the wind and the rain had reduced to a state of ruin. On a board outside was the inscription: "Apply here with reference to Masses, Offerings, and Brotherhoods. Forwarding office for Lourdes water. Subscriptions to the 'Annals of O. L. of Lourdes.'" How many millions of people must have already passed through this wretched shanty, which seemed to date from the innocent days when the foundations of the adjacent Basilica had scarcely been laid!

The whole party went in, eager to see what might be inside. But they simply found a wicket at which Madame Desagneaux had to stop in order to give her friend's name and address; and when she had paid one franc and seventy centimes, a small printed receipt was handed her, such as you receive on registering luggage at a railway station.

As soon as they were outside again Gerard pointed to a large building standing two or three hundred yards away, and resumed: "There, that is where the Fathers reside."

"But we see nothing of them," remarked Pierre.

This observation so astonished the young man that he remained for a moment without replying. "It's true," he at last said, "we do not see them, but then they give up the custody of everything—the Grotto and all the rest—to the Fathers of the Assumption during the national pilgrimage."

Pierre looked at the building which had been pointed out to him, and noticed that it was a massive stone pile resembling a fortress. The windows were closed, and the whole edifice looked lifeless. Yet everything at Lourdes came from it, and to it also everything returned. It seemed, in fact, to the young priest that he could hear the silent, formidable rake-stroke which extended over the entire valley, which caught hold of all who had come to the spot, and placed both the gold and the blood of the throng in the clutches of those reverend Fathers! However, Gerard just then resumed in a low voice "But come, they do show themselves, for here is the reverend superior, Father Capdebarthe himself."

An ecclesiastic was indeed just passing, a man with the appearance of a peasant, a knotty frame, and a large head which looked as though carved with a billhook. His opaque eyes were quite expressionless, and his face, with its worn features, had retained a loamy tint, a gloomy, russet reflection of the earth. Monseigneur Laurence had really made a politic selection in confiding the organisation and management of the Grotto to those Garaison missionaries, who were so tenacious and covetous, for the most part sons of mountain peasants and passionately attached to the soil.

However, the little party now slowly retraced its steps by way of the Plateau de la Merlasse, the broad boulevard which skirts the inclined way on the left hand and leads to the Avenue de la Grotte. It was already past one o'clock, but people were still eating their *dejeuners* from one to the other end of the overflowing town. Many of the fifty thousand pilgrims and sight-seers collected within it had not yet been able to sit down and eat; and Pierre, who had left the *table d'hote* still crowded, who had just seen the hospitallers squeezing together so gaily at the "ordinary," found more and more tables at each step he took. On all sides people were eating, eating without a pause. Hereabouts, however, in the open air, on either side of the broad road, the hungry ones were humble folk who had rushed upon the tables set up on either footway—tables formed of a couple of long boards, flanked by two forms, and shaded from the sun by narrow linen awnings. Broth and coffee were sold at these places at a penny a cup. The little loaves heaped up in high baskets also cost a penny apiece. Hanging from the poles which upheld the awnings were sausages, chitterlings, and hams. Some of the open-air *restaurateurs* were frying potatoes, and others were concocting more or less savoury messes of inferior meat and onions. A pungent smoke, a violent odour, arose into the sunlight, mingling with the dust which was raised by the continuous tramp of the promenaders. Rows of people, moreover, were waiting at each cantine, so that each time a party rose from table fresh customers took possession of the benches ranged beside the oilcloth-covered planks, which were so narrow that there was scarcely room for two bowls of soup to be placed side by side. And one and all made haste, and devoured with the ravenous hunger born of their fatigue, that insatiable appetite which so often follows upon great moral shocks. In fact, when the mind had exhausted itself in prayer, when everything physical had been forgotten amidst the mental flight into the legendary heavens, the human animal suddenly appeared, again asserted itself, and began to gorge. Moreover, under that dazzling Sunday sky, the scene was like that of a fair-field with all the gluttony of a merrymaking community, a display of the delight which they felt in living, despite the multiplicity of their abominable ailments and the dearth of the miracles they hoped for.

"They eat, they amuse themselves; what else can one expect?" remarked Gerard, guessing the thoughts of his amiable companions.

"Ah! poor people!" murmured Pierre, "they have a perfect right to do so."

He was greatly touched to see human nature reassert itself in this fashion. However, when they had got to the lower part of the boulevard near the Grotto, his feelings were hurt at sight of the desperate eagerness displayed by the female vendors of tapers and bouquets, who with the rough fierceness of conquerors assailed the passers-by in bands. They were mostly young women, with bare heads, or with kerchiefs tied over their hair, and they displayed extraordinary effrontery. Even the old ones were scarcely more discreet. With parcels of tapers under their arms, they brandished the one which they offered for sale and even thrust it into the hand of the promenader. "Monsieur," "madame," they called, "buy a taper, buy a taper, it will bring you luck!" One gentleman, who was surrounded and shaken by three of the youngest of these harpies, almost lost the skirts of his frock-coat in attempting to escape their clutches. Then the scene began afresh with the bouquets—large round bouquets they were, carelessly fastened together and looking like cabbages. "A bouquet, madame!" was the cry. "A bouquet for the Blessed Virgin!" If the lady escaped, she heard muttered insults behind her. Trafficking, impudent trafficking, pursued the pilgrims to the very outskirts of the Grotto. Trade was not merely triumphantly installed in every one of the shops, standing close together and transforming each street into a bazaar, but it overran the footways and barred the road with hand-carts full of chaplets, medals, statuettes, and religious prints. On all sides people were buying almost to the same extent as they ate, in order that they might take away with them some souvenir of this holy Kermesse. And the bright gay note of this commercial eagerness, this scramble of hawkers, was supplied by the urchins who rushed about through the crowd, crying the "Journal de la Grotte." Their sharp, shrill voices pierced the ear: "The 'Journal de la Grotte,' this morning's number, two sous, the 'Journal de la Grotte.'"

Amidst the continual pushing which accompanied the eddying of the ever-moving crowd, Gerard's little party became separated. He and Raymonde remained behind the others. They had begun talking together in low tones, with an air of smiling intimacy, lost and isolated as they were in the dense crowd. And Madame Desagneaux at last had to stop, look back, and call to them: "Come on, or we shall lose one another!"

As they drew near, Pierre heard the girl exclaim: "Mamma is so very busy; speak to her before we leave." And Gerard thereupon replied: "It is understood. You have made me very happy, mademoiselle."

Thus the husband had been secured, the marriage decided upon, during this charming promenade among the sights of Lourdes. Raymonde had completed her conquest, and Gerard had at last taken a resolution, realising how gay and sensible she was, as she walked beside him leaning on his arm.

M. de Guersaint, however, had raised his eyes, and was heard inquiring: "Are not those people up there, on that balcony, the rich folk who made the journey in the same train as ourselves?—You know whom I mean, that lady who is so very ill, and whose husband and sister accompany her?"

He was alluding to the Dieulafays; and they indeed were the persons whom he now saw on the balcony of a suite of rooms which they had rented in a new house overlooking the lawns of the Rosary. They here occupied a first-floor, furnished with all the luxury that Lourdes could provide, carpets, hangings, mirrors, and many other things, without mentioning a staff of servants despatched beforehand from Paris. As the weather was so fine that afternoon, the large armchair on which lay the poor ailing woman had been rolled on to the balcony. You could see her there, clad in a lace *peignoir*. Her husband, always correctly attired in a black frock-coat, stood beside her on her right hand, whilst her sister, in a delightful pale mauve gown, sat on her left smiling and leaning over every now and then so as to speak to her, but apparently receiving no reply.

"Oh!" declared little Madame Desagneaux, "I have often heard people speak of Madame Jousseur, that lady in mauve. She is the wife of a diplomatist who neglects her, it seems, in spite of her great beauty; and last year there was a deal of talk about her fancy for a young colonel who is well known in Parisian society. It is said, however, in Catholic *salons* that her religious principles enabled her to conquer it."

They all five remained there, looking up at the balcony. "To think," resumed Madame Desagneaux, "that her sister, poor woman, was once her living portrait." And, indeed, there was an expression of greater kindliness and more gentle gaiety on Madame Dieulafay's face. And now you see her—no different from a dead woman except that she is above instead of under ground—with her flesh wasted away, reduced to a livid, boneless thing which they scarcely dare to move. Ah! the unhappy woman!

Raymonde thereupon assured the others that Madame Dieulafay, who had been married scarcely two years previously, had brought all the jewellery given her on the occasion of her wedding to offer it as a gift to Our Lady of Lourdes; and Gerard confirmed this assertion, saying that the jewellery had been handed over to the treasurer of the Basilica that very morning with a golden lantern studded with gems and a large sum of money destined for the relief of the poor. However, the Blessed Virgin could not have been touched as yet, for the sufferer's condition seemed, if anything, to be worse.

From that moment Pierre no longer beheld aught save that young woman on that handsome balcony, that woeful, wealthy creature lying there high above the merry-making throng, the Lourdes mob which was feasting and laughing in the Sunday sunshine. The two dear ones who were so tenderly watching over her—her sister who had forsaken her society triumphs, her husband who had forgotten his financial business, his millions dispersed throughout the world—increased, by their irreproachable demeanour, the woefulness of the group which they thus formed high above all other heads, and face to face with the lovely valley. For Pierre they alone remained; and they were exceedingly wealthy and exceedingly wretched.

However, lingering in this wise on the footway with their eyes upturned, the five promenaders narrowly escaped being knocked down and run over, for at every moment fresh vehicles were coming up, for the most part landaus drawn by four horses, which were driven at a fast trot, and whose bells jingled merrily. The occupants of these carriages were tourists, visitors to the waters of Pau, Bareges, and Cauterets, whom curiosity had attracted to Lourdes, and who were delighted with the fine weather and quite inspirited by their rapid drive across the mountains. They would remain at Lourdes only a few hours; after hastening to the Grotto and the Basilica in seaside costumes, they would start off again, laughing, and well pleased at having seen it all. In this wise families in light attire, bands of young women with bright parasols, darted hither and thither among the grey, neutral-tinted crowd of pilgrims, imparting to it, in a yet more pronounced manner, the aspect of a fair-day mob, amidst which folks of good society deign to come and amuse themselves.

All at once Madame Desagneaux raised a cry "What, is it you, Berthe?" And thereupon she embraced a tall, charming brunette who had just alighted from a landau with three other young women, the whole party smiling and animated. Everyone began talking at once, and all sorts of merry exclamations rang out, in the delight they felt at meeting in this fashion. "Oh! we are at Cauterets, my dear," said the tall brunette. "And as everybody comes here, we decided to come all four together. And your husband, is he here with you?"

Madame Desagneaux began protesting: "Of course not," said she. "He is at Trouville, as you ought to know. I shall start to join him on Thursday."

"Yes, yes, of course," resumed the tall brunette, who, like her friend, seemed to be an amiable, giddy creature, "I was forgetting; you are here with the pilgrimage."

Then Madame Desagneaux offered to guide her friends, promising to show them everything of interest in less than a couple of hours; and turning to Raymonde, who stood by, smiling, she added "Come with us, my dear; your mother won't be anxious."

The ladies and Pierre and M. de Guersaint thereupon exchanged bows: and Gerard also took leave, tenderly pressing Raymonde's hand, with his eyes fixed on hers, as though to pledge himself definitively. The women swiftly departed, directing their steps towards the Grotto, and when Gerard also had gone off, returning to his duties, M. de Guersaint said to Pierre: "And the hairdresser on the Place du Marcadal, I really must go and see him. You will come with me, won't you?"

"Of course I will go wherever you like. I am quite at your disposal as Marie does not need us."

II. THE "ORDINARY."

Following the pathways between the large lawns which stretch out in front of the Rosary, they reached the new bridge, where they had another encounter, this time with Abbe des Hermoises, who was acting as guide to two young married ladies who had arrived that morning from Tarbes. Walking between them with the gallant air of a society priest, he was showing them Lourdes and explaining it to them, keeping them well away, however, from its more repugnant features, its poor and its ailing folk, its odour of low misery, which, it must be admitted, had well-nigh disappeared that fine, sunshiny day. At the first word which M. de Guersaint addressed to him with respect to the hiring of a vehicle for the trip to Gavarnie, the Abbe was seized with a dread lest he should be obliged to leave his pretty lady-visitors: "As you please, my dear sir," he replied. "Kindly attend to the matter, and—you are quite right, make the cheapest arrangements possible, for I shall have two ecclesiastics of small means with me. There will be four of us. Let me know at the hotel this evening at what hour we shall start."

Thereupon he again joined his lady-friends, and led them towards the Grotto, following the shady path which skirts the Gave, a cool, sequestered path well suited for lovers' walks.

Feeling somewhat tired, Pierre had remained apart from the others, leaning against the parapet of the new bridge. And now for the first time he was struck by the prodigious number of priests among the crowd. He saw all varieties of them swarming across the bridge: priests of correct mien who had come with the pilgrimage and who could be recognised by their air of assurance and their clean cassocks; poor village priests who were far more timid and badly clothed, and who, after making sacrifices in order that they might indulge in the journey, would return home quite scared and, finally, there was the whole crowd of unattached ecclesiastics who had come nobody knew whence, and who enjoyed such absolute liberty that it was difficult to be sure whether they had even said their mass that morning. They doubtless found this liberty very agreeable; and thus the greater number of them, like Abbe des Hermoises, had simply come on a holiday excursion, free from all duties, and happy at being able to live like ordinary men, lost, unnoticed as they were in the multitude around them. And from the young, carefully groomed and perfumed priest, to the old one in a dirty cassock and shoes down at heel, the entire species had its representative in the throng—there were corpulent ones, others but moderately fat, thin ones, tall ones and short ones, some whom faith had brought and whom ardour was consuming, some also who simply plied their calling like worthy men, and some, moreover, who were fond of intriguing, and who were only present in order that they might help the good cause. However, Pierre was quite surprised to see such a stream of priests pass before him, each with his special passion, and one and all hurrying to the Grotto as one hurries to a duty, a belief, a pleasure, or a task. He noticed one among the number, a very short, slim, dark man with a pronounced Italian accent, whose glittering eyes seemed to be taking a plan of Lourdes, who looked, indeed, like one of those spies who come and peer around with a view to conquest; and then he observed another one, an enormous fellow with a paternal air, who was breathing hard through inordinate eating, and who paused in front of a poor sick woman, and ended by slipping a five-franc piece into her hand.

Just then, however, M. de Guersaint returned: "We merely have to go down the boulevard and the Rue Basse," said he.

Pierre followed him without answering. He had just felt his cassock on his shoulders for the first time that afternoon, for never had it seemed so light to him as whilst he was walking about amidst the scramble of the pilgrimage. The young fellow was now living in a state of mingled unconsciousness and dizziness, ever hoping that faith would fall upon him like a lightning flash, in spite of all the vague uneasiness which was growing within him at sight of the things which he beheld. However, the spectacle of that ever-swelling stream of priests no longer wounded his heart; fraternal feelings towards these unknown colleagues had returned to him; how many of them there must be who believed no more than he did himself, and yet, like himself, honestly fulfilled their mission as guides and consolers!

"This boulevard is a new one, you know," said M. de Guersaint, all at once raising his voice. "The number of houses built during the last twenty years is almost beyond belief. There is quite a new town here."

The Lapaca flowed along behind the buildings on their right and, their curiosity inducing them to turn into a narrow lane, they came upon some strange old structures on the margin of the narrow stream. Several ancient mills here displayed their wheels; among them one which Monseigneur Laurence had given to Bernadette's parents after the apparitions. Tourists, moreover, were here shown the pretended abode of Bernadette, a hovel whither the Soubirous family had removed on leaving the Rue des Petits Fosses, and in which the young girl, as she was already boarding with the Sisters of Nevers, can have but seldom slept. At last, by way of the Rue Basse, Pierre and his companion reached the Place du Marcadal.

This was a long, triangular, open space, the most animated and luxurious of the squares of the old town, the one where the cafes, the chemists, all the finest shops were situated. And, among the latter, one showed conspicuously, coloured as it was a lively green, adorned with lofty mirrors, and surmounted by a broad board bearing in gilt letters the inscription: "Cazaban, Hairdresser".

M. de Guersaint and Pierre went in, but there was nobody in the salon and they had to wait. A terrible clatter of forks resounded from the adjoining room, an ordinary dining-room transformed into a *table d'hote*, in which some twenty people were having *dejeuner* although it was already two o'clock. The afternoon was progressing, and yet people were still eating from one to the other end of Lourdes. Like every other householder in the town, whatever his religious convictions might be, Cazaban, in the pilgrimage season, let his bedrooms, surrendered his dining-room, end sought refuge in his cellar, where, heaped up with his family, he ate and slept, although this unventilated hole was no more than three yards square. However, the passion for trading and moneymaking carried all before it; at pilgrimage time the whole population disappeared like that of a conquered city, surrendering even the beds of its women and its children to the pilgrims, seating them at its tables, and supplying them with food.

"Is there nobody here?" called M. de Guersaint after waiting a moment.

At last a little man made his appearance, Cazaban himself, a type of the knotty but active Pyrenean, with a long face, prominent cheek-bones, and a sunburned complexion spotted here and there with red. His big, glittering eyes never remained still; and the whole of his spare little figure quivered with incessant exuberance of speech and gesture.

II. THE "ORDINARY."

"For you, monsieur—a shave, eh?" said he. "I must beg your pardon for keeping you waiting; but my assistant has gone out, and I was in there with my boarders. If you will kindly sit down, I will attend to you at once."

Thereupon, deigning to operate in person, Cazaban began to stir up the lather and strop the razor. He had glanced rather nervously, however, at the cassock worn by Pierre, who without a word had seated himself in a corner and taken up a newspaper in the perusal of which he appeared to be absorbed.

A short interval of silence followed; but it was fraught with suffering for Cazaban, and whilst lathering his customer's chin he began to chatter: "My boarders lingered this morning such a long time at the Grotto, monsieur, that they have scarcely sat down to *dejeuner*. You can hear them, eh? I was staying with them out of politeness. However, I owe myself to my customers as well, do I not? One must try to please everybody."

M. de Guersaint, who also was fond of a chat, thereupon began to question him: "You lodge some of the pilgrims, I suppose?"

"Oh! we all lodge some of them, monsieur; it is necessary for the town," replied the barber.

"And you accompany them to the Grotto?"

At this, however, Cazaban revolted, and, holding up his razor, he answered with an air of dignity "Never, monsieur, never! For five years past I have not been in that new town which they are building."

He was still seeking to restrain himself, and again glanced at Pierre, whose face was hidden by the newspaper. The sight of the red cross pinned on M. de Guersaint's jacket was also calculated to render him prudent; nevertheless his tongue won the victory. "Well, monsieur, opinions are free, are they not?" said he. "I respect yours, but for my part I don't believe in all that phantasmagoria! Oh I've never concealed it! I was already a republican and a freethinker in the days of the Empire. There were barely four men of those views in the whole town at that time. Oh! I'm proud of it."

He had begun to shave M. de Guersaint's left cheek and was quite triumphant. From that moment a stream of words poured forth from his mouth, a stream which seemed to be inexhaustible. To begin with, he brought the same charges as Majeste against the Fathers of the Grotto. He reproached them for their dealings in tapers, chaplets, prints, and crucifixes, for the disloyal manner in which they competed with those who sold those articles as well as with the hotel and lodging-house keepers. And he was also wrathful with the Blue Sisters of the Immaculate Conception, for had they not robbed him of two tenants, two old ladies, who spent three weeks at Lourdes each year? Moreover you could divine within him all the slowly accumulated, overflowing spite with which the old town regarded the new town—that town which had sprung up so quickly on the other side of the castle, that rich city with houses as big as palaces, whither flowed all the life, all the luxury, all the money of Lourdes, so that it was incessantly growing larger and wealthier, whilst its elder sister, the poor, antique town of the mountains, with its narrow, grass-grown, deserted streets, seemed near the point of death. Nevertheless the struggle still continued; the old town seemed determined not to die, and, by lodging pilgrims and opening shops on her side, endeavoured to compel her ungrateful junior to grant her a share of the spoils. But custom only flowed to the shops which were near the Grotto, and only the poorer pilgrims were willing to lodge so far away; so that the unequal conditions of the struggle intensified the rupture and turned the high town and the low town into two irreconcilable enemies, who preyed upon one another amidst continual intrigues.

"Ah, no! They certainly won't see me at their Grotto," resumed Cazaban, with his rageful air. "What an abusive use they make of that Grotto of theirs! They serve it up in every fashion! To think of such idolatry, such gross superstition in the nineteenth century! Just ask them if they have cured a single sufferer belonging to the town during the last twenty years! Yet there are plenty of infirm people crawling about our streets. It was our folk that benefited by the first miracles; but it would seem that the miraculous water has long lost all its power, so far as we are concerned. We are too near it; people have to come from a long distance if they want it to act on them. It's really all too stupid; why, I wouldn't go there even if I were offered a hundred francs!"

Pierre's immobility was doubtless irritating the barber. He had now begun to shave M. de Guersaint's right cheek; and was inveighing against the Fathers of the Immaculate Conception, whose greed for gain was the one cause of all the misunderstanding. These Fathers who were at home there, since they had purchased from the Municipality the land on which they desired to build, did not even carry out the stipulations of the contract they had signed, for there were two clauses in it forbidding all trading, such as the sale of the water and of religious articles. Innumerable actions might have been brought against them. But they snapped their fingers, and felt themselves so powerful that they no longer allowed a single offering to go to the parish, but arranged matters so that the whole harvest of money should be garnered by the Grotto and the Basilica.

And, all at once, Cazaban candidly exclaimed: "If they were only reasonable, if they would only share with us!" Then, when M. de Guersaint had washed his face, and reseated himself, the hairdresser resumed: "And if I were to tell you, monsieur, what they have done with our poor town! Forty years ago all the young girls here conducted themselves properly, I assure you. I remember that in my young days when a young man was wicked he generally had to go elsewhere. But times have changed, our manners are no longer the same. Nowadays nearly all the girls content themselves with selling candles and nosegays; and you must have seen them catching hold of the passers-by and thrusting their goods into their hands! It is really shameful to see so many bold girls about! They make a lot of money, acquire lazy habits, and, instead of working during the winter, simply wait for the return of the pilgrimage season. And I assure you that the young men don't need to go elsewhere nowadays. No, indeed! And add to all this the suspicious floating element which swells the population as soon as the first fine weather sets in—the coachmen, the hawkers, the cantine keepers, all the low-class, wandering folk reeking with grossness and vice—and you can form an idea of the honest new town which they have given us with the crowds that come to their Grotto and their Basilica!"

Greatly struck by these remarks, Pierre had let his newspaper fall and begun to listen. It was now, for the first time, that he fully realised the difference between the two Lourdes—old Lourdes so honest and so pious in its tranquil solitude, and new Lourdes corrupted, demoralised by the circulation of so much money, by such a great enforced increase of wealth, by the ever-growing torrent of strangers sweeping through it, by the fatal rotting influence of the conflux of thousands of people, the contagion of evil examples. And what a terrible result it seemed when one thought of

Bernadette, the pure, candid girl kneeling before the wild primitive grotto, when one thought of all the naive faith, all the fervent purity of those who had first begun the work! Had they desired that the whole countryside should be poisoned in this wise by lucre and human filth? Yet it had sufficed that the nations should flock there for a pestilence to break out.

Seeing that Pierre was listening, Cazaban made a final threatening gesture as though to sweep away all this poisonous superstition. Then, relapsing into silence, he finished cutting M. de Guersaint's hair.

"There you are, monsieur!"

The architect rose, and it was only now that he began to speak of the conveyance which he wished to hire. At first the hairdresser declined to enter into the matter, pretending that they must apply to his brother at the Champ Commun; but at last he consented to take the order. A pair-horse landau for Gavarnie was priced at fifty francs. However, he was so pleased at having talked so much, and so flattered at hearing himself called an honest man, that he eventually agreed to charge only forty francs. There were four persons in the party, so this would make ten francs apiece. And it was agreed that they should start off at about two in the morning, so that they might get back to Lourdes at a tolerably early hour on the Monday evening.

"The landau will be outside the Hotel of the Apparitions at the appointed time," repeated Cazaban in his emphatic way. "You may rely on me, monsieur."

Then he began to listen. The clatter of crockery did not cease in the adjoining room. People were still eating there with that impulsive voracity which had spread from one to the other end of Lourdes. And all at once a voice was heard calling for more bread.

"Excuse me," hastily resumed Cazaban, "my boarders want me." And thereupon he rushed away, his hands still greasy through fingering the comb.

The door remained open for a second, and on the walls of the dining-room Pierre espied various religious prints, and notably a view of the Grotto, which surprised him; in all probability, however, the hairdresser only hung these engravings there during the pilgrimage season by way of pleasing his boarders.

It was now nearly three o'clock. When the young priest and M. de Guersaint got outside they were astonished at the loud pealing of bells which was flying through the air. The parish church had responded to the first stroke of vespers chiming at the Basilica; and now all the convents, one after another, were contributing to the swelling peals. The crystalline notes of the bell of the Carmelites mingled with the grave notes of the bell of the Immaculate Conception; and all the joyous bells of the Sisters of Nevers and the Dominicans were jingling together. In this wise, from morning till evening on fine days of festivity, the chimes winged their flight above the house-roofs of Lourdes. And nothing could have been gayer than that sonorous melody resounding in the broad blue heavens above the gluttonous town, which had at last lunched, and was now comfortably digesting as it strolled about in the sunlight.

III. THE NIGHT PROCESSION

AS soon as night had fallen Marie, still lying on her bed at the Hospital of Our Lady of Dolours, became extremely impatient, for she had learnt from Madame de Jonquiere that Baron Suire had obtained from Father Fourcade the necessary permission for her to spend the night in front of the Grotto. Thus she kept on questioning Sister Hyacinthe, asking her: "Pray, Sister, is it not yet nine o'clock?"

"No, my child, it is scarcely half-past eight," was the reply. "Here is a nice woollen shawl for you to wrap round you at daybreak, for the Gave is close by, and the mornings are very fresh, you know, in these mountainous parts."

"Oh! but the nights are so lovely, Sister, and besides, I sleep so little here!" replied Marie; "I cannot be worse off out-of-doors. *Mon Dieu*, how happy I am; how delightful it will be to spend the whole night with the Blessed Virgin!"

The entire ward was jealous of her; for to remain in prayer before the Grotto all night long was the most ineffable of joys, the supreme beatitude. It was said that in the deep peacefulness of night the chosen ones undoubtedly beheld the Virgin, but powerful protection was needed to obtain such a favour as had been granted to Marie; for nowadays the reverend Fathers scarcely liked to grant it, as several sufferers had died during the long vigil, falling asleep, as it were, in the midst of their ecstasy.

"You will take the Sacrament at the Grotto tomorrow morning, before you are brought back here, won't you, my child?" resumed Sister Hyacinthe.

However, nine o'clock at last struck, and, Pierre not arriving, the girl wondered whether he, usually so punctual, could have forgotten her? The others were now talking to her of the night procession, which she would see from beginning to end if she only started at once. The ceremonies concluded with a procession every night, but the Sunday one was always the finest, and that evening, it was said, would be remarkably splendid, such, indeed, as was seldom seen. Nearly thirty thousand pilgrims would take part in it, each carrying a lighted taper: the nocturnal marvels of the sky would be revealed; the stars would descend upon earth. At this thought the sufferers began to bewail their fate; what a wretched lot was theirs, to be tied to their beds, unable to see any of those wonders.

At last Madame de Jonquiere approached Marie's bed. "My dear girl," said she, "here is your father with Monsieur l'Abbe."

Radiant with delight, the girl at once forgot her weary waiting. "Oh! pray let us make haste, Pierre," she exclaimed; "pray let us make haste!"

III. THE NIGHT PROCESSION

They carried her down the stairs, and the young priest harnessed himself to the little car, which gently rolled along, under the star-studded heavens, whilst M. de Guersaint walked beside it. The night was moonless, but extremely beautiful; the vault above looked like deep blue velvet, spangled with diamonds, and the atmosphere was exquisitely mild and pure, fragrant with the perfumes from the mountains. Many pilgrims were hurrying along the street, all bending their steps towards the Grotto, but they formed a discreet, pensive crowd, with naught of the fair-field, lounging character of the daytime throng. And, as soon as the Plateau de la Merlasse was reached, the darkness spread out, you entered into a great lake of shadows formed by the stretching lawns and lofty trees, and saw nothing rising on high save the black, tapering spire of the Basilica.

Pierre grew rather anxious on finding that the crowd became more and more compact as he advanced. Already on reaching the Place du Rosaire it was difficult to take another forward step. "There is no hope of getting to the Grotto yet awhile," he said. "The best course would be to turn into one of the pathways behind the pilgrims' shelter-house and wait there."

Marie, however, greatly desired to see the procession start. "Oh! pray try to go as far as the Gave," said she. "I shall then see everything from a distance; I don't want to go near."

M. de Guersaint, who was equally inquisitive, seconded this proposal. "Don't be uneasy," he said to Pierre. "I am here behind, and will take care to let nobody jostle her."

Pierre had to begin pulling the little vehicle again. It took him a quarter of an hour to pass under one of the arches of the inclined way on the left hand, so great was the crush of pilgrims at that point. Then, taking a somewhat oblique course, he ended by reaching the quay beside the Gave, where there were only some spectators standing on the sidewalk, so that he was able to advance another fifty yards. At last he halted, and backed the little car against the quay parapet, in full view of the Grotto. "Will you be all right here?" he asked.

"Oh yes, thank you. Only you must sit me up; I shall then be able to see much better."

M. de Guersaint raised her into a sitting posture, and then for his part climbed upon the stonework running from one to the other end of the quay. A mob of inquisitive people had already scaled it in part, like sight-seers waiting for a display of fireworks; and they were all raising themselves on tiptoe, and craning their necks to get a better view. Pierre himself at last grew interested, although there was, so far, little to see.

Some thirty thousand people were assembled, and, every moment there were fresh arrivals. All carried candles, the lower parts of which were wrapped in white paper, on which a picture of Our Lady of Lourdes was printed in blue ink. However, these candles were not yet lighted, and the only illumination that you perceived above the billowy sea of heads was the bright, forge-like glow of the taper-lighted Grotto. A great buzzing arose, whiffs of human breath blew hither and thither, and these alone enabled you to realise that thousands of serried, stifling creatures were gathered together in the black depths, like a living sea that was ever eddying and spreading. There were even people hidden away under the trees beyond the Grotto, in distant recesses of the darkness of which one had no suspicion.

At last a few tapers began to shine forth here and there, like sudden sparks of light spangling the obscurity at random. Their number rapidly increased, eyots of stars were formed, whilst at other points there were meteoric trails, milky ways, so to say, flowing midst the constellations. The thirty thousand tapers were being lighted one by one, their beams gradually increasing in number till they obscured the bright glow of the Grotto and spread, from one to the other end of the promenade, the small yellow flames of a gigantic brasier.

"Oh! how beautiful it is, Pierre!" murmured Marie; "it is like the resurrection of the humble, the bright awakening of the souls of the poor."

"It is superb, superb!" repeated M. de Guersaint, with impassioned artistic satisfaction. "Do you see those two trails of light yonder, which intersect one another and form a cross?"

Pierre's feelings, however, had been touched by what Marie had just said. He was reflecting upon her words. There was truth in them. Taken singly, those slender flames, those mere specks of light, were modest and unobtrusive, like the lowly; it was only their great number that supplied the effulgence, the sun-like resplendency. Fresh ones were continually appearing, farther and farther away, like waifs and strays. "Ah!" murmured the young priest, "do you see that one which has just begun to flicker, all by itself, far away—do you see it, Marie? Do you see how it floats and slowly approaches until it is merged in the great lake of light?"

In the vicinity of the Grotto one could see now as clearly as in the daytime. The trees, illumined from below, were intensely green, like the painted trees in stage scenery. Above the moving brasier were some motionless banners, whose embroidered saints and silken cords showed with vivid distinctness. And the great reflection ascended to the rock, even to the Basilica, whose spire now shone out, quite white, against the black sky; whilst the hillsides across the Gave were likewise brightened, and displayed the pale fronts of their convents amidst their sombre foliage.

There came yet another moment of uncertainty. The flaming lake, in which each burning wick was like a little wave, rolled its starry sparkling as though it were about to burst from its bed and flow away in a river. Then the banners began to oscillate, and soon a regular motion set in.

"Oh! so they won't pass this way!" exclaimed M. de Guersaint in a tone of disappointment.

Pierre, who had informed himself on the matter, thereupon explained that the procession would first of all ascend the serpentine road—constructed at great cost up the hillside—and that it would afterwards pass behind the Basilica, descend by the inclined way on the right hand, and then spread out through the gardens.

"Look!" said he; "you can see the foremost tapers ascending amidst the greenery."

Then came an enchanting spectacle. Little flickering lights detached themselves from the great bed of fire, and began gently rising, without it being possible for one to tell at that distance what connected them with the earth. They moved upward, looking in the darkness like golden particles of the sun. And soon they formed an oblique streak, a streak which suddenly twisted, then extended again until it curved once more. At last the whole hillside was streaked by a flaming zigzag, resembling those lightning flashes which you see falling from black skies in cheap engravings. But, unlike the lightning, the luminous trail did not fade away; the little lights still went onward in the same slow, gentle, gliding manner. Only for a moment, at rare intervals, was there a sudden eclipse; the procession, no doubt, was then passing behind some clump of trees. But, farther on, the tapers beamed forth afresh, rising heavenward by an intricate path, which incessantly diverged and then started upward again. At last, however, the time came when the lights no longer ascended, for they had reached the summit of the hill and had begun to disappear at the last turn of the road.

Exclamations were rising from the crowd. "They are passing behind the Basilica," said one. "Oh! it will take them twenty minutes before they begin coming down on the other side," remarked another. "Yes, madame," said a third, "there are thirty thousand of them, and an hour will go by before the last of them leaves the Grotto."

Ever since the start a sound of chanting had risen above the low rumbling of the crowd. The hymn of Bernadette was being sung, those sixty couplets between which the Angelic Salutation, with its all-besetting rhythm, was ever returning as a refrain. When the sixty couplets were finished they were sung again; and that lullaby of "Ave, ave, ave Maria!" came back incessantly, stupefying the mind, and gradually transporting those thousands of beings into a kind of wide-awake dream, with a vision of Paradise before their eyes. And, indeed, at night-time when they were asleep, their beds would rock to the eternal tune, which they still and ever continued singing.

"Are we going to stop here?" asked M. de Guersaint, who speedily got tired of remaining in any one spot. "We see nothing but the same thing over and over again."

Marie, who had informed herself by listening to what was said in the crowd, thereupon exclaimed: "You were quite right, Pierre; it would be much better to go back yonder under the trees. I so much wish to see everything."

"Yes, certainly; we will seek a spot whence you may see it all," replied the priest. "The only difficulty lies in getting away from here."

Indeed, they were now inclosed within the mob of sight-seers; and, in order to secure a passage, Pierre with stubborn perseverance had to keep on begging a little room for a suffering girl.

M. de Guersaint meantime brought up the rear, screening the little conveyance so that it might not be upset by the jostling; whilst Marie turned her head, still endeavouring to see the sheet of flame spread out before the Grotto, that lake of little sparkling waves which never seemed to diminish, although the procession continued to flow from it without a pause.

At last they all three found themselves out of the crowd, near one of the arches, on a deserted spot where they were able to breathe for a moment. They now heard nothing but the distant canticle with its besetting refrain, and they only saw the reflection of the tapers, hovering like a luminous cloud in the neighbourhood of the Basilica.

"The best plan would be to climb to the Calvary," said M. de Guersaint. "The servant at the hotel told me so this morning. From up there, it seems, the scene is fairy-like."

But they could not think of making the ascent. Pierre at once enumerated the difficulties. "How could we hoist ourselves to such a height with Marie's conveyance?" he asked. "Besides, we should have to come down again, and that would be dangerous work in the darkness amidst all the scrambling."

Marie herself preferred to remain under the trees in the gardens, where it was very mild. So they started off, and reached the esplanade in front of the great crowned statue of the Virgin. It was illuminated by means of blue and yellow globes which encompassed it with a gaudy splendour; and despite all his piety M. de Guersaint could not help finding these decorations in execrable taste.

"There!" exclaimed Marie, "a good place would be near those shrubs yonder."

She was pointing to a shrubbery near the pilgrims' shelter-house; and the spot was indeed an excellent one for their purpose, as it enabled them to see the procession come down by the gradient way on the left, and watch it as it passed between the lawns to the new bridge and back again. Moreover, a delightful freshness prevailed there by reason of the vicinity of the Gave. There was nobody there as yet, and one could enjoy deep peacefulness in the dense shade which fell from the big plane-trees bordering the path.

In his impatience to see the first tapers reappear as soon as they should have passed behind the Basilica, M. de Guersaint had risen on tiptoe. "I see nothing as yet," he muttered, "so whatever the regulations may be I shall sit on the grass for a moment. I've no strength left in my legs." Then, growing anxious about his daughter, he inquired: "Shall I cover you up? It is very cool here."

"Oh, no! I'm not cold, father!" answered Marie; "I feel so happy. It is long since I breathed such sweet air. There must be some roses about—can't you smell that delicious perfume?" And turning to Pierre she asked: "Where are the roses, my friend? Can you see them?"

When M. de Guersaint had seated himself on the grass near the little vehicle, it occurred to Pierre to see if there was not some bed of roses near at hand. But is was in vain that he explored the dark lawns; he could only distinguish sundry clumps of evergreens. And, as he passed in front of the pilgrims' shelter-house on his way back, curiosity prompted him to enter it.

This building formed a long and lofty hall, lighted by large windows upon two sides. With bare walls and a stone pavement, it contained no other furniture than a number of benches, which stood here and there in haphazard fashion. There was neither table nor shelf, so that the homeless pilgrims who had sought refuge there had piled up their baskets, parcels, and valises in the window embrasures. Moreover, the place was apparently empty; the poor folk that it sheltered had no doubt joined the procession. Nevertheless, although the door stood wide open, an almost unbearable smell reigned inside. The very walls seemed impregnated with an odour of poverty, and in spite of the bright sunshine which had prevailed during the day, the flagstones were quite damp, soiled and soaked with expectorations, spilt wine, and grease. This mess had been made by the poorer pilgrims, who with their dirty skins and wretched rags lived in the hall, eating and sleeping in heaps on the benches. Pierre speedily came to the conclusion that the pleasant smell of roses must emanate from some other spot; still, he was making the round of the hall, which was lighted by four smoky lanterns, and which he believed to be altogether unoccupied, when, against the left-hand wall, he was surprised to espy the vague figure of a woman in black, with what seemed to be a white parcel lying on her lap. She was all alone in that solitude, and did not stir; however, her eyes were wide open.

He drew near and recognised Madame Vincent. She addressed him in a deep, broken voice: "Rose has suffered so dreadfully to-day! Since daybreak she has not ceased moaning. And so, as she fell asleep a couple of hours ago, I haven't dared to stir for fear lest she should awake and suffer again."

Thus the poor woman remained motionless, martyr-mother that she was, having for long months held her daughter in her arms in this fashion, in the stubborn hope of curing her. In her arms, too, she had brought her to Lourdes; in her arms she had carried her to the Grotto; in her arms she had rocked her to sleep, having neither a room of her own, nor even a hospital bed at her disposal.

"Isn't the poor little thing any better?" asked Pierre, whose heart ached at the sight.

"No, Monsieur l'Abbe; no, I think not."

"But you are very badly off here on this bench. You should have made an application to the pilgrimage managers instead of remaining like this, in the street, as it were. Some accommodation would have been found for your little girl, at any rate; that's certain."

"Oh! what would have been the use of it, Monsieur l'Abbe? She is all right on my lap. And besides, should I have been allowed to stay with her? No, no, I prefer to have her on my knees; it seems to me that it will end by curing her." Two big tears rolled down the poor woman's motionless cheeks, and in her stifled voice she continued: "I am not penniless. I had thirty sous when I left Paris, and I still have ten left. All I need is a little bread, and she, poor darling, can no longer drink any milk even. I have enough to last me till we go back, and if she gets well again, oh! we shall be rich, rich, rich!"

She had leant forward while speaking, and by the flickering light of a lantern near by, gazed at Rose, who was breathing faintly, with parted lips. "You see how soundly she is sleeping," resumed the unhappy mother. "Surely the Blessed Virgin will take pity on her and cure her, won't she, Monsieur l'Abbe? We only have one day left; still, I don't despair; and I shall again pray all night long without moving from here. She will be cured to-morrow; we must live till then."

Infinite pity was filling the heart of Pierre, who, fearing that he also might weep, now went away. "Yes, yes, my poor woman, we must hope, still hope," said he, as he left her there among the scattered benches, in that deserted, malodorous hall, so motionless in her painful maternal passion as to hold her own breath, fearful lest the heaving of her bosom should awaken the poor little sufferer. And in deepest grief, with closed lips, she prayed ardently.

On Pierre returning to Marie's side, the girl inquired of him: "Well, and those roses? Are there any near here?"

He did not wish to sadden her by telling her what he had seen, so he simply answered: "No, I have searched the lawns; there are none."

"How singular!" she rejoined, in a thoughtful way. "The perfume is both so sweet and penetrating. You can smell it, can't you? At this moment it is wonderfully strong, as though all the roses of Paradise were flowering around us in the darkness."

A low exclamation from her father interrupted her. M. de Guersaint had risen to his feet again on seeing some specks of light shine out above the gradient ways on the left side of the Basilica. "At last! Here they come!" said he.

It was indeed the head of the procession again appearing; and at once the specks of light began to swarm and extend in long, wavering double files. The darkness submerged everything except these luminous points, which seemed to be at a great elevation, and to emerge, as it were, from the black depths of the Unknown. And at the same time the everlasting canticle was again heard, but so lightly, for the procession was far away, that it seemed as yet merely like the rustle of a coming storm, stirring the leaves of the trees.

"Ah! I said so," muttered M. de Guersaint; "one ought to be at the Calvary to see everything." With the obstinacy of a child he kept on returning to his first idea, again and again complaining that they had chosen "the worst possible place."

"But why don't you go up to the Calvary, papa?" at last said Marie. "There is still time. Pierre will stay here with me." And with a mournful laugh she added: "Go; you know very well that nobody will run away with me."

He at first refused to act upon the suggestion, but, unable to resist his desire, he all at once fell in with it. And he had to hasten his steps, crossing the lawns at a run. "Don't move," he called; "wait for me under the trees. I will tell you of all that I may see up there."

Then Pierre and Marie remained alone in that dim, solitary nook, whence came such a perfume of roses, albeit no roses could be found. And they did not speak, but in silence watched the procession, which was now coming down from the hill with a gentle, continuous, gliding motion.

A double file of quivering stars leapt into view on the left-hand side of the Basilica, and then followed the monumental, gradient way, whose curve is gradually described. At that distance you were still unable to see the pilgrims themselves, and you beheld simply those well-disciplined travelling lights tracing geometrical lines amidst the darkness. Under the deep blue heavens, even the buildings at first remained vague, forming but blacker patches against the sky. Little by little, however, as the number of candles increased, the principal architectural lines—the tapering spire of the Basilica, the cyclopean arches of the gradient ways, the heavy, squat facade of the Rosary—became more distinctly visible. And with that ceaseless torrent of bright sparks, flowing slowly downward with the stubborn persistence of a stream which has overflowed its banks and can be stopped by nothing, there came as it were an aurora, a growing, invading mass of light, which would at last spread its glory over the whole horizon.

"Look, look, Pierre!" cried Marie, in an access of childish joy. "There is no end of them; fresh ones are ever shining out."

Indeed, the sudden appearances of the little lights continued with mechanical regularity, as though some inexhaustible celestial source were pouring forth all those solar specks. The head of the procession had just reached the gardens, near the crowned statue of the Virgin, so that as yet the double file of flames merely outlined the curves of the Rosary and the broad inclined way. However, the approach of the multitude was foretokened by the perturbation of the atmosphere, by the gusts of human breath coming from afar; and particularly did the voices swell, the canticle of Bernadette surging with the clamour of a rising tide, through which, with rhythmical persistence, the refrain of "Ave, ave, ave Maria!" rolled ever in a louder key.

"Ah, that refrain!" muttered Pierre; "it penetrates one's very skin. It seems to me as though my whole body were at last singing it."

Again did Marie give vent to that childish laugh of hers. "It is true," said she; "it follows me about everywhere. I heard it the other night whilst I was asleep. And now it is again taking possession of me, rocking me, wafting me above the ground." Then she broke off to say: "Here they come, just across the lawn, in front of us."

III. THE NIGHT PROCESSION

The procession had entered one of the long, straight paths; and then, turning round the lawn by way of the Breton's Cross, it came back by a parallel path. It took more than a quarter of an hour to execute this movement, during which the double file of tapers resembled two long parallel streams of flame. That which ever excited one's admiration was the ceaseless march of this serpent of fire, whose golden coils crept so gently over the black earth, winding, stretching into the far distance, without the immense body ever seeming to end. There must have been some jostling and scrambling every now and then, for some of the luminous lines shook and bent as though they were about to break; but order was soon re-established, and then the slow, regular, gliding movement set in afresh. There now seemed to be fewer stars in the heavens; it was as though a milky way had fallen from on high, rolling its glittering dust of worlds, and transferring the revolutions of the planets from the empyrean to earth. A bluish light streamed all around; there was naught but heaven left; the buildings and the trees assumed a visionary aspect in the mysterious glow of those thousands of tapers, whose number still and ever increased.

A faint sigh of admiration came from Marie. She was at a loss for words, and could only repeat "How beautiful it is! *Mon Dieu*! how beautiful it is! Look, Pierre, is it not beautiful?"

However, since the procession had been going by at so short a distance from them it had ceased to be a rhythmic march of stars which no human hand appeared to guide, for amidst the stream of light they could distinguish the figures of the pilgrims carrying the tapers, and at times even recognise them as they passed. First they espied La Grivotte, who, exaggerating her cure, and repeating that she had never felt in better health, had insisted upon taking part in the ceremony despite the lateness of the hour; and she still retained her excited demeanour, her dancing gait in that cool night air, which often made her shiver. Then the Vignerons appeared; the father at the head of the party, raising his taper on high, and followed by Madame Vigneron and Madame Chaise, who dragged their weary legs; whilst little Gustave, quite worn out, kept on tapping the sanded path with his crutch, his right hand covered meantime with all the wax that had dripped upon it. Every sufferer who could walk was there, among others Elise Rouquet, who, with her bare red face, passed by like some apparition from among the damned. Others were laughing; Sophie Couteau, the little girl who had been miraculously healed the previous year, was quite forgetting herself, playing with her taper as though it were a switch. Heads followed heads without a pause, heads of women especially, more often with sordid, common features, but at times wearing an exalted expression, which you saw for a second ere it vanished amidst the fantastic illumination. And there was no end to that terrible march past; fresh pilgrims were ever appearing. Among them Pierre and Marie noticed yet another little black shadowy figure, gliding along in a discreet, humble way; it was Madame Maze, whom they would not have recognised if she had not for a moment raised her pale face, down which the tears were streaming.

"Look!" exclaimed Pierre; "the first tapers in the procession are reaching the Place du Rosaire, and I am sure that half of the pilgrims are still in front of the Grotto."

Marie had raised her eyes. Up yonder, on the left-hand side of the Basilica, she could see other lights incessantly appearing with that mechanical kind of movement which seemed as though it would never cease. "Ah!" she said, "how many, how many distressed souls there are! For each of those little flames is a suffering soul seeking deliverance, is it not?"

Pierre had to lean over in order to hear her, for since the procession had been streaming by, so near to them, they had been deafened by the sound of the endless canticle, the hymn of Bernadette. The voices of the pilgrims rang out more loudly than ever amidst the increasing vertigo; the couplets became jumbled together—each batch of processionists chanted a different one with the ecstatic voices of beings possessed, who can no longer hear themselves. There was a huge indistinct clamour, the distracted clamour of a multitude intoxicated by its ardent faith. And meantime the refrain of "Ave, ave, ave Maria!" was ever returning, rising, with its frantic, importunate rhythm, above everything else.

All at once Pierre and Marie, to their great surprise, saw M. de Guersaint before them again. "Ah! my children," he said, "I did not want to linger too long up there, I cut through the procession twice in order to get back to you. But what a sight, what a sight it is! It is certainly the first beautiful thing that I have seen since I have been here!" Thereupon he began to describe the procession as he had beheld it from the Calvary height. "Imagine," said he, "another heaven, a heaven down below reflecting that above, a heaven entirely filled by a single immense constellation. The swarming stars seem to be lost, to lie in dim faraway depths; and the trail of fire is in form like a monstrance—yes, a real monstrance, the base of which is outlined by the inclined ways, the stem by the two parallel paths, and the Host by the round lawn which crowns them. It is a monstrance of burning gold, shining out in the depths of the darkness with a perpetual sparkle of moving stars. Nothing else seems to exist; it is gigantic, paramount. I really never saw anything so extraordinary before!"

He was waving his arms, beside himself, overflowing with the emotion of an artist.

"Father dear," said Marie, tenderly, "since you have come back you ought to go to bed. It is nearly eleven o'clock, and you know that you have to start at two in the morning." Then, to render him compliant, she added: "I am so pleased that you are going to make that excursion! Only, come back early to-morrow evening, because you'll see, you'll see—" She stopped short, not daring to express her conviction that she would be cured.

"You are right; I will go to bed," replied M. de Guersaint, quite calmed. "Since Pierre will be with you I sha'n't feel anxious."

"But I don't wish Pierre to pass the night out here. He will join you by-and-by after he has taken me to the Grotto. I sha'n't have any further need of anybody; the first bearer who passes can take me back to the hospital to-morrow morning."

Pierre had not interrupted her, and now he simply said: "No, no, Marie, I shall stay. Like you, I shall spend the night at the Grotto."

She opened her mouth to insist and express her displeasure. But he had spoken those words so gently, and she had detected in them such a dolorous thirst for happiness, that, stirred to the depths of her soul, she stayed her tongue.

"Well, well, my children," replied her father, "settle the matter between you. I know that you are both very sensible. And now good-night, and don't be at all uneasy about me."

He gave his daughter a long, loving kiss, pressed the young priest's hands, and then went off, disappearing among the serried ranks of the procession, which he once more had to cross.

Then they remained alone in their dark, solitary nook under the spreading trees, she still sitting up in her box, and he kneeling on the grass, with his elbow resting on one of the wheels. And it was truly sweet to linger there while the tapers continued marching past, and, after a turning movement, assembled on the Place du Rosaire. What delighted Pierre was that nothing of all the daytime junketing remained. It seemed as though a purifying breeze had come down from the mountains, sweeping away all the odour of strong meats, the greedy Sunday delights, the scorching, pestilential, fair-field dust which, at an earlier hour, had hovered above the town. Overhead there was now only the vast sky, studded with pure stars, and the freshness of the Gave was delicious, whilst the wandering breezes were laden with the perfumes of wild flowers. The mysterious Infinite spread far around in the sovereign peacefulness of night, and nothing of materiality remained save those little candle-flames which the young priest's companion had compared to suffering souls seeking deliverance. All was now exquisitely restful, instinct with unlimited hope. Since Pierre had been there all the heart-rending memories of the afternoon, of the voracious appetites, the impudent simony, and the poisoning of the old town, had gradually left him, allowing him to savour the divine refreshment of that beautiful night, in which his whole being was steeped as in some revivifying water.

A feeling of infinite sweetness had likewise come over Marie, who murmured: "Ah! how happy Blanche would be to see all these marvels."

She was thinking of her sister, who had been left in Paris to all the worries of her hard profession as a teacher forced to run hither and thither giving lessons. And that simple mention of her sister, of whom Marie had not spoken since her arrival at Lourdes, but whose figure now unexpectedly arose in her mind's eye, sufficed to evoke a vision of all the past.

Then, without exchanging a word, Marie and Pierre lived their childhood's days afresh, playing together once more in the neighbouring gardens parted by the quickset hedge. But separation came on the day when he entered the seminary and when she kissed him on the cheeks, vowing that she would never forget him. Years went by, and they found themselves forever parted: he a priest, she prostrated by illness, no longer with any hope of ever being a woman. That was their whole story—an ardent affection of which they had long been ignorant, then absolute severance, as though they were dead, albeit they lived side by side. They again beheld the sorry lodging whence they had started to come to Lourdes after so much battling, so much discussion—his doubts and her passionate faith, which last had conquered. And it seemed to them truly delightful to find themselves once more quite alone together, in that dark nook on that lovely night, when there were as many stars upon earth as there were in heaven.

Marie had hitherto retained the soul of a child, a spotless soul, as her father said, good and pure among the purest. Stricken low in her thirteenth year, she had grown no older in mind. Although she was now three-and-twenty, she was still a child, a child of thirteen, who had retired within herself, absorbed in the bitter catastrophe which had annihilated her. You could tell this by the frigidity of her glance, by her absent expression, by the haunted air she ever wore, unable as she was to bestow a thought on anything but her calamity. And never was woman's soul more pure and candid, arrested as it had been in its development. She had had no other romance in life save that tearful farewell to her friend, which for ten long years had sufficed to fill her heart. During the endless days which she had spent on her couch of wretchedness, she had never gone beyond this dream—that if she had grown up in health, he doubtless would not have become a priest, in order to live near her. She never read any novels. The pious works which she was allowed to peruse maintained her in the excitement of a superhuman love. Even the rumours of everyday life died away at the door of the room where she lived in seclusion; and, in past years, when she had been taken from one to the other end of France, from one inland spa to another, she had passed through the crowds like a somnambulist who neither sees nor hears anything, possessed, as she was, by the idea of the calamity that had befallen her, the bond which made her a sexless thing. Hence her purity and childishness; hence she was but an adorable daughter of suffering, who, despite the growth of her sorry flesh, harboured nothing in her heart save that distant awakening of passion, the unconscious love of her thirteenth year.

Her hand sought Pierre's in the darkness, and when she found it, coming to meet her own, she, for a long time, continued pressing it. Ah! how sweet it was! Never before, indeed, had they tasted such pure and perfect joy in being together, far from the world, amidst the sovereign enchantment of darkness and mystery. Around them nothing subsisted, save the revolving stars. The lulling hymns were like the very vertigo that bore them away. And she knew right well that after spending a night of rapture at the Grotto, she would, on the morrow, be cured. Of this she was, indeed, absolutely convinced; she would prevail upon the Blessed Virgin to listen to her; she would soften her, as soon as she should be alone, imploring her face to face. And she well understood what Pierre had wished to say a short time previously, when expressing his desire to spend the whole night outside the Grotto, like herself. Was it not that he intended to make a supreme effort to believe, that he meant to fall upon his knees like a little child, and beg the all-powerful Mother to restore his lost faith? Without need of any further exchange of words, their clasped hands repeated all those things. They mutually promised that they would pray for each other, and so absorbed in each other did they become that they forgot themselves, with such an ardent desire for one another's cure and happiness, that for a moment they attained to the depths of the love which offers itself in sacrifice. It was divine enjoyment.

"Ah!" murmured Pierre, "how beautiful is this blue night, this infinite darkness, which has swept away all the hideousness of things and beings, this deep, fresh peacefulness, in which I myself should like to bury my doubts!"

His voice died away, and Marie, in her turn, said in a very low voice: "And the roses, the perfume of the roses? Can't you smell them, my friend? Where can they be since you could not see them?"

"Yes, yes, I smell them, but there are none," he replied. "I should certainly have seen them, for I hunted everywhere."

"How can you say that there are no roses when they perfume the air around us, when we are steeped in their aroma? Why, there are moments when the scent is so powerful that I almost faint with delight in inhaling it! They must certainly be here, innumerable, under our very feet."

III. THE NIGHT PROCESSION

"No, no," said Pierre, "I swear to you I hunted everywhere, and there are no roses. They must be invisible, or they may be the very grass we tread and the spreading trees that are around us; their perfume may come from the soil itself, from the torrent which flows along close by, from the woods and the mountains that rise yonder."

For a moment they remained silent. Then, in an undertone, she resumed: "How sweet they smell, Pierre! And it seems to me that even our clasped hands form a bouquet."

"Yes, they smell delightfully sweet; but it is from you, Marie, that the perfume now ascends, as though the roses were budding from your hair."

Then they ceased speaking. The procession was still gliding along, and at the corner of the Basilica bright sparks were still appearing, flashing suddenly from out of the obscurity, as though spurting from some invisible source. The vast train of little flames, marching in double file, threw a riband of light across the darkness. But the great sight was now on the Place du Rosaire, where the head of the procession, still continuing its measured evolutions, was revolving and revolving in a circle which ever grew smaller, with a stubborn whirl which increased the dizziness of the weary pilgrims and the violence of their chants. And soon the circle formed a nucleus, the nucleus of a nebula, so to say, around which the endless riband of fire began to coil itself. And the brasier grew larger and larger—there was first a pool, then a lake of light. The whole vast Place du Rosaire changed at last into a burning ocean, rolling its little sparkling wavelets with the dizzy motion of a whirlpool that never rested. A reflection like that of dawn whitened the Basilica; while the rest of the horizon faded into deep obscurity, amidst which you only saw a few stray tapers journeying alone, like glowworms seeking their way with the help of their little lights. However, a straggling rear-guard of the procession must have climbed the Calvary height, for up there, against the sky, some moving stars could also be seen. Eventually the moment came when the last tapers appeared down below, marched round the lawns, flowed away, and were merged in the sea of flame. Thirty thousand tapers were burning there, still and ever revolving, quickening their sparkles under the vast calm heavens where the planets had grown pale. A luminous glow ascended in company with the strains of the canticle which never ceased. And the roar of voices incessantly repeating the refrain of "Ave, ave, ave Maria!" was like the very crackling of those hearts of fire which were burning away in prayers in order that souls might be saved.

The candles had just been extinguished, one by one, and the night was falling again, paramount, densely black, and extremely mild, when Pierre and Marie perceived that they were still there, hand in hand, hidden away among the trees. In the dim streets of Lourdes, far off, there were now only some stray, lost pilgrims inquiring their way, in order that they might get to bed. Through the darkness there swept a rustling sound—the rustling of those who prowl and fall asleep when days of festivity draw to a close. But the young priest and the girl lingered in their nook forgetfully, never stirring, but tasting delicious happiness amidst the perfume of the invisible roses.

IV. THE VIGIL

WHEN Pierre dragged Marie in her box to the front of the Grotto, and placed her as near as possible to the railing, it was past midnight, and about a hundred persons were still there, some seated on the benches, but the greater number kneeling as though prostrated in prayer. The Grotto shone from afar, with its multitude of lighted tapers, similar to the illumination round a coffin, though all that you could distinguish was a star-like blaze, from the midst of which, with visionary whiteness, emerged the statue of the Virgin in its niche. The hanging foliage assumed an emerald sheen, the hundreds of crutches covering the vault resembled an inextricable network of dead wood on the point of reflowering. And the darkness was rendered more dense by so great a brightness, the surroundings became lost in a deep shadow in which nothing, neither walls nor trees, remained; whilst all alone ascended the angry and continuous murmur of the Gave, rolling along beneath the gloomy, boundless sky, now heavy with a gathering storm.

"Are you comfortable, Marie?" gently inquired Pierre. "Don't you feel chilly?"

She had just shivered. But it was only at a breath from the other world, which had seemed to her to come from the Grotto.

"No, no, I am so comfortable! Only place the shawl over my knees. And—thank you, Pierre—don't be anxious about me. I no longer require anyone now that I am with her."

Her voice died away, she was already falling into an ecstasy, her hands clasped, her eyes raised towards the white statue, in a beatific transfiguration of the whole of her poor suffering face.

Yet Pierre remained a few minutes longer beside her. He would have liked to wrap her in the shawl, for he perceived the trembling of her little wasted hands. But he feared to annoy her, so confined himself to tucking her in like a child; whilst she, slightly raised, with her elbows on the edges of her box, and her eyes fixed on the Grotto, no longer beheld him.

A bench stood near, and he had just seated himself upon it, intending to collect his thoughts, when his glance fell upon a woman kneeling in the gloom. Dressed in black, she was so slim, so discreet, so unobtrusive, so wrapt in darkness, that at first he had not noticed her. After a while, however, he recognised her as Madame Maze. The thought of the letter which she had received during the day then recurred to him. And the sight of her filled him with pity; he could feel for the forlornness of this solitary woman, who had no physical sore to heal, but only implored the Blessed Virgin to relieve her heart-pain by converting her inconstant husband. The letter had no doubt been some harsh reply, for, with bowed head, she seemed almost annihilated, filled with the humility of some poor beaten creature. It was only at night-time that she readily forgot herself there, happy at disappearing, at being able to weep, suffer martyrdom, and implore the return of the lost caresses, for hours together, without anyone suspecting her grievous secret. Her lips did not even move; it was her wounded heart which prayed, which desperately begged for its share of love and happiness.

Ah! that inextinguishable thirst for happiness which brought them all there, wounded either in body or in spirit; Pierre also felt it parching his throat, in an ardent desire to be quenched. He longed to cast himself upon his knees, to beg the divine aid with the same humble faith as that woman. But his limbs were as though tied; he could not find the words he wanted, and it was a relief when he at last felt someone touch him on the arm. "Come with me, Monsieur l'Abbe, if you do not know the Grotto," said a voice. "I will find you a place. It is so pleasant there at this time!"

He raised his head, and recognised Baron Suire, the director of the Hospitality of Our Lady of Salvation. This benevolent and simple man no doubt felt some affection for him. He therefore accepted his offer, and followed him into the Grotto, which was quite empty. The Baron had a key, with which he locked the railing behind them.

"You see, Monsieur l'Abbe," said he, "this is the time when one can really be comfortable here. For my part, whenever I come to spend a few days at Lourdes, I seldom retire to rest before daybreak, as I have fallen into the habit of finishing my night here. The place is deserted, one is quite alone, and is it not pleasant? How well one feels oneself to be in the abode of the Blessed Virgin!"

He smiled with a kindly air, doing the honours of the Grotto like an old frequenter of the place, somewhat enfeebled by age, but full of genuine affection for this delightful nook. Moreover, in spite of his great piety, he was in no way ill at ease there, but talked on and explained matters with the familiarity of a man who felt himself to be the friend of Heaven.

"Ah! you are looking at the tapers," he said. "There are about two hundred of them which burn together night and day; and they end by making the place warm. It is even warm here in winter."

Indeed, Pierre was beginning to feel incommoded by the warm odour of the wax. Dazzled by the brilliant light into which he was penetrating, he gazed at the large, central, pyramidal holder, all bristling with little tapers, and resembling a luminous clipped yew glistening with stars. In the background, a straight holder, on a level with the ground, upheld the large tapers, which, like the pipes of an organ, formed a row of uneven height, some of them being as large as a man's thigh. And yet other holders, resembling massive candelabra, stood here and there on the jutting parts of the rock. The vault of the Grotto sank towards the left, where the stone seemed baked and blackened by the eternal flames which had been heating it for years. And the wax was perpetually dripping like fine snow; the trays of the holders were smothered with it, whitened by its ever-thickening dust. In fact, it coated the whole rock, which had become quite greasy to the touch; and to such a degree did it cover the ground that accidents had occurred, and it had been necessary to spread some mats about to prevent persons from slipping.

"You see those large ones there," obligingly continued Baron Suire. "They are the most expensive and cost sixty francs apiece; they will continue burning for a month.

The smallest ones, which cost but five sous each, only last three hours. Oh! we don't husband them; we never run short. Look here! Here are two more hampers full, which there has not yet been time to remove to the storehouse."

Then he pointed to the furniture, which comprised a harmonium covered with a cloth, a substantial dresser with several large drawers in which the sacred vestments were kept, some benches and chairs reserved for the privileged few who were admitted during the ceremonies, and finally a very handsome movable altar, which was adorned with engraved silver plates, the gift of a great lady, and—for fear of injury from dampness—was only brought out on the occasions of remunerative pilgrimages.

Pierre was disturbed by all this well-meant chatter. His religious emotion lost some of its charm. In spite of his lack of faith, he had, on entering, experienced a feeling of agitation, a heaving of the soul, as though the mystery were about to be revealed to him. It was at the same time both an anxious and a delicious feeling. And he beheld things which deeply stirred him: bunches of flowers, lying in a heap at the Virgin's feet, with the votive offerings of children—little faded shoes, a tiny iron corselet, and a doll-like crutch which almost seemed to be a toy. Beneath the natural ogival cavity in which the apparition had appeared, at the spot where the pilgrims rubbed the chaplets and medals they wished to consecrate, the rock was quite worn away and polished. Millions of ardent lips had pressed kisses on the wall with such intensity of love that the stone was as though calcined, streaked with black veins, shining like marble.

However, he stopped short at last opposite a cavity in which lay a considerable pile of letters and papers of every description.

"Ah! I was forgetting," hastily resumed Baron Suire; "this is the most interesting part of it. These are the letters which the faithful throw into the Grotto through the railing every day. We gather them up and place them there; and in the winter I amuse myself by glancing through them. You see, we cannot burn them without opening them, for they often contain money—francs, half-francs, and especially postage-stamps."

He stirred up the letters, and, selecting a few at random, showed the addresses, and opened them to read. Nearly all of them were letters from illiterate persons, with the superscription, "To Our Lady of Lourdes," scrawled on the envelopes in big, irregular handwriting. Many of them contained requests or thanks, incorrectly worded and wondrously spelt; and nothing was more affecting than the nature of some of the petitions: a little brother to be saved, a lawsuit to be gained, a lover to be preserved, a marriage to be effected. Other letters, however, were angry ones, taking the Blessed Virgin to task for not having had the politeness to acknowledge a former communication by granting the writer's prayers. Then there were still others, written in a finer hand, with carefully worded phrases containing confessions and fervent entreaties; and these were from women who confided to the Queen of Heaven things which they dared not even say to a priest in the shadow of the confessional. Finally, one envelope, selected at random, merely contained a photograph; a young girl had sent her portrait to Our Lady of Lourdes, with this dedication: "To my good Mother." In short, they every day received the correspondence of a most powerful Queen, to whom both prayers and secrets were addressed, and who was expected to reply with favours and kindnesses of every kind. The franc and half-franc pieces were simple tokens of love to propitiate her; while, as for the postage-stamps, these could only be sent for convenience' sake, in lieu of coined money; unless, indeed, they were sent guilelessly, as in the case of a peasant woman who had added a postscript to her letter to say that she enclosed a stamp for the reply.

"I can assure you," concluded the Baron, "that there are some very nice ones among them, much less foolish than you might imagine. During a period of three years I constantly found some very interesting letters from a lady who did nothing without relating it to the Blessed Virgin. She was a married woman, and entertained a most dangerous passion for a friend of her husband's. Well, Monsieur l'Abbe, she overcame it; the Blessed Virgin answered her by sending her an armour for her chastity, an all-divine power to resist the promptings of her heart." Then he broke off to say: "But come and seat yourself here, Monsieur l'Abbe. You will see how comfortable you will be."

Pierre went and placed himself beside him on a bench on the left hand, at the spot where the rock sloped down. This was a deliciously reposeful corner, and neither the one nor the other spoke; a profound silence had ensued, when, behind him, Pierre heard an indistinct murmur, a light crystalline voice, which seemed to come from the Invisible. He gave a start, which Baron Suire understood.

"That is the spring which you hear," said he; "it is there, underground, below this grating. Would you like to see it?"

And without waiting for Pierre's reply, he at once bent down to open one of the iron plates protecting the spring, mentioning that it was thus closed up in order to prevent freethinkers from throwing poison into it. For a moment this extraordinary idea quite amazed the priest; but he ended by attributing it entirely to the Baron, who was, indeed, very childish. The latter, meantime, was vainly struggling with the padlock, which opened by a combination of letters, and refused to yield to his endeavours. "It is singular," he muttered; "the word is *Rome*, and I am positive that it hasn't been changed. The damp destroys everything. Every two years or so we are obliged to replace those crutches up there, otherwise they would all rot away. Be good enough to bring me a taper."

By the light of the candle which Pierre then took from one of the holders, he at last succeeded in unfastening the brass padlock, which was covered with *vert-de-gris*. Then, the plate having been raised, the spring appeared to view. Upon a bed of muddy gravel, in a fissure of the rock, there was a limpid stream, quite tranquil, but seemingly spreading over a rather large surface. The Baron explained that it had been necessary to conduct it to the fountains through pipes coated with cement; and he even admitted that, behind the piscinas, a large cistern had been dug in which the water was collected during the night, as otherwise the small output of the source would not suffice for the daily requirements.

"Will you taste it?" he suddenly asked. "It is much better here, fresh from the earth."

Pierre did not answer; he was gazing at that tranquil, innocent water, which assumed a moire-like golden sheen in the dancing light of the taper. The falling drops of wax now and again ruffled its surface. And, as he gazed at it, the young priest pondered upon all the mystery it brought with it from the distant mountain slopes.

"Come, drink some!" said the Baron, who had already dipped and filled a glass which was kept there handy. The priest had no choice but to empty it; it was good pure, water, fresh and transparent, like that which flows from all the lofty uplands of the Pyrenees.

After refastening the padlock, they both returned to the bench. Now and again Pierre could still hear the spring flowing behind him, with a music resembling the gentle warble of some unseen bird. And now the Baron again raised his voice, giving him the history of the Grotto at all times and seasons, in a pathetic babble, replete with puerile details.

The summer was the roughest season, for then came the great itinerant pilgrimage crowds, with the uproarious fervour of thousands of eager beings, all praying and vociferating together. But with the autumn came the rain, those diluvial rains which beat against the Grotto entrance for days together; and with them arrived the pilgrims from remote countries, small, silent, and ecstatic bands of Indians, Malays, and even Chinese, who fell upon their knees in the mud at the sign from the missionaries accompanying them. Of all the old provinces of France, it was Brittany that sent the most devout pilgrims, whole parishes arriving together, the men as numerous as the women, and all displaying a pious deportment, a simple and unostentatious faith, such as might edify the world. Then came the winter, December with its terrible cold, its dense snow-drifts blocking the mountain ways. But even then families put up at the hotels, and, despite everything, faithful worshippers—all those who, fleeing the noise of the world, wished to speak to the Virgin in the tender intimacy of solitude—still came every morning to the Grotto. Among them were some whom no one knew, who appeared directly they felt certain they would be alone there to kneel and love like jealous lovers; and who departed, frightened away by the first suspicion of a crowd. And how warm and pleasant the place was throughout the foul winter weather! In spite of rain and wind and snow, the Grotto still continued flaring. Even during nights of howling tempest, when not a soul was there, it lighted up the empty darkness, blazing like a brasier of love that nothing could extinguish. The Baron related that, at the time of the heavy snowfall of the previous winter, he had spent whole afternoons there, on the bench where they were then seated. A gentle warmth prevailed, although the spot faced the north and was never reached by a ray of sunshine. No doubt the circumstance of the burning tapers continually heating the rock explained this generous warmth; but might one not also believe in some charming kindness on the part of the Virgin, who endowed the spot with perpetual springtide? And the little birds were well aware of it; when the snow on the ground froze their feet, all the finches of the neighbourhood sought shelter there, fluttering about in the ivy around the holy statue. At length came the awakening of the real spring: the Gave, swollen with melted snow, and rolling on with a voice of thunder: the trees, under the action of their sap, arraying themselves in a mantle of greenery, whilst the crowds, once more returning, noisily invaded the sparkling Grotto, whence they drove the little birds of heaven.

"Yes, yes," repeated Baron Suire, in a declining voice, "I spent some most delightful winter days here all alone. I saw no one but a woman, who leant against the railing to avoid kneeling in the snow. She was quite young, twenty-five perhaps, and very pretty—dark, with magnificent blue eyes. She never spoke, and did not even seem to pray, but remained there for hours together, looking intensely sad. I do not know who she was, nor have I ever seen her since."

He ceased speaking; and when, a couple of minutes later, Pierre, surprised at his silence, looked at him, he perceived that he had fallen asleep. With his hands clasped upon his belly, his chin resting on his chest, he slept as peacefully as a child, a smile hovering the while about his mouth. Doubtless, when he said that he spent the night there, he meant that he came thither to indulge in the early nap of a happy old man, whose dreams are of the angels. And now Pierre tasted all the charms of the solitude. It was indeed true that a feeling of peacefulness and comfort permeated the soul in this rocky nook. It was occasioned by the somewhat stifling fumes of the burning wax, by the transplendent ecstasy into which one sank amidst the glare of the tapers. The young priest could no longer distinctly see the crutches on the roof, the votive offerings hanging from the sides, the altar of engraved silver, and the harmonium in its wrapper, for a slow intoxication seemed to be stealing over him, a gradual prostration of his whole being. And he particularly experienced the divine sensation of having left the living world, of having attained to the far realms of the marvellous and the superhuman, as though that simple iron railing yonder had become the very barrier of the Infinite.

However, a slight noise on his left again disturbed him. It was the spring flowing, ever flowing on, with its bird-like warble. Ah! how he would have liked to fall upon his knees and believe in the miracle, to acquire a certain conviction that that divine water had gushed from the rock solely for the healing of suffering humanity. Had he not come there to prostrate himself and implore the Virgin to restore the faith of his childhood? Why, then, did he not pray, why did he not beseech her to bring him back to grace? His feeling of suffocation increased, the burning tapers dazzled him almost to the point of giddiness. And, all at once, the recollection came to him that for two days past, amidst the great freedom which priests enjoyed at Lourdes, he had neglected to say his mass. He was in a state of sin, and perhaps it was the weight of this transgression which was oppressing his heart. He suffered so much that he was at last compelled to rise from his seat and walk away. He gently closed the gate behind him, leaving Baron Suire still asleep do the bench. Marie, he found, had not stirred, but was still raised on her elbows, with her ecstatic eyes uplifted towards the figure of the Virgin.

"How are you, Marie?" asked Pierre. "Don't you feel cold?"

She did not reply. He felt her hands and found them warm and soft, albeit slightly trembling. "It is not the cold which makes you tremble, is it, Marie?" he asked.

In a voice as gentle as a zephyr she replied: "No, no! let me be; I am so happy! I shall see her, I feel it. Ah! what joy!"

So, after slightly pulling up her shawl, he went forth into the night, a prey to indescribable agitation. Beyond the bright glow of the Grotto was a night as black as ink, a region of darkness, into which he plunged at random. Then, as his eyes became accustomed to this gloom, he found himself near the Gave, and skirted it, following a path shaded by tall trees, where he again came upon a refreshing obscurity. This shade and coolness, both so soothing, now brought him relief. And his only surprise was that he had not fallen on his knees in the Grotto, and prayed, even as Marie was praying, with all the power of his soul. What could be the obstacle within him? Whence came the irresistible revolt which prevented him from surrendering himself to faith even when his overtaxed, tortured being longed to yield? He understood well enough that it was his reason alone which protested, and the time had come when he would gladly have killed that voracious reason, which was devouring his life and preventing him from enjoying the happiness allowed to the ignorant and the simple.

Perhaps, had he beheld a miracle, he might have acquired enough strength of will to believe. For instance, would he not have bowed himself down, vanquished at last, if Marie had suddenly risen up and walked before him. The scene which he conjured up of Marie saved, Marie cured, affected him so deeply that he stopped short, his trembling arms uplifted towards the star-spangled vault of heaven. What a lovely night it was!—so deep and mysterious, so airy and fragrant; and what joy rained down at the hope that eternal health might be restored, that eternal love might ever revive, even as spring returns! Then he continued his walk, following the path to the end. But his doubts were again coming back to him; when you need a miracle to gain belief, it means that you are incapable of believing. There is no need for the Almighty to prove His existence. Pierre also felt uneasy at the thought that, so long as he had not discharged his priestly duties by saying his mass, his prayers would not be answered. Why did he not go at once to the church of the Rosary, whose altars, from midnight till noon, are placed at the disposal of the priests who come from a distance? Thus thinking, he descended by another path, again finding himself beneath the trees, near the leafy spot whence he and Marie had watched the procession of tapers. Not a light now remained, there was but a boundless expanse of gloom.

Here Pierre experienced a fresh attack of faintness, and as though to gain time, he turned mechanically into the pilgrims' shelter-house. Its door had remained wide open; still this failed to sufficiently ventilate the spacious hall, which was now full of people. On the very threshold Pierre felt oppressed by the stifling heat emanating from the multitude of bodies, the dense pestilential smell of human breath and perspiration. The smoking lanterns gave out so bad a light that he had to pick his way with extreme care in order to avoid treading upon outstretched limbs; for the overcrowding was extraordinary, and many persons, unable to find room on the benches, had stretched themselves on the pavement, on the damp stone slabs fouled by all the refuse of the day. And on all sides indescribable promiscuousness prevailed: prostrated by overpowering weariness, men, women, and priests were lying there, pell-mell, at random, open-mouthed and utterly exhausted. A large number were snoring, seated on the slabs, with their backs against the walls and their heads drooping on their chests. Others had slipped down, with limbs intermingled, and one young girl lay prostrate across an old country priest, who in his calm, childlike slumber was smiling at the angels. It was like a cattle-shed sheltering poor wanderers of the roads, all those who were homeless on that beautiful holiday night, and who had dropped in there and fallen fraternally asleep. Still, there were some who found no repose in their feverish excitement, but turned and twisted, or rose up to finish eating the food which remained in their baskets. Others could be seen lying perfectly motionless, their eyes wide open and fixed upon the gloom. The cries of dreamers, the wailing of sufferers, arose amidst general snoring. And pity came to the heart, a pity full of anguish, at sight of this flock of wretches lying there in heaps in loathsome rags, whilst their poor spotless souls no doubt were far away in the blue realm of some mystical dream. Pierre was on the point of withdrawing, feeling sick at heart, when a low continuous moan attracted his attention. He looked, and recognised Madame Vincent, on the same spot and in the same position as before, still nursing little Rose upon her lap. "Ah! Monsieur l'Abbe," the poor woman murmured, "you hear her; she woke up nearly an hour ago, and has been sobbing ever since. Yet I assure you I have not moved even a finger, I felt so happy at seeing her sleep."

The priest bent down, examining the little one, who had not even the strength to raise her eyelids. A plaintive cry no stronger than a breath was coming from her lips; and she was so white that he shuddered, for he felt that death was hovering near.

"Dear me! what shall I do?" continued the poor mother, utterly worn out. "This cannot last; I can no longer bear to hear her cry. And if you knew all that I have been saying to her: 'My jewel, my treasure, my angel, I beseech you cry no more. Be good; the Blessed Virgin will cure you!' And yet she still cries on."

With these words the poor creature burst out sobbing, her big tears falling on the face of the child, whose rattle still continued. "Had it been daylight," she resumed, "I would long ago have left this hall, the more especially as she disturbs the others. There is an old lady yonder who has already complained. But I fear it may be chilly outside; and besides, where could I go in the middle of the night? Ah! Blessed Virgin, Blessed Virgin, take pity upon us!"

Overcome by emotion, Pierre kissed the child's fair head, and then hastened away to avoid bursting into tears like the sorrowing mother. And he went straight to the Rosary, as though he were determined to conquer death.

He had already beheld the Rosary in broad daylight, and had been displeased by the aspect of this church, which the architect, fettered by the rockbound site, had been obliged to make circular and low, so that it seemed crushed beneath its great cupola, which square pillars supported. The worst was that, despite its archaic Byzantine style, it altogether lacked any religious appearance, and suggested neither mystery nor meditation. Indeed, with the glaring light admitted by the cupola and the broad glazed doors it was more like some brand-new corn-market. And then, too, it was not yet completed: the decorations were lacking, the bare walls against which the altars stood had no other embellishment than some artificial roses of coloured paper and a few insignificant votive offerings; and this bareness heightened the resemblance to some vast public hall. Moreover, in time of rain the paved floor became as muddy as that of a general waiting-room at a railway station. The high altar was a temporary structure of painted wood. Innumerable rows of benches filled the central rotunda, benches free to the public, on which people could come and rest at all hours, for night and day alike the Rosary remained open to the swarming pilgrims. Like the shelter-house, it was a cow-shed in which the Almighty received the poor ones of the earth.

On entering, Pierre felt himself to be in some common hall trod by the footsteps of an ever-changing crowd. But the brilliant sunlight no longer streamed on the pallid walls, the tapers burning at every altar simply gleamed like stars amidst the uncertain gloom which filled the building. A solemn high mass had been celebrated at midnight with extraordinary pomp, amidst all the splendour of candles, chants, golden vestments, and swinging, steaming censers; but of all this glorious display there now remained only the regulation number of tapers necessary for the celebration of the masses at each of the fifteen altars ranged around the edifice. These masses began at midnight and did not cease till noon. Nearly four hundred were said during those twelve hours at the Rosary alone. Taking the whole of Lourdes, where there were altogether some fifty altars, more than two thousand masses were celebrated daily. And so great was the abundance of priests, that many had extreme difficulty in fulfilling their duties, having to wait for hours together before they could find an altar unoccupied. What particularly struck Pierre that evening, was the sight of all the altars besieged by rows of priests patiently awaiting their turn in the dim light at the foot of the steps; whilst the officiating minister galloped through the Latin phrases, hastily punctuating them with the prescribed signs of the cross. And the weariness of all the waiting ones was so great, that most of them were seated on the flagstones, some even dozing on the altar steps in heaps, quite overpowered, relying on the beadle to come and rouse them.

For a moment Pierre walked about undecided. Was he going to wait like the others? However, the scene determined him against doing so. At every altar, at every mass, a crowd of pilgrims was gathered, communicating in all haste with a sort of voracious fervour. Each pyx was filled and emptied incessantly; the priests' hands grew tired in thus distributing the bread of life; and Pierre's surprise increased at the sight. Never before had he beheld a corner of this earth so watered by the divine blood, whence faith took wing in such a flight of souls. It was like a return to the heroic days of the Church, when all nations prostrated themselves beneath the same blast of credulity in their terrified ignorance which led them to place their hope of eternal happiness in an Almighty God. He could fancy himself carried back some eight or nine centuries, to the time of great public piety, when people believed in the approaching end of the world; and this he could fancy the more readily as the crowd of simple folk, the whole host that had attended high mass, was still seated on the benches, as much at ease in God's house as at home. Many had no place of refuge. Was not the church their home, the asylum where consolation awaited them both by day and by night? Those who knew not where to sleep, who had not found room even at the shelter place, came to the Rosary, where sometimes they succeeded in finding a vacant seat on a bench, at others sufficient space to lie down on the flagstones. And others who had beds awaiting them lingered there for the joy of passing a whole night in that divine abode, so full of beautiful dreams. Until daylight the concourse and promiscuity were extraordinary; every row of benches was occupied, sleeping persons were scattered in every corner and behind every pillar; men, women, children were leaning against each other, their heads on one another's shoulders, their breath mingling in calm unconsciousness. It was the break-up of a religious gathering overwhelmed by sleep, a church transformed into a chance hospital, its doors wide open to the lovely August night, giving access to all who were wandering in the darkness, the good and the bad, the weary and the lost. And all over the place, from each of the fifteen altars, the bells announcing the elevation of the Host incessantly sounded, whilst from among the mob of sleepers bands of believers now and again arose, went and received the sacrament, and then returned to mingle once more with the nameless, shepherdless flock which the semi-obscurity enveloped like a veil.

With an air of restless indecision, Pierre was still wandering through the shadowy groups, when an old priest, seated on the step of an altar, beckoned to him. For two hours he had been waiting there, and now that his turn was at length arriving he felt so faint that he feared he might not have strength to say the whole of his mass, and preferred, therefore, to surrender his place to another. No doubt the sight of Pierre, wandering so distressfully in the gloom, had moved him. He pointed the vestry out to him, waited until he returned with chasuble and chalice, and then went off and fell into a sound sleep on one of the neighbouring benches. Pierre thereupon said his mass in the same way as he said it at Paris, like a worthy man fulfilling a professional duty. He outwardly maintained an air of sincere faith. But, contrary to what he had expected from the two feverish days through which he had just gone, from the extraordinary and agitating surroundings amidst which he had spent the last few hours, nothing moved him nor touched his heart. He had hoped that a great commotion would overpower him at the moment of the communion, when the divine mystery is accomplished; that he would find himself in view of Paradise, steeped in grace, in the very presence of the Almighty; but there was no manifestation, his chilled heart did not even throb, he went on to the end pronouncing the usual words, making the regulation gestures, with the mechanical accuracy of the profession. In spite of his effort to be fervent, one single idea kept obstinately returning to his mind—that the vestry was far too small, since such an enormous number of masses had to be said. How could the sacristans manage to distribute the holy vestments and the cloths? It puzzled him, and engaged his thoughts with absurd persistency.

At length, to his surprise, he once more found himself outside. Again he wandered through the night, a night which seemed to him utterly void, darker and stiller than before. The town was lifeless, not a light was gleaming. There only remained the growl of the Gave, which his accustomed ears no longer heard. And suddenly, similar to a miraculous apparition, the Grotto blazed before him, illumining the darkness with its everlasting brasier, which burnt with a flame of inextinguishable love. He had returned thither unconsciously, attracted no doubt by thoughts of Marie. Three o'clock was about to strike, the benches before the Grotto were emptying, and only some twenty persons remained there, dark, indistinct forms, kneeling in slumberous ecstasy, wrapped in divine torpor. It seemed as though the night in progressing had increased the gloom, and imparted a remote visionary aspect to the Grotto. All faded away amidst delicious lassitude, sleep reigned supreme over the dim, far-spreading country side; whilst the voice of the invisible waters seemed to be merely the breathing of this pure slumber, upon which the Blessed Virgin, all white with her aureola of tapers, was smiling. And among the few unconscious women was Madame Maze, still kneeling, with clasped hands and bowed head, but so indistinct that she seemed to have melted away amidst her ardent prayer.

Pierre, however, had immediately gone up to Marie. He was shivering, and fancied that she must be chilled by the early morning air. "I beseech you, Marie, cover yourself up," said he. "Do you want to suffer still more?" And thereupon he drew up the shawl which had slipped off her, and endeavoured to fasten it about her neck. "You are cold, Marie," he added; "your hands are like ice."

She did not answer, she was still in the same attitude as when he had left her a couple of hours previously. With her elbows resting on the edges of her box, she kept herself raised, her soul still lifted towards the Blessed Virgin and her face transfigured, beaming with a celestial joy. Her lips moved, though no sound came from them. Perhaps she was still carrying on some mysterious conversation in the world of enchantments, dreaming wide awake, as she had been doing ever since he had placed her there. He spoke to her again, but still she answered not. At last, however, of her own accord, she murmured in a far-away voice: "Oh! I am so happy, Pierre! I have seen her; I prayed to her for you, and she smiled at me, slightly nodding her head to let me know that she heard me and would grant my prayers. And though she did not speak to me, Pierre, I understood what she wished me to know. 'Tis to-day, at four o'clock in the afternoon, when the Blessed Sacrament passes by, that I shall be cured!"

He listened to her in deep agitation. Had she been sleeping with her eyes wide open? Was it in a dream that she had seen the marble figure of the Blessed Virgin bend its head and smile? A great tremor passed through him at the thought that this poor child had prayed for him. And he walked up to the railing, and dropped upon his knees, stammering: "O Marie! O Marie!" without knowing whether this heart-cry were intended for the Virgin or for the beloved friend of his childhood. And he remained there, utterly overwhelmed, waiting for grace to come to him.

Endless minutes went by. This was indeed the superhuman effort, the waiting for the miracle which he had come to seek for himself, the sudden revelation, the thunderclap which was to sweep away his unbelief and restore him, rejuvenated and triumphant, to the faith of the simple-minded. He surrendered himself, he wished that some mighty power might ravage his being and transform it. But, even as before whilst saying his mass, he heard naught within him but an endless silence, felt nothing but a boundless vacuum. There was no divine intervention, his despairing heart almost seemed to cease beating. And although he strove to pray, to fix his mind wholly upon that powerful Virgin, so compassionate to poor humanity, his thoughts none the less wandered, won back by the outside world, and again turning to puerile trifles. Within the Grotto, on the other side of the railing, he had once more caught sight of Baron Suire, still asleep, still continuing his pleasant nap with his hands clasped in front of him. Other things also attracted his attention: the flowers deposited at the feet of the Virgin, the letters cast there as though into a heavenly letter-box, the delicate lace-like work of wax which remained erect around the flames of the larger tapers, looking like some rich silver ornamentation. Then, without any apparent reason, his thoughts flew away to the days of his childhood, and his brother Guillaume's face rose before him with extreme distinctness. He had not seen him since their mother's death. He merely knew that he led a very secluded life, occupying himself with scientific matters, in a little house in which he had buried himself with a mistress and two big dogs; and he would have known nothing more about him, but for having recently read his name in a newspaper in connection with some revolutionary attempt. It was stated that he was passionately devoting himself to the study of explosives, and in constant intercourse with the leaders of the most advanced parties. Why, however, should Guillaume appear to him in this wise, in this ecstatic spot, amidst the mystical light of the tapers,—appear to him, moreover, such as he had formerly known him, so good, affectionate, and brotherly, overflowing with charity for every affliction! The thought haunted him for a moment, and filled him with painful regret for that brotherliness now dead and gone. Then, with hardly a moment's pause, his mind reverted to himself, and he realised that he might stubbornly remain there for hours without regaining faith. Nevertheless, he felt a sort of tremor pass through him, a final hope, a feeling that if the Blessed Virgin should perform the great miracle of curing Marie, he would at last believe. It was like a final delay which he allowed himself, an appointment with Faith for that very day, at four o'clock in the afternoon, when, according to what the girl had told him, the Blessed Sacrament would pass by. And at this thought his anguish at once ceased, he remained kneeling, worn out with fatigue and overcome by invincible drowsiness.

The hours passed by, the resplendent illumination of the Grotto was still projected into the night, its reflection stretching to the neighbouring hillsides and whitening the walls of the convents there. However, Pierre noticed it grow paler and paler, which surprised him, and he roused himself, feeling thoroughly chilled; it was the day breaking, beneath a leaden sky overcast with clouds. He perceived that one of those storms, so sudden in mountainous regions, was rapidly rising from the south. The thunder could already be heard rumbling in the distance, whilst gusts of wind swept along the roads. Perhaps he also had been sleeping, for he no longer beheld Baron Suire, whose departure he did not remember having witnessed. There were scarcely ten persons left before the Grotto, though among them he again recognised Madame Maze with her face hidden in her hands. However, when she noticed that it was daylight and that she could be seen, she rose up, and vanished at a turn of the narrow path leading to the convent of the Blue Sisters.

Feeling anxious, Pierre went up to Marie to tell her she must not remain there any longer, unless she wished to get wet through. "I will take you back to the hospital," said he.

She refused and then entreated: "No, no! I am waiting for mass; I promised to communicate here. Don't trouble about me, return to the hotel at once, and go to bed, I implore you. You know very well that covered vehicles are sent here for the sick whenever it rains."

And she persisted in refusing to leave, whilst on his side he kept on repeating that he did not wish to go to bed. A mass, it should be mentioned, was said at the Grotto early every morning, and it was a divine joy for the pilgrims to be able to communicate, amidst the glory of the rising sun, after a long night of ecstasy. And now, just as some large drops of rain were beginning to fall, there came the priest, wearing a chasuble and accompanied by two acolytes, one of whom, in order to protect the chalice, held a large white silk umbrella, embroidered with gold, over him.

Pierre, after pushing Marie's little conveyance close to the railing, so that the girl might be sheltered by the overhanging rock, under which the few other worshippers had also sought refuge, had just seen her receive the sacrament with ardent fervour, when his attention was attracted by a pitiful spectacle which quite wrung his heart.

Beneath a dense, heavy deluge of rain, he caught sight of Madame Vincent, still with that precious, woeful burden, her little Rose, whom with outstretched arms she was offering to the Blessed Virgin. Unable to stay any longer at the shelter-house owing to the complaints caused by the child's constant moaning, she had carried her off into the night, and during two hours had roamed about in the darkness, lost, distracted, bearing this poor flesh of her flesh, which she pressed to her bosom, unable to give it any relief. She knew not what road she had taken, beneath what trees she had strayed, so absorbed had she been in her revolt against the unjust sufferings which had so sorely stricken this poor little being, so feeble and so pure, and as yet quite incapable of sin. Was it not abominable that the grip of disease should for weeks have been incessantly torturing her child, whose cry she knew not how to quiet? She carried her about, rocking her in her arms as she went wildly along the paths, obstinately hoping that she would at last get her to sleep, and so hush that wail which was rending her heart. And suddenly, utterly worn-out, sharing each of her daughter's death pangs, she found herself opposite the Grotto, at the feet of the miracle-working Virgin, she who forgave and who healed.

"O Virgin, Mother most admirable, heal her! O Virgin, Mother of Divine Grace, heal her!"

She had fallen on her knees, and with quivering, outstretched arms was still offering her expiring daughter, in a paroxysm of hope and desire which seemed to raise her from the ground. And the rain, which she never noticed, beat down behind her with the fury of an escaped torrent, whilst violent claps of thunder shook the mountains. For one moment she thought her prayer was granted, for Rose had slightly shivered as though visited by the archangel, her face becoming quite white, her eyes and mouth opening wide; and with one last little gasp she ceased to cry.

"O Virgin, Mother of Our Redeemer, heal her! O Virgin, All-powerful Mother, heal her!"

But the poor woman felt her child become even lighter in her extended arms. And now she became afraid at no longer hearing her moan, at seeing her so white, with staring eyes and open mouth, without a sign of life. How was it that she did not smile if she were cured? Suddenly a loud heart-rending cry rang out, the cry of the mother, surpassing even the din of the thunder in the storm, whose violence was increasing. Her child was dead. And she rose up erect, turned her back on that deaf Virgin who let little children die, and started off like a madwoman beneath the lashing downpour, going straight before her without knowing whither, and still and ever carrying and nursing that poor little body which she had held in her arms during so many days and nights. A thunderbolt fell, shivering one of the neighbouring trees, as though with the stroke of a giant axe, amidst a great crash of twisted and broken branches.

Pierre had rushed after Madame Vincent, eager to guide and help her. But he was unable to follow her, for he at once lost sight of her behind the blurring curtain of rain. When he returned, the mass was drawing to an end, and, as soon as the rain fell less violently, the officiating priest went off under the white silk umbrella embroidered with gold. Meantime a kind of omnibus awaited the few patients to take them back to the hospital.

Marie pressed Pierre's hands. "Oh! how happy I am!" she said. "Do not come for me before three o'clock this afternoon."

On being left amidst the rain, which had now become an obstinate fine drizzle, Pierre re-entered the Grotto and seated himself on the bench near the spring. He would not go to bed, for in spite of his weariness he dreaded sleep in the state of nervous excitement in which he had been plunged ever since the day before. Little Rose's death had increased his fever; he could not banish from his mind the thought of that heart-broken mother, wandering along the muddy paths with the dead body of her child. What could be the reasons which influenced the Virgin? He was amazed that she could make a choice. Divine Mother as she was, he wondered how her heart could decide upon healing only ten out of a hundred sufferers—that ten per cent. of miracles which Doctor Bonamy had proved by statistics. He, Pierre, had already asked himself the day before which ones he would have chosen had he possessed the power of saving ten. A terrible power in all truth, a formidable selection, which he would never have had the courage to make. Why this one, and not that other? Where was the justice, where the compassion? To be all-powerful and heal every one of them, was not that the desire which rose from each heart? And the Virgin seemed to him to be cruel, badly informed, as harsh and indifferent as even impassible nature, distributing life and death at random, or in accordance with laws which mankind knew nothing of.

The rain was at last leaving off, and Pierre had been there a couple of hours when he felt that his feet were damp. He looked down, and was greatly surprised, for the spring was overflowing through the gratings. The soil of the Grotto was already covered; whilst outside a sheet of water was flowing under the benches, as far as the parapet against the Gave. The late storms had swollen the waters in the neighbourhood. Pierre thereupon reflected that this spring, in spite of its miraculous origin, was subject to the laws that governed other springs, for it certainly communicated with some natural reservoirs, wherein the rain penetrated and accumulated. And then, to keep his ankles dry, he left the place.

V. THE TWO VICTIMS

PIERRE walked along thirsting for fresh air, his head so heavy that he took off his hat to relieve his burning brow. Despite all the fatigue of that terrible night of vigil, he did not think of sleeping. He was kept erect by that rebellion of his whole being which he could not quiet. Eight o'clock was striking, and he walked at random under the glorious morning sun, now shining forth in a spotless sky, which the storm seemed to have cleansed of all the Sunday dust.

All at once, however, he raised his head, anxious to know where he was; and he was quite astonished, for he found that he had already covered a deal of ground, and was now below the station, near the municipal hospital. He was hesitating at a point where the road forked, not knowing which direction to take, when a friendly hand was laid on his shoulder, and a voice inquired: "Where are you going at this early hour?"

It was Doctor Chassaigne who addressed him, drawing up his lofty figure, clad in black from head to foot. "Have you lost yourself?" he added; "do you want to know your way?"

"No, thanks, no," replied Pierre, somewhat disturbed. "I spent the night at the Grotto with that young patient to whom I am so much attached, and my heart was so upset that I have been walking about in the hope it would do me good, before returning to the hotel to take a little sleep."

The doctor continued looking at him, clearly detecting the frightful struggle which was raging within him, the despair which he felt at being unable to sink asleep in faith, the suffering which the futility of all his efforts brought him. "Ah, my poor child!" murmured M. Chassaigne; and in a fatherly way he added: "Well, since you are walking, suppose we take a walk together? I was just going down yonder, to the bank of the Gave. Come along, and on our way back you will see what a lovely view we shall have."

For his part, the doctor took a walk of a couple of hours' duration each morning, ever alone, seeking, as it were, to tire and exhaust his grief. First of all, as soon as he had risen, he repaired to the cemetery, and knelt on the tomb of his wife and daughter, which, at all seasons, he decked with flowers. And afterwards he would roam along the roads, with tearful eyes, never returning home until fatigue compelled him.

With a wave of the hand, Pierre accepted his proposal, and in perfect silence they went, side by side, down the sloping road. They remained for a long time without speaking; the doctor seemed more overcome than was his wont that morning; it was as though his chat with his dear lost ones had made his heart bleed yet more copiously. He walked along with his head bowed; his face, round which his white hair streamed, was very pale, and tears still blurred his eyes. And yet it was so pleasant, so warm in the sunlight on that lovely morning. The road now followed the Gave on its right bank, on the other side of the new town; and you could see the gardens, the inclined ways, and the Basilica. And, all at once, the Grotto appeared, with the everlasting flare of its tapers, now paling in the broad light.

Doctor Chassaigne, who had turned his head, made the sign of the cross, which Pierre did not at first understand. And when, in his turn, he had perceived the Grotto, he glanced in surprise at his old friend, and once more relapsed into the astonishment which had come over him a couple of days previously on finding this man of science, this whilom atheist and materialist, so overwhelmed by grief that he was now a believer, longing for the one delight of meeting his dear ones in another life. His heart had swept his reason away; old and lonely as he was, it was only the illusion that he would live once more in Paradise, where loving souls meet again, that prolonged his life on earth. This thought increased the young priest's discomfort. Must he also wait until he had grown old and endured equal sufferings in order to find a refuge in faith?

Still walking beside the Gave, leaving the town farther and farther behind them, they were lulled as it were by the noise of those clear waters rolling over the pebbles between banks shaded by trees. And they still remained silent, walking on with an equal step, each, on his own side, absorbed in his sorrows.

"And Bernadette," Pierre suddenly inquired; "did you know her?"

The doctor raised his head. "Bernadette? Yes, yes," said he. "I saw her once—afterwards." He relapsed into silence for a moment, and then began chatting: "In 1858, you know, at the time of the apparitions, I was thirty years of age. I was in Paris, still young in my profession, and opposed to all supernatural notions, so that I had no idea of returning to my native mountains to see a girl suffering from hallucinations. Five or six years later, however, some time about 1864, I passed through Lourdes, and was inquisitive enough to pay Bernadette a visit. She was then still at the asylum with the Sisters of Nevers."

Pierre remembered that one of the reasons of his journey had been his desire to complete his inquiry respecting Bernadette. And who could tell if grace might not come to him from that humble, lovable girl, on the day when he should be convinced that she had indeed fulfilled a mission of divine love and forgiveness? For this consummation to ensue it would perhaps suffice that he should know her better and learn to feel that she was really the saint, the chosen one, as others believed her to have been.

"Tell me about her, I pray you," he said; "tell me all you know of her."

A faint smile curved the doctor's lips. He understood, and would have greatly liked to calm and comfort the young priest whose soul was so grievously tortured by doubt. "Oh! willingly, my poor child!" he answered. "I should be so happy to help you on the path to light. You do well to love Bernadette—that may save you; for since all those old-time things I have deeply reflected on her case, and I declare to you that I never met a more charming creature, or one with a better heart."

Then, to the slow rhythm of their footsteps along the well-kept, sunlit road, in the delightful freshness of morning, the doctor began to relate his visit to Bernadette in 1864. She had then just attained her twentieth birthday, the apparitions had taken place six years previously, and she had astonished him by her candid and sensible air, her perfect modesty. The Sisters of Nevers, who had taught her to read, kept her with them at the asylum in order to shield her from public inquisitiveness. She found an occupation there, helping them in sundry petty duties; but she was very often taken ill, and would spend weeks at a time in her bed. The doctor had been particularly struck by her beautiful eyes, pure, candid, and frank, like those of a child. The rest of her face, said he, had become somewhat spoilt; her complexion was losing its clearness, her features had grown less delicate, and her general appearance was that of an ordinary servant-girl, short, puny, and unobtrusive. Her piety was still keen, but she had not seemed to him to be the ecstatical, excitable creature that many might have supposed; indeed, she appeared to have a rather positive mind which did not indulge in flights of fancy; and she invariably had some little piece of needlework, some knitting, some embroidery in her hand. In a word, she appeared to have entered the common path, and in nowise resembled the intensely passionate female worshippers of the Christ. She had no further visions, and never of her own accord spoke of the eighteen apparitions which had decided her life. To learn anything it was necessary to interrogate her, to address precise questions to her. These she would briefly answer, and then seek to change the conversation, as though she did not like to talk of such mysterious things. If wishing to probe the matter further, you asked her the nature of the three secrets which the Virgin had confided to her, she would remain silent, simply averting her eyes. And it was impossible to make her contradict herself; the particulars she gave invariably agreed with her original narrative, and, indeed, she always seemed to repeat the same words, with the same inflections of the voice.

"I had her in hand during the whole of one afternoon," continued Doctor Chassaigne, "and there was not the variation of a syllable in her story. It was disconcerting. Still, I am prepared to swear that she was not lying, that she never lied, that she was altogether incapable of falsehood."

Pierre boldly ventured to discuss this point. "But won't you admit, doctor, the possibility of some disorder of the will?" he asked. "Has it not been proved, is it not admitted nowadays, that when certain degenerate creatures with childish minds fall into an hallucination, a fancy of some kind or other, they are often unable to free themselves from it, especially when they remain in the same environment in which the phenomenon occurred? Cloistered, living alone with her fixed idea, Bernadette, naturally enough, obstinately clung to it."

The doctor's faint smile returned to his lips, and vaguely waving his arm, he replied: "Ah! my child, you ask me too much. You know very well that I am now only a poor old man, who prides himself but little on his science, and no longer claims to be able to explain anything. However, I do of course know of that famous medical-school example of the young girl who allowed herself to waste away with hunger at home, because she imagined that she was suffering from a serious complaint of the digestive organs, but who nevertheless began to eat when she was taken elsewhere. However, that is but one circumstance, and there are so many contradictory cases."

For a moment they became silent, and only the rhythmical sound of their steps was heard along the road. Then the doctor resumed: "Moreover, it is quite true that Bernadette shunned the world, and was only happy in her solitary corner. She was never known to have a single intimate female friend, any particular human love for anybody. She was kind and gentle towards all, but it was only for children that she showed any lively affection. And as, after all, the medical man is not quite dead within me, I will confess to you that I have sometimes wondered if she remained as pure in mind, as, most undoubtedly, she did remain in body. However, I think it quite possible, given her sluggish, poor-blooded temperament, not to speak of the innocent sphere in which she grew up, first Bartres, and then the convent. Still, a doubt came to me when I heard of the tender interest which she took in the orphan asylum built by the Sisters of Nevers, farther along this very road. Poor little girls are received into it, and shielded from the perils of the highways. And if Bernadette wished it to be extremely large, so as to lodge all the little lambs in danger, was it not because she herself remembered having roamed the roads with bare feet, and still trembled at the idea of what might have become of her but for the help of the Blessed Virgin?"

Then, resuming his narrative, he went on telling Pierre of the crowds that flocked to see Bernadette and pay her reverence in her asylum at Lourdes. This had proved a source of considerable fatigue to her. Not a day went by without a stream of visitors appearing before her. They came from all parts of France, some even from abroad; and it soon proved necessary to refuse the applications of those who were actuated by mere inquisitiveness, and to grant admittance only to the genuine believers, the members of the clergy, and the people of mark on whom the doors could not well have been shut. A Sister was always present to protect Bernadette against the excessive indiscretion of some of her visitors, for questions literally rained upon her, and she often grew faint through having to repeat her story so many times. Ladies of high position fell on their knees, kissed her gown, and would have liked to carry a piece of it away as a relic. She also had to defend her chaplet, which in their excitement they all begged her to sell to them for a fabulous amount. One day a certain marchioness endeavoured to secure it by giving her another one which she had brought with her—a chaplet with a golden cross and beads of real pearls. Many hoped that she would consent to work a miracle in their presence; children were brought to her in order that she might lay her hands upon them; she was also consulted in cases of illness, and attempts were made to purchase her influence with the Virgin. Large sums were offered to her. At the slightest sign, the slightest expression of a desire to be a queen, decked with jewels and crowned with gold, she would have been overwhelmed with regal presents. And while the humble remained on their knees on her threshold, the great ones of the earth pressed round her, and would have counted it a glory to act as her escort. It was even related that one among them, the handsomest and wealthiest of princes, came one clear sunny April day to ask her hand in marriage.

"But what always struck and displeased me," said Pierre, "was her departure from Lourdes when she was two-and-twenty, her sudden disappearance and sequestration in the convent of Saint Gildard at Nevers, whence she never emerged. Didn't that give a semblance of truth to those spurious rumours of insanity which were circulated? Didn't it help people to suppose that she was being shut up, whisked away for fear of some indiscretion on her part, some naive remark or other which might have revealed the secret of a prolonged fraud? Indeed, to speak plainly, I will confess to you that for my own part I still believe that she was spirited away."

Doctor Chassaigne gently shook his head. "No, no," said he, "there was no story prepared in advance in this affair, no big melodrama secretly staged and afterwards performed by more or less unconscious actors. The developments came of themselves, by the sole force of circumstances; and they were always very intricate, very difficult to analyse. Moreover, it is certain that it was Bernadette herself who wished to leave Lourdes. Those incessant visits wearied her, she felt ill at ease amidst all that noisy worship. All that *she* desired was a dim nook where she might live in peace, and so fierce was she at times in her disinterestedness, that when money was handed to her, even with the pious intent of having a mass said or a taper burnt, she would fling it upon the floor. She never accepted anything for herself or for her family, which remained in poverty. And with such pride as she possessed, such natural simplicity, such a desire to remain in the background, one can very well understand that she should have wished to disappear and cloister herself in some lonely spot so as to prepare herself to make a good death. Her work was accomplished; she had initiated this great movement scarcely knowing how or why; and she could really be of no further utility. Others were about to conduct matters to an issue and insure the triumph of the Grotto."

"Let us admit, then, that she went off of her own accord," said Pierre; "still, what a relief it must have been for the people you speak of, who thenceforth became the real masters, whilst millions of money were raining down on Lourdes from the whole world."

"Oh! certainly; I don't pretend that any attempt was made to detain her here!" exclaimed the doctor. "Frankly, I even believe that she was in some degree urged into the course she took. She ended by becoming somewhat of an incumbrance. It was not that any annoying revelations were feared from her; but remember that with her extreme timidity and frequent illnesses she was scarcely ornamental. Besides, however small the room which she took up at Lourdes, however obedient she showed herself, she was none the less a power, and attracted the multitude, which made her, so to say, a competitor of the Grotto. For the Grotto to remain alone, resplendent in its glory, it was advisable that Bernadette should withdraw into the background, become as it were a simple legend. Such, indeed, must have been the reasons which induced Monseigneur Laurence, the Bishop of Tarbes, to hasten her departure. The only mistake that was made was in saying that it was a question of screening her from the enterprises of the world, as though it were feared that she might fall into the sin of pride, by growing vain of the saintly fame with which the whole of Christendom re-echoed. And this was doing her a grave injury, for she was as incapable of pride as she was of falsehood. Never, indeed, was there a more candid or more modest child."

The doctor was growing impassioned, excited. But all at once he became calm again, and a pale smile returned to his lips. "'Tis true," said he, "I love her; the more I have thought of her, the more have I learned to love her. But you must not think, Pierre, that I am completely brutified by belief. If I nowadays acknowledge the existence of an unseen power, if I feel a need of believing in another, better, and more just life, I nevertheless know right well that there are men remaining in this world of ours; and at times, even when they wear the cowl or the cassock, the work they do is vile."

There came another interval of silence. Each was continuing his dream apart from the other. Then the doctor resumed: "I will tell you of a fancy which has often haunted me. Suppose we admit that Bernadette was not the shy, simple child we knew her to be; let us endow her with a spirit of intrigue and domination, transform her into a conqueress, a leader of nations, and try to picture what, in that case, would have happened. It is evident that the Grotto would be hers, the Basilica also. We should see her lording it at all the ceremonies, under a dais, with a gold mitre on her head. She would distribute the miracles; with a sovereign gesture her little hand would lead the multitudes to heaven. All the lustre and glory would come from her, she being the saint, the chosen one, the only one that had been privileged to see the Divinity face to face. And indeed nothing would seem more just, for she would triumph after toiling, enjoy the fruit of her labour in all glory. But you see, as it happens, she is defrauded, robbed. The marvellous harvests sown by her are reaped by others. During the twelve years which she lived at Saint Gildard, kneeling in the gloom, Lourdes was full of victors, priests in golden vestments chanting thanksgivings, and blessing churches and monuments erected at a cost of millions. She alone did not behold the triumph of the new faith, whose author she had been. You say that she dreamt it all. Well, at all events, what a beautiful dream it was, a dream which has stirred the whole world, and from which she, dear girl, never awakened!"

They halted and sat down for a moment on a rock beside the road, before returning to the town. In front of them the Gave, deep at this point of its course, was rolling blue waters tinged with dark moire-like reflections, whilst, farther on, rushing hurriedly over a bed of large stones, the stream became so much foam, a white froth, light like snow. Amidst the gold raining from the sun, a fresh breeze came down from the mountains.

Whilst listening to that story of how Bernadette had been exploited and suppressed, Pierre had simply found in it all a fresh motive for revolt; and, with his eyes fixed on the ground, he began to think of the injustice of nature, of that law which wills that the strong should devour the weak. Then, all at once raising his head, he inquired: "And did you also know Abbe Peyramale?"

The doctor's eyes brightened once more, and he eagerly replied: "Certainly I did! He was an upright, energetic man, a saint, an apostle. He and Bernadette were the great makers of Our Lady of Lourdes. Like her, he endured frightful sufferings, and, like her, he died from them. Those who do not know his story can know nothing, understand nothing, of the drama enacted here."

Thereupon he related that story at length. Abbe Peyramale was the parish priest of Lourdes at the time of the apparitions. A native of the region, tall, broad-shouldered, with a powerful leonine head, he was extremely intelligent, very honest and good-hearted, though at times violent and domineering. He seemed built for combat. An enemy of all pious exaggerations, discharging the duties of his ministry in a broad, liberal spirit, he regarded the apparitions with distrust when he first heard of them, refused to believe in Bernadette's stories, questioned her, and demanded proofs. It was only at a later stage, when the blast of faith became irresistible, upsetting the most rebellious minds and mastering the multitude, that he ended, in his turn, by bowing his head; and when he was finally conquered, it was more particularly by his love for the humble and the oppressed which he could not restrain when he beheld Bernadette threatened with imprisonment. The civil authorities were persecuting one of his flock; at this his shepherd's heart awoke, and, in her defence, he gave full reign to his ardent passion for justice. Moreover, the charm which the child diffused had worked upon him; he felt her to be so candid, so truthful, that he began to place a blind faith in her and love her even as everybody else loved her. Moreover, why should he have curtly dismissed all questions of miracles, when miracles abound in the pages of Holy Writ? It was not for a minister of religion, whatever his prudence, to set himself up as a sceptic when entire populations were falling on their knees and the Church seemed to be on the eve of another great triumph. Then, too, he had the nature of one who leads men, who stirs up crowds, who builds, and in this affair he had really found his vocation, the vast field in which he might exercise his energy, the great cause to which he might wholly devote himself with all his passionate ardour and determination to succeed.

From that moment, then, Abbe Peyramale had but one thought, to execute the orders which the Virgin had commissioned Bernadette to transmit to him. He caused improvements to be carried out at the Grotto. A railing was placed in front of it; pipes were laid for the conveyance of the water from the source, and a variety of work was accomplished in order to clear the approaches. However, the Virgin had particularly requested that a chapel might be built; and he wished to have a church, quite a triumphal Basilica. He pictured everything on a grand scale, and, full of confidence in the enthusiastic help of Christendom, he worried the architects, requiring them to design real palaces worthy of the Queen of Heaven. As a matter of fact, offerings already abounded, gold poured from the most distant dioceses, a rain of gold destined to increase and never end. Then came his happy years: he was to be met among the workmen at all hours, instilling activity into them like the jovial, good-natured fellow he was, constantly on the point of taking a pick or trowel in hand himself, such was his eagerness to behold the realisation of his dream. But days of trial were in store for him: he fell ill, and lay in danger of death on the fourth of April, 1864, when the first procession started from his parish church to the Grotto, a procession of sixty thousand pilgrims, which wound along the streets amidst an immense concourse of spectators.

On the day when Abbe Peyramale rose from his bed, saved, a first time, from death, he found himself despoiled. To second him in his heavy task, Monseigneur Laurence, the Bishop, had already given him as assistant a former episcopal secretary, Father Sempe, whom he had appointed warden of the Missionaries of Geraison, a community founded by himself. Father Sempe was a sly, spare little man, to all appearance most disinterested and humble, but in reality consumed by all the thirst of ambition. At the outset he kept in his place, serving the parish priest of Lourdes like a faithful subordinate, attending to matters of all kinds in order to lighten the other's work, and acquiring information on every possible subject in his desire to render himself indispensable. He must soon have realised what a rich farm the Grotto was destined to become, and what a colossal revenue might be derived from it, if only a little skill were exercised. And thenceforth he no longer stirred from the episcopal residence, but ended by acquiring great influence over the calm, practical Bishop, who was in great need of money for the charities of his diocese. And thus it was that during Abbe Peyramale's illness Father Sempe succeeded in effecting a separation between the parish of Lourdes and the domain of the Grotto, which last he was commissioned to manage at the head of a few Fathers of the Immaculate Conception, over whom the Bishop placed him as Father Superior.

The struggle soon began, one of those covert, desperate, mortal struggles which are waged under the cloak of ecclesiastical discipline. There was a pretext for rupture all ready, a field of battle on which the longer purse would necessarily end by conquering. It was proposed to build a new parish church, larger and more worthy of Lourdes than the old one already in existence, which was admitted to have become too small since the faithful had been flocking into the town in larger and larger numbers. Moreover, it was an old idea of Abbe Peyramale, who desired to carry out the Virgin's orders with all possible precision. Speaking of the Grotto, she had said that people would go "thither in procession"; and the Abbe had always seen the pilgrims start in procession from the town, whither they were expected to return in the same fashion, as indeed had been the practice on the first occasions after the apparitions. A central point, a rallying spot, was therefore required, and the Abbe's dream was to erect a magnificent church, a cathedral of gigantic proportions, which would accommodate a vast multitude. Builder as he was by temperament, impassioned artisan working for the glory of Heaven, he already pictured this cathedral springing from the soil, and rearing its clanging belfry in the sunlight. And it was also his own house that he wished to build, the edifice which would be his act of faith and adoration, the temple where he would be the pontiff, and triumph in company with the sweet memory of Bernadette, in full view of the spot of which both he and she had been so cruelly dispossessed. Naturally enough, bitterly as he felt that act of spoliation, the building of this new parish church was in some degree his revenge, his share of all the glory, besides being a task which would enable him to utilise both his militant activity and the fever that had been consuming him ever since he had ceased going to the Grotto, by reason of his soreness of heart.

At the outset of the new enterprise there was again a flash of enthusiasm. At the prospect of seeing all the life and all the money flow into the new city which was springing from the ground around the Basilica, the old town, which felt itself thrust upon one side, espoused the cause of its priest. The municipal council voted a sum of one hundred thousand francs, which, unfortunately, was not to be paid until the new church should be roofed in. Abbe Peyramale had already accepted the plans of his architect—plans which, he had insisted, should be on a grand scale—and had also treated with a contractor of Chartres, who engaged to complete the church in three or four years if the promised supplies of funds should be regularly forthcoming. The Abbe believed that offerings would assuredly continue raining down from all parts, and so he launched into this big enterprise without any anxiety, overflowing with a careless bravery, and fully expecting that Heaven would not abandon him on the road. He even fancied that he could rely upon the support of Monseigneur Jourdan, who had now succeeded Monseigneur Laurence as Bishop of Tarbes, for this prelate, after blessing the foundation-stone of the new church, had delivered an address in which he admitted that the enterprise was necessary and meritorious. And it seemed, too, as though Father Sempe, with his customary humility, had bowed to the inevitable and accepted this vexatious competition, which would compel him to relinquish a share of the plunder; for he now pretended to devote himself entirely to the management of the Grotto, and even allowed a collection-box for contributions to the building of the new parish church to be placed inside the Basilica.

Then, however, the secret, rageful struggle began afresh. Abbe Peyramale, who was a wretched manager, exulted on seeing his new church so rapidly take shape. The work was being carried on at a fast pace, and he troubled about nothing else, being still under the delusion that the Blessed Virgin would find whatever money might be needed. Thus he was quite stupefied when he at last perceived that the offerings were falling off, that the money of the faithful no longer reached him, as though, indeed, someone had secretly diverted its flow. And eventually the day came when he was unable to make the stipulated payments. In all this there had been so much skilfully combined strangulation, of which he only became aware later on. Father Sempe, however, had once more prevailed on the Bishop to grant his favour exclusively to the

Grotto. There was even a talk of some confidential circulars distributed through the various dioceses, so that the many sums of money offered by the faithful should no longer be sent to the parish. The voracious, insatiable Grotto was bent upon securing everything, and to such a point were things carried that five hundred franc notes slipped into the collection-box at the Basilica were kept back; the box was rifled and the parish robbed. Abbe Peyramale, however, in his passion for the rising church, his child, continued fighting most desperately, ready if need were to give his blood. He had at first treated with the contractor in the name of the vestry; then, when he was at a loss how to pay, he treated in his own name. His life was bound up in the enterprise, he wore himself out in the heroic efforts which he made. Of the four hundred thousand francs that he had promised, he had only been able to pay two hundred thousand; and the municipal council still obstinately refused to hand over the hundred thousand francs which it had voted, until the new church should be covered in. This was acting against the town's real interests. However, it was said that Father Sempe was trying to bring influence to bear on the contractor. And, all at once, the work was stopped.

From that moment the death agony began. Wounded in the heart, the Abbe Peyramale, the broad-shouldered mountaineer with the leonine face, staggered and fell like an oak struck down by a thunderbolt. He took to his bed, and never left it alive. Strange stories circulated: it was said that Father Sempe had sought to secure admission to the parsonage under some pious pretext, but in reality to see if his much-dreaded adversary were really mortally stricken; and it was added, that it had been necessary to drive him from the sick-room, where his presence was an outrageous scandal. Then, when the unhappy priest, vanquished and steeped in bitterness, was dead, Father Sempe was seen triumphing at the funeral, from which the others had not dared to keep him away. It was affirmed that he openly displayed his abominable delight, that his face was radiant that day with the joy of victory. He was at last rid of the only man who had been an obstacle to his designs, whose legitimate authority he had feared. He would no longer be forced to share anything with anybody now that both the founders of Our Lady of Lourdes had been suppressed—Bernadette placed in a convent, and Abbe Peyramale lowered into the ground. The Grotto was now his own property, the alms would come to him alone, and he could do what he pleased with the eight hundred thousand francs[1] or so which were at his disposal every year. He would complete the gigantic works destined to make the Basilica a self-supporting centre, and assist in embellishing the new town in order to increase the isolation of the old one and seclude it behind its rock, like an insignificant parish submerged beneath the splendour of its all-powerful neighbour. All the money, all the sovereignty, would be his; he henceforth would reign.

However, although the works had been stopped, and the new parish church was slumbering inside its wooden fence, it was none the less more than half built. The vaulted aisles were already erected. And the imperfect pile remained there like a threat, for the town might some day attempt to finish it. Like Abbe Peyramale, therefore, it must be killed for good, turned into an irreparable ruin. The secret labour therefore continued, a work of refined cruelty and slow destruction. To begin with, the new parish priest, a simple-minded creature, was cowed to such a point that he no

[1] About 145,000 dollars.

longer opened the envelopes containing remittances for the parish; all the registered letters were at once taken to the Fathers. Then the site selected for the new parish church was criticised, and the diocesan architect was induced to draw up a report stating that the old church was still in good condition and of ample size for the require-requirements of the community. Moreover, influence was brought to bear on the Bishop, and representations were made to him respecting the annoying features of the pecuniary difficulties which had arisen with the contractor. With a little imagination poor Peyramale was transformed into a violent, obstinate madman, through whose undisciplined zeal the Church had almost been compromised. And, at last, the Bishop, forgetting that he himself had blessed the foundation-stone, issued a pastoral letter laying the unfinished church under interdict, and prohibiting all religious services in it. This was the supreme blow. Endless lawsuits had already begun; the contractor, who had only received two hundred thousand francs for the five hundred thousand francs' worth of work which had been executed, had taken proceedings against Abbe Peyramale's heir-at-law, the vestry, and the town, for the last still refused to pay over the amount which it had voted. At first the Prefect's Council declared itself incompetent to deal with the case, and when it was sent back to it by the Council of State, it rendered a judgment by which the town was condemned to pay the hundred thousand francs and the heir-at-law to finish the church. At the same time the vestry was put out of court. However, there was a fresh appeal to the Council of State, which quashed this judgment, and condemned the vestry, and, in default, the heir-at-law, to pay the contractor. Neither party being solvent, matters remained in this position. The lawsuits had lasted fifteen years. The town had now resignedly paid over the hundred thousand francs, and only two hundred thousand remained owing to the contractor. However, the costs and the accumulated interest had so increased the amount of indebtedness that it had risen to six hundred thousand francs; and as, on the other hand, it was estimated that four hundred thousand francs would be required to finish the church, a million was needed to save this young ruin from certain destruction. The Fathers of the Grotto were thenceforth able to sleep in peace; they had assassinated the poor church; it was as dead as Abbe Peyramale himself.

The bells of the Basilica rang out triumphantly, and Father Sempe reigned as a victor at the conclusion of that great struggle, that dagger warfare in which not only a man but stones also had been done to death in the shrouding gloom of intriguing sacristies. And old Lourdes, obstinate and unintelligent, paid a hard penalty for its mistake in not giving more support to its minister, who had died struggling, killed by his love for his parish, for now the new town did not cease to grow and prosper at the expense of the old one. All the wealth flowed to the former: the Fathers of the Grotto coined money, financed hotels and candle shops, and sold the water of the source, although a clause of their agreement with the municipality expressly prohibited them from carrying on any commercial pursuits.

The whole region began to rot and fester; the triumph of the Grotto had brought about such a passion for lucre, such a burning, feverish desire to possess and enjoy, that extraordinary perversion set in, growing worse and worse each day, and changing Bernadette's peaceful Bethlehem into a perfect Sodom or Gomorrah. Father Sempe had ensured the triumph of his Divinity by spreading human abominations all around and wrecking thousands of souls. Gigantic buildings rose from the ground, five or six millions of francs had already been expended, everything being sacrificed to the stern determination to leave the poor parish out in the cold and keep the entire plunder for self and friends. Those costly, colossal gradient ways had only been erected in order to avoid compliance with the Virgin's express desire that the faithful should come to the Grotto in procession. For to go down from the Basilica by the incline on the left, and climb up to it again by the incline on the right, could certainly not be called going to the Grotto in procession: it was simply so much revolving in a circle. However, the Fathers cared little about that; they had succeeded in compelling people to start from their premises and return to them, in order that they might be the sole proprietors of the affair, the opulent farmers who garnered the whole harvest. Abbe Peyramale lay buried in the crypt of his unfinished, ruined church, and Bernadette, who had long since dragged out her life of suffering in the depths of a convent far away, was now likewise sleeping the eternal sleep under a flagstone in a chapel.

Deep silence fell when Doctor Chassaigne had finished this long narrative. Then, with a painful effort, he rose to his feet again: "It will soon be ten o'clock, my dear child," said he, "and I want you to take a little rest. Let us go back."

Pierre followed him without speaking; and they retraced their steps toward the town at a more rapid pace.

"Ah! yes," resumed the doctor, "there were great iniquities and great sufferings in it all. But what else could you expect? Man spoils and corrupts the most beautiful things. And you cannot yet understand all the woeful sadness of the things of which I have been talking to you. You must see them, lay your hand on them. Would you like me to show you Bernadette's room and Abbe Peyramale's unfinished church this evening?"

"Yes, I should indeed," replied Pierre.

"Well, I will meet you in front of the Basilica after the four-o'clock procession, and you can come with me."

Then they spoke no further, each becoming absorbed in his reverie once more.

The Gave, now upon their right hand, was flowing through a deep gorge, a kind of cleft into which it plunged, vanishing from sight among the bushes. But at intervals a clear stretch of it, looking like unburnished silver, would appear to view; and, farther on, after a sudden turn in the road, they found it flowing in increased volume across a plain, where it spread at times into glassy sheets which must often have changed their beds, for the gravelly soil was ravined on all sides. The sun was now becoming very hot, and was already high in the heavens, whose limpid azure assumed a deeper tinge above the vast circle of mountains.

And it was at this turn of the road that Lourdes, still some distance away, reappeared to the eyes of Pierre and Doctor Chassaigne. In the splendid morning atmosphere, amid a flying dust of gold and purple rays, the town shone whitely on the horizon, its houses and monuments becoming more and more distinct at each step which brought them nearer. And the doctor, still silent, at last waved his arm with a broad, mournful gesture in order to call his companion's attention to this growing town, as though to a proof of all that he had been telling him. There, indeed, rising up in the dazzling daylight, was the evidence which confirmed his words.

The flare of the Grotto, fainter now that the sun was shining, could already be espied amidst the greenery. And soon afterwards the gigantic monumental works spread out: the quay with its freestone parapet skirting the Gave, whose course had been diverted; the new bridge connecting the new gardens with the recently opened boulevard; the colossal gradient ways, the massive church of the Rosary, and, finally, the slim, tapering Basilica, rising above all else with graceful pride. Of the new town spread all around the monuments, the wealthy city which had sprung, as though by enchantment, from the ancient impoverished soil, the great convents and the great hotels, you could, at this distance, merely distinguish a swarming of white facades and a scintillation of new slates; whilst, in confusion, far away, beyond the rocky mass on which the crumbling castle walls were profiled against the sky, appeared the humble roofs of the old town, a jumble of little time-worn roofs, pressing timorously against one another. And as a background to this vision of the life of yesterday and to-day, the little and the big Gers rose up beneath the splendour of the everlasting sun, and barred the horizon with their bare slopes, which the oblique rays were tingeing with streaks of pink and yellow.

Doctor Chassaigne insisted on accompanying Pierre to the Hotel of the Apparitions, and only parted from him at its door, after reminding him of their appointment for the afternoon. It was not yet eleven o'clock. Pierre, whom fatigue had suddenly mastered, forced himself to eat before going to bed, for he realised that want of food was one of the chief causes of the weakness which had come over him. He fortunately found a vacant seat at the *table d'hote*, and made some kind of a *dejeuner*, half asleep all the time, and scarcely knowing what was served to him. Then he went up-stairs and flung himself on his bed, after taking care to tell the servant to awake him at three o'clock.

However, on lying down, the fever that consumed him at first prevented him from closing his eyes. A pair of gloves, forgotten in the next room, had reminded him of M. de Guersaint, who had left for Gavarnie before daybreak, and would only return in the evening. What a delightful gift was thoughtlessness, thought Pierre. For his own part, with his limbs worn out by weariness and his mind distracted, he was sad unto death. Everything seemed to conspire against his willing desire to regain the faith of his childhood. The tale of Abbe Peyramale's tragic adventures had simply aggravated the feeling of revolt which the story of Bernadette, chosen and martyred, had implanted in his breast. And thus he asked himself whether his search after the truth, instead of restoring his faith, would not rather lead him to yet greater hatred of ignorance and credulity, and to the bitter conviction that man is indeed all alone in the world, with naught to guide him save his reason.

At last he fell asleep, but visions continued hovering around him in his painful slumber. He beheld Lourdes, contaminated by Mammon, turned into a spot of abomination and perdition, transformed into a huge bazaar, where everything was sold, masses and souls alike! He beheld also Abbe Peyramale, dead and slumbering under the ruins of his church, among the nettles which ingratitude had sown there. And he only grew calm again, only tasted the delights of forgetfulness when a last pale, woeful vision had faded from his gaze—a vision of Bernadette upon her knees in a gloomy corner at Nevers, dreaming of her far-away work, which she was never, never to behold.

THE FOURTH DAY

I. THE BITTERNESS OP DEATH

AT the Hospital of Our Lady of Dolours, that morning, Marie remained seated on her bed, propped up by pillows. Having spent the whole night at the Grotto, she had refused to let them take her back there. And, as Madame de Jonquiere approached her, to raise one of the pillows which was slipping from its place, she asked: "What day is it, madame?"

"Monday, my dear child."

"Ah! true. One so soon loses count of time. And, besides, I am so happy! It is to-day that the Blessed Virgin will cure me!"

She smiled divinely, with the air of a day-dreamer, her eyes gazing into vacancy, her thoughts so far away, so absorbed in her one fixed idea, that she beheld nothing save the certainty of her hope. Round about her, the Sainte-Honorine Ward was now quite deserted, all the patients, excepting Madame Vetu, who lay at the last extremity in the next bed, having already started for the Grotto. But Marie did not even notice her neighbour; she was delighted with the sudden stillness which had fallen. One of the windows overlooking the courtyard had been opened, and the glorious morning sunshine entered in one broad beam, whose golden dust was dancing over her bed and streaming upon her pale hands. It was indeed pleasant to find this room, so dismal at nighttime with its many beds of sickness, its unhealthy atmosphere, and its nightmare groans, thus suddenly filled with sunlight, purified by the morning air, and wrapped in such delicious silence! "Why don't you try to sleep a little?" maternally inquired Madame de Jonquiere. "You must be quite worn out by your vigil."

Marie, who felt so light and cheerful that she no longer experienced any pain, seemed surprised.

"But I am not at all tired, and I don't feel a bit sleepy. Go to sleep? Oh! no, that would be too sad. I should no longer know that I was going to be cured!"

At this the superintendent laughed. "Then why didn't you let them take you to the Grotto?" she asked. "You won't know what to do with yourself all alone here."

"I am not alone, madame, I am with her," replied Marie; and thereupon, her vision returning to her, she clasped her hands in ecstasy. "Last night, you know, I saw her bend her head towards me and smile. I quite understood her, I could hear her voice, although she never opened her lips. When the Blessed Sacrament passes at four o'clock I shall be cured."

Madame de Jonquiere tried to calm her, feeling rather anxious at the species of somnambulism in which she beheld her. However, the sick girl went on: "No, no, I am no worse, I am waiting. Only, you must surely see, madame, that there is no need for me to go to the Grotto this morning, since the appointment which she gave me is for four o'clock." And then the girl added in a lower tone: "Pierre will come for me at half-past three. At four o'clock I shall be cured."

The sunbeam slowly made its way up her bare arms, which were now almost transparent, so wasted had they become through illness; whilst her glorious fair hair, which had fallen over her shoulders, seemed like the very effulgence of the great luminary enveloping her. The trill of a bird came in from the courtyard, and quite enlivened the tremulous silence of the ward. Some child who could not be seen must also have been playing close by, for now and again a soft laugh could be heard ascending in the warm air which was so delightfully calm.

"Well," said Madame de Jonquiere by way of conclusion, "don't sleep then, as you don't wish to. But keep quite quiet, and it will rest you all the same."

Meantime Madame Vetu was expiring in the adjoining bed. They had not dared to take her to the Grotto, for fear they should see her die on the way. For some little time she had lain there with her eyes closed; and Sister Hyacinthe, who was watching, had beckoned to Madame Desagneaux in order to acquaint her with the bad opinion she had formed of the case. Both of them were now leaning over the dying woman, observing her with increasing anxiety. The mask upon her face had turned more yellow than ever, and now looked like a coating of mud; her eyes too had become more sunken, her lips seemed to have grown thinner, and the death rattle had begun, a slow, pestilential wheezing, polluted by the cancer which was finishing its destructive work. All at once she raised her eyelids, and was seized with fear on beholding those two faces bent over her own. Could her death be near, that they should thus be gazing at her? Immense sadness showed itself in her eyes, a despairing regret of life. It was not a vehement revolt, for she no longer had the strength to struggle; but what a frightful fate it was to have left her shop, her surroundings, and her husband, merely to come and die so far away; to have braved the abominable torture of such a journey, to have prayed both day and night, and then, instead of having her prayer granted, to die when others recovered!

However, she could do no more than murmur "Oh! how I suffer; oh! how I suffer. Do something, anything, to relieve this pain, I beseech you."

Little Madame Desagneaux, with her pretty milk-white face showing amidst her mass of fair, frizzy hair, was quite upset. She was not used to deathbed scenes, she would have given half her heart, as she expressed it, to see that poor woman recover. And she rose up and began to question Sister Hyacinthe, who was also in tears but already resigned, knowing as she did that salvation was assured when one died well. Could nothing really be done, however? Could not something be tried to ease the dying woman? Abbe Judaine had come and administered the last sacrament to her a couple of hours earlier that very morning. She now only had Heaven to look to; it was her only hope, for she had long since given up expecting aid from the skill of man.

"No, no! we must do something," exclaimed Madame Desagneaux. And thereupon she went and fetched Madame de Jonquiere from beside Marie's bed. "Look how this poor creature is suffering, madame!" she exclaimed. "Sister Hyacinthe says that she can only last a few hours longer. But we cannot leave her moaning like this. There are things which give relief. Why not call that young doctor who is here?"

"Of course we will," replied the superintendent. "We will send for him at once."

I. THE BITTERNESS OP DEATH

They seldom thought of the doctor in the wards. It only occurred to the ladies to send for him when a case was at its very worst, when one of their patients was howling with pain. Sister Hyacinthe, who herself felt surprised at not having thought of Ferrand, whom she believed to be in an adjoining room, inquired if she should fetch him.

"Certainly," was the reply. "Bring him as quickly as possible."

When the Sister had gone off, Madame de Jonquiere made Madame Desagneaux help her in slightly raising the dying woman's head, thinking that this might relieve her. The two ladies happened to be alone there that morning, all the other lady-hospitallers having gone to their devotions or their private affairs. However, from the end of the large deserted ward, where, amidst the warm quiver of the sunlight such sweet tranquillity prevailed, there still came at intervals the light laughter of the unseen child.

"Can it be Sophie who is making such a noise?" suddenly asked the lady-superintendent, whose nerves were somewhat upset by all the worry of the death which she foresaw. Then quickly walking to the end of the ward, she found that it was indeed Sophie Couteau—the young girl so miraculously healed the previous year—who, seated on the floor behind a bed, had been amusing herself, despite her fourteen years, in making a doll out of a few rags. She was now talking to it, so happy, so absorbed in her play, that she laughed quite heartily. "Hold yourself up, mademoiselle," said she. "Dance the polka, that I may see how you can do it! One! two! dance, turn, kiss the one you like best!"

Madame de Jonquiere, however, was now coming up. "Little girl," she said, "we have one of our patients here in great pain, and not expected to recover. You must not laugh so loud."

"Ah! madame, I didn't know," replied Sophie, rising up, and becoming quite serious, although still holding the doll in her hand. "Is she going to die, madame?"

"I fear so, my poor child."

Thereupon Sophie became quite silent. She followed the superintendent, and seated herself on an adjoining bed; whence, without the slightest sign of fear, but with her large eyes burning with curiosity, she began to watch Madame Vetu's death agony. In her nervous state, Madame Desagneaux was growing impatient at the delay in the doctor's arrival; whilst Marie, still enraptured, and resplendent in the sunlight, seemed unconscious of what was taking place about her, wrapt as she was in delightful expectancy of the miracle.

Not having found Ferrand in the small apartment near the linen-room which he usually occupied, Sister Hyacinthe was now searching for him all over the building. During the past two days the young doctor had become more bewildered than ever in that extraordinary hospital, where his assistance was only sought for the relief of death pangs. The small medicine-chest which he had brought with him proved quite useless; for there could be no thought of trying any course of treatment, as the sick were not there to be doctored, but simply to be cured by the lightning stroke of a miracle. And so he mainly confined himself to administering a few opium pills, in order to deaden the severer sufferings. He had been fairly amazed when accompanying Doctor Bonamy on a round through the wards. It had resolved itself into a mere stroll, the doctor, who had only come out of curiosity, taking no interest in the patients, whom he neither questioned nor examined. He solely concerned himself with the pretended cases of cure, stopping opposite those women whom he recognised from having seen them at his office where the miracles were verified. One of them had suffered from three complaints, only one of which the Blessed Virgin had so far deigned to cure; but great hopes were entertained respecting the other two. Sometimes, when a wretched woman, who the day before had claimed to be cured, was questioned with reference to her health, she would reply that her pains had returned to her. However, this never disturbed the doctor's serenity; ever conciliatory, the good man declared that Heaven would surely complete what Heaven had begun. Whenever there was an improvement in health, he would ask if it were not something to be thankful for. And, indeed, his constant saying was: "There's an improvement already; be patient!" What he most dreaded were the importunities of the lady-superintendents, who all wished to detain him to show him sundry extraordinary cases. Each prided herself on having the most serious illnesses, the most frightful, exceptional cases in her ward; so that she was eager to have them medically authenticated, in order that she might share in the triumph should cure supervene. One caught the doctor by the arm and assured him that she felt confident she had a leper in her charge; another entreated him to come and look at a young girl whose back, she said, was covered with fish's scales; whilst a third, whispering in his ear, gave him some terrible details about a married lady of the best society. He hastened away, however, refusing to see even one of them, or else simply promising to come back later on when he was not so busy. As he himself said, if he listened to all those ladies, the day would pass in useless consultations. However, he at last suddenly stopped opposite one of the miraculously cured inmates, and, beckoning Ferrand to his side, exclaimed: "Ah! now here is an interesting cure!" and Ferrand, utterly bewildered, had to listen to him whilst he described all the features of the illness, which had totally disappeared at the first immersion in the piscina.

At last Sister Hyacinthe, still wandering about, encountered Abbe Judaine, who informed her that the young doctor had just been summoned to the Family Ward. It was the fourth time he had gone thither to attend to Brother Isidore, whose sufferings were as acute as ever, and whom he could only fill with opium. In his agony, the Brother merely asked to be soothed a little, in order that he might gather together sufficient strength to return to the Grotto in the afternoon, as he had not been able to do so in the morning. However, his pains increased, and at last he swooned away.

When the Sister entered the ward she found the doctor seated at the missionary's bedside. "Monsieur Ferrand," she said, "come up-stairs with me to the Sainte-Honorine Ward at once. We have a patient there at the point of death."

He smiled at her; indeed, he never beheld her without feeling brighter and comforted. "I will come with you, Sister," he replied. "But you'll wait a minute, won't you? I must try to restore this poor man."

She waited patiently and made herself useful. The Family Ward, situated on the ground-floor, was also full of sunshine and fresh air which entered through three large windows opening on to a narrow strip of garden. In addition to Brother Isidore, only Monsieur Sabathier had remained in bed that morning, with the view of obtaining a little rest; whilst Madame Sabathier, taking advantage of the opportunity, had gone to purchase a few medals and pictures, which she intended for presents. Comfortably seated on his bed, his back supported by some pillows, the ex-professor was rolling the beads of a chaplet between his fingers. He was no longer praying, however, but merely continuing the operation in a mechanical manner, his eyes, meantime, fixed upon his neighbour, whose attack he was following with painful interest.

"Ah! Sister," said he to Sister Hyacinthe, who had drawn near, "that poor Brother fills me with admiration. Yesterday I doubted the Blessed Virgin for a moment, seeing that she did not deign to hear me, though I have been coming here for seven years past; but the example set me by that poor martyr, so resigned amidst his torments, has quite shamed me for my want of faith. You can have no idea how grievously he suffers, and you should see him at the Grotto, with his eyes glowing with divine hope! It is really sublime! I only know of one picture at the Louvre—a picture by some unknown Italian master—in which there is the head of a monk beatified by a similar faith."

The man of intellect, the ex-university-professor, reared on literature and art, was reappearing in this poor old fellow, whose life had been blasted, and who had desired to become a free patient, one of the poor of the earth, in order to move the pity of Heaven. He again began thinking of his own case, and with tenacious hopefulness, which the futility of seven journeys to Lourdes had failed to destroy, he added: "Well, I still have this afternoon, since we sha'n't leave till to-morrow. The water is certainly very cold, but I shall let them dip me a last time; and all the morning I have been praying and asking pardon for my revolt of yesterday. When the Blessed Virgin chooses to cure one of her children, it only takes her a second to do so; is that not so, Sister? May her will be done, and blessed be her name!"

Passing the beads of the chaplet more slowly between his fingers, he again began saying his "Aves" and "Paters," whilst his eyelids drooped on his flabby face, to which a childish expression had been returning during the many years that he had been virtually cut off from the world.

Meantime Ferrand had signalled to Brother Isidore's sister, Marthe, to come to him. She had been standing at the foot of the bed with her arms hanging down beside her, showing the tearless resignation of a poor, narrow-minded girl whilst she watched that dying man whom she worshipped. She was no more than a faithful dog; she had accompanied her brother and spent her scanty savings, without being of any use save to watch him suffer. Accordingly, when the doctor told her to take the invalid in her arms and raise him up a little, she felt quite happy at being of some service at last. Her heavy, freckled, mournful face actually grew bright.

"Hold him," said the doctor, "whilst I try to give him this."

When she had raised him, Ferrand, with the aid of a small spoon, succeeded in introducing a few drops of liquid between his set teeth. Almost immediately the sick man opened his eyes and heaved a deep sigh. He was calmer already; the opium was taking effect and dulling the pain which he felt burning his right side, as though a red-hot iron were being applied to it. However, he remained so weak that, when he wished to speak, it became necessary to place one's ear close to his mouth in order to catch what he said. With a slight sign he had begged Ferrand to bend over him. "You are the doctor, monsieur, are you not?" he faltered. "Give me sufficient strength that I may go once more to the Grotto, this afternoon. I am certain that, if I am able to go, the Blessed Virgin will cure me."

"Why, of course you shall go," replied the young man. "Don't you feel ever so much better?"

"Oh! ever so much better—no! I know very well what my condition is, because I saw many of our Brothers die, out there in Senegal. When the liver is attacked and the abscess has worked its way outside, it means the end. Sweating, fever, and delirium follow. But the Blessed Virgin will touch the sore with her little finger and it will be healed. Oh! I implore you all, take me to the Grotto, even if I should be unconscious!"

Sister Hyacinthe had also approached, and leant over him. "Be easy, dear Brother," said she. "You shall go to the Grotto after *dejeuner*, and we will all pray for you."

At length, in despair at these delays and extremely anxious about Madame Vetu, she was able to get Ferrand away. Still, the Brother's state filled her with pity; and, as they ascended the stairs, she questioned the doctor, asking him if there were really no more hope. The other made a gesture expressive of absolute hopelessness. It was madness to come to Lourdes when one was in such a condition. However, he hastened to add, with a smile: "I beg your pardon, Sister. You know that I am unfortunate enough not to be a believer."

But she smiled in her turn, like an indulgent friend who tolerates the shortcomings of those she loves. "Oh! that doesn't matter," she replied. "I know you; you're all the same a good fellow. Besides, we see so many people, we go amongst such pagans that it would be difficult to shock us."

Up above, in the Sainte-Honorine Ward, they found Madame Vetu still moaning, a prey to most intolerable suffering. Madame de Jonquiere and Madame Desagneaux had remained beside the bed, their faces turning pale, their hearts distracted by that death-cry, which never ceased. And when they consulted Ferrand in a whisper, he merely replied, with a slight shrug of the shoulders, that she was a lost woman, that it was only a question of hours, perhaps merely of minutes. All he could do was to stupefy her also, in order to ease the atrocious death agony which he foresaw. She was watching him, still conscious, and also very obedient, never refusing the medicine offered her. Like the others, she now had but one ardent desire—to go back to the Grotto—and she gave expression to it in the stammering accents of a child who fears that its prayer may not be granted: "To the Grotto—will you? To the Grotto!"

"You shall be taken there by-and-by, I promise you," said Sister Hyacinthe. "But you must be good. Try to sleep a little to gain some strength."

The sick woman appeared to sink into a doze, and Madame de Jonquiere then thought that she might take Madame Desagneaux with her to the other end of the ward to count the linen, a troublesome business, in which they became quite bewildered, as some of the articles were missing. Meantime Sophie, seated on the bed opposite Madame Vetu, had not stirred. She had laid her doll on her lap, and was waiting for the lady's death, since they had told her that she was about to die. Sister Hyacinthe, moreover, had remained beside the dying woman, and, unwilling to waste her time, had taken a needle and cotton to mend some patient's bodice which had a hole in the sleeve.

"You'll stay a little while with us, won't you?" she asked Ferrand.

The latter, who was still watching Madame Vetu, replied: "Yes, yes. She may go off at any moment. I fear hemorrhage." Then, catching sight of Marie on the neighbouring bed, he added in a lower voice: "How is she? Has she experienced any relief?"

"No, not yet. Ah, dear child! we all pray for her very sincerely. She is so young, so sweet, and so sorely afflicted. Just look at her now! Isn't she pretty? One might think her a saint amid all this sunshine, with her large, ecstatic eyes, and her golden hair shining like an aureola!"

Ferrand watched Marie for a moment with interest. Her absent air, her indifference to all about her, the ardent faith, the internal joy which so completely absorbed her, surprised him. "She will recover," he murmured, as though giving utterance to a prognostic. "She will recover."

Then he rejoined Sister Hyacinthe, who had seated herself in the embrasure of the lofty window, which stood wide open, admitting the warm air of the courtyard. The sun was now creeping round, and only a narrow golden ray fell upon her white coif and wimple. Ferrand stood opposite to her, leaning against the window bar and watching her while she sewed. "Do you know, Sister," said he, "this journey to Lourdes, which I undertook to oblige a friend, will be one of the few delights of my life."

She did not understand him, but innocently asked: "Why so?"

"Because I have found you again, because I am here with you, assisting you in your admirable work. And if you only knew how grateful I am to you, what sincere affection and reverence I feel for you!"

She raised her head to look him straight in the face, and began jesting without the least constraint. She was really delicious, with her pure lily-white complexion, her small laughing mouth, and adorable blue eyes which ever smiled. And you could realise that she had grown up in all innocence and devotion, slender and supple, with all the appearance of a girl hardly in her teens.

"What! You are so fond of me as all that!" she exclaimed. "Why?"

"Why I'm fond of you? Because you are the best, the most consoling, the most sisterly of beings. You are the sweetest memory in my life, the memory I evoke whenever I need to be encouraged and sustained. Do you no longer remember the month we spent together, in my poor room, when I was so ill and you so affectionately nursed me?"

"Of course, of course I remember it! Why, I never had so good a patient as you. You took all I offered you; and when I tucked you in, after changing your linen, you remained as still as a little child."

So speaking, she continued looking at him, smiling ingenuously the while. He was very handsome and robust, in the very prime of youth, with a rather pronounced nose, superb eyes, and red lips showing under his black moustache. But she seemed to be simply pleased at seeing him there before her moved almost to tears.

"Ah! Sister, I should have died if it hadn't been for you," he said. "It was through having you that I was cured."

Then, as they gazed at one another, with tender gaiety of heart, the memory of that adorable month recurred to them. They no longer heard Madame Vetu's death moans, nor beheld the ward littered with beds, and, with all its disorder, resembling some infirmary improvised after a public catastrophe. They once more found themselves in a small attic at the top of a dingy house in old Paris, where air and light only reached them through a tiny window opening on to a sea of roofs. And how charming it was to be alone there together—he who had been prostrated by fever, she who had appeared there like a good angel, who had quietly come from her convent like a comrade who fears nothing! It was thus that she nursed women, children, and men, as chance ordained, feeling perfectly happy so long as she had something to do, some sufferer to relieve. She never displayed any consciousness of her sex; and he, on his side, never seemed to have suspected that she might be a woman, except it were for the extreme softness of her hands, the caressing accents of her voice, the beneficent gentleness of her manner; and yet all the tender love of a mother, all the affection of a sister, radiated from her person. During three weeks, as she had said, she had nursed him like a child, helping him in and out of bed, and rendering him every necessary attention, without the slightest embarrassment or repugnance, the holy purity born of suffering and charity shielding them both the while. They were indeed far removed from the frailties of life. And when he became convalescent, what a happy existence began, how joyously they laughed, like two old friends! She still watched over him, scolding him and gently slapping his arms when he persisted in keeping them uncovered. He would watch her standing at the basin, washing him a shirt in order to save him the trifling expense of employing a laundress. No one ever came up there; they were quite alone, thousands of miles away from the world, delighted with this solitude, in which their youth displayed such fraternal gaiety.

"Do you remember, Sister, the morning when I was first able to walk about?" asked Ferrand. "You helped me to get up, and supported me whilst I awkwardly stumbled about, no longer knowing how to use my legs. We did laugh so."

"Yes, yes, you were saved, and I was very pleased."

"And the day when you brought me some cherries—I can see it all again: myself reclining on my pillows, and you seated at the edge of the bed, with the cherries lying between us in a large piece of white paper. I refused to touch them unless you ate some with me. And then we took them in turn, one at a time, until the paper was emptied; and they were very nice."

"Yes, yes, very nice. It was the same with the currant syrup: you would only drink it when I took some also."

Thereupon they laughed yet louder; these recollections quite delighted them. But a painful sigh from Madame Vetu brought them back to the present. Ferrand leant over and cast a glance at the sick woman, who had not stirred. The ward was still full of a quivering peacefulness, which was only broken by the clear voice of Madame Desagneaux counting the linen. Stifling with emotion, the young man resumed in a lower tone: "Ah! Sister, were I to live a hundred years, to know every joy, every pleasure, I should never love another woman as I love you!"

Then Sister Hyacinthe, without, however, showing any confusion, bowed her head and resumed her sewing. An almost imperceptible blush tinged her lily-white skin with pink.

"I also love you well, Monsieur Ferrand," she said, "but you must not make me vain. I only did for you what I do for so many others. It is my business, you see. And there was really only one pleasant thing about it all, that the Almighty cured you."

They were now again interrupted. La Grivotte and Elise Rouquet had returned from the Grotto before the others. La Grivotte at once squatted down on her mattress on the floor, at the foot of Madame Vetu's bed, and, taking a piece of bread from her pocket, proceeded to devour it. Ferrand, since the day before, had felt some interest in this consumptive patient, who was traversing such a curious phase of agitation, a prey to an inordinate appetite and a feverish need of motion. For the moment, however, Elise Rouquet's case interested him still more; for it had now become evident that the lupus, the sore which was eating away her face, was showing signs of cure. She had continued bathing her face at the miraculous fountain, and had just come from the Verification Office, where Doctor Bonamy had triumphed. Ferrand, quite surprised, went and examined the sore, which, although still far from healed, was already paler in colour and slightly desiccated, displaying all the symptoms of gradual cure. And the case seemed to him so curious, that he resolved to make some notes upon it for one of his old masters at the medical college, who was studying the nervous origin of certain skin diseases due to faulty nutrition.

"Have you felt any pricking sensation?" he asked.

"Not at all, monsieur," she replied. "I bathe my face and tell my beads with my whole soul, and that is all."

La Grivotte, who was vain and jealous, and ever since the day before had been going in triumph among the crowds, thereupon called to the doctor. "I say, monsieur, I am cured, cured, cured completely!"

He waved his hand to her in a friendly way, but refused to examine her. "I know, my girl. There is nothing more the matter with you."

Just then Sister Hyacinthe called to him. She had put her sewing down on seeing Madame Vetu raise herself in a frightful fit of nausea. In spite of her haste, however, she was too late with the basin; the sick woman had brought up another discharge of black matter, similar to soot; but, this time, some blood was mixed with it, little specks of violet-coloured blood. It was the hemorrhage coming, the near end which Ferrand had been dreading.

"Send for the superintendent," he said in a low voice, seating himself at the bedside.

Sister Hyacinthe ran for Madame de Jonquiere. The linen having been counted, she found her deep in conversation with her daughter Raymonde, at some distance from Madame Desagneaux, who was washing her hands.

Raymonde had just escaped for a few minutes from the refectory, where she was on duty. This was the roughest of her labours. The long narrow room, with its double row of greasy tables, its sickening smell of food and misery, quite disgusted her. And taking advantage of the half-hour still remaining before the return of the patients, she had hurried up-stairs, where, out of breath, with a rosy face and shining eyes, she had thrown her arms around her mother's neck.

"Ah! mamma," she cried, "what happiness! It's settled!"

Amazed, her head buzzing, busy with the superintendence of her ward, Madame de Jonquiere did not understand. "What's settled, my child?" she asked.

Then Raymonde lowered her voice, and, with a faint blush, replied: "My marriage!"

It was now the mother's turn to rejoice. Lively satisfaction appeared upon her face, the fat face of a ripe, handsome, and still agreeable woman. She at once beheld in her mind's eye their little lodging in the Rue Vaneau, where, since her husband's death, she had reared her daughter with great difficulty upon the few thousand francs he had left her. This marriage, however, meant a return to life, to society, the good old times come back once more.

"Ah! my child, how happy you make me!" she exclaimed.

But a feeling of uneasiness suddenly restrained her. God was her witness that for three years past she had been coming to Lourdes through pure motives of charity, for the one great joy of nursing His beloved invalids. Perhaps, had she closely examined her conscience, she might, behind her devotion, have found some trace of her fondness for authority, which rendered her present managerial duties extremely pleasant to her. However, the hope of finding a husband for her daughter among the suitable young men who swarmed at the Grotto was certainly her last thought. It was a thought which came to her, of course, but merely as something that was possible, though she never mentioned it. However, her happiness, wrung an avowal from her:

"Ah! my child, your success doesn't surprise me. I prayed to the Blessed Virgin for it this morning."

Then she wished to be quite sure, and asked for further information. Raymonde had not yet told her of her long walk leaning on Gerard's arm the day before, for she did not wish to speak of such things until she was triumphant, certain of having at last secured a husband. And now it was indeed settled, as she had exclaimed so gaily: that very morning she had again seen the young man at the Grotto, and he had formally become engaged to her. M. Berthaud would undoubtedly ask for her hand on his cousin's behalf before they took their departure from Lourdes.

"Well," declared Madame de Jonquiere, who was now convinced, smiling, and delighted at heart, "I hope you will be happy, since you are so sensible and do not need my aid to bring your affairs to a successful issue. Kiss me."

It was at this moment that Sister Hyacinthe arrived to announce Madame Vetu's imminent death. Raymonde at once ran off. And Madame Desagneaux, who was wiping her hands, began to complain of the lady-assistants, who had all disappeared precisely on the morning when they were most wanted. "For instance," said she, "there's Madame Volmar. I should like to know where she can have got to. She has not been seen, even for an hour, ever since our arrival."

"Pray leave Madame Volmar alone!" replied Madame de Jonquiere with some asperity. "I have already told you that she is ill."

They both hastened to Madame Vetu. Ferrand stood there waiting; and Sister Hyacinthe having asked him if there were indeed nothing to be done, he shook his head. The dying woman, relieved by her first emesis, now lay inert, with closed eyes. But, a second time, the frightful nausea returned to her, and she brought up another discharge of black matter mingled with violet-coloured blood. Then she had another short interval of calm, during which she noticed La Grivotte, who was greedily devouring her hunk of bread on the mattress on the floor.

"She is cured, isn't she?" the poor woman asked, feeling that she herself was dying.

La Grivotte heard her, and exclaimed triumphantly: "Oh, yes, madame, cured, cured, cured completely!"

For a moment Madame Vetu seemed overcome by a miserable feeling of grief, the revolt of one who will not succumb while others continue to live. But almost immediately she became resigned, and they heard her add very faintly, "It is the young ones who ought to remain."

Then her eyes, which remained wide open, looked round, as though bidding farewell to all those persons, whom she seemed surprised to see about her. She attempted to smile as she encountered the eager gaze of curiosity which little Sophie Couteau still fixed upon her: the charming child had come to kiss her that very morning, in her bed. Elise Rouquet, who troubled herself about nobody, was meantime holding her hand-glass, absorbed in the contemplation of her face, which seemed to her to be growing beautiful, now that the sore was healing. But what especially charmed the dying woman was the sight of Marie, so lovely in her ecstasy. She watched her for a long time, constantly attracted towards her, as towards a vision of light and joy. Perhaps she fancied that she already beheld one of the saints of Paradise amid the glory of the sun.

Suddenly, however, the fits of vomiting returned, and now she solely brought up blood, vitiated blood, the colour of claret. The rush was so great that it bespattered the sheet, and ran all over the bed. In vain did Madame de Jonquiere and Madame Desagneaux bring cloths; they were both very pale and scarce able to remain standing. Ferrand, knowing how powerless he was, had withdrawn to the window, to the very spot where he had so lately experienced such delicious emotion; and with an instinctive movement, of which she was surely unconscious, Sister Hyacinthe had likewise returned to that happy window, as though to be near him.

"Really, can you do nothing?" she inquired.

"No, nothing! She will go off like that, in the same way as a lamp that has burnt out."

Madame Vetu, who was now utterly exhausted, with a thin red stream still flowing from her mouth, looked fixedly at Madame de Jonquiere whilst faintly moving her lips. The lady-superintendent thereupon bent over her and heard these slowly uttered words:

"About my husband, madame—the shop is in the Rue Mouffetard—oh! it's quite a tiny one, not far from the Gobelins.—He's a clockmaker, he is; he couldn't come with me, of course, having to attend to the business; and he will be very much put out when he finds I don't come back.—Yes, I cleaned the jewelry and did the errands—" Then her voice grew fainter, her words disjointed by the death rattle, which began. "Therefore, madame, I beg you will write to him, because I haven't done so, and now here's the end.—Tell him my body had better remain here at Lourdes, on account of the expense.—And he must marry again; it's necessary for one in trade—his cousin—tell him his cousin—"

The rest became a confused murmur. Her weakness was too great, her breath was halting. Yet her eyes continued open and full of life, amid her pale, yellow, waxy mask. And those eyes seemed to fix themselves despairingly on the past, on all that which soon would be no more: the little clockmaker's shop hidden away in a populous neighbourhood; the gentle humdrum existence, with a toiling husband who was ever bending over his watches; the great pleasures of Sunday, such as watching children fly their kites upon the fortifications. And at last these staring eyes gazed vainly into the frightful night which was gathering.

A last time did Madame de Jonquiere lean over her, seeing that her lips were again moving. There came but a faint breath, a voice from far away, which distantly murmured in an accent of intense grief: "She did not cure me."

And then Madame Vetu expired, very gently.

As though this were all that she had been waiting for, little Sophie Couteau jumped from the bed quite satisfied, and went off to play with her doll again at the far end of the ward. Neither La Grivotte, who was finishing her bread, nor Elise Rouquet, busy with her mirror, noticed the catastrophe. However, amidst the cold breath which seemingly swept by, while Madame de Jonquiere and Madame Desagneaux—the latter of whom was unaccustomed to the sight of death—were whispering together in agitation, Marie emerged from the expectant rapture in which the continuous, unspoken prayer of her whole being had plunged her so long. And when she understood what had happened, a feeling of sisterly compassion—the compassion of a suffering companion, on her side certain of cure—brought tears to her eyes.

"Ah! the poor woman!" she murmured; "to think that she has died so far from home, in such loneliness, at the hour when others are being born anew!"

Ferrand, who, in spite of professional indifference, had also been stirred by the scene, stepped forward to verify the death; and it was on a sign from him that Sister Hyacinthe turned up the sheet, and threw it over the dead woman's face, for there could be no question of removing the corpse at that moment. The patients were now returning from the Grotto in bands, and the ward, hitherto so calm, so full of sunshine, was again filling with the tumult of wretchedness and pain—deep coughing and feeble shuffling, mingled with a noisome smell—a pitiful display, in fact, of well-nigh every human infirmity.

II. THE SERVICE AT THE GROTTO

ON that day, Monday, the crowd at the Grotto, was enormous. It was the last day that the national pilgrimage would spend at Lourdes, and Father Fourcade, in his morning address, had said that it would be necessary to make a supreme effort of fervour and faith to obtain from Heaven all that it might be willing to grant in the way of grace and prodigious cure. So, from two o'clock in the afternoon, twenty thousand pilgrims were assembled there, feverish, and agitated by the most ardent hopes. From minute to minute the throng continued increasing, to such a point, indeed, that Baron Suire became alarmed, and came out of the Grotto to say to Berthaud: "My friend, we shall be overwhelmed, that's certain. Double your squads, bring your men closer together."

The Hospitality of Our Lady of Salvation was alone entrusted with the task of keeping order, for there were neither guardians nor policemen, of any sort present; and it was for this reason that the President of the Association was so alarmed. However, Berthaud, under grave circumstances, was a leader whose words commanded attention, and who was endowed with energy that could be relied on.

"Be easy," said he; "I will be answerable for everything. I shall not move from here until the four-o'clock procession has passed by."

Nevertheless, he signalled to Gerard to approach.

"Give your men the strictest instructions," he said to him. "Only those persons who have cards should be allowed to pass. And place your men nearer each other; tell them to hold the cord tight."

Yonder, beneath the ivy which draped the rock, the Grotto opened, with the eternal flaring of its candles. From a distance it looked rather squat and misshapen, a very narrow and modest aperture for the breath of the Infinite which issued from it, turning all faces pale and bowing every head. The statue of the Virgin had become a mere white spot, which seemed to move amid the quiver of the atmosphere, heated by the small yellow flames. To see everything it was necessary to raise oneself; for the silver altar, the harmonium divested of its housing, the heap of bouquets flung there, and the votive offerings streaking the smoky walls were scarcely distinguishable from behind the railing. And the day was lovely; never yet had a purer sky expanded above the immense crowd; the softness of the breeze in particular seemed delicious after the storm of the night, which had brought down the over-oppressive heat of the two first days.

Gerard had to fight his way with his elbows in order to repeat the orders to his men. The crowd had already begun pushing. "Two more men here!" he called. "Come, four together, if necessary, and hold the rope well!"

The general impulse was instinctive and invincible; the twenty thousand persons assembled there were drawn towards the Grotto by an irresistible attraction, in which burning curiosity mingled with the thirst for mystery. All eyes converged, every mouth, hand, and body was borne towards the pale glitter of the candles and the white moving speck of the marble Virgin. And, in order that the large space reserved to the sick, in front of the railings, might not be invaded by the swelling mob, it had been necessary to inclose it with a stout rope which the bearers at intervals of two or three yards grasped with both hands. Their orders were to let nobody pass excepting the sick provided with hospital cards and the few persons to whom special authorisations had been granted. They limited themselves, therefore, to raising the cords and then letting them fall behind the chosen ones, without heeding the supplications of the others. In fact they even showed themselves somewhat rough, taking a certain pleasure in exercising the authority with which they were invested for a day. In truth, however, they were very much pushed about, and had to support each other and resist with all the strength of their loins to avoid being swept away.

While the benches before the Grotto and the vast reserved space were filling with sick people, handcarts, and stretchers, the crowd, the immense crowd, swayed about on the outskirts. Starting from the Place du Rosaire, it extended to the bottom of the promenade along the Gave, where the pavement throughout its entire length was black with people, so dense a human sea that all circulation was prevented. On the parapet was an interminable line of women—most of them seated, but some few standing so as to see the better—and almost all carrying silk parasols, which, with holiday-like gaiety, shimmered in the sunlight. The managers had wished to keep a path open in order that the sick might be brought along; but it was ever being invaded and obstructed, so that the carts and stretchers remained on the road, submerged and lost until a bearer freed them. Nevertheless, the great tramping was that of a docile flock, an innocent, lamb-like crowd; and it was only the involuntary pushing, the blind rolling towards the light of the candles that had to be contended against. No accident had ever happened there, notwithstanding the excitement, which gradually increased and threw the people into the unruly delirium of faith.

However, Baron Suire again forced his way through the throng. "Berthaud! Berthaud!" he called, "see that the *defile* is conducted less rapidly. There are women and children stifling."

This time Berthaud gave a sign of impatience. "Ah! hang it, I can't be everywhere! Close the gate for a moment if it's necessary."

It was a question of the march through the Grotto which went on throughout the afternoon. The faithful were permitted to enter by the door on the left, and made their exit by that on the right.

"Close the gate!" exclaimed the Baron. "But that would be worse; they would all get crushed against it!"

As it happened Gerard was there, thoughtlessly talking for an instant with Raymonde, who was standing on the other side of the cord, holding a bowl of milk which she was about to carry to a paralysed old woman; and Berthaud ordered the young fellow to post two men at the entrance gate of the iron railing, with instructions only to allow the pilgrims to enter by tens. When Gerard had executed this order, and returned, he found Berthaud laughing and joking with Raymonde. She went off on her errand, however, and the two men stood watching her while she made the paralysed woman drink.

"She is charming, and it's settled, eh?" said Berthaud. "You are going to marry her, aren't you?"

"I shall ask her mother to-night. I rely upon you to accompany me."

"Why, certainly. You know what I told you. Nothing could be more sensible. The uncle will find you a berth before six months are over."

A push of the crowd separated them, and Berthaud went off to make sure whether the march through the Grotto was now being accomplished in a methodical manner, without any crushing. For hours the same unbroken tide rolled in—women, men, and children from all parts of the world, all who chose, all who passed that way. As a result, the crowd was singularly mixed: there were beggars in rags beside neat *bourgeois*, peasants of either sex, well dressed ladies, servants with bare hair, young girls with bare feet, and others with pomatumed hair and foreheads bound with ribbons. Admission was free; the mystery was open to all, to unbelievers as well as to the faithful, to those who were solely influenced by curiosity as well as to those who entered with their hearts faint with love. And it was a sight to see them, all almost equally affected by the tepid odour of the wax, half stifling in the heavy tabernacle air which gathered beneath the rocky vault, and lowering their eyes for fear of slipping on the gratings. Many stood there bewildered, not even bowing, examining the things around with the covert uneasiness of indifferent folks astray amidst the redoubtable mysteries of a sanctuary. But the devout crossed themselves, threw letters, deposited candles and bouquets, kissed the rock below the Virgin's statue, or else rubbed their chaplets, medals, and other small objects of piety against it, as the contact sufficed to bless them. And the *defile* continued, continued without end during days and months as it had done for years; and it seemed as if the whole world, all the miseries and sufferings of humanity, came in turn and passed in the same hypnotic, contagious kind of round, through that rocky nook, ever in search of happiness.

When Berthaud had satisfied himself that everything was working well, he walked about like a mere spectator, superintending his men. Only one matter remained to trouble him: the procession of the Blessed Sacrament, during which such frenzy burst forth that accidents were always to be feared.

This last day seemed likely to be a very fervent one, for he already felt a tremor of exalted faith rising among the crowd. The treatment needed for miraculous care was drawing to an end; there had been the fever of the journey, the besetting influence of the same endlessly repeated hymns, and the stubborn continuation of the same religious exercises; and ever and ever the conversation had been turned on miracles, and the mind fixed on the divine illumination of the Grotto. Many, not having slept for three nights, had reached a state of hallucination, and walked about in a rageful dream. No repose was granted them, the continual prayers were like whips lashing their souls. The appeals to the Blessed Virgin never ceased; priest followed priest in the pulpit, proclaiming the universal dolour and directing the despairing supplications of the throng, during the whole time that the sick remained with hands clasped and eyes raised to heaven before the pale, smiling, marble statue.

At that moment the white stone pulpit against the rock on the right of the Grotto was occupied by a priest from Toulouse, whom Berthaud knew, and to whom he listened for a moment with an air of approval. He was a stout man with an unctuous dicdiction, famous for his rhetorical successes. However, all eloquence here consisted in displaying the strength of one's lungs in a violent delivery of the phrase or cry which the whole crowd had to repeat; for the addresses were nothing more than so much vociferation interspersed with "Ayes" and "Paters."

The priest, who had just finished the Rosary, strove to increase his stature by stretching his short legs, whilst shouting the first appeal of the litanies which he improvised, and led in his own way, according to the inspiration which possessed him.

"Mary, we love thee!" he called.

And thereupon the crowd repeated in a lower, confused, and broken tone: "Mary, we love thee!"

From that moment there was no stopping. The voice of the priest rang out at full swing, and the voices of the crowd responded in a dolorous murmur:

"Mary, thou art our only hope!"

"Mary, thou art our only hope!"

"Pure Virgin, make us purer, among the pure!"

"Pure Virgin, make us purer, among the pure!"

"Powerful Virgin, save our sick!"

"Powerful Virgin, save our sick!"

Often, when the priest's imagination failed him, or he wished to thrust a cry home with greater force, he would repeat it thrice; while the docile crowd would do the same, quivering under the enervating effect of the persistent lamentation, which increased the fever.

The litanies continued, and Berthaud went back towards the Grotto. Those who defiled through it beheld an extraordinary sight when they turned and faced the sick. The whole of the large space between the cords was occupied by the thousand or twelve hundred patients whom the national pilgrimage had brought with it; and beneath the vast, spotless sky on that radiant day there was the most heart-rending jumble of sufferers that one could behold. The three hospitals of Lourdes had emptied their chambers of horror. To begin with, those who were still able to remain seated had been piled upon the benches. Many of them, however, were propped up with cushions, whilst others kept shoulder to shoulder, the strong ones supporting the weak. Then, in front of the benches, before the Grotto itself, were the more grievously afflicted sufferers lying at full length; the flagstones disappearing from view beneath this woeful assemblage, which was like a large, stagnant pool of horror. There was an indescribable block of vehicles, stretchers, and mattresses. Some of the invalids in little boxes not unlike coffins had raised themselves up and showed above the others, but the majority lay almost on a level with the ground. There were some lying fully dressed on the check-patterned ticks of mattresses; whilst others had been brought with their bedding, so that only their heads and pale hands were seen outside the sheets. Few of these pallets were clean. Some pillows of dazzling whiteness, which by a last feeling of coquetry had been trimmed with embroidery, alone shone out among all the filthy wretchedness of all the rest—a fearful collection of rags, worn-out blankets, and linen splashed with stains. And all were pushed, squeezed, piled up by chance as they came, women, men, children, and priests, people in nightgowns beside people who were fully attired being jumbled together in the blinding light of day.

And all forms of disease were there, the whole frightful procession which, twice a day, left the hospitals to wend its way through horrified Lourdes. There were the heads eaten away by eczema, the foreheads crowned with roseola, and the noses and mouths which elephantiasis had transformed into shapeless snouts. Next, the dropsical ones, swollen out like leathern bottles; the rheumatic ones with twisted hands and swollen feet, like bags stuffed full of rags; and a sufferer from hydrocephalus, whose huge and weighty skull fell backwards. Then the consumptive ones, with livid skins, trembling with fever, exhausted by dysentery, wasted to skeletons. Then the deformities, the contractions, the twisted trunks, the twisted arms, the necks all awry; all the poor broken, pounded creatures, motionless in their tragic, marionette-like postures. Then the poor rachitic girls displaying their waxen complexions and slender necks eaten into by sores; the yellow-faced, besotted-looking women in the painful stupor which falls on unfortunate creatures devoured by cancer; and the others who turned pale, and dared not move, fearing as they did the shock of the tumours whose weighty pain was stifling them. On the benches sat bewildered deaf women, who heard nothing, but sang on all the same, and blind ones with heads erect, who remained for hours turned toward the statue of the Virgin which they could not see. And there was also the woman stricken with imbecility, whose nose was eaten away, and who laughed with a terrifying laugh, displaying the black, empty cavern of her mouth; and then the epileptic woman, whom a recent attack had left as pale as death, with froth still at the corners of her lips.

But sickness and suffering were no longer of consequence, since they were all there, seated or stretched with their eyes upon the Grotto. The poor, fleshless, earthy-looking faces became transfigured, and began to glow with hope. Anchylosed hands were joined, heavy eyelids found the strength to rise, exhausted voices revived as the priest shouted the appeals. At first there was nothing but indistinct stuttering, similar to slight puffs of air rising, here and there above the multitude. Then the cry ascended and spread through the crowd itself from one to the other end of the immense square.

"Mary, conceived without sin, pray for us!" cried the priest in his thundering voice.

And the sick and the pilgrims repeated louder and louder: "Mary, conceived without sin, pray for us!"

Then the flow of the litany set in, and continued with increasing speed:

"Most pure Mother, most chaste Mother, thy children are at thy feet!"

"Most pure Mother, most chaste Mother, thy children are at thy feet!"

"Queen of the Angels, say but a word, and our sick shall be healed!"

"Queen of the Angels, say but a word, and our sick shall be healed!"

In the second row of sufferers, near the pulpit, was M. Sabathier, who had asked to be brought there early, wishing to choose his place like an old *habitue* who knew the cosy corners. Moreover, it seemed to him that it was of paramount importance that he should be as near as possible, under the very eyes of the Virgin, as though she required to see her faithful in order not to forget them. However, for the seven years that he had been coming there he had nursed this one hope of being some day noticed by her, of touching her, and of obtaining his cure, if not by selection, at least by seniority. This merely needed patience on his part without the firmness of his faith being in the least shaken by his way of thinking. Only, like a poor, resigned man just a little weary of being always put off, he sometimes allowed himself diversions. For instance, he had obtained permission to keep his wife near him, seated on a camp-stool, and he liked to talk to her, and acquaint her with his reflections.

"Raise me a little, my dear," said he. "I am slipping. I am very uncomfortable."

Attired in trousers and a coarse woollen jacket, he was sitting upon his mattress, with his back leaning against a tilted chair.

"Are you better?" asked his wife, when she had raised him.

"Yes, yes," he answered; and then began to take an interest in Brother Isidore, whom they had succeeded in bringing in spite of everything, and who was lying upon a neighbouring mattress, with a sheet drawn up to his chin, and nothing protruding but his wasted hands, which lay clasped upon the blanket.

"Ah! the poor man," said M. Sabathier. "It's very imprudent, but the Blessed Virgin is so powerful when she chooses!"

He took up his chaplet again, but once more broke off from his devotions on perceiving Madame Maze, who had just glided into the reserved space—so slender and unobtrusive that she had doubtless slipped under the ropes without being noticed. She had seated herself at the end of a bench and, very quiet and motionless, did not occupy more room there than a child. And her long face, with its weary features, the face of a woman of two-and-thirty faded before her time, wore an expression of unlimited sadness, infinite abandonment.

"And so," resumed M. Sabathier in a low voice, again addressing his wife after attracting her attention by a slight movement of the chin, "it's for the conversion of her husband that this lady prays. You came across her this morning in a shop, didn't you?"

"Yes, yes," replied Madame Sabathier. "And, besides, I had some talk about her with another lady who knows her. Her husband is a commercial-traveller. He leaves her for six months at a time, and goes about with other people. Oh! he's a very gay fellow, it seems, very nice, and he doesn't let her want for money; only she adores him, she cannot accustom herself to his neglect, and comes to pray the Blessed Virgin to give him back to her. At this moment, it appears, he is close by, at Luchon, with two ladies—two sisters."

M. Sabathier signed to his wife to stop. He was now looking at the Grotto, again becoming a man of intellect, a professor whom questions of art had formerly impassioned. "You see, my dear," he said, "they have spoilt the Grotto by endeavouring to make it too beautiful. I am certain it looked much better in its original wildness. It has lost its characteristic features—and what a frightful shop they have stuck there, on the left!"

However, he now experienced sudden remorse for his thoughtlessness. Whilst he was chatting away, might not the Blessed Virgin be noticing one of his neighbours, more fervent, more sedate than himself? Feeling anxious on the point, he reverted to his customary modesty and patience, and with dull, expressionless eyes again began waiting for the good pleasure of Heaven.

Moreover, the sound of a fresh voice helped to bring him back to this annihilation, in which nothing was left of the cultured reasoner that he had formerly been. It was another preacher who had just entered the pulpit, a Capuchin this time, whose guttural call, persistently repeated, sent a tremor through the crowd.

"Holy Virgin of virgins, be blessed!"

"Holy Virgin of virgins, be blessed!"

"Holy Virgin of virgins, turn not thy face from thy children!"

"Holy Virgin of virgins, turn not thy face from thy children!"

"Holy Virgin of virgins, breathe upon our sores, and our sores shall heal!"

"Holy Virgin of virgins, breathe upon our sores, and our sores shall heal!"

At the end of the first bench, skirting the central path, which was becoming crowded, the Vigneron family had succeeded in finding room for themselves. They were all there: little Gustave, seated in a sinking posture, with his crutch between his legs; his mother, beside him, following the prayers like a punctilious *bourgeoise*; his aunt, Madame Chaise, on the other side, so inconvenienced by the crowd that she was stifling; and M. Vigneron, who remained silent and, for a moment, had been examining Madame Chaise attentively.

"What is the matter with you, my dear?" he inquired. "Do you feel unwell?"

She was breathing with difficulty. "Well, I don't know," she answered; "but I can't feel my limbs, and my breath fails me."

At that very moment the thought had occurred to him that all the agitation, fever, and scramble of a pilgrimage could not be very good for heart-disease. Of course he did not desire anybody's death, he had never asked the Blessed Virgin for any such thing. If his prayer for advancement had already been granted through the sudden death of his chief, it must certainly be because Heaven had already ordained the latter's death. And, in the same way, if Madame Chaise should die first, leaving her fortune to Gustave, he would only have to bow before the will of God, which generally requires that the aged should go off before the young. Nevertheless, his hope unconsciously became so keen that he could not help exchanging a glance with his wife, to whom had come the same involuntary thought.

"Gustave, draw back," he exclaimed; "you are inconveniencing your aunt." And then, as Raymonde passed, he asked; "Do you happen to have a glass of water, mademoiselle? One of our relatives here is losing consciousness."

But Madame Chaise refused the offer with a gesture. She was getting better, recovering her breath with an effort. "No, I want nothing, thank you," she gasped. "There, I'm better—still, I really thought this time that I should stifle!"

Her fright left her trembling, with haggard eyes in her pale face. She again joined her hands, and begged the Blessed Virgin to save her from other attacks and cure her; while the Vignerons, man and wife, honest folk both of them, reverted to the covert prayer for happiness that they had come to offer up at Lourdes: a pleasant old age, deservedly gained by twenty years of honesty, with a respectable fortune which in later years they would go and enjoy in the country, cultivating flowers. On the other hand, little Gustave, who had seen and noted everything with his bright eyes and intelligence sharpened by suffering, was not praying, but smiling at space, with his vague enigmatical smile. What could be the use of his praying? He knew that the Blessed Virgin would not cure him, and that he would die.

However, M. Vigneron could not remain long without busying himself about his neighbours. Madame Dieulafay, who had come late, had been deposited in the crowded central pathway; and he marvelled at the luxury about the young woman, that sort of coffin quilted with white silk, in which she was lying, attired in a pink dressing-gown trimmed with Valenciennes lace. The husband in a frock-coat, and the sister in a black gown of simple but marvellous elegance, were standing by; while Abbe Judaine, kneeling near the sufferer, finished offering up a fervent prayer.

When the priest had risen, M. Vigneron made him a little room on the bench beside him; and he then took the liberty of questioning him. "Well, Monsieur le Cure, does that poor young woman feel a little better?"

Abbe Judaine made a gesture of infinite sadness.

"Alas! no. I was full of so much hope! It was I who persuaded the family to come. Two years ago the Blessed Virgin showed me such extraordinary grace by curing my poor lost eyes, that I hoped to obtain another favour from her. However, I will not despair. We still have until to-morrow."

M. Vigneron again looked towards Madame Dieulafay and examined her face, still of a perfect oval and with admirable eyes; but it was expressionless, with ashen hue, similar to a mask of death, amidst the lace. "It's really very sad," he murmured.

"And if you had seen her last summer!" resumed the priest. "They have their country seat at Saligny, my parish, and I often dined with them. I cannot help feeling sad when I look at her elder sister, Madame Jousseur, that lady in black who stands there, for she bears a strong resemblance to her; and the poor sufferer was even prettier, one of the beauties of Paris. And now compare them together—observe that brilliancy, that sovereign grace, beside that poor, pitiful creature—it oppresses one's heart—ah! what a frightful lesson!"

He became silent for an instant. Saintly man that he was naturally, altogether devoid of passions, with no keen intelligence to disturb him in his faith, he displayed a naive admiration for beauty, wealth, and power, which he had never envied. Nevertheless, he ventured to express a doubt, a scruple, which troubled his usual serenity. "For my part, I should have liked her to come here with more simplicity, without all that surrounding of luxury, because the Blessed Virgin prefers the humble—But I understand very well that there are certain social exigencies. And, then, her husband and sister love her so! Remember that he has forsaken his business and she her pleasures in order to come here with her; and so overcome are they at the idea of losing her that their eyes are never dry, they always have that bewildered look which you can notice. So they must be excused for trying to procure her the comfort of looking beautiful until the last hour."

M. Vigneron nodded his head approvingly. Ah! it was certainly not the wealthy who had the most luck at the Grotto! Servants, country folk, poor beggars, were cured, while ladies returned home with their ailments unrelieved, notwithstanding their gifts and the big candles they had burnt. And, in spite of himself, Vigneron then looked at Madame Chaise, who, having recovered from her attack, was now reposing with a comfortable air.

But a tremor passed through the crowd and Abbe Judaine spoke again: "Here is Father Massias coming towards the pulpit. He is a saint; listen to him."

They knew him, and were aware that he could not make his appearance without every soul being stirred by sudden hope, for it was reported that the miracles were often brought to pass by his great fervour. His voice, full of tenderness and strength, was said to be appreciated by the Virgin.

All heads were therefore uplifted and the emotion yet further increased when Father Fourcade was seen coming to the foot of the pulpit, leaning on the shoulder of his well-beloved brother, the preferred of all; and he stayed there, so that he also might hear him. His gouty foot had been paining him more acutely since the morning, so that it required great courage on his part to remain thus standing and smiling. The increasing exaltation of the crowd made him happy, however; he foresaw prodigies and dazzling cures which would redound to the glory of Mary and Jesus.

Having ascended the pulpit, Father Massias did not at once speak. He seemed, very tall, thin, and pale, with an ascetic face, elongated the more by his discoloured beard. His eyes sparkled, and his large eloquent mouth protruded passionately.

"Lord, save us, for we perish!" he suddenly cried; and in a fever, which increased minute by minute, the transported crowd repeated: "Lord, save us, for we perish!"

Then he opened his arms and again launched forth his flaming cry, as if he had torn it from his glowing heart: "Lord, if it be Thy will, Thou canst heal me!"

"Lord, if it be Thy will, Thou canst heal me!"

"Lord, I am not worthy that Thou shouldst enter under my roof, but only say the word, and I shall be healed!"

"Lord, I am not worthy that Thou shouldst enter under my roof, but only say the word, and I shall be healed!"

Marthe, Brother Isidore's sister, had now begun to talk in a whisper to Madame Sabathier, near whom she had at last seated herself. They had formed an acquaintance at the hospital; and, drawn together by so much suffering, the servant had familiarly confided to the *bourgeoise* how anxious she felt about her brother; for she could plainly see that he had very little breath left in him. The Blessed Virgin must be quick indeed if she desired to save him. It was already a miracle that they had been able to bring him alive as far as the Grotto.

In her resignation, poor, simple creature that she was, she did not weep; but her heart was so swollen that her infrequent words came faintly from her lips. Then a flood of past memories suddenly returned to her; and with her utterance thickened by prolonged silence, she began to relieve her heart: "We were fourteen at home, at Saint Jacut, near Vannes. He, big as he was, has always been delicate, and that was why he remained with our priest, who ended by placing him among the Christian Brothers. The elder ones took over the property, and, for my part, I preferred going out to service. Yes, it was a lady who took me with her to Paris, five years ago already. Ah! what a lot of trouble there is in life! Everyone has so much trouble!"

"You are quite right, my girl," replied Madame Sabathier, looking the while at her husband, who was devoutly repeating each of Father Massias's appeals.

"And then," continued Marthe, "there I learned last month that Isidore, who had returned from a hot climate where he had been on a mission, had brought a bad sickness back with him. And, when I ran to see him, he told me he should die if he did not leave for Lourdes, but that he couldn't make the journey, because he had nobody to accompany him. Then, as I had eighty francs saved up, I gave up my place, and we set out together. You see, madame, if I am so fond of him, it's because he used to bring me gooseberries from the parsonage, whereas all the others beat me."

She relapsed into silence for a moment, her countenance swollen by grief, and her poor eyes so scorched by watching that no tears could come from them. Then she began to stutter disjointed words: "Look at him, madame. It fills one with pity. Ah! my God, his poor cheeks, his poor chin, his poor face—"

It was, in fact, a lamentable spectacle. Madame Sabathier's heart was quite upset when she observed Brother Isidore so yellow, cadaverous, steeped in a cold sweat of agony. Above the sheet he still only showed his clasped hands and his face encircled with long scanty hair; but if those wax-like hands seemed lifeless, if there was not a feature of that long-suffering face that stirred, its eyes were still alive, inextinguishable eyes of love, whose flame sufficed to illumine the whole of his expiring visage—the visage of a Christ upon the cross. And never had the contrast been so clearly marked between his low forehead and unintelligent, loutish, peasant air, and the divine splendour which came from his poor human mask, ravaged and sanctified by suffering, sublime at this last hour in the passionate radiance of his faith. His flesh had melted, as it were; he was no longer a breath, nothing but a look, a light.

Since he had been set down there his eyes had not strayed from the statue of the Virgin. Nothing else existed around him. He did not see the enormous multitude, he did not even hear the wild cries of the priests, the incessant cries which shook this quivering crowd. His eyes alone remained to him, his eyes burning with infinite tenderness, and they were fixed upon the Virgin, never more to turn from her. They drank her in, even unto death; they made a last effort of will to disappear, die out in her. For an instant, however, his mouth half opened and his drawn visage relaxed as an expression of celestial beatitude came over it. Then nothing more stirred, his eyes remained wide open, still obstinately fixed upon the white statue.

A few seconds elapsed. Marthe had felt a cold breath, chilling the roots of her hair. "I say, madame, look!" she stammered.

Madame Sabathier, who felt anxious, pretended that she did not understand. "What is it, my girl?"

"My brother! look! He no longer moves. He opened his mouth, and has not stirred since." Then they both shuddered, feeling certain he was dead. He had, indeed, just passed away, without a rattle, without a breath, as if life had escaped in his glance, through his large, loving eyes, ravenous with passion. He had expired gazing upon the Virgin, and nothing could have been so sweet; and he still continued to gaze upon her with his dead eyes, as though with ineffable delight.

"Try to close his eyes," murmured Madame Sabathier. "We shall soon know then."

Marthe had already risen, and, leaning forward, so as not to be observed, she endeavoured to close the eyes with a trembling finger. But each time they reopened, and again looked at the Virgin with invincible obstinacy. He was dead, and Marthe had to leave his eyes wide open, steeped in unbounded ecstasy.

"Ah! it's finished, it's quite finished, madame!" she stuttered.

Two tears then burst from her heavy eyelids and ran down her cheeks; while Madame Sabathier caught hold of her hand to keep her quiet. There had been whisperings, and uneasiness was already spreading. But what course could be adopted? It was impossible to carry off the corpse amidst such a mob, during the prayers, without incurring the risk of creating a disastrous effect. The best plan would be to leave it there, pending a favourable moment. The poor fellow scandalised no one, he did not seem any more dead now than he had seemed ten minutes previously, and everybody would think that his flaming eyes were still alive, ardently appealing to the divine compassion of the Blessed Virgin.

Only a few persons among those around knew the truth. M. Sabathier, quite scared, had made a questioning sign to his wife, and on being answered by a prolonged affirmative nod, he had returned to his prayers without any rebellion, though he could not help turning pale at the thought of the mysterious almighty power which sent death when life was asked for. The Vignerons, who were very much interested, leaned forward, and whispered as though in presence of some street accident, one of those petty incidents which in Paris the father sometimes related on returning home from the Ministry, and which sufficed to occupy them all, throughout the evening. Madame Jousseur, for her part, had simply turned round and whispered a word or two in M. Dieulafay's ear, and then they had both reverted to the heart-rending contemplation of their own dear invalid; whilst Abbe Judaine, informed by M. Vigneron, knelt down, and in a low, agitated voice recited the prayers for the dead. Was he not a Saint, that missionary who had returned from a deadly climate, with a mortal wound in his side, to die there, beneath the smiling gaze of the Blessed Virgin? And Madame Maze, who also knew what had happened, suddenly felt a taste for death, and resolved that she would implore Heaven to suppress her also, in unobtrusive fashion, if it would not listen to her prayer and give her back her husband.

But the cry of Father Massias rose into a still higher key, burst forth with a strength of terrible despair, with a rending like that of a sob: "Jesus, son of David, I am perishing, save me!"

And the crowd sobbed after him in unison "Jesus, son of David, I am perishing, save me!"

Then, in quick succession, and in higher and higher keys, the appeals went on proclaiming the intolerable misery of the world:

"Jesus, son of David, take pity on Thy sick children!"

"Jesus, son of David, take pity on Thy sick children!"

"Jesus, son of David, come, heal them, that they may live!"

"Jesus, son of David, come, heal them, that they may live!"

It was delirium. At the foot of the pulpit Father Fourcade, succumbing to the extraordinary passion which overflowed from all hearts, had likewise raised his arms, and was shouting the appeals in his thundering voice as though to compel the intervention of Heaven. And the exaltation was still increasing beneath this blast of desire, whose powerful breath bowed every head in turn, spreading even to the young women who, in a spirit of mere curiosity, sat watching the scene from the parapet of the Gave; for these also turned pale under their sunshades.

Miserable humanity was clamouring from the depths of its abyss of suffering, and the clamour swept along, sending a shudder down every spine, for one and all were plunged in agony, refusing to die, longing to compel God to grant them eternal life. Ah! life, life! that was what all those unfortunates, who had come so far, amid so many obstacles, wanted—that was the one boon they asked for in their wild desire to live it over again, to live it always! O Lord, whatever our misery, whatever the torment of our life may be, cure us, grant that we may begin to live again and suffer once more what we have suffered already. However unhappy we may be, to be is what we wish. It is not heaven that we ask Thee for, it is earth; and grant that we may leave it at the latest possible moment, never leave it, indeed, if such be Thy good pleasure. And even when we no longer implore a physical cure, but a moral favour, it is still happiness that we ask Thee for; happiness, the thirst for which alone consumes us. O Lord, grant that we may be happy and healthy; let us live, ay, let us live forever!

This wild cry, the cry of man's furious desire for life, came in broken accents, mingled with tears, from every breast.

"O Lord, son of David, heal our sick!"

"O Lord, son of David, heal our sick!"

Berthaud had twice been obliged to dash forward to prevent the cords from giving way under the unconscious pressure of the crowd. Baron Suire, in despair, kept on making signs, begging someone to come to his assistance; for the Grotto was now invaded, and the march past had become the mere trampling of a flock rushing to its passion. In vain did Gerard again leave Raymonde and post himself at the entrance gate of the iron railing, so as to carry out the orders, which were to admit the pilgrims by tens. He was hustled and swept aside, while with feverish excitement everybody rushed in, passing like a torrent between the flaring candles, throwing bouquets and letters to the Virgin, and kissing the rock, which the pressure of millions of inflamed lips had polished. It was faith run wild, the great power that nothing henceforth could stop.

And now, whilst Gerard stood there, hemmed in against the iron railing, he heard two countrywomen, whom the advance was bearing onward, raise loud exclamations at sight of the sufferers lying on the stretchers before them. One of them was so greatly impressed by the pallid face of Brother Isidore, whose large dilated eyes were still fixed on the statue of the Virgin, that she crossed herself, and, overcome by devout admiration, murmured: "Oh! look at that one; see how he is praying with his whole heart, and how he gazes on Our Lady of Lourdes!"

The other peasant woman thereupon replied "Oh! she will certainly cure him, he is so beautiful!"

Indeed, as the dead man lay there, his eyes still fixedly staring whilst he continued his prayer of love and faith, his appearance touched every heart. No one in that endless, streaming throng could behold him without feeling edified.

III. MARIE'S CURE

IT was good Abbe Judaine who was to carry the Blessed Sacrament in the four-o'clock procession. Since the Blessed Virgin had cured him of a disease of the eyes, a miracle with which the Catholic press still resounded, he had become one of the glories of Lourdes, was given the first place, and honoured with all sorts of attentions.

At half-past three he rose, wishing to leave the Grotto, but the extraordinary concourse of people quite frightened him, and he feared he would be late if he did not succeed in getting out of it. Fortunately help came to him in the person of Berthaud. "Monsieur le Cure," exclaimed the superintendent of the bearers, "don't attempt to pass out by way of the Rosary; you would never arrive in time. The best course is to ascend by the winding paths—and come! follow me; I will go before you."

By means of his elbows, he thereupon parted the dense throng and opened a path for the priest, who overwhelmed him with thanks. "You are too kind. It's my fault; I had forgotten myself. But, good heavens! how shall we manage to pass with the procession presently?"

This procession was Berthaud's remaining anxiety. Even on ordinary days it provoked wild excitement, which forced him to take special measures; and what would now happen, as it wended its way through this dense multitude of thirty thousand persons, consumed by such a fever of faith, already on the verge of divine frenzy? Accordingly, in a sensible way, he took advantage of this opportunity to give Abbe Judaine the best advice.

"Ah! Monsieur le Cure, pray impress upon your colleagues of the clergy that they must not leave any space between their ranks; they should come on slowly, one close behind the other. And, above all, the banners should be firmly grasped, so that they may not be overthrown. As for yourself, Monsieur le Cure, see that the canopy-bearers are strong, tighten the cloth around the monstrance, and don't be afraid to carry it in both hands with all your strength."

A little frightened by this advice, the priest went on expressing his thanks. "Of course, of course; you are very good," said he. "Ah! monsieur, how much I am indebted to you for having helped me to escape from all those people!"

Then, free at last, he hastened towards the Basilica by the narrow serpentine path which climbs the hill; while his companion again plunged into the mob, to return to his post of inspection.

At that same moment Pierre, who was bringing Marie to the Grotto in her little cart, encountered on the other side, that of the Place du Rosaire, the impenetrable wall formed by the crowd. The servant at the hotel had awakened him at three o'clock, so that he might go and fetch the young girl at the hospital. There seemed to be no hurry; they apparently had plenty of time to reach the Grotto before the procession. However, that immense throng, that resisting, living wall, through which he did not know how to break, began to cause him some uneasiness. He would never succeed in passing with the little car if the people did not evince some obligingness. "Come, ladies, come!" he appealed. "I beg of you! You see, it's for a patient!"

The ladies, hypnotised as they were by the spectacle of the Grotto sparkling in the distance, and standing on tiptoe so as to lose nothing of the sight, did not move, however. Besides, the clamour of the litanies was so loud at this moment that they did not even hear the young priest's entreaties.

Then Pierre began again: "Pray stand on one side, gentlemen; allow me to pass. A little room for a sick person. Come, please, listen to what I am saying!"

But the men, beside themselves, in a blind, deaf rapture, would stir no more than the women.

Marie, however, smiled serenely, as if ignorant of the impediments, and convinced that nothing in the world could prevent her from going to her cure. However, when Pierre had found an aperture, and begun to work his way through the moving mass, the situation became more serious. From all parts the swelling human waves beat against the frail chariot, and at times threatened to submerge it. At each step it became necessary to stop, wait, and again entreat the people. Pierre had never before felt such an anxious sensation in a crowd. True, it was not a threatening mob, it was as innocent as a flock of sheep; but he found a troubling thrill in its midst, a peculiar atmosphere that upset him. And, in spite of his affection for the humble, the ugliness of the features around him, the common, sweating faces, the evil breath, and the old clothes, smelling of poverty, made him suffer even to nausea.

"Now, ladies, now, gentlemen, it's for a patient," he repeated. "A little room, I beg of you!"

Buffeted about in this vast ocean, the little vehicle continued to advance by fits and starts, taking long minutes to get over a few yards of ground. At one moment you might have thought it swamped, for no sign of it could be detected. Then, however, it reappeared near the piscinas. Tender sympathy had at length been awakened for this sick girl, so wasted by suffering, but still so beautiful. When people had been compelled to give way before the priest's stubborn pushing, they turned round, but did not dare to get angry, for pity penetrated them at sight of that thin, suffering face, shining out amidst a halo of fair hair. Words of compassion and admiration were heard on all sides: "Ah, the poor child!"—"Was it not cruel to be infirm at her age?"—"Might the Blessed Virgin be merciful to her!" Others, however, expressed surprise, struck as they were by the ecstasy in which they saw her, with her clear eyes open to the spheres beyond, where she had placed her hope. She beheld Heaven, she would assuredly be cured. And thus the little car left, as it were, a feeling of wonder and fraternal charity behind it, as it made its way with so much difficulty through that human ocean.

Pierre, however, was in despair and at the end of his strength, when some of the stretcher-bearers came to his aid by forming a path for the passage of the procession—a path which Berthaud had ordered them to keep clear by means of cords, which they were to hold at intervals of a couple of yards. From that moment the young priest was able to drag Marie along in a fairly easy manner, and at last place her within the reserved space, where he halted, facing the Grotto on the left side. You could no longer move in this reserved space, where the crowd seemed to increase every minute. And, quite exhausted by the painful journey he had just accomplished, Pierre reflected what a prodigious concourse of people there was; it had seemed to him as if he were in the midst of an ocean, whose waves he had heard heaving around him without a pause.

Since leaving the hospital Marie had not opened her lips. He now realised, however, that she wished to speak to him, and accordingly bent over her. "And my father," she inquired, "is he here? Hasn't he returned from his excursion?"

Pierre had to answer that M. de Guersaint had not returned, and that he had doubtless been delayed against his will. And thereupon she merely added with a smile: "Ah I poor father, won't he be pleased when he finds me cured!"

Pierre looked at her with tender admiration. He did not remember having ever seen her looking so adorable since the slow wasting of sickness had begun. Her hair, which alone disease had respected, clothed her in gold. Her thin, delicate face had assumed a dreamy expression, her eyes wandering away to the haunting thought of her sufferings, her features motionless, as if she had fallen asleep in a fixed thought until the expected shock of happiness should waken her. She was absent from herself, ready, however, to return to consciousness whenever God might will it. And, indeed, this delicious infantile creature, this little girl of three-and-twenty, still a child as when an accident had struck her, delaying her growth, preventing her from becoming a woman, was at last ready to receive the visit of the angel, the miraculous shock which would draw her out of her torpor and set her upright once more. Her morning ecstasy continued; she had clasped her hands, and a leap of her whole being had ravished her from earth as soon as she had perceived the image of the Blessed Virgin yonder. And now she prayed and offered herself divinely.

It was an hour of great mental trouble for Pierre. He felt that the drama of his priestly life was about to be enacted, and that if he did not recover faith in this crisis, it would never return to him. And he was without bad thoughts, without resistance, hoping with fervour, he also, that they might both be healed! Oh! that he might be convinced by her cure, that he might believe like her, that they might be saved together! He wished to pray, ardently, as she herself did. But in spite of himself he was preoccupied by the crowd, that limitless crowd, among which he found it so difficult to drown himself, disappear, become nothing more than a leaf in the forest, lost amidst the rustle of all the leaves. He could not prevent himself from analysing and judging it. He knew that for four days past it had been undergoing all the training of suggestion; there had been the fever of the long journey, the excitement of the new landscapes, the days spent before the splendour of the Grotto, the sleepless nights, and all the exasperating suffering, ravenous for illusion. Then, again, there had been the all-besetting prayers, those hymns, those litanies, which agitated it without a pause. Another priest had followed Father Massias in the pulpit, a little thin, dark Abbe, whom Pierre heard hurling appeals to the Virgin and Jesus in a lashing voice which resounded like a whip. Father Massias and Father Fourcade had remained at the foot of the pulpit, and were now directing the cries of the crowd, whose lamentations rose in louder and louder tones beneath the limpid sunlight. The general exaltation had yet increased; it was the hour when the violence done to Heaven at last produced the miracles.

All at once a paralytic rose up and walked towards the Grotto, holding his crutch in the air; and this crutch, waving like a flag above the swaying heads, wrung loud applause from the faithful. They were all on the look-out for prodigies, they awaited them with the certainty that they would take place, innumerable and wonderful. Some eyes seemed to behold them, and feverish voices pointed them out. Another woman had been cured! Another! Yet another! A deaf person had heard, a mute had spoken, a consumptive had revived! What, a consumptive? Certainly, that was a daily occurrence! Surprise was no longer possible; you might have certified that an amputated leg was growing again without astonishing anyone. Miracle-working became the actual state of nature, the usual thing, quite commonplace, such was its abundance. The most incredible stories seemed quite simple to those overheated imaginations, given what they expected from the Blessed Virgin. And you should have heard the tales that went about, the quiet affirmations, the expressions of absolute certainty which were exchanged whenever a delirious patient cried out that she was cured. Another! Yet another! However, a piteous voice would at times exclaim: "Ah! she's cured; that one; she's lucky, she is!"

Already, at the Verification Office, Pierre had suffered from this credulity of the folk among whom he lived. But here it surpassed everything he could have imagined; and he was exasperated by the extravagant things he heard people say in such a placid fashion, with the open smiles of children. Accordingly he tried to absorb himself in his thoughts and listen to nothing. "O God!" he prayed, "grant that my reason may be annihilated, that I may no longer desire to understand, that I may accept the unreal and impossible." For a moment he thought the spirit of inquiry dead within him, and allowed the cry of supplication to carry him away: "Lord, heal our sick! Lord, heal our sick!" He repeated this appeal with all his charity, clasped his hands, and gazed fixedly at the statue of the Virgin, until he became quite giddy, and imagined that the figure moved. Why should he not return to a state of childhood like the others, since happiness lay in ignorance and falsehood? Contagion would surely end by acting; he would become nothing more than a grain of sand among innumerable other grains, one of the humblest among the humble ones under the millstone, who trouble not about the power that crushes them. But just at that second, when he hoped that he had killed the old man in him, that he had annihilated himself along with his will and intelligence, the stubborn work of thought, incessant and invincible, began afresh in the depths of his brain. Little by little, notwithstanding his efforts to the contrary, he returned to his inquiries, doubted, and sought the truth. What was the unknown force thrown off by this crowd, the vital fluid powerful enough to work the few cures that really occurred? There was here a phenomenon that no physiologist had yet studied. Ought one to believe that a multitude became a single being, as it were, able to increase the power of auto-suggestion tenfold upon itself? Might one admit that, under certain circumstances of extreme exaltation, a multitude became an agent of sovereign will compelling the obedience of matter? That would have explained how sudden cure fell at times upon the most sincerely excited of the throng. The breaths of all of them united in one breath, and the power that acted was a power of consolation, hope, and life.

This thought, the outcome of his human charity, filled Pierre with emotion. For another moment he was able to regain possession of himself, and prayed for the cure of all, deeply touched by the belief that he himself might in some degree contribute towards the cure of Marie. But all at once, without knowing what transition of ideas led to it, a recollection returned to him of the medical consultation which he had insisted upon prior to the young girl's departure for Lourdes. The scene rose before him with extraordinary clearness and precision; he saw the room with its grey, blue-flowered wall-paper, and he heard the three doctors discuss and decide. The two who had given certificates diagnosticating paralysis of the marrow spoke discreetly, slowly, like esteemed, well-known, perfectly honourable practitioners; but Pierre still heard the warm, vivacious voice of his cousin Beauclair, the third doctor, a young man of vast and daring intelligence, who was treated coldly by his colleagues as being of an adventurous turn of mind. And at this supreme moment Pierre was surprised to find in his memory things which he did not know were there; but it was only an instance of that singular phenomenon by which it sometimes happens that words scarce listened to, words but imperfectly heard, words stored away in the brain almost in spite of self, will awaken, burst forth, and impose themselves on the mind after they have long been forgotten. And thus it now seemed to him that the very approach of the miracle was bringing him a vision of the conditions under which—according to Beauclair's predictions—the miracle would be accomplished.

In vain did Pierre endeavour to drive away this recollection by praying with an increase of fervour. The scene again appeared to him, and the old words rang out, filling his ears like a trumpet-blast. He was now again in the dining-room, where Beauclair and he had shut themselves up after the departure of the two others, and Beauclair recapitulated the history of the malady: the fall from a horse at the age of fourteen; the dislocation and displacement of the organ, with doubtless a slight laceration of the ligaments, whence the weight which the sufferer had felt, and the weakness of the legs leading to paralysis. Then, a slow healing of the disorder, everything returning to its place of itself, but without the pain ceasing. In fact this big, nervous child, whose mind had been so grievously impressed by her accident, was unable to forget it; her attention remained fixed on the part where she suffered, and she could not divert it, so that, even after cure, her sufferings had continued—a neuropathic state, a consecutive nervous exhaustion, doubtless aggravated by accidents due to faulty nutrition as yet imperfectly understood. And further, Beauclair easily explained the contrary and erroneous diagnosis of the numerous doctors who had attended her, and who, as she would not submit to examination, had groped in the dark, some believing in a tumour, and the others, the more numerous, convinced of some lesion of the marrow. He alone, after inquiring into the girl's parentage, had just begun to suspect a simple state of auto-suggestion, in which she had obstinately remained ever since the first violent shock of pain; and among the reasons which he gave for this belief were the contraction of her visual field, the fixity of her eyes, the absorbed, inattentive expression of her face, and above all the nature of the pain she felt, which, leaving the organ, had borne to the left, where it continued in the form of a crushing, intolerable weight, which sometimes rose to the breast in frightful fits of stifling. A sudden determination to throw off the false notion she had formed of her complaint, the will to rise, breathe freely, and suffer no more, could alone place her on her feet again, cured, transfigured, beneath the lash of some intense emotion.

A last time did Pierre endeavour to see and hear no more, for he felt that the irreparable ruin of all belief in the miraculous was in him. And, in spite of his efforts, in spite of the ardour with which he began to cry, "Jesus, son of David, heal our sick!" he still saw, he still heard Beauclair telling him, in his calm, smiling manner how the miracle would take place, like a lightning flash, at the moment of extreme emotion, under the decisive circumstance which would complete the loosening of the muscles. The patient would rise and walk in a wild transport of joy, her legs would all at once be light again, relieved of the weight which had so long made them like lead, as though this weight had melted, fallen to the ground. But above all, the weight which bore upon the lower part of the trunk, which rose, ravaged the breast, and strangled the throat, would this time depart in a prodigious soaring flight, a tempest blast bearing all the evil away with it. And was it not thus that, in the Middle Ages, possessed women had by the mouth cast up the Devil, by whom their flesh had so long been tortured? And Beauclair had added that Marie would at last become a woman, that in that moment of supreme joy she would cease to be a child, that although seemingly worn out by her prolonged dream of suffering, she would all at once be restored to resplendent health, with beaming face, and eyes full of life.

Pierre looked at her, and his trouble increased still more on seeing her so wretched in her little cart, so distractedly imploring health, her whole being soaring towards Our Lady of Lourdes, who gave life. Ah! might she be saved, at the cost even of his own damnation! But she was too ill; science lied like faith; he could not believe that this child, whose limbs had been dead for so many years, would indeed return to life. And, in the bewildered doubt into which he again relapsed, his bleeding heart clamoured yet more loudly, ever and ever repeating with the delirious crowd: "Lord, son of David, heal our sick!—Lord, son of David, heal our sick!"

At that moment a tumult arose agitating one and all. People shuddered, faces were turned and raised. It was the cross of the four-o'clock procession, a little behind time that day, appearing from beneath one of the arches of the monumental gradient way. There was such applause and such violent, instinctive pushing that Berthaud, waving his arms, commanded the bearers to thrust the crowd back by pulling strongly on the cords. Overpowered for a moment, the bearers had to throw themselves backward with sore hands; however, they ended by somewhat enlarging the reserved path, along which the procession was then able to slowly wend its way. At the head came a superb beadle, all blue and gold, followed by the processional cross, a tall cross shining like a star. Then followed the delegations of the different pilgrimages with their banners, standards of velvet and satin, embroidered with metal and bright silk, adorned with painted figures, and bearing the names of towns: Versailles, Rheims, Orleans, Poitiers, and Toulouse. One, which was quite white, magnificently rich, displayed in red letters the inscription "Association of Catholic Working Men's Clubs." Then came the clergy, two or three hundred priests in simple cassocks, about a hundred in surplices, and some fifty clothed in golden chasubles, effulgent like stars. They all carried lighted candles, and sang the "Laudate Sion Salvatorem" in full voices. And then the canopy appeared in royal pomp, a canopy of purple silk, braided with gold, and upheld by four ecclesiastics, who, it could be seen, had been selected from among the most robust. Beneath it, between two other priests who assisted him, was Abbe Judaine, vigorously clasping the Blessed Sacrament with both hands, as Berthaud had recommended him to do; and the somewhat uneasy glances that he cast on the encroaching crowd right and left showed how anxious he was that no injury should befall the heavy divine monstrance, whose weight was already straining his wrists. When the slanting sun fell upon him in front, the monstrance itself looked like another sun. Choir-boys meantime were swinging censers in the blinding glow which gave splendour to the entire procession; and, finally, in the rear, there was a confused mass of pilgrims, a flock-like tramping of believers and sightseers all aflame, hurrying along, and blocking the track with their ever-rolling waves.

Father Massias had returned to the pulpit a moment previously; and this time he had devised another pious exercise. After the burning cries of faith, hope, and love that he threw forth, he all at once commanded absolute silence, in order that one and all might, with closed lips, speak to God in secret for a few minutes. These sudden spells of silence falling upon the vast crowd, these minutes of mute prayer, in which all souls unbosomed their secrets, were deeply, wonderfully impressive. Their solemnity became formidable; you heard desire, the immense desire for life, winging its flight on high. Then Father Massias invited the sick alone to speak, to implore God to grant them what they asked of His almighty power. And, in response, came a pitiful lamentation, hundreds of tremulous, broken voices rising amidst a concert of sobs. "Lord Jesus, if it please Thee, Thou canst cure me!"—"Lord Jesus take pity on Thy child, who is dying of love!"—"Lord Jesus, grant that I may see, grant that I may hear, grant that I may walk!" And, all at once, the shrill voice of a little girl, light and vivacious as the notes of a flute, rose above the universal sob, repeating in the distance: "Save the others, save the others, Lord Jesus!" Tears streamed from every eye; these supplications upset all hearts, threw the hardest into the frenzy of charity, into a sublime disorder which would have impelled them to open their breasts with both hands, if by doing so they could have given their neighbours their health and youth. And then Father Massias, not letting this enthusiasm abate, resumed his cries, and again lashed the delirious crowd with them; while Father Fourcade himself sobbed on one of the steps of the pulpit, raising his streaming face to heaven as though to command God to descend on earth.

But the procession had arrived; the delegations, the priests, had ranged themselves on the right and left; and, when the canopy entered the space reserved to the sick in front of the Grotto, when the sufferers perceived Jesus the Host, the Blessed Sacrament, shining like a sun, in the hands of Abbe Judaine, it became impossible to direct the prayers, all voices mingled together, and all will was borne away by vertigo. The cries, calls, entreaties broke, lapsing into groans. Human forms rose from pallets of suffering; trembling arms were stretched forth; clenched hands seemingly desired to clutch at the miracle on the way. "Lord Jesus, save us, for we perish!"—"Lord Jesus, we worship Thee; heal us!"—"Lord Jesus, Thou art the Christ, the Son of the living God; heal us!" Thrice did the despairing, exasperated voices give vent to the supreme lamentation in a clamour which rushed up to Heaven; and the tears redoubled, flooding all the burning faces which desire transformed. At one moment, the delirium became so great, the instinctive leap toward the Blessed Sacrament seemed so irresistible, that Berthaud placed the bearers who were there in a chain about it. This was the extreme protective manoeuvre, a hedge of bearers drawn up on either side of the canopy, each placing an arm firmly round his neighbour's neck, so as to establish a sort of living wall. Not the smallest aperture was left in it; nothing whatever could pass. Still, these human barriers staggered under the pressure of the unfortunate creatures who hungered for life, who wished to touch, to kiss Jesus; and, oscillating and recoiling, the bearers were at last thrust against the canopy they were defending, and the canopy itself began swaying among the crowd, ever in danger of being swept away like some holy bark in peril of being wrecked.

Then, at the very climax of this holy frenzy, the miracles began amidst supplications and sobs, as when the heavens open during a storm, and a thunderbolt falls on earth. A paralytic woman rose and cast aside her crutches. There was a piercing yell, and another woman appeared erect on her mattress, wrapped in a white blanket as in a winding sheet; and people said it was a half-dead consumptive who had thus been resuscitated. Then grace fell upon two others in quick succession: a blind woman suddenly perceived the Grotto in a flame; a dumb woman fell on both her knees, thanking the Blessed Virgin in a loud, clear voice. And all in a like way prostrated themselves at the feet of Our Lady of Lourdes, distracted with joy and gratitude.

But Pierre had not taken his eyes off Marie, and he was overcome with tender emotion at what he saw. The sufferer's eyes were still expressionless, but they had dilated, while her poor, pale face, with its heavy mask, was contracted as if she were suffering frightfully. She did not speak in her despair; she undoubtedly thought that she was again in the clutches of her ailment. But all at once, when the Blessed Sacrament passed by, and she saw the star-like monstrance sparkling in the sun, a sensation of dizziness came over her. She imagined herself struck by lightning. Her eyes caught fire from the glare which flashed upon her, and at last regained their flame of life, shining out like stars. And under the influence of a wave of blood her face became animated, suffused with colour, beaming with a smile of joy and health. And, suddenly, Pierre saw her rise, stand upright in her little car, staggering, stuttering, and finding in her mind only these caressing words: "Oh, my friend! Oh, my friend!"

He hurriedly drew near in order to support her. But she drove him back with a gesture. She was regaining strength, looking so touching, so beautiful, in the little black woollen gown and slippers which she always wore; tall and slender, too, and crowned as with a halo of gold by her beautiful flaxen hair, which was covered with a simple piece of lace. The whole of her virgin form was quivering as if some powerful fermentation had regenerated her. First of all, it was her legs that were relieved of the chains that bound them; and then, while she felt the spirit of life—the life of woman, wife, and mother—within her, there came a final agony, an enormous weight that rose to her very throat. Only, this time, it did not linger there, did not stifle her, but burst from her open mouth, and flew away in a cry of sublime joy.

"I am cured!—I am cured!"

Then there was an extraordinary sight. The blanket lay at her feet, she was triumphant, she had a superb, glowing face. And her cry of cure had resounded with such rapturous delight that the entire crowd was distracted by it. She had become the sole point of interest, the others saw none but her, erect, grown so radiant and so divine.

"I am cured!—I am cured!"

Pierre, at the violent shock his heart had received, had begun to weep. Indeed, tears glistened again in every eye. Amidst exclamations of gratitude and praise, frantic enthusiasm passed from one to another, throwing the thousands of pilgrims who pressed forward to see into a state of violent emotion. Applause broke out, a fury of applause, whose thunder rolled from one to the other end of the valley.

However, Father Fourcade began waving his arms, and Father Massias was at last able to make himself heard from the pulpit: "God has visited us, my dear brothers, my dear sisters!" said he. "*Magnificat anima mea Dominum*, My soul doth magnify the Lord, and my spirit hath rejoiced in God my Saviour."

And then all the voices, the thousands of voices, began the chant of adoration and gratitude. The procession found itself at a stand-still. Abbe Judaine had been able to reach the Grotto with the monstrance, but he patiently remained there before giving the Benediction. The canopy was awaiting him outside the railings, surrounded by priests in surplices and chasubles, all a glitter of white and gold in the rays of the setting sun.

Marie, however, had knelt down, sobbing; and, whilst the canticle lasted, a burning prayer of faith and love ascended from her whole being. But the crowd wanted to see her walk, delighted women called to her, a group surrounded her, and swept her towards the Verification Office, so that the miracle might be proved true, as patent as the very light of the sun. Her box was forgotten, Pierre followed her, while she, stammering and hesitating, she who for seven years had not used her legs, advanced with adorable awkwardness, the uneasy, charming gait of a little child making its first steps; and it was so affecting, so delicious, that the young priest thought of nothing but the immense happiness of seeing her thus return to her childhood. Ah! the dear friend of infancy, the dear tenderness of long ago, so she would at last be the beautiful and charming woman that she had promised to be as a young girl when, in the little garden at Neuilly, she had looked so gay and pretty beneath the tall trees flecked with sunlight!

The crowd continued to applaud her furiously, a huge wave of people accompanied her; and all remained awaiting her egress, swarming in a fever before the door, when she had entered the office, whither Pierre only was admitted with her.

That particular afternoon there were few people at the Verification Office. The small square room, with its hot wooden walls and rudimentary furniture, its rush-bottomed chairs, and its two tables of unequal height, contained, apart from the usual staff only some five or six doctors, seated and silent. At the tables were the inspector of the piscinas and two young Abbes making entries in the registers, and consulting the sets of documents; while Father Dargeles, at one end, wrote a paragraph for his newspaper. And, as it happened, Doctor Bonamy was just then examining Elise Rouquet, who, for the third time, had come to have the increasing cicatrisation of her sore certified.

"Anyhow, gentlemen," exclaimed the doctor, "have you ever seen a lupus heal in this way so rapidly? I am aware that a new work has appeared on faith healing in which it is stated that certain sores may have a nervous origin. Only that is by no means proved in the case of lupus, and I defy a committee of doctors to assemble and explain mademoiselle's cure by ordinary means."

He paused, and turning towards Father Dargeles, inquired: "Have you noted, Father, that the suppuration has completely disappeared, and that the skin is resuming its natural colour?"

However, he did not wait for the reply, for just then Marie entered, followed by Pierre; and by her beaming radiance he immediately guessed what good-fortune was befalling him. She looked superb, admirably fitted to transport and convert the multitude. He therefore promptly dismissed Elise Rouquet, inquired the new arrival's name, and asked one of the young priests to look for her papers. Then, as she slightly staggered, he wished to seat her in the arm-chair.

"Oh no! oh no!" she exclaimed. "I am so happy to be able to use my legs!"

Pierre, with a glance, had sought for Doctor Chassaigne, whom he was sorry not to see there. He remained on one side, waiting while they rummaged in the untidy drawers without being able to place their hands on the required papers. "Let's see," repeated Dr. Bonamy; "Marie de Guersaint, Marie de Guersaint. I have certainly seen that name before."

At last Raboin discovered the documents classified under a wrong letter; and when the doctor had perused the two medical certificates he became quite enthusiastic. "Here is something very interesting, gentlemen," said he. "I beg you to listen attentively. This young lady, whom you see standing here, was afflicted with a very serious lesion of the marrow. And, if one had the least doubt of it, these two certificates would suffice to convince the most incredulous, for they are signed by two doctors of the Paris faculty, whose names are well known to us all."

Then he passed the certificates to the doctors present, who read them, wagging their heads the while. It was beyond dispute; the medical men who had drawn up these documents enjoyed the reputation of being honest and clever practitioners.

"Well, gentlemen, if the diagnosis is not disputed—and it cannot be when a patient brings us documents of this value—we will now see what change has taken place in the young lady's condition."

However, before questioning her he turned towards Pierre. "Monsieur l'Abbe," said he, "you came from Paris with Mademoiselle de Guersaint, I think. Did you converse with the doctors before your departure?"

The priest shuddered amidst all his great delight.

"I was present at the consultation, monsieur," he replied.

And again the scene rose up before him. He once more saw the two doctors, so serious and rational, and he once more saw Beauclair smiling, while his colleagues drew up their certificates, which were identical. And was he, Pierre, to reduce these certificates to nothing, reveal the other diagnosis, the one that allowed of the cure being explained scientifically? The miracle had been predicted, shattered beforehand.

"You will observe, gentlemen," now resumed Dr. Bonamy, "that the presence of the Abbe gives these proofs additional weight. However, mademoiselle will now tell us exactly what she felt."

He had leant over Father Dargeles's shoulder to impress upon him that he must not forget to make Pierre play the part of a witness in the narrative.

"*Mon Dieu*! gentlemen, how can I tell you?" exclaimed Marie in a halting voice, broken by her surging happiness. "Since yesterday I had felt certain that I should be cured. And yet, a little while ago, when the pins and needles seized me in the legs again, I was afraid it might only be another attack. For an instant I doubted. Then the feeling stopped. But it began again as soon as I recommenced praying. Oh! I prayed, I prayed with all my soul! I ended by surrendering myself like a child. 'Blessed Virgin, Our Lady of Lourdes, do with me as thou wilt,' I said. But the feeling did not cease, it seemed as if my blood were boiling; a voice cried to me: 'Rise! Rise!' And I felt the miracle fall on me in a cracking of all my bones, of all my flesh, as if I had been struck by lightning."

Pierre, very pale, listened to her. Beauclair had positively told him that the cure would come like a lightning flash, that under the influence of extreme excitement a sudden awakening of will so long somnolent would take place within her.

"It was my legs which the Holy Virgin first of all delivered," she continued. "I could well feel that the iron bands which bound them were gliding along my skin like broken chains. Then the weight which still suffocated me, there, in the left side, began to ascend; and I thought I was going to die, it hurt me so. But it passed my chest, it passed my throat, and I felt it there in my mouth, and spat it out violently. It was all over, I no longer had any pain, it had flown away!"

She had made a gesture expressive of the motion of a night bird beating its wings, and, lapsing into silence, stood smiling at Pierre, who was bewildered. Beauclair had told him all that beforehand, using almost the same words and the same imagery. Point by point, his prognostics were realised, there was nothing more in the case than natural phenomena, which had been foreseen.

Raboin, however, had followed Marie's narrative with dilated eyes and the passion of a pietist of limited intelligence, ever haunted by the idea of hell. "It was the devil," he cried; "it was the devil that she spat out!"

Doctor Bonamy, who was more wary, made him hold his tongue. And turning towards the doctors he said: "Gentlemen, you know that we always avoid pronouncing the big word of miracle here. Only here is a fact, and I am curious to know how any of you can explain it by natural means. Seven years ago this young lady was struck with serious paralysis, evidently due to a lesion of the marrow. And that cannot be denied; the certificates are there, irrefutable. She could no longer walk, she could no longer make a movement without a cry of pain, she had reached that extreme state of exhaustion which precedes but by little an unfortunate issue. All at once, however, here she rises, walks, laughs, and beams on us. The paralysis has completely disappeared, no pain remains, she is as well as you and I. Come, gentlemen, approach, examine her, and tell me what has happened."

He triumphed. Not one of the doctors spoke. Two, who were doubtless true Catholics, had shown their approval of his speech by their vigorous nods, while the others remained motionless, with a constrained air, not caring to mix themselves up in the business. However, a little thin man, whose eyes shone behind the glasses he was wearing, ended by rising to take a closer look at Marie. He caught hold of her hand, examined the pupils of her eyes, and merely seemed preoccupied by the air of transfiguration which she wore. Then, in a very courteous manner, without even showing a desire to discuss the matter, he came back and sat down again.

"The case is beyond science, that is all I can assume," concluded Doctor Bonamy, victoriously. "I will add that we have no convalescence here; health is at once restored, full, entire. Observe the young lady. Her eyes are bright, her colour is rosy, her physiognomy has recovered its lively gaiety. Without doubt, the healing of the tissues will proceed somewhat slowly, but one can already say that mademoiselle has been born again. Is it not so, Monsieur l'Abbe, you who have seen her so frequently; you no longer recognise her, eh?"

"That's true, that's true," stammered Pierre.

And, in fact, she already appeared strong to him, her cheeks full and fresh, gaily blooming. But Beauclair had also foreseen this sudden joyful change, this straightening and resplendency of her invalid frame, when life should re-enter it, with the will to be cured and be happy. Once again, however, had Doctor Bonamy leant over Father Dargeles, who was finishing his note, a brief but fairly complete account of the affair. They exchanged a few words in low tones, consulting together, and the doctor ended by saying: "You have witnessed these marvels, Monsieur l'Abbe, so you will not refuse to sign the careful report which the reverend Father has drawn up for publication in the 'Journal de la Grotte.'"

He—Pierre—sign that page of error and falsehood! A revolt roused him, and he was on the point of shouting out the truth. But he felt the weight of his cassock on his shoulders; and, above all, Marie's divine joy filled his heart. He was penetrated with deep happiness at seeing her saved. Since they had ceased questioning her she had come and leant on his arm, and remained smiling at him with eyes full of enthusiasm.

"Oh, my, friend, thank the Blessed Virgin!" she murmured in a low voice. "She has been so good to me; I am now so well, so beautiful, so young! And how pleased my father, my poor father, will be!"

Then Pierre signed. Everything was collapsing within him, but it was enough that she should be saved; he would have thought it sacrilegious to interfere with the faith of that child, the great pure faith which had healed her.

When Marie reappeared outside the office, the applause began afresh, the crowd clapped their hands. It now seemed that the miracle was official. However, certain charitable persons, fearing that she might again fatigue herself and again require her little car, which she had abandoned before the Grotto, had brought it to the office, and when she found it there she felt deeply moved. Ah! that box in which she had lived so many years, that rolling coffin in which she had sometimes imagined herself buried alive, how many tears, how much despair, how many bad days it had witnessed! And, all at once, the idea occurred to her that it had so long been linked with her sufferings, it ought also to share her triumph. It was a sudden inspiration, a kind of holy folly, that made her seize the handle.

At that moment the procession passed by, returning from the Grotto, where Abbe Judaine had pronounced the Benediction. And thereupon Marie, dragging the little car, placed herself behind the canopy. And, in her slippers, her head covered with a strip of lace, her bosom heaving, her face erect, glowing, and superb, she walked on behind the clergy, dragging after her that car of misery, that rolling coffin, in which she had endured so much agony. And the crowd which acclaimed her, the frantic crowd, followed in her wake.

IV. TRIUMPH—DESPAIR

PIERRE also had followed Marie, and like her was behind the canopy, carried along as it were by the blast of glory which made her drag her little car along in triumph. Every moment, however, there was so much tempestuous pushing that the young priest would assuredly have fallen if a rough hand had not upheld him.

"Don't be alarmed," said a voice; "give me your arm, otherwise you won't be able to remain on your feet."

Pierre turned round, and was surprised to recognise Father Massias, who had left Father Fourcade in the pulpit in order to accompany the procession. An extraordinary fever was sustaining him, throwing him forward, as solid as a rock, with eyes glowing like live coals, and an excited face covered with perspiration.

"Take care, then!" he again exclaimed; "give me your arm."

A fresh human wave had almost swept them away. And Pierre now yielded to the support of this terrible enthusiast, whom he remembered as a fellow-student at the seminary. What a singular meeting it was, and how greatly he would have liked to possess that violent faith, that mad faith, which was making Massias pant, with his throat full of sobs, whilst he continued giving vent to the ardent entreaty "Lord Jesus, heal our sick! Lord Jesus, heal our sick!"

There was no cessation of this cry behind the canopy, where there was always a crier whose duty it was to accord no respite to the slow clemency of Heaven. At times a thick voice full of anguish, and at others a shrill and piercing voice, would arise. The Father's, which was an imperious one, was now at last breaking through sheer emotion.

"Lord Jesus, heal our sick! Lord Jesus, heal our sick!"

The rumour of Marie's wondrous cure, of the miracle whose fame would speedily fill all Christendom, had already spread from one to the other end of Lourdes; and from this had come the increased vertigo of the multitude, the attack of contagious delirium which now caused it to whirl and rush toward the Blessed Sacrament like the resistless flux of a rising tide. One and all yielded to the desire of beholding the Sacrament and touching it, of being cured and becoming happy. The Divinity was passing; and now it was not merely a question of ailing beings glowing with a desire for life, but a longing for happiness which consumed all present and raised them up with bleeding, open hearts and eager hands.

Berthaud, who feared the excesses of this religious adoration, had decided to accompany his men. He commanded them, carefully watching over the double chain of bearers beside the canopy in order that it might not be broken.

"Close your ranks—closer—closer!" he called, "and keep your arms firmly linked!"

These young men, chosen from among the most vigorous of the bearers, had an extremely difficult duty to discharge. The wall which they formed, shoulder to shoulder, with arms linked at the waist and the neck, kept on giving way under the involuntary assaults of the throng. Nobody, certainly, fancied that he was pushing, but there was constant eddying, and deep waves of people rolled towards the procession from afar and threatened to submerge it.

When the canopy had reached the middle of the Place du Rosaire, Abbe Judaine really thought that he would be unable to go any farther. Numerous conflicting currents had set in over the vast expanse, and were whirling, assailing him from all sides, so that he had to halt under the swaying canopy, which shook like a sail in a sudden squall on the open sea. He held the Blessed Sacrament aloft with his numbed hands, each moment fearing that a final push would throw him over; for he fully realised that the golden monstrance, radiant like a sun, was the one passion of all that multitude, the Divinity they demanded to kiss, in order that they might lose themselves in it, even though they should annihilate it in doing so. Accordingly, while standing there, the priest anxiously turned his eyes on Berthaud.

"Let nobody pass!" called the latter to the bearers—"nobody! The orders are precise; you hear me?"

Voices, however, were rising in supplication on all sides, wretched beings were sobbing with arms outstretched and lips protruding, in the wild desire that they might be allowed to approach and kneel at the priest's feet. What divine grace it would be to be thrown upon the ground and trampled under foot by the whole procession![1] An infirm old man displayed his withered hand in the conviction that it would be made sound again were he only allowed to touch the monstrance. A dumb woman wildly pushed her way through the throng with her broad shoulders, in order that she might loosen her tongue by a kiss. Others were shouting, imploring, and even clenching their fists in their rage with those cruel men who denied cure to their bodily sufferings and their mental wretchedness. The orders to keep them back were rigidly enforced, however, for the most serious accidents were feared.

"Nobody, nobody!" repeated Berthaud; "let nobody whatever pass!"

There was a woman there, however, who touched every heart with compassion. Clad in wretched garments, bareheaded, her face wet with tears, she was holding in her arms a little boy of ten years or so, whose limp, paralysed legs hung down inertly. The lad's weight was too great for one so weak as herself, still she did not seem to feel it. She had brought the boy there, and was now entreating the bearers with an invincible obstinacy which neither words nor hustling could conquer.

---

[1] One is here irresistibly reminded of the car of Juggernaut, and of the Hindoo fanatics throwing themselves beneath its wheels in the belief that they would thus obtain an entrance into Paradise.—Trans.

IV. TRIUMPH—DESPAIR

At last, as Abbe Judaine, who felt deeply moved, beckoned to her to approach, two of the bearers, in deference to his compassion, drew apart, despite all the danger of opening a breach, and the woman then rushed forward with her burden, and fell in a heap before the priest. For a moment he rested the foot of the monstrance on the child's head, and the mother herself pressed her eager, longing lips to it; and, as they started off again, she wished to remain behind the canopy, and followed the procession, with streaming hair and panting breast, staggering the while under the heavy burden, which was fast exhausting her strength.

They managed, with great difficulty, to cross the remainder of the Place du Rosaire, and then the ascent began, the glorious ascent by way of the monumental incline; whilst upon high, on the fringe of heaven, the Basilica reared its slim spire, whence pealing bells were winging their flight, sounding the triumphs of Our Lady of Lourdes. And now it was towards an apotheosis that the canopy slowly climbed, towards the lofty portal of the high-perched sanctuary which stood open, face to face with the Infinite, high above the huge multitude whose waves continued soaring across the valley's squares and avenues. Preceding the processional cross, the magnificent beadle, all blue and silver, was already rearing the level of the Rosary cupola, the spacious esplanade formed by the roof of the lower church, across which the pilgrimage deputations began to wind, with their bright-coloured silk and velvet banners waving in the ruddy glow of the sunset. Then came the clergy, the priests in snowy surplices, and the priests in golden chasubles, likewise shining out like a procession of stars. And the censers swung, and the canopy continued climbing, without anything of its bearers being seen, so that it seemed as though a mysterious power, some troop of invisible angels, were carrying it off in this glorious ascension towards the open portal of heaven.

A sound of chanting had burst forth; the voices in the procession no longer called for the healing of the sick, now that the *cortege* had extricated itself from amidst the crowd. The miracle had been worked, and they were celebrating it with the full power of their lungs, amidst the pealing of the bells and the quivering gaiety of the atmosphere.

"*Magnificat anima mea Dominum*"—they began. "My soul doth magnify the Lord."

'Twas the song of gratitude, already chanted at the Grotto, and again springing from every heart: "*Et exsultavit spiritus meus in Deo salutari meo.*" "And my spirit hath rejoiced in God my Saviour."

Meantime it was with increasing, overflowing joy that Marie took part in that radiant ascent, by the colossal gradient way, towards the glowing Basilica. It seemed to her, as she continued climbing, that she was growing stronger and stronger, that her legs, so long lifeless, became firmer at each step. The little car which she victoriously dragged behind her was like the earthly tenement of her illness, the *inferno* whence the Blessed Virgin had extricated her, and although its handle was making her hands sore, she nevertheless wished to pull it up yonder with her, in order that she might cast it at last at the feet of the Almighty. No obstacle could stay her course, she laughed through the big tears which were falling on her cheeks, her bosom was swelling, her demeanour becoming warlike. One of her slippers had become unfastened, and the strip of lace had fallen from her head to her shoulders. Nevertheless, with her lovely fair hair crowning her like a helmet and her face beaming brightly, she still marched on and on with such an awakening of will and strength that, behind her, you could hear her car leap and rattle over the rough slope of the flagstones, as though it had been a mere toy.

Near Marie was Pierre, still leaning on the arm of Father Massias, who had not relinquished his hold. Lost amidst the far-spreading emotion, the young priest was unable to reflect. Moreover his companion's sonorous voice quite deafened him.

"*Deposuit potentes de sede et exaltavit humiles.*" "He hath put down the mighty from their seat, and hath exalted the humble."

On Pierre's other side, the right, Berthaud, who no longer had any cause for anxiety, was now also following the canopy. He had given his bearers orders to break their chain, and was gazing with an expression of delight on the human sea through which the procession had lately passed. The higher they the incline, the more did the Place du Rosaire and the avenues and paths of the gardens expand below them, black with the swarming multitude. It was a bird's-eye view of a whole nation, an ant-hill which ever increased in size, spreading farther and farther away. "Look!" Berthaud at last exclaimed to Pierre. "How vast and how beautiful it is! Ah! well, the year won't have been a bad one after all."

Looking upon Lourdes as a centre of propaganda, where his political rancour found satisfaction, he always rejoiced when there was a numerous pilgrimage, as in his mind it was bound to prove unpleasant to the Government. Ah! thought he, if they had only been able to bring the working classes of the towns thither, and create a Catholic democracy. "Last year we scarcely reached the figure of two hundred thousand pilgrims," he continued, "but we shall exceed it this year, I hope." And then, with the gay air of the jolly fellow that he was, despite his sectarian passions, he added: "Well, 'pon my word, I was really pleased just now when there was such a crush. Things are looking up, I thought, things are looking up."

Pierre, however, was not listening to him; his mind had been struck by the grandeur of the spectacle. That multitude, which spread out more and more as the procession rose higher and higher above it, that magnificent valley which was hollowed out below and ever became more and more extensive, displaying afar off its gorgeous horizon of mountains, filled him with quivering admiration. His mental trouble was increased by it all, and seeking Marie's glance, he waved his arm to draw her attention to the vast circular expanse of country. And his gesture deceived her, for in the purely spiritual excitement that possessed her she did not behold the material spectacle he pointed at, but thought that he was calling earth to witness the prodigious favours which the Blessed Virgin had heaped upon them both; for she imagined that he had had his share of the miracle, and that in the stroke of grace which had set her erect with her flesh healed, he, so near to her that their hearts mingled, had felt himself enveloped and raised by the same divine power, his soul saved from doubt, conquered by faith once more. How could he have witnessed her wondrous cure, indeed, without being convinced? Moreover, she had prayed so fervently for him outside the Grotto on the previous night. And now, therefore, to her excessive delight, she espied him transfigured like herself, weeping and laughing, restored to God again. And this lent increased force to her blissful fever; she dragged her little car along with unwearying hands, and—as though it were their double cross, her own redemption and her friend's redemption which she was carrying up that incline with its resounding flagstones—she would have liked to drag it yet farther, for leagues and leagues, ever higher and higher, to the most inaccessible summits, to the transplendent threshold of Paradise itself.

"O Pierre, Pierre!" she stammered, "how sweet it is that this great happiness should have fallen on us together—yes, together! I prayed for it so fervently, and she granted my prayer, and saved you even in saving me. Yes, I felt your soul mingling with my own. Tell me that our mutual prayers have been granted, tell me that I have won your salvation even as you have won mine!"

He understood her mistake and shuddered.

"If you only knew," she continued, "how great would have been my grief had I thus ascended into light alone. Oh! to be chosen without you, to soar yonder without you! But with you, Pierre, it is rapturous delight! We have been saved together, we shall be happy forever! I feel all needful strength for happiness, yes, strength enough to raise the world!"

And in spite of everything, he was obliged to answer her and lie, revolting at the idea of spoiling, dimming that great and pure felicity. "Yes, yes, be happy, Marie," he said, "for I am very happy myself, and all our sufferings are redeemed."

But even while he spoke he felt a deep rending within him, as though a brutal hatchet-stroke were parting them forever. Amidst their common sufferings, she had hitherto remained the little friend of childhood's days, the first artlessly loved woman, whom he knew to be still his own, since she could belong to none. But now she was cured, and he remained alone in his hell, repeating to himself that she would never more be his! This sudden thought so upset him that he averted his eyes, in despair at reaping such suffering from the prodigious felicity with which she exulted.

However the chant went on, and Father Massias, hearing nothing and seeing nothing, absorbed as he was in his glowing gratitude to God, shouted the final verse in a thundering voice: "*Sicut locutus est ad patres nostros, Abraham, et semini ejus in saecula.*" "As He spake to our fathers, to Abraham, and to his seed for ever!"

Yet another incline had to be climbed, yet another effort had to be made up that rough acclivity, with its large slippery flagstones. And the procession rose yet higher, and the ascent still went on in the full, bright light. There came a last turn, and the wheels of Marie's car grated against a granite curb. Then, still higher, still and ever higher, did it roll until it finally reached what seemed to be the very fringe of heaven.

And all at once the canopy appeared on the summit of the gigantic inclined ways, on the stone balcony overlooking the stretch of country outside the portal of the Basilica. Abbe Judaine stepped forward holding the Blessed Sacrament aloft with both hands. Marie, who had pulled her car up the balcony steps, was near him, her heart beating from her exertion, her face all aglow amidst the gold of her loosened hair. Then all the clergy, the snowy surplices, and the dazzling chasubles ranged themselves behind, whilst the banners waved like bunting decking the white balustrades. And a solemn minute followed.

From on high there could have been no grander spectacle. First, immediately below, there was the multitude, the human sea with its dark waves, its heaving billows, now for a moment stilled, amidst which you only distinguished the small pale specks of the faces uplifted towards the Basilica, in expectation of the Benediction; and as far as the eye could reach, from the place du Rosaire to the Gave, along the paths and avenues and across the open spaces, even to the old town in the distance; those little pale faces multiplied and multiplied, all with lips parted, and eyes fixed upon the august heaven was about to open to their gaze.

Then the vast amphitheatre of slopes and hills and mountains surged aloft, ascended upon all sides, crests following crests, until they faded away in the far blue atmosphere. The numerous convents among the trees on the first of the northern slopes, beyond the torrent—those of the Carmelites, the Dominicans, the Assumptionists, and the Sisters of Nevers—were coloured by a rosy reflection from the fire-like glow of the sunset. Then wooded masses rose one above the other, until they reached the heights of Le Buala, which were surmounted by the Serre de Julos, in its turn capped by the Miramont.

Deep valleys opened on the south, narrow gorges between piles of gigantic rocks whose bases were already steeped in lakes of bluish shadow, whilst the summits sparkled with the smiling farewell of the sun. The hills of Visens upon this side were empurpled, and shewed like a promontory of coral, in front of the stagnant lake of the ether, which was bright with a sapphire-like transparency. But, on the east, in front of you, the horizon again spread out to the very point of intersection of the seven valleys. The castle which had formerly guarded them still stood with its keep, its lofty walls, its black outlines—the outlines of a fierce fortress of feudal time,—upon the rock whose base was watered by the Gave; and upon this side of the stern old pile was the new town, looking quite gay amidst its gardens, with its swarm of white house-fronts, its large hotels, its lodging-houses, and its fine shops, whose windows were glowing like live embers; whilst, behind the castle, the discoloured roofs of old Lourdes spread out in confusion, in a ruddy light which hovered over them like a cloud of dust. At this late hour, when the declining luminary was sinking in royal splendour behind the little Gers and the big Gers, those two huge ridges of bare rock, spotted with patches of short herbage, formed nothing but a neutral, somewhat violet, background, as though, indeed, they were two curtains of sober hue drawn across the margin of the horizon.

And higher and still higher, in front of this immensity, did Abbe Judaine with both hands raise the Blessed Sacrament. He moved it slowly from one to the other horizon, causing it to describe a huge sign of the cross against the vault of heaven. He saluted the convents, the heights of Le Buala, the Serre de Julos, and the Miramont, upon his left; he saluted the huge fallen rocks of the dim valleys, and the empurpled hills of Visens, on his right; he saluted the new and the old town, the castle bathed by the Gave, the big and the little Gers, already drowsy, in front of him; and he saluted the woods, the torrents, the mountains, the faint chains linking the distant peaks, the whole earth, even beyond the visible horizon: Peace upon earth, hope and consolation to mankind! The multitude below had quivered beneath that great sign of the cross which enveloped it. It seemed as though a divine breath were passing, rolling those billows of little pale faces which were as numerous as the waves of an ocean. A loud murmur of adoration ascended; all those parted lips proclaimed the glory of God when, in the rays of the setting sun, the illumined monstrance again shone forth like another sun, a sun of pure gold, describing the sign of the cross in streaks of flame upon the threshold of the Infinite.

The banners, the clergy, with Abbe Judaine under the canopy, were already returning to the Basilica, when Marie, who was also entering it, still dragging her car by the handle, was stopped by two ladies, who kissed her, weeping. They were Madame de

Jonquiere and her daughter Raymonde, who had come thither to witness the Benediction, and had been told of the miracle.

"Ah! my dear child, what happiness!" repeated the lady-hospitaller; "and how proud I am to have you in my ward! It is so precious a favour for all of us that the Blessed Virgin should have been pleased to select you."

Raymonde, meanwhile, had kept one of the young girl's hands in her own. "Will you allow me to call you my friend, mademoiselle?" said she. "I felt so much pity for you, and I am now so pleased to see you walking, so strong and beautiful already. Let me kiss you again. It will bring me happiness."

"Thank you, thank you with all my heart," Marie stammered amidst her rapture. "I am so happy, so very happy!"

"Oh! we will not leave you," resumed Madame de Jonquiere. "You hear me, Raymonde? We must follow her, and kneel beside her, and we will take her back after the ceremony."

Thereupon the two ladies joined the *cortege*, and, following the canopy, walked beside Pierre and Father Massias, between the rows of chairs which the deputations already occupied, to the very centre of the choir. The banners alone were allowed on either side of the high altar; but Marie advanced to its steps, still dragging her car, whose wheels resounded over the flagstones. She had at last brought it to the spot whither the sacred madness of her desire had longingly impelled her to drag it. She had brought it, indeed, woeful, wretched-looking as it was, into the splendour of God's house, so that it might there testify to the truth of the miracle. The threshold had scarcely been crossed when the organs burst into a hymn of triumph, the sonorous acclamation of a happy people, from amidst which there soon arose a celestial, angelic voice, of joyful shrillness and crystalline purity. Abbe Judaine had placed the Blessed Sacrament upon the altar, and the crowd was streaming into the nave, each taking a seat, installing him or herself in a corner, pending the commencement of the ceremony. Marie had at once fallen on her knees between Madame de Jonquiere and Raymonde, whose eyes were moist with tender emotion; whilst Father Massias, exhausted by the extraordinary tension of the nerves which had been sustaining him ever since his departure from the Grotto, had sunk upon the ground, sobbing, with his head between his hands. Behind him Pierre and Berthaud remained standing, the latter still busy with his superintendence, his eyes ever on the watch, seeing that good order was preserved even during the most violent outbursts of emotion.

Then, amidst all his mental confusion, increased by the deafening strains of the organ, Pierre raised his head and examined the interior of the Basilica. The nave was narrow and lofty, and streaked with bright colours, which numerous windows flooded with light. There were scarcely any aisles; they were reduced to the proportions of a mere passage running between the side-chapels and the clustering columns, and this circumstance seemed to increase the slim loftiness of the nave, the soaring of the stonework in perpendicular lines of infantile, graceful slenderness. A gilded railing, as transparent as lace, closed the choir, where the high altar, of white marble richly sculptured, arose in all its lavish chasteness. But the feature of the building which astonished you was the mass of extraordinary ornamentation which transformed the whole of it into an overflowing exhibition of embroidery and jewellery. What with all the banners and votive offerings, the perfect river of gifts which had flowed into it and remained clinging to its walls in a stream of gold and silver, velvet and silk, covering it from top to bottom, it was, so to say, the ever-glowing sanctuary of gratitude, whose thousand rich adornments seemed to be chanting a perpetual canticle of faith and thankfulness.

The banners, in particular, abounded, as innumerable as the leaves of trees. Some thirty hung from the vaulted roof, whilst others were suspended, like pictures, between the little columns around the triforium. And others, again, displayed themselves on the walls, waved in the depths of the side-chapels, and encompassed the choir with a heaven of silk, satin, and velvet. You could count them by hundreds, and your eyes grew weary of admiring them. Many of them were quite celebrated, so renowned for their skilful workmanship that talented embroideresses took the trouble to come to Lourdes on purpose to examine them. Among these were the banner of our Lady of Fourvieres, bearing the arms of the city of Lyons; the banner of Alsace, of black velvet embroidered with gold; the banner of Lorraine, on which you beheld the Virgin casting her cloak around two children; and the white and blue banner of Brittany, on which bled the sacred heart of Jesus in the midst of a halo. All empires and kingdoms of the earth were represented; the most distant lands—Canada, Brazil, Chili, Haiti—here had their flags, which, in all piety, were being offered as a tribute of homage to the Queen of Heaven.

Then, after the banners, there were other marvels, the thousands and thousands of gold and silver hearts which were hanging everywhere, glittering on the walls like stars in the heavens. Some were grouped together in the form of mystical roses, others described festoons and garlands, others, again, climbed up the pillars, surrounded the windows, and constellated the deep, dim chapels. Below the triforium somebody had had the ingenious idea of employing these hearts to trace in tall letters the various words which the Blessed Virgin had addressed to Bernadette; and thus, around the nave, there extended a long frieze of words, the delight of the infantile minds which busied themselves with spelling them. It was a swarming, a prodigious resplendency of hearts, whose infinite number deeply impressed you when you thought of all the hands, trembling with gratitude, which had offered them. Moreover, the adornments comprised many other votive offerings, and some of quite an unexpected description. There were bridal wreaths and crosses of honour, jewels and photographs, chaplets, and even spurs, in glass cases or frames. There were also the epaulets and swords of officers, together with a superb sabre, left there in memory of a miraculous conversion.

But all this was not sufficient; other riches, riches of every kind, shone out on all sides—marble statues, diadems enriched with brilliants, a marvellous carpet designed at Blois and embroidered by ladies of all parts of France, and a golden palm with ornaments of enamel, the gift of the sovereign pontiff. The lamps suspended from the vaulted roof, some of them of massive gold and the most delicate workmanship, were also gifts. They were too numerous to be counted, they studded the nave with stars of great price. Immediately in front of the tabernacle there was one, a masterpiece of chasing, offered by Ireland. Others—one from Lille, one from Valence, one from Macao in far-off China—were veritable jewels, sparkling with precious stones. And how great was the resplendency when the choir's score of chandeliers was illumined, when the hundreds of lamps and the hundreds of candles burned all together, at the great evening ceremonies! The whole church then became a conflagration, the thousands of gold and silver hearts reflecting all the little flames with thousands of fiery scintillations. It was like a huge and wondrous brasier; the walls streamed with live flakes of light; you seemed to be entering into the blinding glory of Paradise itself; whilst on all sides the innumerable banners spread out their silk, their satin, and their velvet, embroidered with sanguifluous sacred hearts, victorious saints, and Virgins whose kindly smiles engendered miracles.

Ah! how many ceremonies had already displayed their pomp in that Basilica! Worship, prayer, chanting, never ceased there. From one end of the year to the other incense smoked, organs roared, and kneeling multitudes prayed there with their whole souls. Masses, vespers, sermons, were continually following one upon another; day by day the religious exercises began afresh, and each festival of the Church was celebrated with unparalleled magnificence. The least noteworthy anniversary supplied a pretext for pompous solemnities. Each pilgrimage was granted its share of the dazzling resplendency. It was necessary that those suffering ones and those humble ones who had come from such long distances should be sent home consoled and enraptured, carrying with them a vision of Paradise espied through its opening portals. They beheld the luxurious surroundings of the Divinity, and would forever remain enraptured by the sight. In the depths of bare, wretched rooms, indeed, by the side of humble pallets of suffering throughout all Christendom, a vision of the Basilica with its blazing riches continually arose like a vision of fortune itself, like a vision of the wealth of that life to be, into which the poor would surely some day enter after their long, long misery in this terrestrial sphere.

Pierre, however, felt no delight; no consolation, no hope, came to him as he gazed upon all the splendour. His frightful feeling of discomfort was increasing, all was becoming black within him, with that blackness of the tempest which gathers when men's thoughts and feelings pant and shriek. He had felt immense desolation rising in his soul ever since Marie, crying that she was healed, had risen from her little car and walked along with such strength and fulness of life. Yet he loved her like a passionately attached brother, and had experienced unlimited happiness on seeing that she no longer suffered. Why, therefore, should her felicity bring him such agony? He could now no longer gaze at her, kneeling there, radiant amidst her tears, with beauty recovered and increased, without his poor heart bleeding as from some mortal wound. Still he wished to remain there, and so, averting his eyes, he tried to interest himself in Father Massias, who was still shaking with violent sobbing on the flagstones, and whose prostration and annihilation, amidst the consuming illusion of divine love, he sorely envied. For a moment, moreover, he questioned Berthaud, feigning to admire some banner and requesting information respecting it.

"Which one?" asked the superintendent of the bearers; "that lace banner over there?"

"Yes, that one on the left."

"Oh! it is a banner offered by Le Puy. The arms are those of Le Puy and Lourdes linked together by the Rosary. The lace is so fine that if you crumpled the banner up, you could hold it in the hollow of your hand."

However, Abbe Judaine was now stepping forward; the ceremony was about to begin. Again did the organs resound, and again was a canticle chanted, whilst, on the altar, the Blessed Sacrament looked like the sovereign planet amidst the scintillations of the gold and silver hearts, as innumerable as stars. And then Pierre lacked the strength to remain there any longer. Since Marie had Madame de Jonquiere and Raymonde with her, and they would accompany her back, he might surely go off by himself, vanish into some shadowy corner, and there, at last, vent his grief. In a few words he excused himself, giving his appointment with Doctor Chassaigne as a pretext for his departure. However, another fear suddenly came to him, that of being unable to leave the building, so densely did the serried throng of believers bar the open doorway. But immediately afterwards he had an inspiration, and, crossing the sacristy, descended into the crypt by the narrow interior stairway.

Deep silence and sepulchral gloom suddenly succeeded to the joyous chants and prodigious radiance of the Basilica above. Cut in the rock, the crypt formed two narrow passages, parted by a massive block of stone which upheld the nave, and conducting to a subterranean chapel under the apse, where some little lamps remained burning both day and night. A dim forest of pillars rose up there, a mystic terror reigned in that semi-obscurity where the mystery ever quivered. The chapel walls remained bare, like the very stones of the tomb, in which all men must some day sleep the last sleep. And along the passages, against their sides, covered from top to bottom with marble votive offerings, you only saw a double row of confessionals; for it was here, in the lifeless tranquillity of the bowels of the earth, that sins were confessed; and there were priests, speaking all languages, to absolve the sinners who came thither from the four corners of the world.

At that hour, however, when the multitude was thronging the Basilica above, the crypt had become quite deserted. Not a soul, save Pierre's, throbbed there ever so faintly; and he, amidst that deep silence, that darkness, that coolness of the grave, fell upon his knees. It was not, however, through any need of prayer and worship, but because his whole being was giving way beneath his crushing mental torment. He felt a torturing longing to be able to see clearly within himself. Ah! why could he not plunge even more deeply into the heart of things, reflect, understand, and at last calm himself.

And it was a fearful agony that he experienced. He tried to remember all the minutes that had gone by since Marie, suddenly springing from her pallet of wretchedness, had raised her cry of resurrection. Why had he even then, despite his fraternal joy in seeing her erect, felt such an awful sensation of discomfort, as though, indeed, the greatest of all possible misfortunes had fallen upon him? Was he jealous of the divine grace? Did he suffer because the Virgin, whilst healing her, had forgotten him, whose soul was so afflicted? He remembered how he had granted himself a last delay, fixed a supreme appointment with Faith for the moment when the Blessed Sacrament should pass by, were Marie only cured; and she was cured, and still he did not believe, and henceforth there was no hope, for never, never would he be able to believe. Therein lay the bare, bleeding sore. The truth burst upon him with blinding cruelty and certainty—she was saved, he was lost. That pretended miracle which had restored her to life had, in him, completed the ruin of all belief in the supernatural. That which he had, for a moment, dreamed of seeking, and perhaps finding, at Lourdes,—naive faith, the happy faith of a little child,—was no longer possible, would never bloom again after that collapse of the miraculous, that cure which Beauclair had foretold, and which had afterwards come to pass, exactly as had been predicted. Jealous! No—he was not jealous; but he was ravaged, full of mortal sadness at thus remaining all alone in the icy desert of his intelligence, regretting the illusion, the lie, the divine love of the simpleminded, for which henceforth there was no room in his heart.

A flood of bitterness stifled him, and tears started from his eyes. He had slipped on to the flagstones, prostrated by his anguish. And, by degrees, he remembered the whole delightful story, from the day when Marie, guessing how he was tortured by doubt, had become so passionately eager for his conversion, taking hold of his hand in the gloom, retaining it in her own, and stammering that she would pray for him—oh! pray for him with her whole soul. She forgot herself, she entreated the Blessed Virgin to save her friend rather than herself if there were but one grace that she could obtain from her Divine Son. Then came another memory, the memory of the delightful hours which they had spent together amid the dense darkness of the trees during the night procession. There, again, they had prayed for one another, mingled one in the other with so ardent a desire for mutual happiness that, for a moment, they had attained to the very depths of the love which gives and immolates itself. And now their long, tear-drenched tenderness, their pure idyl of suffering, was ending in this brutal separation; she on her side saved, radiant amidst the hosannas of the triumphant Basilica; and he lost, sobbing with wretchedness, bowed down in the depths of the dark crypt in an icy, grave-like solitude. It was as though he had just lost her again, and this time forever and forever.

All at once Pierre felt the sharp stab which this thought dealt his heart. He at last understood his pain—a sudden light illumined the terrible crisis of woe amidst which he was struggling. He had lost Marie for the first time on the day when he had become a priest, saying to himself that he might well renounce his manhood since she, stricken in her sex by incurable illness, would never be a woman. But behold! she *was* cured. Behold! she *had* become a woman. She had all at once appeared to him very strong, very beautiful, living, and desirable. He, who was dead, however, could not become a man again. Never more would he be able to raise the tombstone which crushed and imprisoned his flesh. She fled away alone, leaving him in the cold grave. The whole wide world was opening before her with smiling happiness, with the love which laughs in the sunlit paths, with the husband, with children, no doubt. Whereas he, buried, as it were to his shoulders, had naught of his body free, save his brain, and that remained free, no doubt, in order that he might suffer the more. She had still been his so long as she had not belonged to another; and if he had been enduring such agony during the past hour, it was only through this final rending which, this time, parted her from him forever and forever.

Then rage shook Pierre from head to foot. He was tempted to return to the Basilica, and cry the truth aloud to Marie. The miracle was a lie! The helpful beneficence of an all-powerful Divinity was but so much illusion! Nature alone had acted, life had conquered once again. And he would have given proofs: he would have shown how life, the only sovereign, worked for health amid all the sufferings of this terrestrial sphere. And then they would have gone off together; they would have fled far, far away, that they might be happy. But a sudden terror took possession of him. What! lay hands upon that little spotless soul, kill all belief in it, fill it with the ruins which worked such havoc in his own soul? It all at once occurred to him that this would be odious sacrilege. He would afterwards become horrified with himself, he would look upon himself as her murderer were he some day to realise that he was unable to give her a happiness equal to that which she would have lost. Perhaps, too, she would not believe him. And, moreover, would she ever consent to marry a priest who had broken his vows? She who would always retain the sweet and never-to be-forgotten memory of how she had been healed in ecstasy! His design then appeared to him insane, monstrous, polluting. And his revolt rapidly subsided, until he only retained a feeling of infinite weariness, a sensation of a burning, incurable wound—the wound of his poor, bruised, lacerated heart.

Then, however, amidst his abandonment, the void in which he was whirling, a supreme struggle began, filling him again with agony. What should he do? His sufferings made a coward of him, and he would have liked to flee, so that he might never see Marie again. For he understood very well that he would now have to lie to her, since she thought that he was saved like herself, converted, healed in soul, even as she had been healed in body. She had told him of her joy while dragging her car up the colossal gradient way. Oh! to have had that great happiness together, together; to have felt their hearts melt and mingle one in the other! And even then he had already lied, as he would always be obliged to lie in order that he might not spoil her pure and blissful illusion. He let the last throbbings of his veins subside, and vowed that he would find sufficient strength for the sublime charity of feigning peacefulness of soul, the rapture of one who is redeemed. For he wished her to be wholly happy—without a regret, without a doubt—in the full serenity of faith, convinced that the blessed Virgin had indeed given her consent to their purely mystical union. What did his torments matter? Later on, perhaps, he might recover possession of himself. Amidst his desolate solitude of mind would there not always be a little joy to sustain him, all that joy whose consoling falsity he would leave to her?

Several minutes again elapsed, and Pierre, still overwhelmed, remained on the flagstones, seeking to calm his fever. He no longer thought, he no longer lived; he was a prey to that prostration of the entire being which follows upon great crises. But, all at once, he fancied he could hear a sound of footsteps, and thereupon he painfully rose to his feet, and feigned to be reading the inscriptions graven in the marble votive slabs along the walls. He had been mistaken—nobody was there; nevertheless, seeking to divert his mind, he continued perusing the inscriptions, at first in a mechanical kind of way, and then, little by little, feeling a fresh emotion steal over him.

The sight was almost beyond imagination. Faith, love, and gratitude displayed themselves in a hundred, a thousand ways on these marble slabs with gilded lettering. Some of the inscriptions were so artless as to provoke a smile. A colonel had sent a sculptured representation of his foot with the words: "Thou hast preserved it; grant that it may serve Thee." Farther on you read the line: "May Her protection extend to the glass trade." And then, by the frankness of certain expressions of thanks, you realised of what a strange character the appeals had been. "To Mary the Immaculate," ran one inscription, "from a father of a family, in recognition of health restored, a lawsuit won, and advancement gained." However, the memory of these instances faded away amidst the chorus of soaring, fervent cries. There was the cry of the lovers: "Paul and Anna entreat Our Lady of Lourdes to bless their union." There was the cry of the mothers in various forms: "Gratitude to Mary, who has thrice healed my child."—"Gratitude to Mary for the birth of Antoinette, whom I dedicate, like myself and all my kin, to Her."—"P. D., three years old, has been preserved to the love of his parents." And then came the cry of the wives, the cry, too, of the sick restored to health, and of the souls restored to happiness: "Protect my husband; grant that my husband may enjoy good health."—"I was crippled in both legs, and now I am healed."—"We came, and now we hope."—"I prayed, I wept, and She heard me." And there were yet other cries, cries whose veiled glow conjured up thoughts of long romances: "Thou didst join us together; protect us, we pray Thee."—"To Mary, for the greatest of all blessings." And the same cries, the same words—gratitude, thankfulness, homage, acknowledgment,—occurred again and again, ever with the same passionate fervour. All! those hundreds, those thousands of cries which were forever graven on that marble, and from the depths of the crypt rose clamorously to the Virgin, proclaiming the everlasting devotion of the unhappy beings whom she had succoured.

Pierre did not weary of reading them, albeit his mouth was bitter and increasing desolation was filling him. So it was only he who had no succour to hope for! When so many sufferers were listened to, he alone had been unable to make himself heard! And he now began to think of the extraordinary number of prayers which must be said at Lourdes from one end of the year to the other. He tried to cast them up; those said during the days spent at the Grotto and during the nights spent at the Rosary, those said at the ceremonies at the Basilica, and those said at the sunlight and the starlight processions. But this continual entreaty of every second was beyond computation. It seemed as if the faithful were determined to weary the ears of the Divinity, determined to extort favours and forgiveness by the very multitude, the vast multitude of their prayers. The priests said that it was necessary to offer to God the acts of expiation which the sins of France required, and that when the number of these acts of expiation should be large enough, God would smite France no more. What a harsh belief in the necessity of chastisement! What a ferocious idea born of the gloomiest pessimism! How evil life must be if it were indeed necessary that such imploring cries, such cries of physical and moral wretchedness, should ever and ever ascend to Heaven!

In the midst of all his sadness, Pierre felt deep compassion penetrate his heart. He was upset by the thought that mankind should be so wretched, reduced to such a state of woe, so bare, so weak, so utterly forsaken, that it renounced its own reason to place the one sole possibility of happiness in the hallucinatory intoxication of dreams. Tears once more filled his eyes; he wept for himself and for others, for all the poor tortured beings who feel a need of stupefying and numbing their pains in order to escape from the realities of the world. He again seemed to hear the swarming, kneeling crowd of the Grotto, raising the glowing entreaty of its prayer to Heaven, the multitude of twenty and thirty thousand souls from whose midst ascended such a fervour of desire that you seemed to see it smoking in the sunlight like incense. Then another form of the exaltation of faith glowed, beneath the crypt, in the Church of the Rosary, where nights were spent in a paradise of rapture, amidst the silent delights of the communion, the mute appeals in which the whole being pines, burns, and soars aloft. And as though the cries raised before the Grotto and the perpetual adoration of the Rosary were not sufficient, that clamour of ardent entreaty burst forth afresh on the walls of the crypt around him; and here it was eternised in marble, here it would continue shrieking the sufferings of humanity even into the far-away ages. It was the marble, it was the walls themselves praying, seized by that shudder of universal woe which penetrated even the world's stones. And, at last, the prayers ascended yet higher, still higher, soared aloft from the radiant Basilica, which was humming and buzzing above him, full as it now was of a frantic multitude, whose mighty voice, bursting into a canticle of hope, he fancied he could hear through the flagstones of the nave. And it finally seemed to him that he was being whirled away, transported, as though he were indeed amidst the very vibrations of that huge wave of prayer, which, starting from the dust of the earth, ascended the tier of superposed churches, spreading from tabernacle to tabernacle, and filling even the walls with such pity that they sobbed aloud, and that the supreme cry of wretchedness pierced its way into heaven with the white spire, the lofty golden cross, above the steeple. O Almighty God, O Divinity, Helpful Power, whoever, whatever Thou mayst be, take pity upon poor mankind and make human suffering cease!

All at once Pierre was dazzled. He had followed the left-hand passage, and was coming out into broad daylight, above the inclined ways, and two affectionate arms at once caught hold of him and clasped him. It was Doctor Chassaigne, whose appointment he had forgotten, and who had been waiting there to take him to visit Bernadette's room and Abbe Peyramale's church. "Oh! what joy must be yours, my child!" exclaimed the good old man. "I have just learnt the great news, the extraordinary favour which Our Lady of Lourdes has granted to your young friend. Recollect what I told you the day before yesterday. I am now at ease—you are saved!"

A last bitterness came to the young priest who was very pale. However, he was able to smile, and he gently answered: "Yes, we are saved, we are very happy."

It was the lie beginning; the divine illusion which in a spirit of charity he wished to give to others.

And then one more spectacle met Pierre's eyes. The principal door of the Basilica stood wide open, and a red sheet of light from the setting sun was enfilading the nave from one to the other end. Everything was flaring with the splendour of a conflagration—the gilt railings of the choir, the votive offerings of gold and silver, the lamps enriched with precious stones, the banners with their bright embroideries, and the swinging censers, which seemed like flying jewels. And yonder, in the depths of this burning splendour, amidst the snowy surplices and the golden chasubles, he recognised Marie, with hair unbound, hair of gold like all else, enveloping her in a golden mantle. And the organs burst into a hymn of triumph; and the delirious people acclaimed God; and Abbe Judaine, who had again just taken the Blessed Sacrament from off the altar, raised it aloft and presented it to their gaze for the last time; and radiantly magnificent it shone out like a glory amidst the streaming gold of the Basilica, whose prodigious triumph all the bells proclaimed in clanging, flying peals.

V. CRADLE AND GRAVE

IMMEDIATELY afterwards, as they descended the steps, Doctor Chassaigne said to Pierre: "You have just seen the triumph; I will now show you two great injustices."

And he conducted him into the Rue des Petits-Fosses to visit Bernadette's room, that low, dark chamber whence she set out on the day the Blessed Virgin appeared to her.

The Rue des Petits-Fosses starts from the former Rue des Bois, now the Rue de la Grotte, and crosses the Rue du Tribunal. It is a winding lane, slightly sloping and very gloomy. The passers-by are few; it is skirted by long walls, wretched-looking houses, with mournful facades in which never a window opens. All its gaiety consists in an occasional tree in a courtyard.

"Here we are," at last said the doctor.

At the part where he had halted, the street contracted, becoming very narrow, and the house faced the high, grey wall of a barn. Raising their heads, both men looked up at the little dwelling, which seemed quite lifeless, with its narrow casements and its coarse, violet pargeting, displaying the shameful ugliness of poverty. The entrance passage down below was quite black; an old light iron gate was all that closed it; and there was a step to mount, which in rainy weather was immersed in the water of the gutter.

"Go in, my friend, go in," said the doctor. "You have only to push the gate."

The passage was long, and Pierre kept on feeling the damp wall with his hand, for fear of making a false step. It seemed to him as if he were descending into a cellar, in deep obscurity, and he could feel a slippery soil impregnated with water beneath his feet. Then at the end, in obedience to the doctor's direction, he turned to the right.

"Stoop, or you may hurt yourself," said M. Chassaigne; "the door is very low. There, here we are."

The door of the room, like the gate in the street, stood wide open, as if the place had been carelessly abandoned; and Pierre, who had stopped in the middle of the chamber, hesitating, his eyes still full of the bright daylight outside, could distinguish absolutely nothing. He had fallen into complete darkness, and felt an icy chill about the shoulders similar to the sensation that might be caused by a wet towel.

But, little by little, his eyes became accustomed to the dimness. Two windows of unequal size opened on to a narrow, interior courtyard, where only a greenish light descended, as at the bottom of a well; and to read there, in the middle of the day, it would be necessary to have a candle. Measuring about fifteen feet by twelve, the room was flagged with large uneven stones; while the principal beam and the rafters of the roof, which were visible, had darkened with time and assumed a dirty, sooty hue. Opposite the door was the chimney, a miserable plaster chimney, with a mantel-piece formed of a rotten old plank. There was a sink between this chimney and one of the windows. The walls, with their decaying, damp-stained plaster falling off by bits, were full of cracks, and turning a dirty black like the ceiling. There was no longer any furniture there; the room seemed abandoned; you could only catch a glimpse of some confused, strange objects, unrecognisable in the heavy obscurity that hung about the corners.

After a spell of silence, the doctor exclaimed "Yes, this is the room; all came from here. Nothing has been changed, with the exception that the furniture has gone. I have tried to picture how it was placed: the beds certainly stood against this wall, opposite the windows; there must have been three of them at least, for the Soubirouses were seven—the father, mother, two boys, and three girls. Think of that! Three beds filling this room! Seven persons living in this small space! All of them buried alive, without air, without light, almost without bread! What frightful misery! What lowly, pity-awaking poverty!"

But he was interrupted. A shadowy form, which Pierre at first took for an old woman, entered. It was a priest, however, the curate of the parish, who now occupied the house. He was acquainted with the doctor.

"I heard your voice, Monsieur Chassaigne, and came down," said he. "So there you are, showing the room again?"

"Just so, Monsieur l' Abbe; I took the liberty. It does not inconvenience you?"

"Oh! not at all, not at all! Come as often as you please, and bring other people."

He laughed in an engaging manner, and bowed to Pierre, who, astonished by this quiet carelessness, observed: "The people who come, however, must sometimes plague you?"

The curate in his turn seemed surprised. "Indeed, no! Nobody comes. You see the place is scarcely known. Every one remains over there at the Grotto. I leave the door open so as not to be worried. But days and days often pass without my hearing even the sound of a mouse."

Pierre's eyes were becoming more and more accustomed to the obscurity; and among the vague, perplexing objects which filled the corners, he ended by distinguishing some old barrels, remnants of fowl cages, and broken tools, a lot of rubbish such as is swept away and thrown to the bottom of cellars. Hanging from the rafters, moreover, were some provisions, a salad basket full of eggs, and several bunches of big pink onions.

"And, from what I see," resumed Pierre, with a slight shudder, "you have thought that you might make use of the room?"

The curate was beginning to feel uncomfortable. "Of course, that's it," said he. "What can one do? The house is so small, I have so little space. And then you can't imagine how damp it is here; it is altogether impossible to occupy the room. And so, *mon Dieu*, little by little all this has accumulated here by itself, contrary to one's own desire."

"It has become a lumber-room," concluded Pierre.

"Oh no! hardly that. An unoccupied room, and yet in truth, if you insist on it, it is a lumber-room!"

His uneasiness was increasing, mingled with a little shame. Doctor Chassaigne remained silent and did not interfere; but he smiled, and was visibly delighted at his companion's revolt against human ingratitude. Pierre, unable to restrain himself, now continued: "You must excuse me, Monsieur l'Abbe, if I insist. But just reflect that you owe everything to Bernadette; but for her Lourdes would still be one of the least known towns of France. And really it seems to me that out of mere gratitude the parish ought to have transformed this wretched room into a chapel."

"Oh! a chapel!" interrupted the curate. "It is only a question of a human creature: the Church could not make her an object of worship."

"Well, we won't say a chapel, then; but at all events there ought to be some lights and flowers—bouquets of roses constantly renewed by the piety of the inhabitants and the pilgrims. In a word, I should like some little show of affection—a touching souvenir, a picture of Bernadette—something that would delicately indicate that she deserves to have a place in all hearts. This forgetfulness and desertion are shocking. It is monstrous that so much dirt should have been allowed to accumulate!"

The curate, a poor, thoughtless, nervous man, at once adopted Pierre's views: "In reality, you are a thousand times right," said he; "but I myself have no power, I can do nothing. Whenever they ask me for the room, to set it to rights, I will give it up and remove my barrels, although I really don't know where else to put them. Only, I repeat, it does not depend on me. I can do nothing, nothing at all!" Then, under the pretext that he had to go out, he hastened to take leave and run away again, saying to Doctor Chassaigne: "Remain, remain as long as you please; you are never in my way."

When the doctor once more found himself alone with Pierre he caught hold of both his hands with effusive delight. "Ah, my dear child," said he, "how pleased you have made me! How admirably you expressed to him all that has been boiling in my own heart so long! Like you, I thought of bringing some roses here every morning. I should have simply had the room cleaned, and would have contented myself with placing two large bunches of roses on the mantelpiece; for you know that I have long felt deep affection for Bernadette, and it seemed to me that those roses would be like the very flowering and perfume of her memory. Only—only—" and so saying he made a despairing gesture, "only courage failed me. Yes, I say courage, no one having yet dared to declare himself openly against the Fathers of the Grotto. One hesitates and recoils in the fear of stirring up a religious scandal. Fancy what a deplorable racket all this would create. And so those who are as indignant as I am are reduced to the necessity of holding their tongues—preferring a continuance of silence to anything else." Then, by way of conclusion, he added: "The ingratitude and rapacity of man, my dear child, are sad things to see. Each time I come into this dim wretchedness, my heart swells and I cannot restrain my tears."

He ceased speaking, and neither of them said another word, both being overcome by the extreme melancholy which the surroundings fostered. They were steeped in gloom. The dampness made them shudder as they stood there amidst the dilapidated walls and the dust of the old rubbish piled upon either side. And the idea returned to them that without Bernadette none of the prodigies which had made Lourdes a town unique in the world would have existed. It was at her voice that the miraculous spring had gushed forth, that the Grotto, bright with candles, had opened. Immense works were executed, new churches rose from the ground, giant-like causeways led up to

God. An entire new city was built, as if by enchantment, with gardens, walks, quays, bridges, shops, and hotels. And people from the uttermost parts of the earth flocked thither in crowds, and the rain of millions fell with such force and so abundantly that the young city seemed likely to increase indefinitely—to fill the whole valley, from one to the other end of the mountains. If Bernadette had been suppressed none of those things would have existed, the extraordinary story would have relapsed into nothingness, old unknown Lourdes would still have been plunged in the sleep of ages at the foot of its castle. Bernadette was the sole labourer and creatress; and yet this room, whence she had set out on the day she beheld the Virgin, this cradle, indeed, of the miracle and of all the marvellous fortune of the town, was disdained, left a prey to vermin, good only for a lumber-room, where onions and empty barrels were put away.

Then the other side of the question vividly appeared in Pierre's mind, and he again seemed to see the triumph which he had just witnessed, the exaltation of the Grotto and Basilica, while Marie, dragging her little car, ascended behind the Blessed Sacrament, amidst the clamour of the multitude. But the Grotto especially shone out before him. It was no longer the wild, rocky cavity before which the child had formerly knelt on the deserted bank of the torrent; it was a chapel, transformed and enriched, a chapel illumined by a vast number of candles, where nations marched past in procession. All the noise, all the brightness, all the adoration, all the money, burst forth there in a splendour of constant victory. Here, at the cradle, in this dark, icy hole, there was not a soul, not a taper, not a hymn, not a flower. Of the infrequent visitors who came thither, none knelt or prayed. All that a few tender-hearted pilgrims had done in their desire to carry away a souvenir had been to reduce to dust, between their fingers, the half-rotten plank serving as a mantelshelf. The clergy ignored the existence of this spot of misery, which the processions ought to have visited as they might visit a station of glory. It was there that the poor child had begun her dream, one cold night, lying in bed between her two sisters, and seized with a fit of her ailment while the whole family was fast asleep. It was thence, too, that she had set out, unconsciously carrying along with her that dream, which was again to be born within her in the broad daylight and to flower so prettily in a vision such as those of the legends. And no one now followed in her footsteps. The manger was forgotten, and left in darkness—that manger where had germed the little humble seed which over yonder was now yielding such prodigious harvests, reaped by the workmen of the last hour amidst the sovereign pomp of ceremonies.

Pierre, whom the great human emotion of the story moved to tears, at last summed up his thoughts in three words, saying in a low voice, "It is Bethlehem."

"Yes," remarked Doctor Chassaigne, in his turn, "it is the wretched lodging, the chance refuge, where new religions are born of suffering and pity. And at times I ask myself if all is not better thus: if it is not better that this room should remain in its actual state of wretchedness and abandonment. It seems to me that Bernadette has nothing to lose by it, for I love her all the more when I come to spend an hour here."

He again became silent, and then made a gesture of revolt: "But no, no! I cannot forgive it—this ingratitude sets me beside myself. I told you I was convinced that Bernadette had freely gone to cloister herself at Nevers. But although no one smuggled her away, what a relief it was for those whom she had begun to inconvenience here! And they are the same men, so anxious to be the absolute masters, who at the present time endeavour by all possible means to wrap her memory in silence. Ah! my dear child, if I were to tell you all!"

Little by little he spoke out and relieved himself. Those Fathers of the Grotto, who showed such greed in trading on the work of Bernadette, dreaded her still more now that she was dead than they had done whilst she was alive. So long as she had lived, their great terror had assuredly been that she might return to Lourdes to claim a portion of the spoil; and her humility alone reassured them, for she was in nowise of a domineering disposition, and had herself chosen the dim abode of renunciation where she was destined to pass away. But at present their fears had increased at the idea that a will other than theirs might bring the relics of the visionary back to Lourdes; that, thought had, indeed, occurred to the municipal council immediately after her death; the town had wished to raise a tomb, and there had been talk of opening a subscription. The Sisters of Nevers, however, formally refused to give up the body, which they said belonged to them. Everyone felt that the Sisters were acting under the influence of the Fathers, who were very uneasy, and energetically bestirred themselves to prevent by all means in their power the return of those venerated ashes, in whose presence at Lourdes they foresaw a possible competition with the Grotto itself. Could they have imagined some such threatening occurrence as this—a monumental tomb in the cemetery, pilgrims proceeding thither in procession, the sick feverishly kissing the marble, and miracles being worked there amidst a holy fervour? This would have been disastrous rivalry, a certain displacement of all the present devotion and prodigies. And the great, the sole fear, still and ever returned to them, that of having to divide the spoils, of seeing the money go elsewhere should the town, now taught by experience, know how to turn the tomb to account.

The Fathers were even credited with a scheme of profound craftiness. They were supposed to have the secret idea of reserving Bernadette's remains for themselves; the Sisters of Nevers having simply undertaken to keep it for them within the peaceful precincts of their chapel. Only, they were waiting, and would not bring it back until the affluence of the pilgrims should decrease. What was the use of a solemn return at present, when crowds flocked to the place without interruption and in increasing numbers? Whereas, when the extraordinary success of Our Lady of Lourdes should decline, like everything else in this world, one could imagine what a reawakening of faith would attend the solemn, resounding ceremony at which Christendom would behold the relics of the chosen one take possession of the soil whence she had made so many marvels spring. And the miracles would then begin again on the marble of her tomb before the Grotto or in the choir of the Basilica.

"You may search," continued Doctor Chassaigne, "but you won't find a single official picture of Bernadette at Lourdes. Her portrait is sold, but it is hung no where, in no sanctuary. It is systematic forgetfulness, the same sentiment of covert uneasiness as that which has wrought silence and abandonment in this sad chamber where we are. In the same way as they are afraid of worship at her tomb, so are they afraid of crowds coming and kneeling here, should two candles burn or a couple of bouquets of roses bloom upon this chimney. And if a paralytic woman were to rise shouting that she was cured, what a scandal would arise, how disturbed would be those good traders of the Grotto on seeing their monopoly seriously threatened! They are the masters, and the masters they intend to remain; they will not part with any portion of the magnificent farm that they have acquired and are working. Nevertheless they tremble—

yes, they tremble at the memory of the workers of the first hour, of that little girl who is still so great in death, and for whose huge inheritance they burn with such greed that after having sent her to live at Nevers, they dare not even bring back her corpse, but leave it imprisoned beneath the flagstones of a convent!"

Ah! how wretched was the fate of that poor creature, who had been cut off from among the living, and whose corpse in its turn was condemned to exile! And how Pierre pitied her, that daughter of misery, who seemed to have been chosen only that she might suffer in her life and in her death! Even admitting that an unique, persistent will had not compelled her to disappear, still guarding her even in her tomb, what a strange succession of circumstances there had been—how it seemed as if someone, uneasy at the idea of the immense power she might grasp, had jealously sought to keep her out of the way! In Pierre's eyes she remained the chosen one, the martyr; and if he could no longer believe, if the history of this unfortunate girl sufficed to complete within him the ruin of his faith, it none the less upset him in all his brotherly love for mankind by revealing a new religion to him, the only one which might still fill his heart, the religion of life, of human sorrow.

Just then, before leaving the room, Doctor Chassaigne exclaimed: "And it's here that one must believe, my dear child. Do you see this obscure hole, do you think of the resplendent Grotto, of the triumphant Basilica, of the town built, of the world created, the crowds that flock to Lourdes! And if Bernadette was only hallucinated, only an idiot, would not the outcome be more astonishing, more inexplicable still? What! An idiot's dream would have sufficed to stir up nations like this! No! no! The Divine breath which alone can explain prodigies passed here."

Pierre was on the point of hastily replying "Yes!" It was true, a breath had passed there, the sob of sorrow, the inextinguishable yearning towards the Infinite of hope. If the dream of a suffering child had sufficed to attract multitudes, to bring about a rain of millions and raise a new city from the soil, was it not because this dream in a measure appeased the hunger of poor mankind, its insatiable need of being deceived and consoled? She had once more opened the Unknown, doubtless at a favourable moment both socially and historically; and the crowds had rushed towards it. Oh! to take refuge in mystery, when reality is so hard, to abandon oneself to the miraculous, since cruel nature seems merely one long injustice! But although you may organise the Unknown, reduce it to dogmas, make revealed religions of it, there is never anything at the bottom of it beyond the appeal of suffering, the cry of life, demanding health, joy, and fraternal happiness, and ready to accept them in another world if they cannot be obtained on earth. What use is it to believe in dogmas? Does it not suffice to weep and love?

Pierre, however, did not discuss the question. He withheld the answer that was on his lips, convinced, moreover, that the eternal need of the supernatural would cause eternal faith to abide among sorrowing mankind. The miraculous, which could not be verified, must be a food necessary to human despair. Besides, had he not vowed in all charity that he would not wound anyone with his doubts?

"What a prodigy, isn't it?" repeated the doctor.

"Certainly," Pierre ended by answering. "The whole human drama has been played, all the unknown forces have acted in this poor room, so damp and dark."

They remained there a few minutes more in silence; they walked round the walls, raised their eyes toward the smoky ceiling, and cast a final glance at the narrow, greenish yard. Truly it was a heart-rending sight, this poverty of the cobweb level, with its dirty old barrels, its worn-out tools, its refuse of all kinds rotting in the corners in heaps. And without adding a word they at last slowly retired, feeling extremely sad.

It was only in the street that Doctor Chassaigne seemed to awaken. He gave a slight shudder and hastened his steps, saying: "It is not finished, my dear child; follow me. We are now going to look at the other great iniquity." He referred to Abbe Peyramale and his church.

They crossed the Place du Porche and turned into the Rue Saint Pierre; a few minutes would suffice them. But their conversation had again fallen on the Fathers of the Grotto, on the terrible, merciless war waged by Father Sempe against the former Cure of Lourdes. The latter had been vanquished, and had died in consequence, overcome by feelings of frightful bitterness; and, after thus killing him by grief, they had completed the destruction of his church, which he had left unfinished, without a roof, open to the wind and to the rain. With what a glorious dream had that monumental edifice filled the last year of the Cure's life! Since he had been dispossessed of the Grotto, driven from the work of Our Lady of Lourdes, of which he, with Bernadette, had been the first artisan, his church had become his revenge, his protestation, his own share of the glory, the House of the Lord where he would triumph in his sacred vestments, and whence he would conduct endless processions in compliance with the formal desire of the Blessed Virgin. Man of authority and domination as he was at bottom, a pastor of the multitude, a builder of temples, he experienced a restless delight in hurrying on the work, with the lack of foresight of an eager man who did not allow indebtedness to trouble him, but was perfectly contented so long as he always had a swarm of workmen busy on the scaffoldings. And thus he saw his church rise up, and pictured it finished, one bright summer morning, all new in the rising sun.

Ah! that vision constantly evoked gave him courage for the struggle, amidst the underhand, murderous designs by which he felt himself to be enveloped. His church, towering above the vast square, at last rose in all its colossal majesty. He had decided that it should be in the Romanesque style, very large, very simple, its nave nearly three hundred feet long, its steeple four hundred and sixty feet high. It shone out resplendently in the clear sunlight, freed on the previous day of the last scaffolding, and looking quite smart in its newness, with its broad courses of stone disposed with perfect regularity. And, in thought, he sauntered around it, charmed with its nudity, its stupendous candour, its chasteness recalling that of a virgin child, for there was not a piece of sculpture, not an ornament that would have uselessly loaded it. The roofs of the nave, transept, and apse were of equal height above the entablature, which was decorated with simple mouldings. In the same way the apertures in the aisles and nave had no other adornments than archivaults with mouldings, rising above the piers. He stopped in thought before the great coloured glass windows of the transept, whose roses were sparkling; and passing round the building he skirted the semicircular apse against which stood the vestry building with its two rows of little windows; and then he returned, never tiring of his contemplation of that regal ordonnance, those great lines standing out against the blue sky, those superposed roofs, that enormous mass of stone, whose solidity promised to defy centuries. But, when he closed his eyes he, above all else, conjured up, with rapturous pride, a vision of the facade and steeple; down below, the three portals, the roofs of the two lateral ones forming terraces, while from the central one, in the very middle of the facade, the steeple boldly sprang. Here again columns resting on piers supported archivaults with simple mouldings. Against the gable, at a point where there was a pinnacle, and between the two lofty windows lighting the nave, was a statue of Our Lady of Lourdes under a canopy. Up above, were other bays with freshly painted luffer-boards. Buttresses started from the ground at the four corners of the steeple-base, becoming less and less massive from storey to storey, till they reached the spire, a bold, tapering spire in stone, flanked by four turrets and adorned with pinnacles, and soaring upward till it vanished in the sky. And to the parish priest of Lourdes it seemed as if it were his own fervent soul which had grown and flown aloft with this spire, to testify to his faith throughout the ages, there on high, quite close to God.

At other times another vision delighted him still more. He thought he could see the inside of his church on the day of the first solemn mass he would perform there. The coloured windows threw flashes of fire brilliant like precious stones; the twelve chapels, the aisles, were beaming with lighted candles. And he was at the high altar of marble and gold; and the fourteen columns of the nave in single blocks of Pyrenean marble, magnificent marble purchased with money that had come from the four corners of Christendom, rose up supporting the vaulted roof, while the sonorous voices of the organs filled the whole building with a hymn of joy. A multitude of the faithful was gathered there, kneeling on the flags in front of the choir, which was screened by ironwork as delicate as lace, and covered with admirably carved wood. The pulpit, the regal present of a great lady, was a marvel of art cut in massive oak. The baptismal fonts had been hewn out of hard stone by an artist of great talent. Pictures by masters ornamented the walls. Crosses, pyxes, precious monstrances, sacred vestments, similar to suns, were piled up in the vestry cupboards. And what a dream it was to be the pontiff of such a temple, to reign there after having erected it with passion, to bless the crowds who hastened to it from the entire earth, while the flying peals from the steeple told the Grotto and Basilica that they had over there, in old Lourdes, a rival, a victorious sister, in whose great nave God triumphed also!

After following the Rue Saint Pierre for a moment, Doctor Chassaigne and his companion turned into the little Rue de Langelle.

"We are coming to it," said the doctor. But though Pierre looked around him he could see no church. There were merely some wretched hovels, a whole district of poverty, littered with foul buildings. At length, however, at the bottom of a blind alley, he perceived a remnant of the half-rotten palings which still surrounded the vast square site bordered by the Rue Saint Pierre, the Rue de Bagneres, the Rue de Langelle, and the Rue des Jardins.

"We must turn to the left," continued the doctor, who had entered a narrow passage among the rubbish. "Here we are!"

And the ruin suddenly appeared amidst the ugliness and wretchedness that masked it.

The whole great carcase of the nave and the aisles, the transept and the apse was standing. The walls rose on all sides to the point where the vaulting would have begun. You entered as into a real church, you could walk about at ease, identifying all the usual parts of an edifice of this description. Only when you raised your eyes you saw the sky; the roofs were wanting, the rain could fall and the wind blow there freely. Some fifteen years previously the works had been abandoned, and things had remained in the same state as the last workman had left them. What struck you first of all were the ten pillars of the nave and the four pillars of the choir, those magnificent columns of Pyrenean marble, each of a single block, which had been covered with a casing of planks in order to protect them from damage. The bases and capitals were still in the rough, awaiting the sculptors. And these isolated columns, thus cased in wood, had a mournful aspect indeed. Moreover, a dismal sensation filled you at sight of the whole gaping enclosure, where grass had sprung up all over the ravaged, bumpy soil of the aisles and the nave, a thick cemetery grass, through which the women of the neighbourhood had ended by making paths. They came in to spread out their washing there. And even now a collection of poor people's washing—thick sheets, shirts in shreds, and babies' swaddling clothes—was fast drying in the last rays of the sun, which glided in through the broad, empty bays.

Slowly, without speaking, Pierre and Doctor Chassaigne walked round the inside of the church. The ten chapels of the aisles formed a species of compartments full of rubbish and remnants. The ground of the choir had been cemented, doubtless to protect the crypt below against infiltrations; but unfortunately the vaults must be sinking; there was a hollow there which the storm of the previous night had transformed into a little lake. However, it was these portions of the transept and the apse which had the least suffered. Not a stone had moved; the great central rose windows above the triforium seemed to be awaiting their coloured glass, while some thick planks, forgotten atop of the walls of the apse, might have made anyone think that the workmen would begin covering it the next day. But, when Pierre and the doctor had retraced their steps, and went out to look at the facade, the lamentable woefulness of the young ruin was displayed to their gaze. On this side, indeed, the works had not been carried forward to anything like the same extent: the porch with its three portals alone was built, and fifteen years of abandonment had sufficed for the winter weather to eat into the sculptures, the small columns and the archivaults, with a really singular destructive effect, as though the stones, deeply penetrated, destroyed, had melted away beneath tears. The heart grieved at the sight of the decay which had attacked the work before it was even finished. Not yet to be, and nevertheless to crumble away in this fashion under the sky! To be arrested in one's colossal growth, and simply strew the weeds with ruins!

They returned to the nave, and were overcome by the frightful sadness which this assassination of a monument provoked. The spacious plot of waste ground inside was littered with the remains of scaffoldings, which had been pulled down when half rotten, in fear lest their fall might crush people; and everywhere amidst the tall grass were boards, put-logs, moulds for arches, mingled with bundles of old cord eaten away by damp. There was also the long narrow carcase of a crane rising up like a gibbet. Spade-handles, pieces of broken wheelbarrows, and heaps of greenish bricks, speckled with moss and wild convolvuli in bloom, were still lying among the forgotten materials. In the beds of nettles you here and there distinguished the rails of a little railway laid down for the trucks, one of which was lying overturned in a corner. But the saddest sight in all this death of things was certainly the portable engine which had remained in the shed that sheltered it. For fifteen years it had been standing there cold and lifeless. A part of the roof of the shed had ended by falling in upon it, and now the rain drenched it at every shower. A bit of the leather harness by which the crane was worked hung down, and seemed to bind the engine like a thread of some gigantic spider's web. And its metal-work, its steel and copper, was also decaying, as if rusted by lichens, covered with the vegetation of old age, whose yellowish patches made it look like a very ancient, grass-grown machine which the winters had preyed upon. This lifeless engine, this cold engine with its empty firebox and its silent boiler, was like the very soul of the departed labour vainly awaiting the advent of some great charitable heart, whose coming through the eglantine and the brambles would awaken this sleeping church in the wood from its heavy slumber of ruin.

At last Doctor Chassaigne spoke: "Ah!" he said, "when one thinks that fifty thousand francs would have sufficed to prevent such a disaster! With fifty thousand francs the roof could have been put on, the heavy work would have been saved, and one could have waited patiently. But they wanted to kill the work just as they had killed the man." With a gesture he designated the Fathers of the Grotto, whom he avoided naming. "And to think," he continued, "that their annual receipts are eight hundred thousand francs. However, they prefer to send presents to Rome to propitiate powerful friends there."

In spite of himself, he was again opening hostilities against the adversaries of Cure Peyramale. The whole story caused a holy anger of justice to haunt him. Face to face with those lamentable ruins, he returned to the facts—the enthusiastic Cure starting on the building of his beloved church, and getting deeper and deeper into debt, whilst Father Sempe, ever on the lookout, took advantage of each of his mistakes, discrediting him with the Bishop, arresting the flow of offerings, and finally stopping the works. Then, after the conquered man was dead, had come interminable lawsuits, lawsuits lasting fifteen years, which gave the winters time to devour the building. And now it was in such a woeful state, and the debt had risen to such an enormous figure, that all seemed over. The slow death, the death of the stones, was becoming irrevocable. The portable engine beneath its tumbling shed would fall to pieces, pounded by the rain and eaten away by the moss.

"I know very well that they chant victory," resumed the doctor; "that they alone remain. It is just what they wanted—to be the absolute masters, to have all the power, all the money for themselves alone. I may tell you that their terror of competition has even made them intrigue against the religious Orders that have attempted to come to Lourdes. Jesuits, Dominicans, Benedictines, Capuchins, and Carmelites have made applications at various times, and the Fathers of the Grotto have always succeeded in keeping them away. They only tolerate the female Orders, and will only have one flock. And the town belongs to them; they have opened shop there, and sell God there wholesale and retail!"

Walking slowly, he had while speaking returned to the middle of the nave, amidst the ruins, and with a sweeping wave of the arm he pointed to all the devastation surrounding him. "Look at this sadness, this frightful wretchedness! Over yonder the Rosary and Basilica cost them three millions of francs."[1]

Then, as in Bernadette's cold, dark room, Pierre saw the Basilica rise before him, radiant in its triumph. It was not here that you found the realisation of the dream of Cure Peyramale, officiating and blessing kneeling multitudes while the organs resounded joyfully. The Basilica, over yonder, appeared, vibrating with the pealing of

[1] About 580,000 dollars.

its bells, clamorous with the superhuman joy of an accomplished miracle, all sparkling with its countless lights, its banners, its lamps, its hearts of silver and gold, its clergy attired in gold, and its monstrance akin to a golden star. It flamed in the setting sun, it touched the heavens with its spire, amidst the soaring of the milliards of prayers which caused its walls to quiver. Here, however, was the church that had died be-before being born, the church placed under interdict by a mandamus of the Bishop, the church falling into dust, and open to the four winds of heaven. Each storm carried away a little more of the stones, big flies buzzed all alone among the nettles which had invaded the nave; and there were no other devotees than the poor women of the neighbourhood, who came thither to turn their sorry linen, spread upon the grass.

It seemed amidst the mournful silence as though a low voice were sobbing, perhaps the voice of the marble columns weeping over their useless beauty under their wooden shirts. At times birds would fly across the deserted apse uttering a shrill cry. Bands of enormous rats which had taken refuge under bits of the lowered scaffoldings would fight, and bite, and bound out of their holes in a gallop of terror. And nothing could have been more heart-rending than the sight of this pre-determined ruin, face to face with its triumphant rival, the Basilica, which beamed with gold.

Again Doctor Chassaigne curtly said, "Come."

They left the church, and following the left aisle, reached a door, roughly fashioned out of a few planks nailed together; and, when they had passed down a half-demolished wooden staircase, the steps of which shook beneath their feet, they found themselves in the crypt.

It was a low vault, with squat arches, on exactly the same plan as the choir. The thick, stunted columns, left in the rough, also awaited their sculptors. Materials were lying about, pieces of wood were rotting on the beaten ground, the whole vast hall was white with plaster in the abandonment in which unfinished buildings are left. At the far end, three bays, formerly glazed, but in which not a pane of glass remained, threw a clear, cold light upon the desolate bareness of the walls.

And there, in the middle, lay Cure Peyramale's corpse. Some pious friends had conceived the touching idea of thus burying him in the crypt of his unfinished church. The tomb stood on a broad step and was all marble. The inscriptions, in letters of gold, expressed the feelings of the subscribers, the cry of truth and reparation that came from the monument itself. You read on the face: "This tomb has been erected by the aid of pious offerings from the entire universe to the blessed memory of the great servant of Our Lady of Lourdes." On the right side were these words from a Brief of Pope Pius IX.: "You have entirely devoted yourself to erecting a temple to the Mother of God." And on the left were these words from the New Testament: "Happy are they who suffer persecution for justice' sake." Did not these inscriptions embody the true plaint, the legitimate hope of the vanquished man who had fought so long in the sole desire of strictly executing the commands of the Virgin as transmitted to him by Bernadette? She, Our Lady of Lourdes, was there personified by a slender statuette, standing above the commemorative inscription, against the naked wall whose only decorations were a few bead wreaths hanging from nails. And before the tomb, as before the Grotto, were five or six benches in rows, for the faithful who desired to sit down.

But with another gesture of sorrowful compassion, Doctor Chassaigne had silently pointed out to Pierre a huge damp spot which was turning the wall at the far end quite green. Pierre remembered the little lake which he had noticed up above on the cracked cement flooring of the choir—quite a quantity of water left by the storm of the previous night. Infiltration had evidently commenced, a perfect stream ran down, invading the crypt, whenever there was heavy rain. And they both felt a pang at their hearts when they perceived that the water was trickling along the vaulted roof in narrow threads, and thence falling in large, regular rhythmical drops upon the tomb. The doctor could not restrain a groan. "Now it rains," he said; "it rains on him!"

Pierre remained motionless, in a kind of awe. In the presence of that falling water, at the thought of the blasts which must rush at winter time through the glassless windows, that corpse appeared to him both woeful and tragic. It acquired a fierce grandeur, lying there alone in its splendid marble tomb, amidst all the rubbish, at the bottom of the crumbling ruins of its own church. It was the solitary guardian, the dead sleeper and dreamer watching over the empty spaces, open to all the birds of night. It was the mute, obstinate, eternal protest, and it was expectation also. Cure Peyramale, stretched in his coffin, having all eternity before him to acquire patience, there, without weariness, awaited the workmen who would perhaps return thither some fine April morning. If they should take ten years to do so, he would be there, and if it should take them a century, he would be there still. He was waiting for the rotten scaffoldings up above, among the grass of the nave, to be resuscitated like the dead, and by the force of some miracle to stand upright once more, along the walls. He was waiting, too, for the moss-covered engine to become all at once burning hot, recover its breath, and raise the timbers for the roof. His beloved enterprise, his gigantic building, was crumbling about his head, and yet with joined hands and closed eyes he was watching over its ruins, watching and waiting too.

In a low voice, the doctor finished the cruel story, telling how, after persecuting Cure Peyramale and his work, they persecuted his tomb. There had formerly been a bust of the Cure there, and pious hands had kept a little lamp burning before it. But a woman had one day fallen with her face to the earth, saying that she had perceived the soul of the deceased, and thereupon the Fathers of the Grotto were in a flutter. Were miracles about to take place there? The sick already passed entire days there, seated on the benches before the tomb. Others knelt down, kissed the marble, and prayed to be cured. And at this a feeling of terror arose: supposing they should be cured, supposing the Grotto should find a competitor in this martyr, lying all alone, amidst the old tools left there by the masons! The Bishop of Tarbes, informed and influenced, thereupon published the mandamus which placed the church under interdict, forbidding all worship there and all pilgrimages and processions to the tomb of the former priest of Lourdes. As in the case of Bernadette, his memory was proscribed, his portrait could be found, officially, nowhere. In the same manner as they had shown themselves merciless against the living man, so did the Fathers prove merciless to his memory. They pursued him even in his tomb. They alone, again nowadays, prevented the works of the church from being proceeded with, by raising continual obstacles, and absolutely refusing to share their rich harvest of alms. And they seemed to be waiting for the winter rains to fall and complete the work of destruction, for the vaulted roof of the crypt, the walls, the whole gigantic pile to crumble down upon the tomb of the martyr, upon the body of the defeated man, so that he might be buried beneath them and at last pounded to dust!

"Ah!" murmured the doctor, "I, who knew him so valiant, so enthusiastic in all noble labour! Now, you see it, it rains, it rains on him!"

Painfully, he set himself on his knees and found relief in a long prayer.

Pierre, who could not pray, remained standing. Compassionate sorrow was overflowing from his heart. He listened to the heavy drops from the roof as one by one they broke on the tomb with a slow rhythmical pit-a-pat, which seemed to be numbering the seconds of eternity, amidst the profound silence. And he reflected on the eternal misery of this world, on the choice which suffering makes in always falling on the best. The two great makers of Our Lady of Lourdes, Bernadette and Cure Peyramale, rose up in the flesh again before him, like woeful victims, tortured during their lives and exiled after their deaths. That alone, indeed, would have completed within him the destruction of his faith; for the Bernadette, whom he had just found at the end of his researches, was but a human sister, loaded with every dolour. But none the less he preserved a tender brotherly veneration for her, and two tears slowly trickled down his cheeks.

THE FIFTH DAY

I. EGOTISM AND LOVE

AGAIN that night Pierre, at the Hotel of the Apparitions, was unable to obtain a wink of sleep. After calling at the hospital to inquire after Marie, who, since her return from the procession, had been soundly enjoying the delicious, restoring sleep of a child, he had gone to bed himself feeling anxious at the prolonged absence of M. de Guersaint. He had expected him at latest at dinner-time, but probably some mischance had detained him at Gavarnie; and he thought how disappointed Marie would be if her father were not there to embrace her the first thing in the morning. With a man like M. de Guersaint, so pleasantly heedless and so hare-brained, everything was possible, every fear might be realised.

Perhaps this anxiety had at first sufficed to keep Pierre awake in spite of his great fatigue; but afterwards the nocturnal noises of the hotel had really assumed unbearable proportions. The morrow, Tuesday, was the day of departure, the last day which the national pilgrimage would spend at Lourdes, and the pilgrims no doubt were making the most of their time, coming from the Grotto and returning thither in the middle of the night, endeavouring as it were to force the grace of Heaven by their commotion, and apparently never feeling the slightest need of repose. The doors slammed, the floors shook, the entire building vibrated beneath the disorderly gallop of a crowd. Never before had the walls reverberated with such obstinate coughs, such thick, husky voices. Thus Pierre, a prey to insomnia, tossed about on his bed and continually rose up, beset with the idea that the noise he heard must have been made by M. de Guersaint who had returned. For some minutes he would listen feverishly; but he could only hear the extraordinary sounds of the passage, amid which he could distinguish nothing precisely. Was it the priest, the mother and her three daughters, or the old married couple on his left, who were fighting with the furniture? or was it rather the larger family, or the single gentleman, or the young single woman on his right, whom some incomprehensible occurrences were leading into adventures? At one moment he jumped from his bed, wishing to explore his absent friend's empty room, as he felt certain that some deeds of violence were taking place in it. But although he listened very attentively when he got there, the only sound he could distinguish was the tender caressing murmur of two voices. Then a sudden recollection of Madame Volmar came to him, and he returned shuddering to bed.

At length, when it was broad daylight and Pierre had just fallen asleep, a loud knocking at his door awoke him with a start. This time there could be no mistake, a loud voice broken by sobs was calling "Monsieur l'Abbe! Monsieur l'Abbe! for Heaven's sake wake up!"

Surely it must be M. de Guersaint who had been brought back dead, at least. Quite scared, Pierre ran and opened the door, in his night-shirt, and found himself in the presence of his neighbour, M. Vigneron.

"Oh! for Heaven's sake, Monsieur l'Abbe, dress yourself at once!" exclaimed the assistant head-clerk. "Your holy ministry is required." And he began to relate that he had just got up to see the time by his watch on the mantelpiece, when he had heard some most frightful sighs issuing from the adjoining room, where Madame Chaise slept. She had left the communicating door open in order to be more with them, as she pleasantly expressed it. Accordingly he had hastened in, and flung the shutters open so as to admit both light and air. "And what a sight, Monsieur l'Abbe!" he continued. "Our poor aunt lying on her bed, nearly purple in the face already, her mouth wide open in a vain effort to breathe, and her hands fumbling with the sheet. It's her heart complaint, you know. Come, come at once, Monsieur l'Abbe, and help her, I implore you!"

Pierre, utterly bewildered, could find neither his breeches nor his cassock. "Of course, of course I'll come with you," said he. "But I have not what is necessary for administering the last sacraments."

M. Vigneron had assisted him to dress, and was now stooping down looking for his slippers. "Never mind," he said, "the mere sight of you will assist her in her last moments, if Heaven has this affliction in store for us. Here! put these on your feet, and follow me at once—oh! at once!"

He went off like a gust of wind and plunged into the adjoining room. All the doors remained wide open. The young priest, who followed him, noticed nothing in the first room, which was in an incredible state of disorder, beyond the half-naked figure of little Gustave, who sat on the sofa serving him as a bed, motionless, very pale, forgotten, and shivering amid this drama of inexorable death. Open bags littered the floor, the greasy remains of supper soiled the table, the parents' bed seemed devastated by the catastrophe, its coverlets torn off and lying on the floor. And almost immediately afterwards he caught sight of the mother, who had hastily enveloped herself in an old yellow dressing-gown, standing with a terrified look in the inner room.

"Well, my love, well, my love?" repeated M. Vigneron, in stammering accents.

With a wave of her hand and without uttering a word Madame Vigneron drew their attention to Madame Chaise, who lay motionless, with her head sunk in the pillow and her hands stiffened and twisted. She was blue in the face, and her mouth gaped, as though with the last great gasp that had come from her.

Pierre bent over her. Then in a low voice he said: "She is dead!"

Dead! The word rang through the room where a heavy silence reigned, and the husband and wife looked at each other in amazement, bewilderment. So it was over? The aunt had died before Gustave, and the youngster inherited her five hundred thousand francs. How many times had they dwelt on that dream; whose sudden realisation dumfounded them? How many times had despair overcome them when they feared that the poor child might depart before her? Dead! Good heavens! was it their fault? Had they really prayed to the Blessed Virgin for this? She had shown herself so good to them that they trembled at the thought that they had not been able to express a wish without its being granted. In the death of the chief clerk, so suddenly carried off so that they might have his place, they had already recognised the powerful hand of Our Lady of Lourdes. Had she again loaded them with favours, listening even to the unconscious dreams of their desire? Yet they had never desired anyone's death; they were worthy people incapable of any bad action, loving their relations, fulfilling their religious duties, going to confession, partaking of the communion like other people without any ostentation. Whenever they thought of those five hundred thousand francs, of their son who might be the first to go, and of the annoyance it would be to them to see another and far less worthy nephew inherit that fortune, it was merely in the innermost recesses of their hearts, in short, quite innocently and naturally. Certainly they *had* thought of it when they were at the Grotto, but was not the Blessed Virgin wisdom itself? Did she not know far better than ourselves what she ought to do for the happiness of both the living and the dead?

Then Madame Vigneron in all sincerity burst into tears and wept for the sister whom she loved so much. "Ah! Monsieur l'Abbe," she said, "I saw her expire; she passed away before my eyes. What a misfortune that you were not here sooner to receive her soul! She died without a priest; your presence would have consoled her so much."

A prey also to emotion, his eyes full of tears, Vigneron sought to console his wife. "Your sister was a saint," said he; "she communicated again yesterday morning, and you need have no anxiety concerning her; her soul has gone straight to heaven. No doubt, if Monsieur l'Abbe had been here in time she would have been glad to see him. But what would you? Death was quicker. I went at once, and really there is nothing for us to reproach ourselves with."

Then, turning towards the priest, he added "Monsieur l'Abbe, it was her excessive piety which certainly hastened her end. Yesterday, at the Grotto, she had a bad attack, which was a warning. And in spite of her fatigue she obstinately followed the procession afterwards. I thought then that she could not last long. Yet, out of delicacy, one did not like to say anything to her, for fear of frightening her."

Pierre gently knelt down and said the customary prayers, with that human emotion which was his nearest approach to faith in the presence of eternal life and eternal death, both so pitiful. Then, as he remained kneeling a little longer, he overheard snatches of the conversation around him.

Little Gustave, forgotten on his couch amid the disorder of the other room, must have lost patience, for he had begun to cry and call out, "Mamma! mamma! mamma!"

At length Madame Vigneron went to quiet him, and it occurred to her to carry him in her arms to kiss his poor aunt for the last time. But at first he struggled and refused, crying so much that M. Vigneron was obliged to interfere and try to make him ashamed of himself. What! he who was never frightened of anything! who bore suffering with the courage of a grown-up man! And to think it was a question of kissing his poor aunt, who had always been so kind, whose last thought must most certainly have been for him!

"Give him to me," said he to his wife; "he's going to be good."

Gustave ended by clinging to his father's neck. He came shivering in his nightshirt, displaying his wretched little body devoured by scrofula. It seemed indeed as though the miraculous water of the piscinas, far from curing him, had freshened the sore on his back; whilst his scraggy leg hung down inertly like a dry stick.

"Kiss her," resumed M. Vigneron.

The child leant forward and kissed his aunt on the forehead. It was not death which upset him and caused him to struggle. Since he had been in the room he had been looking at the dead woman with an air of quiet curiosity. He did not love her, he had suffered on her account so long. He had the ideas and feelings of a man, and the weight of them was stifling him as, like his complaint, they developed and became more acute. He felt full well that he was too little, that children ought not to understand what only concerns their elders.

However, his father, seating himself out of the way, kept him on his knee, whilst his mother closed the window and lit the two candles on the mantelpiece. "Ah! my poor dear," murmured M. Vigneron, feeling that he must say something, "it's a cruel loss for all of us. Our trip is now completely spoilt; this is our last day, for we start this afternoon. And the Blessed Virgin, too, was showing herself so kind to us."

However, seeing his son's surprised look, a look of infinite sadness and reproach, he hastened to add: "Yes, of course, I know that she hasn't yet quite cured you. But we must not despair of her kindness. She loves us so well, she shows us so many favours that she will certainly end by curing you, since that is now the only favour that remains for her to grant us."

Madame Vigneron, who was listening, drew near and said: "How happy we should have been to have returned to Paris all three hale and hearty! Nothing is ever perfect!"

"I say!" suddenly observed Monsieur Vigneron, "I sha'n't be able to leave with you this afternoon, on account of the formalities which have to be gone through. I hope that my return ticket will still be available to-morrow!"

They were both getting over the frightful shock, feeling a sense of relief in spite of their affection for Madame Chaise; and, in fact, they were already forgetting her, anxious above all things to leave Lourdes as soon as possible, as though the principal object of their journey had been attained. A decorous, unavowed delight was slowly penetrating them.

"When I get back to Paris there will be so much for me to do," continued M. Vigneron. "I, who now only long for repose! All the same I shall remain my three years at the Ministry, until I can retire, especially now that I am certain of the retiring pension of chief clerk. But afterwards—oh! afterwards I certainly hope to enjoy life a bit. Since this money has come to us I shall purchase the estate of Les Billottes, that superb property down at my native place which I have always been dreaming of. And I promise you that I sha'n't find time hanging heavy on my hands in the midst of my horses, my dogs, and my flowers!"

Little Gustave was still on his father's knee, his night-shirt tucked up, his whole wretched misshapen body shivering, and displaying the scragginess of a slowly dying child. When he perceived that his father, now full of his dream of an opulent life, no longer seemed to notice that he was there, he gave one of his enigmatical smiles, in which melancholy was tinged with malice. "But what about me, father?" he asked.

M. Vigneron started, like one aroused from sleep, and did not at first seem to understand. "You, little one? You'll be with us, of course!"

But Gustave gave him a long, straight look, without ceasing to smile with his artful, though woeful lips. "Oh! do you think so?" he asked.

"Of course I think so! You'll be with us, and it will be very nice to be with us."

Uneasy, stammering, unable to find the proper words, M. Vigneron felt a chill come over him when his son shrugged his skinny shoulders with an air of philosophical disdain and answered: "Oh, no! I shall be dead."

And then the terrified father was suddenly able to detect in the child's deep glance the glance of a man who was very aged, very knowing in all things, acquainted with all the abominations of life through having gone through them. What especially alarmed him was the abrupt conviction that this child had always seen into the innermost recesses of his heart, even farther than the things he dared to acknowledge to himself. He could recall that when the little sufferer had been but a baby in his cradle his eyes would frequently be fixed upon his own—and even then those eyes had been rendered so sharp by suffering, endowed, too, with such an extraordinary power of divination, that they had seemed able to dive into the unconscious thoughts buried in the depths of his brain. And by a singular counter-effect all the things that he had never owned to himself he now found in his child's eyes—he beheld them, read them there, against his will. The story of his cupidity lay unfolded before him, his anger at having such a sorry son, his anguish at the idea that Madame Chaise's fortune depended upon such a fragile existence, his eager desire that she might make haste and die whilst the youngster was still there, in order that he might finger the legacy. It was simply a question of days, this duel as to which should go off first. And then, at the end, it still meant death—the youngster must in his turn disappear, whilst he, the father, alone pocketed the cash, and lived joyfully to a good old age. And these frightful things shone forth so clearly from the keen, melancholy, smiling eyes of the poor condemned child, passed from son to father with such evident distinctness, that for a moment it seemed to them that they were shouting them aloud.

However, M. Vigneron struggled against it all, and, averting his head, began energetically protesting: "How! You'll be dead? What an idea! It's absurd to have such ideas as that!"

Meantime, Madame Vigneron was sobbing. "You wicked child," she gasped; "how can you make us so unhappy, when we already have such a cruel loss to deplore?"

Gustave had to kiss them, and to promise them that he would live for their sakes. Yet he did not cease smiling, conscious as he was that a lie is necessary when one does not wish to be too miserable, and quite prepared, moreover, to leave his parents happy behind him, since even the Blessed Virgin herself was powerless to grant him in this world the little happy lot to which each creature should be born.

His mother took him back to bed, and Pierre at length rose up, just as M. Vigneron had finished arranging the chamber of death in a suitable manner. "You'll excuse me, won't you, Monsieur l'Abbe?" said he, accompanying the young priest to the door. "I'm not quite myself. Well, it's an unpleasant time to go through. I must get over it somehow, however."

When Pierre got into the passage he stopped for a moment, listening to a sound of voices which was ascending the stairs. He had just been thinking of M. de Guersaint again, and imagined that he could recognise his voice. However, whilst he stood there waiting, an incident occurred which caused him intense discomfort. The door of the room next to M. de Guersaint's softly opened and a woman, clad in black, slipped into the passage. As she turned, she found herself face to face with Pierre, in such a fashion that it was impossible for them to pretend not to recognise each other.

The woman was Madame Volmar. Six o'clock had not yet struck, and she was going off, hoping that nobody would notice her, with the intention of showing herself at the hospital, and there spending this last morning, in order, in some measure, to justify her journey to Lourdes. When she perceived Pierre, she began to tremble, and, at first, could only stammer: "Oh, Monsieur l'Abbe, Monsieur l'Abbe!"

Then, noticing that the priest had left his door wide open, she seemed to give way to the fever consuming her, to a need of speaking out, explaining things and justifying herself. With her face suffused by a rush of blood she entered the young man's room, whither he had to follow her, greatly disturbed by this strange adventure. And, as he still left the door open, it was she who, in her desire to confide her sorrow and her sin to him, begged that he would close it.

"Oh! I pray you, Monsieur l'Abbe," said she, "do not judge me too harshly."

He made a gesture as though to reply that he did not allow himself the right to pass judgment upon her.

"But yes, but yes," she responded; "I know very well that you are acquainted with my misfortune. You saw me once in Paris behind the church of La Trinite, and the other day you recognised me on the balcony here! You were aware that I was there—in that room. But if you only knew—ah, if you only knew!"

Her lips were quivering, and tears were welling into her eyes. As he looked at her he was surprised by the extraordinary beauty transfiguring her face. This woman, invariably clad in black, extremely simple, with never a jewel, now appeared to him in all the brilliancy of her passion; no longer drawing back into the gloom, no longer seeking to bedim the lustre of her eyes, as was her wont. She, who at first sight did not seem pretty, but too dark and slender, with drawn features, a large mouth and long nose, assumed, as he now examined her, a troubling charm, a powerful, irresistible beauty. Her eyes especially—her large, magnificent eyes, whose brasiers she usually sought to cover with a veil of indifference—were flaring like torches; and he understood that she should be loved, adored, to madness.

"If you only knew, Monsieur l'Abbe," she continued. "If I were only to tell you all that I have suffered. Doubtless you have suspected something of it, since you are acquainted with my mother-in-law and my husband. On the few occasions when you have called on us you cannot but have understood some of the abominable things which go on in my home, though I have always striven to appear happy in my silent little corner. But to live like that for ten years, to have no existence—never to love, never to be loved—no, no, it was beyond my power!"

And then she related the whole painful story: her marriage with the diamond merchant, a disastrous, though it seemed an advantageous one; her mother-in-law, with the stern soul of a jailer or an executioner, and her husband, a monster of physical ugliness and mental villainy. They imprisoned her, they did not even allow her to look out of a window. They had beaten her, they had pitilessly assailed her in her tastes, her inclinations, in all her feminine weaknesses. She knew that her husband wandered in his affections, and yet if she smiled to a relative, if she had a flower in her corsage on some rare day of gaiety, he would tear it from her, enter into the most jealous rage, and seize and bruise her wrists whilst shouting the most fearful threats. For years and years she had lived in that hell, hoping, hoping still, having within her such a power of life, such an ardent need of affection, that she continued waiting for happiness, ever thinking, at the faintest breath, that it was about to enter.

I. EGOTISM AND LOVE

"I swear to you, Monsieur l'Abbe," said she, "that I could not do otherwise than I have done. I was too unhappy: my whole being longed for someone who would care for me. And when my friend the first time told me that he loved me it was all over—I was his forever. Ah! to be loved, to be spoken to gently, to have someone near you who is always solicitous and amiable; to know that in absence he thinks of you, that there is a heart somewhere in which you live... Ah! if it be a crime, Monsieur l'Abbe, I cannot, cannot feel remorse for it. I will not even say that I was urged to it; I simply say that it came to me as naturally as my breath, because it was as necessary to my life!"

She had carried her hand to her lips as though to throw a kiss to the world, and Pierre felt deeply disturbed in presence of this lovely woman, who personified all the ardour of human passion, and at the same time a feeling of deep pity began to arise within him.

"Poor woman!" he murmured.

"It is not to the priest that I am confessing," she resumed; "it is to the man that I am speaking, to a man by whom I should greatly like to be understood. No, I am not a believer: religion has not sufficed me. It is said that some women find contentment in it, a firm protection even against all transgressions. But I have ever felt cold in church, weary unto death. Oh! I know very well that it is wrong to feign piety, to mingle religion with my heart affairs. But what would you? I am forced to it. If you saw me in Paris behind La Trinite it was because that church is the only place to which I am allowed to go alone; and if you find me here at Lourdes it is because, in the whole long year, I have but these three days of happiness and freedom."

Again she began to tremble. Hot tears were coursing down her cheeks. A vision of it all arose in Pierre's mind, and, distracted by the thought of the ardent earthly love which possessed this unhappy creature, he again murmured: "Poor woman!"

"And, Monsieur l'Abbe," she continued, "think of the hell to which I am about to return! For weeks and months I live my life of martyrdom without complaint. Another year, another year must go by without a day, an hour of happiness! Ah! I am indeed very unhappy, Monsieur l'Abbe, yet do you not think all the same that I am a good woman?"

He had been deeply moved by her sincere display of mingled grief and passion. He felt in her the breath of universal desire—a sovereign flame. And his compassion overflowed from his heart, and his words were words of pardon. "Madame," he said, "I pity you and respect you infinitely."

Then she spoke no further, but looked at him with her large tear-blurred eyes. And suddenly catching hold of both his hands, she grasped them tightly with her burning fingers. And then she went off, vanishing down the passage as light, as ethereal, as a shadow.

However, Pierre suffered from her presence in that room even more acutely after she had departed. He opened the window wide that the fresh air might carry off the breath of passion which she had left there. Already on the Sunday when he had seen her on the balcony he had been seized with terror at the thought that she personified the revenge of the world and the flesh amidst all the mystical exaltation of immaculate Lourdes. And now his terror was returning to him. Love seemed stronger than faith, and perhaps it was only love that was divine. To love, to belong to one another, to create and continue life—was not that the one sole object of nature outside of all social and religious policies? For a moment he was conscious of the abyss before him: his chastity was his last prop, the very dignity of his spoilt life; and he realised that, if after yielding to his reason he also yielded to his flesh, he would be utterly lost. All his pride of purity, all his strength which he had placed in professional rectitude, thereupon returned to him, and he again vowed that he would never be a man, since he had voluntarily cut himself off from among men.

Seven o'clock was striking, and Pierre did not go back to bed, but began to wash himself, thoroughly enjoying the cool water, which ended by calming his fever. As he finished dressing, the anxious thought of M. de Guersaint recurred to him on hearing a sound of footsteps in the passage. These steps stopped outside his room and someone knocked. With a feeling of relief he went to open the door, but on doing so exclaimed in great surprise "What, it's you! How is it that you're already up, running about to see people?"

Marie stood on the threshold smiling, whilst behind her was Sister Hyacinthe, who had come with her, and who also was smiling, with her lovely, candid eyes.

"Ah! my friend," said the girl, "I could not remain in bed. I sprang out directly I saw the sunshine. I had such a longing to walk, to run and jump about like a child, and I begged and implored so much that Sister was good enough to come with me. I think I should have got out through the window if the door had been closed against me."

Pierre ushered them in, and an indescribable emotion oppressed him as he heard her jest so gaily and saw her move about so freely with such grace and liveliness. She, good heavens! she whom he had seen for years with lifeless legs and colourless face! Since he had left her the day before at the Basilica she had blossomed into full youth and beauty. One night had sufficed for him to find again, developed it is true, the sweet creature whom he had loved so tenderly, the superb, radiant child whom he had embraced so wildly in the by-gone days behind the flowering hedge, beneath the sun-flecked trees.

"How tall and lovely you are, Marie!" said he, in spite of himself.

Then Sister Hyacinthe interposed: "Hasn't the Blessed Virgin done things well, Monsieur l'Abbe? When she takes us in hand, you see, she turns us out as fresh as roses and smelling quite as sweet."

"Ah!" resumed Marie, "I'm so happy; I feel quite strong and well and spotless, as though I had just been born!"

All this was very delicious to Pierre. It seemed to him that the atmosphere was now truly purified of Madame Volmar's presence. Marie filled the room with her candour, with the perfume and brightness of her innocent youth. And yet the joy he felt at the sight of pure beauty and life reflowering was not exempt from sadness. For, after all, the revolt which he had felt in the crypt, the wound of his wrecked life, must forever leave him a bleeding heart. As he gazed upon all that resuscitated grace, as the woman he loved thus reappeared before him in the flower of her youth, he could not but remember that she would never be his, that he belonged no longer to the world, but to the grave. However, he no longer lamented; he experienced a boundless melancholy—a sensation of utter nothingness as he told himself that he was dead, that this dawn of beauty was rising on the tomb in which his manhood slept. It was renunciation, accepted, resolved upon amidst all the desolate grandeur attaching to those lives which are led contrary to nature's law. Then, like the other woman, the impassioned one, Marie took hold of Pierre's hands. But hers were so soft, so fresh, so soothing! She looked at him with so little confusion and a great longing which she dared not express. After a while, however, she summoned up her courage and said: "Will you kiss me, Pierre? It would please me so much."

He shuddered, his heart crushed by this last torture. Ah! the kisses of other days—those kisses which had ever lingered on his lips! Never since had he kissed her, and to-day she was like a sister flinging her arms around his neck. She kissed him with a loud smack on both his cheeks, and offering her own, insisted on his doing likewise to her. So twice, in his turn, he embraced her.

"I, too, Marie," said he, "am pleased, very pleased, I assure you." And then, overcome by emotion, his courage exhausted, whilst at the same time filled with delight and bitterness, he burst into sobs, weeping with his face buried in his hands, like a child seeking to hide its tears.

"Come, come, we must not give way," said Sister Hyacinthe, gaily. "Monsieur l'Abbe would feel too proud if he fancied that we had merely come on his account. M. de Guersaint is about, isn't he?"

Marie raised a cry of deep affection. "Ah! my dear father! After all, it's he who'll be most pleased!"

Thereupon Pierre had to relate that M. de Guersaint had not returned from his excursion to Gavarnie. His increasing anxiety showed itself while he spoke, although he sought to explain his friend's absence, surmising all sorts of obstacles and unforeseen complications. Marie, however, did not seem afraid, but again laughed, saying that her father never could be punctual. Still she was extremely eager for him to see her walking, to find her on her legs again, resuscitated, in the fresh blossoming of her youth.

All at once Sister Hyacinthe, who had gone to lean over the balcony, returned to the room, saying "Here he comes! He's down below, just alighting from his carriage."

"Ah!" cried Marie, with the eager playfulness of a school-girl, "let's give him a surprise. Yes, we must hide, and when he's here we'll show ourselves all of a sudden."

With these words, she hastily dragged Sister Hyacinthe into the adjoining room.

Almost immediately afterwards, M. de Guersaint entered like a whirlwind from the passage, the door communicating with which had been quickly opened by Pierre, and, shaking the young priest's hand, the belated excursionist exclaimed: "Here I am at last! Ah! my friend, you can't have known what to think since four o'clock yesterday, when you expected me back, eh? But you have no idea of the adventures we have had. To begin with, one of the wheels of our landau came off just as we reached Gavarnie; then, yesterday evening—though we managed to start off again—a frightful storm detained us all night long at Saint-Sauveur. I wasn't able to sleep a wink." Then, breaking off, he inquired, "And you, are you all right?"

"I wasn't able to sleep either," said the priest; "they made such a noise in the hotel."

But M. de Guersaint had already started off again: "All the same, it was delightful. I must tell you; you can't imagine it. I was with three delightful churchmen. Abbe des Hermoises is certainly the most charming man I know. Oh! we did laugh—we did laugh!"

Then he again stopped, to inquire, "And how's my daughter?"

Thereupon a clear laugh behind him caused him to turn round, and he remained with his mouth wide open. Marie was there, and was walking, with a look of rapturous delight upon her face, which was beaming with health. He had never for a momoment doubted the miracle, and was not in the least surprised that it had taken place, for he had returned with the conviction that everything would end well, and that he would surely find her cured. But what so utterly astounded him was the prodigious spectacle which he had not foreseen: his daughter, looking so beautiful, so divine, in her little black gown!—his daughter, who had not even brought a hat with her, and merely had a piece of lace tied over her lovely fair hair!—his daughter, full of life, blooming, triumphant, similar to all the daughters of all the fathers whom he had envied for so many years!

"O my child! O my child!" he exclaimed.

And, as she had flown into his arms, he pressed her to his heart, and then they fell upon their knees together. Everything disappeared from before them in a radiant effusion of faith and love. This heedless, hare-brained man, who fell asleep instead of accompanying his daughter to the Grotto, who went off to Gavarnie on the day the Blessed Virgin was to cure her, overflowed with such paternal affection, with such Christian faith so exalted by thankfulness, that for a moment he appeared sublime.

"O Jesus! O Mary! let me thank you for having restored my child to me! O my child, we shall never have breath enough, soul enough, to render thanks to Mary and Jesus for the great happiness they have vouchsafed us! O my child, whom they have resuscitated, O my child, whom they have made so beautiful again, take my heart to offer it to them with your own! I am yours, I am theirs eternally, O my beloved child, my adored child!"

Kneeling before the open window they both, with uplifted eyes, gazed ardently on heaven. The daughter had rested her head on her father's shoulder; whilst he had passed an arm round her waist. They had become one. Tears slowly trickled down their enraptured faces, which were smiling with superhuman felicity, whilst they stammered together disconnected expressions of gratitude.

"O Jesus, we give Thee thanks! O Holy Mother of Jesus, we give thee thanks! We love you, we adore you both. You have rejuvenated the best blood in our veins; it is yours, it circulates only for you. O All-powerful Mother, O Divine and Well-beloved Son, behold a daughter and a father who bless you, who prostrate themselves with joy at your feet."

So affecting was this mingling of two beings, happy at last after so many dark days, this happiness, which could but stammer as though still tinged with suffering, that Pierre was again moved to tears. But this time they were soothing tears which relieved his heart. Ah! poor pitiable humanity! how pleasant it was to see it somewhat consoled and enraptured! and what did it matter, after all, if its great joys of a few seconds' duration sprang from the eternal illusion! Was not the whole of humanity, pitiable humanity, saved by love, personified by that poor childish man who suddenly became sublime because he found his daughter resuscitated?

Standing a little aside, Sister Hyacinthe was also weeping, her heart very full, full of human emotion which she had never before experienced, she who had known no other parents than the Almighty and the Blessed Virgin. Silence had now fallen in this room full of so much tearful fraternity. And it was she who spoke the first, when the father and the daughter, overcome with emotion, at length rose up.

"Now, mademoiselle," she said, "we must be quick and get back to the hospital."

But they all protested. M. de Guersaint wished to keep his daughter with him, and Marie's eyes expressed an eager desire, a longing to enjoy life, to walk and ramble through the whole vast world.

"Oh! no, no!" said the father, "I won't give her back to you. We'll each have a cup of milk, for I'm dying of thirst; then we'll go out and walk about. Yes, yes, both of us! She shall take my arm, like a little woman!"

Sister Hyacinthe laughed again. "Very well!" said she, "I'll leave her with you, and tell the ladies that you've stolen her from me. But for my own part I must be off. You've no idea what an amount of work we have to get through at the hospital if we are to be ready in time to leave: there are all the patients and things to be seen to; and all is in the greatest confusion!"

"So to-day's really Tuesday, and we leave this afternoon?" asked Monsieur de Guersaint, already absent-minded again.

"Of course we do, and don't forget! The white train starts at 3.40. And if you're sensible you'll bring your daughter back early so that she may have a little rest."

Marie walked with the Sister to the door, saying "Be easy, I will be very good. Besides, I want to go back to the Grotto, to thank the Blessed Virgin once more."

When they found themselves all three alone in the little room full of sunshine, it was delicious. Pierre called the servant and told her to bring them some milk, some chocolate, and cakes, in fact the nicest things he could think of. And although Marie had already broken her fast, she ate again, so great an appetite had come upon her since the night before. They drew the table to the window and made quite a feast amidst the keen air from the mountains, whilst the hundred bells of Lourdes, proclaimed with flying peals the glory of that radiant day. They chattered and laughed, and the young woman told her father the story of the miracle, with all the oft-repeated details. She related, too, how she had left her box at the Basilica, and how she had slept twelve hours without stirring. Then M. de Guersaint on his side wished to relate his excursion, but got mixed and kept coming back to the miracle. Finally, it appeared that the Cirque de Gavarnie was something colossal. Only, when you looked at it from a distance it seemed small, for you lost all sense of proportion. The gigantic snow-covered tiers of cliffs, the topmost ridge standing out against the sky with the outlines of some cyclopean fortress with razed keep and jagged ramparts, the great cascade, whose ceaseless jet seemed so slow when in reality it must have rushed down with a noise like thunder, the whole immensity, the forests on right and left, the torrents and the landslips, looked as though they might have been held in the palm of one's hand, when one gazed upon them from the village market-place. And what had impressed him most, what he repeatedly alluded to, were the strange figures described by the snow, which had remained up there amongst the rocks. Amongst others was a huge crucifix, a white cross, several thousand yards in length, which you might have thought had been thrown across the amphitheatre from one end to the other.

However, all at once M. de Guersaint broke off to inquire: "By the way, what's happening at our neighbour's? As I came up-stairs a little while ago I met Monsieur Vigneron running about like a madman; and, through the open doorway of their room, I fancied I saw Madame Vigneron looking very red. Has their son Gustave had another attack?"

Pierre had quite forgotten Madame Chaise lying dead on the other side of the partition. He seemed to feel a cold breath pass over him. "No, no," he answered, "the child is all right." And he said no more, preferring to remain silent. Why spoil this happy hour of new life and reconquered youth by mingling with it the image of death? However, from that moment he himself could not cease thinking of the proximity of nothingness. And he thought, too, of that other room where Madame Volmar's friend was now alone, stifling his sobs with his lips pressed upon a pair of gloves which he had stolen from her. All the sounds of the hotel were now becoming audible again—the coughs, the sighs, the indistinct voices, the continual slamming of doors, the creaking of the floors beneath the great accumulation of travellers, and all the stir in the passages, along which flying skirts were sweeping, and families galloping distractedly amidst the hurry-scurry of departure.

"On my word! you'll do yourself an injury," all at once cried Monsieur de Guersaint, on seeing his daughter take up another cake.

Marie was quite merry too. But at a sudden thought tears came into her eyes, and she exclaimed: "Ah! how glad I am! but also how sorry when I think that everybody is not as pleased as myself."

II. PLEASANT HOURS

IT was eight o'clock, and Marie was so impatient that she could not keep still, but continued going to the window, as if she wished to inhale all the air of the vast, expanse and the immense sky. Ah! what a pleasure to be able to run about the streets, across the squares, to go everywhere as far as she might wish. And to show how strong she was, to have the pride of walking leagues in the presence of everyone, now that the Blessed Virgin had cured her! It was an irresistible impulsion, a flight of her entire being, her blood, and her heart.

However, just as she was setting out she made up her mind that her first visit with her father ought to be to the Grotto, where both of them had to thank Our Lady of Lourdes. Then they would be free; they would have two long hours before them, and might walk wherever they chose, before she returned to lunch and pack up her few things at the hospital.

"Well, is everyone ready?" repeated M. de Guersaint. "Shall we make a move?"

Pierre took his hat, and all three went down-stairs, talking very loud and laughing on the staircase, like boisterous school-boys going for their holidays. They had almost reached the street, when at the doorway Madame Majeste rushed forward. She had evidently been waiting for them to go out.

"Ah! mademoiselle; ah! gentlemen, allow me to congratulate you," she said. "We have heard of the extraordinary favour that has been granted you; we are so happy, so much flattered, when the Blessed Virgin is pleased to select one of our customers!"

Her dry, harsh face was melting with amiability, and she observed the miraculously healed girl with the fondest of eyes. Then she impulsively called her husband, who was passing: "Look, my dear! It's mademoiselle; it's mademoiselle."

Majeste's clean-shaven face, puffed out with yellow fat, assumed a happy and grateful expression. "Really, mademoiselle, I cannot tell you how honoured we feel," said he. "We shall never forget that your papa put up at our place. It has already excited the envy of many people."

While he spoke Madame Majeste stopped the other travellers who were going out, and with a sign summoned the families already seated in the dining-room; indeed, she would have called in the whole street if they had given her time, to show that she had in her house the miracle at which all Lourdes had been marvelling since the previous day. People ended by collecting there, a crowd gathered little by little, while she whispered in the ear of each "Look! that's she; the young party, you know, the young party who—"

But all at once she exclaimed: "I'll go and fetch Apolline from the shop; I must show mademoiselle to Apolline."

Thereupon, however, Majeste, in a very dignified way, restrained her. "No," he said, "leave Apolline; she has three ladies to serve already. Mademoiselle and these gentlemen will certainly not leave Lourdes without making a few purchases. The little souvenirs that one carries away with one are so pleasant to look at later on! And our customers make a point of never buying elsewhere than here, in the shop which we have annexed to the hotel."

"I have already offered my services," added Madame Majeste, "and I renew them. Apolline will be so happy to show mademoiselle all our prettiest articles, at prices, too, which are incredibly low! Oh! there are some delightful things, delightful!"

Marie was becoming impatient at being detained in this manner, and Pierre was suffering from the increasing curiosity which they were arousing. As for M. de Guersaint, he enjoyed this popularity and triumph of his daughter immensely, and promised to return.

"Certainly," said he, "we will purchase a few little knick-knacks. Some souvenirs for ourselves, and some presents that we shall have to make, but later on, when we come back."

At last they escaped and descended the Avenue de la Grotte. The weather was again superb after the storms of the two preceding nights. Cooled by the rain, the morning air was delicious amidst the gaiety which the bright sun shed around. A busy crowd, well pleased with life, was already hurrying along the pavements. And what pleasure it all was for Marie, to whom everything seemed new, charming, inappreciable! In the morning she had had to allow Raymonde to lend her a pair of boots, for she had taken good care not to put any in her portmanteau, superstitiously fearing that they might bring her bad luck. However, Raymonde's boots fitted her admirably, and she listened with childish delight to the little heels tapping merrily on the flagstones. And she did not remember having ever seen houses so white, trees so green, and passers-by so happy. All her senses seemed holiday-making, endowed with a marvellously delicate sensibility; she heard music, smelt distant perfumes, savoured the air greedily, as though it were some delicious fruit. But what she considered, above all, so nice, so charming, was to walk along in this wise on her father's arm. She had never done so before, although she had felt the desire for years, as for one of those impossible pleasures with which people occupy their minds when invalided. And now her dream was realised and her heart beat with joy. She pressed against her father, and strove to walk very upright and look very handsome, so as to do him honour. And he was quite proud, as happy as she was, showing, exhibiting her, overcome with joy at the thought that she belonged to him, that she was his blood, his flesh, his daughter, henceforth beaming with youth and health.

As they were all three crossing the Plateau de la Merlasse, already obstructed by a band of candle and bouquet sellers running after the pilgrims, M. de Guersaint exclaimed, "We are surely not going to the Grotto empty-handed!"

Pierre, who was walking on the other side of Marie, himself brightened by her merry humour, thereupon stopped, and they were at once surrounded by a crowd of female hawkers, who with eager fingers thrust their goods into their faces. "My beautiful young lady! My good gentleman! Buy of me, of me, of me!" Such was the onslaught that it became necessary to struggle in order to extricate oneself. M. de

Guersaint ended by purchasing the largest nosegay he could see—a bouquet of white marguerites, as round and hard as a cabbage—from a handsome, fair-haired, well developed girl of twenty, who was extremely bold both in look and manner. It only cost twenty sons, and he insisted on paying for it out of his own little purse, somewhat abashed meantime by the girl's unblushing effrontery. Then Pierre in his turn settled for the three candles which Marie had taken from an old woman, candles at two francs each, a very reasonable price, as she repeatedly said. And on being paid, the old creature, who had an angular face, covetous eyes, and a nose like the beak of a bird of prey, returned profuse and mellifluous thanks: "May Our Lady of Lourdes bless you, my beautiful young lady! May she cure you of your complaints, you and yours!" This enlivened them again, and they set out once more, all three laughing, amused like children at the idea that the good woman's wish had already been accomplished.

At the Grotto Marie wished to file off at once, in order to offer the bouquet and candles herself before even kneeling down. There were not many people there as yet, and having gone to the end of the line their turn came after waiting some three or four minutes. And with what enraptured glances did she then examine everything—the altar of engraved silver, the harmonium-organ, the votive offerings, the candle-holders, streaming with wax blazing in broad daylight. She was now inside that Grotto which she had hitherto only seen from her box of misery; she breathed there as in Paradise itself, steeped rapturously in a pleasant warmth and odour, which slightly oppressed her. When she had placed the tapers at the bottom of the large basket, and had raised herself on tiptoe to fix the bouquet on one of the spears of the iron railing, she imprinted a long kiss upon the rock, below the statue of the Blessed Virgin, at the very spot, indeed, which millions of lips had already polished. And the stone received a kiss of love in which she put forth all the strength of her gratitude, a kiss with which her heart melted.

When she was once more outside, Marie prostrated and humbled herself in an almost endless act of thanksgiving. Her father also had knelt down near her, and mingled the fervour of his gratitude with hers. But he could not remain doing the same thing for long. Little by little he became uneasy, and ended by bending down to his daughter's ear to tell her that he had a call to make which he had previously forgotten. Assuredly the best course would be for her to remain where she was, praying, and waiting for him. While she completed her devotions he would hurry along and get his troublesome errand over; and then they might walk about at ease wheresoever they liked. She did not understand him, did not even hear him, but simply nodded her head, promising that she would not move, and then such tender faith again took possession of her that her eyes, fixed on the white statue of the Virgin, filled with tears.

When M. de Guersaint had joined Pierre, who had remained a short distance off, he gave him the following explanation. "My dear fellow," he said, "it's a matter of conscience; I formally promised the coachman who drove us to Gavarnie that I would see his master and tell him the real cause of our delay. You know whom I mean—the hairdresser on the Place du Marcadal. And, besides, I want to get shaved."

Pierre, who felt uneasy at this proposal, had to give way in face of the promise that they would be back within a quarter of an hour. Only, as the distance seemed long, he on his side insisted on taking a trap which was standing at the bottom of the Plateau de la Merlasse. It was a sort of greenish cabriolet, and its driver, a fat fellow of about thirty, with the usual Basque cap on his head, was smoking a cigarette whilst waiting to be hired. Perched sideways on the seat with his knees wide apart, he drove them on with the tranquil indifference of a well-fed man who considers himself the master of the street.

"We will keep you," said Pierre as he alighted, when they had reached the Place du Marcadal.

"Very well, very well, Monsieur l'Abbe! I'll wait for you!" And then, leaving his lean horse in the hot sun, the driver went to chat and laugh with a strong, dishevelled servant-girl who was washing a dog in the basin of the neighbouring fountain.

Cazaban, as it happened, was just then on the threshold of his shop, the lofty windows and pale green painting of which enlivened the dull Place, which was so deserted on week-days. When he was not pressed with work he delighted to parade in this manner, standing between his two windows, which pots of pomatum and bottles of perfumery decorated with bright shades of colour.

He at once recognised the gentlemen. "Very flattered, very much honoured. Pray walk in, I beg of you," he said.

Then, at the first words which M. de Guersaint said to him to excuse the man who had driven him to Gavarnie, he showed himself well disposed. Of course it was not the man's fault; he could not prevent wheels coming to pieces, or storms falling. So long as the travellers did not complain all was well.

"Oh!" thereupon exclaimed M. de Guersaint, "it's a magnificent country, never to be forgotten."

"Well, monsieur, as our neighbourhood pleases you, you must come and see us again; we don't ask anything better," said Cazaban; and, on the architect seating himself in one of the arm-chairs and asking to be shaved, he began to bustle about.

His assistant was still absent, running errands for the pilgrims whom he lodged, a whole family, who were taking a case of chaplets, plaster Virgins, and framed engravings away with them. You heard a confused tramping of feet and violent bursts of conversation coming from the first floor, all the helter-skelter of people whom the approaching departure and the packing of purchases lying hither and thither drove almost crazy. In the adjoining dining-room, the door of which had remained open, two children were draining the dregs of some cups of chocolate which stood about amidst the disorder of the breakfast service. The whole of the house had been let, entirely given over, and now had come the last hours of this invasion which compelled the hairdresser and his wife to seek refuge in the narrow cellar, where they slept on a small camp-bed.

While Cazaban was rubbing M. de Guersaint's cheeks with soap-suds, the architect questioned him. "Well, are you satisfied with the season?"

"Certainly, monsieur, I can't complain. As you hear, my travellers are leaving today, but I am expecting others to-morrow morning; barely sufficient time for a sweep out. It will be the same up to October."

Then, as Pierre remained standing, walking about the shop and looking at the walls with an air of impatience, he turned round politely and said: "Pray be seated, Monsieur l'Abbe; take a newspaper. It will not be long."

The priest having thanked him with a nod, and refusing to sit down, the hairdresser, whose tongue was ever itching to talk, continued: "Oh! as for myself, I am always busy, my house is renowned for the cleanliness of the beds and the excellence of the fare. Only the town is not satisfied. Ah, no! I may even say that I have never known so much discontent here."

He became silent for a moment, and shaved his customer's left cheek; then again pausing in his work he suddenly declared with a cry, wrung from him by conviction, "The Fathers of the Grotto are playing with fire, monsieur, that is all I have to say."

From that moment, however, the vent-plug was withdrawn, and he talked and talked and talked again. His big eyes rolled in his long face with prominent cheekbones and sunburnt complexion sprinkled with red, while the whole of his nervous little body continued on the jump, agitated by his growing exuberance of speech and gesture. He returned to his former indictment, and enumerated all the many grievances that the old town had against the Fathers. The hotel-keepers complained; the dealers in religious fancy articles did not take half the amount they ought to have realised; and, finally, the new town monopolised both the pilgrims and the cash; there was now no possibility for anyone but the keepers of the lodging-houses, hotels, and shops open in the neighbourhood of the Grotto to make any money whatever. It was a merciless struggle, a deadly hostility increasing from day to day, the old city losing a little of its life each season, and assuredly destined to disappear,—to be choked, assassinated, by the young town. Ah! their dirty Grotto! He would rather have his feet cut off than tread there. Wasn't it heart-rending, that knick-knack shop which they had stuck beside it? A shameful thing, at which a bishop had shown himself so indignant that it was said he had written to the Pope! He, Cazaban, who flattered himself with being a freethinker and a Republican of the old days, who already under the Empire had voted for the Opposition candidates, assuredly had the right to declare that he did not believe in their dirty Grotto, and that he did not care a fig for it!

"Look here, monsieur," he continued; "I am going to tell you a fact. My brother belongs to the municipal council, and it's through him that I know it. I must tell you first of all that we now have a Republican municipal council, which is much worried by the demoralisation of the town. You can no longer go out at night without meeting girls in the streets—you know, those candle hawkers! They gad about with the drivers who come here when the season commences, and swell the suspicious floating population which comes no one knows whence. And I must also explain to you the position of the Fathers towards the town. When they purchased the land at the Grotto they signed an agreement by which they undertook not to engage in any business there. Well, they have opened a shop in spite of their signature. Is not that an unfair rivalry, unworthy of honest people? So the new council decided on sending them a deputation to insist on the agreement being respected, and enjoining them to close their shop at once. What do you think they answered, monsieur? Oh! what they have replied twenty times before, what they will always answer, when they are reminded of their engagements: 'Very well, we consent to keep them, but we are masters at our own place, and we'll close the Grotto!'"

He raised himself up, his razor in the air, and, repeating his words, his eyes dilated by the enormity of the thing, he said, "'We'll close the Grotto.'"

Pierre, who was continuing his slow walk, suddenly stopped and said in his face, "Well! the municipal council had only to answer, 'Close it.'"

At this Cazaban almost choked; the blood rushed to his face, he was beside himself, and stammered out "Close the Grotto?—Close the Grotto?"

"Certainly! As the Grotto irritates you and rends your heart; as it's a cause of continual warfare, injustice, and corruption. Everything would be over, we should hear no more about it. That would really be a capital solution, and if the council had the power it would render you a service by forcing the Fathers to carry out their threat."

As Pierre went on speaking, Cazaban's anger subsided. He became very calm and somewhat pale, and in the depths of his big eyes the priest detected an expression of increasing uneasiness. Had he not gone too far in his passion against the Fathers? Many ecclesiastics did not like them; perhaps this young priest was simply at Lourdes for the purpose of stirring-up an agitation against them. Then who knows?—it might possibly result in the Grotto being closed later on. But it was by the Grotto that they all lived. If the old city screeched with rage at only picking up the crumbs, it was well pleased to secure even that windfall; and the freethinkers themselves, who coined money with the pilgrims, like everyone else, held their tongues, ill at ease, and even frightened, when they found people too much of their opinion with regard to the objectionable features of new Lourdes. It was necessary to be prudent.

Cazaban thereupon returned to M. de Guersaint, whose other cheek he began shaving, murmuring the while in an off-hand manner: "Oh! what I say about the Grotto is not because it troubles me much in reality, and, besides, everyone must live."

In the dining-room, the children, amidst deafening shouts, had just broken one of the bowls, and Pierre, glancing through the open doorway, again noticed the engravings of religious subjects and the plaster Virgin with which the hairdresser had ornamented the apartment in order to please his lodgers. And just then, too, a voice shouted from the first floor that the trunk was ready, and that they would be much obliged if the assistant would cord it as soon as he returned.

However, Cazaban, in the presence of these two gentlemen whom, as a matter of fact, he did not know, remained suspicious and uneasy, his brain haunted by all sorts of disquieting suppositions. He was in despair at the idea of having to let them go away without learning anything about them, especially after having exposed himself. If he had only been able to withdraw the more rabid of his biting remarks about the Fathers. Accordingly, when M. de Guersaint rose to wash his chin, he yielded to a desire to renew the conversation.

"Have you heard talk of yesterday's miracle? The town is quite upside down with it; more than twenty people have already given me an account of what occurred. Yes, it seems they obtained an extraordinary miracle, a paralytic young lady got up and dragged her invalid carriage as far as the choir of the Basilica."

M. de Guersaint, who was about to sit down after wiping himself, gave a complacent laugh. "That young lady is my daughter," he said.

Thereupon, under this sudden and fortunate flash of enlightenment, Cazaban became all smiles. He felt reassured, and combed M. de Guersaint's hair with a masterly touch, amid a returning exuberance of speech and gesture. "Ah! monsieur, I congratulate you, I am flattered at having you in my hands. Since the young lady your daughter is cured, your father's heart is at ease. Am I not right?"

And he also found a few pleasant words for Pierre. Then, when he had decided to let them go, he looked at the priest with an air of conviction, and remarked, like a sensible man, desirous of coming to a conclusion on the subject of miracles: "There are some, Monsieur l'Abbe, which are good fortunes for everybody. From time to time we require one of that description."

II. PLEASANT HOURS

Outside, M. de Guersaint had to go and fetch the coachman, who was still laughing with the servant-girl, while her dog, dripping with water, was shaking itself in the sun. In five minutes the trap brought them back to the bottom of the Plateau de la Merlasse. The trip had taken a good half-hour. Pierre wanted to keep the conveyance, with the idea of showing Marie the town without giving her too much fatigue. So, while the father ran to the Grotto to fetch his daughter, he waited there beneath the trees.

The coachman at once engaged in conversation with the priest. He had lit another cigarette and showed himself very familiar. He came from a village in the environs of Toulouse, and did not complain, for he earned good round sums each day at Lourdes. You fed well there, said he, you amused yourself, it was what you might call a good neighbourhood. He said these things with the *abandon* of a man who was not troubled with religious scruples, but yet did not forget the respect which he owed to an ecclesiastic.

At last, from the top of his box, where he remained half lying down, dangling one of his legs, he allowed this remark to fall slowly from his lips: "Ah! yes, Monsieur l'Abbe, Lourdes has caught on well, but the question is whether it will all last long!"

Pierre, who was very much struck by the remark, was pondering on its involuntary profundity, when M. de Guersaint reappeared, bringing Marie with him. He had found her kneeling on the same spot, in the same act of faith and thankfulness, at the feet of the Blessed Virgin; and it seemed as if she had brought all the brilliant light of the Grotto away in her eyes, so vividly did they sparkle with divine joy at her cure. She would not entertain a proposal to keep the trap. No, no! she preferred to go on foot; she did not care about seeing the town, so long as she might for another hour continue walking on her father's arm through the gardens, the streets, the squares, anywhere they pleased! And, when Pierre had paid the driver, it was she who turned into a path of the Esplanade garden, delighted at being able to saunter in this wise beside the turf and the flower beds, under the great trees. The grass, the leaves, the shady solitary walks where you heard the everlasting rippling of the Gave, were so sweet and fresh! But afterwards she wished to return by way of the streets, among the crowd, that she might find the agitation, noise, and life, the need of which possessed her whole being.

In the Rue St. Joseph, on perceiving the panorama, where the former Grotto was depicted, with Bernadette kneeling down before it on the day of the miracle of the candle, the idea occurred to Pierre to go in. Marie became as happy as a child; and even M. de Guersaint was full of innocent delight, especially when he noticed that among the batch of pilgrims who dived at the same time as themselves into the depths of the obscure corridor, several recognised in his daughter the girl so miraculously healed the day before, who was already famous, and whose name flew from mouth to mouth. Up above, on the circular platform, when they came out into the diffuse light, filtering through a vellum, there was a sort of ovation around Marie; soft whispers, beatifical glances, a rapture of delight in seeing, following, and touching her. Now glory had come, she would be loved in that way wherever she went, and it was not until the showman who gave the explanations had placed himself at the head of the little party of visitors, and begun to walk round, relating the incident depicted on the huge circular canvas, nearly five hundred feet in length, that she was in some measure forgotten. The painting represented the seventeenth apparition of the Blessed Virgin to Bernadette, on the day when, kneeling before the Grotto during her vision, she had heedlessly left her hand on the flame of the candle without burning it. The whole of the old primitive landscape of the Grotto was shown, the whole scene was set out with all its historical personages: the doctor verifying the miracle watch in hand, the Mayor, the Commissary of Police, and the Public Prosecutor, whose names the showman gave out, amidst the amazement of the public following him.

Then, by an unconscious transition of ideas, Pierre recalled the remark which the driver of the cabriolet had made a short time previously: "Lourdes has caught on well, but the question is whether it will all last long." That, in fact, was the question. How many venerated sanctuaries had thus been built already, at the bidding of innocent chosen children, to whom the Blessed Virgin had shown herself! It was always the same story beginning afresh: an apparition; a persecuted shepherdess, who was called a liar; next the covert propulsion of human misery hungering after illusion; then propaganda, and the triumph of the sanctuary shining like a star; and afterwards decline, and oblivion, when the ecstatic dream of another visionary gave birth to another sanctuary elsewhere. It seemed as if the power of illusion wore away; that it was necessary in the course of centuries to displace it, set it amidst new scenery, under fresh circumstances, in order to renew its force. La Salette had dethroned the old wooden and stone Virgins that had healed; Lourdes had just dethroned La Salette, pending the time when it would be dethroned itself by Our Lady of to-morrow, she who will show her sweet, consoling features to some pure child as yet unborn. Only, if Lourdes had met with such rapid, such prodigious fortune, it assuredly owed it to the little sincere soul, the delightful charm of Bernadette. Here there was no deceit, no falsehood, merely the blossoming of suffering, a delicate sick child who brought to the afflicted multitude her dream of justice and equality in the miraculous. She was merely eternal hope, eternal consolation. Besides, all historical and social circumstances seem to have combined to increase the need of this mystical flight at the close of a terrible century of positivist inquiry; and that was perhaps the reason why Lourdes would still long endure in its triumph, before becoming a mere legend, one of those dead religions whose powerful perfume has evaporated.

Ah! that ancient Lourdes, that city of peace and belief, the only possible cradle where the legend could come into being, how easily Pierre conjured it up before him, whilst walking round the vast canvas of the Panorama! That canvas said everything; it was the best lesson of things that could be seen. The monotonous explanations of the showman were not heard; the landscape spoke for itself. First of all there was the Grotto, the rocky hollow beside the Gave, a savage spot suitable for reverie—bushy slopes and heaps of fallen stone, without a path among them; and nothing yet in the way of ornamentation—no monumental quay, no garden paths winding among trimly cut shrubs; no Grotto set in order, deformed, enclosed with iron railings; above all, no shop for the sale of religious articles, that simony shop which was the scandal of all pious souls. The Virgin could not have selected a more solitary and charming nook wherein to show herself to the chosen one of her heart, the poor young girl who came thither still possessed by the dream of her painful nights, even whilst gathering dead wood. And on the opposite side of the Gave, behind the rock of the castle, was old Lourdes, confident and asleep. Another age was then conjured up; a small town, with narrow pebble-paved streets, black houses with marble dressings, and an antique, semi-Spanish church, full of old carvings, and peopled with visions of gold and painted flesh. Communication with other places was only kept up by the Bagneres and

Cauterets *diligences*, which twice a day forded the Lapaca to climb the steep causeway of the Rue Basse. The spirit of the century had not breathed on those peaceful roofs sheltering a belated population which had remained childish, enclosed within the narrow limits of strict religious discipline. There was no debauchery; a slow antique commerce sufficed for daily life, a poor life whose hardships were the safeguards of morality. And Pierre had never better understood how Bernadette, born in that land of faith and honesty, had flowered like a natural rose, budding on the briars of the road.

"It's all the same very curious," observed M. de Guersaint when they found themselves in the street again. "I'm not at all sorry I saw it."

Marie was also laughing with pleasure. "One would almost think oneself there. Isn't it so, father? At times it seems as if the people were going to move. And how charming Bernadette looks on her knees, in ecstasy, while the candle flame licks her fingers without burning them."

"Let us see," said the architect; "we have only an hour left, so we must think of making our purchases, if we wish to buy anything. Shall we take a look at the shops? We certainly promised Majeste to give him the preference; but that does not prevent us from making a few inquiries. Eh! Pierre, what do you say?"

"Oh! certainly, as you like," answered the priest. "Besides, it will give us a walk."

And he thereupon followed the young girl and her father, who returned to the Plateau de la Merlasse. Since he had quitted the Panorama he felt as though he no longer knew where he was. It seemed to him as if he had all at once been transported from one to another town, parted by centuries. He had left the solitude, the slumbering peacefulness of old Lourdes, which the dead light of the vellum had increased, to fall at last into new Lourdes, sparkling with brightness and noisy with the crowd. Ten o'clock had just struck, and extraordinary animation reigned on the footways, where before breakfast an entire people was hastening to complete its purchases, so that it might have nothing but its departure to think of afterwards. The thousands of pilgrims of the national pilgrimage streamed along the thoroughfares and besieged the shops in a final scramble. You would have taken the cries, the jostling, and the sudden rushes for those at some fair just breaking up amidst a ceaseless roll of vehicles. Many, providing themselves with provisions for the journey, cleared the open-air stalls where bread and slices of sausages and ham were sold. Others purchased fruit and wine; baskets were filled with bottles and greasy parcels until they almost burst. A hawker who was wheeling some cheeses about on a small truck saw his goods carried off as if swept away by the wind. But what the crowd more particularly purchased were religious articles, and those hawkers whose barrows were loaded with statuettes and sacred engravings were reaping golden gains. The customers at the shops stood in strings on the pavement; the women were belted with immense chaplets, had Blessed Virgins tucked under their arms, and were provided with cans which they meant to fill at the miraculous spring. Carried in the hand or slung from the shoulder, some of them quite plain and others daubed over with a Lady of Lourdes in blue paint, these cans held from one to ten quarts apiece; and, shining with all the brightness of new tin, clashing, too, at times with the sharp jingle of stew-pans, they added a gay note to the aspect of the noisy multitude. And the fever of dealing, the pleasure of spending one's money, of returning home with one's pockets crammed with photographs and medals, lit up all faces with a holiday expression, transforming the radiant gathering into a fair-field crowd with appetites either beyond control or satisfied.

On the Plateau de la Merlasse, M. de Guersaint for a moment felt tempted to enter one of the finest and most patronised shops, on the board over which were these words in large letters: "Soubirous, Brother of Bernadette."

"Eh! what if we were to make our purchases there? It would be more appropriate, more interesting to remember."

However, he passed on, repeating that they must see everything first of all.

Pierre had looked at the shop kept by Bernadette's brother with a heavy heart. It grieved him to find the brother selling the Blessed Virgin whom the sister had beheld. However, it was necessary to live, and he had reason to believe that, beside the triumphant Basilica resplendent with gold, the visionary's relatives were not making a fortune, the competition being so terrible. If on the one hand the pilgrims left millions behind them at Lourdes, on the other there were more than two hundred dealers in religious articles, to say nothing of the hotel and lodging-house keepers, to whom the largest part of the spoils fell; and thus the gain, so eagerly disputed, ended by being moderate enough after all. Along the Plateau on the right and left of the repository kept by Bernadette's brother, other shops appeared, an uninterrupted row of them, pressing one against the other, each occupying a division of a long wooden structure, a sort of gallery erected by the town, which derived from it some sixty thousand francs a year. It formed a regular bazaar of open stalls, encroaching on the pavements so as to tempt people to stop as they passed along. For more than three hundred yards no other trade was plied: a river of chaplets, medals, and statuettes streamed without end behind the windows; and in enormous letters on the boards above appeared the venerated names of Saint Roch, Saint Joseph, Jerusalem, The Immaculate Virgin, The Sacred Heart of Mary, all the names in Paradise that were most likely to touch and attract customers.

"Really," said M. de Guersaint, "I think it's the same thing all over the place. Let us go anywhere." He himself had had enough of it, this interminable display was quite exhausting him.

"But as you promised to make the purchases at Majeste's," said Marie, who was not, in the least tired, "the best thing will be to go back."

"That's it; let's return to Majeste's place."

But the rows of shops began again in the Avenue de la Grotte. They swarmed on both sides; and among them here were jewellers, drapers, and umbrella-makers, who also dealt in religious articles. There was even a confectioner who sold boxes of pastilles *a l'eau de Lourdes*, with a figure of the Virgin on the cover. A photographer's windows were crammed with views of the Grotto and the Basilica, and portraits of Bishops and reverend Fathers of all Orders, mixed up with views of famous sites in the neighbouring mountains. A bookseller displayed the last Catholic publications, volumes bearing devout titles, and among them the innumerable works published on Lourdes during the last twenty years, some of which had had a wonderful success, which was still fresh in memory. In this broad, populous thoroughfare the crowd streamed along in more open order; their cans jingled, everyone was in high spirits, amid the bright sunrays which enfiladed the road from one end to the other. And it seemed as if there would never be a finish to the statuettes, the medals, and the chaplets; one display followed another; and, indeed, there were miles of them running through the streets of the entire town, which was ever the same bazaar selling the same articles.

In front of the Hotel of the Apparitions M. de Guersaint again hesitated. "Then it's decided, we are going to make our purchases there?" he asked.

"Certainly," said Marie. "See what a beautiful shop it is!"

And she was the first to enter the establishment, which was, in fact, one of the largest in the street, occupying the ground-floor of the hotel on the left hand. M. de Guersaint and Pierre followed her.

Apolline, the niece of the Majestes, who was in charge of the place, was standing on a stool, taking some holy-water vases from a top shelf to show them to a young man, an elegant bearer, wearing beautiful yellow gaiters. She was laughing with the cooing sound of a dove, and looked charming with her thick black hair and her superb eyes, set in a somewhat square face, which had a straight forehead, chubby cheeks, and full red lips. Jumping lightly to the ground, she exclaimed: "Then you don't think that this pattern would please madame, your aunt?"

"No, no," answered the bearer, as he went off. "Obtain the other pattern. I shall not leave until to-morrow, and will come back."

When Apolline learnt that Marie was the young person visited by the miracle of whom Madame Majeste had been talking ever since the previous day, she became extremely attentive. She looked at her with her merry smile, in which there was a dash of surprise and covert incredulity. However, like the clever saleswoman that she was, she was profuse in complimentary remarks. "Ah, mademoiselle, I shall be so happy to sell to you! Your miracle is so beautiful! Look, the whole shop is at your disposal. We have the largest choice."

Marie was ill at ease. "Thank you," she replied, "you are very good. But we have only come to buy a few small things."

"If you will allow us," said M. de Guersaint, "we will choose ourselves."

"Very well. That's it, monsieur. Afterwards we will see!"

And as some other customers now came in, Apolline forgot them, returned to her duties as a pretty saleswoman, with caressing words and seductive glances, especially for the gentlemen, whom she never allowed to leave until they had their pockets full of purchases.

M. de Guersaint had only two francs left of the louis which Blanche, his eldest daughter, had slipped into his hand when he was leaving, as pocket-money; and so he did not dare to make any large selection. But Pierre declared that they would cause him great pain if they did not allow him to offer them the few things which they would like to take away with them from Lourdes. It was therefore understood that they would first of all choose a present for Blanche, and then Marie and her father should select the souvenirs that pleased them best.

"Don't let us hurry," repeated M. de Guersaint, who had become very gay. "Come, Marie, have a good look. What would be most likely to please Blanche?"

All three looked, searched, and rummaged. But their indecision increased as they went from one object to another. With its counters, show-cases, and nests of drawers, furnishing it from top to bottom, the spacious shop was a sea of endless billows, overflowing with all the religious knick-knacks imaginable. There were the chaplets: skeins of chaplets hanging along the walls, and heaps of chaplets lying in the drawers, from humble ones costing twenty sons a dozen, to those of sweet-scented wood, agate, and lapis-lazuli, with chains of gold or silver; and some of them, of immense length, made to go twice round the neck or waist, had carved beads, as large as walnuts, separated by death's-heads. Then there were the medals: a shower of medals, boxes full of medals, of all sizes, of all metals, the cheapest and the most precious. They bore different inscriptions, they represented the Basilica, the Grotto, or the Immaculate Conception; they were engraved, *repoussees*, or enamelled, executed with care, or made by the gross, according to the price. And next there were the Blessed Virgins, great and small, in zinc, wood, ivory, and especially plaster; some entirely white, others tinted in bright colours, in accordance with the description given by Bernadette; the amiable and smiling face, the extremely long veil, the blue sash, and the golden roses on the feet, there being, however, some slight modification in each model so as to guarantee the copyright. And there was another flood of other religious objects: a hundred varieties of scapularies, a thousand different sorts of sacred pictures: fine engravings, large chromo-lithographs in glaring colours, submerged beneath a mass of smaller pictures, which were coloured, gilded, varnished, decorated with bouquets of flowers, and bordered with lace paper. And there was also jewellery: rings, brooches, and bracelets, loaded with stars and crosses, and ornamented with saintly figures. Finally, there was the Paris article, which rose above and submerged all the rest: pencil-holders, purses, cigar-holders, paperweights, paper-knives, even snuff-boxes; and innumerable other objects on which the Basilica, Grotto, and Blessed Virgin ever and ever appeared, reproduced in every way, by every process that is known. Heaped together pell-mell in one of the cases reserved to articles at fifty centimes apiece were napkin-rings, egg-cups, and wooden pipes, on which was carved the beaming apparition of Our Lady of Lourdes.

Little by little, M. de Guersaint, with the annoyance of a man who prides himself on being an artist, became disgusted and quite sad. "But all this is frightful, frightful!" he repeated at every new article he took up to look at.

Then he relieved himself by reminding Pierre of the ruinous attempt which he had made to improve the artistic quality of religious prints. The remains of his fortune had been lost in that attempt, and the thought made him all the more angry, in presence of the wretched productions with which the shop was crammed. Had anyone ever seen things of such idiotic, pretentious, and complicated ugliness! The vulgarity of the ideas and the silliness of the expressions portrayed rivalled the commonplace character of the composition. You were reminded of fashion-plates, the covers of boxes of sweets, and the wax dolls' heads that revolve in hairdressers' windows; it was an art abounding in false prettiness, painfully childish, with no really human touch in it, no tone, and no sincerity. And the architect, who was wound up, could not stop, but went on to express his disgust with the buildings of new Lourdes, the pitiable disfigurement of the Grotto, the colossal monstrosity of the inclined ways, the disastrous lack of symmetry in the church of the Rosary and the Basilica, the former looking too heavy, like a corn market, whilst the latter had an anaemical structural leanness with no kind of style but the mongrel.

"Ah! one must really be very fond of God," he at last concluded, "to have courage enough to come and adore Him amidst such horrors! They have failed in everything, spoilt everything, as though out of pleasure. Not one of them has experienced that moment of true feeling, of real naturalness and sincere faith, which gives birth to masterpieces. They are all clever people, but all plagiarists; not one has given his mind and being to the undertaking. And what must they not require to inspire them, since they have failed to produce anything grand even in this land of miracles?"

Pierre did not reply, but he was very much struck by these reflections, which at last gave him an explanation of a feeling of discomfort that he had experienced ever since his arrival at Lourdes. This discomfort arose from the difference between the modern surroundings and the faith of past ages which it sought to resuscitate. He thought of the old cathedrals where quivered that faith of nations; he pictured the former attributes of worship—the images, the goldsmith's work, the saints in wood and stone—all of admirable power and beauty of expression. The fact was that in those ancient times the workmen had been true believers, had given their whole souls and bodies and all the candour of their feelings to their productions, just as M. de Guersaint said. But nowadays architects built churches with the same practical tranquillity that they erected five-storey houses, just as the religious articles, the chaplets, the medals, and the statuettes were manufactured by the gross in the populous quarters of Paris by merrymaking workmen who did not even follow their religion. And thus what slopwork, what toymakers', ironmongers' stuff it all was! of a prettiness fit to make you cry, a silly sentimentality fit to make your heart turn with disgust! Lourdes was inundated, devastated, disfigured by it all to such a point as to quite upset persons with any delicacy of taste who happened to stray through its streets. It clashed jarringly with the attempted resuscitation of the legends, ceremonies, and processions of dead ages; and all at once it occurred to Pierre that the social and historical condemnation of Lourdes lay in this, that faith is forever dead among a people when it no longer introduces it into the churches it builds or the chaplets it manufactures.

However, Marie had continued examining the shelves with the impatience of a child, hesitating, and finding nothing which seemed to her worthy of the great dream of ecstasy which she would ever keep within her.

"Father," she said, "it is getting late; you must take me back to the hospital; and to make up my mind, look, I will give Blanche this medal with the silver chain. After all it's the most simple and prettiest thing here. She will wear it; it will make her a little piece of jewellery. As for myself, I will take this statuette of Our Lady of Lourdes, this small one, which is rather prettily painted. I shall place it in my room and surround it with fresh flowers. It will be very nice, will it not?"

M. de Guersaint approved of her idea, and then busied himself with his own choice. "O dear! oh dear! how embarrassed I am!" said he.

He was examining some ivory-handled penholders capped with pea-like balls, in which were microscopic photographs, and while bringing one of the little holes to his eye to look in it he raised an exclamation of mingled surprise and pleasure. "Hallo! here's the Cirque de Gavarnie! Ah! it's prodigious; everything is there; how can that colossal panorama have been got into so small a space? Come, I'll take this penholder; it's curious, and will remind me of my excursion."

Pierre had simply chosen a portrait of Bernadette, the large photograph which represents her on her knees in a black gown, with a handkerchief tied over her hair, and which is said to be the only one in existence taken from life. He hastened to pay, and they were all three on the point of leaving when Madame Majeste entered, protested, and positively insisted on making Marie a little present, saying that it would bring her establishment good-fortune. "I beg of you, mademoiselle, take a scapulary," said she.

"Look among those there. The Blessed Virgin who chose you will repay me in good luck."

She raised her voice and made so much fuss that the purchasers filling the shop were interested, and began gazing at the girl with envious eyes. It was popularity bursting out again around her, a popularity which ended even by reaching the street when the landlady went to the threshold of the shop, making signs to the tradespeople opposite and putting all the neighbourhood in a flutter.

"Let us go," repeated Marie, feeling more and more uncomfortable.

But her father, on noticing a priest come in, detained her. "Ah! Monsieur l'Abbe des Hermoises!"

It was in fact the handsome Abbe, clad in a cassock of fine cloth emitting a pleasant odour, and with an expression of soft gaiety on his fresh-coloured face. He had not noticed his companion of the previous day, but had gone straight to Apolline and taken her on one side. And Pierre overheard him saying in a subdued tone: "Why didn't you bring me my three-dozen chaplets this morning?"

Apolline again began laughing with the cooing notes of a dove, and looked at him sideways, roguishly, without answering.

"They are for my little penitents at Toulouse. I wanted to place them at the bottom of my trunk; and you offered to help me pack my linen."

She continued laughing, and her pretty eyes sparkled.

"However, I shall not leave before to-morrow. Bring them me to-night, will you not? When you are at liberty. It's at the end of the street, at Duchene's."

Thereupon, with a slight movement of her red lips, and in a somewhat bantering way, which left him in doubt as to whether she would keep her promise, she replied: "Certainly, Monsieur l'Abbe, I will go."

They were now interrupted by M. de Guersaint, who came forward to shake the priest's hand. And the two men at once began talking again of the Cirque de Gavarnie: they had had a delightful trip, a most pleasant time, which they would never forget. Then they enjoyed a laugh at the expense of their two companions, ecclesiastics of slender means, good-natured fellows, who had much amused them. And the architect ended by reminding his new friend that he had kindly promised to induce a personage at Toulouse, who was ten times a millionaire, to interest himself in his studies on navigable balloons. "A first advance of a hundred thousand francs would be sufficient," he said.

"You can rely on me," answered Abbe des Hermoises. "You will not have prayed to the Blessed Virgin in vain."

However, Pierre, who had kept Bernadette's portrait in his hand, had just then been struck by the extraordinary likeness between Apolline and the visionary. It was the same rather massive face, the same full thick mouth, and the same magnificent eyes; and he recollected that Madame Majeste had already pointed out to him this striking resemblance, which was all the more peculiar as Apolline had passed through a similar poverty-stricken childhood at Bartres before her aunt had taken her with her to assist in keeping the shop. Bernadette! Apolline! What a strange association, what an unexpected reincarnation at thirty years' distance! And, all at once, with this Apolline, who was so flightily merry and careless, and in regard to whom there were so many odd rumours, new Lourdes rose before his eyes: the coachmen, the candle-girls, the persons who let rooms and waylaid tenants at the railway station, the hundreds of furnished houses with discreet little lodgings, the crowd of free priests, the lady hospitallers, and the simple passers-by, who came there to satisfy their appetites. Then, too, there was the trading mania excited by the shower of millions, the entire town given up to lucre, the shops transforming the streets into bazaars which devoured one another, the hotels living gluttonously on the pilgrims, even to the Blue Sisters who kept a *table d'hote*, and the Fathers of the Grotto who coined money with their God! What a sad and frightful course of events, the vision of pure Bernadette inflaming multitudes, making them rush to the illusion of happiness, bringing a river of gold to the town, and from that moment rotting everything. The breath of superstition had sufficed to make humanity flock thither, to attract abundance of money, and to corrupt this honest corner of the earth forever. Where the candid lily had formerly bloomed there now grew the carnal rose, in the new loam of cupidity and enjoyment. Bethlehem had become Sodom since an innocent child had seen the Virgin.

"Eh? What did I tell you?" exclaimed Madame Majeste, perceiving that Pierre was comparing her niece with the portrait. "Apolline is Bernadette all over!"

The young girl approached with her amiable smile, flattered at first by the comparison.

"Let's see, let's see!" said Abbe des Hermoises, with an air of lively interest.

He took the photograph in his turn, compared it with the girl, and then exclaimed in amazement: "It's wonderful; the same features. I had not noticed it before. Really I'm delighted—"

"Still I fancy she had a larger nose," Apolline ended by remarking.

The Abbe then raised an exclamation of irresistible admiration: "Oh! you are prettier, much prettier, that's evident. But that does not matter, anyone would take you for two sisters."

Pierre could not refrain from laughing, he thought the remark so peculiar. Ah! poor Bernadette was absolutely dead, and she had no sister. She could not have been born again; it would have been impossible for her to exist in the region of crowded life and passion which she had made.

At length Marie went off leaning on her father's arm, and it was agreed that they would both call and fetch her at the hospital to go to the station together. More than fifty people were awaiting her in the street in a state of ecstasy. They bowed to her and followed her; and one woman even made her infirm child, whom she was bringing back from the Grotto, touch her gown.

III. DEPARTURE

At half-past two o'clock the white train, which was to leave Lourdes at three-forty, was already in the station, alongside the second platform. For three days it had been waiting on a siding, in the same state as when it had come from Paris, and since it had been run into the station again white flags had been waving from the foremost and hindmost of its carriages, by way of preventing any mistakes on the part of the pilgrims, whose entraining was usually a very long and troublesome affair. Moreover, all the fourteen trains of the pilgrimage were timed to leave that day. The green train had started off at ten o'clock, followed by the pink and the yellow trains, and the others—the orange, the grey, and the blue—would start in turn after the white train had taken its departure. It was, indeed, another terrible day's work for the station staff, amidst a tumult and a scramble which altogether distracted them.

However, the departure of the white train was always the event of the day which provoked most interest and emotion, for it took away with it all the more afflicted patients, amongst whom were naturally those loved by the Virgin and chosen by her for the miraculous cures. Accordingly, a large, serried crowd was collected under the roofing of the spacious platform, a hundred yards in length, where all the benches were already covered with waiting pilgrims and their parcels. In the refreshment-room, at one end of the buildings, men were drinking beer and women ordering lemonade at the little tables which had been taken by assault, whilst at the other end bearers stood on guard at the goods entrance so as to keep the way clear for the speedy passage of the patients, who would soon be arriving. And all along the broad platform there was incessant coming and going, poor people rushing hither and thither in bewilderment, priests trotting along to render assistance, gentlemen in frock-coats looking on with quiet inquisitiveness: indeed, all the jumbling and jostling of the most mixed, most variegated throng ever elbowed in a railway station.

At three o'clock, however, the sick had not yet reached the station, and Baron Suire was in despair, his anxiety arising from the dearth of horses, for a number of unexpected tourists had arrived at Lourdes that morning and hired conveyances for Bareges, Cauterets, and Gavarnie. At last, however, the Baron espied Berthaud and Gerard arriving in all haste, after scouring the town; and when he had rushed up to them they soon pacified him by announcing that things were going splendidly. They had been able to procure the needful animals, and the removal of the patients from the hospital was now being carried out under the most favorable circumstances. Squads of bearers with their stretchers and little carts were already in the station yard, watching for the arrival of the vans, breaks, and other vehicles which had been recruited. A reserve supply of mattresses and cushions was, moreover, heaped up beside a lamp-post. Nevertheless, just as the first patients arrived, Baron Suire again lost his head, whilst Berthaud and Gerard hastened to the platform from which the train would start. There they began to superintend matters, and gave orders amidst an increasing scramble.

Father Fourcade was on this platform, walking up and down alongside the train, on Father Massias's arm. Seeing Doctor Bonamy approach, he stopped short to speak to him: "Ah, doctor," said he, "I am pleased to see you. Father Massias, who is about to leave us, was again telling me just now of the extraordinary favor granted by the Blessed Virgin to that interesting young person, Mademoiselle Marie de Guersaint. There has not been such a brilliant miracle for years! It is signal good-fortune for us—a blessing which should render our labours fruitful. All Christendom will be illumined, comforted, enriched by it."

He was radiant with pleasure, and forthwith the doctor with his clean-shaven face, heavy, peaceful features, and usually tired eyes, also began to exult: "Yes, your reverence, it is prodigious, prodigious! I shall write a pamphlet about it. Never was cure produced by supernatural means in a more authentic manner. Ah! what a stir it will create!"

Then, as they had begun walking to and fro again, all three together, he noticed that Father Fourcade was dragging his leg with increased difficulty, leaning heavily the while on his companion's arm. "Is your attack of gout worse, your reverence?" he inquired. "You seem to be suffering a great deal."

"Oh! don't speak of it; I wasn't able to close my eyes all night! It is very annoying that this attack should have come on me the very day of my arrival here! It might as well have waited. But there is nothing to be done, so don't let us talk of it any more. I am, at all events, very pleased with this year's result."

"Ah! yes, yes indeed," in his turn said Father Massias, in a voice which quivered with fervour; "we may all feel proud, and go away with our hearts full of enthusiasm and gratitude. How many prodigies there have been, in addition to the healing of that young woman you spoke of! There is no counting all the miracles: deaf women and dumb women have recovered their faculties, faces disfigured by sores have become as smooth as the hand, moribund consumptives have come to life again and eaten and danced! It is not a train of sufferers, but a train of resurrection, a train of glory, that I am about to take back to Paris!"

He had ceased to see the ailing creatures around him, and in the blindness of his faith was soaring triumphantly.

Then, alongside the carriages, whose compartments were beginning to fill, they all three continued their slow saunter, smiling at the pilgrims who bowed to them, and at times again stopping to address a kind word to some mournful woman who, pale and shivering, passed by upon a stretcher. They boldly declared that she was looking much better, and would assuredly soon get well.

However, the station-master, who was incessantly bustling about, passed by, calling in a shrill voice: "Don't block up the platform, please; don't block up the platform!" And on Berthaud pointing out to him that it was, at all events, necessary to deposit the stretchers on the platform before hoisting the patients into the carriages, he became quite angry: "But, come, come; is it reasonable?" he asked. "Look at that little hand-cart which has been left on the rails over yonder. I expect the train to Toulouse in a few minutes. Do you want your people to be crushed to death?"

Then he went off at a run to instruct some porters to keep the bewildered flock of pilgrims away from the rails. Many of them, old and simple people, did not even recognise the colour of their train, and this was the reason why one and all wore cards of some particular hue hanging from their necks, so that they might be led and entrained like marked cattle. And what a constant state of excitement it was, with the starting of these fourteen special trains, in addition to all the ordinary traffic, in which no change had been made.

Pierre arrived, valise in hand, and found some difficulty in reaching the platform. He was alone, for Marie had expressed an ardent desire to kneel once more at the Grotto, so that her soul might burn with gratitude before the Blessed Virgin until the last moment; and so he had left M. de Guersaint to conduct her thither whilst he himself settled the hotel bill. Moreover, he had made them promise that they would take a fly to the station, and they would certainly arrive within a quarter of an hour. Meantime, his idea was to seek their carriage, and there rid himself of his valise. This, however, was not an easy task, and he only recognised the carriage eventually by the placard which had been swinging from it in the sunlight and the storms during the last three days—a square of pasteboard bearing the names of Madame de Jonquiere and Sisters Hyacinthe and Claire des Anges. There could be no mistake, and Pierre again pictured the compartments full of his travelling companions. Some cushions already marked M. Sabathier's corner, and on the seat where Marie had experienced such suffering he still found some scratches caused by the ironwork of her box. Then, having deposited his valise in his own place, he remained on the platform waiting and looking around him, with a slight feeling of surprise at not perceiving Doctor Chassaigne, who had promised to come and embrace him before the train started.

Now that Marie was well again, Pierre had laid his bearer straps aside, and merely wore the red cross of the pilgrimage on his cassock. The station, of which he had caught but a glimpse, in the livid dawn amidst the anguish of the terrible morning of their arrival, now surprised him by its spacious platforms, its broad exits, and its clear gaiety. He could not see the mountains, but some verdant slopes rose up on the other side, in front of the waiting-rooms; and that afternoon the weather was delightfully mild, the sky of a milky whiteness, with light fleecy clouds veiling the sun, whence there fell a broad diffuse light, like a nacreous, pearly dust: "maiden's weather," as country folk are wont to say.

The big clock had just struck three, and Pierre was looking at it when he saw Madame Desagneaux and Madame Volmar arrive, followed by Madame de Jonquiere and her daughter. These ladies, who had driven from the hospital in a landau, at once began looking for their carriage, and it was Raymonde who first recognised the first-class compartment in which she had travelled from Paris. "Mamma, mamma, here; here it is!" she called. "Stay a little while with us; you have plenty of time to install yourself among your patients, since they haven't yet arrived."

Pierre now again found himself face to face with Madame Volmar, and their glances met. However, he gave no sign of recognition, and on her side there was but a slight sudden drooping of the eyelids. She had again assumed the air of a languid, indolent, black-robed woman, who modestly shrinks back, well pleased to escape notice. Her brasier-like eyes no longer glowed; it was only at long intervals that they kindled into a spark beneath the veil of indifference, the moire-like shade, which dimmed them.

"Oh! it was a fearful sick headache!" she was repeating to Madame Desagneaux. "And, you can see, I've hardly recovered the use of my poor head yet. It's the journey which brings it on. It's the same thing every year."

However, Berthaud and Gerard, who had just perceived the ladies, were hurrying up to them. That morning they had presented themselves at the Hospital of Our Lady of Dolours, and Madame de Jonquiere had received them in a little office near the linen-room. Thereupon, apologising with smiling affability for making his request amidst such a hurly-burly, Berthaud had solicited the hand of Mademoiselle Raymonde for his cousin, Gerard. They at once felt themselves at ease, the mother, with some show of emotion, saying that Lourdes would bring the young couple good luck. And so the marriage was arranged in a few words, amidst general satisfaction. A meeting was even appointed for the fifteenth of September at the Chateau of Berneville, near Caen, an estate belonging to Raymonde's uncle, the diplomatist, whom Berthaud knew, and to whom he promised to introduce Gerard. Then Raymonde was summoned, and blushed with pleasure as she placed her little hand in those of her betrothed.

Binding her now upon the platform, the latter began paying her every attention, and asking, "Would you like some pillows for the night? Don't make any ceremony about it; I can give you plenty, both for yourself and for these ladies who are accompanying you."

However, Raymonde gaily refused the offer, "No, no," said she, "we are not so delicate. Keep them for the poor sufferers."

All the ladies were now talking together. Madame de Jonquiere declared that she was so tired, so tired that she no longer felt alive; and yet she displayed great happiness, her eyes smiling as she glanced at her daughter and the young man she was engaged to. But neither Berthaud nor Gerard could remain there; they had their duties to perform, and accordingly took their leave, after reminding Madame de Jonquiere and Raymonde of the appointed meeting. It was understood, was it not, on September 15th, at the Chateau of Berneville? Yes, yes, it was understood! And then came fresh smiles and handshakes, whilst the eyes of the newly engaged couple—caressing, delighted eyes—added all that they dared not say aloud in the midst of such a throng.

"What!" exclaimed little Madame Desagneaux, "you will go to Berneville on the 15th? But if we stay at Trouville till the 10th, as my husband wishes to do, we will go to see you!" And then, turning towards Madame Volmar, who stood there silent, she added, "You ought to come as well, my dear. It would be so nice to meet there all together."

But, with a slow wave of the hand and an air of weary indifference, Madame Volmar answered, "Oh! my holiday is all over; I am going home."

Just then her eyes again met those of Pierre, who had remained standing near the party, and he fancied that she became confused, whilst an expression of indescribable suffering passed over her lifeless face.

The Sisters of the Assumption were now arriving, and the ladies joined them in front of the cantine van. Ferrand, who had come with the Sisters from the hospital, got into the van, and then helped Sister Saint-Francois to mount upon the somewhat high footboard. Then he remained standing on the threshold of the van—transformed into a kitchen and containing all sorts of supplies for the journey, such as bread, broth, milk, and chocolate,—whilst Sister Hyacinthe and Sister Claire des Anges, who were still on the platform, passed him his little medicine-chest and some small articles of luggage.

"You are sure you have everything?" Sister Hyacinthe asked him. "All right. Well, now you only have to go and lie down in your corner and get to sleep, since you complain that your services are not utilised."

Ferrand began to laugh softly. "I shall help Sister Saint-Francois," said he. "I shall light the oil-stove, wash the crockery, carry the cups of broth and milk to the patients whenever we stop, according to the time-table hanging yonder; and if, all the same, you *should* require a doctor, you will please come to fetch me."

Sister Hyacinthe had also begun to laugh. "But we no longer require a doctor since all our patients are cured," she replied; and, fixing her eyes on his, with her calm, sisterly air, she added, "Good-bye, Monsieur Ferrand."

He smiled again, whilst a feeling of deep emotion brought moisture to his eyes. The tremulous accents of his voice expressed his conviction that he would never be able to forget this journey, his joy at having seen her again, and the souvenir of divine and eternal affection which he was taking away with him. "Good-bye, Sister," said he.

Then Madame de Jonquiere talked of going to her carriage with Sister Claire des Anges and Sister Hyacinthe; but the latter assured her that there was no hurry, since the sick pilgrims were as yet scarcely arriving. She left her, therefore, taking the other Sister with her, and promising to see to everything. Moreover, she even insisted on ridding the superintendent of her little bag, saying that she would find it on her seat when it was time for her to come. Thus the ladies continued walking and chatting gaily on the broad platform, where the atmosphere was so pleasant.

Pierre, however, his eyes fixed upon the big clock, watched the minutes hasten by on the dial, and began to feel surprised at not seeing Marie arrive with her father. It was to be hoped that M. de Guersaint would not lose himself on the road!

The young priest was still watching, when, to his surprise, he caught sight of M. Vigneron, in a state of perfect exasperation, pushing his wife and little Gustave furiously before him.

"Oh, Monsieur l'Abbe," he exclaimed, "tell me where our carriage is! Help me to put our luggage and this child in it. I am at my wit's end! They have made me altogether lose my temper."

Then, on reaching the second-class compartment, he caught hold of Pierre's hands, just as the young man was about to place little Gustave inside, and quite an outburst followed. "Could you believe it? They insist on my starting. They tell me that my return-ticket will not be available if I wait here till to-morrow. It was of no use my telling them about the accident. As it is, it's by no means pleasant to have to stay with that corpse, watch over it, see it put in a coffin, and remove it to-morrow within the regulation time. But they pretend that it doesn't concern them, that they already make large enough reductions on the pilgrimage tickets, and that they can't enter into any questions of people dying."

Madame Vigneron stood all of a tremble listening to him, whilst Gustave, forgotten, staggering on his crutch with fatigue, raised his poor, inquisitive, suffering face.

"But at all events," continued the irate father, "as I told them, it's a case of compulsion. What do they expect me to do with that corpse? I can't take it under my arm, and bring it them to-day, like an article of luggage! I am therefore absolutely obliged to remain behind. But no! ah! how many stupid and wicked people there are!"

"Have you spoken to the station-master?" asked Pierre.

"The station-master! Oh! he's somewhere about, in the midst of the scramble. They were never able to find him. How could you have anything done properly in such a bear-garden? Still, I mean to rout him out, and give him a bit of my mind!"

Then, perceiving his wife standing beside him motionless, glued as it were to the platform, he cried: "What are you doing there? Get in, so that we may pass you the youngster and the parcels!"

With these words he pushed her in, and threw the parcels after her, whilst the young priest took Gustave in his arms. The poor little fellow, who was as light as a bird, seemingly thinner than before, consumed by sores, and so full of pain, raised a faint cry. "Oh, my dear child, have I hurt you?" asked Pierre.

"No, no, Monsieur l'Abbe, but I've been moved about so much to-day, and I'm very tired this afternoon." As he spoke, he smiled with his usual intelligent and mournful expression, and then, sinking back into his corner, closed his eyes, exhausted, indeed done for, by this fearful trip to Lourdes.

"As you can very well understand," now resumed M. Vigneron, "it by no means amuses me to stay here, kicking my heels, while my wife and my son go back to Paris without me. They have to go, however, for life at the hotel is no longer bearable; and besides, if I kept them with me, and the railway people won't listen to reason, I should have to pay three extra fares. And to make matters worse, my wife hasn't got much brains. I'm afraid she won't be able to manage things properly."

Then, almost breathless, he overwhelmed Madame Vigneron with the most minute instructions—what she was to do during the journey, how she was to get back home on arriving in Paris, and what steps she was to take if Gustave was to have another attack. Somewhat scared, she responded, in all docility, to each recommendation: "Yes, yes, dear—of course, dear, of course."

But all at once her husband's rage came back to him. "After all," he shouted, "what I want to know is whether my return ticket be good or not! I must know for certain! They must find that station-master for me!"

He was already on the point of rushing away through the crowd, when he noticed Gustave's crutch lying on the platform. This was disastrous, and he raised his eyes to heaven as though to call Providence to witness that he would never be able to extricate himself from such awful complications. And, throwing the crutch to his wife, he hurried off, distracted and shouting, "There, take it! You forget everything!"

The sick pilgrims were now flocking into the station, and, as on the occasion of their arrival, there was plenty of disorderly carting along the platform and across the lines. All the abominable ailments, all the sores, all the deformities, went past once more, neither their gravity nor their number seeming to have decreased; for the few cures which had been effected were but a faint inappreciable gleam of light amidst the general mourning. They were taken back as they had come. The little carts, laden with helpless old women with their bags at their feet, grated over the rails. The stretchers on which you saw inflated bodies and pale faces with glittering eyes, swayed amidst the jostling of the throng. There was wild and senseless haste, indescribable confusion, questions, calls, sudden running, all the whirling of a flock which cannot find the entrance to the pen. And the bearers ended by losing their heads, no longer knowing which direction to take amidst the warning cries of the porters, who at each moment were frightening people, distracting them with anguish. "Take care, take care over there! Make haste! No, no, don't cross! The Toulouse train, the Toulouse train!"

Retracing his steps, Pierre again perceived the ladies, Madame de Jonquiere and the others, still gaily chatting together. Lingering near them, he listened to Berthaud, whom Father Fourcade had stopped, to congratulate him on the good order which had been maintained throughout the pilgrimage. The ex-public prosecutor was now bowing his thanks, feeling quite flattered by this praise. "Is it not a lesson for their Republic, your reverence?" he asked. "People get killed in Paris when such crowds as these celebrate some bloody anniversary of their hateful history. They ought to come and take a lesson here."

He was delighted with the thought of being disagreeable to the Government which had compelled him to resign. He was never so happy as when women were just saved from being knocked over amidst the great concourse of believers at Lourdes. However, he did not seem to be satisfied with the results of the political propaganda which he came to further there, during three days, every year. Fits of impatience came over him, things did not move fast enough. When did Our Lady of Lourdes mean to bring back the monarchy?

"You see, your reverence," said he, "the only means, the real triumph, would be to bring the working classes of the towns here *en masse*. I shall cease dreaming, I shall devote myself to that entirely. Ah! if one could only create a Catholic democracy!"

Father Fourcade had become very grave. His fine, intelligent eyes filled with a dreamy expression, and wandered far away. How many times already had he himself made the creation of that new people the object of his efforts! But was not the breath of a new Messiah needed for the accomplishment of such a task? "Yes, yes," he murmured, "a Catholic democracy; ah! the history of humanity would begin afresh!"

But Father Massias interrupted him in a passionate voice, saying that all the nations of the earth would end by coming; whilst Doctor Bonamy, who already detected a slight subsidence of fervour among the pilgrims, wagged his head and expressed the opinion that the faithful ones of the Grotto ought to increase their zeal. To his mind, success especially depended on the greatest possible measure of publicity being given to the miracles. And he assumed a radiant air and laughed complacently whilst pointing to the tumultuous *defile* of the sick. "Look at them!" said he. "Don't they go off looking better? There are a great many who, although they don't appear to be cured, are nevertheless carrying the germs of cure away with them; of that you may be certain! Ah! the good people; they do far more than we do all together for the glory of Our Lady of Lourdes!"

However, he had to check himself, for Madame Dieulafay was passing before them, in her box lined with quilted silk. She was deposited in front of the door of the first-class carriage, in which a maid was already placing the luggage. Pity came to all who beheld the unhappy woman, for she did not seem to have awakened from her prostration during her three days' sojourn at Lourdes. What she had been when they had removed her from the carriage on the morning of her arrival, that she also was now when the bearers were about to place her inside it again—clad in lace, covered with jewels, still with the lifeless, imbecile face of a mummy slowly liquefying; and, indeed, one might have thought that she had become yet more wasted, that she was being taken back diminished, shrunken more and more to the proportions of a child, by the march of that horrible disease which, after destroying her bones, was now dissolving the softened fibres of her muscles. Inconsolable, bowed down by the loss of their last hope, her husband and sister, their eyes red, were following her with Abbe Judaine, even as one follows a corpse to the grave.

"No, no! not yet!" said the old priest to the bearers, in order to prevent them from placing the box in the carriage. "She will have time enough to roll along in there. Let her have the warmth of that lovely sky above her till the last possible moment."

Then, seeing Pierre near him, he drew him a few steps aside, and, in a voice broken by grief, resumed: "Ah! I am indeed distressed. Again this morning I had a hope. I had her taken to the Grotto, I said my mass for her, and came back to pray till eleven o'clock. But nothing came of it; the Blessed Virgin did not listen to me. Although she cured me, a poor, useless old man like me, I could not obtain from her the cure of this beautiful, young, and wealthy woman, whose life ought to be a continual *fete*. Undoubtedly the Blessed Virgin knows what she ought to do better than ourselves, and I bow and bless her name. Nevertheless, my soul is full of frightful sadness."

He did not tell everything; he did not confess the thought which was upsetting him, simple, childish, worthy man that he was, whose life had never been troubled by either passion or doubt. But his thought was that those poor weeping people, the husband and the sister, had too many millions, that the presents they had brought were too costly, that they had given far too much money to the Basilica. A miracle is not to be bought. The wealth of the world is a hindrance rather than an advantage when you address yourself to God. Assuredly, if the Blessed Virgin had turned a deaf ear to their entreaties, had shown them but a stern, cold countenance, it was in order that she might the more attentively listen to the weak voices of the lowly ones who had come to her with empty hands, with no other wealth than their love, and these she had loaded with grace, flooded with the glowing affection of her Divine Motherhood. And those poor wealthy ones, who had not been heard, that sister and that husband, both so wretched beside the sorry body they were taking away with them, they themselves felt like pariahs among the throng of the humble who had been consoled or healed; they seemed embarrassed by their very luxury, and recoiled, awkward and ill at ease, covered with shame at the thought that Our Lady of Lourdes had relieved beggars whilst never casting a glance upon that beautiful and powerful lady agonising unto death amidst all her lace!

All at once it occurred to Pierre that he might have missed seeing M. de Guersaint and Marie arrive, and that they were perhaps already in the carriage. He returned thither, but there was still only his valise on the seat. Sister Hyacinthe and Sister Claire des Anges, however, had begun to install themselves, pending the arrival of their charges, and as Gerard just then brought up M. Sabathier in a little handcart, Pierre helped to place him in the carriage, a laborious task which put both the young priest and Gerard into a perspiration. The ex-professor, who looked disconsolate though very calm, at once settled himself in his corner.

"Thank you, gentlemen," said he. "That's over, thank goodness. And now they'll only have to take me out at Paris."

After wrapping a rug round his legs, Madame Sabathier, who was also there, got out of the carriage and remained standing near the open door. She was talking to Pierre when all at once she broke off to say: "Ah! here's Madame Maze coming to take her seat. She confided in me the other day, you know. She's a very unhappy little woman."

Then, in an obliging spirit, she called to her and offered to watch over her things. But Madame Maze shook her head, laughed, and gesticulated as though she were out of her senses.

"No, no, I am not going," said she.

"What! you are not going back?"

"No, no, I am not going—that is, I am, but not with you, not with you!"

She wore such an extraordinary air, she looked so bright, that Pierre and Madame Sabathier found it difficult to recognise her. Her fair, prematurely faded face was radiant, she seemed to be ten years younger, suddenly aroused from the infinite sadness into which desertion had plunged her. And, at last, her joy overflowing, she raised a cry: "I am going off with him! Yes, he has come to fetch me, he is taking me with him. Yes, yes, we are going to Luchon together, together!"

Then, with a rapturous glance, she pointed out a dark, sturdy-looking young man, with gay eyes and bright red lips, who was purchasing some newspapers. "There! that's my husband," said she, "that handsome man who's laughing over there with the newspaper-girl. He turned up here early this morning, and he's carrying me off. We shall take the Toulouse train in a couple of minutes. Ah! dear madame, I told you of all my worries, and you can understand my happiness, can't you?"

However, she could not remain silent, but again spoke of the frightful letter which she had received on Sunday, a letter in which he had declared to her that if she should take advantage of her sojourn at Lourdes to come to Luchon after him, he would not open the door to her. And, think of it, theirs had been a love match! But for ten years he had neglected her, profiting by his continual journeys as a commercial traveller to take friends about with him from one to the other end of France. Ah! that time she had thought it all over, she had asked the Blessed Virgin to let her die, for she knew that the faithless one was at that very moment at Luchon with two friends. What was it then that had happened? A thunderbolt must certainly have fallen from heaven. Those two friends must have received a warning from on high—perhaps they had dreamt that they were already condemned to everlasting punishment. At all events they had fled one evening without a word of explanation, and he, unable to live alone, had suddenly been seized with a desire to fetch his wife and keep her with him for a week. Grace must have certainly fallen on him, though he did not say it, for he was so kind and pleasant that she could not do otherwise than believe in a real beginning of conversion.

"Ah! how grateful I am to the Blessed Virgin," she continued; "she alone can have acted, and I well understood her last evening. It seemed to me that she made me a little sign just at the very moment when my husband was making up his mind to come here to fetch me. I asked him at what time it was that the idea occurred to him, and the hours fit in exactly. Ah! there has been no greater miracle. The others make me smile with their mended legs and their vanished sores. Blessed be Our Lady of Lourdes, who has healed my heart!"

Just then the sturdy young man turned round, and she darted away to join him, so full of delight that she forgot to bid the others good-bye. And it was at this moment, amidst the growing crowd of patients whom the bearers were bringing, that the Toulouse train at last came in. The tumult increased, the confusion became extraordinary.

Bells rang and signals worked, whilst the station-master was seen rushing up, shouting with all the strength of his lungs: "Be careful there! Clear the line at once!"

A railway *employe* had to rush from the platform to push a little vehicle, which had been forgotten on the line, with an old woman in it, out of harm's way; however, yet another scared band of pilgrims ran across when the steaming, growling engine was only thirty yards distant. Others, losing their heads, would have been crushed by the wheels if porters had not roughly caught them by the shoulders. Then, without having pounded anybody, the train at last stopped alongside the mattresses, pillows, and cushions lying hither and thither, and the bewildered, whirling groups of people. The carriage doors opened and a torrent of travellers alighted, whilst another torrent climbed in, these two obstinately contending currents bringing the tumult to a climax. Faces, first wearing an inquisitive expression, and then overcome by stupefaction at the astonishing sight, showed themselves at the windows of the doors which remained closed; and, among them, one especially noticed the faces of two remarkably pretty girls, whose large candid eyes ended by expressing the most dolorous compassion.

Followed by her husband, however, Madame Maze had climbed into one of the carriages, feeling as happy and buoyant as if she were in her twentieth year again, as on the already distant evening of her honeymoon journey. And the doors having been slammed, the engine gave a loud whistle and began to move, going off slowly and heavily between the throng, which, in the rear of the train, flowed on to the lines again like an invading torrent whose flood-gates have been swept away.

"Bar the platform!" shouted the station-master to his men. "Keep watch when the engine comes up!"

The belated patients and pilgrims had arrived during this alert. La Grivotte passed by with her feverish eyes and excited, dancing gait, followed by Elise Rouquet and Sophie Couteau, who were very gay, and quite out of breath through running. All three hastened to their carriage, where Sister Hyacinthe scolded them. They had almost been left behind at the Grotto, where, at times, the pilgrims lingered forgetfully, unable to tear themselves away, still imploring and entreating the Blessed Virgin, when the train was waiting for them at the railway-station.

All at once Pierre, who likewise was anxious, no longer knowing what to think, perceived M. de Guersaint and Marie quietly talking with Abbe Judaine on the covered platform. He hastened to join them, and told them of his impatience. "What have you been doing?" he asked. "I was losing all hope."

"What have we been doing?" responded M. de Guersaint, with quiet astonishment. "We were at the Grotto, as you know very well. There was a priest there, preaching in a most remarkable manner, and we should still be there if I hadn't remembered that we had to leave. And we took a fly here, as we promised you we would do."

He broke off to look at the clock. "But hang it all!" he added, "there's no hurry. The train won't start for another quarter of an hour."

This was true. Then Marie, smiling with divine joy, exclaimed: "Oh! if you only knew, Pierre, what happiness I have brought away from that last visit to the Blessed Virgin. I saw her smile at me, I felt her giving me strength to live. Really, that farewell was delightful, and you must not scold us, Pierre."

He himself had begun to smile, somewhat ill at ease, however, as he thought of his nervous fidgeting. Had he, then, experienced so keen a desire to get far away from Lourdes? Had he feared that the Grotto might keep Marie, that she might never come away from it again? Now that she was there beside him, he was astonished at having indulged such thoughts, and felt himself to be very calm.

However, whilst he was advising them to go and take their seats in the carriage, he recognised Doctor Chassaigne hastily approaching. "Ah! my dear doctor," he said, "I was waiting for you. I should have been sorry indeed to have gone away without embracing you."

But the old doctor, who was trembling with emotion, interrupted him. "Yes, yes, I am late. But ten minutes ago, just as I arrived, I caught sight of that eccentric fellow, the Commander, and had a talk with him over yonder. He was sneering at the sight of your people taking the train again to go and die at home, when, said he, they ought to have done so before coming to Lourdes. Well, all at once, while he was talking like this, he fell on the ground before me. It was his third attack of paralysis; the one he had long been expecting."

"Oh! *mon Dieu,*" murmured Abbe Judaine, who heard the doctor, "he was blaspheming. Heaven has punished him."

M. de Guersaint and Marie were listening, greatly interested and deeply moved.

"I had him carried yonder, into that shed," continued the doctor. "It is all over; I can do nothing. He will doubtless be dead before a quarter of an hour has gone by. But I thought of a priest, and hastened up to you."

Then, turning towards Abbe Judaine, M. Chassaigne added: "Come with me, Monsieur le Cure; you know him. We cannot let a Christian depart unsuccoured. Perhaps he will be moved, recognise his error, and become reconciled with God."

Abbe Judaine quickly followed the doctor, and in the rear went M. de Guersaint, leading Marie and Pierre, whom the thought of this tragedy impassioned. All five entered the goods shed, at twenty paces from the crowd which was still bustling and buzzing, without a soul in it expecting that there was a man dying so near by.

In a solitary corner of the shed, between two piles of sacks filled with oats, lay the Commander, on a mattress borrowed from the Hospitality reserve supply. He wore his everlasting frock-coat, with its buttonhole decked with a broad red riband, and somebody who had taken the precaution to pick up his silver-knobbed walking-stick had carefully placed it on the ground beside the mattress.

Abbe Judaine at once leant over him. "You recognise us, you can hear us, my poor friend, can't you?" asked the priest.

Only the Commander's eyes now appeared to be alive; but they *were* alive, still glittering brightly with a stubborn flame of energy. The attack had this time fallen on his right side, almost entirely depriving him of the power of speech. He could only stammer a few words, by which he succeeded in making them understand that he wished to die there, without being moved or worried any further. He had no relative at Lourdes, where nobody knew anything either of his former life or his family. For three years he had lived there happily on the salary attached to his little post at the station, and now he at last beheld his ardent, his only desire, approaching fulfilment—the desire that he might depart and fall into the eternal sleep. His eyes expressed the great joy he felt at being so near his end.

"Have you any wish to make known to us?" resumed Abbe Judaine. "Cannot we be useful to you in any way?"

No, no; his eyes replied that he was all right, well pleased. For three years past he had never got up in the morning without hoping that by night time he would be sleeping in the cemetery. Whenever he saw the sun shine he was wont to say in an envious tone: "What a beautiful day for departure!" And now that death was at last at hand, ready to deliver him from his hateful existence, it was indeed welcome.

"I can do nothing, science is powerless. He is condemned," said Doctor Chassaigne in a low, bitter tone to the old priest, who begged him to attempt some effort.

However, at that same moment it chanced that an aged woman, a pilgrim of fourscore years, who had lost her way and knew not whither she was going, entered the shed. Lame and humpbacked, reduced to the stature of childhood's days, afflicted with all the ailments of extreme old age, she was dragging herself along with the assistance of a stick, and at her side was slung a can full of Lourdes water, which she was taking away with her, in the hope of yet prolonging her old age, in spite of all its frightful decay. For a moment her senile, imbecile mind was quite scared. She stood looking at that outstretched, stiffened man, who was dying. Then a gleam of grandmotherly kindliness appeared in the depths of her dim, vague eyes; and with the sisterly feelings of one who was very aged and suffered very grievously she drew nearer, and, taking hold of her can with her hands, which never ceased shaking, she offered it to the man.

To Abbe Judaine this seemed like a sudden flash of light, an inspiration from on high. He, who had prayed so fervently and so often for the cure of Madame Dieulafay without being heard by the Blessed Virgin, now glowed with fresh faith in the conviction that if the Commander would only drink that water he would be cured.

The old priest fell upon his knees beside the mattress. "O brother!" he said, "it is God who has sent you this woman. Reconcile yourself with God, drink and pray, whilst we ourselves implore the divine mercy with our whole souls. God will prove His power to you; God will work the great miracle of setting you erect once more, so that you may yet spend many years upon this earth, loving Him and glorifying Him."

No, no! the Commander's sparkling eyes cried no! He, indeed, show himself as cowardly as those flocks of pilgrims who came from afar, through so many fatigues, in order to drag themselves on the ground and sob and beg Heaven to let them live a month, a year, ten years longer! It was so pleasant, so simple to die quietly in your bed. You turned your face to the wall and you died.

"Drink, O my brother, I implore you!" continued the old priest. "It is life that you will drink, it is strength and health, the very joy of living. Drink that you may become young again, that you may begin a new and pious life; drink that you may sing the praises of the Divine Mother, who will have saved both your body and your soul. She is speaking to me, your resurrection is certain."

But no! but no! The eyes refused, repelled the offer of life with growing obstinacy, and in their expression now appeared a covert fear of the miraculous. The Commander did not believe; for three years he had been shrugging his shoulders at the pretended cases of cure. But could one ever tell in this strange world of ours? Such extraordinary things did sometimes happen. And if by chance their water should really have a supernatural power, and if by force they should make him drink some of it, it would be terrible to have to live again—to endure once more the punishment of a galley-slave existence, that abomination which Lazarus—the pitiable object of the great miracle—had suffered twice. No, no, he would not drink; he would not incur the fearful risk of resurrection.

"Drink, drink, my brother," repeated Abbe Judaine, who was now in tears; "do not harden your heart to refuse the favours of Heaven."

And then a terrible thing was seen; this man, already half dead, raised himself, shaking off the stifling bonds of paralysis, loosening for a second his tied tongue, and stammering, growling in a hoarse voice: "No, no, NO!"

Pierre had to lead the stupefied old woman away and put her in the right direction again. She had failed to understand that refusal of the water which she herself was taking home with her like an inestimable treasure, the very gift of God's eternity to the poor who did not wish to die. Lame of one leg, humpbacked, dragging the sorry remnants of her fourscore years along by the assistance of her stick, she disappeared among the tramping crowd, consumed by the passion of being, eager for space, air, sunshine, and noise.

Marie and her father had shuddered in presence of that appetite for death, that greedy hungering for the end which the Commander showed. Ah! to sleep, to sleep without a dream, in the infinite darkness forever and ever—nothing in the world could have seemed so sweet to him. He did not hope in a better life; he had no desire to become happy, at last, in Paradise where equality and justice would reign. His sole longing was for black night and endless sleep, the joy of being no more, of never, never being again. And Doctor Chassaigne also had shuddered, for he also nourished but one thought, the thought of the happy moment when he would depart. But, in his case, on the other side of this earthly existence he would find his dear lost ones awaiting him, at the spot where eternal life began; and how icy cold all would have seemed had he but for a single moment thought that he might not meet them there.

Abbe Judaine painfully rose up. It had seemed to him that the Commander was now fixing his bright eyes upon Marie. Deeply grieved that his entreaties should have been of no avail, the priest wished to show the dying man an example of that goodness of God which he repulsed.

"You recognise her, do you not?" he asked. "Yes, it is the young lady who arrived here on Saturday so ill, with both legs paralysed. And you see her now, so full of health, so strong, so beautiful. Heaven has taken pity on her, and now she is reviving to youth, to the long life she was born to live. Do you feel no regret in seeing her? Would you also like her to be dead? would you have advised her not to drink the water?"

The Commander could not answer; but his eyes no longer strayed from Marie's young face, on which one read such great happiness at having resuscitated, such vast hopes in countless morrows; and tears appeared in those fixed eyes of his, gathered under their lids, and rolled down his cheeks, which were already cold. He was certainly weeping for her; he must have been thinking of that other miracle which he had wished her—that if she should be cured, she might be happy. It was the tenderness of an old man, who knows the miseries of this world, stirred to pity by the thought of all the sorrows which awaited this young creature. Ah! poor woman, how many times; perhaps, might she regret that she had not died in her twentieth year!

Then the Commander's eyes grew very dim, as though those last pitiful tears had dissolved them. It was the end; coma was coming; the mind was departing with the breath. He slightly turned, and died.

Doctor Chassaigne at once drew Marie aside. "The train's starting," he said; "make haste, make haste!"

Indeed, the loud ringing of a bell was clearly resounding above the growing tumult of the crowd. And the doctor, having requested two bearers to watch the body, which would be removed later on when the train had gone, desired to accompany his friends to their carriage.

They hastened their steps. Abbe Judaine, who was in despair, joined them after saying a short prayer for the repose of that rebellious soul. However, while Marie, followed by Pierre and M. de Guersaint, was running along the platform, she was stopped once more, and this time by Doctor Bonamy, who triumphantly presented her to Father Fourcade. "Here is Mademoiselle de Guersaint, your reverence, the young lady who was healed so marvellously yesterday."

The radiant smile of a general who is reminded of his most decisive victory appeared on Father Fourcade's face. "I know, I know; I was there," he replied. "God has blessed you among all women, my dear daughter; go, and cause His name to be worshipped."

Then he congratulated M. de Guersaint, whose paternal pride savoured divine enjoyment. It was the ovation beginning afresh—the concert of loving words and enraptured glances which had followed the girl through the streets of Lourdes that morning, and which again surrounded her at the moment of departure. The bell might go on ringing; a circle of delighted pilgrims still lingered around her; it seemed as if she were carrying away in her person all the glory of the pilgrimage, the triumph of religion, which would echo and echo to the four corners of the earth.

And Pierre was moved as he noticed the dolorous group which Madame Jousseur and M. Dieulafay formed near by. Their eyes were fixed upon Marie; like the others, they were astonished by the resurrection of this beautiful girl, whom they had seen lying inert, emaciated, with ashen face. Why should that child have been healed? Why not the young woman, the dear woman, whom they were taking home in a dying state? Their confusion, their sense of shame, seemed to increase; they drew back, uneasy, like pariahs burdened with too much wealth; and it was a great relief for them when, three bearers having with difficulty placed Madame Dieulafay in the first-class compartment, they themselves were able to vanish into it in company with Abbe Judaine.

The *employes* were already shouting, "Take your seats! take your seats," and Father Massias, the spiritual director of the train, had returned to his compartment, leaving Father Fourcade on the platform leaning on Doctor Bonamy's shoulder. In all haste Gerard and Berthaud again saluted the ladies, while Raymonde got in to join Madame Desagneaux and Madame Volmar in their corner; and Madame de Jonquiere at last ran off to her carriage, which she reached at the same time as the Guersaints. There was hustling, and shouting, and wild running from one to the other end of the long train, to which the engine, a copper engine, glittering like a star, had just been coupled.

Pierre was helping Marie into the carriage, when M. Vigneron, coming back at a gallop, shouted to him: "It'll be good to-morrow, it'll be good tomorrow!" Very red in the face, he showed and waved his ticket, and then galloped off again to the compartment where his wife and son had their seats, in order to announce the good news to them.

When Marie and her father were installed in their places, Pierre lingered for another moment on the platform with Doctor Chassaigne, who embraced him paternally.

The young man wished to induce the doctor to return to Paris and take some little interest in life again. But M. Chassaigne shook his head. "No, no, my dear child," he replied. "I shall remain here. They are here, they keep me here." He was speaking of his dear lost ones. Then, very gently and lovingly, he said, "Farewell."

"Not farewell, my dear doctor; till we meet again."

"Yes, yes, farewell. The Commander was right, you know; nothing can be so sweet as to die, but to die in order to live again."

Baron Suire was now giving orders for the removal of the white flags on the foremost and hindmost carriages of the train; the shouts of the railway *employes* were ringing out in more and more imperious tones, "Take your seats! take your seats!" and now came the supreme scramble, the torrent of belated pilgrims rushing up distracted, breathless, and covered with perspiration. Madame de Jonquiere and Sister Hyacinthe were counting their party in the carriage. La Grivotte, Elise Rouquet, and Sophie Couteau were all three there. Madame Sabathier, too, had taken her seat in front of her husband, who, with his eyes half closed, was patiently awaiting the departure. However, a voice inquired, "And Madame Vincent, isn't she going back with us?"

Thereupon Sister Hyacinthe, who was leaning out of the window exchanging a last smile with Ferrand, who stood at the door of the cantine van, exclaimed: "Here she comes!"

Madame Vincent crossed the lines, rushed up, the last of all, breathless and haggard. And at once, by an involuntary impulse, Pierre glanced at her arms. They carried nothing now.

All the doors were being closed, slammed one after the other; the carriages were full, and only the signal for departure was awaited. Panting and smoking, the engine gave vent to a first loud whistle, shrill and joyous; and at that moment the sun, hitherto veiled from sight, dissipated the light cloudlets and made the whole train resplendent, gilding the engine, which seemed on the point of starting for the legendary Paradise. No bitterness, but a divine, infantile gaiety attended the departure. All the sick appeared to be healed. Though most of them were being taken away in the same condition as they had been brought, they went off relieved and happy, at all events, for an hour. And not the slightest jealousy tainted their brotherly and sisterly feelings; those who were not cured waxed quite gay, triumphant at the cure of the others. Their own turns would surely come; yesterday's miracle was the formal promise of to-morrow's. Even after those three days of burning entreaty their fever of desire remained within them; the faith of the forgotten ones continued as keen as ever in the conviction that the Blessed Virgin had simply deferred a cure for their souls' benefit. Inextinguishable love, invincible hope glowed within all those wretched ones thirsting for life. And so a last outburst of joy, a turbulent display of happiness, laughter and shouts, overflowed from all the crowded carriages. "Till next year! We'll come back, we'll come back again!" was the cry; and then the gay little Sisters of the Assumption clapped their hands, and the hymn of gratitude, the "Magnificat," began, sung by all the eight hundred pilgrims: "*Magnificat anima mea Dominum.*" "My soul doth magnify the Lord."

Thereupon the station-master, his mind at last at ease, his arms hanging beside him, caused the signal to be given. The engine whistled once again and then set out, rolling along in the dazzling sunlight as amidst a glory. Although his leg was causing him great suffering, Father Fourcade had remained on the platform, leaning upon

Doctor Bonamy's shoulder, and, in spite of everything, saluting the departure of his dear children with a smile. Berthaud, Gerard, and Baron Suire formed another group, and near them were Doctor Chassaigne and M. Vigneron waving their handkerchiefs. Heads were looking joyously out of the windows of the fleeing carriages, whence other handkerchiefs were streaming in the current of air produced by the motion of the train. Madame Vigneron compelled Gustave to show his pale little face, and for a long time Raymonde's small hand could be seen waving good wishes; but Marie remained the last, looking back on Lourdes as it grew smaller and smaller amidst the trees.

Across the bright countryside the train triumphantly disappeared, resplendent, growling, chanting at the full pitch of its eight hundred voices: "*Et exsultavit spiritus meus in Deo salutari meo*." "And my spirit hath rejoiced in God my Saviour!"

IV. MARIE'S VOW

ONCE more was the white train rolling, rolling towards Paris on its way home; and the third-class carriage, where the shrill voices singing the "Magnificat" at full pitch rose above the growling of the wheels, had again become a common room, a travelling hospital ward, full of disorder, littered like an improvised ambulance. Basins and brooms and sponges lay about under the seats, which half concealed them. Articles of luggage, all the wretched mass of poor worn-out things, were heaped together, a little bit everywhere; and up above, the litter began again, what with the parcels, the baskets, and the bags hanging from the brass pegs and swinging to and fro without a moment's rest. The same Sisters of the Assumption and the same lady-hospitallers were there with their patients, amidst the contingent of healthy pilgrims, who were already suffering from the overpowering heat and unbearable odour. And at the far end there was again the compartment full of women, the ten close-packed female pilgrims, some young, some old, and all looking pitifully ugly as they violently chanted the canticle in cracked and woeful voices.

"At what time shall we reach Paris?" M. de Guersaint inquired of Pierre.

"To-morrow at about two in the afternoon, I think," the priest replied.

Since starting, Marie had been looking at the latter with an air of anxious preoccupation, as though haunted by a sudden sorrow which she could not reveal. However, she found her gay, healthful smile again to say: "Twenty-two hours' journey! Ah! it won't be so long and trying as it was coming."

"Besides," resumed her father, "we have left some of our people behind. We have plenty of room now."

In fact Madame Maze's absence left a corner free at the end of the seat which Marie, now sitting up like any other passenger, no longer encumbered with her box. Moreover, little Sophie had this time been placed in the next compartment, where there was neither Brother Isidore nor his sister Marthe. The latter, it was said, had remained at Lourdes in service with a pious lady. On the other side, Madame de Jonquiere and Sister Hyacinthe also had the benefit of a vacant seat, that of Madame Vetu; and it had further occurred to them to get rid of Elise Rouquet by placing her with Sophie, so that only La Grivotte and the Sabathier couple were with them in their compartment. Thanks to these new arrangements, they were better able to breathe, and perhaps they might manage to sleep a little.

The last verse of the "Magnificat" having been sung, the ladies finished installing themselves as comfortably as possible by setting their little household in order. One of the most important matters was to put the zinc water-can, which interfered with their legs, out of the way. All the blinds of the left-hand windows had been pulled down, for the oblique sunrays were falling on the train, and had poured into it in sheets of fire. The last storms, however, must have laid the dust, and the night would certainly be cool. Moreover, there was less suffering: death had carried off the most afflicted ones, and only stupefied ailments, numbed by fatigue and lapsing into a slow torpor, remained. The overpowering reaction which always follows great moral shocks was about to declare itself. The souls had made the efforts required of them, the miracles had been worked, and now the relaxing was beginning amidst a hebetude tinged with profound relief.

Until they got to Tarbes they were all very much occupied in setting things in order and making themselves comfortable. But as they left that station Sister Hyacinthe rose up and clapped her hands. "My children," said she, "we must not forget the Blessed Virgin who has been so kind to us. Let us begin the Rosary."

Then the whole carriage repeated the first chaplet—the five joyful mysteries, the Annunciation, the Visitation, the Nativity, the Purification, and the Finding of Jesus in the Temple. And afterwards they intoned the canticle, "Let us contemplate the heavenly Archangel," in such loud voices that the peasants working in the fields raised their heads to look at this singing train as it rushed past them at full speed.

Marie was at the window, gazing with admiration at the vast landscape and the immense stretch of sky, which had gradually freed itself of its mist and was now of a dazzling blue. It was the delicious close of a fine day. However, she at last looked back into the carriage, and her eyes were fixing themselves on Pierre with that mute sadness which had previously dimmed them, when all at once a sound of furious sobbing burst forth in front of her. The canticle was finished, and it was Madame Vincent who was crying, stammering confused words, half-choked by her tears: "Ah, my poor little one!" she gasped. "Ah, my jewel, my treasure, my life!"

She had previously remained in her corner, shrinking back into it as though anxious to disappear. With a fierce face, her lips tightly set, and her eyes closed, as though to isolate herself in the depths of her cruel grief, she had hitherto not said a word. But, chancing to open her eyes, she had espied the leathern window-strap hanging down beside the door, and the sight of that strap, which her daughter had touched, almost played with at one moment during the previous journey, had overwhelmed her with a frantic despair which swept away her resolution to remain silent.

"Ah! my poor little Rose," she continued. "Her little hand touched that strap, she turned it, and looked at it—ah, it was her last plaything! And we were there both together then; she was still alive, I still had her on my lap, in my arms. It was still so nice, so nice! But now I no longer have her; I shall never, never have her again, my poor little Rose, my poor little Rose!"

Distracted, sobbing bitterly, she looked at her knees and her arms, on which nothing now rested, and which she was at a loss how to employ. She had so long rocked her daughter on her knees, so long carried her in her arms, that it now seemed to her as if some portion of her being had been amputated, as if her body had been deprived of one of its functions, leaving her diminished, unoccupied, distracted at being unable to fulfil that function any more. Those useless arms and knees of hers quite embarrassed her.

Pierre and Marie, who were deeply moved, had drawn near, uttering kind words and striving to console the unhappy mother. And, little by little, from the disconnected sentences which mingled with her sobs, they learned what a Calvary she had as-ascended since her daughter's death. On the morning of the previous day, when she had carried the body off in her arms amidst the storm, she must have long continued walking, blind and deaf to everything, whilst the torrential rain beat down upon her. She no longer remembered what squares she had crossed, what streets she had traversed, as she roamed through that infamous Lourdes, that Lourdes which killed little children, that Lourdes which she cursed.

"Ah! I can't remember, I can't remember," she faltered. "But some people took me in, had pity upon me, some people whom I don't know, but who live somewhere. Ah! I can't remember where, but it was somewhere high up, far away, at the other end of the town. And they were certainly very poor folk, for I can still see myself in a poor-looking room with my dear little one who was quite cold, and whom they laid upon their bed."

At this recollection a fresh attack of sobbing shook her, in fact almost stifled her.

"No, no," she at last resumed, "I would not part with her dear little body by leaving it in that abominable town. And I can't tell exactly how it happened, but it must have been those poor people who took me with them. We did a great deal of walking, oh! a great deal of walking; we saw all those gentlemen of the pilgrimage and the railway. 'What can it matter to you?' I repeated to them. 'Let me take her back to Paris in my arms. I brought her here like that when she was alive, I may surely take her back dead? Nobody will notice anything, people will think that she is asleep.'"

"And all of them, all those officials, began shouting and driving me away as though I were asking them to let me do something wicked. Then I ended by telling them my mind. When people make so much fuss, and bring so many agonising sick to a place like that, they surely ought to send the dead ones home again, ought they not? And do you know how much money they ended by asking of me at the station? Three hundred francs! Yes, it appears it is the price! Three hundred francs, good Lord! of me, who came here with thirty sous in my pocket and have only five left. Why, I don't earn that amount of money by six months' sewing. They ought to have asked me for my life; I would have given it so willingly. Three hundred francs! three hundred francs for that poor little bird-like body, which it would have consoled me so much to have brought away on my knees!"

Then she began stammering and complaining in a confused, husky voice: "Ah, if you only knew how sensibly those poor people talked to me to induce me to go back. A work-woman like myself, with work waiting, ought to return to Paris, they said; and, besides, I couldn't afford to sacrifice my return ticket; I must take the three-forty train. And they told me, too, that people are compelled to put up with things when they are not rich. Only the rich can keep their dead, do what they like with them, eh? And I can't remember—no, again I can't remember! I didn't even know the time; I should never have been able to find my way back to the station. After the funeral over there, at a place where there were two trees, it must have been those poor people who led me away, half out of my senses, and brought me to the station, and pushed me into the carriage just at the moment when the train was starting. But what a rending it was—as if my heart had remained there underground, and it is frightful, that it is, frightful, my God!"

"Poor woman!" murmured Marie. "Take courage, and pray to the Blessed Virgin for the succour which she never refuses to the afflicted."

But at this Madame Vincent shook with rage. "It isn't true!" she cried. "The Blessed Virgin doesn't care a rap about me. She doesn't tell the truth! Why did she deceive me? I should never have gone to Lourdes if I hadn't heard that voice in a church. My little girl would still be alive, and perhaps the doctors would have saved her. I, who would never set my foot among the priests formerly! Ah! I was right! I was right! There's no Blessed Virgin at all!"

And in this wise, without resignation, without illusion, without hope, she continued blaspheming with the coarse fury of a woman of the people, shrieking the sufferings of her heart aloud in such rough fashion that Sister Hyacinthe had to intervene: "Be quiet, you unhappy woman! It is God who is making you suffer, to punish you."

The scene had already lasted a long time, and as they passed Riscle at full speed the Sister again clapped her hands and gave the signal for the chanting of the "Laudate Mariam." "Come, come, my children," she exclaimed, "all together, and with all your hearts:

"In heav'n, on earth,
All voices raise,
In concert sing
My Mother's praise:
Laudate, laudate, laudate Mariam!"

Madame Vincent, whose voice was drowned by this canticle of love, now only sobbed, with her hands pressed to her face. Her revolt was over, she was again strengthless, weak like a suffering woman whom grief and weariness have stupefied.

After the canticle, fatigue fell more or less heavily upon all the occupants of the carriage. Only Sister Hyacinthe, so quick and active, and Sister Claire des Anges, so gentle, serious, and slight, retained, as on their departure from Paris and during their sojourn at Lourdes, the professional serenity of women accustomed to everything, amidst the bright gaiety of their white coifs and wimples. Madame de Jonquiere, who had scarcely slept for five days past, had to make an effort to keep her poor eyes open; and yet she was delighted with the journey, for her heart was full of joy at having arranged her daughter's marriage, and at bringing back with her the greatest of all the miracles, a *miraculee* whom everybody was talking of. She decided in her own mind that she would get to sleep that night, however bad the jolting might be; though on the other hand she could not shake off a covert fear with regard to La Grivotte, who looked very strange, excited, and haggard, with dull eyes, and cheeks glowing with patches of violet colour. Madame de Jonquiere had tried a dozen times to keep her from fidgeting, but had not been able to induce her to remain still, with joined hands and closed eyes. Fortunately, the other patients gave her no anxiety; most of them were either so relieved or so weary that they were already dozing off. Elise Rouquet, however, had bought herself a pocket mirror, a large round one, in which she did not weary of contemplating herself, finding herself quite pretty, and verifying from minute to minute the progress of her cure with a coquetry which, now that her monstrous face was becoming human again, made her purse her lips and try a variety of smiles. As for Sophie Couteau, she was playing very prettily; for finding that nobody now asked to examine her foot, she had taken off her shoe and stocking of her own accord, repeating that she must surely have a pebble in one or the other of them; and as her companions still paid no attention to that little foot which the Blessed Virgin had been pleased to visit, she kept it in her hands, caressing it, seemingly delighted to touch it and turn it into a plaything.

M. de Guersaint had meantime risen from his seat, and, leaning on the low partition between the compartments, he was glancing at M. Sabathier, when all of a sudden Marie called: "Oh! father, father, look at this notch in the seat; it was the ironwork of my box that made it!"

The discovery of this trace rendered her so happy that for a moment she forgot the secret sorrow which she seemed anxious to keep to herself. And in the same way as Madame Vincent had burst out sobbing on perceiving the leather strap which her little girl had touched, so she burst into joy at the sight of this scratch, which reminded her of her long martyrdom in this same carriage, all the abomination which had now disappeared, vanished like a nightmare. "To think that four days have scarcely gone by," she said; "I was lying there, I could not stir, and now, now I come and go, and feel so comfortable!"

Pierre and M. de Guersaint were smiling at her; and M. Sabathier, who had heard her, slowly said: "It is quite true. We leave a little of ourselves in things, a little of our sufferings and our hopes, and when we find them again they speak to us, and once more tell us the things which sadden us or make us gay."

He had remained in his corner silent, with an air of resignation, ever since their departure from Lourdes. Even his wife whilst wrapping up his legs had only been able to obtain sundry shakes of the head from him in response to her inquiries whether he was suffering. In point of fact he was not suffering, but extreme dejection was overcoming him.

"Thus for my own part," he continued, "during our long journey from Paris I tried to divert my thoughts by counting the bands in the roofing up there. There were thirteen from the lamp to the door. Well, I have just been counting them again, and naturally enough there are still thirteen. It's like that brass knob beside me. You can't imagine what dreams I had whilst I watched it shining at night-time when Monsieur l'Abbe was reading the story of Bernadette to us. Yes, I saw myself cured; I was making that journey to Rome which I have been talking of for twenty years past; I walked and travelled the world—briefly, I had all manner of wild and delightful dreams. And now here we are on our way back to Paris, and there are thirteen bands across the roofing there, and the knob is still shining—all of which tells me that I am again on the same seat, with my legs lifeless. Well, well, it's understood, I'm a poor, old, used-up animal, and such I shall remain."

Two big tears appeared in his eyes; he must have been passing through an hour of frightful bitterness. However, he raised his big square head, with its jaw typical of patient obstinacy, and added: "This is the seventh year that I have been to Lourdes, and the Blessed Virgin has not listened to me. No matter! It won't prevent me from going back next year. Perhaps she will at last deign to hear me."

For his part he did not revolt. And Pierre, whilst chatting with him, was stupefied to find persistent, tenacious credulity springing up once more, in spite of everything, in the cultivated brain of this man of intellect. What ardent desire of cure and life was it that had led to this refusal to accept evidence, this determination to remain blind?

He stubbornly clung to the resolution to be saved when all human probabilities were against him, when the experiment of the miracle itself had failed so many times already; and he had reached such a point that he wished to explain his fresh rebuff, urging moments of inattention at the Grotto, a lack of sufficient contrition, and all sorts of little transgressions which must have displeased the Blessed Virgin. Moreover, he was already deciding in his mind that he would perform a novena somewhere next year, before again repairing to Lourdes.

"Ah! by the way," he resumed, "do you know of the good-luck which my substitute has had? Yes, you must remember my telling you about that poor fellow suffering from tuberculosis, for whom I paid fifty francs when I obtained *hospitalisation* for myself. Well, he has been thoroughly cured."

"Really! And he was suffering from tuberculosis!" exclaimed M. de Guersaint.

"Certainly, monsieur, perfectly cured I had seen him looking so low, so yellow, so emaciated, when we started; but when he came to pay me a visit at the hospital he was quite a new man; and, dear me, I gave him five francs."

Pierre had to restrain a smile, for be had heard the story from Doctor Chassaigne. This miraculously healed individual was a feigner, who had eventually been recognised at the Medical Verification Office. It was, apparently, the third year that he had presented himself there, the first time alleging paralysis and the second time a tumour, both of which had been as completely healed as his pretended tuberculosis. On each occasion he obtained an outing, lodging and food, and returned home loaded with alms. It appeared that he had formerly been a hospital nurse, and that he transformed himself, "made-up" a face suited to his pretended ailment, in such an extremely artistic manner that it was only by chance that Doctor Bonamy had detected the imposition. Moreover, the Fathers had immediately required that the incident should be kept secret. What was the use of stirring up a scandal which would only have led to jocular remarks in the newspapers? Whenever any fraudulent miracles of this kind were discovered, the Fathers contented themselves with forcing the guilty parties to go away. Moreover, these feigners were far from numerous, despite all that was related of them in the amusing stories concocted by Voltairean humourists. Apart from faith, human stupidity and ignorance, alas! were quite sufficient to account for the miracles.

M. Sabathier, however, was greatly stirred by the idea that Heaven had healed this man who had gone to Lourdes at his expense, whereas he himself was returning home still helpless, still in the same woeful state. He sighed, and, despite all his resignation, could not help saying, with a touch of envy: "What would you, however? The Blessed Virgin must know very well what she's about. Neither you nor I can call her to account to us for her actions. Whenever it may please her to cast her eyes on me she will find me at her feet."

After the "Angelus" when they got to Mont-de-Marsan, Sister Hyacinthe made them repeat the second chaplet, the five sorrowful mysteries, Jesus in the Garden of Olives, Jesus scourged, Jesus crowned with thorns, Jesus carrying the cross, and Jesus crucified. Then they took dinner in the carriage, for there would be no stopping until they reached Bordeaux, where they would only arrive at eleven o'clock at night. All the pilgrims' baskets were crammed with provisions, to say nothing of the milk, broth, chocolate, and fruit which Sister Saint-Francois had sent from the cantine. Then, too, there was fraternal sharing: they sat with their food on their laps and drew close together, every compartment becoming, as it were, the scene of a picnic, to which each contributed his share. And they had finished their meal and were packing up the remaining bread again when the train passed Morceux.

"My children," now said Sister Hyacinthe, rising up, "the evening prayer!"

Thereupon came a confused murmuring made up of "Paters" and "Aves," self-examinations, acts of contrition and vows of trustful reliance in God, the Blessed Virgin, and the Saints, with thanksgivings for that happy day, and, at last, a prayer for the living and for the faithful departed.

"I warn you," then resumed the Sister, "that when we get to Lamothe, at ten o'clock, I shall order silence. However, I think you will all be very good and won't require any rocking to get to sleep."

This made them laugh. It was now half-past eight o'clock, and the night had slowly covered the country-side. The hills alone retained a vague trace of the twilight's farewell, whilst a dense sheet of darkness blotted out all the low ground. Rushing on at full speed, the train entered an immense plain, and then there was nothing but a sea of darkness, through which they ever and ever rolled under a blackish sky, studded with stars.

For a moment or so Pierre had been astonished by the demeanour of La Grivotte. While the other pilgrims and patients were already dozing off, sinking down amidst the luggage, which the constant jolting shook, she had risen to her feet and was clinging to the partition in a sudden spasm of agony. And under the pale, yellow, dancing gleam of the lamp she once more looked emaciated, with a livid, tortured face.

"Take care, madame, she will fall!" the priest called to Madame de Jonquiere, who, with eyelids lowered, was at last giving way to sleep.

She made all haste to intervene, but Sister Hyacinthe had turned more quickly and caught La Grivotte in her arms. A frightful fit of coughing, however, prostrated the unhappy creature upon the seat, and for five minutes she continued stifling, shaken by such an attack that her poor body seemed to be actually cracking and rending. Then a red thread oozed from between her lips, and at last she spat up blood by the throatful.

"Good heavens! good heavens! it's coming on her again!" repeated Madame de Jonquiere in despair. "I had a fear of it; I was not at ease, seeing her looking so strange. Wait a moment; I will sit down beside her."

But the Sister would not consent: "No, no, madame, sleep a little. I'll watch over her. You are not accustomed to it: you would end by making yourself ill as well."

Then she settled herself beside La Grivotte, made her rest her head against her shoulder, and wiped the blood from her lips. The attack subsided, but weakness was coming back, so extreme that the wretched woman was scarcely able to stammer: "Oh, it is nothing, nothing at all; I am cured, I am cured, completely cured!"

Pierre was thoroughly upset: This sudden, overwhelming relapse had sent an icy chill through the whole carriage. Many of the passengers raised themselves up and looked at La Grivotte with terror in their eyes. Then they dived down into their corners again, and nobody spoke, nobody stirred any further. Pierre, for his part, reflected on the curious medical aspect of this girl's case. Her strength had come back to her over yonder. She had displayed a ravenous appetite, she had walked long distances with a dancing gait, her face quite radiant the while; and now she had spat blood, her cough had broken out afresh, she again had the heavy ashen face of one in the last agony. Her ailment had returned to her with brutal force, victorious over everything. Was this, then, some special case of phthisis complicated by neurosis? Or was it some other malady, some unknown disease, quietly continuing its work in the midst of contradictory diagnosis? The sea of error and ignorance, the darkness amidst which human science is still struggling, again appeared to Pierre. And he once more saw Doctor Chassaigne shrugging his shoulders with disdain, whilst Doctor Bonamy, full of serenity, quietly continued his verification work, absolutely convinced that nobody would be able to prove to him the impossibility of his miracles any more than he himself could have proved their possibility.

"Oh! I am not frightened," La Grivotte continued, stammering. "I am cured, completely cured; they all told me so, over yonder."

Meantime the carriage was rolling, rolling along, through the black night. Each of its occupants was making preparations, stretching himself out in order to sleep more comfortably. They compelled Madame Vincent to lie down on the seat, and gave her a pillow on which to rest her poor pain-racked head; and then, as docile as a child, quite stupefied, she fell asleep in a nightmare-like torpor, with big, silent tears still flowing from her closed eyes. Elise Rouquet, who had a whole seat to herself, was also getting ready to lie down, but first of all she made quite an elaborate toilet, tying the black wrap which had served to hide her sore about her head, and then again peering into her glass to see if this headgear became her, now that the swelling of her lip had subsided. And again did Pierre feel astonished at sight of that sore, which was certainly healing, if not already healed—that face, so lately a monster's face, which one could now look at without feeling horrified. The sea of incertitude stretched before him once more. Was it even a real lupus? Might it not rather be some unknown form of ulcer of hysterical origin? Or ought one to admit that certain forms of lupus, as yet but imperfectly studied and arising from faulty nutrition of the skin, might be benefited by a great moral shock? At all events there here seemed to be a miracle, unless, indeed, the sore should reappear again in three weeks', three months', or three years' time, like La Grivotte's phthisis.

It was ten o'clock, and the people in the carriage were falling asleep when they left Lamothe. Sister Hyacinthe, upon whose knees La Grivotte was now drowsily resting her head, was unable to rise, and, for form's sake, merely said, "Silence, silence, my children!" in a low voice, which died away amidst the growling rumble of the wheels.

However, something continued stirring in an adjoining compartment; she heard a noise which irritated her nerves, and the cause of which she at last fancied she could understand.

"Why do you keep on kicking the seat, Sophie?" she asked. "You must get to sleep, my child."

"I'm not kicking, Sister. It's a key that was rolling about under my foot."

"A key!—how is that? Pass it to me."

Then she examined it. A very old, poor-looking key it was—blackened, worn away, and polished by long use, its ring bearing the mark of where it had been broken and resoldered. However, they all searched their pockets, and none of them, it seemed, had lost a key.

"I found it in the corner," now resumed Sophie; "it must have belonged to the man."

"What man?" asked Sister Hyacinthe.

"The man who died there."

They had already forgotten him. But it had surely been his, for Sister Hyacinthe recollected that she had heard something fall while she was wiping his forehead. And she turned the key over and continued looking at it, as it lay in her hand, poor, ugly, wretched key that it was, no longer of any use, never again to open the lock it belonged to—some unknown lock, hidden far away in the depths of the world. For a moment she was minded to put it in her pocket, as though by a kind of compassion for this little bit of iron, so humble and so mysterious, since it was all that remained of that unknown man. But then the pious thought came to her that it is wrong to show attachment to any earthly thing; and, the window being half-lowered, she threw out the key, which fell into the black night.

"You must not play any more, Sophie," she resumed. "Come, come, my children, silence!"

It was only after the brief stay at Bordeaux, however, at about half-past eleven o'clock, that sleep came back again and overpowered all in the carriage. Madame de Jonquiere had been unable to contend against it any longer, and her head was now resting against the partition, her face wearing an expression of happiness amidst all her fatigue. The Sabathiers were, in a like fashion, calmly sleeping; and not a sound now came from the compartment which Sophie Couteau and Elise Rouquet occupied, stretched in front of each other, on the seats. From time to time a low plaint would rise, a strangled cry of grief or fright, escaping from the lips of Madame Vincent, who, amidst her prostration, was being tortured by evil dreams. Sister Hyacinthe was one of the very few who still had their eyes open, anxious as she was respecting La Grivotte, who now lay quite motionless, like a felled animal, breathing painfully, with a continuous wheezing sound. From one to the other end of this travelling dormitory, shaken by the rumbling of the train rolling on at full speed, the pilgrims and the sick surrendered themselves to sleep, and limbs dangled and heads swayed under the pale, dancing gleams from the lamps. At the far end, in the compartment occupied by the ten female pilgrims, there was a woeful jumbling of poor, ugly faces, old and young, and all open-mouthed, as though sleep had suddenly fallen upon them at the moment they were finishing some hymn. Great pity came to the heart at the sight of all those mournful, weary beings, prostrated by five days of wild hope and infinite ecstasy, and destined to awaken, on the very morrow, to the stern realities of life.

And now Pierre once more felt himself to be alone with Marie. She had not consented to stretch herself on the seat—she had been lying down too long, she said, for seven years, alas! And in order that M. de Guersaint, who on leaving Bordeaux had again fallen into his childlike slumber, might be more at ease, Pierre came and sat down beside the girl. As the light of the lamp annoyed her he drew the little screen, and they thus found themselves in the shade, a soft and transparent shade. The train must now have been crossing a plain, for it glided through the night as in an endless flight, with a sound like the regular flapping of huge wings. Through the window, which they had opened, a delicious coolness came from the black fields, the fathomless fields, where not even any lonely little village lights could be seen gleaming. For a moment Pierre had turned towards Marie and had noticed that her eyes were closed. But he could divine that she was not sleeping, that she was savouring the deep peacefulness which prevailed around them amidst the thundering roar of their rush through the darkness, and, like her, he closed his eyelids and began dreaming.

IV. MARIE'S VOW

Yet once again did the past arise before him: the little house at Neuilly, the embrace which they had exchanged near the flowering hedge under the trees flecked with sunlight. How far away all that already was, and with what perfume had it not filled his life! Then bitter thoughts returned to him at the memory of the day when he had become a priest. Since she would never be a woman, he had consented to be a man no more; and that was to prove their eternal misfortune, for ironical Nature was to make her a wife and a mother after all. Had he only been able to retain his faith he might have found eternal consolation in it. But all his attempts to regain it had been in vain. He had gone to Lourdes, he had striven his utmost at the Grotto, he had hoped for a moment that he would end by believing should Marie be miraculously healed; but total and irremediable ruin had come when the predicted cure had taken place even as science had foretold. And their idyl, so pure and so painful, the long story of their affection bathed in tears, likewise spread out before him. She, having penetrated his sad secret, had come to Lourdes to pray to Heaven for the miracle of his conversion. When they had remained alone under the trees amidst the perfume of the invisible roses, during the night procession, they had prayed one for the other, mingling one in the other, with an ardent desire for their mutual happiness. Before the Grotto, too, she had entreated the Blessed Virgin to forget her and to save him, if she could obtain but one favour from her Divine Son. Then, healed, beside herself, transported with love and gratitude, whirled with her little car up the inclined ways to the Basilica, she had thought her prayers granted, and had cried aloud the joy she felt that they should have both been saved, together, together! Ah! that lie which he, prompted by affection and charity, had told, that error in which he had from that moment suffered her to remain, with what a weight did it oppress his heart! It was the heavy slab which walled him in his voluntarily chosen sepulchre. He remembered the frightful attack of grief which had almost killed him in the gloom of the crypt, his sobs, his brutal revolt, his longing to keep her for himself alone, to possess her since he knew her to be his own—all that rising passion of his awakened manhood, which little by little had fallen asleep again, drowned by the rushing river of his tears; and in order that he might not destroy the divine illusion which possessed her, yielding to brotherly compassion, he had taken that heroic vow to lie to her, that vow which now filled him with such anguish.

Pierre shuddered amidst his reverie. Would he have the strength to keep that vow forever? Had he not detected a feeling of impatience in his heart even whilst he was waiting for her at the railway station, a jealous longing to leave that Lourdes which she loved too well, in the vague hope that she might again become his own, somewhere far away? If he had not been a priest he would have married her. And what rapture, what felicity would then have been his! He would have given himself wholly unto her, she would have been wholly his own, and he and she would have lived again in the dear child that would doubtless have been born to them. Ah! surely that alone was divine, the life which is complete, the life which creates life! And then his reverie strayed: he pictured himself married, and the thought filled him with such delight that he asked why such a dream should be unrealisable? She knew no more than a child of ten; he would educate her, form her mind. She would then understand that this cure for which she thought herself indebted to the Blessed Virgin, had in reality come to her from the Only Mother, serene and impassive Nature. But even whilst he was thus settling things in his mind, a kind of terror, born of his religious education, arose within him. Could he tell if that human happiness with which he desired to endow her would ever be worth as much as the holy ignorance, the infantile candour in which she now lived? How bitterly he would reproach himself afterwards if she should not be happy. Then, too, what a drama it would all be; he to throw off the cassock, and marry this girl healed by an alleged miracle—ravage her faith sufficiently to induce her to consent to such sacrilege? Yet therein lay the brave course; there lay reason, life, real manhood, real womanhood. Why, then, did he not dare? Horrible sadness was breaking upon his reverie, he became conscious of nothing beyond the sufferings of his poor heart.

The train was still rolling along with its great noise of flapping wings. Beside Pierre and Marie, only Sister Hyacinthe was still awake amidst the weary slumber of the carriage; and just then, Marie leant towards Pierre, and softly said to him: "It's strange, my friend; I am so sleepy, and yet I can't sleep." Then, with alight laugh, she added: "I've got Paris in my head!"

"How is that—Paris?"

"Yes, yes. I'm thinking that it's waiting for me, that I am about to return to it—that Paris which I know nothing of, and where I shall have to live!"

These words brought fresh anguish to Pierre's heart. He had well foreseen it; she could no longer belong to him, she would belong to others. If Lourdes had restored her to him, Paris was about to take her from him again. And he pictured this ignorant little being fatally acquiring all the education of woman. That little spotless soul which had remained so candid in the frame of a big girl of three-and-twenty, that soul which illness had kept apart from others, far from life, far even from novels, would soon ripen, now that it could fly freely once more. He beheld her, a gay, healthy young girl, running everywhere, looking and learning, and, some day, meeting the husband who would finish her education.

"And so," said he, "you propose to amuse yourself in Paris?"

"Oh! what are you saying, my friend? Are we rich enough to amuse ourselves?" she replied. "No, I was thinking of my poor sister Blanche, and wondering what I should be able to do in Paris to help her a little. She is so good, she works so hard; I don't wish that she should have to continue earning all the money."

And, after a fresh pause, as he, deeply moved, remained silent, she added: "Formerly, before I suffered so dreadfully, I painted miniatures rather nicely. You remember, don't you, that I painted a portrait of papa which was very like him, and which everybody praised. You will help me, won't you? You will find me customers?"

Then she began talking of the new life which she was about to live. She wanted to arrange her room and hang it with cretonne, something pretty, with a pattern of little blue flowers. She would buy it out of the first money she could save. Blanche had spoken to her of the big shops where things could be bought so cheaply. To go out with Blanche and run about a little would be so amusing for her, who, confined to her bed since childhood, had never seen anything. Then Pierre, who for a moment had been calmer, again began to suffer, for he could divine all her glowing desire to live, her ardour to see everything, know everything, and taste everything. It was at last the awakening of the woman whom she was destined to be, whom he had divined in childhood's days—a dear creature of gaiety and passion, with blooming lips, starry eyes, a milky complexion, golden hair, all resplendent with the joy of being.

"Oh! I shall work, I shall work," she resumed; "but you are right, Pierre, I shall also amuse myself, because it cannot be a sin to be gay, can it?"

"No, surely not, Marie."

"On Sundays we will go into the country, oh very far away, into the woods where there are beautiful trees. And we will sometimes go to the theatre, too, if papa will take us. I have been told that there are many plays that one may see. But, after all, it's not all that. Provided I can go out and walk in the streets and see things, I shall be so happy; I shall come home so gay. It is so nice to live, is it not, Pierre?"

"Yes, yes, Marie, it is very nice."

A chill like that of death was coming over him; his regret that he was no longer a man was filling him with agony. But since she tempted him like this with her irritating candour, why should he not confess to her the truth which was ravaging his being? He would have won her, have conquered her. Never had a more frightful struggle arisen between his heart and his will. For a moment he was on the point of uttering irrevocable words.

But with the voice of a joyous child she was already resuming: "Oh! look at poor papa; how pleased he must be to sleep so soundly!"

On the seat in front of them M. de Guersaint was indeed slumbering with a comfortable expression on his face, as though he were in his bed, and had no consciousness of the continual jolting of the train. This monotonous rolling and heaving seemed, in fact, a lullaby rocking the whole carriage to sleep. All surrendered themselves to it, sinking powerless on to the piles of bags and parcels, many of which had also fallen; and the rhythmical growling of the wheels never ceased in the unknown darkness through which the train was still rolling. Now and again, as they passed through a station or under a bridge, there would be a loud rush of wind, a tempest would suddenly sweep by; and then the lulling, growling sound would begin again, ever the same for hours together.

Marie gently took hold of Pierre's hands; he and she were so lost, so completely alone among all those prostrated beings, in the deep, rumbling peacefulness of the train flying across the black night. And sadness, the sadness which she had hitherto hidden, had again come back to her, casting a shadow over her large blue eyes.

"You will often come with us, my good Pierre, won't you?" she asked.

He had started on feeling her little hand pressing his own. His heart was on his lips, he was making up his mind to speak. However, he once again restrained himself and stammered: "I am not always at liberty, Marie; a priest cannot go everywhere."

"A priest?" she repeated. "Yes, yes, a priest. I understand."

Then it was she who spoke, who confessed the mortal secret which had been oppressing her heart ever since they had started. She leant nearer, and in a lower voice resumed: "Listen, my good Pierre; I am fearfully sad. I may look pleased, but there is death in my soul. You did not tell me the truth yesterday."

He became quite scared, but did not at first understand her. "I did not tell you the truth—About what?" he asked.

A kind of shame restrained her, and she again hesitated at the moment of descending into the depths of another conscience than her own. Then, like a friend, a sister, she continued: "No, you let me believe that you had been saved with me, and it was not true, Pierre, you have not found your lost faith again."

Good Lord! she knew. For him this was desolation, such a catastrophe that he forgot his torments. And, at first, he obstinately clung to the falsehood born of his fraternal charity. "But I assure you, Marie. How can you have formed such a wicked idea?"

"Oh! be quiet, my friend, for pity's sake. It would grieve me too deeply if you were to speak to me falsely again. It was yonder, at the station, at the moment when we were starting, and that unhappy man had died. Good Abbe Judaine had knelt down to pray for the repose of that rebellious soul. And I divined everything, I understood everything when I saw that you did not kneel as well, that prayer did not rise to your lips as to his."

"But, really, I assure you, Marie—"

"No, no, you did not pray for the dead; you no longer believe. And besides, there is something else; something I can guess, something which comes to me from you, a despair which you can't hide from me, a melancholy look which comes into your poor eyes directly they meet mine. The Blessed Virgin did not grant my prayer, she did not restore your faith, and I am very, very wretched."

She was weeping, a hot tear fell upon the priest's hand, which she was still holding. It quite upset him, and he ceased struggling, confessing, in his turn letting his tears flow, whilst, in a very low voice, he stammered: "Ah! Marie, I am very wretched also. Oh! so very wretched."

For a moment they remained silent, in their cruel grief at feeling that the abyss which parts different beliefs was yawning between them. They would never belong to one another again, and they were in despair at being so utterly unable to bring themselves nearer to one another; but the severance was henceforth definitive, since Heaven itself had been unable to reconnect the bond. And thus, side by side, they wept over their separation.

"I who prayed so fervently for your conversion," she said in a dolorous voice, "I who was so happy. It had seemed to me that your soul was mingling with mine; and it was so delightful to have been saved together, together. I felt such strength for life; oh, strength enough to raise the world!"

He did not answer; his tears were still flowing, flowing without end.

"And to think," she resumed, "that I was saved all alone; that this great happiness fell upon me without you having any share in it. And to see you so forsaken, so desolate, when I am loaded with grace and joy, rends my heart. Ah! how severe the Blessed Virgin has been! Why did she not heal your soul at the same time that she healed my body?"

The last opportunity was presenting itself; he ought to have illumined this innocent creature's mind with the light of reason, have explained the miracle to her, in order that life, after accomplishing its healthful work in her body, might complete its triumph by throwing them into one another's arms. He also was healed, his mind was healthy now, and it was not for the loss of faith, but for the loss of herself, that he was weeping. However, invincible compassion was taking possession of him amidst all his grief. No, no, he would not trouble that dear soul; he would not rob her of her belief, which some day might prove her only stay amidst the sorrows of this world. One cannot yet require of children and women the bitter heroism of reason. He had not the strength to do it; he even thought that he had not the right. It would have seemed to him violation, abominable murder. And he did not speak out, but his tears flowed, hotter and hotter, in this immolation of his love, this despairing sacrifice of his own happiness in order that she might remain candid and ignorant and gay at heart.

"Oh, Marie, how wretched I am! Nowhere on the roads, nowhere at the galleys even, is there a man more wretched than myself! Oh, Marie, if you only knew; if you only knew how wretched I am!"

She was distracted, and caught him in her trembling arms, wishing to console him with a sisterly embrace. And at that moment the woman awaking within her understood everything, and she herself sobbed with sorrow that both human and divine will should thus part them. She had never yet reflected on such things, but suddenly she caught a glimpse of life, with its passions, its struggles, and its sufferings; and then, seeking for what she might say to soothe in some degree that broken heart, she stammered very faintly, distressed that she could find nothing sweet enough, "I know, I know—"

Then the words it was needful she should speak came to her; and as though that which she had to say ought only to be heard by the angels, she became anxious and looked around her. But the slumber which reigned in the carriage seemed more heavy even than before. Her father was still sleeping, with the innocent look of a big child. Not one of the pilgrims, not one of the ailing ones, had stirred amidst the rough rocking which bore them onward. Even Sister Hyacinthe, giving way to her overpowering weariness, had just closed her eyes, after drawing the lamp-screen in her own compartment. And now there were only vague shadows there, ill-defined bodies amidst nameless things, ghostly forms scarce visible, which a tempest blast, a furious rush, was carrying on and on through the darkness. And she likewise distrusted that black country-side whose unknown depths went by on either side of the train without one even being able to tell what forests, what rivers, what hills one was crossing. A short time back some bright sparks of light had appeared, possibly the lights of some distant forges, or the woeful lamps of workers or sufferers. Now, however, the night again streamed deeply all around, the obscure, infinite, nameless sea, farther and farther through which they ever went, not knowing where they were.

Then, with a chaste confusion, blushing amidst her tears, Marie placed her lips near Pierre's ear. "Listen, my friend; there is a great secret between the Blessed Virgin and myself. I had sworn that I would never tell it to anybody. But you are too unhappy, you are suffering too bitterly; she will forgive me; I will confide it to you."

And in a faint breath she went on: "During that night of love, you know, that night of burning ecstasy which I spent before the Grotto, I engaged myself by a vow: I promised the Blessed Virgin the gift of my chastity if she would but heal me.... She has healed me, and never—you hear me, Pierre, never will I marry anybody."

Ah! what unhoped-for sweetness! He thought that a balmy dew was falling on his poor wounded heart. It was a divine enchantment, a delicious relief. If she belonged to none other she would always be a little bit his own. And how well she had known his torment and what it was needful she should say in order that life might yet be possible for him.

In his turn he wished to find happy words and promise that he also would ever be hers, ever love her as he had loved her since childhood, like the dear creature she was, whose one kiss, long, long ago, had sufficed to perfume his entire life. But she made him stop, already anxious, fearing to spoil that pure moment. "No, no, my friend," she murmured, "let us say nothing more; it would be wrong, perhaps. I am very weary; I shall sleep quietly now."

And, with her head against his shoulder, she fell asleep at once, like a sister who is all confidence. He for a moment kept himself awake in that painful happiness of renunciation which they had just tasted together. It was all over, quite over now; the sacrifice was consummated. He would live a solitary life, apart from the life of other men. Never would he know woman, never would any child be born to him. And there remained to him only the consoling pride of that accepted and desired suicide, with the desolate grandeur that attaches to lives which are beyond the pale of nature.

But fatigue overpowered him also; his eyes closed, and in his turn he fell asleep. And afterwards his head slipped down, and his cheek touched the cheek of his dear friend, who was sleeping very gently with her brow against his shoulder. Then their hair mingled. She had her golden hair, her royal hair, half unbound, and it streamed over his face, and he dreamed amidst its perfume. Doubtless the same blissful dream fell upon them both, for their loving faces assumed the same expression of rapture; they both seemed to be smiling to the angels. It was chaste and passionate abandon, the innocence of chance slumber placing them in one another's arms, with warm, close lips so that their breath mingled, like the breath of two babes lying in the same cradle. And such was their bridal night, the consummation of the spiritual marriage in which they were to live, a delicious annihilation born of extreme fatigue, with scarcely a fleeting dream of mystical possession, amidst that carriage of wretchedness and suffering, which still and ever rolled along through the dense night. Hours and hours slipped by, the wheels growled, the bags and baskets swung from the brass hooks, whilst from the piled-up, crushed bodies there only arose a sense of terrible fatigue, the great physical exhaustion brought back from the land of miracles when the overworked souls returned home.

At last, at five o'clock, whilst the sun was rising, there was a sudden awakening, a resounding entry into a large station, with porters calling, doors opening, and people scrambling together. They were at Poitiers, and at once the whole carriage was on foot, amidst a chorus of laughter and exclamations. Little Sophie Couteau alighted here, and was bidding everybody farewell. She embraced all the ladies, even passing over the partition to take leave of Sister Claire des Anges, whom nobody had seen since the previous evening, for, silent and slight of build, with eyes full of mystery, she had vanished into her corner. Then the child came back again, took her little parcel, and showed herself particularly amiable towards Sister Hyacinthe and Madame de Jonquiere.

"*Au revoir*, Sister! *Au revoir*, madame! I thank you for all your kindness."

"You must come back again next year, my child."

"Oh, I sha'n't fail, Sister; it's my duty."

"And be good, my dear child, and take care of your health, so that the Blessed Virgin may be proud of you."

"To be sure, madame, she was so good to me, and it amuses me so much to go to see her."

When she was on the platform, all the pilgrims in the carriage leaned out, and with happy faces watched her go off.

"Till next year!" they called to her; "till next year!"

"Yes, yes, thank you kindly. Till next year."

IV. MARIE'S VOW

The morning prayer was only to be said at Chatelherault. After the stoppage at Poitiers, when the train was once more rolling on in the fresh breeze of morning, M. de Guersaint gaily declared that he had slept delightfully, in spite of the hardness of the seat. Madame de Jonquiere also congratulated herself on the good rest which she had had, and of which she had been in so much need; though, at the same time, she was somewhat annoyed at having left Sister Hyacinthe all alone to watch over La Grivotte, who was now shivering with intense fever, again attacked by her horrible cough. Meanwhile the other female pilgrims were tidying themselves. The ten women at the far end were fastening their *fichus* and tying their cap strings, with a kind of modest nervousness displayed on their mournfully ugly faces. And Elise Rouquet, all attention, with her face close to her pocket glass, did not cease examining her nose, mouth, and cheeks, admiring herself with the thought that she was really and truly becoming nice-looking.

And it was then that Pierre and Marie again experienced a feeling of deep compassion on glancing at Madame Vincent, whom nothing had been able to rouse from a state of torpor, neither the tumultuous stoppage at Poitiers, nor the noise of voices which had continued ever since they had started off again. Prostrate on the seat, she had not opened her eyes, but still and ever slumbered, tortured by atrocious dreams. And, with big tears still streaming from her closed eyes, she had caught hold of the pillow which had been forced upon her, and was closely pressing it to her breast in some nightmare born of her suffering. Her poor arms, which had so long carried her dying daughter, her arms now unoccupied, forever empty, had found this cushion whilst she slept, and had coiled around them, as around a phantom, with a blind and frantic embrace.

On the other hand, M. Sabathier had woke up feeling quite joyous. Whilst his wife was pulling up his rug, carefully wrapping it round his lifeless legs; he began to chat with sparkling eyes, once more basking in illusion. He had dreamt of Lourdes, said he, and had seen the Blessed Virgin leaning towards him with a smile of kindly promise. And then, although he had before him both Madame Vincent, that mother whose daughter the Virgin had allowed to die, and La Grivotte, the wretched woman whom she had healed and who had so cruelly relapsed into her mortal disease, he nevertheless rejoiced and made merry, repeating to M. de Guersaint, with an air of perfect conviction: "Oh! I shall return home quite easy in mind, monsieur—I shall be cured next year. Yes, yes, as that dear little girl said just now: 'Till next year, till next year!'"

It was indestructible illusion, victorious even over certainty, eternal hope determined not to die, but shooting up with more life than ever, after each defeat, upon the ruins of everything.

At Chatelherault, Sister Hyacinthe made them say the morning prayer, the "Pater," the "Ave," the "Credo," and an appeal to God begging Him for the happiness of a glorious day: "O God, grant me sufficient strength that I may avoid all that is evil, do all that is good, and suffer without complaint every pain."

V. THE DEATH OP BERNADETTE—THE NEW RELIGION

AND the journey continued; the train rolled, still rolled along. At Sainte-Maure the prayers of the mass were said, and at Sainte-Pierre-des-Corps the "Credo" was chanted. However, the religious exercises no longer proved so welcome; the pilgrims' zeal was flagging somewhat in the increasing fatigue of their return journey, after such prolonged mental excitement. It occurred to Sister Hyacinthe that the happiest way of entertaining these poor worn-out folks would be for someone to read aloud; and she promised that she would allow Monsieur l'Abbe to read them the finish of Bernadette's life, some of the marvellous episodes of which he had already on two occasions related to them. However, they must wait until they arrived at Les Aubrais; there would be nearly two hours between Les Aubrais and Etampes, ample time to finish the story without being disturbed.

Then the various religious exercises followed one after the other, in a monotonous repetition of the order which had been observed whilst they crossed the same plains on their way to Lourdes. They again began the Rosary at Amboise, where they said the first chaplet, the five joyful mysteries; then, after singing the canticle, "O loving Mother, bless," at Blois, they recited the second chaplet, the five sorrowful mysteries, at Beaugency. Some little fleecy clouds had veiled the sun since morning, and the landscapes, very sweet and somewhat sad, flew by with a continuous fan-like motion. The trees and houses on either side of the line disappeared in the grey light with the fleetness of vague visions, whilst the distant hills, enveloped in mist, vanished more slowly, with the gentle rise and fall of a swelling sea. Between Beaugency and Les Aubrais the train seemed to slacken speed, though it still kept up its rhythmical, persistent rumbling, which the deafened pilgrims no longer even heard.

At length, when Les Aubrais had been left behind, they began to lunch in the carriage. It was then a quarter to twelve, and when they had said the "Angelus," and the three "Aves" had been thrice repeated, Pierre took from Marie's bag the little book whose blue cover was ornamented with an artless picture of Our Lady of Lourdes. Sister Hyacinthe clapped her hands as a signal for silence, and amidst general wakefulness and ardent curiosity like that of big children impassioned by the marvellous story, the priest was able to begin reading in his fine, penetrating voice. Now came the narrative of Bernadette's sojourn at Nevers, and then her death there. Pierre, however, as on the two previous occasions, soon ceased following the exact text of the little book, and added charming anecdotes of his own, both what he knew and what he could divine; and, for himself alone, he again evolved the true story, the human, pitiful story, that which none had ever told, but which he felt so deeply.

It was on the 8th July, 1866, that Bernadette left Lourdes. She went to take the veil at Nevers, in the convent of Saint-Gildard, the chief habitation of the Sisters on duty at the Asylum where she had learnt to read and had been living for eight years. She was then twenty-two years of age, and it was eight years since the Blessed Virgin had appeared to her. And her farewells to the Grotto, to the Basilica, to the whole town which she loved, were watered with tears. But she could no longer remain there, owing to the continuous persecution of public curiosity, the visits, the homage, and the adoration paid to her, from which, on account of her delicate health, she suffered cruelly. Her sincere humility, her timid love of shade and silence, had at last produced in her an ardent desire to disappear, to hide her resounding glory—the glory of one whom heaven had chosen and whom the world would not leave in peace—in the depth of some unknown darkness; and she longed only for simple-mindedness, for a quiet humdrum life devoted to prayer and petty daily occupations. Her departure was therefore a relief both to her and to the Grotto, which she was beginning to embarrass with her excessive innocence and burdensome complaints.

At Nevers, Saint-Gildard ought to have proved a paradise. She there found fresh air, sunshine, spacious apartments, and an extensive garden planted with fine trees. Yet she did not enjoy peace,—that utter forgetfulness of the world for which one flees to the far-away desert. Scarcely twenty days after her arrival, she donned the garb of the Order and assumed the name of Sister Marie-Bernard, for the time simply engaging herself by partial vows. However, the world still flocked around her, the persecution of the multitude began afresh. She was pursued even into the cloister through an irresistible desire to obtain favours from her saintly person. Ah! to see her, touch her, become lucky by gazing on her or surreptitiously rubbing some medal against her dress. It was the credulous passion of fetishism, a rush of believers pursuing this poor beatified being in the desire which each felt to secure a share of hope and divine illusion. She wept at it with very weariness, with impatient revolt, and often repeated: "Why do they torment me like this? What more is there in me than in others?" And at last she felt real grief at thus becoming "the raree-show," as she ended by calling herself with a sad, suffering smile. She defended herself as far as she could, refusing to see anyone. Her companions defended her also, and sometimes very sternly, showing her only to such visitors as were authorised by the Bishop. The doors of the Convent remained closed, and ecclesiastics almost alone succeeded in effecting an entrance. Still, even this was too much for her desire for solitude, and she often had to be obstinate, to request that the priests who had called might be sent away, weary as she was of always telling the same story, of ever answering the same questions. She was incensed, wounded, on behalf of the Blessed Virgin herself. Still, she sometimes had to yield, for the Bishop in person would bring great personages, dignitaries, and prelates; and she would then appear with her grave air, answering politely and as briefly as possible; only feeling at ease when she was allowed to return to her shadowy corner. Never, indeed, had distinction weighed more heavily on a mortal. One day, when she was asked if she was not proud of the continual visits paid her by the Bishop, she answered simply: "Monseigneur does not come to see me, he comes to show me." On another occasion some princes of the Church, great militant Catholics, who wished to see her, were overcome with emotion and sobbed before her; but, in her horror of being shown, in the vexation they caused her simple mind, she left them without comprehending, merely feeling very weary and very sad.

At length, however, she grew accustomed to Saint-Gildard, and spent a peaceful existence there, engaged in avocations of which she became very fond. She was so delicate, so frequently ill, that she was employed in the infirmary. In addition to the little assistance she rendered there, she worked with her needle, with which she became rather skilful, embroidering albs and altar-cloths in a delicate manner. But at times she, would lose all strength, and be unable to do even this light work. When she was not confined to her bed she spent long days in an easy-chair, her only diversion being to recite her rosary or to read some pious work. Now that she had learnt to read, books interested her, especially the beautiful stories of conversion, the delightful legends in which saints of both sexes appear, and the splendid and terrible dramas in which the devil is baffled and cast back into hell. But her great favourite, the book at which she continually marvelled, was the Bible, that wonderful New Testament of whose perpetual miracle she never wearied. She remembered the Bible at Bartres, that old book which had been in the family a hundred years, and whose pages had turned yellow; she could again see her foster-father slip a pin between the leaves to open the book at random, and then read aloud from the top of the right-hand page; and even at that time she had already known those beautiful stories so well that she could have continued repeating the narrative by heart, whatever might be the passage at which the perusal had ceased. And now that she read the book herself, she found in it a constant source of surprise, an ever-increasing delight. The story of the Passion particularly upset her, as though it were some extraordinary tragical event that had happened only the day before. She sobbed with pity; it made her poor suffering body quiver for hours. Mingled with her tears, perhaps, there was the unconscious dolour of her own passion, the desolate Calvary which she also had been ascending ever since her childhood.

When Bernadette was well and able to perform her duties in the infirmary, she bustled about, filling the building with childish liveliness. Until her death she remained an innocent, infantile being, fond of laughing, romping, and play. She was very little, the smallest Sister of the community, so that her companions always treated her somewhat like a child. Her face grew long and hollow, and lost its bloom of youth; but she retained the pure divine brightness of her eyes, the beautiful eyes of a visionary, in which, as in a limpid sky, you detected the flight of her dreams. As she grew older and her sufferings increased, she became somewhat sour-tempered and violent, cross-grained, anxious, and at times rough; little imperfections which after each attack filled her with remorse. She would humble herself, think herself damned, and beg pardon of everyone. But, more frequently, what a good little daughter of Providence she was! She became lively, alert, quick at repartee, full of mirth-provoking remarks, with a grace quite her own, which made her beloved. In spite of her great devotion, although she spent days in prayer, she was not at all bigoted or over-exacting with regard to others, but tolerant and compassionate. In fact, no nun was ever so much a woman, with distinct features, a decided personality, charming even in its puerility. And this gift of childishness which she had retained, the simple innocence of the child she still was, also made children love her, as though they recognised in her one of themselves. They all ran to her, jumped upon her lap, and passed their tiny arms round her neck, and the garden would then fill with the noise of joyous games, races, and cries; and it was not she who ran or cried the least, so happy was she at once more feeling herself a poor unknown little girl as in the far-away days of Bartres! Later on it was related that a mother had one day brought her paralysed child to the convent for the saint to touch and cure it. The woman sobbed so much that the Superior ended by consenting to make the attempt. However, as Bernadette indignantly protested whenever she was asked to perform a miracle, she was not forewarned, but simply called to take the sick child to the infirmary. And she did so, and when she stood the child on the ground it walked. It was cured.

Ah! how many times must Bartres and her free childhood spent watching her lambs—the years passed among the hills, in the long grass, in the leafy woods—have returned to her during the hours she gave to her dreams when weary of praying for sinners! No one then fathomed her soul, no one could say if involuntary regrets did not rend her wounded heart. One day she spoke some words, which her historians have preserved, with the view of making her passion more touching. Cloistered far away from her mountains, confined to a bed of sickness, she exclaimed: "It seems to me that I was made to live, to act, to be ever on the move, and yet the Lord will have me remain motionless." What a revelation, full of terrible testimony and immense sadness! Why should the Lord wish that dear being, all grace and gaiety, to remain motionless? Could she not have honoured Him equally well by living the free, healthy life that she had been born to live? And would she not have done more to increase the world's happiness and her own if, instead of praying for sinners, her constant occupation, she had given her love to the husband who might have been united to her and to the children who might have been born to her? She, so gay and so active, would, on certain evenings, become extremely depressed. She turned gloomy and remained wrapped in herself, as though overcome by excess of pain. No doubt the cup was becoming too bitter. The thought of her life's perpetual renunciation was killing her.

Did Bernadette often think of Lourdes whilst she was at Saint-Gildard? What knew she of the triumph of the Grotto, of the prodigies which were daily transforming the land of miracles? These questions were never thoroughly elucidated. Her companions were forbidden to talk to her of such matters, which remained enveloped in absolute, continual silence. She herself did not care to speak of them; she kept silent with regard to the mysterious past, and evinced no desire to know the present, however triumphant it might be. But all the same did not her heart, in imagination, fly away to the enchanted country of her childhood, where lived her kith and kin, where all her life-ties had been formed, where she had left the most extraordinary dream that ever human being dreamt? Surely she must have sometimes travelled the beautiful journey of memory, she must have known the main features of the great events that had taken place at Lourdes. What she most dreaded was to go there herself, and, she always refused to do so, knowing full well that she could not remain unrecognised, and fearful of meeting the crowds whose adoration awaited her. What glory would have been hers had she been headstrong, ambitious, domineering! She would have returned to the holy spot of her visions, have worked miracles there, have become a priestess, a female pope, with the infallibility and sovereignty of one of the elect, a friend of the Blessed Virgin. But the Fathers never really feared this, although express orders had been given to withdraw her from the world for her salvation's sake. In reality they were easy, for they knew her, so gentle and so humble in her fear of becoming divine, in her ignorance of the colossal machine which she had put in motion, and the working of which would have made her recoil with affright had she understood it. No, no! that was no longer her land, that place of crowds, of violence and trafficking. She would have suffered too much there, she would have been out of her element, bewildered, ashamed. And so, when pilgrims bound thither asked her with a smile, "Will you come with us?" she shivered slightly, and then hastily replied, "No, no! but how I should like to, were I a little bird!"

Her reverie alone was that little travelling bird, with rapid flight and noiseless wings, which continually went on pilgrimage to the Grotto. In her dreams, indeed, she must have continually lived at Lourdes, though in the flesh she had not even gone there for either her father's or her mother's funeral. Yet she loved her kin; she was anxious to procure work for her relations who had remained poor, and she had insisted on seeing her eldest brother, who, coming to Nevers to complain, had been refused admission to the convent. However, he found her weary and resigned, and she did not ask him a single question about New Lourdes, as though that rising town were no longer her own. The year of the crowning of the Virgin, a priest whom she had deputed to pray for her before the Grotto came back and told her of the never-to-be forgotten wonders of the ceremony, the hundred thousand pilgrims who had flocked to it, and the five-and-thirty bishops in golden vestments who had assembled in the resplendent Basilica. Whilst listening, she trembled with her customary little quiver of desire and anxiety. And when the priest exclaimed, "Ah! if you had only seen that pomp!" she answered: "Me! I was much better here in my little corner in the infirmary." They had robbed her of her glory; her work shone forth resplendently amidst a continuous hosanna, and she only tasted joy in forgetfulness, in the gloom of the cloister, where the opulent farmers of the Grotto forgot her. It was never the re-echoing solemnities that prompted her mysterious journeys; the little bird of her soul only winged its lonesome flight to Lourdes on days of solitude, in the peaceful hours when no one could there disturb its devotions. It was before the wild primitive Grotto that she returned to kneel, amongst the bushy eglantine, as in the days when the Gave was not walled in by a monumental quay. And it was the old town that she visited at twilight, when the cool, perfumed breezes came down from the mountains, the old painted and gilded semi-Spanish church where she had made her first communion, the old Asylum so full of suffering where during eight years she had grown accustomed to solitude—all that poor, innocent old town, whose every paving-stone awoke old affections in her memory's depths.

And did Bernadette ever extend the pilgrimage of her dreams as far as Bartres? Probably, at times when she sat in her invalid-chair and let some pious book slip from her tired hands, and closed her eyes, Bartres did appear to her, lighting up the darkness of her view. The little antique Romanesque church with sky-blue nave and blood-red altar screens stood there amidst the tombs of the narrow cemetery. Then she would find herself once more in the house of the Lagues, in the large room on the left, where the fire was burning, and where, in winter-time, such wonderful stories were told whilst the big clock gravely ticked the hours away. At times the whole countryside spread out before her, meadows without end, giant chestnut-trees beneath which you lost yourself, deserted table-lands whence you descried the distant mountains, the Pic du Midi and the Pic de Viscos soaring aloft as airy and as rose-coloured as dreams, in a paradise such as the legends have depicted. And afterwards, afterwards came her free childhood, when she scampered off whither she listed in the open air, her lonely, dreamy thirteenth year, when with all the joy of living she wandered through the immensity of nature. And now, too, perhaps, she again beheld herself roaming in the tall grass among the hawthorn bushes beside the streams on a warm sunny day in June. Did she not picture herself grown, with a lover of her own age, whom she would have loved with all the simplicity and affection of her heart? Ah! to be a child again, to be free, unknown, happy once more, to love afresh, and to love differently! The vision must have passed confusedly before her—a husband who worshipped her, children gaily growing up around her, the life that everybody led, the joys and sorrows that her own parents had known, and which her children would have had to know in their turn. But little by little all vanished, and she again found herself in her chair of suffering, imprisoned between four cold walls, with no other desire than a longing one for a speedy death, since she had been denied a share of the poor common happiness of this world.

Bernadette's ailments increased each year. It was, in fact, the commencement of her passion, the passion of this new child-Messiah, who had come to bring relief to the unhappy, to announce to mankind the religion of divine justice and equality in the face of miracles which flouted the laws of impassible nature. If she now rose it was only to drag herself from chair to chair for a few days at a time, and then she would have a relapse and be again forced to take to her bed. Her sufferings became terrible. Her hereditary nervousness, her asthma, aggravated by cloister life, had probably turned into phthisis. She coughed frightfully, each fit rending her burning chest and leaving her half dead. To complete her misery, caries of the right knee-cap supervened, a gnawing disease, the shooting pains of which caused her to cry aloud. Her poor body, to which dressings were continually being applied, became one great sore, which was irritated by the warmth of her bed, by her prolonged sojourn between sheets whose friction ended by breaking her skin. One and all pitied her; those who beheld her martyrdom said that it was impossible to suffer more, or with greater fortitude. She tried some of the Lourdes water, but it brought her no relief. Lord, Almighty King, why cure others and not cure her? To save her soul? Then dost Thou not save the souls of the others? What an inexplicable selection! How absurd that in the eternal evolution of worlds it should be necessary for this poor being to be tortured! She sobbed, and again and again said in order to keep up her courage: "Heaven is at the end, but how long the end is in coming!" There was ever the idea that suffering is the test, that it is necessary to suffer upon earth if one would triumph elsewhere, that suffering is indispensable, enviable, and blessed. But is this not blasphemous, O Lord? Hast Thou not created youth and joy? Is it Thy wish that Thy creatures should enjoy neither the sun, nor the smiling Nature which Thou hast created, nor the human affections with which Thou hast endowed their flesh? She dreaded the feeling of revolt which maddened her at times, and wished also to strengthen herself against the disease which made her groan, and she crucified herself in thought, extending her arms so as to form a cross and unite herself to Jesus, her limbs against His limbs, her mouth against His mouth, streaming the while with blood like Him, and steeped like Him in bitterness! Jesus died in three hours, but a longer agony fell to her, who again brought redemption by pain, who died to give others life. When her bones ached with agony she would sometimes utter complaints, but she reproached herself immediately. "Oh! how I suffer, oh! how I suffer! but what happiness it is to bear this pain!" There can be no more frightful words, words pregnant with a blacker pessimism. Happy to suffer, O Lord! but why, and to what unknown and senseless end? Where is the reason in this useless cruelty, in this revolting glorification of suffering, when from the whole of humanity there ascends but one desperate longing for health and happiness?

In the midst of her frightful sufferings, however, Sister Marie-Bernard took the final vows on September 22, 1878. Twenty years had gone by since the Blessed Virgin had appeared to her, visiting her as the Angel had visited the Virgin, choosing her as the Virgin had been chosen, amongst the most lowly and the most candid, that she might hide within her the secret of King Jesus. Such was the mystical explanation of that election of suffering, the *raison d'etre* of that being who was so harshly separated from her fellows, weighed down by disease, transformed into the pitiable field of every human affliction. She was the "garden inclosed"[1] that brings such pleasure to the gaze of the Spouse. He had chosen her, then buried her in the death of her hidden life. And even when the unhappy creature staggered beneath the weight of her cross, her companions would say to her: "Do you forget that the Blessed Virgin promised you that you should be happy, not in this world, but in the next?" And with renewed strength, and striking her forehead, she would answer: "Forget? no, no! it is here!" She only recovered temporary energy by means of this illusion of a paradise of glory, into which she would enter escorted by seraphims, to be forever and ever happy. The three personal secrets which the Blessed Virgin had confided to her, to arm her against evil, must have been promises of beauty, felicity, and immortality in heaven. What monstrous dupery if there were only the darkness of the earth beyond the grave, if the Blessed Virgin of her dream were not there to meet her with the prodigious guerdons she had promised! But Bernadette had not a doubt; she willingly undertook all the little commissions with which her companions naively entrusted her for Heaven: "Sister Marie-Bernard, you'll say this, you'll say that, to the Almighty." "Sister Marie-Bernard, you'll kiss my brother if you meet him in Paradise." "Sister Marie-Bernard, give me a little place beside you when I die." And she obligingly answered each one: "Have no fear, I will do it!" Ah! all-powerful illusion, delicious repose, power ever reviving and consolatory!

And then came the last agony, then came death.

On Friday, March 28, 1879, it was thought that she would not last the night. She had a despairing longing for the tomb, in order that she might suffer no more, and live again in heaven. And thus she obstinately refused to receive extreme unction, saying that twice already it had cured her. She wished, in short, that God would let her die, for it was more than she could bear; it would have been unreasonable to require that she should suffer longer. Yet she ended by consenting to receive the sacraments, and her last agony was thereby prolonged for nearly three weeks. The priest who attended her frequently said: "My daughter, you must make the sacrifice of your life"; and one day, quite out of patience, she sharply answered him: "But, Father, it is no sacrifice." A terrible saying, that also, for it implied disgust at *being*, furious contempt for existence, and an immediate ending of her humanity, had she had the power to suppress herself by a gesture. It is true that the poor girl had nothing to regret, that she had been compelled to banish everything from her life, health, joy, and love, so that she might leave it as one casts off a soiled, worn, tattered garment. And she was right; she

[1] Song of Solomon iv. 12.

condemned her useless, cruel life when she said: "My passion will finish only at my death; it will not cease until I enter into eternity." And this idea of her passion pursued her, attaching her more closely to the cross with her Divine Master. She had induced them to give her a large crucifix; she pressed it vehemently against her poor maidenly breast, exclaiming that she would like to thrust it into her bosom and leave it there. Towards the end, her strength completely forsook her, and she could no longer grasp the crucifix with her trembling hands. "Let it be tightly tied to me," she prayed, "that I may feel it until my last breath!" The Redeemer upon that crucifix was the only spouse that she was destined to know; His bleeding kiss was to be the only one bestowed upon her womanhood, diverted from nature's course. The nuns took cords, passed them under her aching back, and fastened the crucifix so roughly to her bosom that it did indeed penetrate it.

At last death took pity upon her. On Easter Monday she was seized with a great fit of shivering. Hallucinations perturbed her, she trembled with fright, she beheld the devil jeering and prowling around her. "Be off, be off, Satan!" she gasped; "do not touch me, do not carry me away!" And amidst her delirium she related that the fiend had sought to throw himself upon her, that she had felt his mouth scorching her with all the flames of hell. The devil in a life so pure, in a soul without sin! what for, O Lord! and again I ask it, why this relentless suffering, intense to the very last, why this nightmare-like ending, this death troubled with such frightful fancies, after so beautiful a life of candour, purity, and innocence? Could she not fall asleep serenely in the peacefulness of her chaste soul? But doubtless so long as breath remained in her body it was necessary to leave her the hatred and dread of life, which is the devil. It was life which menaced her, and it was life which she cast out, in the same way that she denied life when she reserved to the Celestial Bridegroom her tortured, crucified womanhood. That dogma of the Immaculate Conception, which her dream had come to strengthen, was a blow dealt by the Church to woman, both wife and mother. To decree that woman is only worthy of worship on condition that she be a virgin, to imagine that virgin to be herself born without sin, is not this an insult to Nature, the condemnation of life, the denial of womanhood, whose true greatness consists in perpetuating life? "Be off, be off, Satan! let me die without fulfilling Nature's law." And she drove the sunshine from the room and the free air that entered by the window, the air that was sweet with the scent of flowers, laden with all the floating germs which transmit love throughout the whole vast world.

On the Wednesday after Easter (April 16th), the death agony commenced. It is related that on the morning of that day one of Bernadette's companions, a nun attacked with a mortal illness and lying in the infirmary in an adjoining bed, was suddenly healed upon drinking a glass of Lourdes water. But she, the privileged one, had drunk of it in vain. God at last granted her the signal favour which she desired by sending her into the good sound sleep of the earth, in which there is no more suffering. She asked pardon of everyone. Her passion was consummated; like the Saviour, she had the nails and the crown of thorns, the scourged limbs, the pierced side. Like Him she raised her eyes to heaven, extended her arms in the form of a cross, and uttered a loud cry: "My God!" And, like Him, she said, towards three o'clock: "I thirst." She moistened her lips in the glass, then bowed her head and expired.

Thus, very glorious and very holy, died the Visionary of Lourdes, Bernadette Soubirous, Sister Marie-Bernard, one of the Sisters of Charity of Nevers. During three days her body remained exposed to view, and vast crowds passed before it; a whole people hastened to the convent, an interminable procession of devotees hungering after hope, who rubbed medals, chaplets, pictures, and missals against the dead woman's dress, to obtain from her one more favour, a fetish bringing happiness. Even in death her dream of solitude was denied her: a mob of the wretched ones of this world rushed to the spot, drinking in illusion around her coffin. And it was noticed that her left eye, the eye which at the time of the apparitions had been nearest to the Blessed Virgin, remained obstinately open. Then a last miracle amazed the convent: the body underwent no change, but was interred on the third day, still supple, warm, with red lips, and a very white skin, rejuvenated as it were, and smelling sweet. And to-day Bernadette Soubirous, exiled from Lourdes, obscurely sleeps her last sleep at Saint Gildard, beneath a stone slab in a little chapel, amidst the shade and silence of the old trees of the garden, whilst yonder the Grotto shines resplendently in all its triumph.

Pierre ceased speaking; the beautiful, marvellous story was ended. And yet the whole carriage was still listening, deeply impressed by that death, at once so tragic and so touching. Compassionate tears fell from Marie's eyes, while the others, Elise Rouquet, La Grivotte herself, now calmer, clasped their hands and prayed to her who was in heaven to intercede with the Divinity to complete their cure. M. Sabathier made a big sign of the cross, and then ate a cake which his wife had bought him at Poitiers.

M. de Guersaint, whom sad things always upset, had fallen asleep again in the middle of the story. And there was only Madame Vincent, with her face buried in her pillow, who had not stirred, like a deaf and blind creature, determined to see and hear nothing more.

Meanwhile the train rolled, still rolled along. Madame de Jonquiere, after putting her head out of the window, informed them that they were approaching Etampes. And, when they had left that station behind them, Sister Hyacinthe gave the signal, and they recited the third chaplet of the Rosary, the five glorious mysteries—the Resurrection of Our Lord, the Ascension of Our Lord, the Mission of the Holy Ghost, the Assumption of the Most Blessed Virgin, and the Crowning of the Most Blessed Virgin. And afterwards they sang the canticle:

"O Virgin, in thy help I put my trust."

Then Pierre fell into a deep reverie. His glance had turned towards the now sunlit landscape, the continual flight of which seemed to lull his thoughts. The noise of the wheels was making him dizzy, and he ended by no longer recognising the familiar horizon of this vast suburban expanse with which he had once been acquainted. They still had to pass Bretigny and Juvisy, and then, in an hour and a half at the utmost, they would at last be at Paris. So the great journey was finished! the inquiry, which he had so much desired to make, the experiment which he had attempted with so much passion, were over! He had wished to acquire certainty, to study Bernadette's case on the spot, and see if grace would not come back to him in a lightning flash, restoring him his faith. And now he had settled the point—Bernadette had dreamed through the continual torments of her flesh, and he himself would never believe again. And this forced itself upon his mind like a brutal fact: the simple faith of the child who kneels and prays, the primitive faith of young people, bowed down by an awe born of their ignorance, was dead. Though thousands of pilgrims might each year go to Lourdes, the nations were no longer with them; this attempt to bring about the resurrection of absolute faith, the faith of dead-and-gone centuries, without revolt or examination, was fatally doomed to fail. History never retraces its steps, humanity cannot return to childhood, times have too much changed, too many new inspirations have sown new harvests for the men of to-day to become once more like the men of olden time. It was decisive; Lourdes was only an explainable accident, whose reactionary violence was even a proof of the extreme agony in which belief under the antique form of Catholicism was struggling. Never again, as in the cathedrals of the twelfth century, would the entire nation kneel like a docile flock in the hands of the Master. To blindly, obstinately cling to the attempt to bring that to pass would mean to dash oneself against the impossible, to rush, perhaps, towards great moral catastrophes.

And of his journey there already only remained to Pierre an immense feeling of compassion. Ah! his heart was overflowing with pity; his poor heart was returning wrung by all that he had seen. He recalled the words of worthy Abbe Judaine; and he had seen those thousands of unhappy beings praying, weeping, and imploring God to take pity on their suffering; and he had wept with them, and felt within himself, like an open wound, a sorrowful fraternal feeling for all their ailments. He could not think of those poor people without burning with a desire to relieve them. If it were true that the faith of the simple-minded no longer sufficed; if one ran the risk of going astray in wishing to turn back, would it become necessary to close the Grotto, to preach other efforts, other sufferings? However, his compassion revolted at that thought. No, no! it would be a crime to snatch their dream of Heaven from those poor creatures who suffered either in body or in mind, and who only found relief in kneeling yonder amidst the splendour of tapers and the soothing repetition of hymns. He had not taken the murderous course of undeceiving Marie, but had sacrificed himself in order to leave her the joy of her fancy, the divine consolation of having been healed by the Virgin. Where was the man hard enough, cruel enough, to prevent the lowly from believing, to rob them of the consolation of the supernatural, the hope that God troubled Himself about them, that He held a better life in His paradise in reserve for them? All humanity was weeping, desperate with anguish, like some despairing invalid, irrevocably condemned, and whom only a miracle could save. He felt mankind to be unhappy indeed, and he shuddered with fraternal affection in the presence of such pitiable humility, ignorance, poverty in its rags, disease with its sores and evil odour, all the lowly sufferers, in hospital, convent, and slums, amidst vermin and dirt, with ugliness and imbecility written on their faces, an immense protest against health, life, and Nature, in the triumphal name of justice, equality, and benevolence. No, no! it would never do to drive the wretched to despair. Lourdes must be tolerated, in the same way that you tolerate a falsehood which makes life possible. And, as he had already said in Bernadette's chamber, she remained the martyr, she it was who revealed to him the only religion which still filled his heart, the religion of human suffering. Ah! to be good and kindly, to alleviate all ills, to lull pain, to sleep in a dream, to lie even, so that no one might suffer any more!

The train passed at full speed through a village, and Pierre vaguely caught sight of a church nestling amidst some large apple trees. All the pilgrims in the carriage crossed themselves. But he was now becoming uneasy, scruples were tingeing his reverie with anxiety. This religion of human suffering, this redemption by pain, was not this yet another lure, a continual aggravation of pain and misery? It is cowardly and dangerous to allow superstition to live. To tolerate and accept it is to revive the dark evil ages afresh. It weakens and stupefies; the sanctimoniousness bequeathed by heredity produces humiliated, timorous generations, decadent and docile nations, who are an easy prey to the powerful of the earth. Whole nations are imposed upon, robbed, devoured, when they have devoted the whole effort of their will to the mere conquest of a future existence. Would it not, therefore, be better to cure humanity at once by boldly closing the miraculous Grottos whither it goes to weep, and thus restore to it the courage to live the real life, even in the midst of tears? And it was the same prayer, that incessant flood of prayer which ascended from Lourdes, the endless supplication in which he had been immersed and softened: was it not after all but puerile lullaby, a debasement of all one's energies? It benumbed the will, one's very being became dissolved in it and acquired disgust for life and action. Of what use could it be to will anything, do anything, when you totally resigned yourself to the caprices of an unknown almighty power? And, in another respect, what a strange thing was this mad desire for prodigies, this anxiety to drive the Divinity to transgress the laws of Nature established by Himself in His infinite wisdom! Therein evidently lay peril and unreasonableness; at the risk even of losing illusion, that divine comforter, only the habit of personal effort and the courage of truth should have been developed in man, and especially in the child.

Then a great brightness arose in Pierre's mind and dazzled him. It was Reason, protesting against the glorification of the absurd and the deposition of common-sense. Ah! reason, it was through her that he had suffered, through her alone that he was happy. As he had told Doctor Chassaigne, his one consuming longing was to satisfy reason ever more and more, although it might cost him happiness to do so. It was reason, he now well understood it, whose continual revolt at the Grotto, at the Basilica, throughout entire Lourdes, had prevented him from believing. Unlike his old friend—that stricken old man, who was afflicted with such dolorous senility, who had fallen into second childhood since the shipwreck of his affections,—he had been unable to kill reason and humiliate and annihilate himself. Reason remained his sovereign mistress, and she it was who buoyed him up even amidst the obscurities and failures of science. Whenever he met with a thing which he could not understand, it was she who whispered to him, "There is certainly a natural explanation which escapes me." He repeated that there could be no healthy ideal outside the march towards the discovery of the unknown, the slow victory of reason amidst all the wretchedness of body and mind. In the clashing of the twofold heredity which he had derived from his father, all brain, and his mother, all faith, he, a priest, found it possible to ravage his life in order that he might keep his vows. He had acquired strength enough to master his flesh, but he felt that his paternal heredity had now definitely gained the upper hand, for henceforth the sacrifice of his reason had become an impossibility; this he would not renounce and would not master. No, no, even human suffering, the hallowed suffering of the poor, ought not to prove an obstacle, enjoining the necessity of ignorance and folly. Reason before all; in her alone lay salvation. If at Lourdes, whilst bathed in tears, softened by the sight of so much affliction, he had said that it was sufficient to weep and love, he had made a dangerous mistake. Pity was but a convenient expedient. One must live, one must act; reason must combat suffering, unless it be desired that the latter should last forever.

V. THE DEATH OP BERNADETTE—THE NEW RELIGION

However, as the train rolled on and the landscape flew by, a church once more appeared, this time on the fringe of heaven, some votive chapel perched upon a hill and surmounted by a lofty statue of the Virgin. And once more all the pilgrims made the sign of the cross, and once more Pierre's reverie strayed, a fresh stream of reflections bringing his anguish back to him. What was this imperious need of the things beyond, which tortured suffering humanity? Whence came it? Why should equality and justice be desired when they did not seem to exist in impassive nature? Man had set them in the unknown spheres of the Mysterious, in the supernatural realms of religious paradises, and there contented his ardent thirst for them. That unquenchable thirst for happiness had ever consumed, and would consume him always. If the Fathers of the Grotto drove such a glorious trade, it was simply because they made motley out of what was divine. That thirst for the Divine, which nothing had quenched through the long, long ages, seemed to have returned with increased violence at the close of our century of science. Lourdes was a resounding and undeniable proof that man could never live without the dream of a Sovereign Divinity, re-establishing equality and re-creating happiness by dint of miracles. When man has reached the depths of life's misfortunes, he returns to the divine illusion, and the origin of all religions lies there. Man, weak and bare, lacks the strength to live through his terrestrial misery without the everlasting lie of a paradise. To-day, thought Pierre, the experiment had been made; it seemed that science alone could not suffice, and that one would be obliged to leave a door open on the Mysterious.

All at once in the depths of his deeply absorbed mind the words rang out, A new religion! The door which must be left open on the Mysterious was indeed a new religion. To subject mankind to brutal amputation, lop off its dream, and forcibly deprive it of the Marvellous, which it needed to live as much as it needed bread, would possibly kill it. Would it ever have the philosophical courage to take life as it is, and live it for its own sake, without any idea of future rewards and penalties? It certainly seemed that centuries must elapse before the advent of a society wise enough to lead a life of rectitude without the moral control of some cultus and the consolation of superhuman equality and justice. Yes, a new religion! The call burst forth, resounded within Pierre's brain like the call of the nations, the eager, despairing desire of the modern soul. The consolation and hope which Catholicism had brought the world seemed exhausted after eighteen hundred years full of so many tears, so much blood, so much vain and barbarous agitation. It was an illusion departing, and it was at least necessary that the illusion should be changed. If mankind had long ago darted for refuge into the Christian paradise, it was because that paradise then opened before it like a fresh hope. But now a new religion, a new hope, a new paradise, yes, that was what the world thirsted for, in the discomfort in which it was struggling. And Father Fourcade, for his part, fully felt such to be the case; he had not meant to imply anything else when he had given rein to his anxiety, entreating that the people of the great towns, the dense mass of the humble which forms the nation, might be brought to Lourdes. One hundred thousand, two hundred thousand pilgrims at Lourdes each year, that was, after all, but a grain of sand. It was the people, the whole people, that was required. But the people has forever deserted the churches, it no longer puts any soul in the Blessed Virgins which it manufactures, and nothing nowadays could restore its lost faith. A Catholic democracy—yes, history would then begin afresh; only were it possible to create a new Christian people, would not the advent of a new Saviour, the mighty breath of a new Messiah, have been needed for such a task?

However, the words still sounded, still rang out in Pierre's mind with the growing clamour of pealing bells. A new religion; a new religion. Doubtless it must be a religion nearer to life, giving a larger place to the things of the world, and taking the acquired truths into due account. And, above all, it must be a religion which was not an appetite for death—Bernadette living solely in order that she might die, Doctor Chassaigne aspiring to the tomb as to the only happiness—for all that spiritualistic abandonment was so much continuous disorganisation of the will to live. At bottom of it was hatred to life, disgust with and cessation of action. Every religion, it is true, is but a promise of immortality, an embellishment of the spheres beyond, an enchanted garden to be entered on the morrow of death. Could a new religion ever place such a garden of eternal happiness on earth? Where was the formula, the dogma, that would satisfy the hopes of the mankind of to-day? What belief should be sown to blossom forth in a harvest of strength and peace? How could one fecundate the universal doubt so that it should give birth to a new faith? and what sort of illusion, what divine falsehood of any kind could be made to germinate in the contemporary world, ravaged as it had been upon all sides, broken up by a century of science?

At that moment, without any apparent transition, Pierre saw the face of his brother Guillaume arise in the troublous depths of his mind. Still, he was not surprised; some secret link must have brought that vision there. Ah! how fond they had been of one another long ago, and what a good brother that elder brother, so upright and gentle, had been! Henceforth, also, the rupture was complete; Pierre no longer saw Guillaume, since the latter had cloistered himself in his chemical studies, living like a savage in a little suburban house, with a mistress and two big dogs. Then Pierre's reverie again diverged, and he thought of that trial in which Guillaume had been mentioned, like one suspected of having compromising friendships amongst the most violent revolutionaries. It was related, too, that the young man had, after long researches, discovered the formula of a terrible explosive, one pound of which would suffice to blow up a cathedral. And Pierre then thought of those Anarchists who wished to renew and save the world by destroying it. They were but dreamers, horrible dreamers; yet dreamers in the same way as those innocent pilgrims whom he had seen kneeling at the Grotto in an enraptured flock. If the Anarchists, if the extreme Socialists, demanded with violence the equality of wealth, the sharing of all the enjoyments of the world, the pilgrims on their side demanded with tears equality of health and an equitable sharing of moral and physical peace. The latter relied on miracles, the former appealed to brute force. At bottom, however, it was but the same exasperated dream of fraternity and justice, the eternal desire for happiness—neither poor nor sick left, but bliss for one and all. And, in fact, had not the primitive Christians been terrible revolutionaries for the pagan world, which they threatened, and did, indeed, destroy? They who were persecuted, whom the others sought to exterminate, are to-day inoffensive, because they have become the Past. The frightful Future is ever the man who dreams of a future society; even as to-day it is the madman so wildly bent on social renovation that he harbours the great black dream of purifying everything by the flame of conflagrations. This seemed monstrous to Pierre. Yet, who could tell? Therein, perchance, lay the rejuvenated world of to-morrow.

V. THE DEATH OP BERNADETTE—THE NEW RELIGION

Astray, full of doubts, he nevertheless, in his horror of violence, made common cause with old society now reduced to defend itself, unable though he was to say whence would come the new Messiah of Gentleness, in whose hands he would have liked to place poor ailing mankind. A new religion, yes, a new religion. But it is not easy to invent one, and he knew not to what conclusion to come between the ancient faith, which was dead, and the young faith of to-morrow, as yet unborn. For his part, in his desolation, he was only sure of keeping his vow, like an unbelieving priest watching over the belief of others, chastely and honestly discharging his duties, with the proud sadness that he had been unable to renounce his reason as he had renounced his flesh. And for the rest, he would wait.

However, the train rolled on between large parks, and the engine gave a prolonged whistle, a joyful flourish, which drew Pierre from his reflections. The others were stirring, displaying emotion around him. The train had just left Juvisy, and Paris was at last near at hand, within a short half-hour's journey. One and all were getting their things together: the Sabathiers were remaking their little parcels, Elise Rouquet was giving a last glance at her mirror. For a moment Madame de Jonquiere again became anxious concerning La Grivotte, and decided that as the girl was in such a pitiful condition she would have her taken straight to a hospital on arriving; whilst Marie endeavoured to rouse Madame Vincent from the torpor in which she seemed determined to remain. M. de Guersaint, who had been indulging in a little siesta, also had to be awakened. And at last, when Sister Hyacinthe had clapped her hands, the whole carriage intonated the "Te Deum," the hymn of praise and thanksgiving. "*Te Deum, laudamus, te Dominum confitemur*." The voices rose amidst a last burst of fervour. All those glowing souls returned thanks to God for the beautiful journey, the marvellous favours that He had already bestowed on them, and would bestow on them yet again.

At last came the fortifications. The two o'clock sun was slowly descending the vast, pure heavens, so serenely warm. Distant smoke, a ruddy smoke, was rising in light clouds above the immensity of Paris like the scattered, flying breath of that toiling colossus. It was Paris in her forge, Paris with her passions, her battles, her ever-growling thunder, her ardent life ever engendering the life of to-morrow. And the white train, the woeful train of every misery and every dolour, was returning into it all at full speed, sounding in higher and higher strains the piercing flourishes of its whistle-calls. The five hundred pilgrims, the three hundred patients, were about to disappear in the vast city, fall again upon the hard pavement of life after the prodigious dream in which they had just indulged, until the day should come when their need of the consolation of a fresh dream would irresistibly impel them to start once more on the everlasting pilgrimage to mystery and forgetfulness.

Ah! unhappy mankind, poor ailing humanity, hungering for illusion, and in the weariness of this waning century distracted and sore from having too greedily acquired science; it fancies itself abandoned by the physicians of both the mind and the body, and, in great danger of succumbing to incurable disease, retraces its steps and asks the miracle of its cure of the mystical Lourdes of a past forever dead! Yonder, however, Bernadette, the new Messiah of suffering, so touching in her human reality, constitutes the terrible lesson, the sacrifice cut off from the world, the victim condemned to abandonment, solitude, and death, smitten with the penalty of being neither woman, nor wife, nor mother, because she beheld the Blessed Virgin.

ROME

Of the Three Cities

Translated By Ernest A. Vizetelly

PREFACE

IN submitting to the English-speaking public this second volume of M. Zola's trilogy "Lourdes, Rome, Paris," I have no prefatory remarks to offer on behalf of the author, whose views on Rome, its past, present, and future, will be found fully expounded in the following pages. That a book of this character will, like its forerunner "Lourdes," provoke considerable controversy is certain, but comment or rejoinder may well be postponed until that controversy has arisen. At present then I only desire to say, that in spite of the great labour which I have bestowed on this translation, I am sensible of its shortcomings, and in a work of such length, such intricacy, and such a wide range of subject, it will not be surprising if some slips are discovered. Any errors which may be pointed out to me, however, shall be rectified in subsequent editions. I have given, I think, the whole essence of M. Zola's text; but he himself has admitted to me that he has now and again allowed his pen to run away with him, and thus whilst sacrificing nothing of his sense I have at times abbreviated his phraseology so as slightly to condense the book. I may add that there are no chapter headings in the original, and that the circumstances under which the translation was made did not permit me to supply any whilst it was passing through the press; however, as some indication of the contents of the book—which treats of many more things than are usually found in novels—may be a convenience to the reader, I have prepared a table briefly epitomising the chief features of each successive chapter.

E. A. V.

MERTON, SURREY, ENGLAND,
April, 1896.

PART I.

I.

THE train had been greatly delayed during the night between Pisa and Civita Vecchia, and it was close upon nine o'clock in the morning when, after a fatiguing journey of twenty-five hours' duration, Abbe Pierre Froment at last reached Rome. He had brought only a valise with him, and, springing hastily out of the railway carriage amidst the scramble of the arrival, he brushed the eager porters aside, intent on carrying his trifling luggage himself, so anxious was he to reach his destination, to be alone, and look around him. And almost immediately, on the Piazza dei Cinquecento, in front of the railway station, he climbed into one of the small open cabs ranged alongside the footwalk, and placed the valise near him after giving the driver this address:

"Via Giulia, Palazzo Boccanera."[1]

It was a Monday, the 3rd of September, a beautifully bright and mild morning, with a clear sky overhead. The cabby, a plump little man with sparkling eyes and white teeth, smiled on realising by Pierre's accent that he had to deal with a French priest. Then he whipped up his lean horse, and the vehicle started off at the rapid pace customary to the clean and cheerful cabs of Rome. However, on reaching the Piazza delle Terme, after skirting the greenery of a little public garden, the man turned round, still smiling, and pointing to some ruins with his whip,

"The baths of Diocletian," said he in broken French, like an obliging driver who is anxious to court favour with foreigners in order to secure their custom.

Then, at a fast trot, the vehicle descended the rapid slope of the Via Nazionale, which dips down from the summit of the Viminalis,[2] where the railway station is situated. And from that moment the driver scarcely ceased turning round and pointing at the monuments with his whip. In this broad new thoroughfare there were only buildings of recent erection. Still, the wave of the cabman's whip became more pronounced and his voice rose to a higher key, with a somewhat ironical inflection, when he gave the name of a huge and still chalky pile on his left, a gigantic erection of stone, overladen with sculptured work-pediments and statues.

---

[1] Boccanera mansion, Julia Street.

[2] One of the seven hills on which Rome is built. The other six are the Capitoline, Aventine, Quirinal, Esquiline, Coelian, and Palatine. These names will perforce frequently occur in the present narrative.

"The National Bank!" he said.

Pierre, however, during the week which had followed his resolve to make the journey, had spent wellnigh every day in studying Roman topography in maps and books. Thus he could have directed his steps to any given spot without inquiring his way, and he anticipated most of the driver's explanations. At the same time he was disconcerted by the sudden slopes, the perpetually recurring hills, on which certain districts rose, house above house, in terrace fashion. On his right-hand clumps of greenery were now climbing a height, and above them stretched a long bare yellow building of barrack or convent-like aspect.

"The Quirinal, the King's palace," said the driver.

Lower down, as the cab turned across a triangular square, Pierre, on raising his eyes, was delighted to perceive a sort of aerial garden high above him—a garden which was upheld by a lofty smooth wall, and whence the elegant and vigorous silhouette of a parasol pine, many centuries old, rose aloft into the limpid heavens. At this sight he realised all the pride and grace of Rome.

"The Villa Aldobrandini," the cabman called.

Then, yet lower down, there came a fleeting vision which decisively impassioned Pierre. The street again made a sudden bend, and in one corner, beyond a short dim alley, there was a blazing gap of light. On a lower level appeared a white square, a well of sunshine, filled with a blinding golden dust; and amidst all that morning glory there arose a gigantic marble column, gilt from base to summit on the side which the sun in rising had laved with its beams for wellnigh eighteen hundred years. And Pierre was surprised when the cabman told him the name of the column, for in his mind he had never pictured it soaring aloft in such a dazzling cavity with shadows all around. It was the column of Trajan.

The Via Nazionale turned for the last time at the foot of the slope. And then other names fell hastily from the driver's lips as his horse went on at a fast trot. There was the Palazzo Colonna, with its garden edged by meagre cypresses; the Palazzo Torlonia, almost ripped open by recent "improvements"; the Palazzo di Venezia, bare and fearsome, with its crenelated walls, its stern and tragic appearance, that of some fortress of the middle ages, forgotten there amidst the commonplace life of nowadays. Pierre's surprise increased at the unexpected aspect which certain buildings and streets presented; and the keenest blow of all was dealt him when the cabman with his whip triumphantly called his attention to the Corso, a long narrow thoroughfare, about as broad as Fleet Street,[1] white with sunshine on the left, and black with shadows on the right, whilst at the far end the Piazza del Popolo (the Square of the People) showed like a bright star. Was this, then, the heart of the city, the vaunted promenade, the street brimful of life, whither flowed all the blood of Rome?

However, the cab was already entering the Corso Vittorio Emanuele, which follows the Via Nazionale, these being the two piercings effected right across the olden city from the railway station to the bridge of St. Angelo. On the left-hand the rounded apsis of the Gesu church looked quite golden in the morning brightness. Then, between the church and the heavy Altieri palace which the "improvers" had not dared to

---

[1] M. Zola likens the Corso to the Rue St. Honore in Paris, but I have thought that an English comparison would be preferable in the present version.—Trans.

demolish, the street became narrower, and one entered into cold, damp shade. But a moment afterwards, before the facade of the Gesu, when the square was reached, the sun again appeared, dazzling, throwing golden sheets of light around; whilst afar off at the end of the Via di Ara Coeli, steeped in shadow, a glimpse could be caught of some sunlit palm-trees.

"That's the Capitol yonder," said the cabman.

The priest hastily leant to the left, but only espied the patch of greenery at the end of the dim corridor-like street. The sudden alternations of warm light and cold shade made him shiver. In front of the Palazzo di Venezia, and in front of the Gesu, it had seemed to him as if all the night of ancient times were falling icily upon his shoulders; but at each fresh square, each broadening of the new thoroughfares, there came a return to light, to the pleasant warmth and gaiety of life. The yellow sunflashes, in falling from the house fronts, sharply outlined the violescent shadows. Strips of sky, very blue and very benign, could be perceived between the roofs. And it seemed to Pierre that the air he breathed had a particular savour, which he could not yet quite define, but it was like that of fruit, and increased the feverishness which had possessed him ever since his arrival.

The Corso Vittorio Emanuele is, in spite of its irregularity, a very fine modern thoroughfare; and for a time Pierre might have fancied himself in any great city full of huge houses let out in flats. But when he passed before the Cancelleria,[1] Bramante's masterpiece, the typical monument of the Roman Renascence, his astonishment came back to him and his mind returned to the mansions which he had previously espied, those bare, huge, heavy edifices, those vast cubes of stone-work resembling hospitals or prisons. Never would he have imagined that the famous Roman "palaces" were like that, destitute of all grace and fancy and external magnificence. However, they were considered very fine and must be so; he would doubtless end by understanding things, but for that he would require reflection.[2]

All at once the cab turned out of the populous Corso Vittorio Emanuele into a succession of winding alleys, through which it had difficulty in making its way. Quietude and solitude now came back again; the olden city, cold and somniferous, followed the new city with its bright sunshine and its crowds. Pierre remembered the maps which he had consulted, and realised that he was drawing near to the Via Giulia, and thereupon his curiosity, which had been steadily increasing, augmented to such a point that he suffered from it, full of despair at not seeing more and learning more at once. In the feverish state in which he had found himself ever since leaving the station, his astonishment at not finding things such as he had expected, the many shocks that his imagination had received, aggravated his passion beyond endurance, and brought him an acute desire to satisfy himself immediately. Nine o'clock had struck but a few minutes previously, he had the whole morning before him to repair to the Boccanera palace, so why should he not at once drive to the classic spot, the summit whence one perceives the whole of Rome spread out upon her seven hills? And when once this

---

[1] Formerly the residence of the Papal Vice-Chancellors.

[2] It is as well to point out at once that a palazzo is not a palace as we understand the term, but rather a mansion.—Trans.

thought had entered into his mind it tortured him until he was at last compelled to yield to it.

The driver no longer turned his head, so that Pierre rose up to give him this new address: "To San Pietro in Montorio!"

On hearing him the man at first looked astonished, unable to understand. He indicated with his whip that San Pietro was yonder, far away. However, as the priest insisted, he again smiled complacently, with a friendly nod of his head. All right! For his own part he was quite willing.

The horse then went on at a more rapid pace through the maze of narrow streets. One of these was pent between high walls, and the daylight descended into it as into a deep trench. But at the end came a sudden return to light, and the Tiber was crossed by the antique bridge of Sixtus IV, right and left of which stretched the new quays, amidst the ravages and fresh plaster-work of recent erections. On the other side of the river the Trastevere district also was ripped open, and the vehicle ascended the slope of the Janiculum by a broad thoroughfare where large slabs bore the name of Garibaldi. For the last time the driver made a gesture of good-natured pride as he named this triumphal route.

"Via Garibaldi!"

The horse had been obliged to slacken its pace, and Pierre, mastered by childish impatience, turned round to look at the city as by degrees it spread out and revealed itself behind him. The ascent was a long one; fresh districts were ever rising up, even to the most distant hills. Then, in the increasing emotion which made his heart beat, the young priest felt that he was spoiling the contentment of his desire by thus gradually satisfying it, slowly and but partially effecting his conquest of the horizon. He wished to receive the shock full in the face, to behold all Rome at one glance, to gather the holy city together, and embrace the whole of it at one grasp. And thereupon he mustered sufficient strength of mind to refrain from turning round any more, in spite of the impulses of his whole being.

There is a spacious terrace on the summit of the incline. The church of San Pietro in Montorio stands there, on the spot where, as some say, St. Peter was crucified. The square is bare and brown, baked by the hot summer suns; but a little further away in the rear, the clear and noisy waters of the Acqua Paola fall bubbling from the three basins of a monumental fountain amidst sempiternal freshness. And alongside the terrace parapet, on the very crown of the Trastevere, there are always rows of tourists, slim Englishmen and square-built Germans, agape with traditional admiration, or consulting their guide-books in order to identify the monuments.

Pierre sprang lightly from the cab, leaving his valise on the seat, and making a sign to the driver, who went to join the row of waiting cabs, and remained philosophically seated on his box in the full sunlight, his head drooping like that of his horse, both resigning themselves to the customary long stoppage.

Meantime Pierre, erect against the parapet, in his tight black cassock, and with his bare feverish hands nervously clenched, was gazing before him with all his eyes, with all his soul. Rome! Rome! the city of the Caesars, the city of the Popes, the Eternal City which has twice conquered the world, the predestined city of the glowing dream in which he had indulged for months! At last it was before him, at last his eyes beheld it! During the previous days some rainstorms had abated the intense August heat, and on that lovely September morning the air had freshened under the pale blue of the spotless far-spreading heavens. And the Rome that Pierre beheld was a Rome steeped in mildness, a visionary Rome which seemed to evaporate in the clear sunshine. A fine bluey haze, scarcely perceptible, as delicate as gauze, hovered over the roofs of the low-lying districts; whilst the vast Campagna, the distant hills, died away in a pale pink flush. At first Pierre distinguished nothing, sought no particular edifice or spot, but gave sight and soul alike to the whole of Rome, to the living colossus spread out below him, on a soil compounded of the dust of generations. Each century had renewed the city's glory as with the sap of immortal youth. And that which struck Pierre, that which made his heart leap within him, was that he found Rome such as he had desired to find her, fresh and youthful, with a volatile, almost incorporeal, gaiety of aspect, smiling as at the hope of a new life in the pure dawn of a lovely day.

And standing motionless before the sublime vista, with his hands still clenched and burning, Pierre in a few minutes again lived the last three years of his life. Ah! what a terrible year had the first been, spent in his little house at Neuilly, with doors and windows ever closed, burrowing there like some wounded animal suffering unto death. He had come back from Lourdes with his soul desolate, his heart bleeding, with nought but ashes within him. Silence and darkness fell upon the ruins of his love and his faith. Days and days went by, without a pulsation of his veins, without the faintest gleam arising to brighten the gloom of his abandonment. His life was a mechanical one; he awaited the necessary courage to resume the tenor of existence in the name of sovereign reason, which had imposed upon him the sacrifice of everything. Why was he not stronger, more resistant, why did he not quietly adapt his life to his new opinions? As he was unwilling to cast off his cassock, through fidelity to the love of one and disgust of backsliding, why did he not seek occupation in some science suited to a priest, such as astronomy or archaeology? The truth was that something, doubtless his mother's spirit, wept within him, an infinite, distracted love which nothing had yet satisfied and which ever despaired of attaining contentment. Therein lay the perpetual suffering of his solitude: beneath the lofty dignity of reason regained, the wound still lingered, raw and bleeding.

One autumn evening, however, under a dismal rainy sky, chance brought him into relations with an old priest, Abbe Rose, who was curate at the church of Ste. Marguerite, in the Faubourg St. Antoine. He went to see Abbe Rose in the Rue de Charonne, where in the depths of a damp ground floor he had transformed three rooms into an asylum for abandoned children, whom he picked up in the neighbouring streets. And from that moment Pierre's life changed, a fresh and all-powerful source of interest had entered into it, and by degrees he became the old priest's passionate helper. It was a long way from Neuilly to the Rue de Charonne, and at first he only made the journey twice a week. But afterwards he bestirred himself every day, leaving home in the morning and not returning until night. As the three rooms no longer sufficed for the asylum, he rented the first floor of the house, reserving for himself a chamber in which ultimately he often slept. And all his modest income was expended there, in the prompt succouring of poor children; and the old priest, delighted, touched to tears by the young devoted help which had come to him from heaven, would often embrace Pierre, weeping, and call him a child of God.

It was then that Pierre knew want and wretchedness—wicked, abominable wretchedness; then that he lived amidst it for two long years. The acquaintance began with the poor little beings whom he picked up on the pavements, or whom kind-hearted neighbours brought to him now that the asylum was known in the district—little boys, little girls, tiny mites stranded on the streets whilst their fathers and mothers were toiling, drinking, or dying. The father had often disappeared, the mother had gone wrong, drunkenness and debauchery had followed slack times into the home; and then the brood was swept into the gutter, and the younger ones half perished of cold and hunger on the footways, whilst their elders betook themselves to courses of vice and crime. One evening Pierre rescued from the wheels of a stone-dray two little nippers, brothers, who could not even give him an address, tell him whence they had come. On another evening he returned to the asylum with a little girl in his arms, a fair-haired little angel, barely three years old, whom he had found on a bench, and who sobbed, saying that her mother had left her there. And by a logical chain of circumstances, after dealing with the fleshless, pitiful fledglings ousted from their nests, he came to deal with the parents, to enter their hovels, penetrating each day further and further into a hellish sphere, and ultimately acquiring knowledge of all its frightful horror, his heart meantime bleeding, rent by terrified anguish and impotent charity.

Oh! the grievous City of Misery, the bottomless abyss of human suffering and degradation—how frightful were his journeys through it during those two years which distracted his whole being! In that Ste. Marguerite district of Paris, in the very heart of that Faubourg St. Antoine, so active and so brave for work, however hard, he discovered no end of sordid dwellings, whole lanes and alleys of hovels without light or air, cellar-like in their dampness, and where a multitude of wretches wallowed and suffered as from poison. All the way up the shaky staircases one's feet slipped upon filth. On every story there was the same destitution, dirt, and promiscuity. Many windows were paneless, and in swept the wind howling, and the rain pouring torrentially. Many of the inmates slept on the bare tiled floors, never unclothing themselves. There was neither furniture nor linen, the life led there was essentially an animal life, a commingling of either sex and of every age—humanity lapsing into animality through lack of even indispensable things, through indigence of so complete a character that men, women, and children fought even with tooth and nail for the very crumbs swept from the tables of the rich. And the worst of it all was the degradation of the human being; this was no case of the free naked savage, hunting and devouring his prey in the primeval forests; here civilised man was found, sunk into brutishness, with all the stigmas of his fall, debased, disfigured, and enfeebled, amidst the luxury and refinement of that city of Paris which is one of the queens of the world.

In every household Pierre heard the same story. There had been youth and gaiety at the outset, brave acceptance of the law that one must work. Then weariness had come; what was the use of always toiling if one were never to get rich? And so, by way of snatching a share of happiness, the husband turned to drink; the wife neglected her home, also drinking at times, and letting the children grow up as they might. Sordid surroundings, ignorance, and overcrowding did the rest. In the great majority of cases, prolonged lack of work was mostly to blame; for this not only empties the drawers of the savings hidden away in them, but exhausts human courage, and tends to confirmed habits of idleness. During long weeks the workshops empty, and the arms of the toilers lose strength. In all Paris, so feverishly inclined to action, it is impossible to find the slightest thing to do. And then the husband comes home in the evening with tearful eyes, having vainly offered his arms everywhere, having failed even to get a job at street-sweeping, for that employment is much sought after, and to secure it one needs influence and protectors. Is it not monstrous to see a man seeking work that he may eat, and finding no work and therefore no food in this great city resplendent and resonant with wealth? The wife does not eat, the children do not eat. And then comes black famine, brutishness, and finally revolt and the snapping of all social ties under the frightful injustice meted out to poor beings who by their weakness are condemned to death. And the old workman, he whose limbs have been worn out by half a century of hard toil, without possibility of saving a copper, on what pallet of agony, in what dark hole must he not sink to die? Should he then be finished off with a mallet, like a crippled beast of burden, on the day when ceasing to work he also ceases to eat? Almost all pass away in the hospitals, others disappear, unknown, swept off by the muddy flow of the streets. One morning, on some rotten straw in a loathsome hovel, Pierre found a poor devil who had died of hunger and had been forgotten there for a week. The rats had devoured his face.

But it was particularly on an evening of the last winter that Pierre's heart had overflowed with pity. Awful in winter time are the sufferings of the poor in their fireless hovels, where the snow penetrates by every chink. The Seine rolls blocks of ice, the soil is frost-bound, in all sorts of callings there is an enforced cessation of work. Bands of urchins, barefooted, scarcely clad, hungry and racked by coughing, wander about the ragpickers' "rents" and are carried off by sudden hurricanes of consumption. Pierre found families, women with five and six children, who had not eaten for three days, and who huddled together in heaps to try to keep themselves warm. And on that terrible evening, before anybody else, he went down a dark passage and entered a room of terror, where he found that a mother had just committed suicide with her five little ones—driven to it by despair and hunger—a tragedy of misery which for a few hours would make all Paris shudder! There was not an article of furniture or linen left in the place; it had been necessary to sell everything bit by bit to a neighbouring dealer. There was nothing but the stove where the charcoal was still smoking and a half-emptied palliasse on which the mother had fallen, suckling her last-born, a babe but three months old. And a drop of blood had trickled from the nipple of her breast, towards which the dead infant still protruded its eager lips. Two little girls, three and five years old, two pretty little blondes, were also lying there, sleeping the eternal sleep side by side; whilst of the two boys, who were older, one had succumbed crouching against the wall with his head between his hands, and the other had passed through the last throes on the floor, struggling as though he had sought to crawl on his knees to the window in order to open it. Some neighbours, hurrying in, told Pierre the fearful commonplace story; slow ruin, the father unable to find work, perchance taking to drink, the landlord weary of waiting, threatening the family with expulsion, and the mother losing her head, thirsting for death, and prevailing on her little ones to die with her, while her husband, who had been out since the morning, was vainly scouring the streets. Just as the Commissary of Police arrived to verify what had happened, the poor devil returned, and when he had seen and understood things, he fell to the ground like a stunned ox, and raised a prolonged, plaintive howl, such a poignant cry of death that the whole terrified street wept at it.

Both in his ears and in his heart Pierre carried away with him that horrible cry, the plaint of a condemned race expiring amidst abandonment and hunger; and that night he could neither eat nor sleep. Was it possible that such abomination, such absolute destitution, such black misery leading straight to death should exist in the heart of that great city of Paris, brimful of wealth, intoxicated with enjoyment, flinging millions out of the windows for mere pleasure? What! there should on one side be such colossal fortunes, so many foolish fancies gratified, with lives endowed with every happiness, whilst on the other was found inveterate poverty, lack even of bread, absence of every hope, and mothers killing themselves with their babes, to whom they had nought to offer but the blood of their milkless breast! And a feeling of revolt stirred Pierre; he was for a moment conscious of the derisive futility of charity. What indeed was the use of doing that which he did—picking up the little ones, succouring the parents, prolonging the sufferings of the aged? The very foundations of the social edifice were rotten; all would soon collapse amid mire and blood. A great act of justice alone could sweep the old world away in order that the new world might be built. And at that moment he realised so keenly how irreparable was the breach, how irremediable the evil, how deathly the cancer of misery, that he understood the actions of the violent, and was himself ready to accept the devastating and purifying whirlwind, the regeneration of the world by flame and steel, even as when in the dim ages Jehovah in His wrath sent fire from heaven to cleanse the accursed cities of the plains.

However, on hearing him sob that evening, Abbe Rose came up to remonstrate in fatherly fashion. The old priest was a saint, endowed with infinite gentleness and infinite hope. Why despair indeed when one had the Gospel? Did not the divine commandment, "Love one another," suffice for the salvation of the world? He, Abbe Rose, held violence in horror and was wont to say that, however great the evil, it would soon be overcome if humanity would but turn backward to the age of humility, simplicity, and purity, when Christians lived together in innocent brotherhood. What a delightful picture he drew of evangelical society, of whose second coming he spoke with quiet gaiety as though it were to take place on the very morrow! And Pierre, anxious to escape from his frightful recollections, ended by smiling, by taking pleasure in Abbe Rose's bright consoling tale. They chatted until a late hour, and on the following days reverted to the same subject of conversation, one which the old priest was very fond of, ever supplying new particulars, and speaking of the approaching reign of love and justice with the touching confidence of a good if simple man, who is convinced that he will not die till he shall have seen the Deity descend upon earth.

And now a fresh evolution took place in Pierre's mind. The practice of benevolence in that poor district had developed infinite compassion in his breast, his heart failed him, distracted, rent by contemplation of the misery which he despaired of healing. And in this awakening of his feelings he often thought that his reason was giving way, he seemed to be retracing his steps towards childhood, to that need of universal love which his mother had implanted in him, and dreamt of chimerical solutions, awaiting help from the unknown powers. Then his fears, his hatred of the brutality of facts at last brought him an increasing desire to work salvation by love. No time should be lost in seeking to avert the frightful catastrophe which seemed inevitable, the fratricidal war of classes which would sweep the old world away beneath the accumulation of its crimes. Convinced that injustice had attained its apogee, that but little time remained before the vengeful hour when the poor would compel the rich to part with their possessions, he took pleasure in dreaming of a peaceful solution, a kiss of peace exchanged by all men, a return to the pure morals of the Gospel as it had been preached by Jesus.

I.

Doubts tortured him at the outset. Could olden Catholicism be rejuvenated, brought back to the youth and candour of primitive Christianity? He set himself to study things, reading and questioning, and taking a more and more passionate interest in that great problem of Catholic socialism which had made no little noise for some years past. And quivering with pity for the wretched, ready as he was for the miracle of fraternisation, he gradually lost such scruples as intelligence might have prompted, and persuaded himself that once again Christ would work the redemption of suffering humanity. At last a precise idea took possession of him, a conviction that Catholicism purified, brought back to its original state, would prove the one pact, the supreme law that might save society by averting the sanguinary crisis which threatened it.

When he had quitted Lourdes two years previously, revolted by all its gross idolatry, his faith for ever dead, but his mind worried by the everlasting need of the divine which tortures human creatures, a cry had arisen within him from the deepest recesses of his being: "A new religion! a new religion!" And it was this new religion, or rather this revived religion which he now fancied he had discovered in his desire to work social salvation—ensuring human happiness by means of the only moral authority that was erect, the distant outcome of the most admirable implement ever devised for the government of nations.

During the period of slow development through which Pierre passed, two men, apart from Abbe Rose, exercised great influence on him. A benevolent action brought him into intercourse with Monseigneur Bergerot, a bishop whom the Pope had recently created a cardinal, in reward for a whole life of charity, and this in spite of the covert opposition of the papal *curia* which suspected the French prelate to be a man of open mind, governing his diocese in paternal fashion. Pierre became more impassioned by his intercourse with this apostle, this shepherd of souls, in whom he detected one of the good simple leaders that he desired for the future community. However, his apostolate was influenced even more decisively by meeting Viscount Philibert de la Choue at the gatherings of certain workingmen's Catholic associations. A handsome man, with military manners, and a long noble-looking face, spoilt by a small and broken nose which seemed to presage the ultimate defeat of a badly balanced mind, the Viscount was one of the most active agitators of Catholic socialism in France. He was the possessor of vast estates, a vast fortune, though it was said that some unsuccessful agricultural enterprises had already reduced his wealth by nearly one-half. In the department where his property was situated he had been at great pains to establish model farms, at which he had put his ideas on Christian socialism into practice, but success did not seem to follow him. However, it had all helped to secure his election as a deputy, and he spoke in the Chamber, unfolding the programme of his party in long and stirring speeches.

Unwearying in his ardour, he also led pilgrimages to Rome, presided over meetings, and delivered lectures, devoting himself particularly to the people, the conquest of whom, so he privately remarked, could alone ensure the triumph of the Church. And thus he exercised considerable influence over Pierre, who in him admired qualities which himself did not possess—an organising spirit and a militant if somewhat blundering will, entirely applied to the revival of Christian society in France. However, though the young priest learnt a good deal by associating with him, he nevertheless remained a sentimental dreamer, whose imagination, disdainful of political requirements, straightway winged its flight to the future abode of universal happiness;

whereas the Viscount aspired to complete the downfall of the liberal ideas of 1789 by utilising the disillusion and anger of the democracy to work a return towards the past.

Pierre spent some delightful months. Never before had neophyte lived so entirely for the happiness of others. He was all love, consumed by the passion of his apostolate. The sight of the poor wretches whom he visited, the men without work, the women, the children without bread, filled him with a keener and keener conviction that a new religion must arise to put an end to all the injustice which otherwise would bring the rebellious world to a violent death. And he was resolved to employ all his strength in effecting and hastening the intervention of the divine, the resuscitation of primitive Christianity. His Catholic faith remained dead; he still had no belief in dogmas, mysteries, and miracles; but a hope sufficed him, the hope that the Church might still work good, by connecting itself with the irresistible modern democratic movement, so as to save the nations from the social catastrophe which impended. His soul had grown calm since he had taken on himself the mission of replanting the Gospel in the hearts of the hungry and growling people of the Faubourgs. He was now leading an active life, and suffered less from the frightful void which he had brought back from Lourdes; and as he no longer questioned himself, the anguish of uncertainty no longer tortured him. It was with the serenity which attends the simple accomplishment of duty that he continued to say his mass. He even finished by thinking that the mystery which he thus celebrated—indeed, that all the mysteries and all the dogmas were but symbols—rites requisite for humanity in its childhood, which would be got rid of later on, when enlarged, purified, and instructed humanity should be able to support the brightness of naked truth.

And in his zealous desire to be useful, his passion to proclaim his belief aloud, Pierre one morning found himself at his table writing a book. This had come about quite naturally; the book proceeded from him like a heart-cry, without any literary idea having crossed his mind. One night, whilst he lay awake, its title suddenly flashed before his eyes in the darkness: "NEW ROME." That expressed everything, for must not the new redemption of the nations originate in eternal and holy Rome? The only existing authority was found there; rejuvenescence could only spring from the sacred soil where the old Catholic oak had grown. He wrote his book in a couple of months, having unconsciously prepared himself for the work by his studies in contemporary socialism during a year past. There was a bubbling flow in his brain as in a poet's; it seemed to him sometimes as if he dreamt those pages, as if an internal distant voice dictated them to him.

When he read passages written on the previous day to Viscount Philibert de la Choue, the latter often expressed keen approval of them from a practical point of view, saying that one must touch the people in order to lead them, and that it would also be a good plan to compose pious and yet amusing songs for singing in the workshops. As for Monseigneur Bergerot, without examining the book from the dogmatic standpoint, he was deeply touched by the glowing breath of charity which every page exhaled, and was even guilty of the imprudence of writing an approving letter to the author, which letter he authorised him to insert in his work by way of preface. And yet now the Congregation of the Index Expurgatorius was about to place this book, issued in the previous June, under interdict; and it was to defend it that the young priest had hastened to Rome, inflamed by the desire to make his ideas prevail, and resolved to plead his cause in person before the Holy Father, having, he was convinced of it, simply given expression to the pontiff's views.

Pierre had not stirred whilst thus living his three last years afresh: he still stood erect before the parapet, before Rome, which he had so often dreamt of and had so keenly desired to see. There was a constant succession of arriving and departing vehicles behind him; the slim Englishmen and the heavy Germans passed away after bestowing on the classic view the five minutes prescribed by their guidebooks; whilst the driver and the horse of Pierre's cab remained waiting complacently, each with his head drooping under the bright sun, which was heating the valise on the seat of the vehicle. And Pierre, in his black cassock, seemed to have grown slimmer and elongated, very slight of build, as he stood there motionless, absorbed in the sublime spectacle. He had lost flesh after his journey to Lourdes, his features too had become less pronounced. Since his mother's part in his nature had regained ascendency, the broad, straight forehead, the intellectual air which he owed to his father seemed to have grown less conspicuous, while his kind and somewhat large mouth, and his delicate chin, bespeaking infinite affection, dominated, revealing his soul, which also glowed in the kindly sparkle of his eyes.

Ah! how tender and glowing were the eyes with which he gazed upon the Rome of his book, the new Rome that he had dreamt of! If, first of all, the *ensemble* had claimed his attention in the soft and somewhat veiled light of that lovely morning, at present he could distinguish details, and let his glance rest upon particular edifices. And it was with childish delight that he identified them, having long studied them in maps and collections of photographs. Beneath his feet, at the bottom of the Janiculum, stretched the Trastevere district with its chaos of old ruddy houses, whose sunburnt tiles hid the course of the Tiber. He was somewhat surprised by the flattish aspect of everything as seen from the terraced summit. It was as though a bird's-eye view levelled the city, the famous hills merely showing like bosses, swellings scarcely perceptible amidst the spreading sea of house-fronts. Yonder, on the right, distinct against the distant blue of the Alban mountains, was certainly the Aventine with its three churches half-hidden by foliage; there, too, was the discrowned Palatine, edged as with black fringe by a line of cypresses. In the rear, the Coelian hill faded away, showing only the trees of the Villa Mattei paling in the golden sunshine. The slender spire and two little domes of Sta. Maria Maggiore alone indicated the summit of the Esquiline, right in front and far away at the other end of the city; whilst on the heights of the neighbouring Viminal, Pierre only perceived a confused mass of whitish blocks, steeped in light and streaked with fine brown lines—recent erections, no doubt, which at that distance suggested an abandoned stone quarry. He long sought the Capitol without being able to discover it; he had to take his bearings, and ended by convincing himself that the square tower, modestly lost among surrounding house-roofs, which he saw in front of Sta. Maria Maggiore was its campanile. Next, on the left, came the Quirinal, recognisable by the long facade of the royal palace, a barrack or hospital-like facade, flat, crudely yellow in hue, and pierced by an infinite number of regularly disposed windows. However, as Pierre was completing the circuit, a sudden vision made him stop short. Without the city, above the trees of the Botanical Garden, the dome of St. Peter's appeared to him. It seemed to be poised upon the greenery, and rose up into the pure blue sky, sky-blue itself and so ethereal that it mingled with the azure of the infinite. The stone lantern which surmounts it, white and dazzling, looked as though it were suspended on high.

Pierre did not weary, and his glances incessantly travelled from one end of the horizon to the other. They lingered on the noble outlines, the proud gracefulness of the town-sprinkled Sabine and Alban mountains, whose girdle limited the expanse. The Roman Campagna spread out in far stretches, bare and majestic, like a desert of death, with the glaucous green of a stagnant sea; and he ended by distinguishing "the stern round tower" of the tomb of Cecilia Metella, behind which a thin pale line indicated the ancient Appian Way. Remnants of aqueducts strewed the short herbage amidst the dust of the fallen worlds. And, bringing his glance nearer in, the city again appeared with its jumble of edifices, on which his eyes lighted at random. Close at hand, by its loggia turned towards the river, he recognised the huge tawny cube of the Palazzo Farnese. The low cupola, farther away and scarcely visible, was probably that of the Pantheon. Then by sudden leaps came the freshly whitened walls of San Paolo-fuori-le-Mura,[1] similar to those of some huge barn, and the statues crowning San Giovanni in Laterano, delicate, scarcely as big as insects. Next the swarming of domes, that of the Gesu, that of San Carlo, that of St'. Andrea della Valle, that of San Giovanni dei Fiorentini; then a number of other sites and edifices, all quivering with memories, the castle of St'. Angelo with its glittering statue of the Destroying Angel, the Villa Medici dominating the entire city, the terrace of the Pincio with its marbles showing whitely among its scanty verdure; and the thick-foliaged trees of the Villa Borghese, whose green crests bounded the horizon. Vainly however did Pierre seek the Colosseum.

The north wind, which was blowing very mildly, had now begun to dissipate the morning haze. Whole districts vigorously disentangled themselves, and showed against the vaporous distance like promontories in a sunlit sea. Here and there, in the indistinct swarming of houses, a strip of white wall glittered, a row of window panes flared, or a garden supplied a black splotch, of wondrous intensity of hue. And all the rest, the medley of streets and squares, the endless blocks of buildings, scattered about on either hand, mingled and grew indistinct in the living glory of the sun, whilst long coils of white smoke, which had ascended from the roofs, slowly traversed the pure sky.

Guided by a secret influence, however, Pierre soon ceased to take interest in all but three points of the mighty panorama. That line of slender cypresses which set a black fringe on the height of the Palatine yonder filled him with emotion: beyond it he saw only a void: the palaces of the Caesars had disappeared, had fallen, had been razed by time; and he evoked their memory, he fancied he could see them rise like vague, trembling phantoms of gold amidst the purple of that splendid morning. Then his glances reverted to St. Peter's, and there the dome yet soared aloft, screening the Vatican which he knew was beside the colossus, clinging to its flanks. And that dome, of the same colour as the heavens, appeared so triumphant, so full of strength, so vast, that it seemed to him like a giant king, dominating the whole city and seen from every spot throughout eternity. Then he fixed his eyes on the height in front of him, on the

---

[1] St. Paul-beyond-the-walls.

Quirinal, and there the King's palace no longer appeared aught but a flat low barracks bedaubed with yellow paint.

And for him all the secular history of Rome, with its constant convulsions and successive resurrections, found embodiment in that symbolical triangle, in those three summits gazing at one another across the Tiber. Ancient Rome blossoming forth in a piling up of palaces and temples, the monstrous florescence of imperial power and splendour; Papal Rome, victorious in the middle ages, mistress of the world, bringing that colossal church, symbolical of beauty regained, to weigh upon all Christendom; and the Rome of to-day, which he knew nothing of, which he had neglected, and whose royal palace, so bare and so cold, brought him disparaging ideas—the idea of some out-of-place, bureaucratic effort, some sacrilegious attempt at modernity in an exceptional city which should have been left entirely to the dreams of the future. However, he shook off the almost painful feelings which the importunate present brought to him, and would not let his eyes rest on a pale new district, quite a little town, in course of erection, no doubt, which he could distinctly see near St. Peter's on the margin of the river. He had dreamt of his own new Rome, and still dreamt of it, even in front of the Palatine whose edifices had crumbled in the dust of centuries, of the dome of St. Peter's whose huge shadow lulled the Vatican to sleep, of the Palace of the Quirinal repaired and repainted, reigning in homely fashion over the new districts which swarmed on every side, while with its ruddy roofs the olden city, ripped up by improvements, coruscated beneath the bright morning sun.

Again did the title of his book, "NEW ROME," flare before Pierre's eyes, and another reverie carried him off; he lived his book afresh even as he had just lived his life. He had written it amid a flow of enthusiasm, utilising the *data* which he had accumulated at random; and its division into three parts, past, present, and future, had at once forced itself upon him.

The PAST was the extraordinary story of primitive Christianity, of the slow evolution which had turned this Christianity into present-day Catholicism. He showed that an economical question is invariably hidden beneath each religious evolution, and that, upon the whole, the everlasting evil, the everlasting struggle, has never been aught but one between the rich and the poor. Among the Jews, when their nomadic life was over, and they had conquered the land of Canaan, and ownership and property came into being, a class warfare at once broke out. There were rich, and there were poor; thence arose the social question. The transition had been sudden, and the new state of things so rapidly went from bad to worse that the poor suffered keenly, and protested with the greater violence as they still remembered the golden age of the nomadic life. Until the time of Jesus the prophets are but rebels who surge from out the misery of the people, proclaim its sufferings, and vent their wrath upon the rich, to whom they prophesy every evil in punishment for their injustice and their harshness. Jesus Himself appears as the claimant of the rights of the poor. The prophets, whether socialists or anarchists, had preached social equality, and called for the destruction of the world if it were unjust. Jesus likewise brings to the wretched hatred of the rich. All His teaching threatens wealth and property; and if by the Kingdom of Heaven which He promised one were to understand peace and fraternity upon this earth, there would only be a question of returning to a life of pastoral simplicity, to the dream of the Christian community, such as after Him it would seem to have been realised by His disciples. During the first three centuries each Church was an experiment in communism, a real association whose members possessed all in common—wives excepted. This is shown to us by the apologists and early fathers of the Church. Christianity was then but the religion of the humble and the poor, a form of democracy, of socialism struggling against Roman society. And when the latter toppled over, rotted by money, it succumbed far more beneath the results of frantic speculation, swindling banks, and financial disasters, than beneath the onslaught of barbarian hordes and the stealthy, termite-like working of the Christians.

The money question will always be found at the bottom of everything. And a new proof of this was supplied when Christianity, at last triumphing by virtue of historical, social, and human causes, was proclaimed a State religion. To ensure itself complete victory it was forced to range itself on the side of the rich and the powerful; and one should see by means of what artfulness and sophistry the fathers of the Church succeeded in discovering a defence of property and wealth in the Gospel of Jesus. All this, however, was a vital political necessity for Christianity; it was only at this price that it became Catholicism, the universal religion. From that time forth the powerful machine, the weapon of conquest and rule, was reared aloft: up above were the powerful and the wealthy, those whose duty it was to share with the poor, but who did not do so; while down below were the poor, the toilers, who were taught resignation and obedience, and promised the kingdom of futurity, the divine and eternal reward—an admirable monument which has lasted for ages, and which is entirely based on the promise of life beyond life, on the inextinguishable thirst for immortality and justice that consumes mankind.

Pierre had completed this first part of his book, this history of the past, by a broad sketch of Catholicism until the present time. First appeared St. Peter, ignorant and anxious, coming to Rome by an inspiration of genius, there to fulfil the ancient oracles which had predicted the eternity of the Capitol. Then came the first popes, mere heads of burial associations, the slow rise of the all-powerful papacy ever struggling to conquer the world, unremittingly seeking to realise its dream of universal domination. At the time of the great popes of the middle ages it thought for a moment that it had attained its goal, that it was the sovereign master of the nations. Would not absolute truth and right consist in the pope being both pontiff and ruler of the world, reigning over both the souls and the bodies of all men, even like the Deity whose vicar he is? This, the highest and mightiest of all ambitions, one, too, that is perfectly logical, was attained by Augustus, emperor and pontiff, master of all the known world; and it is the glorious figure of Augustus, ever rising anew from among the ruins of ancient Rome, which has always haunted the popes; it is his blood which has pulsated in their veins.

But power had become divided into two parts amidst the crumbling of the Roman empire; it was necessary to content oneself with a share, and leave temporal government to the emperor, retaining over him, however, the right of coronation by divine grant. The people belonged to God, and in God's name the pope gave the people to the emperor, and could take it from him; an unlimited power whose most terrible weapon was excommunication, a superior sovereignty, which carried the papacy towards real and final possession of the empire. Looking at things broadly, the everlasting quarrel between the pope and the emperor was a quarrel for the people, the inert mass of humble and suffering ones, the great silent multitude whose irremediable wretchedness was only revealed by occasional covert growls. It was disposed of, for its good, as one might dispose of a child. Yet the Church really contributed to civilisation, rendered constant services to humanity, diffused abundant alms. In the convents, at any rate, the old dream of the Christian community was ever coming back: one-third of the wealth accumulated for the purposes of worship, the adornment and glorification of the shrine, one-third for the priests, and one-third for the poor. Was not this a simplification of life, a means of rendering existence possible to the faithful who had no earthly desires, pending the marvellous contentment of heavenly life? Give us, then, the whole earth, and we will divide terrestrial wealth into three such parts, and you shall see what a golden age will reign amidst the resignation and the obedience of all!

However, Pierre went on to show how the papacy was assailed by the greatest dangers on emerging from its all-powerfulness of the middle ages. It was almost swept away amidst the luxury and excesses of the Renascence, the bubbling of living sap which then gushed from eternal nature, downtrodden and regarded as dead for ages past. More threatening still were the stealthy awakenings of the people, of the great silent multitude whose tongue seemed to be loosening. The Reformation burst forth like the protest of reason and justice, like a recall to the disregarded truths of the Gospel; and to escape total annihilation Rome needed the stern defence of the Inquisition, the slow stubborn labour of the Council of Trent, which strengthened the dogmas and ensured the temporal power. And then the papacy entered into two centuries of peace and effacement, for the strong absolute monarchies which had divided Europe among themselves could do without it, and had ceased to tremble at the harmless thunderbolts of excommunication or to look on the pope as aught but a master of ceremonies, controlling certain rites. The possession of the people was no longer subject to the same rules. Allowing that the kings still held the people from God, it was the pope's duty to register the donation once for all, without ever intervening, whatever the circumstances, in the government of states. Never was Rome farther away from the realisation of its ancient dream of universal dominion. And when the French Revolution burst forth, it may well have been imagined that the proclamation of the rights of man would kill that papacy to which the exercise of divine right over the nations had been committed. And so how great at first was the anxiety, the anger, the desperate resistance with which the Vatican opposed the idea of freedom, the new *credo* of liberated reason, of humanity regaining self-possession and control. It was the apparent *denouement* of the long struggle between the pope and the emperor for possession of the people: the emperor vanished, and the people, henceforward free to dispose of itself, claimed to escape from the pope—an unforeseen solution, in which it seemed as though all the ancient scaffolding of the Catholic world must fall to the very ground.

At this point Pierre concluded the first part of his book by contrasting primitive Christianity with present-day Catholicism, which is the triumph of the rich and the powerful. That Roman society which Jesus had come to destroy in the name of the poor and humble, had not Catholic Rome steadily continued rebuilding it through all the centuries, by its policy of cupidity and pride? And what bitter irony it was to find, after eighteen hundred years of the Gospel, that the world was again collapsing through frantic speculation, rotten banks, financial disasters, and the frightful injustice of a few men gorged with wealth whilst thousands of their brothers were dying of hunger! The whole redemption of the wretched had to be worked afresh. However,

Pierre gave expression to all these terrible things in words so softened by charity, so steeped in hope, that they lost their revolutionary danger. Moreover, he nowhere attacked the dogmas. His book, in its sentimental, somewhat poetic form, was but the cry of an apostle glowing with love for his fellow-men.

Then came the second part of the work, the PRESENT, a study of Catholic society as it now exists. Here Pierre had painted a frightful picture of the misery of the poor, the misery of a great city, which he knew so well and bled for, through having laid his hands upon its poisonous wounds. The present-day injustice could no longer be tolerated, charity was becoming powerless, and so frightful was the suffering that all hope was dying away from the hearts of the people. And was it not the monstrous spectacle presented by Christendom, whose abominations corrupted the people, and maddened it with hatred and vengeance, that had largely destroyed its faith? However, after this picture of rotting and crumbling society, Pierre returned to history, to the period of the French Revolution, to the mighty hope with which the idea of freedom had filled the world. The middle classes, the great Liberal party, on attaining power had undertaken to bring happiness to one and all. But after a century's experience it really seemed that liberty had failed to bring any happiness whatever to the outcasts. In the political sphere illusions were departing. At all events, if the reigning third estate declares itself satisfied, the fourth estate, that of the toilers,[1] still suffers and continues to demand its share of fortune. The working classes have been proclaimed free; political equality has been granted them, but the gift has been valueless, for economically they are still bound to servitude, and only enjoy, as they did formerly, the liberty of dying of hunger. All the socialist revendications have come from that; between labour and capital rests the terrifying problem, the solution of which threatens to sweep away society. When slavery disappeared from the olden world to be succeeded by salaried employment the revolution was immense, and certainly the Christian principle was one of the great factors in the destruction of slavery. Nowadays, therefore, when the question is to replace salaried employment by something else, possibly by the participation of the workman in the profits of his work, why should not Christianity again seek a new principle of action? The fatal and proximate accession of the democracy means the beginning of another phase in human history, the creation of the society of to-morrow. And Rome cannot keep away from the arena; the papacy must take part in the quarrel if it does not desire to disappear from the world like a piece of mechanism that has become altogether useless.

Hence it followed that Catholic socialism was legitimate. On every side the socialist sects were battling with their various solutions for the privilege of ensuring the happiness of the people, and the Church also must offer her solution of the problem. Here it was that New Rome appeared, that the evolution spread into a renewal of boundless hope. Most certainly there was nothing contrary to democracy in the principles of the Roman Catholic Church. Indeed she had only to return to the evangelical traditions, to become once more the Church of the humble and the poor, to re-establish the universal Christian community. She is undoubtedly of democratic essence, and if she sided with the rich and the powerful when Christianity became

---

[1] In England we call the press the fourth estate, but in France and elsewhere the term is applied to the working classes, and in that sense must be taken here.—Trans.

Catholicism, she only did so perforce, that she might live by sacrificing some portion of her original purity; so that if to-day she should abandon the condemned governing classes in order to make common cause with the multitude of the wretched, she would simply be drawing nearer to Christ, thereby securing a new lease of youth and purifying herself of all the political compromises which she formerly was compelled to acaccept. Without renouncing aught of her absolutism the Church has at all times known how to bow to circumstances; but she reserves her perfect sovereignty, simply tolerating that which she cannot prevent, and patiently waiting, even through long centuries, for the time when she shall again become the mistress of the world.

Might not that time come in the crisis which was now at hand? Once more, all the powers are battling for possession of the people. Since the people, thanks to liberty and education, has become strong, since it has developed consciousness and will, and claimed its share of fortune, all rulers have been seeking to attach it to themselves, to reign by it, and even with it, should that be necessary. Socialism, therein lies the future, the new instrument of government; and the kings tottering on their thrones, the middle-class presidents of anxious republics, the ambitious plotters who dream of power, all dabble in socialism! They all agree that the capitalist organisation of the State is a return to pagan times, to the olden slave-market; and they all talk of breaking for ever the iron law by which the labour of human beings has become so much merchandise, subject to supply and demand, with wages calculated on an estimate of what is strictly necessary to keep a workman from dying of hunger. And, down in the sphere below, the evil increases, the workmen agonise with hunger and exasperation, while above them discussion still goes on, systems are bandied about, and well-meaning persons exhaust themselves in attempting to apply ridiculously inadequate remedies. There is much stir without any progress, all the wild bewilderment which precedes great catastrophes. And among the many, Catholic socialism, quite as ardent as Revolutionary socialism, enters the lists and strives to conquer.

After these explanations Pierre gave an account of the long efforts made by Catholic socialism throughout the Christian world. That which particularly struck one in this connection was that the warfare became keener and more victorious whenever it was waged in some land of propaganda, as yet not completely conquered by Roman Catholicism. For instance, in the countries where Protestantism confronted the latter, the priests fought with wondrous passion, as for dear life itself, contending with the schismatical clergy for possession of the people by dint of daring, by unfolding the most audacious democratic theories. In Germany, the classic land of socialism, Mgr. Ketteler was one of the first to speak of adequately taxing the rich; and later he fomented a wide-spread agitation which the clergy now directs by means of numerous associations and newspapers. In Switzerland Mgr. Mermillod pleaded the cause of the poor so loudly that the bishops there now almost make common cause with the democratic socialists, whom they doubtless hope to convert when the day for sharing arrives. In England, where socialism penetrates so very slowly, Cardinal Manning achieved considerable success, stood by the working classes on the occasion of a famous strike, and helped on a popular movement, which was signalised by numerous conversions. But it was particularly in the United States of America that Catholic socialism proved triumphant, in a sphere of democracy where the bishops, like Mgr. Ireland, were forced to set themselves at the head of the working-class agitation. And there across the Atlantic a new Church seems to be germinating, still in confusion but overflowing with sap, and upheld by intense hope, as at the aurora of the rejuvenated Christianity of to-morrow.

Passing thence to Austria and Belgium, both Catholic countries, one found Catholic socialism mingling in the first instance with anti-semitism, while in the second it had no precise sense. And all movement ceased and disappeared when one came to Spain and Italy, those old lands of faith. The former with its intractable bishops who contented themselves with hurling excommunication at unbelievers as in the days of the Inquisition, seemed to be abandoned to the violent theories of revolutionaries, whilst Italy, immobilised in the traditional courses, remained without possibility of initiative, reduced to silence and respect by the presence of the Holy See. In France, however, the struggle remained keen, but it was more particularly a struggle of ideas. On the whole, the war was there being waged against the revolution, and to some it seemed as though it would suffice to re-establish the old organisation of monarchical times in order to revert to the golden age. It was thus that the question of working-class corporations had become the one problem, the panacea for all the ills of the toilers. But people were far from agreeing; some, those Catholics who rejected State interference and favoured purely moral action, desired that the corporations should be free; whilst others, the young and impatient ones, bent on action, demanded that they should be obligatory, each with capital of its own, and recognised and protected by the State.

Viscount Philibert de la Choue had by pen and speech carried on a vigorous campaign in favour of the obligatory corporations; and his great grief was that he had so far failed to prevail on the Pope to say whether in his opinion these corporations should be closed or open. According to the Viscount, herein lay the fate of society, a peaceful solution of the social question or the frightful catastrophe which must sweep everything away. In reality, though he refused to own it, the Viscount had ended by adopting State socialism. And, despite the lack of agreement, the agitation remained very great; attempts, scarcely happy in their results, were made; co-operative associations, companies for erecting workmen's dwellings, popular savings' banks were started; many more or less disguised efforts to revert to the old Christian community organisation were tried; while day by day, amidst the prevailing confusion, in the mental perturbation and political difficulties through which the country passed, the militant Catholic party felt its hopes increasing, even to the blind conviction of soon resuming sway over the whole world.

The second part of Pierre's book concluded by a picture of the moral and intellectual uneasiness amidst which the end of the century is struggling. While the toiling multitude suffers from its hard lot and demands that in any fresh division of wealth it shall be ensured at least its daily bread, the *elite* is no better satisfied, but complains of the void induced by the freeing of its reason and the enlargement of its intelligence. It is the famous bankruptcy of rationalism, of positivism, of science itself which is in question. Minds consumed by need of the absolute grow weary of groping, weary of the delays of science which recognises only proven truths; doubt tortures them, they need a complete and immediate synthesis in order to sleep in peace; and they fall on their knees, overcome by the roadside, distracted by the thought that science will never tell them all, and preferring the Deity, the mystery revealed and affirmed by faith. Even to-day, it must be admitted, science calms neither our thirst for justice, our desire for safety, nor our everlasting idea of happiness after life in an eternity of enjoyment. To one and all it only brings the austere duty to live, to be a mere contributor in the universal toil; and how well one can understand that hearts should revolt and sigh for the Christian heaven, peopled with lovely angels, full of light and music and perfumes! Ah! to embrace one's dead, to tell oneself that one will meet them again, that one will live with them once more in glorious immortality! And to possess the certainty of sovereign equity to enable one to support the abominations of terrestrial life! And in this wise to trample on the frightful thought of annihilation, to escape the horror of the disappearance of the *ego*, and to tranquillise oneself with that unshakable faith which postpones until the portal of death be crossed the solution of all the problems of destiny! This dream will be dreamt by the nations for ages yet. And this it is which explains why, in these last days of the century, excessive mental labour and the deep unrest of humanity, pregnant with a new world, have awakened religious feeling, anxious, tormented by thoughts of the ideal and the infinite, demanding a moral law and an assurance of superior justice. Religions may disappear, but religious feelings will always create new ones, even with the help of science. A new religion! a new religion! Was it not the ancient Catholicism, which in the soil of the present day, where all seemed conducive to a miracle, was about to spring up afresh, throw out green branches and blossom in a young yet mighty florescence?

At last, in the third part of his book and in the glowing language of an apostle, Pierre depicted the FUTURE: Catholicism rejuvenated, and bringing health and peace, the forgotten golden age of primitive Christianity, back to expiring society. He began with an emotional and sparkling portrait of Leo XIII, the ideal Pope, the Man of Destiny entrusted with the salvation of the nations. He had conjured up a presentment of him and beheld him thus in his feverish longing for the advent of a pastor who should put an end to human misery. It was perhaps not a close likeness, but it was a portrait of the needed saviour, with open heart and mind, and inexhaustible benevolence, such as he had dreamed. At the same time he had certainly searched documents, studied encyclical letters, based his sketch upon facts: first Leo's religious education at Rome, then his brief nunciature at Brussels, and afterwards his long episcopate at Perugia. And as soon as Leo became pope in the difficult situation bequeathed by Pius IX, the duality of his nature appeared: on one hand was the firm guardian of dogmas, on the other the supple politician resolved to carry conciliation to its utmost limits. We see him flatly severing all connection with modern philosophy, stepping backward beyond the Renascence to the middle ages and reviving Christian philosophy, as expounded by "the angelic doctor," St. Thomas Aquinas, in Catholic schools. Then the dogmas being in this wise sheltered, he adroitly maintains himself in equilibrium by giving securities to every power, striving to utilise every opportunity. He displays extraordinary activity, reconciles the Holy See with Germany, draws nearer to Russia, contents Switzerland, asks the friendship of Great Britain, and writes to the Emperor of China begging him to protect the missionaries and Christians in his dominions. Later on, too, he intervenes in France and acknowledges the legitimacy of the Republic.

From the very outset an idea becomes apparent in all his actions, an idea which will place him among the great papal politicians. It is moreover the ancient idea of the papacy—the conquest of every soul, Rome capital and mistress of the world. Thus Leo XIII has but one desire, one object, that of unifying the Church, of drawing all the dissident communities to it in order that it may be invincible in the coming social struggle. He seeks to obtain recognition of the moral authority of the Vatican in Russia; he dreams of disarming the Anglican Church and of drawing it into a sort of fraternal truce; and he particularly seeks to come to an understanding with the Schismatical Churches of the East, which he regards as sisters, simply living apart, whose return his paternal heart entreats. Would not Rome indeed dispose of victorious strength if she exercised uncontested sway over all the Christians of the earth?

And here the social ideas of Leo XIII come in. Whilst yet Bishop of Perugia he wrote a pastoral letter in which a vague humanitarian socialism appeared. As soon, however, as he had assumed the triple crown his opinions changed and he anathematised the revolutionaries whose audacity was terrifying Italy. But almost at once he corrected himself, warned by events and realising the great danger of leaving socialism in the hands of the enemies of the Church. Then he listened to the bishops of the lands of propaganda, ceased to intervene in the Irish quarrel, withdrew the excommunications which he had launched against the American "knights of labour," and would not allow the bold works of Catholic socialist writers to be placed in the Index. This evolution towards democracy may be traced through his most famous encyclical letters: *Immortale Dei*, on the constitution of States; *Libertas*, on human liberty; *Sapientoe*, on the duties of Christian citizens; *Rerum novarum*, on the condition of the working classes; and it is particularly this last which would seem to have rejuvenated the Church. The Pope herein chronicles the undeserved misery of the toilers, the undue length of the hours of labour, the insufficiency of salaries. All men have the right to live, and all contracts extorted by threats of starvation are unjust. Elsewhere he declares that the workman must not be left defenceless in presence of a system which converts the misery of the majority into the wealth of a few. Compelled to deal vaguely with questions of organisation, he contents himself with encouraging the corporative movement, placing it under State patronage; and after thus contributing to restore the secular power, he reinstates the Deity on the throne of sovereignty, and discerns the path to salvation more particularly in moral measures, in the ancient respect due to family ties and ownership. Nevertheless, was not the helpful hand which the august Vicar of Christ thus publicly tendered to the poor and the humble, the certain token of a new alliance, the announcement of a new reign of Jesus upon earth? Thenceforward the people knew that it was not abandoned. And from that moment too how glorious became Leo XIII, whose sacerdotal jubilee and episcopal jubilee were celebrated by all Christendom amidst the coming of a vast multitude, of endless offerings, and of flattering letters from every sovereign!

Pierre next dealt with the question of the temporal power, and this he thought he might treat freely. Naturally, he was not ignorant of the fact that the Pope in his quarrel with Italy upheld the rights of the Church over Rome as stubbornly as his predecessor; but he imagined that this was merely a necessary conventional attitude, imposed by political considerations, and destined to be abandoned when the times were ripe. For his own part he was convinced that if the Pope had never appeared greater than he did now, it was to the loss of the temporal power that he owed it; for thence had come the great increase of his authority, the pure splendour of moral omnipotence which he diffused.

What a long history of blunders and conflicts had been that of the possession of the little kingdom of Rome during fifteen centuries! Constantine quits Rome in the fourth century, only a few forgotten functionaries remaining on the deserted Palatine, and the Pope naturally rises to power, and the life of the city passes to the Lateran. However, it is only four centuries later that Charlemagne recognises accomplished facts and formally bestows the States of the Church upon the papacy. From that time warfare between the spiritual power and the temporal powers has never ceased; though often latent it has at times become acute, breaking forth with blood and fire. And to-day, in the midst of Europe in arms, is it not unreasonable to dream of the papacy ruling a strip of territory where it would be exposed to every vexation, and where it could only maintain itself by the help of a foreign army? What would become of it in the general massacre which is apprehended? Is it not far more sheltered, far more dignified, far more lofty when disentangled from all terrestrial cares, reigning over the world of souls?

In the early times of the Church the papacy from being merely local, merely Roman, gradually became catholicised, universalised, slowly acquiring dominion over all Christendom. In the same way the Sacred College, at first a continuation of the Roman Senate, acquired an international character, and in our time has ended by becoming the most cosmopolitan of assemblies, in which representatives of all the nations have seats. And is it not evident that the Pope, thus leaning on the cardinals, has become the one great international power which exercises the greater authority since it is free from all monarchical interests, and can speak not merely in the name of country but in that of humanity itself? The solution so often sought amidst such long wars surely lies in this: Either give the Pope the temporal sovereignty of the world, or leave him only the spiritual sovereignty. Vicar of the Deity, absolute and infallible sovereign by divine delegation, he can but remain in the sanctuary if, ruler already of the human soul, he is not recognised by every nation as the one master of the body also—the king of kings.

But what a strange affair was this new incursion of the papacy into the field sown by the French Revolution, an incursion conducting it perhaps towards the domination, which it has striven for with a will that has upheld it for centuries! For now it stands alone before the people. The kings are down. And as the people is henceforth free to give itself to whomsoever it pleases, why should it not give itself to the Church? The depreciation which the idea of liberty has certainly undergone renders every hope permissible. The liberal party appears to be vanquished in the sphere of economics. The toilers, dissatisfied with 1789 complain of the aggravation of their misery, bestir themselves, seek happiness despairingly. On the other hand the new *regimes* have increased the international power of the Church; Catholic members are numerous in the parliaments of the republics and the constitutional monarchies. All circumstances seem therefore to favour this extraordinary return of fortune, Catholicism reverting to the vigour of youth in its old age. Even science, remember, is accused of bankruptcy, a charge which saves the *Syllabus* from ridicule, troubles the minds of men, and throws the limitless sphere of mystery and impossibility open once more. And then a prophecy is recalled, a prediction that the papacy shall be mistress of the world on the day when she marches at the head of the democracy after reuniting the Schismatical Churches of the East to the Catholic, Apostolic, and Roman Church. And, in Pierre's opinion, assuredly the times had come since Pope Leo XIII, dismissing the great and the wealthy of the world, left the kings driven from their thrones in exile to place himself like Jesus on the side of the foodless toilers and the beggars of the high roads. Yet a few more years, perhaps, of frightful misery, alarming confusion, fearful social danger, and the people, the great silent multitude which others have so far disposed of, will return to the cradle, to the unified Church of Rome, in order to escape the destruction which threatens human society.

Pierre concluded his book with a passionate evocation of New Rome, the spiritual Rome which would soon reign over the nations, reconciled and fraternising as in another golden age. Herein he even saw the end of superstitions. Without making a direct attack on dogma, he allowed himself to dream of an enlargement of religious feeling, freed from rites, and absorbed in the one satisfaction of human charity. And still smarting from his journey to Lourdes, he felt the need of contenting his heart. Was not that gross superstition of Lourdes the hateful symptom of the excessive suffering of the times? On the day when the Gospel should be universally diffused and practised, suffering ones would cease seeking an illusory relief so far away, assured as they would be of finding assistance, consolation, and cure in their homes amidst their brothers. At Lourdes there was an iniquitous displacement of wealth, a spectacle so frightful as to make one doubt of God, a perpetual conflict which would disappear in the truly Christian society of to-morrow. Ah! that society, that Christian community, all Pierre's work ended in an ardent longing for its speedy advent: Christianity becoming once more the religion of truth and justice which it had been before it allowed itself to be conquered by the rich and the powerful! The little ones and the poor ones reigning, sharing the wealth of earth, and owing obedience to nought but the levelling law of work! The Pope alone erect at the head of the federation of nations, prince of peace, with the simple mission of supplying the moral rule, the link of charity and love which was to unite all men! And would not this be the speedy realisation of the promises of Christ? The times were near accomplishment, secular and religious society would mingle so closely that they would form but one; and it would be the age of triumph and happiness predicted by all the prophets, no more struggles possible, no more antagonism between the mind and the body, but a marvellous equilibrium which would kill evil and set the kingdom of heaven upon earth. New Rome, the centre of the world, bestowing on the world the new religion!

Pierre felt that tears were coming to his eyes, and with an unconscious movement, never noticing how much he astonished the slim Englishmen and thick-set Germans passing along the terrace, he opened his arms and extended them towards the *real* Rome, steeped in such lovely sunshine and stretched out at his feet. Would she prove responsive to his dream? Would he, as he had written, find within her the remedy for our impatience and our alarms? Could Catholicism be renewed, could it return to the spirit of primitive Christianity, become the religion of the democracy, the faith which the modern world, overturned and in danger of perishing, awaits in order to be pacified and to live?

Pierre was full of generous passion, full of faith. He again beheld good Abbe Rose weeping with emotion as he read his book. He heard Viscount Philibert de la Choue telling him that such a book was worth an army. And he particularly felt strong in the approval of Cardinal Bergerot, that apostle of inexhaustible charity. Why should the Congregation of the Index threaten his work with interdiction? Since he had been officiously advised to go to Rome if he desired to defend himself, he had been turning this question over in his mind without being able to discover which of his pages were attacked. To him indeed they all seemed to glow with the purest Christianity. However, he had arrived quivering with enthusiasm and courage: he was all eagerness to kneel before the Pope, and place himself under his august protection, assuring him that he had not written a line without taking inspiration from his ideas, without desiring the triumph of his policy. Was it possible that condemnation should be passed on a book in which he imagined in all sincerity that he had exalted Leo XIII by striving to help him in his work of Christian reunion and universal peace?

For a moment longer Pierre remained standing before the parapet. He had been there for nearly an hour, unable to drink in enough of the grandeur of Rome, which, given all the unknown things she hid from him, he would have liked to possess at once. Oh! to seize hold of her, know her, ascertain at once the true word which he had come to seek from her! This again, like Lourdes, was an experiment, but a graver one, a decisive one, whence he would emerge either strengthened or overcome for evermore. He no longer sought the simple, perfect faith of the little child, but the superior faith of the intellectual man, raising himself above rites and symbols, working for the greatest happiness of humanity as based on its need of certainty. His temples throbbed responsive to his heart. What would be the answer of Rome?

The sunlight had increased and the higher districts now stood out more vigorously against the fiery background. Far away the hills became gilded and empurpled, whilst the nearer house-fronts grew very distinct and bright with their thousands of windows sharply outlined. However, some morning haze still hovered around; light veils seemed to rise from the lower streets, blurring the summits for a moment, and then evaporating in the ardent heavens where all was blue. For a moment Pierre fancied that the Palatine had vanished, for he could scarcely see the dark fringe of cypresses; it was as though the dust of its ruins concealed the hill. But the Quirinal was even more obscured; the royal palace seemed to have faded away in a fog, so paltry did it look with its low flat front, so vague in the distance that he no longer distinguished it; whereas above the trees on his left the dome of St. Peter's had grown yet larger in the limpid gold of the sunshine, and appeared to occupy the whole sky and dominate the whole city!

Ah! the Rome of that first meeting, the Rome of early morning, whose new districts he had not even noticed in the burning fever of his arrival—with what boundless hopes did she not inspirit him, this Rome which he believed he should find alive, such indeed as he had dreamed! And whilst he stood there in his thin black cassock, thus gazing on her that lovely day, what a shout of coming redemption seemed to arise from her house-roofs, what a promise of universal peace seemed to issue from that sacred soil, twice already Queen of the world! It was the third Rome, it was New Rome whose maternal love was travelling across the frontiers to all the nations to console them and reunite them in a common embrace. In the passionate candour of his dream he beheld her, he heard her, rejuvenated, full of the gentleness of childhood, soaring, as it were, amidst the morning freshness into the vast pure heavens.

But at last Pierre tore himself away from the sublime spectacle. The driver and the horse, their heads drooping under the broad sunlight, had not stirred. On the seat the valise was almost burning, hot with rays of the sun which was already heavy. And once more Pierre got into the vehicle and gave this address:

"Via Giulia, Palazzo Boccanera."

II.

THE Via Giulia, which runs in a straight line over a distance of five hundred yards from the Farnese palace to the church of St. John of the Florentines, was at that hour steeped in bright sunlight, the glow streaming from end to end and whitening the small square paving stones. The street had no footways, and the cab rolled along it almost to the farther extremity, passing the old grey sleepy and deserted residences whose large windows were barred with iron, while their deep porches revealed sombre courts resembling wells. Laid out by Pope Julius II, who had dreamt of lining it with magnificent palaces, the street, then the most regular and handsome in Rome, had served as Corso[1] in the sixteenth century. One could tell that one was in a former luxurious district, which had lapsed into silence, solitude, and abandonment, instinct with a kind of religious gentleness and discretion. The old house-fronts followed one after another, their shutters closed and their gratings occasionally decked with climbing plants. At some doors cats were seated, and dim shops, appropriated to humble trades, were installed in certain dependencies. But little traffic was apparent. Pierre only noticed some bare-headed women dragging children behind them, a hay cart drawn by a mule, a superb monk draped in drugget, and a bicyclist speeding along noiselessly, his machine sparkling in the sun.

At last the driver turned and pointed to a large square building at the corner of a lane running towards the Tiber.

"Palazzo Boccanera."

Pierre raised his head and was pained by the severe aspect of the structure, so bare and massive and blackened by age. Like its neighbours the Farnese and Sacchetti palaces, it had been built by Antonio da Sangallo in the early part of the sixteenth century, and, as with the former of those residences, the tradition ran that in raising the pile the architect had made use of stones pilfered from the Colosseum and the Theatre of Marcellus. The vast, square-looking facade had three upper stories, each with seven windows, and the first one very lofty and noble. Down below, the only sign of decoration was that the high ground-floor windows, barred with huge projecting gratings as though from fear of siege, rested upon large consoles, and were crowned by attics which smaller consoles supported. Above the monumental en-

---

[1] The Corso was so called on account of the horse races held in it at carnival time.—Trans.

trance, with folding doors of bronze, there was a balcony in front of the central first-floor window. And at the summit of the facade against the sky appeared a sumptuous entablature, whose frieze displayed admirable grace and purity of ornamentation. The frieze, the consoles, the attics, and the door-case were of white marble, but marble whose surface had so crumbled and so darkened that it now had the rough yellowish grain of stone. Right and left of the entrance were two antique seats upheld by griffons also of marble; and incrusted in the wall at one corner, a lovely Renascence fountain, its source dried up, still lingered; and on it a cupid riding a dolphin could with difficulty be distinguished, to such a degree had the wear and tear of time eaten into the sculpture.

Pierre's eyes, however, had been more particularly attracted by an escutcheon carved above one of the ground-floor windows, the escutcheon of the Boccaneras, a winged dragon venting flames, and underneath it he could plainly read the motto which had remained intact: "*Bocca nera, Alma rossa*" (black mouth, red soul). Above another window, as a pendant to the escutcheon, there was one of those little shrines which are still common in Rome, a satin-robed statuette of the Blessed Virgin, before which a lantern burnt in the full daylight.

The cabman was about to drive through the dim and gaping porch, according to custom, when the young priest, overcome by timidity, stopped him. "No, no," he said; "don't go in, it's useless."

Then he alighted from the vehicle, paid the man, and, valise in hand, found himself first under the vaulted roof, and then in the central court without having met a living soul.

It was a square and fairly spacious court, surrounded by a porticus like a cloister. Some remnants of statuary, marbles discovered in excavating, an armless Apollo, and the trunk of a Venus, were ranged against the walls under the dismal arcades; and some fine grass had sprouted between the pebbles which paved the soil as with a black and white mosaic. It seemed as if the sun-rays could never reach that paving, mouldy with damp. A dimness and a silence instinct with departed grandeur and infinite mournfulness reigned there.

Surprised by the emptiness of this silent mansion, Pierre continued seeking somebody, a porter, a servant; and, fancying that he saw a shadow flit by, he decided to pass through another arch which led to a little garden fringing the Tiber. On this side the facade of the building was quite plain, displaying nothing beyond its three rows of symmetrically disposed windows. However, the abandonment reigning in the garden brought Pierre yet a keener pang. In the centre some large box-plants were growing in the basin of a fountain which had been filled up; while among the mass of weeds, some orange-trees with golden, ripening fruit alone indicated the tracery of the paths which they had once bordered. Between two huge laurel-bushes, against the right-hand wall, there was a sarcophagus of the second century—with fauns offering violence to nymphs, one of those wild *baccanali*, those scenes of eager passion which Rome in its decline was wont to depict on the tombs of its dead; and this marble sarcophagus, crumbling with age and green with moisture, served as a tank into which a streamlet of water fell from a large tragic mask incrusted in the wall. Facing the Tiber there had formerly been a sort of colonnaded loggia, a terrace whence a double flight of steps descended to the river. For the construction of the new quays, however, the river bank was being raised, and the terrace was already lower than the new ground level, and stood there crumbling and useless amidst piles of rubbish and blocks of stone, all the wretched chalky confusion of the improvements which were ripping up and overturning the district.

Pierre, however, was suddenly convinced that he could see somebody crossing the court. So he returned thither and found a woman somewhat short of stature, who must have been nearly fifty, though as yet she had not a white hair, but looked very bright and active. At sight of the priest, however, an expression of distrust passed over her round face and clear eyes.

Employing the few words of broken Italian which he knew, Pierre at once sought to explain matters: "I am Abbe Pierre Froment, madame—" he began.

However, she did not let him continue, but exclaimed in fluent French, with the somewhat thick and lingering accent of the province of the Ile-de-France: "Ah! yes, Monsieur l'Abbe, I know, I know—I was expecting you, I received orders about you." And then, as he gazed at her in amazement, she added: "Oh! I'm a Frenchwoman! I've been here for five and twenty years, but I haven't yet been able to get used to their horrible lingo!"

Pierre thereupon remembered that Viscount Philibert de la Choue had spoken to him of this servant, one Victorine Bosquet, a native of Auneau in La Beauce, who, when two and twenty, had gone to Rome with a consumptive mistress. The latter's sudden death had left her in as much terror and bewilderment as if she had been alone in some land of savages; and so she had gratefully devoted herself to the Countess Ernesta Brandini, a Boccanera by birth, who had, so to say, picked her up in the streets. The Countess had at first employed her as a nurse to her daughter Benedetta, hoping in this way to teach the child some French; and Victorine—remaining for some five and twenty years with the same family—had by degrees raised herself to the position of housekeeper, whilst still remaining virtually illiterate, so destitute indeed of any linguistic gift that she could only jabber a little broken Italian, just sufficient for her needs in her intercourse with the other servants.

"And is Monsieur le Vicomte quite well?" she resumed with frank familiarity. "He is so very pleasant, and we are always so pleased to see him. He stays here, you know, each time he comes to Rome. I know that the Princess and the Contessina received a letter from him yesterday announcing you."

It was indeed Viscount Philibert de la Choue who had made all the arrangements for Pierre's sojourn in Rome. Of the ancient and once vigorous race of the Boccaneras, there now only remained Cardinal Pio Boccanera, the Princess his sister, an old maid who from respect was called "Donna" Serafina, their niece Benedetta—whose mother Ernesta had followed her husband, Count Brandini, to the tomb—and finally their nephew, Prince Dario Boccanera, whose father, Prince Onofrio, was likewise dead, and whose mother, a Montefiori, had married again. It so chanced that the Viscount de la Choue was connected with the family, his younger brother having married a Brandini, sister to Benedetta's father; and thus, with the courtesy rank of uncle, he had, in Count Brandini's time, frequently sojourned at the mansion in the Via Giulia. He had also become attached to Benedetta, especially since the advent of a private family drama, consequent upon an unhappy marriage which the young woman had contracted, and which she had petitioned the Holy Father to annul. Since Benedetta had left her husband to live with her aunt Serafina and her uncle the Cardinal, M. de la Choue had often written to her and sent her parcels of French books. Among others he had forwarded her a copy of Pierre's book, and the whole affair had originated in that wise. Several letters on the subject had been exchanged when at last Benedetta sent word that the work had been denounced to the Congregation of the Index, and that it was advisable the author should at once repair to Rome, where she graciously offered him the hospitality of the Boccanera mansion.

The Viscount was quite as much astonished as the young priest at these tidings, and failed to understand why the book should be threatened at all; however, he prevailed on Pierre to make the journey as a matter of good policy, becoming himself impassioned for the achievement of a victory which he counted in anticipation as his own. And so it was easy to understand the bewildered condition of Pierre, on tumbling into this unknown mansion, launched into an heroic adventure, the reasons and circumstances of which were beyond him.

Victorine, however, suddenly resumed: "But I am leaving you here, Monsieur l'Abbe. Let me conduct you to your rooms. Where is your luggage?"

Then, when he had shown her his valise which he had placed on the ground beside him, and explained that having no more than a fortnight's stay in view he had contented himself with bringing a second cassock and some linen, she seemed very much surprised.

"A fortnight! You only expect to remain here a fortnight? Well, well, you'll see."

And then summoning a big devil of a lackey who had ended by making his appearance, she said: "Take that up into the red room, Giacomo. Will you kindly follow me, Monsieur l'Abbe?"

Pierre felt quite comforted and inspirited by thus unexpectedly meeting such a lively, good-natured compatriot in this gloomy Roman "palace." Whilst crossing the court he listened to her as she related that the Princess had gone out, and that the Contessina—as Benedetta from motives of affection was still called in the house, despite her marriage—had not yet shown herself that morning, being rather poorly. However, added Victorine, she had her orders.

The staircase was in one corner of the court, under the porticus. It was a monumental staircase with broad, low steps, the incline being so gentle that a horse might easily have climbed it. The stone walls, however, were quite bare, the landings empty and solemn, and a death-like mournfulness fell from the lofty vault above.

As they reached the first floor, noticing Pierre's emotion, Victorine smiled. The mansion seemed to be uninhabited; not a sound came from its closed chambers. Simply pointing to a large oaken door on the right-hand, the housekeeper remarked: "The wing overlooking the court and the river is occupied by his Eminence. But he doesn't use a quarter of the rooms. All the reception-rooms on the side of the street have been shut. How could one keep up such a big place, and what, too, would be the use of it? We should need somebody to lodge."

With her lithe step she continued ascending the stairs. She had remained essentially a foreigner, a Frenchwoman, too different from those among whom she lived to be influenced by her environment. On reaching the second floor she resumed: "There, on the left, are Donna Serafina's rooms; those of the Contessina are on the right. This is the only part of the house where there's a little warmth and life. Besides, it's Monday to-day, the Princess will be receiving visitors this evening. You'll see."

Then, opening a door, beyond which was a second and very narrow staircase, she went on: "We others have our rooms on the third floor. I must ask Monsieur l'Abbe to let me go up before him."

The grand staircase ceased at the second floor, and Victorine explained that the third story was reached exclusively by this servants' staircase, which led from the lane running down to the Tiber on one side of the mansion. There was a small private entrance in this lane, which was very convenient.

At last, reaching the third story, she hurried along a passage, again calling Pierre's attention to various doors. "These are the apartments of Don Vigilio, his Eminence's secretary. These are mine. And these will be yours. Monsieur le Vicomte will never have any other rooms when he comes to spend a few days in Rome. He says that he enjoys more liberty up here, as he can come in and go out as he pleases. I gave him a key to the door in the lane, and I'll give you one too. And, besides, you'll see what a nice view there is from here!"

Whilst speaking she had gone in. The apartments comprised two rooms: a somewhat spacious *salon*, with wall-paper of a large scroll pattern on a red ground, and a bed-chamber, where the paper was of a flax grey, studded with faded blue flowers. The sitting-room was in one corner of the mansion overlooking the lane and the Tiber, and Victorine at once went to the windows, one of which afforded a view over the distant lower part of the river, while the other faced the Trastevere and the Janiculum across the water.

"Ah! yes, it's very pleasant!" said Pierre, who had followed and stood beside her.

Giaccomo, who did not hurry, came in behind them with the valise. It was now past eleven o'clock; and seeing that the young priest looked tired, and realising that he must be hungry after such a journey, Victorine offered to have some breakfast served at once in the sitting-room. He would then have the afternoon to rest or go out, and would only meet the ladies in the evening at dinner. At the mere suggestion of resting, however, Pierre began to protest, declaring that he should certainly go out, not wishing to lose an entire afternoon. The breakfast he readily accepted, for he was indeed dying of hunger.

However, he had to wait another full half hour. Giaccomo, who served him under Victorine's orders, did everything in a most leisurely way. And Victorine, lacking confidence in the man, remained with the young priest to make sure that everything he might require was provided.

"Ah! Monsieur l'Abbe," said she, "what people! What a country! You can't have an idea of it. I should never get accustomed to it even if I were to live here for a hundred years. Ah! if it were not for the Contessina, but she's so good and beautiful."

Then, whilst placing a dish of figs on the table, she astonished Pierre by adding that a city where nearly everybody was a priest could not possibly be a good city. Thereupon the presence of this gay, active, unbelieving servant in the queer old palace again scared him.

"What! you are not religious?" he exclaimed.

"No, no, Monsieur l'Abbe, the priests don't suit me," said Victorine; "I knew one in France when I was very little, and since I've been here I've seen too many of them. It's all over. Oh! I don't say that on account of his Eminence, who is a holy man worthy of all possible respect. And besides, everybody in the house knows that I've nothing to reproach myself with. So why not leave me alone, since I'm fond of my employers and attend properly to my duties?"

She burst into a frank laugh. "Ah!" she resumed, "when I was told that another priest was coming, just as if we hadn't enough already, I couldn't help growling to myself. But you look like a good young man, Monsieur l'Abbe, and I feel sure we shall get on well together.... I really don't know why I'm telling you all this—probably it's because you've come from yonder, and because the Contessina takes an interest in you. At all events, you'll excuse me, won't you, Monsieur l'Abbe? And take my advice, stay here and rest to-day; don't be so foolish as to go running about their tiring city. There's nothing very amusing to be seen in it, whatever they may say to the contrary."

When Pierre found himself alone, he suddenly felt overwhelmed by all the fatigue of his journey coupled with the fever of enthusiasm that had consumed him during the morning. And as though dazed, intoxicated by the hasty meal which he had just made—a couple of eggs and a cutlet—he flung himself upon the bed with the idea of taking half an hour's rest. He did not fall asleep immediately, but for a time thought of those Boccaneras, with whose history he was partly acquainted, and of whose life in that deserted and silent palace, instinct with such dilapidated and melancholy grandeur, he began to dream. But at last his ideas grew confused, and by degrees he sunk into sleep amidst a crowd of shadowy forms, some tragic and some sweet, with vague faces which gazed at him with enigmatical eyes as they whirled before him in the depths of dreamland.

The Boccaneras had supplied two popes to Rome, one in the thirteenth, the other in the fifteenth century, and from those two favoured ones, those all-powerful masters, the family had formerly derived its vast fortune—large estates in the vicinity of Viterbo, several palaces in Rome, enough works of art to fill numerous spacious galleries, and a pile of gold sufficient to cram a cellar. The family passed as being the most pious of the Roman *patriziato*, a family of burning faith whose sword had always been at the service of the Church; but if it were the most believing family it was also the most violent, the most disputatious, constantly at war, and so fiercely savage that the anger of the Boccaneras had become proverbial. And thence came their arms, the winged dragon spitting flames, and the fierce, glowing motto, with its play on the name "*Bocca sera, Alma rossa*" (black mouth, red soul), the mouth darkened by a roar, the soul flaming like a brazier of faith and love.

Legends of endless passion, of terrible deeds of justice and vengeance still circulated. There was the duel fought by Onfredo, the Boccanera by whom the present palazzo had been built in the sixteenth century on the site of the demolished antique residence of the family. Onfredo, learning that his wife had allowed herself to be kissed on the lips by young Count Costamagna, had caused the Count to be kidnapped one evening and brought to the palazzo bound with cords. And there in one of the large halls, before freeing him, he compelled him to confess himself to a monk. Then he severed the cords with a stiletto, threw the lamps over and extinguished them, calling to the Count to keep the stiletto and defend himself. During more than an hour, in complete obscurity, in this hall full of furniture, the two men sought one another, fled from one another, seized hold of one another, and pierced one another with their blades. And when the doors were broken down and the servants rushed in they found among the pools of blood, among the overturned tables and broken seats, Costamagna with his nose sliced off and his hips pierced with two and thirty wounds, whilst Onfredo had lost two fingers of his right hand, and had both shoulders riddled with holes! The wonder was that neither died of the encounter.

A century later, on that same bank of the Tiber, a daughter of the Boccaneras, a girl barely sixteen years of age, the lovely and passionate Cassia, filled all Rome with terror and admiration. She loved Flavio Corradini, the scion of a rival and hated house, whose alliance her father, Prince Boccanera, roughly rejected, and whom her elder brother, Ercole, swore to slay should he ever surprise him with her. Nevertheless the young man came to visit her in a boat, and she joined him by the little staircase descending to the river. But one evening Ercole, who was on the watch, sprang into the boat and planted his dagger full in Flavio's heart. Later on the subsequent incidents were unravelled; it was understood that Cassia, wrathful and frantic with despair, unwilling to survive her love and bent on wreaking justice, had thrown herself upon her brother, had seized both murderer and victim with the same grasp whilst overturning the boat; for when the three bodies were recovered Cassia still retained her hold upon the two men, pressing their faces one against the other with her bare arms, which had remained as white as snow.

But those were vanished times. Nowadays, if faith remained, blood violence seemed to be departing from the Boccaneras. Their huge fortune also had been lost in the slow decline which for a century past has been ruining the Roman *patriziato*. It had been necessary to sell the estates; the palace had emptied, gradually sinking to the mediocrity and bourgeois life of the new times. For their part the Boccaneras obstinately declined to contract any alien alliances, proud as they were of the purity of their Roman blood. And poverty was as nothing to them; they found contentment in their immense pride, and without a plaint sequestered themselves amidst the silence and gloom in which their race was dwindling away.

Prince Ascanio, dead since 1848, had left four children by his wife, a Corvisieri; first Pio, the Cardinal; then Serafina, who, in order to remain with her brother, had not married; and finally Ernesta and Onofrio, both of whom were deceased. As Ernesta had merely left a daughter, Benedetta, behind her, it followed that the only male heir, the only possible continuator of the family name was Onofrio's son, young Prince Dario, now some thirty years of age. Should he die without posterity, the Boccaneras, once so full of life and whose deeds had filled Roman history in papal times, must fatally disappear.

Dario and his cousin Benedetta had been drawn together by a deep, smiling, natural passion ever since childhood. They seemed born one for the other; they could not imagine that they had been brought into the world for any other purpose than that of becoming husband and wife as soon as they should be old enough to marry. When Prince Onofrio—an amiable man of forty, very popular in Rome, where he spent his modest fortune as his heart listed—espoused La Montefiori's daughter, the little Marchesa Flavia, whose superb beauty, suggestive of a youthful Juno, had maddened him, he went to reside at the Villa Montefiori, the only property, indeed the only belonging, that remained to the two ladies. It was in the direction of St'. Agnese-fuori-le-Mura,[1] and there were vast grounds, a perfect park in fact, planted with centenarian

[1] St. Agnes-without-the-walls, N.E. of Rome.

trees, among which the villa, a somewhat sorry building of the seventeenth century, was falling into ruins.

Unfavourable reports were circulated about the ladies, the mother having almost lost caste since she had become a widow, and the girl having too bold a beauty, too conquering an air. Thus the marriage had not met with the approval of Serafina, who was very rigid, or of Onofrio's elder brother Pio, at that time merely a *Cameriere segreto* of the Holy Father and a Canon of the Vatican basilica. Only Ernesta kept up a regular intercourse with Onofrio, fond of him as she was by reason of his gaiety of disposition; and thus, later on, her favourite diversion was to go each week to the Villa Montefiori with her daughter Benedetta, there to spend the day. And what a delightful day it always proved to Benedetta and Dario, she ten years old and he fifteen, what a fraternal loving day in that vast and almost abandoned garden with its parasol pines, its giant box-plants, and its clumps of evergreen oaks, amidst which one lost oneself as in a virgin forest.

The poor stifled soul of Ernesta was a soul of pain and passion. Born with a mighty longing for life, she thirsted for the sun—for a free, happy, active existence in the full daylight. She was noted for her large limpid eyes and the charming oval of her gentle face. Extremely ignorant, like all the daughters of the Roman nobility, having learnt the little she knew in a convent of French nuns, she had grown up cloistered in the black Boccanera palace, having no knowledge of the world than by those daily drives to the Corso and the Pincio on which she accompanied her mother. Eventually, when she was five and twenty, and was already weary and desolate, she contracted the customary marriage of her caste, espousing Count Brandini, the last-born of a very noble, very numerous and poor family, who had to come and live in the Via Giulia mansion, where an entire wing of the second floor was got ready for the young couple. And nothing changed, Ernesta continued to live in the same cold gloom, in the midst of the same dead past, the weight of which, like that of a tombstone, she felt pressing more and more heavily upon her.

The marriage was, on either side, a very honourable one. Count Brandini soon passed as being the most foolish and haughty man in Rome. A strict, intolerant formalist in religious matters, he became quite triumphant when, after innumerable intrigues, secret plottings which lasted ten long years, he at last secured the appointment of grand equerry to the Holy Father. With this appointment it seemed as if all the dismal majesty of the Vatican entered his household. However, Ernesta found life still bearable in the time of Pius IX—that is until the latter part of 1870—for she might still venture to open the windows overlooking the street, receive a few lady friends otherwise than in secrecy, and accept invitations to festivities. But when the Italians had conquered Rome and the Pope declared himself a prisoner, the mansion in the Via Giulia became a sepulchre. The great doors were closed and bolted, even nailed together in token of mourning; and during ten years the inmates only went out and came in by the little staircase communicating with the lane. It was also forbidden to open the window shutters of the facade. This was the sulking, the protest of the black world, the mansion sinking into death-like immobility, complete seclusion; no more receptions, barely a few shadows, the intimates of Donna Serafina who on Monday evenings slipped in by the little door in the lane which was scarcely set ajar. And during those ten lugubrious years, overcome by secret despair, the young woman wept every night, suffered untold agony at thus being buried alive.

Ernesta had given birth to her daughter Benedetta rather late in life, when three and thirty years of age. At first the little one helped to divert her mind. But afterwards her wonted existence, like a grinding millstone, again seized hold of her, and she had to place the child in the charge of the French nuns, by whom she herself had been educated, at the convent of the Sacred Heart of La Trinita de' Monti. When Benedetta left the convent, grown up, nineteen years of age, she was able to speak and write French, knew a little arithmetic and her catechism, and possessed a few hazy notions of history. Then the life of the two women was resumed, the life of a *gynoeceum*, suggestive of the Orient; never an excursion with husband or father, but day after day spent in closed, secluded rooms, with nought to cheer one but the sole, everlasting, obligatory promenade, the daily drive to the Corso and the Pincio.

At home, absolute obedience was the rule; the tie of relationship possessed an authority, a strength, which made both women bow to the will of the Count, without possible thought of rebellion; and to the Count's will was added that of Donna Serafina and that of Cardinal Pio, both of whom were stern defenders of the old-time customs. Since the Pope had ceased to show himself in Rome, the post of grand equerry had left the Count considerable leisure, for the number of equipages in the pontifical stables had been very largely reduced; nevertheless, he was constant in his attendance at the Vatican, where his duties were now a mere matter of parade, and ever increased his devout zeal as a mark of protest against the usurping monarchy installed at the Quirinal. However, Benedetta had just attained her twentieth year, when one evening her father returned coughing and shivering from some ceremony at St. Peter's. A week later he died, carried off by inflammation of the lungs. And despite their mourning, the loss was secretly considered a deliverance by both women, who now felt that they were free.

Thenceforward Ernesta had but one thought, that of saving her daughter from that awful life of immurement and entombment. She herself had sorrowed too deeply: it was no longer possible for her to remount the current of existence; but she was unwilling that Benedetta should in her turn lead a life contrary to nature, in a voluntary grave. Moreover, similar lassitude and rebellion were showing themselves among other patrician families, which, after the sulking of the first years, were beginning to draw nearer to the Quirinal. Why indeed should the children, eager for action, liberty, and sunlight, perpetually keep up the quarrel of the fathers? And so, though no reconciliation could take place between the black world and the white world,[1] intermediate tints were already appearing, and some unexpected matrimonial alliances were contracted.

Ernesta for her part was indifferent to the political question; she knew next to nothing about it; but that which she passionately desired was that her race might at last emerge from that hateful sepulchre, that black, silent Boccanera mansion, where her woman's joys had been frozen by so long a death. She had suffered very grievously in her heart, as girl, as lover, and as wife, and yielded to anger at the thought that her life should have been so spoiled, so lost through idiotic resignation. Then, too, her mind was greatly influenced by the choice of a new confessor at this period; for she

---

[1] The "blacks" are the supporters of the papacy, the "whites" those of the King of Italy.—Trans.

had remained very religious, practising all the rites of the Church, and ever docile to the advice of her spiritual director. To free herself the more, however, she now quitted the Jesuit father whom her husband had chosen for her, and in his stead took Abbe Pisoni, the rector of the little church of Sta. Brigida, on the Piazza Farnese, close by. He was a man of fifty, very gentle, and very good-hearted, of a benevolence seldom found in the Roman world; and archaeology, a passion for the old stones of the past, had made him an ardent patriot. Humble though his position was, folks whispered that he had on several occasions served as an intermediary in delicate matters between the Vatican and the Quirinal. And, becoming confessor not only of Ernesta but of Benedetta also, he was fond of discoursing to them about the grandeur of Italian unity, the triumphant sway that Italy would exercise when the Pope and the King should agree together.

Meantime Benedetta and Dario loved as on the first day, patiently, with the strong tranquil love of those who know that they belong to one another. But it happened that Ernesta threw herself between them and stubbornly opposed their marriage. No, no! her daughter must not espouse that Dario, that cousin, the last of the name, who in his turn would immure his wife in the black sepulchre of the Boccanera palace! Their union would be a prolongation of entombment, an aggravation of ruin, a repetition of the haughty wretchedness of the past, of the everlasting peevish sulking which depressed and benumbed one! She was well acquainted with the young man's character; she knew that he was egotistical and weak, incapable of thinking and acting, predestined to bury his race with a smile on his lips, to let the last remnant of the house crumble about his head without attempting the slightest effort to found a new family. And that which she desired was fortune in another guise, a new birth for her daughter with wealth and the florescence of life amid the victors and powerful ones of to-morrow.

From that moment the mother did not cease her stubborn efforts to ensure her daughter's happiness despite herself. She told her of her tears, entreated her not to renew her own deplorable career. Yet she would have failed, such was the calm determination of the girl who had for ever given her heart, if certain circumstances had not brought her into connection with such a son-in-law as she dreamt of. At that very Villa Montefiori where Benedetta and Dario had plighted their troth, she met Count Prada, son of Orlando, one of the heroes of the reunion of Italy. Arriving in Rome from Milan, with his father, when eighteen years of age, at the time of the occupation of the city by the Italian Government, Prada had first entered the Ministry of Finances as a mere clerk, whilst the old warrior, his sire, created a senator, lived scantily on a petty income, the last remnant of a fortune spent in his country's service. The fine war-like madness of the former comrade of Garibaldi had, however, in the son turned into a fierce appetite for booty, so that the young man became one of the real conquerors of Rome, one of those birds of prey that dismembered and devoured the city. Engaged in vast speculations on land, already wealthy according to popular report, he had—at the time of meeting Ernesta—just become intimate with Prince Onofrio, whose head he had turned by suggesting to him the idea of selling the far-spreading grounds of the Villa Montefiori for the erection of a new suburban district on the site. Others averred that he was the lover of the princess, the beautiful Flavia, who, although nine years his senior, was still superb. And, truth to tell, he was certainly a man of violent desires, with an eagerness to rush on the spoils of conquest which rendered him utterly unscrupulous with regard either to the wealth or to the wives of others.

From the first day that he beheld Benedetta he desired her. But she, at any rate, could only become his by marriage. And he did not for a moment hesitate, but broke off all connection with Flavia, eager as he was for the pure virgin beauty, the patrician youth of the other. When he realised that Ernesta, the mother, favoured him, he asked her daughter's hand, feeling certain of success. And the surprise was great, for he was some fifteen years older than the girl. However, he was a count, he bore a name which was already historical, he was piling up millions, he was regarded with favour at the Quirinal, and none could tell to what heights he might not attain. All Rome became impassioned.

Never afterwards was Benedetta able to explain to herself how it happened that she had eventually consented. Six months sooner, six months later, such a marriage would certainly have been impossible, given the fearful scandal which it raised in the black world. A Boccanera, the last maiden of that antique papal race, given to a Prada, to one of the despoilers of the Church! Was it credible? In order that the wild project might prove successful it had been necessary that it should be formed at a particular brief moment—a moment when a supreme effort was being made to conciliate the Vatican and the Quirinal. A report circulated that an agreement was on the point of being arrived at, that the King consented to recognise the Pope's absolute sovereignty over the Leonine City,[1] and a narrow band of territory extending to the sea. And if such were the case would not the marriage of Benedetta and Prada become, so to say, a symbol of union, of national reconciliation? That lovely girl, the pure lily of the black world, was she not the acquiescent sacrifice, the pledge granted to the whites?

For a fortnight nothing else was talked of; people discussed the question, allowed their emotion rein, indulged in all sorts of hopes. The girl, for her part, did not enter into the political reasons, but simply listened to her heart, which she could not bestow since it was hers no more. From morn till night, however, she had to encounter her mother's prayers entreating her not to refuse the fortune, the life which offered. And she was particularly exercised by the counsels of her confessor, good Abbe Pisoni, whose patriotic zeal now burst forth. He weighed upon her with all his faith in the Christian destinies of Italy, and returned heartfelt thanks to Providence for having chosen one of his penitents as the instrument for hastening the reconciliation which would work God's triumph throughout the world. And her confessor's influence was certainly one of the decisive factors in shaping Benedetta's decision, for she was very pious, very devout, especially with regard to a certain Madonna whose image she went to adore every Sunday at the little church on the Piazza Farnese. One circumstance in particular struck her: Abbe Pisoni related that the flame of the lamp before the image in question whitened each time that he himself knelt there to beg the Virgin to incline his penitent to the all-redeeming marriage. And thus superior forces intervened; and she yielded in obedience to her mother, whom the Cardinal and Donna

---

[1] The Vatican suburb of Rome, called the Civitas Leonina, because Leo IV, to protect it from the Saracens and Arabs, enclosed it with walls in the ninth century.—Trans.

Serafina had at first opposed, but whom they left free to act when the religious question arose.

Benedetta had grown up in such absolute purity and ignorance, knowing nothing of herself, so shut off from existence, that marriage with another than Dario was to her simply the rupture of a long-kept promise of life in common. It was not the violent wrenching of heart and flesh that it would have been in the case of a woman who knew the facts of life. She wept a good deal, and then in a day of self-surrender she married Prada, lacking the strength to continue resisting everybody, and yielding to a union which all Rome had conspired to bring about.

But the clap of thunder came on the very night of the nuptials. Was it that Prada, the Piedmontese, the Italian of the North, the man of conquest, displayed towards his bride the same brutality that he had shown towards the city he had sacked? Or was it that the revelation of married life filled Benedetta with repulsion since nothing in her own heart responded to the passion of this man? On that point she never clearly explained herself; but with violence she shut the door of her room, locked it and bolted it, and refused to admit her husband. For a month Prada was maddened by her scorn. He felt outraged; both his pride and his passion bled; and he swore to master her, even as one masters a colt, with the whip. But all his virile fury was impotent against the indomitable determination which had sprung up one evening behind Benedetta's small and lovely brow. The spirit of the Boccaneras had awoke within her; nothing in the world, not even the fear of death, would have induced her to become her husband's wife.[1] And then, love being at last revealed to her, there came a return of her heart to Dario, a conviction that she must reserve herself for him alone, since it was to him that she had promised herself.

Ever since that marriage, which he had borne like a bereavement, the young man had been travelling in France. She did not hide the truth from him, but wrote to him, again vowing that she would never be another's. And meantime her piety increased, her resolve to reserve herself for the lover she had chosen mingled in her mind with constancy of religious faith. The ardent heart of a great *amorosa* had ignited within her, she was ready for martyrdom for faith's sake. And when her despairing mother with clasped hands entreated her to resign herself to her conjugal duties, she replied that she owed no duties, since she had known nothing when she married. Moreover, the times were changing; the attempts to reconcile the Quirinal and the Vatican had failed, so completely, indeed, that the newspapers of the rival parties had, with renewed violence, resumed their campaign of mutual insult and outrage; and thus that triumphal marriage, to which every one had contributed as to a pledge of peace, crumbled amid the general smash-up, became but a ruin the more added to so many others.

Ernesta died of it. She had made a mistake. Her spoilt life—the life of a joyless wife—had culminated in this supreme maternal error. And the worst was that she alone had to bear all the responsibility of the disaster, for both her brother, the Cardi-

---

[1] Many readers will doubtless remember that the situation as here described is somewhat akin to that of the earlier part of M. George Ohnet's Ironmaster, which, in its form as a novel, I translated into English many years ago. However, all resemblance between Rome and the Ironmaster is confined to this one point.—Trans.

nal, and her sister, Donna Serafina, overwhelmed her with reproaches. For consolation she had but the despair of Abbe Pisoni, whose patriotic hopes had been destroyed, and who was consumed with grief at having contributed to such a catastrophe. And one morning Ernesta was found, icy white and cold, in her bed. Folks talked of the rupture of a blood-vessel, but grief had been sufficient, for she had suffered frightfully, secretly, without a plaint, as indeed she had suffered all her life long.

At this time Benedetta had been married about a twelvemonth: still strong in her resistance to her husband, but remaining under the conjugal roof in order to spare her mother the terrible blow of a public scandal. However, her aunt Serafina had brought influence to bear on her, by opening to her the hope of a possible nullification of her marriage, should she throw herself at the feet of the Holy Father and entreat his intervention. And Serafina ended by persuading her of this, when, deferring to certain advice, she removed her from the spiritual control of Abbe Pisoni, and gave her the same confessor as herself. This was a Jesuit father named Lorenza, a man scarce five and thirty, with bright eyes, grave and amiable manners, and great persuasive powers. However, it was only on the morrow of her mother's death that Benedetta made up her mind, and returned to the Palazzo Boccanera, to occupy the apartments where she had been born, and where her mother had just passed away.

Immediately afterwards proceedings for annulling the marriage were instituted, in the first instance, for inquiry, before the Cardinal Vicar charged with the diocese of Rome. It was related that the Contessina had only taken this step after a secret audience with his Holiness, who had shown her the most encouraging sympathy. Count Prada at first spoke of applying to the law courts to compel his wife to return to the conjugal domicile; but, yielding to the entreaties of his old father Orlando, whom the affair greatly grieved, he eventually consented to accept the ecclesiastical jurisdiction. He was infuriated, however, to find that the nullification of the marriage was solicited on the ground of its non-consummation through *impotentia mariti*; this being one of the most valid and decisive pleas on which the Church of Rome consents to part those whom she has joined. And far more unhappy marriages than might be imagined are severed on these grounds, though the world only gives attention to those cases in which people of title or renown are concerned, as it did, for instance, with the famous Martinez Campos suit.

In Benedetta's case, her counsel, Consistorial-Advocate Morano, one of the leading authorities of the Roman bar, simply neglected to mention, in his memoir, that if she was still merely a wife in name, this was entirely due to herself. In addition to the evidence of friends and servants, showing on what terms the husband and wife had lived since their marriage, the advocate produced a certificate of a medical character, showing that the non-consummation of the union was certain. And the Cardinal Vicar, acting as Bishop of Rome, had thereupon remitted the case to the Congregation of the Council. This was a first success for Benedetta, and matters remained in this position. She was waiting for the Congregation to deliver its final pronouncement, hoping that the ecclesiastical dissolution of the marriage would prove an irresistible argument in favour of the divorce which she meant to solicit of the civil courts. And meantime, in the icy rooms where her mother Ernesta, submissive and desolate, had lately died, the Contessina resumed her girlish life, showing herself calm, yet very firm in her passion, having vowed that she would belong to none but Dario, and that she would not belong to him until the day when a priest should have joined them together in God's holy name.

As it happened, some six months previously, Dario also had taken up his abode at the Boccanera palace in consequence of the death of his father and the catastrophe which had ruined him. Prince Onofrio, after adopting Prada's advice and selling the Villa Montefiori to a financial company for ten million *lire*,[1] had, instead of prudently keeping his money in his pockets, succumbed to the fever of speculation which was consuming Rome. He began to gamble, buying back his own land, and ending by losing everything in the formidable *krach* which was swallowing up the wealth of the entire city. Totally ruined, somewhat deeply in debt even, the Prince nevertheless continued to promenade the Corso, like the handsome, smiling, popular man he was, when he accidentally met his death through falling from his horse; and four months later his widow, the ever beautiful Flavia—who had managed to save a modern villa and a personal income of forty thousand *lire*[2] from the disaster—was remarried to a man of magnificent presence, her junior by some ten years. This was a Swiss named Jules Laporte, originally a sergeant in the Papal Swiss Guard, then a traveller for a shady business in "relics," and finally Marchese Montefiore, having secured that title in securing his wife, thanks to a special brief of the Holy Father. Thus the Princess Boccanera had again become the Marchioness Montefiori.

It was then that Cardinal Boccanera, feeling greatly hurt, insisted on his nephew Dario coming to live with him, in a small apartment on the first floor of the palazzo. In the heart of that holy man, who seemed dead to the world, there still lingered pride of name and lineage, with a feeling of affection for his young, slightly built nephew, the last of the race, the only one by whom the old stock might blossom anew. Moreover, he was not opposed to Dario's marriage with Benedetta, whom he also loved with a paternal affection; and so proud was he of the family honour, and so convinced of the young people's pious rectitude that, in taking them to live with him, he absolutely scorned the abominable rumours which Count Prada's friends in the white world had begun to circulate ever since the two cousins had resided under the same roof. Donna Serafina guarded Benedetta, as he, the Cardinal, guarded Dario, and in the silence and the gloom of the vast deserted mansion, ensanguined of olden time by so many tragic deeds of violence, there now only remained these four with their restrained, stilled passions, last survivors of a crumbling world upon the threshold of a new one.

When Abbe Pierre Froment all at once awoke from sleep, his head heavy with painful dreams, he was worried to find that the daylight was already waning. His watch, which he hastened to consult, pointed to six o'clock. Intending to rest for an hour at the utmost, he had slept on for nearly seven hours, overcome beyond power of resistance. And even on awaking he remained on the bed, helpless, as though he were conquered before he had fought. Why, he wondered, did he experience this prostration, this unreasonable discouragement, this quiver of doubt which had come he knew not whence during his sleep, and which was annihilating his youthful enthusiasm of the morning? Had the Boccaneras any connection with this sudden weakening of his powers? He had espied dim disquieting figures in the black night of his dreams; and

---

[1] 400,000 pounds.

[2] 1,800 pounds.

the anguish which they had brought him continued, and he again evoked them, scared as he was at thus awaking in a strange room, full of uneasiness in presence of the unknown. Things no longer seemed natural to him. He could not understand why Bene-Benedetta should have written to Viscount Philibert de la Choue to tell him that his, Pierre's, book had been denounced to the Congregation of the Index. What interest too could she have had in his coming to Rome to defend himself; and with what object had she carried her amiability so far as to desire that he should take up his quarters in the mansion? Pierre's stupefaction indeed arose from his being there, on that bed in that strange room, in that palace whose deep, death-like silence encompassed him. As he lay there, his limbs still overpowered and his brain seemingly empty, a flash of light suddenly came to him, and he realised that there must be certain circumstances that he knew nothing of that, simple though things appeared, they must really hide some complicated intrigue. However, it was only a fugitive gleam of enlightenment; his suspicions faded; and he rose up shaking himself and accusing the gloomy twilight of being the sole cause of the shivering and the despondency of which he felt ashamed.

In order to bestir himself, Pierre began to examine the two rooms. They were furnished simply, almost meagrely, in mahogany, there being scarcely any two articles alike, though all dated from the beginning of the century. Neither the bed nor the windows nor the doors had any hangings. On the floor of bare tiles, coloured red and polished, there were merely some little foot-mats in front of the various seats. And at sight of this middle-class bareness and coldness Pierre ended by remembering a room where he had slept in childhood—a room at Versailles, at the abode of his grandmother, who had kept a little grocer's shop there in the days of Louis Philippe. However, he became interested in an old painting which hung in the bed-room, on the wall facing the bed, amidst some childish and valueless engravings. But partially discernible in the waning light, this painting represented a woman seated on some projecting stone-work, on the threshold of a great stern building, whence she seemed to have been driven forth. The folding doors of bronze had for ever closed behind her, yet she remained there in a mere drapery of white linen; whilst scattered articles of clothing, thrown forth chance-wise with a violent hand, lay upon the massive granite steps. Her feet were bare, her arms were bare, and her hands, distorted by bitter agony, were pressed to her face—a face which one saw not, veiled as it was by the tawny gold of her rippling, streaming hair. What nameless grief, what fearful shame, what hateful abandonment was thus being hidden by that rejected one, that lingering victim of love, of whose unknown story one might for ever dream with tortured heart? It could be divined that she was adorably young and beautiful in her wretchedness, in the shred of linen draped about her shoulders; but a mystery enveloped everything else—her passion, possibly her misfortune, perhaps even her transgression—unless, indeed, she were there merely as a symbol of all that shivers and that weeps visageless before the ever closed portals of the unknown. For a long time Pierre looked at her, and so intently that he at last imagined he could distinguish her profile, divine in its purity and expression of suffering. But this was only an illusion; the painting had greatly suffered, blackened by time and neglect; and he asked himself whose work it might be that it should move him so intensely. On the adjoining wall a picture of a Madonna, a bad copy of an eighteenth-century painting, irritated him by the banality of its smile.

II.

Night was falling faster and faster, and, opening the sitting-room window, Pierre leant out. On the other bank of the Tiber facing him arose the Janiculum, the height whence he had gazed upon Rome that morning. But at this dim hour Rome was no longer the city of youth and dreamland soaring into the early sunshine. The night was raining down, grey and ashen; the horizon was becoming blurred, vague, and mournful. Yonder, to the left, beyond the sea of roofs, Pierre could still divine the presence of the Palatine; and yonder, to the right, there still arose the Dome of St. Peter's, now grey like slate against the leaden sky; whilst behind him the Quirinal, which he could not see, must also be fading away into the misty night. A few minutes went by, and everything became yet more blurred; he realised that Rome was fading, departing in its immensity of which he knew nothing. Then his causeless doubt and disquietude again came on him so painfully that he could no longer remain at the window. He closed it and sat down, letting the darkness submerge him with its flood of infinite sadness. And his despairing reverie only ceased when the door gently opened and the glow of a lamp enlivened the room.

It was Victorine who came in quietly, bringing the light. "Ah! so you are up, Monsieur l'Abbe," said she; "I came in at about four o'clock but I let you sleep on. You have done quite right to take all the rest you required."

Then, as he complained of pains and shivering, she became anxious. "Don't go catching their nasty fevers," she said. "It isn't at all healthy near their river, you know. Don Vigilio, his Eminence's secretary, is always having the fever, and I assure you that it isn't pleasant."

She accordingly advised him to remain upstairs and lie down again. She would excuse his absence to the Princess and the Contessina. And he ended by letting her do as she desired, for he was in no state to have any will of his own. By her advice he dined, partaking of some soup, a wing of a chicken, and some preserves, which Giaccomo, the big lackey, brought up to him. And the food did him a great deal of good; he felt so restored that he refused to go to bed, desiring, said he, to thank the ladies that very evening for their kindly hospitality. As Donna Serafina received on Mondays he would present himself before her.

"Very good," said Victorine approvingly. "As you are all right again it can do you no harm, it will even enliven you. The best thing will be for Don Vigilio to come for you at nine o'clock and accompany you. Wait for him here."

Pierre had just washed and put on the new cassock he had brought with him, when, at nine o'clock precisely, he heard a discreet knock at his door. A little priest came in, a man scarcely thirty years of age, but thin and debile of build, with a long, seared, saffron-coloured face. For two years past attacks of fever, coming on every day at the same hour, had been consuming him. Nevertheless, whenever he forgot to control the black eyes which lighted his yellow face, they shone out ardently with the glow of his fiery soul. He bowed, and then in fluent French introduced himself in this simple fashion: "Don Vigilio, Monsieur l'Abbe, who is entirely at your service. If you are willing, we will go down."

Pierre immediately followed him, expressing his thanks, and Don Vigilio, relapsing into silence, answered his remarks with a smile. Having descended the small staircase, they found themselves on the second floor, on the spacious landing of the grand staircase. And Pierre was surprised and saddened by the scanty illumination, which, as in some dingy lodging-house, was limited to a few gas-jets, placed far apart, their yellow splotches but faintly relieving the deep gloom of the lofty, endless corridors. All was gigantic and funereal. Even on the landing, where was the entrance to Donna Serafina's apartments, facing those occupied by her niece, nothing indicated that a reception was being held that evening. The door remained closed, not a sound came from the rooms, a death-like silence arose from the whole palace. And Don Vigilio did not even ring, but, after a fresh bow, discreetly turned the door-handle.

A single petroleum lamp, placed on a table, lighted the ante-room, a large apartment with bare fresco-painted walls, simulating hangings of red and gold, draped regularly all around in the antique fashion. A few men's overcoats and two ladies' mantles lay on the chairs, whilst a pier table was littered with hats, and a servant sat there dozing, with his back to the wall.

However, as Don Vigilio stepped aside to allow Pierre to enter a first reception-room, hung with red *brocatelle*, a room but dimly lighted and which he imagined to be empty, the young priest found himself face to face with an apparition in black, a woman whose features he could not at first distinguish. Fortunately he heard his companion say, with a low bow, "Contessina, I have the honour to present to you Monsieur l'Abbe Pierre Froment, who arrived from France this morning."

Then, for a moment, Pierre remained alone with Benedetta in that deserted *salon*, in the sleepy glimmer of two lace-veiled lamps. At present, however, a sound of voices came from a room beyond, a larger apartment whose doorway, with folding doors thrown wide open, described a parallelogram of brighter light.

The young woman at once showed herself very affable, with perfect simplicity of manner: "Ah! I am happy to see you, Monsieur l'Abbe. I was afraid that your indisposition might be serious. You are quite recovered now, are you not?"

Pierre listened to her, fascinated by her slow and rather thick voice, in which restrained passion seemed to mingle with much prudent good sense. And at last he saw her, with her hair so heavy and so dark, her skin so white, the whiteness of ivory. She had a round face, with somewhat full lips, a small refined nose, features as delicate as a child's. But it was especially her eyes that lived, immense eyes, whose infinite depths none could fathom. Was she slumbering? Was she dreaming? Did her motionless face conceal the ardent tension of a great saint and a great *amorosa*? So white, so young, and so calm, her every movement was harmonious, her appearance at once very staid, very noble, and very rhythmical. In her ears she wore two large pearls of matchless purity, pearls which had come from a famous necklace of her mother's, known throughout Rome.

Pierre apologised and thanked her. "You see me in confusion, madame," said he; "I should have liked to express to you this morning my gratitude for your great kindness."

He had hesitated to call her madame, remembering the plea brought forward in the suit for the dissolution of her marriage. But plainly enough everybody must call her madame. Moreover, her face had retained its calm and kindly expression.

"Consider yourself at home here, Monsieur l'Abbe," she responded, wishing to put him at his ease. "It is sufficient that our relative, Monsieur de la Choue, should be fond of you, and take interest in your work. I have, you know, much affection for him." Then her voice faltered slightly, for she realised that she ought to speak of the book, the one reason of Pierre's journey and her proffered hospitality. "Yes," she added, "the Viscount sent me your book. I read it and found it very beautiful. It disturbed me. But I am only an ignoramus, and certainly failed to understand everything in it. We must talk it over together; you will explain your ideas to me, won't you, Monsieur l'Abbe?"

In her large clear eyes, which did not know how to lie, Pierre then read the surprise and emotion of a child's soul when confronted by disquieting and undreamt-of problems. So it was not she who had become impassioned and had desired to have him near her that she might sustain him and assist his victory. Once again, and this time very keenly, he suspected a secret influence, a hidden hand which was directing everything towards some unknown goal. However, he was charmed by so much simplicity and frankness in so beautiful, young, and noble a creature; and he gave himself to her after the exchange of those few words, and was about to tell her that she might absolutely dispose of him, when he was interrupted by the advent of another woman, whose tall, slight figure, also clad in black, stood out strongly against the luminous background of the further reception-room as seen through the open doorway.

"Well, Benedetta, have you sent Giaccomo up to see?" asked the newcomer. "Don Vigilio has just come down and he is quite alone. It is improper."

"No, no, aunt. Monsieur l'Abbe is here," was the reply of Benedetta, hastening to introduce the young priest. "Monsieur l'Abbe Pierre Froment—The Princess Boccanera."

Ceremonious salutations were exchanged. The Princess must have been nearly sixty, but she laced herself so tightly that from behind one might have taken her for a young woman. This tight lacing, however, was her last coquetry. Her hair, though still plentiful, was quite white, her eyebrows alone remaining black in her long, wrinkled face, from which projected the large obstinate nose of the family. She had never been beautiful, and had remained a spinster, wounded to the heart by the selection of Count Brandini, who had preferred her younger sister, Ernesta. From that moment she had resolved to seek consolation and satisfaction in family pride alone, the hereditary pride of the great name which she bore. The Boccaneras had already supplied two Popes to the Church, and she hoped that before she died her brother would become the third. She had transformed herself into his housekeeper, as it were, remaining with him, watching over him, and advising him, managing all the household affairs herself, and accomplishing miracles in order to conceal the slow ruin which was bringing the ceilings about their heads. If every Monday for thirty years past she had continued receiving a few intimates, all of them folks of the Vatican, it was from high political considerations, so that her drawing-room might remain a meeting-place of the black world, a power and a threat.

And Pierre divined by her greeting that she deemed him of little account, petty foreign priest that he was, not even a prelate. This too again surprised him, again brought the puzzling question to the fore: Why had he been invited, what was expected of him in this society from which the humble were usually excluded? Knowing the Princess to be austerely devout, he at last fancied that she received him solely out of regard for her kinsman, the Viscount, for in her turn she only found these words of welcome: "We are so pleased to receive good news of Monsieur de la Choue! He brought us such a beautiful pilgrimage two years ago."

Passing the first through the doorway, she at last ushered the young priest into the adjoining reception-room. It was a spacious square apartment, hung with old yellow *brocatelle* of a flowery Louis XIV pattern. The lofty ceiling was adorned with a very fine panelling, carved and coloured, with gilded roses in each compartment. The furniture, however, was of all sorts. There were some high mirrors, a couple of superb gilded pier tables, and a few handsome seventeenth-century arm-chairs; but all the rest was wretched. A heavy round table of first-empire style, which had come nobody knew whence, caught the eye with a medley of anomalous articles picked up at some bazaar, and a quantity of cheap photographs littered the costly marble tops of the pier tables. No interesting article of *virtu* was to be seen. The old paintings on the walls were with two exceptions feebly executed. There was a delightful example of an unknown primitive master, a fourteenth-century Visitation, in which the Virgin had the stature and pure delicacy of a child of ten, whilst the Archangel, huge and superb, inundated her with a stream of dazzling, superhuman love; and in front of this hung an antique family portrait, depicting a very beautiful young girl in a turban, who was thought to be Cassia Boccanera, the *amorosa* and avengeress who had flung herself into the Tiber with her brother Ercole and the corpse of her lover, Flavio Corradini. Four lamps threw a broad, peaceful glow over the faded room, and, like a melancholy sunset, tinged it with yellow. It looked grave and bare, with not even a flower in a vase to brighten it.

In a few words Donna Serafina at once introduced Pierre to the company; and in the silence, the pause which ensued in the conversation, he felt that every eye was fixed upon him as upon a promised and expected curiosity. There were altogether some ten persons present, among them being Dario, who stood talking with little Princess Celia Buongiovanni, whilst the elderly relative who had brought the latter sat whispering to a prelate, Monsignor Nani, in a dim corner. Pierre, however, had been particularly struck by the name of Consistorial-Advocate Morano, of whose position in the house Viscount de la Choue had thought proper to inform him in order to avert any unpleasant blunder. For thirty years past Morano had been Donna Serafina's *amico*. Their connection, formerly a guilty one, for the advocate had wife and children of his own, had in course of time, since he had been left a widower, become one of those *liaisons* which tolerant people excuse and except. Both parties were extremely devout and had certainly assured themselves of all needful "indulgences." And thus Morano was there in the seat which he had always taken for a quarter of a century past, a seat beside the chimney-piece, though as yet the winter fire had not been lighted, and when Donna Serafina had discharged her duties as mistress of the house, she returned to her own place in front of him, on the other side of the chimney.

When Pierre in his turn had seated himself near Don Vigilio, who, silent and discreet, had already taken a chair, Dario resumed in a louder voice the story which he had been relating to Celia. Dario was a handsome man, of average height, slim and elegant. He wore a full beard, dark and carefully tended, and had the long face and pronounced nose of the Boccaneras, but the impoverishment of the family blood over a course of centuries had attenuated, softened as it were, any sharpness or undue prominence of feature.

"Oh! a beauty, an astounding beauty!" he repeated emphatically.

"Whose beauty?" asked Benedetta, approaching him.

Celia, who resembled the little Virgin of the primitive master hanging above her head, began to laugh. "Oh! Dario's speaking of a poor girl, a work-girl whom he met to-day," she explained.

II.

Thereupon Dario had to begin his narrative again. It appeared that while passing along a narrow street near the Piazza Navona, he had perceived a tall, shapely girl of twenty, who was weeping and sobbing violently, prone upon a flight of steps. Touched particularly by her beauty, he had approached her and learnt that she had been working in the house outside which she was, a manufactory of wax beads, but that, slack times having come, the workshops had closed and she did not dare to return home, so fearful was the misery there. Amidst the downpour of her tears she raised such beautiful eyes to his that he ended by drawing some money from his pocket. But at this, crimson with confusion, she sprang to her feet, hiding her hands in the folds of her skirt, and refusing to take anything. She added, however, that he might follow her if it so pleased him, and give the money to her mother. And then she hurried off towards the Ponte St'. Angelo.[1]

"Yes, she was a beauty, a perfect beauty," repeated Dario with an air of ecstasy. "Taller than I, and slim though sturdy, with the bosom of a goddess. In fact, a real antique, a Venus of twenty, her chin rather bold, her mouth and nose of perfect form, and her eyes wonderfully pure and large! And she was bare-headed too, with nothing but a crown of heavy black hair, and a dazzling face, gilded, so to say, by the sun."

They had all begun to listen to him, enraptured, full of that passionate admiration for beauty which, in spite of every change, Rome still retains in her heart.

"Those beautiful girls of the people are becoming very rare," remarked Morano. "You might scour the Trastevere without finding any. However, this proves that there is at least one of them left."

"And what was your goddess's name?" asked Benedetta, smiling, amused and enraptured like the others.

"Pierina," replied Dario, also with a laugh.

"And what did you do with her?"

At this question the young man's excited face assumed an expression of discomfort and fear, like the face of a child on suddenly encountering some ugly creature amidst its play.

"Oh! don't talk of it," said he. "I felt very sorry afterwards. I saw such misery—enough to make one ill."

Yielding to his curiosity, it seemed, he had followed the girl across the Ponte St'. Angelo into the new district which was being built over the former castle meadows[2]; and there, on the first floor of an abandoned house which was already falling into ruins, though the plaster was scarcely dry, he had come upon a frightful spectacle which still stirred his heart: a whole family, father and mother, children, and an infirm old uncle, dying of hunger and rotting in filth! He selected the most dignified words he could think of to describe the scene, waving his hand the while with a gesture of fright, as if to ward off some horrible vision.

"At last," he concluded, "I ran away, and you may be sure that I shan't go back again."

---

[1] Bridge of St. Angelo.

[2] The meadows around the Castle of St. Angelo. The district, now covered with buildings, is quite flat and was formerly greatly subject to floods. It is known as the Quartiere dei Prati.—Trans.

A general wagging of heads ensued in the cold, irksome silence which fell upon the room. Then Morano summed up the matter in a few bitter words, in which he accused the despoilers, the men of the Quirinal, of being the sole cause of all the frightful misery of Rome. Were not people even talking of the approaching nomination of Deputy Sacco as Minister of Finances—Sacco, that intriguer who had engaged in all sorts of underhand practices? His appointment would be the climax of impudence; bankruptcy would speedily and infallibly ensue.

Meantime Benedetta, who had fixed her eyes on Pierre, with his book in her mind, alone murmured: "Poor people, how very sad! But why not go back to see them?"

Pierre, out of his element and absent-minded during the earlier moments, had been deeply stirred by the latter part of Dario's narrative. His thoughts reverted to his apostolate amidst the misery of Paris, and his heart was touched with compassion at being confronted by the story of such fearful sufferings on the very day of his arrival in Rome. Unwittingly, impulsively, he raised his voice, and said aloud: "Oh! we will go to see them together, madame; you will take me. These questions impassion me so much."

The attention of everybody was then again turned upon the young priest. The others questioned him, and he realised that they were all anxious about his first impressions, his opinion of their city and of themselves. He must not judge Rome by mere outward appearances, they said. What effect had the city produced on him? How had he found it, and what did he think of it? Thereupon he politely apologised for his inability to answer them. He had not yet gone out, said he, and had seen nothing. But this answer was of no avail; they pressed him all the more keenly, and he fully understood that their object was to gain him over to admiration and love. They advised him, adjured him not to yield to any fatal disillusion, but to persist and wait until Rome should have revealed to him her soul.

"How long do you expect to remain among us, Monsieur l'Abbe?" suddenly inquired a courteous voice, with a clear but gentle ring.

It was Monsignor Nani, who, seated in the gloom, thus raised his voice for the first time. On several occasions it had seemed to Pierre that the prelate's keen blue eyes were steadily fixed upon him, though all the while he pretended to be attentively listening to the drawling chatter of Celia's aunt. And before replying Pierre glanced at him. In his crimson-edged cassock, with a violet silk sash drawn tightly around his waist, Nani still looked young, although he was over fifty. His hair had remained blond, he had a straight refined nose, a mouth very firm yet very delicate of contour, and beautifully white teeth.

"Why, a fortnight or perhaps three weeks, Monsignor," replied Pierre.

The whole *salon* protested. What, three weeks! It was his pretension to know Rome in three weeks! Why, six weeks, twelve months, ten years were required! The first impression was always a disastrous one, and a long sojourn was needed for a visitor to recover from it.

"Three weeks!" repeated Donna Serafina with her disdainful air. "Is it possible for people to study one another and get fond of one another in three weeks? Those who come back to us are those who have learned to know us."

Instead of launching into exclamations like the others, Nani had at first contented himself with smiling, and gently waving his shapely hand, which bespoke his aristocratic origin. Then, as Pierre modestly explained himself, saying that he had come to

Rome to attend to certain matters and would leave again as soon as those matters should have been concluded, the prelate, still smiling, summed up the argument with the remark: "Oh! Monsieur l'Abbe will stay with us for more than three weeks; we shall have the happiness of his presence here for a long time, I hope."

These words, though spoken with quiet cordiality, strangely disturbed the young priest. What was known, what was meant? He leant towards Don Vigilio, who had remained near him, still and ever silent, and in a whisper inquired: "Who is Monsignor Nani?"

The secretary, however, did not at once reply. His feverish face became yet more livid. Then his ardent eyes glanced round to make sure that nobody was watching him, and in a breath he responded: "He is the Assessor of the Holy Office."[1]

This information sufficed, for Pierre was not ignorant of the fact that the assessor, who was present in silence at the meetings of the Holy Office, waited upon his Holiness every Wednesday evening after the sitting, to render him an account of the matters dealt with in the afternoon. This weekly audience, this hour spent with the Pope in a privacy which allowed of every subject being broached, gave the assessor an exceptional position, one of considerable power. Moreover the office led to the cardinalate; the only "rise" that could be given to the assessor was his promotion to the Sacred College.

Monsignor Nani, who seemed so perfectly frank and amiable, continued to look at the young priest with such an encouraging air that the latter felt obliged to go and occupy the seat beside him, which Celia's old aunt at last vacated. After all, was there not an omen of victory in meeting, on the very day of his arrival, a powerful prelate whose influence would perhaps open every door to him? He therefore felt very touched when Monsignor Nani, immediately after the first words, inquired in a tone of deep interest, "And so, my dear child, you have published a book?"

After this, gradually mastered by his enthusiasm and forgetting where he was, Pierre unbosomed himself, and recounted the birth and progress of his burning love amidst the sick and the humble, gave voice to his dream of a return to the olden Christian community, and triumphed with the rejuvenescence of Catholicism, developing into the one religion of the universal democracy. Little by little he again raised his voice, and silence fell around him in the stern, antique reception-room, every one lending ear to his words with increasing surprise, with a growing coldness of which he remained unconscious.

At last Nani gently interrupted him, still wearing his perpetual smile, the faint irony of which, however, had departed. "No doubt, no doubt, my dear child," he said, "it is very beautiful, oh! very beautiful, well worthy of the pure and noble imagination of a Christian. But what do you count on doing now?"

"I shall go straight to the Holy Father to defend myself," answered Pierre.

A light, restrained laugh went round, and Donna Serafina expressed the general opinion by exclaiming: "The Holy Father isn't seen as easily as that."

Pierre, however, was quite impassioned. "Well, for my part," he rejoined, "I hope I shall see him. Have I not expressed his views? Have I not defended his policy? Can

---

[1] Otherwise the Inquisition.

he let my book be condemned when I believe that I have taken inspiration from all that is best in him?"

"No doubt, no doubt," Nani again hastily replied, as if he feared that the others might be too brusque with the young enthusiast. "The Holy Father has such a lofty mind. And of course it would be necessary to see him. Only, my dear child, you must not excite yourself so much; reflect a little; take your time." And, turning to Benedetta, he added, "Of course his Eminence has not seen Abbe Froment yet. It would be well, however, that he should receive him to-morrow morning to guide him with his wise counsel."

Cardinal Boccanera never attended his sister's Monday-evening receptions. Still, he was always there in the spirit, like some absent sovereign master.

"To tell the truth," replied the Contessina, hesitating, "I fear that my uncle does not share Monsieur l'Abbe's views."

Nani again smiled. "Exactly; he will tell him things which it is good he should hear."

Thereupon it was at once settled with Don Vigilio that the latter would put down the young priest's name for an audience on the following morning at ten o'clock.

However, at that moment a cardinal came in, clad in town costume—his sash and his stockings red, but his simar black, with a red edging and red buttons. It was Cardinal Sarno, a very old intimate of the Boccaneras; and whilst he apologised for arriving so late, through press of work, the company became silent and deferentially clustered round him. This was the first cardinal Pierre had seen, and he felt greatly disappointed, for the newcomer had none of the majesty, none of the fine port and presence to which he had looked forward. On the contrary, he was short and somewhat deformed, with the left shoulder higher than the right, and a worn, ashen face with lifeless eyes. To Pierre he looked like some old clerk of seventy, half stupefied by fifty years of office work, dulled and bent by incessantly leaning over his writing desk ever since his youth. And indeed that was Sarno's story. The puny child of a petty middle-class family, he had been educated at the Seminario Romano. Then later he had for ten years professed Canon Law at that same seminary, afterwards becoming one of the secretaries of the Congregation for the Propagation of the Faith. Finally, five and twenty years ago, he had been created a cardinal, and the jubilee of his cardinalate had recently been celebrated. Born in Rome, he had always lived there; he was the perfect type of the prelate who, through growing up in the shade of the Vatican, has become one of the masters of the world. Although he had never occupied any diplomatic post, he had rendered such important services to the Propaganda, by his methodical habits of work, that he had become president of one of the two commissions which furthered the interests of the Church in those vast countries of the west which are not yet Catholic. And thus, in the depths of his dim eyes, behind his low, dull-looking brow, the huge map of Christendom was stored away.

Nani himself had risen, full of covert respect for the unobtrusive but terrible man whose hand was everywhere, even in the most distant corners of the earth, although he had never left his office. As Nani knew, despite his apparent nullity, Sarno, with his slow, methodical, ably organised work of conquest, possessed sufficient power to set empires in confusion.

"Has your Eminence recovered from that cold which distressed us so much?" asked Nani.

"No, no, I still cough. There is a most malignant passage at the offices. I feel as cold as ice as soon as I leave my room."

From that moment Pierre felt quite little, virtually lost. He was not even introduced to the Cardinal. And yet he had to remain in the room for nearly another hour, looking around and observing. That antiquated world then seemed to him puerile, as though it had lapsed into a mournful second childhood. Under all the apparent haughtiness and proud reserve he could divine real timidity, unacknowledged distrust, born of great ignorance. If the conversation did not become general, it was because nobody dared to speak out frankly; and what he heard in the corners was simply so much childish chatter, the petty gossip of the week, the trivial echoes of sacristies and drawing-rooms. People saw but little of one another, and the slightest incidents assumed huge proportions. At last Pierre ended by feeling as though he were transported into some *salon* of the time of Charles X, in one of the episcopal cities of the French provinces. No refreshments were served. Celia's old aunt secured possession of Cardinal Sarno; but, instead of replying to her, he simply wagged his head from time to time. Don Vigilio had not opened his mouth the whole evening. However, a conversation in a very low tone was started by Nani and Morano, to whom Donna Serafina listened, leaning forward and expressing her approval by slowly nodding her head. They were doubtless speaking of the dissolution of Benedetta's marriage, for they glanced at the young woman gravely from time to time. And in the centre of the spacious room, in the sleepy glow of the lamps, there was only the young people, Benedetta, Dario, and Celia who seemed to be at all alive, chattering in undertones and occasionally repressing a burst of laughter.

All at once Pierre was struck by the great resemblance between Benedetta and the portrait of Cassia hanging on the wall. Each displayed the same delicate youth, the same passionate mouth, the same large, unfathomable eyes, set in the same round, sensible, healthy-looking face. In each there was certainly the same upright soul, the same heart of flame. Then a recollection came to Pierre, that of a painting by Guido Reni, the adorable, candid head of Beatrice Cenci, which, at that moment and to his thinking, the portrait of Cassia closely resembled. This resemblance stirred him and he glanced at Benedetta with anxious sympathy, as if all the fierce fatality of race and country were about to fall on her. But no, it could not be; she looked so calm, so resolute, and so patient! Besides, ever since he had entered that room he had noticed none other than signs of gay fraternal tenderness between her and Dario, especially on her side, for her face ever retained the bright serenity of a love which may be openly confessed. At one moment, it is true, Dario in a joking way had caught hold of her hands and pressed them; but while he began to laugh rather nervously, with a brighter gleam darting from his eyes, she on her side, all composure, slowly freed her hands, as though theirs was but the play of old and affectionate friends. She loved him, though, it was visible, with her whole being and for her whole life.

At last when Dario, after stifling a slight yawn and glancing at his watch, had slipped off to join some friends who were playing cards at a lady's house, Benedetta and Celia sat down together on a sofa near Pierre; and the latter, without wishing to listen, overheard a few words of their confidential chat. The little Princess was the eldest daughter of Prince Matteo Buongiovanni, who was already the father of five children by an English wife, a Mortimer, to whom he was indebted for a dowry of two hundred thousand pounds. Indeed, the Buongiovannis were known as one of the few patrician families of Rome that were still rich, still erect among the ruins of the past, now crumbling on every side. They also numbered two popes among their forerunners, yet this had not prevented Prince Matteo from lending support to the Quirinal without quarrelling with the Vatican. Son of an American woman, no longer having the pure Roman blood in his veins, he was a more supple politician than other aristocrats, and was also, folks said, extremely grasping, struggling to be one of the last to retain the wealth and power of olden times, which he realised were condemned to death. Yet it was in his family, renowned for its superb pride and its continued magnificence, that a love romance had lately taken birth, a romance which was the subject of endless gossip: Celia had suddenly fallen in love with a young lieutenant to whom she had never spoken; her love was reciprocated, and the passionate attachment of the officer and the girl only found vent in the glances they exchanged on meeting each day during the usual drive through the Corso. Nevertheless Celia displayed a tenacious will, and after declaring to her father that she would never take any other husband, she was waiting, firm and resolute, in the certainty that she would ultimately secure the man of her choice. The worst of the affair was that the lieutenant, Attilio Sacco, happened to be the son of Deputy Sacco, a parvenu whom the black world looked down upon, as upon one sold to the Quirinal and ready to undertake the very dirtiest job.

"It was for me that Morano spoke just now," Celia murmured in Benedetta's ear. "Yes, yes, when he spoke so harshly of Attilio's father and that ministerial appointment which people are talking about. He wanted to give me a lesson."

The two girls had sworn eternal affection in their school-days, and Benedetta, the elder by five years, showed herself maternal. "And so," she said, "you've not become a whit more reasonable. You still think of that young man?"

"What! are you going to grieve me too, dear?" replied Celia. "I love Attilio and mean to have him. Yes, him and not another! I want him and I'll have him, because I love him and he loves me. It's simple enough."

Pierre glanced at her, thunderstruck. With her gentle virgin face she was like a candid, budding lily. A brow and a nose of blossom-like purity; a mouth all innocence with its lips closing over pearly teeth, and eyes like spring water, clear and fathomless. And not a quiver passed over her cheeks of satiny freshness, no sign, however faint, of anxiety or inquisitiveness appeared in her candid glance. Did she think? Did she know? Who could have answered? She was virginity personified with all its redoubtable mystery.

"Ah! my dear," resumed Benedetta, "don't begin my sad story over again. One doesn't succeed in marrying the Pope and the King."

All tranquillity, Celia responded: "But you didn't love Prada, whereas I love Attilio. Life lies in that: one must love."

These words, spoken so naturally by that ignorant child, disturbed Pierre to such a point that he felt tears rising to his eyes. Love! yes, therein lay the solution of every quarrel, the alliance between the nations, the reign of peace and joy throughout the world! However, Donna Serafina had now risen, shrewdly suspecting the nature of the conversation which was impassioning the two girls. And she gave Don Vigilio a glance, which the latter understood, for he came to tell Pierre in an undertone that it was time to retire. Eleven o'clock was striking, and Celia went off with her aunt. Advocate Morano, however, doubtless desired to retain Cardinal Sarno and Nani for a few moments in order that they might privately discuss some difficulty which had arisen in the divorce proceedings. On reaching the outer reception-room, Benedetta, after kissing Celia on both cheeks, took leave of Pierre with much good grace.

"In answering the Viscount to-morrow morning," said she, "I shall tell him how happy we are to have you with us, and for longer than you think. Don't forget to come down at ten o'clock to see my uncle, the Cardinal."

Having climbed to the third floor again, Pierre and Don Vigilio, each carrying a candlestick which the servant had handed to them, were about to part for the night, when the former could not refrain from asking the secretary a question which had been worrying him for hours: "Is Monsignor Nani a very influential personage?"

Don Vigilio again became quite scared, and simply replied by a gesture, opening his arms as if to embrace the world. Then his eyes flashed, and in his turn he seemed to yield to inquisitiveness. "You already knew him, didn't you?" he inquired.

"I? not at all!"

"Really! Well, he knows you very well. Last Monday I heard him speak of you in such precise terms that he seemed to be acquainted with the slightest particulars of your career and your character."

"Why, I never even heard his name before."

"Then he must have procured information."

Thereupon Don Vigilio bowed and entered his room; whilst Pierre, surprised to find his door open, saw Victorine come out with her calm active air.

"Ah! Monsieur l'Abbe, I wanted to make sure that you had everything you were likely to want. There are candles, water, sugar, and matches. And what do you take in the morning, please? Coffee? No, a cup of milk with a roll. Very good; at eight o'clock, eh? And now rest and sleep well. I was awfully afraid of ghosts during the first nights I spent in this old palace! But I never saw a trace of one. The fact is, when people are dead, they are too well pleased, and don't want to break their rest!"

Then off she went, and Pierre at last found himself alone, glad to be able to shake off the strain imposed on him, to free himself from the discomfort which he had felt in that reception-room, among those people who in his mind still mingled and vanished like shadows in the sleepy glow of the lamps. Ghosts, thought he, are the old dead ones of long ago whose distressed spirits return to love and suffer in the breasts of the living of to-day. And, despite his long afternoon rest, he had never felt so weary, so desirous of slumber, confused and foggy as was his mind, full of the fear that he had hitherto not understood things aright. When he began to undress, his astonishment at being in that room returned to him with such intensity that he almost fancied himself another person. What did all those people think of his book? Why had he been brought to this cold dwelling whose hostility he could divine? Was it for the purpose of helping him or conquering him? And again in the yellow glimmer, the dismal sunset of the drawing-room, he perceived Donna Serafina and Advocate Morano on either side of the chimney-piece, whilst behind the calm yet passionate visage of Benedetta appeared the smiling face of Monsignor Nani, with cunning eyes and lips bespeaking indomitable energy.

He went to bed, but soon got up again, stifling, feeling such a need of fresh, free air that he opened the window wide in order to lean out. But the night was black as ink, the darkness had submerged the horizon. A mist must have hidden the stars in the firmament; the vault above seemed opaque and heavy like lead; and yonder in front the houses of the Trastevere had long since been asleep. Not one of all their windows glittered; there was but a single gaslight shining, all alone and far away, like a lost spark. In vain did Pierre seek the Janiculum. In the depths of that ocean of nihility all sunk and vanished, Rome's four and twenty centuries, the ancient Palatine and the modern Quirinal, even the giant dome of St. Peter's, blotted out from the sky by the flood of gloom. And below him he could not see, he could not even hear the Tiber, the dead river flowing past the dead city.

III.

AT a quarter to ten o'clock on the following morning Pierre came down to the first floor of the mansion for his audience with Cardinal Boccanera. He had awoke free of all fatigue and again full of courage and candid enthusiasm; nothing remaining of his strange despondency of the previous night, the doubts and suspicions which had then come over him. The morning was so fine, the sky so pure and so bright, that his heart once more palpitated with hope.

On the landing he found the folding doors of the first ante-room wide open. While closing the gala saloons which overlooked the street, and which were rotting with old age and neglect, the Cardinal still used the reception-rooms of one of his grand-uncles, who in the eighteenth century had risen to the same ecclesiastical dignity as himself. There was a suite of four immense rooms, each sixteen feet high, with windows facing the lane which sloped down towards the Tiber; and the sun never entered them, shut off as it was by the black houses across the lane. Thus the installation, in point of space, was in keeping with the display and pomp of the old-time princely dignitaries of the Church. But no repairs were ever made, no care was taken of anything, the hangings were frayed and ragged, and dust preyed on the furniture, amidst an unconcern which seemed to betoken some proud resolve to stay the course of time.

Pierre experienced a slight shock as he entered the first room, the servants' ante-chamber. Formerly two pontifical *gente d'armi* in full uniform had always stood there amidst a stream of lackeys; and the single servant now on duty seemed by his phantom-like appearance to increase the melancholiness of the vast and gloomy hall. One was particularly struck by an altar facing the windows, an altar with red drapery surmounted by a *baldacchino* with red hangings, on which appeared the escutcheon of the Boccaneras, the winged dragon spitting flames with the device, *Bocca nera, Alma rossa.* And the grand-uncle's red hat, the old huge ceremonial hat, was also there, with the two cushions of red silk, and the two antique parasols which were taken in the coach each time his Eminence went out. And in the deep silence it seemed as if one could almost hear the faint noise of the moths preying for a century past upon all this dead splendour, which would have fallen into dust at the slightest touch of a feather broom.

The second ante-room, that was formerly occupied by the secretary, was also empty, and it was only in the third one, the *anticamera nobile*, that Pierre found Don Vigilio. With his retinue reduced to what was strictly necessary, the Cardinal had preferred to have his secretary near him—at the door, so to say, of the old throne-room, where he gave audience. And Don Vigilio, so thin and yellow, and quivering with fever, sat there like one lost, at a small, common, black table covered with papers. Raising his head from among a batch of documents, he recognised Pierre, and in a low voice, a faint murmur amidst the silence, he said, "His Eminence is engaged. Please wait."

Then he again turned to his reading, doubtless to escape all attempts at conversation.

Not daring to sit down, Pierre examined the apartment. It looked perhaps yet more dilapidated than the others, with its hangings of green damask worn by age and resembling the faded moss on ancient trees. The ceiling, however, had remained superb. Within a frieze of gilded and coloured ornaments was a fresco representing the Triumph of Amphitrite, the work of one of Raffaelle's pupils. And, according to antique usage, it was here that the *berretta*, the red cap, was placed, on a credence, below a large crucifix of ivory and ebony.

As Pierre grew used to the half-light, however, his attention was more particularly attracted by a recently painted full-length portrait of the Cardinal in ceremonial costume—cassock of red moire, rochet of lace, and *cappa* thrown like a royal mantle over his shoulders. In these vestments of the Church the tall old man of seventy retained the proud bearing of a prince, clean shaven, but still boasting an abundance of white hair which streamed in curls over his shoulders. He had the commanding visage of the Boccaneras, a large nose and a large thin-lipped mouth in a long face intersected by broad lines; and the eyes which lighted his pale countenance were indeed the eyes of his race, very dark, yet sparkling with ardent life under bushy brows which had remained quite black. With laurels about his head he would have resembled a Roman emperor, very handsome and master of the world, as though indeed the blood of Augustus pulsated in his veins.

Pierre knew his story which this portrait recalled. Educated at the College of the Nobles, Pio Boccanera had but once absented himself from Rome, and that when very young, hardly a deacon, but nevertheless appointed oblegate to convey a *berretta* to Paris. On his return his ecclesiastical career had continued in sovereign fashion. Honours had fallen on him naturally, as by right of birth. Ordained by Pius IX himself, afterwards becoming a Canon of the Vatican Basilica, and *Cameriere segreto*, he had risen to the post of Majordomo about the time of the Italian occupation, and in 1874 had been created a Cardinal. For the last four years, moreover, he had been Papal Chamberlain (*Camerlingo*), and folks whispered that Leo XIII had appointed him to that post, even as he himself had been appointed to it by Pius IX, in order to lessen his chance of succeeding to the pontifical throne; for although the conclave in choosing Leo had set aside the old tradition that the Camerlingo was ineligible for the papacy, it was not probable that it would again dare to infringe that rule. Moreover, people asserted that, even as had been the case in the reign of Pius, there was a secret warfare between the Pope and his Camerlingo, the latter remaining on one side, condemning the policy of the Holy See, holding radically different opinions on all things, and silently waiting for the death of Leo, which would place power in his hands with the duty of summoning the conclave, and provisionally watching over the affairs and interests of the Church until a new Pope should be elected. Behind Cardinal Pio's broad, stern brow, however, in the glow of his dark eyes, might there not also be the ambition of actually rising to the papacy, of repeating the career of Gioachino Pecci,

Camerlingo and then Pope, all tradition notwithstanding? With the pride of a Roman prince Pio knew but Rome; he almost gloried in being totally ignorant of the modern world; and verily he showed himself very pious, austerely religious, with a full firm faith into which the faintest doubt could never enter.

But a whisper drew Pierre from his reflections. Don Vigilio, in his prudent way, invited him to sit down: "You may have to wait some time: take a stool."

Then he began to cover a large sheet of yellowish paper with fine writing, while Pierre seated himself on one of the stools ranged alongside the wall in front of the portrait. And again the young man fell into a reverie, picturing in his mind a renewal of all the princely pomp of the old-time cardinals in that antique room. To begin with, as soon as nominated, a cardinal gave public festivities, which were sometimes very splendid. During three days the reception-rooms remained wide open, all could enter, and from room to room ushers repeated the names of those who came—patricians, people of the middle class, poor folks, all Rome indeed, whom the new cardinal received with sovereign kindliness, as a king might receive his subjects. Then there was quite a princely retinue; some cardinals carried five hundred people about with them, had no fewer than sixteen distinct offices in their households, lived, in fact, amidst a perfect court. Even when life subsequently became simplified, a cardinal, if he were a prince, still had a right to a gala train of four coaches drawn by black horses. Four servants preceded him in liveries, emblazoned with his arms, and carried his hat, cushion, and parasols. He was also attended by a secretary in a mantle of violet silk, a train-bearer in a gown of violet woollen stuff, and a gentleman in waiting, wearing an Elizabethan style of costume, and bearing the *berretta* with gloved hands. Although the household had then become smaller, it still comprised an *auditore* specially charged with the congregational work, a secretary employed exclusively for correspondence, a chief usher who introduced visitors, a gentleman in attendance for the carrying of the *berretta*, a train-bearer, a chaplain, a majordomo and a *valet-de-chambre*, to say nothing of a flock of underlings, lackeys, cooks, coachmen, grooms, quite a population, which filled the vast mansions with bustle. And with these attendants Pierre mentally sought to fill the three spacious ante-rooms now so deserted; the stream of lackeys in blue liveries broidered with emblazonry, the world of abbes and prelates in silk mantles appeared before him, again setting magnificent and passionate life under the lofty ceilings, illumining all the semi-gloom with resuscitated splendour.

But nowadays—particularly since the Italian occupation of Rome—nearly all the great fortunes of the Roman princes have been exhausted, and the pomp of the great dignitaries of the Church has disappeared. The ruined patricians have kept aloof from badly remunerated ecclesiastical offices to which little renown attaches, and have left them to the ambition of the petty *bourgeoisie*. Cardinal Boccanera, the last prince of ancient nobility invested with the purple, received scarcely more than 30,000 *lire*[1] a year to enable him to sustain his rank, that is 22,000 *lire*,[2] the salary of his post as Camerlingo, and various small sums derived from other functions. And he would never have made both ends meet had not Donna Serafina helped him with the rem-

---

[1] 1,200 pounds.

[2] 880 pounds.

nants of the former family fortune which he had long previously surrendered to his sisters and his brother. Donna Serafina and Benedetta lived apart, in their own rooms, having their own table, servants, and personal expenses. The Cardinal only had his nephew Dario with him, and he never gave a dinner or held a public reception. His greatest source of expense was his carriage, the heavy pair-horse coach, which ceremonial usage compelled him to retain, for a cardinal cannot go on foot through the streets of Rome. However, his coachman, an old family servant, spared him the necessity of keeping a groom by insisting on taking entire charge of the carriage and the two black horses, which, like himself, had grown old in the service of the Boccaneras. There were two footmen, father and son, the latter born in the house. And the cook's wife assisted in the kitchen. However, yet greater reductions had been made in the ante-rooms, where the staff, once so brilliant and numerous, was now simply composed of two petty priests, Don Vigilio, who was at once secretary, auditore, and majordomo, and Abbe Paparelli, who acted as train-bearer, chaplain, and chief usher. There, where a crowd of salaried people of all ranks had once moved to and fro, filling the vast halls with bustle and colour, one now only beheld two little black cassocks gliding noiselessly along, two unobtrusive shadows flitting about amidst the deep gloom of the lifeless rooms.

And Pierre now fully understood the haughty unconcern of the Cardinal, who suffered time to complete its work of destruction in that ancestral mansion, to which he was powerless to restore the glorious life of former times! Built for that shining life, for the sovereign display of a sixteenth-century prince, it was now deserted and empty, crumbling about the head of its last master, who had no servants left him to fill it, and would not have known how to pay for the materials which repairs would have necessitated. And so, since the modern world was hostile, since religion was no longer sovereign, since men had changed, and one was drifting into the unknown, amidst the hatred and indifference of new generations, why not allow the old world to collapse in the stubborn, motionless pride born of its ancient glory? Heroes alone died standing, without relinquishing aught of their past, preserving the same faith until their final gasp, beholding, with pain-fraught bravery and infinite sadness, the slow last agony of their divinity. And the Cardinal's tall figure, his pale, proud face, so full of sovereign despair and courage, expressed that stubborn determination to perish beneath the ruins of the old social edifice rather than change a single one of its stones.

Pierre was roused by a rustling of furtive steps, a little mouse-like trot, which made him raise his head. A door in the wall had just opened, and to his surprise there stood before him an abbe of some forty years, fat and short, looking like an old maid in a black skirt, a very old maid in fact, so numerous were the wrinkles on his flabby face. It was Abbe Paparelli, the train-bearer and usher, and on seeing Pierre he was about to question him, when Don Vigilio explained matters.

"Ah! very good, very good, Monsieur l'Abbe Froment. His Eminence will condescend to receive you, but you must wait, you must wait."

Then, with his silent rolling walk, he returned to the second ante-room, where he usually stationed himself.

Pierre did not like his face—the face of an old female devotee, whitened by celibacy, and ravaged by stern observance of the rites; and so, as Don Vigilio—his head weary and his hands burning with fever—had not resumed his work, the young man ventured to question him. Oh! Abbe Paparelli, he was a man of the liveliest faith, who from simple humility remained in a modest post in his Eminence's service. On the other hand, his Eminence was pleased to reward him for his devotion by occasionally condescending to listen to his advice.

As Don Vigilio spoke, a faint gleam of irony, a kind of veiled anger appeared in his ardent eyes. However, he continued to examine Pierre, and gradually seemed reassured, appreciating the evident frankness of this foreigner who could hardly belong to any clique. And so he ended by departing somewhat from his continual sickly distrust, and even engaged in a brief chat.

"Yes, yes," he said, "there is a deal of work sometimes, and rather hard work too. His Eminence belongs to several Congregations, the Consistorial, the Holy Office, the Index, the Rites. And all the documents concerning the business which falls to him come into my hands. I have to study each affair, prepare a report on it, clear the way, so to say. Besides which all the correspondence is carried on through me. Fortunately his Eminence is a holy man, and intrigues neither for himself nor for others, and this enables us to taste a little peace."

Pierre took a keen interest in these particulars of the life led by a prince of the Church. He learnt that the Cardinal rose at six o'clock, summer and winter alike. He said his mass in his chapel, a little room which simply contained an altar of painted wood, and which nobody but himself ever entered. His private apartments were limited to three rooms—a bed-room, dining-room, and study—all very modest and small, contrived indeed by partitioning off portions of one large hall. And he led a very retired life, exempt from all luxury, like one who is frugal and poor. At eight in the morning he drank a cup of cold milk for his breakfast. Then, when there were sittings of the Congregations to which he belonged, he attended them; otherwise he remained at home and gave audience. Dinner was served at one o'clock, and afterwards came the siesta, lasting until five in summer and until four at other seasons—a sacred moment when a servant would not have dared even to knock at the door. On awaking, if it were fine, his Eminence drove out towards the ancient Appian Way, returning at sunset when the *Ave Maria* began to ring. And finally, after again giving audience between seven and nine, he supped and retired into his room, where he worked all alone or went to bed. The cardinals wait upon the Pope on fixed days, two or three times each month, for purposes connected with their functions. For nearly a year, however, the Camerlingo had not been received in private audience by his Holiness, and this was a sign of disgrace, a proof of secret warfare, of which the entire black world spoke in prudent whispers.

"His Eminence is sometimes a little rough," continued Don Vigilio in a soft voice. "But you should see him smile when his niece the Contessina, of whom he is very fond, comes down to kiss him. If you have a good reception, you know, you will owe it to the Contessina."

At this moment the secretary was interrupted. A sound of voices came from the second ante-room, and forthwith he rose to his feet, and bent very low at sight of a stout man in a black cassock, red sash, and black hat, with twisted cord of red and gold, whom Abbe Paparelli was ushering in with a great display of deferential genuflections. Pierre also had risen at a sign from Don Vigilio, who found time to whisper to him, "Cardinal Sanguinetti, Prefect of the Congregation of the Index."

Meantime Abbe Paparelli was lavishing attentions on the prelate, repeating with an expression of blissful satisfaction: "Your most reverend Eminence was expected. I have orders to admit your most reverend Eminence at once. His Eminence the Grand Penitentiary is already here."

Sanguinetti, loud of voice and sonorous of tread, spoke out with sudden familiarity, "Yes, yes, I know. A number of importunate people detained me! One can never do as one desires. But I am here at last."

He was a man of sixty, squat and fat, with a round and highly coloured face distinguished by a huge nose, thick lips, and bright eyes which were always on the move. But he more particularly struck one by his active, almost turbulent, youthful vivacity, scarcely a white hair as yet showing among his brown and carefully tended locks, which fell in curls about his temples. Born at Viterbo, he had studied at the seminary there before completing his education at the Universita Gregoriana in Rome. His ecclesiastical appointments showed how rapidly he had made his way, how supple was his mind: first of all secretary to the nunciature at Lisbon; then created titular Bishop of Thebes, and entrusted with a delicate mission in Brazil; on his return appointed nuncio first at Brussels and next at Vienna; and finally raised to the cardinalate, to say nothing of the fact that he had lately secured the suburban episcopal see of Frascati.[1] Trained to business, having dealt with every nation in Europe, he had nothing against him but his ambition, of which he made too open a display, and his spirit of intrigue, which was ever restless. It was said that he was now one of the irreconcilables who demanded that Italy should surrender Rome, though formerly he had made advances to the Quirinal. In his wild passion to become the next Pope he rushed from one opinion to the other, giving himself no end of trouble to gain people from whom he afterwards parted. He had twice already fallen out with Leo XIII, but had deemed it politic to make his submission. In point of fact, given that he was an almost openly declared candidate to the papacy, he was wearing himself out by his perpetual efforts, dabbling in too many things, and setting too many people agog.

Pierre, however, had only seen in him the Prefect of the Congregation of the Index; and the one idea which struck him was that this man would decide the fate of his book. And so, when the Cardinal had disappeared and Abbe Paparelli had returned to the second ante-room, he could not refrain from asking Don Vigilio, "Are their Eminences Cardinal Sanguinetti and Cardinal Boccanera very intimate, then?"

An irrepressible smile contracted the secretary's lips, while his eyes gleamed with an irony which he could no longer subdue: "Very intimate—oh! no, no—they see one another when they can't do otherwise."

Then he explained that considerable deference was shown to Cardinal Boccanera's high birth, and that his colleagues often met at his residence, when, as happened to be the case that morning, any grave affair presented itself, requiring an interview apart from the usual official meetings. Cardinal Sanguinetti, he added, was the son of a petty medical man of Viterbo. "No, no," he concluded, "their Eminences are not at all intimate. It is difficult for men to agree when they have neither the same ideas nor the same character, especially too when they are in each other's way."

Don Vigilio spoke these last words in a lower tone, as if talking to himself and still retaining his sharp smile. But Pierre scarcely listened, absorbed as he was in his own

[1] Cardinals York and Howard were Bishops of Frascati.—Trans.

worries. "Perhaps they have met to discuss some affair connected with the Index?" said he.

Don Vigilio must have known the object of the meeting. However, he merely replied that, if the Index had been in question, the meeting would have taken place at the residence of the Prefect of that Congregation. Thereupon Pierre, yielding to his impatience, was obliged to put a straight question. "You know of my affair—the affair of my book," he said. "Well, as his Eminence is a member of the Congregation, and all the documents pass through your hands, you might be able to give me some useful information. I know nothing as yet and am so anxious to know!"

At this Don Vigilio relapsed into scared disquietude. He stammered, saying that he had not seen any documents, which was true. "Nothing has yet reached us," he added; "I assure you I know nothing."

Then, as the other persisted, he signed to him to keep quiet, and again turned to his writing, glancing furtively towards the second ante-room as if he believed that Abbe Paparelli was listening. He had certainly said too much, he thought, and he made himself very small, crouching over the table, and melting, fading away in his dim corner.

Pierre again fell into a reverie, a prey to all the mystery which enveloped him—the sleepy, antique sadness of his surroundings. Long minutes went by; it was nearly eleven when the sound of a door opening and a buzz of voices roused him. Then he bowed respectfully to Cardinal Sanguinetti, who went off accompanied by another cardinal, a very thin and tall man, with a grey, bony, ascetic face. Neither of them, however, seemed even to see the petty foreign priest who bent low as they went by. They were chatting aloud in familiar fashion.

"Yes! the wind is falling; it is warmer than yesterday."

"We shall certainly have the sirocco to-morrow."

Then solemn silence again fell on the large, dim room. Don Vigilio was still writing, but his pen made no noise as it travelled over the stiff yellow paper. However, the faint tinkle of a cracked bell was suddenly heard, and Abbe Paparelli, after hastening into the throne-room for a moment, returned to summon Pierre, whom he announced in a restrained voice: "Monsieur l'Abbe Pierre Froment."

The spacious throne-room was like the other apartments, a virtual ruin. Under the fine ceiling of carved and gilded wood-work, the red wall-hangings of *brocatelle*, with a large palm pattern, were falling into tatters. A few holes had been patched, but long wear had streaked the dark purple of the silk—once of dazzling magnificence—with pale hues. The curiosity of the room was its old throne, an arm-chair upholstered in red silk, on which the Holy Father had sat when visiting Cardinal Pio's grand-uncle. This chair was surmounted by a canopy, likewise of red silk, under which hung the portrait of the reigning Pope. And, according to custom, the chair was turned towards the wall, to show that none might sit on it. The other furniture of the apartment was made up of sofas, arm-chairs, and chairs, with a marvellous Louis Quatorze table of gilded wood, having a top of mosaic-work representing the rape of Europa.

But at first Pierre only saw Cardinal Boccanera standing by the table which he used for writing. In his simple black cassock, with red edging and red buttons, the Cardinal seemed to him yet taller and prouder than in the portrait which showed him in ceremonial costume. There was the same curly white hair, the same long, strongly marked face, with large nose and thin lips, and the same ardent eyes, illumining the pale countenance from under bushy brows which had remained black. But the portrait did not express the lofty tranquil faith which shone in this handsome face, a complete certainty of what truth was, and an absolute determination to abide by it for ever.

Boccanera had not stirred, but with black, fixed glance remained watching his visitor's approach; and the young priest, acquainted with the usual ceremonial, knelt and kissed the large ruby which the prelate wore on his hand. However, the Cardinal immediately raised him.

"You are welcome here, my dear son. My niece spoke to me about you with so much sympathy that I am happy to receive you." With these words Pio seated himself near the table, as yet not telling Pierre to take a chair, but still examining him whilst speaking slowly and with studied politeness: "You arrived yesterday morning, did you not, and were very tired?"

"Your Eminence is too kind—yes, I was worn out, as much through emotion as fatigue. This journey is one of such gravity for me."

The Cardinal seemed indisposed to speak of serious matters so soon. "No doubt; it is a long way from Paris to Rome," he replied. "Nowadays the journey may be accomplished with fair rapidity, but formerly how interminable it was!" Then speaking yet more slowly: "I went to Paris once—oh! a long time ago, nearly fifty years ago—and then for barely a week. A large and handsome city; yes, yes, a great many people in the streets, extremely well-bred people, a nation which has accomplished great and admirable things. Even in these sad times one cannot forget that France was the eldest daughter of the Church. But since that one journey I have not left Rome—"

Then he made a gesture of quiet disdain, expressive of all he left unsaid. What was the use of journeying to a land of doubt and rebellion? Did not Rome suffice—Rome, which governed the world—the Eternal City which, when the times should be accomplished, would become the capital of the world once more?

Silently glancing at the Cardinal's lofty stature, the stature of one of the violent war-like princes of long ago, now reduced to wearing that simple cassock, Pierre deemed him superb with his proud conviction that Rome sufficed unto herself. But that stubborn resolve to remain in ignorance, that determination to take no account of other nations excepting to treat them as vassals, disquieted him when he reflected on the motives that had brought him there. And as silence had again fallen he thought it politic to approach the subject he had at heart by words of homage.

"Before taking any other steps," said he, "I desired to express my profound respect for your Eminence; for in your Eminence I place my only hope; and I beg your Eminence to be good enough to advise and guide me."

With a wave of the hand Boccanera thereupon invited Pierre to take a chair in front of him. "I certainly do not refuse you my counsel, my dear son," he replied. "I owe my counsel to every Christian who desires to do well. But it would be wrong for you to rely on my influence. I have none. I live entirely apart from others; I cannot and will not ask for anything. However, this will not prevent us from chatting." Then, approaching the question in all frankness, without the slightest artifice, like one of brave and absolute mind who fears no responsibility however great, he continued: "You have written a book, have you not?—'New Rome,' I believe—and you have come to defend this book which has been denounced to the Congregation of the Index. For my own part I have not yet read it. You will understand that I cannot read everything. I only see the works that are sent to me by the Congregation which I have belonged to since last year; and, besides, I often content myself with the reports which my secretary draws up for me. However, my niece Benedetta has read your book, and has told me that it is not lacking in interest. It first astonished her somewhat, and then greatly moved her. So I promise you that I will go through it and study the incriminated passages with the greatest care."

Pierre profited by the opportunity to begin pleading his cause. And it occurred to him that it would be best to give his references at once. "Your Eminence will realise how stupefied I was when I learnt that proceedings were being taken against my book," he sàid. "Monsieur le Vicomte Philibert de la Choue, who is good enough to show me some friendship, does not cease repeating that such a book is worth the best of armies to the Holy See."

"Oh! De la Choue, De la Choue!" repeated the Cardinal with a pout of good-natured disdain. "I know that De la Choue considers himself a good Catholic. He is in a slight degree our relative, as you know. And when he comes to Rome and stays here, I willingly see him, on condition however that no mention is made of certain subjects on which it would be impossible for us to agree. To tell the truth, the Catholicism preached by De la Choue—worthy, clever man though he is—his Catholicism, I say, with his corporations, his working-class clubs, his cleansed democracy and his vague socialism, is after all merely so much literature!"

This pronouncement struck Pierre, for he realised all the disdainful irony contained in it—an irony which touched himself. And so he hastened to name his other reference, whose authority he imagined to be above discussion: "His Eminence Cardinal Bergerot has been kind enough to signify his full approval of my book."

At this Boccanera's face suddenly changed. It no longer wore an expression of derisive blame, tinged with the pity that is prompted by a child's ill-considered action fated to certain failure. A flash of anger now lighted up the Cardinal's dark eyes, and a pugnacious impulse hardened his entire countenance. "In France," he slowly resumed, "Cardinal Bergerot no doubt has a reputation for great piety. We know little of him in Rome. Personally, I have only seen him once, when he came to receive his hat. And I would not therefore allow myself to judge him if his writings and actions had not recently saddened my believing soul. Unhappily, I am not the only one; you will find nobody here, of the Sacred College, who approves of his doings." Boccanera paused, then in a firm voice concluded: "Cardinal Bergerot is a Revolutionary!"

This time Pierre's surprise for a moment forced him to silence. A Revolutionary—good heavens! a Revolutionary—that gentle pastor of souls, whose charity was inexhaustible, whose one dream was that Jesus might return to earth to ensure at last the reign of peace and justice! So words did not have the same signification in all places; into what religion had he now tumbled that the faith of the poor and the humble should be looked upon as a mere insurrectional, condemnable passion? As yet unable to understand things aright, Pierre nevertheless realised that discussion would be both discourteous and futile, and his only remaining desire was to give an account of his book, explain and vindicate it. But at his first words the Cardinal interposed.

"No, no, my dear son. It would take us too long and I wish to read the passages. Besides, there is an absolute rule. All books which meddle with the faith are condemnable and pernicious. Does your book show perfect respect for dogma?"

"I believe so, and I assure your Eminence that I have had no intention of writing a work of negation."

"Good: I may be on your side if that is true. Only, in the contrary case, I have but one course to advise you, which is to withdraw your work, condemn it, and destroy it without waiting until a decision of the Index compels you to do so. Whosoever has given birth to scandal must stifle it and expiate it, even if he have to cut into his own flesh. The only duties of a priest are humility and obedience, the complete annihilation of self before the sovereign will of the Church. And, besides, why write at all? For there is already rebellion in expressing an opinion of one's own. It is always the temptation of the devil which puts a pen in an author's hand. Why, then, incur the risk of being for ever damned by yielding to the pride of intelligence and domination? Your book again, my dear son—your book is literature, literature!"

This expression again repeated was instinct with so much contempt that Pierre realised all the wretchedness that would fall upon the poor pages of his apostolate on meeting the eyes of this prince who had become a saintly man. With increasing fear and admiration he listened to him, and beheld him growing greater and greater.

"Ah! faith, my dear son, everything is in faith—perfect, disinterested faith—which believes for the sole happiness of believing! How restful it is to bow down before the mysteries without seeking to penetrate them, full of the tranquil conviction that, in accepting them, one possesses both the certain and the final! Is not the highest intellectual satisfaction that which is derived from the victory of the divine over the mind, which it disciplines, and contents so completely that it knows desire no more? And apart from that perfect equilibrium, that explanation of the unknown by the divine, no durable peace is possible for man. If one desires that truth and justice should reign upon earth, it is in God that one must place them. He that does not believe is like a battlefield, the scene of every disaster. Faith alone can tranquillise and deliver."

For an instant Pierre remained silent before the great figure rising up in front of him. At Lourdes he had only seen suffering humanity rushing thither for health of the body and consolation of the soul; but here was the intellectual believer, the mind that needs certainty, finding satisfaction, tasting the supreme enjoyment of doubting no more. He had never previously heard such a cry of joy at living in obedience without anxiety as to the morrow of death. He knew that Boccanera's youth had been somewhat stormy, traversed by acute attacks of sensuality, a flaring of the red blood of his ancestors; and he marvelled at the calm majesty which faith had at last implanted in this descendant of so violent a race, who had no passion remaining in him but that of pride.

"And yet," Pierre at last ventured to say in a timid, gentle voice, "if faith remains essential and immutable, forms change. From hour to hour evolution goes on in all things—the world changes."

"That is not true!" exclaimed the Cardinal, "the world does not change. It continually tramps over the same ground, loses itself, strays into the most abominable courses, and it continually has to be brought back into the right path. That is the truth. In order that the promises of Christ may be fulfilled, is it not necessary that the world should return to its starting point, its original innocence? Is not the end of time fixed for the day when men shall be in possession of the full truth of the Gospel? Yes, truth is in the past, and it is always to the past that one must cling if one would avoid the pitfalls which evil imaginations create. All those fine novelties, those mirages of that famous so-called progress, are simply traps and snares of the eternal tempter, causes of perdition and death. Why seek any further, why constantly incur the risk of error, when for eighteen hundred years the truth has been known? Truth! why it is in Apostolic and Roman Catholicism as created by a long succession of generations! What madness to desire to change it when so many lofty minds, so many pious souls have made of it the most admirable of monuments, the one instrument of order in this world, and of salvation in the next!"

Pierre, whose heart had contracted, refrained from further protest, for he could no longer doubt that he had before him an implacable adversary of his most cherished ideas. Chilled by a covert fear, as though he felt a faint breath, as of a distant wind from a land of ruins, pass over his face, bringing with it the mortal cold of a sepulchre, he bowed respectfully whilst the Cardinal, rising to his full height, continued in his obstinate voice, resonant with proud courage: "And if Catholicism, as its enemies pretend, be really stricken unto death, it must die standing and in all its glorious integrality. You hear me, Monsieur l'Abbe—not one concession, not one surrender, not a single act of cowardice! Catholicism is such as it is, and cannot be otherwise. No modification of the divine certainty, the entire truth, is possible. The removal of the smallest stone from the edifice could only prove a cause of instability. Is this not evident? You cannot save old houses by attacking them with the pickaxe under pretence of decorating them. You only enlarge the fissures. Even if it were true that Rome were on the eve of falling into dust, the only result of all the repairing and patching would be to hasten the catastrophe. And instead of a noble death, met unflinchingly, we should then behold the basest of agonies, the death throes of a coward who struggles and begs for mercy! For my part I wait. I am convinced that all that people say is but so much horrible falsehood, that Catholicism has never been firmer, that it imbibes eternity from the one and only source of life. But should the heavens indeed fall, on that day I should be here, amidst these old and crumbling walls, under these old ceilings whose beams are being devoured by the worms, and it is here, erect, among the ruins, that I should meet my end, repeating my *credo* for the last time."

His final words fell more slowly, full of haughty sadness, whilst with a sweeping gesture he waved his arms towards the old, silent, deserted palace around him, whence life was withdrawing day by day. Had an involuntary presentiment come to him, did the faint cold breath from the ruins also fan his own cheeks? All the neglect into which the vast rooms had fallen was explained by his words; and a superb, despondent grandeur enveloped this prince and cardinal, this uncompromising Catholic who, withdrawing into the dim half-light of the past, braved with a soldier's heart the inevitable downfall of the olden world.

Deeply impressed, Pierre was about to take his leave when, to his surprise, a little door opened in the hangings. "What is it? Can't I be left in peace for a moment?" exclaimed Boccanera with sudden impatience.

Nevertheless, Abbe Paparelli, fat and sleek, glided into the room without the faintest sign of emotion. And he whispered a few words in the ear of the Cardinal, who, on seeing him, had become calm again. "What curate?" asked Boccanera. "Oh! yes, Santobono, the curate of Frascati. I know—tell him I cannot see him just now."

Paparelli, however, again began whispering in his soft voice, though not in so low a key as previously, for some of his words could be overheard. The affair was urgent, the curate was compelled to return home, and had only a word or two to say. And then, without awaiting consent, the train-bearer ushered in the visitor, a *protege* of his, whom he had left just outside the little door. And for his own part he withdrew with the tranquillity of a retainer who, whatever the modesty of his office, knows himself to be all powerful.

Pierre, who was momentarily forgotten, looked at the visitor—a big fellow of a priest, the son of a peasant evidently, and still near to the soil. He had an ungainly, bony figure, huge feet and knotted hands, with a seamy tanned face lighted by extremely keen black eyes. Five and forty and still robust, his chin and cheeks bristling, and his cassock, overlarge, hanging loosely about his big projecting bones, he suggested a bandit in disguise. Still there was nothing base about him; the expression of his face was proud. And in one hand he carried a small wicker basket carefully covered over with fig-leaves.

Santobono at once bent his knees and kissed the Cardinal's ring, but with hasty unconcern, as though only some ordinary piece of civility were in question. Then, with that commingling of respect and familiarity which the little ones of the world often evince towards the great, he said, "I beg your most reverend Eminence's forgiveness for having insisted. But there were people waiting, and I should not have been received if my old friend Paparelli had not brought me by way of that door. Oh! I have a very great service to ask of your Eminence, a real service of the heart. But first of all may I be allowed to offer your Eminence a little present?"

The Cardinal listened with a grave expression. He had been well acquainted with Santobono in the years when he had spent the summer at Frascati, at a princely residence which the Boccaneras had possessed there—a villa rebuilt in the seventeenth century, surrounded by a wonderful park, whose famous terrace overlooked the Campagna, stretching far and bare like the sea. This villa, however, had since been sold, and on some vineyards, which had fallen to Benedetta's share, Count Prada, prior to the divorce proceedings, had begun to erect quite a district of little pleasure houses. In former times, when walking out, the Cardinal had condescended to enter and rest in the dwelling of Santobono, who officiated at an antique chapel dedicated to St. Mary of the Fields, without the town. The priest had his home in a half-ruined building adjoining this chapel, and the charm of the place was a walled garden which he cultivated himself with the passion of a true peasant.

"As is my rule every year," said he, placing his basket on the table, "I wished that your Eminence might taste my figs. They are the first of the season. I gathered them expressly this morning. You used to be so fond of them, your Eminence, when you condescended to gather them from the tree itself. You were good enough to tell me that there wasn't another tree in the world that produced such fine figs."

The Cardinal could not help smiling. He was indeed very fond of figs, and Santobono spoke truly: his fig-tree was renowned throughout the district. "Thank you, my dear Abbe," said Boccanera, "you remember my little failings. Well, and what can I do for you?"

Again he became grave, for, in former times, there had been unpleasant discussions between him and the curate, a lack of agreement which had angered him. Born at Nemi, in the core of a fierce district, Santobono belonged to a violent family, and his eldest brother had died of a stab. He himself had always professed ardently patriotic opinions. It was said that he had all but taken up arms for Garibaldi; and, on the day when the Italians had entered Rome, force had been needed to prevent him from raising the flag of Italian unity above his roof. His passionate dream was to behold Rome mistress of the world, when the Pope and the King should have embraced and made cause together. Thus the Cardinal looked on him as a dangerous revolutionary, a renegade who imperilled Catholicism.

"Oh! what your Eminence can do for me, what your Eminence can do if only condescending and willing!" repeated Santobono in an ardent voice, clasping his big knotty hands. And then, breaking off, he inquired, "Did not his Eminence Cardinal Sanguinetti explain my affair to your most reverend Eminence?"

"No, the Cardinal simply advised me of your visit, saying that you had something to ask of me."

Whilst speaking Boccanera's face had clouded over, and it was with increased sternness of manner that he again waited. He was aware that the priest had become Sanguinetti's "client" since the latter had been in the habit of spending weeks together at his suburban see of Frascati. Walking in the shadow of every cardinal who is a candidate to the papacy, there are familiars of low degree who stake the ambition of their life on the possibility of that cardinal's election. If he becomes Pope some day, if they themselves help him to the throne, they enter the great pontifical family in his train. It was related that Sanguinetti had once already extricated Santobono from a nasty difficulty: the priest having one day caught a marauding urchin in the act of climbing his wall, had beaten the little fellow with such severity that he had ultimately died of it. However, to Santobono's credit it must be added that his fanatical devotion to the Cardinal was largely based upon the hope that he would prove the Pope whom men awaited, the Pope who would make Italy the sovereign nation of the world.

"Well, this is my misfortune," he said. "Your Eminence knows my brother Agostino, who was gardener at the villa for two years in your Eminence's time. He is certainly a very pleasant and gentle young fellow, of whom nobody has ever complained. And so it is hard to understand how such an accident can have happened to him, but it seems that he has killed a man with a knife at Genzano, while walking in the street in the evening. I am dreadfully distressed about it, and would willingly give two fingers of my right hand to extricate him from prison. However, it occurred to me that your Eminence would not refuse me a certificate stating that Agostino was formerly in your Eminence's service, and that your Eminence was always well pleased with his quiet disposition."

But the Cardinal flatly protested: "I was not at all pleased with Agostino. He was wildly violent, and I had to dismiss him precisely because he was always quarrelling with the other servants."

"Oh! how grieved I am to hear your Eminence say that! So it is true, then, my poor little Agostino's disposition has really changed! Still there is always a way out of a difficulty, is there not? You can still give me a certificate, first arranging the wording of it. A certificate from your Eminence would have such a favourable effect upon the law officers."

"No doubt," replied Boccanera; "I can understand that, but I will give no certificate."

"What! does your most reverend Eminence refuse my prayer?"

"Absolutely! I know that you are a priest of perfect morality, that you discharge the duties of your ministry with strict punctuality, and that you would be deserving of high commendation were it not for your political fancies. Only your fraternal affection is now leading you astray. I cannot tell a lie to please you."

Santobono gazed at him in real stupefaction, unable to understand that a prince, an all-powerful cardinal, should be influenced by such petty scruples, when the entire question was a mere knife thrust, the most commonplace and frequent of incidents in the yet wild land of the old Roman castles.

"A lie! a lie!" he muttered; "but surely it isn't lying just to say what is good of a man, leaving out all the rest, especially when a man has good points as Agostino certainly has. In a certificate, too, everything depends on the words one uses."

He stubbornly clung to that idea; he could not conceive that a person should refuse to soften the rigour of justice by an ingenious presentation of the facts. However, on acquiring a certainty that he would obtain nothing, he made a gesture of despair, his livid face assuming an expression of violent rancour, whilst his black eyes flamed with restrained passion.

"Well, well! each looks on truth in his own way," he said. "I shall go back to tell his Eminence Cardinal Sanguinetti. And I beg your Eminence not to be displeased with me for having disturbed your Eminence to no purpose. By the way, perhaps the figs are not yet quite ripe; but I will take the liberty to bring another basketful towards the end of the season, when they will be quite nice and sweet. A thousand thanks and a thousand felicities to your most reverend Eminence."

Santobono went off backwards, his big bony figure bending double with repeated genuflections. Pierre, whom the scene had greatly interested, in him beheld a specimen of the petty clergy of Rome and its environs, of whom people had told him before his departure from Paris. This was not the *scagnozzo*, the wretched famished priest whom some nasty affair brings from the provinces, who seeks his daily bread on the pavements of Rome; one of the herd of begowned beggars searching for a livelihood among the crumbs of Church life, voraciously fighting for chance masses, and mingling with the lowest orders in taverns of the worst repute. Nor was this the country priest of distant parts, a man of crass ignorance and superstition, a peasant among the peasants, treated as an equal by his pious flock, which is careful not to mistake him for the Divinity, and which, whilst kneeling in all humility before the parish saint, does not bend before the man who from that saint derives his livelihood. At Frascati the officiating minister of a little church may receive a stipend of some nine hundred *lire* a year,[1] and he has only bread and meat to buy if his garden yields him wine and fruit and vegetables. This one, Santobono, was not without education; he knew a little theology and a little history, especially the history of the past grandeur of Rome, which had inflamed his patriotic heart with the mad dream that universal domination would soon fall to the portion of renascent Rome, the capital of united Italy. But what an insuperable distance still remained between this petty Roman clergy, often very worthy and intelligent, and the high clergy, the high dignitaries of the Vatican! Nobody that was not at least a prelate seemed to count.

"A thousand thanks to your most reverend Eminence, and may success attend all your Eminence's desires."

With these words Santobono finally disappeared, and the Cardinal returned to Pierre, who also bowed preparatory to taking his leave.

---

[1] About 36 pounds. One is reminded of Goldsmith's line: "And passing rich with forty pounds a year."—Trans.

III.

"To sum up the matter, Monsieur l'Abbe," said Boccanera, "the affair of your book presents certain difficulties. As I have told you, I have no precise information, I have seen no documents. But knowing that my niece took an interest in you, I said a few words on the subject to Cardinal Sanguinetti, the Prefect of the Index, who was here just now. And he knows little more than I do, for nothing has yet left the Secretary's hands. Still he told me that the denunciation emanated from personages of rank and influence, and applied to numerous pages of your work, in which it was said there were passages of the most deplorable character as regards both discipline and dogma."

Greatly moved by the idea that he had hidden foes, secret adversaries who pursued him in the dark, the young priest responded: "Oh! denounced, denounced! If your Eminence only knew how that word pains my heart! And denounced, too, for offences which were certainly involuntary, since my one ardent desire was the triumph of the Church! All I can do, then, is to fling myself at the feet of the Holy Father and entreat him to hear my defence."

Boccanera suddenly became very grave again. A stern look rested on his lofty brow as he drew his haughty figure to its full height. "His Holiness," said he, "can do everything, even receive you, if such be his good pleasure, and absolve you also. But listen to me. I again advise you to withdraw your book yourself, to destroy it, simply and courageously, before embarking in a struggle in which you will reap the shame of being overwhelmed. Reflect on that."

Pierre, however, had no sooner spoken of the Pope than he had regretted it, for he realised that an appeal to the sovereign authority was calculated to wound the Cardinal's feelings. Moreover, there was no further room for doubt. Boccanera would be against his book, and the utmost that he could hope for was to gain his neutrality by bringing pressure to bear on him through those about him. At the same time he had found the Cardinal very plain spoken, very frank, far removed from all the secret intriguing in which the affair of his book was involved, as he now began to realise; and so it was with deep respect and genuine admiration for the prelate's strong and lofty character that he took leave of him.

"I am infinitely obliged to your Eminence," he said, "and I promise that I will carefully reflect upon all that your Eminence has been kind enough to say to me."

On returning to the ante-room, Pierre there found five or six persons who had arrived during his audience, and were now waiting. There was a bishop, a domestic prelate, and two old ladies, and as he drew near to Don Vigilio before retiring, he was surprised to find him conversing with a tall, fair young fellow, a Frenchman, who, also in astonishment, exclaimed, "What! are you here in Rome, Monsieur l'Abbe?"

For a moment Pierre had hesitated. "Ah! I must ask your pardon, Monsieur Narcisse Habert," he replied, "I did not at first recognise you! It was the less excusable as I knew that you had been an *attache* at our embassy here ever since last year."

Tall, slim, and elegant of appearance, Narcisse Habert had a clear complexion, with eyes of a bluish, almost mauvish, hue, a fair frizzy beard, and long curling fair hair cut short over the forehead in the Florentine fashion. Of a wealthy family of militant Catholics, chiefly members of the bar or bench, he had an uncle in the diplomatic profession, and this had decided his own career. Moreover, a place at Rome was marked out for him, for he there had powerful connections. He was a nephew by marriage of Cardinal Sarno, whose sister had married another of his uncles, a Paris notary; and he was also cousin german of Monsignor Gamba del Zoppo, a *Cameriere segreto*, and son of one of his aunts, who had married an Italian colonel. And in some measure for these reasons he had been attached to the embassy to the Holy See, his superiors tolerating his somewhat fantastic ways, his everlasting passion for art which sent him wandering hither and thither through Rome. He was moreover very amiable and extremely well-bred; and it occasionally happened, as was the case that morning, that with his weary and somewhat mysterious air he came to speak to one or another of the cardinals on some real matter of business in the ambassador's name.

So as to converse with Pierre at his ease, he drew him into the deep embrasure of one of the windows. "Ah! my dear Abbe, how pleased I am to see you!" said he. "You must remember what pleasant chats we had when we met at Cardinal Bergerot's! I told you about some paintings which you were to see for your book, some miniatures of the fourteenth and fifteenth centuries. And now, you know, I mean to take possession of you. I'll show you Rome as nobody else could show it to you. I've seen and explored everything. Ah! there are treasures, such treasures! But in truth there is only one supreme work; one always comes back to one's particular passion. The Botticelli in the Sixtine Chapel—ah, the Botticelli!"

His voice died away, and he made a faint gesture as if overcome by admiration. Then Pierre had to promise that he would place himself in his hands and accompany him to the Sixtine Chapel. "You know why I am here," at last said the young priest. "Proceedings have been taken against my book; it has been denounced to the Congregation of the Index."

"Your book! is it possible?" exclaimed Narcisse: "a book like that with pages recalling the delightful St. Francis of Assisi!" And thereupon he obligingly placed himself at Pierre's disposal. "But our ambassador will be very useful to you," he said. "He is the best man in the world, of charming affability, and full of the old French spirit. I will present you to him this afternoon or to-morrow morning at the latest; and since you desire an immediate audience with the Pope, he will endeavour to obtain one for you. His position naturally designates him as your intermediary. Still, I must confess that things are not always easily managed. Although the Holy Father is very fond of him, there are times when his Excellency fails, for the approaches are so extremely intricate."

Pierre had not thought of employing the ambassador's good offices, for he had naively imagined that an accused priest who came to defend himself would find every door open. However, he was delighted with Narcisse's offer, and thanked him as warmly as if the audience were already obtained.

"Besides," the young man continued, "if we encounter any difficulties I have relatives at the Vatican, as you know. I don't mean my uncle the Cardinal, who would be of no use to us, for he never stirs out of his office at the Propaganda, and will never apply for anything. But my cousin, Monsignor Gamba del Zoppo, is very obliging, and he lives in intimacy with the Pope, his duties requiring his constant attendance on him. So, if necessary, I will take you to see him, and he will no doubt find a means of procuring you an interview, though his extreme prudence keeps him perpetually afraid of compromising himself. However, it's understood, you may rely on me in every respect."

"Ah! my dear sir," exclaimed Pierre, relieved and happy, "I heartily accept your offer. You don't know what balm your words have brought me; for ever since my arrival everybody has been discouraging me, and you are the first to restore my strength by looking at things in the true French way."

Then, lowering his voice, he told the *attache* of his interview with Cardinal Boccanera, of his conviction that the latter would not help him, of the unfavourable information which had been given by Cardinal Sanguinetti, and of the rivalry which he had divined between the two prelates. Narcisse listened, smiling, and in his turn began to gossip confidentially. The rivalry which Pierre had mentioned, the premature contest for the tiara which Sanguinetti and Boccanera were waging, impelled to it by a furious desire to become the next Pope, had for a long time been revolutionising the black world. There was incredible intricacy in the depths of the affair; none could exactly tell who was pulling the strings, conducting the vast intrigue. As regards generalities it was simply known that Boccanera represented absolutism—the Church freed from all compromises with modern society, and waiting in immobility for the Deity to triumph over Satan, for Rome to be restored to the Holy Father, and for repentant Italy to perform penance for its sacrilege; whereas Sanguinetti, extremely politic and supple, was reported to harbour bold and novel ideas: permission to vote to be granted to all true Catholics,[1] a majority to be gained by this means in the Legislature; then, as a fatal corollary, the downfall of the House of Savoy, and the proclamation of a kind of republican federation of all the former petty States of Italy under the august protectorate of the Pope. On the whole, the struggle was between these two antagonistic elements—the first bent on upholding the Church by a rigorous maintenance of the old traditions, and the other predicting the fall of the Church if it did not follow the bent of the coming century. But all was steeped in so much mystery that people ended by thinking that, if the present Pope should live a few years longer, his successor would certainly be neither Boccanera nor Sanguinetti.

All at once Pierre interrupted Narcisse: "And Monsignor Nani, do you know him? I spoke with him yesterday evening. And there he is coming in now!"

Nani was indeed just entering the ante-room with his usual smile on his amiable pink face. His cassock of fine texture, and his sash of violet silk shone with discreet soft luxury. And he showed himself very amiable to Abbe Paparelli, who, accompanying him in all humility, begged him to be kind enough to wait until his Eminence should be able to receive him.

"Oh! Monsignor Nani," muttered Narcisse, becoming serious, "he is a man whom it is advisable to have for a friend."

Then, knowing Nani's history, he related it in an undertone. Born at Venice, of a noble but ruined family which had produced heroes, Nani, after first studying under the Jesuits, had come to Rome to perfect himself in philosophy and theology at the Collegio Romano, which was then also under Jesuit management. Ordained when three and twenty, he had at once followed a nuncio to Bavaria as private secretary;

---

[1] Since the occupation of Rome by the Italian authorities, the supporters of the Church, obedient to the prohibition of the Vatican, have abstained from taking part in the political elections, this being their protest against the new order of things which they do not recognise. Various attempts have been made, however, to induce the Pope to give them permission to vote, many members of the Roman aristocracy considering the present course impolitic and even harmful to the interests of the Church.—Trans.

and then had gone as *auditore* to the nunciatures of Brussels and Paris, in which latter city he had lived for five years. Everything seemed to predestine him to diplomacy, his brilliant beginnings and his keen and encyclopaedical intelligence; but all at once he had been recalled to Rome, where he was soon afterwards appointed Assessor to the Holy Office. It was asserted at the time that this was done by the Pope himself, who, being well acquainted with Nani, and desirous of having a person he could depend upon at the Holy Office, had given instructions for his recall, saying that he could render far more services at Rome than abroad. Already a domestic prelate, Nani had also lately become a Canon of St. Peter's and an apostolic prothonotary, with the prospect of obtaining a cardinal's hat whenever the Pope should find some other favourite who would please him better as assessor.

"Oh, Monsignor Nani!" continued Narcisse. "He's a superior man, thoroughly well acquainted with modern Europe, and at the same time a very saintly priest, a sincere believer, absolutely devoted to the Church, with the substantial faith of an intelligent politician—a belief different, it is true, from the narrow gloomy theological faith which we know so well in France. And this is one of the reasons why you will hardly understand things here at first. The Roman prelates leave the Deity in the sanctuary and reign in His name, convinced that Catholicism is the human expression of the government of God, the only perfect and eternal government, beyond the pales of which nothing but falsehood and social danger can be found. While we in our country lag behind, furiously arguing whether there be a God or not, they do not admit that God's existence can be doubted, since they themselves are his delegated ministers; and they entirely devote themselves to playing their parts as ministers whom none can dispossess, exercising their power for the greatest good of humanity, and devoting all their intelligence, all their energy to maintaining themselves as the accepted masters of the nations. As for Monsignor Nani, after being mixed up in the politics of the whole world, he has for ten years been discharging the most delicate functions in Rome, taking part in the most varied and most important affairs. He sees all the foreigners who come to Rome, knows everything, has a hand in everything. Add to this that he is extremely discreet and amiable, with a modesty which seems perfect, though none can tell whether, with his light silent footstep, he is not really marching towards the highest ambition, the purple of sovereignty."

"Another candidate for the tiara," thought Pierre, who had listened passionately; for this man Nani interested him, caused him an instinctive disquietude, as though behind his pink and smiling face he could divine an infinity of obscure things. At the same time, however, the young priest but ill understood his friend, for he again felt bewildered by all this strange Roman world, so different from what he had expected.

Nani had perceived the two young men and came towards them with his hand cordially outstretched "Ah! Monsieur l'Abbe Froment, I am happy to meet you again. I won't ask you if you have slept well, for people always sleep well at Rome. Good-day, Monsieur Habert; your health has kept good I hope, since I met you in front of Bernini's Santa Teresa, which you admire so much.[1] I see that you know one another.

---

[1] The allusion is to a statue representing St. Theresa in ecstasy, with the Angel of Death descending to transfix her with his dart. It stands in a transept of Sta. Maria della Vittoria.—Trans.

That is very nice. I must tell you, Monsieur l'Abbe, that Monsieur Habert is a passionate lover of our city; he will be able to show you all its finest sights."

Then, in his affectionate way, he at once asked for information respecting Pierre's interview with the Cardinal. He listened attentively to the young man's narrative, nodding his head at certain passages, and occasionally restraining his sharp smile. The Cardinal's severity and Pierre's conviction that he would accord him no support did not at all astonish Nani. It seemed as if he had expected that result. However, on hearing that Cardinal Sanguinetti had been there that morning, and had pronounced the affair of the book to be very serious, he appeared to lose his self-control for a moment, for he spoke out with sudden vivacity:

"It can't be helped, my dear child, my intervention came too late. Directly I heard of the proceedings I went to his Eminence Cardinal Sanguinetti to tell him that the result would be an immense advertisement for your book. Was it sensible? What was the use of it? We know that you are inclined to be carried away by your ideas, that you are an enthusiast, and are prompt to do battle. So what advantage should we gain by embarrassing ourselves with the revolt of a young priest who might wage war against us with a book of which some thousands of copies have been sold already? For my part I desired that nothing should be done. And I must say that the Cardinal, who is a man of sense, was of the same mind. He raised his arms to heaven, went into a passion, and exclaimed that he was never consulted, that the blunder was already committed beyond recall, and that it was impossible to prevent process from taking its course since the matter had already been brought before the Congregation, in consequence of denunciations from authoritative sources, based on the gravest motives. Briefly, as he said, the blunder was committed, and I had to think of something else."

All at once Nani paused. He had just noticed that Pierre's ardent eyes were fixed upon his own, striving to penetrate his meaning. A faint flush then heightened the pinkiness of his complexion, whilst in an easy way he continued, unwilling to reveal how annoyed he was at having said too much: "Yes, I thought of helping you with all the little influence I possess, in order to extricate you from the worries in which this affair will certainly land you."

An impulse of revolt was stirring Pierre, who vaguely felt that he was perhaps being made game of. Why should he not be free to declare his faith, which was so pure, so free from personal considerations, so full of glowing Christian charity? "Never," said he, "will I withdraw; never will I myself suppress my book, as I am advised to do. It would be an act of cowardice and falsehood, for I regret nothing, I disown nothing. If I believe that my book brings a little truth to light I cannot destroy it without acting criminally both towards myself and towards others. No, never! You hear me—never!"

Silence fell. But almost immediately he resumed: "It is at the knees of the Holy Father that I desire to make that declaration. He will understand me, he will approve me."

Nani no longer smiled; henceforth his face remained as it were closed. He seemed to be studying the sudden violence of the young priest with curiosity; then sought to calm him with his own tranquil kindliness. "No doubt, no doubt," said he. "There is certainly great sweetness in obedience and humility. Still I can understand that, before anything else, you should desire to speak to his Holiness. And afterwards you will see—is that not so?—you will see—"

Then he evinced a lively interest in the suggested application for an audience. He expressed keen regret that Pierre had not forwarded that application from Paris, before even coming to Rome: in that course would have rested the best chance of a favourable reply. Bother of any kind was not liked at the Vatican, and if the news of the young priest's presence in Rome should only spread abroad, and the motives of his journey be discussed, all would be lost. Then, on learning that Narcisse had offered to present Pierre to the French ambassador, Nani seemed full of anxiety, and deprecated any such proceeding: "No, no! don't do that—it would be most imprudent. In the first place you would run the risk of embarrassing the ambassador, whose position is always delicate in affairs of this kind. And then, too, if he failed—and my fear is that he might fail—yes, if he failed it would be all over; you would no longer have the slightest chance of obtaining an audience by any other means. For the Vatican would not like to hurt the ambassador's feelings by yielding to other influence after resisting his."

Pierre anxiously glanced at Narcisse, who wagged his head, embarrassed and hesitating. "The fact is," the *attache* at last murmured, "we lately solicited an audience for a high French personage and it was refused, which was very unpleasant for us. Monsignor is right. We must keep our ambassador in reserve, and only utilise him when we have exhausted all other means." Then, noticing Pierre's disappointment, he added obligingly: "Our first visit therefore shall be for my cousin at the Vatican."

Nani, his attention again roused, looked at the young man in astonishment. "At the Vatican? You have a cousin there?"

"Why, yes—Monsignor Gamba del Zoppo."

"Gamba! Gamba! Yes, yes, excuse me, I remember now. Ah! so you thought of Gamba to bring influence to bear on his Holiness? That's an idea, no doubt; one must see—one must see."

He repeated these words again and again as if to secure time to see into the matter himself, to weigh the pros and cons of the suggestion. Monsignor Gamba del Zoppo was a worthy man who played no part at the Papal Court, whose nullity indeed had become a byword at the Vatican. His childish stories, however, amused the Pope, whom he greatly flattered, and who was fond of leaning on his arm while walking in the gardens. It was during these strolls that Gamba easily secured all sorts of little favours. However, he was a remarkable poltroon, and had such an intense fear of losing his influence that he never risked a request without having convinced himself by long meditation that no possible harm could come to him through it.

"Well, do you know, the idea is not a bad one," Nani at last declared. "Yes, yes, Gamba can secure the audience for you, if he is willing. I will see him myself and explain the matter."

At the same time Nani did not cease advising extreme caution. He even ventured to say that it was necessary to be on one's guard with the papal *entourage*, for, alas! it was a fact his Holiness was so good, and had such a blind faith in the goodness of others, that he had not always chosen his familiars with the critical care which he ought to have displayed. Thus one never knew to what sort of man one might be applying, or in what trap one might be setting one's foot. Nani even allowed it to be understood that on no account ought any direct application to be made to his Eminence the Secretary of State, for even his Eminence was not a free agent, but found himself encompassed by intrigues of such intricacy that his best intentions were paralysed. And as Nani went on discoursing in this fashion, in a very gentle, extremely unctuous manner, the Vatican appeared like some enchanted castle, guarded by jealous and treacherous dragons—a castle where one must not take a step, pass through a doorway, risk a limb, without having carefully assured oneself that one would not leave one's whole body there to be devoured.

Pierre continued listening, feeling colder and colder at heart, and again sinking into uncertainty. "*Mon Dieu*!" he exclaimed, "I shall never know how to act. You discourage me, Monsignor."

At this Nani's cordial smile reappeared. "I, my dear child? I should be sorry to do so. I only want to repeat to you that you must wait and do nothing. Avoid all feverishness especially. There is no hurry, I assure you, for it was only yesterday that a *consultore* was chosen to report upon your book, so you have a good full month before you. Avoid everybody, live in such a way that people shall be virtually ignorant of your existence, visit Rome in peace and quietness—that is the best course you can adopt to forward your interests." Then, taking one of the priest's hands between both his own, so aristocratic, soft, and plump, he added: "You will understand that I have my reasons for speaking to you like this. I should have offered my own services; I should have made it a point of honour to take you straight to his Holiness, had I thought it advisable. But I do not wish to mix myself up in the matter at this stage; I realise only too well that at the present moment we should simply make sad work of it. Later on—you hear me—later on, in the event of nobody else succeeding, I myself will obtain you an audience; I formally promise it. But meanwhile, I entreat you, refrain from using those words 'a new religion,' which, unfortunately, occur in your book, and which I heard you repeat again only last night. There can be no new religion, my dear child; there is but one eternal religion, which is beyond all surrender and compromise—the Catholic, Apostolic, and Roman religion. And at the same time leave your Paris friends to themselves. Don't rely too much on Cardinal Bergerot, whose lofty piety is not sufficiently appreciated in Rome. I assure you that I am speaking to you as a friend."

Then, seeing how disabled Pierre appeared to be, half overcome already, no longer knowing in what direction to begin his campaign, he again strove to comfort him: "Come, come, things will right themselves; everything will end for the best, both for the welfare of the Church and your own. And now you must excuse me, I must leave you; I shall not be able to see his Eminence to-day, for it is impossible for me to wait any longer."

Abbe Paparelli, whom Pierre had noticed prowling around with his ears cocked, now hastened forward and declared to Monsignor Nani that there were only two persons to be received before him. But the prelate very graciously replied that he would come back again at another time, for the affair which he wished to lay before his Eminence was in no wise pressing. Then he withdrew, courteously bowing to everybody.

Narcisse Habert's turn came almost immediately afterwards. However, before entering the throne-room he pressed Pierre's hand, repeating, "So it is understood. I will go to see my cousin at the Vatican to-morrow, and directly I get a reply I will let you know. We shall meet again soon I hope."

It was now past twelve o'clock, and the only remaining visitor was one of the two old ladies who seemed to have fallen asleep. At his little secretarial table Don Vigilio still sat covering huge sheets of yellow paper with fine handwriting, from which he only lifted his eyes at intervals to glance about him distrustfully, and make sure that nothing threatened him.

In the mournful silence which fell around, Pierre lingered for yet another moment in the deep embrasure of the window. Ah! what anxiety consumed his poor, tender, enthusiastic heart! On leaving Paris things had seemed so simple, so natural to him! He was unjustly accused, and he started off to defend himself, arrived and flung himself at the feet of the Holy Father, who listened to him indulgently. Did not the Pope personify living religion, intelligence to understand, justice based upon truth? And was he not, before aught else, the Father, the delegate of divine forgiveness and mercy, with arms outstretched towards all the children of the Church, even the guilty ones? Was it not meet, then, that he should leave his door wide open so that the humblest of his sons might freely enter to relate their troubles, confess their transgressions, explain their conduct, imbibe comfort from the source of eternal loving kindness? And yet on the very first day of his, Pierre's, arrival, the doors closed upon him with a bang; he felt himself sinking into a hostile sphere, full of traps and pitfalls. One and all cried out to him "Beware!" as if he were incurring the greatest dangers in setting one foot before the other. His desire to see the Pope became an extraordinary pretension, so difficult of achievement that it set the interests and passions and influences of the whole Vatican agog. And there was endless conflicting advice, long-discussed manoeuvring, all the strategy of generals leading an army to victory, and fresh complications ever arising in the midst of a dim stealthy swarming of intrigues. Ah! good Lord! how different all this was from the charitable reception that Pierre had anticipated: the pastor's house standing open beside the high road for the admission of all the sheep of the flock, both those that were docile and those that had gone astray.

That which began to frighten Pierre, however, was the evil, the wickedness, which he could divine vaguely stirring in the gloom: Cardinal Bergerot suspected, dubbed a Revolutionary, deemed so compromising that he, Pierre, was advised not to mention his name again! The young priest once more saw Cardinal Boccanera's pout of disdain while speaking of his colleague. And then Monsignor Nani had warned him not to repeat those words "a new religion," as if it were not clear to everybody that they simply signified the return of Catholicism to the primitive purity of Christianity! Was that one of the crimes denounced to the Congregation of the Index? He had begun to suspect who his accusers were, and felt alarmed, for he was now conscious of secret subterranean plotting, a great stealthy effort to strike him down and suppress his work. All that surrounded him became suspicious. If he listened to advice and temporised, it was solely to follow the same politic course as his adversaries, to learn to know them before acting. He would spend a few days in meditation, in surveying and studying that black world of Rome which to him had proved so unexpected. But, at the same time, in the revolt of his apostle-like faith, he swore, even as he had said to Nani, that he would never yield, never change either a page or a line of his book, but maintain it in its integrity in the broad daylight as the unshakable testimony of his belief. Even were the book condemned by the Index, he would not tender submission, withdraw aught of it. And should it become necessary he would quit the Church, he would go even as far as schism, continuing to preach the new religion and writing a new book, *Real Rome*, such as he now vaguely began to espy.

III.

However, Don Vigilio had ceased writing, and gazed so fixedly at Pierre that the latter at last stepped up to him politely in order to take leave. And then the secretary, yielding, despite his fears, to a desire to confide in him, murmured, "He came simply on your account, you know; he wanted to ascertain the result of your interview with his Eminence."

It was not necessary for Don Vigilio to mention Nani by name; Pierre understood. "Really, do you think so?" he asked.

"Oh! there is no doubt of it. And if you take my advice you will do what he desires with a good grace, for it is absolutely certain that you will do it later on."

These words brought Pierre's disquietude and exasperation to a climax. He went off with a gesture of defiance. They would see if he would ever yield.

The three ante-rooms which he again crossed appeared to him blacker, emptier, more lifeless than ever. In the second one Abbe Paparelli saluted him with a little silent bow; in the first the sleepy lackey did not even seem to see him. A spider was weaving its web between the tassels of the great red hat under the *baldacchino*. Would not the better course have been to set the pick at work amongst all that rotting past, now crumbling into dust, so that the sunlight might stream in freely and restore to the purified soil the fruitfulness of youth?

PART II.

IV.

ON the afternoon of that same day Pierre, having leisure before him, at once thought of beginning his peregrinations through Rome by a visit on which he had set his heart. Almost immediately after the publication of "New Rome" he had been deeply moved and interested by a letter addressed to him from the Eternal City by old Count Orlando Prada, the hero of Italian independence and reunion, who, although unacquainted with him, had written spontaneously after a first hasty perusal of his book. And the letter had been a flaming protest, a cry of the patriotic faith still young in the heart of that aged man, who accused him of having forgotten Italy and claimed Rome, the new Rome, for the country which was at last free and united. Correspondence had ensued, and the priest, while clinging to his dream of Neo-Catholicism saving the world, had from afar grown attached to the man who wrote to him with such glowing love of country and freedom. He had eventually informed him of his journey, and promised to call upon him. But the hospitality which he had accepted at the Boccanera mansion now seemed to him somewhat of an impediment; for after Benedetta's kindly, almost affectionate, greeting, he felt that he could not, on the very first day and with out warning her, sally forth to visit the father of the man from whom she had fled and from whom she now asked the Church to part her for ever. Moreover, old Orlando was actually living with his son in a little palazzo which the latter had erected at the farther end of the Via Venti Settembre.

Before venturing on any step Pierre resolved to confide in the Contessina herself; and this seemed the easier as Viscount Philibert de la Choue had told him that the young woman still retained a filial feeling, mingled with admiration, for the old hero. And indeed, at the very first words which he uttered after lunch, Benedetta promptly retorted: "But go, Monsieur l'Abbe, go at once! Old Orlando, you know, is one of our national glories—you must not be surprised to hear me call him by his Christian name. All Italy does so, from pure affection and gratitude. For my part I grew up among people who hated him, who likened him to Satan. It was only later that I learned to know him, and then I loved him, for he is certainly the most just and gentle man in the world."

She had begun to smile, but timid tears were moistening her eyes at the recollection, no doubt, of the year of suffering she had spent in her husband's house, where her only peaceful hours had been those passed with the old man. And in a lower and somewhat tremulous voice she added: "As you are going to see him, tell him from me that I still love him, and, whatever happens, shall never forget his goodness."

So Pierre set out, and whilst he was driving in a cab towards the Via Venti Settembre, he recalled to mind the heroic story of old Orlando's life which had been told him in Paris. It was like an epic poem, full of faith, bravery, and the disinterestedness of another age.

Born of a noble house of Milan, Count Orlando Prada had learnt to hate the foreigner at such an early age that, when scarcely fifteen, he already formed part of a secret society, one of the ramifications of the antique Carbonarism. This hatred of Austrian domination had been transmitted from father to son through long years, from the olden days of revolt against servitude, when the conspirators met by stealth in abandoned huts, deep in the recesses of the forests; and it was rendered the keener by the eternal dream of Italy delivered, restored to herself, transformed once more into a great sovereign nation, the worthy daughter of those who had conquered and ruled the world. Ah! that land of whilom glory, that unhappy, dismembered, parcelled Italy, the prey of a crowd of petty tyrants, constantly invaded and appropriated by neighbouring nations—how superb and ardent was that dream to free her from such long opprobrium! To defeat the foreigner, drive out the despots, awaken the people from the base misery of slavery, to proclaim Italy free and Italy united—such was the passion which then inflamed the young with inextinguishable ardour, which made the youthful Orlando's heart leap with enthusiasm. He spent his early years consumed by holy indignation, proudly and impatiently longing for an opportunity to give his blood for his country, and to die for her if he could not deliver her.

Quivering under the yoke, wasting his time in sterile conspiracies, he was living in retirement in the old family residence at Milan, when, shortly after his marriage and his twenty-fifth birthday, tidings came to him of the flight of Pius IX and the Revolution of Rome.[1] And at once he quitted everything, wife and hearth, and hastened to Rome as if summoned thither by the call of destiny. This was the first time that he set out scouring the roads for the attainment of independence; and how frequently, yet again and again, was he to start upon fresh campaigns, never wearying, never disheartened! And now it was that he became acquainted with Mazzini, and for a moment was inflamed with enthusiasm for that mystical unitarian Republican. He himself indulged in an ardent dream of a Universal Republic, adopted the Mazzinian device, "*Dio e popolo*" (God and the people), and followed the procession which wended its way with great pomp through insurrectionary Rome. The time was one of vast hopes, one when people already felt a need of renovated religion, and looked to the coming of a humanitarian Christ who would redeem the world yet once again. But before long a man, a captain of the ancient days, Giuseppe Garibaldi, whose epic glory was dawning, made Orlando entirely his own, transformed him into a soldier whose sole cause was freedom and union. Orlando loved Garibaldi as though the latter were a demi-god, fought beside him in defence of Republican Rome, took part in the victory of Rieti over the Neapolitans, and followed the stubborn patriot in his retreat when he sought to succour Venice, compelled as he was to relinquish the Eternal City to the French army of General Oudinot, who came thither to reinstate Pius IX. And what an extraordinary and madly heroic adventure was that of Garibaldi and

---

[1] It was on November 24, 1848, that the Pope fled to Gaeta, consequent upon the insurrection which had broken out nine days previously.—Trans.

Venice! Venice, which Manin, another great patriot, a martyr, had again transformed into a republican city, and which for long months had been resisting the Austrians! And Garibaldi starts with a handful of men to deliver the city, charters thirteen fishing barks, loses eight in a naval engagement, is compelled to return to the Roman shores, and there in all wretchedness is bereft of his wife, Anita, whose eyes he closes before returning to America, where, once before, he had awaited the hour of insurrection. Ah! that land of Italy, which in those days rumbled from end to end with the internal fire of patriotism, where men of faith and courage arose in every city, where riots and insurrections burst forth on all sides like eruptions—it continued, in spite of every check, its invincible march to freedom!

Orlando returned to his young wife at Milan, and for two years lived there, almost in concealment, devoured by impatience for the glorious morrow which was so long in coming. Amidst his fever a gleam of happiness softened his heart; a son, Luigi, was born to him, but the birth killed the mother, and joy was turned into mourning. Then, unable to remain any longer at Milan, where he was spied upon, tracked by the police, suffering also too grievously from the foreign occupation, Orlando decided to realise the little fortune remaining to him, and to withdraw to Turin, where an aunt of his wife took charge of the child. Count di Cavour, like a great statesman, was then already seeking to bring about independence, preparing Piedmont for the decisive *role* which it was destined to play. It was the time when King Victor Emmanuel evinced flattering cordiality towards all the refugees who came to him from every part of Italy, even those whom he knew to be Republicans, compromised and flying the consequences of popular insurrection. The rough, shrewd House of Savoy had long been dreaming of bringing about Italian unity to the profit of the Piedmontese monarchy, and Orlando well knew under what master he was taking service; but in him the Republican already went behind the patriot, and indeed he had begun to question the possibility of a united Republican Italy, placed under the protectorate of a liberal Pope, as Mazzini had at one time dreamed. Was that not indeed a chimera beyond realisation which would devour generation after generation if one obstinately continued to pursue it? For his part, he did not wish to die without having slept in Rome as one of the conquerors. Even if liberty was to be lost, he desired to see his country united and erect, returning once more to life in the full sunlight. And so it was with feverish happiness that he enlisted at the outset of the war of 1859; and his heart palpitated with such force as almost to rend his breast, when, after Magenta, he entered Milan with the French army—Milan which he had quitted eight years previously, like an exile, in despair. The treaty of Villafranca which followed Solferino proved a bitter deception: Venetia was not secured, Venice remained enthralled. Nevertheless the Milanese was conquered from the foe, and then Tuscany and the duchies of Parma and Modena voted for annexation. So, at all events, the nucleus of the Italian star was formed; the country had begun to build itself up afresh around victorious Piedmont.

Then, in the following year, Orlando plunged into epopoeia once more. Garibaldi had returned from his two sojourns in America, with the halo of a legend round him—paladin-like feats in the pampas of Uruguay, an extraordinary passage from Canton to Lima—and he had returned to take part in the war of 1859, forestalling the French army, overthrowing an Austrian marshal, and entering Como, Bergamo, and Brescia. And now, all at once, folks heard that he had landed at Marsala with only a thousand men—the Thousand of Marsala, the ever illustrious handful of braves! Orlando fought in the first rank, and Palermo after three days' resistance was carried. Becoming the dictator's favourite lieutenant, he helped him to organise a government, then crossed the straits with him, and was beside him on the triumphal entry into Naples, whose king had fled. There was mad audacity and valour at that time, an explosion of the inevitable; and all sorts of supernatural stories were current—Garibaldi invulnerable, protected better by his red shirt than by the strongest armour, Garibaldi routing opposing armies like an archangel, by merely brandishing his flaming sword! The Piedmontese on their side had defeated General Lamoriciere at Castelfidardo, and were invading the States of the Church. And Orlando was there when the dictator, abdicating power, signed the decree which annexed the Two Sicilies to the Crown of Italy; even as subsequently he took part in that forlorn attempt on Rome, when the rageful cry was "Rome or Death!"—an attempt which came to a tragic issue at Aspromonte, when the little army was dispersed by the Italian troops, and Garibaldi, wounded, was taken prisoner, and sent back to the solitude of his island of Caprera, where he became but a fisherman and a tiller of the rocky soil.[1]

Six years of waiting again went by, and Orlando still dwelt at Turin, even after Florence had been chosen as the new capital. The Senate had acclaimed Victor Emmanuel, King of Italy; and Italy was indeed almost built, it lacked only Rome and Venice. But the great battles seemed all over, the epic era was closed; Venice was to be won by defeat. Orlando took part in the unlucky battle of Custozza, where he received two wounds, full of furious grief at the thought that Austria should be triumphant. But at that same moment the latter, defeated at Sadowa, relinquished Venetia, and five months later Orlando satisfied his desire to be in Venice participating in the joy of triumph, when Victor Emmanuel made his entry amidst the frantic acclamations of the people. Rome alone remained to be won, and wild impatience urged all Italy towards the city; but friendly France had sworn to maintain the Pope, and this acted as a check. Then, for the third time, Garibaldi dreamt of renewing the feats of the old-world legends, and threw himself upon Rome like a soldier of fortune illumined by patriotism and free from every tie. And for the third time Orlando shared in that fine heroic madness destined to be vanquished at Mentana by the Pontifical Zouaves supported by a small French corps. Again wounded, he came back to Turin in almost a dying condition. But, though his spirit quivered, he had to resign himself; the situation seemed to have no outlet; only an upheaval of the nations could give Rome to Italy.

All at once the thunderclap of Sedan, of the downfall of France, resounded through the world; and then the road to Rome lay open, and Orlando, having returned to service in the regular army, was with the troops who took up position in the Campagna to ensure the safety of the Holy See, as was said in the letter which Victor

---

[1] M. Zola's brief but glowing account of Garibaldi's glorious achievements has stirred many memories in my mind. My uncle, Frank Vizetelly, the war artist of the Illustrated London News, whose bones lie bleaching somewhere in the Soudan, was one of Garibaldi's constant companions throughout the memorable campaign of the Two Sicilies, and afterwards he went with him to Caprera. Later, in 1870, my brother, Edward Vizetelly, acted as orderly-officer to the general when he offered the help of his sword to France.—Trans.

Emmanuel wrote to Pius IX. There was, however, but the shadow of an engagement: General Kanzler's Pontifical Zouaves were compelled to fall back, and Orlando was one of the first to enter the city by the breach of the Porta Pia. Ah! that twentieth of September—that day when he experienced the greatest happiness of his life—a day of delirium, of complete triumph, which realised the dream of so many years of terrible contest, the dream for which he had sacrificed rest and fortune, and given both body and mind!

Then came more than ten happy years in conquered Rome—in Rome adored, flattered, treated with all tenderness, like a woman in whom one has placed one's entire hope. From her he awaited so much national vigour, such a marvellous resurrection of strength and glory for the endowment of the young nation. Old Republican, old insurrectional soldier that he was, he had been obliged to adhere to the monarchy, and accept a senatorship. But then did not Garibaldi himself—Garibaldi his divinity—likewise call upon the King and sit in parliament? Mazzini alone, rejecting all compromises, was unwilling to rest content with a united and independent Italy that was not Republican. Moreover, another consideration influenced Orlando, the future of his son Luigi, who had attained his eighteenth birthday shortly after the occupation of Rome. Though he, Orlando, could manage with the crumbs which remained of the fortune he had expended in his country's service, he dreamt of a splendid destiny for the child of his heart. Realising that the heroic age was over, he desired to make a great politician of him, a great administrator, a man who should be useful to the mighty nation of the morrow; and it was on this account that he had not rejected royal favour, the reward of long devotion, desiring, as he did, to be in a position to help, watch, and guide Luigi. Besides, was he himself so old, so used-up, as to be unable to assist in organisation, even as he had assisted in conquest? Struck by his son's quick intelligence in business matters, perhaps also instinctively divining that the battle would now continue on financial and economic grounds, he obtained him employment at the Ministry of Finances. And again he himself lived on, dreaming, still enthusiastically believing in a splendid future, overflowing with boundless hope, seeing Rome double her population, grow and spread with a wild vegetation of new districts, and once more, in his loving enraptured eyes, become the queen of the world.

But all at once came a thunderbolt. One morning, as he was going downstairs, Orlando was stricken with paralysis. Both his legs suddenly became lifeless, as heavy as lead. It was necessary to carry him up again, and never since had he set foot on the street pavement. At that time he had just completed his fifty-sixth year, and for fourteen years since he had remained in his arm-chair, as motionless as stone, he who had so impetuously trod every battlefield of Italy. It was a pitiful business, the collapse of a hero. And worst of all, from that room where he was for ever imprisoned, the old soldier beheld the slow crumbling of all his hopes, and fell into dismal melancholy, full of unacknowledged fear for the future. Now that the intoxication of action no longer dimmed his eyes, now that he spent his long and empty days in thought, his vision became clear. Italy, which he had desired to see so powerful, so triumphant in her unity, was acting madly, rushing to ruin, possibly to bankruptcy. Rome, which to him had ever been the one necessary capital, the city of unparalleled glory, requisite for the sovereign people of to-morrow, seemed unwilling to take upon herself the part of a great modern metropolis; heavy as a corpse she weighed with all her centuries on the bosom of the young nation. Moreover, his son Luigi distressed him. Rebellious to all guidance, the young man had become one of the devouring offsprings of conquest, eager to despoil that Italy, that Rome, which his father seemed to have desired solely in order that he might pillage them and batten on them. Orlando had vainly opposed Luigi's departure from the ministry, his participation in the frantic speculations on land and house property to which the mad building of the new districts had given rise. But at the same time he loved his son, and was reduced to silence, especially now when everything had succeeded with Luigi, even his most risky financial ventures, such as the transformation of the Villa Montefiori into a perfect town—a colossal enterprise in which many of great wealth had been ruined, but whence he himself had emerged with millions. And it was in part for this reason that Orlando, sad and silent, had obstinately restricted himself to one small room on the third floor of the little palazzo erected by Luigi in the Via Venti Settembre—a room where he lived cloistered with a single servant, subsisting on his own scanty income, and accepting nothing but that modest hospitality from his son.

As Pierre reached that new Via Venti Settembre[1] which climbs the side and summit of the Viminal hill, he was struck by the heavy sumptuousness of the new "palaces," which betokened among the moderns the same taste for the huge that marked the ancient Romans. In the warm afternoon glow, blent of purple and old gold, the broad, triumphant thoroughfare, with its endless rows of white house-fronts, bore witness to new Rome's proud hope of futurity and sovereign power. And Pierre fairly gasped when he beheld the Palazzo delle Finanze, or Treasury, a gigantic erection, a cyclopean cube with a profusion of columns, balconies, pediments, and sculptured work, to which the building mania had given birth in a day of immoderate pride. And on the other side of the street, a little higher up, before reaching the Villa Bonaparte, stood Count Prada's little palazzo.

After discharging his driver, Pierre for a moment remained somewhat embarrassed. The door was open, and he entered the vestibule; but, as at the mansion in the Via Giulia, no door porter or servant was to be seen. So he had to make up his mind to ascend the monumental stairs, which with their marble balustrades seemed to be copied, on a smaller scale, from those of the Palazzo Boccanera. And there was much the same cold bareness, tempered, however, by a carpet and red door-hangings, which contrasted vividly with the white stucco of the walls. The reception-rooms, sixteen feet high, were on the first floor, and as a door chanced to be ajar he caught a glimpse of two *salons*, one following the other, and both displaying quite modern richness, with a profusion of silk and velvet hangings, gilt furniture, and lofty mirrors reflecting a pompous assemblage of stands and tables. And still there was nobody, not a soul, in that seemingly forsaken abode, which exhaled nought of woman's presence. Indeed Pierre was on the point of going down again to ring, when a footman at last presented himself.

"Count Prada, if you please."

The servant silently surveyed the little priest, and seemed to understand. "The father or the son?" he asked.

---

[1] The name—Twentieth September Street—was given to the thoroughfare to commemorate the date of the occupation of Rome by Victor Emmanuel's army.—Trans.

IV.

"The father, Count Orlando Prada."

"Oh! that's on the third floor." And he condescended to add: "The little door on the right-hand side of the landing. Knock loudly if you wish to be admitted."

Pierre indeed had to knock twice, and then a little withered old man of military appearance, a former soldier who had remained in the Count's service, opened the door and apologised for the delay by saying that he had been attending to his master's legs. Immediately afterwards he announced the visitor, and the latter, after passing through a dim and narrow ante-room, was lost in amazement on finding himself in a relatively small chamber, extremely bare and bright, with wall-paper of a light hue studded with tiny blue flowers. Behind a screen was an iron bedstead, the soldier's pallet, and there was no other furniture than the arm-chair in which the cripple spent his days, with a table of black wood placed near him, and covered with books and papers, and two old straw-seated chairs which served for the accommodation of the infrequent visitors. A few planks, fixed to one of the walls, did duty as book-shelves. However, the broad, clear, curtainless window overlooked the most admirable panorama of Rome that could be desired.

Then the room disappeared from before Pierre's eyes, and with a sudden shock of deep emotion he only beheld old Orlando, the old blanched lion, still superb, broad, and tall. A forest of white hair crowned his powerful head, with its thick mouth, fleshy broken nose, and large, sparkling, black eyes. A long white beard streamed down with the vigour of youth, curling like that of an ancient god. By that leonine muzzle one divined what great passions had growled within; but all, carnal and intellectual alike, had erupted in patriotism, in wild bravery, and riotous love of independence. And the old stricken hero, his torso still erect, was fixed there on his straw-seated arm-chair, with lifeless legs buried beneath a black wrapper. Alone did his arms and hands live, and his face beam with strength and intelligence.

Orlando turned towards his servant, and gently said to him: "You can go away, Batista. Come back in a couple of hours." Then, looking Pierre full in the face, he exclaimed in a voice which was still sonorous despite his seventy years: "So it's you at last, my dear Monsieur Froment, and we shall be able to chat at our ease. There, take that chair, and sit down in front of me."

He had noticed the glance of surprise which the young priest had cast upon the bareness of the room, and he gaily added: "You will excuse me for receiving you in my cell. Yes, I live here like a monk, like an old invalided soldier, henceforth withdrawn from active life. My son long begged me to take one of the fine rooms downstairs. But what would have been the use of it? I have no needs, and I scarcely care for feather beds, for my old bones are accustomed to the hard ground. And then too I have such a fine view up here, all Rome presenting herself to me, now that I can no longer go to her."

With a wave of the hand towards the window he sought to hide the embarrassment, the slight flush which came to him each time that he thus excused his son; unwilling as he was to tell the true reason, the scruple of probity which had made him obstinately cling to his bare pauper's lodging.

"But it is very nice, the view is superb!" declared Pierre, in order to please him. "I am for my own part very glad to see you, very glad to be able to grasp your valiant hands, which accomplished so many great things."

Orlando made a fresh gesture, as though to sweep the past away. "Pooh! pooh! all that is dead and buried. Let us talk about you, my dear Monsieur Froment, you who are young and represent the present; and especially about your book, which represents the future! Ah! if you only knew how angry your book, your 'New Rome,' made me first of all."

He began to laugh, and took the book from off the table near him; then, tapping on its cover with his big, broad hand, he continued: "No, you cannot imagine with what starts of protest I read your book. The Pope, and again the Pope, and always the Pope! New Rome to be created by the Pope and for the Pope, to triumph thanks to the Pope, to be given to the Pope, and to fuse its glory in the glory of the Pope! But what about us? What about Italy? What about all the millions which we have spent in order to make Rome a great capital? Ah! only a Frenchman, and a Frenchman of Paris, could have written such a book! But let me tell you, my dear sir, if you are ignorant of it, that Rome has become the capital of the kingdom of Italy, that we here have King Humbert, and the Italian people, a whole nation which must be taken into account, and which means to keep Rome—glorious, resuscitated Rome—for itself!"

This juvenile ardour made Pierre laugh in turn. "Yes, yes," said he, "you wrote me that. Only what does it matter from my point of view? Italy is but one nation, a part of humanity, and I desire concord and fraternity among all the nations, mankind reconciled, believing, and happy. Of what consequence, then, is any particular form of government, monarchy or republic, of what consequence is any question of a united and independent country, if all mankind forms but one free people subsisting on truth and justice?"

To only one word of this enthusiastic outburst did Orlando pay attention. In a lower tone, and with a dreamy air, he resumed: "Ah! a republic. In my youth I ardently desired one. I fought for one; I conspired with Mazzini, a saintly man, a believer, who was shattered by collision with the absolute. And then, too, one had to bow to practical necessities; the most obstinate ended by submitting. And nowadays would a republic save us? In any case it would differ but little from our parliamentary monarchy. Just think of what goes on in France! And so why risk a revolution which would place power in the hands of the extreme revolutionists, the anarchists? We fear all that, and this explains our resignation. I know very well that a few think they can detect salvation in a republican federation, a reconstitution of all the former little states in so many republics, over which Rome would preside. The Vatican would gain largely by any such transformation; still one cannot say that it endeavours to bring it about; it simply regards the eventuality without disfavour. But it is a dream, a dream!"

At this Orlando's gaiety came back to him, with even a little gentle irony: "You don't know, I suppose, what it was that took my fancy in your book—for, in spite of all my protests, I have read it twice. Well, what pleased me was that Mazzini himself might almost have written it at one time. Yes! I found all my youth again in your pages, all the wild hope of my twenty-fifth year, the new religion of a humanitarian Christ, the pacification of the world effected by the Gospel! Are you aware that, long before your time, Mazzini desired the renovation of Christianity? He set dogma and discipline on one side and only retained morals. And it was new Rome, the Rome of the people, which he would have given as see to the universal Church, in which all the churches of the past were to be fused—Rome, the eternal and predestined city, the mother and queen, whose domination was to arise anew to ensure the definitive happiness of mankind! Is it not curious that all the present-day Neo-Catholicism, the vague, spiritualistic awakening, the evolution towards communion and Christian charity, with which some are making so much stir, should be simply a return of the mystical and humanitarian ideas of 1848? Alas! I saw all that, I believed and burned, and I know in what a fine mess those flights into the azure of mystery landed us! So it cannot be helped, I lack confidence."

Then, as Pierre on his side was growing impassioned and sought to reply, he stopped him: "No, let me finish. I only want to convince you how absolutely necessary it was that we should take Rome and make her the capital of Italy. Without Rome new Italy could not have existed; Rome represented the glory of ancient time; in her dust lay the sovereign power which we wished to re-establish; she brought strength, beauty, eternity to those who possessed her. Standing in the middle of our country, she was its heart, and must assuredly become its life as soon as she should be awakened from the long sleep of ruin. Ah! how we desired her, amidst victory and amidst defeat, through years and years of frightful impatience! For my part I loved her, and longed for her, far more than for any woman, with my blood burning, and in despair that I should be growing old. And when we possessed her, our folly was a desire to behold her huge, magnificent, and commanding all at once, the equal of the other great capitals of Europe—Berlin, Paris, and London. Look at her! she is still my only love, my only consolation now that I am virtually dead, with nothing alive in me but my eyes."

With the same gesture as before, he directed Pierre's attention to the window. Under the glowing sky Rome stretched out in its immensity, empurpled and gilded by the slanting sunrays. Across the horizon, far, far away, the trees of the Janiculum stretched a green girdle, of a limpid emerald hue, whilst the dome of St. Peter's, more to the left, showed palely blue, like a sapphire bedimmed by too bright a light. Then came the low town, the old ruddy city, baked as it were by centuries of burning summers, soft to the eye and beautiful with the deep life of the past, an unbounded chaos of roofs, gables, towers, *campanili*, and cupolas. But, in the foreground under the window, there was the new city—that which had been building for the last five and twenty years—huge blocks of masonry piled up side by side, still white with plaster, neither the sun nor history having as yet robed them in purple. And in particular the roofs of the colossal Palazzo delle Finanze had a disastrous effect, spreading out like far, bare steppes of cruel hideousness. And it was upon the desolation and abomination of all the newly erected piles that the eyes of the old soldier of conquest at last rested.

Silence ensued. Pierre felt the faint chill of hidden, unacknowledged sadness pass by, and courteously waited.

"I must beg your pardon for having interrupted you just now," resumed Orlando; "but it seems to me that we cannot talk about your book to any good purpose until you have seen and studied Rome closely. You only arrived yesterday, did you not? Well, stroll about the city, look at things, question people, and I think that many of your ideas will change. I shall particularly like to know your impression of the Vatican since you have cone here solely to see the Pope and defend your book against the Index. Why should we discuss things to-day, if facts themselves are calculated to bring you to other views, far more readily than the finest speeches which I might make? It is understood, you will come to see me again, and we shall then know what we are talking about, and, maybe, agree together."

"Why certainly, you are too kind," replied Pierre. "I only came to-day to express my gratitude to you for having read my book so attentively, and to pay homage to one of the glories of Italy."

Orlando was not listening, but remained for a moment absorbed in thought, with his eyes still resting upon Rome. And overcome, despite himself, by secret disquietude, he resumed in a low voice as though making an involuntary confession: "We have gone too fast, no doubt. There were expenses of undeniable utility—the roads, ports, and railways. And it was necessary to arm the country also; I did not at first disapprove of the heavy military burden. But since then how crushing has been the war budget—a war which has never come, and the long wait for which has ruined us. Ah! I have always been the friend of France. I only reproach her with one thing, that she has failed to understand the position in which we were placed, the vital reasons which compelled us to ally ourselves with Germany. And then there are the thousand millions of *lire*[1] swallowed up in Rome! That was the real madness; pride and enthusiasm led us astray. Old and solitary as I've been for many years now, given to deep reflection, I was one of the first to divine the pitfall, the frightful financial crisis, the deficit which would bring about the collapse of the nation. I shouted it from the housetops, to my son, to all who came near me; but what was the use? They didn't listen; they were mad, still buying and selling and building, with no thought but for gambling booms and bubbles. But you'll see, you'll see. And the worst is that we are not situated as you are; we haven't a reserve of men and money in a dense peasant population, whose thrifty savings are always at hand to fill up the gaps caused by big catastrophes. There is no social rise among our people as yet; fresh men don't spring up out of the lower classes to reinvigorate the national blood, as they constantly do in your country. And, besides, the people are poor; they have no stockings to empty. The misery is frightful, I must admit it. Those who have any money prefer to spend it in the towns in a petty way rather than to risk it in agricultural or manufacturing enterprise. Factories are but slowly built, and the land is almost everywhere tilled in the same primitive manner as it was two thousand years ago. And then, too, take Rome—Rome, which didn't make Italy, but which Italy made its capital to satisfy an ardent, overpowering desire—Rome, which is still but a splendid bit of scenery, picturing the glory of the centuries, and which, apart from its historical splendour, has only given us its degenerate papal population, swollen with ignorance and pride! Ah! I loved Rome too well, and I still love it too well to regret being now within its walls. But, good heavens! what insanity its acquisition brought us, what piles of money it has cost us, and how heavily and triumphantly it weighs us down! Look! look!"

He waved his hand as he spoke towards the livid roofs of the Palazzo delle Finanze, that vast and desolate steppe, as though he could see the harvest of glory all stripped off and bankruptcy appear with its fearful, threatening bareness. Restrained tears were dimming his eyes, and he looked superbly pitiful with his expression of baffled hope and grievous disquietude, with his huge white head, the muzzle of an old blanched lion henceforth powerless and caged in that bare, bright room, whose pov-

[1] 40,000,000 pounds.

erty-stricken aspect was instinct with so much pride that it seemed, as it were, a protest against the monumental splendour of the whole surrounding district! So those were the purposes to which the conquest had been put! And to think that he was impotent, henceforth unable to give his blood and his soul as he had done in the days gone by.

"Yes, yes," he exclaimed in a final outburst; "one gave everything, heart and brain, one's whole life indeed, so long as it was a question of making the country one and independent. But, now that the country is ours, just try to stir up enthusiasm for the reorganisation of its finances! There's no ideality in that! And this explains why, whilst the old ones are dying off, not a new man comes to the front among the young ones—"

All at once he stopped, looking somewhat embarrassed, yet smiling at his feverishness. "Excuse me," he said, "I'm off again, I'm incorrigible. But it's understood, we'll leave that subject alone, and you'll come back here, and we'll chat together when you've seen everything."

From that moment he showed himself extremely pleasant, and it was apparent to Pierre that he regretted having said so much, by the seductive affability and growing affection which he now displayed. He begged the young priest to prolong his sojourn, to abstain from all hasty judgments on Rome, and to rest convinced that, at bottom, Italy still loved France. And he was also very desirous that France should love Italy, and displayed genuine anxiety at the thought that perhaps she loved her no more. As at the Boccanera mansion, on the previous evening, Pierre realised that an attempt was being made to persuade him to admiration and affection. Like a susceptible woman with secret misgivings respecting the attractive power of her beauty, Italy was all anxiety with regard to the opinion of her visitors, and strove to win and retain their love.

However, Orlando again became impassioned when he learnt that Pierre was staying at the Boccanera mansion, and he made a gesture of extreme annoyance on hearing, at that very moment, a knock at the outer door. "Come in!" he called; but at the same time he detained Pierre, saying, "No, no, don't go yet; I wish to know—"

But a lady came in—a woman of over forty, short and extremely plump, and still attractive with her small features and pretty smile swamped in fat. She was a blonde, with green, limpid eyes; and, fairly well dressed in a sober, nicely fitting mignonette gown, she looked at once pleasant, modest, and shrewd.

"Ah! it's you, Stefana," said the old man, letting her kiss him.

"Yes, uncle, I was passing by and came up to see how you were getting on."

The visitor was the Signora Sacco, niece of Prada and a Neapolitan by birth, her mother having quitted Milan to marry a certain Pagani, a Neapolitan banker, who had afterwards failed. Subsequent to that disaster Stefana had married Sacco, then merely a petty post-office clerk. He, later on, wishing to revive his father-in-law's business, had launched into all sorts of terrible, complicated, suspicious affairs, which by unforeseen luck had ended in his election as a deputy. Since he had arrived in Rome, to conquer the city in his turn, his wife had been compelled to assist his devouring ambition by dressing well and opening a *salon*; and, although she was still a little awkward, she rendered him many real services, being very economical and prudent, a thorough good housewife, with all the sterling, substantial qualities of Northern Italy which she had inherited from her mother, and which showed conspicuously beside the turbulence and carelessness of her husband, in whom flared Southern Italy with its perpetual, rageful appetite.

Despite his contempt for Sacco, old Orlando had retained some affection for his niece, in whose veins flowed blood similar to his own. He thanked her for her kind inquiries, and then at once spoke of an announcement which he had read in the morning papers, for he suspected that the deputy had sent his wife to ascertain his opinion.

"Well, and that ministry?" he asked.

The Signora had seated herself and made no haste to reply, but glanced at the newspapers strewn over the table. "Oh! nothing is settled yet," she at last responded; "the newspapers spoke out too soon. The Prime Minister sent for Sacco, and they had a talk together. But Sacco hesitates a good deal; he fears that he has no aptitude for the Department of Agriculture. Ah! if it were only the Finances—However, in any case, he would not have come to a decision without consulting you. What do you think of it, uncle?"

He interrupted her with a violent wave of the hand: "No, no, I won't mix myself up in such matters!"

To him the rapid success of that adventurer Sacco, that schemer and gambler who had always fished in troubled waters, was an abomination, the beginning of the end. His son Luigi certainly distressed him; but it was even worse to think that—whilst Luigi, with his great intelligence and many remaining fine qualities, was nothing at all—Sacco, on the other hand, Sacco, blunderhead and ever-famished battener that he was, had not merely slipped into parliament, but was now, it seemed, on the point of securing office! A little, swarthy, dry man he was, with big, round eyes, projecting cheekbones, and prominent chin. Ever dancing and chattering, he was gifted with a showy eloquence, all the force of which lay in his voice—a voice which at will became admirably powerful or gentle! And withal an insinuating man, profiting by every opportunity, wheedling and commanding by turn.

"You hear, Stefana," said Orlando; "tell your husband that the only advice I have to give him is to return to his clerkship at the post-office, where perhaps he may be of use."

What particularly filled the old soldier with indignation and despair was that such a man, a Sacco, should have fallen like a bandit on Rome—on that Rome whose conquest had cost so many noble efforts. And in his turn Sacco was conquering the city, was carrying it off from those who had won it by such hard toil, and was simply using it to satisfy his wild passion for power and its attendant enjoyments. Beneath his wheedling air there was the determination to devour everything. After the victory, while the spoil lay there, still warm, the wolves had come. It was the North that had made Italy, whereas the South, eager for the quarry, simply rushed upon the country, preyed upon it. And beneath the anger of the old stricken hero of Italian unity there was indeed all the growing antagonism of the North towards the South—the North industrious, economical, shrewd in politics, enlightened, full of all the great modern ideas, and the South ignorant and idle, bent on enjoying life immediately, amidst childish disorder in action, and an empty show of fine sonorous words.

Stefana had begun to smile in a placid way while glancing at Pierre, who had approached the window. "Oh, you say that, uncle," she responded; "but you love us well all the same, and more than once you have given me myself some good advice, for which I'm very thankful to you. For instance, there's that affair of Attilio's—"

She was alluding to her son, the lieutenant, and his love affair with Celia, the little Princess Buongiovanni, of which all the drawing-rooms, white and black alike, were talking.

"Attilio—that's another matter!" exclaimed Orlando. "He and you are both of the same blood as myself, and it's wonderful how I see myself again in that fine fellow. Yes, he is just the same as I was at his age, good-looking and brave and enthusiastic! I'm paying myself compliments, you see. But, really now, Attilio warms my heart, for he is the future, and brings me back some hope. Well, and what about his affair?"

"Oh! it gives us a lot of worry, uncle. I spoke to you about it before, but you shrugged your shoulders, saying that in matters of that kind all that the parents had to do was to let the lovers settle their affairs between them. Still, we don't want everybody to repeat that we are urging our son to get the little princess to elope with him, so that he may afterwards marry her money and title."

At this Orlando indulged in a frank outburst of gaiety: "That's a fine scruple! Was it your husband who instructed you to tell me of it? I know, however, that he affects some delicacy in this matter. For my own part, I believe myself to be as honest as he is, and I can only repeat that, if I had a son like yours, so straightforward and good, and candidly loving, I should let him marry whomsoever he pleased in his own way. The Buongiovannis—good heavens! the Buongiovannis—why, despite all their rank and lineage and the money they still possess, it will be a great honour for them to have a handsome young man with a noble heart as their son-in-law!"

Again did Stefana assume an expression of placid satisfaction. She had certainly only come there for approval. "Very well, uncle," she replied, "I'll repeat that to my husband, and he will pay great attention to it; for if you are severe towards him he holds you in perfect veneration. And as for that ministry—well, perhaps nothing will be done, Sacco will decide according to circumstances."

She rose and took her leave, kissing the old soldier very affectionately as on her arrival. And she complimented him on his good looks, declaring that she found him as handsome as ever, and making him smile by speaking of a lady who was still madly in love with him. Then, after acknowledging the young priest's silent salutation by a slight bow, she went off, once more wearing her modest and sensible air.

For a moment Orlando, with his eyes turned towards the door, remained silent, again sad, reflecting no doubt on all the difficult, equivocal present, so different from the glorious past. But all at once he turned to Pierre, who was still waiting. "And so, my friend," said he, "you are staying at the Palazzo Boccanera? Ah! what a grievous misfortune there has been on that side too!"

However, when the priest had told him of his conversation with Benedetta, and of her message that she still loved him and would never forget his goodness to her, no matter whatever happened, he appeared moved and his voice trembled: "Yes, she has a good heart, she has no spite. But what would you have? She did not love Luigi, and he was possibly violent. There is no mystery about the matter now, and I can speak to you freely, since to my great grief everybody knows what has happened."

Then Orlando abandoned himself to his recollections, and related how keen had been his delight on the eve of the marriage at the thought that so lovely a creature would become his daughter, and set some youth and charm around his invalid's armchair. He had always worshipped beauty, and would have had no other love than woman, if his country had not seized upon the best part of him. And Benedetta on her side loved him, revered him, constantly coming up to spend long hours with him, sharing his poor little room, which at those times became resplendent with all the divine grace that she brought with her. With her fresh breath near him, the pure scent she diffused, the caressing womanly tenderness with which she surrounded him, he lived anew. But, immediately afterwards, what a frightful drama and how his heart had bled at his inability to reconcile the husband and the wife! He could not possibly say that his son was in the wrong in desiring to be the loved and accepted spouse. At first indeed he had hoped to soften Benedetta, and throw her into Luigi's arms. But when she had confessed herself to him in tears, owning her old love for Dario, and her horror of belonging to another, he realised that she would never yield. And a whole year had then gone by; he had lived for a whole year imprisoned in his arm-chair, with that poignant drama progressing beneath him in those luxurious rooms whence no sound even reached his ears. How many times had he not listened, striving to hear, fearing atrocious quarrels, in despair at his inability to prove still useful by creating happiness. He knew nothing by his son, who kept his own counsel; he only learnt a few particulars from Benedetta at intervals when emotion left her defenceless; and that marriage in which he had for a moment espied the much-needed alliance between old and new Rome, that unconsummated marriage filled him with despair, as if it were indeed the defeat of every hope, the final collapse of the dream which had filled his life. And he himself had ended by desiring the divorce, so unbearable had become the suffering caused by such a situation.

"Ah! my friend!" he said to Pierre; "never before did I so well understand the fatality of certain antagonism, the possibility of working one's own misfortune and that of others, even when one has the most loving heart and upright mind!"

But at that moment the door again opened, and this time, without knocking, Count Luigi Prada came in. And after rapidly bowing to the visitor, who had risen, he gently took hold of his father's hands and felt them, as if fearing that they might be too warm or too cold.

"I've just arrived from Frascati, where I had to sleep," said he; "for the interruption of all that building gives me a lot of worry. And I'm told that you spent a bad night!"

"No, I assure you."

"Oh! I knew you wouldn't own it. But why will you persist in living up here without any comfort? All this isn't suited to your age. I should be so pleased if you would accept a more comfortable room where you might sleep better."

"No, no—I know that you love me well, my dear Luigi. But let me do as my old head tells me. That's the only way to make me happy."

Pierre was much struck by the ardent affection which sparkled in the eyes of the two men as they gazed at one another, face to face. This seemed to him very touching and beautiful, knowing as he did how many contrary ideas and actions, how many moral divergencies separated them. And he next took an interest in comparing them physically. Count Luigi Prada, shorter, more thick-set than his father, had, however, much the same strong energetic head, crowned with coarse black hair, and the same frank but somewhat stern eyes set in a face of clear complexion, barred by thick moustaches. But his mouth differed—a sensual, voracious mouth it was, with wolfish teeth—a mouth of prey made for nights of rapine, when the only question is to bite, and tear, and devour others. And for this reason, when some praised the frankness in his eyes, another would retort: "Yes, but I don't like his mouth." His feet were large, his hands plump and over-broad, but admirably cared for.

And Pierre marvelled at finding him such as he had anticipated. He knew enough of his story to picture in him a hero's son spoilt by conquest, eagerly devouring the harvest garnered by his father's glorious sword. And he particularly studied how the father's virtues had deflected and become transformed into vices in the son—the most noble qualities being perverted, heroic and disinterested energy lapsing into a ferocious appetite for possession, the man of battle leading to the man of booty, since the great gusts of enthusiasm no longer swept by, since men no longer fought, since they remained there resting, pillaging, and devouring amidst the heaped-up spoils. And the pity of it was that the old hero, the paralytic, motionless father beheld it all—beheld the degeneration of his son, the speculator and company promoter gorged with millions!

However, Orlando introduced Pierre. "This is Monsieur l'Abbe Pierre Froment, whom I spoke to you about," he said, "the author of the book which I gave you to read."

Luigi Prada showed himself very amiable, at once talking of home with an intelligent passion like one who wished to make the city a great modern capital. He had seen Paris transformed by the Second Empire; he had seen Berlin enlarged and embellished after the German victories; and, according to him, if Rome did not follow the movement, if it did not become the inhabitable capital of a great people, it was threatened with prompt death: either a crumbling museum or a renovated, resuscitated city—those were the alternatives.[1]

Greatly struck, almost gained over already, Pierre listened to this clever man, charmed with his firm, clear mind. He knew how skilfully Prada had manoeuvred in the affair of the Villa Montefiori, enriching himself when every one else was ruined, having doubtless foreseen the fatal catastrophe even while the gambling passion was maddening the entire nation. However, the young priest could already detect marks of weariness, precocious wrinkles and a fall of the lips, on that determined, energetic face, as though its possessor were growing tired of the continual struggle that he had to carry on amidst surrounding downfalls, the shock of which threatened to bring the most firmly established fortunes to the ground. It was said that Prada had recently had grave cause for anxiety; and indeed there was no longer any solidity to be found; everything might be swept away by the financial crisis which day by day was becoming more and more serious. In the case of Luigi, sturdy son though he was of Northern Italy, a sort of degeneration had set in, a slow rot, caused by the softening, perversive influence of Rome. He had there rushed upon the satisfaction of every appetite, and prolonged enjoyment was exhausting him. This, indeed, was one of the causes of the deep silent sadness of Orlando, who was compelled to witness the swift deterioration of his conquering race, whilst Sacco, the Italian of the South—served as it were by

[1] Personally I should have thought the example of Berlin a great deterrent. The enlargement and embellishment of the Prussian capital, after the war of 1870, was attended by far greater roguery and wholesale swindling than even the previous transformation of Paris. Thousands of people too were ruined, and instead of an increase of prosperity the result was the very reverse.—Trans.

the climate, accustomed to the voluptuous atmosphere, the life of those sun-baked cities compounded of the dust of antiquity—bloomed there like the natural vegetation of a soil saturated with the crimes of history, and gradually grasped everything, both wealth and power.

As Orlando spoke of Stefana's visit to his son, Sacco's name was mentioned. Then, without another word, the two men exchanged a smile. A rumour was current that the Minister of Agriculture, lately deceased, would perhaps not be replaced immediately, and that another minister would take charge of the department pending the next session of the Chamber.

Next the Palazzo Boccanera was mentioned, and Pierre, his interest awakened, became more attentive. "Ah!" exclaimed Count Luigi, turning to him, "so you are staying in the Via Giulia? All the Rome of olden time sleeps there in the silence of forgetfulness."

With perfect ease he went on to speak of the Cardinal and even of Benedetta—"the Countess," as he called her. But, although he was careful to let no sign of anger escape him, the young priest could divine that he was secretly quivering, full of suffering and spite. In him the enthusiastic energy of his father appeared in a baser, degenerate form. Quitting the yet handsome Princess Flavia in his passion for Benedetta, her divinely beautiful niece, he had resolved to make the latter his own at any cost, determined to marry her, to struggle with her and overcome her, although he knew that she loved him not, and that he would almost certainly wreck his entire life. Rather than relinquish her, however, he would have set Rome on fire. And thus his hopeless suffering was now great indeed: this woman was but his wife in name, and so torturing was the thought of her disdain, that at times, however calm his outward demeanour, he was consumed by a jealous vindictive sensual madness that did not even recoil from the idea of crime.

"Monsieur l'Abbe is acquainted with the situation," sadly murmured old Orlando.

His son responded by a wave of the hand, as though to say that everybody was acquainted with it. "Ah! father," he added, "but for you I should never have consented to take part in those proceedings for annulling the marriage! The Countess would have found herself compelled to return here, and would not nowadays be deriding us with her lover, that cousin of hers, Dario!"

At this Orlando also waved his hand, as if in protest.

"Oh! it's a fact, father," continued Luigi. "Why did she flee from here if it wasn't to go and live with her lover? And indeed, in my opinion, it's scandalous that a Cardinal's palace should shelter such goings-on!"

This was the report which he spread abroad, the accusation which he everywhere levelled against his wife, of publicly carrying on a shameless *liaison*. In reality, however, he did not believe a word of it, being too well acquainted with Benedetta's firm rectitude, and her determination to belong to none but the man she loved, and to him only in marriage. However, in Prada's eyes such accusations were not only fair play but also very efficacious.

And now, although he turned pale with covert exasperation, and laughed a hard, vindictive, cruel laugh, he went on to speak in a bantering tone of the proceedings for annulling the marriage, and in particular of the plea put forward by Benedetta's advocate Morano. And at last his language became so free that Orlando, with a glance towards the priest, gently interposed: "Luigi! Luigi!"

IV.

"Yes, you are right, father, I'll say no more," thereupon added the young Count. "But it's really abominable and ridiculous. Lisbeth, you know, is highly amused at it."

Orlando again looked displeased, for when visitors were present he did not like his son to refer to the person whom he had just named. Lisbeth Kauffmann, very blonde and pink and merry, was barely thirty years of age, and belonged to the Roman foreign colony. For two years past she had been a widow, her husband having died at Rome whither he had come to nurse a complaint of the lungs. Thenceforward free, and sufficiently well off, she had remained in the city by taste, having a marked predilection for art, and painting a little, herself. In the Via Principe Amadeo, in the new Viminal district, she had purchased a little palazzo, and transformed a large apartment on its second floor into a studio hung with old stuffs, and balmy in every season with the scent of flowers. The place was well known to tolerant and intellectual society. Lisbeth was there found in perpetual jubilation, clad in a long blouse, somewhat of a *gamine* in her ways, trenchant too and often bold of speech, but nevertheless capital company, and as yet compromised with nobody but Prada. Their *liaison* had begun some four months after his wife had left him, and now Lisbeth was near the time of becoming a mother. This she in no wise concealed, but displayed such candid tranquillity and happiness that her numerous acquaintances continued to visit her as if there were nothing in question, so facile and free indeed is the life of the great cosmopolitan continental cities. Under the circumstances which his wife's suit had created, Prada himself was not displeased at the turn which events had taken with regard to Lisbeth, but none the less his incurable wound still bled.

There could be no compensation for the bitterness of Benedetta's disdain, it was she for whom his heart burned, and he dreamt of one day wreaking on her a tragic punishment.

Pierre, knowing nothing of Lisbeth, failed to understand the allusions of Orlando and his son. But realising that there was some embarrassment between them, he sought to take countenance by picking from off the littered table a thick book which, to his surprise, he found to be a French educational work, one of those manuals for the *baccalaureat*,[1] containing a digest of the knowledge which the official programmes require. It was but a humble, practical, elementary work, yet it necessarily dealt with all the mathematical, physical, chemical, and natural sciences, thus broadly outlining the intellectual conquests of the century, the present phase of human knowledge.

"Ah!" exclaimed Orlando, well pleased with the diversion, "you are looking at the book of my old friend Theophile Morin. He was one of the thousand of Marsala, you know, and helped us to conquer Sicily and Naples. A hero! But for more than thirty years now he has been living in France again, absorbed in the duties of his petty professorship, which hasn't made him at all rich. And so he lately published that book, which sells very well in France it seems; and it occurred to him that he might increase his modest profits on it by issuing translations, an Italian one among others. He and I have remained brothers, and thinking that my influence would prove decisive, he

---

[1] The examination for the degree of bachelor, which degree is the necessary passport to all the liberal professions in France. M. Zola, by the way, failed to secure it, being ploughed for "insufficiency in literature"!—Trans.

wishes to utilise it. But he is mistaken; I fear, alas! that I shall be unable to get anybody to take up his book."

At this Luigi Prada, who had again become very composed and amiable, shrugged his shoulders slightly, full as he was of the scepticism of his generation which desired to maintain things in their actual state so as to derive the greatest profit from them. "What would be the good of it?" he murmured; "there are too many books already!"

"No, no!" the old man passionately retorted, "there can never be too many books! We still and ever require fresh ones! It's by literature, not by the sword, that mankind will overcome falsehood and injustice and attain to the final peace of fraternity among the nations—Oh! you may smile; I know that you call these ideas my fancies of '48, the fancies of a greybeard, as people say in France. But it is none the less true that Italy is doomed, if the problem be not attacked from down below, if the people be not properly fashioned. And there is only one way to make a nation, to create men, and that is to educate them, to develop by educational means the immense lost force which now stagnates in ignorance and idleness. Yes, yes, Italy is made, but let us make an Italian nation. And give us more and more books, and let us ever go more and more forward into science and into light, if we wish to live and to be healthy, good, and strong!"

With his torso erect, with his powerful leonine muzzle flaming with the white brightness of his beard and hair, old Orlando looked superb. And in that simple, candid chamber, so touching with its intentional poverty, he raised his cry of hope with such intensity of feverish faith, that before the young priest's eyes there arose another figure—that of Cardinal Boccanera, erect and black save for his snow-white hair, and likewise glowing with heroic beauty in his crumbling palace whose gilded ceilings threatened to fall about his head! Ah! the magnificent stubborn men of the past, the believers, the old men who still show themselves more virile, more ardent than the young! Those two represented the opposite poles of belief; they had not an idea, an affection in common, and in that ancient city of Rome, where all was being blown away in dust, they alone seemed to protest, indestructible, face to face like two parted brothers, standing motionless on either horizon. And to have seen them thus, one after the other, so great and grand, so lonely, so detached from ordinary life, was to fill one's day with a dream of eternity.

Luigi, however, had taken hold of the old man's hands to calm him by an affectionate filial clasp. "Yes, yes, you are right, father, always right, and I'm a fool to contradict you. Now, pray don't move about like that, for you are uncovering yourself, and your legs will get cold again."

So saying, he knelt down and very carefully arranged the wrapper; and then remaining on the floor like a child, albeit he was two and forty, he raised his moist eyes, full of mute, entreating worship towards the old man who, calmed and deeply moved, caressed his hair with a trembling touch.

Pierre had been there for nearly two hours, when he at last took leave, greatly struck and affected by all that he had seen and heard. And again he had to promise that he would return and have a long chat with Orlando. Once out of doors he walked along at random. It was barely four o'clock, and it was his idea to ramble in this wise, without any predetermined programme, through Rome at that delightful hour when the sun sinks in the refreshed and far blue atmosphere. Almost immediately, however, he found himself in the Via Nazionale, along which he had driven on arriving the previous day. And he recognised the huge livid Banca d'Italia, the green gardens climbing to the Quirinal, and the heaven-soaring pines of the Villa Aldobrandini. Then, at the turn of the street, as he stopped short in order that he might again contemplate the column of Trajan which now rose up darkly from its low piazza, already full of twilight, he was surprised to see a victoria suddenly pull up, and a young man courteously beckon to him.

"Monsieur l'Abbe Froment! Monsieur l'Abbe Froment!"

It was young Prince Dario Boccanera, on his way to his daily drive along the Corso. He now virtually subsisted on the liberality of his uncle the Cardinal, and was almost always short of money. But, like all the Romans, he would, if necessary, have rather lived on bread and water than have forgone his carriage, horse, and coachman. An equipage, indeed, is the one indispensable luxury of Rome.

"If you will come with me, Monsieur l'Abbe Froment," said the young Prince, "I will show you the most interesting part of our city."

He doubtless desired to please Benedetta, by behaving amiably towards her protege. Idle as he was, too, it seemed to him a pleasant occupation to initiate that young priest, who was said to be so intelligent, into what he deemed the inimitable side, the true florescence of Roman life.

Pierre was compelled to accept, although he would have preferred a solitary stroll. Yet he was interested in this young man, the last born of an exhausted race, who, while seemingly incapable of either thought or action, was none the less very seductive with his high-born pride and indolence. Far more a Roman than a patriot, Dario had never had the faintest inclination to rally to the new order of things, being well content to live apart and do nothing; and passionate though he was, he indulged in no follies, being very practical and sensible at heart, as are all his fellow-citizens, despite their apparent impetuosity. As soon as his carriage, after crossing the Piazza di Venezia, entered the Corso, he gave rein to his childish vanity, his desire to shine, his passion for gay, happy life in the open under the lovely sky. All this, indeed, was clearly expressed in the simple gesture which he made whilst exclaiming: "The Corso!"

As on the previous day, Pierre was filled with astonishment. The long narrow street again stretched before him as far as the white dazzling Piazza del Popolo, the only difference being that the right-hand houses were now steeped in sunshine, whilst those on the left were black with shadow. What! was that the Corso then, that semi-obscure trench, close pressed by high and heavy house-fronts, that mean roadway where three vehicles could scarcely pass abreast, and which serried shops lined with gaudy displays? There was neither space, nor far horizon, nor refreshing greenery such as the fashionable drives of Paris could boast! Nothing but jostling, crowding, and stifling on the little footways under the narrow strip of sky. And although Dario named the pompous and historical palaces, Bonaparte, Doria, Odescalchi, Sciarra, and Chigi; although he pointed out the column of Marcus Aurelius on the Piazza Colonna, the most lively square of the whole city with its everlasting throng of lounging, gazing, chattering people; although, all the way to the Piazza del Popolo, he never ceased calling attention to churches, houses, and side-streets, notably the Via dei Condotti, at the far end of which the Trinity de' Monti, all golden in the glory of the sinking sun, appeared above that famous flight of steps, the triumphal Scala di Spagna—Pierre still and ever retained the impression of disillusion which the narrow, airless thoroughfare had conveyed to him: the "palaces" looked to him like mournful hospitals or barracks, the Piazza Colonna suffered terribly from a lack of trees, and the Trinity de' Monti alone took his fancy by its distant radiance of fairyland.

But it was necessary to come back from the Piazza del Popolo to the Piazza di Venezia, then return to the former square, and come back yet again, following the entire Corso three and four times without wearying. The delighted Dario showed himself and looked about him, exchanging salutations. On either footway was a compact crowd of promenaders whose eyes roamed over the equipages and whose hands could have shaken those of the carriage folks. So great at last became the number of vehicles that both lines were absolutely unbroken, crowded to such a point that the coachmen could do no more than walk their horses. Perpetually going up and coming down the Corso, people scrutinised and jostled one another. It was open-air promiscuity, all Rome gathered together in the smallest possible space, the folks who knew one another and who met here as in a friendly drawing-room, and the folks belonging to adverse parties who did not speak together but who elbowed each other, and whose glances penetrated to each other's soul. Then a revelation came to Pierre, and he suddenly understood the Corso, the ancient custom, the passion and glory of the city. Its pleasure lay precisely in the very narrowness of the street, in that forced elbowing which facilitated not only desired meetings but the satisfaction of curiosity, the display of vanity, and the garnering of endless tittle-tattle. All Roman society met here each day, displayed itself, spied on itself, offering itself in spectacle to its own eyes, with such an indispensable need of thus beholding itself that the man of birth who missed the Corso was like one out of his element, destitute of newspapers, living like a savage. And withal the atmosphere was delightfully balmy, and the narrow strip of sky between the heavy, rusty mansions displayed an infinite azure purity.

Dario never ceased smiling, and slightly inclining his head while he repeated to Pierre the names of princes and princesses, dukes and duchesses—high-sounding names whose flourish had filled history, whose sonorous syllables conjured up the shock of armour on the battlefield and the splendour of papal pomp with robes of purple, tiaras of gold, and sacred vestments sparkling with precious stones. And as Pierre listened and looked he was pained to see merely some corpulent ladies or undersized gentlemen, bloated or shrunken beings, whose ill-looks seemed to be increased by their modern attire. However, a few pretty women went by, particularly some young, silent girls with large, clear eyes. And just as Dario had pointed out the Palazzo Buongiovanni, a huge seventeenth-century facade, with windows encompassed by foliaged ornamentation deplorably heavy in style, he added gaily:

"Ah! look—that's Attilio there on the footway. Young Lieutenant Sacco—you know, don't you?"

Pierre signed that he understood. Standing there in uniform, Attilio, so young, so energetic and brave of appearance, with a frank countenance softly illumined by blue eyes like his mother's, at once pleased the priest. He seemed indeed the very personification of youth and love, with all their enthusiastic, disinterested hope in the future.

"You'll see by and by, when we pass the palace again," said Dario. "He'll still be there and I'll show you something."

Then he began to talk gaily of the girls of Rome, the little princesses, the little duchesses, so discreetly educated at the convent of the Sacred Heart, quitting it for the most part so ignorant and then completing their education beside their mothers, never going out but to accompany the latter on the obligatory drive to the Corso, and living through endless days, cloistered, imprisoned in the depths of sombre mansions. Nevertheless what tempests raged in those mute souls to which none had ever penetrated! what stealthy growth of will suddenly appeared from under passive obedience, apparent unconsciousness of surroundings! How many there were who stubbornly set their minds on carving out their lives for themselves, on choosing the man who might please them, and securing him despite the opposition of the entire world! And the lover was chosen there from among the stream of young men promenading the Corso, the lover hooked with a glance during the daily drive, those candid eyes speaking aloud and sufficing for confession and the gift of all, whilst not a breath was wafted from the lips so chastely closed. And afterwards there came love letters, furtively exchanged in church, and the winning-over of maids to facilitate stolen meetings, at first so innocent. In the end, a marriage often resulted.

Celia, for her part, had determined to win Attilio on the very first day when their eyes had met. And it was from a window of the Palazzo Buongiovanni that she had perceived him one afternoon of mortal weariness. He had just raised his head, and she had taken him for ever and given herself to him with those large, pure eyes of hers as they rested on his own. She was but an *amorosa*—nothing more; he pleased her; she had set her heart on him—him and none other. She would have waited twenty years for him, but she relied on winning him at once by quiet stubbornness of will. People declared that the terrible fury of the Prince, her father, had proved impotent against her respectful, obstinate silence. He, man of mixed blood as he was, son of an American woman, and husband of an English woman, laboured but to retain his own name and fortune intact amidst the downfall of others; and it was rumoured that as the result of a quarrel which he had picked with his wife, whom he accused of not sufficiently watching over their daughter, the Princess had revolted, full not only of the pride of a foreigner who had brought a huge dowry in marriage, but also of such plain, frank egotism that she had declared she no longer found time enough to attend to herself, let alone another. Had she not already done enough in bearing him five children? She thought so; and now she spent her time in worshipping herself, letting Celia do as she listed, and taking no further interest in the household through which swept stormy gusts.

However, the carriage was again about to pass the Buongiovanni mansion, and Dario forewarned Pierre. "You see," said he, "Attilio has come back. And now look up at the third window on the first floor."

It was at once rapid and charming. Pierre saw the curtain slightly drawn aside and Celia's gentle face appear. Closed, candid lily, she did not smile, she did not move. Nothing could be read on those pure lips, or in those clear but fathomless eyes of hers. Yet she was taking Attilio to herself, and giving herself to him without reserve. And soon the curtain fell once more.

"Ah, the little mask!" muttered Dario. "Can one ever tell what there is behind so much innocence?"

As Pierre turned round he perceived Attilio, whose head was still raised, and whose face was also motionless and pale, with closed mouth, and widely opened eyes. And the young priest was deeply touched, for this was love, absolute love in its sudden omnipotence, true love, eternal and juvenescent, in which ambition and calculation played no part.

Then Dario ordered the coachman to drive up to the Pincio; for, before or after the Corso, the round of the Pincio is obligatory on fine, clear afternoons. First came the Piazza del Popolo, the most airy and regular square of Rome, with its conjunction of thoroughfares, its churches and fountains, its central obelisk, and its two clumps of trees facing one another at either end of the small white paving-stones, betwixt the severe and sun-gilt buildings. Then, turning to the right, the carriage began to climb the inclined way to the Pincio—a magnificent winding ascent, decorated with bas-reliefs, statues, and fountains—a kind of apotheosis of marble, a commemoration of ancient Rome, rising amidst greenery. Up above, however, Pierre found the garden small, little better than a large square, with just the four necessary roadways to enable the carriages to drive round and round as long as they pleased. An uninterrupted line of busts of the great men of ancient and modern Italy fringed these roadways. But what Pierre most admired was the trees—trees of the most rare and varied kinds, chosen and tended with infinite care, and nearly always evergreens, so that in winter and summer alike the spot was adorned with lovely foliage of every imaginable shade of verdure. And beside these trees, along the fine, breezy roadways, Dario's victoria began to turn, following the continuous, unwearying stream of the other carriages.

Pierre remarked one young woman of modest demeanour and attractive simplicity who sat alone in a dark-blue victoria, drawn by a well-groomed, elegantly harnessed horse. She was very pretty, short, with chestnut hair, a creamy complexion, and large gentle eyes. Quietly robed in dead-leaf silk, she wore a large hat, which alone looked somewhat extravagant. And seeing that Dario was staring at her, the priest inquired her name, whereat the young Prince smiled. Oh! she was nobody, La Tonietta was the name that people gave her; she was one of the few *demi-mondaines* that Roman society talked of. Then, with the freeness and frankness which his race displays in such matters, Dario added some particulars. La Tonietta's origin was obscure; some said that she was the daughter of an innkeeper of Tivoli, and others that of a Neapolitan banker. At all events, she was very intelligent, had educated herself, and knew thoroughly well how to receive and entertain people at the little palazzo in the Via dei Mille, which had been given to her by old Marquis Manfredi now deceased. She made no scandalous show, had but one protector at a time, and the princesses and duchesses who paid attention to her at the Corso every afternoon, considered her nice-looking. One peculiarity had made her somewhat notorious. There was some one whom she loved and from whom she never accepted aught but a bouquet of white roses; and folks would smile indulgently when at times for weeks together she was seen driving round the Pincio with those pure, white bridal flowers on the carriage seat.

Dario, however, suddenly paused in his explanations to address a ceremonious bow to a lady who, accompanied by a gentleman, drove by in a large landau. Then he simply said to the priest: "My mother."

Pierre already knew of her. Viscount de la Choue had told him her story, how, after Prince Onofrio Boccanera's death, she had married again, although she was already fifty; how at the Corso, just like some young girl, she had hooked with her eyes a handsome man to her liking—one, too, who was fifteen years her junior. And Pierre also knew who that man was, a certain Jules Laporte, an ex-sergeant of the papal Swiss Guard, an ex-traveller in relics, compromised in an extraordinary "false relic" fraud; and he was further aware that Laporte's wife had made a fine-looking

Marquis Montefiori of him, the last of the fortunate adventurers of romance, triumphing as in the legendary lands where shepherds are wedded to queens.

At the next turn, as the large landau again went by, Pierre looked at the couple. The Marchioness was really wonderful, blooming with all the classical Roman beauty, tall, opulent, and very dark, with the head of a goddess and regular if somewhat massive features, nothing as yet betraying her age except the down upon her upper lip. And the Marquis, the Romanised Swiss of Geneva, really had a proud bearing, with his solid soldierly figure and long wavy moustaches. People said that he was in no wise a fool but, on the contrary, very gay and very supple, just the man to please women. His wife so gloried in him that she dragged him about and displayed him everywhere, having begun life afresh with him as if she were still but twenty, spending on him the little fortune which she had saved from the Villa Montefiori disaster, and so completely forgetting her son that she only saw the latter now and again at the promenade and acknowledged his bow like that of some chance acquaintance.

"Let us go to see the sun set behind St. Peter's," all at once said Dario, conscientiously playing his part as a showman of curiosities.

The victoria thereupon returned to the terrace, where a military band was now playing with a terrific blare of brass instruments. In order that their occupants might hear the music, a large number of carriages had already drawn up, and a growing crowd of loungers on foot had assembled there. And from that beautiful terrace, so broad and lofty, one of the most wonderful views of Rome was offered to the gaze. Beyond the Tiber, beyond the pale chaos of the new district of the castle meadows,[1] and between the greenery of Monte Mario and the Janiculum arose St. Peter's. Then on the left came all the olden city, an endless stretch of roofs, a rolling sea of edifices as far as the eye could reach. But one's glances always came back to St. Peter's, towering into the azure with pure and sovereign grandeur. And, seen from the terrace, the slow sunsets in the depths of the vast sky behind the colossus were sublime.

Sometimes there are topplings of sanguineous clouds, battles of giants hurling mountains at one another and succumbing beneath the monstrous ruins of flaming cities. Sometimes only red streaks or fissures appear on the surface of a sombre lake, as if a net of light has been flung to fish the submerged orb from amidst the seaweed. Sometimes, too, there is a rosy mist, a kind of delicate dust which falls, streaked with pearls by a distant shower, whose curtain is drawn across the mystery of the horizon. And sometimes there is a triumph, a *cortege* of gold and purple chariots of cloud rolling along a highway of fire, galleys floating upon an azure sea, fantastic and extravagant pomps slowly sinking into the less and less fathomable abyss of the twilight.

But that night the sublime spectacle presented itself to Pierre with a calm, blinding, desperate grandeur. At first, just above the dome of St. Peter's, the sun, descending in a spotless, deeply limpid sky, proved yet so resplendent that one's eyes could not face its brightness. And in this resplendency the dome seemed to be incandescent, you would have said a dome of liquid silver; whilst the surrounding districts, the house-roofs of the Borgo, were as though changed into a lake of live embers. Then, as the sun was by degrees inclined, it lost some of its blaze, and one could look;

---

[1] See ante note on castle meadows.

and soon afterwards sinking with majestic slowness it disappeared behind the dome, which showed forth darkly blue, while the orb, now entirely hidden, set an aureola around it, a glory like a crown of flaming rays. And then began the dream, the dazzling symbol, the singular illumination of the row of windows beneath the cupola which were transpierced by the light and looked like the ruddy mouths of furnaces, in such wise that one might have imagined the dome to be poised upon a brazier, isolated, in the air, as though raised and upheld by the violence of the fire. It all lasted barely three minutes. Down below the jumbled roofs of the Borgo became steeped in violet vapour, sank into increasing gloom, whilst from the Janiculum to Monte Mario the horizon showed its firm black line. And it was the sky then which became all purple and gold, displaying the infinite placidity of a supernatural radiance above the earth which faded into nihility. Finally the last window reflections were extinguished, the glow of the heavens departed, and nothing remained but the vague, fading roundness of the dome of St. Peter's amidst the all-invading night.

And, by some subtle connection of ideas, Pierre at that moment once again saw rising before him the lofty, sad, declining figures of Cardinal Boccanera and old Orlando. On the evening of that day when he had learnt to know them, one after the other, both so great in the obstinacy of their hope, they seemed to be there, erect on the horizon above their annihilated city, on the fringe of the heavens which death apparently was about to seize. Was everything then to crumble with them? was everything to fade away and disappear in the falling night following upon accomplished Time?

V.

ON the following day Narcisse Habert came in great worry to tell Pierre that Monsignor Gamba del Zoppo complained of being unwell, and asked for a delay of two or three days before receiving the young priest and considering the matter of his audience. Pierre was thus reduced to inaction, for he dared not make any attempt elsewhere in view of seeing the Pope. He had been so frightened by Nani and others that he feared he might jeopardise everything by inconsiderate endeavours. And so he began to visit Rome in order to occupy his leisure.

His first visit was for the ruins of the Palatine. Going out alone one clear morning at eight o'clock, he presented himself at the entrance in the Via San Teodoro, an iron gateway flanked by the lodges of the keepers. One of the latter at once offered his services, and though Pierre would have preferred to roam at will, following the bent of his dream, he somehow did not like to refuse the offer of this man, who spoke French very distinctly, and smiled in a very good-natured way. He was a squatly built little man, a former soldier, some sixty years of age, and his square-cut, ruddy face was barred by thick white moustaches.

"Then will you please follow me, Monsieur l'Abbe," said he. "I can see that you are French, Monsieur l'Abbe. I'm a Piedmontese myself, but I know the French well enough; I was with them at Solferino. Yes, yes, whatever people may say, one can't forget old friendships. Here, this way, please, to the right."

Raising his eyes, Pierre had just perceived the line of cypresses edging the plateau of the Palatine on the side of the Tiber; and in the delicate blue atmosphere the intense greenery of these trees showed like a black fringe. They alone attracted the eye; the slope, of a dusty, dirty grey, stretched out bare and devastated, dotted by a few bushes, among which peeped fragments of ancient walls. All was instinct with the ravaged, leprous sadness of a spot handed over to excavation, and where only men of learning could wax enthusiastic.

"The palaces of Tiberius, Caligula, and the Flavians are up above," resumed the guide. "We must keep then for the end and go round." Nevertheless he took a few steps to the left, and pausing before an excavation, a sort of grotto in the hillside, exclaimed: "This is the Lupercal den where the wolf suckled Romulus and Remus. Just here at the entry used to stand the Ruminal fig-tree which sheltered the twins."

Pierre could not restrain a smile, so convinced was the tone in which the old soldier gave these explanations, proud as he was of all the ancient glory, and wont to regard the wildest legends as indisputable facts. However, when the worthy man pointed out some vestiges of Roma Quadrata—remnants of walls which really seemed to date from the foundation of the city—Pierre began to feel interested, and a first touch of emotion made his heart beat. This emotion was certainly not due to any beauty of scene, for he merely beheld a few courses of tufa blocks, placed one upon the other and uncemented. But a past which had been dead for seven and twenty centuries seemed to rise up before him, and those crumbling, blackened blocks, the foundation of such a mighty eclipse of power and splendour, acquired extraordinary majesty.

Continuing their inspection, they went on, skirting the hillside. The outbuildings of the palaces must have descended to this point; fragments of porticoes, fallen beams, columns and friezes set up afresh, edged the rugged path which wound through wild weeds, suggesting a neglected cemetery; and the guide repeated the words which he had used day by day for ten years past, continuing to enunciate suppositions as facts, and giving a name, a destination, a history, to every one of the fragments.

"The house of Augustus," he said at last, pointing towards some masses of earth and rubbish.

Thereupon Pierre, unable to distinguish anything, ventured to inquire: "Where do you mean?"

"Oh!" said the man, "it seems that the walls were still to be seen at the end of the last century. But it was entered from the other side, from the Sacred Way. On this side there was a huge balcony which overlooked the Circus Maximus so that one could view the sports. However, as you can see, the greater part of the palace is still buried under that big garden up above, the garden of the Villa Mills. When there's money for fresh excavations it will be found again, together with the temple of Apollo and the shrine of Vesta which accompanied it."

Turning to the left, he next entered the Stadium, the arena erected for foot-racing, which stretched beside the palace of Augustus; and the priest's interest was now once more awakened. It was not that he found himself in presence of well-preserved and monumental remains, for not a column had remained erect, and only the right-hand walls were still standing. But the entire plan of the building had been traced, with the goals at either end, the porticus round the course, and the colossal imperial tribune which, after being on the left, annexed to the house of Augustus, had afterwards opened on the right, fitting into the palace of Septimius Severus. And while Pierre looked on all the scattered remnants, his guide went on chattering, furnishing the most copious and precise information, and declaring that the gentlemen who directed the excavations had mentally reconstructed the Stadium in each and every particular, and were even preparing a most exact plan of it, showing all the columns in their proper order and the statues in their niches, and even specifying the divers sorts of marble which had covered the walls.

"Oh! the directors are quite at ease," the old soldier eventually added with an air of infinite satisfaction. "There will be nothing for the Germans to pounce on here. They won't be allowed to set things topsy-turvy as they did at the Forum, where everybody's at sea since they came along with their wonderful science!"

Pierre—a Frenchman—smiled, and his interest increased when, by broken steps and wooden bridges thrown over gaps, he followed the guide into the great ruins of the palace of Severus. Rising on the southern point of the Palatine, this palace had overlooked the Appian Way and the Campagna as far as the eye could reach. Nowadays, almost the only remains are the substructures, the subterranean halls contrived under the arches of the terraces, by which the plateau of the hill was enlarged; and yet these dismantled substructures suffice to give some idea of the triumphant palace which they once upheld, so huge and powerful have they remained in their indestructible massiveness. Near by arose the famous Septizonium, the tower with the seven tiers of arcades, which only finally disappeared in the sixteenth century. One of the palace terraces yet juts out upon cyclopean arches and from it the view is splendid. But all the rest is a commingling of massive yet crumbling walls, gaping depths whose ceilings have fallen, endless corridors and vast halls of doubtful destination. Well cared for by the new administration, swept and cleansed of weeds, the ruins have lost their romantic wildness and assumed an aspect of bare and mournful grandeur. However, flashes of living sunlight often gild the ancient walls, penetrate by their breaches into the black halls, and animate with their dazzlement the mute melancholy of all this dead splendour now exhumed from the earth in which it slumbered for centuries. Over the old ruddy masonry, stripped of its pompous marble covering, is the purple mantle of the sunlight, draping the whole with imperial glory once more.

For more than two hours already Pierre had been walking on, and yet he still had to visit all the earlier palaces on the north and east of the plateau. "We must go back," said the guide, "the gardens of the Villa Mills and the convent of San Bonaventura stop the way. We shall only be able to pass on this side when the excavations have made a clearance. Ah! Monsieur l'Abbe, if you had walked over the Palatine merely some fifty years ago! I've seen some plans of that time. There were only some vineyards and little gardens with hedges then, a real campagna, where not a soul was to be met. And to think that all these palaces were sleeping underneath!"

Pierre followed him, and after again passing the house of Augustus, they ascended the slope and reached the vast Flavian palace,[1] still half buried by the neighbouring villa, and composed of a great number of halls large and small, on the nature of which scholars are still arguing. The aula regia, or throne-room, the basilica, or hall of justice, the triclinium, or dining-room, and the peristylium seem certainties; but for all the rest, and especially the small chambers of the private part of the structure, only more or less fanciful conjectures can be offered. Moreover, not a wall is entire; merely foundations peep out of the ground, mutilated bases describing the plan of the edifice. The only ruin preserved, as if by miracle, is the house on a lower level which some assert to have been that of Livia,[2] a house which seems very small beside all the huge palaces, and where are three halls comparatively intact, with mural paintings of mythological scenes, flowers, and fruits, still wonderfully fresh. As for the palace of Tiberius, not one of its stones can be seen; its remains lie buried beneath a lovely public garden; whilst of the neighbouring palace of Caligula, overhanging the Forum, there are only some huge substructures, akin to those of the house of Severus—buttresses, lofty arcades, which upheld the palace, vast basements, so to say, where the praetorians were posted and gorged themselves with continual junketings. And thus this lofty plateau dominating the city merely offered some scarcely recognisable

---

[1] Begun by Vespasian and finished by Domitian.—Trans.

[2] Others assert it to have been the house of Germanicus, father of Caligula.—Trans.

vestiges to the view, stretches of grey, bare soil turned up by the pick, and dotted with fragments of old walls; and it needed a real effort of scholarly imagination to conjure up the ancient imperial splendour which once had triumphed there.

Nevertheless Pierre's guide, with quiet conviction, persisted in his explanations, pointing to empty space as though the edifices still rose before him. "Here," said he, "we are in the Area Palatina. Yonder, you see, is the facade of Domitian's palace, and there you have that of Caligula's palace, while on turning round the temple of Jupiter Stator is in front of you. The Sacred Way came up as far as here, and passed under the Porta Mugonia, one of the three gates of primitive Rome."

He paused and pointed to the northwest portion of the height. "You will have noticed," he resumed, "that the Caesars didn't build yonder. And that was evidently because they had to respect some very ancient monuments dating from before the foundation of the city and greatly venerated by the people. There stood the temple of Victory built by Evander and his Arcadians, the Lupercal grotto which I showed you, and the humble hut of Romulus constructed of reeds and clay. Oh! everything has been found again, Monsieur l'Abbe; and, in spite of all that the Germans say there isn't the slightest doubt of it."

Then, quite abruptly, like a man suddenly remembering the most interesting thing of all, he exclaimed: "Ah! to wind up we'll just go to see the subterranean gallery where Caligula was murdered."

Thereupon they descended into a long crypto-porticus, through the breaches of which the sun now casts bright rays. Some ornaments of stucco and fragments of mosaic-work are yet to be seen. Still the spot remains mournful and desolate, well fitted for tragic horror. The old soldier's voice had become graver as he related how Caligula, on returning from the Palatine games, had been minded to descend all alone into this gallery to witness certain sacred dances which some youths from Asia were practising there. And then it was that the gloom gave Cassius Chaereas, the chief of the conspirators, an opportunity to deal him the first thrust in the abdomen. Howling with pain, the emperor sought to flee; but the assassins, his creatures, his dearest friends, rushed upon him, threw him down, and dealt him blow after blow, whilst he, mad with rage and fright, filled the dim, deaf gallery with the howling of a slaughtered beast. When he had expired, silence fell once more, and the frightened murderers fled.

The classical visit to the Palatine was now over, and when Pierre came up into the light again, he wished to rid himself of his guide and remain alone in the pleasant, dreamy garden on the summit of the height. For three hours he had been tramping about with the guide's voice buzzing in his ears. The worthy man was now talking of his friendship for France and relating the battle of Magenta in great detail. He smiled as he took the piece of silver which Pierre offered him, and then started on the battle of Solferino. Indeed, it seemed impossible to stop him, when fortunately a lady came up to ask for some information. And, thereupon, he went off with her. "Good-evening, Monsieur l'Abbe," he said; "you can go down by way of Caligula's palace."

Delightful was Pierre's relief when he was at last able to rest for a moment on one of the marble seats in the garden. There were but few clumps of trees, cypresses, box-trees, palms, and some fine evergreen oaks; but the latter, sheltering the seat, cast a dark shade of exquisite freshness around. The charm of the spot was also largely due to its dreamy solitude, to the low rustle which seemed to come from that ancient soil saturated with resounding history. Here formerly had been the pleasure grounds of the

Villa Farnese which still exists though greatly damaged, and the grace of the Renascence seems to linger here, its breath passing caressingly through the shiny foliage of the old evergreen oaks. You are, as it were, enveloped by the soul of the past, an ethereal conglomeration of visions, and overhead is wafted the straying breath of innumerable generations buried beneath the sod.

After a time, however, Pierre could no longer remain seated, so powerful was the attraction of Rome, scattered all around that august summit. So he rose and approached the balustrade of a terrace; and beneath him appeared the Forum, and beyond it the Capitoline hill. To the eye the latter now only presented a commingling of grey buildings, lacking both grandeur and beauty. On the summit one saw the rear of the Palace of the Senator, flat, with little windows, and surmounted by a high, square campanile. The large, bare, rusty-looking walls hid the church of Santa Maria in Ara Coeli and the spot where the temple of Capitoline Jove had formerly stood, radiant in all its royalty. On the left, some ugly houses rose terrace-wise upon the slope of Monte Caprino, where goats were pastured in the middle ages; while the few fine trees in the grounds of the Caffarelli palace, the present German embassy, set some greenery above the ancient Tarpeian rock now scarcely to be found, lost, hidden as it is, by buttress walls. Yet this was the Mount of the Capitol, the most glorious of the seven hills, with its citadel and its temple, the temple to which universal dominion was promised, the St. Peter's of pagan Rome; this indeed was the hill—steep on the side of the Forum, and a precipice on that of the Campus Martius—where the thunder of Jupiter fell, where in the dimmest of the far-off ages the Asylum of Romulus rose with its sacred oaks, a spot of infinite savage mystery. Here, later, were preserved the public documents of Roman grandeur inscribed on tablets of brass; hither climbed the heroes of the triumphs; and here the emperors became gods, erect in statues of marble. And nowadays the eye inquires wonderingly how so much history and so much glory can have had for their scene so small a space, such a rugged, jumbled pile of paltry buildings, a mole-hill, looking no bigger, no loftier than a hamlet perched between two valleys.

Then another surprise for Pierre was the Forum, starting from the Capitol and stretching out below the Palatine: a narrow square, close pressed by the neighbouring hills, a hollow where Rome in growing had been compelled to rear edifice close to edifice till all stifled for lack of breathing space. It was necessary to dig very deep—some fifty feet—to find the venerable republican soil, and now all you see is a long, clean, livid trench, cleared of ivy and bramble, where the fragments of paving, the bases of columns, and the piles of foundations appear like bits of bone. Level with the ground the Basilica Julia, entirely mapped out, looks like an architect's ground plan. On that side the arch of Septimius Severus alone rears itself aloft, virtually intact, whilst of the temple of Vespasian only a few isolated columns remain still standing, as if by miracle, amidst the general downfall, soaring with a proud elegance, with sovereign audacity of equilibrium, so slender and so gilded, into the blue heavens. The column of Phocas is also erect; and you see some portions of the Rostra fitted together out of fragments discovered near by. But if the eye seeks a sensation of extraordinary vastness, it must travel beyond the three columns of the temple of Castor and Pollux, beyond the vestiges of the house of the Vestals, beyond the temple of Faustina, in which the Christian Church of San Lorenzo has so composedly installed itself, and even beyond the round temple of Romulus, to light upon the Basilica of

Constantine with its three colossal, gaping archways. From the Palatine they look like porches built for a nation of giants, so massive that a fallen fragment resembles some huge rock hurled by a whirlwind from a mountain summit. And there, in that illustrious, narrow, overflowing Forum the history of the greatest of nations held for centuries, from the legendary time of the Sabine women, reconciling their relatives and their ravishers, to that of the proclamation of public liberty, so slowly wrung from the patricians by the plebeians. Was not the Forum at once the market, the exchange, the tribunal, the open-air hall of public meeting? The Gracchi there defended the cause of the humble; Sylla there set up the lists of those whom he proscribed; Cicero there spoke, and there, against the rostra, his bleeding head was hung. Then, under the emperors, the old renown was dimmed, the centuries buried the monuments and temples with such piles of dust that all that the middle ages could do was to turn the spot into a cattle market! Respect has come back once more, a respect which violates tombs, which is full of feverish curiosity and science, which is dissatisfied with mere hypotheses, which loses itself amidst this historical soil where generations rise one above the other, and hesitates between the fifteen or twenty restorations of the Forum that have been planned on paper, each of them as plausible as the other. But to the mere passer-by, who is not a professional scholar and has not recently re-perused the history of Rome, the details have no significance. All he sees on this searched and scoured spot is a city's cemetery where old exhumed stones are whitening, and whence rises the intense sadness that envelops dead nations. Pierre, however, noting here and there fragments of the Sacred Way, now turning, now running down, and now ascending with their pavement of silex indented by the chariot-wheels, thought of the triumphs, of the ascent of the triumpher, so sorely shaken as his chariot jolted over that rough pavement of glory.

But the horizon expanded towards the southeast, and beyond the arches of Titus and Constantine he perceived the Colosseum. Ah! that colossus, only one-half or so of which has been destroyed by time as with the stroke of a mighty scythe, it rises in its enormity and majesty like a stone lace-work with hundreds of empty bays agape against the blue of heaven! There is a world of halls, stairs, landings, and passages, a world where one loses oneself amidst death-like silence and solitude. The furrowed tiers of seats, eaten into by the atmosphere, are like shapeless steps leading down into some old extinct crater, some natural circus excavated by the force of the elements in indestructible rock. The hot suns of eighteen hundred years have baked and scorched this ruin, which has reverted to a state of nature, bare and golden-brown like a mountain-side, since it has been stripped of its vegetation, the flora which once made it like a virgin forest. And what an evocation when the mind sets flesh and blood and life again on all that dead osseous framework, fills the circus with the 90,000 spectators which it could hold, marshals the games and the combats of the arena, gathers a whole civilisation together, from the emperor and the dignitaries to the surging plebeian sea, all aglow with the agitation and brilliancy of an impassioned people, assembled under the ruddy reflection of the giant purple velum. And then, yet further, on the horizon, were other cyclopean ruins, the baths of Caracalla, standing there like relics of a race of giants long since vanished from the world: halls extravagantly and inexplicably spacious and lofty; vestibules large enough for an entire population; a *frigidarium* where five hundred people could swim together; a *tepidarium* and a *calidarium*[1] on the same proportions, born of a wild craving for the huge; and then the terrific massiveness of the structures, the thickness of the piles of brick-work, such as no feudal castle ever knew; and, in addition, the general immensity which makes passing visitors look like lost ants; such an extraordinary riot of the great and the mighty that one wonders for what men, for what multitudes, this monstrous edifice was reared. To-day, you would say a mass of rocks in the rough, thrown from some height for building the abode of Titans.

And as Pierre gazed, he became more and more immersed in the limitless past which encompassed him. On all sides history rose up like a surging sea. Those bluey plains on the north and west were ancient Etruria; those jagged crests on the east were the Sabine Mountains; while southward, the Alban Mountains and Latium spread out in the streaming gold of the sunshine. Alba Longa was there, and so was Monte Cavo, with its crown of old trees, and the convent which has taken the place of the ancient temple of Jupiter. Then beyond the Forum, beyond the Capitol, the greater part of Rome stretched out, whilst behind Pierre, on the margin of the Tiber, was the Janiculum. And a voice seemed to come from the whole city, a voice which told him of Rome's eternal life, resplendent with past greatness. He remembered just enough of what he had been taught at school to realise where he was; he knew just what every one knows of Rome with no pretension to scholarship, and it was more particularly his artistic temperament which awoke within him and gathered warmth from the flame of memory. The present had disappeared, and the ocean of the past was still rising, buoying him up, carrying him away.

And then his mind involuntarily pictured a resurrection instinct with life. The grey, dismal Palatine, razed like some accursed city, suddenly became animated, peopled, crowned with palaces and temples. There had been the cradle of the Eternal City, founded by Romulus on that summit overlooking the Tiber. There assuredly the seven kings of its two and a half centuries of monarchical rule had dwelt, enclosed within high, strong walls, which had but three gateways. Then the five centuries of republican sway spread out, the greatest, the most glorious of all the centuries, those which brought the Italic peninsula and finally the known world under Roman dominion. During those victorious years of social and war-like struggle, Rome grew and peopled the seven hills, and the Palatine became but a venerable cradle with legendary temples, and was even gradually invaded by private residences. But at last Caesar, the incarnation of the power of his race, after Gaul and after Pharsalia triumphed in the name of the whole Roman people, having completed the colossal task by which the five following centuries of imperialism were to profit, with a pompous splendour and a rush of every appetite. And then Augustus could ascend to power; glory had reached its climax; millions of gold were waiting to be filched from the depths of the provinces; and the imperial gala was to begin in the world's capital, before the eyes of the dazzled and subjected nations. Augustus had been born on the Palatine, and after Actium had given him the empire, he set his pride in reigning from the summit of that sacred mount, venerated by the people. He bought up private houses and there built his palace with luxurious splendour: an atrium upheld by four pilasters and eight col-

[1] Tepidarium, warm bath; calidarium, vapour bath.—Trans.

umns; a peristylium encompassed by fifty-six Ionic columns; private apartments all around, and all in marble; a profusion of marble, brought at great cost from foreign lands, and of the brightest hues, resplendent like gems. And he lodged himself with the gods, building near his own abode a large temple of Apollo and a shrine of Vesta in order to ensure himself divine and eternal sovereignty. And then the seed of the imperial palaces was sown; they were to spring up, grow and swarm, and cover the entire mount.

Ah! the all-powerfulness of Augustus, his four and forty years of total, absolute, superhuman power, such as no despot has known even in his dreams! He had taken to himself every title, united every magistracy in his person. Imperator and consul, he commanded the armies and exercised executive power; pro-consul, he was supreme in the provinces; perpetual censor and princeps, he reigned over the senate; tribune, he was the master of the people. And, formerly called Octavius, he had caused himself to be declared Augustus, sacred, god among men, having his temples and his priests, worshipped in his lifetime like a divinity deigning to visit the earth. And finally he had resolved to be supreme pontiff, annexing religious to civil power, and thus by a stroke of genius attaining to the most complete dominion to which man can climb. As the supreme pontiff could not reside in a private house, he declared his abode to be State property. As the supreme pontiff could not leave the vicinity of the temple of Vesta, he built a temple to that goddess near his own dwelling, leaving the guardianship of the ancient altar below the Palatine to the Vestal virgins. He spared no effort, for he well realised that human omnipotence, the mastery of mankind and the world, lay in that reunion of sovereignty, in being both king and priest, emperor and pope. All the sap of a mighty race, all the victories achieved, and all the favours of fortune yet to be garnered, blossomed forth in Augustus, in a unique splendour which was never again to shed such brilliant radiance. He was really the master of the world, amidst the conquered and pacified nations, encompassed by immortal glory in literature and in art. In him would seem to have been satisfied the old intense ambition of his people, the ambition which it had pursued through centuries of patient conquest, to become the people-king. The blood of Rome, the blood of Augustus, at last coruscated in the sunlight, in the purple of empire. And the blood of Augustus, of the divine, triumphant, absolute sovereign of bodies and souls, of the man in whom seven centuries of national pride had culminated, was to descend through the ages, through an innumerable posterity with a heritage of boundless pride and ambition. For it was fatal: the blood of Augustus was bound to spring into life once more and pulsate in the veins of all the successive masters of Rome, ever haunting them with the dream of ruling the whole world. And later on, after the decline and fall, when power had once more become divided between the king and the priest, the popes—their hearts burning with the red, devouring blood of their great forerunner—had no other passion, no other policy, through the centuries, than that of attaining to civil dominion, to the totality of human power.

But Augustus being dead, his palace having been closed and consecrated, Pierre saw that of Tiberius spring up from the soil. It had stood where his feet now rested, where the beautiful evergreen oaks sheltered him. He pictured it with courts, porticoes, and halls, both substantial and grand, despite the gloomy bent of the emperor who betook himself far from Rome to live amongst informers and debauchees, with his heart and brain poisoned by power to the point of crime and most extraordinary insanity. Then the palace of Caligula followed, an enlargement of that of Tiberius, with arcades set up to increase its extent, and a bridge thrown over the Forum to the Capitol, in order that the prince might go thither at his ease to converse with Jove, whose son he claimed to be. And sovereignty also rendered this one ferocious—a madman with omnipotence to do as he listed! Then, after Claudius, Nero, not finding the Palatine large enough, seized upon the delightful gardens climbing the Esquiline in order to set up his Golden House, a dream of sumptuous immensity which he could not complete and the ruins of which disappeared in the troubles following the death of this monster whom pride demented. Next, in eighteen months, Galba, Otho, and Vitellius fell one upon the other, in mire and in blood, the purple converting them also into imbeciles and monsters, gorged like unclean beasts at the trough of imperial enjoyment. And afterwards came the Flavians, at first a respite, with commonsense and human kindness: Vespasian; next Titus, who built but little on the Palatine; but then Domitian, in whom the sombre madness of omnipotence burst forth anew amidst a *regime* of fear and spying, idiotic atrocities and crimes, debauchery contrary to nature, and building enterprises born of insane vanity instinct with a desire to outvie the temples of the gods. The palace of Domitian, parted by a lane from that of Tiberius, arose colossal-like—a palace of fairyland. There was the hall of audience, with its throne of gold, its sixteen columns of Phrygian and Numidian marble and its eight niches containing colossal statues; there were the hall of justice, the vast dining-room, the peristylium, the sleeping apartments, where granite, porphyry, and alabaster overflowed, carved and decorated by the most famous artists, and lavished on all sides in order to dazzle the world. And finally, many years later, a last palace was added to all the others—that of Septimius Severus: again a building of pride, with arches supporting lofty halls, terraced storeys, towers o'er-topping the roofs, a perfect Babylonian pile, rising up at the extreme point of the mount in view of the Appian Way, so that the emperor's compatriots—those from the province of Africa, where he was born—might, on reaching the horizon, marvel at his fortune and worship him in his glory.

And now Pierre beheld all those palaces which he had conjured up around him, resuscitated, resplendent in the full sunlight. They were as if linked together, parted merely by the narrowest of passages. In order that not an inch of that precious summit might be lost, they had sprouted thickly like the monstrous florescence of strength, power, and unbridled pride which satisfied itself at the cost of millions, bleeding the whole world for the enjoyment of one man. And in truth there was but one palace altogether, a palace enlarged as soon as one emperor died and was placed among the deities, and another, shunning the consecrated pile where possibly the shadow of death frightened him, experienced an imperious need to build a house of his own and perpetuate in everlasting stone the memory of his reign. All the emperors were seized with this building craze; it was like a disease which the very throne seemed to carry from one occupant to another with growing intensity, a consuming desire to excel all predecessors by thicker and higher walls, by a more and more wonderful profusion of marbles, columns, and statues. And among all these princes there was the idea of a glorious survival, of leaving a testimony of their greatness to dazzled and stupefied generations, of perpetuating themselves by marvels which would not perish but for ever weigh heavily upon the earth, when their own light ashes should long since have been swept away by the winds. And thus the Palatine became but the venerable base of a monstrous edifice, a thick vegetation of adjoining buildings, each new pile being like a fresh eruption of feverish pride; while the whole, now showing the snowy brightness of white marble and now the glowing hues of coloured marble, ended by crowning Rome and the world with the most extraordinary and most insolent abode of sovereignty—whether palace, temple, basilica, or cathedral—that omnipotence and dominion have ever reared under the heavens.

But death lurked beneath this excess of strength and glory. Seven hundred and thirty years of monarchy and republic had sufficed to make Rome great; and in five centuries of imperial sway the people-king was to be devoured down to its last muscles. There was the immensity of the territory, the more distant provinces gradually pillaged and exhausted; there was the fisc consuming everything, digging the pit of fatal bankruptcy; and there was the degeneration of the people, poisoned by the scenes of the circus and the arena, fallen to the sloth and debauchery of their masters, the Caesars, while mercenaries fought the foe and tilled the soil. Already at the time of Constantine, Rome had a rival, Byzantium; disruption followed with Honorius; and then some ten emperors sufficed for decomposition to be complete, for the bones of the dying prey to be picked clean, the end coming with Romulus Augustulus, the sorry creature whose name is, so to say, a mockery of the whole glorious history, a buffet for both the founder of Rome and the founder of the empire.

The palaces, the colossal assemblage of walls, storeys, terraces, and gaping roofs, still remained on the deserted Palatine; many ornaments and statues, however, had already been removed to Byzantium. And the empire, having become Christian, had afterwards closed the temples and extinguished the fire of Vesta, whilst yet respecting the ancient Palladium. But in the fifth century the barbarians rush upon Rome, sack and burn it, and carry the spoils spared by the flames away in their chariots. As long as the city was dependent on Byzantium a custodian of the imperial palaces remained there watching over the Palatine. Then all fades and crumbles in the night of the middle ages. It would really seem that the popes then slowly took the place of the Caesars, succeeding them both in their abandoned marble halls and their ever-subsisting passion for domination. Some of them assuredly dwelt in the palace of Septimius Severus; a council of the Church was held in the Septizonium; and, later on, Gelasius II was elected in a neighbouring monastery on the sacred mount. It was as if Augustus were again rising from the tomb, once more master of the world, with a Sacred College of Cardinals resuscitating the Roman Senate. In the twelfth century the Septizonium belonged to some Benedictine monks, and was sold by them to the powerful Frangipani family, who fortified it as they had already fortified the Colosseum and the arches of Constantine and Titus, thus forming a vast fortress round about the venerable cradle of the city. And the violent deeds of civil war and the ravages of invasion swept by like whirlwinds, throwing down the walls, razing the palaces and towers. And afterwards successive generations invaded the ruins, installed themselves in them by right of trover and conquest, turned them into cellars, store-places for forage, and stables for mules. Kitchen gardens were formed, vines were planted on the spots where fallen soil had covered the mosaics of the imperial halls. All around nettles and brambles grew up, and ivy preyed on the overturned porticoes, till there came a day when the colossal assemblage of palaces and temples, which marble was to have rendered eternal, seemed to dive beneath the dust, to disappear under the surging soil and vegetation which impassive Nature threw over it. And then, in the hot sunlight, among the wild flowerets, only big, buzzing flies remained, whilst herds of goats strayed in freedom through the throne-room of Domitian and the fallen sanctuary of Apollo.

A great shudder passed through Pierre. To think of so much strength, pride, and grandeur, and such rapid ruin—a world for ever swept away! He wondered how entire palaces, yet peopled by admirable statuary, could thus have been gradually buried without any one thinking of protecting them. It was no sudden catastrophe which had swallowed up those masterpieces, subsequently to be disinterred with exclamations of admiring wonder; they had been drowned, as it were—caught progressively by the legs, the waist, and the neck, till at last the head had sunk beneath the rising tide. And how could one explain that generations had heedlessly witnessed such things without thought of putting forth a helping hand? It would seem as if, at a given moment, a black curtain were suddenly drawn across the world, as if mankind began afresh, with a new and empty brain which needed moulding and furnishing. Rome had become depopulated; men ceased to repair the ruins left by fire and sword; the edifices which by their very immensity had become useless were utterly neglected, allowed to crumble and fall. And then, too, the new religion everywhere hunted down the old one, stole its temples, overturned its gods. Earthly deposits probably completed the disaster—there were, it is said, both earthquakes and inundations—and the soil was ever rising, the alluvia of the young Christian world buried the ancient pagan society. And after the pillaging of the temples, the theft of the bronze roofs and marble columns, the climax came with the filching of the stones torn from the Colosseum and the Theatre of Marcellus, with the pounding of the statuary and sculpture-work, thrown into kilns to procure the lime needed for the new monuments of Catholic Rome.

It was nearly one o'clock, and Pierre awoke as from a dream. The sun-rays were streaming in a golden rain between the shiny leaves of the ever-green oaks above him, and down below Rome lay dozing, overcome by the great heat. Then he made up his mind to leave the garden, and went stumbling over the rough pavement of the Clivus Victoriae, his mind still haunted by blinding visions. To complete his day, he had resolved to visit the old Appian Way during the afternoon, and, unwilling to return to the Via Giulia, he lunched at a suburban tavern, in a large, dim room, where, alone with the buzzing flies, he lingered for more than two hours, awaiting the sinking of the sun.

Ah! that Appian Way, that ancient queen of the high roads, crossing the Campagna in a long straight line with rows of proud tombs on either hand—to Pierre it seemed like a triumphant prolongation of the Palatine. He there found the same passion for splendour and domination, the same craving to eternise the memory of Roman greatness in marble and daylight. Oblivion was vanquished; the dead refused to rest, and remained for ever erect among the living, on either side of that road which was traversed by multitudes from the entire world. The deified images of those who were now but dust still gazed on the passers-by with empty eyes; the inscriptions still spoke, proclaiming names and titles. In former times the rows of sepulchres must have extended without interruption along all the straight, level miles between the tomb of Caecilia Metella and that of Casale Rotondo, forming an elongated cemetery where the powerful and wealthy competed as to who should leave the most colossal and lavishly decorated mausoleum: such, indeed, was the craving for survival, the passion for pompous immortality, the desire to deify death by lodging it in temples; whereof the present-day monumental splendour of the Genoese Campo Santo and the

Roman Campo Verano is, so to say, a remote inheritance. And what a vision it was to picture all the tremendous tombs on the right and left of the glorious pavement which the legions trod on their return from the conquest of the world! That tomb of Caecilia Metella, with its bond-stones so huge, its walls so thick that the middle ages transformed it into the battlemented keep of a fortress! And then all the tombs which follow, the modern structures erected in order that the marble fragments discovered might be set in place, the old blocks of brick and concrete, despoiled of their sculptured-work and rising up like seared rocks, yet still suggesting their original shapes as shrines, *cippi*, and *sarcophagi*. There is a wondrous succession of high reliefs figuring the dead in groups of three and five; statues in which the dead live deified, erect; seats contrived in niches in order that wayfarers may rest and bless the hospitality of the dead; laudatory epitaphs celebrating the dead, both the known and the unknown, the children of Sextius Pompeius Justus, the departed Marcus Servilius Quartus, Hilarius Fuscus, Rabirius Hermodorus; without counting the sepulchres venturously ascribed to Seneca and the Horatii and Curiatii. And finally there is the most extraordinary and gigantic of all the tombs, that known as Casale Rotondo, which is so large that it has been possible to establish a farmhouse and an olive garden on its substructures, which formerly upheld a double rotunda, adorned with Corinthian pilasters, large candelabra, and scenic masks.[1]

Pierre, having driven in a cab as far as the tomb of Caecilia Metella, continued his excursion on foot, going slowly towards Casale Rotondo. In many places the old pavement appears—large blocks of basaltic lava, worn into deep ruts that jolt the best-hung vehicles. Among the ruined tombs on either hand run bands of grass, the neglected grass of cemeteries, scorched by the summer suns and sprinkled with big violet thistles and tall sulphur-wort. Parapets of dry stones, breast high, enclose the russet roadsides, which resound with the crepitation of grasshoppers; and, beyond, the Campagna stretches, vast and bare, as far as the eye can see. A parasol pine, a eucalyptus, some olive or fig trees, white with dust, alone rise up near the road at infrequent intervals. On the left the ruddy arches of the Acqua Claudia show vigorously in the meadows, and stretches of poorly cultivated land, vineyards, and little farms, extend to the blue and lilac Sabine and Alban hills, where Frascati, Rocca di Papa, and Albano set bright spots, which grow and whiten as one gets nearer to them. Then, on the right, towards the sea, the houseless, treeless plain grows and spreads with vast, broad ripples, extraordinary ocean-like simplicity and grandeur, a long, straight line alone parting it from the sky. At the height of summer all burns and flares on this limitless prairie, then of a ruddy gold; but in September a green tinge begins to suffuse the ocean of herbage, which dies away in the pink and mauve and vivid blue of the fine sunsets.

As Pierre, quite alone and in a dreary mood, slowly paced the endless, flat highway, that resurrection of the past which he had beheld on the Palatine again confronted his mind's eye. On either hand the tombs once more rose up intact, with marble of dazzling whiteness. Had not the head of a colossal statue been found, min-

---

[1] Some believe this tomb to have been that of Messalla Corvinus, the historian and poet, a friend of Augustus and Horace; others ascribe it to his son, Aurelius Messallinus Cotta.—Trans.

gled with fragments of huge sphinxes, at the foot of yonder vase-shaped mass of bricks? He seemed to see the entire colossal statue standing again between the huge, crouching beasts. Farther on a beautiful headless statue of a woman had been discovered in the cella of a sepulchre, and he beheld it, again whole, with features expressive of grace and strength smiling upon life. The inscriptions also became perfect; he could read and understand them at a glance, as if living among those dead ones of two thousand years ago. And the road, too, became peopled: the chariots thundered, the armies tramped along, the people of Rome jostled him with the feverish agitation of great communities. It was a return of the times of the Flavians or the Antonines, the palmy years of the empire, when the pomp of the Appian Way, with its grand sepulchres, carved and adorned like temples, attained its apogee. What a monumental Street of Death, what an approach to Rome, that highway, straight as an arrow, where with the extraordinary pomp of their pride, which had survived their dust, the great dead greeted the traveller, ushered him into the presence of the living! He may well have wondered among what sovereign people, what masters of the world, he was about to find himself—a nation which had committed to its dead the duty of telling strangers that it allowed nothing whatever to perish—that its dead, like its city, remained eternal and glorious in monuments of extraordinary vastness! To think of it—the foundations of a fortress, and a tower sixty feet in diameter, that one woman might be laid to rest! And then, far away, at the end of the superb, dazzling highway, bordered with the marble of its funereal palaces, Pierre, turning round, distinctly beheld the Palatine, with the marble of its imperial palaces—the huge assemblage of palaces whose omnipotence had dominated the world!

But suddenly he started: two carabiniers had just appeared among the ruins. The spot was not safe; the authorities watched over tourists even in broad daylight. And later on came another meeting which caused him some emotion. He perceived an ecclesiastic, a tall old man, in a black cassock, edged and girt with red; and was surprised to recognise Cardinal Boccanera, who had quitted the roadway, and was slowly strolling along the band of grass, among the tall thistles and sulphur-wort. With his head lowered and his feet brushing against the fragments of the tombs, the Cardinal did not even see Pierre. The young priest courteously turned aside, surprised to find him so far from home and alone. Then, on perceiving a heavy coach, drawn by two black horses, behind a building, he understood matters. A footman in black livery was waiting motionless beside the carriage, and the coachman had not quitted his box. And Pierre remembered that the Cardinals were not expected to walk in Rome, so that they were compelled to drive into the country when they desired to take exercise. But what haughty sadness, what solitary and, so to say, ostracised grandeur there was about that tall, thoughtful old man, thus forced to seek the desert, and wander among the tombs, in order to breathe a little of the evening air!

Pierre had lingered there for long hours; the twilight was coming on, and once again he witnessed a lovely sunset. On his left the Campagna became blurred, and assumed a slaty hue, against which the yellowish arcades of the aqueduct showed very plainly, while the Alban hills, far away, faded into pink. Then, on the right, towards the sea, the planet sank among a number of cloudlets, figuring an archipelago of gold in an ocean of dying embers. And excepting the sapphire sky, studded with rubies, above the endless line of the Campagna, which was likewise changed into a sparkling lake, the dull green of the herbage turning to a liquid emerald tint, there was nothing to be seen, neither a hillock nor a flock—nothing, indeed, but Cardinal Boccanera's black figure, erect among the tombs, and looking, as it were, enlarged as it stood out against the last purple flush of the sunset.

Early on the following morning Pierre, eager to see everything, returned to the Appian Way in order to visit the catacomb of St. Calixtus, the most extensive and remarkable of the old Christian cemeteries, and one, too, where several of the early popes were buried. You ascend through a scorched garden, past olives and cypresses, reach a shanty of boards and plaster in which a little trade in "articles of piety" is carried on, and there a modern and fairly easy flight of steps enables you to descend. Pierre fortunately found there some French Trappists, who guard these catacombs and show them to strangers. One brother was on the point of going down with two French ladies, the mother and daughter, the former still comely and the other radiant with youth. They stood there smiling, though already slightly frightened, while the monk lighted some long, slim candles. He was a man with a bossy brow, the large, massive jaw of an obstinate believer and pale eyes bespeaking an ingenuous soul.

"Ah! Monsieur l'Abbe," he said to Pierre, "you've come just in time. If the ladies are willing, you had better come with us; for three Brothers are already below with people, and you would have a long time to wait. This is the great season for visitors."

The ladies politely nodded, and the Trappist handed a candle to the priest. In all probability neither mother nor daughter was devout, for both glanced askance at their new companion's cassock, and suddenly became serious. Then they all went down and found themselves in a narrow subterranean corridor. "Take care, mesdames," repeated the Trappist, lighting the ground with his candle. "Walk slowly, for there are projections and slopes."

Then, in a shrill voice full of extraordinary conviction, he began his explanations. Pierre had descended in silence, his heart beating with emotion. Ah! how many times, indeed, in his innocent seminary days, had he not dreamt of those catacombs of the early Christians, those asylums of the primitive faith! Even recently, while writing his book, he had often thought of them as of the most ancient and venerable remains of that community of the lowly and simple, for the return of which he called. But his brain was full of pages written by poets and great prose writers. He had beheld the catacombs through the magnifying glass of those imaginative authors, and had believed them to be vast, similar to subterranean cities, with broad highways and spacious halls, fit for the accommodation of vast crowds. And now how poor and humble the reality!

"Well, yes," said the Trappist in reply to the ladies' questions, "the corridor is scarcely more than a yard in width; two persons could not pass along side by side. How they dug it? Oh! it was simple enough. A family or a burial association needed a place of sepulchre. Well, a first gallery was excavated with pickaxes in soil of this description—granular tufa, as it is called—a reddish substance, as you can see, both soft and yet resistant, easy to work and at the same time waterproof. In a word, just the substance that was needed, and one, too, that has preserved the remains of the buried in a wonderful way." He paused and brought the flamelet of his candle near to the compartments excavated on either hand of the passage. "Look," he continued, "these are the *loculi*. Well, a subterranean gallery was dug, and on both sides these compartments were hollowed out, one above the other. The bodies of the dead were laid in them, for the most part simply wrapped in shrouds. Then the aperture was closed with tiles or marble slabs, carefully cemented. So, as you can see, everything explains itself. If other families joined the first one, or the burial association became more numerous, fresh galleries were added to those already filled. Passages were excavated on either hand, in every sense; and, indeed, a second and lower storey, at times even a third, was dug out. And here, you see, we are in a gallery which is certainly thirteen feet high. Now, you may wonder how they raised the bodies to place them in the compartments of the top tier. Well, they did not raise them to any such height; in all their work they kept on going lower and lower, removing more and more of the soil as the compartments became filled. And in this wise, in these catacombs of St. Calixtus, in less than four centuries, the Christians excavated more than ten miles of galleries, in which more than a million of their dead must have been laid to rest. Now, there are dozens of catacombs; the environs of Rome are honeycombed with them. Think of that, and perhaps you will be able to form some idea of the vast number of people who were buried in this manner."

Pierre listened, feeling greatly impressed. He had once visited a coal pit in Belgium, and he here found the same narrow passages, the same heavy, stifling atmosphere, the same nihility of darkness and silence. The flamelets of the candles showed merely like stars in the deep gloom; they shed no radiance around. And he at last understood the character of this funereal, termite-like labour—these chance burrowings continued according to requirements, without art, method, or symmetry. The rugged soil was ever ascending and descending, the sides of the gallery snaked: neither plumb-line nor square had been used. All this, indeed, had simply been a work of charity and necessity, wrought by simple, willing grave-diggers, illiterate craftsmen, with the clumsy handiwork of the decline and fall. Proof thereof was furnished by the inscriptions and emblems on the marble slabs. They reminded one of the childish drawings which street urchins scrawl upon blank walls.

"You see," the Trappist continued, "most frequently there is merely a name; and sometimes there is no name, but simply the words *In Pace*. At other times there is an emblem, the dove of purity, the palm of martyrdom, or else the fish whose name in Greek is composed of five letters which, as initials, signify: 'Jesus Christ, Son of God, Saviour.'"

He again brought his candle near to the marble slabs, and the palm could be distinguished: a central stroke, whence started a few oblique lines; and then came the dove or the fish, roughly outlined, a zigzag indicating a tail, two bars representing the bird's feet, while a round point simulated an eye. And the letters of the short inscriptions were all askew, of various sizes, often quite misshapen, as in the coarse handwriting of the ignorant and simple.

However, they reached a crypt, a sort of little hall, where the graves of several popes had been found; among others that of Sixtus II, a holy martyr, in whose honour there was a superbly engraved metrical inscription set up by Pope Damasus. Then, in another hall, a family vault of much the same size, decorated at a later stage, with naive mural paintings, the spot where St. Cecilia's body had been discovered was shown. And the explanations continued. The Trappist dilated on the paintings, drawing from them a confirmation of every dogma and belief, baptism, the Eucharist, the resurrection, Lazarus arising from the tomb, Jonas cast up by the whale, Daniel in the lions' den, Moses drawing water from the rock, and Christ—shown beardless, as was the practice in the early ages—accomplishing His various miracles.

"You see," repeated the Trappist, "all those things are shown there; and remember that none of the paintings was specially prepared: they are absolutely authentic."

At a question from Pierre, whose astonishment was increasing, he admitted that the catacombs had been mere cemeteries at the outset, when no religious ceremonies had been celebrated in them. It was only later, in the fourth century, when the martyrs were honoured, that the crypts were utilised for worship. And in the same way they only became places of refuge during the persecutions, when the Christians had to conceal the entrances to them. Previously they had remained freely and legally open. This was indeed their true history: cemeteries four centuries old becoming places of asylum, ravaged at times during the persecutions; afterwards held in veneration till the eighth century; then despoiled of their holy relics, and subsequently blocked up and forgotten, so that they remained buried during more than seven hundred years, people thinking of them so little that at the time of the first searches in the fifteenth century they were considered an extraordinary discovery—an intricate historical problem—one, moreover, which only our own age has solved.

"Please stoop, mesdames," resumed the Trappist. "In this compartment here is a skeleton which has not been touched. It has been lying here for sixteen or seventeen hundred years, and will show you how the bodies were laid out. Savants say that it is the skeleton of a female, probably a young girl. It was still quite perfect last spring; but the skull, as you can see, is now split open. An American broke it with his walking stick to make sure that it was genuine."

The ladies leaned forward, and the flickering light illumined their pale faces, expressive of mingled fright and compassion. Especially noticeable was the pitiful, pain-fraught look which appeared on the countenance of the daughter, so full of life with her red lips and large black eyes. Then all relapsed into gloom, and the little candles were borne aloft and went their way through the heavy darkness of the galleries. The visit lasted another hour, for the Trappist did not spare a detail, fond as he was of certain nooks and corners, and as zealous as if he desired to work the redemption of his visitors.

While Pierre followed the others, a complete evolution took place within him. As he looked about him, and formed a more and more complete idea of his surroundings, his first stupefaction at finding the reality so different from the embellished accounts of story-tellers and poets, his disillusion at being plunged into such rudely excavated mole-burrows, gave way to fraternal emotion. It was not that he thought of the fifteen hundred martyrs whose sacred bones had rested there. But how humble, resigned, yet full of hope had been those who had chosen such a place of sepulchre! Those low, darksome galleries were but temporary sleeping-places for the Christians. If they did not burn the bodies of their dead, as the Pagans did, it was because, like the Jews, they believed in the resurrection of the body; and it was that lovely idea of sleep, of tranquil rest after a just life, whilst awaiting the celestial reward, which imparted such intense peacefulness, such infinite charm, to the black, subterranean city. Everything there spoke of calm and silent night; everything there slumbered in rapturous quiescence, patient until the far-off awakening. What could be more touching than those terra-cotta tiles, those marble slabs, which bore not even a name—nothing but the words *In Pace*—at peace. Ah! to be at peace—life's work at last accomplished; to sleep in peace, to hope in peace for the advent of heaven! And the peacefulness seemed the more delightful as it was enjoyed in such deep humility. Doubtless the diggers worked chance-wise and clumsily; the craftsmen no longer knew how to engrave a name or carve a palm or a dove. Art had vanished; but all the feebleness and ignorance were instinct with the youth of a new humanity. Poor and lowly and meek ones swarmed there, reposing beneath the soil, whilst up above the sun continued its everlasting task. You found there charity and fraternity and death; husband and wife often lying together with their offspring at their feet; the great mass of the unknown submerging the personage, the bishop, or the martyr; the most touching equality—that springing from modesty—prevailing amidst all that dust, with compartments ever similar and slabs destitute of ornament, so that rows and rows of the sleepers mingled without distinctive sign. The inscriptions seldom ventured on a word of praise, and then how prudent, how delicate it was: the men were very worthy, very pious: the women very gentle, very beautiful, very chaste. A perfume of infancy arose, unlimited human affection spread: this was death as understood by the primitive Christians—death which hid itself to await the resurrection, and dreamt no more of the empire of the world!

And all at once before Pierre's eyes arose a vision of the sumptuous tombs of the Appian Way, displaying the domineering pride of a whole civilisation in the sunlight—tombs of vast dimensions, with a profusion of marbles, grandiloquent inscriptions, and masterpieces of sculptured-work. Ah! what an extraordinary contrast between that pompous avenue of death, conducting, like a highway of triumph, to the regal Eternal City, when compared with the subterranean necropolis of the Christians, that city of hidden death, so gentle, so beautiful, and so chaste! Here only quiet slumber, desired and accepted night, resignation and patience were to be found. Millions of human beings had here laid themselves to rest in all humility, had slept for centuries, and would still be sleeping here, lulled by the silence and the gloom, if the living had not intruded on their desire to remain in oblivion so long as the trumpets of the Judgment Day did not awaken them. Death had then spoken of Life: nowhere had there been more intimate and touching life than in these buried cities of the unknown, lowly dead. And a mighty breath had formerly come from them—the breath of a new humanity destined to renew the world. With the advent of meekness, contempt for the flesh, terror and hatred of nature, relinquishment of terrestrial joys, and a passion for death, which delivers and opens the portals of Paradise, another world had begun. And the blood of Augustus, so proud of purpling in the sunlight, so fired by the passion for sovereign dominion, seemed for a moment to disappear, as if, indeed, the new world had sucked it up in the depths of its gloomy sepulchres.

However, the Trappist insisted on showing the ladies the steps of Diocletian, and began to tell them the legend. "Yes," said he, "it was a miracle. One day, under that emperor, some soldiers were pursuing several Christians, who took refuge in these catacombs; and when the soldiers followed them inside the steps suddenly gave way, and all the persecutors were hurled to the bottom. The steps remain broken to this day. Come and see them; they are close by."

But the ladies were quite overcome, so affected by their prolonged sojourn in the gloom and by the tales of death which the Trappist had poured into their ears that they insisted on going up again. Moreover, the candles were coming to an end. They were all dazzled when they found themselves once more in the sunlight, outside the little hut where articles of piety and souvenirs were sold. The girl bought a paper weight, a piece of marble on which was engraved the fish symbolical of "Jesus Christ, Son of God, Saviour of Mankind."

On the afternoon of that same day Pierre decided to visit St. Peter's. He had as yet only driven across the superb piazza with its obelisk and twin fountains, encircled by Bernini's colonnades, those four rows of columns and pilasters which form a girdle of monumental majesty. At the far end rises the basilica, its facade making it look smaller and heavier than it really is, but its sovereign dome nevertheless filling the heavens.

Pebbled, deserted inclines stretched out, and steps followed steps, worn and white, under the burning sun; but at last Pierre reached the door and went in. It was three o'clock. Broad sheets of light streamed in through the high square windows, and some ceremony—the vesper service, no doubt—was beginning in the Capella Clementina on the left. Pierre, however, heard nothing; he was simply struck by the immensity of the edifice, as with raised eyes he slowly walked along. At the entrance came the giant basins for holy water with their boy-angels as chubby as Cupids; then the nave, vaulted and decorated with sunken coffers; then the four cyclopean buttress-piers upholding the dome, and then again the transepts and apsis, each as large as one of our churches. And the proud pomp, the dazzling, crushing splendour of everything, also astonished him: he marvelled at the cupola, looking like a planet, resplendent with the gold and bright colours of its mosaic-work, at the sumptuous *baldacchino* of bronze, crowning the high altar raised above the very tomb of St. Peter, and whence descend the double steps of the Confession, illumined by seven and eighty lamps, which are always kept burning. And finally he was lost in astonishment at the extraordinary profusion of marble, both white and coloured. Oh! those polychromatic marbles, Bernini's luxurious passion! The splendid pavement reflecting the entire edifice, the facings of the pilasters with their medallions of popes, the tiara and the keys borne aloft by chubby angels, the walls covered with emblems, particularly the dove of Innocent X, the niches with their colossal statues uncouth in taste, the *loggie* and their balconies, the balustrade and double steps of the Confession, the rich altars and yet richer tombs—all, nave, aisles, transepts, and apsis, were in marble, resplendent with the wealth of marble; not a nook small as the palm of one's hand appearing but it showed the insolent opulence of marble. And the basilica triumphed, beyond discussion, recognised and admired by every one as the largest and most splendid church in the whole world—the personification of hugeness and magnificence combined.

Pierre still wandered on, gazing, overcome, as yet not distinguishing details. He paused for a moment before the bronze statue of St. Peter, seated in a stiff, hierarchical attitude on a marble pedestal. A few of the faithful were there kissing the large toe of the Saint's right foot. Some of them carefully wiped it before applying their lips; others, with no thought of cleanliness, kissed it, pressed their foreheads to it, and then kissed it again. Next, Pierre turned into the transept on the left, where stand the confessionals. Priests are ever stationed there, ready to confess penitents in every language. Others wait, holding long staves, with which they lightly tap the heads of kneeling sinners, who thereby obtain thirty days' indulgence. However, there were few people present, and inside the small wooden boxes the priests occupied their leisure time in reading and writing, as if they were at home. Then Pierre again found himself before the Confession, and gazed with interest at the eighty lamps, scintillating like stars. The high altar, at which the Pope alone can officiate, seemed wrapped in the haughty melancholy of solitude under its gigantic, flowery *baldacchino*, the casting and gilding of which cost two and twenty thousand pounds. But suddenly Pierre remembered the ceremony in the Capella Clementina, and felt astonished, for he could hear nothing of it. As he drew near a faint breath, like the far-away piping of a flute, was wafted to him. Then the volume of sound slowly increased, but it was only on reaching the chapel that he recognised an organ peal. The sunlight here filtered through red curtains drawn before the windows, and thus the chapel glowed like a furnace whilst resounding with the grave music. But in that huge pile all became so slight, so weak, that at sixty paces neither voice nor organ could be distinguished.

On entering the basilica Pierre had fancied that it was quite empty and lifeless. There were, however, some people there, but so few and far between that their presence was not noticed. A few tourists wandered about wearily, guide-book in hand. In the grand nave a painter with his easel was taking a view, as in a public gallery. Then a French seminary went by, conducted by a prelate who named and explained the tombs. But in all that space these fifty or a hundred people looked merely like a few black ants who had lost themselves and were vainly seeking their way. And Pierre pictured himself in some gigantic gala hall or tremendous vestibule in an immeasurable palace of reception. The broad sheets of sunlight streaming through the lofty square windows of plain white glass illumined the church with blending radiance. There was not a single stool or chair: nothing but the superb, bare pavement, such as you might find in a museum, shining mirror-like under the dancing shower of sunrays. Nor was there a single corner for solitary reflection, a nook of gloom and mystery, where one might kneel and pray. In lieu thereof the sumptuous, sovereign dazzlement of broad daylight prevailed upon every side. And, on thus suddenly finding himself in this deserted opera-house, all aglow with flaring gold and purple, Pierre could but remember the quivering gloom of the Gothic cathedrals of France, where dim crowds sob and supplicate amidst a forest of pillars. In presence of all this ceremonial majesty—this huge, empty pomp, which was all Body—he recalled with a pang the emaciate architecture and statuary of the middle ages, which were all Soul. He vainly sought for some poor, kneeling woman, some creature swayed by faith or suffering, yielding in a modest half-light to thoughts of the unknown, and with closed lips holding communion with the invisible. These he found not: there was but the weary wandering of the tourists, and the bustle of the prelates conducting the young priests to the obligatory stations; while the vesper service continued in the left-hand chapel, nought of it reaching the ears of the visitors save, perhaps, a confused vibration, as of the peal of a bell penetrating from outside through the vaults above.

And Pierre then understood that this was the splendid skeleton of a colossus whence life was departing. To fill it, to animate it with a soul, all the gorgeous display of great religious ceremonies was needed; the eighty thousand worshippers which it could hold, the great pontifical pomps, the festivals of Christmas and Easter, the processions and *corteges* displaying all the luxury of the Church amidst operatic scenery and appointments. And he tried to conjure up a picture of the past magnificence—the basilica overflowing with an idolatrous multitude, and the superhuman *cortege* passing along whilst every head was lowered; the cross and the sword opening the march, the cardinals going two by two, like twin divinities, in their rochets of lace and their mantles and robes of red moire, which train-bearers held up behind them; and at last, with Jove-like pomp, the Pope, carried on a stage draped with red velvet, seated in an arm-chair of red velvet and gold, and dressed in white velvet, with cope of gold, stole of gold, and tiara of gold. The bearers of the *Sedia gestatoria*[1] shone bravely in red tunics broidered with gold. Above the one and only Sovereign Pontiff of the world the *flabelli* waved those huge fans of feathers which formerly were waved before the idols of pagan Rome. And around the seat of triumph what a dazzling, glorious court there was! The whole pontifical family, the stream of assistant prelates, the patriarchs, the archbishops, and the bishops, with vestments and mitres of gold, the *Camerieri segreti partecipanti* in violet silk, the *Camerieri partecipanti* of the cape and the sword in black velvet Renascence costumes, with ruffs and golden chains, the whole innumerable ecclesiastical and laical suite, which not even a hundred pages of the "Gerarchia" can completely enumerate, the prothonotaries, the chaplains, the prelates of every class and degree, without mentioning the military household, the gendarmes with their busbies, the Palatine Guards in blue trousers and black tunics, the Swiss Guards costumed in red, yellow, and black, with breastplates of silver, suggesting the men at arms of some drama of the Romantic school, and the Noble Guards, superb in their high boots, white pigskins, red tunics, gold lace, epaulets, and helmets! However, since Rome had become the capital of Italy the doors were no longer thrown wide open; on the rare occasions when the Pope yet came down to officiate, to show himself as the supreme representative of the Divinity on earth, the basilica was filled with chosen ones. To enter it you needed a card of invitation. You no longer saw the people—a throng of fifty, even eighty, thousand Christians—flocking to the Church and swarming within it promiscuously; there was but a select gathering, a congregation of friends convened as for a private function. Even when, by dint of effort, thousands were collected together there, they formed but a picked audience invited to the performance of a monster concert.

And as Pierre strolled among the bright, crude marbles in that cold if gorgeous museum, the feeling grew upon him that he was in some pagan temple raised to the deity of Light and Pomp. The larger temples of ancient Rome were certainly similar piles, upheld by the same precious columns, with walls covered with the same polychromatic marbles and vaulted ceilings having the same gilded panels. And his feeling was destined to become yet more acute after his visits to the other basilicas, which could but reveal the truth to him. First one found the Christian Church quietly, audaciously quartering itself in a pagan church, as, for instance, San Lorenzo in Miranda installed in the temple of Antoninus and Faustina, and retaining the latter's rare porticus in *cipollino* marble and its handsome white marble entablature. Then there was the Christian Church springing from the ruins of the destroyed pagan edifice, as, for example, San Clemente, beneath which centuries of contrary beliefs are stratified: a very ancient edifice of the time of the kings or the republic, then another of the days of the empire identified as a temple of Mithras, and next a basilica of the primitive faith. Then, too, there was the Christian Church, typified by that of Saint Agnes-beyond-the-walls which had been built on exactly the same pattern as the Roman secular basilica—that Tribunal and Exchange which accompanied every Forum. And, in particular, there was the Christian Church erected with material stolen from the demolished pagan temples. To this testified the sixteen superb columns of that same Saint Agnes, columns of various marbles filched from various gods; the one and

[1] The chair and stage are known by that name.—Trans.

twenty columns of Santa Maria in Trastevere, columns of all sorts of orders torn from a temple of Isis and Serapis, who even now are represented on their capitals; also the six and thirty white marble Ionic columns of Santa Maria Maggiore derived from the temple of Juno Lucina; and the two and twenty columns of Santa Maria in Ara Coeli, these varying in substance, size, and workmanship, and certain of them said to have been stolen from Jove himself, from the famous temple of Jupiter Capitolinus which rose upon the sacred summit. In addition, the temples of the opulent Imperial period seemed to resuscitate in our times at San Giovanni in Laterano and San Paolo-fuori-le-mura. Was not that Basilica of San Giovanni—"the Mother and Head of all the churches of the city and the earth"—like the abode of honour of some pagan divinity whose splendid kingdom was of this world? It boasted five naves, parted by four rows of columns; it was a profusion of bas-reliefs, friezes, and entablatures, and its twelve colossal statues of the Apostles looked like subordinate deities lining the approach to the master of the gods! And did not San Paolo, lately completed, its new marbles shimmering like mirrors, recall the abode of the Olympian immortals, typical temple as it was with its majestic colonnade, its flat, gilt-panelled ceiling, its marble pavement incomparably beautiful both in substance and workmanship, its violet columns with white bases and capitals, and its white entablature with violet frieze: everywhere, indeed, you found, the mingling of those two colours so divinely carnal in their harmony. And there, as at St. Peter's, not one patch of gloom, not one nook of mystery where one might peer into the invisible, could be found! And, withal, St. Peter's remained the monster, the colossus, larger than the largest of all others, an extravagant testimony of what the mad passion for the huge can achieve when human pride, by dint of spending millions, dreams of lodging the divinity in an over-vast, over-opulent palace of stone, where in truth that pride itself, and not the divinity, triumphs!

And to think that after long centuries that gala colossus had been the outcome of the fervour of primitive faith! You found there a blossoming of that ancient sap, peculiar to the soil of Rome, which in all ages has thrown up preposterous edifices, of exaggerated hugeness and dazzling and ruinous luxury. It would seem as if the absolute masters successively ruling the city brought that passion for cyclopean building with them, derived it from the soil in which they grew, for they transmitted it one to the other, without a pause, from civilisation to civilisation, however diverse and contrary their minds. It has all been, so to say, a continuous blossoming of human vanity, a passionate desire to set one's name on an imperishable wall, and, after being master of the world, to leave behind one an indestructible trace, a tangible proof of one's passing glory, an eternal edifice of bronze and marble fit to attest that glory until the end of time. At the bottom the spirit of conquest, the proud ambition to dominate the world, subsists; and when all has crumbled, and a new society has sprung up from the ruins of its predecessor, men have erred in imagining it to be cured of the sin of pride, steeped in humility once more, for it has had the old blood in its veins, and has yielded to the same insolent madness as its ancestors, a prey to all the violence of its heredity directly it has become great and strong. Among the illustrious popes there has not been one that did not seek to build, did not revert to the traditions of the Caesars, eternising their reigns in stone and raising temples for resting-places, so as to rank among the gods. Ever the same passion for terrestrial immortality has burst forth: it has been a battle as to who should leave the highest, most substantial, most gorgeous monument; and so acute has been the disease that those who, for lack of means and opportunity, have been unable to build, and have been forced to content themselves with repairing, have, nevertheless, desired to bequeath the memory of their modest achievements to subsequent generations by commemorative marble slabs engraved with pompous inscriptions! These slabs are to be seen on every side: not a wall has ever been strengthened but some pope has stamped it with his arms, not a ruin has been restored, not a palace repaired, not a fountain cleaned, but the reigning pope has signed the work with his Roman and pagan title of "Pontifex Maximus." It is a haunting passion, a form of involuntary debauchery, the fated florescence of that compost of ruins, that dust of edifices whence new edifices are ever arising. And given the perversion with which the old Roman soil almost immediately tarnished the doctrines of Jesus, that resolute passion for domination and that desire for terrestrial glory which wrought the triumph of Catholicism in scorn of the humble and pure, the fraternal and simple ones of the primitive Church, one may well ask whether Rome has ever been Christian at all!

And whilst Pierre was for the second time walking round the huge basilica, admiring the tombs of the popes, truth, like a sudden illumination, burst upon him and filled him with its glow. Ah! those tombs! Yonder in the full sunlight, in the rosy Campagna, on either side of the Appian Way—that triumphal approach to Rome, conducting the stranger to the august Palatine with its crown of circling palaces—there arose the gigantic tombs of the powerful and wealthy, tombs of unparalleled artistic splendour, perpetuating in marble the pride and pomp of a strong race that had mastered the world. Then, near at hand, beneath the sod, in the shrouding night of wretched mole-holes, other tombs were hidden—the tombs of the lowly, the poor, and the suffering—tombs destitute of art or display, but whose very humility proclaimed that a breath of affection and resignation had passed by, that One had come preaching love and fraternity, the relinquishment of the wealth of the earth for the everlasting joys of a future life, and committing to the soil the good seed of His Gospel, sowing the new humanity which was to transform the olden world. And, behold, from that seed, buried in the soil for centuries, behold, from those humble, unobtrusive tombs, where martyrs slept their last and gentle sleep whilst waiting for the glorious call, yet other tombs had sprung, tombs as gigantic and as pompous as the ancient, destroyed sepulchres of the idolaters, tombs uprearing their marbles among a pagan-temple-like splendour, proclaiming the same superhuman pride, the same mad passion for universal sovereignty. At the time of the Renascence Rome became pagan once more; the old imperial blood frothed up and swept Christianity away with the greatest onslaught ever directed against it. Ah! those tombs of the popes at St. Peter's, with their impudent, insolent glorification of the departed, their sumptuous, carnal hugeness, defying death and setting immortality upon this earth. There are giant popes of bronze, allegorical figures and angels of equivocal character wearing the beauty of lovely girls, of passion-compelling women with the thighs and the breasts of pagan goddesses! Paul III is seated on a high pedestal, Justice and Prudence are almost prostrate at his feet. Urban VIII is between Prudence and Religion, Innocent XI between Religion and Justice, Innocent XII between Justice and Charity, Gregory XIII between Religion and Strength. Attended by Prudence and Justice, Alexander VII appears kneeling, with Charity and Truth before him, and a skeleton rises up displaying an empty hourglass. Clement XIII, also on his knees, triumphs above a monumental sarcophagus, against which leans Religion bearing the Cross; while the Genius of Death, his elbow resting on the right-hand corner, has two huge, superb lions, emblems of omnipotence, beneath him. Bronze bespeaks the eternity of the figures, white marble dedescribes opulent flesh, and coloured marble winds around in rich draperies, deifying the monuments under the bright, golden glow of nave and aisles.

And Pierre passed from one tomb to the other on his way through the magnificent, deserted, sunlit basilica. Yes, these tombs, so imperial in their ostentation, were meet companions for those of the Appian Way. Assuredly it was Rome, the soil of Rome, that soil where pride and domination sprouted like the herbage of the fields that had transformed the humble Christianity of primitive times, the religion of fraternity, justice, and hope into what it now was: victorious Catholicism, allied to the rich and powerful, a huge implement of government, prepared for the conquest of every nation. The popes had awoke as Caesars. Remote heredity had acted, the blood of Augustus had bubbled forth afresh, flowing through their veins and firing their minds with immeasurable ambition. As yet none but Augustus had held the empire of the world, had been both emperor and pontiff, master of the body and the soul. And thence had come the eternal dream of the popes in despair at only holding the spiritual power, and obstinately refusing to yield in temporal matters, clinging for ever to the ancient hope that their dream might at last be realised, and the Vatican become another Palatine, whence they might reign with absolute despotism over all the conquered nations.

VI.

PIERRE had been in Rome for a fortnight, and yet the affair of his book was no nearer solution. He was still possessed by an ardent desire to see the Pope, but could in no wise tell how to satisfy it, so frequent were the delays and so greatly had he been frightened by Monsignor Nani's predictions of the dire consequences which might attend any imprudent action. And so, foreseeing a prolonged sojourn, he at last betook himself to the Vicariate in order that his "celebret" might be stamped, and afterwards said his mass each morning at the Church of Santa Brigida, where he received a kindly greeting from Abbe Pisoni, Benedetta's former confessor.

One Monday evening he resolved to repair early to Donna Serafina's customary reception in the hope of learning some news and expediting his affairs. Perhaps Monsignor Nani would look in; perhaps he might be lucky enough to come across some cardinal or domestic prelate willing to help him. It was in vain that he had tried to extract any positive information from Don Vigilio, for, after a short spell of affability and willingness, Cardinal Pio's secretary had relapsed into distrust and fear, and avoided Pierre as if he were resolved not to meddle in a business which, all considered, was decidedly suspicious and dangerous. Moreover, for a couple of days past a violent attack of fever had compelled him to keep his room.

Thus the only person to whom Pierre could turn for comfort was Victorine Bosquet, the old Beauceronne servant who had been promoted to the rank of housekeeper, and who still retained a French heart after thirty years' residence in Rome. She often spoke to the young priest of Auneau, her native place, as if she had left it only the previous day; but on that particular Monday even she had lost her wonted gay vivacity, and when she heard that he meant to go down in the evening to see the ladies she wagged her head significantly. "Ah! you won't find them very cheerful," said she. "My poor Benedetta is greatly worried. Her divorce suit is not progressing at all well."

All Rome, indeed, was again talking of this affair. An extraordinary revival of tittle-tattle had set both white and black worlds agog. And so there was no need for reticence on Victorine's part, especially in conversing with a compatriot. It appeared, then, that, in reply to Advocate Morano's memoir setting forth that the marriage had not been consummated, there had come another memoir, a terrible one, emanating from Monsignor Palma, a doctor in theology, whom the Congregation of the Council had selected to defend the marriage. As a first point, Monsignor Palma flatly disputed the alleged non-consummation, questioned the certificate put forward on Benedetta's behalf, and quoted instances recorded in scientific text-books which showed how deceptive appearances often were. He strongly insisted, moreover, on the narrative which Count Prada supplied in another memoir, a narrative well calculated to inspire doubt; and, further, he so turned and twisted the evidence of Benedetta's own maid as to make that evidence also serve against her. Finally he argued in a decisive way that, even supposing the marriage had not been consummated, this could only be ascribed to the resistance of the Countess, who had thus set at defiance one of the elementary laws of married life, which was that a wife owed obedience to her husband.

Next had come a fourth memoir, drawn up by the reporter of the Congregation, who analysed and discussed the three others, and subsequently the Congregation itself had dealt with the matter, opining in favour of the dissolution of the marriage by a majority of one vote—such a bare majority, indeed, that Monsignor Palma, exercising his rights, had hastened to demand further inquiry, a course which brought the whole *procedure* again into question, and rendered a fresh vote necessary.

"Ah! the poor Contessina!" exclaimed Victorine, "she'll surely die of grief, for, calm as she may seem, there's an inward fire consuming her. It seems that Monsignor Palma is the master of the situation, and can make the affair drag on as long as he likes. And then a deal of money had already been spent, and one will have to spend a lot more. Abbe Pisoni, whom you know, was very badly inspired when he helped on that marriage; and though I certainly don't want to soil the memory of my good mistress, Countess Ernesta, who was a real saint, it's none the less true that she wrecked her daughter's life when she gave her to Count Prada."

The housekeeper paused. Then, impelled by an instinctive sense of justice, she resumed. "It's only natural that Count Prada should be annoyed, for he's really being made a fool of. And, for my part, as there is no end to all the fuss, and this divorce is so hard to obtain, I really don't see why the Contessina shouldn't live with her Dario without troubling any further. Haven't they loved one another ever since they were children? Aren't they both young and handsome, and wouldn't they be happy together, whatever the world might say? Happiness, *mon Dieu*! one finds it so seldom that one can't afford to let it pass."

Then, seeing how greatly surprised Pierre was at hearing such language, she began to laugh with the quiet composure of one belonging to the humble classes of France, whose only desire is a quiet and happy life, irrespective of matrimonial ties. Next, in more discreet language, she proceeded to lament another worry which had fallen on the household, another result of the divorce affair. A rupture had come about between Donna Serafina and Advocate Morano, who was very displeased with the ill success of his memoir to the congregation, and accused Father Lorenza—the confessor of the Boccanera ladies—of having urged them into a deplorable lawsuit, whose only fruit could be a wretched scandal affecting everybody. And so great had been Morano's annoyance that he had not returned to the Boccanera mansion, but had severed a connection of thirty years' standing, to the stupefaction of all the Roman drawing-rooms, which altogether disapproved of his conduct. Donna Serafina was, for her part, the more grieved as she suspected the advocate of having purposely picked the quarrel in order to secure an excuse for leaving her; his real motive, in her estimation, being a sudden, disgraceful passion for a young and intriguing woman of the middle classes.

That Monday evening, when Pierre entered the drawing-room, hung with yellow brocatelle of a flowery Louis XIV pattern, he at once realised that melancholy reigned in the dim light radiating from the lace-veiled lamps. Benedetta and Celia, seated on a sofa, were chatting with Dario, whilst Cardinal Sarno, ensconced in an arm-chair, listened to the ceaseless chatter of the old relative who conducted the little Princess to each Monday gathering. And the only other person present was Donna Serafina, seated all alone in her wonted place on the right-hand side of the chimney-piece, and consumed with secret rage at seeing the chair on the left-hand side unoccupied—that chair which Morano had always taken during the thirty years that he had been faithful to her. Pierre noticed with what anxious and then despairing eyes she observed his entrance, her glance ever straying towards the door, as though she even yet hoped for the fickle one's return. Withal her bearing was erect and proud; she seemed to be more tightly laced than ever; and there was all the wonted haughtiness on her hard-featured face, with its jet-black eyebrows and snowy hair.

Pierre had no sooner paid his respects to her than he allowed his own worry to appear by inquiring whether they would not have the pleasure of seeing Monsignor Nani that evening. Thereupon Donna Serafina could not refrain from answering: "Oh! Monsignor Nani is forsaking us like the others. People always take themselves off when they can be of service."

She harboured a spite against the prelate for having done so little to further the divorce in spite of his many promises. Beneath his outward show of extreme willingness and caressing affability he doubtless concealed some scheme of his own which he was tenaciously pursuing. However, Donna Serafina promptly regretted the confession which anger had wrung from her, and resumed: "After all, he will perhaps come. He is so good-natured, and so fond of us."

In spite of the vivacity of her temperament she really wished to act diplomatically, so as to overcome the bad luck which had recently set in. Her brother the Cardinal had told her how irritated he was by the attitude of the Congregation of the Council; he had little doubt that the frigid reception accorded to his niece's suit had been due in part to the desire of some of his brother cardinals to be disagreeable to him. Personally, he desired the divorce, as it seemed to him the only means of ensuring the perpetuation of the family; for Dario obstinately refused to marry any other woman than his cousin. And thus there was an accumulation of disasters; the Cardinal was wounded in his pride, his sister shared his sufferings and on her own side was stricken in the heart, whilst both lovers were plunged in despair at finding their hopes yet again deferred.

As Pierre approached the sofa where the young folks were chatting he found that they were speaking of the catastrophe. "Why should you be so despondent?" asked Celia in an undertone. "After all, there was a majority of a vote in favour of annulling the marriage. Your suit hasn't been rejected; there is only a delay."

But Benedetta shook her head. "No, no! If Monsignor Palma proves obstinate his Holiness will never consent. It's all over."

"Ah! if one were only rich, very rich!" murmured Dario, with such an air of conviction that no one smiled. And, turning to his cousin, he added in a whisper: "I must really have a talk with you. We cannot go on living like this."

In a breath she responded: "Yes, you are right. Come down to-morrow evening at five. I will be here alone."

Then dreariness set in; the evening seemed to have no end. Pierre was greatly touched by the evident despair of Benedetta, who as a rule was so calm and sensible.

The deep eyes which illumined her pure, delicate, infantile face were now blurred as by restrained tears. He had already formed a sincere affection for her, pleased as he was with her equable if somewhat indolent disposition, the semblance of discreet good sense with which she veiled her soul of fire. That Monday even she certainly tried to smile while listening to the pretty secrets confided to her by Celia, whose love affairs were prospering far more than her own. There was only one brief interval of general conversation, and that was brought about by the little Princess's aunt, who, suddenly raising her voice, began to speak of the infamous manner in which the Italian newspapers referred to the Holy Father. Never, indeed, had there been so much bad feeling between the Vatican and the Quirinal. Cardinal Sarno felt so strongly on the subject that he departed from his wonted silence to announce that on the occasion of the sacrilegious festivities of the Twentieth of September, celebrating the capture of Rome, the Pope intended to cast a fresh letter of protest in the face of all the Christian powers, whose indifference proved their complicity in the odious spoliation of the Church.

"Yes, indeed! what folly to try and marry the Pope and the King," bitterly exclaimed Donna Serafina, alluding to her niece's deplorable marriage.

The old maid now seemed quite beside herself; it was already so late that neither Monsignor Nani nor anybody else was expected. However, at the unhoped-for sound of footsteps her eyes again brightened and turned feverishly towards the door. But it was only to encounter a final disappointment. The visitor proved to be Narcisse Habert, who stepped up to her, apologising for making so late a call. It was Cardinal Sarno, his uncle by marriage, who had introduced him into this exclusive *salon*, where he had received a cordial reception on account of his religious views, which were said to be most uncompromising. If, however, despite the lateness of the hour, he had ventured to call there that evening, it was solely on account of Pierre, whom he at once drew on one side.

"I felt sure I should find you here," he said. "Just now I managed to see my cousin, Monsignor Gamba del Zoppo, and I have some good news for you. He will see us to-morrow at about eleven in his rooms at the Vatican." Then, lowering his voice: "I think he will endeavour to conduct you to the Holy Father. Briefly, the audience seems to me assured."

Pierre was greatly delighted by this promised certainty, which came to him so suddenly in that dreary drawing-room, where for a couple of hours he had been gradually sinking into despair! So at last a solution was at hand!

Meantime Narcisse, after shaking hands with Dario and bowing to Benedetta and Celia, approached his uncle the Cardinal, who, having rid himself of the old relation, made up his mind to talk. But his conversation was confined to the state of his health, and the weather, and sundry insignificant anecdotes which he had lately heard. Not a word escaped him respecting the thousand complicated matters with which he dealt at the Propaganda. It was as though, once outside his office, he plunged into the commonplace and the unimportant by way of resting from the anxious task of governing the world. And after he had spoken for a time every one got up, and the visitors took leave.

"Don't forget," Narcisse repeated to Pierre, "you will find me at the Sixtine Chapel to-morrow at ten. And I will show you the Botticellis before we go to our appointment."

At half-past nine on the following morning Pierre, who had come on foot, was already on the spacious Piazza of St. Peter's; and before turning to the right, towards the bronze gate near one corner of Bernini's colonnade, he raised his eyes and lingered, gazing at the Vatican. Nothing to his mind could be less monumental than the jumble of buildings which, without semblance of architectural order or regularity of any kind, had grown up in the shadow cast by the dome of the basilica. Roofs rose one above the other and broad, flat walls stretched out chance-wise, just as wings and storeys had been added. The only symmetry observable above the colonnade was that of the three sides of the court of San Damaso, where the lofty glass-work which now encloses the old *loggie* sparkled in the sun between the ruddy columns and pilasters, suggesting, as it were, three huge conservatories.

And this was the most beautiful palace in the world, the largest of all palaces, comprising no fewer than eleven thousand apartments and containing the most admirable masterpieces of human genius! But Pierre, disillusioned as he was, had eyes only for the lofty facade on the right, overlooking the piazza, for he knew that the second-floor windows there were those of the Pope's private apartments. And he contemplated those windows for a long time, and remembered having been told that the fifth one on the right was that of the Pope's bed-room, and that a lamp could always be seen burning there far into the night.

What was there, too, behind that gate of bronze which he saw before him—that sacred portal by which all the kingdoms of the world communicated with the kingdom of heaven, whose august vicar had secluded himself behind those lofty, silent walls? From where he stood Pierre gazed on that gate with its metal panels studded with large square-headed nails, and wondered what it defended, what it concealed, what it shut off from the view, with its stern, forbidding air, recalling that of the gate of some ancient fortress. What kind of world would he find behind it, what treasures of human charity jealously preserved in yonder gloom, what revivifying hope for the new nations hungering for fraternity and justice? He took pleasure in fancying, in picturing the one holy pastor of humanity, ever watching in the depths of that closed palace, and, while the nations strayed into hatred, preparing all for the final reign of Jesus, and at last proclaiming the advent of that reign by transforming our democracies into the one great Christian community promised by the Saviour. Assuredly the world's future was being prepared behind that bronze portal; assuredly it was that future which would issue forth.

But all at once Pierre was amazed to find himself face to face with Monsignor Nani, who had just left the Vatican on his way to the neighbouring Palace of the Inquisition, where, as Assessor, he had his residence.

"Ah! Monsignor," said Pierre, "I am very pleased. My friend Monsieur Habert is going to present me to his cousin, Monsignor Gamba del Zoppo, and I think I shall obtain the audience I so greatly desire."

Monsignor Nani smiled with his usual amiable yet keen expression. "Yes, yes, I know." But, correcting himself as it were, he added: "I share your satisfaction, my dear son. Only, you must be prudent." And then, as if fearing that the young priest might have understood by his first words that he had just seen Monsignor Gamba, the most easily terrified prelate of the whole prudent pontifical family, he related that he had been running about since an early hour on behalf of two French ladies, who likewise were dying of a desire to see the Pope. However, he greatly feared that the help he was giving them would not prove successful.

"I will confess to you, Monsignor," replied Pierre, "that I myself was getting very discouraged. Yes, it is high time I should find a little comfort, for my sojourn here is hardly calculated to brace my soul."

He went on in this strain, allowing it to be seen that the sights of Rome were finally destroying his faith. Such days as those which he had spent on the Palatine and along the Appian Way, in the Catacombs and at St. Peter's, grievously disturbed him, spoilt his dream of Christianity rejuvenated and triumphant. He emerged from them full of doubt and growing lassitude, having already lost much of his usually rebellious enthusiasm.

Still smiling, Monsignor Nani listened and nodded approvingly. Yes, no doubt that was the fatal result. He seemed to have foreseen it, and to be well satisfied thereat. "At all events, my dear son," said he, "everything is going on well, since you are now certain that you will see his Holiness."

"That is true, Monsignor; I have placed my only hope in the very just and perspicacious Leo XIII. He alone can judge me, since he alone can recognise in my book his own ideas, which I think I have very faithfully set forth. Ah! if he be willing he will, in Jesus' name and by democracy and science, save this old world of ours!"

Pierre's enthusiasm was returning again, and Nani, smiling more and more affably with his piercing eyes and thin lips, again expressed approval: "Certainly; quite so, my dear son. You will speak to him, you will see."

Then as they both raised their heads and looked towards the Vatican, Nani carried his amiability so far as to undeceive Pierre with respect to the Pope's bed-room. No, the window where a light was seen every evening was simply that of a landing where the gas was kept burning almost all night. The window of his Holiness's bed-chamber was the second one farther on. Then both relapsed into silence, equally grave as they continued to gaze at the facade.

"Well, till we meet again, my dear son," said Nani at last. "You will tell me of your interview, I hope."

As soon as Pierre was alone he went in by the bronze portal, his heart beating violently, as if he were entering some redoubtable sanctuary where the future happiness of mankind was elaborated. A sentry was on duty there, a Swiss guard, who walked slowly up and down in a grey-blue cloak, below which one only caught a glimpse of his baggy red, black, and yellow breeches; and it seemed as if this cloak of sober hue were purposely cast over a disguise in order to conceal its strangeness, which had become irksome. Then, on the right-hand, came the covered stairway conducting to the Court of San Damaso; but to reach the Sixtine Chapel it was necessary to follow a long gallery, with columns on either hand, and ascend the royal staircase, the Scala Regia. And in this realm of the gigantic, where every dimension is exaggerated and replete with overpowering majesty, Pierre's breath came short as he ascended the broad steps.

He was much surprised on entering the Sixtine Chapel, for it at first seemed to him small, a sort of rectangular and lofty hall, with a delicate screen of white marble separating the part where guests congregate on the occasion of great ceremonies from the choir where the cardinals sit on simple oaken benches, while the inferior prelates remain standing behind them. On a low platform to the right of the soberly adorned altar is the pontifical throne; while in the wall on the left opens the narrow singing gallery with its balcony of marble. And for everything suddenly to spread out and soar into the infinite one must raise one's head, allow one's eyes to ascend from the huge fresco of the Last Judgment, occupying the whole of the end wall, to the paintings which cover the vaulted ceiling down to the cornice extending between the twelve windows of white glass, six on either hand.

Fortunately there were only three or four quiet tourists there; and Pierre at once perceived Narcisse Habert occupying one of the cardinals' seats above the steps where the train-bearers crouch. Motionless, and with his head somewhat thrown back, the young man seemed to be in ecstasy. But it was not the work of Michael Angelo that he thus contemplated. His eyes never strayed from one of the earlier frescoes below the cornice; and on recognising the priest he contented himself with murmuring: "Ah! my friend, just look at the Botticelli." Then, with dreamy eyes, he relapsed into a state of rapture.

Pierre, for his part, had received a great shock both in heart and in mind, overpowered as he was by the superhuman genius of Michael Angelo. The rest vanished; there only remained, up yonder, as in a limitless heaven, the extraordinary creations of the master's art. That which at first surprised one was that the painter should have been the sole artisan of the mighty work. No marble cutters, no bronze workers, no gilders, no one of another calling had intervened. The painter with his brush had sufficed for all—for the pilasters, columns, and cornices of marble, for the statues and the ornaments of bronze, for the *fleurons* and roses of gold, for the whole of the wondrously rich decorative work which surrounded the frescoes. And Pierre imagined Michael Angelo on the day when the bare vault was handed over to him, covered with plaster, offering only a flat white surface, hundreds of square yards to be adorned. And he pictured him face to face with that huge white page, refusing all help, driving all inquisitive folks away, jealously, violently shutting himself up alone with his gigantic task, spending four and a half years in fierce solitude, and day by day adding to his colossal work of creation. Ah! that mighty work, a task to fill a whole lifetime, a task which he must have begun with quiet confidence in his own will and power, drawing, as it were, an entire world from his brain and flinging it there with the ceaseless flow of creative virility in the full heyday of its omnipotence.

And Pierre was yet more overcome when he began to examine these presentments of humanity, magnified as by the eyes of a visionary, overflowing in mighty sympathetic pages of cyclopean symbolisation. Royal grace and nobility, sovereign peacefulness and power—every beauty shone out like natural florescence. And there was perfect science, the most audacious foreshortening risked with the certainty of success—an everlasting triumph of technique over the difficulty which an arched surface presented. And, in particular, there was wonderful simplicity of medium; matter was reduced almost to nothingness; a few colours were used broadly without any studied search for effect or brilliancy. Yet that sufficed, the blood seethed freely, the muscles projected, the figures became animated and stood out of their frames with such energy and dash that it seemed as if a flame were flashing by aloft, endowing all those beings with superhuman and immortal life. Life, aye, it was life, which burst forth and triumphed—mighty, swarming life, miraculous life, the creation of one sole hand possessed of the supreme gift—simplicity blended with power.

VI.

That a philosophical system, a record of the whole of human destiny, should have been found therein, with the creation of the world, of man, and of woman, the fall, the chastisement, then the redemption, and finally God's judgment on the last day—this was a matter on which Pierre was unable to dwell, at this first visit, in the wondering stupor into which the paintings threw him. But he could not help noticing how the human body, its beauty, its power, and its grace were exalted! Ah! that regal Jehovah, at once terrible and paternal, carried off amid the whirlwind of his creation, his arms outstretched and giving birth to worlds! And that superb and nobly outlined Adam, with extended hand, whom Jehovah, though he touch him not, animates with his finger—a wondrous and admirable gesture, leaving a sacred space between the finger of the Creator and that of the created—a tiny space, in which, nevertheless, abides all the infinite of the invisible and the mysterious. And then that powerful yet adorable Eve, that Eve with the sturdy flanks fit for the bearing of humanity, that Eve with the proud, tender grace of a woman bent on being loved even to perdition, that Eve embodying the whole of woman with her fecundity, her seductiveness, her empire! Moreover, even the decorative figures of the pilasters at the corners of the frescoes celebrate the triumph of the flesh: there are the twenty young men radiant in their nakedness, with incomparable splendour of torso and of limb, and such intensity of life that a craze for motion seems to carry them off, bend them, throw them over in superb attitudes. And between the windows are the giants, the prophets and the sibyls—man and woman deified, with inordinate wealth of muscle and grandeur of intellectual expression. There is Jeremiah with his elbow resting on his knee and his chin on his hand, plunged as he is in reflection—in the very depths of his visions and his dreams; there is the Sibylla Erithraea, so pure of profile, so young despite the opulence of her form, and with one finger resting on the open book of destiny; there is Isaiah with the thick lips of truth, virile and haughty, his head half turned and his hand raised with a gesture of command; there is the Sibylla Cumaea, terrifying with her science and her old age, her wrinkled countenance, her vulture's nose, her square protruding chin; there is Jonah cast forth by the whale, and wondrously foreshortened, his torso twisted, his arms bent, his head thrown back, and his mouth agape and shouting: and there are the others, all of the same full-blown, majestic family, reigning with the sovereignty of eternal health and intelligence, and typifying the dream of a broader, loftier, and indestructible humanity. Moreover, in the lunettes and the arches over the windows other figures of grace, power, and beauty appear and throng, the ancestors of the Christ, thoughtful mothers with lovely nude infants, men with wondering eyes peering into the future, representatives of the punished weary race longing for the promised Redeemer; while in the pendentives of the four corners various biblical episodes, the victories of Israel over the Spirit of Evil, spring into life. And finally there is the gigantic fresco at the far end, the Last Judgment with its swarming multitude, so numerous that days and days are needed to see each figure aright, a distracted crowd, full of the hot breath of life, from the dead rising in response to the furious trumpeting of the angels, from the fearsome groups of the damned whom the demons fling into hell, even to Jesus the justiciar, surrounded by the saints and apostles, and to the radiant concourse of the blessed who ascend upheld by angels, whilst higher and still higher other angels, bearing the instruments of the Passion, triumph as in full glory. And yet, above this gigantic composition, painted thirty years subsequently, in the full ripeness of age, the ceiling retains its ethereality, its unquestionable superiority, for on it the artist bestowed all his virgin power, his whole youth, the first great flare of his genius.

And Pierre found but one word to express his feelings: Michael Angelo was the monster dominating and crushing all others. Beneath his immense achievement you had only to glance at the works of Perugino, Pinturicchio, Roselli, Signorelli, and Botticelli, those earlier frescoes, admirable in their way, which below the cornice spread out around the chapel.

Narcisse for his part had not raised his eyes to the overpowering splendour of the ceiling. Wrapt in ecstasy, he did not allow his gaze to stray from one of the three frescoes of Botticelli. "Ah! Botticelli," he at last murmured; "in him you have the elegance and the grace of the mysterious; a profound feeling of sadness even in the midst of voluptuousness, a divination of the whole modern soul, with the most troublous charm that ever attended artist's work."

Pierre glanced at him in amazement, and then ventured to inquire: "You come here to see the Botticellis?"

"Yes, certainly," the young man quietly replied; "I only come here for him, and five hours every week I only look at his work. There, just study that fresco, Moses and the daughters of Jethro. Isn't it the most penetrating work that human tenderness and melancholy have produced?"

Then, with a faint, devout quiver in his voice and the air of a priest initiating another into the delightful but perturbing atmosphere of a sanctuary, he went on repeating the praises of Botticelli's art; his women with long, sensual, yet candid faces, supple bearing, and rounded forms showing from under light drapery; his young men, his angels of doubtful sex, blending stateliness of muscle with infinite delicacy of outline; next the mouths he painted, fleshy, fruit-like mouths, at times suggesting irony, at others pain, and often so enigmatical with their sinuous curves that one knew not whether the words they left unuttered were words of purity or filth; then, too, the eyes which he bestowed on his figures, eyes of languor and passion, of carnal or mystical rapture, their joy at times so instinct with grief as they peer into the nihility of human things that no eyes in the world could be more impenetrable. And finally there were Botticelli's hands, so carefully and delicately painted, so full of life, wantoning so to say in a free atmosphere, now joining, caressing, and even, as it were, speaking, the whole evincing such intense solicitude for gracefulness that at times there seems to be undue mannerism, though every hand has its particular expression, each varying expression of the enjoyment or pain which the sense of touch can bring. And yet there was nothing effeminate or false about the painter's work: on all sides a sort of virile pride was apparent, an atmosphere of superb passionate motion, absolute concern for truth, direct study from life, conscientiousness, veritable realism, corrected and elevated by a genial strangeness of feeling and character that imparted a never-to-be-forgotten charm even to ugliness itself.

Pierre's stupefaction, however, increased as he listened to Narcisse, whose somewhat studied elegance, whose curly hair cut in the Florentine fashion, and whose blue, mauvish eyes paling with enthusiasm he now for the first time remarked. "Botticelli," he at last said, "was no doubt a marvellous artist, only it seems to me that here, at any rate, Michael Angelo—"

But Narcisse interrupted him almost with violence. "No! no! Don't talk of him! He spoilt everything, ruined everything! A man who harnessed himself to his work like an ox, who laboured at his task like a navvy, at the rate of so many square yards a day! And a man, too, with no sense of the mysterious and the unknown, who saw everything so huge as to disgust one with beauty, painting girls like the trunks of oak-trees, women like giant butchers, with heaps and heaps of stupid flesh, and never a gleam of a divine or infernal soul! He was a mason—a colossal mason, if you like—but he was nothing more."

Weary "modern" that Narcisse was, spoilt by the pursuit of the original and the rare, he thus unconsciously gave rein to his fated hate of health and power. That Michael Angelo who brought forth without an effort, who had left behind him the most prodigious of all artistic creations, was the enemy. And his crime precisely was that he had created life, produced life in such excess that all the petty creations of others, even the most delightful among them, vanished in presence of the overflowing torrent of human beings flung there all alive in the sunlight.

"Well, for my part," Pierre courageously declared, "I'm not of your opinion. I now realise that life is everything in art; that real immortality belongs only to those who create. The case of Michael Angelo seems to me decisive, for he is the superhuman master, the monster who overwhelms all others, precisely because he brought forth that magnificent living flesh which offends your sense of delicacy. Those who are inclined to the curious, those who have minds of a pretty turn, whose intellects are ever seeking to penetrate things, may try to improve on the equivocal and invisible, and set all the charm of art in some elaborate stroke or symbolisation; but, none the less, Michael Angelo remains the all-powerful, the maker of men, the master of clearness, simplicity, and health."

At this Narcisse smiled with indulgent and courteous disdain. And he anticipated further argument by remarking: "It's already eleven. My cousin was to have sent a servant here as soon as he could receive us. I am surprised to have seen nobody as yet. Shall we go up to see the *stanze* of Raffaelle while we wait?"

Once in the rooms above, he showed himself perfect, both lucid in his remarks and just in his appreciations, having recovered all his easy intelligence as soon as he was no longer upset by his hatred of colossal labour and cheerful decoration.

It was unfortunate that Pierre should have first visited the Sixtine Chapel; for it was necessary he should forget what he had just seen and accustom himself to what he now beheld in order to enjoy its pure beauty. It was as if some potent wine had confused him, and prevented any immediate relish of a lighter vintage of delicate fragrance. Admiration did not here fall upon one with lightning speed; it was slowly, irresistibly that one grew charmed. And the contrast was like that of Racine beside Corneille, Lamartine beside Hugo, the eternal pair, the masculine and feminine genius coupled through centuries of glory. With Raffaelle it is nobility, grace, exquisiteness, and correctness of line, and divineness of harmony that triumph. You do not find in him merely the materialist symbolism so superbly thrown off by Michael Angelo; he introduces psychological analysis of deep penetration into the painter's art. Man is shown more purified, idealised; one sees more of that which is within him. And though one may be in presence of an artist of sentimental bent, a feminine genius whose quiver of tenderness one can feel, it is also certain that admirable firmness of workmanship confronts one, that the whole is very strong and very great. Pierre gradually yielded to such sovereign masterliness, such virile elegance, such a vision of supreme beauty set in supreme perfection. But if the "Dispute on the Sacrament" and the so-called "School of Athens," both prior to the paintings of the Sixtine Chapel, seemed to him to be Raffaelle's masterpieces, he felt that in the "Burning of the Borgo," and particularly in the "Expulsion of Heliodorus from the Temple," and "Pope St. Leo staying Attila at the Gates of Rome," the artist had lost the flower of his divine grace, through the deep impression which the overwhelming grandeur of Michael Angelo had wrought upon him. How crushing indeed had been the blow when the Sixtine Chapel was thrown open and the rivals entered! The creations of the monster then appeared, and the greatest of the humanisers lost some of his soul at sight of them, thenceforward unable to rid himself of their influence.

From the *stanze* Narcisse took Pierre to the *loggie*, those glazed galleries which are so high and so delicately decorated. But here you only find work which pupils executed after designs left by Raffaelle at his death. The fall was sudden and complete, and never had Pierre better understood that genius is everything—that when it disappears the school collapses. The man of genius sums up his period; at a given hour he throws forth all the sap of the social soil, which afterwards remains exhausted often for centuries. So Pierre became more particularly interested in the fine view that the *loggie* afford, and all at once he noticed that the papal apartments were in front of him, just across the Court of San Damaso. This court, with its porticus, fountain, and white pavement, had an aspect of empty, airy, sunlit solemnity which surprised him. There was none of the gloom or pent-up religious mystery that he had dreamt of with his mind full of the surroundings of the old northern cathedrals. Right and left of the steps conducting to the rooms of the Pope and the Cardinal Secretary of State four or five carriages were ranged, the coachmen stiffly erect and the horses motionless in the brilliant light; and nothing else peopled that vast square desert of a court which, with its bareness gilded by the coruscations of its glass-work and the ruddiness of its stones, suggested a pagan temple dedicated to the sun. But what more particularly struck Pierre was the splendid panorama of Rome, for he had not hitherto imagined that the Pope from his windows could thus behold the entire city spread out before him as if he merely had to stretch forth his hand to make it his own once more.

While Pierre contemplated the scene a sound of voices caused him to turn; and he perceived a servant in black livery who, after repeating a message to Narcisse, was retiring with a deep bow. Looking much annoyed, the *attache* approached the young priest. "Monsignor Gamba del Zoppo," said he, "has sent word that he can't see us this morning. Some unexpected duties require his presence." However, Narcisse's embarrassment showed that he did not believe in the excuse, but rather suspected some one of having so terrified his cousin that the latter was afraid of compromising himself. Obliging and courageous as Habert himself was, this made him indignant. Still he smiled and resumed: "Listen, perhaps there's a means of forcing an entry. If your time is your own we can lunch together and then return to visit the Museum of Antiquities. I shall certainly end by coming across my cousin and we may, perhaps, be lucky enough to meet the Pope should he go down to the gardens."

At the news that his audience was yet again postponed Pierre had felt keenly disappointed. However, as the whole day was at his disposal, he willingly accepted the *attache's* offer. They lunched in front of St. Peter's, in a little restaurant of the Borgo, most of whose customers were pilgrims, and the fare, as it happened, was far from good. Then at about two o'clock they set off for the museum, skirting the basilica by way of the Piazza della Sagrestia. It was a bright, deserted, burning district; and again, but in a far greater degree, did the young priest experience that sensation of bare, tawny, sun-baked majesty which had come upon him while gazing into the Court of San Damaso. Then, as he passed the apse of St. Peter's, the enormity of the colossus was brought home to him more strongly than ever: it rose like a giant bouquet of architecture edged by empty expanses of pavement sprinkled with fine weeds. And in all the silent immensity there were only two children playing in the shadow of a wall. The old papal mint, the Zecca, now an Italian possession, and guarded by soldiers of the royal army, is on the left of the passage leading to the museums, while on the right, just in front, is one of the entrances of honour to the Vatican where the papal Swiss Guard keeps watch and ward; and this is the entrance by which, according to etiquette, the pair-horse carriages convey the Pope's visitors into the Court of San Damaso.

Following the long lane which ascends between a wing of the palace and its garden wall, Narcisse and Pierre at last reached the Museum of Antiquities. Ah! what a museum it is, with galleries innumerable, a museum compounded of three museums, the Pio-Clementino, Chiaramonti, and the Braccio-Nuovo, and containing a whole world found beneath the soil, then exhumed, and now glorified in full sunlight. For more than two hours Pierre went from one hall to another, dazzled by the masterpieces, bewildered by the accumulation of genius and beauty. It was not only the celebrated examples of statuary, the Laocoon and the Apollo of the cabinets of the Belvedere, the Meleager, or even the torso of Hercules—that astonished him. He was yet more impressed by the *ensemble*, by the innumerable quantities of Venuses, Bacchuses, and deified emperors and empresses, by the whole superb growth of beautiful or August flesh celebrating the immortality of life. Three days previously he had visited the Museum of the Capitol, where he had admired the Venus, the Dying Gaul,[1] the marvellous Centaurs of black marble, and the extraordinary collection of busts, but here his admiration became intensified into stupor by the inexhaustible wealth of the galleries. And, with more curiosity for life than for art, perhaps, he again lingered before the busts which so powerfully resuscitate the Rome of history—the Rome which, whilst incapable of realising the ideal beauty of Greece, was certainly well able to create life. The emperors, the philosophers, the learned men, the poets are all there, and live such as they really were, studied and portrayed in all scrupulousness with their deformities, their blemishes, the slightest peculiarities of their features. And from this extreme solicitude for truth springs a wonderful wealth of character and an incomparable vision of the past. Nothing, indeed, could be loftier: the very men live once more, and retrace the history of their city, that history which has been so falsified that the teaching of it has caused generations of school-boys to hold antiquity in horror. But on seeing the men, how well one understands, how fully one can sympathise! And indeed the smallest bits of marble, the maimed statues, the bas-reliefs in fragments, even the isolated limbs—whether the divine arm of a nymph or the sinewy, shaggy thigh of a satyr—evoke the splendour of a civilisation full of light, grandeur, and strength.

---

[1] Best known in England, through Byron's lines, as the Dying Gladiator, though that appellation is certainly erroneous.—Trans.

At last Narcisse brought Pierre back into the Gallery of the Candelabra, three hundred feet in length and full of fine examples of sculpture. "Listen, my dear Abbe," said he. "It is scarcely more than four o'clock, and we will sit down here for a while, as I am told that the Holy Father sometimes passes this way to go down to the gardens. It would be really lucky if you could see him, perhaps even speak to him—who can tell? At all events, it will rest you, for you must be tired out."

Narcisse was known to all the attendants, and his relationship to Monsignor Gamba gave him the run of almost the entire Vatican, where he was fond of spending his leisure time. Finding two chairs, they sat down, and the *attache* again began to talk of art.

How astonishing had been the destiny of Rome, what a singular, borrowed royalty had been hers! She seemed like a centre whither the whole world converged, but where nothing grew from the soil itself, which from the outset appeared to be stricken with sterility. The arts required to be acclimatised there; it was necessary to transplant the genius of neighbouring nations, which, once there, however, flourished magnificently. Under the emperors, when Rome was the queen of the earth, the beauty of her monuments and sculpture came to her from Greece. Later, when Christianity arose in Rome, it there remained impregnated with paganism; it was on another soil that it produced Gothic art, the Christian Art *par excellence*. Later still, at the Renascence, it was certainly at Rome that the age of Julius II and Leo X shone forth; but the artists of Tuscany and Umbria prepared the evolution, brought it to Rome that it might thence expand and soar. For the second time, indeed, art came to Rome from without, and gave her the royalty of the world by blossoming so triumphantly within her walls. Then occurred the extraordinary awakening of antiquity, Apollo and Venus resuscitated worshipped by the popes themselves, who from the time of Nicholas V dreamt of making papal Rome the equal of the imperial city. After the precursors, so sincere, tender, and strong in their art—Fra Angelico, Perugino, Botticelli, and so many others—came the two sovereigns, Michael Angelo and Raffaelle, the superhuman and the divine. Then the fall was sudden, years elapsed before the advent of Caravaggio with power of colour and modelling, all that the science of painting could achieve when bereft of genius. And afterwards the decline continued until Bernini was reached—Bernini, the real creator of the Rome of the present popes, the prodigal child who at twenty could already show a galaxy of colossal marble wenches, the universal architect who with fearful activity finished the facade, built the colonnade, decorated the interior of St. Peter's, and raised fountains, churches, and palaces innumerable. And that was the end of all, for since then Rome has little by little withdrawn from life, from the modern world, as though she, who always lived on what she derived from others, were dying of her inability to take anything more from them in order to convert it to her own glory.

"Ah! Bernini, that delightful Bernini!" continued Narcisse with his rapturous air. "He is both powerful and exquisite, his verve always ready, his ingenuity invariably awake, his fecundity full of grace and magnificence. As for their Bramante with his masterpiece, that cold, correct Cancelleria, we'll dub him the Michael Angelo and Raffaelle of architecture and say no more about it. But Bernini, that exquisite Bernini, why, there is more delicacy and refinement in his pretended bad taste than in all the hugeness and perfection of the others! Our own age ought to recognise itself in his art, at once so varied and so deep, so triumphant in its mannerisms, so full of a perturbing solicitude for the artificial and so free from the baseness of reality. Just go to the Villa Borghese to see the group of Apollo and Daphne which Bernini executed when he was eighteen,[1] and in particular see his statue of Santa Teresa in ecstasy at Santa Maria della Vittoria! Ah! that Santa Teresa! It is like heaven opening, with the quiver that only a purely divine enjoyment can set in woman's flesh, the rapture of faith carried to the point of spasm, the creature losing breath and dying of pleasure in the arms of the Divinity! I have spent hours and hours before that work without exhausting the infinite scope of its precious, burning symbolisation."

Narcisse's voice died away, and Pierre, no longer astonished at his covert, unconscious hatred of health, simplicity, and strength, scarcely listened to him. The young priest himself was again becoming absorbed in the idea he had formed of pagan Rome resuscitating in Christian Rome and turning it into Catholic Rome, the new political, sacerdotal, domineering centre of earthly government. Apart from the primitive age of the Catacombs, had Rome ever been Christian? The thoughts that had come to him on the Palatine, in the Appian Way, and in St. Peter's were gathering confirmation. Genius that morning had brought him fresh proof. No doubt the paganism which reappeared in the art of Michael Angelo and Raffaelle was tempered, transformed by the Christian spirit. But did it not still remain the basis? Had not the former master peered across Olympus when snatching his great nudities from the terrible heavens of Jehovah? Did not the ideal figures of Raffaelle reveal the superb, fascinating flesh of Venus beneath the chaste veil of the Virgin? It seemed so to Pierre, and some embarrassment mingled with his despondency, for all those beautiful forms glorifying the ardent passions of life, were in opposition to his dream of rejuvenated Christianity giving peace to the world and reviving the simplicity and purity of the early ages.

All at once he was surprised to hear Narcisse, by what transition he could not tell, speaking to him of the daily life of Leo XIII. "Yes, my dear Abbe, at eighty-four[2] the Holy Father shows the activity of a young man and leads a life of determination and hard work such as neither you nor I would care for! At six o'clock he is already up, says his mass in his private chapel, and drinks a little milk for breakfast. Then, from eight o'clock till noon, there is a ceaseless procession of cardinals and prelates, all the affairs of the congregations passing under his eyes, and none could be more numerous or intricate. At noon the public and collective audiences usually begin. At two he dines. Then comes the siesta which he has well earned, or else a promenade in the gardens until six o'clock. The private audiences then sometimes keep him for an hour or two. He sups at nine and scarcely eats, lives on nothing, in fact, and is always alone at his little table. What do you think, eh, of the etiquette which compels him to such loneliness? There you have a man who for eighteen years has never had a guest at his table, who day by day sits all alone in his grandeur! And as soon as ten o'clock strikes, after saying the Rosary with his familiars, he shuts himself up in his room. But, although he may go to bed, he sleeps very little; he is frequently troubled by in-

---

[1] There is also at the Villa Borghese Bernini's Anchises carried by Aeneas, which he sculptured when only sixteen. No doubt his faults were many; but it was his misfortune to belong to a decadent period.—Trans.

[2] The reader should remember that the period selected for this narrative is the year 1894. Leo XIII was born in 1810.—Trans.

somnia, and gets up and sends for a secretary to dictate memoranda or letters to him. When any interesting matter requires his attention he gives himself up to it heart and soul, never letting it escape his thoughts. And his life, his health, lies in all this. His mind is always busy; his will and strength must always be exerting themselves. You may know that he long cultivated Latin verse with affection; and I believe that in his days of struggle he had a passion for journalism, inspired the articles of the newspapers he subsidised, and even dictated some of them when his most cherished ideas were in question."

Silence fell. At every moment Narcisse craned his neck to see if the little papal *cortege* were not emerging from the Gallery of the Tapestries to pass them on its way to the gardens. "You are perhaps aware," he resumed, "that his Holiness is brought down on a low chair which is small enough to pass through every doorway. It's quite a journey, more than a mile, through the *loggie*, the *stanze* of Raffaelle, the painting and sculpture galleries, not to mention the numerous staircases, before he reaches the gardens, where a pair-horse carriage awaits him. It's quite fine this evening, so he will surely come. We must have a little patience."

Whilst Narcisse was giving these particulars Pierre again sank into a reverie and saw the whole extraordinary history pass before him. First came the worldly, ostentatious popes of the Renascence, those who resuscitated antiquity with so much passion and dreamt of draping the Holy See with the purple of empire once more. There was Paul II, the magnificent Venetian who built the Palazzo di Venezia; Sixtus IV, to whom one owes the Sixtine Chapel; and Julius II and Leo X, who made Rome a city of theatrical pomp, prodigious festivities, tournaments, ballets, hunts, masquerades, and banquets. At that time the papacy had just rediscovered Olympus amidst the dust of buried ruins, and as though intoxicated by the torrent of life which arose from the ancient soil, it founded the museums, thus reviving the superb temples of the pagan age, and restoring them to the cult of universal admiration. Never had the Church been in such peril of death, for if the Christ was still honoured at St. Peter's, Jupiter and all the other gods and goddesses, with their beauteous, triumphant flesh, were enthroned in the halls of the Vatican. Then, however, another vision passed before Pierre, one of the modern popes prior to the Italian occupation—notably Pius IX, who, whilst yet free, often went into his good city of Rome. His huge red and gold coach was drawn by six horses, surrounded by Swiss Guards and followed by Noble Guards; but now and again he would alight in the Corso, and continue his promenade on foot, and then the mounted men of the escort galloped forward to give warning and stop the traffic. The carriages drew up, the gentlemen had to alight and kneel on the pavement, whilst the ladies simply rose and devoutly inclined their heads, as the Holy Father, attended by his Court, slowly wended his way to the Piazza del Popolo, smiling and blessing at every step. And now had come Leo XIII, the voluntary prisoner, shut up in the Vatican for eighteen years, and he, behind the high, silent walls, in the unknown sphere where each of his days flowed by so quietly, had acquired a more exalted majesty, instinct with sacred and redoubtable mysteriousness.

Ah! that Pope whom you no longer meet or see, that Pope hidden from the common of mankind like some terrible divinity whom the priests alone dare to approach! It is in that sumptuous Vatican which his forerunners of the Renascence built and adorned for giant festivities that he has secluded himself; it is there he lives, far from the crowd, in prison with the handsome men and the lovely women of Michael Angelo and Raffaelle, with the gods and goddesses of marble, with the whole of resplendent Olympus celebrating around him the religion of life and light. With him the entire Papacy is there steeped in paganism. What a spectacle when the slender, weak old man, all soul, so purely white, passes along the galleries of the Museum of Antiquities on his way to the gardens. Right and left the statues behold him pass with all their bare flesh. There is Jupiter, there is Apollo, there is Venus the *dominatrix*, there is Pan, the universal god in whose laugh the joys of earth ring out. Nereids bathe in transparent water. Bacchantes roll, unveiled, in the warm grass. Centaurs gallop by carrying lovely girls, faint with rapture, on their steaming haunches. Ariadne is surprised by Bacchus, Ganymede fondles the eagle, Adonis fires youth and maiden with his flame. And on and on passes the weak, white old man, swaying on his low chair, amidst that splendid triumph, that display and glorification of the flesh, which shouts aloud the omnipotence of Nature, of everlasting matter! Since they have found it again, exhumed it, and honoured it, that it is which once more reigns there imperishable; and in vain have they set vine leaves on the statues, even as they have swathed the huge figures of Michael Angelo; sex still flares on all sides, life overflows, its germs course in torrents through the veins of the world. Near by, in that Vatican library of incomparable wealth, where all human science lies slumbering, there lurks a yet more terrible danger—the danger of an explosion which would sweep away everything, Vatican and St. Peter's also, if one day the books in their turn were to awake and speak aloud as speak the beauty of Venus and the manliness of Apollo. But the white, diaphanous old man seems neither to see nor to hear, and the huge heads of Jupiter, the trunks of Hercules, the equivocal statues of Antinous continue to watch him as he passes on!

However, Narcisse had become impatient, and, going in search of an attendant, he learnt from him that his Holiness had already gone down. To shorten the distance, indeed, the *cortege* often passes along a kind of open gallery leading towards the Mint. "Well, let us go down as well," said Narcisse to Pierre; "I will try to show you the gardens."

Down below, in the vestibule, a door of which opened on to a broad path, he spoke to another attendant, a former pontifical soldier whom he personally knew. The man at once let him pass with Pierre, but was unable to tell him whether Monsignor Gamba del Zoppo had accompanied his Holiness that day.

"No matter," resumed Narcisse when he and his companion were alone in the path; "I don't despair of meeting him—and these, you see, are the famous gardens of the Vatican."

They are very extensive grounds, and the Pope can go quite two and a half miles by passing along the paths of the wood, the vineyard, and the kitchen garden. Occupying the plateau of the Vatican hill, which the medieval wall of Leo IV still girdles, the gardens are separated from the neighbouring valleys as by a fortified rampart. The wall formerly stretched to the castle of Sant' Angelo, thereby forming what was known as the Leonine City. No inquisitive eyes can peer into the grounds excepting from the dome of St. Peter's, which casts its huge shadow over them during the hot summer weather. They are, too, quite a little world, which each pope has taken pleasure in embellishing. There is a large parterre with lawns of geometrical patterns, planted with handsome palms and adorned with lemon and orange trees in pots; there is a less formal, a shadier garden, where, amidst deep plantations of yoke-elms, you find Giovanni Vesanzio's fountain, the Aquilone, and Pius IV's old Casino; then, too, there are the woods with their superb evergreen oaks, their thickets of plane-trees, acacias, and pines, intersected by broad avenues, which are delightfully pleasant for leisurely strolls; and finally, on turning to the left, beyond other clumps of trees, come the kitchen garden and the vineyard, the last well tended.

Whilst walking through the wood Narcisse told Pierre of the life led by the Holy Father in these gardens. He strolls in them every second day when the weather allows. Formerly the popes left the Vatican for the Quirinal, which is cooler and healthier, as soon as May arrived; and spent the dog days at Castle Gandolfo on the margins of the Lake of Albano. But nowadays the only summer residence possessed by his Holiness is a virtually intact tower of the old rampart of Leo IV. He here spends the hottest days, and has even erected a sort of pavilion beside it for the accommodation of his suite. Narcisse, like one at home, went in and secured permission for Pierre to glance at the one room occupied by the Pope, a spacious round chamber with semispherical ceiling, on which are painted the heavens with symbolical figures of the constellations; one of the latter, the lion, having two stars for eyes—stars which a system of lighting causes to sparkle during the night. The walls of the tower are so thick that after blocking up a window, a kind of room, for the accommodation of a couch, has been contrived in the embrasure. Beside this couch the only furniture is a large work-table, a dining-table with flaps, and a large regal arm-chair, a mass of gilding, one of the gifts of the Pope's episcopal jubilee. And you dream of the days of solitude and perfect silence, spent in that low donjon hall, where the coolness of a tomb prevails whilst the heavy suns of August are scorching overpowered Rome.

An astronomical observatory has been installed in another tower, surmounted by a little white cupola, which you espy amidst the greenery; and under the trees there is also a Swiss chalet, where Leo XIII is fond of resting. He sometimes goes on foot to the kitchen garden, and takes much interest in the vineyard, visiting it to see if the grapes are ripening and if the vintage will be a good one. What most astonished Pierre, however, was to learn that the Holy Father had been very fond of "sport" before age had weakened him. He was indeed passionately addicted to bird snaring. Broad-meshed nets were hung on either side of a path on the fringe of a plantation, and in the middle of the path were placed cages containing the decoys, whose songs soon attracted all the birds of the neighbourhood—red-breasts, white-throats, black-caps, nightingales, fig-peckers of all sorts. And when a numerous company of them was gathered together Leo XIII, seated out of sight and watching, would suddenly clap his hands and startle the birds, which flew up and were caught by the wings in the meshes of the nets. All that then remained to be done was to take them out of the nets and stifle them by a touch of the thumb. Roast fig-peckers are delicious.[1]

As Pierre came back through the wood he had another surprise. He suddenly lighted on a "Grotto of Lourdes," a miniature imitation of the original, built of rocks and blocks of cement. And such was his emotion at the sight that he could not conceal it. "It's true, then!" said he. "I was told of it, but I thought that the Holy Father was of loftier mind—free from all such base superstitions!"

---

[1] Perhaps so; but what a delightful pastime for the Vicar of the Divinity!—Trans.

"Oh!" replied Narcisse, "I fancy that the grotto dates from Pius IX, who evinced especial gratitude to our Lady of Lourdes. At all events, it must be a gift, and Leo XIII simply keeps it in repair."

For a few moments Pierre remained motionless and silent before that imitation grotto, that childish plaything. Some zealously devout visitors had left their visiting cards in the cracks of the cement-work! For his part, he felt very sad, and followed his companion with bowed head, lamenting the wretched idiocy of the world. Then, on emerging from the wood, on again reaching the parterre, he raised his eyes.

Ah! how exquisite in spite of everything was that decline of a lovely day, and what a victorious charm ascended from the soil in that part of the gardens. There, in front of that bare, noble, burning parterre, far more than under the languishing foliage of the wood or among the fruitful vines, Pierre realised the strength of Nature. Above the grass growing meagrely over the compartments of geometrical pattern which the pathways traced there were barely a few low shrubs, dwarf roses, aloes, rare tufts of withering flowers. Some green bushes still described the escutcheon of Pius IX in accordance with the strange taste of former times. And amidst the warm silence one only heard the faint crystalline murmur of the water trickling from the basin of the central fountain. But all Rome, its ardent heavens, sovereign grace, and conquering voluptuousness, seemed with their own soul to animate this vast rectangular patch of decorative gardening, this mosaic of verdure, which in its semi-abandonment and scorched decay assumed an aspect of melancholy pride, instinct with the ever returning quiver of a passion of fire that could not die. Some antique vases and statues, whitely nude under the setting sun, skirted the parterres. And above the aroma of eucalyptus and of pine, stronger even than that of the ripening oranges, there rose the odour of the large, bitter box-shrubs, so laden with pungent life that it disturbed one as one passed as if indeed it were the very scent of the fecundity of that ancient soil saturated with the dust of generations.

"It's very strange that we have not met his Holiness," exclaimed Narcisse. "Perhaps his carriage took the other path through the wood while we were in the tower."

Then, reverting to Monsignor Gamba del Zoppo, the *attache* explained that the functions of *Copiere*, or papal cup-bearer, which his cousin should have discharged as one of the four *Camerieri segreti partecipanti* had become purely honorary since the dinners offered to diplomatists or in honour of newly consecrated bishops had been given by the Cardinal Secretary of State. Monsignor Gamba, whose cowardice and nullity were legendary, seemed therefore to have no other *role* than that of enlivening Leo XIII, whose favour he had won by his incessant flattery and the anecdotes which he was ever relating about both the black and the white worlds. Indeed this fat, amiable man, who could even be obliging when his interests were not in question, was a perfect newspaper, brimful of tittle-tattle, disdaining no item of gossip whatever, even if it came from the kitchens. And thus he was quietly marching towards the cardinalate, certain of obtaining the hat without other exertion than that of bringing a budget of gossip to beguile the pleasant hours of the promenade. And Heaven knew that he was always able to garner an abundant harvest of news in that closed Vatican swarming with prelates of every kind, in that womanless pontifical family of old begowned bachelors, all secretly exercised by vast ambitions, covert and revolting rivalries, and ferocious hatreds, which, it is said, are still sometimes carried as far as the good old poison of ancient days.

All at once Narcisse stopped. "Ah!" he exclaimed, "I was certain of it. There's the Holy Father! But we are not in luck. He won't even see us; he is about to get into his carriage again."

As he spoke a carriage drew up at the verge of the wood, and a little *cortege* emerging from a narrow path, went towards it.

Pierre felt as if he had received a great blow in the heart. Motionless beside his companion, and half hidden by a lofty vase containing a lemon-tree, it was only from a distance that he was able to see the white old man, looking so frail and slender in the wavy folds of his white cassock, and walking so very slowly with short, gliding steps. The young priest could scarcely distinguish the emaciated face of old diaphanous ivory, emphasised by a large nose which jutted out above thin lips. However, the Pontiff's black eyes were glittering with an inquisitive smile, while his right ear was inclined towards Monsignor Gamba del Zoppo, who was doubtless finishing some story at once rich and short, flowery and dignified. And on the left walked a Noble Guard; and two other prelates followed.

It was but a familiar apparition; Leo XIII was already climbing into the closed carriage. And Pierre, in the midst of that large, odoriferous, burning garden, again experienced the singular emotion which had come upon him in the Gallery of the Candelabra while he was picturing the Pope on his way between the Apollos and Venuses radiant in their triumphant nudity. There, however, it was only pagan art which had celebrated the eternity of life, the superb, almighty powers of Nature. But here he had beheld the Pontiff steeped in Nature itself, in Nature clad in the most lovely, most voluptuous, most passionate guise. Ah! that Pope, that old man strolling with his Divinity of grief, humility, and renunciation along the paths of those gardens of love, in the languid evenings of the hot summer days, beneath the caressing scents of pine and eucalyptus, ripe oranges, and tall, acrid box-shrubs! The whole atmosphere around him proclaimed the powers of the great god Pan. How pleasant was the thought of living there, amidst that magnificence of heaven and of earth, of loving the beauty of woman and of rejoicing in the fruitfulness of all! And suddenly the decisive truth burst forth that from a land of such joy and light it was only possible for a temporal religion of conquest and political domination to rise; not the mystical, painfraught religion of the North—the religion of the soul!

However, Narcisse led the young priest away, telling him other anecdotes as they went—anecdotes of the occasional *bonhomie* of Leo XIII, who would stop to chat with the gardeners, and question them about the health of the trees and the sale of the oranges. And he also mentioned the Pope's former passion for a pair of gazelles, sent him from Africa, two graceful creatures which he had been fond of caressing, and at whose death he had shed tears. But Pierre no longer listened. When they found themselves on the Piazza of St. Peter's, he turned round and gazed at the Vatican once more.

His eyes had fallen on the gate of bronze, and he remembered having wondered that morning what there might be behind these metal panels ornamented with big nails. And he did not yet dare to answer the question, and decide if the new nations thirsting for fraternity and justice would really find there the religion necessary for the democracies of to-morrow; for he had not been able to probe things, and only carried a first impression away with him. But how keen it was, and how ill it boded for his dreams! A gate of bronze! Yes, a hard, impregnable gate, so completely shutting the

Vatican off from the rest of the world that nothing new had entered the palace for three hundred years. Behind that portal the old centuries, as far as the sixteenth, remained immutable. Time seemed to have stayed its course there for ever; nothing more stirred; the very costumes of the Swiss Guards, the Noble Guards, and the prelates themselves were unchanged; and you found yourself in the world of three hundred years ago, with its etiquette, its costumes, and its ideas. That the popes in a spirit of haughty protest should for five and twenty years have voluntarily shut themselves up in their palace was already regrettable; but this imprisonment of centuries within the past, within the grooves of tradition, was far more serious and dangerous. It was all Catholicism which was thus imprisoned, whose dogmas and sacerdotal organisation were obstinately immobilised. Perhaps, in spite of its apparent flexibility, Catholicism was really unable to yield in anything, under peril of being swept away, and therein lay both its weakness and its strength. And then what a terrible world was there, how great the pride and ambition, how numerous the hatreds and rivalries! And how strange the prison, how singular the company assembled behind the bars—the Crucified by the side of Jupiter Capitolinus, all pagan antiquity fraternising with the Apostles, all the splendours of the Renascence surrounding the pastor of the Gospel who reigns in the name of the humble and the poor!

The sun was sinking, the gentle, luscious sweetness of the Roman evenings was falling from the limpid heavens, and after that splendid day spent with Michael Angelo, Raffaelle, the ancients, and the Pope, in the finest palace of the world, the young priest lingered, distracted, on the Piazza of St. Peter's.

"Well, you must excuse me, my dear Abbe," concluded Narcisse. "But I will now confess to you that I suspect my worthy cousin of a fear that he might compromise himself by meddling in your affair. I shall certainly see him again, but you will do well not to put too much reliance on him."

It was nearly six o'clock when Pierre got back to the Boccanera mansion. As a rule, he passed in all modesty down the lane, and entered by the little side door, a key of which had been given him. But he had that morning received a letter from M. de la Choue, and desired to communicate it to Benedetta. So he ascended the grand staircase, and on reaching the anteroom was surprised to find nobody there. As a rule, whenever the man-servant went out Victorine installed herself in his place and busied herself with some needlework. Her chair was there, and Pierre even noticed some linen which she had left on a little table when probably summoned elsewhere. Then, as the door of the first reception-room was ajar, he at last ventured in. It was almost night there already, the twilight was softly dying away, and all at once the young priest stopped short, fearing to take another step, for, from the room beyond, the large yellow *salon*, there came a murmur of feverish, distracted words, ardent entreaties, fierce panting, a rustling and a shuffling of footsteps. And suddenly Pierre no longer hesitated, urged on despite himself by the conviction that the sounds he heard were those of a struggle, and that some one was hard pressed.

And when he darted into the further room he was stupefied, for Dario was there, no longer showing the degenerate elegance of the last scion of an exhausted race, but maddened by the hot, frantic blood of the Boccaneras which had bubbled up within him. He had clasped Benedetta by the shoulders in a frenzy of passion and was scorching her face with his hot, entreating words: "But since you say, my darling, that it is all over, that your marriage will never be dissolved—oh! why should we be wretched for ever! Love me as you do love me, and let me love you—let me love you!"

But the Contessina, with an indescribable expression of tenderness and suffering on her tearful face, repulsed him with her outstretched arms, she likewise evincing a fierce energy as she repeated: "No, no; I love you, but it must not, it must not be."

At that moment, amidst the roar of his despair, Dario became conscious that some one was entering the room. He turned and gazed at Pierre with an expression of stupefied insanity, scarce able even to recognise him. Then he carried his two hands to his face, to his bloodshot eyes and his cheeks wet with scalding tears, and fled, heaving a terrible, pain-fraught sigh in which baffled passion mingled with grief and repentance.

Benedetta seated herself, breathing hard, her strength and courage wellnigh exhausted. But as Pierre, too much embarrassed to speak, turned towards the door, she addressed him in a calmer voice: "No, no, Monsieur l'Abbe, do not go away—sit down, I pray you; I should like to speak to you for a moment."

He thereupon thought it his duty to account for his sudden entrance, and explained that he had found the door of the first *salon* ajar, and that Victorine was not in the ante-room, though he had seen her work lying on the table there.

"Yes," exclaimed the Contessina, "Victorine ought to have been there; I saw her there but a short time ago. And when my poor Dario lost his head I called her. Why did she not come?" Then, with sudden expansion, leaning towards Pierre, she continued: "Listen, Monsieur l'Abbe, I will tell you what happened, for I don't want you to form too bad an opinion of my poor Dario. It was all in some measure my fault. Last night he asked me for an appointment here in order that we might have a quiet chat, and as I knew that my aunt would be absent at this time to-day I told him to come. It was only natural—wasn't it?—that we should want to see one another and come to an agreement after the grievous news that my marriage will probably never be annulled. We suffer too much, and must form a decision. And so when he came this evening we began to weep and embrace, mingling our tears together. I kissed him again and again, telling him how I adored him, how bitterly grieved I was at being the cause of his sufferings, and how surely I should die of grief at seeing him so unhappy. Ah! no doubt I did wrong; I ought not to have caught him to my heart and embraced him as I did, for it maddened him, Monsieur l'Abbe; he lost his head, and would have made me break my vow to the Blessed Virgin."

She spoke these words in all tranquillity and simplicity, without sign of embarrassment, like a young and beautiful woman who is at once sensible and practical. Then she resumed: "Oh! I know my poor Dario well, but it does not prevent me from loving him; perhaps, indeed, it only makes me love him the more. He looks delicate, perhaps rather sickly, but in truth he is a man of passion. Yes, the old blood of my people bubbles up in him. I know something of it myself, for when I was a child I sometimes had fits of angry passion which left me exhausted on the floor, and even now, when the gusts arise within me, I have to fight against myself and torture myself in order that I may not act madly. But my poor Dario does not know how to suffer. He is like a child whose fancies must be gratified. And yet at bottom he has a good deal of common sense; he waits for me because he knows that the only real happiness lies with the woman who adores him."

As Pierre listened he was able to form a more precise idea of the young prince, of whose character he had hitherto had but a vague perception. Whilst dying of love for his cousin, Dario had ever been a man of pleasure. Though he was no doubt very amiable, the basis of his temperament was none the less egotism. And, in particular, he was unable to endure suffering; he loathed suffering, ugliness, and poverty, whether they affected himself or others. Both his flesh and his soul required gaiety, brilliancy, show, life in the full sunlight. And withal he was exhausted, with no strength left him but for the idle life he led, so incapable of thought and will that the idea of joining the new *regime* had not even occurred to him. Yet he had all the unbounded pride of a Roman; sagacity—a keen, practical perception of the real—was mingled with his indolence; while his inveterate love of woman, more frequently displayed in charm of manner, burst forth at times in attacks of frantic sensuality.

"After all he is a man," concluded Benedetta in a low voice, "and I must not ask impossibilities of him." Then, as Pierre gazed at her, his notions of Italian jealousy quite upset, she exclaimed, aglow with passionate adoration: "No, no. Situated as we are, I am not jealous. I know very well that he will always return to me, and that he will be mine alone whenever I please, whenever it may be possible."

Silence followed; shadows were filling the room, the gilding of the large pier tables faded away, and infinite melancholy fell from the lofty, dim ceiling and the old hangings, yellow like autumn leaves. But soon, by some chance play of the waning light, a painting stood out above the sofa on which the Contessina was seated. It was the portrait of the beautiful young girl with the turban—Cassia Boccanera the forerunner, the *amorosa* and avengeress. Again was Pierre struck by the portrait's resemblance to Benedetta, and, thinking aloud, he resumed: "Passion always proves the stronger; there invariably comes a moment when one succumbs—"

But Benedetta violently interrupted him: "I! I! Ah! you do not know me; I would rather die!" And with extraordinary exaltation, all aglow with love, as if her superstitious faith had fired her passion to ecstasy, she continued: "I have vowed to the Madonna that I will belong to none but the man I love, and to him only when he is my husband. And hitherto I have kept that vow, at the cost of my happiness, and I will keep it still, even if it cost me my life! Yes, we will die, my poor Dario and I, if it be necessary; but the holy Virgin has my vow, and the angels shall not weep in heaven!"

She was all in those words, her nature all simplicity, intricate, inexplicable though it might seem. She was doubtless swayed by that idea of human nobility which Christianity has set in renunciation and purity; a protest, as it were, against eternal matter, against the forces of Nature, the everlasting fruitfulness of life. But there was more than this; she reserved herself, like a divine and priceless gift, to be bestowed on the one being whom her heart had chosen, he who would be her lord and master when God should have united them in marriage. For her everything lay in the blessing of the priest, in the religious solemnisation of matrimony. And thus one understood her long resistance to Prada, whom she did not love, and her despairing, grievous resistance to Dario, whom she did love, but who was not her husband. And how torturing it was for that soul of fire to have to resist her love; how continual was the combat waged by duty in the Virgin's name against the wild, passionate blood of her race! Ignorant, indolent though she might be, she was capable of great fidelity of heart, and, moreover, she was not given to dreaming: love might have its immaterial charms, but she desired it complete.

As Pierre looked at her in the dying twilight he seemed to see and understand her for the first time. The duality of her nature appeared in her somewhat full, fleshy lips, in her big black eyes, which suggested a dark, tempestuous night illumined by flashes of lightning, and in the calm, sensible expression of the rest of her gentle, infantile face. And, withal, behind those eyes of flame, beneath that pure, candid skin, one divined the internal tension of a superstitious, proud, and self-willed woman, who was obstinately intent on reserving herself for her one love. And Pierre could well understand that she should be adored, that she should fill the life of the man she chose with passion, and that to his own eyes she should appear like the younger sister of that lovely, tragic Cassia who, unwilling to survive the blow that had rendered self-bestowal impossible, had flung herself into the Tiber, dragging her brother Ercole and the corpse of her lover Flavio with her.

However, with a gesture of kindly affection Benedetta caught hold of Pierre's hands. "You have been here a fortnight, Monsieur l'Abbe," said she, "and I have come to like you very much, for I feel you to be a friend. If at first you do not understand us, at least pray do not judge us too severely. Ignorant as I may be, I always strive to act for the best, I assure you."

Pierre was greatly touched by her affectionate graciousness, and thanked her whilst for a moment retaining her beautiful hands in his own, for he also was becoming much attached to her. A fresh dream was carrying him off, that of educating her, should he have the time, or, at all events, of not returning home before winning her soul over to his own ideas of future charity and fraternity. Did not that adorable, unoccupied, indolent, ignorant creature, who only knew how to defend her love, personify the Italy of yesterday? The Italy of yesterday, so lovely and so sleepy, instinct with a dying grace, charming one even in her drowsiness, and retaining so much mystery in the fathomless depths of her black, passionate eyes! And what a *role* would be that of awakening her, instructing her, winning her over to truth, making her the rejuvenated Italy of to-morrow such as he had dreamt of! Even in that disastrous marriage with Count Prada he tried to see merely a first attempt at revival which had failed, the modern Italy of the North being over-hasty, too brutal in its eagerness to love and transform that gentle, belated Rome which was yet so superb and indolent. But might he not take up the task? Had he not noticed that his book, after the astonishment of the first perusal, had remained a source of interest and reflection with Benedetta amidst the emptiness of her days given over to grief? What! was it really possible that she might find some appeasement for her own wretchedness by interesting herself in the humble, in the happiness of the poor? Emotion already thrilled her at the idea, and he, quivering at the thought of all the boundless love that was within her and that she might bestow, vowed to himself that he would draw tears of pity from her eyes.

But the night had now almost completely fallen, and Benedetta rose to ask for a lamp. Then, as Pierre was about to take leave, she detained him for another moment in the gloom. He could no longer see her; he only heard her grave voice: "You will not go away with too bad an opinion of us, will you, Monsieur l'Abbe? We love one another, Dario and I, and that is no sin when one behaves as one ought. Ah! yes, I love him, and have loved him for years. I was barely thirteen, he was eighteen, and we already loved one another wildly in those big gardens of the Villa Montefiori which are now all broken up. Ah! what days we spent there, whole afternoons among the trees, hours in secret hiding-places, where we kissed like little angels. When the oranges ripened their perfume intoxicated us. And the large box-plants, ah, *Dio!* how they enveloped us, how their strong, acrid scent made our hearts beat! I can never smell then nowadays without feeling faint!"

A man-servant brought in the lamp, and Pierre ascended to his room. But when half-way up the little staircase he perceived Victorine, who started slightly, as if she had posted herself there to watch his departure from the *salon*. And now, as she followed him up, talking and seeking for information, he suddenly realised what had happened. "Why did you not go to your mistress instead of running off," he asked, "when she called you, while you were sewing in the ante-room?"

At first she tried to feign astonishment and reply that she had heard nothing. But her good-natured, frank face did not know how to lie, and she ended by confessing, with a gay, courageous air. "Well," she said, "it surely wasn't for me to interfere between lovers! Besides, my poor little Benedetta is simply torturing herself to death with those ideas of hers. Why shouldn't they be happy, since they love one another? Life isn't so amusing as some may think. And how bitterly one regrets not having seized hold of happiness when the time for it has gone!"

Once alone in his room, Pierre suddenly staggered, quite overcome. The great box-plants, the great box-plants with their acrid, perturbing perfume! She, Benedetta, like himself, had quivered as she smelt them; and he saw them once more in a vision of the pontifical gardens, the voluptuous gardens of Rome, deserted, glowing under the August sun. And now his whole day crystallised, assumed clear and full significance. It spoke to him of the fruitful awakening, of the eternal protest of Nature and life, Venus and Hercules, whom one may bury for centuries beneath the soil, but who, nevertheless, one day arise from it, and though one may seek to wall them up within the domineering, stubborn, immutable Vatican, reign yet even there, and rule the whole, wide world with sovereign power!

PART III.

VII.

On the following day as Pierre, after a long ramble, once more found himself in front of the Vatican, whither a harassing attraction ever led him, he again encountered Monsignor Nani. It was a Wednesday evening, and the Assessor of the Holy Office had just come from his weekly audience with the Pope, whom he had acquainted with the proceedings of the Congregation at its meeting that morning. "What a fortunate chance, my dear sir," said he; "I was thinking of you. Would you like to see his Holiness in public while you are waiting for a private audience?"

Nani had put on his pleasant expression of smiling civility, beneath which one would barely detect the faint irony of a superior man who knew everything, prepared everything, and could do everything.

"Why, yes, Monsignor," Pierre replied, somewhat astonished by the abruptness of the offer. "Anything of a nature to divert one's mind is welcome when one loses one's time in waiting."

"No, no, you are not losing your time," replied the prelate. "You are looking round you, reflecting, and enlightening yourself. Well, this is the point. You are doubtless aware that the great international pilgrimage of the Peter's Pence Fund will arrive in Rome on Friday, and be received on Saturday by his Holiness. On Sunday, moreover, the Holy Father will celebrate mass at the Basilica. Well, I have a few cards left, and here are some very good places for both ceremonies." So saying he produced an elegant little pocketbook bearing a gilt monogram and handed Pierre two cards, one green and the other pink. "If you only knew how people fight for them," he resumed. "You remember that I told you of two French ladies who are consumed by a desire to see his Holiness. Well, I did not like to support their request for an audience in too pressing a way, and they have had to content themselves with cards like these. The fact is, the Holy Father is somewhat fatigued at the present time. I found him looking yellow and feverish just now. But he has so much courage; he nowadays only lives by force of soul." Then Nani's smile came back with its almost imperceptible touch of derision as he resumed: "Impatient ones ought to find a great example in him, my dear son. I heard that Monsignor Gamba del Zoppo had been unable to help you. But you must not be too much distressed on that account. This long delay is assuredly a grace of Providence in order that you may instruct yourself and come to understand certain things which you French priests do not, unfortunately, realise when you arrive in Rome. And perhaps it will prevent you from making certain mistakes. Come, calm yourself, and remember that the course of events is in the hands of God, who, in His sovereign wisdom, fixes the hour for all things."

Thereupon Nani offered Pierre his plump, supple, shapely hand, a hand soft like a woman's but with the grasp of a vice. And afterwards he climbed into his carriage, which was waiting for him.

It so happened that the letter which Pierre had received from Viscount Philibert de la Choue was a long cry of spite and despair in connection with the great international pilgrimage of the Peter's Pence Fund. The Viscount wrote from his bed, to which he was confined by a very severe attack of gout, and his grief at being unable to come to Rome was the greater as the President of the Committee, who would naturally present the pilgrims to the Pope, happened to be Baron de Fouras, one of his most bitter adversaries of the old conservative, Catholic party. M. de la Choue felt certain that the Baron would profit by his opportunity to win the Pope over to the theory of free corporations; whereas he, the Viscount, believed that the salvation of Catholicism and the world could only be worked by a system in which the corporations should be closed and obligatory. And so he urged Pierre to exert himself with such cardinals as were favourable, to secure an audience with the Holy Father whatever the obstacles, and to remain in Rome until he should have secured the Pontiff's approbation, which alone could decide the victory. The letter further mentioned that the pilgrimage would be made up of a number of groups headed by bishops and other ecclesiastical dignitaries, and would comprise three thousand people from France, Belgium, Spain, Austria, and even Germany. Two thousand of these would come from France alone. An international committee had assembled in Paris to organise everything and select the pilgrims, which last had proved a delicate task, as a representative gathering had been desired, a commingling of members of the aristocracy, sisterhood of middle-class ladies, and associations of the working classes, among whom all social differences would be forgotten in the union of a common faith. And the Viscount added that the pilgrimage would bring the Pope a large sum of money, and had settled the date of its arrival in the Eternal City in such wise that it would figure as a solemn protest of the Catholic world against the festivities of September 20, by which the Quirinal had just celebrated the anniversary of the occupation of Rome.

The reception of the pilgrimage being fixed for noon, Pierre in all simplicity thought that he would be sufficiently early if he reached St. Peter's at eleven. The function was to take place in the Hall of Beatifications, which is a large and handsome apartment over the portico, and has been arranged as a chapel since 1890. One of its windows opens on to the central balcony, whence the popes formerly blessed the people, the city, and the world. To reach the apartment you pass through two other halls of audience, the Sala Regia and Sala Ducale, and when Pierre wished to gain the place to which his green card entitled him he found both those rooms so extremely crowded that he could only elbow his way forward with the greatest difficulty. For an hour already the three or four thousand people assembled there had been stifling, full of growing emotion and feverishness. At last the young priest managed to reach the threshold of the third hall, but was so discouraged at sight of the extraordinary multitude of heads before him that he did not attempt to go any further.

The apartment, which he could survey at a glance by rising on tip-toe, appeared to him to be very rich of aspect, with walls gilded and painted under a severe and lofty ceiling. On a low platform, where the altar usually stood, facing the entry, the pontifical throne had now been set: a large arm-chair upholstered in red velvet with glittering golden back and arms; whilst the hangings of the *baldacchino*, also of red velvet, fell behind and spread out on either side like a pair of huge purple wings. However, what more particularly interested Pierre was the wildly passionate concourse of people whose hearts he could almost hear beating and whose eyes sought to beguile their feverish impatience by contemplating and adoring the empty throne. As if it had been some golden monstrance which the Divinity in person would soon deign to occupy, that throne dazzled them, disturbed them, filled them all with devout rapture. Among the throng were workmen rigged out in their Sunday best, with clear childish eyes and rough ecstatic faces; ladies of the upper classes wearing black, as the regulations required, and looking intensely pale from the sacred awe which mingled with their excessive desire; and gentlemen in evening dress, who appeared quite glorious, inflated with the conviction that they were saving both the Church and the nations. One cluster of dress-coats assembled near the throne, was particularly noticeable; it comprised the members of the International Committee, headed by Baron de Fouras, a very tall, stout, fair man of fifty, who bestirred and exerted himself and issued orders like some commander on the morning of a decisive victory. Then, amidst the general mass of grey, neutral hue, there gleamed the violet silk of some bishop's cassock, for each pastor had desired to remain with his flock; whilst members of various religious orders, superiors in brown, black, and white habits, rose up above all others with lofty bearded or shaven heads. Right and left drooped banners which associations and congregations had brought to present to the Pope. And the sea of pilgrims ever waved and surged with a growing clamour: so much impatient love being exhaled by those perspiring faces, burning eyes, and hungry mouths that the atmosphere, reeking with the odour of the throng, seemed thickened and darkened.

All at once, however, Pierre perceived Monsignor Nani standing near the throne and beckoning him to approach; and although the young priest replied by a modest gesture, implying that he preferred to remain where he was, the prelate insisted and even sent an usher to make way for him. Directly the usher had led him forward, Nani inquired: "Why did you not come to take your place? Your card entitled you to be here, on the left of the throne."

"The truth is," answered the priest, "I did not like to disturb so many people. Besides, this is an undue honour for me."

"No, no; I gave you that place in order that you should occupy it. I want you to be in the first rank, so that you may see everything of the ceremony."

Pierre could not do otherwise than thank him. Then, on looking round, he saw that several cardinals and many other prelates were likewise waiting on either side of the throne. But it was in vain that he sought Cardinal Boccanera, who only came to St. Peter's and the Vatican on the days when his functions required his presence there. However, he recognised Cardinal Sanguinetti, who, broad and sturdy and red of face, was talking in a loud voice to Baron de Fouras. And Nani, with his obliging air, stepped up again to point out two other Eminences who were high and mighty personages—the Cardinal Vicar, a short, fat man, with a feverish countenance scorched by ambition, and the Cardinal Secretary, who was robust and bony, fashioned as with a hatchet, suggesting a romantic type of Sicilian bandit, who, to other courses, had preferred the discreet, smiling diplomacy of the Church. A few steps further on, and quite alone, the Grand Penitentiary, silent and seemingly suffering, showed his grey, lean, ascetic profile.

Noon had struck. There was a false alert, a burst of emotion, which swept in like a wave from the other halls. But it was merely the ushers opening a passage for the *cortege*. Then, all at once, acclamations arose in the first hall, gathered volume, and drew nearer. This time it was the *cortege* itself. First came a detachment of the Swiss Guard in undress, headed by a sergeant; then a party of chair-bearers in red; and next the domestic prelates, including the four *Camerieri segreti partecipanti*. And finally, between two rows of Noble Guards, in semi-gala uniforms, walked the Holy Father, alone, smiling a pale smile, and slowly blessing the pilgrims on either hand. In his wake the clamour which had risen in the other apartments swept into the Hall of Beatifications with the violence of delirious love; and, under his slender, white, benedictive hand, all those distracted creatures fell upon both knees, nought remaining but the prostration of a devout multitude, overwhelmed, as it were, by the apparition of its god.

Quivering, carried away, Pierre had knelt like the others. Ah! that omnipotence, that irresistible contagion of faith, of the redoubtable current from the spheres beyond, increased tenfold by a *scenario* and a pomp of sovereign grandeur! Profound silence fell when Leo XIII was seated on the throne surrounded by the cardinals and his court; and then the ceremony proceeded according to rite and usage. First a bishop spoke, kneeling and laying the homage of the faithful of all Christendom at his Holiness's feet. The President of the Committee, Baron de Fouras, followed, remaining erect whilst he read a long address in which he introduced the pilgrimage and explained its motive, investing it with all the gravity of a political and religious protest. This stout man had a shrill and piercing voice, and his words jarred like the grating of a gimlet as he proclaimed the grief of the Catholic world at the spoliation which the Holy See had endured for a quarter of a century, and the desire of all the nations there represented by the pilgrims to console the supreme and venerated Head of the Church by bringing him the offerings of rich and poor, even to the mites of the humblest, in order that the Papacy might retain the pride of independence and be able to treat its enemies with contempt. And he also spoke of France, deplored her errors, predicted her return to healthy traditions, and gave it to be understood that she remained in spite of everything the most opulent and generous of the Christian nations, the donor whose gold and presents flowed into Rome in a never ending stream. At last Leo XIII arose to reply to the bishop and the baron. His voice was full, with a strong nasal twang, and surprised one coming from a man so slight of build. In a few sentences he expressed his gratitude, saying how touched he was by the devotion of the nations to the Holy See. Although the times might be bad, the final triumph could not be delayed much longer. There were evident signs that mankind was returning to faith, and that iniquity would soon cease under the universal dominion of the Christ. As for France, was she not the eldest daughter of the Church, and had she not given too many proofs of her affection for the Holy See for the latter ever to cease loving her? Then, raising his arm, he bestowed on all the pilgrims present, on the societies and enterprises they represented, on their families and friends, on France, on all the nations of the Catholic world, his apostolic benediction, in gratitude for the precious help which they sent him. And whilst he was again seating himself applause burst forth, frantic salvoes of applause lasting for ten minutes and mingling with vivats and inarticulate cries—a passionate, tempestuous outburst, which made the very building shake.

Amidst this blast of frantic adoration Pierre gazed at Leo XIII, now again motionless on his throne. With the papal cap on his head and the red cape edged with ermine about his shoulders, he retained in his long white cassock the rigid, sacerdotal attitude of an idol venerated by two hundred and fifty millions of Christians. Against the purple background of the hangings of the *baldacchino*, between the wing-like drapery on either side, enclosing, as it were, a brasier of glory, he assumed real majesty of aspect. He was no longer the feeble old man with the slow, jerky walk and the slender, scraggy neck of a poor ailing bird. The simious ugliness of his face, the largeness of his nose, the long slit of his mouth, the hugeness of his ears, the conflicting jumble of his withered features disappeared. In that waxen countenance you only distinguished the admirable, dark, deep eyes, beaming with eternal youth, with extraordinary intelligence and penetration. And then there was a resolute bracing of his entire person, a consciousness of the eternity which he represented, a regal nobility, born of the very circumstance that he was now but a mere breath, a soul set in so pellucid a body of ivory that it became visible as though it were already freed from the bonds of earth. And Pierre realised what such a man—the Sovereign Pontiff, the king obeyed by two hundred and fifty millions of subjects—must be for the devout and dolent creatures who came to adore him from so far, and who fell at his feet awestruck by the splendour of the powers incarnate in him. Behind him, amidst the purple of the hangings, what a gleam was suddenly afforded of the spheres beyond, what an Infinite of ideality and blinding glory! So many centuries of history from the Apostle Peter downward, so much strength and genius, so many struggles and triumphs to be summed up in one being, the Elect, the Unique, the Superhuman! And what a miracle, incessantly renewed, was that of Heaven deigning to descend into human flesh, of the Deity fixing His abode in His chosen servant, whom He consecrated above and beyond all others, endowing him with all power and all science! What sacred perturbation, what emotion fraught with distracted love might one not feel at the thought of the Deity being ever there in the depths of that man's eyes, speaking with his voice and emanating from his hand each time that he raised it to bless! Could one imagine the exorbitant absoluteness of that sovereign who was infallible, who disposed of the totality of authority in this world and of salvation in the next! At all events, how well one understood that souls consumed by a craving for faith should fly towards him, that those who at last found the certainty they had so ardently sought should seek annihilation in him, the consolation of self-bestowal and disappearance within the Deity Himself.

Meantime, the ceremony was drawing to an end; Baron de Fouras was now presenting the members of the committee and a few other persons of importance. There was a slow procession with trembling genuflections and much greedy kissing of the papal ring and slipper. Then the banners were offered, and Pierre felt a pang on seeing that the finest and richest of them was one of Lourdes, an offering no doubt from the Fathers of the Immaculate Conception. On one side of the white, gold-bordered silk Our Lady of Lourdes was painted, while on the other appeared a portrait of Leo XIII. Pierre saw the Pope smile at the presentment of himself, and was greatly grieved thereat, as though, indeed, his whole dream of an intellectual, evangelical Pope, disentangled from all low superstition, were crumbling away. And just then his eyes met those of Nani, who from the outset had been watching him with the inquisitive air of a man who is making an experiment.

"That banner is superb, isn't it?" said Nani, drawing near. "How it must please his Holiness to be so nicely painted in company with so pretty a virgin." And as the young priest, turning pale, did not reply, the prelate added, with an air of devout enjoyment: "We are very fond of Lourdes in Rome; that story of Bernadette is so delightful."

However, the scene which followed was so extraordinary that for a long time Pierre remained overcome by it. He had beheld never-to-be-forgotten idolatry at Lourdes, incidents of naive faith and frantic religious passion which yet made him quiver with alarm and grief. But the crowds rushing on the grotto, the sick dying of divine love before the Virgin's statue, the multitudes delirious with the contagion of the miraculous—nothing of all that gave an idea of the blast of madness which suddenly inflamed the pilgrims at the feet of the Pope. Some bishops, superiors of religious orders, and other delegates of various kinds had stepped forward to deposit near the throne the offerings which they brought from the whole Catholic world, the universal "collection" of St. Peter's Pence. It was the voluntary tribute of the nations to their sovereign: silver, gold, and bank notes in purses, bags, and cases. Ladies came and fell on their knees to offer silk and velvet alms-bags which they themselves had embroidered. Others had caused the note cases which they tendered to be adorned with the monogram of Leo XIII in diamonds. And at one moment the enthusiasm became so intense that several women stripped themselves of their adornments, flung their own purses on to the platform, and emptied their pockets even to the very coppers they had about them. One lady, tall and slender, very beautiful and very dark, wrenched her watch from about her neck, pulled off her rings, and threw everything upon the carpet. Had it been possible, they would have torn away their flesh to pluck out their love-burnt hearts and fling them likewise to the demi-god. They would even have flung themselves, have given themselves without reserve. It was a rain of presents, an explosion of the passion which impels one to strip oneself for the object of one's cult, happy at having nothing of one's own that shall not belong to him. And meantime the clamour grew, vivats and shrill cries of adoration arose amidst pushing and jostling of increased violence, one and all yielding to the irresistible desire to kiss the idol!

But a signal was given, and Leo XIII made haste to quit the throne and take his place in the *cortege* in order to return to his apartments. The Swiss Guards energetically thrust back the throng, seeking to open a way through the three halls. But at sight of his Holiness's departure a lamentation of despair arose and spread, as if heaven had suddenly closed again and shut out those who had not yet been able to approach. What a frightful disappointment—to have beheld the living manifestation of the Deity and to see it disappear before gaining salvation by just touching it! So terrible became the scramble, so extraordinary the confusion, that the Swiss Guards were swept away. And ladies were seen to dart after the Pope, to drag themselves on all fours over the marble slabs and kiss his footprints and lap up the dust of his steps! The tall dark lady suddenly fell at the edge of the platform, raised a loud shriek, and fainted; and two gentlemen of the committee had to hold her so that she might not do herself an injury in the convulsions of the hysterical fit which had come upon her. Another, a plump blonde, was wildly, desperately kissing one of the golden arms of the throne-chair, on which the old man's poor, bony elbow had just rested. And others, on seeing her, came to dispute possession, seized both arms, gilding and velvet, and pressed their mouths to wood-work or upholstery, their bodies meanwhile shaking with their sobs. Force had to be employed in order to drag them away.

When it was all over Pierre went off, emerging as it were from a painful dream, sick at heart, and with his mind revolting. And again he encountered Nani's glance, which never left him. "It was a superb ceremony, was it not?" said the prelate. "It consoles one for many iniquities."

"Yes, no doubt; but what idolatry!" the young priest murmured despite himself.

Nani, however, merely smiled, as if he had not heard the last word. At that same moment the two French ladies whom he had provided with tickets came up to thank him, and. Pierre was surprised to recognise the mother and daughter whom he had met at the Catacombs. Charming, bright, and healthy as they were, their enthusiasm was only for the spectacle: they declared that they were well pleased at having seen it—that it was really astonishing, unique.

As the crowd slowly withdrew Pierre all at once felt a tap on his shoulder, and, on turning his head, perceived Narcisse Habert, who also was very enthusiastic. "I made signs to you, my dear Abbe," said he, "but you didn't see me. Ah! how superb was the expression of that dark woman who fell rigid beside the platform with her arms outstretched. She reminded me of a masterpiece of one of the primitives, Cimabue, Giotto, or Fra Angelico. And the others, those who devoured the chair arms with their kisses, what suavity, beauty, and love! I never miss these ceremonies: there are always some fine scenes, perfect pictures, in which souls reveal themselves."

The long stream of pilgrims slowly descended the stairs, and Pierre, followed by Nani and Narcisse, who had begun to chat, tried to bring the ideas which were tumultuously throbbing in his brain into something like order. There was certainly grandeur and beauty in that Pope who had shut himself up in his Vatican, and who, the more he became a purely moral, spiritual authority, freed from all terrestrial cares, had grown in the adoration and awe of mankind. Such a flight into the ideal deeply stirred Pierre, whose dream of rejuvenated Christianity rested on the idea of the supreme Head of the Church exercising only a purified, spiritual authority. He had just seen what an increase of majesty and power was in that way gained by the Supreme Pontiff of the spheres beyond, at whose feet the women fainted, and behind whom they beheld a vision of the Deity. But at the same moment the pecuniary side of the question had risen before him and spoilt his joy. If the enforced relinquishment of the temporal power had exalted the Pope by freeing him from the worries of a petty sovereignty which was ever threatened, the need of money still remained like a chain about his feet tying him to earth. As he could not accept the proffered subvention of the Italian Government,[1] there was certainly in the Peter's Pence a means of placing the Holy See above all material cares, provided, however, that this Peter's Pence were really the Catholic *sou*, the mite of each believer, levied on his daily income and sent direct to Rome. Such a voluntary tribute paid by the flock to its pastor would, moreover, suffice for the wants of the Church if each of the 250,000,000 of Catholics gave his or

[1] 110,000 pounds per annum. It has never been accepted, and the accumulations lapse to the Government every five years, and cannot afterwards be recovered.—Trans.

her *sou* every week. In this wise the Pope, indebted to each and all of his children, would be indebted to none in particular. A *sou* was so little and so easy to give, and there was also something so touching about the idea. But, unhappily, things were not worked in that way; the great majority of Catholics gave nothing whatever, while the rich ones sent large sums from motives of political passion; and a particular objection was that the gifts were centralised in the hands of certain bishops and religious orders, so that these became ostensibly the benefactors of the papacy, the indispensable cashiers from whom it drew the sinews of life. The lowly and humble whose mites filled the collection boxes were, so to say, suppressed, and the Pope became dependent on the intermediaries, and was compelled to act cautiously with them, listen to their remonstrances, and even at times obey their passions, lest the stream of gifts should suddenly dry up. And so, although he was disburdened of the dead weight of the temporal power, he was not free; but remained the tributary of his clergy, with interests and appetites around him which he must needs satisfy. And Pierre remembered the "Grotto of Lourdes" in the Vatican gardens, and the banner which he had just seen, and he knew that the Lourdes fathers levied 200,000 francs a year on their receipts to send them as a present to the Holy Father. Was not that the chief reason of their great power? He quivered, and suddenly became conscious that, do what he might, he would be defeated, and his book would be condemned.

At last, as he was coming out on to the Piazza of St. Peter's, he heard Narcisse asking Monsignor Nani: "Indeed! Do you really think that to-day's gifts exceeded that figure?"

"Yes, more than three millions,[1] I'm convinced of it," the prelate replied.

For a moment the three men halted under the right-hand colonnade and gazed at the vast, sunlit piazza where the pilgrims were spreading out like little black specks hurrying hither and thither—an ant-hill, as it were, in revolution.

Three millions! The words had rung in Pierre's ears. And, raising his head, he gazed at the Vatican, all golden in the sunlight against the expanse of blue sky, as if he wished to penetrate its walls and follow the steps of Leo XIII returning to his apartments. He pictured him laden with those millions, with his weak, slender arms pressed to his breast, carrying the silver, the gold, the bank notes, and even the jewels which the women had flung him. And almost unconsciously the young priest spoke aloud: "What will he do with those millions? Where is he taking them?"

Narcisse and even Nani could not help being amused by this strangely expressed curiosity. It was the young *attache* who replied. "Why, his Holiness is taking them to his room; or, at least, is having them carried there before him. Didn't you see two persons of his suite picking up everything and filling their pockets? And now his Holiness has shut himself up quite alone; and if you could see him you would find him counting and recounting his treasure with cheerful care, ranging the rolls of gold in good order, slipping the bank notes into envelopes in equal quantities, and then putting everything away in hiding-places which are only known to himself."

While his companion was speaking Pierre again raised his eyes to the windows of the Pope's apartments, as if to follow the scene. Moreover, Narcisse gave further ex-

---

[1] All the amounts given on this and the following pages are calculated in francs. The reader will bear in mind that a million francs is equivalent to 40,000 pounds.—Trans.

planations, asserting that the money was put away in a certain article of furniture, standing against the right-hand wall in the Holy Father's bedroom. Some people, he added, also spoke of a writing table or secretaire with deep drawers; and others declared that the money slumbered in some big padlocked trunks stored away in the depths of the alcove, which was very roomy. Of course, on the left side of the passage leading to the Archives there was a large room occupied by a general cashier and a monumental safe; but the funds kept there were simply those of the Patrimony of St. Peter, the administrative receipts of Rome; whereas the Peter's Pence money, the voluntary donations of Christendom, remained in the hands of Leo XIII: he alone knew the exact amount of that fund, and lived alone with its millions, which he disposed of like an absolute master, rendering account to none. And such was his prudence that he never left his room when the servants cleaned and set it in order. At the utmost he would consent to remain on the threshold of the adjoining apartment in order to escape the dust. And whenever he meant to absent himself for a few hours, to go down into the gardens, for instance, he double-locked the doors and carried the keys away with him, never confiding them to another.

At this point Narcisse paused and, turning to Nani, inquired: "Is not that so, Monsignor? These are things known to all Rome."

The prelate, ever smiling and wagging his head without expressing either approval or disapproval, had begun to study on Pierre's face the effect of these curious stories. "No doubt, no doubt," he responded; "so many things are said! I know nothing myself, but you seem to be certain of it all, Monsieur Habert."

"Oh!" resumed the other, "I don't accuse his Holiness of sordid avarice, such as is rumoured. Some fabulous stories are current, stories of coffers full of gold in which the Holy Father is said to plunge his hands for hours at a time; treasures which he has heaped up in corners for the sole pleasure of counting them over and over again. Nevertheless, one may well admit that his Holiness is somewhat fond of money for its own sake, for the pleasure of handling it and setting it in order when he happens to be alone—and after all that is a very excusable mania in an old man who has no other pastime. But I must add that he is yet fonder of money for the social power which it brings, the decisive help which it will give to the Holy See in the future, if the latter desires to triumph."

These words evoked the lofty figure of a wise and prudent Pope, conscious of modern requirements, inclined to utilise the powers of the century in order to conquer it, and for this reason venturing on business and speculation. As it happened, the treasure bequeathed by Pius IX had nearly been lost in a financial disaster, but ever since that time Leo XIII had sought to repair the breach and make the treasure whole again, in order that he might leave it to his successor intact and even enlarged. Economical he certainly was, but he saved for the needs of the Church, which, as he knew, increased day by day; and money was absolutely necessary if Atheism was to be met and fought in the sphere of the schools, institutions, and associations of all sorts. Without money, indeed, the Church would become a vassal at the mercy of the civil powers, the Kingdom of Italy and other Catholic states; and so, although he liberally helped every enterprise which might contribute to the triumph of the Faith, Leo XIII had a contempt for all expenditure without an object, and treated himself and others with stern closeness. Personally, he had no needs. At the outset of his pontificate he had set his small private patrimony apart from the rich patrimony of St. Peter, refusing to take aught from the latter for the purpose of assisting his relatives. Never had pontiff displayed less nepotism: his three nephews and his two nieces had remained poor—in fact, in great pecuniary embarrassment. Still he listened neither to complaints nor accusations, but remained inflexible, proudly resolved to bequeath the sinews of life, the invincible weapon money, to the popes of future times, and therefore vigorously defending the millions of the Holy See against the desperate covetousness of one and all.

"But, after all, what are the receipts and expenses of the Holy See?" inquired Pierre.

In all haste Nani again made his amiable, evasive gesture. "Oh! I am altogether ignorant in such matters," he replied. "Ask Monsieur Habert, who is so well informed."

"For my part," responded the *attache*, "I simply know what is known to all the embassies here, the matters which are the subject of common report. With respect to the receipts there is, first of all, the treasure left by Pius IX, some twenty millions, invested in various ways and formerly yielding about a million a year in interest. But, as I said before, a disaster happened, and there must then have been a falling off in the income. Still, nowadays it is reported that nearly all deficiencies have been made good. Well, besides the regular income from the invested money, a few hundred thousand francs are derived every year from chancellery dues, patents of nobility, and all sorts of little fees paid to the Congregations. However, as the annual expenses exceed seven millions, it has been necessary to find quite six millions every year; and certainly it is the Peter's Pence Fund that has supplied, not the six millions, perhaps, but three or four of them, and with these the Holy See has speculated in the hope of doubling them and making both ends meet. It would take me too long just now to relate the whole story of these speculations, the first huge gains, then the catastrophe which almost swept everything away, and finally the stubborn perseverance which is gradually supplying all deficiencies. However, if you are anxious on the subject, I will one day tell you all about it."

Pierre had listened with deep interest. "Six millions—even four!" he exclaimed, "what does the Peter's Pence Fund bring in, then?"

"Oh! I can only repeat that nobody has ever known the exact figures. In former times the Catholic Press published lists giving the amounts of different offerings, and in this way one could frame an approximate estimate. But the practice must have been considered unadvisable, for no documents nowadays appear, and it is absolutely impossible for people to form any real idea of what the Pope receives. He alone knows the correct amount, keeps the money, and disposes of it with absolute authority. Still I believe that in good years the offerings have amounted to between four and five millions. Originally France contributed one-half of the sum; but nowadays it certainly gives much less. Then come Belgium and Austria, England and Germany. As for Spain and Italy—oh! Italy—"

Narcisse paused and smiled at Monsignor Nani, who was wagging his head with the air of a man delighted at learning some extremely curious things of which he had previously had no idea.

"Oh, you may proceed, you may proceed, my dear son," said he.

"Well, then, Italy scarcely distinguishes itself. If the Pope had to provide for his living out of the gifts of the Italian Catholics there would soon be a famine at the Vatican. Far from helping him, indeed, the Roman nobility has cost him dear; for one of the chief causes of his pecuniary losses was his folly in lending money to the princes who speculated. It is really only from France and England that rich people, noblemen and so forth, have sent royal gifts to the imprisoned and martyred Pontiff. Among others there was an English nobleman who came to Rome every year with a large offering, the outcome of a vow which he had made in the hope that Heaven would cure his unhappy idiot son. And, of course, I don't refer to the extraordinary harvest garnered during the sacerdotal and the episcopal jubilees—the forty millions which then fell at his Holiness's feet."

"And the expenses?" asked Pierre.

"Well, as I told you, they amount to about seven millions. We may reckon two of them for the pensions paid to former officials of the pontifical government who were unwilling to take service under Italy; but I must add that this source of expense is diminishing every year as people die off and their pensions become extinguished. Then, broadly speaking, we may put down one million for the Italian sees, another for the Secretariate and the Nunciatures, and another for the Vatican. In this last sum I include the expenses of the pontifical Court, the military establishment, the museums, and the repair of the palace and the Basilica. Well, we have reached five millions, and the two others may be set down for the various subsidised enterprises, the Propaganda, and particularly the schools, which Leo XIII, with great practical good sense, subsidises very handsomely, for he is well aware that the battle and the triumph be in that direction—among the children who will be men to-morrow, and who will then defend their mother the Church, provided that they have been inspired with horror for the abominable doctrines of the age."

A spell of silence ensued, and the three men slowly paced the majestic colonnade. The swarming crowd had gradually disappeared, leaving the piazza empty, so that only the obelisk and the twin fountains now arose from the burning desert of symmetrical paving; whilst on the entablature of the porticus across the square a noble line of motionless statues stood out in the bright sunlight. And Pierre, with his eyes still raised to the Pope's windows, again fancied that he could see Leo XIII amidst all the streaming gold that had been spoken of, his whole, white, pure figure, his poor, waxen, transparent form steeped amidst those millions which he hid and counted and expended for the glory of God alone. "And so," murmured the young priest, "he has no anxiety, he is not in any pecuniary embarrassment."

"Pecuniary embarrassment!" exclaimed Monsignor Nani, his patience so sorely tried by the remark that he could no longer retain his diplomatic reserve. "Oh! my dear son! Why, when Cardinal Mocenni, the treasurer, goes to his Holiness every month, his Holiness always gives him the sum he asks for; he would give it, and be able to give it, however large it might be! His Holiness has certainly had the wisdom to effect great economies; the Treasure of St. Peter is larger than ever. Pecuniary embarrassment, indeed! Why, if a misfortune should occur, and the Sovereign Pontiff were to make a direct appeal to all his children, the Catholics of the entire world, do you know that in that case a thousand millions would fall at his feet just like the gold and the jewels which you saw raining on the steps of his throne just now?" Then suddenly calming himself and recovering his pleasant smile, Nani added: "At least, that is what I sometimes hear said; for, personally, I know nothing, absolutely nothing; and it is fortunate that Monsieur Habert should have been here to give you information. Ah! Monsieur Habert, Monsieur Habert! Why, I fancied that you were always in the skies absorbed in your passion for art, and far removed from all base mundane interests! But you really understand these things like a banker or a notary. Nothing escapes you, nothing. It is wonderful."

Narcisse must have felt the sting of the prelate's delicate sarcasm. At bottom, beneath this make-believe Florentine all-angelicalness, with long curly hair and mauve eyes which grew dim with rapture at sight of a Botticelli, there was a thoroughly practical, business-like young man, who took admirable care of his fortune and was even somewhat miserly. However, he contented himself with lowering his eyelids and assuming a languorous air. "Oh!" said he, "I'm all reverie; my soul is elsewhere."

"At all events," resumed Nani, turning towards Pierre, "I am very glad that you were able to see such a beautiful spectacle. A few more such opportunities and you will understand things far better than you would from all the explanations in the world. Don't miss the grand ceremony at St. Peter's to-morrow. It will be magnificent, and will give you food for useful reflection; I'm sure of it. And now allow me to leave you, delighted at seeing you in such a fit frame of mind."

Darting a last glance at Pierre, Nani seemed to have observed with pleasure the weariness and uncertainty which were paling his face. And when the prelate had gone off, and Narcisse also had taken leave with a gentle hand-shake, the young priest felt the ire of protest rising within him. What fit frame of mind did Nani mean? Did that man hope to weary him and drive him to despair by throwing him into collision with obstacles, so that he might afterwards overcome him with perfect ease? For the second time Pierre became suddenly and briefly conscious of the stealthy efforts which were being made to invest and crush him. But, believing as he did in his own strength of resistance, pride filled him with disdain. Again he swore that he would never yield, never withdraw his book, no matter what might happen. And then, before crossing the piazza, he once more raised his eyes to the windows of the Vatican, all his impressions crystallising in the thought of that much-needed money which like a last bond still attached the Pope to earth. Its chief evil doubtless lay in the manner in which it was provided; and if indeed the only question were to devise an improved method of collection, his dream of a pope who should be all soul, the bond of love, the spiritual leader of the world, would not be seriously affected. At this thought, Pierre felt comforted and was unwilling to look on things otherwise than hopefully, moved as he was by the extraordinary scene which he had just beheld, that feeble old man shining forth like the symbol of human deliverance, obeyed and venerated by the multitudes, and alone among all men endowed with the moral omnipotence that might at last set the reign of charity and peace on earth.

For the ceremony on the following day, it was fortunate that Pierre held a private ticket which admitted him to a reserved gallery, for the scramble at the entrances to the Basilica proved terrible. The mass, which the Pope was to celebrate in person, was fixed for ten o'clock, but people began to pour into St. Peter's four hours earlier, as soon, indeed, as the gates had been thrown open. The three thousand members of the International Pilgrimage were increased tenfold by the arrival of all the tourists in Italy, who had hastened to Rome eager to witness one of those great pontifical functions which nowadays are so rare. Moreover, the devotees and partisans whom the Holy See numbered in Rome itself and in other great cities of the kingdom, helped to swell the throng, all alacrity at the prospect of a demonstration. Judging by the tickets distributed, there would be a concourse of 40,000 people. And, indeed, at nine o'clock, when Pierre crossed the piazza on his way to the Canons' Entrance in the Via Santa Marta, where the holders of pink tickets were admitted, he saw the portico of the facade still thronged with people who were but slowly gaining admittance, while several gentlemen in evening dress, members of some Catholic association, bestirred themselves to maintain order with the help of a detachment of Pontifical Guards. Nevertheless, violent quarrels broke out in the crowd, and blows were exchanged amidst the involuntary scramble. Some people were almost stifled, and two women were carried off half crushed to death.

A disagreeable surprise met Pierre on his entry into the Basilica. The huge edifice was draped; coverings of old red damask with bands of gold swathed the columns and pilasters, seventy-five feet high; even the aisles were hung with the same old and faded silk; and the shrouding of those pompous marbles, of all the superb dazzling ornamentation of the church bespoke a very singular taste, a tawdry affectation of pomposity, extremely wretched in its effect. However, he was yet more amazed on seeing that even the statue of St. Peter was clad, costumed like a living pope in sumptuous pontifical vestments, with a tiara on its metal head. He had never imagined that people could garment statues either for their glory or for the pleasure of the eyes, and the result seemed to him disastrous.

The Pope was to say mass at the papal altar of the Confession, the high altar which stands under the dome. On a platform at the entrance of the left-hand transept was the throne on which he would afterwards take his place. Then, on either side of the nave, tribunes had been erected for the choristers of the Sixtine Chapel, the Corps Diplomatique, the Knights of Malta, the Roman nobility, and other guests of various kinds. And, finally, in the centre, before the altar, there were three rows of benches covered with red rugs, the first for the cardinals and the other two for the bishops and the prelates of the pontifical court. All the rest of the congregation was to remain standing.

Ah! that huge concert-audience, those thirty, forty thousand believers from here, there, and everywhere, inflamed with curiosity, passion, or faith, bestirring themselves, jostling one another, rising on tip-toe to see the better! The clamour of a human sea arose, the crowd was as gay and familiar as if it had found itself in some heavenly theatre where it was allowable for one to chat aloud and recreate oneself with the spectacle of religious pomp! At first Pierre was thunderstruck, he who only knew of nervous, silent kneeling in the depths of dim cathedrals, who was not accustomed to that religion of light, whose brilliancy transformed a religious celebration into a morning festivity. Around him, in the same tribune as himself, were gentlemen in dress-coats and ladies gowned in black, carrying glasses as in an opera-house. There were German and English women, and numerous Americans, all more or less charming, displaying the grace of thoughtless, chirruping birds. In the tribune of the Roman nobility on the left he recognised Benedetta and Donna Serafina, and there the simplicity of the regulation attire for ladies was relieved by large lace veils rivalling one another in richness and elegance. Then on the right was the tribune of the Knights of Malta, where the Grand Master stood amidst a group of commanders: while across the nave rose the diplomatic tribune where Pierre perceived the ambassadors of all the Catholic nations, resplendent in gala uniforms covered with gold lace. However, the young priest's eyes were ever returning to the crowd, the great surging throng in which the three thousand pilgrims were lost amidst the multitude of other spectators. And yet as the Basilica was so vast that it could easily contain eighty thousand people, it did not seem to be more than half full. People came and went along the aisles and took up favourable positions without impediment. Some could be seen gesticulating, and calls rang out above the ceaseless rumble of voices. From the lofty windows of plain white glass fell broad sheets of sunlight, which set a gory glow upon the faded damask hangings, and these cast a reflection as of fire upon all the tumultuous, feverish, impatient faces. The multitude of candles, and the seven-and-eighty lamps of the Confession paled to such a degree that they seemed but glimmering night-lights in the blinding radiance; and everything proclaimed the worldly gala of the imperial Deity of Roman pomp.

All at once there came a premature shock of delight, a false alert. Cries burst forth and circulated through the crowd: "Eccolo! eccolo! Here he comes!" And then there was pushing and jostling, eddying which made the human sea whirl and surge, all craning their necks, raising themselves to their full height, darting forward in a frenzied desire to see the Holy Father and the *cortege*. But only a detachment of Noble Guards marched by and took up position right and left of the altar. A flattering murmur accompanied them, their fine impassive bearing with its exaggerated military stiffness, provoking the admiration of the throng. An American woman declared that they were superb-looking fellows; and a Roman lady gave an English friend some particulars about the select corps to which they belonged. Formerly, said she, young men of the aristocracy had greatly sought the honour of forming part of it, for the sake of wearing its rich uniform and caracoling in front of the ladies. But recruiting was now such a difficult matter that one had to content oneself with good-looking young men of doubtful or ruined nobility, whose only care was for the meagre "pay" which just enabled them to live.

When another quarter of an hour of chatting and scrutinising had elapsed, the papal *cortege* at last made its appearance, and no sooner was it seen than applause burst forth as in a theatre—furious applause it was which rose and rolled along under the vaulted ceilings, suggesting the acclamations which ring out when some popular, idolised actor makes his entry on the stage. As in a theatre, too, everything had been very skilfully contrived so as to produce all possible effect amidst the magnificent scenery of the Basilica. The *cortege* was formed in the wings, that is in the Cappella della Pieta, the first chapel of the right aisle, and in order to reach it, the Holy Father, coming from his apartments by the way of the Chapel of the Blessed Sacrament, had been stealthily carried behind the hangings of the aisle which served the purpose of a drop-scene. Awaiting him in all readiness in the Cappella della Pieta were the cardinals, archbishops, and bishops, the whole pontifical prelacy, hierarchically classified and grouped. And then, as at a signal from a ballet master, the *cortege* made its entry, reaching the nave and ascending it in triumph from the closed Porta Santa to the altar of the Confession. On either hand were the rows of spectators whose applause at the sight of so much magnificence grew louder and louder as their delirious enthusiasm increased.

It was the *cortege* of the olden solemnities, the cross and sword, the Swiss Guard in full uniform, the valets in scarlet simars, the Knights of the Cape and the Sword in Renascence costumes, the Canons in rochets of lace, the superiors of the religious communities, the apostolic prothonotaries, the archbishops, and bishops, all the pontifical prelates in violet silk, the cardinals, each wearing the *cappa magna* and draped in purple, walking solemnly two by two with long intervals between each pair. Finally, around his Holiness were grouped the officers of the military household, the chamber prelates, Monsignor the Majordomo, Monsignor the Grand Chamberlain, and all the other high dignitaries of the Vatican, with the Roman prince assistant of the throne, the traditional, symbolical defender of the Church. And on the *sedia gestatoria,* screened by the *flabelli* with their lofty triumphal fans of feathers and carried on high by the bearers in red tunics broidered with silk, sat the Pope, clad in the sacred vestments which he had assumed in the Chapel of the Blessed Sacrament, the amict, the alb, the stole, and the white chasuble and white mitre enriched with gold, two gifts of extraordinary sumptuousness that had come from France. And, as his Holiness drew near, all hands were raised and clapped yet more loudly amidst the waves of living sunlight which streamed from the lofty windows.

Then a new and different impression of Leo XIII came to Pierre. The Pope, as he now beheld him, was no longer the familiar, tired, inquisitive old man, leaning on the arm of a talkative prelate as he strolled through the loveliest gardens in the world. He no longer recalled the Holy Father, in red cape and papal cap, giving a paternal welcome to a pilgrimage which brought him a fortune. He was here the Sovereign Pontiff, the all-powerful Master whom Christendom adored. His slim waxen form seemed to have stiffened within his white vestments, heavy with golden broidery, as in a reliquary of precious metal; and he retained a rigid, haughty, hieratic attitude, like that of some idol, gilded, withered for centuries past by the smoke of sacrifices. Amidst the mournful stiffness of his face only his eyes lived—eyes like black sparkling diamonds gazing afar, beyond earth, into the infinite. He gave not a glance to the crowd, he lowered his eyes neither to right nor to left, but remained soaring in the heavens, ignoring all that took place at his feet.

And as that seemingly embalmed idol, deaf and blind, in spite of the brilliancy of his eyes, was carried through the frantic multitude which it appeared neither to hear nor to see, it assumed fearsome majesty, disquieting grandeur, all the rigidity of dogma, all the immobility of tradition exhumed with its *fascioe* which alone kept it erect. Still Pierre fancied he could detect that the Pope was ill and weary, suffering from the attack of fever which Nani had spoken of when glorifying the courage of that old man of eighty-four, whom strength of soul alone now kept alive.

The service began. Alighting from the *sedia gestatoria* before the altar of the Confession, his Holiness slowly celebrated a low mass, assisted by four prelates and the pro-prefect of the ceremonies. When the time came for washing his fingers, Monsignor the Majordomo and Monsignor the Grand Chamberlain, accompanied by two cardinals, poured the water on his august hands; and shortly before the elevation of the host all the prelates of the pontifical court, each holding a lighted taper, came and knelt around the altar. There was a solemn moment, the forty thousand believers there assembled shuddered as if they could feel the terrible yet delicious blast of the invisible sweeping over them when during the elevation the silver clarions sounded the famous chorus of angels which invariably makes some women swoon. Almost immediately an aerial chant descended from the cupola, from a lofty gallery where one hundred and twenty choristers were concealed, and the enraptured multitude marvelled as though the angels had indeed responded to the clarion call. The voices descended, taking their flight under the vaulted ceilings with the airy sweetness of celestial harps; then in suave harmony they died away, reascended to the heavens as with a faint flapping of wings. And, after the mass, his Holiness, still standing at the altar, in person started the *Te Deum*, which the singers of the Sixtine Chapel and the other choristers took up, each party chanting a verse alternately. But soon the whole congregation joined them, forty thousand voices were raised, and a hymn of joy and glory spread through the vast nave with incomparable splendour of effect. And then the scene became one of extraordinary magnificence: there was Bernini's triumphal, flowery, gilded *baldacchino*, surrounded by the whole pontifical court with the lighted tapers showing like starry constellations, there was the Sovereign Pontiff in the centre, radiant like a planet in his gold-broidered chasuble, there were the benches crowded with cardinals in purple and archbishops and bishops in violet silk, there were the tribunes glittering with official finery, the gold lace of the diplomatists, the variegated uniforms of foreign officers, and then there was the throng flowing and eddying on all sides, rolling billows after billows of heads from the most distant depths of the Basilica. And the hugeness of the temple increased one's amazement; and even the glorious hymn which the multitude repeated became colossal, ascended like a tempest blast amidst the great marble tombs, the superhuman statues and gigantic pillars, till it reached the vast vaulted heavens of stone, and penetrated into the firmament of the cupola where the Infinite seemed to open resplendent with the goldwork of the mosaics.

A long murmur of voices followed the *Te Deum*, whilst Leo XIII, after donning the tiara in lieu of the mitre, and exchanging the chasuble for the pontifical cope, went to occupy his throne on the platform at the entry of the left transept. He thence dominated the whole assembly, through which a quiver sped when after the prayers of the ritual, he once more rose erect. Beneath the symbolic, triple crown, in the golden sheathing of his cope, he seemed to have grown taller. Amidst sudden and profound silence, which only feverish heart-beats interrupted, he raised his arm with a very noble gesture and pronounced the papal benediction in a slow, loud, full voice, which seemed, as it were, the very voice of the Deity, so greatly did its power astonish one, coming from such waxen lips, from such a bloodless, lifeless frame. And the effect was prodigious: as soon as the *cortege* reformed to return whence it had come, applause again burst forth, a frenzy of enthusiasm which the clapping of hands could no longer content. Acclamations resounded and gradually gained upon the whole multitude. They began among a group of ardent partisans stationed near the statue of St. Peter: *"Evviva il Papa-Re! evviva il Papa-Re*! Long live the Pope-King!" as the *cortege* went by the shout rushed along like leaping fire, inflaming heart after heart, and at last springing from every mouth in a thunderous protest against the theft of the states of the Church. All the faith, all the love of those believers, overexcited by the regal spectacle they had just beheld, returned once more to the dream, to the rageful desire that the Pope should be both King and Pontiff, master of men's bodies as he was of their souls—in one word, the absolute sovereign of the earth. Therein lay the only truth, the only happiness, the only salvation! Let all be given to him, both mankind and the world! "*Evviva il Papa-Re! evviva il Papa-Re*! Long live the Pope-King!"

Ah! that cry, that cry of war which had caused so many errors and so much bloodshed, that cry of self-abandonment and blindness which, realised, would have brought back the old ages of suffering, it shocked Pierre, and impelled him in all haste to quit the tribune where he was in order that he might escape the contagion of idolatry. And while the *cortege* still went its way and the deafening clamour of the crowd continued, he for a moment followed the left aisle amidst the general scramble. This, however, made him despair of reaching the street, and anxious to escape the crush of the general departure, it occurred to him to profit by a door which he saw open and which led him into a vestibule, whence ascended the steps conducting to the dome. A sacristan standing in the doorway, both bewildered and delighted at the demonstration, looked at him for a moment, hesitating whether he should stop him or not. However, the sight of the young priest's cassock combined with his own emotion rendered the man tolerant. Pierre was allowed to pass, and at once began to climb the staircase as rapidly as he could, in order that he might flee farther and farther away, ascend higher and yet higher into peace and silence.

And the silence suddenly became profound, the walls stifled the cry of the multitude. The staircase was easy and light, with broad paved steps turning within a sort of tower. When Pierre came out upon the roofs of nave and aisles, he was delighted to find himself in the bright sunlight and the pure keen air which blew there as in the open country. And it was with astonishment that he gazed upon the huge expanse of lead, zinc, and stone-work, a perfect aerial city living a life of its own under the blue sky. He saw cupolas, spires, terraces, even houses and gardens, houses bright with flowers, the residences of the workmen who live atop of the Basilica, which is ever and ever requiring repair. A little population here bestirs itself, labours, loves, eats, and sleeps. However, Pierre desired to approach the balustrade so as to get a near view of the colossal statues of the Saviour and the Apostles which surmount the facade on the side of the piazza. These giants, some nineteen feet in height, are constantly being mended; their arms, legs, and heads, into which the atmosphere is ever eating, nowadays only hold together by the help of cement, bars, and hooks. And having examined them, Pierre was leaning forward to glance at the Vatican's jumble of ruddy roofs, when it seemed to him that the shout from which he had fled was rising from the piazza, and thereupon, in all haste, he resumed his ascent within the pillar conducting to the dome. There was first a staircase, and then came some narrow, oblique passages, inclines intersected by a few steps, between the inner and outer walls of the cupola. Yielding to curiosity, Pierre pushed a door open, and suddenly found himself inside the Basilica again, at nearly 200 feet from the ground. A narrow gallery there ran round the dome just above the frieze, on which, in letters five feet high, appeared the famous inscription: *Tu es Petrus et super hanc petram oedificabo ecclesiam meam et tibi dabo claves regni coelorum.*[1] And then, as Pierre leant over to gaze into the fearful cavity beneath him and the wide openings of nave, and aisles, and transepts, the cry, the delirious cry of the multitude, yet clamorously swarming below, struck him full in the face. He fled once more; but, higher up, yet a second time he pushed another door open and found another gallery, one perched above the windows, just where the splendid mosaics begin, and whence the crowd seemed to him lost in the depths of a dizzy abyss, altar and *baldacchino* alike looking no larger than toys. And yet the cry of idolatry and warfare arose again, and smote him like the buffet of a tempest which gathers increase of strength the farther it rushes. So to es-

[1] Thou art Peter (Petrus) and on that rock (Petram) will I build my church, and to thee will I give the keys of the Kingdom of Heaven.

cape it he had to climb higher still, even to the outer gallery which encircles the lantern, hovering in the very heavens.

How delightful was the relief which that bath of air and sunlight at first brought him! Above him now there only remained the ball of gilt copper into which emperors and queens have ascended, as is testified by the pompous inscriptions in the passages; a hollow ball it is, where the voice crashes like thunder, where all the sounds of space reverberate. As he emerged on the side of the apse, his eyes at first plunged into the papal gardens, whose clumps of trees seemed mere bushes almost level with the soil; and he could retrace his recent stroll among them, the broad *parterre* looking like a faded Smyrna rug, the large wood showing the deep glaucous greenery of a stagnant pool. Then there were the kitchen garden and the vineyard easily identified and tended with care. The fountains, the observatory, the casino, where the Pope spent the hot days of summer, showed merely like little white spots in those undulating grounds, walled in like any other estate, but with the fearsome rampart of the fourth Leo, which yet retained its fortress-like aspect. However, Pierre took his way round the narrow gallery and abruptly found himself in front of Rome, a sudden and immense expanse, with the distant sea on the west, the uninterrupted mountain chains on the east and the south, the Roman Campagna stretching to the horizon like a bare and greenish desert, while the city, the Eternal City, was spread out at his feet. Never before had space impressed him so majestically. Rome was there, as a bird might see it, within the glance, as distinct as some geographical plan executed in relief. To think of it, such a past, such a history, so much grandeur, and Rome so dwarfed and contracted by distance! Houses as lilliputian and as pretty as toys; and the whole a mere mouldy speck upon the earth's face! What impassioned Pierre was that he could at a glance understand the divisions of Rome: the antique city yonder with the Capitol, the Forum, and the Palatine; the papal city in that Borgo which he overlooked, with St. Peter's and the Vatican gazing across the city of the middle ages—which was huddled together in the right angle described by the yellow Tiber—towards the modern city, the Quirinal of the Italian monarchy. And particularly did he remark the chalky girdle with which the new districts encompassed the ancient, central, sun-tanned quarters, thus symbolising an effort at rejuvenescence, the old heart but slowly mended, whereas the outlying limbs were renewed as if by miracle.

In that ardent noontide glow, however, Pierre no longer beheld the pure ethereal Rome which had met his eyes on the morning of his arrival in the delightfully soft radiance of the rising sun. That smiling, unobtrusive city, half veiled by golden mist, immersed as it were in some dream of childhood, now appeared to him flooded with a crude light, motionless, hard of outline and silent like death. The distance was as if devoured by too keen a flame, steeped in a luminous dust in which it crumbled. And against that blurred background the whole city showed with violent distinctness in great patches of light and shade, their tracery harshly conspicuous. One might have fancied oneself above some very ancient, abandoned stone quarry, which a few clumps of trees spotted with dark green. Of the ancient city one could see the sunburnt tower of the Capitol, the black cypresses of the Palatine, and the ruins of the palace of Septimius Severus, suggesting the white osseous carcase of some fossil monster, left there by a flood. In front, was enthroned the modern city with the long, renovated buildings of the Quirinal, whose yellow walls stood forth with wondrous crudity amidst the vigorous crests of the garden trees. And to right and left on the

Viminal, beyond the palace, the new districts appeared like a city of chalk and plaster mottled by innumerable windows as with a thousand touches of black ink. Then here and there were the Pincio showing like a stagnant mere, the Villa Medici uprearing its campanili, the castle of Sant' Angelo brown like rust, the spire of Santa Maria Maggiore aglow like a burning taper, the three churches of the Aventine drowsy amidst verdure, the Palazzo Farnese with its summer-baked tiles showing like old gold, the domes of the Gesu, of Sant' Andrea della Valle, of San Giovanni dei Fiorentini, and yet other domes and other domes, all in fusion, incandescent in the brazier of the heavens. And Pierre again felt a heart-pang in presence of that harsh, stern Rome, so different from the Rome of his dream, the Rome of rejuvenescence and hope, which he had fancied he had found on his first morning, but which had now faded away to give place to the immutable city of pride and domination, stubborn under the sun even unto death.

And there on high, all alone with his thoughts, Pierre suddenly understood. It was as if a dart of flaming light fell on him in that free, unbounded expanse where he hovered. Had it come from the ceremony which he had just beheld, from the frantic cry of servitude still ringing in his ears? Had it come from the spectacle of that city beneath him, that city which suggested an embalmed queen still reigning amidst the dust of her tomb? He knew not; but doubtless both had acted as factors, and at all events the light which fell upon his mind was complete: he felt that Catholicism could not exist without the temporal power, that it must fatally disappear whenever it should no longer be king over this earth. A first reason of this lay in heredity, in the forces of history, the long line of the heirs of the Caesars, the popes, the great pontiffs, in whose veins the blood of Augustus, demanding the empire of the world, had never ceased to flow. Though they might reside in the Vatican they had come from the imperial abodes on the Palatine, from the palace of Septimius Severus, and throughout the centuries their policy had ever pursued the dream of Roman mastery, of all the nations vanquished, submissive, and obedient to Rome. If its sovereignty were not universal, extending alike over bodies and over souls, Catholicism would lose its *raison d'etre*; for the Church cannot recognise any empire or kingdom otherwise than politically—the emperors and the kings being purely and simply so many temporary delegates placed in charge of the nations pending the time when they shall be called upon to relinquish their trust. All the nations, all humanity, and the whole world belong to the Church to whom they have been given by God. And if real and effective possession is not hers to-day, this is only because she yields to force, compelled to face accomplished facts, but with the formal reserve that she is in presence of guilty usurpation, that her possessions are unjustly withheld from her, and that she awaits the realisation of the promises of the Christ, who, when the time shall be accomplished, will for ever restore to her both the earth and mankind. Such is the real future city which time is to bring: Catholic Rome, sovereign of the world once more. And Rome the city forms a substantial part of the dream, Rome whose eternity has been predicted, Rome whose soil has imparted to Catholicism the inextinguishable thirst of absolute power. And thus the destiny of the papacy is linked to that of Rome, to such a point indeed that a pope elsewhere than at Rome would no longer be a Catholic pope. The thought of all this frightened Pierre; a great shudder passed through him as he leant on the light iron balustrade, gazing down into the abyss where the stern mournful city was even now crumbling away under the fierce sun.

There was, however, evidence of the facts which had dawned on him. If Pius IX and Leo XIII had resolved to imprison themselves in the Vatican, it was because necessity bound them to Rome. A pope is not free to leave the city, to be the head of the Church elsewhere; and in the same way a pope, however well he may understand the modern world, has not the right to relinquish the temporal power. This is an inalienable inheritance which he must defend, and it is moreover a question of life, peremptory, above discussion. And thus Leo XIII has retained the title of Master of the temporal dominions of the Church, and this he has done the more readily since as a cardinal—like all the members of the Sacred College when elected—he swore that he would maintain those dominions intact. Italy may hold Rome as her capital for another century or more, but the coming popes will never cease to protest and claim their kingdom. If ever an understanding should be arrived at, it must be based on the gift of a strip of territory. Formerly, when rumours of reconciliation were current, was it not said that the papacy exacted, as a formal condition, the possession of at least the Leonine City with the neutralisation of a road leading to the sea? Nothing is not enough, one cannot start from nothing to attain to everything, whereas that Civitas Leonina, that bit of a city, would already be a little royal ground, and it would then only be necessary to conquer the rest, first Rome, next Italy, then the neighbouring states, and at last the whole world. Never has the Church despaired, even when, beaten and despoiled, she seemed to be at the last gasp. Never will she abdicate, never will she renounce the promises of the Christ, for she believes in a boundless future and declares herself to be both indestructible and eternal. Grant her but a pebble on which to rest her head, and she will hope to possess, first the field in which that pebble lies, and then the empire in which the field is situated. If one pope cannot achieve the recovery of the inheritance, another pope, ten, twenty other popes will continue the work. The centuries do not count. And this explains why an old man of eighty-four has undertaken colossal enterprises whose achievement requires several lives, certain as he is that his successors will take his place, and that the work will ever and ever be carried forward and completed.

As these thoughts coursed through his mind, Pierre, overlooking that ancient city of glory and domination, so stubbornly clinging to its purple, realised that he was an imbecile with his dream of a purely spiritual pope. The notion seemed to him so different from the reality, so out of place, that he experienced a sort of shame-fraught despair. The new pope, consonant to the teachings of the Gospel, such as a purely spiritual pope reigning over souls alone, would be, was virtually beyond the ken of a Roman prelate. At thought of that papal court congealed in ritual, pride, and authority, Pierre suddenly understood what horror and repugnance such a pastor would inspire. How great must be the astonishment and contempt of the papal prelates for that singular notion of the northern mind, a pope without dominions or subjects, military household or royal honours, a pope who would be, as it were, a spirit, exercising purely moral authority, dwelling in the depths of God's temple, and governing the world solely with gestures of benediction and deeds of kindliness and love! All that was but a misty Gothic invention for this Latin clergy, these priests of light and magnificence, who were certainly pious and even superstitious, but who left the Deity well sheltered within the tabernacle in order to govern in His name, according to what they considered the interests of Heaven. Thence it arose that they employed craft and artifice like mere politicians, and lived by dint of expedients amidst the great battle of human appetites, marching with the prudent, stealthy steps of diplomatists towards the final terrestrial victory of the Christ, who, in the person of the Pope, was one day to reign over all the nations. And how stupefied must a French prelate have been—a prelate like Monseigneur Bergerot, that apostle of renunciation and charity—when he lighted amidst that world of the Vatican! How difficult must it have been for him to understand and focus things, and afterwards how great his grief at finding himself unable to come to any agreement with those men without country, without fatherland, those "internationals," who were ever poring over the maps of both hemispheres, ever absorbed in schemes which were to bring them empire. Days and days were necessary, one needed to live in Rome, and he, Pierre himself, had only seen things clearly after a month's sojourn, whilst labouring under the violent shock of the royal pomp of St. Peter's, and standing face to face with the ancient city as it slumbered heavily in the sunlight and dreamt its dream of eternity.

But on lowering his eyes to the piazza in front of the Basilica he perceived the multitude, the 40,000 believers streaming over the pavement like insects. And then he thought that he could hear the cry again rising: "*Evviva il Papa-Re! evviva il Papa-Re*! Long live the Pope-King!" Whilst ascending those endless staircases a moment previously it had seemed to him as if the colossus of stone were quivering with the frantic shout raised beneath its ceilings. And now that he had climbed even into cloudland that shout apparently was traversing space. If the colossal pile beneath him still vibrated with it, was it not as with a last rise of sap within its ancient walls, a re-invigoration of that Catholic blood which formerly had demanded that the pile should be a stupendous one, the veritable king of temples, and which now was striving to reanimate it with the powerful breath of life, and this at the very hour when death was beginning to fall upon its over-vast, deserted nave and aisles? The crowd was still streaming forth, filling the piazza, and Pierre's heart was wrung by frightful anguish, for that throng with its shout had just swept his last hope away. On the previous afternoon, after the reception of the pilgrimage, he had yet been able to deceive himself by overlooking the necessity for money which bound the Pope to earth in order that he might see nought but the feeble old man, all spirituality, resplendent like the symbol of moral authority. But his faith in such a pastor of the Gospel, free from all considerations of earthly wealth, and king of none other than a heavenly kingdom, had fled. Not only did the Peter's Pence impose hard servitude upon Leo XIII but he was also the prisoner of papal tradition—the eternal King of Rome, riveted to the soil of Rome, unable either to quit the city or to renounce the temporal power. The fatal end would be collapse on the spot, the dome of St. Peter's falling even as the temple of Olympian Jupiter had fallen, Catholicism strewing the grass with its ruins whilst elsewhere schism burst forth: a new faith for the new nations. Of this Pierre had a grandiose and tragical vision: he beheld his dream destroyed, his book swept away amidst that cry which spread around him as if flying to the four corners of the Catholic world "*Evviva il Papa-Re! evviva il Papa-Re!* Long live the Pope-King!" But even in that hour of the papacy's passing triumph he already felt that the giant of gold and marble on which he stood was oscillating, even as totter all old and rotten societies.

At last he took his way down again, and a fresh shock of emotion came to him as he reached the roofs, that sunlit expanse of lead and zinc, large enough for the site of a town. Monsignor Nani was there, in company with the two French ladies, the mother and the daughter, both looking very happy and highly amused. No doubt the prelate had good-naturedly offered to conduct them to the dome. However, as soon as he recognised the young priest he went towards him: "Well, my dear son," he inquired, "are you pleased? Have you been impressed, edified?" As he spoke, his searching eyes dived into Pierre's soul, as if to ascertain the present result of his experiments. Then, satisfied with what he detected, he began to laugh softly: "Yes, yes, I see—come, you are a sensible fellow after all. I begin to think that the unfortunate affair which brought you here will have a happy ending."

VIII.

WHEN Pierre remained in the morning at the Boccanera mansion he often spent some hours in the little neglected garden which had formerly ended with a sort of colonnaded *loggia*, whence two flights of steps descended to the Tiber. This garden was a delightful, solitary nook, perfumed by the ripe fruit of the centenarian orange-trees, whose symmetrical lines were the only indication of the former pathways, now hidden beneath rank weeds. And Pierre also found there the acrid scent of the large box-shrubs growing in the old central fountain basin, which had been filled up with loose earth and rubbish.

On those luminous October mornings, full of such tender and penetrating charm, the spot was one where all the joy of living might well be savoured, but Pierre brought thither his northern dreaminess, his concern for suffering, his steadfast feeling of compassion, which rendered yet sweeter the caress of the sunlight pervading that atmosphere of love. He seated himself against the right-hand wall on a fragment of a fallen column over which a huge laurel cast a deep-black shadow, fresh and aromatic. In the antique greenish sarcophagus beside him, on which fauns offered violence to nymphs, the streamlet of water trickling from the mask incrusted in the wall, set the unchanging music of its crystal note, whilst he read the newspapers and the letters which he received, all the communications of good Abbe Rose, who kept him informed of his mission among the wretched ones of gloomy Paris, now already steeped in fog and mud.

One morning however, Pierre unexpectedly found Benedetta seated on the fallen column which he usually made his chair. She raised a light cry of surprise on seeing him, and for a moment remained embarrassed, for she had with her his book "New Rome," which she had read once already, but had then imperfectly understood. And overcoming her embarrassment she now hastened to detain him, making him sit down beside her, and frankly owning that she had come to the garden in order to be alone and apply herself to an attentive study of the book, in the same way as some ignorant school-girl. Then they began to chat like a pair of friends, and the young priest spent a delightful hour. Although Benedetta did not speak of herself, he realised that it was her grief alone which brought her nearer to him, as if indeed her own sufferings enlarged her heart and made her think of all who suffered in the world. Patrician as she was, regarding social hierarchy as a divine law, she had never previously thought of such things, and some pages of Pierre's book greatly astonished her. What! one ought to take interest in the lowly, realise that they had the same souls and the same griefs as oneself, and seek in brotherly or sisterly fashion to make them happy? She certainly sought to acquire such an interest, but with no great success, for she secretly feared that it might lead her into sin, as it could not be right to alter aught of the social system which had been established by God and consecrated by the Church. Charitable she undoubtedly was, wont to bestow small sums in alms, but she did not give her heart, she felt no true sympathy for the humble, belonging as she did to such a different race, which looked to a throne in heaven high above the seats of all the plebeian elect.

She and Pierre, however, found themselves on other mornings side by side in the shade of the laurels near the trickling, singing water; and he, lacking occupation, weary of waiting for a solution which seemed to recede day by day, fervently strove to animate this young and beautiful woman with some of his own fraternal feelings. He was impassioned by the idea that he was catechising Italy herself, the queen of beauty, who was still slumbering in ignorance, but who would recover all her past glory if she were to awake to the new times with soul enlarged, swelling with pity for men and things. Reading good Abbe Rose's letters to Benedetta, he made her shudder at the frightful wail of wretchedness which ascends from all great cities. With such deep tenderness in her eyes, with the happiness of love reciprocated emanating from her whole being, why should she not recognise, even as he did, that the law of love was the sole means of saving suffering humanity, which, through hatred, incurred the danger of death? And to please him she did try to believe in democracy, in the fraternal remodelling of society, but among other nations only—not at Rome, for an involuntary, gentle laugh came to her lips whenever his words evoked the idea of the poor still remaining in the Trastevere district fraternising with those who yet dwelt in the old princely palaces. No, no, things had been as they were so long; they could not, must not, be altered! And so, after all, Pierre's pupil made little progress: she was, in reality, simply touched by the wealth of ardent love which the young priest had chastely transferred from one alone to the whole of human kind. And between him and her, as those sunlit October mornings went by, a tie of exquisite sweetness was formed; they came to love one another with deep, pure, fraternal affection, amidst the great glowing passion which consumed them both.

Then, one day, Benedetta, her elbow resting on the sarcophagus, spoke of Dario, whose name she had hitherto refrained from mentioning. Ah! poor *amico*, how circumspect and repentant he had shown himself since that fit of brutal insanity! At first, to conceal his embarrassment, he had gone to spend three days at Naples, and it was said that La Tonietta, the sentimental *demi-mondaine*, had hastened to join him there, wildly in love with him. Since his return to the mansion he had avoided all private meetings with his cousin, and scarcely saw her except at the Monday receptions, when he wore a submissive air, and with his eyes silently entreated forgiveness.

"Yesterday, however," continued Benedetta, "I met him on the staircase and gave him my hand. He understood that I was no longer angry with him and was very happy. What else could I have done? One must not be severe for ever. Besides, I do not want things to go too far between him and that woman. I want him to remember that I still love him, and am still waiting for him. Oh! he is mine, mine alone. But alas! I cannot say the word: our affairs are in such sorry plight."

She paused, and two big tears welled into her eyes. The divorce proceedings to which she alluded had now come to a standstill, fresh obstacles ever arising to stay their course.

Pierre was much moved by her tears, for she seldom wept. She herself sometimes confessed, with her calm smile, that she did not know how to weep. But now her heart was melting, and for a moment she remained overcome, leaning on the mossy, crumbling sarcophagus, whilst the clear water falling from the gaping mouth of the tragic mask still sounded its flutelike note. And a sudden thought of death came to the priest as he saw her, so young and so radiant with beauty, half fainting beside that marble resting-place where fauns were rushing upon nymphs in a frantic bacchanal which proclaimed the omnipotence of love—that omnipotence which the ancients were fond of symbolising on their tombs as a token of life's eternity. And meantime a faint, warm breeze passed through the sunlit, silent garden, wafting hither and thither the penetrating scent of box and orange.

"One has so much strength when one loves," Pierre at last murmured.

"Yes, yes, you are right," she replied, already smiling again. "I am childish. But it is the fault of your book. It is only when I suffer that I properly understand it. But all the same I am making progress, am I not? Since you desire it, let all the poor, all those who suffer, as I do, be my brothers and sisters."

Then for a while they resumed their chat.

On these occasions Benedetta was usually the first to return to the house, and Pierre would linger alone under the laurels, vaguely dreaming of sweet, sad things. Often did he think how hard life proved for poor creatures whose only thirst was for happiness!

One Monday evening, at a quarter-past ten, only the young folks remained in Donna Serafina's reception-room. Monsignor Nani had merely put in an appearance that night, and Cardinal Sarno had just gone off.

Even Donna Serafina, in her usual seat by the fireplace, seemed to have withdrawn from the others, absorbed as she was in contemplation of the chair which the absent Morano still stubbornly left unoccupied. Chatting and laughing in front of the sofa on which sat Benedetta and Celia were Dario, Pierre, and Narcisse Habert, the last of whom had begun to twit the young Prince, having met him, so he asserted, a few days previously, in the company of a very pretty girl.

"Oh! don't deny it, my dear fellow," continued Narcisse, "for she was really superb. She was walking beside you, and you turned into a lane together—the Borgo Angelico, I think."

Dario listened smiling, quite at his ease and incapable of denying his passionate predilection for beauty. "No doubt, no doubt; it was I, I don't deny it," he responded. "Only the inferences you draw are not correct." And turning towards Benedetta, who, without a thought of jealous anxiety, wore as gay a look as himself, as though delighted that he should have enjoyed that passing pleasure of the eyes, he went on: "It was the girl, you know, whom I found in tears six weeks ago. Yes, that bead-worker who was sobbing because the workshop was shut up, and who rushed along, all blushing, to conduct me to her parents when I offered her a bit of silver. Pierina her name is, as you, perhaps, remember."

"Oh! yes, Pierina."

"Well, since then I've met her in the street on four or five occasions. And, to tell the truth, she is so very beautiful that I've stopped and spoken to her. The other day, for instance, I walked with her as far as a manufacturer's. But she hasn't yet found any work, and she began to cry, and so, to console her a little, I kissed her. She was quite taken aback at it, but she seemed very well pleased."

At this all the others began to laugh. But suddenly Celia desisted and said very gravely, "You know, Dario, she loves you; you must not be hard on her."

Dario, no doubt, was of Celia's opinion, for he again looked at Benedetta, but with a gay toss of the head, as if to say that, although the girl might love him, he did not love her. A bead-worker indeed, a girl of the lowest classes, pooh! She might be a Venus, but she could be nothing to him. And he himself made merry over his romantic adventure, which Narcisse sought to arrange in a kind of antique sonnet: A beautiful bead-worker falling madly in love with a young prince, as fair as sunlight, who, touched by her misfortune, hands her a silver crown; then the beautiful bead-worker, quite overcome at finding him as charitable as handsome, dreaming of him incessantly, and following him everywhere, chained to his steps by a link of flame; and finally the beautiful bead-worker, who has refused the silver crown, so entreating the handsome prince with her soft, submissive eyes, that he at last deigns to grant her the alms of his heart. This pastime greatly amused Benedetta; but Celia, with her angelic face and the air of a little girl who ought to have been ignorant of everything, remained very grave and repeated sadly, "Dario, Dario, she loves you; you must not make her suffer."

Then the Contessina, in her turn, was moved to pity. "And those poor folks are not happy!" said she.

"Oh!" exclaimed the Prince, "it's misery beyond belief. On the day she took me to the Quartiere dei Prati[1] I was quite overcome; it was awful, astonishingly awful!"

"But I remember that we promised to go to see the poor people," resumed Benedetta, "and we have done wrong in delaying our visit so long. For your studies, Monsieur l'Abbe Froment, you greatly desired to accompany us and see the poor of Rome—was that not so?"

As she spoke she raised her eyes to Pierre, who for a moment had been silent. He was much moved by her charitable thought, for he realised, by the faint quiver of her voice, that she desired to appear a docile pupil, progressing in affection for the lowly and the wretched. Moreover, his passion for his apostolate had at once returned to him. "Oh!" said he, "I shall not quit Rome without having seen those who suffer, those who lack work and bread. Therein lies the malady which affects every nation; salvation can only be attained by the healing of misery. When the roots of the tree cannot find sustenance the tree dies."

"Well," resumed the Contessina, "we will fix an appointment at once; you shall come with us to the Quartiere dei Prati—Dario will take us there."

At this the Prince, who had listened to the priest with an air of stupefaction, unable to understand the simile of the tree and its roots, began to protest distressfully, "No, no, cousin, take Monsieur l'Abbe for a stroll there if it amuses you. But I've been, and

---

[1] The district of the castle meadows—see ante note.—Trans.

don't want to go back. Why, when I got home the last time I was so upset that I almost took to my bed. No, no; such abominations are too awful—it isn't possible."

At this moment a voice, bitter with displeasure, arose from the chimney corner. Donna Serafina was emerging from her long silence. "Dario is quite right! Send your alms, my dear, and I will gladly add mine. There are other places where you might take Monsieur l'Abbe, and which it would be far more useful for him to see. With that idea of yours you would send him away with a nice recollection of our city."

Roman pride rang out amidst the old lady's bad temper. Why, indeed, show one's sores to foreigners, whose visit is possibly prompted by hostile curiosity? One always ought to look beautiful; Rome should not be shown otherwise than in the garb of glory.

Narcisse, however, had taken possession of Pierre. "It's true, my dear Abbe," said he; "I forgot to recommend that stroll to you. You really must visit the new district built over the castle meadows. It's typical, and sums up all the others. And you won't lose your time there, I'll warrant you, for nowhere can you learn more about the Rome of the present day. It's extraordinary, extraordinary!" Then, addressing Benedetta, he added, "Is it decided? Shall we say to-morrow morning? You'll find the Abbe and me over there, for I want to explain matters to him beforehand, in order that he may understand them. What do you say to ten o'clock?"

Before answering him the Contessina turned towards her aunt and respectfully opposed her views. "But Monsieur l'Abbe, aunt, has met enough beggars in our streets already, so he may well see everything. Besides, judging by his book, he won't see worse things than he has seen in Paris. As he says in one passage, hunger is the same all the world over." Then, with her sensible air, she gently laid siege to Dario. "You know, Dario," said she, "you would please me very much by taking me there. We can go in the carriage and join these gentlemen. It will be a very pleasant outing for us. It is such a long time since we went out together."

It was certainly that idea of going out with Dario, of having a pretext for a complete reconciliation with him, that enchanted her; he himself realised it, and, unable to escape, he tried to treat the matter as a joke. "Ah! cousin," he said, "it will be your fault; I shall have the nightmare for a week. An excursion like that spoils all the enjoyment of life for days and days."

The mere thought made him quiver with revolt. However, laughter again rang out around him, and, in spite of Donna Serafina's mute disapproval, the appointment was finally fixed for the following morning at ten o'clock. Celia as she went off expressed deep regret that she could not form one of the party; but, with the closed candour of a budding lily, she really took interest in Pierina alone. As she reached the ante-room she whispered in her friend's ear: "Take a good look at that beauty, my dear, so as to tell me whether she is so very beautiful—beautiful beyond compare."

When Pierre met Narcisse near the Castle of Sant' Angelo on the morrow, at nine o'clock, he was surprised to find him again languid and enraptured, plunged anew in artistic enthusiasm. At first not a word was said of the excursion. Narcisse related that he had risen at sunrise in order that he might spend an hour before Bernini's "Santa Teresa." It seemed that when he did not see that statue for a week he suffered as acutely as if he were parted from some cherished mistress. And his adoration varied with the time of day, according to the light in which he beheld the figure: in the morning, when the pale glow of dawn steeped it in whiteness, he worshipped it with quite a mystical transport of the soul, whilst in the afternoon, when the glow of the declining sun's oblique rays seemed to permeate the marble, his passion became as fiery red as the blood of martyrs. "Ah! my friend," said he with a weary air whilst his dreamy eyes faded to mauve, "you have no idea how delightful and perturbing her awakening was this morning—how languorously she opened her eyes, like a pure, candid virgin, emerging from the embrace of the Divinity. One could die of rapture at the sight!"

Then, growing calm again when he had taken a few steps, he resumed in the voice of a practical man who does not lose his balance in the affairs of life: "We'll walk slowly towards the castle-fields district—the buildings yonder; and on our way I'll tell you what I know of the things we shall see there. It was the maddest affair imaginable, one of those delirious frenzies of speculation which have a splendour of their own, just like the superb, monstrous masterpiece of a man of genius whose mind is unhinged. I was told of it all by some relatives of mine, who took part in the gambling, and, in point of fact, made a good deal of money by it."

Thereupon, with the clearness and precision of a financier, employing technical terms with perfect ease, he recounted the extraordinary adventure. That all Italy, on the morrow of the occupation of Rome, should have been delirious with enthusiasm at the thought of at last possessing the ancient and glorious city, the eternal capital to which the empire of the world had been promised, was but natural. It was, so to say, a legitimate explosion of the delight and the hopes of a young nation anxious to show its power. The question was to make Rome a modern capital worthy of a great kingdom, and before aught else there were sanitary requirements to be dealt with: the city needed to be cleansed of all the filth which disgraced it. One cannot nowadays imagine in what abominable putrescence the city of the popes, the *Roma sporca* which artists regret, was then steeped: the vast majority of the houses lacked even the most primitive arrangements, the public thoroughfares were used for all purposes, noble ruins served as store-places for sewage, the princely palaces were surrounded by filth, and the streets were perfect manure beds which fostered frequent epidemics. Thus vast municipal works were absolutely necessary, the question was one of health and life itself. And in much the same way it was only right to think of building houses for the newcomers, who would assuredly flock into the city. There had been a precedent at Berlin, whose population, after the establishment of the German empire, had suddenly increased by some hundreds of thousands. In the same way the population of Rome would certainly be doubled, tripled, quadrupled, for as the new centre of national life the city would necessarily attract all the *vis viva* of the provinces. And at this thought pride stepped in: the fallen government of the Vatican must be shown what Italy was capable of achieving, what splendour she would bestow on the new and third Rome, which, by the magnificence of its thoroughfares and the multitude of its people, would far excel either the imperial or the papal city.

True, during the early years some prudence was observed; wisely enough, houses were only built in proportion as they were required. The population had doubled at one bound, rising from two to four hundred thousand souls, thanks to the arrival of the little world of employees and officials of the public services—all those who live on the State or hope to live on it, without mentioning the idlers and enjoyers of life whom a Court always carries in its train. However, this influx of newcomers was a first cause of intoxication, for every one imagined that the increase would continue, and, in fact, become more and more rapid. And so the city of the day before no longer seemed large enough; it was necessary to make immediate preparations for the morrow's need by enlarging Rome on all sides. Folks talked, too, of the Paris of the secsecond empire, which had been so extended and transformed into a city of light and health. But unfortunately on the banks of the Tiber there was neither any preconcerted general plan nor any clear-seeing man, master of the situation, supported by powerful financial organisations. And the work, begun by pride, prompted by the ambition of surpassing the Rome of the Caesars and the Popes, the determination to make the eternal, predestined city the queen and centre of the world once more, was completed by speculation, one of those extraordinary gambling frenzies, those tempests which arise, rage, destroy, and carry everything away without premonitory warning or possibility of arresting their course. All at once it was rumoured that land bought at five francs the metre had been sold again for a hundred francs the metre; and thereupon the fever arose—the fever of a nation which is passionately fond of gambling. A flight of speculators descending from North Italy swooped down upon Rome, the noblest and easiest of preys. Those needy, famished mountaineers found spoils for every appetite in that voluptuous South where life is so benign, and the very delights of the climate helped to corrupt and hasten moral gangrene. At first, too; it was merely necessary to stoop; money was to be found by the shovelful among the rubbish of the first districts which were opened up. People who were clever enough to scent the course which the new thoroughfares would take and purchase buildings threatened with demolition increased their capital tenfold in a couple of years. And after that the contagion spread, infecting all classes—the princes, burgesses, petty proprietors, even the shop-keepers, bakers, grocers, and boot-makers; the delirium rising to such a pitch that a mere baker subsequently failed for forty-five millions.[1] Nothing, indeed, was left but rageful gambling, in which the stakes were millions, whilst the lands and the houses became mere fictions, mere pretexts for stock-exchange operations. And thus the old hereditary pride, which had dreamt of transforming Rome into the capital of the world, was heated to madness by the high fever of speculation—folks buying, and building, and selling without limit, without a pause, even as one might throw shares upon the market as fast and as long as presses can be found to print them.

No other city in course of evolution has ever furnished such a spectacle. Nowadays, when one strives to penetrate things one is confounded. The population had increased to five hundred thousand, and then seemingly remained stationary; nevertheless, new districts continued to sprout up more thickly than ever. Yet what folly it was not to wait for a further influx of inhabitants! Why continue piling up accommodation for thousands of families whose advent was uncertain? The only excuse lay in having beforehand propounded the proposition that the third Rome, the triumphant capital of Italy, could not count less than a million souls, and in regarding that proposition as indisputable fact. The people had not come, but they surely would come: no patriot could doubt it without being guilty of treason. And so houses were built and built without a pause, for the half-million citizens who were coming. There was no anxiety as to the date of their arrival; it was sufficient that they should be expected. Inside Rome the companies which had been formed in connection with the new thoroughfares passing through the old, demolished, pestiferous districts, certainly sold or

---

[1] 1,800,000 pounds. See ante note.—Trans.

let their house property, and thereby realised large profits. But, as the craze increased, other companies were established for the purpose of erecting yet more and more districts outside Rome—veritable little towns, of which there was no need whatever. Beyond the Porta San Giovanni and the Porta San Lorenzo, suburbs sprang up as by miracle. A town was sketched out over the vast estate of the Villa Ludovisi, from the Porta Pia to the Porta Salaria and even as far as Sant' Agnese. And then came an attempt to make quite a little city, with church, school, and market, arise all at once on the fields of the Castle of Sant' Angelo. And it was no question of small dwellings for labourers, modest flats for employees, and others of limited means; no, it was a question of colossal mansions three and four storeys high, displaying uniform and endless facades which made these new excentral quarters quite Babylonian, such districts, indeed, as only capitals endowed with intense life, like Paris and London, could contrive to populate. However, such were the monstrous products of pride and gambling; and what a page of history, what a bitter lesson now that Rome, financially ruined, is further disgraced by that hideous girdle of empty, and, for the most part, uncompleted carcases, whose ruins already strew the grassy streets!

The fatal collapse, the disaster proved a frightful one. Narcisse explained its causes and recounted its phases so clearly that Pierre fully understood. Naturally enough, numerous financial companies had sprouted up: the Immobiliere, the Society d'Edilizia e Construzione, the Fondaria, the Tiberiana, and the Esquilino. Nearly all of them built, erected huge houses, entire streets of them, for purposes of sale; but they also gambled in land, selling plots at large profit to petty speculators, who also dreamt of making large profits amidst the continuous, fictitious rise brought about by the growing fever of agiotage. And the worst was that the petty speculators, the middle-class people, the inexperienced shop-keepers without capital, were crazy enough to build in their turn by borrowing of the banks or applying to the companies which had sold them the land for sufficient cash to enable them to complete their structures. As a general rule, to avoid the loss of everything, the companies were one day compelled to take back both land and buildings, incomplete though the latter might be, and from the congestion which resulted they were bound to perish. If the expected million of people had arrived to occupy the dwellings prepared for them the gains would have been fabulous, and in ten years Rome might have become one of the most flourishing capitals of the world. But the people did not come, and the dwellings remained empty. Moreover, the buildings erected by the companies were too large and costly for the average investor inclined to put his money into house property. Heredity had acted, the builders had planned things on too huge a scale, raising a series of magnificent piles whose purpose was to dwarf those of all other ages; but, as it happened, they were fated to remain lifeless and deserted, testifying with wondrous eloquence to the impotence of pride.

So there was no private capital that dared or could take the place of that of the companies. Elsewhere, in Paris for instance, new districts have been erected and embellishments have been carried out with the capital of the country—the money saved by dint of thrift. But in Rome all was built on the credit system, either by means of bills of exchange at ninety days, or—and this was chiefly the case—by borrowing money abroad. The huge sum sunk in these enterprises is estimated at a milliard, four-fifths of which was French money. The bankers did everything; the French ones lent to the Italian bankers at 3 1-2 or 4 per cent.; and the Italian bankers accommodated the speculators, the Roman builders, at 6, 7, and even 8 per cent. And thus the disaster was great indeed when France, learning of Italy's alliance with Germany, withdrew her 800,000,000 francs in less than two years. The Italian banks were drained of their specie, and the land and building companies, being likewise compelled to reimburse their loans, were compelled to apply to the banks of issue, those privileged to issue notes. At the same time they intimidated the Government, threatening to stop all work and throw 40,000 artisans and labourers starving on the pavement of Rome if it did not compel the banks of issue to lend them the five or six millions of paper which they needed. And this the Government at last did, appalled by the possibility of universal bankruptcy. Naturally, however, the five or six millions could not be paid back at maturity, as the newly built houses found neither purchasers nor tenants; and so the great fall began, and continued with a rush, heaping ruin upon ruin. The petty speculators fell on the builders, the builders on the land companies, the land companies on the banks of issue, and the latter on the public credit, ruining the nation. And that was how a mere municipal crisis became a frightful disaster: a whole milliard sunk to no purpose, Rome disfigured, littered with the ruins of the gaping and empty dwellings which had been prepared for the five or six hundred thousand inhabitants for whom the city yet waits in vain!

Moreover, in the breeze of glory which swept by, the state itself took a colossal view of things. It was a question of at once making Italy triumphant and perfect, of accomplishing in five and twenty years what other nations have required centuries to effect. So there was feverish activity and a prodigious outlay on canals, ports, roads, railway lines, and improvements in all the great cities. Directly after the alliance with Germany, moreover, the military and naval estimates began to devour millions to no purpose. And the ever growing financial requirements were simply met by the issue of paper, by a fresh loan each succeeding year. In Rome alone, too, the building of the Ministry of War cost ten millions, that of the Ministry of Finances fifteen, whilst a hundred was spent on the yet unfinished quays, and two hundred and fifty were sunk on works of defence around the city. And all this was a flare of the old hereditary pride, springing from that soil whose sap can only blossom in extravagant projects; the determination to dazzle and conquer the world which comes as soon as one has climbed to the Capitol, even though one's feet rest amidst the accumulated dust of all the forms of human power which have there crumbled one above the other.

"And, my dear friend," continued Narcisse, "if I could go into all the stories that are current, that are whispered here and there, you would be stupefied at the insanity which overcame the whole city amidst the terrible fever to which the gambling passion gave rise. Folks of small account, and fools and ignorant people were not the only ones to be ruined; nearly all the Roman nobles lost their ancient fortunes, their gold and their palaces and their galleries of masterpieces, which they owed to the munificence of the popes. The colossal wealth which it had taken centuries of nepotism to pile up in the hands of a few melted away like wax, in less than ten years, in the levelling fire of modern speculation." Then, forgetting that he was speaking to a priest, he went on to relate one of the whispered stories to which he had alluded: "There's our good friend Dario, Prince Boccanera, the last of the name, reduced to live on the crumbs which fall to him from his uncle the Cardinal, who has little beyond his stipend left him. Well, Dario would be a rich man had it not been for that extraordinary affair of the Villa Montefiori. You have heard of it, no doubt; how

Prince Onofrio, Dario's father, speculated, sold the villa grounds for ten millions, then bought them back and built on them, and how, at last, not only the ten millions were lost, but also all that remained of the once colossal fortune of the Boccaneras. What you haven't been told, however, is the secret part which Count Prada—our Contessina's husband—played in the affair. He was the lover of Princess Boccanera, the beautiful Flavia Montefiori, who had brought the villa as dowry to the old Prince. She was a very fine woman, much younger than her husband, and it is positively said that it was through her that Prada mastered the Prince—for she held her old doting husband at arm's length whenever he hesitated to give a signature or go farther into the affair of which he scented the danger. And in all this Prada gained the millions which he now spends, while as for the beautiful Flavia, you are aware, no doubt, that she saved a little fortune from the wreck and bought herself a second and much younger husband, whom she turned into a Marquis Montefiori. In the whole affair the only victim is our good friend Dario, who is absolutely ruined, and wishes to marry his cousin, who is as poor as himself. It's true that she's determined to have him, and that it's impossible for him not to reciprocate her love. But for that he would have already married some American girl with a dowry of millions, like so many of the ruined princes, on the verge of starvation, have done; that is, unless the Cardinal and Donna Serafina had opposed such a match, which would not have been surprising, proud and stubborn as they are, anxious to preserve the purity of their old Roman blood. However, let us hope that Dario and the exquisite Benedetta will some day be happy together."

Narcisse paused; but, after taking a few steps in silence, he added in a lower tone: "I've a relative who picked up nearly three millions in that Villa Montefiori affair. Ah! I regret that I wasn't here in those heroic days of speculation. It must have been very amusing; and what strokes there were for a man of self-possession to make!"

However, all at once, as he raised his head, he saw before him the Quartiere dei Prati—the new district of the castle fields; and his face thereupon changed: he again became an artist, indignant with the modern abominations with which old Rome had been disfigured. His eyes paled, and a curl of his lips expressed the bitter disdain of a dreamer whose passion for the vanished centuries was sorely hurt: "Look, look at it all!" he exclaimed. "To think of it, in the city of Augustus, the city of Leo X, the city of eternal power and eternal beauty!"

Pierre himself was thunderstruck. The meadows of the Castle of Sant' Angelo, dotted with a few poplar trees, had here formerly stretched alongside the Tiber as far as the first slopes of Monte Mario, thus supplying, to the satisfaction of artists, a foreground or greenery to the Borgo and the dome of St. Peter's. But now, amidst the white, leprous, overturned plain, there stood a town of huge, massive houses, cubes of stone-work, invariably the same, with broad streets intersecting one another at right angles. From end to end similar facades appeared, suggesting series of convents, barracks, or hospitals. Extraordinary and painful was the impression produced by this town so suddenly immobilised whilst in course of erection. It was as if on some accursed morning a wicked magician had with one touch of his wand stopped the works and emptied the noisy stone-yards, leaving the buildings in mournful abandonment. Here on one side the soil had been banked up; there deep pits dug for foundations had remained gaping, overrun with weeds. There were houses whose halls scarcely rose above the level of the soil; others which had been raised to a second or third floor;

others, again, which had been carried as high as was intended, and even roofed in, suggesting skeletons or empty cages. Then there were houses finished excepting that their walls had not been plastered, others which had been left without window frames, shutters, or doors; others, again, which had their doors and shutters, but were nailed up like coffins with not a soul inside them; and yet others which were partly, and in a few cases fully, inhabited—animated by the most unexpected of populations. And no words could describe the fearful mournfulness of that City of the Sleeping Beauty, hushed into mortal slumber before it had even lived, lying annihilated beneath the heavy sun pending an awakening which, likely enough, would never come.

Following his companion, Pierre walked along the broad, deserted streets, where all was still as in a cemetery. Not a vehicle nor a pedestrian passed by. Some streets had no foot ways; weeds were covering the unpaved roads, turning them once more into fields; and yet there were temporary gas lamps, mere leaden pipes bound to poles, which had been there for years. To avoid payment of the door and window tax, the house owners had generally closed all apertures with planks; while some houses, of which little had been built, were surrounded by high palings for fear lest their cellars should become the dens of all the bandits of the district. But the most painful sight of all was that of the young ruins, the proud, lofty structures, which, although unfinished, were already cracking on all sides, and required the support of an intricate arrangement of timbers to prevent them from falling in dust upon the ground. A pang came to one's heart as though one was in a city which some scourge had depopulated—pestilence, war, or bombardment, of which these gaping carcases seem to retain the mark. Then at the thought that this was abortment, not death—that destruction would complete its work before the dreamt-of, vainly awaited denizens would bring life to the still-born houses, one's melancholy deepened to hopeless discouragement. And at each corner, moreover, there was the frightful irony of the magnificent marble slabs which bore the names of the streets, illustrious historical names, Gracchus, Scipio, Pliny, Pompey, Julius Caesar, blazing forth on those unfinished, crumbling walls like a buffet dealt by the Past to modern incompetency.

Then Pierre was once more struck by this truth—that whosoever possesses Rome is consumed by the building frenzy, the passion for marble, the boastful desire to build and leave his monument of glory to future generations. After the Caesars and the Popes had come the Italian Government, which was no sooner master of the city than it wished to reconstruct it, make it more splendid, more huge than it had ever been before. It was the fatal suggestion of the soil itself—the blood of Augustus rushing to the brain of these last-comers and urging them to a mad desire to make the third Rome the queen of the earth. Thence had come all the vast schemes such as the cyclopean quays and the mere ministries struggling to outvie the Colosseum; and thence had come all the new districts of gigantic houses which had sprouted like towns around the ancient city. It was not only on the castle fields, but at the Porta San Giovanni, the Porta San Lorenzo, the Villa Ludovisi, and on the heights of the Viminal and the Esquiline that unfinished, empty districts were already crumbling amidst the weeds of their deserted streets. After two thousand years of prodigious fertility the soil really seemed to be exhausted. Even as in very old fruit gardens newly planted plum and cherry trees wither and die, so the new walls, no doubt, found no life in that old dust of Rome, impoverished by the immemorial growth of so many temples, circuses, arches, basilicas, and churches. And thus the modern houses, which men had sought to render fruitful, the useless, over-huge houses, swollen with hereditary ambition, had been unable to attain maturity, and remained there sterile like dry bushes on a plot of land exhausted by over-cultivation. And the frightful sadness that one felt arose from the fact that so creative and great a past had culminated in such present-day impotency—Rome, who had covered the world with indestructible monuments, now so reduced that she could only generate ruins.

"Oh, they'll be finished some day!" said Pierre.

Narcisse gazed at him in astonishment: "For whom?"

That was the cruel question! Only by dint of patriotic enthusiasm on the morrow of the conquest had one been able to indulge in the hope of a mighty influx of population, and now singular blindness was needed for the belief that such an influx would ever take place. The past experiments seemed decisive; moreover, there was no reason why the population should double: Rome offered neither the attraction of pleasure nor that of gain to be amassed in commerce and industry for those she had not, nor of intensity of social and intellectual life, since of this she seemed no longer capable. In any case, years and years would be requisite. And, meantime, how could one people those houses which were finished; and for whom was one to finish those which had remained mere skeletons, falling to pieces under sun and rain? Must they all remain there indefinitely, some gaunt and open to every blast and others closed and silent like tombs, in the wretched hideousness of their inutility and abandonment? What a terrible proof of error they offered under the radiant sky! The new masters of Rome had made a bad start, and even if they now knew what they ought to have done would they have the courage to undo what they had done? Since the milliard sunk there seemed to be definitely lost and wasted, one actually hoped for the advent of a Nero, endowed with mighty, sovereign will, who would take torch and pick and burn and raze everything in the avenging name of reason and beauty.

"Ah!" resumed Narcisse, "here are the Contessina and the Prince."

Benedetta had told the coachman to pull up in one of the open spaces intersecting the deserted streets, and now along the broad, quiet, grassy road—well fitted for a lovers' stroll—she was approaching on Dario's arm, both of them delighted with their outing, and no longer thinking of the sad things which they had come to see. "What a nice day it is!" the Contessina gaily exclaimed as she reached Pierre and Narcisse. "How pleasant the sunshine is! It's quite a treat to be able to walk about a little as if one were in the country!"

Dario was the first to cease smiling at the blue sky, all the delight of his stroll with his cousin on his arm suddenly departing. "My dear," said he, "we must go to see those people, since you are bent on it, though it will certainly spoil our day. But first I must take my bearings. I'm not particularly clever, you know, in finding my way in places where I don't care to go. Besides, this district is idiotic with all its dead streets and dead houses, and never a face or a shop to serve as a reminder. Still I think the place is over yonder. Follow me; at all events, we shall see."

The four friends then wended their way towards the central part of the district, the part facing the Tiber, where a small nucleus of a population had collected. The landlords turned the few completed houses to the best advantage they could, letting the rooms at very low rentals, and waiting patiently enough for payment. Some needy employees, some poverty-stricken families—had thus installed themselves there, and in the long run contrived to pay a trifle for their accommodation. In consequence, however, of the demolition of the ancient Ghetto and the opening of the new streets by which air had been let into the Trastevere district, perfect hordes of tatterdemalions, famished and homeless, and almost without garments, had swooped upon the unfinished houses, filling them with wretchedness and vermin; and it had been necessary to tolerate this lawless occupation lest all the frightful misery should remain displayed in the public thoroughfares. And so it was to those frightful tenants that had fallen the huge four and five storeyed palaces, entered by monumental doorways flanked by lofty statues and having carved balconies upheld by caryatides all along their fronts. Each family had made its choice, often closing the frameless windows with boards and the gaping doorways with rags, and occupying now an entire princely flat and now a few small rooms, according to its taste. Horrid-looking linen hung drying from the carved balconies, foul stains already degraded the white walls, and from the magnificent porches, intended for sumptuous equipages, there poured a stream of filth which rotted in stagnant pools in the roads, where there was neither pavement nor footpath.

On two occasions already Dario had caused his companions to retrace their steps. He was losing his way and becoming more and more gloomy. "I ought to have taken to the left," said he, "but how is one to know amidst such a set as that!"

Parties of verminous children were now to be seen rolling in the dust; they were wondrously dirty, almost naked, with black skins and tangled locks as coarse as horsehair. There were also women in sordid skirts and with their loose jackets unhooked. Many stood talking together in yelping voices, whilst others, seated on old chairs with their hands on their knees, remained like that idle for hours. Not many men were met; but a few lay on the scorched grass, sleeping heavily in the sunlight. However, the stench was becoming unbearable—a stench of misery as when the human animal eschews all cleanliness to wallow in filth. And matters were made worse by the smell from a small, improvised market—the emanations of the rotting fruit, cooked and sour vegetables, and stale fried fish which a few poor women had set out on the ground amidst a throng of famished, covetous children.

"Ah! well, my dear, I really don't know where it is," all at once exclaimed the Prince, addressing his cousin. "Be reasonable; we've surely seen enough; let's go back to the carriage."

He was really suffering, and, as Benedetta had said, he did not know how to suffer. It seemed to him monstrous that one should sadden one's life by such an excursion as this. Life ought to be buoyant and benign under the clear sky, brightened by pleasant sights, by dance and song. And he, with his naive egotism, had a positive horror of ugliness, poverty, and suffering, the sight of which caused him both mental and physical pain.

Benedetta shuddered even as he did, but in presence of Pierre she desired to be brave. Glancing at him, and seeing how deeply interested and compassionate he looked, she desired to persevere in her effort to sympathise with the humble and the wretched. "No, no, Dario, we must stay. These gentlemen wish to see everything—is it not so?"

"Oh, the Rome of to-day is here," exclaimed Pierre; "this tells one more about it than all the promenades among the ruins and the monuments."

"You exaggerate, my dear Abbe," declared Narcisse. "Still, I will admit that it is very interesting. Some of the old women are particularly expressive."

At this moment Benedetta, seeing a superbly beautiful girl in front of her, could not restrain a cry of enraptured admiration: "*O che bellezza!*"

And then Dario, having recognised the girl, exclaimed with the same delight: "Why, it's La Pierina; she'll show us the way."

The girl had been following the party for a moment already without daring to approach. Her eyes, glittering with the joy of a loving slave, had at first darted towards the Prince, and then had hastily scrutinised the Contessina—not, however, with any show of jealous anger, but with an expression of affectionate submission and resigned happiness at seeing that she also was very beautiful. And the girl fully answered to the Prince's description of her—tall, sturdy, with the bust of a goddess, a real antique, a Juno of twenty, her chin somewhat prominent, her mouth and nose perfect in contour, her eyes large and full like a heifer's, and her whole face quite dazzling—gilded, so to say, by a sunflash—beneath her casque of heavy jet-black hair.

"So you will show us the way?" said Benedetta, familiar and smiling, already consoled for all the surrounding ugliness by the thought that there should be such beautiful creatures in the world.

"Oh yes, signora, yes, at once!" And thereupon Pierina ran off before them, her feet in shoes which at any rate had no holes, whilst the old brown woollen dress which she wore appeared to have been recently washed and mended. One seemed to divine in her a certain coquettish care, a desire for cleanliness, which none of the others displayed; unless, indeed, it were simply that her great beauty lent radiance to her humble garments and made her appear a goddess.

"*Che bellezza! the bellezza!*" the Contessina repeated without wearying. "That girl, Dario *mio*, is a real feast for the eyes!"

"I knew she would please you," he quietly replied, flattered at having discovered such a beauty, and no longer talking of departure, since he could at last rest his eyes on something pleasant.

Behind them came Pierre, likewise full of admiration, whilst Narcisse spoke to him of the scrupulosity of his own tastes, which were for the rare and the subtle. "She's beautiful, no doubt," said he; "but at bottom nothing can be more gross than the Roman style of beauty; there's no soul, none of the infinite in it. These girls simply have blood under their skins without ever a glimpse of heaven."

Meantime Pierina had stopped, and with a wave of the hand directed attention to her mother, who sat on a broken box beside the lofty doorway of an unfinished mansion. She also must have once been very beautiful, but at forty she was already a wreck, with dim eyes, drawn mouth, black teeth, broadly wrinkled countenance, and huge fallen bosom. And she was also fearfully dirty, her grey wavy hair dishevelled and her skirt and jacket soiled and slit, revealing glimpses of grimy flesh. On her knees she held a sleeping infant, her last-born, at whom she gazed like one overwhelmed and courageless, like a beast of burden resigned to her fate.

"*Bene, bene,*" said she, raising her head, "it's the gentleman who came to give me a crown because he saw you crying. And he's come back to see us with some friends. Well, well, there are some good hearts in the world after all."

Then she related their story, but in a spiritless way, without seeking to move her visitors. She was called Giacinta, it appeared, and had married a mason, one Tomaso Gozzo, by whom she had had seven children, Pierina, then Tito, a big fellow of eighteen, then four more girls, each at an interval of two years, and finally the infant, a boy, whom she now had on her lap. They had long lived in the Trastevere district, in an old house which had lately been pulled down; and their existence seemed to have then been shattered, for since they had taken refuge in the Quartiere dei Prati the crisis in the building trade had reduced Tomaso and Tito to absolute idleness, and the bead factory where Pierina had earned as much as tenpence a day—just enough to prevent them from dying of hunger—had closed its doors. At present not one of them had any work; they lived purely by chance.

"If you like to go up," the woman added, "you'll find Tomaso there with his brother Ambrogio, whom we've taken to live with us. They'll know better than I what to say to you. Tomaso is resting; but what else can he do? It's like Tito—he's dozing over there."

So saying she pointed towards the dry grass amidst which lay a tall young fellow with a pronounced nose, hard mouth, and eyes as admirable as Pierina's. He had raised his head to glance suspiciously at the visitors, a fierce frown gathering on his forehead when he remarked how rapturously his sister contemplated the Prince. Then he let his head fall again, but kept his eyes open, watching the pair stealthily.

"Take the lady and gentlemen upstairs, Pierina, since they would like to see the place," said the mother.

Other women had now drawn near, shuffling along with bare feet in old shoes; bands of children, too, were swarming around; little girls but half clad, amongst whom, no doubt, were Giacinta's four. However, with their black eyes under their tangled mops they were all so much alike that only their mothers could identify them. And the whole resembled a teeming camp of misery pitched on that spot of majestic disaster, that street of palaces, unfinished yet already in ruins.

With a soft, loving smile, Benedetta turned to her cousin. "Don't you come up," she gently said; "I don't desire your death, Dario *mio*. It was very good of you to come so far. Wait for me here in the pleasant sunshine: Monsieur l'Abbe and Monsieur Habert will go up with me."

Dario began to laugh, and willingly acquiesced. Then lighting a cigarette, he walked slowly up and down, well pleased with the mildness of the atmosphere.

La Pierina had already darted into the spacious porch whose lofty, vaulted ceiling was adorned with coffers displaying a rosaceous pattern. However, a veritable manure heap covered such marble slabs as had already been laid in the vestibule, whilst the steps of the monumental stone staircase with sculptured balustrade were already cracked and so grimy that they seemed almost black. On all sides appeared the greasy stains of hands; the walls, whilst awaiting the painter and gilder, had been smeared with repulsive filth.

On reaching the spacious first-floor landing Pierina paused, and contented herself with calling through a gaping portal which lacked both door and framework: "Father, here's a lady and two gentlemen to see you." Then to the Contessina she added: "It's the third room at the end." And forthwith she herself rapidly descended the stairs, hastening back to her passion.

Benedetta and her companions passed through two large rooms, bossy with plaster under foot and having frameless windows wide open upon space; and at last they reached a third room, where the whole Gozzo family had installed itself with the remnants it used as furniture. On the floor, where the bare iron girders showed, no boards having been laid down, were five or six leprous-looking palliasses. A long table, which was still strong, occupied the centre of the room, and here and there were a few old, damaged, straw-seated chairs mended with bits of rope. The great business had been to close two of the three windows with boards, whilst the third one and the door were screened with some old mattress ticking studded with stains and holes.

Tomaso's face expressed the surprise of a man who is unaccustomed to visits of charity. Seated at the table, with his elbows resting on it and his chin supported by his hands, he was taking repose, as his wife Giacinta had said. He was a sturdy fellow of five and forty, bearded and long-haired; and, in spite of all his misery and idleness, his large face had remained as serene as that of a Roman senator. However, the sight of the two foreigners—for such he at once judged Pierre and Narcisse to be, made him rise to his feet with sudden distrust. But he smiled on recognising Benedetta, and as she began to speak of Dario, and to explain the charitable purpose of their visit, he interrupted her: "Yes, yes, I know, Contessina. Oh! I well know who you are, for in my father's time I once walled up a window at the Palazzo Boccanera."

Then he complaisantly allowed himself to be questioned, telling Pierre, who was surprised, that although they were certainly not happy they would have found life tolerable had they been able to work two days a week. And one could divine that he was, at heart, fairly well content to go on short commons, provided that he could live as he listed without fatigue. His narrative and his manner suggested the familiar locksmith who, on being summoned by a traveller to open his trunk, the key of which was lost, sent word that he could not possibly disturb himself during the hour of the siesta. In short, there was no rent to pay, as there were plenty of empty mansions open to the poor, and a few coppers would have sufficed for food, easily contented and sober as one was.

"But oh, sir," Tomaso continued, "things were ever so much better under the Pope. My father, a mason like myself, worked at the Vatican all his life, and even now, when I myself get a job or two, it's always there. We were spoilt, you see, by those ten years of busy work, when we never left our ladders and earned as much as we pleased. Of course, we fed ourselves better, and bought ourselves clothes, and took such pleasure as we cared for; so that it's all the harder nowadays to have to stint ourselves. But if you'd only come to see us in the Pope's time! No taxes, everything to be had for nothing, so to say—why, one merely had to let oneself live."

At this moment a growl arose from one of the palliasses lying in the shade of the boarded windows, and the mason, in his slow, quiet way, resumed: "It's my brother Ambrogio, who isn't of my opinion.

"He was with the Republicans in '49, when he was fourteen. But it doesn't matter; we took him with us when we heard that he was dying of hunger and sickness in a cellar."

The visitors could not help quivering with pity. Ambrogio was the elder by some fifteen years; and now, though scarcely sixty, he was already a ruin, consumed by fever, his legs so wasted that he spent his days on his palliasse without ever going out. Shorter and slighter, but more turbulent than his brother, he had been a carpenter by trade. And, despite his physical decay, he retained an extraordinary head—the head of an apostle and martyr, at once noble and tragic in its expression, and encompassed by bristling snowy hair and beard.

VIII.

"The Pope," he growled; "I've never spoken badly of the Pope. Yet it's his fault if tyranny continues. He alone in '49 could have given us the Republic, and then we shouldn't have been as we are now."

Ambrogio had known Mazzini, whose vague religiosity remained in him—the dream of a Republican pope at last establishing the reign of liberty and fraternity. But later on his passion for Garibaldi had disturbed these views, and led him to regard the papacy as worthless, incapable of achieving human freedom. And so, between the dream of his youth and the stern experience of his life, he now hardly knew in which direction the truth lay. Moreover, he had never acted save under the impulse of violent emotion, but contented himself with fine words—vague, indeterminate wishes.

"Brother Ambrogio," replied Tomaso, all tranquillity, "the Pope is the Pope, and wisdom lies in putting oneself on his side, because he will always be the Pope—that is to say, the stronger. For my part, if we had to vote to-morrow I'd vote for him."

Calmed by the shrewd prudence characteristic of his race, the old carpenter made no haste to reply. At last he said, "Well, as for me, brother Tomaso, I should vote against him—always against him. And you know very well that we should have the majority. The Pope-king indeed! That's all over. The very Borgo would revolt. Still, I won't say that we oughtn't to come to an understanding with him, so that everybody's religion may be respected."

Pierre listened, deeply interested, and at last ventured to ask: "Are there many socialists among the Roman working classes?"

This time the answer came after a yet longer pause. "Socialists? Yes, there are some, no doubt, but much fewer than in other places. All those things are novelties which impatient fellows go in for without understanding much about them. We old men, we were for liberty; we don't believe in fire and massacre."

Then, fearing to say too much in presence of that lady and those gentlemen, Ambrogio began to moan on his pallet, whilst the Contessina, somewhat upset by the smell of the place, took her departure, after telling the young priest that it would be best for them to leave their alms with the wife downstairs. Meantime Tomaso resumed his seat at the table, again letting his chin rest on his hands as he nodded to his visitors, no more impressed by their departure than he had been by their arrival: "To the pleasure of seeing you again, and am happy to have been able to oblige you."

On the threshold, however, Narcisse's enthusiasm burst forth; he turned to cast a final admiring glance at old Ambrogio's head, "a perfect masterpiece," which he continued praising whilst he descended the stairs.

Down below Giacinta was still sitting on the broken box with her infant across her lap, and a few steps away Pierina stood in front of Dario, watching him with an enchanted air whilst he finished his cigarette. Tito, lying low in the grass like an animal on the watch for prey, did not for a moment cease to gaze at them.

"Ah, signora!" resumed the woman, in her resigned, doleful voice, "the place is hardly inhabitable, as you must have seen. The only good thing is that one gets plenty of room. But there are draughts enough to kill me, and I'm always so afraid of the children falling down some of the holes."

Thereupon she related a story of a woman who had lost her life through mistaking a window for a door one evening and falling headlong into the street. Then, too, a little girl had broken both arms by tumbling from a staircase which had no banisters. And you could die there without anybody knowing how bad you were and coming to help you. Only the previous day the corpse of an old man had been found lying on the plaster in a lonely room. Starvation must have killed him quite a week previously, yet he would still have been stretched there if the odour of his remains had not attracted the attention of neighbours.

"If one only had something to eat things wouldn't be so bad!" continued Giacinta. "But it's dreadful when there's a baby to suckle and one gets no food, for after a while one has no milk. This little fellow wants his titty and gets angry with me because I can't give him any. But it isn't my fault. He has sucked me till the blood came, and all I can do is to cry."

As she spoke tears welled into her poor dim eyes. But all at once she flew into a tantrum with Tito, who was still wallowing in the grass like an animal instead of rising by way of civility towards those fine people, who would surely leave her some alms. "Eh! Tito, you lazy fellow, can't you get up when people come to see you?" she called.

After some pretence of not hearing, the young fellow at last rose with an air of great ill-humour; and Pierre, feeling interested in him, tried to draw him out as he had done with the father and uncle upstairs. But Tito only returned curt answers, as if both bored and suspicious. Since there was no work to be had, said he, the only thing was to sleep. It was of no use to get angry; that wouldn't alter matters. So the best was to live as one could without increasing one's worry. As for socialists—well, yes, perhaps there were a few, but he didn't know any. And his weary, indifferent manner made it quite clear that, if his father was for the Pope and his uncle for the Republic, he himself was for nothing at all. In this Pierre divined the end of a nation, or rather the slumber of a nation in which democracy has not yet awakened. However, as the priest continued, asking Tito his age, what school he had attended, and in what district he had been born, the young man suddenly cut the questions short by pointing with one finger to his breast and saying gravely, "*Io son' Romano di Roma.*"

And, indeed, did not that answer everything? "I am a Roman of Rome." Pierre smiled sadly and spoke no further. Never had he more fully realised the pride of that race, the long-descending inheritance of glory which was so heavy to bear. The sovereign vanity of the Caesars lived anew in that degenerate young fellow who was scarcely able to read and write. Starveling though he was, he knew his city, and could instinctively have recounted the grand pages of its history. The names of the great emperors and great popes were familiar to him. And why should men toil and moil when they had been the masters of the world? Why not live nobly and idly in the most beautiful of cities, under the most beautiful of skies? "*Io son' Romano di Roma*!"

Benedetta had slipped her alms into the mother's hand, and Pierre and Narcisse were following her example when Dario, who had already done so, thought of Pierina. He did not like to offer her money, but a pretty, fanciful idea occurred to him. Lightly touching his lips with his finger-tips, he said, with a faint laugh, "For beauty!"

There was something really pretty and pleasing in the kiss thus wafted with a slightly mocking laugh by that familiar, good-natured young Prince who, as in some love story of the olden time, was touched by the beautiful bead-worker's mute adoration. Pierina flushed with pleasure, and, losing her head, darted upon Dario's hand and pressed her warm lips to it with unthinking impulsiveness, in which there was as much divine gratitude as tender passion. But Tito's eyes flashed with anger at the sight, and, brutally seizing his sister by the skirt, he threw her back, growling between his teeth, "None of that, you know, or I'll kill you, and him too!"

It was high time for the visitors to depart, for other women, scenting the presence of money, were now coming forward with outstretched hands, or despatching tearful children in their stead. The whole wretched, abandoned district was in a flutter, a distressful wail ascended from those lifeless streets with high resounding names. But what was to be done? One could not give to all. So the only course lay in flight—amidst deep sadness as one realised how powerless was charity in presence of such appalling want.

When Benedetta and Dario had reached their carriage they hastened to take their seats and nestle side by side, glad to escape from all such horrors. Still the Contessina was well pleased with her bravery in the presence of Pierre, whose hand she pressed with the emotion of a pupil touched by the master's lesson, after Narcisse had told her that he meant to take the young priest to lunch at the little restaurant on the Piazza of St. Peter's whence one obtained such an interesting view of the Vatican.

"Try some of the light white wine of Genzano," said Dario, who had become quite gay again. "There's nothing better to drive away the blues."

However, Pierre's curiosity was insatiable, and on the way he again questioned Narcisse about the people of modern Rome, their life, habits, and manners. There was little or no education, he learnt; no large manufactures and no export trade existed. The men carried on the few trades that were current, all consumption being virtually limited to the city itself. Among the women there were bead-workers and embroiderers; and the manufacture of religious articles, such as medals and chaplets, and of certain popular jewellery had always occupied a fair number of hands. But after marriage the women, invariably burdened with numerous offspring, attempted little beyond household work. Briefly, the population took life as it came, working just sufficiently to secure food, contenting itself with vegetables, pastes, and scraggy mutton, without thought of rebellion or ambition. The only vices were gambling and a partiality for the red and white wines of the Roman province—wines which excited to quarrel and murder, and on the evenings of feast days, when the taverns emptied, strewed the streets with groaning men, slashed and stabbed with knives. The girls, however, but seldom went wrong; one could count those who allowed themselves to be seduced; and this arose from the great union prevailing in each family, every member of which bowed submissively to the father's absolute authority. Moreover, the brothers watched over their sisters even as Tito did over Pierina, guarding them fiercely for the sake of the family honour. And amidst all this there was no real religion, but simply a childish idolatry, all hearts going forth to Madonna and the Saints, who alone were entreated and regarded as having being: for it never occurred to anybody to think of God.

Thus the stagnation of the lower orders could easily be understood. Behind them were the many centuries during which idleness had been encouraged, vanity flattered, and nerveless life willingly accepted. When they were neither masons, nor carpenters, nor bakers, they were servants serving the priests, and more or less directly in the pay of the Vatican. Thence sprang the two antagonistic parties, on the one hand the more numerous party composed of the old Carbonari, Mazzinians, and Garibaldians, the *elite* of the Trastevere; and on the other the "clients" of the Vatican, all who lived on or by the Church and regretted the Pope-King. But, after all, the antagonism was confined to opinions; there was no thought of making an effort or incurring a risk. For that, some sudden flare of passion, strong enough to overcome the sturdy calmness of the race, would have been needed. But what would have been the use of it? The wretchedness had lasted for so many centuries, the sky was so blue, the siesta preferable to aught else during the hot hours! And only one thing seemed positive—that the majority was certainly in favour of Rome remaining the capital of Italy. Indeed, rebellion had almost broken out in the Leonine City when the cession of the latter to the Holy See was rumoured. As for the increase of want and poverty, this was largely due to the circumstance that the Roman workman had really gained nothing by the many works carried on in his city during fifteen years. First of all, over 40,000 provincials, mostly from the North, more spirited and resistant than himself, and working at cheaper rates, had invaded Rome; and when he, the Roman, had secured his share of the labour, he had lived in better style, without thought of economy; so that after the crisis, when the 40,000 men from the provinces were sent home again, he had found himself once more in a dead city where trade was always slack. And thus he had relapsed into his antique indolence, at heart well pleased at no longer being hustled by press of work, and again accommodating himself as best he could to his old mistress, Want, empty in pocket yet always a *grand seigneur*.

However, Pierre was struck by the great difference between the want and wretchedness of Rome and Paris. In Rome the destitution was certainly more complete, the food more loathsome, the dirt more repulsive. Yet at the same time the Roman poor retained more ease of manner and more real gaiety. The young priest thought of the fireless, breadless poor of Paris, shivering in their hovels at winter time; and suddenly he understood. The destitution of Rome did not know cold. What a sweet and eternal consolation; a sun for ever bright, a sky for ever blue and benign out of charity to the wretched! And what mattered the vileness of the dwelling if one could sleep under the sky, fanned by the warm breeze! What mattered even hunger if the family could await the windfall of chance in sunlit streets or on the scorched grass! The climate induced sobriety; there was no need of alcohol or red meat to enable one to face treacherous fogs. Blissful idleness smiled on the golden evenings, poverty became like the enjoyment of liberty in that delightful atmosphere where the happiness of living seemed to be all sufficient. Narcisse told Pierre that at Naples, in the narrow odoriferous streets of the port and Santa Lucia districts, the people spent virtually their whole lives out-of-doors, gay, childish, and ignorant, seeking nothing beyond the few pence that were needed to buy food. And it was certainly the climate which fostered the prolonged infancy of the nation, which explained why such a democracy did not awaken to social ambition and consciousness of itself. No doubt the poor of Naples and Rome suffered from want; but they did not know the rancour which cruel winter implants in men's hearts, the dark rancour which one feels on shivering with cold while rich people are warming themselves before blazing fires. They did not know the infuriated reveries in snow-swept hovels, when the guttering dip burns low, the passionate need which then comes upon one to wreak justice, to revolt, as from a sense of duty, in order that one may save wife and children from consumption, in order that they also may have a warm nest where life shall be a possibility! Ah! the want that shivers with the bitter cold—therein lies the excess of social injustice, the most terrible of schools, where the poor learn to realise their sufferings, where they are roused to indignation, and swear to make those sufferings cease, even if in doing so they annihilate all olden society!

And in that same clemency of the southern heavens Pierre also found an explanation of the life of St. Francis,[1] that divine mendicant of love who roamed the high roads extolling the charms of poverty. Doubtless he was an unconscious revolutionary, protesting against the overflowing luxury of the Roman court by his return to the love of the humble, the simplicity of the primitive Church. But such a revival of innocence and sobriety would never have been possible in a northern land. The enchantment of Nature, the frugality of a people whom the sunlight nourished, the benignity of mendicancy on roads for ever warm, were needed to effect it. And yet how was it possible that a St. Francis, glowing with brotherly love, could have appeared in a land which nowadays so seldom practises charity, which treats the lowly so harshly and contemptuously, and cannot even bestow alms on its own Pope? Is it because ancient pride ends by hardening all hearts, or because the experience of very old races leads finally to egotism, that one now beholds Italy seemingly benumbed amidst dogmatic and pompous Catholicism, whilst the return to the ideals of the Gospel, the passionate interest in the poor and the suffering comes from the woeful plains of the North, from the nations whose sunlight is so limited? Yes, doubtless all that has much to do with the change, and the success of St. Francis was in particular due to the circumstance that, after so gaily espousing his lady, Poverty, he was able to lead her, bare-footed and scarcely clad, during endless and delightful spring-tides, among communities whom an ardent need of love and compassion then consumed.

While conversing, Pierre and Narcisse had reached the Piazza of St. Peter's, and they sat down at one of the little tables skirting the pavement outside the restaurant where they had lunched once before. The linen was none too clean, but the view was splendid. The Basilica rose up in front of them, and the Vatican on the right, above the majestic curve of the colonnade. Just as the waiter was bringing the *hors-d'oeuvre*, some *finocchio*[2] and anchovies, the young priest, who had fixed his eyes on the Vatican, raised an exclamation to attract Narcisse's attention: "Look, my friend, at that window, which I am told is the Holy Father's. Can't you distinguish a pale figure standing there, quite motionless?"

The young man began to laugh. "Oh! well," said he, "it must be the Holy Father in person. You are so anxious to see him that your very anxiety conjures him into your presence."

"But I assure you," repeated Pierre, "that he is over there behind the window-pane. There is a white figure looking this way."

Narcisse, who was very hungry, began to eat whilst still indulging in banter. All at once, however, he exclaimed: "Well, my dear Abbe, as the Pope is looking at us, this is the moment to speak of him. I promised to tell you how he sunk several millions of St. Peter's Patrimony in the frightful financial crisis of which you have just seen the ruins; and, indeed, your visit to the new district of the castle fields would not be complete without this story by way of appendix."

---

[1] St. Francis of Assisi, the founder of the famous order of mendicant friars.—Trans.

[2] Fennel-root, eaten raw, a favourite "appetiser" in Rome during the spring and autumn.—Trans.

Thereupon, without losing a mouthful, Narcisse spoke at considerable length. At the death of Pius IX the Patrimony of St. Peter, it seemed, had exceeded twenty millions of francs. Cardinal Antonelli, who speculated, and whose ventures were usually successful, had for a long time left a part of this money with the Rothschilds and a part in the hands of different nuncios, who turned it to profit abroad. After Antonelli's death, however, his successor, Cardinal Simeoni, withdrew the money from the nuncios to invest it at Rome; and Leo XIII on his accession entrusted the administration of the Patrimony to a commission of cardinals, of which Monsignor Folchi was appointed secretary. This prelate, who for twelve years played such an important *role*, was the son of an employee of the Dataria, who, thanks to skilful financial operations, had left a fortune of a million francs. Monsignor Folchi inherited his father's cleverness, and revealed himself to be a financier of the first rank in such wise that the commission gradually relinquished its powers to him, letting him act exactly as he pleased and contenting itself with approving the reports which he laid before it at each meeting. The Patrimony, however, yielded scarcely more than a million francs per annum, and, as the expenditure amounted to seven millions, six had to be found. Accordingly, from that other source of income, the Peter's Pence, the Pope annually gave three million francs to Monsignor Folchi, who, by skilful speculations and investments, was able to double them every year, and thus provide for all disbursements without ever breaking into the capital of the Patrimony. In the earlier times he realised considerable profit by gambling in land in and about Rome. He took shares also in many new enterprises, speculated in mills, omnibuses, and water-services, without mentioning all the gambling in which he participated with the Banca di Roma, a Catholic institution. Wonderstruck by his skill, the Pope, who, on his own side, had hitherto speculated through the medium of a confidential employee named Sterbini, dismissed the latter, and entrusted Monsignor Folchi with the duty of turning his money to profit in the same way as he turned that of the Holy See. This was the climax of the prelate's favour, the apogee of his power. Bad days were dawning, things were tottering already, and the great collapse was soon to come, sudden and swift like lightning. One of Leo XIII's practices was to lend large sums to the Roman princes who, seized with the gambling frenzy, and mixed up in land and building speculations, were at a loss for money. To guarantee the Pope's advances they deposited shares with him, and thus, when the downfall came, he was left with heaps of worthless paper on his hands. Then another disastrous affair was an attempt to found a house of credit in Paris in view of working off the shares which could not be disposed of in Italy among the French aristocracy and religious people. To egg these on it was said that the Pope was interested in the venture; and the worst was that he dropped three millions of francs in it.[1] The situation then became the more critical as he had

---

[1] The allusion is evidently to the famous Union Generale, on which the Pope bestowed his apostolic benediction, and with which M. Zola deals at length in his novel Money. Certainly a very brilliant idea was embodied in the Union Generale, that of establishing a great international Catholic bank which would destroy the Jewish financial autocracy throughout Europe, and provide both the papacy and the Legitimist cause in several countries with the sinews of war. But in the battle which ensued the great Jew financial houses

gradually risked all the money he disposed of in the terrible agiotage going on in Rome, tempted thereto by the prospect of huge profits and perhaps indulging in the hope that he might win back by money the city which had been torn from him by force. His own responsibility remained complete, for Monsignor Folchi never made an important venture without consulting him; and he must have been therefore the real artisan of the disaster, mastered by his passion for gain, his desire to endow the Church with a huge capital, that great source of power in modern times. As always happens, however, the prelate was the only victim. He had become imperious and difficult to deal with; and was no longer liked by the cardinals of the commission, who were merely called together to approve such transactions as he chose to entrust to them. So, when the crisis came, a plot was laid; the cardinals terrified the Pope by telling him of all the evil rumours which were current, and then forced Monsignor Folchi to render a full account of his speculations. The situation proved to be very bad; it was no longer possible to avoid heavy losses. And so Monsignor Folchi was disgraced, and since then has vainly solicited an audience of Leo XIII, who has always refused to receive him, as if determined to punish him for their common fault—that passion for lucre which blinded them both. Very pious and submissive, however, Monsignor Folchi has never complained, but has kept his secrets and bowed to fate. Nobody can say exactly how many millions the Patrimony of St. Peter lost when Rome was changed into a gambling-hell, but if some prelates only admit ten, others go as far as thirty. The probability is that the loss was about fifteen millions.[1]

Whilst Narcisse was giving this account he and Pierre had despatched their cutlets and tomatoes, and the waiter was now serving them some fried chicken. "At the present time," said Narcisse by way of conclusion, "the gap has been filled up; I told you of the large sums yielded by the Peter's Pence Fund, the amount of which is only known by the Pope, who alone fixes its employment. And, by the way, he isn't cured of speculating: I know from a good source that he still gambles, though with more prudence. Moreover, his confidential assistant is still a prelate. And, when all is said, my dear Abbe, he's in the right: a man must belong to his times—dash it all!"

Pierre had listened with growing surprise, in which terror and sadness mingled. Doubtless such things were natural, even legitimate; yet he, in his dream of a pastor of souls free from all terrestrial cares, had never imagined that they existed. What! the Pope—the spiritual father of the lowly and the suffering—had speculated in land and in stocks and shares! He had gambled, placed funds in the hands of Jew bankers, practised usury, extracted hard interest from money—he, the successor of the Apostle, the Pontiff of Christ, the representative of Jesus, of the Gospel, that divine friend of the poor! And, besides, what a painful contrast: so many millions stored away in those rooms of the Vatican, and so many millions working and fructifying, constantly being diverted from one speculation to another in order that they might yield the more gain; and then down below, near at hand, so much want and misery in those abominable unfinished buildings of the new districts, so many poor folks dying of hunger amidst filth, mothers without milk for their babes, men reduced to idleness by lack of work,

---

proved the stronger, and the disaster which overtook the Catholic speculators was a terrible one.—Trans.

[1] That is 600,000 pounds.

old ones at the last gasp like beasts of burden who are pole-axed when they are of no more use! Ah! God of Charity, God of Love, was it possible! The Church doubtless had material wants; she could not live without money; prudence and policy had dictated the thought of gaining for her such a treasure as would enable her to fight her adversaries victoriously. But how grievously this wounded one's feelings, how it soiled the Church, how she descended from her divine throne to become nothing but a party, a vast international association organised for the purpose of conquering and possessing the world!

And the more Pierre thought of the extraordinary adventure the greater was his astonishment. Could a more unexpected, startling drama be imagined? That Pope shutting himself up in his palace—a prison, no doubt, but one whose hundred windows overlooked immensity; that Pope who, at all hours of the day and night, in every season, could from his window see his capital, the city which had been stolen from him, and the restitution of which he never ceased to demand; that Pope who, day by day, beheld the changes effected in the city—the opening of new streets, the demolition of ancient districts, the sale of land, and the gradual erection of new buildings which ended by forming a white girdle around the old ruddy roofs; that Pope who, in presence of this daily spectacle, this building frenzy, which he could follow from morn till eve, was himself finally overcome by the gambling passion, and, secluded in his closed chamber, began to speculate on the embellishments of his old capital, seeking wealth in the spurt of work and trade brought about by that very Italian Government which he reproached with spoliation; and finally that Pope losing millions in a catastrophe which he ought to have desired, but had been unable to foresee! No, never had dethroned monarch yielded to a stranger idea, compromised himself in a more tragical venture, the result of which fell upon him like divine punishment. And it was no mere king who had done this, but the delegate of God, the man who, in the eyes of idolatrous Christendom, was the living manifestation of the Deity!

Dessert had now been served—a goat's cheese and some fruit—and Narcisse was just finishing some grapes when, on raising his eyes, he in turn exclaimed: "Well, you are quite right, my dear Abbe, I myself can see a pale figure at the window of the Holy Father's room."

Pierre, who scarcely took his eyes from the window, answered slowly: "Yes, yes, it went away, but has just come back, and stands there white and motionless."

"Well, after all, what would you have the Pope do?" resumed Narcisse with his languid air. "He's like everybody else; he looks out of the window when he wants a little distraction, and certainly there's plenty for him to look at."

The same idea had occurred to Pierre, and was filling him with emotion. People talked of the Vatican being closed, and pictured a dark, gloomy palace, encompassed by high walls, whereas this palace overlooked all Rome, and the Pope from his window could see the world. Pierre himself had viewed the panorama from the summit of the Janiculum, the *loggie* of Raffaelle, and the dome of St. Peter's, and so he well knew what it was that Leo XIII was able to behold. In the centre of the vast desert of the Campagna, bounded by the Sabine and Alban mountains, the seven illustrious hills appeared to him with their trees and edifices. His eyes ranged also over all the basilicas, Santa Maria Maggiore, San Giovanni in Laterano, the cradle of the papacy, San Paolo-fuori-le-Mura, Santa Croce in Gerusalemme, Sant' Agnese, and the others; they beheld, too, the domes of the Gesu of Sant' Andrea della Valle, San Carlo and

San Giovanni dei Fiorentini, and indeed all those four hundred churches of Rome which make the city like a *campo santo* studded with crosses. And Leo XIII could moreover see the famous monuments testifying to the pride of successive centuries—the Castle of Sant' Angelo, that imperial mausoleum which was transformed into a papal fortress, the distant white line of the tombs of the Appian Way, the scattered ruins of the baths of Caracalla and the abode of Septimius Severus; and then, after the innumerable columns, porticoes, and triumphal arches, there were the palaces and villas of the sumptuous cardinals of the Renascence, the Palazzo Farnese, the Palazzo Borghese, the Villa Medici, and others, amidst a swarming of facades and roofs. But, in particular, just under his window, on the left, the Pope was able to see the abominations of the unfinished district of the castle fields. In the afternoon, when he strolled through his gardens, bastioned by the wall of the fourth Leo like the plateau of a citadel, his view stretched over the ravaged valley at the foot of Monte Mario, where so many brick-works were established during the building frenzy. The green slopes are still ripped up, yellow trenches intersect them in all directions, and the closed works and factories have become wretched ruins with lofty, black, and smokeless chimneys. And at any other hour of the day Leo XIII could not approach his window without beholding the abandoned houses for which all those brick-fields had worked, those houses which had died before they even lived, and where there was now nought but the swarming misery of Rome, rotting there like some decomposition of olden society.

However, Pierre more particularly thought of Leo XIII, forgetting the rest of the city to let his thoughts dwell on the Palatine, now bereft of its crown of palaces and rearing only its black cypresses towards the blue heavens. Doubtless in his mind he rebuilt the palaces of the Caesars, whilst before him rose great shadowy forms arrayed in purple, visions of his real ancestors, those emperors and Supreme Pontiffs who alone could tell him how one might reign over every nation and be the absolute master of the world. Then, however, his glances strayed to the Quirinal, and there he could contemplate the new and neighbouring royalty. How strange the meeting of those two palaces, the Quirinal and the Vatican, which rise up and gaze at one another across the Rome of the middle ages and the Renascence, whose roofs, baked and gilded by the burning sun, are jumbled in confusion alongside the Tiber. When the Pope and the King go to their windows they can with a mere opera-glass see each other quite distinctly. True, they are but specks in the boundless immensity, and what a gulf there is between them—how many centuries of history, how many generations that battled and suffered, how much departed greatness, and how much new seed for the mysterious future! Still, they can see one another, and they are yet waging the eternal fight, the fight as to which of them—the pontiff and shepherd of the soul or the monarch and master of the body—shall possess the people whose stream rolls beneath them, and in the result remain the absolute sovereign. And Pierre wondered also what might be the thoughts and dreams of Leo XIII behind those window-panes where he still fancied he could distinguish his pale, ghostly figure. On surveying new Rome, the ravaged olden districts and the new ones laid waste by the blast of disaster, the Pope must certainly rejoice at the colossal failure of the Italian Government. His city had been stolen from him; the newcomers had virtually declared that they would show him how a great capital was created, and their boast had ended in that catastrophe—a multitude of hideous and useless buildings which they did not even know how to finish! He, the Pope, could moreover only be delighted with the terrible worries into which the usurping *regime* had fallen, the political crisis, and the financial crisis, the whole growing national unrest amidst which that *regime* seemed likely to sink some day; and yet did not he himself possess a patriotic soul? was he not a loving son of that Italy whose genius and ancient ambition coursed in the blood of his veins? Ah! no, nothing against Italy; rather everything that would enable her to become once more the mistress of the world. And so, even amidst the joy of hope, he must have been grieved to see her thus ruined, threatened with bankruptcy, displaying like a sore that overturned, unfinished Rome which was a confession of her impotency. But, on the other hand, if the House of Savoy were to be swept away, would he not be there to take its place, and at last resume possession of his capital, which, from his window, for fifteen years past, he had beheld in the grip of masons and demolishers? And then he would again be the master and reign over the world, enthroned in the predestined city to which prophecy has ensured eternity and universal dominion.

But the horizon spread out, and Pierre wondered what Leo XIII beheld beyond Rome, beyond the Campagna and the Sabine and Alban mountains. What had he seen for eighteen years past from that window whence he obtained his only view of the world? What echoes of modern society, its truths and certainties, had reached his ears? From the heights of the Viminal, where the railway terminus stands, the prolonged whistling of engines must have occasionally been carried towards him, suggesting our scientific civilisation, the nations brought nearer together, free humanity marching on towards the future. Did he himself ever dream of liberty when, on turning to the right, he pictured the sea over yonder, past the tombs of the Appian Way? Had he ever desired to go off, quit Rome and her traditions, and found the Papacy of the new democracies elsewhere? As he was said to possess so clear and penetrating a mind he ought to have understood and trembled at the far-away stir and noise that came from certain lands of battle, from those United States of America, for instance, where revolutionary bishops were conquering, winning over the people. Were they working for him or for themselves? If he could not follow them, if he remained stubborn within his Vatican, bound on every side by dogma and tradition, might not rupture some day become unavoidable? And, indeed, the fear of a blast of schism, coming from afar, must have filled him with growing anguish. It was assuredly on that account that he had practised the diplomacy of conciliation, seeking to unite in his hands all the scattered forces of the Church, overlooking the audacious proceedings of certain bishops as far as possible, and himself striving to gain the support of the people by putting himself on its side against the fallen monarchies. But would he ever go any farther? Shut up in that Vatican, behind that bronze portal, was he not bound to the strict formulas of Catholicism, chained to them by the force of centuries? There obstinacy was fated; it was impossible for him to resign himself to that which was his real and surpassing power, the purely spiritual power, the moral authority which brought mankind to his feet, made thousands of pilgrims kneel and women swoon. Departure from Rome and the renunciation of the temporal power would not displace the centre of the Catholic world, but would transform him, the head of the Catholic Church, into the head of something else. And how anxious must have been his thoughts if the evening breeze ever brought him a vague presentiment of that something else, a fear of the new religion which was yet dimly, confusedly dawning amidst the tramp of the nations on the march, and the sound of which must have reached him at one and the same time from every point of the compass.

At this precise moment, however, Pierre felt that the white and motionless shadow behind those windowpanes was held erect by pride, by the ever present conviction of victory. If man could not achieve it, a miracle would intervene. He, the Pope, was absolutely convinced that he or some successor would recover possession of Rome. Had not the Church all eternity before it? And, moreover, why should not the victor be himself? Could not God accomplish the impossible? Why, if it so pleased God, on the very morrow his city would be restored to him, in spite of all the objections of human reason, all the apparent logic of facts. Ah! how he would welcome the return of that prodigal daughter whose equivocal adventures he had ever watched with tears bedewing his paternal eyes! He would soon forget the excesses which he had beheld during eighteen years at all hours and in all seasons. Perhaps he dreamt of what he would do with those new districts with which the city had been soiled. Should they be razed, or left as evidence of the insanity of the usurpers? At all events, Rome would again become the august and lifeless city, disdainful of such vain matters as material cleanliness and comfort, and shining forth upon the world like a pure soul encompassed by the traditional glory of the centuries. And his dream continued, picturing the course which events would take on the very morrow, no doubt. Anything, even a republic was preferable to that House of Savoy. Why not a federal republic, reviving the old political divisions of Italy, restoring Rome to the Church, and choosing him, the Pope, as the natural protector of the country thus reorganised? But his eyes travelled beyond Rome and Italy, and his dream expanded, embracing republican France, Spain which might become republican again, Austria which would some day be won, and indeed all the Catholic nations welded into the United States of Europe, and fraternising in peace under his high presidency as Sovereign Pontiff. And then would follow the supreme triumph, all the other churches at last vanishing, and all the dissident communities coming to him as to the one and only pastor, who would reign in the name of Jesus over the universal democracy.

However, whilst Pierre was immersed in this dream which he attributed to Leo XIII, he was all at once interrupted by Narcisse, who exclaimed: "Oh! my dear Abbe, just look at those statues on the colonnade." The young fellow had ordered a cup of coffee and was languidly smoking a cigar, deep once more in the subtle aesthetics which were his only preoccupation. "They are rosy, are they not?" he continued; "rosy, with a touch of mauve, as if the blue blood of angels circulated in their stone veins. It is the sun of Rome which gives them that supra-terrestrial life; for they live, my friend; I have seen them smile and hold out their arms to me during certain fine sunsets. Ah! Rome, marvellous, delicious Rome! One could live here as poor as Job, content with the very atmosphere, and in everlasting delight at breathing it!"

This time Pierre could not help feeling surprised at Narcisse's language, for he remembered his incisive voice and clear, precise, financial acumen when speaking of money matters. And, at this recollection, the young priest's mind reverted to the castle fields, and intense sadness filled his heart as for the last time all the want and suffering rose before him. Again he beheld the horrible filth which was tainting so many human beings, that shocking proof of the abominable social injustice which condemns the greater number to lead the joyless, breadless lives of accursed beasts. And as his glance returned yet once more to the window of the Vatican, and he fancied he could see a pale hand uplifted behind the glass panes, he thought of that papal benediction which Leo XIII gave from that height, over Rome, and over the plain and the hills, to the faithful of all Christendom. And that papal benediction suddenly seemed to him a mockery, destitute of all power, since throughout such a multitude of centuries it had not once been able to stay a single one of the sufferings of mankind, and could not even bring a little justice for those poor wretches who were agonising yonder beneath the very window.

IX.

THAT evening at dusk, as Benedetta had sent Pierre word that she desired to see him, he went down to her little *salon*, and there found her chatting with Celia.

"I've seen your Pierina, you know," exclaimed the latter, just as the young priest came in. "And with Dario, too. Or rather, she must have been watching for him; he found her waiting in a path on the Pincio and smiled at her. I understood at once. What a beauty she is!"

Benedetta smiled at her friend's enthusiasm; but her lips twitched somewhat painfully, for, however sensible she might be, this passion, which she realised to be so naive and so strong, was beginning to make her suffer. She certainly made allowances for Dario, but the girl was too much in love with him, and she feared the consequences. Even in turning the conversation she allowed the secret of her heart to escape her. "Pray sit down, Monsieur l'Abbe," she said, "we are talking scandal, you see. My poor Dario is accused of making love to every pretty woman in Rome. People say that it's he who gives La Tonietta those white roses which she has been exhibiting at the Corso every afternoon for a fortnight past."

"That's certain, my dear," retorted Celia impetuously. "At first people were in doubt, and talked of little Pontecorvo and Lieutenant Moretta. But every one now knows that La Tonietta's caprice is Dario. Besides, he joined her in her box at the Costanzi the other evening."

Pierre remembered that the young Prince had pointed out La Tonietta at the Pincio one afternoon. She was one of the few *demi-mondaines* that the higher-class society of Rome took an interest in. For a month or so the rich Englishman to whom she owed her means had been absent, travelling.

"Ah!" resumed Benedetta, whose budding jealousy was entirely confined to La Pierina, "so my poor Dario is ruining himself in white roses! Well, I shall have to twit him about it. But one or another of these beauties will end by robbing me of him if our affairs are not soon settled. Fortunately, I have had some better news. Yes, my suit is to be taken in hand again, and my aunt has gone out to-day on that very account."

Then, as Victorine came in with a lamp, and Celia rose to depart, Benedetta turned towards Pierre, who also was rising from his chair: "Please stay," said she; "I wish to speak to you."

However, Celia still lingered, interested by the mention of the divorce suit, and eager to know if the cousins would soon be able to marry. And at last throwing her arms round Benedetta, she kissed her passionately. "So you are hopeful, my dear," she exclaimed. "You think that the Holy Father will give you back your liberty? Oh! I am so pleased; it will be so nice for you to marry Dario! And I'm well pleased on my own account, for my father and mother are beginning to yield. Only yesterday I said to them with that quiet little air of mine, 'I want Attilio, and you must give him me.' And then my father flew into a furious passion and upbraided me, and shook his fist at me, saying that if he'd made my head as hard as his own he would know how to break it. My mother was there quite silent and vexed, and all at once he turned to her and said: 'Here, give her that Attilio she wants, and then perhaps we shall have some peace!' Oh yes! I'm well pleased, very well pleased indeed!"

As she spoke her pure virginal face beamed with so much innocent, celestial joy that Pierre and Benedetta could not help laughing. And at last she went off attended by a maid who had waited for her in the first *salon.*

When they were alone Benedetta made the priest sit down again: "I have been asked to give you some important advice, my friend," she said. "It seems that the news of your presence in Rome is spreading, and that bad reports of you are circulated. Your book is said to be a fierce appeal to schism, and you are spoken of as a mere ambitious, turbulent schismatic. After publishing your book in Paris you have come to Rome, it is said, to raise a fearful scandal over it in order to make it sell. Now, if you still desire to see his Holiness, so as to plead your cause before him, you are advised to make people forget you, to disappear altogether for a fortnight or three weeks."

Pierre was stupefied. Why, they would end by maddening him with all the obstacles they raised to exhaust his patience; they would actually implant in him an idea of schism, of an avenging, liberating scandal! He wished to protest and refuse the advice, but all at once he made a gesture of weariness. What would be the good of it, especially with that young woman, who was certainly sincere and affectionate. "Who asked you to give me this advice?" he inquired. She did not answer, but smiled, and with sudden intuition he resumed: "It was Monsignor Nani, was it not?"

Thereupon, still unwilling to give a direct reply, she began to praise the prelate. He had at last consented to guide her in her divorce affair; and Donna Serafina had gone to the Palace of the Inquisition that very afternoon in order to acquaint him with the result of certain steps she had taken. Father Lorenza, the confessor of both the Boccanera ladies, was to be present at the interview, for the idea of the divorce was in reality his own. He had urged the two women to it in his eagerness to sever the bond which the patriotic priest Pisoni had tied full of such fine illusions. Benedetta became quite animated as she explained the reasons of her hopefulness. "Monsignor Nani can do everything," she said, "and I am very happy that my affair should be in his hands. You must be reasonable also, my friend; do as you are requested. I'm sure you will some day be well pleased at having taken this advice."

Pierre had bowed his head and remained thoughtful. There was nothing unpleasant in the idea of remaining for a few more weeks in Rome, where day by day his curiosity found so much fresh food. Of course, all these delays were calculated to discourage him and bend his will. Yet what did he fear, since he was still determined to relinquish nothing of his book, and to see the Holy Father for the sole purpose of proclaiming his new faith? Once more, in silence, he took that oath, then yielded to Benedetta's entreaties. And as he apologised for being a source of embarrassment in the house she exclaimed: "No, no, I am delighted to have you here. I fancy that your presence will bring us good fortune now that luck seems to be changing in our favour."

It was then agreed that he would no longer prowl around St. Peter's and the Vatican, where his constant presence must have attracted attention. He even promised that he would virtually spend a week indoors, desirous as he was of reperusing certain books, certain pages of Rome's history. Then he went on chatting for a moment, lulled by the peacefulness which reigned around him, since the lamp had illumined the *salon* with its sleepy radiance. Six o'clock had just struck, and outside all was dark.

"Wasn't his Eminence indisposed to-day?" the young man asked.

"Yes," replied the Contessina. "But we are not anxious: it is only a little fatigue. He sent Don Vigilio to tell me that he intended to shut himself up in his room and dictate some letters. So there can be nothing much the matter, you see."

Silence fell again. For a while not a sound came from the deserted street or the old empty mansion, mute and dreamy like a tomb. But all at once the soft somnolence, instinct with all the sweetness of a dream of hope, was disturbed by a tempestuous entry, a whirl of skirts, a gasp of terror. It was Victorine, who had gone off after bringing the lamp, but now returned, scared and breathless: "Contessina! Contessina!"

Benedetta had risen, suddenly quite white and cold, as at the advent of a blast of misfortune. "What, what is it? Why do you run and tremble?" she asked.

"Dario, Monsieur Dario—down below. I went down to see if the lantern in the porch were alight, as it is so often forgotten. And in the dark, in the porch, I stumbled against Monsieur Dario. He is on the ground; he has a knife-thrust somewhere."

A cry leapt from the *amorosa's* heart: "Dead!"

"No, no, wounded."

But Benedetta did not hear; in a louder and louder voice she cried: "Dead! dead!"

"No, no, I tell you, he spoke to me. And for Heaven's sake, be quiet. He silenced me because he did not want any one to know; he told me to come and fetch you—only you. However, as Monsieur l'Abbe is here, he had better help us. We shall be none too many."

Pierre listened, also quite aghast. And when Victorine wished to take the lamp her trembling hand, with which she had no doubt felt the prostrate body, was seen to be quite bloody. The sight filled Benedetta with so much horror that she again began to moan wildly.

"Be quiet, be quiet!" repeated Victorine. "We ought not to make any noise in going down. I shall take the lamp, because we must at all events be able to see. Now, quick, quick!"

Across the porch, just at the entrance of the vestibule, Dario lay prone upon the slabs, as if, after being stabbed in the street, he had only had sufficient strength to take a few steps before falling. And he had just fainted, and lay there with his face very pale, his lips compressed, and his eyes closed. Benedetta, recovering the energy of her race amidst her excessive grief, no longer lamented or cried out, but gazed at him with wild, tearless, dilated eyes, as though unable to understand. The horror of it all was the suddenness and mysteriousness of the catastrophe, the why and wherefore of this murderous attempt amidst the silence of the old deserted palace, black with the shades of night. The wound had as yet bled but little, for only the Prince's clothes were stained.

"Quick, quick!" repeated Victorine in an undertone after lowering the lamp and moving it around. "The porter isn't there—he's always at the carpenter's next door—and you see that he hasn't yet lighted the lantern. Still he may come back at any moment. So the Abbe and I will carry the Prince into his room at once." She alone retained her head, like a woman of well-balanced mind and quiet activity. The two others, whose stupor continued, listened to her and obeyed her with the docility of children. "Contessina," she continued, "you must light us. Here, take the lamp and lower it a little so that we may see the steps. You, Abbe, take the feet; I'll take hold of him under the armpits. And don't be alarmed, the poor dear fellow isn't heavy."

Ah! that ascent of the monumental staircase with its low steps and its landings as spacious as guardrooms. They facilitated the cruel journey, but how lugubrious looked the little *cortege* under the flickering glimmer of the lamp which Benedetta held with arm outstretched, stiffened by determination! And still not a sound came from the old lifeless dwelling, nothing but the silent crumbling of the walls, the slow decay which was making the ceilings crack. Victorine continued to whisper words of advice whilst Pierre, afraid of slipping on the shiny slabs, put forth an excess of strength which made his breath come short. Huge, wild shadows danced over the big expanse of bare wall up to the very vaults decorated with sunken panels. So endless seemed the ascent that at last a halt became necessary; but the slow march was soon resumed. Fortunately Dario's apartments—bed-chamber, dressing-room, and sitting-room—were on the first floor adjoining those of the Cardinal in the wing facing the Tiber; so, on reaching the landing, they only had to walk softly along the corridor, and at last, to their great relief, laid the wounded man upon his bed.

Victorine vented her satisfaction in a light laugh. "That's done," said she; "put the lamp on that table, Contessina. I'm sure nobody heard us. It's lucky that Donna Serafina should have gone out, and that his Eminence should have shut himself up with Don Vigilio. I wrapped my skirt round Monsieur Dario's shoulders, you know, so I don't think any blood fell on the stairs. By and by, too, I'll go down with a sponge and wipe the slabs in the porch—" She stopped short, looked at Dario, and then quickly added: "He's breathing—now I'll leave you both to watch over him while I go for good Doctor Giordano, who saw you come into the world, Contessina. He's a man to be trusted."

Alone with the unconscious sufferer in that dim chamber, which seemed to quiver with the frightful horror that filled their hearts, Benedetta and Pierre remained on either side of the bed, as yet unable to exchange a word. The young woman first opened her arms and wrung her hands whilst giving vent to a hollow moan, as if to relieve and exhale her grief; and then, leaning forward, she watched for some sign of life on that pale face whose eyes were closed. Dario was certainly breathing, but his respiration was slow and very faint, and some time went by before a touch of colour returned to his cheeks. At last, however, he opened his eyes, and then she at once took hold of his hand and pressed it, instilling into the pressure all the anguish of her heart. Great was her happiness on feeling that he feebly returned the clasp.

"Tell me," she said, "you can see me and hear me, can't you? What has happened, good God?"

He did not at first answer, being worried by the presence of Pierre. On recognising the young priest, however, he seemed content that he should be there, and then glanced apprehensively round the room to see if there were anybody else. And at last he murmured: "No one saw me, no one knows?"

"No, no; be easy. We carried you up with Victorine without meeting a soul. Aunt has just gone out, uncle is shut up in his rooms."

At this Dario seemed relieved, and he even smiled. "I don't want anybody to know, it is so stupid," he murmured.

"But in God's name what has happened?" she again asked him.

"Ah! I don't know, I don't know," was his response, as he lowered his eyelids with a weary air as if to escape the question. But he must have realised that it was best for him to confess some portion of the truth at once, for he resumed: "A man was hidden in the shadow of the porch—he must have been waiting for me. And so, when I came in, he dug his knife into my shoulder, there."

Forthwith she again leant over him, quivering, and gazing into the depths of his eyes: "But who was the man, who was he?" she asked. Then, as he, in a yet more weary way, began to stammer that he didn't know, that the man had fled into the darkness before he could recognise him, she raised a terrible cry: "It was Prada! it was Prada, confess it, I know it already!" And, quite delirious, she went on: "I tell you that I know it! Ah! I would not be his, and he is determined that we shall never belong to one another. Rather than have that he will kill you on the day when I am free to be your wife! Oh! I know him well; I shall never, never be happy. Yes, I know it well, it was Prada, Prada!"

But sudden energy upbuoyed the wounded man, and he loyally protested: "No, no, it was not Prada, nor was it any one working for him. That I swear to you. I did not recognise the man, but it wasn't Prada—no, no!"

There was such a ring of truth in Dario's words that Benedetta must have been convinced by them. But terror once more overpowered her, for the hand she held was suddenly growing soft, moist, and powerless. Exhausted by his effort, Dario had fallen back, again fainting, his face quite white and his eyes closed. And it seemed to her that he was dying. Distracted by her anguish, she felt him with trembling, groping hands: "Look, look, Monsieur l'Abbe!" she exclaimed. "But he is dying, he is dying; he is already quite cold. Ah! God of heaven, he is dying!"

Pierre, terribly upset by her cries, sought to reassure her, saying: "He spoke too much; he has lost consciousness, as he did before. But I assure you that I can feel his heart beating. Here, put your hand here, Contessina. For mercy's sake don't distress yourself like that; the doctor will soon be here, and everything will be all right."

But she did not listen to him, and all at once he was lost in amazement, for she flung herself upon the body of the man she adored, caught it in a frantic embrace, bathed it with tears and covered it with kisses whilst stammering words of fire: "Ah! if I were to lose you, if I were to lose you! And to think that I repulsed you, that I would not accept happiness when it was yet possible! Yes, that idea of mine, that vow I made to the Madonna! Yet how could she be offended by our happiness? And then, and then, if she has deceived me, if she takes you from me, ah! then I can have but one regret—that I did not damn myself with you—yes, yes, damnation rather than that we should never, never be each other's!"

Was this the woman who had shown herself so calm, so sensible, so patient the better to ensure her happiness? Pierre was terrified, and no longer recognised her. He had hitherto seen her so reserved, so modest, with a childish charm that seemed to come from her very nature! But under the threatening blow she feared, the terrible blood of the Boccaneras had awoke within her with a long heredity of violence, pride, frantic and exasperated longings. She wished for her share of life, her share of love! And she moaned and she clamoured, as if death, in taking her lover from her, were tearing away some of her own flesh.

"Calm yourself, I entreat you, madame," repeated the priest. "He is alive, his heart beats. You are doing yourself great harm."

But she wished to die with her lover: "O my darling! if you must go, take me, take me with you. I will lay myself on your heart, I will clasp you so tightly with my arms that they shall be joined to yours, and then we must needs be buried together. Yes, yes, we shall be dead, and we shall be wedded all the same—wedded in death! I promised that I would belong to none but you, and I will be yours in spite of everything, even in the grave. O my darling, open your eyes, open your mouth, kiss me if you don't want me to die as soon as you are dead!"

A blaze of wild passion, full of blood and fire, had passed through that mournful chamber with old, sleepy walls. But tears were now overcoming Benedetta, and big gasping sobs at last threw her, blinded and strengthless, on the edge of the bed. And fortunately an end was put to the terrible scene by the arrival of the doctor whom Victorine had fetched.

Doctor Giordano was a little old man of over sixty, with white curly hair, and fresh-looking, clean-shaven countenance. By long practice among Churchmen he had acquired the paternal appearance and manner of an amiable prelate. And he was said to be a very worthy man, tending the poor for nothing, and displaying ecclesiastical reserve and discretion in all delicate cases. For thirty years past the whole Boccanera family, children, women, and even the most eminent Cardinal himself, had in all cases of sickness been placed in the hands of this prudent practitioner. Lighted by Victorine and helped by Pierre, he undressed Dario, who was roused from his swoon by pain; and after examining the wound he declared with a smile that it was not at all dangerous. The young Prince would at the utmost have to spend three weeks in bed, and no complications were to be feared. Then, like all the doctors of Rome, enamoured of the fine thrusts and cuts which day by day they have to dress among chance patients of the lower classes, he complacently lingered over the wound, doubtless regarding it as a clever piece of work, for he ended by saying to the Prince in an undertone: "That's what we call a warning. The man didn't want to kill, the blow was dealt downwards so that the knife might slip through the flesh without touching the bone. Ah! a man really needs to be skilful to deal such a stab; it was very neatly done."

"Yes, yes," murmured Dario, "he spared me; had he chosen he could have pierced me through."

Benedetta did not hear. Since the doctor had declared the case to be free from danger, and had explained that the fainting fits were due to nervous shock, she had fallen in a chair, quite prostrated. Gradually, however, some gentle tears coursed from her eyes, bringing relief after her frightful despair, and then, rising to her feet, she came and kissed Dario with mute and passionate delight.

"I say, my dear doctor," resumed the Prince, "it's useless for people to know of this. It's so ridiculous. Nobody has seen anything, it seems, excepting Monsieur l'Abbe, whom I ask to keep the matter secret. And in particular I don't want anybody to alarm the Cardinal or my aunt, or indeed any of our friends."

Doctor Giordano indulged in one of his placid smiles. "*Bene, bene*," said he, "that's natural; don't worry yourself. We will say that you have had a fall on the stairs and have dislocated your shoulder. And now that the wound is dressed you must try to sleep, and don't get feverish. I will come back to-morrow morning."

That evening of excitement was followed by some very tranquil days, and a new life began for Pierre, who at first remained indoors, reading and writing, with no other recreation than that of spending his afternoons in Dario's room, where he was certain to find Benedetta. After a somewhat intense fever lasting for eight and forty hours, cure took its usual course, and the story of the dislocated shoulder was so generally believed, that the Cardinal insisted on Donna Serafina departing from her habits of strict economy, to have a second lantern lighted on the landing in order that no such accident might occur again. And then the monotonous peacefulness was only disturbed by a final incident, a threat of trouble, as it were, with which Pierre found himself mixed up one evening when he was lingering beside the convalescent patient.

Benedetta had absented herself for a few minutes, and as Victorine, who had brought up some broth, was leaning towards the Prince to take the empty cup from him, she said in a low voice: "There's a girl, Monsieur, La Pierina, who comes here every day, crying and asking for news of you. I can't get rid of her, she's always prowling about the place, so I thought it best to tell you of it."

Unintentionally, Pierre heard her and understood everything. Dario, who was looking at him, at once guessed his thoughts, and without answering Victorine exclaimed: "Yes, Abbe, it was that brute Tito! How idiotic, eh?" At the same time, although the young man protested that he had done nothing whatever for the girl's brother to give him such a "warning," he smiled in an embarrassed way, as if vexed and even somewhat ashamed of being mixed up in an affair of the kind. And he was evidently relieved when the priest promised that he would see the girl, should she come back, and make her understand that she ought to remain at home.

"It was such a stupid affair!" the Prince repeated, with an exaggerated show of anger. "Such things are not of our times."

But all at once he ceased speaking, for Benedetta entered the room. She sat down again beside her dear patient, and the sweet, peaceful evening then took its course in the old sleepy chamber, the old, lifeless palace, whence never a sound arose.

When Pierre began to go out again he at first merely took a brief airing in the district. The Via Giulia interested him, for he knew how splendid it had been in the time of Julius II, who had dreamt of lining it with sumptuous palaces. Horse and foot races then took place there during the carnival, the Palazzo Farnese being the starting-point, and the Piazza of St. Peter's the goal. Pierre had also lately read that a French ambassador, D'Estree, Marquis de Coure, had resided at the Palazzo Sacchetti, and in 1638 had given some magnificent entertainments in honour of the birth of the Dauphin,[1] when on three successive days there had been racing from the Ponte Sisto to San Giovanni dei Fiorentini amidst an extraordinary display of sumptuosity: the street being strewn with flowers, and rich hangings adorning every window. On the second even-

---

[1] Afterwards Louis XIV.—Trans.

ing there had been fireworks on the Tiber, with a machine representing the ship Argo carrying Jason and his companions to the recovery of the Golden Fleece; and, on another occasion, the Farnese fountain, the Mascherone, had flowed with wine. Nowadays, however, all was changed. The street, bright with sunshine or steeped in shadow according to the hour, was ever silent and deserted. The heavy, ancient palatial houses, their old doors studded with plates and nails, their windows barred with huge iron gratings, always seemed to be asleep, whole storeys showing nothing but closed shutters as if to keep out the daylight for evermore. Now and again, when a door was open, you espied deep vaults, damp, cold courts, green with mildew, and encompassed by colonnades like cloisters. Then, in the outbuildings of the mansions, the low structures which had collected more particularly on the side of the Tiber, various small silent shops had installed themselves. There was a baker's, a tailor's, and a bookbinder's, some fruiterers' shops with a few tomatoes and salad plants set out on boards, and some wine-shops which claimed to sell the vintages of Frascati and Genzano, but whose customers seemed to be dead. Midway along the street was a modern prison, whose horrid yellow wall in no wise enlivened the scene, whilst, overhead, a flight of telegraph wires stretched from the arcades of the Farnese palace to the distant vista of trees beyond the river. With its infrequent traffic the street, even in the daytime, was like some sepulchral corridor where the past was crumbling into dust, and when night fell its desolation quite appalled Pierre. You did not meet a soul, you did not see a light in any window, and the glimmering gas lamps, few and far between, seemed powerless to pierce the gloom. On either hand the doors were barred and bolted, and not a sound, not a breath came from within. Even when, after a long interval, you passed a lighted wine-shop, behind whose panes of frosted glass a lamp gleamed dim and motionless, not an exclamation, not a suspicion of a laugh ever reached your ear. There was nothing alive save the two sentries placed outside the prison, one before the entrance and the other at the corner of the right-hand lane, and they remained erect and still, coagulated, as it were, in that dead street.

Pierre's interest, however, was not merely confined to the Via Giulia; it extended to the whole district, once so fine and fashionable, but now fallen into sad decay, far removed from modern life, and exhaling a faint musty odour of monasticism. Towards San Giovanni dei Fiorentini, where the new Corso Vittorio Emanuele has ripped up every olden district, the lofty five-storeyed houses with their dazzling sculptured fronts contrasted violently with the black sunken dwellings of the neighbouring lanes. In the evening the globes of the electric lamps on the Corso shone out with such dazzling whiteness that the gas lamps of the Via Giulia and other streets looked like smoky lanterns. There were several old and famous thoroughfares, the Via Banchi Vecchi, the Via del Pellegrino, the Via di Monserrato, and an infinity of cross-streets which intersected and connected the others, all going towards the Tiber, and for the most part so narrow that vehicles scarcely had room to pass. And each street had its church, a multitude of churches all more or less alike, highly decorated, gilded, and painted, and open only at service time when they were full of sunlight and incense. In the Via Giulia, in addition to San Giovanni dei Fiorentini, San Biagio della Pagnotta, San Eligio degli Orefici, and three or four others, there was the so-called Church of the Dead, Santa Maria dell' Orazione; and this church, which is at the lower end behind the Farnese palace, was often visited by Pierre, who liked to dream there of the wild life of Rome, and of the pious brothers of the Confraternita della Morte, who officiate there, and whose mission is to search for and bury such poor outcasts as die in the Campagna. One evening he was present at the funeral of two unknown men, whose bodies, after remaining unburied for quite a fortnight, had been discovered in a field near the Appian Way.

However, Pierre's favourite promenade soon became the new quay of the Tiber beyond the Palazzo Boccanera. He had merely to take the narrow lane skirting the mansion to reach a spot where he found much food for reflection. Although the quay was not yet finished, the work seemed to be quite abandoned. There were heaps of rubbish, blocks of stone, broken fences, and dilapidated tool-sheds all around. To such a height had it been necessary to carry the quay walls—designed to protect the city from floods, for the river bed has been rising for centuries past—that the old terrace of the Boccanera gardens, with its double flight of steps to which pleasure boats had once been moored, now lay in a hollow, threatened with annihilation whenever the works should be finished. But nothing had yet been levelled; the soil, brought thither for making up the bank, lay as it had fallen from the carts, and on all sides were pits and mounds interspersed with the abandoned building materials. Wretched urchins came to play there, workmen without work slept in the sunshine, and women after washing ragged linen spread it out to dry upon the stones. Nevertheless the spot proved a happy, peaceful refuge for Pierre, one fruitful in inexhaustible reveries when for hours at a time he lingered gazing at the river, the quays, and the city, stretching in front of him and on either hand.

At eight in the morning the sun already gilded the vast opening. On turning to the left he perceived the roofs of the Trastevere, of a misty, bluish grey against the dazzling sky. Then, just beyond the apse of San Giovanni, on the right, the river curved, and on its other bank the poplars of the Ospedale di Santo Spirito formed a green curtain, while the castle of Sant' Angelo showed brightly in the distance. But Pierre's eyes dwelt more particularly on the bank just in front of him, for there he found some lingering vestiges of old Rome. On that side indeed between the Ponte Sisto and the Ponte Sant' Angelo, the quays, which were to imprison the river within high, white, fortress-like walls, had not yet been raised, and the bank with its remnants of the old papal city conjured up an extraordinary vision of the middle ages. The houses, descending to the river brink, were cracked, scorched, rusted by innumerable burning summers, like so many antique bronzes. Down below there were black vaults into which the water flowed, piles upholding walls, and fragments of Roman stone-work plunging into the river bed; then, rising from the shore, came steep, broken stairways, green with moisture, tiers of terraces, storeys with tiny windows pierced here and their in hap-hazard fashion, houses perched atop of other houses, and the whole jumbled together with a fantastic commingling of balconies and wooden galleries, footbridges spanning courtyards, clumps of trees growing apparently on the very roofs, and attics rising from amidst pinky tiles. The contents of a drain fell noisily into the river from a worn and soiled gorge of stone; and wherever the houses stood back and the bank appeared, it was covered with wild vegetation, weeds, shrubs, and mantling ivy, which trailed like a kingly robe of state. And in the glory of the sun the wretchedness and dirt vanished, the crooked, jumbled houses seemed to be of gold, draped with the purple of the red petticoats and the dazzling white of the shifts which hung drying from their windows; while higher still, above the district, the Janiculum rose into all the luminary's dazzlement, uprearing the slender profile of Sant' Onofrio amidst cypresses and pines.

Leaning on the parapet of the quay wall, Pierre sadly gazed at the Tiber for hours at a time. Nothing could convey an idea of the weariness of those old waters, the mournful slowness of their flow along that Babylonian trench where they were confined within huge, bare, livid prison-like walls. In the sunlight their yellowness was gilded, and the faint quiver of the current brought ripples of green and blue; but as soon as the shade spread over it the stream became opaque like mud, so turbid in its venerable old age that it no longer even gave back a reflection of the houses lining it. And how desolate was its abandonment, what a stream of silence and solitude it was! After the winter rains it might roll furiously and threateningly, but during the long months of bright weather it traversed Rome without a sound, and Pierre could remain there all day long without seeing either a skiff or a sail. The two or three little steamboats which arrived from the coast, the few tartanes which brought wine from Sicily, never came higher than the Aventine, beyond which there was only a watery desert in which here and there, at long intervals, a motionless angler let his line dangle. All that Pierre ever saw in the way of shipping was a sort of ancient, covered pinnace, a rotting Noah's ark, moored on the right beside the old bank, and he fancied that it might be used as a washhouse, though on no occasion did he see any one in it. And on a neck of mud there also lay a stranded boat with one side broken in, a lamentable symbol of the impossibility and the relinquishment of navigation. Ah! that decay of the river, that decay of father Tiber, as dead as the famous ruins whose dust he is weary of laving! And what an evocation! all the centuries of history, so many things, so many men, that those yellow waters have reflected till, full of lassitude and disgust, they have grown heavy, silent and deserted, longing only for annihilation.

One morning on the river bank Pierre found La Pierina standing behind an abandoned tool-shed. With her neck extended, she was looking fixedly at the window of Dario's room, at the corner of the quay and the lane. Doubtless she had been frightened by Victorine's severe reception, and had not dared to return to the mansion; but some servant, possibly, had told her which was the young Prince's window, and so she now came to this spot, where without wearying she waited for a glimpse of the man she loved, for some sign of life and salvation, the mere hope of which made her heart leap. Deeply touched by the way in which she hid herself, all humility and quivering with adoration, the priest approached her, and instead of scolding her and driving her away as he had been asked to do, spoke to her in a gentle, cheerful manner, asking her for news of her people as though nothing had happened, and at last contriving to mention Dario's name in order that she might understand that he would be up and about again within a fortnight. On perceiving Pierre, La Pierina had started with timidity and distrust as if anxious to flee; but when she understood him, tears of happiness gushed from her eyes, and with a bright smile she kissed her hand to him, calling: "*Grazie, grazie*, thanks, thanks!" And thereupon she darted away, and he never saw her again.

On another morning at an early hour, as Pierre was going to say mass at Santa Brigida on the Piazza Farnese, he was surprised to meet Benedetta coming out of the church and carrying a small phial of oil. She evinced no embarrassment, but frankly told him that every two or three days she went thither to obtain from the beadle a few drops of the oil used for the lamp that burnt before an antique wooden statue of the

Madonna, in which she had perfect confidence. She even confessed that she had never had confidence in any other Madonna, having never obtained anything from any other, though she had prayed to several of high repute, Madonnas of marble and even of silver. And so her heart was full of ardent devotion for the holy image which refused her nothing. And she declared in all simplicity, as though the matter were quite natural and above discussion, that the few drops of oil which she applied, morning and evening, to Dario's wound, were alone working his cure, so speedy a cure as to be quite miraculous. Pierre, fairly aghast, distressed indeed to find such childish, superstitious notions in one so full of sense and grace and passion, did not even venture to smile.

In the evenings, when he came back from his strolls and spent an hour or so in Dario's room, he would for a time divert the patient by relating what he had done and seen and thought of during the day. And when he again ventured to stray beyond the district, and became enamoured of the lovely gardens of Rome, which he visited as soon as they opened in the morning in order that he might be virtually alone, he delighted the young prince and Benedetta with his enthusiasm, his rapturous passion for the splendid trees, the plashing water, and the spreading terraces whence the views were so sublime. It was not the most extensive of these gardens which the more deeply impressed his heart. In the grounds of the Villa Borghese, the little Roman Bois de Boulogne, there were certainly some majestic clumps of greenery, some regal avenues where carriages took a turn in the afternoon before the obligatory drive to the Pincio; but Pierre was more touched by the reserved garden of the villa—that villa dazzling with marble and now containing one of the finest museums in the world. There was a simple lawn of fine grass with a vast central basin surmounted by a figure of Venus, nude and white; and antique fragments, vases, statues, columns, and *sarcophagi* were ranged symmetrically all around the deserted, sunlit yet melancholy, sward. On returning on one occasion to the Pincio Pierre spent a delightful morning there, penetrated by the charm of this little nook with its scanty evergreens, and its admirable vista of all Rome and St. Peter's rising up afar off in the soft limpid radiance. At the Villa Albani and the Villa Pamphili he again came upon superb parasol pines, tall, stately, and graceful, and powerful elm-trees with twisted limbs and dusky foliage. In the Pamphili grounds, the elm-trees steeped the paths in a delicious half-light, the lake with its weeping willows and tufts of reeds had a dreamy aspect, while down below the *parterre* displayed a fantastic floral mosaic bright with the various hues of flowers and foliage. That which most particularly struck Pierre, however, in this, the noblest, most spacious, and most carefully tended garden of Rome, was the novel and unexpected view that he suddenly obtained of St. Peter's, whilst skirting a low wall: a view whose symbolism for ever clung to him. Rome had completely vanished, and between the slopes of Monte Mario and another wooded height which hid the city, there only appeared the colossal dome which seemed to be poised on an infinity of scattered blocks, now white, now red. These were the houses of the Borgo, the jumbled piles of the Vatican and the Basilica which the huge dome surmounted and annihilated, showing greyly blue in the light blue of the heavens, whilst far away stretched a delicate, boundless vista of the Campagna, likewise of a bluish tint.

It was, however, more particularly in the less sumptuous gardens, those of a more homely grace, that Pierre realised that even things have souls. Ah! that Villa Mattei on one side of the Coelius with its terraced grounds, its sloping alleys edged with laurel, aloe, and spindle tree, its box-plants forming arbours, its oranges, its roses, and its fountains! Pierre spent some delicious hours there, and only found a similar charm on visiting the Aventine, where three churches are embowered in verdure. The little garden of Santa Sabina, the birthplace of the Dominican order, is closed on all sides and affords no view: it slumbers in quiescence, warm and perfumed by its orange-trees, amongst which that planted by St. Dominic stands huge and gnarled but still laden with ripe fruit. At the adjoining Priorato, however, the garden, perched high above the Tiber, overlooks a vast expanse, with the river and the buildings on either bank as far as the summit of the Janiculum. And in these gardens of Rome Pierre ever found the same clipped box-shrubs, the same eucalypti with white trunks and pale leaves long like hair, the same ilex-trees squat and dusky, the same giant pines, the same black cypresses, the same marbles whitening amidst tufts of roses, and the same fountains gurgling under mantling ivy. Never did he enjoy more gentle, sorrow-tinged delight than at the Villa of Pope Julius, where all the life of a gay and sensual period is suggested by the semi-circular porticus opening on the gardens, a porticus decorated with paintings, golden trellis-work laden with flowers, amidst which flutter flights of smiling Cupids. Then, on the evening when he returned from the Farnesina, he declared that he had brought all the dead soul of ancient Rome away with him, and it was not the paintings executed after Raffaelle's designs that had touched him, it was rather the pretty hall on the river side decorated in soft blue and pink and lilac, with an art devoid of genius yet so charming and so Roman; and in particular it was the abandoned garden once stretching down to the Tiber, and now shut off from it by the new quay, and presenting an aspect of woeful desolation, ravaged, bossy and weedy like a cemetery, albeit the golden fruit of orange and citron tree still ripened there.

And for the last time a shock came to Pierre's heart on the lovely evening when he visited the Villa Medici. There he was on French soil.[1] And again what a marvellous garden he found with box-plants, and pines, and avenues full of magnificence and charm! What a refuge for antique reverie was that wood of ilex-trees, so old and so sombre, where the sun in declining cast fiery gleams of red gold amidst the sheeny bronze of the foliage. You ascend by endless steps, and from the crowning belvedere on high you embrace all Rome at a glance as though by opening your arms you could seize it in its entirety. From the villa's dining-room, decorated with portraits of all the artists who have successfully sojourned there, and from the spacious peaceful library one beholds the same splendid, broad, all-conquering panorama, a panorama of unlimited ambition, whose infinite ought to set in the hearts of the young men dwelling there a determination to subjugate the world. Pierre, who came thither opposed to the principle of the "Prix de Rome," that traditional, uniform education so dangerous for originality, was for a moment charmed by the warm peacefulness, the limpid solitude of the garden, and the sublime horizon where the wings of genius seemed to flutter. Ah! how delightful, to be only twenty and to live for three years amidst such infinite sweetness, encompassed by the finest works of man; to say to oneself that one is as yet too young to produce, and to reflect, and seek, and learn how to enjoy, suffer, and

---

[1] Here is the French Academy, where winners of the "Prix de Rome" in painting, sculpture, architecture, engraving, and music are maintained by the French Government for three years. The creation dates from Louis XIV.—Trans.

love! But Pierre afterwards reflected that this was not a fit task for youth, and that to appreciate the divine enjoyment of such a retreat, all art and blue sky, ripe age was needed, age with victories already gained and weariness following upon the accomplishment of work. He chatted with some of the young pensioners, and remarked that if those who were inclined to dreaminess and contemplation, like those who could merely claim mediocrity, accommodated themselves to this life cloistered in the art of the past, on the other hand artists of active bent and personal temperament pined with impatience, their eyes ever turned towards Paris, their souls eager to plunge into the furnace of battle and production.

All those gardens of which Pierre spoke to Dario and Benedetta with so much rapture, awoke within them the memory of the garden of the Villa Montefiori, now a waste, but once so green, planted with the finest orange-trees of Rome, a grove of centenarian orange-trees where they had learnt to love one another. And the memory of their early love brought thoughts of their present situation and their future prospects. To these the conversation always reverted, and evening after evening Pierre witnessed their delight, and heard them talk of coming happiness like lovers transported to the seventh heaven. The suit for the dissolution of Benedetta's marriage was now assuming a more and more favourable aspect. Guided by a powerful hand, Donna Serafina was apparently acting very vigorously, for almost every day she had some further good news to report. She was indeed anxious to finish the affair both for the continuity and for the honour of the name, for on the one hand Dario refused to marry any one but his cousin, and on the other this marriage would explain everything and put an end to an intolerable situation. The scandalous rumours which circulated both in the white and the black world quite incensed her, and a victory was the more necessary as Leo XIII, already so aged, might be snatched away at any moment, and in the Conclave which would follow she desired that her brother's name should shine forth with untarnished, sovereign radiance. Never had the secret ambition of her life, the hope that her race might give a third pope to the Church, filled her with so much passion. It was as if she therein sought a consolation for the harsh abandonment of Advocate Morano. Invariably clad in sombre garb, ever active and slim, so tightly laced that from behind one might have taken her for a young girl, she was so to say the black soul of that old palace; and Pierre, who met her everywhere, prowling and inspecting like a careful house-keeper, and jealously watching over her brother the Cardinal, bowed to her in silence, chilled to the heart by the stern look of her withered wrinkled face in which was set the large, opiniative nose of her family. However she barely returned his bows, for she still disdained that paltry foreign priest, and only tolerated him in order to please Monsignor Nani and Viscount Philibert de la Choue.

A witness every evening of the anxious delight and impatience of Benedetta and Dario, Pierre by degrees became almost as impassioned as themselves, as desirous for an early solution. Benedetta's suit was about to come before the Congregation of the Council once more. Monsignor Palma, the defender of the marriage, had demanded a supplementary inquiry after the favourable decision arrived at in the first instance by a bare majority of one vote—a majority which the Pope would certainly not have thought sufficient had he been asked for his ratification. So the question now was to gain votes among the ten cardinals who formed the Congregation, to persuade and convince them, and if possible ensure an almost unanimous pronouncement. The task was arduous, for, instead of facilitating matters, Benedetta's relationship to Cardinal

Boccanera raised many difficulties, owing to the intriguing spirit rife at the Vatican, the spite of rivals who, by perpetuating the scandal, hoped to destroy Boccanera's chance of ever attaining to the papacy. Every afternoon, however, Donna Serafina devoted herself to the task of winning votes under the direction of her confessor, Father Lorenza, whom she saw daily at the Collegio Germanico, now the last refuge of the Jesuits in Rome, for they have ceased to be masters of the Gesu. The chief hope of success lay in Prada's formal declaration that he would not put in an appearance. The whole affair wearied and irritated him; the imputations levelled against him as a man, seemed to him supremely odious and ridiculous; and he no longer even took the trouble to reply to the assignations which were sent to him. He acted indeed as if he had never been married, though deep in his heart the wound dealt to his passion and his pride still lingered, bleeding afresh whenever one or another of the scandalous rumours in circulation reached his ears. However, as their adversary desisted from all action, one can understand that the hopes of Benedetta and Dario increased, the more so as hardly an evening passed without Donna Serafina telling them that she believed she had gained the support of another cardinal.

But the man who terrified them all was Monsignor Palma, whom the Congregation had appointed to defend the sacred ties of matrimony. His rights and privileges were almost unlimited, he could appeal yet again, and in any case would make the affair drag on as long as it pleased him. His first report, in reply to Morano's memoir, had been a terrible blow, and it was now said that a second one which he was preparing would prove yet more pitiless, establishing as a fundamental principle of the Church that it could not annul a marriage whose nonconsummation was purely and simply due to the action of the wife in refusing obedience to her husband. In presence of such energy and logic, it was unlikely that the cardinals, even if sympathetic, would dare to advise the Holy Father to dissolve the marriage. And so discouragement was once more overcoming Benedetta when Donna Serafina, on returning from a visit to Monsignor Nani, calmed her somewhat by telling her that a mutual friend had undertaken to deal with Monsignor Palma. However, said she, even if they succeeded, it would doubtless cost them a large sum.

Monsignor Palma, a theologist expert in all canonical affairs, and a perfectly honest man in pecuniary matters, had met with a great misfortune in his life. He had a niece, a poor and lovely girl, for whom, unhappily, in his declining years he conceived an insensate passion, with the result that to avoid a scandal he was compelled to marry her to a rascal who now preyed upon her and even beat her. And the prelate was now passing through a fearful crisis, weary of reducing himself to beggary, and indeed no longer having the money necessary to extricate his nephew by marriage from a very nasty predicament, the result of cheating at cards. So the idea was to save the young man by a considerable pecuniary payment, and then to procure him employment without asking aught of his uncle, who, as if offering complicity, came in tears one evening, when night had fallen, to thank Donna Serafina for her exceeding goodness.

Pierre was with Dario that evening when Benedetta entered the room, laughing and joyfully clapping her bands. "It's done, it's done!" she said, "he has just left aunt, and vowed eternal gratitude to her. He will now be obliged to show himself amiable."

However Dario distrustfully inquired: "But was he made to sign anything, did he enter into a formal engagement?"

"Oh! no; how could one do that? It's such a delicate matter," replied Benedetta. "But people say that he is a very honest man." Nevertheless, in spite of these words, she herself became uneasy. What if Monsignor Palma should remain incorruptible in spite of the great service which had been rendered him? Thenceforth this idea haunted them, and their suspense began once more.

Dario, eager to divert his mind, was imprudent enough to get up before he was perfectly cured, and, his wound reopening, he was obliged to take to his bed again for a few days. Every evening, as previously, Pierre strove to enliven him with an account of his strolls. The young priest was now getting bolder, rambling in turn through all the districts of Rome, and discovering the many "classical" curiosities catalogued in the guide-books. One evening he spoke with a kind of affection of the principal squares of the city which he had first thought commonplace, but which now seemed to him very varied, each with original features of its own. There was the noble Piazza del Popolo of such monumental symmetry and so full of sunlight; there was the Piazza di Spagna, the lively meeting-place of foreigners, with its double flight of a hundred and thirty steps gilded by the sun; there was the vast Piazza Colonna, always swarming with people, and the most Italian of all the Roman squares from the presence of the idle, careless crowd which ever lounged round the column of Marcus Aurelius as if waiting for fortune to fall from heaven; there was also the long and regular Piazza Navona, deserted since the market was no longer held there, and retaining a melancholy recollection of its former bustling life; and there was the Campo dei Fiori, which was invaded each morning by the tumultuous fruit and vegetable markets, quite a plantation of huge umbrellas sheltering heaps of tomatoes, pimentoes, and grapes amidst a noisy stream of dealers and housewives. Pierre's great surprise, however, was the Piazza del Campidoglio—the "Square of the Capitol"—which to him suggested a summit, an open spot overlooking the city and the world, but which he found to be small and square, and on three sides enclosed by palaces, whilst on the fourth side the view was of little extent.[1] There are no passers-by there; visitors usually come up by a flight of steps bordered by a few palm-trees, only foreigners making use of the winding carriage-ascent. The vehicles wait, and the tourists loiter for a while with their eyes raised to the admirable equestrian statue of Marcus Aurelius, in antique bronze, which occupies the centre of the piazza. Towards four o'clock, when the sun gilds the left-hand palace, and the slender statues of its entablature show vividly against the blue sky, you might think yourself in some warm cosy square of a little provincial town, what with the women of the neighbourhood who sit knitting under the arcade, and the bands of ragged urchins who disport themselves on all sides like school-boys in a playground.

Then, on another evening Pierre told Benedetta and Dario of his admiration for the Roman fountains, for in no other city of the world does water flow so abundantly and magnificently in fountains of bronze and marble, from the boat-shaped Fontana della Barcaccia on the Piazza di Spagna, the Triton on the Piazza Barberini, and the Tortoises which give their name to the Piazza delle Tartarughe, to the three fountains of

[1] The Piazza del Campidoglio is really a depression between the Capitolium proper and the northern height called the Arx. It is supposed to have been the exact site of Romulus's traditional Asylum.—Trans.

the Piazza Navona where Bernini's vast central composition of rock and river-gods rises so triumphantly, and to the colossal and pompous fountain of Trevi, where King Neptune stands on high attended by lofty figures of Health and Fruitfulness. And on yet another evening Pierre came home quite pleased, relating that he had at last discovered why it was that the old streets around the Capitol and along the Tiber seemed to him so strange: it was because they had no footways, and pedestrians, instead of skirting the walls, invariably took the middle of the road, leisurely wending their way among the vehicles. Pierre was very fond of those old districts with their winding lanes, their tiny squares so irregular in shape, and their huge square mansions swamped by a multitudinous jumble of little houses. He found a charm, too, in the district of the Esquiline, where, besides innumerable flights of ascending steps, each of grey pebbles edged with white stone, there were sudden sinuous slopes, tiers of terraces, seminaries and convents, lifeless, with their windows ever closed, and lofty, blank walls above which a superb palm-tree would now and again soar into the spotless blue of the sky. And on yet another evening, having strolled into the Campagna beside the Tiber and above the Ponte Molle, he came back full of enthusiasm for a form of classical art which hitherto he had scarcely appreciated. Along the river bank, however, he had found the very scenery that Poussin so faithfully depicted: the sluggish, yellow stream fringed with reeds; low riven cliffs, whose chalky whiteness showed against the ruddy background of a far-stretching, undulating plain, bounded by blue hills; a few spare trees with a ruined porticus opening on to space atop of the bank, and a line of pale-hued sheep descending to drink, whilst the shepherd, with an elbow resting on the trunk of an ilex-tree, stood looking on. It was a special kind of beauty, broad and ruddy, made up of nothing, sometimes simplified into a series of low, horizontal lines, but ever ennobled by the great memories it evoked: the Roman legions marching along the paved highways across the bare Campagna; the long slumber of the middle ages; and then the awakening of antique nature in the midst of Catholicism, whereby, for the second time, Rome became ruler of the world.

One day when Pierre came back from seeing the great modern cemetery, the Campo Verano, he found Celia, as well as Benedetta, by the side of Dario's bed. "What, Monsieur l'Abbe!" exclaimed the little Princess when she learnt where he had been; "it amuses you to visit the dead?"

"Oh those Frenchmen," remarked Dario, to whom the mere idea of a cemetery was repulsive; "those Frenchmen seem to take a pleasure in making their lives wretched with their partiality for gloomy scenes."

"But there is no escaping the reality of death," gently replied Pierre; "the best course is to look it in the face."

This made the Prince quite angry. "Reality, reality," said he, "when reality isn't pleasant I don't look at it; I try never to think of it even."

In spite of this rejoinder, Pierre, with his smiling, placid air, went on enumerating the things which had struck him: first, the admirable manner in which the cemetery was kept, then the festive appearance which it derived from the bright autumn sun, and the wonderful profusion in which marble was lavished in slabs, statues, and chapels. The ancient atavism had surely been at work, the sumptuous mausoleums of the Appian Way had here sprung up afresh, making death a pretext for the display of pomp and pride. In the upper part of the cemetery the Roman nobility had a district of its own, crowded with veritable temples, colossal statues, groups of several figures;

and if at times the taste shown in these monuments was deplorable, it was none the less certain that millions had been expended on them. One charming feature of the place, said Pierre, was that the marbles, standing among yews and cypresses were remarkably well preserved, white and spotless; for, if the summer sun slowly gilded them, there were none of those stains of moss and rain which impart an aspect of melancholy decay to the statues of northern climes.

Touched by the discomfort of Dario, Benedetta, hitherto silent, ended by interrupting Pierre. "And was the hunt interesting?" she asked, turning to Celia.

The little Princess had been taken by her mother to see a fox-hunt, and had been speaking of it when the priest entered the room.

"Yes, it was very interesting, my dear," she replied; "the meet was at noon near the tomb of Caecilia Metella, where a buffet had been arranged under a tent. And there was such a number of people—the foreign colony, the young men of the embassies, and some officers, not to mention ourselves—all the men in scarlet and a great many ladies in habits. The 'throw-off' was at one o'clock, and the gallop lasted more than two hours and a half, so that the fox had a very long run. I wasn't able to follow, but all the same I saw some extraordinary things—a great wall which the whole hunt had to leap, and then ditches and hedges—a mad race indeed in the rear of the hounds. There were two accidents, but nothing serious; one gentleman, who was unseated, sprained his wrist badly, and another broke his leg."[1]

Dario had listened to Celia with passionate interest, for fox-hunting is one of the great pleasures of Rome, and the Campagna, flat and yet bristling with obstacles, is certainly well adapted to the sport. "Ah!" said the young Prince in a despairing tone, "how idiotic it is to be riveted to this room! I shall end by dying of *ennui*!"

Benedetta contented herself with smiling; neither reproach nor expression of sadness came from her at this candid display of egotism. Her own happiness at having him all to herself in the room where she nursed him was great indeed; still her love, at once full of youth and good sense, included a maternal element, and she well understood that he hardly amused himself, deprived as he was of his customary pleasures and severed from his friends, few of whom he was willing to receive, for he feared that they might think the story of the dislocated shoulder suspicious. Of course there were no more *fetes*, no more evenings at the theatre, no more flirtations. But above everything else Dario missed the Corso, and suffered despairingly at no longer seeing or learning anything by watching the procession of Roman society from four to five each afternoon. Accordingly, as soon as an intimate called, there were endless questions: Had the visitor seen so and so? Had such a one reappeared? How had a certain friend's love affair ended? Was any new adventure setting the city agog? And so forth; all the petty frivolities, nine days' wonders, and puerile intrigues in which the young Prince had hitherto expended his manly energy.

After a pause Celia, who was fond of coming to him with innocent gossip, fixed her candid eyes on him—the fathomless eyes of an enigmatical virgin, and resumed: "How long it takes to set a shoulder right!"

---

[1] The Roman Hunt, which counts about one hundred subscribers, has flourished since 1840. There is a kennel of English hounds, an English huntsman and whip, and a stable of English hunters.—Trans.

Had she, child as she was, with love her only business, divined the truth? Dario in his embarrassment glanced at Benedetta, who still smiled. However, the little Princess was already darting to another subject: "Ah! you know, Dario, at the Corso yesterday I saw a lady—" Then she stopped short, surprised and embarrassed that these words should have escaped her. However, in all bravery she resumed like one who had been a friend since childhood, sharing many a little love secret: "Yes, a very pretty person whom you know. Well, she had a bouquet of white roses with her all the same."

At this Benedetta indulged in a burst of frank merriment, and Dario, still looking at her, also laughed. She had twitted him during the early days because no young woman ever sent to make inquiries about him. For his part, he was not displeased with the rupture, for the continuance of the connection might have proved embarrassing; and so, although his vanity may have been slightly hurt, the news that he was already replaced in La Tonietta's affections was welcome rather than otherwise. "Ah!" he contented himself with saying, "the absent are always in the wrong."

"The man one loves is never absent," declared Celia with her grave, candid air.

However, Benedetta had stepped up to the bed to raise the young man's pillows: "Never mind, Dario *mio*," said she, "all those things are over; I mean to keep you, and you will only have me to love."

He gave her a passionate glance and kissed her hair. She spoke the truth: he had never loved any one but her, and she was not mistaken in her anticipation of keeping him always to herself alone, as soon as they should be wedded. To her great delight, since she had been nursing him he had become quite childish again, such as he had been when she had learnt to love him under the orange-trees of the Villa Montefiori. He retained a sort of puerility, doubtless the outcome of impoverished blood, that return to childhood which one remarks amongst very ancient races; and he toyed on his bed with pictures, gazed for hours at photographs, which made him laugh. Moreover, his inability to endure suffering had yet increased; he wished Benedetta to be gay and sing, and amused her with his petty egotism which led him to dream of a life of continual joy with her. Ah! how pleasant it would be to live together and for ever in the sunlight, to do nothing and care for nothing, and even if the world should crumble somewhere to heed it not!

"One thing which greatly pleases me," suddenly said the young Prince, "is that Monsieur l'Abbe has ended by falling in love with Rome."

Pierre admitted it with a good grace.

"We told you so," remarked Benedetta. "A great deal of time is needed for one to understand and love Rome. If you had only stayed here for a fortnight you would have gone off with a deplorable idea of us, but now that you have been here for two full months we are quite at ease, for you will never think of us without affection."

She looked exceedingly charming as she spoke these words, and Pierre again bowed. However, he had already given thought to the phenomenon, and fancied he could explain it. When a stranger comes to Rome he brings with him a Rome of his own, a Rome such as he dreams of, so ennobled by imagination that the real Rome proves a terrible disenchantment. And so it is necessary to wait for habituation, for the mediocrity of the reality to soften, and for the imagination to have time to kindle again, and only behold things such as they are athwart the prodigious splendour of the past.

IX.

However, Celia had risen and was taking leave. "Good-bye, dear," she said; "I hope the wedding will soon take place. You know, Dario, that I mean to be betrothed before the end of the month. Oh yes, I intend to make my father give a grand entertainment. And how nice it would be if the two weddings could take place at the same time!"

Two days later, after a long ramble through the Trastevere district, followed by a visit to the Palazzo Farnese, Pierre felt that he could at last understand the terrible, melancholy truth about Rome. He had several times already strolled through the Trastevere, attracted towards its wretched denizens by his compassion for all who suffered. Ah! that quagmire of wretchedness and ignorance! He knew of abominable nooks in the faubourgs of Paris, frightful "rents" and "courts" where people rotted in heaps, but there was nothing in France to equal the listless, filthy stagnation of the Trastevere. On the brightest days a dank gloom chilled the sinuous, cellar-like lanes, and the smell of rotting vegetables, rank oil, and human animality brought on fits of nausea. Jumbled together in a confusion which artists of romantic turn would admire, the antique, irregular houses had black, gaping entrances diving below ground, outdoor stairways conducting to upper floors, and wooden balconies which only a miracle upheld. There were crumbling fronts, shored up with beams; sordid lodgings whose filth and bareness could be seen through shattered windows; and numerous petty shops, all the open-air cook-stalls of a lazy race which never lighted a fire at home: you saw frying-shops with heaps of polenta, and fish swimming in stinking oil, and dealers in cooked vegetables displaying huge turnips, celery, cauliflowers, and spinach, all cold and sticky. The butcher's meat was black and clumsily cut up; the necks of the animals bristled with bloody clots, as though the heads had simply been torn away. The baker's loaves, piled on planks, looked like little round paving stones; at the beggarly greengrocers' merely a few pimentoes and fir-apples were shown under the strings of dry tomatoes which festooned the doorways; and the only shops which were at all attractive were those of the pork butchers with their salted provisions and their cheese, whose pungent smell slightly attenuated the pestilential reek of the gutters. Lottery offices, displaying lists of winning numbers, alternated with wine-shops, of which latter there was a fresh one every thirty yards with large inscriptions setting forth that the best wines of Genzano, Marino, and Frascati were to be found within. And the whole district teemed with ragged, grimy denizens, children half naked and devoured by vermin, bare-headed, gesticulating and shouting women, whose skirts were stiff with grease, old men who remained motionless on benches amidst swarms of hungry flies; idleness and agitation appearing on all sides, whilst cobblers sat on the sidewalks quietly plying their trade, and little donkeys pulled carts hither and thither, and men drove turkeys along, whip in hand, and hands of beggars rushed upon the few anxious tourists who had timorously ventured into the district. At the door of a little tailor's shop an old house-pail dangled full of earth, in which a succulent plant was flowering. And from every window and balcony, as from the many cords which stretched across the street from house to house, all the household washing hung like bunting, nameless drooping rags, the symbolical banners of abominable misery.

Pierre's fraternal, soul filled with pity at the sight. Ah! yes, it was necessary to demolish all those pestilential districts where the populace had wallowed for centuries as in a poisonous gaol! He was for demolition and sanitary improvement, even if old

Rome were killed and artists scandalised. Doubtless the Trastevere was already greatly changed, pierced with several new thoroughfares which let the sun stream in. And amidst the *abattis* of rubbish and the spacious clearings, where nothing new had yet been erected, the remaining portions of the old district seemed even blacker and more loathsome. Some day, no doubt, it would all be rebuilt, but how interesting was this phase of the city's evolution: old Rome expiring and new Rome just dawning amidst countless difficulties! To appreciate the change it was necessary to have known the filthy Rome of the past, swamped by sewage in every form. The recently levelled Ghetto had, over a course of centuries, so rotted the soil on which it stood that an awful pestilential odour yet arose from its bare site. It was only fitting that it should long remain waste, so that it might dry and become purified in the sun. In all the districts on either side of the Tiber where extensive improvements have been undertaken you find the same scenes. You follow some narrow, damp, evil-smelling street with black house-fronts and overhanging roofs, and suddenly come upon a clearing as in a forest of ancient leprous hovels. There are squares, broad footways; lofty white carved buildings yet in the rough, littered with rubbish and fenced off. On every side you find as it were a huge building yard, which the financial crisis perpetuates; the city of to-morrow arrested in its growth, stranded there in its monstrous, precocious, surprising infancy. Nevertheless, therein lies good and healthful work, such as was and is absolutely necessary if Rome is to become a great modern city, instead of being left to rot, to dwindle into a mere ancient curiosity, a museum show-piece.

That day, as Pierre went from the Trastevere to the Palazzo Farnese, where he was expected, he chose a roundabout route, following the Via di Pettinari and the Via dei Giubbonari, the former so dark and narrow with a great hospital wall on one side and a row of wretched houses on the other, and the latter animated by a constant stream of people and enlivened by the jewellers' windows, full of big gold chains, and the displays of the drapers' shops, where stuffs hung in bright red, blue, green, and yellow lengths. And the popular district through which he had roamed and the trading district which he was now crossing reminded him of the castle fields with their mass of workpeople reduced to mendicity by lack of employment and forced to camp in the superb, unfinished, abandoned mansions. Ah! the poor, sad people, who were yet so childish, kept in the ignorance and credulity of a savage race by centuries of theocracy, so habituated to mental night and bodily suffering that even to-day they remained apart from the social awakening, simply desirous of enjoying their pride, indolence, and sunlight in peace! They seemed both blind and deaf in their decadence, and whilst Rome was being overturned they continued to lead the stagnant life of former times, realising nought but the worries of the improvements, the demolition of the old favourite districts, the consequent change in habits, and the rise in the cost of food, as if indeed they would rather have gone without light, cleanliness, and health, since these could only be secured by a great financial and labour crisis. And yet, at bottom, it was solely for the people, the populace, that Rome was being cleansed and rebuilt with the idea of making it a great modern capital, for democracy lies at the end of these present day transformations; it is the people who will inherit the cities whence dirt and disease are being expelled, and where the law of labour will end by prevailing and killing want. And so, though one may curse the dusting and repairing of the ruins and the stripping of all the wild flora from the Colosseum, though one may wax indignant at sight of the hideous fortress like ramparts which imprison the Tiber, and bewail the old romantic banks with their greenery and their antique dwellings dipping into the stream, one must at the same time acknowledge that life springs from death, and that to-morrow must perforce blossom in the dust of the past.

While thinking of all these things Pierre had reached the deserted, stern-looking Piazza Farnese, and for a moment he looked up at the bare monumental facade of the heavy square Palazzo, its lofty entrance where hung the tricolour, its rows of windows and its famous cornice sculptured with such marvellous art. Then he went in. A friend of Narcisse Habert, one of the *attaches* of the embassy to the King of Italy, was waiting for him, having offered to show him over the huge pile, the finest palace in Rome, which France had leased as a lodging for her ambassador.[1] Ah! that colossal, sumptuous, deadly dwelling, with its vast court whose porticus is so dark and damp, its giant staircase with low steps, its endless corridors, its immense galleries and halls. All was sovereign pomp blended with death. An icy, penetrating chill fell from the walls. With a discreet smile the *attache* owned that the embassy was frozen in winter and baked in summer. The only part of the building which was at all lively and pleasant was the first storey, overlooking the Tiber, which the ambassador himself occupied. From the gallery there, containing the famous frescoes of Annibale Caracci, one can see the Janiculum, the Corsini gardens, and the Acqua Paola above San Pietro in Montorio. Then, after a vast drawing-room comes the study, peaceful and pleasant, and enlivened by sunshine. But the dining-room, the bed-chambers, and other apartments occupied by the *personnel* look out on to the mournful gloom of a side street. All these vast rooms, twenty and four-and-twenty feet high, have admirable carved or painted ceilings, bare walls, a few of them decorated with frescoes, and incongruous furniture, superb pier tables mingling with modern *bric-a-brac*. And things become abominable when you enter the gala reception-rooms overlooking the piazza, for there you no longer find an article of furniture, no longer a hanging, nothing but disaster, a series of magnificent deserted halls given over to rats and spiders. The embassy occupies but one of them, where it heaps up its dusty archives. Near by is a huge hall occupying the height of two floors, and thus sixty feet in elevation. Reserved by the owner of the palace, the ex-King of Naples, it has become a mere lumber-room where *maquettes*, unfinished statues, and a very fine sarcophagus are stowed away amidst all kinds of remnants. And this is but a part of the palace. The ground floor is altogether uninhabited; the French "Ecole de Rome" occupies a corner of the second floor; while the embassy huddles in chilly fashion in the most habitable corner of the first floor, compelled to abandon everything else and lock the doors to spare itself the useless trouble of sweeping. No doubt it is grand to live in the Palazzo Farnese, built by Pope Paul III and for more than a century inhabited by cardinals; but how cruel the discomfort and how frightful the melancholy of this huge ruin, three-fourths of whose rooms are dead, useless, impossible, cut off from life. And the evenings, oh! the evenings, when porch, court, stairs, and corridors are invaded by dense gloom, against which a few smoky gas lamps struggle in vain, when a long, long journey lies before one through the lugubrious desert of stone, before one reaches the ambassador's warm and cheerful drawing-room!

---

[1] The French have two embassies at Rome: one at the Palazzo Farnese, to the Italian Court, and the other at the Palazzo Rospigliosi, to the Vatican.—Trans.

Pierre came away quite aghast. And, as he walked along, the many other grand palaces which he had seen during his strolls rose before him, one and all of them stripped of their splendour, shorn of their princely establishments, let out in uncomfortable flats! What could be done with those grandiose galleries and halls now that no fortune could defray the cost of the pompous life for which they had been built, or even feed the retinue needed to keep them up? Few indeed were the nobles who, like Prince Aldobrandini, with his numerous progeny, still occupied their entire mansions. Almost all of them let the antique dwellings of their forefathers to companies or individual tenants, reserving only a storey, and at times a mere lodging in some dark corner, for themselves. The Palazzo Chigi was let: the ground floor to bankers and the first floor to the Austrian ambassador, while the Prince and his family divided the second floor with a cardinal. The Palazzo Sciarra was let: the first floor to the Minister of Foreign Affairs and the second to a senator, while the Prince and his mother merely occupied the ground floor. The Palazzo Barberini was let: its ground floor, first floor, and second floor to various families, whilst the Prince found a refuge on the third floor in the rooms which had been occupied by his ancestors' lackeys. The Palazzo Borghese was let: the ground floor to a dealer in antiquities, the first floor to a Lodge of Freemasons, and the rest to various households, whilst the Prince only retained the use of a small suite of apartments. And the Palazzo Odescalchi, the Palazzo Colonna, the Palazzo Doria were let: their Princes reduced to the position of needy landlords eager to derive as much profit as possible from their property in order to make both ends meet. A blast of ruin was sweeping over the Roman patriziato, the greatest fortunes had crumbled in the financial crisis, very few remained wealthy, and what a wealth it was, stagnant and dead, which neither commerce nor industry could renew. The numerous princes who had tried speculation were stripped of their fortunes. The others, terrified, called upon to pay enormous taxes, amounting to nearly one-third of their incomes, could henceforth only wait and behold their last stagnant millions dwindle away till they were exhausted or distributed according to the succession laws. Such wealth as remained to these nobles must perish, for, like everything else, wealth perishes when it lacks a soil in which it may fructify. In all this there was solely a question of time: eventual ruin was a foregone and irremediable conclusion, of absolute, historical certainty. Those who resigned themselves to the course of letting their deserted mansions still struggled for life, seeking to accommodate themselves to present-day exigencies; whilst death already dwelt among the others, those stubborn, proud ones who immured themselves in the tombs of their race, like that appalling Palazzo Boccanera, which was falling into dust amidst such chilly gloom and silence, the latter only broken at long intervals when the Cardinal's old coach rumbled over the grassy court.

The point which most struck Pierre, however, was that his visits to the Trastevere and the Palazzo Farnese shed light one on the other, and led him to a conclusion which had never previously seemed so manifest. As yet no "people," and soon no aristocracy. He had found the people so wretched, ignorant, and resigned in its long infancy induced by historic and climatic causes that many years of instruction and culture were necessary for it to become a strong, healthy, and laborious democracy, conscious of both its rights and its duties. As for the aristocracy, it was dwindling to death in its crumbling palaces, no longer aught than a finished, degenerate race, with such an admixture also of American, Austrian, Polish, and Spanish blood that pure

Roman blood became a rare exception; and, moreover, it had ceased to belong either to sword or gown, unwilling to serve constitutional Italy and forsaking the Sacred College, where only *parvenus* now donned the purple. And between the lowly and the aristocracy there was as yet no firmly seated middle class, with the vigour of fresh sap and sufficient knowledge, and good sense to act as the transitional educator of the nation. The middle class was made up in part of the old servants and clients of the princes, the farmers who rented their lands, the stewards, notaries, and solicitors who managed their fortunes; in part, too, of all the employees, the functionaries of every rank and class, the deputies and senators, whom the new Government had brought from the provinces; and, in particular, of the voracious hawks who had swooped down upon Rome, the Pradas, the men of prey from all parts of the kingdom, who with beak and talon devoured both people and aristocracy. For whom, then, had one laboured? For whom had those gigantic works of new Rome been undertaken? A shudder of fear sped by, a crack as of doom was heard, arousing pitiful disquietude in every fraternal heart. Yes, a threat of doom and annihilation: as yet no people, soon no aristocracy, and only a ravenous middle class, quarrying, vulture-like, among the ruins.

On the evening of that day, when all was dark, Pierre went to spend an hour on the river quay beyond the Boccanera mansion. He was very fond of meditating on that deserted spot in spite of the warnings of Victorine, who asserted that it was not safe. And, indeed, on such inky nights as that one, no cutthroat place ever presented a more tragic aspect. Not a soul, not a passer-by; a dense gloom, a void in front and on either hand. At a corner of the mansion, now steeped in darkness, there was a gas lamp which stood in a hollow since the river margin had been banked up, and this lamp cast an uncertain glimmer upon the quay, level with the latter's bossy soil. Thus long vague shadows stretched from the various materials, piles of bricks and piles of stone, which were strewn around. On the right a few lights shone upon the bridge near San Giovanni and in the windows of the hospital of the Santo Spirito. On the left, amidst the dim recession of the river, the distant districts were blotted out. Then yonder, across the stream, was the Trastevere, the houses on the bank looking like vague, pale phantoms, with infrequent window-panes showing a blurred yellow glimmer, whilst on high only a dark band shadowed the Janiculum, near whose summit the lamps of some promenade scintillated like a triangle of stars. But it was the Tiber which impassioned Pierre; such was its melancholy majesty during those nocturnal hours. Leaning over the parapet, he watched it gliding between the new walls, which looked like those of some black and monstrous prison built for a giant. So long as lights gleamed in the windows of the houses opposite he saw the sluggish water flow by, showing slow, moire-like ripples there where the quivering reflections endowed it with a mysterious life. And he often mused on the river's famous past and evoked the legends which assert that fabulous wealth lies buried in its muddy bed. At each fresh invasion of the barbarians, and particularly when Rome was sacked, the treasures of palaces and temples are said to have been cast into the water to prevent them from falling into the hands of the conquerors. Might not those golden bars trembling yonder in the glaucous stream be the branches of the famous candelabrum which Titus brought from Jerusalem? Might not those pale patches whose shape remained uncertain amidst the frequent eddies indicate the white marble of statues and columns? And those deep moires glittering with little flamelets, were they not promiscuous heaps of precious metal, cups, vases, ornaments enriched with gems? What a dream was that of the swarming riches espied athwart the old river's bosom, of the hidden life of the treasures which were said to have slumbered there for centuries; and what a hope for the nation's pride and enrichment centred in the miraculous finds which might be made in the Tiber if one could some day dry it up and search its bed, as had already been suggested! Therein, perchance, lay Rome's new fortune.

However, on that black night, whilst Pierre leant over the parapet, it was stern reality alone which occupied his mind. He was still pursuing the train of thought suggested by his visits to the Trastevere and the Farnese palace, and in presence of that lifeless water was coming to the conclusion that the selection of Rome for transformation into a modern capital was the great misfortune to which the sufferings of young Italy were due. He knew right well that the selection had been inevitable: Rome being the queen of glory, the antique ruler of the world to whom eternity had been promised, and without whom the national unity had always seemed an impossibility. And so the problem was a terrible one, since without Rome Italy could not exist, and with Rome it seemed difficult for it to exist. Ah! that dead river, how it symbolised disaster! Not a boat upon its surface, not a quiver of the commercial and industrial activity of those waters which bear life to the very hearts of great modern cities! There had been fine schemes, no doubt—Rome a seaport, gigantic works, canalisation to enable vessels of heavy tonnage to come up to the Aventine; but these were mere delusions; the authorities would scarcely be able to clear the river mouth, which deposits were continually choking. And there was that other cause of mortal languishment, the Campagna—the desert of death which the dead river crossed and which girdled Rome with sterility. There was talk of draining and planting it; much futile discussion on the question whether it had been fertile in the days of the old Romans; and even a few experiments were made; but, all the same, Rome remained in the midst of a vast cemetery like a city of other times, for ever separated from the modern world by that *lande* or moor where the dust of centuries had accumulated. The geographical considerations which once gave the city the empire of the world no longer exist. The centre of civilisation has been displaced. The basin of the Mediterranean has been divided among powerful nations. In Italy all roads now lead to Milan, the city of industry and commerce, and Rome is but a town of passage. And so the most valiant efforts have failed to rouse it from its invincible slumber. The capital which the newcomers sought to improvise with such extreme haste has remained unfinished, and has almost ruined the nation. The Government, legislators, and functionaries only camp there, fleeing directly the warm weather sets in so as to escape the pernicious climate. The hotels and shops even put up their shutters, and the streets and promenades become deserts, the city having failed to acquire any life of its own, and relapsing into death as soon as the artificial life instilled into it is withdrawn. So all remains in suspense in this purely decorative capital, where only a fresh growth of men and money can finish and people the huge useless piles of the new districts. If it be true that to-morrow always blooms in the dust of the past, one ought to force oneself to hope; but Pierre asked himself if the soil were not exhausted, and since mere buildings could no longer grow on it, if it were not for ever drained of the sap which makes a race healthy, a nation powerful.

As the night advanced the lights in the houses of the Trastevere went out one by one: yet Pierre for a long time lingered on the quay, leaning over the blackened river and yielding to hopelessness. There was now no distance to the gloom; all had become dense; no longer did any reflections set a moire-like, golden quiver in the water, or reveal beneath its mystery-concealing current a fantastic, dancing vision of fabulous wealth. Gone was the legend, gone the seven-branched golden candelabrum, gone the golden vases, gone the golden jewellery, the whole dream of antique treasure that had vanished into night, even like the antique glory of Rome. Not a glimmer, nothing but slumber, disturbed solely by the heavy fall of sewage from the drain on the right-hand, which could not be seen. The very water had disappeared, and Pierre no longer espied its leaden flow through the darkness, no longer had any perception of the sluggish senility, the long-dating weariness, the intense sadness of that ancient and glorious Tiber, whose waters now rolled nought but death. Only the vast, opulent sky, the eternal, pompous sky displayed the dazzling life of its milliards of planets above that river of darkness, bearing away the ruins of wellnigh three thousand years.

Before returning to his own chamber that evening Pierre entered Dario's room, and found Victorine there preparing things for the night. And as soon as she heard where he had been she raised her voice in protest: "What! you have again been to the quay at this time of night, Monsieur l'Abbe? You want to get a good knife thrust yourself, it seems. Well, for my part, I certainly wouldn't take the air at such a late hour in this dangerous city." Then, with her wonted familiarity, she turned and spoke to the Prince, who was lying back in an arm-chair and smiling: "That girl, La Pierina," she said, "hasn't been back here, but all the same I've lately seen her prowling about among the building materials."

Dario raised his hand to silence her, and, addressing Pierre, exclaimed: "But you spoke to her, didn't you? It's becoming idiotic! Just fancy that brute Tito coming back to dig his knife into my other shoulder—"

All at once he paused, for he had just perceived Benedetta standing there and listening to him; she had slipped into the room a moment previously in order to wish him good-night. At sight of her his embarrassment was great indeed; he wished to speak, explain his words, and swear that he was wholly innocent in the affair. But she, with a smiling face, contented herself with saying, "I knew all about it, Dario *mio*. I am not so foolish as not to have thought it all over and understood the truth. If I ceased questioning you it was because I knew, and loved you all the same."

The young woman looked very happy as she spoke, and for this she had good cause, for that very evening she had learnt that Monsignor Palma had shown himself grateful for the service rendered to his nephew by laying a fresh and favourable memoir on the marriage affair before the Congregation of the Council. He had been unwilling to recall his previous opinions so far as to range himself completely on the Contessina's side, but the certificates of two doctors whom she had recently seen had enabled him to conclude that her own declarations were accurate. And gliding over the question of wifely obedience, on which he had previously laid stress, he had skilfully set forth the reasons which made a dissolution of the marriage desirable. No hope of reconciliation could be entertained, so it was certain that both parties were constantly exposed to temptation and sin. He discreetly alluded to the fact that the husband had already succumbed to this danger, and praised the wife's lofty morality and piety, all the virtues which she displayed, and which guaranteed her veracity. Then, without formulating any conclusion of his own, he left the decision to the wisdom of the Congregation. And as he virtually repeated Advocate Morano's arguments, and Prada stubbornly refused to enter an appearance, it now seemed certain that the Congregation would by a great majority pronounce itself in favour of dissolution, a result which would enable the Holy Father to act benevolently.

"Ah! Dario *mio*!" said Benedetta, "we are at the end of our worries. But what a lot of money, what a lot of money it all costs! Aunt says that they will scarcely leave us water to drink."

So speaking she laughed with the happy heedlessness of an impassioned *amorosa*. It was not that the jurisdiction of the Congregations was in itself ruinous; indeed, in principle, it was gratuitous. Still there were a multitude of petty expenses, payments to subaltern employees, payments for medical consultations and certificates, copies of documents, and the memoirs and addresses of counsel. And although the votes of the cardinals were certainly not bought direct, some of them ended by costing considerable sums, for it often became necessary to win over dependants, to induce quite a little world to bring influence to bear upon their Eminences; without mentioning that large pecuniary gifts, when made with tact, have a decisive effect in clearing away the greatest difficulties in that sphere of the Vatican. And, briefly, Monsignor Palma's nephew by marriage had cost the Boccaneras a large sum.

"But it doesn't matter, does it, Dario *mio*?" continued Benedetta. "Since you are now cured, they must make haste to give us permission to marry. That's all we ask of them. And if they want more, well, I'll give them my pearls, which will be all I shall have left me."

He also laughed, for money had never held any place in his life. He had never had it at his pleasure, and simply hoped that he would always live with his uncle the cardinal, who would certainly not leave him and his young wife in the streets. Ruined as the family was, one or two hundred thousand francs represented nothing to his mind, and he had heard that certain dissolutions of marriage had cost as much as half a million. So, by way of response, he could only find a jest: "Give them my ring as well," said he; "give them everything, my dear, and we shall still be happy in this old palace even if we have to sell the furniture!"

His words filled her with enthusiasm; she took his head between both hands and kissed him madly on the eyes in an extraordinary transport of passion. Then, suddenly turning to Pierre, she said: "Oh! excuse me, Monsieur l'Abbe. I was forgetting that I have a commission for you. Yes, Monsignor Nani, who brought us that good news, bade me tell you that you are making people forget you too much, and that you ought to set to work to defend your book."

The priest listened in astonishment; then replied: "But it was he who advised me to disappear."

"No doubt—only it seems that the time has now come for you to see people and plead your cause. And Monsignor Nani has been able to learn that the reporter appointed to examine your book is Monsignor Fornaro, who lives on the Piazza Navona."

Pierre's stupefaction was increasing, for a reporter's name is never divulged, but kept quite secret, in order to ensure a free exercise of judgment. Was a new phase of his sojourn in Rome about to begin then? His mind was all wonderment. However, he simply answered: "Very good, I will set to work and see everybody."

PART IV.

X.

IN his anxiety to bring things to a finish, Pierre wished to begin his campaign on the very next day. But on whom should he first call if he were to steer clear of blunders in that intricate and conceited ecclesiastical world? The question greatly perplexed him; however, on opening his door that morning he luckily perceived Don Vigilio in the passage, and with a sudden inspiration asked him to step inside. He realised that this thin little man with the saffron face, who always trembled with fever and displayed such exaggerated, timorous discretion, was in reality well informed, mixed up in everything. At one period it had seemed to Pierre that the secretary purposely avoided him, doubtless for fear of compromising himself; but recently Don Vigilio had proved less unsociable, as though he were not far from sharing the impatience which must be consuming the young Frenchman amidst his long enforced inactivity. And so, on this occasion, he did not seek to avoid the chat on which Pierre was bent.

"I must apologise," said the latter, "for asking you in here when things are in such disorder. But I have just received some more linen and some winter clothing from Paris. I came, you know, with just a little valise, meaning to stay for a fortnight, and yet I've now been here for nearly three months, and am no more advanced than I was on the morning of my arrival."

Don Vigilio nodded. "Yes, yes, I know," said he.

Thereupon Pierre explained to him that Monsignor Nani had informed him, through the Contessina, that he now ought to act and see everybody for the defence of his book. But he was much embarrassed, as he did not know in what order to make his visits so that they might benefit him. For instance, ought he to call in the first place on Monsignor Fornaro, the *consultore* selected to report on his book, and whose name had been given him?

"Ah!" exclaimed Don Vigilio, quivering; "has Monsignor Nani gone as far as that—given you the reporter's name? That's even more than I expected." Then, forgetting his prudence, yielding to his secret interest in the affair, he resumed: "No, no; don't begin with Monsignor Fornaro. Your first visit should be a very humble one to the Prefect of the Congregation of the Index—his Eminence Cardinal Sanguinetti; for he would never forgive you for having offered your first homage to another should he some day hear of it." And, after a pause, Don Vigilio added, in a low voice, amidst a faint, feverish shiver: "And he *would* hear of it; everything becomes known."

Again he hesitated, and then, as if yielding to sudden, sympathetic courage, he took hold of the young Frenchman's hands. "I swear to you, my dear Monsieur Froment," he said, "that I should be very happy to help you, for you are a man of simple soul, and I really begin to feel worried for you. But you must not ask me for impossibilities. Ah! if you only knew—if I could only tell you of all the perils which surround us! However, I think I can repeat to you that you must in no wise rely on my patron, his Eminence Cardinal Boccanera. He has expressed absolute disapproval of your book in my presence on several occasions. Only he is a saint, a most worthy, honourable man; and, though he won't defend you, he won't attack you—he will remain neutral out of regard for his niece, whom he loves so dearly, and who protects you. So, when you see him, don't plead your cause; it would be of no avail, and might even irritate him."

Pierre was not particularly distressed by this news, for at his first interview with the Cardinal, and on the few subsequent occasions when he had respectfully visited him, he had fully understood that his Eminence would never be other than an adversary. "Well," said he, "I will wait on him to thank him for his neutrality."

But at this all Don Vigilio's terrors returned. "No, no, don't do that; he would perhaps realise that I have spoken to you, and then what a disaster—my position would be compromised. I've said nothing, nothing! See the cardinals to begin with, see all the cardinals. Let it be understood between us that I've said nothing more." And, on that occasion at any rate, Don Vigilio would speak no further, but left the room shuddering and darting fiery, suspicious glances on either side of the corridor.

Pierre at once went out to call on Cardinal Sanguinetti. It was ten o'clock, and there was a chance that he might find him at home. This cardinal resided on the first floor of a little palazzo in a dark, narrow street near San Luigi dei Francesi.[1] There was here none of the giant ruin full of princely and melancholy grandeur amidst which Cardinal Boccanera so stubbornly remained. The old regulation gala suite of rooms had been cut down just like the number of servants. There was no throne-room, no red hat hanging under a *baldacchino*, no arm-chair turned to the wall pending a visit from the Pope. A couple of apartments served as ante-rooms, and then came a *salon* where the Cardinal received; and there was no luxury, indeed scarcely any comfort; the furniture was of mahogany, dating from the empire period, and the hangings and carpets were dusty and faded by long use. Moreover, Pierre had to wait a long time for admittance, and when a servant, leisurely putting on his jacket, at last set the door ajar, it was only to say that his Eminence had been away at Frascati since the previous day.

Pierre then remembered that Cardinal Sanguinetti was one of the suburban bishops. At his see of Frascati he had a villa where he occasionally spent a few days whenever a desire for rest or some political motive impelled him to do so.

"And will his Eminence soon return?" Pierre inquired.

"Ah! we don't know. His Eminence is poorly, and expressly desired us to send nobody to worry him."

---

[1] This is the French church of Rome, and is under the protection of the French Government.—Trans.

X.

When Pierre reached the street again he felt quite bewildered by this disappointment. At first he wondered whether he had not better call on Monsignor Fornaro without more ado, but he recollected Don Vigilio's advice to see the cardinals first of all, and, an inspiration coming to him, he resolved that his next visit should be for Cardinal Sarno, whose acquaintance he had eventually made at Donna Serafina's Mondays. In spite of Cardinal Sarno's voluntary self-effacement, people looked upon him as one of the most powerful and redoubtable members of the Sacred College, albeit his nephew Narcisse Habert declared that he knew no man who showed more obtuseness in matters which did not pertain to his habitual occupations. At all events, Pierre thought that the Cardinal, although not a member of the Congregation of the Index, might well give him some good advice, and possibly bring his great influence to bear on his colleagues.

The young man straightway betook himself to the Palace of the Propaganda, where he knew he would find the Cardinal. This palace, which is seen from the Piazza di Spagna, is a bare, massive corner pile between two streets. And Pierre, hampered by his faulty Italian, quite lost himself in it, climbing to floors whence he had to descend again, and finding himself in a perfect labyrinth of stairs, passages, and halls. At last he luckily came across the Cardinal's secretary, an amiable young priest, whom he had already seen at the Boccanera mansion. "Why, yes," said the secretary, "I think that his Eminence will receive you. You did well to come at this hour, for he is always here of a morning. Kindly follow me, if you please."

Then came a fresh journey. Cardinal Sarno, long a Secretary of the Propaganda, now presided over the commission which controlled the organisation of worship in those countries of Europe, Africa, America, and Oceanica where Catholicism had lately gained a footing; and he thus had a private room of his own with special officers and assistants, reigning there with the ultra-methodical habits of a functionary who had grown old in his arm-chair, closely surrounded by nests of drawers, and knowing nothing of the world save the usual sights of the street below his window.

The secretary left Pierre on a bench at the end of a dark passage, which was lighted by gas even in full daylight. And quite a quarter of an hour went by before he returned with his eager, affable air. "His Eminence is conferring with some missionaries who are about to leave Rome," he said; "but it will soon be over, and he told me to take you to his room, where you can wait for him."

As soon as Pierre was alone in the Cardinal's sanctum he examined it with curiosity. Fairly spacious, but in no wise luxurious, it had green paper on its walls, and its furniture was of black wood and green damask. From two windows overlooking a narrow side street a mournful light reached the dark wall-paper and faded carpets. There were a couple of pier tables and a plain black writing-table, which stood near one window, its worn mole-skin covering littered with all sorts of papers. Pierre drew near to it for a moment, and glanced at the arm-chair with damaged, sunken seat, the screen which sheltered it from draughts, and the old inkstand splotched with ink. And then, in the lifeless and oppressive atmosphere, the disquieting silence, which only the low rumbles from the street disturbed, he began to grow impatient.

However, whilst he was softly walking up and down he suddenly espied a map affixed to one wall, and the sight of it filled him with such absorbing thoughts that he soon forgot everything else. It was a coloured map of the world, the different tints indicating whether the territories belonged to victorious Catholicism or whether Catholicism was still warring there against unbelief; these last countries being classified as vicariates or prefectures, according to the general principles of organisation. And the whole was a graphic presentment of the long efforts of Catholicism in striving for the universal dominion which it has sought so unremittingly since its earliest hour. God has given the world to His Church, but it is needful that she should secure possession of it since error so stubbornly abides. From this has sprung the eternal battle, the fight which is carried on, even in our days, to win nations over from other religions, as it was in the days when the Apostles quitted Judaea to spread abroad the tidings of the Gospel. During the middle ages the great task was to organise conquered Europe, and this was too absorbing an enterprise to allow of any attempt at reconciliation with the dissident churches of the East. Then the Reformation burst forth, schism was added to schism, and the Protestant half of Europe had to be reconquered as well as all the orthodox East.

War-like ardour, however, awoke at the discovery of the New World. Rome was ambitious of securing that other side of the earth, and missions were organised for the subjection of races of which nobody had known anything the day before, but which God had, nevertheless, given to His Church, like all the others. And by degrees the two great divisions of Christianity were formed, on one hand the Catholic nations, those where the faith simply had to be kept up, and which the Secretariate of State installed at the Vatican guided with sovereign authority, and on the other the schismatical or pagan nations which were to be brought back to the fold or converted, and over which the Congregation of the Propaganda sought to reign. Then this Congregation had been obliged to divide itself into two branches in order to facilitate its work—the Oriental branch, which dealt with the dissident sects of the East, and the Latin branch, whose authority extended over all the other lands of mission: the two forming a vast organisation—a huge, strong, closely meshed net cast over the whole world in order that not a single soul might escape.

It was in presence of that map that Pierre for the first time became clearly conscious of the mechanism which for centuries had been working to bring about the absorption of humanity. The Propaganda, richly dowered by the popes, and disposing of a considerable revenue, appeared to him like a separate force, a papacy within the papacy, and he well understood that the Prefect of the Congregation should be called the "Red Pope," for how limitless were the powers of that man of conquest and domination, whose hands stretched from one to the other end of the earth. Allowing that the Cardinal Secretary held Europe, that diminutive portion of the globe, did not he, the Prefect, hold all the rest—the infinity of space, the distant countries as yet almost unknown? Besides, statistics showed that Rome's uncontested dominion was limited to 200 millions of Apostolic and Roman Catholics; whereas the schismatics of the East and the Reformation, if added together, already exceeded that number, and how small became the minority of the true believers when, besides the schismatics, one brought into line the 1000 millions of infidels who yet remained to be converted. The figures struck Pierre with a force which made him shudder. What! there were 5 million Jews, nearly 200 million Mahommedans, more than 700 million Brahmanists and Buddhists, without counting another 100 million pagans of divers creeds, the whole making 1000 millions, and against these the Christians could marshal barely more than 400 millions, who were divided among themselves, ever in conflict, one half with Rome and the other half against her?[1] Was it possible that in 1800 years Christianity had not proved victorious over even one-third of mankind, and that Rome, the eternal and all-powerful, only counted a sixth part of the nations among her subjects? Only one soul saved out of every six—how fearful was the disproportion! However, the map spoke with brutal eloquence: the red-tinted empire of Rome was but a speck when compared with the yellow-hued empire of the other gods—the endless countries which the Propaganda still had to conquer. And the question arose: How many centuries must elapse before the promises of the Christ were realised, before the whole world were gained to Christianity, before religious society spread over secular society, and there remained but one kingdom and one belief? And in presence of this question, in presence of the prodigious labour yet to be accomplished, how great was one's astonishment when one thought of Rome's tranquil serenity, her patient stubbornness, which has never known doubt or weariness, her bishops and ministers toiling without cessation in the conviction that she alone will some day be the mistress of the world!

Narcisse had told Pierre how carefully the embassies at Rome watched the doings of the Propaganda, for the missions were often the instruments of one or another nation, and exercised decisive influence in far-away lands. And so there was a continual struggle, in which the Congregation did all it could to favour the missionaries of Italy and her allies. It had always been jealous of its French rival, "L'Oeuvre de la Propagation de la Foi," installed at Lyons, which is as wealthy in money as itself, and richer in men of energy and courage. However, not content with levelling tribute on this French association, the Propaganda thwarted it, sacrificed it on every occasion when it had reason to think it might achieve a victory. Not once or twice, but over and over again had the French missionaries, the French orders, been driven from the scenes of their labours to make way for Italians or Germans. And Pierre, standing in that mournful, dusty room, which the sunlight never brightened, pictured the secret hotbed of political intrigue masked by the civilising ardour of faith. Again he shuddered as one shudders when monstrous, terrifying things are brought home to one. And might not the most sensible be overcome? Might not the bravest be dismayed by the thought of that universal engine of conquest and domination, which worked with the stubbornness of eternity, not merely content with the gain of souls, but ever seeking to ensure its future sovereignty over the whole of corporeal humanity, and—pending the time when it might rule the nations itself—disposing of them, handing them over to the charge of this or that temporary master, in accordance with its good pleasure. And then, too, what a prodigious dream! Rome smiling and tranquilly awaiting the day

[1] Some readers may question certain of the figures given by M. Zola, but it must be remembered that all such calculations (even those of the best "authorities") are largely guesswork. I myself think that there are more than 5 million Jews, and more than 200 millions of Mahommedans, but I regard the alleged number of Brahmanists and Buddhists as exaggerated. On the other hand, some statistical tables specify 80 millions of Confucianists, of whom M. Zola makes no separate mention. However, as regards the number of Christians in the world, the figures given above are, within a few millions, probably accurate.—Trans.

when she will have united Christians, Mahommedans, Brahmanists, and Buddhists into one sole nation, of whom she will be both the spiritual and the temporal queen!

However, a sound of coughing made Pierre turn, and he started on perceiving Cardinal Sarno, whom he had not heard enter. Standing in front of that map, he felt like one caught in the act of prying into a secret, and a deep flush overspread his face. The Cardinal, however, after looking at him fixedly with his dim eyes, went to his writing-table, and let himself drop into the arm-chair without saying a word. With a gesture he dispensed Pierre of the duty of kissing his ring.

"I desired to offer my homage to your Eminence," said the young man. "Is your Eminence unwell?"

"No, no, it's nothing but a dreadful cold which I can't get rid of. And then, too, I have so many things to attend to just now."

Pierre looked at the Cardinal as he appeared in the livid light from the window, puny, lopsided, with the left shoulder higher than the right, and not a sign of life on his worn and ashen countenance. The young priest was reminded of one of his uncles, who, after thirty years spent in the offices of a French public department, displayed the same lifeless glance, parchment-like skin, and weary hebetation. Was it possible that this withered old man, so lost in his black cassock with red edging, was really one of the masters of the world, with the map of Christendom so deeply stamped on his mind, albeit he had never left Rome, that the Prefect of the Propaganda did not take a decision without asking his opinion?

"Sit down, Monsieur l'Abbe," said the Cardinal. "So you have come to see me—you have something to ask of me!" And, whilst disposing himself to listen, he stretched out his thin bony hands to finger the documents heaped up before him, glancing at each of them like some general, some strategist, profoundly versed in the science of his profession, who, although his army is far away, nevertheless directs it to victory from his private room, never for a moment allowing it to escape his mind.

Pierre was somewhat embarrassed by such a plain enunciation of the interested object of his visit; still, he decided to go to the point. "Yes, indeed," he answered, "it is a liberty I have taken to come and appeal to your Eminence's wisdom for advice. Your Eminence is aware that I am in Rome for the purpose of defending a book of mine, and I should be grateful if your Eminence would help and guide me." Then he gave a brief account of the present position of the affair, and began to plead his cause; but as he continued speaking he noticed that the Cardinal gave him very little attention, as though indeed he were thinking of something else, and failed to understand.

"Ah! yes," the great man at last muttered, "you have written a book. There was some question of it at Donna Serafina's one evening. But a priest ought not to write; it is a mistake for him to do so. What is the good of it? And the Congregation of the Index must certainly be in the right if it is prosecuting your book. At all events, what can I do? I don't belong to the Congregation, and I know nothing, nothing about the matter."

Pierre, pained at finding him so listless and indifferent, went on trying to enlighten and move him. But he realised that this man's mind, so far-reaching and penetrating in the field in which it had worked for forty years, closed up as soon as one sought to divert it from its specialty. It was neither an inquisitive nor a supple mind. All trace of life faded from the Cardinal's eyes, and his entire countenance assumed an expression of mournful imbecility. "I know nothing, nothing," he repeated, "and I never recommend anybody." However, at last he made an effort: "But Nani is mixed up in this," said he. "What does Nani advise you to do?"

"Monsignor Nani has been kind enough to reveal to me that the reporter is Monsignor Fornaro, and advises me to see him."

At this Cardinal Sarno seemed surprised and somewhat roused. A little light returned to his eyes. "Ah! really," he rejoined, "ah! really—Well, if Nani has done that he must have some idea. Go and see Monsignor Fornaro." Then, after rising and dismissing his visitor, who was compelled to thank him, bowing deeply, he resumed his seat, and a moment later the only sound in the lifeless room was that of his bony fingers turning over the documents before him.

Pierre, in all docility, followed the advice given him, and immediately betook himself to the Piazza Navona, where, however, he learnt from one of Monsignor Fornaro's servants that the prelate had just gone out, and that to find him at home it was necessary to call in the morning at ten o'clock. Accordingly it was only on the following day that Pierre was able to obtain an interview. He had previously made inquiries and knew what was necessary concerning Monsignor Fornaro. Born at Naples, he had there begun his studies under the Barnabites, had finished them at the Seminario Romano, and had subsequently, for many years, been a professor at the University Gregoriana. Nowadays Consultor to several Congregations and a Canon of Santa Maria Maggiore, he placed his immediate ambition in a Canonry at St. Peter's, and harboured the dream of some day becoming Secretary of the Consistorial Congregation, a post conducting to the cardinalate. A theologian of remarkable ability, Monsignor Fornaro incurred no other reproach than that of occasionally sacrificing to literature by contributing articles, which he carefully abstained from signing, to certain religious reviews. He was also said to be very worldly.

Pierre was received as soon as he had sent in his card, and perhaps he would have fancied that his visit was expected had not an appearance of sincere surprise, blended with a little anxiety, marked his reception.

"Monsieur l'Abbe Froment, Monsieur l'Abbe Froment," repeated the prelate, looking at the card which he still held. "Kindly step in—I was about to forbid my door, for I have some urgent work to attend to. But no matter, sit down."

Pierre, however, remained standing, quite charmed by the blooming appearance of this tall, strong, handsome man who, although five and forty years of age, was quite fresh and rosy, with moist lips, caressing eyes, and scarcely a grey hair among his curly locks. Nobody more fascinating and decorative could be found among the whole Roman prelacy. Careful of his person undoubtedly, and aiming at a simple elegance, he looked really superb in his black cassock with violet collar. And around him the spacious room where he received his visitors, gaily lighted as it was by two large windows facing the Piazza Navona, and furnished with a taste nowadays seldom met with among the Roman clergy, diffused a pleasant odour and formed a setting instinct with kindly cheerfulness.

"Pray sit down, Monsieur l'Abbe Froment," he resumed, "and tell me to what I am indebted for the honour of your visit."

He had already recovered his self-possession and assumed a *naif*, purely obliging air; and Pierre, though the question was only natural, and he ought to have foreseen it, suddenly felt greatly embarrassed, more embarrassed indeed than in Cardinal Sarno's presence. Should he go to the point at once, confess the delicate motive of his visit? A moment's reflection showed him that this would be the best and worthier course. "Dear me, Monseigneur," he replied, "I know very well that the step I have taken in calling on you is not usually taken, but it has been advised me, and it has seemed to me that among honest folks there can never be any harm in seeking in all good faith to elucidate the truth."

"What is it, what is it, then?" asked the prelate with an expression of perfect candour, and still continuing to smile.

"Well, simply this. I have learnt that the Congregation of the Index has handed you my book 'New Rome,' and appointed you to examine it; and I have ventured to present myself before you in case you should have any explanations to ask of me."

But Monsignor Fornaro seemed unwilling to hear any more. He had carried both hands to his head and drawn back, albeit still courteous. "No, no," said he, "don't tell me that, don't continue, you would grieve me dreadfully. Let us say, if you like, that you have been deceived, for nothing ought to be known, in fact nothing is known, either by others or myself. I pray you, do not let us talk of such matters."

Pierre, however, had fortunately remarked what a decisive effect was produced when he had occasion to mention the name of the Assessor of the Holy Office. So it occurred to him to reply: "I most certainly do not desire to give you the slightest cause for embarrassment, Monseigneur, and I repeat to you that I would never have ventured to importune you if Monsignor Nani himself had not acquainted me with your name and address."

This time the effect was immediate, though Monsignor Fornaro, with that easy grace which he introduced into all things, made some ceremony about surrendering. He began by a demurrer, speaking archly with subtle shades of expression. "What! is Monsignor Nani the tattler! But I shall scold him, I shall get angry with him! And what does he know? He doesn't belong to the Congregation; he may have been led into error. You must tell him that he has made a mistake, and that I have nothing at all to do with your affair. That will teach him not to reveal needful secrets which everybody respects!" Then, in a pleasant way, with winning glance and flowery lips, he went on: "Come, since Monsignor Nani desires it, I am willing to chat with you for a moment, my dear Monsieur Froment, but on condition that you shall know nothing of my report or of what may have been said or done at the Congregation."

Pierre in his turn smiled, admiring how easy things became when forms were respected and appearances saved. And once again he began to explain his case, the profound astonishment into which the prosecution of his book had thrown him, and his ignorance of the objections which were taken to it, and for which he had vainly sought a cause.

"Really, really," repeated the prelate, quite amazed at so much innocence. "The Congregation is a tribunal, and can only act when a case is brought before it. Proceedings have been taken against your book simply because it has been denounced."

"Yes, I know, denounced."

"Of course. Complaint was laid by three French bishops, whose names you will allow me to keep secret, and it consequently became necessary for the Congregation to examine the incriminated work."

Pierre looked at him quite scared. Denounced by three bishops? Why? With what object? Then he thought of his protector. "But Cardinal Bergerot," said he, "wrote me a letter of approval, which I placed at the beginning of my work as a preface. Ought not a guarantee like that to have been sufficient for the French episcopacy?"

Monsignor Fornaro wagged his head in a knowing way before making up his mind to reply: "Ah! yes, no doubt, his Eminence's letter, a very beautiful letter. I think, however, that it would have been much better if he had not written it, both for himself and for you especially." Then as the priest, whose surprise was increasing, opened his mouth to urge him to explain himself, he went on: "No, no, I know nothing, I say nothing. His Eminence Cardinal Bergerot is a saintly man whom everybody venerates, and if it were possible for him to sin it would only be through pure goodness of heart."

Silence fell. Pierre could divine that an abyss was opening, and dared not insist. However, he at last resumed with some violence: "But, after all, why should my book be prosecuted, and the books of others be left untouched? I have no intention of acting as a denouncer myself, but how many books there are to which Rome closes her eyes, and which are far more dangerous than mine can be!"

This time Monsignor Fornaro seemed glad to be able to support Pierre's views. "You are right," said he, "we cannot deal with every bad book, and it greatly distresses us. But you must remember what an incalculable number of works we should be compelled to read. And so we have to content ourselves with condemning the worst *en bloc*."

Then he complacently entered into explanations. In principle, no printer ought to send any work to press without having previously submitted the manuscript to the approval of the bishop of the diocese. Nowadays, however, with the enormous output of the printing trade, one could understand how terribly embarrassed the bishops would be if the printers were suddenly to conform to the Church's regulation. There was neither the time nor the money, nor were there the men necessary for such colossal labour. And so the Congregation of the Index condemned *en masse*, without examination, all works of certain categories: first, books which were dangerous for morals, all erotic writings, and all novels; next the various bibles in the vulgar tongue, for the perusal of Holy Writ without discretion was not allowable; then the books on magic and sorcery, and all works on science, history, or philosophy that were in any way contrary to dogma, as well as the writings of heresiarchs or mere ecclesiastics discussing religion, which should never be discussed. All these were wise laws made by different popes, and were set forth in the preface to the catalogue of forbidden books which the Congregation published, and without them this catalogue, to have been complete, would in itself have formed a large library. On turning it over one found that the works singled out for interdiction were chiefly those of priests, the task being so vast and difficult that Rome's concern extended but little beyond the observance of good order within the Church. And Pierre and his book came within the limit.

"You will understand," continued Monsignor Fornaro, "that we have no desire to advertise a heap of unwholesome writings by honouring them with special condemnation. Their name is legion in every country, and we should have neither enough paper nor enough ink to deal with them all. So we content ourselves with condemning one from time to time, when it bears a famous name and makes too much noise, or contains disquieting attacks on the faith. This suffices to remind the world that we exist and defend ourselves without abandoning aught of our rights or duties."

"But my book, my book," exclaimed Pierre, "why these proceedings against my book?"

"I am explaining that to you as far as it is allowable for me to do, my dear Monsieur Froment. You are a priest, your book is a success, you have published a cheap edition of it which sells very readily; and I don't speak of its literary merit, which is remarkable, for it contains a breath of real poetry which transported me, and on which I must really compliment you. However, under the circumstances which I have enumerated, how could we close our eyes to such a work as yours, in which the conclusion arrived at is the annihilation of our holy religion and the destruction of Rome?"

Pierre remained open-mouthed, suffocating with surprise. "The destruction of Rome!" he at last exclaimed; "but I desire to see Rome rejuvenated, eternal, again the queen of the world." And, once more mastered by his glowing enthusiasm, he defended himself and confessed his faith: Catholicism reverting to the principles and practices of the primitive Church, drawing the blood of regeneration from the fraternal Christianity of Jesus; the Pope, freed from all terrestrial royalty, governing the whole of humanity with charity and love, and saving the world from the frightful social cataclysm that threatens it by leading it to the real Kingdom of God: the Christian communion of all nations united in one nation only. "And can the Holy Father disavow me?" he continued. "Are not these his secret ideas, which people are beginning to divine, and does not my only offence lie in having expressed them perhaps too soon and too freely? And if I were allowed to see him should I not at once obtain from him an order to stop these proceedings?"

Monsignor Fornaro no longer spoke, but wagged his head without appearing offended by the priest's juvenile ardour. On the contrary, he smiled with increasing amiability, as though highly amused by so much innocence and imagination. At last he gaily responded, "Oh! speak on, speak on; it isn't I who will stop you. I'm forbidden to say anything. But the temporal power, the temporal power."

"Well, what of the temporal power?" asked Pierre.

The prelate had again become silent, raising his amiable face to heaven and waving his white hands with a pretty gesture. And when he once more opened his mouth it was to say: "Then there's your new religion—for the expression occurs twice: the new religion, the new religion—ah, *Dio*!"

Again he became restless, going off into an ecstasy of wonderment, at sight of which Pierre impatiently exclaimed: "I do not know what your report will be, Monseigneur, but I declare to you that I have had no desire to attack dogma. And, candidly now, my whole book shows that I only sought to write a work of pity and salvation. It is only justice that some account should be taken of one's intentions."

Monsignor Fornaro had become very calm and paternal again. "Oh! intentions! intentions!" he said as he rose to dismiss his visitor. "You may be sure, my dear Monsieur Froment, that I feel much honoured by your visit. Naturally I cannot tell you what my report will be; as it is, we have talked too much about it, and, in fact, I ought to have refused to listen to your defence. At the same time, you will always find me ready to be of service to you in anything that does not go against my duty. But I greatly fear that your book will be condemned." And then, as Pierre again started, he added: "Well, yes. It is facts that are judged, you know, not intentions. So all defence is useless; the book is there, and we take it such as it is. However much you may try to explain it, you cannot alter it. And this is why the Congregation never calls the accused parties before it, and never accepts from them aught but retraction pure and simple. And, indeed, the wisest course would be for you to withdraw your book and make your submission. No? You won't? Ah! how young you are, my friend!"

He laughed yet more loudly at the gesture of revolt, of indomitable pride which had just escaped his young friend, as he called him. Then, on reaching the door, he again threw off some of his reserve, and said in a low voice, "Come, my dear Abbe, there is something I will do for you. I will give you some good advice. At bottom, I myself am nothing. I deliver my report, and it is printed, and the members of the Congregation read it, but are quite free to pay no attention to it. However, the Secretary of the Congregation, Father Dangelis, can accomplish everything, even impossibilities. Go to see him; you will find him at the Dominican convent behind the Piazza di Spagna. Don't name me. And for the present good-bye, my dear fellow, good-bye."

Pierre once more found himself on the Piazza Navona, quite dazed, no longer knowing what to believe or hope. A cowardly idea was coming over him; why should he continue this struggle, in which his adversaries remained unknown and indiscernible? Why carry obstinacy any further, why linger any longer in that impassionating but deceptive Rome? He would flee that very evening, return to Paris, disappear there, and forget his bitter disillusion in the practice of humble charity. He was traversing one of those hours of weakness when the long-dreamt-of task suddenly seems to be an impossibility. However, amidst his great confusion he was nevertheless walking on, going towards his destination. And when he found himself in the Corso, then in the Via dei Condotti, and finally in the Piazza di Spagna, he resolved that he would at any rate see Father Dangelis. The Dominican convent is there, just below the Trinity de' Monti.

Ah! those Dominicans! Pierre had never thought of them without a feeling of respect with which mingled a little fear. What vigorous pillars of the principle of authority and theocracy they had for centuries proved themselves to be! To them the Church had been indebted for its greatest measure of authority; they were the glorious soldiers of its triumph. Whilst St. Francis won the souls of the humble over to Rome, St. Dominic, on Rome's behalf, subjected all the superior souls—those of the intelligent and powerful. And this he did with passion, amidst a blaze of faith and determination, making use of all possible means, preachings, writings, and police and judicial pressure. Though he did not found the Inquisition, its principles were his, and it was with fire and sword that his fraternal, loving heart waged war on schism. Living like his monks, in poverty, chastity, and obedience—the great virtues of those times of pride and licentiousness—he went from city to city, exhorting the impious, striving to bring them back to the Church and arraigning them before the ecclesiastical courts when his preachings did not suffice. He also laid siege to science, sought to make it his own, dreamt of defending God with the weapons of reason and human knowledge like a true forerunner of the angelic St. Thomas, that light of the middle ages, who joined the Dominican order and set everything in his "Summa Theologiae," psychology, logic, policy, and morals. And thus it was that the Dominicans filled the world, upholding the doctrines of Rome in the most famous pulpits of every nation, and contending almost everywhere against the free sprit of the Universities, like the vigilant guardians of dogma that they were, the unwearying artisans of the fortunes of the popes, the most powerful amongst all the artistic, scientific, and literary workers who raised the huge edifice of Catholicism such as it exists to-day.

However, Pierre, who could feel that this edifice was even now tottering, though it had been built, people fancied, so substantially as to last through all eternity, asked himself what could be the present use of the Dominicans, those toilers of another age, whose police system and whose tribunals had perished beneath universal execration, whose voices were no longer listened to, whose books were but seldom read, and whose *role* as *savants* and civilisers had come to an end in presence of latter-day science, the truths of which were rending dogma on all sides. Certainly the Dominicans still form an influential and prosperous order; but how far one is from the times when their general reigned in Rome, Master of the Holy Palace, with convents and schools, and subjects throughout Europe! Of all their vast inheritance, so far as the Roman curia is concerned, only a few posts now remain to them, and among others the Secretaryship of the Congregation of the Index, a former dependency of the Holy Office where they once despotically ruled.

Pierre was immediately ushered into the presence of Father Dangelis. The convent parlour was vast, bare, and white, flooded with bright sunshine. The only furniture was a table and some stools; and a large brass crucifix hung from the wall. Near the table stood the Father, a very thin man of about fifty, severely draped in his ample white habit and black mantle. From his long ascetic face, with thin lips, thin nose, and pointed, obstinate chin, his grey eyes shone out with a fixity that embarrassed one. And, moreover, he showed himself very plain and simple of speech, and frigidly polite in manner.

"Monsieur l'Abbe Froment—the author of 'New Rome,' I suppose?" Then seating himself on one stool and pointing to another, he added: "Pray acquaint me with the object of your visit, Monsieur l'Abbe."

Thereupon Pierre had to begin his explanation, his defence, all over again; and the task soon became the more painful as his words fell from his lips amidst death-like silence and frigidity. Father Dangelis did not stir; with his hands crossed upon his knees he kept his sharp, penetrating eyes fixed upon those of the priest. And when the latter had at last ceased speaking, he slowly said: "I did not like to interrupt you, Monsieur l'Abbe, but it was not for me to hear all this. Process against your book has begun, and no power in the world can stay or impede its course. I do not therefore realise what it is that you apparently expect of me."

In a quivering voice Pierre was bold enough to answer: "I look for some kindness and justice."

A pale smile, instinct with proud humility, arose to the Dominican's lips. "Be without fear," he replied, "God has ever deigned to enlighten me in the discharge of my modest duties. Personally, be it said, I have no justice to render; I am but an employee whose duty is to classify matters and draw up documents concerning them. Their Eminences, the members of the Congregation, will alone pronounce judgment on your book. And assuredly they will do so with the help of the Holy Spirit. You will only have to bow to their sentence when it shall have been ratified by his Holiness."

Then he broke off the interview by rising, and Pierre was obliged to do the same. The Dominican's words were virtually identical with those that had fallen from Monsignor Fornaro, but they were spoken with cutting frankness, a sort of tranquil bravery. On all sides Pierre came into collision with the same anonymous force, the same powerful engine whose component parts sought to ignore one another. For a long time yet, no doubt, he would be sent from one to the other, without ever finding the volitional element which reasoned and acted. And the only thing that he could do was to bow to it all.

However, before going off, it occurred to him once more to mention the name of Monsignor Nani, the powerful effect of which he had begun to realise. "I ask your pardon," he said, "for having disturbed you to no purpose, but I simply deferred to the kind advice of Monsignor Nani, who has condescended to show me some interest."

The effect of these words was unexpected. Again did Father Dangelis's thin face brighten into a smile, but with a twist of the lips, sharp with ironical contempt. He had become yet paler, and his keen intelligent eyes were flaming. "Ah! it was Monsignor Nani who sent you!" he said. "Well, if you think you need a protector, it is useless for you to apply to any other than himself. He is all-powerful. Go to see him; go to see him!"

And that was the only encouragement Pierre derived from his visit: the advice to go back to the man who had sent him. At this he felt that he was losing ground, and he resolved to return home in order to reflect on things and try to understand them before taking any further steps. The idea of questioning Don Vigilio at once occurred to him, and that same evening after supper he luckily met the secretary in the corridor, just as, candle in hand, he was on his way to bed.

"I have so many things that I should like to say to you," Pierre said to him. "Can you kindly come to my rooms for a moment?"

But the other promptly silenced him with a gesture, and then whispered: "Didn't you see Abbe Paparelli on the first floor? He was following us, I'm sure."

Pierre often saw the train-bearer roaming about the house, and greatly disliked his stealthy, prying ways. However, he had hitherto attached no importance to him, and was therefore much surprised by Don Vigilio's question. The other, without awaiting his reply, had returned to the end of the corridor, where for a long while he remained listening. Then he came back on tip-toe, blew out his candle, and darted into Pierre's sitting-room. "There—that's done," he murmured directly the door was shut. "But if it is all the same to you, we won't stop in this sitting-room. Let us go into your bed-room. Two walls are better than one."

When the lamp had been placed on the table and they found themselves seated face to face in that bare, faded bed-chamber, Pierre noticed that the secretary was suffering from a more violent attack of fever than usual. His thin puny figure was shivering from head to foot, and his ardent eyes had never before blazed so blackly in his ravaged, yellow face. "Are you poorly?" asked Pierre. "I don't want to tire you."

"Poorly, yes, I am on fire—but I want to talk. I can't bear it any longer. One always has to relieve oneself some day or other."

Was it his complaint that he desired to relieve; or was he anxious to break his long silence in order that it might not stifle him? This at first remained uncertain. He immediately asked for an account of the steps that Pierre had lately taken, and became yet more restless when he heard how the other had been received by Cardinal Sarno, Monsignor Fornaro, and Father Dangelis. "Yes, that's quite it," he repeated, "nothing astonishes me nowadays, and yet I feel indignant on your account. Yes, it doesn't concern me, but all the same it makes me ill, for it reminds me of all my own troubles. You must not rely on Cardinal Sarno, remember, for he is always elsewhere, with his mind far away, and has never helped anybody. But that Fornaro, that Fornaro!"

"He seemed to me very amiable, even kindly disposed," replied Pierre; "and I really think that after our interview, he will considerably soften his report."

"He! Why, the gentler he was with you the more grievously he will saddle you! He will devour you, fatten himself with such easy prey. Ah! you don't know him, *dilizioso* that he is, ever on the watch to rear his own fortune on the troubles of poor devils whose defeat is bound to please the powerful. I prefer the other one, Father Dangelis, a terrible man, no doubt, but frank and brave and of superior mind. I must admit, however, that he would burn you like a handful of straw if he were the master. And ah! if I could tell you everything, if I could show you the frightful under-side of this world of ours, the monstrous, ravenous ambition, the abominable network of intrigues, venality, cowardice, treachery, and even crime!"

On seeing Don Vigilio so excited, in such a blaze of spite, Pierre thought of extracting from him some of the many items of information which he had hitherto sought in vain. "Well, tell me merely what is the position of my affair," he responded. "When I questioned you on my arrival here you said that nothing had yet reached Cardinal Boccanera. But all information must now have been collected, and you must know of it. And, by the way, Monsignor Fornaro told me that three French bishops had asked that my book should be prosecuted. Three bishops, is it possible?"

Don Vigilio shrugged his shoulders. "Ah!" said he, "yours is an innocent soul! I'm surprised that there were *only* three! Yes, several documents relating to your affair are in our hands; and, moreover, things have turned out much as I suspected. The three bishops are first the Bishop of Tarbes, who evidently carries out the vengeance of the Fathers of Lourdes; and then the Bishops of Poitiers and Evreux, who are both known as uncompromising Ultramontanists and passionate adversaries of Cardinal Bergerot. The Cardinal, you know, is regarded with disfavour at the Vatican, where his Gallican ideas and broad liberal mind provoke perfect anger. And don't seek for anything else. The whole affair lies in that: an execution which the powerful Fathers of Lourdes demand of his Holiness, and a desire to reach and strike Cardinal Bergerot through your book, by means of the letter of approval which he imprudently wrote to you and which you published by way of preface. For a long time past the condemnations of the Index have largely been secret knock-down blows levelled at Churchmen. Denunciation reigns supreme, and the law applied is that of good pleasure. I could tell you some almost incredible things, how perfectly innocent books have been selected among a hundred for the sole object of killing an idea or a man; for the blow is almost always levelled at some one behind the author, some one higher than he is. And there is such a hot-bed of intrigue, such a source of abuses in this institution of the Index, that it is tottering, and even among those who surround the Pope it is felt that it must soon be freshly regulated if it is not to fall into complete discredit. I well understand that the Church should endeavour to retain universal power, and govern by every fit weapon, but the weapons must be such as one can use without their injustice leading to revolt, or their antique childishness provoking merriment!"

Pierre listened with dolorous astonishment in his heart. Since he had been at Rome and had seen the Fathers of the Grotto saluted and feared there, holding an authoritative position, thanks to the large alms which they contributed to the Peter's Pence, he had felt that they were behind the proceedings instituted against him, and realised that he would have to pay for a certain page of his book in which he had called attention to an iniquitous displacement of fortune at Lourdes, a frightful spectacle which made one doubt the very existence of the Divinity, a continual cause of battle and conflict which would disappear in the truly Christian society of to-morrow. And he could also now understand that his delight at the loss of the temporal power must have caused a scandal, and especially that the unfortunate expression "a new religion" had alone been sufficient to arm *delatores* against him. But that which amazed and grieved him was to learn that Cardinal Bergerot's letter was looked upon as a crime, and that his (Pierre's) book was denounced and condemned in order that adversaries who dared not attack the venerable pastor face to face might, deal him a cowardly blow from behind. The thought of afflicting that saintly man, of serving as the implement to strike him in his ardent charity, cruelly grieved Pierre. And how bitter and disheartening it was to find the most hideous questions of pride and money, ambition and appetite, running riot with the most ferocious egotism, beneath the quarrels of those leaders of the Church who ought only to have contended together in love for the poor!

And then Pierre's mind revolted against that supremely odious and idiotic Index. He now understood how it worked, from the arrival of the denunciations to the public posting of the titles of the condemned works. He had just seen the Secretary of the Congregation, Father Dangelis, to whom the denunciations came, and who then investigated the affair, collecting all documents and information concerning it with the passion of a cultivated authoritarian monk, who dreamt of ruling minds and consciences as in the heroic days of the Inquisition. Then, too, Pierre had visited one of the consultive prelates, Monsignor Fornaro, who was so ambitious and affable, and so subtle a theologian that he would have discovered attacks against the faith in a treatise on algebra, had his interests required it. Next there were the infrequent meetings of the cardinals, who at long intervals voted for the interdiction of some hostile book, deeply regretting that they could not suppress them all; and finally came the Pope, approving and signing the decrees, which was a mere formality, for were not all books guilty? But what an extraordinary wretched Bastille of the past was that aged Index, that senile institution now sunk into second childhood. One realised that it must have been a formidable power when books were rare and the Church had tribunals of blood and fire to enforce her edicts. But books had so greatly multiplied, the written, printed thoughts of mankind had swollen into such a deep broad river, that they had swept all opposition away, and now the Index was swamped and reduced to powerlessness, compelled more and more to limit its field of action, to confine itself to the examination of the writings of ecclesiastics, and even in this respect it was becoming corrupt, fouled by the worst passions and changed into an instrument of intrigue, hatred, and vengeance. Ah! that confession of decay, of paralysis which grew more and more complete amidst the scornful indifference of the nations. To think that Catholicism, the once glorious agent of civilisation, had come to such a pass that it cast books into hell-fire by the heap; and what books they were, almost the entire literature, history, philosophy, and science of the past and the present! Few works, indeed, are published nowadays that would not fall under the ban of the Church. If she seems to close her eyes, it is in order to avoid the impossible task of hunting out and destroying everything. Yet she stubbornly insists on retaining a semblance of sovereign authority over human intelligence, just as some very aged queen, dispossessed of her states and henceforth without judges or executioners, might continue to deliver vain sentences to which only an infinitesimal minority would pay heed. But imagine the Church momentarily victorious, miraculously mastering the modern world, and ask yourself what she, with her tribunals to condemn and her gendarmes to enforce, would do with human thought. Imagine a strict application of the Index regulations: no printer able to put anything whatever to press without the approval of his bishop, and even then every book laid before the Congregation, the past expunged, the present throttled, subjected to an intellectual Reign of Terror! Would not the closing of every library perforce ensue, would not the long heritage of written thought be cast into prison, would not the future be barred, would not all progress, all conquest of knowledge, be totally arrested? Rome herself is nowadays a terrible example of such a disastrous experiment—Rome with her congealed soil, her dead sap, killed by centuries of papal government, Rome which has become so barren that not a man, not a work has sprung from her midst even after five and twenty years of awakening and liberty! And who would accept such a state of things, not among people of revolutionary mind, but among those of religious mind that might possess any culture and breadth of view? Plainly enough it was all mere childishness and absurdity.

Deep silence reigned, and Pierre, quite upset by his reflections, made a gesture of despair whilst glancing at Don Vigilio, who sat speechless in front of him. For a moment longer, amidst the death-like quiescence of that old sleeping mansion, both continued silent, seated face to face in the closed chamber which the lamp illumined with a peaceful glow. But at last Don Vigilio leant forward, his eyes sparkling, and with a feverish shiver murmured: "It is they, you know, always they, at the bottom of everything."

Pierre, who did not understand, felt astonished, indeed somewhat anxious at such a strange remark coming without any apparent transition. "Who are *they*?" he asked.

"The Jesuits!"

In this reply the little, withered, yellow priest had set all the concentrated rage of his exploding passion. Ah! so much the worse if he had perpetrated a fresh act of folly. The cat was out of the bag at last! Nevertheless, he cast a final suspicious glance around the walls. And then he relieved his mind at length, with a flow of words which gushed forth the more irresistibly since he had so long held them in check. "Ah! the Jesuits, the Jesuits! You fancy that you know them, but you haven't even an idea of their abominable actions and incalculable power. They it is whom one always comes upon, everywhere, in every circumstance. Remember *that* whenever you fail to understand anything, if you wish to understand it. Whenever grief or trouble comes upon you, whenever you suffer, whenever you weep, say to yourself at once: 'It is they; they are there!' Why, for all I know, there may be one of them under that bed, inside that cupboard. Ah! the Jesuits, the Jesuits! They have devoured me, they are devouring me still, they will leave nothing of me at last, neither flesh nor bone."

Then, in a halting voice, he related the story of his life, beginning with his youth, which had opened so hopefully. He belonged to the petty provincial nobility, and had been dowered with a fairly large income, besides a keen, supple intelligence, which looked smilingly towards the future. Nowadays, he would assuredly have been a prelate, on the road to high dignities, but he had been foolish enough to speak ill of the Jesuits and to thwart them in two or three circumstances. And from that moment, if he were to be believed, they had caused every imaginable misfortune to rain upon him: his father and mother had died, his banker had robbed him and fled, good positions had escaped him at the very moment when he was about to occupy them, the most awful misadventures had pursued him amidst the duties of his ministry to such a point indeed, that he had narrowly escaped interdiction. It was only since Cardinal Boccanera, compassionating his bad luck, had taken him into his house and attached him to his person, that he had enjoyed a little repose. "Here I have a refuge, an asylum," he continued. "They execrate his Eminence, who has never been on their side, but they haven't yet dared to attack him or his servants. Oh! I have no illusions, they will end by catching me again, all the same. Perhaps they will even hear of our conversation this evening, and make me pay dearly for it; for I do wrong to speak, I speak in spite of myself. They have stolen all my happiness, and brought all possible misfortune on me, everything that was possible, everything—you hear me!"

Increasing discomfort was taking possession of Pierre, who, seeking to relieve himself by a jest, exclaimed: "Come, come, at any rate it wasn't the Jesuits who gave you the fever."

"Yes, yes, it was!" Don Vigilio violently declared. "I caught it on the bank of the Tiber one evening, when I went to weep there in my grief at having been driven from the little church where I officiated."

Pierre, hitherto, had never believed in the terrible legend of the Jesuits. He belonged to a generation which laughed at the idea of wehr-wolves, and considered the *bourgeois* fear of the famous black men, who hid themselves in walls and terrorised families, to be a trifle ridiculous. To him all such things seemed to be nursery tales, exaggerated by religious and political passion. And so it was with amazement that he examined Don Vigilio, suddenly fearing that he might have to deal with a maniac.

Nevertheless he could not help recalling the extraordinary story of the Jesuits. If St. Francis of Assisi and St. Dominic are the very soul and spirit of the middle ages, its masters and teachers, the former a living expression of all the ardent, charitable faith of the humble, and the other defending dogma and fixing doctrines for the intelligent and the powerful, on the other hand Ignatius de Loyola appeared on the threshold of modern times to save the tottering heritage by accommodating religion to the new developments of society, thereby ensuring it the empire of the world which was about to appear.

At the advent of the modern era it seemed as if the Deity were to be vanquished in the uncompromising struggle with sin, for it was certain that the old determination to suppress Nature, to kill the man within man, with his appetites, passions, heart, and blood, could only result in a disastrous defeat, in which, indeed, the Church found herself on the very eve of sinking; and it was the Jesuits who came to extricate her from this peril and reinvigorate her by deciding that it was she who now ought to go to the world, since the world seemed unwilling to go any longer to her. All lay in that; you find the Jesuits declaring that one can enter into arrangements with heaven; they bend and adjust themselves to the customs, prejudices, and even vices of the times; they smile, all condescension, cast rigourism aside, and practice the diplomacy of amiability, ever ready to turn the most awful abominations "to the greater glory of God." That is their motto, their battle-cry, and thence springs the moral principle which many regard as their crime: that all means are good to attain one's end, especially when that end is the furtherance of the Deity's interests as represented by those of the Church. And what overwhelming success attends the efforts of the Jesuits! they swarm and before long cover the earth, on all sides becoming uncontested masters.

They shrive kings, they acquire immense wealth, they display such victorious power of invasion that, however humbly they may set foot in any country, they soon wholly possess it: souls, bodies, power, and fortune alike falling to them. And they are particularly zealous in founding schools, they show themselves to be incomparable moulders of the human brain, well understanding that power always belongs to the morrow, to the generations which are growing up and whose master one must be if one desire to reign eternally. So great is their power, based on the necessity of compromise with sin, that, on the morrow of the Council of Trent, they transform the very spirit of Catholicism, penetrate it, identify it with themselves and become the indispensable soldiers of the papacy which lives by them and for them. And from that moment Rome is theirs, Rome where their general so long commands, whence so long go forth the directions for the obscure tactics which are blindly followed by their innumerable army, whose skilful organisation covers the globe as with an iron network hidden by the velvet of hands expert in dealing gently with poor suffering humanity. But, after all, the most prodigious feature is the stupefying vitality of the Jesuits who are incessantly tracked, condemned, executed, and yet still and ever erect. As soon as their power asserts itself, their unpopularity begins and gradually becomes universal. Hoots of execration arise around them, abominable accusations, scandalous law cases in which they appear as corruptors and felons. Pascal devotes them to public contempt, parliaments condemn their books to be burnt, universities denounce their system of morals and their teaching as poisonous. They foment such disturbances, such struggles in every kingdom, that organised persecution sets in, and they are soon driven from everywhere. During more than a century they become wanderers, expelled, then recalled, passing and repassing frontiers, leaving a country amidst cries of hatred to return to it as soon as quiet has been restored. Finally, for supreme disaster, they are suppressed by one pope, but another re-establishes them, and since then they have been virtually tolerated everywhere. And in the diplomatic self-effacement, the shade in which they have the prudence to sequester themselves, they are none the less triumphant, quietly confident of their victory like soldiers who have once and for ever subdued the earth.

Pierre was aware that, judging by mere appearances, the Jesuits were nowadays dispossessed of all influence in Rome. They no longer officiated at the Gesu, they no longer directed the Collegio Romano, where they formerly fashioned so many souls; and with no abode of their own, reduced to accept foreign hospitality, they had modestly sought a refuge at the Collegio Germanico, where there is a little chapel. There they taught and there they still confessed, but without the slightest bustle or display. Was one to believe, however, that this effacement was but masterly cunning, a feigned disappearance in order that they might really remain secret, all-powerful masters, the hidden hand which directs and guides everything? People certainly said that the proclamation of papal Infallibility had been their work, a weapon with which they had armed themselves whilst feigning to bestow it on the papacy, in readiness for the coming decisive task which their genius foresaw in the approaching social upheavals. And thus there might perhaps be some truth in what Don Vigilio, with a shiver of mystery, related about their occult sovereignty, a seizin, as it were, of the government of the Church, a royalty ignored but nevertheless complete.

As this idea occurred to Pierre, a dim connection between certain of his experiences arose in his mind and he all at once inquired: "Is Monsignor Nani a Jesuit, then?"

These words seemed to revive all Don Vigilio's anxious passion. He waved his trembling hand, and replied: "He? Oh, he's too clever, too skilful by far to have taken the robe. But he comes from that Collegio Romano where his generation grew up, and he there imbibed that Jesuit genius which adapted itself so well to his own. Whilst fully realising the danger of wearing an unpopular and embarrassing livery, and wishing to be free, he is none the less a Jesuit in his flesh, in his bones, in his very soul. He is evidently convinced that the Church can only triumph by utilising the passions of mankind, and withal he is very fond of the Church, very pious at bottom, a very good priest, serving God without weakness in gratitude for the absolute power which God gives to His ministers. And besides, he is so charming, incapable of any brutal action, full of the good breeding of his noble Venetian ancestors, and deeply versed in knowledge of the world, thanks to his experiences at the nunciatures of Paris, Vienna, and other places, without mentioning that he knows everything that goes on by reason of the delicate functions which he has discharged for ten years past as Assessor of the Holy Office. Yes, he is powerful, all-powerful, and in him you do not have the furtive Jesuit whose robe glides past amidst suspicion, but the head, the brain, the leader whom no uniform designates."

This reply made Pierre grave, for he was quite willing to admit that an opportunist code of morals, like that of the Jesuits, was inoculable and now predominated throughout the Church. Indeed, the Jesuits might disappear, but their doctrine would survive them, since it was the one weapon of combat, the one system of strategy which might again place the nations under the dominion of Rome. And in reality the struggle which continued lay precisely in the attempts to accommodate religion to the century, and the century to religion. Such being the case, Pierre realised that such men as Monsignor Nani might acquire vast and even decisive importance.

"Ah! if you knew, if you knew," continued Don Vigilio, "he's everywhere, he has his hand in everything. For instance, nothing has ever happened here, among the Boccaneras, but I've found him at the bottom of it, tangling or untangling the threads according to necessities with which he alone is acquainted."

Then, in the unquenchable fever for confiding things which was now consuming him, the secretary related how Monsignor Nani had most certainly brought on Benedetta's divorce case. The Jesuits, in spite of their conciliatory spirit, have always taken up a hostile position with regard to Italy, either because they do not despair of reconquering Rome, or because they wait to treat in due season with the ultimate and real victor, whether King or Pope. And so Nani, who had long been one of Donna Serafina's intimates, had helped to precipitate the rupture with Prada as soon as Benedetta's mother was dead. Again, it was he who, to prevent any interference on the part of the patriotic Abbe Pisoni, the young woman's confessor and the artisan of her marriage, had urged her to take the same spiritual director as her aunt, Father Lorenza, a handsome Jesuit with clear and kindly eyes, whose confessional in the chapel of the Collegio Germanico was incessantly besieged by penitents. And it seemed certain that this manoeuvre had brought about everything; what one cleric working for Italy had done, was to be undone by another working against Italy. Why was it, however, that Nani, after bringing about the rupture, had momentarily ceased to show all interest in the affair to the point even of jeopardising the suit for the dissolution of the marriage? And why was he now again busying himself with it, setting Donna Serafina in action, prompting her to buy Monsignor Palma's support, and bringing his own influence to bear on the cardinals of the Congregation? There was mystery in all this, as there was in everything he did, for his schemes were always complicated and distant in their effects. However, one might suppose that he now wished to hasten the marriage of Benedetta and Dario, in order to stop all the abominable rumours which were circulating in the white world; unless, indeed, this divorce secured by pecuniary payments and the pressure of notorious influences were an intentional scandal at first spun out and now hastened, in order to harm Cardinal Boccanera, whom the Jesuits might desire to brush aside in certain eventualities which were possibly near at hand.

"To tell the truth, I rather incline to the latter view," said Don Vigilio, "the more so indeed as I learnt this evening that the Pope is not well. With an old man of eighty-four the end may come at any moment, and so the Pope can never catch cold but what the Sacred College and the prelacies are all agog, stirred by sudden ambitious rivalries. Now, the Jesuits have always opposed Cardinal Boccanera's candidature. They ought to be on his side, on account of his rank, and his uncompromising attitude towards Italy, but the idea of giving themselves such a master disquiets them, for they consider him unseasonably rough and stern, too violent in his faith, which unbending as it is would prove dangerous in these diplomatic times through which the Church is passing. And so I should in no wise be astonished if there were an attempt to discredit him and render his candidature impossible, by employing the most underhand and shameful means."

A little quiver of fear was coming over Pierre. The contagion of the unknown, of the black intrigues plotted in the dark, was spreading amidst the silence of the night in the depths of that palace, near that Tiber, in that Rome so full of legendary tragedies. But all at once the young man's mind reverted to himself, to his own affair. "But what is my part in all this?" he asked: "why does Monsignor Nani seem to take an interest in me? Why is he mixed up in the proceedings against my book?"

"Oh! one never knows, one never knows exactly!" replied Don Vigilio, waving his arms. "One thing I can say, that he only knew of the affair when the denunciations of the three bishops were already in the hands of Father Dangelis; and I have also learnt that he then tried to stop the proceedings, which he no doubt thought both useless and impolitic. But when a matter is once before the Congregation it is almost impossible for it to be withdrawn, and Monsignor Nani must also have come into collision with Father Dangelis who, like a faithful Dominican, is the passionate adversary of the Jesuits. It was then that he caused the Contessina to write to Monsieur de la Choue, requesting him to tell you to hasten here in order to defend yourself, and to arrange for your acceptance of hospitality in this mansion, during your stay."

This revelation brought Pierre's emotion to a climax. "You are sure of that?" he asked.

"Oh! quite sure. I heard Nani speak of you one Monday, and some time ago I told you that he seemed to know all about you, as if he had made most minute inquiries. My belief is that he had already read your book, and was extremely preoccupied about it."

"Do you think that he shares my ideas, then? Is he sincere, is he defending himself while striving to defend me?"

"Oh! no, no, not at all. Your ideas, why he certainly hates them, and your book and yourself as well. You have no idea what contempt for the weak, what hatred of the poor, and love of authority and domination he conceals under his caressing amiability. Lourdes he might abandon to you, though it embodies a marvellous weapon of government; but he will never forgive you for being on the side of the little ones of the world, and for pronouncing against the temporal power. If you only heard with what gentle ferocity he derides Monsieur de la Choue, whom he calls the weeping willow of Neo-Catholicism!"

Pierre carried his hands to his temples and pressed his head despairingly. "Then why, why, tell me I beg of you, why has he brought me here and kept me here in this house at his disposal? Why has he promenaded me up and down Rome for three long months, throwing me against obstacles and wearying me, when it was so easy for him to let the Index condemn my book if it embarrassed him? It's true, of course, that things would not have gone quietly, for I was disposed to refuse submission and openly confess my new faith, even against the decisions of Rome."

Don Vigilio's black eyes flared in his yellow face: "Perhaps it was that which he wished to prevent. He knows you to be very intelligent and enthusiastic, and I have often heard him say that intelligence and enthusiasm should not be fought openly."

Pierre, however, had risen to his feet, and instead of listening, was striding up and down the room as though carried away by the whirlwind of his thoughts. "Come, come," he said at last, "it is necessary that I should know and understand things if I am to continue the struggle. You must be kind enough to give me some detailed particulars about each of the persons mixed up in my affair. Jesuits, Jesuits everywhere? *Mon Dieu*, it may be so, you are perhaps right! But all the same you must point out the different shades to me. Now, for instance, what of that Fornaro?"

"Monsignor Fornaro, oh! he's whatever you like. Still he also was brought up at the Collegio Romano, so you may be certain that he is a Jesuit, a Jesuit by education, position, and ambition. He is longing to become a cardinal, and if he some day becomes one, he'll long to be the next pope. Besides, you know, every one here is a candidate to the papacy as soon as he enters the seminary."

"And Cardinal Sanguinetti?"

"A Jesuit, a Jesuit! To speak plainly, he was one, then ceased to be one, and is now undoubtedly one again. Sanguinetti has flirted with every influence. It was long thought that he was in favour of conciliation between the Holy See and Italy; but things drifted into a bad way, and he violently took part against the usurpers. In the same style he has frequently fallen out with Leo XIII and then made his peace. To-day at the Vatican, he keeps on a footing of diplomatic reserve. Briefly he only has one object, the tiara, and even shows it too plainly, which is a mistake, for it uses up a candidate. Still, just at present the struggle seems to be between him and Cardinal Boccanera. And that's why he has gone over to the Jesuits again, utilising their hatred of his rival, and anticipating that they will be forced to support *him* in order to defeat the other. But I doubt it, they are too shrewd, they will hesitate to patronise a candidate who is already so compromised. He, blunder-head, passionate and proud as he is, doubts nothing, and since you say that he is now at Frascati, I'm certain that he made all haste to shut himself up there with some grand strategical object in view, as soon as he heard of the Pope's illness."

"Well, and the Pope himself, Leo XIII?" asked Pierre.

This time Don Vigilio slightly hesitated, his eyes blinking. Then he said: "Leo XIII? He is a Jesuit, a Jesuit! Oh! I know it is said that he sides with the Dominicans, and this is in a measure true, for he fancies that he is animated with their spirit and he has brought St. Thomas into favour again, and has restored all the ecclesiastical teaching of doctrine. But there is also the Jesuit, remember, who is one involuntarily and without knowing it, and of this category the present Pope will prove the most famous example. Study his acts, investigate his policy, and you will find that everything in it emanates from the Jesuit spirit. The fact is that he has unwittingly become impregnated with that spirit, and that all the influence, directly or indirectly brought to bear on him comes from a Jesuit centre. Ah! why don't you believe me? I repeat that the Jesuits have conquered and absorbed everything, that all Rome belongs to them from the most insignificant cleric to his Holiness in person."

Then he continued, replying to each fresh name that Pierre gave with the same obstinate, maniacal cry: "Jesuit, Jesuit!" It seemed as if a Churchman could be nothing else, as if each answer were a confirmation of the proposition that the clergy must compound with the modern world if it desired to preserve its Deity. The heroic age of Catholicism was accomplished, henceforth it could only live by dint of diplomacy and ruses, concessions and arrangements. "And that Paparelli, he's a Jesuit too, a Jesuit!" Don Vigilio went on, instinctively lowering his voice. "Yes, the humble but terrible Jesuit, the Jesuit in his most abominable *role* as a spy and a perverter! I could swear that he has merely been placed here in order to keep watch on his Eminence! And you should see with what supple talent and craft he has performed his task, to such a point indeed that it is now he alone who wills and orders things. He opens the door to whomsoever he pleases, uses his master like something belonging to him, weighs on each of his resolutions, and holds him in his power by dint of his stealthy unremitting efforts. Yes! it's the lion conquered by the insect; the infinitesimally small disposing of the infinitely great; the train-bearer—whose proper part is to sit at his cardinal's feet like a faithful hound—in reality reigning over him, and impelling him in whatsoever direction he chooses. Ah! the Jesuit! the Jesuit! Mistrust him when you see him gliding by in his shabby old cassock, with the flabby wrinkled face of a devout old maid. And make sure that he isn't behind the doors, or in the cupboards, or under the beds. Ah! I tell you that they'll devour you as they've devoured me; and they'll give you the fever too, perhaps even the plague if you are not careful!"

Pierre suddenly halted in front of his companion. He was losing all assurance, both fear and rage were penetrating him. And, after all, why not? These extraordinary stories must be true. "But in that case give me some advice," he exclaimed, "I asked you to come in here this evening precisely because I no longer know what to do, and need to be set in the right path—" Then he broke off and again paced to and fro, as if urged into motion by his exploding passion. "Or rather no, tell me nothing!" he abruptly resumed. "It's all over; I prefer to go away. The thought occurred to me before, but it was in a moment of cowardice and with the idea of disappearing and of returning to live in peace in my little nook: whereas now, if I go off, it will be as an avenger, a judge, to cry aloud to all the world from Paris, to proclaim what I have seen in Rome, what men have done there with the Christianity of Jesus, the Vatican falling into dust, the corpse-like odour which comes from it, the idiotic illusions of those who hope that they will one day see a renascence of the modern soul arise from a sepulchre where the remnants of dead centuries rot and slumber. Oh! I will not yield, I will not make my submission, I will defend my book by a fresh one. And that book, I promise you, will make some noise in the world, for it will sound the last agony of a dying religion, which one must make all haste to bury lest its remains should poison the nations!"

All this was beyond Don Vigilio's mind. The Italian priest, with narrow belief and ignorant terror of the new ideas, awoke within him. He clasped his hands, affrighted. "Be quiet, be quiet! You are blaspheming! And, besides, you cannot go off like that without again trying to see his Holiness. He alone is sovereign. And I know that I shall surprise you; but Father Dangelis has given you in jest the only good advice that can be given: Go back to see Monsignor Nani, for he alone will open the door of the Vatican for you."

Again did Pierre give a start of anger: "What! It was with Monsignor Nani that I began, from him that I set out; and I am to go back to him? What game is that? Can I consent to be a shuttlecock sent flying hither and thither by every battledore? People are having a game with me!"

Then, harassed and distracted, the young man fell on his chair in front of Don Vigilio, who with his face drawn by his prolonged vigil, and his hands still and ever faintly trembling, remained for some time silent. At last he explained that he had another idea. He was slightly acquainted with the Pope's confessor, a Franciscan father, a man of great simplicity, to whom he might recommend Pierre. This Franciscan, despite his self-effacement, would perhaps prove of service to him. At all events he might be tried. Then, once more, silence fell, and Pierre, whose dreamy eyes were turned towards the wall, ended by distinguishing the old picture which had touched him so deeply on the day of his arrival. In the pale glow of the lamp it gradually showed forth and lived, like an incarnation of his own case, his own futile despair before the sternly closed portal of truth and justice. Ah! that outcast woman, that stubborn victim of love, weeping amidst her streaming hair, her visage hidden whilst with pain and grief she sank upon the steps of that palace whose door was so pitilessly shut—how she resembled him! Draped with a mere strip of linen, she was shivering, and amidst the overpowering distress of her abandonment she did not reveal her secret, misfortune, or transgression, whichever it might be. But he, behind her close-pressed hands, endowed her with a face akin to his own: she became his sister, as were all the poor creatures without roof or certainty who weep because they are naked and alone, and wear out their strength in seeking to force the wicked thresholds of men. He could never gaze at her without pitying her, and it stirred him so much that evening to find her ever so unknown, nameless and visageless, yet steeped in the most bitter tears, that he suddenly began to question his companion.

"Tell me," said he, "do you know who painted that old picture? It stirs me to the soul like a masterpiece."

Stupefied by this unexpected question, the secretary raised his head and looked, feeling yet more astonished when he had examined the blackened, forsaken panel in its sorry frame.

"Where did it come from?" resumed Pierre; "why has it been stowed away in this room?"

"Oh!" replied Don Vigilio, with a gesture of indifference, "it's nothing. There are heaps of valueless old paintings everywhere. That one, no doubt, has always been here. But I don't know; I never noticed it before."

Whilst speaking he had at last risen to his feet, and this simple action had brought on such a fit of shivering that he could scarcely take leave, so violently did his teeth chatter with fever. "No, no, don't show me out," he stammered, "keep the lamp here. And to conclude: the best course is for you to leave yourself in the hands of Monsignor Nani, for he, at all events, is a superior man. I told you on your arrival that, whether you would or not, you would end by doing as he desired. And so what's the use of struggling? And mind, not a word of our conversation to-night; it would mean my death."

Then he noiselessly opened the doors, glanced distrustfully into the darkness of the passage, and at last ventured out and disappeared, regaining his own room with such soft steps that not the faintest footfall was heard amidst the tomb-like slumber of the old mansion.

On the morrow, Pierre, again mastered by a desire to fight on to the very end, got Don Vigilio to recommend him to the Pope's confessor, the Franciscan friar with whom the secretary was slightly acquainted. However, this friar proved to be an extremely timid if worthy man, selected precisely on account of his great modesty, simplicity, and absolute lack of influence in order that he might not abuse his position with respect to the Holy Father. And doubtless there was an affectation of humility on the latter's part in taking for confessor a member of the humblest of the regular orders, a friend of the poor, a holy beggar of the roads. At the same time the friar certainly enjoyed a reputation for oratory; and hidden by a veil the Pope at times listened to his sermons; for although as infallible Sovereign Pontiff Leo XIII could not receive lessons from any priest, it was admitted that as a man he might reap profit by listening to good discourse. Nevertheless apart from his natural eloquence, the worthy friar was really a mere washer of souls, a confessor who listens and absolves without even remembering the impurities which he removes in the waters of penitence. And Pierre, finding him really so poor and such a cipher, did not insist on an intervention which he realised would be futile.

All that day the young priest was haunted by the figure of that ingenuous lover of poverty, that delicious St. Francis, as Narcisse Habert was wont to say. Pierre had often wondered how such an apostle, so gentle towards both animate and inanimate creation, and so full of ardent charity for the wretched, could have arisen in a country of egotism and enjoyment like Italy, where the love of beauty alone has remained queen. Doubtless the times have changed; yet what a strong sap of love must have been needed in the old days, during the great sufferings of the middle ages, for such a consoler of the humble to spring from the popular soil and preach the gift of self to others, the renunciation of wealth, the horror of brutal force, the equality and obedience which would ensure the peace of the world. St. Francis trod the roads clad as one of the poorest, a rope girdling his grey gown and his bare feet shod with sandals, and he carried with him neither purse nor staff. And he and his brethren spoke aloud and freely, with sovereign florescence of poetry and boldness of truth, attacking the rich and the powerful, and daring even to denounce the priests of evil life, the debauched, simoniacal, and perjured bishops. A long cry of relief greeted the Franciscans, the people followed them in crowds—they were the friends, the liberators of all the humble ones who suffered. And thus, like revolutionaries, they at first so alarmed Rome, that the popes hesitated to authorise their Order. When they at last gave way it was assuredly with the hope of using this new force for their own profit, by conquering the whole vague mass of the lowly whose covert threats have ever growled through the ages, even in the most despotic times. And thenceforward in the sons of St. Francis the Church possessed an ever victorious army—a wandering army which spread over the roads, in the villages and through the towns, penetrating to the firesides of artisan and peasant, and gaining possession of all simple hearts. How great the democratic power of such an Order which had sprung from the very entrails of the people! And thence its rapid prosperity, its teeming growth in a few years, friaries arising upon all sides, and the third Order[1] so invading the secular population as to impregnate and absorb it. And that there was here a genuine growth of the soil, a vigorous vegetation of the plebeian stock was shown by an entire national art arising from it—the precursors of the Renascence in painting and even Dante himself, the soul of Italia's genius.

For some days now, in the Rome of the present time, Pierre had been coming into contact with those great Orders of the past. The Franciscans and the Dominicans were there face to face in their vast convents of prosperous aspect. But it seemed as if the humility of the Franciscans had in the long run deprived them of influence. Perhaps, too, their *role* as friends and liberators of the people was ended since the people now undertook to liberate itself. And so the only real remaining battle was between the Dominicans and the Jesuits, both of whom still claimed to mould the world according to their particular views. Warfare between them was incessant, and Rome—the supreme power at the Vatican—was ever the prize for which they contended. But, although the Dominicans had St. Thomas on their side, they must have felt that their old dogmatic science was crumbling, compelled as they were each day to surrender a little ground to the Jesuits whose principles accorded better with the spirit of the century. And, in addition to these, there were the white-robed Carthusians, those very holy, pure, and silent meditators who fled from the world into quiet cells and cloisters, those despairing and consoled ones whose numbers may decrease but whose Order will live for ever, even as grief and desire for solitude will live. And then there were the Benedictines whose admirable rules have sanctified labour, passionate toilers in literature and science, once powerful instruments of civilisation, enlarging universal knowledge by their immense historical and critical works. These Pierre loved, and with them would have sought a refuge two centuries earlier, yet he was astonished to find them building on the Aventine a huge dwelling, for which Leo XIII has already given millions, as if the science of to-day and to-morrow were yet a field where they might garner harvests. But *cui bono*, when the workmen have changed, and dogmas are there to bar the road—dogmas which totter, no doubt, but which believers may not fling aside in order to pass onward? And finally came the swarm of less important Orders, hundreds in number; there were the Carmelites, the Trappists, the Minims, the Barnabites, the Lazzarists, the Eudists, the Mission Fathers, the Servites, the Brothers of the Christian Doctrine; there were the Bernadines, the Augustinians, the Theatines, the Observants, the Passionists, the Celestines, and the Capuchins, without counting the corresponding Orders of women or the Poor Clares, or the innumerable nuns like those of the Visitation and the Calvary. Each community had its modest or sumptuous dwelling, certain districts of Rome were entirely composed of convents, and behind the silent lifeless facades all those people buzzed,

---

[1] The Franciscans, like the Dominicans and others, admit, in addition to the two Orders of friars and nuns, a third Order comprising devout persons of either sex who have neither the vocation nor the opportunity for cloistered life, but live in the world, privately observing the chief principles of the fraternity with which they are connected. In central and southern Europe members of these third Orders are still numerous.—Trans.

intrigued, and waged the everlasting warfare of rival interests and passions. The social evolution which produced them had long since ceased, still they obstinately sought to prolong their life, growing weaker and more useless day by day, destined to a slow agony until the time shall come when the new development of society will leave them neither foothold nor breathing space.

And it was not only with the regulars that Pierre came in contact during his peregrinations through Rome; indeed, he more particularly had to deal with the secular clergy, and learnt to know them well. A hierarchical system which was still vigorously enforced maintained them in various ranks and classes. Up above, around the Pope, reigned the pontifical family, the high and noble cardinals and prelates whose conceit was great in spite of their apparent familiarity. Below them the parish clergy formed a very worthy middle class of wise and moderate minds; and here patriot priests were not rare. Moreover, the Italian occupation of a quarter of a century, by installing in the city a world of functionaries who saw everything that went on, had, curiously enough, greatly purified the private life of the Roman priesthood, in which under the popes women, beyond all question, played a supreme part. And finally one came to the plebeian clergy whom Pierre studied with curiosity, a collection of wretched, grimy, half-naked priests who like famished animals prowled around in search of masses, and drifted into disreputable taverns in the company of beggars and thieves. However, he was more interested by the floating population of foreign priests from all parts of Christendom—the adventurers, the ambitious ones, the believers, the madmen whom Rome attracted just as a lamp at night time attracts the insects of the gloom. Among these were men of every nationality, position, and age, all lashed on by their appetites and scrambling from morn till eve around the Vatican, in order to snap at the prey which they hoped to secure. He found them everywhere, and told himself with some shame that he was one of them, that the unit of his own personality served to increase the incredible number of cassocks that one encountered in the streets. Ah! that ebb and flow, that ceaseless tide of black gowns and frocks of every hue! With their processions of students ever walking abroad, the seminaries of the different nations would alone have sufficed to drape and decorate the streets, for there were the French and the English all in black, the South Americans in black with blue sashes, the North Americans in black with red sashes, the Poles in black with green sashes, the Greeks in blue, the Germans in red, the Scots in violet, the Romans in black or violet or purple, the Bohemians with chocolate sashes, the Irish with red lappets, the Spaniards with blue cords, to say nothing of all the others with broidery and bindings and buttons in a hundred different styles. And in addition there were the confraternities, the penitents, white, black, blue, and grey, with sleeveless frocks and capes of different hue, grey, blue, black, or white. And thus even nowadays Papal Rome at times seemed to resuscitate, and one could realise how tenaciously and vivaciously she struggled on in order that she might not disappear in the cosmopolitan Rome of the new era. However, Pierre, whilst running about from one prelate to another, frequenting priests and crossing churches, could not accustom himself to the worship, the Roman piety which astonished him when it did not wound him. One rainy Sunday morning, on entering Santa Maria Maggiore, he fancied himself in some waiting-room, a very splendid one, no doubt, but where God seemed to have no habitation. There was not a bench, not a chair in the nave, across which people passed, as they might pass through a railway station, wetting and soiling the precious mosaic pavement with their muddy shoes; and tired women and children sat round the bases of the columns, even as in railway stations one sees people sitting and waiting for their trains during the great crushes of the holiday season. And for this tramping throng of folks of small degree, who had looked in *en passant*, a priest was saying a low mass in a side chapel, before which a narrow file of standing people had gathered, extending across the nave, and recalling the crowds which wait in front of theatres for the opening of the doors. At the elevation of the host one and all inclined themselves devoutly, but almost immediately afterwards the gathering dispersed. And indeed why linger? The mass was said. Pierre everywhere found the same form of attendance, peculiar to the countries of the sun; the worshippers were in a hurry and only favoured the Deity with short familiar visits, unless it were a question of some gala scene at San Paolo or San Giovanni in Laterano or some other of the old basilicas. It was only at the Gesu, on another Sunday morning, that the young priest came upon a high-mass congregation, which reminded him of the devout throngs of the North. Here there were benches and women seated, a worldly warmth and cosiness under the luxurious, gilded, carved, and painted roof, whose tawny splendour is very fine now that time has toned down the eccentricities of the decoration. But how many of the churches were empty, among them some of the most ancient and venerable, San Clemente, Sant' Agnese, Santa Croce in Gerusalemme, where during the offices one saw but a few believers of the neighbourhood. Four hundred churches were a good many for even Rome to people; and, indeed, some were merely attended on fixed ceremonial occasions, and a good many merely opened their doors once every year—on the feast day, that is, of their patron saint. Some also subsisted on the lucky possession of a fetish, an idol compassionate to human sufferings. Santa Maria in Ara Coeli possessed the miraculous little Jesus, the "Bambino," who healed sick children, and Sant' Agostino had the "Madonna del Parto," who grants a happy delivery to mothers. Then others were renowned for the holy water of their fonts, the oil of their lamps, the power of some wooden saint or marble virgin. Others again seemed forsaken, given up to tourists and the perquisites of beadles, like mere museums peopled with dead gods: Finally others disturbed one's faith by the suggestiveness of their aspects, as, for instance, that Santa Maria Rotonda, which is located in the Pantheon, a circular hall recalling a circus, where the Virgin remains the evident tenant of the Olympian deities.

Pierre took no little interest in the churches of the poor districts, but did not find there the keen faith and the throngs he had hoped for. One afternoon, at Santa Maria in Trastevere, he heard the choir in full song, but the church was quite empty, and the chant had a most lugubrious sound in such a desert. Then, another day, on entering San Crisogono, he found it draped, probably in readiness for some festival on the morrow. The columns were cased with red damask, and between them were hangings and curtains alternately yellow and blue, white and red; and the young man fled from such a fearful decoration as gaudy as that of a fair booth. Ah! how far he was from the cathedrals where in childhood he had believed and prayed! On all sides he found the same type of church, the antique basilica accommodated to the taste of eighteenth-century Rome. Though the style of San Luigi dei Francesi is better, more soberly elegant, the only thing that touched him even there was the thought of the heroic or saintly Frenchmen, who sleep in foreign soil beneath the flags. And as he sought for something Gothic, he ended by going to see Santa Maria sopra Minerva,[1] which, he was told, was the only example of the Gothic style in Rome. Here his stupefaction attained a climax at sight of the clustering columns cased in stucco imitating marble, the ogives which dared not soar, the rounded vaults condemned to the heavy majesty of the dome style. No, no, thought he, the faith whose cooling cinders lingered there was no longer that whose brazier had invaded and set all Christendom aglow! However, Monsignor Fornaro whom he chanced to meet as he was leaving the church, inveighed against the Gothic style as rank heresy. The first Christian church, said the prelate, had been the basilica, which had sprung from the temple, and it was blasphemy to assert that the Gothic cathedral was the real Christian house of prayer, for Gothic embodied the hateful Anglo-Saxon spirit, the rebellious genius of Luther. At this a passionate reply rose to Pierre's lips, but he said nothing for fear that he might say too much. However, he asked himself whether in all this there was not a decisive proof that Catholicism was the very vegetation of Rome, Paganism modified by Christianity. Elsewhere Christianity has grown up in quite a different spirit, to such a point that it has risen in rebellion and schismatically turned against the mother-city. And the breach has ever gone on widening, the dissemblance has become more and more marked; and amidst the evolution of new societies, yet a fresh schism appears inevitable and proximate in spite of all the despairing efforts to maintain union.

While Pierre thus visited the Roman churches, he also continued his efforts to gain support in the matter of his book, his irritation tending to such stubbornness, that if in the first instance he failed to obtain an interview, he went back again and again to secure one, steadfastly keeping his promise to call in turn upon each cardinal of the Congregation of the Index. And as a cardinal may belong to several Congregations, it resulted that he gradually found himself roaming through those former ministries of the old pontifical government which, if less numerous than formerly, are still very intricate institutions, each with its cardinal-prefect, its cardinal-members, its consultative prelates, and its numerous employees. Pierre repeatedly had to return to the Cancelleria, where the Congregation of the Index meets, and lost himself in its world of staircases, corridors, and halls. From the moment he passed under the porticus he was overcome by the icy shiver which fell from the old walls, and was quite unable to appreciate the bare, frigid beauty of the palace, Bramante's masterpiece though it be, so purely typical of the Roman Renascence. He also knew the Propaganda where he had seen Cardinal Sarno; and, sent as he was hither and thither, in his efforts to gain over influential prelates, chance made him acquainted with the other Congregations, that of the Bishops and Regulars, that of the Rites and that of the Council. He even obtained a glimpse of the Consistorial, the Dataria,[2] and the sacred Penitentiary. All these formed part of the administrative mechanism of the Church under its several aspects—the government of the Catholic world, the enlargement of the Church's conquests, the administration of its affairs in conquered countries, the decision of all

---

[1] So called because it occupies the site of a temple to Minerva.—Trans.

[2] It is from the Dataria that bulls, rescripts, letters of appointment to benefices, and dispensations of marriage, are issued, after the affixture of the date and formula Datum Romae, "Given at Rome."—Trans.

questions touching faith, morals, and individuals, the investigation and punishment of offences, the grant of dispensations and the sale of favours. One can scarcely imagine what a fearful number of affairs are each morning submitted to the Vatican, questions of the greatest gravity, delicacy, and intricacy, the solution of which gives rise to endless study and research. It is necessary to reply to the innumerable visitors who flock to Rome from all parts, and to the letters, the petitions, and the batches of documents which are submitted and require to be distributed among the various offices. And Pierre was struck by the deep and discreet silence in which all this colossal labour was accomplished; not a sound reaching the streets from the tribunals, parliaments, and factories for the manufacture of saints and nobles, whose mechanism was so well greased, that in spite of the rust of centuries and the deep and irremediable wear and tear, the whole continued working without clank or creak to denote its presence behind the walls. And did not that silence embody the whole policy of the Church, which is to remain mute and await developments? Nevertheless what a prodigious mechanism it was, antiquated no doubt, but still so powerful! And amidst those Congregations how keenly Pierre felt himself to be in the grip of the most absolute power ever devised for the domination of mankind. However much he might notice signs of decay and coming ruin he was none the less seized, crushed, and carried off by that huge engine made up of vanity and venality, corruption and ambition, meanness and greatness. And how far, too, he now was from the Rome that he had dreamt of, and what anger at times filled him amidst his weariness, as he persevered in his resolve to defend himself!

All at once certain things which he had never understood were explained to him. One day, when he returned to the Propaganda, Cardinal Sarno spoke to him of Freemasonry with such icy rage that he was abruptly enlightened. Freemasonry had hitherto made him smile; he had believed in it no more than he had believed in the Jesuits. Indeed, he had looked upon the ridiculous stories which were current—the stories of mysterious, shadowy men who governed the world with secret incalculable power—as mere childish legends. In particular he had been amazed by the blind hatred which maddened certain people as soon as Freemasonry was mentioned. However, a very distinguished and intelligent prelate had declared to him, with an air of profound conviction, that at least on one occasion every year each masonic Lodge was presided over by the Devil in person, incarnate in a visible shape! And now, by Cardinal Sarno's remarks, he understood the rivalry, the furious struggle of the Roman Catholic Church against that other Church, the Church of over the way.[1] Although the former counted on her own triumph, she none the less felt that the other, the Church of Freemasonry, was a competitor, a very ancient enemy, who indeed

[1] Some readers may think the above passages an exaggeration, but such is not the case. The hatred with which the Catholic priesthood, especially in Italy, Spain, and France, regards Freemasonry is remarkable. At the moment of writing these lines I have before me several French clerical newspapers, which contain the most abusive articles levelled against President Faure solely because he is a Freemason. One of these prints, a leading journal of Lyons, tells the French President that he cannot serve both God and the Devil; and that if he cannot give up Freemasonry he would do well to cease desecrating the abode of the Deity by his attendance at divine service.—Trans.

claimed to be more ancient than herself, and whose victory always remained a possibility. And the friction between them was largely due to the circumstance that they both aimed at universal sovereignty, and had a similar international organisation, a similar net thrown over the nations, and in a like way mysteries, dogmas, and rites. It was deity against deity, faith against faith, conquest against conquest: and so, like competing tradesmen in the same street, they were a source of mutual embarrassment, and one of them was bound to kill the other. But if Roman Catholicism seemed to Pierre to be worn out and threatened with ruin, he remained quite as sceptical with regard to the power of Freemasonry. He had made inquiries as to the reality of that power in Rome, where both Grand Master and Pope were enthroned, one in front of the other. He was certainly told that the last Roman princes had thought themselves compelled to become Freemasons in order to render their own difficult position somewhat easier and facilitate the future of their sons. But was this true? had they not simply yielded to the force of the present social evolution? And would not Freemasonry eventually be submerged by its own triumph—that of the ideas of justice, reason, and truth, which it had defended through the dark and violent ages of history? It is a thing which constantly happens; the victory of an idea kills the sect which has propagated it, and renders the apparatus with which the members of the sect surrounded themselves, in order to fire imaginations, both useless and somewhat ridiculous. Carbonarism did not survive the conquest of the political liberties which it demanded; and on the day when the Catholic Church crumbles, having accomplished its work of civilisation, the other Church, the Freemasons' Church of across the road, will in a like way disappear, its task of liberation ended. Nowadays the famous power of the Lodges, hampered by traditions, weakened by a ceremonial which provokes laughter, and reduced to a simple bond of brotherly agreement and mutual assistance, would be but a sorry weapon of conquest for humanity, were it not that the vigorous breath of science impels the nations onwards and helps to destroy the old religions.

However, all Pierre's journeyings and applications brought him no certainty; and, while stubbornly clinging to Rome, intent on fighting to the very end, like a soldier who will not believe in the possibility of defeat, he remained as anxious as ever. He had seen all the cardinals whose influence could be of use to him. He had seen the Cardinal Vicar, entrusted with the diocese of Rome, who, like the man of letters he was, had spoken to him of Horace, and, like a somewhat blundering politician, had questioned him about France, the Republic, the Army, and the Navy Estimates, without dealing in the slightest degree with the incriminated book. He had also seen the Grand Penitentiary, that tall old man, with fleshless, ascetic face, of whom he had previously caught a glimpse at the Boccanera mansion, and from whom he now only drew a long and severe sermon on the wickedness of young priests, whom the century had perverted and who wrote most abominable books. Finally, at the Vatican, he had seen the Cardinal Secretary, in some wise his Holiness's Minister of Foreign Affairs, the great power of the Holy See, whom he had hitherto been prevented from approaching by terrifying warnings as to the possible result of an unfavourable reception. However, whilst apologising for calling at such a late stage, he had found himself in presence of a most amiable man, whose somewhat rough appearance was softened by diplomatic affability, and who, after making him sit down, questioned him with an air of interest, listened to him, and even spoke some words of comfort. Nevertheless, on again reaching the Piazza of St. Peter's, Pierre well understood that his affair had not made the slightest progress, and that if he ever managed to force the Pope's door, it would not be by way of the Secretariate of State. And that evening he returned home quite exhausted by so many visits, in such distraction at feeling that little by little he had been wholly caught in that huge mechanism with its hundred wheels, that he asked himself in terror what he should do on the morrow now that there remained nothing for him to do—unless, indeed, it were to go mad.

However, meeting Don Vigilio in a passage of the house, he again wished to ask him for some good advice. But the secretary, who had a gleam of terror in his eyes, silenced him, he knew not why, with an anxious gesture. And then in a whisper, in Pierre's ear, he said: "Have you seen Monsignor Nani? No! Well, go to see him, go to see him. I repeat that you have nothing else to do!"

Pierre yielded. And indeed why should he have resisted? Apart from the motives of ardent charity which had brought him to Rome to defend his book, was he not there for a self-educating, experimental purpose? It was necessary that he should carry his attempts to the very end.

On the morrow, when he reached the colonnade of St. Peter's, the hour was so early that he had to wait there awhile. He had never better realised the enormity of those four curving rows of columns, forming a forest of gigantic stone trunks among which nobody ever promenades. In fact, the spot is a grandiose and dreary desert, and one asks oneself the why and wherefore of such a majestic porticus. Doubtless, however, it was for its sole majesty, for the mere pomp of decoration, that this colonnade was reared; and therein, again, one finds the whole Roman spirit. However, Pierre at last turned into the Via di Sant' Offizio, and passing the sacristy of St. Peter's, found himself before the Palace of the Holy Office in a solitary silent district, which the footfall of pedestrians or the rumble of wheels but seldom disturbs. The sun alone lives there, in sheets of light which spread slowly over the small, white paving. You divine the vicinity of the Basilica, for there is a smell as of incense, a cloisteral quiescence as of the slumber of centuries. And at one corner the Palace of the Holy Office rises up with heavy, disquieting bareness, only a single row of windows piercing its lofty, yellow front. The wall which skirts a side street looks yet more suspicious with its row of even smaller casements, mere peep-holes with glaucous panes. In the bright sunlight this huge cube of mud-coloured masonry ever seems asleep, mysterious, and closed like a prison, with scarcely an aperture for communication with the outer world.

Pierre shivered, but then smiled as at an act of childishness, for he reflected that the Holy Roman and Universal Inquisition, nowadays the Sacred Congregation of the Holy Office, was no longer the institution it had been, the purveyor of heretics for the stake, the occult tribunal beyond appeal which had right of life and death over all mankind. True, it still laboured in secrecy, meeting every Wednesday, and judging and condemning without a sound issuing from within its walls. But on the other hand if it still continued to strike at the crime of heresy, if it smote men as well as their works, it no longer possessed either weapons or dungeons, steel or fire to do its bidding, but was reduced to a mere *role* of protest, unable to inflict aught but disciplinary penalties even upon the ecclesiastics of its own Church.

When Pierre on entering was ushered into the reception-room of Monsignor Nani who, as assessor, lived in the palace, he experienced an agreeable surprise. The apartment faced the south, and was spacious and flooded with sunshine. And stiff as was the furniture, dark as were the hangings, an exquisite sweetness pervaded the room, as though a woman had lived in it and accomplished the prodigy of imparting some of her own grace to all those stern-looking things. There were no flowers, yet there was a pleasant smell. A charm expanded and conquered every heart from the very threshold.

Monsignor Nani at once came forward, with a smile on his rosy face, his blue eyes keenly glittering, and his fine light hair powdered by age. With hands outstretched, he exclaimed: "Ah! how kind of you to have come to see me, my dear son! Come, sit down, let us have a friendly chat." Then with an extraordinary display of affection, he began to question Pierre: "How are you getting on? Tell me all about it, exactly what you have done."

Touched in spite of Don Vigilio's revelations, won over by the sympathy which he fancied he could detect, Pierre thereupon confessed himself, relating his visits to Cardinal Sarno, Monsignor Fornaro and Father Dangelis, his applications to all the influential cardinals, those of the Index, the Grand Penitentiary, the Cardinal Vicar, and the Cardinal Secretary; and dwelling on his endless journeys from door to door through all the Congregations and all the clergy, that huge, active, silent bee-hive amidst which he had wearied his feet, exhausted his limbs, and bewildered his poor brain. And at each successive Station of this Calvary of entreaty, Monsignor Nani, who seemed to listen with an air of rapture, exclaimed: "But that's very good, that's capital! Oh! your affair is progressing. Yes, yes, it's progressing marvellously well."

He was exultant, though he allowed no unseemly irony to appear, while his pleasant, penetrating eyes fathomed the young priest, to ascertain if he had been brought to the requisite degree of obedience. Had he been sufficiently wearied, disillusioned and instructed in the reality of things, for one to finish with him? Had three months' sojourn in Rome sufficed to turn the somewhat mad enthusiast of the first days into an unimpassioned or at least resigned being?

However, all at once Monsignor Nani remarked: "But, my dear son, you tell me nothing of his Eminence Cardinal Sanguinetti."

"The fact is, Monseigneur, that his Eminence is at Frascati, so I have been unable to see him."

Thereupon the prelate, as if once more postponing the *denouement* with the secret enjoyment of an artistic *diplomate*, began to protest, raising his little plump hands with the anxious air of a man who considers everything lost: "Oh! but you must see his Eminence; it is absolutely necessary! Think of it! The Prefect of the Index! We can only act after your visit to him, for as you have not seen *him* it is as if you had seen nobody. Go, go to Frascati, my dear son."

And thereupon Pierre could only bow and reply: "I will go, Monseigneur."

XI.

ALTHOUGH Pierre knew that he would be unable to see Cardinal Sanguinetti before eleven o'clock, he nevertheless availed himself of an early train, so that it was barely nine when he alighted at the little station of Frascati. He had already visited the place during his enforced idleness, when he had made the classical excursion to the Roman castles which extend from Frascati to Rocco di Papa, and from Rocco di Papa to Monte Cavo, and he was now delighted with the prospect of strolling for a couple of hours along those first slopes of the Alban hills, where, amidst rushes, olives, and vines, Frascati, like a promontory, overlooks the immense ruddy sea of the Campagna even as far as Rome, which, six full leagues away, wears the whitish aspect of a marble isle.

Ah! that charming Frascati, on its greeny knoll at the foot of the wooded Tusculan heights, with its famous terrace whence one enjoys the finest view in the world, its old patrician villas with proud and elegant Renascence facades and magnificent parks, which, planted with cypress, pine, and ilex, are for ever green! There was a sweetness, a delight, a fascination about the spot, of which Pierre would have never wearied. And for more than an hour he had wandered blissfully along roads edged with ancient, knotty olive-trees, along dingle ways shaded by the spreading foliage of neighbouring estates, and along perfumed paths, at each turn of which the Campagna was seen stretching far away, when all at once he was accosted by a person whom he was both surprised and annoyed to meet. He had strolled down to some low ground near the railway station, some old vineyards where a number of new houses had been built of recent years, and suddenly saw a stylish pair-horse victoria, coming from the direction of Rome, draw up close by, whilst its occupant called to him: "What! Monsieur l'Abbe Froment, are you taking a walk here, at this early hour?"

Thereupon Pierre recognised Count Luigi Prada, who alighted, shook hands with him and began to walk beside him, whilst the empty carriage went on in advance. And forthwith the Count explained his tastes: "I seldom take the train," he said, "I drive over. It gives my horses an outing. I have interests over here as you may know, a big building enterprise which is unfortunately not progressing very well. And so, although the season is advanced, I'm obliged to come rather more frequently than I care to do."

As Prada suggested, Pierre was acquainted with the story. The Boccaneras had been obliged to sell a sumptuous villa which a cardinal of their family had built at Frascati in accordance with the plans of Giacomo della Porta, during the latter part of the sixteenth century: a regal summer-residence it had been, finely wooded, with groves and basins and cascades, and in particular a famous terrace projecting like a cape above the Roman Campagna whose expanse stretches from the Sabine mountains to the Mediterranean sands. Through the division of the property, Benedetta had inherited from her mother some very extensive vineyards below Frascati, and these she had brought as dowry to Prada at the very moment when the building mania was extending from Rome into the provinces. And thereupon Prada had conceived the idea of erecting on the spot a number of middle-class villas like those which litter the suburbs of Paris. Few purchasers, however, had come forward, the financial crash had supervened, and he was now with difficulty liquidating this unlucky business, having indemnified his wife at the time of their separation.

"And then," he continued, addressing Pierre, "one can come and go as one likes with a carriage, whereas, on taking the train, one is at the mercy of the time table. This morning, for instance, I have appointments with contractors, experts, and lawyers, and I have no notion how long they will keep me. It's a wonderful country, isn't it? And we are quite right to be proud of it in Rome. Although I may have some worries just now, I can never set foot here without my heart beating with delight."

A circumstance which he did not mention, was that his *amica*, Lisbeth Kauffmann, had spent the summer in one of the newly erected villas, where she had installed her studio and had been visited by all the foreign colony, which tolerated her irregular position on account of her gay spirits and artistic talent. Indeed, people had even ended by accepting the outcome of her connection with Prada, and a fortnight previously she had returned to Rome, and there given birth to a son—an event which had again revived all the scandalous tittle-tattle respecting Benedetta's divorce suit. And Prada's attachment to Frascati doubtless sprang from the recollection of the happy hours he had spent there, and the joyful pride with which the birth of the boy inspired him.

Pierre, for his part, felt ill at ease in the young Count's presence, for he had an instinctive hatred of money-mongers and men of prey. Nevertheless, he desired to respond to his amiability, and so inquired after his father, old Orlando, the hero of the Liberation.

"Oh!" replied Prada, "excepting for his legs he's in wonderfully good health. He'll live a hundred years. Poor father! I should so much have liked to install him in one of these little houses, last summer. But I could not get him to consent; he's determined not to leave Rome; he's afraid, perhaps, that it might be taken away from him during his absence." Then the young Count burst into a laugh, quite merry at the thought of jeering at the heroic but no longer fashionable age of independence. And afterwards he said, "My father was speaking of you again only yesterday, Monsieur l'Abbe. He is astonished that he has not seen you lately."

This distressed Pierre, for he had begun to regard Orlando with respectful affection. Since his first visit, he had twice called on the old hero, but the latter had refused to broach the subject of Rome so long as his young friend should not have seen, felt, and understood everything. There would be time for a talk later on, said he, when they were both in a position to formulate their conclusions.

"Pray tell Count Orlando," responded Pierre, "that I have not forgotten him, and that, if I have deferred a fresh visit, it is because I desire to satisfy him. However, I certainly will not leave Rome without going to tell him how deeply his kind greeting has touched me."

XI.

Whilst talking, the two men slowly followed the ascending road past the newly erected villas, several of which were not yet finished. And when Prada learned that the priest had come to call on Cardinal Sanguinetti, he again laughed, with the laugh of a good-natured wolf, showing his white fangs. "True," he exclaimed, "the Cardinal has been here since the Pope has been laid up. Ah! you'll find him in a pretty fever."

"Why?"

"Why, because there's bad news about the Holy Father this morning. When I left Rome it was rumoured that he had spent a fearful night."

So speaking, Prada halted at a bend of the road, not far from an antique chapel, a little church of solitary, mournful grace of aspect, on the verge of an olive grove. Beside it stood a ruinous building, the old parsonage, no doubt, whence there suddenly emerged a tall, knotty priest with coarse and earthy face, who, after roughly locking the door, went off in the direction of the town.

"Ah!" resumed the Count in a tone of raillery, "that fellow's heart also must be beating violently; he's surely gone to your Cardinal in search of news."

Pierre had looked at the priest. "I know him," he replied; "I saw him, I remember, on the day after my arrival at Cardinal Boccanera's. He brought the Cardinal a basket of figs and asked him for a certificate in favour of his young brother, who had been sent to prison for some deed of violence—a knife thrust if I recollect rightly. However, the Cardinal absolutely refused him the certificate."

"It's the same man," said Prada, "you may depend on it. He was often at the Villa Boccanera formerly; for his young brother was gardener there. But he's now the client, the creature of Cardinal Sanguinetti. Santobono his name is, and he's a curious character, such as you wouldn't find in France, I fancy. He lives all alone in that falling hovel, and officiates at that old chapel of St. Mary in the Fields, where people don't go to hear mass three times in a year. Yes, it's a perfect sinecure, which with its stipend of a thousand francs enables him to live there like a peasant philosopher, cultivating the somewhat extensive garden whose big walls you see yonder."

The close to which he called attention stretched down the slope behind the parsonage, without an aperture, like some savage place of refuge into which not even the eye could penetrate. And all that could be seen above the left-hand wall was a superb, gigantic fig-tree, whose big leaves showed blackly against the clear sky. Prada had moved on again, and continued to speak of Santobono, who evidently interested him. Fancy, a patriot priest, a Garibaldian! Born at Nemi, in that yet savage nook among the Alban hills, he belonged to the people and was still near to the soil. However, he had studied, and knew sufficient history to realise the past greatness of Rome, and dream of the re-establishment of Roman dominion as represented by young Italy. And he had come to believe, with passionate fervour, that only a great pope could realise his dream by seizing upon power, and then conquering all the other nations. And what could be easier, since the Pope commanded millions of Catholics? Did not half Europe belong to him? France, Spain, and Austria would give way as soon as they should see him powerful, dictating laws to the world. Germany and Great Britain, indeed all the Protestant countries, would also inevitably be conquered, for the papacy was the only dike that could be opposed to error, which must some day fatally succumb in its efforts against such a barrier. Politically, however, Santobono had declared himself for Germany, for he considered that France needed to be crushed before she would throw herself into the arms of the Holy Father. And thus contradictions and fancies clashed in his foggy brain, whose burning ideas swiftly turned to violence under the influence of primitive, racial fierceness. Briefly, the priest was a barbarian upholder of the Gospel, a friend of the humble and woeful, a sectarian of that school which is capable alike of great virtues and great crimes.

"Yes," concluded Prada, "he is now devoted to Cardinal Sanguinetti because he believes that the latter will prove the great pope of to-morrow, who is to make Rome the one capital of the nations. At the same time he doubtless harbours a lower personal ambition, that of attaining to a canonry or of gaining assistance in the little worries of life, as when he wished to extricate his brother from trouble. Here, you know, people stake their luck on a cardinal just as they nurse a 'trey' in the lottery, and if their cardinal proves the winning number and becomes pope they gain a fortune. And that's why you now see Santobono striding along yonder, all anxiety to know if Leo XIII will die and Sanguinetti don the tiara."

"Do you think the Pope so very ill, then?" asked Pierre, both anxious and interested.

The Count smiled and raised both arms: "Ah!" said he, "can one ever tell? They all get ill when their interest lies that way. However, I believe that the Pope is this time really indisposed; a complaint of the bowels, it is said; and at his age, you know, the slightest indisposition may prove fatal."

The two men took a few steps in silence, then the priest again asked a question: "Would Cardinal Sanguinetti have a great chance if the Holy See were vacant?"

"A great chance! Ah! that's another of those things which one never knows. The truth is people class Sanguinetti among the acceptable candidates, and if personal desire sufficed he would certainly be the next pope, for ambition consumes him to the marrow, and he displays extraordinary passion and determination in his efforts to succeed. But therein lies his very weakness; he is using himself up, and he knows it. And so he must be resolved to every step during the last days of battle. You may be quite sure that if he has shut himself up here at this critical time, it is in order that he may the better direct his operations from a distance, whilst at the same time feigning a retreat, a disinterestedness which is bound to have a good effect."

Then Prada began to expatiate on Sanguinetti with no little complacency, for he liked the man's spirit of intrigue, his keen, conquering appetite, his excessive, and even somewhat blundering activity. He had become acquainted with him on his return from the nunciature at Vienna, when he had already resolved to win the tiara. That ambition explained everything, his quarrels and reconciliations with the reigning pope, his affection for Germany, followed by a sudden evolution in the direction of France, his varying attitude with regard to Italy, at first a desire for agreement, and then absolute rejection of all compromises, a refusal to grant any concession, so long as Rome should not be evacuated. This, indeed, seemed to be Sanguinetti's definite position; he made a show of disliking the wavering sway of Leo XIII, and of retaining a fervent admiration for Pius IX, the great, heroic pope of the days of resistance, whose goodness of heart had proved no impediment to unshakable firmness. And all this was equivalent to a promise that he, Sanguinetti, would again make kindliness exempt from weakness, the rule of the Church, and would steer clear of the dangerous compounding of politics. At bottom, however, politics were his only dream, and he had even formulated a complete programme of intentional vagueness, which his clients and creatures spread abroad with an air of rapturous mystery. However, since a previous indisposition of the Pope's, during the spring, he had been living in mortal disquietude, for it had then been rumoured that the Jesuits would resign themselves to support Cardinal Pio Boccanera, although the latter scarcely favoured them. He was rough and stern, no doubt, and his extreme bigotry might be a source of danger in this tolerant age; but, on the other hand, was he not a patrician, and would not his election imply that the papacy would never cease to claim the temporal power? From that moment Boccanera had been the one man whom Sanguinetti feared, for he beheld himself despoiled of his prize, and spent his time in devising plans to rid himself of such a powerful rival, repeating abominable stories of Cardinal Pio's alleged complaisance with regard to Benedetta and Dario, and incessantly representing him as Antichrist, the man of sin, whose reign would consummate the ruin of the papacy. Finally, to regain the support of the Jesuits, Sanguinetti's last idea was to repeat through his familiars that for his part he would not merely maintain the principle of the temporal power intact, but would even undertake to regain that power. And he had a full plan on the subject, which folks confided to one another in whispers, a plan which, in spite of its apparent concessions, would lead to the overwhelming victory of the Church. It was to raise the prohibition which prevented Catholics from voting or becoming candidates at the Italian elections; to send a hundred, then two hundred, and then three hundred deputies to the Chamber, and in that wise to overthrow the House of Savoy, and establish a Federation of the Italian provinces, whereof the Holy Father, once more placed in possession of Rome, would become the august and sovereign President.

As Prada finished he again laughed, showing his white teeth—teeth which would never readily relinquish the prey they held. "So you see," he added, "we need to defend ourselves, since it's a question of turning us out. Fortunately, there are some little obstacles in the way of that. Nevertheless, such dreams naturally have great influence on excited minds, such as that of Santobono, for instance. He's a man whom one word from Sanguinetti would lead far indeed. Ah! he has good legs. Look at him up yonder, he has already reached the Cardinal's little palace—that white villa with the sculptured balconies."

Pierre raised his eyes and perceived the episcopal residence, which was one of the first houses of Frascati. Of modern construction and Renascence style, it overlooked the immensity of the Roman Campagna.

It was now eleven o'clock, and as the young priest, before going up to pay his own visit, bade the Count good-bye, the latter for a moment kept hold of his hand. "Do you know," said he, "it would be very kind of you to lunch with me—will you? Come and join me at that restaurant yonder with the pink front as soon as you are at liberty. I shall have settled my own business in an hour's time, and I shall be delighted to have your company at table."

Pierre began by declining, but he could offer no possible excuse, and at last surrendered, won over, despite himself, by Prada's real charm of manner. When they had parted, the young priest only had to climb a street in order to reach the Cardinal's door. With his natural expansiveness and craving for popularity, Sanguinetti was easy of access, and at Frascati in particular his doors were flung open even to the most humble cassocks. So Pierre was at once ushered in, a circumstance which somewhat surprised him, for he remembered the bad humour of the servant whom he had seen on calling at the Cardinal's residence in Rome, when he had been advised to forego the journey, as his Eminence did not like to be disturbed when he was ill. However, nothing spoke of illness in that pleasant villa, flooded with sunshine. True, the waiting-room, where he was momentarily left alone, displayed neither luxury nor comfort; but it was brightened by the finest light in the world, and overlooked that extraordinary Campagna, so flat, so bare, and so unique in its beauty, for in front of it one ever dreams and sees the past arise. And so, whilst waiting, Pierre stationed himself at an open window, conducting on to a balcony, and his eyes roamed over the endless sea of herbage to the far-away whiteness of Rome, above which rose the dome of St. Peter's, at that distance a mere sparkling speck, barely as large as the nail of one's little finger.

However, the young man had scarcely taken up this position when he was surprised to hear some people talking, their words reaching him with great distinctness. And on leaning forward he realised that his Eminence in person was standing on another balcony close by, and conversing with a priest, only a portion of whose cassock could be seen. Still, this sufficed for Pierre to recognise Santobono. His first impulse, dictated by natural discretion, was to withdraw from the window, but the words he next heard riveted him to the spot.

"We shall know in a moment," his Eminence was saying in his full voice. "I sent Eufemio to Rome, for he is the only person in whom I've any confidence. And see, there is the train bringing him back."

A train, still as small as a plaything, could in fact be seen approaching over the vast plain, and doubtless it was to watch for its arrival that Sanguinetti had stationed himself on the balcony. And there he lingered, with his eyes fixed on distant Rome. Then Santobono, in a passionate voice, spoke some words which Pierre imperfectly understood, but the Cardinal with clear articulation rejoined, "Yes, yes, my dear fellow, a catastrophe would be a great misfortune. Ah! may his Holiness long be preserved to us." Then he paused, and as he was no hypocrite, gave full expression to the thoughts which were in his mind: "At least, I hope that he will be preserved just now, for the times are bad, and I am in frightful anguish. The partisans of Antichrist have lately gained much ground."

A cry escaped Santobono: "Oh! your Eminence will act and triumph."

"I, my dear fellow? What would you have me do? I am simply at the disposal of my friends, those who are willing to believe in me, with the sole object of ensuring the victory of the Holy See. It is they who ought to act, it is they—each according to the measure of his means—who ought to bar the road to the wicked in order that the righteous may succeed. Ah! if Antichrist should reign—"

The recurrence of this word Antichrist greatly disturbed Pierre; but he suddenly remembered what the Count had told him: Antichrist was Cardinal Boccanera.

"Think of that, my dear fellow," continued Sanguinetti. "Picture Antichrist at the Vatican, consummating the ruin of religion by his implacable pride, his iron will, his gloomy passion for nihility; for there can be no doubt of it, he is the Beast of Death announced by the prophecies, the Beast who will expose one and all to the danger of being swallowed up with him in his furious rush into abysmal darkness. I know him; he only dreams of obstinacy and destruction, he will seize the pillars of the temple and shake them in order that he may sink beneath the ruins, he and the whole Catholic world! In less than six months he will be driven from Rome, at strife with all the nations, execrated by Italy, and roaming the world like the phantom of the last pope!"

XI.

It was with a low growl, suggestive of a stifled oath, that Santobono responded to this frightful prediction. But the train had now reached the station, and among the few passengers who had alighted, Pierre could distinguish a little Abbe, who was walking so fast that his cassock flapped against his hips. It was Abbe Eufemio, the Cardinal's secretary, and when he had perceived his Eminence on the balcony he lost all self-respect, and broke into a run, in order that he might the sooner ascend the sloping street. "Ah! here's Eufemio," exclaimed the Cardinal, quivering with anxiety. "We shall know now, we shall know now."

The secretary had plunged into the doorway below, and he climbed the stairs with such rapidity that almost immediately afterwards Pierre saw him rush breathlessly across the waiting-room, and vanish into the Cardinal's sanctum. Sanguinetti had quitted the balcony to meet his messenger, but soon afterwards he returned to it asking questions, venting exclamations, raising, in fact, quite a tumult over the news which he had received. "And so it's really true, the night was a bad one. His Holiness scarcely slept! Colic, you were told? But nothing could be worse at his age; it might carry him off in a couple of hours. And the doctors, what do they say?"

The answer did not reach Pierre, but he understood its purport as the Cardinal in his naturally loud voice resumed: "Oh! the doctors never know. Besides, when they refuse to speak death is never far off. *Dio*! what a misfortune if the catastrophe cannot be deferred for a few days!"

Then he became silent, and Pierre realised that his eyes were once more travelling towards Rome, gazing with ambitious anguish at the dome of St. Peter's, that little, sparkling speck above the vast, ruddy plain. What a commotion, what agitation if the Pope were dead! And he wished that it had merely been necessary for him to stretch forth his arm in order to take and hold the Eternal City, the Holy City, which, yonder on the horizon, occupied no more space than a heap of gravel cast there by a child's spade. And he was already dreaming of the coming Conclave, when the canopy of each other cardinal would fall, and his own, motionless and sovereign, would crown him with purple.

"But you are right, my friend!" he suddenly exclaimed, addressing Santobono, "one must act, the salvation of the Church is at stake. And, besides, it is impossible that Heaven should not be with us, since our sole desire is its triumph. If necessary, at the supreme moment, Heaven will know how to crush Antichrist."

Then, for the first time, Pierre distinctly heard the voice of Santobono, who, gruffly, with a sort of savage decision, responded: "Oh! if Heaven is tardy it shall be helped."

That was all; the young man heard nothing further save a confused murmur of voices. The speakers quitted the balcony, and his spell of waiting began afresh in the sunlit *salon* so peaceful and delightful in its brightness. But all at once the door of his Eminence's private room was thrown wide open and a servant ushered him in; and he was surprised to find the Cardinal alone, for he had not witnessed the departure of the two priests, who had gone off by another door. The Cardinal, with his highly coloured face, big nose, thick lips, square-set, vigorous figure, which still looked young despite his sixty years, was standing near a window in the bright golden light. He had put on the paternal smile with which he greeted even the humblest from motives of good policy, and as soon as Pierre had knelt and kissed his ring, he motioned him to a chair.

"Sit down, dear son, sit down. You have come of course about that unfortunate affair of your book. I am very pleased indeed to be able to speak with you about it."

He himself then took a chair in front of that window overlooking Rome whence he seemed unable to drag himself. And the young priest, whilst apologising for coming to disturb his rest, perceived that he scarcely listened, for his eyes again sought the prey which he so ardently coveted. Yet the semblance of good-natured attention was perfect, and Pierre marvelled at the force of will which this man must possess to appear so calm, so interested in the affairs of others, when such a tempest was raging in him.

"Your Eminence will, I hope, kindly forgive me," continued the young priest.

"But you have done right to come, since I am kept here by my failing health," said the Cardinal. "Besides, I am somewhat better, and it is only natural that you should wish to give me some explanations and defend your work and enlighten my judgment. In fact, I was astonished at not yet having seen you, for I know that your faith in your cause is great and that you spare no steps to convert your judges. So speak, my dear son, I am listening and shall be pleased indeed if I can absolve you."

Pierre was caught by these kind words, and a hope returned to him, that of winning the support of the all-powerful Prefect of the Index. He already regarded this ex-nuncio—who at Brussels and Vienna had acquired the worldly art of sending people away satisfied with indefinite promises though he meant to grant them nothing—as a man of rare intelligence and exquisite cordiality. And so once more he regained the fervour of his apostolate to express his views respecting the future Rome, the Rome he dreamt of, which was destined yet again to become the mistress of the world if she would return to the Christianity of Jesus, to an ardent love for the weak and the humble.

Sanguinetti smiled, wagged his head, and raised exclamations of rapture: "Very good, very good indeed, perfect! Oh! I agree with you, dear son. One cannot put things better. It is quite evident; all good minds must agree with you." And then, said he, the poetic side deeply touched him. Like Leo XIII—and doubtless in a spirit of rivalry—he courted the reputation of being a very distinguished Latinist, and professed a special and boundless affection for Virgil. "I know, I know," he exclaimed, "I remember your page on the return of spring, which consoles the poor whom winter has frozen. Oh! I read it three times over! And are you aware that your writing is full of Latin turns of style. I noticed more than fifty expressions which could be found in the 'Bucolics.' Your book is a charm, a perfect charm!"

As he was no fool, and realised that the little priest before him was a man of high intelligence, he ended by interesting himself, not in Pierre personally, but in the profit which he might possibly derive from him. Amidst his feverish intrigues, he unceasingly sought to utilise all the qualities possessed by those whom God sent to him that might in any way be conducive to his own triumph. So, for a moment, he turned away from Rome and looked his companion in the face, listening to him and asking himself in what way he might employ him—either at once in the crisis through which he was passing, or later on when he should be pope. But the young priest again made the mistake of attacking the temporal power, and of employing that unfortunate expression, "a new religion." Thereupon the Cardinal stopped him with a gesture, still smiling, still retaining all his amiability, although the resolution which he had long since formed became from that moment definitive. "You are certainly in the right on many points, my dear son," he said, "and I often share your views—share them completely. But come, you are doubtless not aware that I am the protector of Lourdes here at Rome. And so, after the page which you have written about the Grotto, how can I possibly pronounce in your favour and against the Fathers?"

Pierre was utterly overcome by this announcement, for he was indeed unaware of the Cardinal's position with respect to Lourdes, nobody having taken the precaution to warn him. However, each of the Catholic enterprises distributed throughout the world has a protector at Rome, a cardinal who is designated by the Pope to represent it and, if need be, to defend it.

"Those good Fathers!" Sanguinetti continued in a gentle voice, "you have caused them great grief, and really our hands are tied, we cannot add to their sorrow. If you only knew what a number of masses they send us! I know more than one of our poor priests who would die of hunger if it were not for them."

Pierre could only bow beneath the blow. Once more he found himself in presence of the pecuniary question, the necessity in which the Holy See is placed to secure the revenue it requires one year with another. And thus the Pope was ever in servitude, for if the loss of Rome had freed him of the cares of state, his enforced gratitude for the alms he received still riveted him to earth. So great, indeed, were the requirements, that money was the ruler, the sovereign power, before which all bowed at the Court of Rome.

And now Sanguinetti rose to dismiss his visitor. "You must not despair, dear son," he said effusively. "I have only my own vote, you know, and I promise you that I will take into account the excellent explanations which you have just given me. And who can tell? If God be with you, He will save you even in spite of all!" This speech formed part of the Cardinal's usual tactics; for one of his principles was never to drive people to extremes by sending them away hopeless. What good, indeed, would it do to tell this one that the condemnation of his book was a foregone conclusion, and that his only prudent course would be to disavow it? Only a savage like Boccanera breathed anger upon fiery souls and plunged them into rebellion. "You must hope, hope!" repeated Sanguinetti with a smile, as if implying a multitude of fortunate things which he could not plainly express.

Thereupon Pierre, who was deeply touched, felt born anew. He even forgot the conversation he had surprised, the Cardinal's keen ambition and covert rage with his redoubtable rival. Besides, might not intelligence take the place of heart among the powerful? If this man should some day become pope, and had understood him, might he not prove the pope who was awaited, the pope who would accept the task of reorganising the Church of the United States of Europe, and making it the spiritual sovereign of the world? So he thanked him with emotion, bowed, and left him to his dream, standing before that widely open window whence Rome appeared to him, glittering like a jewel, even indeed as the tiara of gold and gems, in the splendour of the autumn sun.

It was nearly one o'clock when Pierre and Count Prada were at last able to sit down to *dejeuner* in the little restaurant where they had agreed to meet. They had both been delayed by their affairs. However, the Count, having settled some worrying matters to his own advantage, was very lively, whilst the priest on his side was again hopeful, and yielded to the delightful charm of that last fine day. And so the meal proved a very pleasant one in the large, bright room, which, as usual at that season of the year, was quite deserted. Pink and blue predominated in the decoration, but Cupids fluttered on the ceiling, and landscapes, vaguely recalling the Roman castles, adorned the walls. The things they ate were fresh, and they drank the wine of Frascati, to which the soil imparts a kind of burnt flavour as if the old volcanoes of the region had left some little of their fire behind.

For a long while the conversation ranged over those wild and graceful Alban hills, which, fortunately for the pleasure of the eye, overlook the flat Roman Campagna. Pierre, who had made the customary carriage excursion from Frascati to Nemi, still felt its charm and spoke of it in glowing language. First came the lovely road from Frascati to Albano, ascending and descending hillsides planted with reeds, vines, and olive-trees, amongst which one obtained frequent glimpses of the Campagna's wavy immensity. On the right-hand the village of Rocca di Papa arose in amphitheatrical fashion, showing whitely on a knoll below Monte Cavo, which was crowned by lofty and ancient trees. And from this point of the road, on looking back towards Frascati, one saw high up, on the verge of a pine wood the ruins of Tusculum, large ruddy ruins, baked by centuries of sunshine, and whence the boundless panorama must have been superb. Next one passed through Marino, with its sloping streets, its large cathedral, and its black decaying palace belonging to the Colonnas. Then, beyond a wood of ilex-trees, the lake of Albano was skirted with scenery which has no parallel in the world. In front, beyond the clear mirror of motionless water, were the ruins of Alba Longa; on the left rose Monte Cavo with Rocca di Papa and Palazzuolo; whilst on the right Castel Gandolfo overlooked the lake as from the summit of a cliff. Down below in the extinct crater, as in the depths of a gigantic cup of verdure, the lake slept heavy and lifeless: a sheet of molten metal, which the sun on one side streaked with gold, whilst the other was black with shade. And the road then ascended all the way to Castel Gandolfo, which was perched on its rock, like a white bird betwixt the lake and the sea. Ever refreshed by breezes, even in the most burning hours of summer, the little place was once famous for its papal villa, where Pius IX loved to spend hours of indolence, and whither Leo XIII has never come. And next the road dipped down, and the ilex-trees appeared again, ilex-trees famous for their size, a double row of monsters with twisted limbs, two and three hundred years old. Then one at last reached Albano, a small town less modernised and less cleansed than Frascati, a patch of the old land which has retained some of its ancient wildness; and afterwards there was Ariccia with the Palazzo Chigi, and hills covered with forests and viaducts spanning ravines which overflowed with foliage; and there was yet Genzano, and yet Nemi, growing still wilder and more remote, lost in the midst of rocks and trees.

Ah! how ineffaceable was the recollection which Pierre had retained of Nemi, Nemi on the shore of its lake, Nemi so delicious and fascinating from afar, conjuring up all the ancient legends of fairy towns springing from amidst the greenery of mysterious waters, but so repulsively filthy when one at last reaches it, crumbling on all sides but yet dominated by the Orsini tower, as by the evil genius of the middle ages, which there seems to perpetuate the ferocious habits, the violent passions, the knife thrusts of the past! Thence came that Santobono whose brother had killed, and who himself, with his eyes of crime glittering like live embers, seemed to be consumed by a murderous flame. And the lake, that lake round like an extinguished moon fallen into the depths of a former crater, a deeper and less open cup than that of the lake of Albano, a cup rimmed with trees of wondrous vigour and density! Pines, elms, and willows descend to the very margin, with a green mass of tangled branches which weigh each other down. This formidable fecundity springs from the vapour which constantly arises from the water under the parching action of the sun, whose rays accumulate in this hollow till it becomes like a furnace. There is a warm, heavy dampness, the paths of the adjacent gardens grow green with moss, and in the morning dense mists often fill the large cup with white vapour, as with the steaming milk of some sorceress of malevolent craft. And Pierre well remembered how uncomfortable he had felt before that lake where ancient atrocities, a mysterious religion with abominable rites, seemed to slumber amidst the superb scenery. He had seen it at the approach of evening, looking, in the shade of its forest girdle, like a plate of dull metal, black and silver, motionless by reason of its weight. And that water, clear and yet so deep, that water deserted, without a bark upon its surface, that water august, lifeless, and sepulchral, had left him a feeling of inexpressible sadness, of mortal melancholy, the hopelessness of great solitary passion, earth and water alike swollen by the mute spasms of germs, troublous in their fecundity. Ah! those black and plunging banks, and that black mournful lake prone at the bottom![1]

Count Prada began to laugh when Pierre told him of these impressions. "Yes, yes," said he, "it's true, Nemi isn't always gay. In dull weather I have seen the lake looking like lead, and even the full sunshine scarcely animates it. For my part, I know I should die of *ennui* if I had to live face to face with that bare water. But it is admired by poets and romantic women, those who adore great tragedies of passion."

Then, as he and Pierre rose from the table to go and take coffee on the terrace of the restaurant, the conversation changed: "Do you mean to attend Prince Buongiovanni's reception this evening?" the Count inquired. "It will be a curious sight, especially for a foreigner, and I advise you not to miss it."

"Yes, I have an invitation," Pierre replied. "A friend of mine, Monsieur Narcisse Habert, an *attache* at our embassy, procured it for me, and I am going with him."

That evening, indeed, there was to be a *fete* at the Palazzo Buongiovanni on the Corso, one of the few galas that take place in Rome each winter. People said that this one would surpass all others in magnificence, for it was to be given in honour of the betrothal of little Princess Celia. The Prince, her father, after boxing her ears, it was rumoured, and narrowly escaping an attack of apoplexy as the result of a frightful fit of anger, had, all at once, yielded to her quiet, gentle stubbornness, and consented to her marriage with Lieutenant Attilio, the son of Minister Sacco. And all the drawing-rooms of Rome, those of the white world quite as much as those of the black, were thoroughly upset by the tidings.

---

[1] Some literary interest attaches to M. Zola's account of Nemi, whose praises have been sung by a hundred poets. It will be observed that he makes no mention of Egeria. The religion distinguished by abominable practices to which he alludes, may perhaps be the worship of the Egyptian Diana, who had a famous temple near Nemi, which was excavated by Lord Savile some ten years ago, when all the smaller objects discovered were presented to the town of Nottingham. At this temple, according to some classical writers, the chief priest was required to murder his predecessor, and there were other abominable usages.—Trans.

Count Prada made merry over the affair. "Ah! you'll see a fine sight!" he exclaimed. "Personally, I'm delighted with it all for the sake of my good cousin Attilio, who is really a very nice and worthy fellow. And nothing in the world would keep me from going to see my dear uncle Sacco make his entry into the ancient *salons* of the Buongiovanni. It will be something extraordinary and superb. He has at last become Minister of Agriculture, you know. My father, who always takes things so seriously, told me this morning that the affair so worried him he hadn't closed his eyes all night."

The Count paused, but almost immediately added: "I say, it is half-past two and you won't have a train before five o'clock. Do you know what you ought to do? Why, drive back to Rome with me in my carriage."

"No, no," rejoined Pierre, "I'm deeply obliged to you but I'm to dine with my friend Narcisse this evening, and I mustn't be late."

"But you won't be late—on the contrary! We shall start at three and reach Rome before five o'clock. There can't be a more pleasant promenade when the light falls; and, come, I promise you a splendid sunset."

He was so pressing that the young priest had to accept, quite subjugated by so much amiability and good humour. They spent another half-hour very pleasantly in chatting about Rome, Italy, and France. Then, for a moment, they went up into Frascati where the Count wished to say a few words to a contractor, and just as three o'clock was striking they started off, seated side by side on the soft cushions and gently rocked by the motion of the victoria as the two horses broke into a light trot. As Prada had predicted, that return to Rome across the bare Campagna under the vast limpid heavens at the close of such a mild autumn day proved most delightful. First of all, however, the victoria had to descend the slopes of Frascati between vineyards and olive-trees. The paved road snaked, and was but little frequented; they merely saw a few peasants in old felt hats, a white mule, and a cart drawn by a donkey, for it is only upon Sundays that the *osterie* or wine-shops are filled and that artisans in easy circumstances come to eat a dish of kid at the surrounding *bastides*. However, at one turn of the road they passed a monumental fountain. Then a flock of sheep momentarily barred the way before defiling past. And beyond the gentle undulations of the ruddy Campagna Rome appeared amidst the violet vapours of evening, sinking by degrees as the carriage itself descended to a lower and lower level. There came a moment when the city was a mere thin grey streak, speckled whitely here and there by a few sunlit house-fronts. And then it seemed to plunge below the ground—to be submerged by the swell of the far-spreading fields.

The victoria was now rolling over the plain, leaving the Alban hills behind, whilst before it and on either hand came the expanse of meadows and stubbles. And then it was that the Count, after leaning forward, exclaimed: "Just look ahead, yonder, there's our man of this morning, Santobono in person—what a strapping fellow he is, and how fast he walks! My horses can scarcely overtake him."

Pierre in his turn leant forward and likewise perceived the priest of St. Mary in the Fields, looking tall and knotty, fashioned as it were with a bill-hook. Robed in a long black cassock, he showed like a vigorous splotch of ink amidst the bright sunshine streaming around him; and he was walking on at such a fast, stern, regular pace that he suggested Destiny on the march. Something, which could not be well distinguished, was hanging from his right arm.

XI.

When the carriage had at last overtaken him Prada told the coachman to slacken speed, and then entered into conversation.

"Good-day, Abbe; you are well, I hope?" he asked.

"Very well, Signor Conte, I thank you."

"And where are you going so bravely?"

"Signor Conte, I am going to Rome."

"What! to Rome, at this late hour?"

"Oh! I shall be there nearly as soon as yourself. The distance doesn't frighten me, and money's quickly earned by walking."

Scarcely turning his head to reply, stepping out beside the wheels, Santobono did not miss a stride. And Prada, diverted by the meeting, whispered to Pierre: "Wait a bit, he'll amuse us." Then he added aloud: "Since you are going to Rome, Abbe, you had better get in here; there's room for you."

Santobono required no pressing, but at once accepted the offer. "Willingly; a thousand thanks," he said. "It's still better to save one's shoe leather."

Then he got in and installed himself on the bracket-seat, declining with abrupt humility the place which Pierre politely offered him beside the Count. The young priest and the latter now saw that the object he was carrying was a little basket of fresh figs, nicely arranged and covered with leaves.

The horses set off again at a faster trot, and the carriage rolled on and on over the superb, flat plain. "So you are going to Rome?" the Count resumed in order to make Santobono talk.

"Yes," the other replied, "I am taking his Eminence Cardinal Boccanera these few figs, the last of the season: a little present which I had promised him." He had placed the basket on his knees and was holding it between his big knotty hands as if it were something rare and fragile.

"Ah! some of the famous figs of your garden," said Prada. "It's quite true, they are like honey. But why don't you rid yourself of them. You surely don't mean to keep them on your knees all the way to Rome. Give them to me, I'll put them in the hood."

However, Santobono became quite agitated, and vigorously declined the offer. "No, no, a thousand thanks! They don't embarrass me in the least; they are very well here; and in this way I shall be sure that no accident will befall them."

His passion for the fruit he grew quite amused Prada, who nudged Pierre, and then inquired: "Is the Cardinal fond of your figs?"

"Oh! his Eminence condescends to adore them. In former years, when he spent the summer at the villa, he would never touch the figs from other trees. And so, you see, knowing his tastes, it costs me very little to gratify him."

Whilst making this reply Santobono had shot such a keen glance in the direction of Pierre that the Count felt it necessary to introduce them to one another. This he did saying: "As it happens, Monsieur l'Abbe Froment is stopping at the Palazzo Boccanera; he has been there for three months or so."

"Yes, I'm aware of it," Santobono quietly replied; "I found Monsieur l'Abbe with his Eminence one day when I took some figs to the Palazzo. Those were less ripe, but these are perfect." So speaking he gave the little basket a complacent glance, and seemed to press it yet more closely between his huge and hairy fingers.

Then came a spell of silence, whilst on either hand the Campagna spread out as far as the eye could reach. All houses had long since disappeared; there was not a wall, not a tree, nothing but the undulating expanse whose sparse, short herbage was, with the approach of winter, beginning to turn green once more. A tower, a half-fallen ruin which came into sight on the left, rising in solitude into the limpid sky above the flat, boundless line of the horizon, suddenly assumed extraordinary importance. Then, on the right, the distant silhouettes of cattle and horses were seen in a large enclosure with wooden rails. Urged on by the goad, oxen, still yoked, were slowly coming back from ploughing; whilst a farmer, cantering beside the ploughed land on a little sorrel nag, gave a final look round for the night. Now and again the road became peopled. A *biroccino*, an extremely light vehicle with two huge wheels and a small seat perched upon the springs, whisked by like a gust of wind. From time to time also the victoria passed a *carrotino*, one of the low carts in which peasants, sheltered by a kind of bright-hued tent, bring the wine, vegetables, and fruit of the castle-lands to Rome. The shrill tinkling of horses' bells was heard afar off as the animals followed the well-known road of their own accord, their peasant drivers usually being sound asleep. Women with bare, black hair, scarlet neckerchiefs, and skirts caught up, were seen going home in groups of three and four. And then the road again emptied, and the solitude became more and more complete, without a wayfarer or an animal appearing for miles and miles, whilst yonder, at the far end of the lifeless sea, so grandiose and mournful in its monotony, the sun continued to descend from the infinite vault of heaven.

"And the Pope, Abbe, is he dead?" Prada suddenly inquired.

Santobono did not even start. "I trust," he replied in all simplicity, "that his Holiness still has many long years to live for the triumph of the Church."

"So you had good news this morning when you called on your bishop, Cardinal Sanguinetti?"

This time the priest was unable to restrain a slight start. Had he been seen, then? In his haste he had failed to notice the two men following the road behind him. However, he at once regained self-possession, and replied: "Oh! one can never tell exactly whether news is good or bad. It seems that his Holiness passed a somewhat painful night, but I devoutly hope that the next will be a better one." Then he seemed to meditate for a moment, and added: "Moreover, if God should have deemed it time to call his Holiness to Himself, He would not leave His flock without a shepherd. He would have already chosen and designated the Sovereign Pontiff of to-morrow."

This superb answer increased Prada's gaiety. "You are really extraordinary, Abbe," he said. "So you think that popes are solely created by the grace of the Divinity! The pope of to-morrow is chosen up in heaven, eh, and simply waits? Well, I fancied that men had something to do with the matter. But perhaps you already know which cardinal it is that the divine favour has thus elected in advance?"

Then, like the unbeliever he was, he went on with his facile jests, which left the priest unruffled. In fact, the latter also ended by laughing when the Count, after alluding to the gambling passion which at each fresh Conclave sets wellnigh the whole population of Rome betting for or against this or that candidate, told him that he might easily make his fortune if he were in the divine secret. Next the talk turned on the three white cassocks of different sizes which are always kept in readiness in a cupboard at the Vatican. Which of them would be required on this occasion?—the short one, the long one, or the one of medium size? Each time that the reigning pope falls somewhat seriously ill there is in this wise an extraordinary outburst of emotion, a keen awakening of all ambitions and intrigues, to such a point that not merely in the black world, but throughout the city, people have no other subject of curiosity, conversation, and occupation than that of discussing the relative claims of the cardinals and predicting which of them will be elected.

"Come, come," Prada resumed, "since you know the truth, I'm determined that you shall tell me. Will it be Cardinal Moretta?"

Santobono, in spite of his evident desire to remain dignified and disinterested, like a good, pious priest, was gradually growing impassioned, yielding to the hidden fire which consumed him. And this interrogatory finished him off; he could no longer restrain himself, but replied: "Moretta! What an idea! Why, he is sold to all Europe!"

"Well, will it be Cardinal Bartolini?"

"Oh! you can't think that. Bartolini has used himself up in striving for everything and getting nothing."

"Will it be Cardinal Dozio, then?"

"Dozio, Dozio! Why, if Dozio were to win one might altogether despair of our Holy Church, for no man can have a baser mind than he!"

Prada raised his hands, as if he had exhausted the serious candidates. In order to increase the priest's exasperation he maliciously refrained from naming Cardinal Sanguinetti, who was certainly Santobono's nominee. All at once, however, he pretended to make a good guess, and gaily exclaimed: "Ah! I have it; I know your man—Cardinal Boccanera!"

The blow struck Santobono full in the heart, wounding him both in his rancour and his patriotic faith. His terrible mouth was already opening, and he was about to shout "No! no!" with all his strength, but he managed to restrain the cry, compelled as he was to silence by the present on his knees—that little basket of figs which he pressed so convulsively with both hands; and the effort which he was obliged to make left him quivering to such a point that he had to wait some time before he could reply in a calm voice: "His most reverend Eminence Cardinal Boccanera is a saintly man, well worthy of the throne, and my only fear is that, with his hatred of new Italy, he might bring us warfare."

Prada, however, desired to enlarge the wound. "At all events," said he, "you accept him and love him too much not to rejoice over his chances of success. And I really think that we have arrived at the truth, for everybody is convinced that the Conclave's choice cannot fall elsewhere. Come, come; Boccanera is a very tall man, so it's the long white cassock which will be required."

"The long cassock, the long cassock," growled Santobono, despite himself; "that's all very well, but—"

Then he stopped short, and, again overcoming his passion, left his sentence unfinished. Pierre, listening in silence, marvelled at the man's self-restraint, for he remembered the conversation which he had overheard at Cardinal Sanguinetti's. Those figs were evidently a mere pretext for gaining admission to the Boccanera mansion, where some friend—Abbe Paparelli, no doubt—could alone supply certain positive information which was needed. But how great was the command which the hot-blooded priest exercised over himself amidst the riotous impulses of his soul!

On either side of the road the Campagna still and ever spread its expanse of verdure, and Prada, who had become grave and dreamy, gazed before him without seeing anything. At last, however, he gave expression to his thoughts. "You know, Abbe, what will be said if the Pope should die this time. That sudden illness, those colics, those refusals to make any information public, mean nothing good—Yes, yes, poison, just as for the others!"

Pierre gave a start of stupefaction. The Pope poisoned! "What! Poison? Again?" he exclaimed as he gazed at his companions with dilated eyes. Poison at the end of the nineteenth century, as in the days of the Borgias, as on the stage in a romanticist melodrama! To him the idea appeared both monstrous and ridiculous.

Santobono, whose features had become motionless and impenetrable, made no reply. But Prada nodded, and the conversation was henceforth confined to him and the young priest. "Why, yes, poison," he replied. "The fear of it has remained very great in Rome. Whenever a death seems inexplicable, either by reason of its suddenness or the tragic circumstances which attend it, the unanimous thought is poison. And remark this: in no city, I believe, are sudden deaths so frequent. The causes I don't exactly know, but some doctors put everything down to the fevers. Among the people, however, the one thought is poison, poison with all its legends, poison which kills like lightning and leaves no trace, the famous recipe bequeathed from age to age, through the emperors and the popes, down to these present times of middle-class democracy."

As he spoke he ended by smiling, for he was inclined to be somewhat sceptical on the point, despite the covert terror with which he was inspired by racial and educational causes. However, he quoted instances. The Roman matrons had rid themselves of their husbands and lovers by employing the venom of red toads. Locusta, in a more practical spirit, sought poison in plants, one of which, probably aconite, she was wont to boil. Then, long afterwards, came the age of the Borgias, and subsequently, at Naples, La Toffana sold a famous water, doubtless some preparation of arsenic, in phials decorated with a representation of St. Nicholas of Bari. There were also extraordinary stories of pins, a prick from which killed one like lightning, of cups of wine poisoned by the infusion of rose petals, of woodcocks cut in half with prepared knives, which poisoned but one-half of the bird, so that he who partook of that half was killed. "I myself, in my younger days," continued Prada, "had a friend whose bride fell dead in church during the marriage service through simply inhaling a bouquet of flowers. And so isn't it possible that the famous recipe may really have been handed down, and have remained known to a few adepts?"

"But chemistry has made too much progress," Pierre replied. "If mysterious poisons were believed in by the ancients and remained undetected in their time it was because there were no means of analysis. But the drug of the Borgias would now lead the simpleton who might employ it straight to the Assizes. Such stories are mere nonsense, and at the present day people scarcely tolerate them in newspaper serials and shockers."

"Perhaps so," resumed the Count with his uneasy smile. "You are right, no doubt—only go and tell that to your host, for instance, Cardinal Boccanera, who last summer held in his arms an old and deeply-loved friend, Monsignor Gallo, who died after a seizure of a couple of hours."

"But apoplexy may kill one in two hours, and aneurism only takes two minutes."

"True, but ask the Cardinal what he thought of his friend's prolonged shudders, the leaden hue which overcame his face, the sinking of his eyes, and the expression of terror which made him quite unrecognisable. The Cardinal is convinced that Monsignor Gallo was poisoned, because he was his dearest confidant, the counsellor to whom he always listened, and whose wise advice was a guarantee of success."

Pierre's bewilderment was increasing, and, irritated by the impassibility of Santobono, he addressed him direct. "It's idiotic, it's awful! Does your reverence also believe in these frightful stories?"

But the priest of Frascati gave no sign. His thick, passionate lips remained closed while his black glowing eyes never ceased to gaze at Prada. The latter, moreover, was quoting other instances. There was the case of Monsignor Nazzarelli, who had been found in bed, shrunken and calcined like carbon. And there was that of Monsignor Brando, struck down in his sacerdotal vestments at St. Peter's itself, in the very sacristy, during vespers!

"Ah! *Mon Dieu*!" sighed Pierre, "you will tell me so much that I myself shall end by trembling, and sha'n't dare to eat anything but boiled eggs as long as I stay in this terrible Rome of yours."

For a moment this whimsical reply enlivened both the Count and Pierre. But it was quite true that their conversation showed Rome under a terrible aspect, for it conjured up the Eternal City of Crime, the city of poison and the knife, where for more than two thousand years, ever since the raising of the first bit of wall, the lust of power, the frantic hunger for possession and enjoyment, had armed men's hands, ensanguined the pavements, and cast victims into the river and the ground. Assassinations and poisonings under the emperors, poisonings and assassinations under the popes, ever did the same torrent of abominations strew that tragic soil with death amidst the sovereign glory of the sun.

"All the same," said the Count, "those who take precautions are perhaps not ill advised. It is said that more than one cardinal shudders and mistrusts people. One whom I know will never eat anything that has not been bought and prepared by his own cook. And as for the Pope, if he is anxious—"

Pierre again raised a cry of stupefaction. "What, the Pope himself! The Pope afraid of being poisoned!"

"Well, my dear Abbe, people commonly assert it. There are certainly days when he considers himself more menaced than anybody else. And are you not aware of the old Roman view that a pope ought never to live till too great an age, and that when he is so obstinate as not to die at the right time he ought to be assisted? As soon as a pope begins to fall into second childhood, and by reason of his senility becomes a source of embarrassment, and possibly even danger, to the Church, his right place is heaven. Moreover, matters are managed in a discreet manner; a slight cold becomes a decent pretext to prevent him from tarrying any longer on the throne of St. Peter."

Prada then gave some curious details. One prelate, it was said, wishing to dispel his Holiness's fears, had devised an elaborate precautionary system which, among other things, was to comprise a little padlocked vehicle, in which the food destined for the frugal pontifical table was to be securely placed before leaving the kitchen, so that it might not be tampered with on its way to the Pope's apartments. However, this project had not yet been carried into effect.

"After all," the Count concluded with a laugh, "every pope has to die some day, especially when his death is needful for the welfare of the Church. Isn't that so, Abbe?"

Santobono, whom he addressed, had a moment previously lowered his eyes as if to contemplate the little basket of figs which he held on his lap with as much care as if it had been the Blessed Sacrament. On being questioned in such a direct, sharp fashion he could not do otherwise than look up. However, he did not depart from his prolonged silence, but limited his answer to a slow nod.

"And it is God alone, and not poison, who causes one to die. Is that not so, Abbe?" repeated Prada. "It is said that those were the last words of poor Monsignor Gallo before he expired in the arms of his friend Cardinal Boccanera."

For the second time Santobono nodded without speaking. And then silence fell, all three sinking into a dreamy mood.

Meantime, without a pause, the carriage rolled on across the immensity of the Campagna. The road, straight as an arrow, seemed to extend into the infinite. As the sun descended towards the horizon the play of light and shade became more marked on the broad undulations of the ground which stretched away, alternately of a pinky green and a violet grey, till they reached the distant fringe of the sky. At the roadside on either hand there were still and ever tall withered thistles and giant fennel with yellow umbels. Then, after a time, came a team of four oxen, that had been kept ploughing until late, and stood forth black and huge in the pale atmosphere and mournful solitude. Farther on some flocks of sheep, whence the breeze wafted a tallowy odour, set patches of brown amidst the herbage, which once more was becoming verdant; whilst at intervals a dog was heard to bark, his voice the only distinct sound amidst the low quivering of that silent desert where the sovereign peacefulness of death seemed to reign. But all at once a light melody arose and some larks flew up, one of them soaring into the limpid golden heavens. And ahead, at the far extremity of the pure sky, Rome, with her towers and domes, grew larger and larger, like a city of white marble springing from a mirage amidst the greenery of some enchanted garden.

"Matteo!" Prada called to his coachman, "pull up at the Osteria Romana." And to his companions he added: "Pray excuse me, but I want to see if I can get some new-laid eggs for my father. He is so fond of them."

A few minutes afterwards the carriage stopped. At the very edge of the road stood a primitive sort of inn, bearing the proud and sonorous name of "Antica Osteria Romana." It had now become a mere house of call for carters and chance sportsmen, who ventured to drink a flagon of white wine whilst eating an omelet and a slice of ham. Occasionally, on Sundays, some of the humble classes would walk over from Rome and make merry there; but the week days often went by without a soul entering the place, such was its isolation amidst the bare Campagna.

The Count was already springing from the carriage. "I shall only be a minute," said he as he turned away.

The *osteria* was a long, low pile with a ground floor and one upper storey, the last being reached by an outdoor stairway built of large blocks of stone which had been scorched by the hot suns. The entire place, indeed, was corroded, tinged with the hue of old gold. On the ground floor one found a common room, a cart-house, and a stable with adjoining sheds. At one side, near a cluster of parasol pines—the only trees that could grow in that ungrateful soil—there was an arbour of reeds where five or six rough wooden tables were set out. And, as a background to this sorry, mournful nook of life, there arose a fragment of an ancient aqueduct whose arches, half fallen and opening on to space, alone interrupted the flat line of the horizon.

All at once, however, the Count retraced his steps, and, addressing Santobono, exclaimed: "I say, Abbe, you'll surely accept a glass of white wine. I know that you are a bit of a vine grower, and they have a little white wine here which you ought to make acquaintance with."

Santobono again required no pressing, but quietly alighted. "Oh! I know it," said he; "it's a wine from Marino; it's grown in a lighter soil than ours at Frascati."

Then, as he would not relax his hold on his basket of figs, but even now carried it along with him, the Count lost patience. "Come, you don't want that basket," said he; "leave it in the carriage."

The priest gave no reply, but walked ahead, whilst Pierre also made up his mind to descend from the carriage in order to see what a suburban *osteria* was like. Prada was known at this place, and an old woman, tall, withered, but looking quite queenly in her wretched garments, had at once presented herself. On the last occasion when the Count had called she had managed to find half a dozen eggs. This time she said she would go to see, but could promise nothing, for the hens laid here and there all over the place, and she could never tell what eggs there might be.

"All right!" Prada answered, "go and look; and meantime we will have a *caraffa* of white wine."

The three men entered the common room, which was already quite dark. Although the hot weather was now over, one heard the buzzing of innumerable flies immediately one reached the threshold, and a pungent odour of acidulous wine and rancid oil caught one at the throat. As soon as their eyes became accustomed to the dimness they were able to distinguish the spacious, blackened, malodorous chamber, whose only furniture consisted of some roughly made tables and benches. It seemed to be quite empty, so complete was the silence, apart from the buzz of the flies. However, two men were seated there, two wayfarers who remained mute and motionless before their untouched, brimming glasses. Moreover, on a low chair near the door, in the little light which penetrated from without, a thin, sallow girl, the daughter of the house, sat idle, trembling with fever, her hands close pressed between her knees.

Realising that Pierre felt uncomfortable there, the Count proposed that they should drink their wine outside. "We shall be better out of doors," said he, "it's so very in mild this evening."

Accordingly, whilst the mother looked for the eggs, and the father mended a wheel in an adjacent shed, the daughter was obliged to get up shivering to carry the flagon of wine and the three glasses to the arbour, where she placed them on one of the tables. And, having pocketed the price of the wine—threepence—in silence, she went back to her seat with a sullen look, as if annoyed at having been compelled to make such a long journey. Meanwhile the three men had sat down, and Prada gaily filled each of the glasses, although Pierre declared that he was quite unable to drink wine between his meals. "Pooh, pooh," said the Count, "you can always clink glasses with us. And now, Abbe, isn't this little wine droll? Come, here's to the Pope's better health, since he's unwell!"

Santobono at one gulp emptied his glass and clacked his tongue. With gentle, paternal care he had deposited his basket on the ground beside him: and, taking off his hat, he drew a long breath. The evening was really delightful. A superb sky of a soft golden hue stretched over that endless sea of the Campagna which was soon to fall asleep with sovereign quiescence. And the light breeze which went by amidst the deep silence brought with it an exquisite odour of wild herbs and flowers.

"How pleasant it is!" muttered Pierre, affected by the surrounding charm. "And what a desert for eternal rest, forgetfulness of all the world!"

Prada, who had emptied the flagon by filling Santobono's glass a second time, made no reply; he was silently amusing himself with an occurrence which at first he was the only one to observe. However, with a merry expression of complicity, he gave the young priest a wink, and then they both watched the dramatic incidents of the affair. Some scraggy fowls were wandering round them searching the yellow turf for grasshoppers; and one of these birds, a little shiny black hen with an impudent manner, had caught sight of the basket of figs and was boldly approaching it. When she got near, however, she took fright, and retreated somewhat, with neck stiffened and head turned, so as to cast suspicious glances at the basket with her round sparkling eye. But at last covetousness gained the victory, for she could see one of the figs between the leaves, and so she slowly advanced, lifting her feet very high at each step; and, all at once, stretching out her neck, she gave the fig a formidable peck, which ripped it open and made the juice exude.

Prada, who felt as happy as a child, was then able to give vent to the laughter which he had scarcely been able to restrain: "Look out, Abbe," he called, "mind your figs!"

At that very moment Santobono was finishing his second glass of wine with his head thrown back and his eyes blissfully raised to heaven. He gave a start, looked round, and on seeing the hen at once understood the position. And then came a terrible outburst of anger, with sweeping gestures and terrible invectives. But the hen, who was again pecking, would not be denied; she dug her beak into the fig and carried it off, flapping her wings, so quick and so comical that Prada, and Pierre as well, laughed till tears came into their eyes, their merriment increasing at sight of the impotent fury of Santobono, who, for a moment, pursued the thief, threatening her with his fist.

"Ah!" said the Count, "that's what comes of not leaving the basket in the carriage. If I hadn't warned you the hen would have eaten all the figs."

The priest did not reply, but, growling out vague imprecations, placed the basket on the table, where he raised the leaves and artistically rearranged the fruit so as to fill up the void. Then, the harm having been repaired as far as was possible, he at last calmed down.

It was now time for them to resume their journey, for the sun was sinking towards the horizon, and night would soon fall. Thus the Count ended by getting impatient. "Well, and those eggs?" he called.

Then, as the woman did not return, he went to seek her. He entered the stable, and afterwards the cart-house, but she was neither here nor there. Next he went towards the rear of the *osteria* in order to look in the sheds. But all at once an unexpected spectacle made him stop short. The little black hen was lying on the ground, dead, killed as by lightning. She showed no sign of hurt; there was nothing but a little streamlet of violet blood still trickling from her beak. Prada was at first merely astonished. He stooped and touched the hen. She was still warm and soft like a rag. Doubtless some apoplectic stroke had killed her. But immediately afterwards he became fearfully pale; the truth appeared to him, and turned him as cold as ice. In a moment he conjured up everything: Leo XIII attacked by illness, Santobono hurrying to Cardinal Sanguinetti for tidings, and then starting for Rome to present a basket of figs to Cardinal Boccanera. And Prada also remembered the conversation in the carriage: the possibility of the Pope's demise, the candidates for the tiara, the legendary stories of poison which still fostered terror in and around the Vatican; and he once more saw the priest, with his little basket on his knees, lavishing paternal attention on it, and he saw the little black hen pecking at the fruit and fleeing with a fig on her beak. And now that little black hen lay there, suddenly struck down, dead!

His conviction was immediate and absolute. But he did not have time to decide what course he should take, for a voice behind him exclaimed: "Why, it's the little hen; what's the matter with her?"

The voice was that of Pierre, who, letting Santobono climb into the carriage alone, had in his turn come round to the rear of the house in order to obtain a better view of the ruined aqueduct among the parasol pines.

Prada, who shuddered as if he himself were the culprit, answered him with a lie, a lie which he did not premeditate, but to which he was impelled by a sort of instinct. "But she's dead," he said.... "Just fancy, there was a fight. At the moment when I got here that other hen, which you see yonder, sprang upon this one to get the fig, which she was still holding, and with a thrust of the beak split her head open.... The blood's flowing, as you can see yourself."

Why did he say these things? He himself was astonished at them whilst he went on inventing them. Was it then that he wished to remain master of the situation, keep the abominable secret entirely to himself, in order that he might afterwards act in accordance with his own desires? Certainly his feelings partook of shame and embarrassment in presence of that foreigner, whilst his personal inclination for violence set some admiration amidst the revolt of his conscience, and a covert desire arose within him to examine the matter from the standpoint of his interests before he came to a decision. But, on the other hand, he claimed to be a man of integrity, and would assuredly not allow people to be poisoned.

Pierre, who was compassionately inclined towards all creation, looked at the hen with the emotion which he always felt at the sudden severance of life. However, he at once accepted Prada's story. "Ah! those fowls!" said he. "They treat one another with an idiotic ferocity which even men can scarcely equal. I kept fowls at home at one time, and one of the hens no sooner hurt her leg than all the others, on seeing the blood oozing, would flock round and peck at the limb till they stripped it to the bone."

Prada, however, did not listen, but at once went off; and it so happened that the woman was, on her side, looking for him in order to hand him four eggs which, after a deal of searching, she had discovered in odd corners about the house. The Count made haste to pay for them, and called to Pierre, who was lingering behind: "We must look sharp! We sha'n't reach Rome now until it is quite dark."

They found Santobono quietly waiting in the carriage, where he had again installed himself on the bracket with his spine resting against the box-seat and his long legs drawn back under him, and he again had the little basket of figs on his knees, and clasped it with his big knotty hands as though it were something fragile and rare which the slightest jolting might damage. His cassock showed like a huge blot, and in his coarse ashen face, that of a peasant yet near to the wild soil and but slightly polished by a few years of theological studies, his eyes alone seemed to live, glowing with the dark flame of a devouring passion. On seeing him seated there in such composure Prada could not restrain a slight shudder. Then, as soon as the victoria was again rolling along the road, he exclaimed: "Well, Abbe, that glass of wine will guarantee us against the malaria. The Pope would soon be cured if he could imitate our example."

Santobono's only reply was a growl. He was in no mood for conversation, but wrapped himself in perfect silence, as in the night which was slowly falling. And Prada in his turn ceased to speak, and, with his eyes still fixed upon the other, reflected on the course that he should follow.

The road turned, and then the carriage rolled on and on over another interminable straight highway with white paving, whose brilliancy made the road look like a ribbon of snow stretching across the Campagna, where delicate shadows were slowly falling. Gloom gathered in the hollows of the broad undulations whence a tide of violet hue seemed to spread over the short herbage until all mingled and the expanse became an indistinct swell of neutral hue from one to the other horizon. And the solitude was now yet more complete; a last indolent cart had gone by and a last tinkling of horses' bells had subsided in the distance. There was no longer a passer-by, no longer a beast of the fields to be seen, colour and sound died away, all forms of life sank into slumber, into the serene stillness of nihility. Some fragments of an aqueduct were still to be seen at intervals on the right hand, where they looked like portions of gigantic millepeds severed by the scythe of time; next, on the left, came another tower, whose dark and ruined pile barred the sky as with a huge black stake; and then the remains of another aqueduct spanned the road, assuming yet greater dimensions against the sunset glow. Ah! that unique hour, the hour of twilight in the Campagna, when all is blotted out and simplified, the hour of bare immensity, of the infinite in its simplest expression! There is nothing, nothing all around you, but the flat line of the horizon with the one splotch of an isolated tower, and yet that nothing is instinct with sovereign majesty.

However, on the left, towards the sea, the sun was setting, descending in the limpid sky like a globe of fire of blinding redness. It slowly plunged beneath the horizon, and the only sign of cloud was some fiery vapour, as if indeed the distant sea had seethed at contact with that royal and flaming visit. And directly the sun had disappeared the heavens above it purpled and became a lake of blood, whilst the Campagna turned to grey. At the far end of the fading plain there remained only that purple lake whose brasier slowly died out behind the black arches of the aqueduct, while in the opposite direction the scattered arches remained bright and rosy against a pewter-like sky. Then the fiery vapour was dissipated, and the sunset ended by fading away. One by one the stars came out in the pacified vault, now of an ashen blue, while the lights of Rome, still far away on the verge of the horizon, scintillated like the lamps of lighthouses.

And Prada, amidst the dreamy silence of his companions and the infinite melancholy of the evening and the inexpressible distress which even he experienced, continued to ask himself what course he should adopt. Again and again he mentally repeated that he could not allow people to be poisoned. The figs were certainly intended for Cardinal Boccanera, and on the whole it mattered little to him whether there were a cardinal the more or the fewer in the world. Moreover, it had always seemed to him best to let Destiny follow its course; and, infidel that he was, he saw no harm in one priest devouring another. Again, it might be dangerous for him to intervene in that abominable affair, to mix himself up in the base, fathomless intrigues of the black world. But on the other hand the Cardinal was not the only person who lived in the Boccanera mansion, and might not the figs go to others, might they not be eaten by people to whom no harm was intended? This idea of a treacherous chance haunted him, and in spite of every effort the figures of Benedetta and Dario rose up before him, returned and imposed themselves on him though he again and again sought to banish them from his mind. What if Benedetta, what if Dario should partake of that fruit? For Benedetta he felt no fear, for he knew that she and her aunt ate their meals by themselves, and that their cuisine and the Cardinal's had nothing in common. But Dario sat at his uncle's table every day, and for a moment Prada, pictured the young Prince suddenly seized with a spasm, then falling, like poor Monsignor Gallo, into the Cardinal's arms with livid face and receding eyes, and dying within two hours.

But no, no! That would be frightful, he could not suffer such an abomination. And thereupon he made up his mind. He would wait till the night had completely gathered round and would then simply take the basket from Santobono's lap and fling it into some dark hollow without saying a word. The priest would understand him. The other one, the young Frenchman, would perhaps not even notice the incident. Besides, that mattered little, for he would not even attempt to explain his action. And he felt quite calm again when the idea occurred to him to throw the basket away while the carriage passed through the Porta Furba, a couple of miles or so before reaching Rome. That would suit him exactly; in the darkness of the gateway nothing whatever would be seen.

"We stopped too long at that *osteria*," he suddenly exclaimed aloud, turning towards Pierre. "We sha'n't reach Rome much before six o'clock. Still you will have time to dress and join your friend." And then without awaiting the young man's reply he said to Santobono: "Your figs will arrive very late, Abbe."

"Oh!" answered the priest, "his Eminence receives until eight o'clock. And, besides, the figs are not for this evening. People don't eat figs in the evening. They will be for to-morrow morning." And thereupon he again relapsed into silence.

"For to-morrow morning—yes, yes, no doubt," repeated Prada. "And the Cardinal will be able to thoroughly regale himself if nobody helps him to eat the fruit."

Thereupon Pierre, without pausing to reflect, exclaimed: "He will no doubt eat it by himself, for his nephew, Prince Dario, must have started to-day for Naples on a little convalescence trip to rid himself of the effects of the accident which laid him up during the last month." Then, having got so far, the young priest remembered to whom he was speaking, and abruptly stopped short.

The Count noticed his embarrassment. "Oh! speak on, my dear Monsieur Froment," said he, "you don't offend me. It's an old affair now. So that young man has left, you say?"

"Yes, unless he has postponed his departure. However, I don't expect to find him at the palazzo when I get there."

For a moment the only sound was that of the continuous rumble of the wheels. Prada again felt worried, a prey to the discomfort of uncertainty. Why should he mix himself up in the affair if Dario were really absent? All the ideas which came to him tired his brain, and he ended by thinking aloud: "If he has gone away it must be for propriety's sake, so as to avoid attending the Buongiovanni reception, for the Congregation of the Council met this morning to give its decision in the suit which the Countess has brought against me. Yes, I shall know by and by whether our marriage is to be dissolved."

It was in a somewhat hoarse voice that he spoke these words, and one could realise that the old wound was again bleeding within him. Although Lisbeth had borne him a son, the charge levelled against him in his wife's petition for divorce still filled him with blind fury each time that he thought of it. And all at once he shuddered violently, as if an icy blast had darted through his frame. Then, turning the conversation, he added: "It's not at all warm this evening. This is the dangerous hour of the Roman climate, the twilight hour when it's easy to catch a terrible fever if one isn't prudent. Here, pull the rug over your legs, wrap it round you as carefully as you can."

Then, as they drew near the Porta Furba, silence again fell, more profound, like the slumber which was invincibly spreading over the Campagna, now steeped in night. And at last, in the bright starlight, appeared the gate, an arch of the Acqua Felice, under which the road passed. From a distance, this fragment seemed to bar the way with its mass of ancient half-fallen walls. But afterwards the gigantic arch where all was black opened like a gaping porch. And the carriage passed under it in darkness whilst the wheels rumbled with increased sonority.

When the victoria emerged on the other side, Santobono still had the little basket of figs upon his knees and Prada looked at it, quite overcome, asking himself what sudden paralysis of the hands had prevented him from seizing it and throwing it into the darkness. Such had still been his intention but a few seconds before they passed under the arch. He had even given the basket a final glance in order that he might the better realise what movements he should make. What had taken place within him then? At present he was yielding to increasing irresolution, henceforth incapable of decisive action, feeling a need of delay in order that he might, before everything else, fully satisfy himself as to what was likely to happen. And as Dario had doubtless gone away and the figs would certainly not be eaten until the following morning, what reason was there for him to hurry? He would know that evening if the Congregation of the Council had annulled his marriage, he would know how far the so-called "Justice of God" was venal and mendacious! Certainly he would suffer nobody to be poisoned, not even Cardinal Boccanera, though the latter's life was of little account to him personally. But had not that little basket, ever since leaving Frascati, been like Destiny on the march? And was it not enjoyment, the enjoyment of omnipotence, to be able to say to himself that he was the master who could stay that basket's course, or allow it to go onward and accomplish its deadly purpose? Moreover, he yielded to the dimmest of mental struggles, ceasing to reason, unable to raise his hand, and yet convinced that he would drop a warning note into the letter-box at the palazzo before he went to bed, though at the same time he felt happy in the thought that if his interest directed otherwise he would not do so.

And the remainder of the journey was accomplished in silent weariness, amidst the shiver of evening which seemed to have chilled all three men. In vain did the Count endeavour to escape from the battle of his thoughts, by reverting to the Buongiovanni reception, and giving particulars of the splendours which would be witnessed at it: his words fell sparsely in an embarrassed and absent-minded way. Then he sought to inspirit Pierre by speaking to him of Cardinal Sanguinetti's amiable manner and fair words, but although the young priest was returning home well pleased with his journey, in the idea that with a little help he might yet triumph, he scarcely answered the Count, so wrapt he was in his reverie. And Santobono, on his side, neither spoke nor moved. Black like the night itself, he seemed to have vanished. However, the lights of Rome were increasing in number, and houses again appeared on either hand, at first at long intervals, and then in close succession. They were suburban houses, and there were yet more fields of reeds, quickset hedges, olive-trees overtopping long walls, and big gateways with vase-surmounted pillars; but at last came the city with its rows of small grey houses, its petty shops and its dingy taverns, whence at times came shouts and rumours of battle.

Prada insisted on setting his companions down in the Via Giulia, at fifty paces from the palazzo. "It doesn't inconvenience me at all," said he to Pierre. "Besides, with the little time you have before you, it would never do for you to go on foot."

The Via Giulia was already steeped in slumber, and wore a melancholy aspect of abandonment in the dreary light of the gas lamps standing on either hand. And as soon as Santobono had alighted from the carriage, he took himself off without waiting for Pierre, who, moreover, always went in by the little door in the side lane.

"Good-bye, Abbe," exclaimed Prada.

"Good-bye, Count, a thousand thanks," was Santobono's response.

Then the two others stood watching him as he went towards the Boccanera mansion, whose old, monumental entrance, full of gloom, was still wide open. For a moment they saw his tall, rugged figure erect against that gloom. Then in he plunged, he and his little basket, bearing Destiny.

XII.

IT was ten o'clock when Pierre and Narcisse, after dining at the Caffe di Roma, where they had long lingered chatting, at last walked down the Corso towards the Palazzo Buongiovanni. They had the greatest difficulty to reach its entrance, for carriages were coming up in serried files, and the inquisitive crowd of on-lookers, who pressed even into the roadway, in spite of the injunctions of the police, was growing so compact that even the horses could no longer approach. The ten lofty windows on the first floor of the long monumental facade shone with an intense white radiance, the radiance of electric lamps, which illumined the street like sunshine, spreading over the equipages aground in that human sea, whose billows of eager, excited faces rolled to and fro amidst an extraordinary tumult.

And in all this there was not merely the usual curiosity to see uniforms go by and ladies in rich attire alight from their carriages, for Pierre soon gathered from what he heard that the crowd had come to witness the arrival of the King and Queen, who had promised to appear at the ball given by Prince Buongiovanni, in celebration of the betrothal of his daughter Celia to Lieutenant Attilio Sacco, the son of one of his Majesty's ministers. Moreover, people were enraptured with this marriage, the happy ending of a love story which had impassioned the whole city: to begin with, love at first sight, with the suddenness of a lightning-flash, and then stubborn fidelity triumphing over all obstacles, amidst romantic circumstances whose story sped from lip to lip, moistening every eye and stirring every heart.

It was this story that Narcisse had related at dessert to Pierre, who already knew some portion of it. People asserted that if the Prince had ended by yielding after a final terrible scene, it was only from fear of seeing Celia elope from the palace with her lover. She did not threaten to do so, but, amidst her virginal calmness, there was so much contempt for everything foreign to her love, that her father felt her to be capable of acting with the greatest folly in all ingenuousness. Only indifference was manifested by the Prince's wife, a phlegmatic and still beautiful Englishwoman, who considered that she had done quite enough for the household by bringing her husband a dowry of five millions, and bearing him five children. The Prince, anxious and weak despite his violence, in which one found a trace of the old Roman blood, already spoilt by mixture with that of a foreign race, was nowadays ever influenced in his actions by the fear that his house and fortune—which hitherto had remained intact amidst the accumulated ruins of the *patriziato*—might suddenly collapse. And in finally yielding to Celia, he must have been guided by the idea of rallying to the new *regime* through his daughter, so as to have one foot firmly set at the Quirinal, without withdrawing the other from the Vatican. It was galling, no doubt; his pride must have bled at the idea of allying his name with that of such low folks as the Saccos. But then Sacco was a minister, and had sped so quickly from success to success that it seemed likely he would rise yet higher, and, after the portfolio of Agriculture, secure that of Finances, which he had long coveted. And an alliance with Sacco meant the certain favour of the King, an assured retreat in that direction should the papacy some day collapse. Then, too, the Prince had made inquiries respecting the son, and was somewhat disarmed by the good looks, bravery, and rectitude of young Attilio, who represented the future, and possibly the glorious Italy of to-morrow. He was a soldier, and could be helped forward to the highest rank. And people spitefully added that the last reason which had influenced the Prince, who was very avaricious, and greatly worried by the thought that his fortune must be divided among his five children,[1] was that an opportunity presented itself for him to bestow a ridiculously small dowry on Celia. However, having consented to the marriage, he resolved to give a splendid *fete*, such as was now seldom witnessed in Rome, throwing his doors open to all the rival sections of society, inviting the sovereigns, and setting the palazzo ablaze as in the grand days of old. In doing this he would necessarily have to expend some of the money to which he clung, but a boastful spirit incited him to show the world that he at any rate had not been vanquished by the financial crisis, and that the Buongiovannis had nothing to hide and nothing to blush for. To tell the truth, some people asserted that this bravado had not originated with himself, but had been instilled into him without his knowledge by the quiet and innocent Celia, who wished to exhibit her happiness to all applauding Rome.

"Dear me!" said Narcisse, whom the throng prevented from advancing. "We shall never get in. Why, they seem to have invited the whole city." And then, as Pierre seemed surprised to see a prelate drive up in his carriage, the *attache* added: "Oh! you will elbow more than one of them upstairs. The cardinals won't like to come on account of the presence of the King and Queen, but the prelates are sure to be here. This, you know, is a neutral drawing-room where the black and the white worlds can fraternise. And then too, there are so few *fetes* that people rush on them."

He went on to explain that there were two grand balls at Court every winter, but that it was only under exceptional circumstances that the *patriziato* gave similar *galas*. Two or three of the black *salons* were opened once in a way towards the close of the Carnival, but little dances among intimates replaced the pompous entertainments of former times. Some princesses moreover merely had their day. And as for the few white *salons* that existed, these likewise retained the same character of intimacy, more or less mixed, for no lady had yet become the undisputed queen of the new society.

"Well, here we are at last," resumed Narcisse as they eventually climbed the stairs.

"Let us keep together," Pierre somewhat anxiously replied. "My only acquaintance is with the *fiancee*, and I want you to introduce me."

---

[1] The Italian succession law is similar to the French. Children cannot be disinherited. All property is divided among them, and thus the piling up of large hereditary fortunes is prevented.—Trans.

However, a considerable effort was needed even to climb the monumental staircase, so great was the crush of arriving guests. Never, in the old days of wax candles and oil lamps, had this staircase offered such a blaze of light. Electric lamps, burning in clusters in superb bronze candelabra on the landings, steeped everything in a white radiance. The cold stucco of the walls was hidden by a series of lofty tapestries depicting the story of Cupid and Psyche, marvels which had remained in the family since the days of the Renascence. And a thick carpet covered the worn marble steps, whilst clumps of evergreens and tall spreading palms decorated every corner. An affluence of new blood warmed the antique mansion that evening; there was a resurrection of life, so to say, as the women surged up the staircase, smiling and perfumed, bare-shouldered, and sparkling with diamonds.

At the entrance of the first reception-room Pierre at once perceived Prince and Princess Buongiovanni, standing side by side and receiving their guests. The Prince, a tall, slim man with fair complexion and hair turning grey, had the pale northern eyes of his American mother in an energetic face such as became a former captain of the popes. The Princess, with small, delicate, and rounded features, looked barely thirty, though she had really passed her fortieth year. And still pretty, displaying a smiling serenity which nothing could disconcert, she purely and simply basked in self-adoration. Her gown was of pink satin, and a marvellous parure of large rubies set flamelets about her dainty neck and in her fine, fair hair. Of her five children, her son, the eldest, was travelling, and three of the girls, mere children, were still at school, so that only Celia was present, Celia in a modest gown of white muslin, fair like her mother, quite bewitching with her large innocent eyes and her candid lips, and retaining to the very end of her love story the semblance of a closed lily of impenetrable, virginal mysteriousness. The Saccos had but just arrived, and Attilio, in his simple lieutenant's uniform, had remained near his betrothed, so naively and openly delighted with his great happiness that his handsome face, with its caressing mouth and brave eyes, was quite resplendent with youth and strength. Standing there, near one another, in the triumph of their passion they appeared like life's very joy and health, like the personification of hope in the morrow's promises; and the entering guests who saw them could not refrain from smiling and feeling moved, momentarily forgetting their loquacious and malicious curiosity to give their hearts to those chosen ones of love who looked so handsome and so enraptured.

Narcisse stepped forward in order to present Pierre, but Celia anticipated him. Going to meet the young priest she led him to her father and mother, saying: "Monsieur l'Abbe Pierre Froment, a friend of my dear Benedetta." Ceremonious salutations followed. Then the young girl, whose graciousness greatly touched Pierre, said to him: "Benedetta is coming with her aunt and Dario. She must be very happy this evening! And you will also see how beautiful she will be."

Pierre and Narcisse next began to congratulate her, but they could not remain there, the throng was ever jostling them; and the Prince and Princess, quite lost in the crush, had barely time to answer the many salutations with amiable, continuous nods. And Celia, after conducting the two friends to Attilio, was obliged to return to her parents so as to take her place beside them as the little queen of the *fete*.

Narcisse was already slightly acquainted with Attilio, and so fresh congratulations ensued. Then the two friends manoeuvred to find a spot where they might momentarily tarry and contemplate the spectacle which this first *salon* presented. It was a vast hall, hung with green velvet broidered with golden flowers, and contained a very remarkable collection of weapons and armour, breast-plates, battle-axes, and swords, almost all of which had belonged to the Buongiovannis of the fifteenth and sixteenth centuries. And amidst those stern implements of war there was a lovely sedan-chair of the last century, gilded and decorated with delicate paintings. It was in this chair that the Prince's great-grandmother, the celebrated Bettina, whose beauty was historical, had usually been carried to mass. On the walls, moreover, there were numerous historical paintings: battles, peace congresses, and royal receptions in which the Buongiovannis had taken part, without counting the many family portraits, tall and proud figures of sea-captains, commanders in the field, great dignitaries of the Church, prelates and cardinals, amongst whom, in the place of honour, appeared the family pope, the white-robed Buongiovanni whose accession to the pontifical throne had enriched a long line of descendants. And it was among those armours, near that coquettish sedan, and below those antique portraits, that the Saccos, husband and wife, had in their turn just halted, at a few steps from the master and mistress of the house, in order to secure their share of congratulations and bows.

"Look over there!" Narcisse whispered to Pierre, "those are the Saccos in front of us, that dark little fellow and the lady in mauve silk."

Pierre promptly recognised the bright face and pleasant smile of Stefana, whom he had already met at old Orlando's. But he was more interested in her husband, a dark dry man, with big eyes, sallow complexion, prominent chin, and vulturine nose. Like some gay Neapolitan "Pulcinello," he was dancing, shouting, and displaying such infectious good humour that it spread to all around him. He possessed a wonderful gift of speech, with a voice that was unrivalled as an instrument of fascination and conquest; and on seeing how easily he ingratiated himself with the people in that drawing-room, one could understand his lightning-like successes in the political world. He had manoeuvered with rare skill in the matter of his son's marriage, affecting such exaggerated delicacy of feeling as to set himself against the lovers, and declare that he would never consent to their union, as he had no desire to be accused of stealing a dowry and a title. As a matter of fact, he had only yielded after the Buongiovannis had given their consent, and even then he had desired to take the opinion of old Orlando, whose lofty integrity was proverbial. However, he knew right well that he would secure the old hero's approval in this particular affair, for Orlando made no secret of his opinion that the Buongiovannis ought to be glad to admit his grand-nephew into their family, as that handsome young fellow, with brave and healthy heart, would help to regenerate their impoverished blood. And throughout the whole affair, Sacco had shrewdly availed himself of Orlando's famous name, for ever talking of the relationship between them, and displaying filial veneration for this glorious founder of the country, as if indeed he had no suspicion that the latter despised and execrated him and mourned his accession to power in the conviction that he would lead Italy to shame and ruin.

"Ah!" resumed Narcisse addressing Pierre, "he's one of those supple, practical men who care nothing for a smack in the face. It seems that unscrupulous individuals like himself become necessary when states get into trouble and have to pass through political, financial, and moral crises. It is said that Sacco with his imperturbable assurance and ingenious and resourceful mind has quite won the King's favour. Just look at him!

Why, with that crowd of courtiers round him, one might think him the master of this palace!"

And indeed the guests, after passing the Prince and Princess with a bow, at once congregated around Sacco, for he represented power, emoluments, pensions, and crosses; and if folks still smiled at seeing his dark, turbulent, and scraggy figure amidst that framework of family portraits which proclaimed the mighty ancestry of the Buongiovannis, they none the less worshipped him as the personification of the new power, the democratic force which was confusedly rising even from the old Roman soil where the *patriziato* lay in ruins.

"What a crowd!" muttered Pierre. "Who are all these people?"

"Oh!" replied Narcisse, "it is a regular mixture. These people belong neither to the black nor the white world; they form a grey world as it were. The evolution was certain; a man like Cardinal Boccanera may retain an uncompromising attitude, but a whole city, a nation can't. The Pope alone will always say no and remain immutable. But everything around him progresses and undergoes transformation, so that in spite of all resistance, Rome will become Italian in a few years' time. Even now, whenever a prince has two sons only one of them remains on the side of the Vatican, the other goes over to the Quirinal. People must live, you see; and the great families threatened with annihilation have not sufficient heroism to carry obstinacy to the point of suicide. And I have already told you that we are here on neutral ground, for Prince Buongiovanni was one of the first to realise the necessity of conciliation. He feels that his fortune is perishing, he does not care to risk it either in industry or in speculation, and already sees it portioned out among his five children, by whose descendants it will be yet further divided; and this is why he prudently makes advances to the King without, however, breaking with the Pope. In this *salon*, therefore, you see a perfect picture of the *debacle*, the confusion which reigns in the Prince's ideas and opinions." Narcisse paused, and then began to name some of the persons who were coming in. "There's a general," said he, "who has become very popular since his last campaign in Africa. There will be a great many military men here this evening, for all Attilio's superiors have been invited, so as to give the young man an *entourage* of glory. Ah! and there's the German ambassador. I fancy that nearly all the Corps Diplomatique will come on account of their Majesties' presence. But, by way of contrast, just look at that stout fellow yonder. He's a very influential deputy, a *parvenu* of the new middle class. Thirty years ago he was merely one of Prince Albertini's farmers, one of those *mercanti di campagna* who go about the environs of Rome in stout boots and a soft felt hat. And now look at that prelate coming in—"

"Oh! I know him," Pierre interrupted. "He's Monsignor Fornaro."

"Exactly, Monsignor Fornaro, a personage of some importance. You told me, I remember, that he is the reporter of the Congregation in that affair of your book. A most delightful man! Did you see how he bowed to the Princess? And what a noble and graceful bearing he has in his little mantle of violet silk!"

Then Narcisse went on enumerating the princes and princesses, the dukes and duchesses, the politicians and functionaries, the diplomatists and ministers, and the officers and well-to-do middle-class people, who of themselves made up a most wonderful medley of guests, to say nothing of the representatives of the various foreign colonies, English people, Americans, Germans, Spaniards, and Russians, in a word, all ancient Europe, and both Americas. And afterwards the young man reverted to the

Saccos, to the little Signora Sacco in particular, in order to tell Pierre of the heroic efforts which she had made to open a *salon* for the purpose of assisting her husband's ambition. Gentle and modest as she seemed, she was also very shrewd, endowed with genuine qualities, Piedmontese patience and strength of resistance, orderly habits and thriftiness. And thus it was she who re-established the equilibrium in household affairs which her husband by his exuberance so often disturbed. He was indeed greatly indebted to her, though nobody suspected it. At the same time, however, she had so far failed in her attempts to establish a white *salon* which should take the lead in influencing opinion. Only the people of her own set visited her, not a single prince ever came, and her Monday dances were the same as in a score of other middle-class homes, having no brilliancy and no importance. In fact, the real white *salon*, which should guide men and things and sway all Rome was still in dreamland.

"Just notice her keen smile as she examines everything here," resumed Narcisse. "She's teaching herself and forming plans, I'm sure of it. Now that she is about to be connected with a princely family she probably hopes to receive some of the best society."

Large as was the room, the crowd in it had by this time grown so dense that the two friends were pressed back to a wall, and felt almost stifled. The *attache* therefore decided to lead the priest elsewhere, and as they walked along he gave him some particulars concerning the palace, which was one of the most sumptuous in Rome, and renowned for the magnificence of its reception-rooms. Dancing took place in the picture gallery, a superb apartment more than sixty feet long, with eight windows overlooking the Corso; while the buffet was installed in the Hall of the Antiques, a marble hall, which among other precious things contained a statue of Venus, rivalling the one at the Capitol. Then there was a suite of marvellous *salons*, still resplendent with ancient luxury, hung with the rarest stuffs, and retaining some unique specimens of old-time furniture, on which covetous antiquaries kept their eyes fixed, whilst waiting and hoping for the inevitable future ruin. And one of these apartments, the little Saloon of the Mirrors, was particularly famous. Of circular shape and Louis XV style, it was surrounded by mirrors in *rococo* frames, extremely rich, and most exquisitely carved.

"You will see all that by and by," continued Narcisse. "At present we had better go in here if we want to breathe a little. It is here that the arm-chairs from the adjacent gallery have been brought for the accommodation of the ladies who desire to sit down and be seen and admired."

The apartment they entered was a spacious one, draped with the most superb Genoese velvet, that antique *jardiniere* velvet with pale satin ground, and flowers once of dazzling brightness, whose greens and blues and reds had now become exquisitely soft, with the subdued, faded tones of old floral love-tokens. On the pier tables and in the cabinets all around were some of the most precious curios in the palace, ivory caskets, gilt and painted wood carvings, pieces of antique plate—briefly, a collection of marvels. And several ladies, fleeing the crush, had already taken refuge on the numerous seats, clustering in little groups, and laughing and chatting with the few gentlemen who had discovered this retreat of grace and *galanterie*. In the bright glow of the lamps nothing could be more delightful than the sight of all those bare, sheeny shoulders, and those supple necks, above whose napes were coiled tresses of fair or raven hair. Bare arms emerged like living flowers of flesh from amidst the mingling lace and silk of soft-hued bodices. The fans played slowly, as if to heighten the fires of the precious stones, and at each beat wafted around an *odore di femina* blended with a predominating perfume of violets.

"Hallo!" exclaimed Narcisse, "there's our good friend Monsignor Nani bowing to the Austrian ambassadress."

As soon as Nani perceived the young priest and his companion he came towards them, and the trio then withdrew into the embrasure of a window in order that they might chat for a moment at their ease. The prelate was smiling like one enchanted with the beauty of the *fete*, but at the same time he retained all the serenity of innocence, as if he had not even noticed the exhibition of bare shoulders by which he was surrounded. "Ah, my dear son!" he said to Pierre, "I am very pleased to see you! Well, and what do you think of our Rome when she makes up her mind to give *fetes*?"

"Why, it is superb, Monseigneur."

Then, in an emotional manner, Nani spoke of Celia's lofty piety; and, in order to give the Vatican the credit of this sumptuous *gala*, affected to regard the Prince and Princess as staunch adherents of the Church, as if he were altogether unaware that the King and Queen were presently coming. And afterwards he abruptly exclaimed: "I have been thinking of you all day, my dear son. Yes, I heard that you had gone to see his Eminence Cardinal Sanguinetti. Well, and how did he receive you?"

"Oh! in a most paternal manner," Pierre replied. "At first he made me understand the embarrassment in which he was placed by his position as protector of Lourdes; but just as I was going off he showed himself charming, and promised me his help with a delicacy which deeply touched me."

"Did he indeed, my dear son? But it doesn't surprise me, his Eminence is so good-hearted!"

"And I must add, Monseigneur, that I came back with a light and hopeful heart. It now seems to me as if my suit were half gained."

"Naturally, I understand it," replied Nani, who was still smiling with that keen, intelligent smile of his, sharpened by a touch of almost imperceptible irony. And after a short pause he added in a very simple way: "The misfortune is that on the day before yesterday your book was condemned by the Congregation of the Index, which was convoked by its Secretary expressly for that purpose. And the judgment will be laid before his Holiness, for him to sign it, on the day after to-morrow."

Pierre looked at the prelate in bewilderment. Had the old mansion fallen on his head he would not have felt more overcome. What! was it all over? His journey to Rome, the experiment he had come to attempt there, had resulted in that defeat, of which he was thus suddenly apprised amidst that betrothal *fete*. And he had not even been able to defend himself, he had sacrificed his time without finding any one to whom he might speak, before whom he might plead his cause! Anger was rising within him, and he could not prevent himself from muttering bitterly: "Ah! how I have been duped! And that Cardinal who said to me only this morning: 'If God be with you he will save you in spite of everything.' Yes, yes, I now understand him; he was juggling with words, he only desired a disaster in order that submission might lead me to Heaven! Submit, indeed, ah! I cannot, I cannot yet! My heart is too full of indignation and grief."

Nani examined and studied him with curiosity. "But my dear son," he said, "nothing is final so long as the Holy Father has not signed the judgment. You have all to-morrow and even the morning of the day after before you. A miracle is always possible." Then, lowering his voice and drawing Pierre on one side whilst Narcisse in an aesthetical spirit examined the ladies, he added: "Listen, I have a communication to make to you in great secrecy. Come and join me in the little Saloon of the Mirrors by and by, during the Cotillon. We shall be able to talk there at our ease."

Pierre nodded, and thereupon the prelate discreetly withdrew and disappeared in the crowd. However, the young man's ears were buzzing; he could no longer hope; what indeed could he accomplish in one day since he had lost three months without even being able to secure an audience with the Pope? And his bewilderment increased as he suddenly heard Narcisse speaking to him of art. "It's astonishing how the feminine figure has deteriorated in these dreadful democratic days. It's all fat and horribly common. Not one of those women yonder shows the Florentine contour, with small bosom and slender, elegant neck. Ah! that one yonder isn't so bad perhaps, the fair one with her hair coiled up, whom Monsignor Fornaro has just approached."

For a few minutes indeed Monsignor Fornaro had been fluttering from beauty to beauty, with an amiable air of conquest. He looked superb that evening with his lofty decorative figure, blooming cheeks, and victorious affability. No unpleasant scandal was associated with his name; he was simply regarded as a prelate of gallant ways who took pleasure in the society of ladies. And he paused and chatted, and leant over their bare shoulders with laughing eyes and humid lips as if experiencing a sort of devout rapture. However, on perceiving Narcisse whom he occasionally met, he at once came forward and the *attache* had to bow to him. "You have been in good health I hope, Monseigneur, since I had the honour of seeing you at the embassy."

"Oh! yes, I am very well, very well indeed. What a delightful *fete*, is it not?"

Pierre also had bowed. This was the man whose report had brought about the condemnation of his book; and it was with resentment that he recalled his caressing air and charming greeting, instinct with such lying promise. However, the prelate, who was very shrewd, must have guessed that the young priest was already acquainted with the decision of the Congregation, and have thought it more dignified to abstain from open recognition; for on his side he merely nodded and smiled at him. "What a number of people!" he went on, "and how many charming persons there are! It will soon be impossible for one to move in this room."

All the seats in fact were now occupied by ladies, and what with the strong perfume of violets and the exhalations of warm necks and shoulders the atmosphere was becoming most oppressive. The fans flapped more briskly, and clear laughter rang out amidst a growing hubbub of conversation in which the same words constantly recurred. Some news, doubtless, had just arrived, some rumour was being whispered from group to group, throwing them all into feverish excitement. As it happened, Monsignor Fornaro, who was always well informed, desired to be the proclaimer of this news, which nobody as yet had ventured to announce aloud.

"Do you know what is exciting them all?" he inquired.

"Is it the Holy Father's illness?" asked Pierre in his anxiety. "Is he worse this evening?"

The prelate looked at him in astonishment, and then somewhat impatiently replied: "Oh, no, no. His Holiness is much better, thank Heaven. A person belonging to the Vatican was telling me just now that he was able to get up this afternoon and receive his intimates as usual."

"All the same, people have been alarmed," interrupted Narcisse. "I must confess that we did not feel easy at the embassy, for a Conclave at the present time would be a great worry for France. She would exercise no influence at it. It is a great mistake on the part of our Republican Government to treat the Holy See as of no importance! However, can one ever tell whether the Pope is ill or not? I know for a certainty that he was nearly carried off last winter when nobody breathed a word about any illness, whereas on the last occasion when the newspapers killed him and talked about a dreadful attack of bronchitis, I myself saw him quite strong and in the best of spirits! His reported illnesses are mere matters of policy, I fancy."[1]

With a hasty gesture, however, Monsignor Fornaro brushed this importunate subject aside. "No, no," said he, "people are tranquillised and no longer talk of it. What excites all those ladies is that the Congregation of the Council to-day voted the dissolution of the Prada marriage by a great majority."

Again did Pierre feel moved. However, not having had time to see any members of the Boccanera family on his return from Frascati he feared that the news might be false and said so. Thereupon the prelate gave his word of honour that things were as he stated. "The news is certain," he declared. "I had it from a member of the Congregation." And then, all at once, he apologised and hurried off: "Excuse me but I see a lady whom I had not yet caught sight of, and desire to pay my respects to her."

He at once hastened to the lady in question, and, being unable to sit down, inclined his lofty figure as if to envelop her with his gallant courtesy; whilst she, young, fresh, and bare-shouldered, laughed with a pearly laugh as his cape of violet silk lightly brushed her sheeny skin.

"You know that person, don't you?" Narcisse inquired of Pierre. "No! Really? Why, that is Count Prada's *inamorata*, the charming Lisbeth Kauffmann, by whom he has just had a son. It's her first appearance in society since that event. She's a German, you know, and lost her husband here. She paints a little; in fact, rather nicely. A great deal is forgiven to the ladies of the foreign colony, and this one is particularly popular on account of the very affable manner in which she receives people at her little palazzo in the Via Principe Amedeo. As you may imagine, the news of the dissolution of that marriage must amuse her!"

She looked really exquisite, that Lisbeth, very fair, rosy, and gay, with satiny skin, soft blue eyes, and lips wreathed in an amiable smile, which was renowned for its grace. And that evening, in her gown of white silk spangled with gold, she showed herself so delighted with life, so securely happy in the thought that she was free, that she loved and was loved in return, that the whispered tidings, the malicious remarks exchanged behind the fans of those around her, seemed to turn to her personal triumph. For a moment all eyes had sought her, and people talked of the outcome of her connection with Prada, the man whose manhood the Church solemnly denied by its decision of that very day! And there came stifled laughter and whispered jests, whilst she, radiant in her insolent serenity, accepted with a rapturous air the gallantry of Monsignor Fornaro, who congratulated her on a painting of the Virgin with the lily, which she had lately sent to a fine-art show.

---

[1] There is much truth in this; but the reader must not imagine that the Pope is never ill. At his great age, indispositions are only natural.—Trans.

XII.

Ah! that matrimonial nullity suit, which for a year had supplied Rome with scandal, what a final hubbub it occasioned as the tidings of its termination burst forth amidst that ball! The black and white worlds had long chosen it as a battlefield for the exchange of incredible slander, endless gossip, the most nonsensical tittle-tattle. And now it was over; the Vatican with imperturbable impudence had pronounced the marriage null and void on the ground that the husband was no man, and all Rome would laugh over the affair, with that free scepticism which it displayed as soon as the pecuniary affairs of the Church came into question. The incidents of the struggle were already common property: Prada's feelings revolting to such a point that he had withdrawn from the contest, the Boccaneras moving heaven and earth in their feverish anxiety, the money which they had distributed among the creatures of the various cardinals in order to gain their influence, and the large sum which they had indirectly paid for the second and favourable report of Monsignor Palma. People said that, altogether, more than a hundred thousand francs had been expended, but this was not thought over-much, as a well-known French countess had been obliged to disburse nearly ten times that amount to secure the dissolution of her marriage. But then the Holy Father's need was so great! And, moreover, nobody was angered by this venality; it merely gave rise to malicious witticisms; and the fans continued waving in the increasing heat, and the ladies quivered with contentment as the whispered pleasantries took wing and fluttered over their bare shoulders.

"Oh! how pleased the Contessina must be!" Pierre resumed. "I did not understand what her little friend, Princess Celia, meant by saying when we came in that she would be so happy and beautiful this evening. It is doubtless on that account that she is coming here, after cloistering herself all the time the affair lasted, as if she were in mourning."

However, Lisbeth's eyes had chanced to meet those of Narcisse, and as she smiled at him he was, in his turn, obliged to pay his respects to her, for, like everybody else of the foreign colony, he knew her through having visited her studio. He was again returning to Pierre when a fresh outburst of emotion stirred the diamond aigrettes and the flowers adorning the ladies' hair. People turned to see what was the matter, and again did the hubbub increase. "Ah! it's Count Prada in person!" murmured Narcisse, with an admiring glance. "He has a fine bearing, whatever folks may say. Dress him up in velvet and gold, and what a splendid, unscrupulous, fifteenth-century adventurer he would make!"

Prada entered the room, looking quite gay, in fact, almost triumphant. And above his large, white shirtfront, edged by the black of his coat, he really had a commanding, predacious expression, with his frank, stern eyes, and his energetic features barred by a large black moustache. Never had a more rapturous smile of sensuality revealed the wolfish teeth of his voracious mouth. With rapid glances he took stock of the women, dived into their very souls. Then, on seeing Lisbeth, who looked so pink, and fair, and girlish, his expression softened, and he frankly went up to her, without troubling in the slightest degree about the ardent, inquisitive eyes which were turned upon him. As soon as Monsignor Fornaro had made room, he stooped and conversed with the young woman in a low tone. And she no doubt confirmed the news which was circulating, for as he again drew himself erect, he laughed a somewhat forced laugh, and made an involuntary gesture.

However, he then caught sight of Pierre, and joined him in the embrasure of the window; and when he had also shaken hands with Narcisse, he said to the young priest with all his wonted *bravura*: "You recollect what I told you as we were coming back from Frascati? Well, it's done, it seems, they've annulled my marriage. It's such an impudent, such an imbecile decision, that I still doubted it a moment ago!"

"Oh! the news is certain," Pierre made bold to reply. "It has just been confirmed to us by Monsignor Fornaro, who had it from a member of the Congregation. And it is said that the majority was very large."

Prada again shook with laughter. "No, no," said he, "such a farce is beyond belief! It's the finest smack given to justice and common-sense that I know of. Ah! if the marriage can also be annulled by the civil courts, and if my friend whom you see yonder be only willing, we shall amuse ourselves in Rome! Yes, indeed, I'd marry her at Santa Maria Maggiore with all possible pomp. And there's a dear little being in the world who would take part in the *fete* in his nurse's arms!"

He laughed too loud as he spoke, alluded in too brutal a fashion to his child, that living proof of his manhood. Was it suffering that made his lips curve upwards and reveal his white teeth? It could be divined that he was quivering, fighting against an awakening of covert, tumultuous passion, which he would not acknowledge even to himself.

"And you, my dear Abbe?" he hastily resumed. "Do you know the other report? Do you know that the Countess is coming here?" It was thus, by force of habit, that he designated Benedetta, forgetting that she was no longer his wife.

"Yes, I have just been told so," Pierre replied; and then he hesitated for a moment before adding, with a desire to prevent any disagreeable surprise: "And we shall no doubt see Prince Dario also, for he has not started for Naples as I told you. Something prevented his departure at the last moment, I believe. At least so I gathered from a servant."

Prada no longer laughed. His face suddenly became grave, and he contented himself with murmuring: "Ah! so the cousin is to be of the party. Well, we shall see them, we shall see them both!"

Then, whilst the two friends went on chatting, he became silent, as if serious considerations impelled him to reflect. And suddenly making a gesture of apology he withdrew yet farther into the embrasure in which he stood, pulled a note-book out of his pocket, and tore from it a leaf on which, without modifying his handwriting otherwise than by slightly enlarging it, he pencilled these four lines: "A legend avers that the fig tree of Judas now grows at Frascati, and that its fruit is deadly for him who may desire to become Pope. Eat not the poisoned figs, nor give them either to your servants or your fowls." Then he folded the paper, fastened it with a postage stamp, and wrote on it the address: "To his most Reverend and most Illustrious Eminence, Cardinal Boccanera." And when he had placed everything in his pocket again, he drew a long breath and once more called back his laugh.

A kind of invincible discomfort, a far-away terror had momentarily frozen him. Without being guided by any clear train of reasoning, he had felt the need of protecting himself against any cowardly temptation, any possible abomination. He could not have told what course of ideas had induced him to write those four lines without a moment's delay, on the very spot where he stood, under penalty of contributing to a great catastrophe. But one thought was firmly fixed in his brain, that on leaving the ball he would go to the Via Giulia and throw that note into the letter-box at the Palazzo Boccanera. And that decided, he was once more easy in mind.

"Why, what is the matter with you, my dear Abbe?" he inquired on again joining in the conversation of the two friends. "You are quite gloomy." And on Pierre telling him of the bad news which he had received, the condemnation of his book, and the single day which remained to him for action if he did not wish his journey to Rome to result in defeat, he began to protest as if he himself needed agitation and diversion in order to continue hopeful and bear the ills of life. "Never mind, never mind, don't worry yourself," said he, "one loses all one's strength by worrying. A day is a great deal, one can do ever so many things in a day. An hour, a minute suffices for Destiny to intervene and turn defeat into victory!" He grew feverish as he spoke, and all at once added, "Come, let's go to the ball-room. It seems that the scene there is something prodigious."

Then he exchanged a last loving glance with Lisbeth whilst Pierre and Narcisse followed him, the three of them extricating themselves from their corner with the greatest difficulty, and then wending their way towards the adjoining gallery through a sea of serried skirts, a billowy expanse of necks and shoulders whence ascended the passion which makes life, the odour alike of love and of death.

With its eight windows overlooking the Corso, their panes uncurtained and throwing a blaze of light upon the houses across the road, the picture gallery, sixty-five feet in length and more than thirty in breadth, spread out with incomparable splendour. The illumination was dazzling. Clusters of electric lamps had changed seven pairs of huge marble candelabra into gigantic *torcheres*, akin to constellations; and all along the cornice up above, other lamps set in bright-hued floral glasses formed a marvellous garland of flaming flowers: tulips, paeonies, and roses. The antique red velvet worked with gold, which draped the walls, glowed like a furnace fire. About the doors and windows there were hangings of old lace broidered with flowers in coloured silk whose hues had the very intensity of life. But the sight of sights beneath the sumptuous panelled ceiling adorned with golden roses, the unique spectacle of a richness not to be equalled, was the collection of masterpieces such as no museum could excel. There were works of Raffaelle and Titian, Rembrandt and Rubens, Velasquez and Ribera, famous works which in this unexpected illumination suddenly showed forth, triumphant with youth regained, as if awakened to the immortal life of genius. And, as their Majesties would not arrive before midnight, the ball had just been opened, and flights of soft-hued gowns were whirling in a waltz past all the pompous throng, the glittering jewels and decorations, the gold-broidered uniforms and the pearl-broidered robes, whilst silk and satin and velvet spread and overflowed upon every side.

"It is prodigious, really!" declared Prada with his excited air; "let us go this way and place ourselves in a window recess again. There is no better spot for getting a good view without being too much jostled."

They lost Narcisse somehow or other, and on reaching the desired recess found themselves but two, Pierre and the Count. The orchestra, installed on a little platform at the far end of the gallery, had just finished the waltz, and the dancers, with an air of giddy rapture, were slowly walking through the crowd when a fresh arrival caused every head to turn. Donna Serafina, arrayed in a robe of purple silk as if she had worn the colours of her brother the Cardinal, was making a royal entry on the arm of Consistorial-Advocate Morano. And never before had she laced herself so tightly, never had her waist looked so slim and girlish; and never had her stern, wrinkled face, which her white hair scarcely softened, expressed such stubborn and victorious domination. A discreet murmur of approval ran round, a murmur of public relief as it were, for all Roman society had condemned the unworthy conduct of Morano in severing a connection of thirty years to which the drawing-rooms had grown as accustomed as if it had been a legal marriage. The rupture had lasted for two months, to the great scandal of Rome where the cult of long and faithful affections still abides. And so the reconciliation touched every heart and was regarded as one of the happiest consequences of the victory which the Boccaneras had that day gained in the affair of Benedetta's marriage. Morano repentant and Donna Serafina reappearing on his arm, nothing could have been more satisfactory; love had conquered, decorum was preserved and good order re-established.

But there was a deeper sensation as soon as Benedetta and Dario were seen to enter, side by side, behind the others. This tranquil indifference for the ordinary forms of propriety, on the very day when the marriage with Prada had been annulled, this victory of love, confessed and celebrated before one and all, seemed so charming in its audacity, so full of the bravery of youth and hope, that the pair were at once forgiven amidst a murmur of universal admiration. And as in the case of Celia and Attilio, all hearts flew to them, to their radiant beauty, to the wondrous happiness that made their faces so resplendent. Dario, still pale after his long convalescence, somewhat slight and delicate of build, with the fine clear eyes of a big child, and the dark curly beard of a young god, bore himself with a light pride, in which all the old princely blood of the Boccaneras could be traced. And Benedetta, she so white under her casque of jetty hair, she so calm and so sensible, wore her lovely smile, that smile so seldom seen on her face but which was irresistibly fascinating, transfiguring her, imparting the charm of a flower to her somewhat full mouth, and filling the infinite of her dark and fathomless eyes with a radiance as of heaven. And in this gay return of youth and happiness, an exquisite instinct had prompted her to put on a white gown, a plain girlish gown which symbolised her maidenhood, which told that she had remained through all a pure untarnished lily for the husband of her choice. And nothing of her form was to be seen, not a glimpse of bosom or shoulder. It was as if the impenetrable, redoubtable mystery of love, the sovereign beauty of woman slumbered there, all powerful, but veiled with white. Again, not a jewel appeared on her fingers or in her ears. There was simply a necklace falling about her *corsage*, but a necklace fit for royalty, the famous pearl necklace of the Boccaneras, which she had inherited from her mother, and which was known to all Rome—pearls of fabulous size cast negligently about her neck, and sufficing, simply as she was gowned, to make her queen of all.

"Oh!" murmured Pierre in ecstasy, "how happy and how beautiful she is!"

But he at once regretted that he had expressed his thoughts aloud, for beside him he heard a low plaint, an involuntary growl which reminded him of the Count's presence. However, Prada promptly stifled this cry of returning anguish, and found strength enough to affect a brutish gaiety: "The devil!" said he, "they have plenty of impudence. I hope we shall see them married and bedded at once!" Then regretting this coarse jest which had been prompted by the revolt of passion, he sought to appear indifferent: "She looks very nice this evening," he said; "she has the finest shoulders in the world, you know, and its a real success for her to hide them and yet appear more beautiful than ever."

He went on speaking, contriving to assume an easy tone, and giving various little particulars about the Countess as he still obstinately called the young woman. However, he had drawn rather further into the recess, for fear, no doubt, that people might remark his pallor, and the painful twitch which contracted his mouth. He was in no state to fight, to show himself gay and insolent in presence of the joy which the lovers so openly and naively expressed. And he was glad of the respite which the arrival of the King and Queen at this moment offered him. "Ah! here are their Majesties!" he exclaimed, turning towards the window. "Look at the scramble in the street!"

Although the windows were closed, a tumult could be heard rising from the footways. And Pierre on looking down saw, by the light of the electric lamps, a sea of human heads pour over the road and encompass the carriages. He had several times already seen the King during the latter's daily drives to the grounds of the Villa Borghese, whither he came like any private gentleman—unguarded, unescorted, with merely an aide-de-camp accompanying him in his victoria. At other times he drove a light phaeton with only a footman in black livery to attend him. And on one occasion Pierre had seen him with the Queen, the pair of them seated side by side like worthy middle-class folks driving abroad for pleasure. And, as the royal couple went by, the busy people in the streets and the promenaders in the public gardens contented themselves with wafting them an affectionate wave of the hand, the most expansive simply approaching to smile at them, and no one importuning them with acclamations. Pierre, who harboured the traditional idea of kings closely guarded and passing processionally with all the accompaniment of military pomp, was therefore greatly surprised and touched by the amiable *bonhomie* of this royal pair, who went wherever they listed in full security amidst the smiling affection of their people. Everybody, moreover, had told him of the King's kindliness and simplicity, his desire for peace, and his passion for sport, solitude, and the open air, which, amidst the worries of power, must often have made him dream of a life of freedom far from the imperious duties of royalty for which he seemed unfitted.[1] But the Queen was yet more tenderly loved. So naturally and serenely virtuous that she alone remained ignorant of the scandals of Rome, she was also a woman of great culture and great refinement, conversant with every field of literature, and very happy in being so intelligent, so superior to those around her—a pre-eminence which she realised and which she was fond of showing, but in the most natural and most graceful of ways.

Like Pierre, Prada had remained with his face to the window, and suddenly pointing to the crowd he said: "Now that they have seen the Queen they will go to bed well pleased. And there isn't a single police agent there, I'm sure. Ah! to be loved, to be loved!" Plainly enough his distress of spirit was coming back, and so, turning towards the gallery again, he tried to play the jester. "Attention, my dear Abbe, we mustn't miss their Majesties' entry. That will be the finest part of the *fete*!"

---

[1] King Humbert inherited these tastes from his father Victor Emanuel, who was likewise a great sportsman and had a perfect horror of court life, pageantry, and the exigencies of politics.—Trans.

A few minutes went by, and then, in the very midst of a polka, the orchestra suddenly ceased playing. But a moment afterwards, with all the blare of its brass instruments, it struck up the Royal March. The dancers fled in confusion, the centre of the gallery was cleared, and the King and Queen entered, escorted by the Prince and Princess Buongiovanni, who had received them at the foot of the staircase. The King was in ordinary evening dress, while the Queen wore a robe of straw-coloured satin, covered with superb white lace; and under the diadem of brilliants which encircled her beautiful fair hair, she looked still young, with a fresh and rounded face, whose expression was all amiability, gentleness, and wit. The music was still sounding with the enthusiastic violence of welcome. Behind her father and mother, Celia appeared amidst the press of people who were following to see the sight; and then came Attilio, the Saccos, and various relatives and official personages. And, pending the termination of the Royal March, only salutations, glances, and smiles were exchanged amidst the sonorous music and dazzling light; whilst all the guests crowded around on tiptoe, with outstretched necks and glittering eyes—a rising tide of heads and shoulders, flashing with the fires of precious stones.

At last the march ended and the presentations began. Their Majesties were already acquainted with Celia, and congratulated her with quite affectionate kindliness. However, Sacco, both as minister and father, was particularly desirous of presenting his son Attilio. He bent his supple spine, and summoned to his lips the fine words which were appropriate, in such wise that he contrived to make the young man bow to the King in the capacity of a lieutenant in his Majesty's army, whilst his homage as a handsome young man, so passionately loved by his betrothed was reserved for Queen Margherita. Again did their Majesties show themselves very gracious, even towards the Signora Sacco who, ever modest and prudent, had remained in the background. And then occurred an incident that was destined to give rise to endless gossip. Catching sight of Benedetta, whom Count Prada had presented to her after his marriage, the Queen, who greatly admired her beauty and charm of manner, addressed her a smile in such wise that the young woman was compelled to approach. A conversation of some minutes' duration ensued, and the Contessina was favoured with some extremely amiable expressions which were perfectly audible to all around. Most certainly the Queen was ignorant of the event of the day, the dissolution of Benedetta's marriage with Prada, and her coming union with Dario so publicly announced at this *gala*, which now seemed to have been given to celebrate a double betrothal. Nevertheless that conversation caused a deep impression; the guests talked of nothing but the compliments which Benedetta had received from the most virtuous and intelligent of queens, and her triumph was increased by it all, she became yet more beautiful and more victorious amidst the happiness she felt at being at last able to bestow herself on the spouse of her choice, that happiness which made her look so radiant.

But, on the other hand, the torture which Prada experienced now became intense. Whilst the sovereigns continued conversing, the Queen with the ladies who came to pay her their respects, the King with the officers, diplomatists, and other important personages who approached him, Prada saw none but Benedetta—Benedetta congratulated, caressed, exalted by affection and glory. Dario was near her, flushing with pleasure, radiant like herself. It was for them that this ball had been given, for them that the lamps shone out, for them that the music played, for them that the most beautiful women of Rome had bared their bosoms and adorned them with precious stones.

It was for them that their Majesties had entered to the strains of the Royal March, for them that the *fete* was becoming like an apotheosis, for them that a fondly loved queen was smiling, appearing at that betrothal *gala* like the good fairy of the nursery tales, whose coming betokens life-long happiness. And for Prada, this wondrously brilliant hour when good fortune and joyfulness attained their apogee, was one of defeat. It was fraught with the victory of that woman who had refused to be his wife in aught but name, and of that man who now was about to take her from him: such a public, ostentatious, insulting victory that it struck him like a buffet in the face. And not merely did his pride and passion bleed for that: he felt that the triumph of the Saccos dealt a blow to his fortune. Was it true, then, that the rough conquerors of the North were bound to deteriorate in the delightful climate of Rome, was that the reason why he already experienced such a sensation of weariness and exhaustion? That very morning at Frascati in connection with that disastrous building enterprise he had realised that his millions were menaced, albeit he refused to admit that things were going badly with him, as some people rumoured. And now, that evening, amidst that *fete* he beheld the South victorious, Sacco winning the day like one who feeds at his ease on the warm prey so gluttonously pounced upon under the flaming sun.

And the thought of Sacco being a minister, an intimate of the King, allying himself by marriage to one of the noblest families of the Roman aristocracy, and already laying hands on the people and the national funds with the prospect of some day becoming the master of Rome and Italy—that thought again was a blow for the vanity of this man of prey, for the ever voracious appetite of this enjoyer, who felt as if he were being pushed away from table before the feast was over! All crumbled and escaped him, Sacco stole his millions, and Benedetta tortured his flesh, stirring up that awful wound of unsatisfied passion which never would be healed.

Again did Pierre hear that dull plaint, that involuntary despairing growl, which had upset him once before. And he looked at the Count, and asked him: "Are you suffering?" But on seeing how livid was the face of Prada, who only retained his calmness by a superhuman effort, he regretted his indiscreet question, which, moreover, remained unanswered. And then to put the other more at ease, the young priest went on speaking, venting the thoughts which the sight before him inspired: "Your father was right," said he, "we Frenchmen whose education is so full of the Catholic spirit, even in these days of universal doubt, we never think of Rome otherwise than as the old Rome of the popes. We scarcely know, we can scarcely understand the great changes which, year by year, have brought about the Italian Rome of the present day. Why, when I arrived here, the King and his government and the young nation working to make a great capital for itself, seemed to me of no account whatever! Yes, I dismissed all that, thought nothing of it, in my dream of resuscitating a Christian and evangelical Rome, which should assure the happiness of the world."

He laughed as he spoke, pitying his own artlessness, and then pointed towards the gallery where Prince Buongiovanni was bowing to the King whilst the Princess listened to the gallant remarks of Sacco: a scene full of symbolism, the old papal aristocracy struck down, the *parvenus* accepted, the black and white worlds so mixed together that one and all were little else than subjects, on the eve of forming but one united nation. That conciliation between the Quirinal and the Vatican which in principle was regarded as impossible, was it not in practice fatal, in face of the evolution which went on day by day? People must go on living, loving, and creating life throughout the ages. And the marriage of Attilio and Celia would be the symbol of the needful union: youth and love triumphing over ancient hatred, all quarrels forgotten as a handsome lad goes by, wins a lovely girl, and carries her off in his arms in order that the world may last.

"Look at them!" resumed Pierre, "how handsome and young and gay both the *fiances* are, all confidence in the future. Ah! I well understand that your King should have come here to please his minister and win one of the old Roman families over to his throne; it is good, brave, and fatherly policy. But I like to think that he has also realised the touching significance of that marriage—old Rome, in the person of that candid, loving child giving herself to young Italy, that upright, enthusiastic young man who wears his uniform so jauntily. And may their nuptials be definitive and fruitful; from them and from all the others may there arise the great nation which, now that I begin to know you, I trust you will soon become!"

Amidst the tottering of his former dream of an evangelical and universal Rome, Pierre expressed these good wishes for the Eternal City's future fortune with such keen and deep emotion that Prada could not help replying: "I thank you; that wish of yours is in the heart of every good Italian."

But his voice quavered, for even whilst he was looking at Celia and Attilio, who stood smiling and talking together, he saw Benedetta and Dario approach them, wearing the same joyful expression of perfect happiness. And when the two couples were united, so radiant and so triumphant, so full of superb and happy life, he no longer had strength to stay there, see them, and suffer.

"I am frightfully thirsty," he hoarsely exclaimed. "Let's go to the buffet to drink something." And, thereupon, in order to avoid notice, he so manoeuvred as to glide behind the throng, skirting the windows in the direction of the entrance to the Hall of the Antiques, which was beyond the gallery.

Whilst Pierre was following him they were parted by an eddy of the crowd, and the young priest found himself carried towards the two loving couples who still stood chatting together. And Celia, on recognising him, beckoned to him in a friendly way. With her passionate cult for beauty, she was enraptured with the appearance of Benedetta, before whom she joined her little lily hands as before the image of the Madonna. "Oh! Monsieur l'Abbe," said she, "to please me now, do tell her how beautiful she is, more beautiful than anything on earth, more beautiful than even the sun, and the moon and stars. If you only knew, my dear, it makes me quiver to see you so beautiful as that, as beautiful as happiness, as beautiful as love itself!"

Benedetta began to laugh, while the two young men made merry. "But you are as beautiful as I am, darling," said the Contessina. "And if we are beautiful it is because we are happy."

"Yes, yes, happy," Celia gently responded. "Do you remember the evening when you told me that one didn't succeed in marrying the Pope and the King? But Attilio and I are marrying them, and yet we are very happy."

"But we don't marry them, Dario and I! On the contrary!" said Benedetta gaily. "No matter; as you answered me that same evening, it is sufficient that we should love one another, love saves the world."

When Pierre at last succeeded in reaching the door of the Hall of the Antiques, where the buffet was installed, he found Prada there, motionless, gazing despite himself on the galling spectacle which he desired to flee. A power stronger than his will had kept him there, forcing him to turn round and look, and look again. And thus, with a bleeding heart, he still lingered and witnessed the resumption of the dancing, the first figure of a quadrille which the orchestra began to play with a lively flourish of its brass instruments. Benedetta and Dario, Celia and Attilio were *vis-à-vis*. And so charming and delightful was the sight which the two couples presented dancing in the white blaze, all youth and joy, that the King and Queen drew near to them and became interested. And soon bravos of admiration rang out, while from every heart spread a feeling of infinite tenderness.

"I'm dying of thirst, let's go!" repeated Prada, at last managing to wrench himself away from the torturing sight.

He called for some iced lemonade and drank the glassful at one draught, gulping it down with the greedy eagerness of a man stricken with fever, who will never more be able to quench the burning fire within him.

The Hall of the Antiques was a spacious room with mosaic pavement, and decorations of stucco; and a famous collection of vases, bas-reliefs, and statues, was disposed along its walls. The marbles predominated, but there were a few bronzes, and among them a dying gladiator of extreme beauty. The marvel however was the famous statue of Venus, a companion to that of the Capitol, but with a more elegant and supple figure and with the left arm falling loosely in a gesture of voluptuous surrender. That evening a powerful electric reflector threw a dazzling light upon the statue, which, in its divine and pure nudity, seemed to be endowed with superhuman, immortal life. Against the end-wall was the buffet, a long table covered with an embroidered cloth and laden with fruit, pastry, and cold meats. Sheaves of flowers rose up amidst bottles of champagne, hot punch, and iced *sorbetto*, and here and there were marshalled armies of glasses, tea-cups, and broth-bowls, a perfect wealth of sparkling crystal, porcelain, and silver. And a happy innovation had been to fill half of the hall with rows of little tables, at which the guests, in lieu of being obliged to refresh themselves standing, were able to sit down and order what they desired as in a cafe.

At one of these little tables, Pierre perceived Narcisse seated near a young woman, whom Prada, on approaching, recognised to be Lisbeth. "You find me, you see, in delightful company," gallantly exclaimed the *attache*. "As we lost one another, I could think of nothing better than of offering madame my arm to bring her here."

"It was, in fact, a good idea," said Lisbeth with her pretty laugh, "for I was feeling very thirsty."

They had ordered some iced coffee, which they were slowly sipping out of little silver-gilt spoons.

"I have a terrible thirst, too," declared the Count, "and I can't quench it. You will allow us to join you, will you not, my dear sir? Some of that coffee will perhaps calm me." And then to Lisbeth he added, "Ah! my dear, allow me to introduce to you Monsieur l'Abbe Froment, a young French priest of great distinction."

Then for a long time they all four remained seated at that table, chatting and making merry over certain of the guests who went by. Prada, however, in spite of his usual gallantry towards Lisbeth, frequently became absent-minded; at times he quite forgot her, being again mastered by his anguish, and, in spite of all his efforts, his eyes ever turned towards the neighbouring gallery whence the sound of music and dancing reached him.

"Why, what are you thinking of, *caro mio*?" Lisbeth asked in her pretty way, on seeing him at one moment so pale and lost. "Are you indisposed?"

He did not reply, however, but suddenly exclaimed, "Ah! look there, that's the real pair, there's real love and happiness for you!"

With a jerk of the hand he designated Dario's mother, the Marchioness Montefiori and her second husband, Jules Laporte—that ex-sergeant of the papal Swiss Guard, her junior by fifteen years, whom she had one day hooked at the Corso with her eyes of fire, which yet had remained superb, and whom she had afterwards triumphantly transformed into a Marquis Montefiori in order to have him entirely to herself. Such was her passion that she never relaxed her hold on him whether at ball or reception, but, despite all usages, kept him beside her, and even made him escort her to the buffet, so much did she delight in being able to exhibit him and say that this handsome man was her own exclusive property. And standing there side by side, the pair of them began to drink champagne and eat sandwiches, she yet a marvel of massive beauty although she was over fifty, and he with long wavy moustaches, and proud bearing, like a fortunate adventurer whose jovial impudence pleased the ladies.

"You know that she had to extricate him from a nasty affair," resumed the Count in a lower tone. "Yes, he travelled in relics; he picked up a living by supplying relics on commission to convents in France and Switzerland; and he had launched quite a business in false relics with the help of some Jews here who concocted little ancient reliquaries out of mutton bones, with everything sealed and signed by the most genuine authorities. The affair was hushed up, as three prelates were also compromised in it! Ah! the happy man! Do you see how she devours him with her eyes? And he, doesn't he look quite a *grand seigneur* by the mere way in which he holds that plate for her whilst she eats the breast of a fowl out of it!"

Then, in a rough way and with biting irony, he went on to speak of the *amours* of Rome. The Roman women, said he, were ignorant, obstinate, and jealous. When a woman had managed to win a man, she kept him for ever, he became her property, and she disposed of him as she pleased. By way of proof, he cited many interminable *liaisons*, such as that of Donna Serafina and Morano which, in time became virtual marriages; and he sneered at such a lack of fancy, such an excess of fidelity whose only ending, when it did end, was some very disagreeable unpleasantness.

At this, Lisbeth interrupted him. "But what is the matter with you this evening, my dear?" she asked with a laugh. "What you speak of is on the contrary very nice and pretty! When a man and a woman love one another they ought to do so for ever!"

She looked delightful as she spoke, with her fine wavy blonde hair and delicate fair complexion; and Narcisse with a languorous expression in his half-closed eyes compared her to a Botticelli which he had seen at Florence. However, the night was now far advanced, and Pierre had once more sunk into gloomy thoughtfulness when he heard a passing lady remark that they had already begun to dance the Cotillon in the gallery; and thereupon he suddenly remembered that Monsignor Nani had given him an appointment in the little Saloon of the Mirrors.

"Are you leaving?" hastily inquired Prada on seeing him rise and bow to Lisbeth.

"No, no, not yet," Pierre answered.

"Oh! all right. Don't go away without me. I want to walk a little, and I'll see you home. It's agreed, eh? You will find me here."

XII.

The young priest had to cross two rooms, one hung with yellow and the other with blue, before he at last reached the mirrored *salon*. This was really an exquisite example of the *rococo* style, a rotunda as it were of pale mirrors framed with superb gilded carvings. Even the ceiling was covered with mirrors disposed slantwise so that on every side things multiplied, mingled, and appeared under all possible aspects. Discreetly enough no electric lights had been placed in the room, the only illumination being that of some pink tapers burning in a pair of candelabra. The hangings and upholstery were of soft blue silk, and the impression on entering was very sweet and charming, as if one had found oneself in the abode of some fairy queen of the rills, a palace of limpid water, illumined to its farthest depths by clusters of stars.

Pierre at once perceived Monsignor Nani, who was sitting on a low couch, and, as the prelate had hoped, he was quite alone, for the Cotillon had attracted almost everybody to the picture gallery. And the silence in the little *salon* was nearly perfect, for at that distance the blare of the orchestra subsided into a faint, flute-like murmur. The young priest at once apologised to the prelate for having kept him waiting.

"No, no, my dear son," said Nani, with his inexhaustible amiability. "I was very comfortable in this retreat—when the press of the crowd became over-threatening I took refuge here." He did not speak of the King and Queen, but he allowed it to be understood that he had politely avoided their company. If he had come to the *fete* it was on account of his sincere affection for Celia and also with a very delicate diplomatic object, for the Church wished to avoid any appearance of having entirely broken with the Buongiovanni family, that ancient house which was so famous in the annals of the papacy. Doubtless the Vatican was unable to subscribe to this marriage which seemed to unite old Rome with the young Kingdom of Italy, but on the other hand it did not desire people to think that it abandoned old and faithful supporters and took no interest in what befell them.

"But come, my dear son," the prelate resumed, "it is you who are now in question. I told you that although the Congregation of the Index had pronounced itself for the condemnation of your book, the sentence would only be submitted to the Holy Father and signed by him on the day after to-morrow. So you still have a whole day before you."

At this Pierre could not refrain from a dolorous and vivacious interruption.

"Alas! Monseigneur, what can I do?" said he; "I have thought it all over, and I see no means, no opportunity of defending myself. How could I even see his Holiness now that he is so ill?"

"Oh! ill, ill!" muttered Nani with his shrewd expression. "His Holiness is ever so much better, for this very day, like every other Wednesday, I had the honour to be received by him. When his Holiness is a little tired and people say that he is very ill, he often lets them do so, for it gives him a rest and enables him to judge certain ambitions and manifestations of impatience around him."

Pierre, however, was too upset to listen attentively. "No, it's all over," he continued, "I'm in despair. You spoke to me of the possibility of a miracle, but I am no great believer in miracles. Since I am defeated here at Rome, I shall go away, I shall return to Paris, and continue the struggle there. Oh! I cannot resign myself, my hope in salvation by the practice of love cannot die, and I shall answer my denouncers in a new book, in which I shall tell in what new soil the new religion will grow up!"

Silence fell. Nani looked at him with his clear eyes in which intelligence shone distinct and sharp like steel. And amidst the deep calm, the warm heavy atmosphere of the little *salon*, whose mirrors were starred with countless reflections of candles, a more sonorous burst of music was suddenly wafted from the gallery, a rhythmical waltz melody, which slowly expanded, then died away.

"My dear son," said Nani, "anger is always harmful. You remember that on your arrival here I promised that if your own efforts to obtain an interview with the Holy Father should prove unavailing, I would myself endeavour to secure an audience for you." Then, seeing how agitated the young priest was getting, he went on: "Listen to me and don't excite yourself. His Holiness, unfortunately, is not always prudently advised. Around him are persons whose devotion, however great, is at times deficient in intelligence. I told you that, and warned you against inconsiderate applications. And this is why, already three weeks ago, I myself handed your book to his Holiness in the hope that he would deign to glance at it. I rightly suspected that it had not been allowed to reach him. And this is what I am instructed to tell you: his Holiness, who has had the great kindness to read your book, expressly desires to see you."

A cry of joy and gratitude died away in Pierre's throat: "Ah! Monseigneur. Ah! Monseigneur!"

But Nani quickly silenced him and glanced around with an expression of keen anxiety as if he feared that some one might hear them. "Hush! Hush!" said he, "it is a secret. His Holiness wishes to see you privately, without taking anybody else into his confidence. Listen attentively. It is now two o'clock in the morning. Well, this very day, at nine in the evening precisely, you must present yourself at the Vatican and at every door ask for Signor Squadra. You will invariably be allowed to pass. Signor Squadra will be waiting for you upstairs, and will introduce you. And not a word, mind; not a soul must have the faintest suspicion of these things."

Pierre's happiness and gratitude at last flowed forth. He had caught hold of the prelate's soft, plump hands, and stammered, "Ah! Monseigneur, how can I express my gratitude to you? If you only knew how full my soul was of night and rebellion since I realised that I had been a mere plaything in the hands of those powerful cardinals. But you have saved me, and again I feel sure that I shall win the victory, for I shall at last be able to fling myself at the feet of his Holiness the father of all truth and all justice. He can but absolve me, I who love him, I who admire him, I who have never battled for aught but his own policy and most cherished ideas. No, no, it is impossible; he will not sign that judgment; he will not condemn my book!"

Releasing his hands, Nani sought to calm him with a fatherly gesture, whilst retaining a faint smile of contempt for such a useless expenditure of enthusiasm. At last he succeeded, and begged him to retire. The orchestra was again playing more loudly in the distance. And when the young priest at last withdrew, thanking him once more, he said very simply, "Remember, my dear son, that only obedience is great."

Pierre, whose one desire now was to take himself off, found Prada almost immediately afterwards in the first reception-room. Their Majesties had just left the ball in grand ceremony, escorted to the threshold by the Buongiovannis and the Saccos. And before departing the Queen had maternally kissed Celia, whilst the King shook hands with Attilio—honours instinct with a charming good nature which made the members of both families quite radiant. However, a good many of the guests were following the example of the sovereigns and disappearing in small batches. And the Count, who seemed strangely nervous, and showed more sternness and bitterness than ever, was, on his side, also eager to be gone. "Ah! it's you at last. I was waiting for you," he said to Pierre. "Well, let's get off at once, eh? Your compatriot Monsieur Narcisse Habert asked me to tell you not to look for him. The fact is, he has gone to see my friend Lisbeth to her carriage. I myself want a breath of fresh air, a stroll, and so I'll go with you as far as the Via Giulia."

Then, as they took their things from the cloak-room, he could not help sneering and saying in his brutal way: "I saw your good friends go off, all four together. It's lucky that you prefer to go home on foot, for there was no room for you in the carriage. What superb impudence it was on the part of that Donna Serafina to drag herself here, at her age, with that Morano of hers, so as to triumph over the return of the fickle one! And the two others, the two young ones—ah! I confess that I can hardly speak calmly of *them*, for in parading here together as they did this evening, they have shown an impudence and a cruelty such as is rarely seen!" Prada's hands trembled, and he murmured: "A good journey, a good journey to the young man, since he is going to Naples. Yes, I heard Celia say that he was starting for Naples this evening at six o'clock. Well, my wishes go with him; a good journey!"

The two men found the change delightful when they at last emerged from the stifling heat of the reception-rooms into the lovely, cool, and limpid night. It was a night illumined by a superb full moon, one of those matchless Roman nights when the city slumbers in Elysian radiance, steeped in a dream of the Infinite, under the vast vault of heaven. And they took the most agreeable route, going down the Corso proper and then turning into the Corso Vittorio Emanuele.

Prada had grown somewhat calmer, but remained full of irony. To divert his mind, no doubt, he talked on in the most voluble manner, reverting to the women of Rome and to that *fete* which he had at first found splendid, but at which he now began to rail.

"Oh! of course they have very fine gowns," said he, speaking of the women; "but gowns which don't fit them, gowns which are sent them from Paris, and which, of course, they can't try on. It's just the same with their jewels; they still have diamonds and pearls, in particular, which are very fine, but they are so wretchedly, so heavily mounted that they look frightful. And if you only knew how ignorant and frivolous these women are, despite all their conceit! Everything is on the surface with them, even religion: there's nothing beneath. I looked at them eating at the buffet. Oh! they at least have fine appetites. This evening some decorum was observed, there wasn't too much gorging. But at one of the Court balls you would see a general pillage, the buffets besieged, and everything swallowed up amidst a scramble of amazing voracity!"

To all this talk Pierre only returned monosyllabic responses. He was wrapped in overflowing delight at the thought of that audience with the Pope, which, unable as he was to confide in any one, he strove to arrange and picture in his own mind, even in its pettiest details. And meantime the footsteps of the two men rang out on the dry pavement of the clear, broad, deserted thoroughfare, whose black shadows were sharply outlined by the moonlight.

All at once Prada himself became silent. His loquacious *bravura* was exhausted, the frightful struggle going on in his mind wholly possessed and paralysed him. Twice already he had dipped his hand into his coat pocket and felt the pencilled note whose four lines he mentally repeated: "A legend avers that the fig-tree of Judas now grows at Frascati, and that its fruit is deadly for him who may desire to become pope. Eat not the poisoned figs, nor give them either to your servants or your fowls." The note was there; he could feel it; and if he had desired to accompany Pierre, it was in order that he might drop it into the letter-box at the Palazzo Boccanera. And he continued to step out briskly, so that within another ten minutes that note would surely be in the box, for no power in the world could prevent it, since such was his express determination. Never would he commit such a crime as to allow people to be poisoned.

But he was suffering such abominable torture. That Benedetta and that Dario had raised such a tempest of jealous hatred within him! For them he forgot Lisbeth whom he loved, and even that flesh of his flesh, the child of whom he was so proud. All sex as he was, eager to conquer and subdue, he had never cared for facile loves. His passion was to overcome. And now there was a woman in the world who defied him, a woman forsooth whom he had bought, whom he had married, who had been handed over to him, but who would never, never be his. Ah! in the old days, to subdue her, he would if needful have fired Rome like a Nero; but now he asked himself what he could possibly do to prevent her from belonging to another. That galling thought made the blood gush from his gaping wound. How that woman and her lover must deride him! And to think that they had sought to turn him to ridicule by a baseless charge, an arrant lie which still and ever made him smart, all proof of its falsity to the contrary. He, on his side, had accused them in the past without much belief in what he said, but now the charges he had imputed to them must come true, for they were free, freed at all events of the religious bond, and that no doubt was their only care. And then visions of their happiness passed before his eyes, infuriating him. Ah! no, ah! no, it was impossible, he would rather destroy the world!

Then, as he and Pierre turned out of the Corso Vittorio Emanuele to thread the old narrow tortuous streets leading to the Via Giulia, he pictured himself dropping the note into the letter-box at the palazzo. And next he conjured up what would follow. The note would lie in the letter-box till morning. At an early hour Don Vigilio, the secretary, who by the Cardinal's express orders kept the key of the box, would come down, find the note, and hand it to his Eminence, who never allowed another to open any communication addressed to him. And then the figs would be thrown away, there would be no further possibility of crime, the black world would in all prudence keep silent. But if the note should not be in the letter-box, what would happen then? And admitting that supposition he pictured the figs placed on the table at the one o'clock meal, in their pretty little leaf-covered basket. Dario would be there as usual, alone with his uncle, since he was not to leave for Naples till the evening. And would both the uncle and the nephew eat the figs, or would only one of them partake of the fruit, and which of them would that be? At this point Prada's clearness of vision failed him; again he conjured up Destiny on the march, that Destiny which he had met on the road from Frascati, going on towards its unknown goal, athwart all obstacles without possibility of stoppage. Aye, the little basket of figs went ever on and on to accomplish its fateful purpose, which no hand in the world had power enough to prevent.

And at last, on either hand of Pierre and Prada, the Via Giulia stretched away in a long line white with moonlight, and the priest emerged as if from a dream at sight of the Palazzo Boccanera rising blackly under the silver sky. Three o'clock struck at a neighbouring church. And he felt himself quivering slightly as once again he heard near him the dolorous moan of a lion wounded unto death, that low involuntary growl which the Count, amidst the frightful struggle of his feelings, had for the third time allowed to escape him. But immediately afterwards he burst into a sneering laugh, and pressing the priest's hands, exclaimed: "No, no, I am not going farther. If I were seen here at this hour, people would think that I had fallen in love with my wife again."

And thereupon he lighted a cigar, and retraced his steps in the clear night, without once looking round.

XIII.

WHEN Pierre awoke he was much surprised to hear eleven o'clock striking. Fatigued as he was by that ball where he had lingered so long, he had slept like a child in delightful peacefulness, and as soon as he opened his eyes the radiant sunshine filled him with hope. His first thought was that he would see the Pope that evening at nine o'clock. Ten more hours to wait! What would he be able to do with himself during that lovely day, whose radiant sky seemed to him of such happy augury? He rose and opened the windows to admit the warm air which, as he had noticed on the day of his arrival, had a savour of fruit and flowers, a blending, as it were, of the perfume of rose and orange. Could this possibly be December? What a delightful land, that the spring should seem to flower on the very threshold of winter! Then, having dressed, he was leaning out of the window to glance across the golden Tiber at the evergreen slopes of the Janiculum, when he espied Benedetta seated in the abandoned garden of the mansion. And thereupon, unable to keep still, full of a desire for life, gaiety, and beauty, he went down to join her.

With radiant visage and outstretched hands, she at once vented the cry he had expected: "Ah! my dear Abbe, how happy I am!"

They had often spent their mornings in that quiet, forsaken nook; but what sad mornings those had been, hopeless as they both were! To-day, however, the weed-grown paths, the box-plants growing in the old basin, the orange-trees which alone marked the outline of the beds—all seemed full of charm, instinct with a sweet and dreamy cosiness in which it was very pleasant to lull one's joy. And it was so warm, too, beside the big laurel-bush, in the corner where the streamlet of water ever fell with flute-like music from the gaping, tragic mask.

"Ah!" repeated Benedetta, "how happy I am! I was stifling upstairs, and my heart felt such a need of space, and air, and sunlight, that I came down here!"

She was seated on the fallen column beside the old marble sarcophagus, and desired the priest to place himself beside her. Never had he seen her looking so beautiful, with her black hair encompassing her pure face, which in the sunshine appeared pinky and delicate as a flower. Her large, fathomless eyes showed in the light like braziers rolling gold, and her childish mouth, all candour and good sense, laughed the laugh of one who was at last free to love as her heart listed, without offending either God or man. And, dreaming aloud, she built up plans for the future. "It's all simple enough," said she; "I have already obtained a separation, and shall easily get that changed into civil divorce now that the Church has annulled my marriage. And I shall marry Dario next spring, perhaps sooner, if the formalities can be hastened. He is going to Naples this evening about the sale of some property which we still possess there, but which must now be sold, for all this business has cost us a lot of money. Still, that doesn't matter since we now belong to one another. And when he comes back in a few days, what a happy time we shall have! I could not sleep when I got back from that splendid ball last night, for my head was so full of plans—oh! splendid plans, as you shall see, for I mean to keep you in Rome until our marriage."

Like herself, Pierre began to laugh, so gained upon by this explosion of youth and happiness that he had to make a great effort to refrain from speaking of his own delight, his hopefulness at the thought of his coming interview with the Pope. Of that, however, he had sworn to speak to nobody.

Every now and again, amidst the quivering silence of the sunlit garden, the cry of a bird persistently rang out; and Benedetta, raising her head and looking at a cage hanging beside one of the first-floor windows, jestingly exclaimed: "Yes, yes, Tata, make a good noise, show that you are pleased, my dear. Everybody in the house must be pleased now." Then, turning towards Pierre, she added gaily: "You know Tata, don't you? What! No? Why, Tata is my uncle's parrot. I gave her to him last spring; he's very fond of her, and lets her help herself out of his plate. And he himself attends to her, puts her out and takes her in, and keeps her in his dining-room, for fear lest she should take cold, as that is the only room of his which is at all warm."

Pierre in his turn looked up and saw the bird, one of those pretty little parrots with soft, silky, dull-green plumage. It was hanging by the beak from a bar of its cage, swinging itself and flapping its wings, all mirth in the bright sunshine.

"Does the bird talk?" he asked.

"No, she only screams," replied Benedetta, laughing. "Still my uncle pretends that he understands her." And then the young woman abruptly darted to another subject, as if this mention of her uncle the Cardinal had made her think of the uncle by marriage whom she had in Paris. "I suppose you have heard from Viscount de la Choue," said she. "I had a letter from him yesterday, in which he said how grieved he was that you were unable to see the Holy Father, as he had counted on you for the triumph of his ideas."

Pierre indeed frequently heard from the Viscount, who was greatly distressed by the importance which his adversary, Baron de Fouras, had acquired since his success with the International Pilgrimage of the Peter's Pence. The old, uncompromising Catholic party would awaken, said the Viscount, and all the conquests of Neo-Catholicism would be threatened, if one could not obtain the Holy Father's formal adhesion to the proposed system of free guilds, in order to overcome the demand for closed guilds which was brought forward by the Conservatives. And the Viscount overwhelmed Pierre with injunctions, and sent him all sorts of complicated plans in his eagerness to see him received at the Vatican. "Yes, yes," muttered the young priest in reply to Benedetta. "I had a letter on Sunday, and found another waiting for me on my return from Frascati yesterday. Ah! it would make me very happy to be able to send the Viscount some good news." Then again Pierre's joy overflowed at the thought that he would that evening see the Pope, and, on opening his loving heart to the Pontiff, receive the supreme encouragement which would strengthen him in his mission to work social salvation in the name of the lowly and the poor. And he could not restrain himself any longer, but let his secret escape him: "It's settled, you know," said he. "My audience is for this evening."

Benedetta did not understand at first. "What audience?" she asked.

"Oh! Monsignor Nani was good enough to tell me at the ball this morning, that the Holy Father has read my book and desires to see me. I shall be received this evening at nine o'clock."

At this the Contessina flushed with pleasure, participating in the delight of the young priest to whom she had grown much attached. And this success of his, coming in the midst of her own felicity, acquired extraordinary importance in her eyes as if it were an augury of complete success for one and all. Superstitious as she was, she raised a cry of rapture and excitement: "Ah! *Dio*, that will bring us good luck. How happy I am, my friend, to see happiness coming to you at the same time as to me! You cannot think how pleased I am! And all will go well now, it's certain, for a house where there is any one whom the Pope welcomes is blessed, the thunder of Heaven falls on it no more!"

She laughed yet more loudly as she spoke, and clapped her hands with such exuberant gaiety that Pierre became anxious. "Hush! hush!" said he, "it's a secret. Pray don't mention it to any one, either your aunt or even his Eminence. Monsignor Nani would be much annoyed."

She thereupon promised to say nothing, and in a kindly voice spoke of Nani as a benefactor, for was she not indebted to him for the dissolution of her marriage? Then, with a fresh explosion of gaiety, she went on: "But come, my friend, is not happiness the only good thing? You don't ask me to weep over the suffering poor to-day! Ah! the happiness of life, that's everything. People don't suffer or feel cold or hungry when they are happy."

He looked at her in stupefaction at the idea of that strange solution of the terrible question of human misery. And suddenly he realised that, with that daughter of the sun who had inherited so many centuries of sovereign aristocracy, all his endeavours at conversion were vain. He had wished to bring her to a Christian love for the lowly and the wretched, win her over to the new, enlightened, and compassionate Italy that he had dreamt of; but if she had been moved by the sufferings of the multitude at the time when she herself had suffered, when grievous wounds had made her own heart bleed, she was no sooner healed than she proclaimed the doctrine of universal felicity like a true daughter of a clime of burning summers, and winters as mild as spring. "But everybody is not happy!" said he.

"Yes, yes, they are!" she exclaimed. "You don't know the poor! Give a girl of the Trastevere the lad she loves, and she becomes as radiant as a queen, and finds her dry bread quite sweet. The mothers who save a child from sickness, the men who conquer in a battle, or who win at the lottery, one and all in fact are like that, people only ask for good fortune and pleasure. And despite all your striving to be just and to arrive at a more even distribution of fortune, the only satisfied ones will be those whose hearts sing—often without their knowing the cause—on a fine sunny day like this."

Pierre made a gesture of surrender, not wishing to sadden her by again pleading the cause of all the poor ones who at that very moment were somewhere agonising with physical or mental pain. But, all at once, through the luminous mild atmosphere a shadow seemed to fall, tingeing joy with sadness, the sunshine with despair. And the sight of the old sarcophagus, with its bacchanal of satyrs and nymphs, brought back the memory that death lurks even amidst the bliss of passion, the unsatiated kisses of love. For a moment the clear song of the water sounded in Pierre's ears like a long-drawn sob, and all seemed to crumble in the terrible shadow which had fallen from the invisible.

Benedetta, however, caught hold of his hands and roused him once more to the delight of being there beside her. "Your pupil is rebellious, is she not, my friend?" said she. "But what would you have? There are ideas which can't enter into our heads. No, you will never get those things into the head of a Roman girl. So be content with loving us as we are, beautiful with all our strength, as beautiful as we can be."

She herself, in her resplendent happiness, looked at that moment so beautiful that he trembled as in presence of a divinity whose all-powerfulness swayed the world. "Yes, yes," he stammered, "beauty, beauty, still and ever sovereign. Ah! why can it not suffice to satisfy the eternal longings of poor suffering men?"

"Never mind!" she gaily responded. "Do not distress yourself; it is pleasant to live. And now let us go upstairs, my aunt must be waiting."

The midday meal was served at one o'clock, and on the few occasions when Pierre did not eat at one or another restaurant a cover was laid for him at the ladies' table in the little dining-room of the second floor, overlooking the courtyard. At the same hour, in the sunlit dining-room of the first floor, whose windows faced the Tiber, the Cardinal likewise sat down to table, happy in the society of his nephew Dario, for his secretary, Don Vigilio, who also was usually present, never opened his mouth unless to reply to some question. And the two services were quite distinct, each having its own kitchen and servants, the only thing at all common to them both being a large room downstairs which served as a pantry and store-place.

Although the second-floor dining-room was so gloomy, saddened by the greeny half-light of the courtyard, the meal shared that day by the two ladies and the young priest proved a very gay one. Even Donna Serafina, usually so rigid, seemed to relax under the influence of great internal felicity. She was no doubt still enjoying her triumph of the previous evening, and it was she who first spoke of the ball and sung its praises, though the presence of the King and Queen had much embarrassed her, said she. According to her account, she had only avoided presentation by skilful strategy; however she hoped that her well-known affection for Celia, whose god-mother she was, would explain her presence in that neutral mansion where Vatican and Quirinal had met. At the same time she must have retained certain scruples, for she declared that directly after dinner she was going to the Vatican to see the Cardinal Secretary, to whom she desired to speak about an enterprise of which she was lady-patroness. This visit would compensate for her attendance at the Buongiovanni entertainment. And on the other hand never had Donna Serafina seemed so zealous and hopeful of her brother's speedy accession to the throne of St. Peter: therein lay a supreme triumph, an elevation of her race, which her pride deemed both needful and inevitable; and indeed during Leo XIII's last indisposition she had actually concerned herself about the trousseau which would be needed and which would require to be marked with the new Pontiff's arms.

On her side, Benedetta was all gaiety during the repast, laughing at everything, and speaking of Celia and Attilio with the passionate affection of a woman whose own happiness delights in that of her friends. Then, just as the dessert had been served, she turned to the servant with an air of surprise: "Well, and the figs, Giacomo?" she asked.

Giacomo, slow and sleepy of notion, looked at her without understanding. However, Victorine was crossing the room, and Benedetta's next question was for her: "Why are the figs not served, Victorine?" she inquired.

"What figs, Contessina?"

"Why the figs I saw in the pantry as I passed through it this morning on my way to the garden. They were in a little basket and looked superb. I was even astonished to see that there were still some fresh figs left at this season. I'm very fond of them, and felt quite pleased at the thought that I should eat some at dinner."

Victorine began to laugh: "Ah! yes, Contessina, I understand," she replied. "They were some figs which that priest of Frascati, whom you know very well, brought yesterday evening as a present for his Eminence. I was there, and I heard him repeat three or four times that they were a present, and were to be put on his Eminence's table without a leaf being touched. And so one did as he said."

"Well, that's nice," retorted Benedetta with comical indignation. "What *gourmands* my uncle and Dario are to regale themselves without us! They might have given us a share!"

Donna Serafina thereupon intervened, and asked Victorine: "You are speaking, are you not, of that priest who used to come to the villa at Frascati?"

"Yes, yes, Abbe Santobono his name is, he officiates at the little church of St. Mary in the Fields. He always asks for Abbe Paparelli when he calls; I think they were at the seminary together. And it was Abbe Paparelli who brought him to the pantry with his basket last night. To tell the truth, the basket was forgotten there in spite of all the injunctions, so that nobody would have eaten the figs to-day if Abbe Paparelli hadn't run down just now and carried them upstairs as piously as if they were the Blessed Sacrament. It's true though that his Eminence is so fond of them."

"My brother won't do them much honour to-day," remarked the Princess. "He is slightly indisposed. He passed a bad night." The repeated mention of Abbe Paparelli had made the old lady somewhat thoughtful. She had regarded the train-bearer with displeasure ever since she had noticed the extraordinary influence he was gaining over the Cardinal, despite all his apparent humility and self-effacement. He was but a servant and apparently a very insignificant one, yet he governed, and she could feel that he combated her own influence, often undoing things which she had done to further her brother's interests. Twice already, moreover, she had suspected him of having urged the Cardinal to courses which she looked upon as absolute blunders. But perhaps she was wrong; she did the train-bearer the justice to admit that he had great merits and displayed exemplary piety.

However, Benedetta went on laughing and jesting, and as Victorine had now withdrawn, she called the man-servant: "Listen, Giacomo, I have a commission for you." Then she broke off to say to her aunt and Pierre: "Pray let us assert our rights. I can see them at table almost underneath us. Uncle is taking the leaves off the basket and serving himself with a smile; then he passes the basket to Dario, who passes it on to Don Vigilio. And all three of them eat and enjoy the figs. You can see them, can't you?" She herself could see them well. And it was her desire to be near Dario, the constant flight of her thoughts to him that now made her picture him at table with the others. Her heart was down below, and there was nothing there that she could not see, and hear, and smell, with such keenness of the senses did her love endow her. "Giacomo," she resumed, "you are to go down and tell his Eminence that we are longing to taste his figs, and that it will be very kind of him if he will send us such as he can spare."

Again, however, did Donna Serafina intervene, recalling her wonted severity of voice: "Giacomo, you will please stay here." And to her niece she added: "That's enough childishness! I dislike such silly freaks."

"Oh! aunt," Benedetta murmured. "But I'm so happy, it's so long since I laughed so good-heartedly."

Pierre had hitherto remained listening, enlivened by the sight of her gaiety. But now, as a little chill fell, he raised his voice to say that on the previous day he himself had been astonished to see the famous fig-tree of Frascati still bearing fruit so late in the year. This was doubtless due, however, to the tree's position and the protection of a high wall.

"Ah! so you saw the tree?" said Benedetta.

"Yes, and I even travelled with those figs which you would so much like to taste."

"Why, how was that?"

The young man already regretted the reply which had escaped him. However, having gone so far, he preferred to say everything. "I met somebody at Frascati who had come there in a carriage and who insisted on driving me back to Rome," said he. "On the way we picked up Abbe Santobono, who was bravely making the journey on foot with his basket in his hand. And afterwards we stopped at an *osteria*—" Then he went on to describe the drive and relate his impressions whilst crossing the Campagna amidst the falling twilight. But Benedetta gazed at him fixedly, aware as she was of Prada's frequent visits to the land and houses which he owned at Frascati; and suddenly she murmured: "Somebody, somebody, it was the Count, was it not?"

"Yes, madame, the Count," Pierre answered. "I saw him again last night; he was overcome, and really deserves to be pitied."

The two women took no offence at this charitable remark which fell from the young priest with such deep and natural emotion, full as he was of overflowing love and compassion for one and all. Donna Serafina remained motionless as if she had not even heard him, and Benedetta made a gesture which seemed to imply that she had neither pity nor hatred to express for a man who had become a perfect stranger to her. However, she no longer laughed, but, thinking of the little basket which had travelled in Prada's carriage, she said: "Ah! I don't care for those figs at all now, I am even glad that I haven't eaten any of them."

Immediately after the coffee Donna Serafina withdrew, saying that she was at once going to the Vatican; and the others, being left to themselves, lingered at table, again full of gaiety, and chatting like friends. The priest, with his feverish impatience, once more referred to the audience which he was to have that evening. It was now barely two o'clock, and he had seven more hours to wait. How should he employ that endless afternoon? Thereupon Benedetta good-naturedly made him a proposal. "I'll tell you what," said she, "as we are all in such good spirits we mustn't leave one another. Dario has his victoria, you know. He must have finished lunch by now, and I'll ask him to take us for a long drive along the Tiber."

This fine project so delighted her that she began to clap her hands; but just then Don Vigilio appeared with a scared look on his face. "Isn't the Princess here?" he inquired.

"No, my aunt has gone out. What is the matter?"

"His Eminence sent me. The Prince has just felt unwell on rising from table. Oh! it's nothing—nothing serious, no doubt."

Benedetta raised a cry of surprise rather than anxiety: "What, Dario! Well, we'll all go down. Come with me, Monsieur l'Abbe. He mustn't get ill if he is to take us for a drive!" Then, meeting Victorine on the stairs, she bade her follow. "Dario isn't well," she said. "You may be wanted."

They all four entered the spacious, antiquated, and simply furnished bed-room where the young Prince had lately been laid up for a whole month. It was reached by way of a small *salon*, and from an adjoining dressing-room a passage conducted to the Cardinal's apartments, the relatively small dining-room, bed-room, and study, which had been devised by subdividing one of the huge galleries of former days. In addition, the passage gave access to his Eminence's private chapel, a bare, uncarpeted, chairless room, where there was nothing beyond the painted, wooden altar, and the hard, cold tiles on which to kneel and pray.

On entering, Benedetta hastened to the bed where Dario was lying, still fully dressed. Near him, in fatherly fashion, stood Cardinal Boccanera, who, amidst his dawning anxiety, retained his proud and lofty bearing—the calmness of a soul beyond reproach. "Why, what is the matter, Dario *mio*?" asked the young woman.

He smiled, eager to reassure her. One only noticed that he was very pale, with a look as of intoxication on his face.

"Oh! it's nothing, mere giddiness," he replied. "It's just as if I had drunk too much. All at once things swam before my eyes, and I thought I was going to fall. And then I only had time to come and fling myself on the bed."

Then he drew a long breath, as though talking exhausted him, and the Cardinal in his turn gave some details. "We had just finished our meal," said he, "I was giving Don Vigilio some orders for this afternoon, and was about to rise when I saw Dario get up and reel. He wouldn't sit down again, but came in here, staggering like a somnambulist, and fumbling at the doors to open them. We followed him without understanding. And I confess that I don't yet comprehend it."

So saying, the Cardinal punctuated his surprise by waving his arm towards the rooms, through which a gust of misfortune seemed to have suddenly swept. All the doors had remained wide open: the dressing-room could be seen, and then the passage, at the end of which appeared the dining-room, in a disorderly state, like an apartment suddenly vacated; the table still laid, the napkins flung here and there, and the chairs pushed back. As yet, however, there was no alarm.

Benedetta made the remark which is usually made in such cases: "I hope you haven't eaten anything which has disagreed with you."

The Cardinal, smiling, again waved his hand as if to attest the frugality of his table. "Oh!" said he, "there were only some eggs, some lamb cutlets, and a dish of sorrel—they couldn't have overloaded his stomach. I myself only drink water; he takes just a sip of white wine. No, no, the food has nothing to do with it."

"Besides, in that case his Eminence and I would also have felt indisposed," Don Vigilio made bold to remark.

XIII.

Dario, after momentarily closing his eyes, opened them again, and once more drew a long breath, whilst endeavouring to laugh. "Oh, it will be nothing;" he said. "I feel more at ease already. I must get up and stir myself."

"In that case," said Benedetta, "this is what I had thought of. You will take Monsieur l'Abbe Froment and me for a long drive in the Campagna."

"Willingly. It's a nice idea. Victorine, help me."

Whilst speaking he had raised himself by means of one arm; but, before the servant could approach, a slight convulsion seized him, and he fell back again as if overcome by a fainting fit. It was the Cardinal, still standing by the bedside, who caught him in his arms, whilst the Contessina this time lost her head: "*Dio, Dio*! It has come on him again. Quick, quick, a doctor!"

"Shall I run for one?" asked Pierre, whom the scene was also beginning to upset.

"No, no, not you; stay with me. Victorine will go at once. She knows the address. Doctor Giordano, Victorine."

The servant hurried away, and a heavy silence fell on the room where the anxiety became more pronounced every moment. Benedetta, now quite pale, had again approached the bed, whilst the Cardinal looked down at Dario, whom he still held in his arms. And a terrible suspicion, vague, indeterminate as yet, had just awoke in the old man's mind: Dario's face seemed to him to be ashen, to wear that mask of terrified anguish which he had already remarked on the countenance of his dearest friend, Monsignor Gallo, when he had held him in his arms, in like manner, two hours before his death. There was also the same swoon and the same sensation of clasping a cold form whose heart ceases to beat. And above everything else there was in Boccanera's mind the same growing thought of poison, poison coming one knew not whence or how, but mysteriously striking down those around him with the suddenness of lightning. And for a long time he remained with his head bent over the face of his nephew, that last scion of his race, seeking, studying, and recognising the signs of the mysterious, implacable disorder which once already had rent his heart atwain.

But Benedetta addressed him in a low, entreating voice: "You will tire yourself, uncle. Let me take him a little, I beg you. Have no fear, I'll hold him very gently, he will feel that it is I, and perhaps that will rouse him."

At last the Cardinal raised his head and looked at her, and allowed her to take his place after kissing her with distracted passion, his eyes the while full of tears—a sudden burst of emotion in which his great love for the young woman melted the stern frigidity which he usually affected. "Ah! my poor child, my poor child!" he stammered, trembling from head to foot like an oak-tree about to fall. Immediately afterwards, however, he mastered himself, and whilst Pierre and Don Vigilio, mute and motionless, regretted that they could be of no help, he walked slowly to and fro. Soon, moreover, that bed-chamber became too small for all the thoughts revolving in his mind, and he strayed first into the dressing-room and then down the passage as far as the dining-room. And again and again he went to and fro, grave and impassible, his head low, ever lost in the same gloomy reverie. What were the multitudinous thoughts stirring in the brain of that believer, that haughty Prince who had given himself to God and could do naught to stay inevitable Destiny? From time to time he returned to the bedside, observed the progress of the disorder, and then started off again at the same slow regular pace, disappearing and reappearing, carried along as it were by the monotonous alternations of forces which man cannot control. Possibly he was mistaken, possibly this was some mere indisposition at which the doctor would smile. One must hope and wait. And again he went off and again he came back; and amidst the heavy silence nothing more clearly bespoke the torture of anxious fear than the rhythmical footsteps of that tall old man who was thus awaiting Destiny.

The door opened, and Victorine came in breathless. "I found the doctor, here he is," she gasped.

With his little pink face and white curls, his discreet paternal bearing which gave him the air of an amiable prelate, Doctor Giordano came in smiling; but on seeing that room and all the anxious people waiting in it, he turned very grave, at once assuming the expression of profound respect for all ecclesiastical secrets which he had acquired by long practice among the clergy. And when he had glanced at the sufferer he let but a low murmur escape him: "What, again! Is it beginning again!"

He was probably alluding to the knife thrust for which he had recently tended Dario. Who could be thus relentlessly pursuing that poor and inoffensive young prince? However no one heard the doctor unless it were Benedetta, and she was so full of feverish impatience, so eager to be tranquillised, that she did not listen but burst into fresh entreaties: "Oh! doctor, pray look at him, examine him, tell us that it is nothing. It can't be anything serious, since he was so well and gay but a little while ago. It's nothing serious, is it?"

"You are right no doubt, Contessina, it can be nothing dangerous. We will see."

However, on turning round, Doctor Giordano perceived the Cardinal, who with regular, thoughtful footsteps had come back from the dining-room to place himself at the foot of the bed. And while bowing, the doctor doubtless detected a gleam of mortal anxiety in the dark eyes fixed upon his own, for he added nothing but began to examine Dario like a man who realises that time is precious. And as his examination progressed the affable optimism which usually appeared upon his countenance gave place to ashen gravity, a covert terror which made his lips slightly tremble. It was he who had attended Monsignor Gallo when the latter had been carried off so mysteriously; it was he who for imperative reasons had then delivered a certificate stating the cause of death to be infectious fever; and doubtless he now found the same terrible symptoms as in that case, a leaden hue overspreading the sufferer's features, a stupor as of excessive intoxication; and, old Roman practitioner that he was, accustomed to sudden deaths, he realised that the *malaria* which kills was passing, that *malaria* which science does not yet fully understand, which may come from the putrescent exhalations of the Tiber unless it be but a name for the ancient poison of the legends.

As the doctor raised his head his glance again encountered the black eyes of the Cardinal, which never left him. "Signor Giordano," said his Eminence, "you are not over-anxious, I hope? It is only some case of indigestion, is it not?"

The doctor again bowed. By the slight quiver of the Cardinal's voice he understood how acute was the anxiety of that powerful man, who once more was stricken in his dearest affections.

"Your Eminence must be right," he said, "there's a bad digestion certainly. Such accidents sometimes become dangerous when fever supervenes. I need not tell your Eminence how thoroughly you may rely on my prudence and zeal." Then he broke off and added in a clear professional voice: "We must lose no time; the Prince must be undressed. I should prefer to remain alone with him for a moment."

XIII.

Whilst speaking in this way, however, Doctor Giordano detained Victorine, who would be able to help him, said he; should he need any further assistance he would take Giacomo. His evident desire was to get rid of the members of the family in order that he might have more freedom of action. And the Cardinal, who understood him, gently led Benedetta into the dining-room, whither Pierre and Don Vigilio followed.

When the doors had been closed, the most mournful and oppressive silence reigned in that dining-room, which the bright sun of winter filled with such delightful warmth and radiance. The table was still laid, its cloth strewn here and there with bread-crumbs; and a coffee cup had remained half full. In the centre stood the basket of figs, whose covering of leaves had been removed. However, only two or three of the figs were missing. And in front of the window was Tata, the female parrot, who had flown out of her cage and perched herself on her stand, where she remained, dazzled and enraptured, amidst the dancing dust of a broad yellow sunray. In her astonishment however, at seeing so many people enter, she had ceased to scream and smooth her feathers, and had turned her head the better to examine the newcomers with her round and scrutinising eye.

The minutes went by slowly amidst all the feverish anxiety as to what might be occurring in the neighbouring room. Don Vigilio had taken a corner seat in silence, whilst Benedetta and Pierre, who had remained standing, preserved similar muteness, and immobility. But the Cardinal had reverted to that instinctive, lulling tramp by which he apparently hoped to quiet his impatience and arrive the sooner at the explanation for which he was groping through a tumultuous maze of ideas. And whilst his rhythmical footsteps resounded with mechanical regularity, dark fury was taking possession of his mind, exasperation at being unable to understand the why and wherefore of that sickness. As he passed the table he had twice glanced at the things lying on it in confusion, as if seeking some explanation from them. Perhaps the harm had been done by that unfinished coffee, or by that bread whose crumbs lay here and there, or by those cutlets, a bone of which remained? Then as for the third time he passed by, again glancing, his eyes fell upon the basket of figs, and at once he stopped, as if beneath the shock of a revelation. An idea seized upon him and mastered him, without any plan, however, occurring to him by which he might change his sudden suspicion into certainty. For a moment he remained puzzled with his eyes fixed upon the basket. Then he took a fig and examined it, but, noticing nothing strange, was about to put it back when Tata, the parrot, who was very fond of figs, raised a strident cry. And this was like a ray of light; the means of changing suspicion into certainty was found.

Slowly, with grave air and gloomy visage, the Cardinal carried the fig to the parrot and gave it to her without hesitation or regret. She was a very pretty bird, the only being of the lower order of creation to which he had ever really been attached. Stretching out her supple, delicate form, whose silken feathers of dull green here and there assumed a pinky tinge in the sunlight, she took hold of the fig with her claws, then ripped it open with her beak. But when she had raked it she ate but little, and let all the rest fall upon the floor. Still grave and impassible, the Cardinal looked at her and waited. Quite three minutes went by, and then feeling reassured, he began to scratch the bird's poll, whilst she, taking pleasure in the caress, turned her neck and fixed her bright ruby eye upon her master. But all at once she sank back without even a flap of the wings, and fell like a bullet. She was dead, killed as by a thunderbolt.

Boccanera made but a gesture, raising both hands to heaven as if in horror at what he now knew. Great God! such a terrible crime, and such a fearful mistake, such an abominable trick of Destiny! No cry of grief came from him, but the gloom upon his face grew black and fierce. Yet there was a cry, a piercing cry from Benedetta, who like Pierre and Don Vigilio had watched the Cardinal with an astonishment which had changed into terror: "Poison! poison! Ah! Dario, my heart, my soul!"

But the Cardinal violently caught his niece by the wrist, whilst darting a suspicious glance at the two petty priests, the secretary and the foreigner, who were present: "Be quiet, be quiet!" said he.

She shook herself free, rebelling, frantic with rage and hatred: "Why should I be quiet!" she cried. "It is Prada's work, I shall denounce him, he shall die as well! I tell you it is Prada, I know it, for yesterday Abbe Froment came back with him from Frascati in his carriage with that priest Santobono and that basket of figs! Yes, yes, I have witnesses, it is Prada, Prada!"

"No, no, you are mad, be quiet!" said the Cardinal, who had again taken hold of the young woman's hands and sought to master her with all his sovereign authority. He, who knew the influence which Cardinal Sanguinetti exercised over Santobono's excitable mind, had just understood the whole affair; no direct complicity but covert propulsion, the animal excited and then let loose upon the troublesome rival at the moment when the pontifical throne seemed likely to be vacant. The probability, the certainty of all this flashed upon Boccanera who, though some points remained obscure, did not seek to penetrate them. It was not necessary indeed that he should know every particular: the thing was as he said, since it was bound to be so. "No, no, it was not Prada," he exclaimed, addressing Benedetta. "That man can bear me no personal grudge, and I alone was aimed at, it was to me that those figs were given. Come, think it out! Only an unforeseen indisposition prevented me from eating the greater part of the fruit, for it is known that I am very fond of figs, and while my poor Dario was tasting them, I jested and told him to leave the finer ones for me to-morrow. Yes, the abominable blow was meant for me, and it is on him that it has fallen by the most atrocious of chances, the most monstrous of the follies of fate. Ah! Lord God, Lord God, have you then forsaken us!"

Tears came into the old man's eyes, whilst she still quivered and seemed unconvinced: "But you have no enemies, uncle," she said. "Why should that Santobono try to take your life?"

For a moment he found no fitting reply. With supreme grandeur he had already resolved to keep the truth secret. Then a recollection came to him, and he resigned himself to the telling of a lie: "Santobono's mind has always been somewhat unhinged," said he, "and I know that he has hated me ever since I refused to help him to get a brother of his, one of our former gardeners, out of prison. Deadly spite often has no more serious cause. He must have thought that he had reason to be revenged on me."

Thereupon Benedetta, exhausted, unable to argue any further, sank upon a chair with a despairing gesture: "Ah! God, God! I no longer know—and what matters it now that my Dario is in such danger? There's only one thing to be done, he must be saved. How long they are over what they are doing in that room—why does not Victorine come for us!"

The silence again fell, full of terror. Without speaking the Cardinal took the basket of figs from the table and carried it to a cupboard in which he locked it. Then he put the key in his pocket. No doubt, when night had fallen, he himself would throw the proofs of the crime into the Tiber. However, on coming back from the cupboard he noticed the two priests, who naturally had watched him; and with mingled grandeur and simplicity he said to them: "Gentlemen, I need not ask you to be discreet. There are scandals which we must spare the Church, which is not, cannot be guilty. To deliver one of ourselves, even when he is a criminal, to the civil tribunals, often means a blow for the whole Church, for men of evil mind may lay hold of the affair and seek to impute the responsibility of the crime even to the Church itself. We therefore have but to commit the murderer to the hands of God, who will know more surely how to punish him. Ah! for my part, whether I be struck in my own person or whether the blow be directed against my family, my dearest affections, I declare in the name of the Christ who died upon the cross, that I feel neither anger, nor desire for vengeance, that I efface the murderer's name from my memory and bury his abominable act in the eternal silence of the grave."

Tall as he was, he seemed of yet loftier stature whilst with hand upraised he took that oath to leave his enemies to the justice of God alone; for he did not refer merely to Santobono, but to Cardinal Sanguinetti, whose evil influence he had divined. And amidst all the heroism of his pride, he was rent by tragic dolour at thought of the dark battle which was waged around the tiara, all the evil hatred and voracious appetite which stirred in the depths of the gloom. Then, as Pierre and Don Vigilio bowed to him as a sign that they would preserve silence, he almost choked with invincible emotion, a sob of loving grief which he strove to keep down rising to his throat, whilst he stammered: "Ah! my poor child, my poor child, the only scion of our race, the only love and hope of my heart! Ah! to die, to die like this!"

But Benedetta, again all violence, sprang up: "Die! Who, Dario? I won't have it! We'll nurse him, we'll go back to him. We will take him in our arms and save him. Come, uncle, come at once! I won't, I won't, I won't have him die!"

She was going towards the door, and nothing would have prevented her from re-entering the bed-room, when, as it happened, Victorine appeared with a wild look on her face, for, despite her wonted serenity, all her courage was now exhausted. "The doctor begs madame and his Eminence to come at once, at once," said she.

Stupefied by all these things, Pierre did not follow the others, but lingered for a moment in the sunlit dining-room with Don Vigilio. What! poison? Poison as in the time of the Borgias, elegantly hidden away, served up with luscious fruit by a crafty traitor, whom one dared not even denounce! And he recalled the conversation on his way back from Frascati, and his Parisian scepticism with respect to those legendary drugs, which to his mind had no place save in the fifth acts of melodramas. Yet those abominable stories were true, those tales of poisoned knives and flowers, of prelates and even dilatory popes being suppressed by a drop or a grain of something administered to them in their morning chocolate. That passionate tragical Santobono was really a poisoner, Pierre could no longer doubt it, for a lurid light now illumined the whole of the previous day: there were the words of ambition and menace which had been spoken by Cardinal Sanguinetti, the eagerness to act in presence of the probable death of the reigning pope, the suggestion of a crime for the sake of the Church's salvation, then that priest with his little basket of figs encountered on the road, then that basket carried for hours so carefully, so devoutly, on the priest's knees, that basket which now haunted Pierre like a nightmare, and whose colour, and odour, and shape he would ever recall with a shudder. Aye, poison, poison, there was truth in it; it existed and still circulated in the depths of the black world, amidst all the ravenous, rival longings for conquest and sovereignty.

And all at once the figure of Prada likewise arose in Pierre's mind. A little while previously, when Benedetta had so violently accused the Count, he, Pierre, had stepped forward to defend him and cry aloud what he knew, whence the poison had come, and what hand had offered it. But a sudden thought had made him shiver: though Prada had not devised the crime, he had allowed it to be perpetrated. Another memory darted keen like steel through the young priest's mind—that of the little black hen lying lifeless beside the shed, amidst the dismal surroundings of the *osteria*, with a tiny streamlet of violet blood trickling from her beak. And here again, Tata, the parrot, lay still soft and warm at the foot of her stand, with her beak stained by oozing blood. Why had Prada told that lie about a battle between two fowls? All the dim intricacy of passion and contention bewildered Pierre, he could not thread his way through it; nor was he better able to follow the frightful combat which must have been waged in that man's mind during the night of the ball. At the same time he could not again picture him by his side during their nocturnal walk towards the Boccanera mansion without shuddering, dimly divining what a frightful decision had been taken before that mansion's door. Moreover, whatever the obscurities, whether Prada had expected that the Cardinal alone would be killed, or had hoped that some chance stroke of fate might avenge him on others, the terrible fact remained—he had known, he had been able to stay Destiny on the march, but had allowed it to go onward and blindly accomplish its work of death.

Turning his head Pierre perceived Don Vigilio still seated on the corner chair whence he had not stirred, and looking so pale and haggard that perhaps he also had swallowed some of the poison. "Do you feel unwell?" the young priest asked.

At first the secretary could not reply, for terror had gripped him at the throat. Then in a low voice he said: "No, no, I didn't eat any. Ah, Heaven, when I think that I so much wanted to taste them, and that merely deference kept me back on seeing that his Eminence did not take any!" Don Vigilio's whole body shivered at the thought that his humility alone had saved him; and on his face and his hands there remained the icy chill of death which had fallen so near and grazed him as it passed.

Then twice he heaved a sigh, and with a gesture of affright sought to brush the horrid thing away while murmuring: "Ah! Paparelli, Paparelli!"

Pierre, deeply stirred, and knowing what he thought of the train-bearer, tried to extract some information from him: "What do you mean?" he asked. "Do you accuse him too? Do you think they urged him on, and that it was they at bottom?"

The word Jesuits was not even spoken, but a big black shadow passed athwart the gay sunlight of the dining-room, and for a moment seemed to fill it with darkness. "They! ah yes!" exclaimed Don Vigilio, "they are everywhere; it is always they! As soon as one weeps, as soon as one dies, they are mixed up in it. And this is intended for me too; I am quite surprised that I haven't been carried off." Then again he raised a dull moan of fear, hatred, and anger: "Ah! Paparelli, Paparelli!" And he refused to reply any further, but darted scared glances at the walls as if from one or another of them he expected to see the train-bearer emerge, with his wrinkled flabby face like that of an old maid, his furtive mouse-like trot, and his mysterious, invading hands which had gone expressly to bring the forgotten figs from the pantry and deposit them on the table.

At last the two priests decided to return to the bedroom, where perhaps they might be required; and Pierre on entering was overcome by the heart-rending scene which the chamber now presented. Doctor Giordano, suspecting poison, had for half an hour been trying the usual remedies, an emetic and then magnesia. Just then, too, he had made Victorine whip some whites of eggs in water. But the disorder was progressing with such lightning-like rapidity that all succour was becoming futile. Undressed and lying on his back, his bust propped up by pillows and his arms lying outstretched over the sheets, Dario looked quite frightful in the sort of painful intoxication which characterised that redoubtable and mysterious disorder to which already Monsignor Gallo and others had succumbed. The young man seemed to be stricken with a sort of dizzy stupor, his eyes receded farther and farther into the depth of their dark sockets, whilst his whole face became withered, aged as it were, and covered with an earthy pallor. A moment previously he had closed his eyes, and the only sign that he still lived was the heaving of his chest induced by painful respiration. And leaning over his poor dying face stood Benedetta, sharing his sufferings, and mastered by such impotent grief that she also was unrecognisable, so white, so distracted by anguish, that it seemed as if death were gradually taking her at the same time as it was taking him.

In the recess by the window whither Cardinal Boccanera had led Doctor Giordano, a few words were exchanged in low tones. "He is lost, is he not?"

The doctor made the despairing gesture of one who is vanquished: "Alas! yes. I must warn your Eminence that in an hour all will be over."

A short interval of silence followed. "And the same malady as Gallo, is it not?" asked the Cardinal; and as the doctor trembling and averting his eyes did not answer he added: "At all events of an infectious fever!"

Giordano well understood what the Cardinal thus asked of him: silence, the crime for ever hidden away for the sake of the good renown of his mother, the Church. And there could be no loftier, no more tragical grandeur than that of this old man of seventy, still so erect and sovereign, who would neither suffer a slur to be cast upon his spiritual family, nor consent to his human family being dragged into the inevitable mire of a sensational murder trial. No, no, there must be none of that, there must be silence, the eternal silence in which all becomes forgotten.

At last the doctor bowed with his gentle air of discretion. "Evidently, of an infectious fever as your Eminence so well says," he replied.

Two big tears then again appeared in Boccanera's eyes. Now that he had screened the Deity from attack in the person of the Church, his heart as a man again bled. He begged the doctor to make a supreme effort, to attempt the impossible; but, pointing to the dying man with trembling hands, Giordano shook his head. For his own father, his own mother he could have done nothing. Death was there. So why weary, why torture a dying man, whose sufferings he would only have increased? And then, as the Cardinal, finding the end so near at hand, thought of his sister Serafina, and lamented that she would not be able to kiss her nephew for the last time if she lingered at the Vatican, the doctor offered to fetch her in his carriage which was waiting below. It would not take him more than twenty minutes, said he, and he would be back in time for the end, should he then be needed.

Left to himself in the window recess the Cardinal remained there motionless for another moment. With eyes blurred by tears, he gazed towards heaven. And his quivering arms were suddenly raised in a gesture of ardent entreaty. O God, since the science of man was so limited and vain, since that doctor had gone off happy to escape the embarrassment of his impotence, O God, why not a miracle which should proclaim the splendour of Thy Almighty Power! A miracle, a miracle! that was what the Cardinal asked from the depths of his believing soul, with the insistence, the imperious entreaty of a Prince of the Earth, who deemed that he had rendered considerable services to Heaven by dedicating his whole life to the Church. And he asked for that miracle in order that his race might be perpetuated, in order that its last male scion might not thus miserably perish, but be able to marry that fondly loved cousin, who now stood there all woe and tears. A miracle, a miracle for the sake of those two dear children! A miracle which would endow the family with fresh life: a miracle which would eternise the glorious name of Boccanera by enabling an innumerable posterity of valiant ones and faithful ones to spring from that young couple!

When the Cardinal returned to the centre of the room he seemed transfigured. Faith had dried his eyes, his soul had become strong and submissive, exempt from all human weakness. He had placed himself in the hands of God, and had resolved that he himself would administer extreme unction to Dario. With a gesture he summoned Don Vigilio and led him into the little room which served as a chapel, and the key of which he always carried. A cupboard had been contrived behind the altar of painted wood, and the Cardinal went to it to take both stole and surplice. The coffer containing the Holy Oils was likewise there, a very ancient silver coffer bearing the Boccanera arms. And on Don Vigilio following the Cardinal back into the bed-room they in turn pronounced the Latin words:

"*Pax huic domui.*"

"*Et omnibus habitantibus in ea.*"[1]

Death was coming so fast and threatening, that all the usual preparations were perforce dispensed with. Neither the two lighted tapers, nor the little table covered with white cloth had been provided. And, in the same way, Don Vigilio the assistant, having failed to bring the Holy Water basin and sprinkler, the Cardinal, as officiating priest, could merely make the gesture of blessing the room and the dying man, whilst pronouncing the words of the ritual: "*Asperges me, Domine, hyssopo, et mundabor; lavabis me, et super nivem dealbabor.*"[2]

Benedetta on seeing the Cardinal appear carrying the Holy Oils, had with a long quiver fallen on her knees at the foot of the bed, whilst, somewhat farther away, Pierre and Victorine likewise knelt, overcome by the dolorous grandeur of the scene. And the dilated eyes of the Contessina, whose face was pale as snow, never quitted her Dario, whom she no longer recognised, so earthy was his face, its skin tanned and wrinkled like that of an old man. And it was not for their marriage which he so much desired that their uncle, the all-powerful Prince of the Church, was bringing the Sacrament, but for the supreme rupture, the end of all pride, Death which finishes off the

---

[1] "Peace unto this house and unto all who dwell in it."—Trans.

[2] "Sprinkle me, Lord, with hyssop, and purify me; wash me, and make me whiter than snow."—Trans.

haughtiest races, and sweeps them away, even as the wind sweeps the dust of the roads.

It was needful that there should be no delay, so the Cardinal promptly repeated the Credo in an undertone, "*Credo in unum Deum*—"

"*Amen*," responded Don Vigilio, who, after the prayers of the ritual, stammered the Litanies in order that Heaven might take pity on the wretched man who was about to appear before God, if God by a prodigy did not spare him.

Then, without taking time to wash his fingers, the Cardinal opened the case containing the Holy Oils, and limiting himself to one anointment, as is permissible in pressing cases, he deposited a single drop of the oil on Dario's parched mouth which was already withered by death. And in doing so he repeated the words of the formula, his heart all aglow with faith as he asked that the divine mercy might efface each and every sin that the young man had committed by either of his five senses, those five portals by which everlasting temptation assails the soul. And the Cardinal's fervour was also instinct with the hope that if God had smitten the poor sufferer for his offences, perhaps He would make His indulgence entire and even restore him to life as soon as He should have forgiven his sins. Life, O Lord, life in order that the ancient line of the Boccaneras might yet multiply and continue to serve Thee in battle and at the altar until the end of time!

For a moment the Cardinal remained with quivering hands, gazing at the mute face, the closed eyes of the dying man, and waiting for the miracle. But no sign appeared, not the faintest glimmer brightened that haggard countenance, nor did a sigh of relief come from the withered lips as Don Vigilio wiped them with a little cotton wool. And the last prayer was said, and whilst the frightful silence fell once more the Cardinal, followed by his assistant, returned to the chapel. There they both knelt, the Cardinal plunging into ardent prayer upon the bare tiles. With his eyes raised to the brass crucifix upon the altar he saw nothing, heard nothing, but gave himself wholly to his entreaties, supplicating God to take him in place of his nephew, if a sacrifice were necessary, and yet clinging to the hope that so long as Dario retained a breath of life and he himself thus remained on his knees addressing the Deity, he might succeed in pacifying the wrath of Heaven. He was both so humble and so great. Would not accord surely be established between God and a Boccanera? The old palace might have fallen to the ground, he himself would not even have felt the toppling of its beams.

In the bed-room, however, nothing had yet stirred beneath the weight of tragic majesty which the ceremony had left there. It was only now that Dario raised his eyelids, and when on looking at his hands he saw them so aged and wasted the depths of his eyes kindled with an expression of immense regretfulness that life should be departing. Doubtless it was at this moment of lucidity amidst the kind of intoxication with which the poison overwhelmed him, that he for the first time realised his perilous condition. Ah! to die, amidst such pain, such physical degradation, what a revolting horror for that frivolous and egotistical man, that lover of beauty, joy, and light, who knew not how to suffer! In him ferocious fate chastised racial degeneracy with too heavy a hand. He became horrified with himself, seized with childish despair and terror, which lent him strength enough to sit up and gaze wildly about the room, in order to see if every one had not abandoned him. And when his eyes lighted on Benedetta still kneeling at the foot of the bed, a supreme impulse carried him towards her, he stretched forth both arms as passionately as his strength allowed and stammered her name: "O Benedetta, Benedetta!"

She, motionless in the stupor of her anxiety, had not taken her eyes from his face. The horrible disorder which was carrying off her lover, seemed also to possess and annihilate her more and more, even as he himself grew weaker and weaker. Her features were assuming an immaterial whiteness; and through the void of her clear eyeballs one began to espy her soul. However, when she perceived him thus resuscitating and calling her with arms outstretched, she in her turn arose and standing beside the bed made answer: "I am coming, my Dario, here I am."

And then Pierre and Victorine, still on their knees, beheld a sublime deed of such extraordinary grandeur that they remained rooted to the floor, spell-bound as in the presence of some supra-terrestrial spectacle in which human beings may not intervene. Benedetta herself spoke and acted like one freed from all social and conventional ties, already beyond life, only seeing and addressing beings and things from a great distance, from the depths of the unknown in which she was about to disappear.

"Ah! my Dario, so an attempt has been made to part us! It was in order that I might never belong to you—that we might never be happy, that your death was resolved upon, and it was known that with your life my own must cease! And it is that man who is killing you! Yes, he is your murderer, even if the actual blow has been dealt by another. He is the first cause—he who stole me from you when I was about to become yours, he who ravaged our lives, and who breathed around us the hateful poison which is killing us. Ah! how I hate him, how I hate him; how I should like to crush him with my hate before I die with you!"

She did not raise her voice, but spoke those terrible words in a deep murmur, simply and passionately. Prada was not even named, and she scarcely turned towards Pierre—who knelt, paralysed, behind her—to add with a commanding air: "You will see his father, I charge you to tell him that I cursed his son! That kind-hearted hero loved me well—I love him even now, and the words you will carry to him from me will rend his heart. But I desire that he should know—he must know, for the sake of truth and justice."

Distracted by terror, sobbing amidst a last convulsion, Dario again stretched forth his arms, feeling that she was no longer looking at him, that her clear eyes were no longer fixed upon his own: "Benedetta, Benedetta!"

"I am coming, I am coming, my Dario—I am here!" she responded, drawing yet nearer to the bedside and almost touching him. "Ah!" she went on, "that vow which I made to the Madonna to belong to none, not even you, until God should allow it by the blessing of one of his priests! Ah! I set a noble, a divine pride in remaining immaculate for him who should be the one master of my soul and body. And that chastity which I was so proud of, I defended it against the other as one defends oneself against a wolf, and I defended it against you with tears for fear of sacrilege. And if you only knew what terrible struggles I was forced to wage with myself, for I loved you and longed to be yours, like a woman who accepts the whole of love, the love that makes wife and mother! Ah! my vow to the Madonna—with what difficulty did I keep it when the old blood of our race arose in me like a tempest; and now what a disaster!" She drew yet nearer, and her low voice became more ardent: "You remember that evening when you came back with a knife-thrust in your shoulder. I thought you dead, and cried aloud with rage at the idea of losing you like that. I insulted the Madonna and regretted that I had not damned myself with you that we might die together, so tightly clasped that we must needs be buried together also. And to think that such a terrible warning was of no avail! I was blind and foolish; and now you are again stricken, again being taken from my love. Ah! my wretched pride, my idiotic dream!"

That which now rang out in her stifled voice was the anger of the practical woman that she had ever been, all superstition notwithstanding. Could the Madonna, who was so maternal, desire the woe of lovers? No, assuredly not. Nor did the angels make the mere absence of a priest a cause for weeping over the transports of true and mutual love. Was not such love holy in itself, and did not the angels rather smile upon it and burst into gladsome song! And ah! how one cheated oneself by not loving to heart's content under the sun, when the blood of life coursed through one's veins!

"Benedetta! Benedetta!" repeated the dying man, full of child-like terror at thus going off all alone into the depths of the black and everlasting night.

"Here I am, my Dario, I am coming!"

Then, as she fancied that the servant, albeit motionless, had stirred, as if to rise and interfere, she added: "Leave me, leave me, Victorine, nothing in the world can henceforth prevent it. A moment ago, when I was on my knees, something roused me and urged me on. I know whither I am going. And besides, did I not swear on the night of the knife thrust? Did I not promise to belong to him alone, even in the earth if it were necessary? I must embrace him, and he will carry me away! We shall be dead, and we shall be wedded in spite of all, and for ever and for ever!"

She stepped back to the dying man, and touched him: "Here I am, my Dario, here I am!"

Then came the apogee. Amidst growing exaltation, buoyed up by a blaze of love, careless of glances, candid like a lily, she divested herself of her garments and stood forth so white, that neither marble statue, nor dove, nor snow itself was ever whiter. "Here I am, my Dario, here I am!"

Recoiling almost to the ground as at sight of an apparition, the glorious flash of a holy vision, Pierre and Victorine gazed at her with dazzled eyes. The servant had not stirred to prevent this extraordinary action, seized as she was with that shrinking reverential terror which comes upon one in presence of the wild, mad deeds of faith and passion. And the priest, whose limbs were paralysed, felt that something so sublime was passing that he could only quiver in distraction. And no thought of impurity came to him on beholding that lily, snowy whiteness. All candour and all nobility as she was, that virgin shocked him no more than some sculptured masterpiece of genius.

"Here I am, my Dario, here I am."

She had lain herself down beside the spouse whom she had chosen, she had clasped the dying man whose arms only had enough strength left to fold themselves around her. Death was stealing him from her, but she would go with him; and again she murmured: "My Dario, here I am."

And at that moment, against the wall at the head of the bed, Pierre perceived the escutcheon of the Boccaneras, embroidered in gold and coloured silks on a groundwork of violet velvet. There was the winged dragon belching flames, there was the fierce and glowing motto "*Bocca nera, Alma rossa*" (black mouth, red soul), the mouth darkened by a roar, the soul flaming like a brazier of faith and love. And behold! all that old race of passion and violence with its tragic legends had reappeared, its blood bubbling up afresh to urge that last and adorable daughter of the line to those terrifying and prodigious nuptials in death. And to Pierre that escutcheon recalled another memory, that of the portrait of Cassia Boccanera the *amorosa* and avengeress who had flung herself into the Tiber with her brother Ercole and the corpse of her lover Flavio. Was there not here even with Benedetta the same despairing clasp seeking to vanquish death, the same savagery in hurling oneself into the abyss with the corpse of the one's only love? Benedetta and Cassia were as sisters, Cassia, who lived anew in the old painting in the *salon* overhead, Benedetta who was here dying of her lover's death, as though she were but the other's spirit. Both had the same delicate childish features, the same mouth of passion, the same large dreamy eyes set in the same round, practical, and stubborn head.

"My Dario, here I am!"

For a second, which seemed an eternity, they clasped one another, she neither repelled nor terrified by the disorder which made him so unrecognisable, but displaying a delirious passion, a holy frenzy as if to pass beyond life, to penetrate with him into the black Unknown. And beneath the shock of the felicity at last offered to him he expired, with his arms yet convulsively wound around her as though indeed to carry her off. Then, whether from grief or from bliss amidst that embrace of death, there came such a rush of blood to her heart that the organ burst: she died on her lover's neck, both tightly and for ever clasped in one another's arms.

There was a faint sigh. Victorine understood and drew near, while Pierre, also erect, remained quivering with the tearful admiration of one who has beheld the sublime.

"Look, look!" whispered the servant, "she no longer moves, she no longer breathes. Ah! my poor child, my poor child, she is dead!"

Then the priest murmured: "Oh! God, how beautiful they are."

It was true, never had loftier and more resplendent beauty appeared on the faces of the dead. Dario's countenance, so lately aged and earthen, had assumed the pallor and nobility of marble, its features lengthened and simplified as by a transport of ineffable joy. Benedetta remained very grave, her lips curved by ardent determination, whilst her whole face was expressive of dolorous yet infinite beatitude in a setting of infinite whiteness. Their hair mingled, and their eyes, which had remained open, continued gazing as into one another's souls with eternal, caressing sweetness. They were for ever linked, soaring into immortality amidst the enchantment of their union, vanquishers of death, radiant with the rapturous beauty of love, the conqueror, the immortal.

But Victorine's sobs at last burst forth, mingled with such lamentations that great confusion followed. Pierre, now quite beside himself, in some measure failed to understand how it was that the room suddenly became invaded by terrified people. The Cardinal and Don Vigilio, however, must have hastened in from the chapel; and at the same moment, no doubt, Doctor Giordano must have returned with Donna Serafina, for both were now there, she stupefied by the blows which had thus fallen on the house in her absence, whilst he, the doctor, displayed the perturbation and astonishment which comes upon the oldest practitioners when facts seem to give the lie to their experience. However, he sought an explanation of Benedetta's death, and hesitatingly ascribed it to aneurism, or possibly embolism.

XIII.

Thereupon Victorine, like a servant whose grief makes her the equal of her employers, boldly interrupted him: "Ah! Sir," said she, "they loved each other too fondly; did not that suffice for them to die together?"

Meantime Donna Serafina, after kissing the poor children on the brow, desired to close their eyes; but she could not succeed in doing so, for the lids lifted directly she removed her finger and once more the eyes began to smile at one another, to exchange in all fixity their loving and eternal glance. And then as she spoke of parting the bodies, Victorine again protested: "Oh! madame, oh! madame," she said, "you would have to break their arms. Cannot you see that their fingers are almost dug into one another's shoulders? No, they can never be parted!"

Thereupon Cardinal Boccanera intervened. God had not granted the miracle; and he, His minister, was livid, tearless, and full of icy despair. But he waved his arm with a sovereign gesture of absolution and sanctification, as if, Prince of the Church that he was, disposing of the will of Heaven, he consented that the lovers should appear in that embrace before the supreme tribunal. In presence of such wondrous love, indeed, profoundly stirred by the sufferings of their lives and the beauty of their death, he showed a broad and lofty contempt for mundane proprieties. "Leave them, leave me, my sister," said he, "do not disturb their slumber. Let their eyes remain open since they desire to gaze on one another till the end of time without ever wearying. And let them sleep in one another's arms since in their lives they did not sin, and only locked themselves in that embrace in order that they might be laid together in the ground."

And then, again becoming a Roman Prince whose proud blood was yet hot with old-time deeds of battle and passion, he added: "Two Boccaneras may well sleep like that; all Rome will admire them and weep for them. Leave them, leave them together, my sister. God knows them and awaits them!"

All knelt, and the Cardinal himself repeated the prayers for the dead. Night was coming, increasing gloom stole into the chamber, where two burning tapers soon shone out like stars.

And then, without knowing how, Pierre again found himself in the little deserted garden on the bank of the Tiber. Suffocating with fatigue and grief, he must have come thither for fresh air. Darkness shrouded the charming nook where the streamlet of water falling from the tragic mask into the ancient sarcophagus ever sang its shrill and flute-like song; and the laurel-bush which shaded it, and the bitter box-plants and the orange-trees skirting the paths now formed but vague masses under the blue-black sky. Ah! how gay and sweet had that melancholy garden been in the morning, and what a desolate echo it retained of Benedetta's winsome laughter, all that fine delight in coming happiness which now lay prone upstairs, steeped in the nothingness of things and beings! So dolorous was the pang which came to Pierre's heart that he burst into sobs, seated on the same broken column where she had sat, and encompassed by the same atmosphere that she had breathed, in which still lingered the perfume of her presence.

But all at once a distant clock struck six, and the young priest started on remembering that he was to be received by the Pope that very evening at nine. Yet three more hours! He had not thought of that interview during the terrifying catastrophe, and it seemed to him now as if months and months had gone by, as if the appointment were some very old one which a man is only able to keep after years of absence, when he has grown aged and had his heart and brain modified by innumerable experiences.

However, he made an effort and rose to his feet. In three hours' time he would go to the Vatican and at last he would see the Pope.

PART V.

XIV.

THAT evening, when Pierre emerged from the Borgo in front of the Vatican, a sonorous stroke rang out from the clock amidst the deep silence of the dark and sleepy district. It was only half-past eight, and being in advance the young priest resolved to wait some twenty minutes in order to reach the doors of the papal apartments precisely at nine, the hour fixed for his audience.

This respite brought him some relief amidst the infinite emotion and grief which gripped his heart. That tragic afternoon which he had spent in the chamber of death, where Dario and Benedetta now slept the eternal sleep in one another's arms, had left him very weary. He was haunted by a wild, dolorous vision of the two lovers, and involuntary sighs came from his lips whilst tears continually moistened his eyes. He had been altogether unable to eat that evening. Ah! how he would have liked to hide himself and weep at his ease! His heart melted at each fresh thought. The pitiful death of the lovers intensified the grievous feeling with which his book was instinct, and impelled him to yet greater compassion, a perfect anguish of charity for all who suffered in the world. And he was so distracted by the thought of the many physical and moral sores of Paris and of Rome, where he had beheld so much unjust and abominable suffering, that at each step he took he feared lest he should burst into sobs with arms upstretched towards the blackness of heaven.

In the hope of somewhat calming himself he began to walk slowly across the Piazza of St. Peter's, now all darkness and solitude. On arriving he had fancied that he was losing himself in a murky sea, but by degrees his eyes grew accustomed to the dimness. The vast expanse was only lighted by the four candelabra at the corners of the obelisk and by infrequent lamps skirting the buildings which run on either hand towards the Basilica. Under the colonnade, too, other lamps threw yellow gleams across the forest of pillars, showing up their stone trunks in fantastic fashion; while on the piazza only the pale, ghostly obelisk was at all distinctly visible. Pierre could scarcely perceive the dim, silent facade of St. Peter's; whilst of the dome he merely divined a gigantic, bluey roundness faintly shadowed against the sky. In the obscurity he at first heard the plashing of the fountains without being at all able to see them, but on approaching he at last distinguished the slender phantoms of the ever rising jets which fell again in spray. And above the vast square stretched the vast and moonless sky of a deep velvety blue, where the stars were large and radiant like carbuncles; Charles's Wain, with golden wheels and golden shaft tilted back as it were, over the roof of the Vatican, and Orion, bedizened with the three bright stars of his belt, showing magnificently above Rome, in the direction of the Via Giulia.

At last Pierre raised his eyes to the Vatican, but facing the piazza there was here merely a confused jumble of walls, amidst which only two gleams of light appeared on the floor of the papal apartments. The Court of San Damaso was, however, lighted, for the conservatory-like glass-work of two of its sides sparkled as with the reflection of gas lamps which could not be seen. For a time there was not a sound or sign of movement, but at last two persons crossed the expanse of the piazza, and then came a third who in his turn disappeared, nothing remaining but a rhythmical far-away echo of steps. The spot was indeed a perfect desert, there were neither promenaders nor passers-by, nor was there even the shadow of a prowler in the pillared forest of the colonnade, which was as empty as the wild primeval forests of the world's infancy. And what a solemn desert it was, full of the silence of haughty desolation. Never had so vast and black a presentment of slumber, so instinct with the sovereign nobility of death, appeared to Pierre.

At ten minutes to nine he at last made up his mind and went towards the bronze portal. Only one of the folding doors was now open at the end of the right-hand porticus, where the increasing density of the gloom steeped everything in night. Pierre remembered the instructions which Monsignor Nani had given him; at each door that he reached he was to ask for Signor Squadra without adding a word, and thereupon each door would open and he would have nothing to do but to let himself be guided on. No one but the prelate now knew that he was there, since Benedetta, the only being to whom he had confided the secret, was dead. When he had crossed the threshold of the bronze doors and found himself in presence of the motionless, sleeping Swiss Guard, who was on duty there, he simply spoke the words agreed upon: "Signor Squadra." And as the Guard did not stir, did not seek to bar his way, he passed on, turning into the vestibule of the Scala Pia, the stone stairway which ascends to the Court of San Damaso. And not a soul was to be seen: there was but the faint sound of his own light footsteps and the sleepy glow of the gas jets whose light was softly whitened by globes of frosted glass. Up above, on reaching the courtyard he found it a solitude, whose slumber seemed sepulchral amidst the mournful gleams of the gas lamps which cast a pallid reflection on the lofty glass-work of the facades. And feeling somewhat nervous, affected by the quiver which pervaded all that void and silence, Pierre hastened on, turning to the right, towards the low flight of steps which leads to the staircase of the Pope's private apartments.

Here stood a superb gendarme in full uniform. "Signor Squadra," said Pierre, and without a word the gendarme pointed to the stairs.

The young man went up. It was a broad stairway, with low steps, balustrade of white marble, and walls covered with yellowish stucco. The gas, burning in globes of round glass, seemed to have been already turned down in a spirit of prudent economy. And in the glimmering light nothing could have been more mournfully solemn than that cold and pallid staircase. On each landing there was a Swiss Guard, halbard in hand, and in the heavy slumber spreading through the palace one only heard the regular monotonous footsteps of these men, ever marching up and down, in order no doubt that they might not succumb to the benumbing influence of their surroundings.

Amidst the invading dimness and the quivering silence the ascent of the stairs seemed interminable to Pierre, who by the time he reached the second-floor landing imagined that he had been climbing for ages. There, outside the glass door of the Sala Clementina, only the right-hand half of which was open, a last Swiss Guard stood watching.

"Signor Squadra," Pierre said again, and the Guard drew back to let him pass.

The Sala Clementina, spacious enough by daylight, seemed immense at that nocturnal hour, in the twilight glimmer of its lamps. All the opulent decorative-work, sculpture, painting, and gilding became blended, the walls assuming a tawny vagueness amidst which appeared bright patches like the sparkle of precious stones. There was not an article of furniture, nothing but the endless pavement stretching away into the semi-darkness. At last, however, near a door at the far end Pierre espied some men dozing on a bench. They were three Swiss Guards. "Signor Squadra," he said to them.

One of the Guards thereupon slowly rose and left the hall, and Pierre understood that he was to wait. He did not dare to move, disturbed as he was by the sound of his own footsteps on the paved floor, so he contented himself with gazing around and picturing the crowds which at times peopled that vast apartment, the first of the many papal ante-chambers. But before long the Guard returned, and behind him, on the threshold of the adjoining room, appeared a man of forty or thereabouts, who was clad in black from head to foot and suggested a cross between a butler and a beadle. He had a good-looking, clean-shaven face, with somewhat pronounced nose and large, clear, fixed eyes. "Signor Squadra," said Pierre for the last time.

The man bowed as if to say that he was Signor Squadra, and then, with a fresh reverence, he invited the priest to follow him. Thereupon at a leisurely step, one behind the other, they began to thread the interminable suite of waiting-rooms. Pierre, who was acquainted with the ceremonial, of which he had often spoken with Narcisse, recognised the different apartments as he passed through them, recalling their names and purpose, and peopling them in imagination with the various officials of the papal retinue who have the right to occupy them. These according to their rank cannot go beyond certain doors, so that the persons who are to have audience of the Pope are passed on from the servants to the Noble Guards, from the Noble Guards to the honorary *Camerieri*, and from the latter to the *Camerieri segreti*, until they at last reach the presence of the Holy Father. At eight o'clock, however, the ante-rooms empty and become both deserted and dim, only a few lamps being left alight upon the pier tables standing here and there against the walls.

And first Pierre came to the ante-room of the *bussolanti*, mere ushers clad in red velvet broidered with the papal arms, who conduct visitors to the door of the anteroom of honour. At that late hour only one of them was left there, seated on a bench in such a dark corner that his purple tunic looked quite black. Then the Hall of the Gendarmes was crossed, where according to the regulations the secretaries of cardinals and other high personages await their masters' return; and this was now completely empty, void both of the handsome blue uniforms with white shoulder belts and the cassocks of fine black cloth which mingled in it during the brilliant reception hours. Empty also was the following room, a smaller one reserved to the Palatine Guards, who are recruited among the Roman middle class and wear black tunics with gold epaulets and shakoes surmounted by red plumes. Then Pierre and his guide turned into another series of apartments, and again was the first one empty. This was the Hall of the Arras, a superb waiting-room with lofty painted ceiling and admirable Gobelins tapestry designed by Audran and representing the miracles of Jesus. And empty also was the ante-chamber of the Noble Guards which followed, with its wooden stools, its pier table on the right-hand surmounted by a large crucifix standing between two lamps, and its large door opening at the far end into another but smaller room, a sort of alcove indeed, where there is an altar at which the Holy Father says mass by himself whilst those privileged to be present remain kneeling on the marble slabs of the outer apartment which is resplendent with the dazzling uniforms of the Guards. And empty likewise was the ensuing ante-room of honour, otherwise the grand throne-room, where the Pope receives two or three hundred people at a time in public audience. The throne, an arm-chair of elaborate pattern, gilded, and upholstered with red velvet, stands under a velvet canopy of the same hue, in front of the windows. Beside it is the cushion on which the Pope rests his foot in order that it may be kissed. Then facing one another, right and left of the room, there are two pier tables, on one of which is a clock and on the other a crucifix between lofty candelabra with feet of gilded wood. The wall hangings, of red silk damask with a Louis XIV palm pattern, are topped by a pompous frieze, framing a ceiling decorated with allegorical figures and attributes, and it is only just in front of the throne that a Smyrna carpet covers the magnificent marble pavement. On the days of private audience, when the Pope remains in the little throne-room or at times in his bed-chamber, the grand throne-room becomes simply the ante-room of honour, where high dignitaries of the Church, ambassadors, and great civilian personages, wait their turns. Two *Camerieri*, one in violet coat, the other of the Cape and the Sword, here do duty, receiving from the *bussolanti* the persons who are to be honoured with audiences and conducting them to the door of the next room, the secret or private ante-chamber, where they hand them over to the *Camerieri segreti*.

Signor Squadra who, walking on with slow and silent steps, had not yet once turned round, paused for a moment on reaching the door of the *anticamera segreta* so as to give Pierre time to breathe and recover himself somewhat before crossing the threshold of the sanctuary. The *Camerieri segreti* alone had the right to occupy that last ante-chamber, and none but the cardinals might wait there till the Pope should condescend to receive them. And so when Signor Squadra made up his mind to admit Pierre, the latter could not restrain a slight nervous shiver as if he were passing into some redoubtable mysterious sphere beyond the limits of the lower world. In the daytime a Noble Guard stood on sentry duty before the door, but the latter was now free of access, and the room within proved as empty as all the others. It was rather narrow, almost like a passage, with two windows overlooking the new district of the castle fields and a third one facing the Piazza of St. Peter's. Near the last was a door conducting to the little throne-room, and between this door and the window stood a small table at which a secretary, now absent, usually sat. And here again, as in all the other rooms, one found a gilded pier table surmounted by a crucifix flanked by a pair of lamps. In a corner too there was a large clock, loudly ticking in its ebony case incrusted with brass-work. Still there was nothing to awaken curiosity under the panelled and gilded ceiling unless it were the wall-hangings of red damask, on which yellow scutcheons displaying the Keys and the Tiara alternated with armorial lions, each with a paw resting on a globe.

Signor Squadra, however, now noticed that Pierre still carried his hat in his hand, whereas according to etiquette he should have left it in the hall of the *bussolanti*, only cardinals being privileged to carry their hats with them into the Pope's presence. Accordingly he discreetly took the young priest's from him, and deposited it on the pier table to indicate that it must at least remain there. Then, without a word, by a simple bow he gave Pierre to understand that he was about to announce him to his Holiness, and that he must be good enough to wait for a few minutes in that room.

On being left to himself Pierre drew a long breath. He was stifling; his heart was beating as though it would burst. Nevertheless his mind remained clear, and in spite of the semi-obscurity he had been able to form some idea of the famous and magnificent apartments of the Pope, a suite of splendid *salons* with tapestried or silken walls, gilded or painted friezes, and frescoed ceilings. By way of furniture, however, there were only pier table, stools,[1] and thrones. And the lamps and the clocks, and the crucifixes, even the thrones, were all presents brought from the four quarters of the world in the great fervent days of jubilee. There was no sign of comfort, everything was pompous, stiff, cold, and inconvenient. All olden Italy was there, with its perpetual display and lack of intimate, cosy life. It had been necessary to lay a few carpets over the superb marble slabs which froze one's feet; and some *caloriferes* had even lately been installed, but it was not thought prudent to light them lest the variations of temperature should give the Pope a cold. However, that which more particularly struck Pierre now that he stood there waiting was the extraordinary silence which prevailed all around, silence so deep that it seemed as if all the dark quiescence of that huge, somniferous Vatican were concentrated in that one suite of lifeless, sumptuous rooms, which the motionless flamelets of the lamps as dimly illumined.

All at once the ebony clock struck nine and the young man felt astonished. What! had only ten minutes elapsed since he had crossed the threshold of the bronze doors below? He felt as if he had been walking on for days and days. Then, desiring to overcome the nervous feeling which oppressed him—for he ever feared lest his enforced calmness should collapse amidst a flood of tears—he began to walk up and down, passing in front of the clock, glancing at the crucifix on the pier table, and the globe of the lamp on which had remained the mark of a servant's greasy fingers. And the light was so faint and yellow that he felt inclined to turn the lamp up, but did not dare. Then he found himself with his brow resting against one of the panes of the window facing the Piazza of St. Peter's, and for a moment he was thunderstruck, for between the imperfectly closed shutters he could see all Rome, as he had seen it one day from the *loggie* of Raffaelle, and as he had pictured Leo XIII contemplating it from the window of his bed-room. However, it was now Rome by night, Rome spreading out into the depths of the gloom, as limitless as the starry sky. And in that sea of black waves one could only with certainty identify the larger thoroughfares which the white brightness of electric lights turned, as it were, into Milky Ways. All the rest showed but a swarming of little yellow sparks, the crumbs, as it were, of a half-extinguished heaven swept down upon the earth. Occasional constellations of bright stars, tracing mysterious figures, vainly endeavoured to show forth distinctly, but they were submerged, blotted out by the general chaos which suggested the dust

[1] M. Zola seems to have fallen into error here. Many of the seats, which are of peculiar antique design, do, in the lower part, resemble stools, but they have backs, whereas a stool proper has none. Briefly, these seats, which are entirely of wood, are not unlike certain old-fashioned hall chairs.—Trans.

of some old planet that had crumbled there, losing its splendour and reduced to mere phosphorescent sand. And how immense was the blackness thus sprinkled with light, how huge the mass of obscurity and mystery into which the Eternal City with its seven and twenty centuries, its ruins, its monuments, its people, its history seemed to have been merged. You could no longer tell where it began or where it ended, whether it spread to the farthest recesses of the gloom, or whether it were so reduced that the sun on rising would illumine but a little pile of ashes.

However, in spite of all Pierre's efforts, his nervous anguish increased each moment, even in presence of that ocean of darkness which displayed such sovereign quiescence. He drew away from the window and quivered from head to foot on hearing a faint footfall and thinking it was that of Signor Squadra approaching to fetch him. The sound came from an adjacent apartment, the little throne-room, whose door, he now perceived, had remained ajar. And at last, as he heard nothing further, he yielded to his feverish impatience and peeped into this room which he found to be fairly spacious, again hung with red damask, and containing a gilded arm-chair, covered with red velvet under a canopy of the same material. And again there was the inevitable pier table, with a tall ivory crucifix, a clock, a pair of lamps, a pair of candelabra, a pair of large vases on pedestals, and two smaller ones of Sevres manufacture decorated with the Holy Father's portrait. At the same time, however, the room displayed rather more comfort, for a Smyrna carpet covered the whole of the marble floor, while a few arm-chairs stood against the walls, and an imitation chimney-piece, draped with damask, served as counterpart to the pier table. As a rule the Pope, whose bed-chamber communicated with this little throne-room, received in the latter such persons as he desired to honour. And Pierre's shiver became more pronounced at the idea that in all likelihood he would merely have the throne-room to cross and that Leo XIII was yonder behind its farther door. Why was he kept waiting, he wondered? He had been told of mysterious audiences granted at a similar hour to personages who had been received in similar silent fashion, great personages whose names were only mentioned in the lowest whispers. With regard to himself no doubt, it was because he was considered compromising that there was a desire to receive him in this manner unknown to the personages of the Court, and so as to speak with him at ease. Then, all at once, he understood the cause of the noise he had recently heard, for beside the lamp on the pier table of the little throne-room he saw a kind of butler's tray containing some soiled plates, knives, forks, and spoons, with a bottle and a glass, which had evidently just been removed from a supper table. And he realised that Signor Squadra, having seen these things in the Pope's room, had brought them there, and had then gone in again, perhaps to tidy up. He knew also of the Pope's frugality, how he took his meals all alone at a little round table, everything being brought to him in that tray, a plate of meat, a plate of vegetables, a little Bordeaux claret as prescribed by his doctor, and a large allowance of beef broth of which he was very fond. In the same way as others might offer a cup of tea, he was wont to offer cups of broth to the old cardinals his friends and favourites, quite an invigorating little treat which these old bachelors much enjoyed. And, O ye orgies of Alexander VI, ye banquets and *galas* of Julius II and Leo X, only eight *lire* a day—six shillings and fourpence—were allowed to defray the cost of Leo XIII's table! However, just as that recollection occurred to Pierre, he again heard a slight noise, this time in his Holiness's bed-chamber, and thereupon, terrified by his indiscretion, he hastened to withdraw from the entrance of the throne-room which, lifeless and quiescent though it was, seemed in his agitation to flare as with sudden fire.

Then, quivering too violently to be able to remain still, he began to walk up and down the ante-chamber. He remembered that Narcisse had spoken to him of that Signor Squadra, his Holiness's cherished valet, whose importance and influence were so great. He alone, on reception days, was able to prevail on the Pope to don a clean cassock if the one he was wearing happened to be soiled by snuff. And though his Holiness stubbornly shut himself up alone in his bed-room every night from a spirit of independence, which some called the anxiety of a miser determined to sleep alone with his treasure, Signor Squadra at all events occupied an adjoining chamber, and was ever on the watch, ready to respond to the faintest call. Again, it was he who respectfully intervened whenever his Holiness sat up too late or worked too long. But on this point it was difficult to induce the Pope to listen to reason. During his hours of insomnia he would often rise and send Squadra to fetch a secretary in order that he might detail some memoranda or sketch out an encyclical letter. When the drafting of one of the latter impassioned him he would have spent days and nights over it, just as formerly, when claiming proficiency in Latin verse, he had often let the dawn surprise him whilst he was polishing a line. But, indeed, he slept very little, his brain ever being at work, ever scheming out the realisation of some former ideas. His memory alone seemed to have slightly weakened during recent times.

Pierre, as he slowly paced to and fro, gradually became absorbed in his thoughts of that lofty and sovereign personality. From the petty details of the Pope's daily existence, he passed to his intellectual life, to the *role* which he was certainly bent on playing as a great pontiff. And Pierre asked himself which of his two hundred and fifty-seven predecessors, the long line of saints and criminals, men of mediocrity and men of genius, he most desired to resemble. Was it one of the first humble popes, those who followed on during the first three centuries, mere heads of burial guilds, fraternal pastors of the Christian community? Was it Pope Damasus, the first great builder, the man of letters who took delight in intellectual matters, the ardent believer who is said to have opened the Catacombs to the piety of the faithful? Was it Leo III, who by crowning Charlemagne boldly consummated the rupture with the schismatic East and conveyed the Empire to the West by the all-powerful will of God and His Church, which thenceforth disposed of the crowns of monarchs? Was it the terrible Gregory VII, the purifier of the temple, the sovereign of kings; was it Innocent III or Boniface VIII, those masters of souls, nations, and thrones, who, armed with the fierce weapon of excommunication, reigned with such despotism over the terrified middle ages that Catholicism was never nearer the attainment of its dream of universal dominion? Was it Urban II or Gregory IX or another of those popes in whom flared the red Crusading passion which urged the nations on to the conquest of the unknown and the divine? Was it Alexander III, who defended the Holy See against the Empire, and at last conquered and set his foot on the neck of Frederick Barbarossa? Was it, long after the sorrows of Avignon, Julius II, who wore the cuirass and once more strengthened the political power of the papacy? Was it Leo X, the pompous, glorious patron of the Renascence, of a whole great century of art, whose mind, however, was possessed of so little penetration and foresight that he looked on Luther as a mere rebellious monk? Was it Pius V, who personified dark and avenging reaction, the fire of the stakes that punished the heretic world? Was it some other of the popes who reigned after the Council of Trent with faith absolute, belief re-established in its full integrity, the Church saved by pride and the stubborn upholding of every dogma? Or was it a pope of the decline, such as Benedict XIV, the man of vast intelligence, the learned theologian who, as his hands were tied, and he could not dispose of the kingdoms of the world, spent a worthy life in regulating the affairs of heaven?

In this wise, in Pierre's mind there spread out the whole history of the popes, the most prodigious of all histories, showing fortune in every guise, the lowest, the most wretched, as well as the loftiest and most dazzling; whilst an obstinate determination to live enabled the papacy to survive everything—conflagrations, massacres, and the downfall of many nations, for always did it remain militant and erect in the persons of its popes, that most extraordinary of all lines of absolute, conquering, and domineering sovereigns, every one of them—even the puny and humble—masters of the world, every one of them glorious with the imperishable glory of heaven when they were thus evoked in that ancient Vatican, where their spirits assuredly awoke at night and prowled about the endless galleries and spreading halls in that tomb-like silence whose quiver came no doubt from the light touch of their gliding steps over the marble slabs.

However, Pierre was now thinking that he indeed knew which of the great popes Leo XIII most desired to resemble. It was first Gregory the Great, the conqueror and organiser of the early days of Catholic power. He had come of ancient Roman stock, and in his heart there was a little of the blood of the emperors. He administered Rome after it had been saved from the Goths, cultivated the ecclesiastical domains, and divided earthly wealth into thirds, one for the poor, one for the clergy, and one for the Church. Then too he was the first to establish the Propaganda, sending his priests forth to civilise and pacify the nations, and carrying his conquests so far as to win Great Britain over to the divine law of Christ. And the second pope whom Leo XIII took as model was one who had arisen after a long lapse of centuries, Sixtus V, the pope financier and politician, the vine-dresser's son, who, when he had donned the tiara, revealed one of the most extensive and supple minds of a period fertile in great diplomatists. He heaped up treasure and displayed stern avarice, in order that he might ever have in his coffers all the money needful for war or for peace. He spent years and years in negotiations with kings, never despairing of his own triumph; and never did he display open hostility for his times, but took them as they were and then sought to modify them in accordance with the interests of the Holy See, showing himself conciliatory in all things and with every one, already dreaming of an European balance of power which he hoped to control. And withal a very saintly pope, a fervent mystic, yet a pope of the most absolute and domineering mind blended with a politician ready for whatever courses might most conduce to the rule of God's Church on earth.

And, after all, Pierre amidst his rising enthusiasm, which despite his efforts at calmness was sweeping away all prudence and doubt, Pierre asked himself why he need question the past. Was not Leo XIII the pope whom he had depicted in his book, the great pontiff, who was desired and expected? No doubt the portrait which he had sketched was not accurate in every detail, but surely its main lines must be correct if mankind were to retain a hope of salvation. Whole pages of that book of his arose before him, and he again beheld the Leo XIII that he had portrayed, the wise and conciliatory politician, labouring for the unity of the Church and so anxious to make it strong and invincible against the day of the inevitable great struggle. He again beheld him freed from the cares of the temporal power, elevated, radiant with moral splendour, the only authority left erect above the nations; he beheld him realising what mortal danger would be incurred if the solution of the social question were left to the enemies of Christianity, and therefore resolving to intervene in contemporary quarrels for the defence of the poor and the lowly, even as Jesus had intervened once before. And he again beheld him putting himself on the side of the democracies, accepting the Republic in France, leaving the dethroned kings in exile, and verifying the prediction which promised the empire of the world to Rome once more when the papacy should have unified belief and have placed itself at the head of the people. The times indeed were near accomplishment, Caesar was struck down, the Pope alone remained, and would not the people, the great silent multitude, for whom the two powers had so long contended, give itself to its Father now that it knew him to be both just and charitable, with heart aglow and hand outstretched to welcome all the penniless toilers and beggars of the roads! Given the catastrophe which threatened our rotten modern societies, the frightful misery which ravaged every city, there was surely no other solution possible: Leo XIII, the predestined, necessary redeemer, the pastor sent to save the flock from coming disaster by re-establishing the true Christian community, the forgotten golden age of primitive Christianity. The reign of justice would at last begin, all men would be reconciled, there would be but one nation living in peace and obeying the equalising law of work, under the high patronage of the Pope, sole bond of charity and love on earth!

And at this thought Pierre was upbuoyed by fiery enthusiasm. At last he was about to see the Holy Father, empty his heart and open his soul to him! He had so long and so passionately looked for the advent of that moment! To secure it he had fought with all his courage through ever recurring obstacles, and the length and difficulty of the struggle and the success now at last achieved, increased his feverishness, his desire for final victory. Yes, yes, he would conquer, he would confound his enemies. As he had said to Monsignor Fornaro, could the Pope disavow him? Had he not expressed the Holy Father's secret ideas? Perhaps he might have done so somewhat prematurely, but was not that a fault to be forgiven? And then too, he remembered his declaration to Monsignor Nani, that he himself would never withdraw and suppress his book, for he neither regretted nor disowned anything that was in it. At this very moment he again questioned himself, and felt that all his valour and determination to defend his book, all his desire to work the triumph of his belief, remained intact. Yet his mental perturbation was becoming great, he had to seek for ideas, wondering how he should enter the Pope's presence, what he should say, what precise terms he should employ. Something heavy and mysterious which he could hardly account for seemed to weigh him down. At bottom he was weary, already exhausted, only held up by his dream, his compassion for human misery. However, he would enter in all haste, he would fall upon his knees and speak as he best could, letting his heart flow forth. And assuredly the Holy Father would smile on him, and dismiss him with a promise that he would not sign the condemnation of a work in which he had found the expression of his own most cherished thoughts.

Then, again, such an acute sensation as of fainting came over Pierre that he went up to the window to press his burning brow against the cold glass. His ears were buzzing, his legs staggering, whilst his brain throbbed violently. And he was striving to forget his thoughts by gazing upon the black immensity of Rome, longing to be steeped in night himself, total, healing night, the night in which one sleeps on for ever, knowing neither pain nor wretchedness, when all at once he became conscious that somebody was standing behind him; and thereupon, with a start, he turned round.

And there, indeed, stood Signor Squadra in his black livery. Again he made one of his customary bows to invite the visitor to follow him, and again he walked on in front, crossing the little throne-room, and slowly opening the farther door. Then he drew aside, allowed Pierre to enter, and noiselessly closed the door behind him.

Pierre was in his Holiness's bed-room. He had feared one of those overwhelming attacks of emotion which madden or paralyse one. He had been told of women reaching the Pope's presence in a fainting condition, staggering as if intoxicated, while others came with a rush, as though upheld and borne along by invisible pinions. And suddenly the anguish of his own spell of waiting, his intense feverishness, ceased in a sort of astonishment, a reaction which rendered him very calm and so restored his clearness of vision, that he could see everything. As he entered he distinctly realised the decisive importance of such an audience, he, a mere petty priest in presence of the Supreme Pontiff, the Head of the Church. All his religious and moral life would depend on it; and possibly it was this sudden thought that thus chilled him on the threshold of the redoubtable sanctuary, which he had approached with such quivering steps, and which he would not have thought to enter otherwise than with distracted heart and loss of senses, unable to do more than stammer the simple prayers of childhood.

Later on, when he sought to classify his recollections he remembered that his eyes had first lighted on Leo XIII, not, however, to the exclusion of his surroundings, but in conjunction with them, that spacious room hung with yellow damask whose alcove, adorned with fluted marble columns, was so deep that the bed was quite hidden away in it, as well as other articles of furniture, a couch, a wardrobe, and some trunks, those famous trunks in which the treasure of the Peter's Pence was said to be securely locked. A sort of Louis XIV writing-desk with ornaments of engraved brass stood face to face with a large gilded and painted Louis XV pier table on which a lamp was burning beside a lofty crucifix. The room was virtually bare, only three arm-chairs and four or five other chairs, upholstered in light silk, being disposed here and there over the well-worn carpet. And on one of the arm-chairs sat Leo XIII, near a small table on which another lamp with a shade had been placed. Three newspapers, moreover, lay there, two of them French and one Italian, and the last was half unfolded as if the Pope had momentarily turned from it to stir a glass of syrup, standing beside him, with a long silver-gilt spoon.

In the same way as Pierre saw the Pope's room, he saw his costume, his cassock of white cloth with white buttons, his white skull-cap, his white cape and his white sash fringed with gold and broidered at either end with golden keys. His stockings were white, his slippers were of red velvet, and these again were broidered with golden keys. What surprised the young priest, however, was his Holiness's face and figure, which now seemed so shrunken that he scarcely recognised them. This was his fourth meeting with the Pope. He had seen him walking in the Vatican gardens, enthroned in the Hall of Beatifications, and pontifying at St. Peter's, and now he beheld him on that arm-chair, in privacy, and looking so slight and fragile that he could not restrain a feeling of affectionate anxiety. Leo's neck was particularly remarkable, slender beyond belief, suggesting the neck of some little, aged, white bird. And his face, of the pallor of alabaster, was characteristically transparent, to such a degree, indeed, that one could see the lamplight through his large commanding nose, as if the blood had entirely withdrawn from that organ. A mouth of great length, with white bloodless lips, streaked the lower part of the papal countenance, and the eyes alone had remained young and handsome. Superb eyes they were, brilliant like black diamonds, endowed with sufficient penetration and strength to lay souls open and force them to confess the truth aloud. Some scanty white curls emerged from under the white skull-cap, thus whitely crowning the thin white face, whose ugliness was softened by all this whiteness, this spiritual whiteness in which Leo XIII's flesh seemed as it were but pure lily-white florescence.

At the first glance, however, Pierre noticed that if Signor Squadra had kept him waiting, it had not been in order to compel the Holy Father to don a clean cassock, for the one he was wearing was badly soiled by snuff. A number of brown stains had trickled down the front of the garment beside the buttons, and just like any good *bourgeois*, his Holiness had a handkerchief on his knees to wipe himself. Apart from all this he seemed in good health, having recovered from his recent indisposition as easily as he usually recovered from such passing illnesses, sober, prudent old man that he was, quite free from organic disease, and simply declining by reason of progressive natural exhaustion.

Immediately on entering Pierre had felt that the Pope's sparkling eyes, those two black diamonds, were fixed upon him. The silence was profound, and the lamps burned with motionless, pallid flames. He had to approach, and after making the three genuflections prescribed by etiquette, he stooped over one of the Pope's feet resting on a cushion in order to kiss the red velvet slipper. And on the Pope's side there was not a word, not a gesture, not a movement. When the young man drew himself up again he found the two black diamonds, those two eyes which were all brightness and intelligence, still riveted on him.

But at last Leo XIII, who had been unwilling to spare the young priest the humble duty of kissing his foot and who now left him standing, began to speak, whilst still examining him, probing, as it were, his very soul. "My son," he said, "you greatly desired to see me, and I consented to afford you that satisfaction."

He spoke in French, somewhat uncertain French, pronounced after the Italian fashion, and so slowly did he articulate each sentence that one could have written it down like so much dictation. And his voice, as Pierre had previously noticed, was strong and nasal, one of those full voices which people are surprised to hear coming from debile and apparently bloodless and breathless frames.

In response to the Holy Father's remark Pierre contented himself with bowing, knowing that respect required him to wait for a direct answer before speaking. However, this question promptly came. "You live in Paris?" asked Leo XIII.

"Yes, Holy Father."

"Are you attached to one of the great parishes of the city?"

"No, Holy Father. I simply officiate at the little church of Neuilly."

"Ah, yes, Neuilly, that is in the direction of the Bois de Boulogne, is it not? And how old are you, my son?"

"Thirty-four, Holy Father."

A short interval followed. Leo XIII had at last lowered his eyes. With frail, ivory hand he took up the glass beside him, again stirred the syrup with the long spoon, and then drank a little of it. And all this he did gently and slowly, with a prudent, judicious air, as was his wont no doubt in everything. "I have read your book, my son," he resumed. "Yes, the greater part of it. As a rule only fragments are submitted to me. But a person who is interested in you handed me the volume, begging me to glance through it. And that is how I was able to look into it."

As he spoke he made a slight gesture in which Pierre fancied he could detect a protest against the isolation in which he was kept by those surrounding him, who, as Monsignor Nani had said, maintained a strict watch in order that nothing they objected to might reach him. And thereupon the young priest ventured to say: "I thank your Holiness for having done me so much honour. No greater or more desired happiness could have befallen me." He was indeed so happy! On seeing the Pope so calm, so free from all signs of anger, and on hearing him speak in that way of his book, like one well acquainted with it, he imagined that his cause was won.

"You are in relations with Monsieur le Vicomte Philibert de la Choue, are you not, my son?" continued Leo XIII. "I was struck by the resemblance between some of your ideas and those of that devoted servant of the Church, who has in other ways given us previous testimony of his good feelings."

"Yes, indeed, Holy Father, Monsieur de la Choue is kind enough to show me some affection. We have often talked together, so it is not surprising that I should have given expression to some of his most cherished ideas."

"No doubt, no doubt. For instance, there is that question of the working-class guilds with which he largely occupies himself—with which, in fact, he occupies himself rather too much. At the time of his last journey to Rome he spoke to me of it in the most pressing manner. And in the same way, quite recently, another of your compatriots, one of the best and worthiest of men, Monsieur le Baron de Fouras, who brought us that superb pilgrimage of the St. Peter's Pence Fund, never ceased his efforts until I consented to receive him, when he spoke to me on the same subject during nearly an hour. Only it must be said that they do not agree in the matter, for one begs me to do things which the other will not have me do on any account."

Pierre realised that the conversation was straying away from his book, but he remembered having promised the Viscount that if he should see the Pope he would make an attempt to obtain from him a decisive expression of opinion on the famous question as to whether the working-class guilds or corporations should be free or obligatory, open or closed. And the unhappy Viscount, kept in Paris by the gout, had written the young priest letter after letter on the subject, whilst his rival the Baron, availing himself of the opportunity offered by the international pilgrimage, endeavoured to wring from the Pope an approval of his own views, with which he would have returned in triumph to France. Pierre conscientiously desired to keep his promise, and so he answered: "Your Holiness knows better than any of us in which direction true wisdom lies. Monsieur de Fouras is of opinion that salvation, the solution of the labour question, lies simply in the re-establishment of the old free corporations, whilst Monsieur de la Choue desires the corporations to be obligatory, protected by the state and governed by new regulations. This last conception is certainly more in agreement with the social ideas now prevalent in France. Should your Holiness condescend to express a favourable opinion in that sense, the young French

Catholic party would certainly know how to turn it to good result, by producing quite a movement of the working classes in favour of the Church."

In his quiet way Leo XIII responded: "But I cannot. Frenchmen always ask things of me which I cannot, will not do. What I will allow you to say on my behalf to Monsieur de la Choue is, that though I cannot content him I have not contented Monsieur de Fouras. He obtained from me nothing beyond the expression of my sincere goodwill for the French working classes, who are so dear to me and who can do so much for the restoration of the faith. You must surely understand, however, that among you Frenchmen there are questions of detail, of mere organisation, so to say, into which I cannot possibly enter without imparting to them an importance which they do not have, and at the same time greatly discontenting some people should I please others."

As the Pope pronounced these last words he smiled a pale smile, in which the shrewd, conciliatory politician, who was determined not to allow his infallibility to be compromised in useless and risky ventures, was fully revealed. And then he drank a little more syrup and wiped his mouth with his handkerchief, like a sovereign whose Court day is over and who takes his ease, having chosen this hour of solitude and silence to chat as long as he may be so inclined.

Pierre, however, sought to bring him back to the subject of his book. "Monsieur de la Choue," said he, "has shown me so much kindness and is so anxious to know the fate reserved to my book—as if, indeed, it were his own—that I should have been very happy to convey to him an expression of your Holiness's approval."

However, the Pope continued wiping his mouth and did not reply.

"I became acquainted with the Viscount," continued Pierre, "at the residence of his Eminence Cardinal Bergerot, another great heart whose ardent charity ought to suffice to restore the faith in France."

This time the effect was immediate. "Ah! yes, Monsieur le Cardinal Bergerot!" said Leo XIII. "I read that letter of his which is printed at the beginning of your book. He was very badly inspired in writing it to you; and you, my son, acted very culpably on the day you published it. I cannot yet believe that Monsieur le Cardinal Bergerot had read some of your pages when he sent you an expression of his complete and full approval. I prefer to charge him with ignorance and thoughtlessness. How could he approve of your attacks on dogma, your revolutionary theories which tend to the complete destruction of our holy religion? If it be a fact that he had read your book, the only excuse he can invoke is sudden and inexplicable aberration. It is true that a very bad spirit prevails among a small portion of the French clergy. What are called Gallican ideas are ever sprouting up like noxious weeds; there is a malcontent Liberalism rebellious to our authority which continually hungers for free examination and sentimental adventures."

The Pope grew animated as he spoke. Italian words mingled with his hesitating French, and every now and again his full nasal voice resounded with the sonority of a brass instrument. "Monsieur le Cardinal Bergerot," he continued, "must be given to understand that we shall crush him on the day when we see in him nothing but a rebellious son. He owes the example of obedience; we shall acquaint him with our displeasure, and we hope that he will submit. Humility and charity are great virtues doubtless, and we have always taken pleasure in recognising them in him. But they must not be the refuge of a rebellious heart, for they are as nothing unless accompanied by obedience—obedience, obedience, the finest adornment of the great saints!"

Pierre listened thunderstruck, overcome. He forgot himself to think of the apostle of kindliness and tolerance upon whose head he had drawn this all-powerful anger. So Don Vigilio had spoken the truth: over and above his—Pierre's—head the denunciations of the Bishops of Evreux and Poitiers were about to fall on the man who opposed their Ultramontane policy, that worthy and gentle Cardinal Bergerot, whose heart was open to all the woes of the lowly and the poor. This filled the young priest with despair; he could accept the denunciation of the Bishop of Tarbes acting on behalf of the Fathers of the Grotto, for that only fell on himself, as a reprisal for what he had written about Lourdes; but the underhand warfare of the others exasperated him, filled him with dolorous indignation. And from that puny old man before him with the slender, scraggy neck of an aged bird, he had suddenly seen such a wrathful, formidable Master arise that he trembled. How could he have allowed himself to be deceived by appearances on entering? How could he have imagined that he was simply in presence of a poor old man, worn out by age, desirous of peace, and ready for every concession? A blast had swept through that sleepy chamber, and all his doubts and his anguish awoke once more. Ah! that Pope, how thoroughly he answered to all the accounts that he, Pierre, had heard but had refused to believe; so many people had told him in Rome that he would find Leo XIII a man of intellect rather than of sentiment, a man of the most unbounded pride, who from his very youth had nourished the supreme ambition, to such a point indeed that he had promised eventual triumph to his relatives in order that they might make the necessary sacrifices for him, while since he had occupied the pontifical throne his one will and determination had been to reign, to reign in spite of all, to be the sole absolute and omnipotent master of the world! And now here was reality arising with irresistible force and confirming everything. And yet Pierre struggled, stubbornly clutching at his dream once more.

"Oh! Holy Father," said he, "I should be grieved indeed if his Eminence should have a moment's worry on account of my unfortunate book. If I be guilty I can answer for my error, but his Eminence only obeyed the dictates of his heart and can only have transgressed by excess of love for the disinherited of the world!"

Leo XIII made no reply. He had again raised his superb eyes, those eyes of ardent life, set, as it were, in the motionless countenance of an alabaster idol; and once more he was fixedly gazing at the young priest.

And Pierre, amidst his returning feverishness, seemed to behold him growing in power and splendour, whilst behind him arose a vision of the ages, a vision of that long line of popes whom the young priest had previously evoked, the saintly and the proud ones, the warriors and the ascetics, the theologians and the diplomatists, those who had worn armour, those who had conquered by the Cross, those who had disposed of empires as of mere provinces which God had committed to their charge. And in particular Pierre beheld the great Gregory, the conqueror and founder, and Sixtus V, the negotiator and politician, who had first foreseen the eventual victory of the papacy over all the vanquished monarchies. Ah! what a throng of magnificent princes, of sovereign masters with powerful brains and arms, there was behind that pale, motionless, old man! What an accumulation of inexhaustible determination, stubborn genius, and boundless domination! The whole history of human ambition, the whole effort of the ages to subject the nations to the pride of one man, the greatest force that has ever conquered, exploited, and fashioned mankind in the name of its happiness! And even now, when territorial sovereignty had come to an end, how great was the spiritual sovereignty of that pale and slender old man, in whose presence women fainted, as if overcome by the divine splendour radiating from his person. Not only did all the resounding glories, the masterful triumphs of history spread out behind him, but heaven opened, the very spheres beyond life shone out in their dazzling mystery. He—the Pope—stood at the portals of heaven, holding the keys and opening those portals to human souls; all the ancient symbolism was revived, freed at last from the stains of royalty here below.

"Oh! I beg you, Holy Father," resumed Pierre, "if an example be needed strike none other than myself. I have come, and am here; decide my fate, but do not aggravate my punishment by filling me with remorse at having brought condemnation on the innocent."

Leo XIII still refrained from replying, though he continued to look at the young priest with burning eyes. And he, Pierre, no longer beheld Leo XIII, the last of a long line of popes, the Vicar of Jesus Christ, the Successor of the Prince of the Apostles, the Supreme Pontiff of the Universal Church, Patriarch of the East, Primate of Italy, Archbishop and Metropolitan of the Roman Province, Sovereign of the Temporal Domains of the Holy Church; he saw the Leo XIII that he had dreamt of, the awaited saviour who would dispel the frightful cataclysm in which rotten society was sinking. He beheld him with his supple, lofty intelligence and fraternal, conciliatory tactics, avoiding friction and labouring to bring about unity whilst with his heart overflowing with love he went straight to the hearts of the multitude, again giving the best of his blood in sign of the new alliance. He raised him aloft as the sole remaining moral authority, the sole possible bond of charity and peace—as the Father, in fact, who alone could stamp out injustice among his children, destroy misery, and re-establish the liberating Law of Work by bringing the nations back to the faith of the primitive Church, the gentleness and the wisdom of the true Christian community. And in the deep silence of that room the great figure which he thus set up assumed invincible all-powerfulness, extraordinary majesty.

"Oh, I beseech you, Holy Father, listen to me," he said. "Do not even strike me, strike no one, neither a being nor a thing, anything that can suffer under the sun. Show kindness and indulgence to all, show all the kindness and indulgence which the sight of the world's sufferings must have set in you!"

And then, seeing that Leo XIII still remained silent and still left him standing there, he sank down upon his knees, as if felled by the growing emotion which rendered his heart so heavy. And within him there was a sort of *debacle*; all his doubts, all his anguish and sadness burst forth in an irresistible stream. There was the memory of the frightful day that he had just spent, the tragic death of Dario and Benedetta, which weighed on him like lead; there were all the sufferings that he had experienced since his arrival in Rome, the destruction of his illusions, the wounds dealt to his delicacy, the buffets with which men and things had responded to his young enthusiasm; and, lying yet more deeply within his heart, there was the sum total of human wretchedness, the thought of famished ones howling for food, of mothers whose breasts were drained and who sobbed whilst kissing their hungry babes, of fathers without work, who clenched their fists and revolted—indeed, the whole of that hateful misery which is as old as mankind itself, which has preyed upon mankind since its earliest hour, and which he now had everywhere found increasing in horror and havoc, without a gleam of hope that it would ever be healed. And withal, yet more immense and more incurable, he felt within him a nameless sorrow to which he could assign no precise cause or name—an universal, an illimitable sorrow with which he melted despairingly, and which was perhaps the very sorrow of life.

"O Holy Father!" he exclaimed, "I myself have no existence and my book has no existence. I desired, passionately desired to see your Holiness that I might explain and defend myself. But I no longer know, I can no longer recall a single one of the things that I wished to say, I can only weep, weep the tears which are stifling me. Yes, I am but a poor man, and the only need I feel is to speak to you of the poor. Oh! the poor ones, oh! the lowly ones, whom for two years past I have seen in our faubourgs of Paris, so wretched and so full of pain; the poor little children that I have picked out of the snow, the poor little angels who had eaten nothing for two days; the women too, consumed by consumption, without bread or fire, shivering in filthy hovels; and the men thrown on the street by slackness of trade, weary of begging for work as one begs for alms, sinking back into night, drunken with rage and harbouring the sole avenging thought of setting the whole city afire! And that night too, that terrible night, when in a room of horror I beheld a mother who had just killed herself with her five little ones, she lying on a palliasse suckling her last-born, and two little girls, two pretty little blondes, sleeping the last sleep beside her, while the two boys had succumbed farther away, one of them crouching against a wall, and the other lying upon the floor, distorted as though by a last effort to avoid death!... O Holy Father! I am but an ambassador, the messenger of those who suffer and who sob, the humble delegate of the humble ones who die of want beneath the hateful harshness, the frightful injustice of our present-day social system! And I bring your Holiness their tears, and I lay their tortures at your Holiness's feet, I raise their cry of woe, like a cry from the abyss, that cry which demands justice unless indeed the very heavens are to fall! Oh! show your loving kindness, Holy Father, show compassion!"

The young man had stretched out his arms and implored Leo XIII with a gesture as of supreme appeal to the divine compassion. Then he continued: "And here, Holy Father, in this splendid and eternal Rome, is not the want and misery as frightful! During the weeks that I have roamed hither and thither among the dust of famous ruins, I have never ceased to come in contact with evils which demand cure. Ah! to think of all that is crumbling, all that is expiring, the agony of so much glory, the fearful sadness of a world which is dying of exhaustion and hunger! Yonder, under your Holiness's windows, have I not seen a district of horrors, a district of unfinished palaces stricken like rickety children who cannot attain to full growth, palaces which are already in ruins and have become places of refuge for all the woeful misery of Rome? And here, as in Paris, what a suffering multitude, what a shameless exhibition too of the social sore, the devouring cancer openly tolerated and displayed in utter heedlessness! There are whole families leading idle and hungry lives in the splendid sunlight; fathers waiting for work to fall to them from heaven; sons listlessly spending their days asleep on the dry grass; mothers and daughters, withered before their time, shuffling about in loquacious idleness. O Holy Father, already to-morrow at dawn may your Holiness open that window yonder and with your benediction awaken that great childish people, which still slumbers in ignorance and poverty! May your Holiness give it the soul it lacks, a soul with the consciousness of human dignity, of the necessary law of work, of free and fraternal life regulated by justice only! Yes, may your Holiness make a people out of that heap of wretches, whose excuse lies in all their bodily suffering and mental night, who live like the beasts that go by and die, never knowing nor understanding, yet ever lashed onward with the whip!"

Pierre's sobs were gradually choking him, and it was only the impulse of his passion which still enabled him to speak. "And, Holy Father," he continued, "is it not to you that I ought to address myself in the name of all these wretched ones? Are you not the Father, and is it not before the Father that the messenger of the poor and the lowly should kneel as I am kneeling now? And is it not to the Father that he should bring the huge burden of their sorrows and ask for pity and help and justice? Yes, particularly for justice! And since you are the Father throw the doors wide open so that all may enter, even the humblest of your children, the faithful, the chance passers, even the rebellious ones and those who have gone astray but who will perhaps enter and whom you will save from the errors of abandonment! Be as the house of refuge on the dangerous road, the loving greeter of the wayfarer, the lamp of hospitality which ever burns, and is seen afar off and saves one in the storm! And since, O Father, you are power be salvation also! You can do all; you have centuries of domination behind you; you have nowadays risen to a moral authority which has rendered you the arbiter of the world; you are there before me like the very majesty of the sun which illumines and fructifies! Oh! be the star of kindness and charity, be the redeemer; take in hand once more the purpose of Jesus, which has been perverted by being left in the hands of the rich and the powerful who have ended by transforming the work of the Gospel into the most hateful of all monuments of pride and tyranny! And since the work has been spoilt, take it in hand, begin it afresh, place yourself on the side of the little ones, the lowly ones, the poor ones, and bring them back to the peace, the fraternity, and the justice of the original Christian communion. And say, O Father, that I have understood you, that I have sincerely expressed in this respect your most cherished ideas, the sole living desire of your reign! The rest, oh! the rest, my book, myself, what matter they! I do not defend myself, I only seek your glory and the happiness of mankind. Say that from the depths of this Vatican you have heard the rending of our corrupt modern societies! Say that you have quivered with loving pity, say that you desire to prevent the awful impending catastrophe by recalling the Gospel to the hearts of your children who are stricken with madness, and by bringing them back to the age of simplicity and purity when the first Christians lived together in innocent brotherhood! Yes, it is for that reason, is it not, that you have placed yourself, Father, on the side of the poor, and for that reason I am here and entreat you for pity and kindness and justice with my whole soul!"

Then the young man gave way beneath his emotion, and fell all of a heap upon the floor amidst a rush of sobs—loud, endless sobs, which flowed forth in billows, coming as it were not only from himself but from all the wretched, from the whole world in whose veins sorrow coursed mingled with the very blood of life. He was there as the ambassador of suffering, as he had said. And indeed, at the foot of that mute and motionless pope, he was like the personification of the whole of human woe.

Leo XIII, who was extremely fond of talking and could only listen to others with an effort, had twice raised one of his pallid hands to interrupt the young priest. Then, gradually overcome by astonishment, touched by emotion himself, he had allowed him to continue, to go on to the end of his outburst. A little blood even had suffused the snowy whiteness of the Pontiff's face whilst his eyes shone out yet more brilliantly. And as soon as he saw the young man speechless at his feet, shaken by those sobs which seemed to be wrenching away his heart, he became anxious and leant forward: "Calm yourself, my son, raise yourself," he said.

But the sobs still continued, still flowed forth, all reason and respect being swept away amidst that distracted plaint of a wounded soul, that moan of suffering, dying flesh.

"Raise yourself, my son, it is not proper," repeated Leo XIII. "There, take that chair." And with a gesture of authority he at last invited the young man to sit down.

Pierre rose with pain, and at once seated himself in order that he might not fall. He brushed his hair back from his forehead, and wiped his scalding tears away with his hands, unable to understand what had just happened, but striving to regain his self-possession.

"You appeal to the Holy Father," said Leo XIII. "Ah! rest assured that his heart is full of pity and affection for those who are unfortunate. But that is not the point, it is our holy religion which is in question. I have read your book, a bad book, I tell you so at once, the most dangerous and culpable of books, precisely on account of its qualities, the pages in which I myself felt interested. Yes, I was often fascinated, I should not have continued my perusal had I not felt carried away, transported by the ardent breath of your faith and enthusiasm. The subject 'New Rome' is such a beautiful one and impassions me so much! and certainly there is a book to be written under that title, but in a very different spirit to yours. You think that you have understood me, my son, that you have so penetrated yourself with my writings and actions that you simply express my most cherished ideas. But no, no, you have not understood me, and that is why I desired to see you, explain things to you, and convince you."

It was now Pierre who sat listening, mute and motionless. Yet he had only come thither to defend himself; for three months past he had been feverishly desiring this interview, preparing his arguments and feeling confident of victory; and now although he heard his book spoken of as dangerous and culpable he did not protest, did not reply with any one of those good reasons which he had deemed so irresistible. But the fact was that intense weariness had come upon him, the appeal that he had made, the tears that he had shed had left him utterly exhausted. By and by, however, he would be brave and would say what he had resolved to say.

"People do not understand me, do not understand me!" resumed Leo XIII with an air of impatient irritation. "It is incredible what trouble I have to make myself understood, in France especially! Take the temporal power for instance; how can you have fancied that the Holy See would ever enter into any compromise on that question? Such language is unworthy of a priest, it is the chimerical dream of one who is ignorant of the conditions in which the papacy has hitherto lived and in which it must still live if it does not desire to disappear. Cannot you see the sophistry of your argument that the Church becomes the loftier the more it frees itself from the cares of terrestrial sovereignty? A purely spiritual royalty, a sway of charity and love, indeed, 'tis a fine imaginative idea! But who will ensure us respect? Who will grant us the alms of a stone on which to rest our head if we are ever driven forth and forced to roam the highways? Who will guarantee our independence when we are at the mercy of every state?... No, no! this soil of Rome is ours, we have inherited it from the long line of our ancestors, and it is the indestructible, eternal soil on which the Church is built, so that any relinquishment would mean the downfall of the Holy Catholic Apostolic and

Roman Church. And, moreover, we could not relinquish it; we are bound by our oath to God and man."

He paused for a moment to allow Pierre to answer him. But the latter to his stupefaction could say nothing, for he perceived that this pope spoke as he was bound to speak. All the heavy mysterious things which had weighed the young priest down whilst he was waiting in the ante-room, now became more and more clearly defined. They were, indeed, the things which he had seen and learnt since his arrival in Rome, the disillusions, the rebuffs which he had experienced, all the many points of difference between existing reality and imagination, whereby his dream of a return to primitive Christianity was already half shattered. And in particular he remembered the hour which he had spent on the dome of St. Peter's, when, in presence of the old city of glory so stubbornly clinging to its purple, he had realised that he was an imbecile with his idea of a purely spiritual pope. He had that day fled from the furious shouts of the pilgrims acclaiming the Pope-King. He had only accepted the necessity for money, that last form of servitude still binding the Pope to earth. But all had crumbled afterwards, when he had beheld the real Rome, the ancient city of pride and domination where the papacy can never be complete without the temporal power. Too many bonds, dogma, tradition, environment, the very soil itself rendered the Church for ever immutable. It was only in appearances that she could make concessions, and a time would even arrive when her concessions would cease, in presence of the impossibility of going any further without committing suicide. If his, Pierre's, dream of a New Rome were ever to be realised, it would only be faraway from ancient Rome. Only in some distant region could the new Christianity arise, for Catholicism was bound to die on the spot when the last of the popes, riveted to that land of ruins, should disappear beneath the falling dome of St. Peter's, which would fall as surely as the temple of Jupiter had fallen! And, as for that pope of the present day, though he might have no kingdom, though age might have made him weak and fragile, though his bloodless pallor might be that of some ancient idol of wax, he none the less flared with the red passion for universal sovereignty, he was none the less the stubborn scion of his ancestry, the Pontifex Maximus, the Caesar Imperator in whose veins flowed the blood of Augustus, master of the world.

"You must be fully aware," resumed Leo XIII, "of the ardent desire for unity which has always possessed us. We were very happy on the day when we unified the rite, by imposing the Roman rite throughout the whole Catholic world. This is one of our most cherished victories, for it can do much to uphold our authority. And I hope that our efforts in the East will end by bringing our dear brethren of the dissident communions back to us, in the same way as I do not despair of convincing the Anglican sects, without speaking of the other so-called Protestant sects who will be compelled to return to the bosom of the only Church, the Catholic, Apostolic, and Roman Church, when the times predicted by the Christ shall be accomplished. But a thing which you did not say in your book is that the Church can relinquish nothing whatever of dogma. On the contrary, you seem to fancy that an agreement might be effected, concessions made on either side, and that, my son, is a culpable thought, such language as a priest cannot use without being guilty of a crime. No, the truth is absolute, not a stone of the edifice shall be changed. Oh! in matters of form, we will do whatever may be asked. We are ready to adopt the most conciliatory courses if it be only a question of turning certain difficulties and weighing expressions in order to facilitate agreement.. .. Again, there is the part we have taken in contemporary socialism, and here too it is necessary that we should be understood. Those whom you have so well called the disinherited of the world, are certainly the object of our solicitude. If socialism be simply a desire for justice, and a constant determination to come to the help of the weak and the suffering, who can claim to give more thought to the matter and work with more energy than ourselves? Has not the Church always been the mother of the afflicted, the helper and benefactress of the poor? We are for all reasonable progress, we admit all new social forms which will promote peace and fraternity.... Only we can but condemn that socialism which begins by driving away God as a means of ensuring the happiness of mankind. Therein lies simple savagery, an abominable relapse into the primitive state in which there can only be catastrophe, conflagration, and massacre. And that again is a point on which you have not laid sufficient stress, for you have not shown in your book that there can be no progress outside the pale of the Church, that she is really the only initiatory and guiding power to whom one may surrender oneself without fear. Indeed, and in this again you have sinned, it seemed to me as if you set God on one side, as if for you religion lay solely in a certain bent of the soul, a florescence of love and charity, which sufficed one to work one's salvation. But that is execrable heresy. God is ever present, master of souls and bodies; and religion remains the bond, the law, the very governing power of mankind, apart from which there can only be barbarism in this world and damnation in the next. And, once again, forms are of no importance; it is sufficient that dogma should remain. Thus our adhesion to the French Republic proves that we in no wise mean to link the fate of religion to that of any form of government, however august and ancient the latter may be. Dynasties may have done their time, but God is eternal. Kings may perish, but God lives! And, moreover, there is nothing anti-Christian in the republican form of government; indeed, on the contrary, it would seem like an awakening of that Christian commonwealth to which you have referred in some really charming pages. The worst is that liberty at once becomes license, and that our desire for conciliation is often very badly requited.... But ah! what a wicked book you have written, my son,—with the best intentions, I am willing to believe,—and how your silence shows that you are beginning to recognise the disastrous consequences of your error."

Pierre still remained silent, overcome, feeling as if his arguments would fall against some deaf, blind, and impenetrable rock, which it was useless to assail since nothing could enter it. And only one thing now preoccupied him; he wondered how it was that a man of such intelligence and such ambition had not formed a more distinct and exact idea of the modern world. He could divine that the Pope possessed much information and carried the map of Christendom with many of the needs, deeds, and hopes of the nations, in his mind amidst his complicated diplomatic enterprises; but at the same time what gaps there were in his knowledge! The truth, no doubt, was that his personal acquaintance with the world was confined to his brief nunciature at Brussels.[1]

During his occupation of the see of Perugia, which had followed, he had only mingled with the dawning life of young Italy. And for eighteen years now he had

[1] That too, was in 1843-44, and the world is now utterly unlike what it was then!—Trans.

been shut up in the Vatican, isolated from the rest of mankind and communicating with the nations solely through his *entourage*, which was often most unintelligent, most mendacious, and most treacherous. Moreover, he was an Italian priest, a superstitious and despotic High Pontiff, bound by tradition, subjected to the influences of race environment, pecuniary considerations, and political necessities, not to speak of his great pride, the conviction that he ought to be implicitly obeyed in all things as the one sole legitimate power upon earth. Therein lay fatal causes of mental deformity, of errors and gaps in his extraordinary brain, though the latter certainly possessed many admirable qualities, quickness of comprehension and patient stubbornness of will and strength to draw conclusions and act. Of all his powers, however, that of intuition was certainly the most wonderful, for was it not this alone which, owing to his voluntary imprisonment, enabled him to divine the vast evolution of humanity at the present day? He was thus keenly conscious of the dangers surrounding him, of the rising tide of democracy and the boundless ocean of science which threatened to submerge the little islet where the dome of St. Peter's yet triumphed. And the object of all his policy, of all his labour, was to conquer so that he might reign. If he desired the unity of the Church it was in order that the latter might become strong and inexpugnable in the contest which he foresaw. If he preached conciliation, granting concessions in matters of form, tolerating audacious actions on the part of American bishops, it was because he deeply and secretly feared the dislocation of the Church, some sudden schism which might hasten disaster. And this fear explained his returning affection for the people, the concern which he displayed respecting socialism, and the Christian solution which he offered to the woes of earthly life. As Caesar was stricken low, was not the long contest for possession of the people over, and would not the people, the great silent multitude, speak out, and give itself to him, the Pope? He had begun experiments with France, forsaking the lost cause of the monarchy and recognising the Republic which he hoped might prove strong and victorious, for in spite of everything France remained the eldest daughter of the Church, the only Catholic nation which yet possessed sufficient strength to restore the temporal power at some propitious moment. And briefly Leo's desire was to reign. To reign by the support of France since it seemed impossible to do so by the support of Germany! To reign by the support of the people, since the people was now becoming the master, the bestower of thrones! To reign by means even of an Italian Republic, if only that Republic could wrest Rome from the House of Savoy and restore her to him, a federal Republic which would make him President of the United States of Italy pending the time when he should be President of the United States of Europe! To reign in spite of everybody and everything, such was his ambition, to reign over the world, even as Augustus had reigned, Augustus whose devouring blood alone upheld this expiring old man, yet so stubbornly clinging to power!

"And another crime of yours, my son," resumed Leo XIII, "is that you have dared to ask for a new religion. That is impious, blasphemous, sacrilegious. There is but one religion in the world, our Holy Catholic Apostolic and Roman Religion, apart from which there can be but darkness and damnation. I quite understand that what you mean to imply is a return to early Christianity. But the error of so-called Protestantism, so culpable and so deplorable in its consequences, never had any other pretext. As soon as one departs from the strict observance of dogma and absolute respect for tradition one sinks into the most frightful precipices.... Ah! schism, schism, my son, is a crime beyond forgiveness, an assassination of the true God, a device of the loathsome Beast of Temptation which Hell sends into the world to work the ruin of the faithful! If your book contained nothing beyond those words 'a new religion,' it would be necessary to destroy and burn it like so much poison fatal in its effects upon the human soul."

He continued at length on this subject, while Pierre recalled what Don Vigilio had told him of those all-powerful Jesuits who at the Vatican as elsewhere remained in the background, secretly but none the less decisively governing the Church. Was it true then that this pope, whose opportunist tendencies were so freely displayed, was one of them, a mere docile instrument in their hands, though he fancied himself penetrated with the doctrines of St. Thomas Aquinas? In any case, like them he compounded with the century, made approaches to the world, and was willing to flatter it in order that he might possess it. Never before had Pierre so cruelly realised that the Church was now so reduced that she could only live by dint of concessions and diplomacy. And he could at last distinctly picture that Roman clergy which at first is so difficult of comprehension to a French priest, that Government of the Church, represented by the pope, the cardinals, and the prelates, whom the Deity has appointed to govern and administer His mundane possessions—mankind and the earth. They begin by setting that very Deity on one side, in the depths of the tabernacle, and impose whatever dogmas they please as so many essential truths. That the Deity exists is evident, since they govern in His name which is sufficient for everything. And being by virtue of their charge the masters, if they consent to sign covenants, Concordats, it is only as matters of form; they do not observe them, and never yield to anything but force, always reserving the principle of their absolute sovereignty which must some day finally triumph. Pending that day's arrival, they act as diplomatists, slowly carrying on their work of conquest as the Deity's functionaries; and religion is but the public homage which they pay to the Deity, and which they organise with all the pomp and magnificence that is likely to influence the multitude. Their only object is to enrapture and conquer mankind in order that the latter may submit to the rule of the Deity, that is the rule of themselves, since they are the Deity's visible representatives, expressly delegated to govern the world. In a word, they straightway descend from Roman law, they are still but the offspring of the old pagan soul of Rome, and if they have lasted until now and if they rely on lasting for ever, until the awaited hour when the empire of the world shall be restored to them, it is because they are the direct heirs of the purple-robed Caesars, the uninterrupted and living progeny of the blood of Augustus.

And thereupon Pierre felt ashamed of his tears. Ah! those poor nerves of his, that outburst of sentiment and enthusiasm to which he had given way! His very modesty was appalled, for he felt as if he had exhibited his soul in utter nakedness. And so uselessly too, in that room where nothing similar had ever been said before, and in presence of that Pontiff-King who could not understand him. His plan of the popes reigning by means of the poor and lowly now horrified him. His idea of the papacy going to the people, at last rid of its former masters, seemed to him a suggestion worthy of a wolf, for if the papacy should go to the people it would only be to prey upon it as the others had done. And really he, Pierre, must have been mad when he had imagined that a Roman prelate, a cardinal, a pope, was capable of admitting a return to the Christian commonwealth, a fresh florescence of primitive Christianity to pacify the aged nations whom hatred consumed. Such a conception indeed was beyond the comprehension of men who for centuries had regarded themselves as masters of the world, so heedless and disdainful of the lowly and the suffering, that they had at last become altogether incapable of either love or charity.[1]

Leo XIII, however, was still holding forth in his full, unwearying voice. And the young priest heard him saying: "Why did you write that page on Lourdes which shows such a thoroughly bad spirit? Lourdes, my son, has rendered great services to religion. To the persons who have come and told me of the touching miracles which are witnessed at the Grotto almost daily, I have often expressed my desire to see those miracles confirmed, proved by the most rigorous scientific tests. And, indeed, according to what I have read, I do not think that the most evilly disposed minds can entertain any further doubt on the matter, for the miracles *are* proved scientifically in the most irrefutable manner. Science, my son, must be God's servant. It can do nothing against Him, it is only by His grace that it arrives at the truth. All the solutions which people nowadays pretend to discover and which seemingly destroy dogma will some day be recognised as false, for God's truth will remain victorious when the times shall be accomplished. That is a very simple certainty, known even to little children, and it would suffice for the peace and salvation of mankind, if mankind would content itself with it. And be convinced, my son, that faith and reason are not incompatible. Have we not got St. Thomas who foresaw everything, explained everything, regulated everything? Your faith has been shaken by the onslaught of the spirit of examination, you have known trouble and anguish which Heaven has been pleased to spare our priests in this land of ancient belief, this city of Rome which the blood of so many martyrs has sanctified. However, we have no fear of the spirit of examination, study St. Thomas, read him thoroughly and your faith will return, definitive and triumphant, firmer than ever."

These remarks caused Pierre as much dismay as if fragments of the celestial vault were raining on his head. O God of truth, miracles—the miracles of Lourdes!—proved scientifically, faith in the dogmas compatible with reason, and the writings of St. Thomas Aquinas sufficient to instil certainty into the minds of this present generation! How could one answer that, and indeed why answer it at all?

"Yes, yours is a most culpable and dangerous book," concluded Leo XIII; "its very title 'New Rome' is mendacious and poisonous, and the work is the more to be condemned as it offers every fascination of style, every perversion of generous fancy. Briefly it is such a book that a priest, if he conceived it in an hour of error, can have no other duty than that of burning it in public with the very hand which traced the pages of error and scandal."

All at once Pierre rose up erect. He was about to exclaim: "'Tis true, I had lost my faith, but I thought I had found it again in the compassion which the woes of the world set in my heart. You were my last hope, the awaited saviour. But, behold, that again is a dream, you cannot take the work of Jesus in hand once more and pacify mankind so as to avert the frightful fratricidal war which is preparing. You cannot leave your throne and come along the roads with the poor and the humble to carry out the supreme work of fraternity. Well, it is all over with you, your Vatican and your St.

---

[1] The reader should bear in mind that these remarks apply to the Italian cardinals and prelates, whose vanity and egotism are remarkable.—Trans.

Peter's. All is falling before the onslaught of the rising multitude and growing science. You no longer exist, there are only ruins and remnants left here."

However, he did not speak those words. He simply bowed and said: "Holy Father, I make my submission and reprobate my book." And as he thus replied his voice trembled with disgust, and his open hands made a gesture of surrender as though he were yielding up his soul. The words he had chosen were precisely those of the required formula: *Auctor laudabiliter se subjecit et opus reprobavit.* "The author has laudably made his submission and reprobated his work." No error could have been confessed, no hope could have accomplished self-destruction with loftier despair, more sovereign grandeur. But what frightful irony: that book which he had sworn never to withdraw, and for whose triumph he had fought so passionately, and which he himself now denied and suppressed, not because he deemed it guilty, but because he had just realised that it was as futile, as chimerical as a lover's desire, a poet's dream. Ah! yes, since he had been mistaken, since he had merely dreamed, since he had found there neither the Deity nor the priest that he had desired for the happiness of mankind, why should he obstinately cling to the illusion of an awakening which was impossible! 'Twere better to fling his book on the ground like a dead leaf, better to deny it, better to cut it away like a dead limb that could serve no purpose whatever!

Somewhat surprised by such a prompt victory Leo XIII raised a slight exclamation of content. "That is well said, my son, that is well said! You have spoken the only words that can become a priest."

And in his evident satisfaction, he who left nothing to chance, who carefully prepared each of his audiences, deciding beforehand what words he would say, what gestures even he would make, unbent somewhat and displayed real *bonhomie*. Unable to understand, mistaking the real motives of this rebellious priest's submission, he tasted positive delight in having so easily reduced him to silence, the more so as report had stated the young man to be a terrible revolutionary. And thus his Holiness felt quite proud of such a conversion. "Moreover, my son," he said, "I did not expect less of one of your distinguished mind. There can be no loftier enjoyment than that of owning one's error, doing penance, and submitting."

He had again taken the glass off the little table beside him and was stirring the last spoonful of syrup before drinking it. And Pierre was amazed at again finding him as he had found him at the outset, shrunken, bereft of sovereign majesty, and simply suggestive of some aged *bourgeois* drinking his glass of sugared water before getting into bed. It was as if after growing and radiating, like a planet ascending to the zenith, he had again sunk to the level of the soil in all human mediocrity. Again did Pierre find him puny and fragile, with the slender neck of a little sick bird, and all those marks of senile ugliness which rendered him so exacting with regard to his portraits, whether they were oil paintings or photographs, gold medals, or marble busts, for of one and the other he would say that the artist must not portray "Papa Pecci" but Leo XIII, the great Pope, of whom he desired to leave such a lofty image to posterity. And Pierre, after momentarily ceasing to see them, was again embarrassed by the handkerchief which lay on the Pope's lap, and the dirty cassock soiled by snuff. His only feelings now were affectionate pity for such white old age, deep admiration for the stubborn power of life which had found a refuge in those dark black eyes, and respectful deference, such as became a worker, for that large brain which harboured such vast projects and overflowed with such innumerable ideas and actions.

XIV.

The audience was over, and the young man bowed low: "I thank your Holiness for having deigned to give me such a fatherly reception," he said.

However, Leo XIII detained him for a moment longer, speaking to him of France and expressing his sincere desire to see her prosperous, calm, and strong for the greater advantage of the Church. And Pierre, during that last moment, had a singular vision, a strange haunting fancy. As he gazed at the Holy Father's ivory brow and thought of his great age and of his liability to be carried off by the slightest chill, he involuntarily recalled the scene instinct with a fierce grandeur which is witnessed each time a pope dies. He recalled Pius IX, Giovanni Mastai, two hours after death, his face covered by a white linen cloth, while the pontifical family surrounded him in dismay; and then Cardinal Pecci, the *Camerlingo*, approaching the bed, drawing aside the veil and dealing three taps with his silver hammer on the forehead of the deceased, repeating at each tap the call, "Giovanni! Giovanni! Giovanni!" And as the corpse made no response, turning, after an interval of a few seconds, and saying: "The Pope is dead!" And at the same time, yonder in the Via Giulia Pierre pictured Cardinal Boccanera, the present *Camerlingo*, awaiting his turn with his silver hammer, and he imagined Leo XIII, otherwise Gioachino Pecci, dead, like his predecessor, his face covered by a white linen cloth and his corpse surrounded by his prelates in that very room. And he saw the *Camerlingo* approach, draw the veil aside and tap the ivory forehead, each time repeating the call: "Gioachino! Gioachino! Gioachino!" Then, as the corpse did not answer, he waited for a few seconds and turned and said "The Pope is dead!" Did Leo XIII remember how he had thrice tapped the forehead of Pius IX, and did he ever feel on the brow an icy dread of the silver hammer with which he had armed his own *Camerlingo*, the man whom he knew to be his implacable adversary, Cardinal Boccanera?

"Go in peace, my son," at last said his Holiness by way of parting benediction. "Your transgression will be forgiven you since you have confessed and testify your horror for it."

With distressful spirit, accepting humiliation as well-deserved chastisement for his chimerical fancies, Pierre retired, stepping backwards according to the customary ceremonial. He made three deep bows and crossed the threshold without turning, followed by the black eyes of Leo XIII, which never left him. Still he saw the Pope stretch his arm towards the table to take up the newspaper which he had been reading prior to the audience, for Leo retained a great fancy for newspapers, and was very inquisitive as to news, though in the isolation in which he lived he frequently made mistakes respecting the relative importance of articles. And once more the chamber sank into deep quietude, whilst the two lamps continued to diffuse a soft and steady light.

In the centre of the *anticamera segreta* Signor Squadra stood waiting black and motionless. And on noticing that Pierre in his flurry forgot to take his hat from the pier table, he himself discreetly fetched it and handed it to the young priest with a silent bow. Then without any appearance of haste, he walked ahead to conduct the visitor back to the Sala Clementina. The endless promenade through the interminable ante-rooms began once more, and there was still not a soul, not a sound, not a breath. In each empty room stood the one solitary lamp, burning low amidst a yet deeper silence than before. The wilderness seemed also to have grown larger as the night advanced, casting its gloom over the few articles of furniture scattered under the lofty gilded ceilings, the thrones, the stools, the pier tables, the crucifixes, and the candelabra which recurred in each succeeding room. And at last the Sala Clementina which the Swiss Guards had just quitted was reached again, and Signor Squadra, who hitherto had not turned his head, thereupon drew aside without word or gesture, and, saluting Pierre with a last bow, allowed him to pass on. Then he himself disappeared.

And Pierre descended the two flights of the monumental staircase where the gas jets in their globes of ground glass glimmered like night lights amidst a wondrously heavy silence now that the footsteps of the sentries no longer resounded on the landings. And he crossed the Court of St. Damasus, empty and lifeless in the pale light of the lamps above the steps, and descended the Scala Pia, that other great stairway as dim, deserted, and void of life as all the rest, and at last passed beyond the bronze door which a porter slowly shut behind him. And with what a rumble, what a fierce roar did the hard metal close upon all that was within; all the accumulated darkness and silence; the dead, motionless centuries perpetuated by tradition; the indestructible idols, the dogmas, bound round for preservation like mummies; every chain which may weigh on one or hamper one, the whole apparatus of bondage and sovereign domination, with whose formidable clang all the dark, deserted halls re-echoed.

Once more the young man found himself alone on the gloomy expanse of the Piazza of St. Peter's. Not a single belated pedestrian was to be seen. There was only the lofty, livid, ghost-like obelisk, emerging between its four candelabra, from the mosaic pavement of red and serpentine porphyry. The facade of the Basilica also showed vaguely, pale as a vision, whilst from it on either side like a pair of giant arms stretched the quadruple colonnade, a thicket of stone, steeped in obscurity. The dome was but a huge roundness scarcely discernible against the moonless sky; and only the jets of the fountains, which could at last be detected rising like slim phantoms ever on the move, lent a voice to the silence, the endless murmur of a plaint of sorrow coming one knew not whence. Ah! how great was the melancholy grandeur of that slumber, that famous square, the Vatican and St. Peter's, thus seen by night when wrapped in silence and darkness! But suddenly the clock struck ten with so slow and loud a chime that never, so it seemed, had more solemn and decisive an hour rung out amidst blacker and more unfathomable gloom. All Pierre's poor weary frame quivered at the sound as he stood motionless in the centre of the expanse. What! had he spent barely three-quarters of an hour, chatting up yonder with that white old man who had just wrenched all his soul away from him! Yes, it was the final wrench; his last belief had been torn from his bleeding heart and brain. The supreme experiment had been made, a world had collapsed within him. And all at once he thought of Monsignor Nani, and reflected that he alone had been right. He, Pierre, had been told that in any case he would end by doing what Monsignor Nani might desire, and he was now stupefied to find that he had done so.

But sudden despair seized upon him, such atrocious distress of spirit that, from the depths of the abyss of darkness where he stood, he raised his quivering arms into space and spoke aloud: "No, no, Thou art not here, O God of life and love, O God of Salvation! But come, appear since Thy children are perishing because they know neither who Thou art, nor where to find Thee amidst the Infinite of the worlds!"

Above the vast square spread the vast sky of dark-blue velvet, the silent disturbing Infinite, where the constellations palpitated. Over the roofs of the Vatican, Charles's Wain seemed yet more tilted, its golden wheels straying from the right path, its golden shaft upreared in the air; whilst yonder, over Rome towards the Via Giulia, Orion was about to disappear and already showed but one of the three golden stars which bedecked his belt.

XV.

IT was nearly daybreak when Pierre fell asleep, exhausted by emotion and hot with fever. And at nine o'clock, when he had risen and breakfasted, he at once wished to go down into Cardinal Boccanera's rooms where the bodies of Dario and Benedetta had been laid in state in order that the members of the family, its friends and clients, might bring them their tears and prayers.

Whilst he breakfasted, Victorine who, showing an active bravery amidst her despair, had not been to bed at all, told him of what had taken place in the house during the night and early morning. Donna Serafina, prude that she was, had again made an attempt to have the bodies separated; but this had proved an impossibility, as *rigor mortis* had set in, and to part the lovers it would have been necessary to break their limbs. Moreover, the Cardinal, who had interposed once before, almost quarrelled with his sister on the subject, unwilling as he was that any one should disturb the lovers' last slumber, their union of eternity. Beneath his priestly garb there coursed the blood of his race, a pride in the passions of former times; and he remarked that if the family counted two popes among its forerunners, it had also been rendered illustrious by great captains and ardent lovers. Never would he allow any one to touch those two children, whose dolorous lives had been so pure and whom the grave alone had united. He was the master in his house, and they should be sewn together in the same shroud, and nailed together in the same coffin. Then too the religious service should take place at the neighbouring church of San Carlo, of which he was Cardinal-priest and where again he was the master. And if needful he would address himself to the Pope. And such being his sovereign will, so authoritatively expressed, everybody in the house had to bow submissively.

Donna Serafina at once occupied herself with the laying-out. According to the Roman custom the servants were present, and Victorine as the oldest and most appreciated of them, assisted the relatives. All that could be done in the first instance was to envelop both corpses in Benedetta's unbound hair, thick and odorous hair, which spread out into a royal mantle; and they were then laid together in one shroud of white silk, fastened about their necks in such wise that they formed but one being in death. And again the Cardinal imperatively ordered that they should be brought into his apartments and placed on a state bed in the centre of the throne-room, so that a supreme homage might be rendered to them as to the last scions of the name, the two tragic lovers with whom the once resounding glory of the Boccaneras was about to return to earth. The story which had been arranged was already circulating through

Rome; folks related how Dario had been carried off in a few hours by infectious fever, and how Benedetta, maddened by grief, had expired whilst clasping him in her arms to bid him a last farewell; and there was talk too of the royal honours which the bodies were to receive, the superb funeral nuptials which were to be accorded them as they lay clasped on their bed of eternal rest. All Rome, quite overcome by this tragic story of love and death, would talk of nothing else for several weeks.

Pierre would have started for France that same night, eager as he was to quit the city of disaster where he had lost the last shreds of his faith, but he desired to attend the obsequies, and therefore postponed his departure until the following evening. And thus he would spend one more day in that old crumbling palace, near the corpse of that unhappy young woman to whom he had been so much attached and for whom he would try to find some prayers in the depths of his empty and lacerated heart.

When he reached the threshold of the Cardinal's reception-rooms, he suddenly remembered his first visit to them. They still presented the same aspect of ancient princely pomp falling into decay and dust. The doors of the three large ante-rooms were wide open, and the rooms themselves were at that early hour still empty. In the first one, the servants' anteroom, there was nobody but Giacomo who stood motionless in his black livery in front of the old red hat hanging under the *baldacchino* where spiders spun their webs between the crumbling tassels. In the second room, which the secretary formerly had occupied, Abbe Paparelli, the train-bearer, was softly walking up and down whilst waiting for visitors; and with his conquering humility, his all-powerful obsequiousness, he had never before so closely resembled an old maid, whitened and wrinkled by excess of devout observances. Finally, in the third ante-room, the *anticamera nobile*, where the red cap lay on a credence facing the large imperious portrait of the Cardinal in ceremonial costume, there was Don Vigilio who had left his little work-table to station himself at the door of the throne-room and there bow to those who crossed the threshold. And on that gloomy winter morning the rooms appeared more mournful and dilapidated than ever, the hangings frayed and ragged, the few articles of furniture covered with dust, the old wood-work crumbling beneath the continuous onslaught of worms, and the ceilings alone retaining their pompous show of gilding and painting.

However, Pierre, to whom Abbe Paparelli addressed a profound bow, in which one divined the irony of a sort of dismissal given to one who was vanquished, felt more impressed by the mournful grandeur which those three dilapidated rooms presented that day, conducting as they did to the old throne-room, now a chamber of death, where the two last children of the house slept their last sleep. What a superb and sorrowful *gala* of death! Every door wide open and all the emptiness of those over-spacious rooms, void of the throngs of ancient days and leading to the supreme affliction—the end of a race! The Cardinal had shut himself up in his little work-room where he received the relatives and intimates who desired to present their condolences to him, whilst Donna Serafina had chosen an adjoining apartment to await her lady friends who would come in procession until evening. And Pierre, informed of the ceremonial by Victorine, had in the first place to enter the throne-room, greeted as he passed by a deep bow from Don Vigilio who, pale and silent, did not seem to recognise him.

A surprise awaited the young priest. He had expected such a lying-in-state as is seen in France and elsewhere, all windows closed so as to steep the room in night, and hundreds of candles burning round a *catafalco*, whilst from ceiling to floor the walls were hung with black drapery. He had been told that the bodies would lie in the throne-room because the antique chapel on the ground floor of the palazzo had been shut up for half a century and was in no condition to be used, whilst the Cardinal's little private chapel was altogether too small for any such ceremony. And thus it had been necessary to improvise an altar in the throne-room, an altar at which masses had been said ever since dawn. Masses and other religious services were moreover to be celebrated all day long in the private chapel; and two additional altars had even been set up, one in a small room adjoining the *anticamera nobile* and the other in a sort of alcove communicating with the second anteroom: and in this wise priests, Franciscans, and members of other Orders bound by the vow of poverty, would simultaneously and without intermission celebrate the divine sacrifice on those four altars. The Cardinal, indeed, had desired that the Divine Blood should flow without pause under his roof for the redemption of those two dear souls which had flown away together. And thus in that mourning mansion, through those funeral halls the bells scarcely stopped tinkling for the elevation of the host, whilst the quivering murmur of Latin words ever continued, and consecrated wafers were continually broken and chalices drained, in such wise that the Divine Presence could not for a moment quit the heavy atmosphere all redolent of death.

On the other hand, however, Pierre, to his great astonishment, found the throne-room much as it had been on the day of his first visit. The curtains of the four large windows had not even been drawn, and the grey, cold, subdued light of the gloomy winter morning freely entered. Under the ceiling of carved and gilded wood-work there were the customary red wall-hangings of *brocatelle*, worn away by long usage; and there was the old throne with the arm-chair turned to the wall, uselessly waiting for a visit from the Pope which would never more come. The principal changes in the aspect of the room were that its seats and tables had been removed, and that, in addition to the improvised altar arranged beside the throne, it now contained the state bed on which lay the bodies of Benedetta and Dario, amidst a profusion of flowers. The bed stood in the centre of the room on a low platform, and at its head were two lighted candles, one on either side. There was nothing else, nothing but that wealth of flowers, such a harvest of white roses that one wondered in what fairy garden they had been culled, sheaves of them on the bed, sheaves of them toppling from the bed, sheaves of them covering the step of the platform, and falling from that step on to the magnificent marble paving of the room.

Pierre drew near to the bed, his heart faint with emotion. Those tapers whose little yellow flamelets scarcely showed in the pale daylight, that continuous low murmur of the mass being said at the altar, that penetrating perfume of roses which rendered the atmosphere so heavy, filled the antiquated, dusty room with a spirit of infinite woe, a lamentation of boundless mourning. And there was not a gesture, not a word spoken, save by the priest officiating at the altar, nothing but an occasional faint sound of stifled sobbing among the few persons present. Servants of the house constantly relieved one another, four always standing erect and motionless at the head of the bed, like faithful, familiar guards. From time to time Consistorial-Advocate Morano who, since early morning had been attending to everything, crossed the room with a silent step and the air of a man in a hurry. And at the edge of the platform all who entered, knelt, prayed, and wept. Pierre perceived three ladies there, their faces hidden by their handkerchiefs; and there was also an old priest who trembled with grief and hung his head in such wise that his face could not be distinguished. However, the young man was most moved by the sight of a poorly clad girl, whom he took for a servant, and whom sorrow had utterly prostrated on the marble slabs.

Then in his turn he knelt down, and with the professional murmur of the lips sought to repeat the Latin prayers which, as a priest, he had so often said at the bed-side of the departed. But his growing emotion confused his memory, and he became wrapt in contemplation of the lovers whom his eyes were unable to quit. Under the wealth of flowers which covered them the clasped bodies could scarcely be distinguished, but the two heads emerged from the silken shroud, and lying there on the same cushion, with their hair mingling, they were still beautiful, beautiful as with satisfied passion. Benedetta had kept her divinely gay, loving, and faithful face for eternity, transported with rapture at having rendered up her last breath in a kiss of love; whilst Dario retained a more dolorous expression amidst his final joy. And their eyes were still wide open, gazing at one another with a persistent and caressing sweetness which nothing would ever more disturb.

Oh! God, was it true that yonder lay that Benedetta whom he, Pierre, had loved with such pure, brotherly affection? He was stirred to the very depths of his soul by the recollection of the delightful hours which he had spent with her. She had been so beautiful, so sensible, yet so full of passion! And he had indulged in so beautiful a dream, that of animating with his own liberating fraternal feelings that admirable creature with soul of fire and indolent air, in whom he had pictured all ancient Rome, and whom he would have liked to awaken and win over to the Italy of to-morrow. He had dreamt of enlarging her brain and heart by filling her with love for the lowly and the poor, with all present-day compassion for things and beings. How he would now have smiled at such a dream had not his tears been flowing! Yet how charming she had shown herself in striving to content him despite the invincible obstacles of race, education, and environment. She had been a docile pupil, but was incapable of any real progress. One day she had certainly seemed to draw nearer to him, as though her own sufferings had opened her soul to every charity; but the illusion of happiness had come back, and then she had lost all understanding of the woes of others, and had gone off in the egotism of her own hope and joy. Did that mean then that this Roman race must finish in that fashion, beautiful as it still often is, and fondly adored but so closed to all love for others, to those laws of charity and justice which, by regulating labour, can henceforth alone save this world of ours?

Then there came another great sorrow to Pierre which left him stammering, unable to speak any precise prayer. He thought of the overwhelming reassertion of Nature's powers which had attended the death of those two poor children. Was it not awful? To have taken that vow to the Virgin, to have endured torment throughout life, and to end by plunging into death, on the loved one's neck, distracted by vain regret and eager for self-bestowal! The brutal fact of impending separation had sufficed for Benedetta to realise how she had duped herself, and to revert to the universal instinct of love. And therein, again once more, was the Church vanquished; therein again appeared the great god Pan, mating the sexes and scattering life around! If in the days of the Renascence the Church did not fall beneath the assault of the Venuses and Hercules then exhumed from the old soil of Rome, the struggle at all events continued as bitterly as ever; and at each and every hour new nations, overflowing with sap, hungering for life, and warring against a religion which was nothing more than an appetite for death, threatened to sweep away that old Holy Apostolic Roman and Catholic edifice whose walls were already tottering on all sides.

And at that moment Pierre felt that the death of that adorable Benedetta was for him the supreme disaster. He was still looking at her and tears were scorching his eyes. She was carrying off his chimera. This time 'twas really the end. Rome the Catholic and the Princely was dead, lying there like marble on that funeral bed. She had been unable to go to the humble, the suffering ones of the world, and had just expired amidst the impotent cry of her egotistical passion when it was too late either to love or to create. Never more would children be born of her, the old Roman house was henceforth empty, sterile, beyond possibility of awakening. Pierre whose soul mourned such a splendid dream, was so grieved at seeing her thus motionless and frigid, that he felt himself fainting. He feared lest he might fall upon the step beside the bed, and so struggled to his feet and drew aside.

Then, as he sought refuge in a window recess in order that he might try to recover self-possession, he was astonished to perceive Victorine seated there on a bench which the hangings half concealed. She had come thither by Donna Serafina's orders, and sat watching her two dear children as she called them, whilst keeping an eye upon all who came in and went out. And, on seeing the young priest so pale and nearly swooning, she at once made room for him to sit down beside her. "Ah!" he murmured after drawing a long breath, "may they at least have the joy of being together elsewhere, of living a new life in another world."

Victorine, however, shrugged her shoulders, and in an equally low voice responded, "Oh! live again, Monsieur l'Abbe, why? When one's dead the best is to remain so and to sleep. Those poor children had enough torments on earth, one mustn't wish that they should begin again elsewhere."

This naive yet deep remark on the part of an ignorant unbelieving woman sent a shudder through Pierre's very bones. To think that his own teeth had chattered with fear at night time at the sudden thought of annihilation. He deemed her heroic at remaining so undisturbed by any ideas of eternity and the infinite. And she, as she felt he was quivering, went on: "What can you suppose there should be after death? We've deserved a right to sleep, and nothing to my thinking can be more desirable and consoling."

"But those two did not live," murmured Pierre, "so why not allow oneself the joy of believing that they now live elsewhere, recompensed for all their torments?"

Victorine, however, again shook her head; "No, no," she replied. "Ah! I was quite right in saying that my poor Benedetta did wrong in torturing herself with all those superstitious ideas of hers when she was really so fond of her lover. Yes, happiness is rarely found, and how one regrets having missed it when it's too late to turn back! That's the whole story of those poor little ones. It's too late for them, they are dead." Then in her turn she broke down and began to sob. "Poor little ones! poor little ones! Look how white they are, and think what they will be when only the bones of their heads lie side by side on the cushion, and only the bones of their arms still clasp one another. Ah! may they sleep, may they sleep; at least they know nothing and feel nothing now."

A long interval of silence followed. Pierre, amidst the quiver of his own doubts, the anxious desire which in common with most men he felt for a new life beyond the grave, gazed at this woman who did not find priests to her fancy, and who retained all her Beauceronne frankness of speech, with the tranquil, contented air of one who has ever done her duty in her humble station as a servant, lost though she had been for five and twenty years in a land of wolves, whose language she had not even been able to learn. Ah! yes, tortured as the young man was by his doubts, he would have liked to be as she was, a well-balanced, healthy, ignorant creature who was quite content with what the world offered, and who, when she had accomplished her daily task, went fully satisfied to bed, careless as to whether she might never wake again!

However, as Pierre's eyes once more sought the state bed, he suddenly recognised the old priest, who was kneeling on the step of the platform, and whose features he had hitherto been unable to distinguish. "Isn't that Abbe Pisoni, the priest of Santa Brigida, where I sometimes said mass?" he inquired. "The poor old man, how he weeps!"

In her quiet yet desolate voice Victorine replied, "He has good reason to weep. He did a fine thing when he took it into his head to marry my poor Benedetta to Count Prada. All those abominations would never have happened if the poor child had been given her Dario at once. But in this idiotic city they are all mad with their politics; and that old priest, who is none the less a very worthy man, thought he had accomplished a real miracle and saved the world by marrying the Pope and the King as he said with a soft laugh, poor old *savant* that he is, who for his part has never been in love with anything but old stones—you know, all that antiquated rubbish of theirs of a hundred thousand years ago. And now, you see, he can't keep from weeping. The other one too came not twenty minutes ago, Father Lorenza, the Jesuit who became the Contessina's confessor after Abbe Pisoni, and who undid what the other had done. Yes, a handsome man he is, but a fine bungler all the same, a perfect killjoy with all the crafty hindrances which he brought into that divorce affair. I wish you had been here to see what a big sign of the cross he made after he had knelt down. He didn't cry, he didn't: he seemed to be saying that as things had ended so badly it was evident that God had withdrawn from all share in the business. So much the worse for the dead!"

Victorine spoke gently and without a pause, as it relieved her, to empty her heart after the terrible hours of bustle and suffocation which she had spent since the previous day. "And that one yonder," she resumed in a lower voice, "don't you recognise her?"

She glanced towards the poorly clad girl whom Pierre had taken for a servant, and whom intensity of grief had prostrated beside the bed. With a gesture of awful suffering this girl had just thrown back her head, a head of extraordinary beauty, enveloped by superb black hair.

"La Pierina!" said Pierre. "Ah! poor girl."

Victorine made a gesture of compassion and tolerance.

"What would you have?" said she, "I let her come up. I don't know how she heard of the trouble, but it's true that she is always prowling round the house. She sent and asked me to come down to her, and you should have heard her sob and entreat me to let her see her Prince once more! Well, she does no harm to anybody there on the floor, looking at them both with her beautiful loving eyes full of tears. She's been there for half an hour already, and I had made up my mind to turn her out if she didn't behave properly. But since she's so quiet and doesn't even move, she may well stop and fill her heart with the sight of them for her whole life long."

It was really sublime to see that ignorant, passionate, beautiful Pierina thus overwhelmed below the nuptial couch on which the lovers slept for all eternity. She had sunk down on her heels, her arms hanging heavily beside her, and her hands open. And with raised face, motionless as in an ecstasy of suffering, she did not take her eyes from that adorable and tragic pair. Never had human face displayed such beauty, such a dazzling splendour of suffering and love; never had there been such a portrayal of ancient Grief, not however cold like marble but quivering with life. What was she thinking of, what were her sufferings, as she thus fixedly gazed at her Prince now and for ever locked in her rival's arms? Was it some jealousy which could have no end that chilled the blood of her veins? Or was it mere suffering at having lost him, at realising that she was looking at him for the last time, without thought of hatred for that other woman who vainly sought to warm him with her arms as icy cold as his own? There was still a soft gleam in the poor girl's blurred eyes, and her lips were still lips of love though curved in bitterness by grief. She found the lovers so pure and beautiful as they lay there amidst that profusion of flowers! And beautiful herself, beautiful like a queen, ignorant of her own charms, she remained there breathless, a humble servant, a loving slave as it were, whose heart had been wrenched away and carried off by her dying master.

People were now constantly entering the room, slowly approaching with mournful faces, then kneeling and praying for a few minutes, and afterwards retiring with the same mute, desolate mien. A pang came to Pierre's heart when he saw Dario's mother, the ever beautiful Flavia, enter, accompanied by her husband, the handsome Jules Laporte, that ex-sergeant of the Swiss Guard whom she had turned into a Marquis Montefiori. Warned of the tragedy directly it had happened, she had already come to the mansion on the previous evening; but now she returned in grand ceremony and full mourning, looking superb in her black garments which were well suited to her massive, Juno-like style of beauty. When she had approached the bed with a queenly step, she remained for a moment standing with two tears at the edges of her eyelids, tears which did not fall. Then, at the moment of kneeling, she made sure that Jules was beside her, and glanced at him as if to order him to kneel as well. They both sank down beside the platform and remained in prayer for the proper interval, she very dignified in her grief and he even surpassing her, with the perfect sorrow-stricken bearing of a man who knew how to conduct himself in every circumstance of life, even the gravest. And afterwards they rose together, and slowly betook themselves to the entrance of the private apartments where the Cardinal and Donna Serafina were receiving their relatives and friends.

Five ladies then came in one after the other, while two Capuchins and the Spanish ambassador to the Holy See went off. And Victorine, who for a few minutes had remained silent, suddenly resumed. "Ah! there's the little Princess, she's much afflicted too, and, no wonder, she was so fond of our Benedetta."

Pierre himself had just noticed Celia coming in. She also had attired herself in full mourning for this abominable visit of farewell. Behind her was a maid, who carried on either arm a huge sheaf of white roses.

"The dear girl!" murmured Victorine, "she wanted her wedding with her Attilio to take place on the same day as that of the poor lovers who lie there. And they, alas! have forestalled her, their wedding's over; there they sleep in their bridal bed."

XV.

Celia had at once crossed herself and knelt down beside the bed, but it was evident that she was not praying. She was indeed looking at the lovers with desolate stupefaction at finding them so white and cold with a beauty as of marble. What! had a few hours sufficed, had life departed, would those lips never more exchange a kiss! She could again see them at the ball of that other night, so resplendent and triumphant with their living love. And a feeling of furious protest rose from her young heart, so open to life, so eager for joy and sunlight, so angry with the hateful idiocy of death. And her anger and affright and grief, as she thus found herself face to face with the annihilation which chills every passion, could be read on her ingenuous, candid, lily-like face. She herself stood on the threshold of a life of passion of which she yet knew nothing, and behold! on that very threshold she encountered the corpses of those dearly loved ones, the loss of whom racked her soul with grief.

She gently closed her eyes and tried to pray, whilst big tears fell from under her lowered eyelids. Some time went by amidst the quivering silence, which only the murmur of the mass near by disturbed. At last she rose and took the sheaves of flowers from her maid; and standing on the platform she hesitated for a moment, then placed the roses to the right and left of the cushion on which the lovers' heads were resting, as if she wished to crown them with those blossoms, perfume their young brows with that sweet and powerful aroma. Then, though her hands remained empty she did not retire, but remained there leaning over the dead ones, trembling and seeking what she might yet say to them, what she might leave them of herself for ever more. An inspiration came to her, and she stooped forward, and with her whole, deep, loving soul set a long, long kiss on the brow of either spouse.

"Ah! the dear girl!" said Victorine, whose tears were again flowing. "You saw that she kissed them, and nobody had yet thought of that, not even the poor young Prince's mother. Ah! the dear little heart, she surely thought of her Attilio."

However, as Celia turned to descend from the platform she perceived La Pierina, whose figure was still thrown back in an attitude of mute and dolorous adoration. And she recognised the girl and melted with pity on seeing such a fit of sobbing come over her that her whole body, her goddess-like hips and bosom, shook as with frightful anguish. That agony of love quite upset the little Princess, and she could be heard murmuring in a tone of infinite compassion, "Calm yourself, my dear, calm yourself. Be reasonable, my dear, I beg you."

Then as La Pierina, thunderstruck at thus being pitied and succoured, began to sob yet more loudly so as to create quite a stir in the room, Celia raised her and held her up with both arms, for fear lest she should fall again. And she led her away in a sisterly clasp, like a sister of affection and despair, lavishing the most gentle, consoling words upon her as they went.

"Follow them, go and see what becomes of them," Victorine said to Pierre. "I do not want to stir from here, it quiets me to watch over my two poor children."

A Capuchin was just beginning a fresh mass at the improvised altar, and the low Latin psalmody went on again, while in the adjoining ante-chamber, where another mass was being celebrated, a bell was heard tinkling for the elevation of the host. The perfume of the flowers was becoming more violent and oppressive amidst the motionless and mournful atmosphere of the spacious throne-room. The four servants standing at the head of the bed, as for a *gala* reception, did not stir, and the procession of visitors ever continued, men and women entering in silence, suffocating there for a moment, and then withdrawing, carrying away with them the never-to-be-forgotten vision of the two tragic lovers sleeping their eternal sleep.

Pierre joined Celia and La Pierina in the *anticamera nobile*, where stood Don Vigilio. The few seats belonging to the throne-room had there been placed in a corner, and the little Princess had just compelled the work-girl to sit down in an arm-chair, in order that she might recover self-possession. Celia was in ecstasy before her, enraptured at finding her so beautiful, more beautiful than any other, as she said. Then she spoke of the two dead ones, who also had seemed to her very beautiful, endowed with an extraordinary beauty, at once superb and sweet; and despite all her tears, she still remained in a transport of admiration. On speaking with La Pierina, Pierre learnt that her brother Tito was at the hospital in great danger from the effects of a terrible knife thrust dealt him in the side; and since the beginning of the winter, said the girl, the misery in the district of the castle fields had become frightful. It was a source of great suffering to every one, and those whom death carried off had reason to rejoice.

Celia, however, with a gesture of invincible hopefulness, brushed all idea of suffering, even of death, aside. "No, no, we must live," she said. "And beauty is sufficient for life. Come, my dear, do not remain here, do not weep any more; live for the delight of being beautiful."

Then she led La Pierina away, and Pierre remained seated in one of the armchairs, overcome by such sorrow and weariness that he would have liked to remain there for ever. Don Vigilio was still bowing to each fresh visitor that arrived. A severe attack of fever had come on him during the night, and he was shivering from it, with his face very yellow, and his eyes ablaze and haggard. He constantly glanced at Pierre, as if anxious to speak to him, but his dread lest he should be seen by Abbe Paparelli, who stood in the next ante-room, the door of which was wide open, doubtless restrained him, for he did not cease to watch the train-bearer. At last the latter was compelled to absent himself for a moment, and the secretary thereupon approached the young Frenchman.

"You saw his Holiness last night," he said; and as Pierre gazed at him in stupefaction he added: "Oh! everything gets known, I told you so before. Well, and you purely and simply withdrew your book, did you not?" The young priest's increasing stupor was sufficient answer, and without leaving him time to reply, Don Vigilio went on: "I suspected it, but I wished to make certain. Ah! that's just the way they work! Do you believe me now, have you realised that they stifle those whom they don't poison?"

He was no doubt referring to the Jesuits. However, after glancing into the adjoining room to make sure that Abbe Paparelli had not returned thither, he resumed: "And what has Monsignor Nani just told you?"

"But I have not yet seen Monsignor Nani," was Pierre's reply.

"Oh! I thought you had. He passed through before you arrived. If you did not see him in the throne-room he must have gone to pay his respects to Donna Serafina and his Eminence. However, he will certainly pass this way again; you will see him by and by." Then with the bitterness of one who was weak, ever terror-smitten and vanquished, Don Vigilio added: "I told you that you would end by doing what Monsignor Nani desired."

With these words, fancying that he heard the light footfall of Abbe Paparelli, he hastily returned to his place and bowed to two old ladies who just then walked in. And Pierre, still seated, overcome, his eyes wearily closing, at last saw the figure of

Nani arise before him in all its reality so typical of sovereign intelligence and address. He remembered what Don Vigilio, on the famous night of his revelations, had told him of this man who was far too shrewd to have labelled himself, so to say, with an unpopular robe, and who, withal, was a charming prelate with thorough knowledge of the world, acquired by long experience at different nunciatures and at the Holy Office, mixed up in everything, informed with regard to everything, one of the heads, one of the chief minds in fact of that modern black army, which by dint of Opportunism hopes to bring this century back to the Church. And all at once, full enlightenment fell on Pierre, he realised by what supple, clever strategy that man had led him to the act which he desired of him, the pure and simple withdrawal of his book, accomplished with every appearance of free will. First there had been great annoyance on Nani's part on learning that the book was being prosecuted, for he feared lest its excitable author might be prompted to some dangerous revolt; then plans had at once been formed, information had been collected concerning this young priest who seemed so capable of schism, he had been urged to come to Rome, invited to stay in an ancient mansion whose very walls would chill and enlighten him. And afterwards had come the ever recurring obstacles, the system of prolonging his sojourn in Rome by preventing him from seeing the Pope, but promising him the much-desired interview when the proper time should come, that is after he had been sent hither and thither and brought into collision with one and all. And finally, when every one and everything had shaken, wearied, and disgusted him, and he was restored once more to his old doubts, there had come the audience for which he had undergone all this preparation, that visit to the Pope which was destined to shatter whatever remained to him of his dream. Pierre could picture Nani smiling at him and speaking to him, declaring that the repeated delays were a favour of Providence, which would enable him to visit Rome, study and understand things, reflect, and avoid blunders. How delicate and how profound had been the prelate's diplomacy in thus crushing his feelings beneath his reason, appealing to his intelligence to suppress his work without any scandalous struggle as soon as his knowledge of the real Rome should have shown him how supremely ridiculous it was to dream of a new one!

At that moment Pierre perceived Nani in person just coming from the throne-room, and did not feel the irritation and rancour which he had anticipated. On the contrary he was glad when the prelate, in his turn seeing him, drew near and held out his hand. Nani, however, did not wear his wonted smile, but looked very grave, quite grief-stricken. "Ah! my dear son," he said, "what a frightful catastrophe! I have just left his Eminence, he is in tears. It is horrible, horrible!"

He seated himself on one of the chairs, inviting the young priest, who had risen, to do the same; and for a moment he remained silent, weary with emotion no doubt, and needing a brief rest to free himself of the weight of thoughts which visibly darkened his usually bright face. Then, with a gesture, he strove to dismiss that gloom, and recover his amiable cordiality. "Well, my dear son," he began, "you saw his Holiness?"

"Yes, Monseigneur, yesterday evening; and I thank you for your great kindness in satisfying my desire."

Nani looked at him fixedly, and his invincible smile again returned to his lips. "You thank me.... I can well see that you behaved sensibly and laid your full submission at his Holiness's feet. I was certain of it, I did not expect less of your fine intelligence. But, all the same, you render me very happy, for I am delighted to find that I was not mistaken concerning you." And then, setting aside his reserve, the prelate went on: "I never discussed things with you. What would have been the good of it, since facts were there to convince you? And now that you have withdrawn your book a discussion would be still more futile. However, just reflect that if it were possible for you to bring the Church back to her early period, to that Christian community which you have sketched so delightfully, she could only again follow the same evolutions as those in which God the first time guided her; so that, at the end of a similar number of centuries, she would find herself exactly in the position which she occupies to-day. No, what God has done has been well done, the Church such as she is must govern the world, such as it is; it is for her alone to know how she will end by firmly establishing her reign here below. And this is why your attack upon the temporal power was an unpardonable fault, a crime even, for by dispossessing the papacy of her domains you hand her over to the mercy of the nations. Your new religion is but the final downfall of all religion, moral anarchy, the liberty of schism, in a word, the destruction of the divine edifice, that ancient Catholicism which has shown such prodigious wisdom and solidity, which has sufficed for the salvation of mankind till now, and will alone be able to save it to-morrow and always."

Pierre felt that Nani was sincere, pious even, and really unshakable in his faith, loving the Church like a grateful son, and convinced that she was the only social organisation which could render mankind happy. And if he were bent on governing the world, it was doubtless for the pleasure of governing, but also in the conviction that no one could do so better than himself.

"Oh! certainly," said he, "methods are open to discussion. I desire them to be as affable and humane as possible, as conciliatory as can be with this present century, which seems to be escaping us, precisely because there is a misunderstanding between us. But we shall bring it back, I am sure of it. And that is why, my dear son, I am so pleased to see you return to the fold, thinking as we think, and ready to battle on our side, is that not so?"

In Nani's words the young priest once more found the arguments of Leo XIII. Desiring to avoid a direct reply, for although he now felt no anger the wrenching away of his dream had left him a smarting wound, he bowed, and replied slowly in order to conceal the bitter tremble of his voice: "I repeat, Monseigneur, that I deeply thank you for having amputated my vain illusions with the skill of an accomplished surgeon. A little later, when I shall have ceased to suffer, I shall think of you with eternal gratitude."

Monsignor Nani still looked at him with a smile. He fully understood that this young priest would remain on one side, that as an element of strength he was lost to the Church. What would he do now? Something foolish no doubt. However, the prelate had to content himself with having helped him to repair his first folly; he could not foresee the future. And he gracefully waved his hand as if to say that sufficient unto the day was the evil thereof.

"Will you allow me to conclude, my dear son?" he at last exclaimed. "Be sensible, your happiness as a priest and a man lies in humility. You will be terribly unhappy if you use the great intelligence which God has given you against Him."

Then with another gesture he dismissed this affair, which was all over, and with which he need busy himself no more. And thereupon the other affair came back to make him gloomy, that other affair which also was drawing to a close, but so tragically, with those two poor children slumbering in the adjoining room. "Ah!" he resumed, "that poor Princess and that poor Cardinal quite upset my heart! Never did catastrophe fall so cruelly on a house. No, no, it is indeed too much, misfortune goes too far—it revolts one's soul!"

Just as he finished a sound of voices came from the second ante-room, and Pierre was thunderstruck to see Cardinal Sanguinetti go by, escorted with the greatest obsequiousness by Abbe Paparelli.

"If your most Reverend Eminence will have the extreme kindness to follow me," the train-bearer was saying, "I will conduct your most Reverend Eminence myself."

"Yes," replied Sanguinetti, "I arrived yesterday evening from Frascati, and when I heard the sad news, I at once desired to express my sorrow and offer consolation."

"Your Eminence will perhaps condescend to remain for a moment near the bodies. I will afterwards escort your Eminence to the private apartments."

"Yes, by all means. I desire every one to know how greatly I participate in the sorrow which has fallen on this illustrious house."

Then Sanguinetti entered the throne-room, leaving Pierre quite aghast at his quiet audacity. The young priest certainly did not accuse him of direct complicity with Santobono, he did not even dare to measure how far his moral complicity might go. But on seeing him pass by like that, his brow so lofty, his speech so clear, he had suddenly felt convinced that he knew the truth. How or through whom, he could not have told; but doubtless crimes become known in those shady spheres by those whose interest it is to know of them. And Pierre remained quite chilled by the haughty fashion in which that man presented himself, perhaps to stifle suspicion and certainly to accomplish an act of good policy by giving his rival a public mark of esteem and affection.

"The Cardinal! Here!" Pierre murmured despite himself.

Nani, who followed the young man's thoughts in his childish eyes, in which all could be read, pretended to mistake the sense of his exclamation. "Yes," said he, "I learnt that the Cardinal returned to Rome yesterday evening. He did not wish to remain away any longer; the Holy Father being so much better that he might perhaps have need of him."

Although these words were spoken with an air of perfect innocence, Pierre was not for a moment deceived by them. And having in his turn glanced at the prelate, he was convinced that the latter also knew the truth. Then, all at once, the whole affair appeared to him in its intricacy, in the ferocity which fate had imparted to it. Nani, an old intimate of the Palazzo Boccanera, was not heartless, he had surely loved Benedetta with affection, charmed by so much grace and beauty. One could thus explain the victorious manner in which he had at last caused her marriage to be annulled. But if Don Vigilio were to be believed, that divorce, obtained by pecuniary outlay, and under pressure of the most notorious influences, was simply a scandal which he, Nani, had in the first instance spun out, and then precipitated towards a resounding finish with the sole object of discrediting the Cardinal and destroying his chances of the tiara on the eve of the Conclave which everybody thought imminent. It seemed certain, too, that the Cardinal, uncompromising as he was, could not be the candidate of Nani, who was so desirous of universal agreement, and so the latter's long labour in that house, whilst conducing to the happiness of the Contessina, had been designed to frustrate Donna Serafina and Cardinal Pio in their burning ambition, that third triumphant elevation to the papacy which they sought to secure for their ancient family.

However, if Nani had always desired to baulk this ambition, and had even at one moment placed his hopes in Sanguinetti and fought for him, he had never imagined that Boccanera's foes would go to the point of crime, to such an abomination as poison which missed its mark and killed the innocent. No, no, as he himself said, that was too much, and made one's soul rebel. He employed more gentle weapons; such brutality filled him with indignation; and his face, so pinky and carefully tended, still wore the grave expression of his revolt in presence of the tearful Cardinal and those poor lovers stricken in his stead.

Believing that Sanguinetti was still the prelate's secret candidate, Pierre was worried to know how far their moral complicity in this baleful affair might go. So he resumed the conversation by saying: "It is asserted that his Holiness is on bad terms with his Eminence Cardinal Sanguinetti. Of course the reigning pope cannot look on the future pope with a very kindly eye."

At this, Nani for a moment became quite gay in all frankness. "Oh," said he, "the Cardinal has quarrelled and made things up with the Vatican three or four times already. And, in any event, the Holy Father has no motive for posthumous jealousy; he knows very well that he can give his Eminence a good greeting." Then, regretting that he had thus expressed a certainty, he added: "I am joking, his Eminence is altogether worthy of the high fortune which perhaps awaits him."

Pierre knew what to think however; Sanguinetti was certainly Nani's candidate no longer. It was doubtless considered that he had used himself up too much by his impatient ambition, and was too dangerous by reason of the equivocal alliances which in his feverishness he had concluded with every party, even that of patriotic young Italy. And thus the situation became clearer. Cardinals Sanguinetti and Boccanera devoured and suppressed one another; the first, ever intriguing, accepting every compromise, dreaming of winning Rome back by electoral methods; and the other, erect and motionless in his stern maintenance of the past, excommunicating the century, and awaiting from God alone the miracle which would save the Church. And, indeed, why not leave the two theories, thus placed face to face, to destroy one another, including all the extreme, disquieting views which they respectively embodied? If Boccanera had escaped the poison, he had none the less become an impossible candidate, killed by all the stories which had set Rome buzzing; while if Sanguinetti could say that he was rid of a rival, he had at the same time dealt a mortal blow to his own candidature, by displaying such passion for power, and such unscrupulousness with regard to the methods he employed, as to be a danger for every one. Monsignor Nani was visibly delighted with this result; neither candidate was left, it was like the legendary story of the two wolves who fought and devoured one another so completely that nothing of either of them was found left, not even their tails! And in the depths of the prelate's pale eyes, in the whole of his discreet person, there remained nothing but redoubtable mystery: the mystery of the yet unknown, but definitively selected candidate who would be patronised by the all-powerful army of which he was one of the most skilful leaders. A man like him always had a solution ready. Who, then, who would be the next pope?

However, he now rose and cordially took leave of the young priest. "I doubt if I shall see you again, my dear son," he said; "I wish you a good journey."

Still he did not go off, but continued to look at Pierre with his penetrating eyes, and finally made him sit down again and did the same himself. "I feel sure," he said, "that you will go to pay your respects to Cardinal Bergerot as soon as you have returned to France. Kindly tell him that I respectfully desired to be reminded to him. I knew him a little at the time when he came here for his hat. He is one of the great luminaries of the French clergy. Ah! a man of such intelligence would only work for a good understanding in our holy Church. Unfortunately I fear that race and environment have instilled prejudices into him, for he does not always help us."

Pierre, who was surprised to hear Nani speak of the Cardinal for the first time at this moment of farewell, listened with curiosity. Then in all frankness he replied: "Yes, his Eminence has very decided ideas about our old Church of France. For instance, he professes perfect horror of the Jesuits."

With a light exclamation Nani stopped the young man. And he wore the most sincerely, frankly astonished air that could be imagined. "What! horror of the Jesuits! In what way can the Jesuits disquiet him? The Jesuits, there are none, that's all over! Have you seen any in Rome? Have they troubled you in any way, those poor Jesuits who haven't even a stone of their own left here on which to lay their heads? No, no, that bogey mustn't be brought up again, it's childish."

Pierre in his turn looked at him, marvelling at his perfect ease, his quiet courage in dealing with this burning subject. He did not avert his eyes, but displayed an open face like a book of truth. "Ah!" he continued, "if by Jesuits you mean the sensible priests who, instead of entering into sterile and dangerous struggles with modern society, seek by human methods to bring it back to the Church, why, then of course we are all of us more or less Jesuits, for it would be madness not to take into account the times in which one lives. And besides, I won't haggle over words; they are of no consequence! Jesuits, well, yes, if you like, Jesuits!" He was again smiling with that shrewd smile of his in which there was so much raillery and so much intelligence. "Well, when you see Cardinal Bergerot tell him that it is unreasonable to track the Jesuits and treat them as enemies of the nation. The contrary is the truth. The Jesuits are for France, because they are for wealth, strength, and courage. France is the only great Catholic country which has yet remained erect and sovereign, the only one on which the papacy can some day lean. Thus the Holy Father, after momentarily dreaming of obtaining support from victorious Germany, has allied himself with France, the vanquished, because he has understood that apart from France there can be no salvation for the Church. And in this he has only followed the policy of the Jesuits, those frightful Jesuits, whom your Parisians execrate. And tell Cardinal Bergerot also that it would be grand of him to work for pacification by making people understand how wrong it is for your Republic to help the Holy Father so little in his conciliatory efforts. It pretends to regard him as an element in the world's affairs that may be neglected; and that is dangerous, for although he may seem to have no political means of action he remains an immense moral force, and can at any moment raise consciences in rebellion and provoke a religious agitation of the most far-reaching consequences. It is still he who disposes of the nations, since he disposes of their souls, and the Republic acts most inconsiderately, from the standpoint of its own interests, in showing that it no longer even suspects it. And tell the Cardinal too, that it is really pitiful to see in what a wretched way your Republic selects its bishops, as though it intentionally desired to weaken its episcopacy. Leaving out a few fortunate exceptions, your bishops are men of small brains, and as a result your cardinals, likewise mere mediocrities, have no influence, play no part here in Rome. Ah! what a sorry figure you Frenchmen will cut at the next Conclave! And so why do you show such blind and foolish hatred of those Jesuits, who, politically, are your friends? Why don't you employ their intelligent zeal, which is ready to serve you, so that you may assure yourselves the help of the next, the coming pope? It is necessary for you that he should be on your side, that he should continue the work of Leo XIII, which is so badly judged and so much opposed, but which cares little for the petty results of to-day, since its purpose lies in the future, in the union of all the nations under their holy mother the Church. Tell Cardinal Bergerot, tell him plainly that he ought to be with us, that he ought to work for his country by working for us. The coming pope, why the whole question lies in that, and woe to France if in him she does not find a continuator of Leo XIII!"

Nani had again risen, and this time he was going off. Never before had he unbosomed himself at such length. But most assuredly he had only said what he desired to say, for a purpose that he alone knew of, and in a firm, gentle, and deliberate voice by which one could tell that each word had been weighed and determined beforehand. "Farewell, my dear son," he said, "and once again think over all you have seen and heard in Rome. Be as sensible as you can, and do not spoil your life."

Pierre bowed, and pressed the small, plump, supple hand which the prelate offered him. "Monseigneur," he replied, "I again thank you for all your kindness; you may be sure that I shall forget nothing of my journey."

Then he watched Nani as he went off, with a light and conquering step as if marching to all the victories of the future. No, no, he, Pierre, would forget nothing of his journey! He well knew that union of all the nations under their holy mother the Church, that temporal bondage in which the law of Christ would become the dictatorship of Augustus, master of the world! And as for those Jesuits, he had no doubt that they did love France, the eldest daughter of the Church, and the only daughter that could yet help her mother to reconquer universal sovereignty, but they loved her even as the black swarms of locusts love the harvests which they swoop upon and devour. Infinite sadness had returned to the young man's heart as he dimly realised that in that sorely-stricken mansion, in all that mourning and downfall, it was they, they again, who must have been the artisans of grief and disaster.

As this thought came to him he turned round and perceived Don Vigilio leaning against the credence in front of the large portrait of the Cardinal. Holding his hands to his face as if he desired to annihilate himself, the secretary was shivering in every limb as much with fear as with fever. At a moment when no fresh visitors were arriving he had succumbed to an attack of terrified despair.

"*Mon Dieu*! What is the matter with you?" asked Pierre stepping forward, "are you ill, can I help you?"

But Don Vigilio, suffocating and still hiding his face, could only gasp between his close-pressed hands "Ah! Paparelli, Paparelli!"

"What is it? What has he done to you?" asked the other astonished.

Then the secretary disclosed his face, and again yielded to his quivering desire to confide in some one. "Eh? what he has done to me? Can't you feel anything, can't you see anything then? Didn't you notice the manner in which he took possession of Cardinal Sanguinetti so as to conduct him to his Eminence? To impose that suspected, hateful rival on his Eminence at such a moment as this, what insolent audacity! And a few minutes previously did you notice with what wicked cunning he bowed out an old lady, a very old family friend, who only desired to kiss his Eminence's hand and show a little real affection which would have made his Eminence so happy! Ah! I tell you that he's the master here, he opens or closes the door as he pleases, and holds us all between his fingers like a pinch of dust which one throws to the wind!"

Pierre became anxious, seeing how yellow and feverish Don Vigilio was: "Come, come, my dear fellow," he said, "you are exaggerating!"

"Exaggerating? Do you know what happened last night, what I myself unwillingly witnessed? No, you don't know it; well, I will tell you."

Thereupon he related that Donna Serafina, on returning home on the previous day to face the terrible catastrophe awaiting her, had already been overcome by the bad news which she had learnt when calling on the Cardinal Secretary and various prelates of her acquaintance. She had then acquired a certainty that her brother's position was becoming extremely bad, for he had made so many fresh enemies among his colleagues of the Sacred College, that his election to the pontifical throne, which a year previously had seemed probable, now appeared an impossibility. Thus, all at once, the dream of her life collapsed, the ambition which she had so long nourished lay in dust at her feet. On despairingly seeking the why and wherefore of this change, she had been told of all sorts of blunders committed by the Cardinal, acts of rough sternness, unseasonable manifestations of opinion, inconsiderate words or actions which had sufficed to wound people, in fact such provoking demeanour that one might have thought it adopted with the express intention of spoiling everything. And the worst was that in each of the blunders she had recognised errors of judgment which she herself had blamed, but which her brother had obstinately insisted on perpetrating under the unacknowledged influence of Abbe Paparelli, that humble and insignificant train-bearer, in whom she detected a baneful and powerful adviser who destroyed her own vigilant and devoted influence. And so, in spite of the mourning in which the house was plunged, she did not wish to delay the punishment of the traitor, particularly as his old friendship with that terrible Santobono, and the story of that basket of figs which had passed from the hands of the one to those of the other, chilled her blood with a suspicion which she even recoiled from elucidating. However, at the first words she spoke, directly she made a formal request that the traitor should be immediately turned out of the house, she was confronted by invincible resistance on her brother's part. He would not listen to her, but flew into one of those hurricane-like passions which swept everything away, reproaching her for laying blame on so modest, pious, and saintly a man, and accusing her of playing into the hands of his enemies, who, after killing Monsignor Gallo, were seeking to poison his sole remaining affection for that poor, insignificant priest. He treated all the stories he was told as abominable inventions, and swore that he would keep the train-bearer in his service if only to show his disdain for calumny. And she was thereupon obliged to hold her peace.

However, Don Vigilio's shuddering fit had again come back; he carried his hands to his face stammering: "Ah! Paparelli, Paparelli!" And muttered invectives followed: the train-bearer was an artful hypocrite who feigned modesty and humility, a vile spy appointed to pry into everything, listen to everything, and pervert everything that went on in the palace; he was a loathsome, destructive insect, feeding on the most noble prey, devouring the lion's mane, a Jesuit—the Jesuit who is at once lackey and tyrant, in all his base horror as he accomplishes the work of vermin.

"Calm yourself, calm yourself," repeated Pierre, who whilst allowing for foolish exaggeration on the secretary's part could not help shivering at thought of all the threatening things which he himself could divine astir in the gloom.

However, since Don Vigilio had so narrowly escaped eating those horrible figs, his fright was such that nothing could calm it. Even when he was alone at night, in bed, with his door locked and bolted, sudden terror fell on him and made him hide his head under the sheet and vent stifled cries as if he thought that men were coming through the wall to strangle him. In a faint, breathless voice, as if just emerging from a struggle, he now resumed: "I told you what would happen on the evening when we had a talk together in your room. Although all the doors were securely shut, I did wrong to speak of them to you, I did wrong to ease my heart by telling you all that they were capable of. I was sure they would learn it, and you see they did learn it, since they tried to kill me.... Why it's even wrong of me to tell you this, for it will reach their ears and they won't miss me the next time. Ah! it's all over, I'm as good as dead; this house which I thought so safe will be my tomb."

Pierre began to feel deep compassion for this ailing man, whose feverish brain was haunted by nightmares, and whose life was being finally wrecked by the anguish of persecution mania. "But you must run away in that case!" he said. "Don't stop here; come to France."

Don Vigilio looked at him, momentarily calmed by surprise. "Run away, why? Go to France? Why, they are there! No matter where I might go, they would be there. They are everywhere, I should always be surrounded by them! No, no, I prefer to stay here and would rather die at once if his Eminence can no longer defend me." With an expression of ardent entreaty in which a last gleam of hope tried to assert itself, he raised his eyes to the large painting in which the Cardinal stood forth resplendent in his cassock of red moire; but his attack came back again and overwhelmed him with increased intensity of fever. "Leave me, I beg you, leave me," he gasped. "Don't make me talk any more. Ah! Paparelli, Paparelli! If he should come back and see us and hear me speak.... Oh! I'll never say anything again. I'll tie up my tongue, I'll cut it off. Leave me, you are killing me, I tell you, he'll be coming back and that will mean my death. Go away, oh! for mercy's sake, go away!"

Thereupon Don Vigilio turned towards the wall as if to flatten his face against it, and immure his lips in tomb-like silence; and Pierre resolved to leave him to himself, fearing lest he should provoke a yet more serious attack if he went on endeavouring to succour him.

On returning to the throne-room the young priest again found himself amidst all the frightful mourning. Mass was following mass; without cessation murmured prayers entreated the divine mercy to receive the two dear departed souls with loving kindness. And amidst the dying perfume of the fading roses, in front of the pale stars of the lighted candles, Pierre thought of that supreme downfall of the Boccaneras. Dario was the last of the name, and one could well understand that the Cardinal, whose only sin was family pride, should have loved that one remaining scion by whom alone the old stock might yet blossom afresh. And indeed, if he and Donna Serafina had desired the divorce, and then the marriage of the cousins, it had been less with the view of putting an end to scandal than with the hope of seeing a new line of Boccaneras spring up. But the lovers were dead, and the last remains of a long series of dazzling princes of sword and of gown lay there on that bed, soon to rot in the grave. It was all over; that old maid and that aged Cardinal could leave no posterity. They remained face to face like two withered oaks, sole remnants of a vanished forest, and their fall would soon leave the plain quite clear. And how terrible the grief of surviving in impotence, what anguish to have to tell oneself that one is the end of everything, that with oneself all life, all hope for the morrow will depart! Amidst the murmur of the prayers, the dying perfume of the roses, the pale gleams of the two candies, Pierre realised what a downfall was that bereavement, how heavy was the gravestone which fell for ever on an extinct house, a vanished world.

He well understood that as one of the familiars of the mansion he must pay his respects to Donna Serafina and the Cardinal, and he at once sought admission to the neighbouring room where the Princess was receiving her friends. He found her robed in black, very slim and very erect in her arm-chair, whence she rose with slow dignity to respond to the bow of each person that entered. She listened to the condolences but answered never a word, overcoming her physical pain by rigidity of bearing. Pierre, who had learnt to know her, could divine, however, by the hollowness of her cheeks, the emptiness of her eyes, and the bitter twinge of her mouth, how frightful was the collapse within her. Not only was her race ended, but her brother would never be pope, never secure the elevation which she had so long fancied she was winning for him by dint of devotion, dint of feminine renunciation, giving brain and heart, care and money, foregoing even wifehood and motherhood, spoiling her whole life, in order to realise that dream. And amidst all the ruin of hope, it was perhaps the nonfulfilment of that ambition which most made her heart bleed. She rose for the young priest, her guest, as she rose for the other persons who presented themselves; but she contrived to introduce shades of meaning into the manner in which she quitted her chair, and Pierre fully realised that he had remained in her eyes a mere petty French priest, an insignificant domestic of the Divinity who had not known how to acquire even the title of prelate. When she had again seated herself after acknowledging his compliment with a slight inclination of the head, he remained for a moment standing, out of politeness. Not a word, not a sound disturbed the mournful quiescence of the room, for although there were four or five lady visitors seated there they remained motionless and silent as with grief. Pierre was most struck, however, by the sight of Cardinal Sarno, who was lying back in an arm-chair with his eyes closed. The poor puny lopsided old man had lingered there forgetfully after expressing his condolences, and, overcome by the heavy silence and close atmosphere, had just fallen asleep. And everybody respected his slumber. Was he dreaming as he dozed of that map of Christendom which he carried behind his low obtuse-looking brow? Was he continuing in dreamland his terrible work of conquest, that task of subjecting and governing the earth which he directed from his dark room at the Propaganda? The ladies glanced at him affectionately and deferentially; he was gently scolded at times for over-working himself, the sleepiness which nowadays frequently overtook him in all sorts of places being attributed to excess of genius and zeal. And of this all-powerful Eminence Pierre was destined to carry off only this last impression: an exhausted old man, resting amidst the emotion of a mourning-gathering, sleeping there like a candid child, without any one knowing whether this were due to the approach of senile imbecility, or to the fatigues of a night spent in organising the reign of God over some distant continent.

Two ladies went off and three more arrived. Donna Serafina rose, bowed, and then reseated herself, reverting to her rigid attitude, her bust erect, her face stern and full of despair. Cardinal Sarno was still asleep. Then Pierre felt as if he would stifle, a kind of vertigo came on him, and his heart beat violently. So he bowed and withdrew: and on passing through the dining-room on his way to the little study where Cardinal Boccanera received his visitors, he found himself in the presence of Paparelli who was jealously guarding the door. When the train-bearer had sniffed at the young man, he seemed to realise that he could not refuse him admittance. Moreover, as this intruder was going away the very next day, defeated and covered with shame, there was nothing to be feared from him.

"You wish to see his Eminence?" said Paparelli. "Good, good. By and by, wait." And opining that Pierre was too near the door, he pushed him back to the other end of the room, for fear no doubt lest he should overhear anything. "His Eminence is still engaged with his Eminence Cardinal Sanguinetti. Wait, wait there!"

Sanguinetti indeed had made a point of kneeling for a long time in front of the bodies in the throne-room, and had then spun out his visit to Donna Serafina in order to mark how largely he shared the family sorrow. And for more than ten minutes now he had been closeted with Cardinal Boccanera, nothing but an occasional murmur of their voices being heard through the closed door.

Pierre, however, on finding Paparelli there, was again haunted by all that Don Vigilio had told him. He looked at the train-bearer, so fat and short, puffed out with bad fat in his dirty cassock, his face flabby and wrinkled, and his whole person at forty years of age suggestive of that of a very old maid: and he felt astonished. How was it that Cardinal Boccanera, that superb prince who carried his head so high, and who was so supremely proud of his name, had allowed himself to be captured and swayed by such a frightful creature reeking of baseness and abomination? Was it not the man's very physical degradation and profound humility that had struck him, disturbed him, and finally fascinated him, as wondrous gifts conducing to salvation, which he himself lacked? Paparelli's person and disposition were like blows dealt to his own handsome presence and his own pride. He, who could not be so deformed, he who could not vanquish his passion for glory, must, by an effort of faith, have grown jealous of that man who was so extremely ugly and so extremely insignificant, he must have come to admire him as a superior force of penitence and human abasement which threw the portals of heaven wide open. Who can ever tell what ascendency is exercised by the monster over the hero; by the horrid-looking saint covered with vermin over the powerful of this world in their terror at having to endure everlasting flames in payment of their terrestrial joys? And 'twas indeed the lion devoured by the insect, vast strength and splendour destroyed by the invisible. Ah! to have that fine soul which was so certain of paradise, which for its welfare was enclosed in such a disgusting body, to possess the happy humility of that wide intelligence, that remarkable theologian, who scourged himself with rods each morning on rising, and was content to be the lowest of servants.

Standing there a heap of livid fat, Paparelli on his side watched Pierre with his little grey eyes blinking amidst the myriad wrinkles of his face. And the young priest began to feel uneasy, wondering what their Eminences could be saying to one another, shut up together like that for so long a time. And what an interview it must be if Boccanera suspected Sanguinetti of counting Santobono among his clients. What serene audacity it was on Sanguinetti's part to have dared to present himself in that house, and what strength of soul there must be on Boccanera's part, what empire over himself, to prevent all scandal by remaining silent and accepting the visit as a simple mark of esteem and affection! What could they be saying to one another, however? How interesting it would have been to have seen them face to face, and have heard them exchange the diplomatic phrases suited to such an interview, whilst their souls were raging with furious hatred!

All at once the door opened and Cardinal Sanguinetti appeared with calm face, no ruddier than usual, indeed a trifle paler, and retaining the fitting measure of sorrow which he had thought it right to assume. His restless eyes alone revealed his delight at being rid of a difficult task. And he was going off, all hope, in the conviction that he was the only eligible candidate to the papacy that remained.

Abbe Paparelli had darted forward: "If your Eminence will kindly follow me—I will escort your Eminence to the door." Then, turning towards Pierre, he added: "You may go in now."

Pierre watched them walk away, the one so humble behind the other, who was so triumphant. Then he entered the little work-room, furnished simply with a table and three chairs, and in the centre of it he at once perceived Cardinal Boccanera still standing in the lofty, noble attitude which he had assumed to take leave of Sanguinetti, his hated rival to the pontifical throne. And, visibly, Boccanera also believed himself the only possible pope, the one whom the coming Conclave would elect.

However, when the door had been closed, and the Cardinal beheld that young priest, his guest, who had witnessed the death of those two dear children lying in the adjoining room, he was again mastered by emotion, an unexpected attack of weakness in which all his energy collapsed. His human feelings were taking their revenge now that his rival was no longer there to see him. He staggered like an old tree smitten with the axe, and sank upon a chair, stifling with sobs.

And as Pierre, according to usage, was about to stoop and kiss his ring, he raised him and at once made him sit down, stammering in a halting voice: "No, no, my dear son! Seat yourself there, wait—Excuse me, leave me to myself for a moment, my heart is bursting."

He sobbed with his hands to his face, unable to master himself, unable to drive back his grief with those yet vigorous fingers which were pressed to his cheeks and temples.

Tears came into Pierre's eyes, for he also lived through all that woe afresh, and was much upset by the weeping of that tall old man, that saint and prince, usually so haughty, so fully master of himself, but now only a poor, suffering, agonising man, as weak and as lost as a child. However, although the young priest was likewise stifling with grief, he desired to present his condolences, and sought for kindly words by which he might soothe the other's despair. "I beg your Eminence to believe in my profound grief," he said. "I have been overwhelmed with kindness here, and desired at once to tell your Eminence how much that irreparable loss—"

But with a brave gesture the Cardinal silenced him. "No, no, say nothing, for mercy's sake say nothing!"

And silence reigned while he continued weeping, shaken by the struggle he was waging, his efforts to regain sufficient strength to overcome himself. At last he mastered his quiver and slowly uncovered his face, which had again become calm, like that of a believer strong in his faith, and submissive to the will of God. In refusing a miracle, in dealing so hard a blow to that house, God had doubtless had His reasons, and he, the Cardinal, one of God's ministers, one of the high dignitaries of His terrestrial court, was in duty bound to bow to it. The silence lasted for another moment, and then, in a voice which he managed to render natural and cordial, Boccanera said: "You are leaving us, you are going back to France to-morrow, are you not, my dear son?"

"Yes, I shall have the honour to take leave of your Eminence to-morrow, again thanking your Eminence for your inexhaustible kindness."

"And you have learnt that the Congregation of the Index has condemned your book, as was inevitable?"

"Yes, I obtained the signal favour of being received by his Holiness, and in his presence made my submission and reprobated my book."

The Cardinal's moist eyes again began to sparkle. "Ah! you did that, ah! you did well, my dear son," he said. "It was only your strict duty as a priest, but there are so many nowadays who do not even do their duty! As a member of the Congregation I kept the promise I gave you to read your book, particularly the incriminated pages. And if I afterwards remained neutral, to such a point even as to miss the sitting in which judgment was pronounced, it was only to please my poor, dear niece, who was so fond of you, and who pleaded your cause to me."

Tears were coming into his eyes again, and he paused, feeling that he would once more be overcome if he evoked the memory of that adored and lamented Benedetta. And so it was with a pugnacious bitterness that he resumed: "But what an execrable book it was, my dear son, allow me to tell you so. You told me that you had shown respect for dogma, and I still wonder what aberration can have come over you that you should have been so blind to all consciousness of your offences. Respect for dogma—good Lord! when the entire work is the negation of our holy religion! Did you not realise that by asking for a new religion you absolutely condemned the old one, the only true one, the only good one, the only one that can be eternal? And that sufficed to make your book the most deadly of poisons, one of those infamous books which in former times were burnt by the hangman, and which one is nowadays compelled to leave in circulation after interdicting them and thereby designating them to evil curiosity, which explains the contagious rottenness of the century. Ah! I well recognised there some of the ideas of our distinguished and poetical relative, that dear Viscount Philibert de la Choue. A man of letters, yes! a man of letters! Literature, mere literature! I beg God to forgive him, for he most surely does not know what he is doing, or whither he is going with his elegiac Christianity for talkative working men and young persons of either sex, to whom scientific notions have given vagueness of soul. And I only feel angry with his Eminence Cardinal Bergerot, for he at any rate knows what he does, and does as he pleases. No, say nothing, do not defend him. He personifies Revolution in the Church, and is against God."

Although Pierre had resolved that he would not reply or argue, he had allowed a gesture of protest to escape him on hearing this furious attack upon the man whom he most respected in the whole world. However, he yielded to Cardinal Boccanera's injunction and again bowed.

"I cannot sufficiently express my horror," the Cardinal roughly continued; "yes, my horror for all that hollow dream of a new religion! That appeal to the most hideous passions which stir up the poor against the rich, by promising them I know not what division of wealth, what community of possession which is nowadays impossible! That base flattery shown to the lower orders to whom equality and justice are promised but never given, for these can come from God alone, it is only He who can finally make them reign on the day appointed by His almighty power! And there is even that interested charity which people abuse of to rail against Heaven itself and accuse it of iniquity and indifference, that lackadaisical weakening charity and compassion, unworthy of strong firm hearts, for it is as if human suffering were not necessary for salvation, as if we did not become more pure, greater and nearer to the supreme happiness, the more and more we suffer!"

He was growing excited, full of anguish, and superb. It was his bereavement, his heart wound, which thus exasperated him, the great blow which had felled him for a moment, but against which he again rose erect, defying grief, and stubborn in his stoic belief in an omnipotent God, who was the master of mankind, and reserved felicity to those whom He selected. Again, however, he made an effort to calm himself, and resumed in a more gentle voice: "At all events the fold is always open, my dear son, and here you are back in it since you have repented. You cannot imagine how happy it makes me."

In his turn Pierre strove to show himself conciliatory in order that he might not further ulcerate that violent, grief-stricken soul: "Your Eminence," said he, "may be sure that I shall endeavour to remember every one of the kind words which your Eminence has spoken to me, in the same way as I shall remember the fatherly greeting of his Holiness Leo XIII."

This sentence seemed to throw Boccanera into agitation again. At first only murmured, restrained words came from him, as if he were struggling against a desire to question the young priest. "Ah yes! you saw his Holiness, you spoke to him, and he told you I suppose, as he tells all the foreigners who go to pay their respects to him, that he desires conciliation and peace. For my part I now only see him when it is absolutely necessary; for more than a year I have not been received in private audience."

This proof of disfavour, of the covert struggle which as in the days of Pius IX kept the Holy Father and the *Camerlingo* at variance, filled the latter with bitterness. He was unable to restrain himself and spoke out, reflecting no doubt that he had a familiar before him, one whose discretion was certain, and who moreover was leaving Rome on the morrow. "One may go a long way," said he, "with those fine words, peace and conciliation, which are so often void of real wisdom and courage. The terrible truth is that Leo XIII's eighteen years of concessions have shaken everything in the Church, and should he long continue to reign Catholicism would topple over and crumble into dust like a building whose pillars have been undermined."

Interested by this remark, Pierre in his desire for knowledge began to raise objections. "But hasn't his Holiness shown himself very prudent?" he asked; "has he not placed dogma on one side in an impregnable fortress? If he seems to have made concessions on many points, have they not always been concessions in mere matters of form?"

"Matters of form; ah, yes!" the Cardinal resumed with increasing passion. "He told you, no doubt, as he tells others, that whilst in substance he will make no surrender, he will readily yield in matters of form! It's a deplorable axiom, an equivocal form of diplomacy even when it isn't so much low hypocrisy! My soul revolts at the thought of that Opportunism, that Jesuitism which makes artifice its weapon, and only serves to cast doubt among true believers, the confusion of a *sauve-qui-peut*, which by and by must lead to inevitable defeat. It is cowardice, the worst form of cowardice, abandonment of one's weapons in order that one may retreat the more speedily, shame of oneself, assumption of a mask in the hope of deceiving the enemy, penetrating into his camp, and overcoming him by treachery! No, no, form is everything in a traditional and immutable religion, which for eighteen hundred years has been, is now, and till the end of time will be the very law of God!"

The Cardinal's feelings so stirred him that he was unable to remain seated, and began to walk about the little room. And it was the whole reign, the whole policy of Leo XIII which he discussed and condemned. "Unity too," he continued, "that famous unity of the Christian Church which his Holiness talks of bringing about, and his desire for which people turn to his great glory, why, it is only the blind ambition of a conqueror enlarging his empire without asking himself if the new nations that he subjects may not disorganise, adulterate, and impregnate his old and hitherto faithful people with every error. What if all the schismatical nations on returning to the Catholic Church should so transform it as to kill it and make it a new Church? There is only one wise course, which is to be what one is, and that firmly. Again, isn't there both shame and danger in that pretended alliance with the democracy which in itself gives the lie to the ancient spirit of the papacy? The right of kings is divine, and to abandon the monarchical principle is to set oneself against God, to compound with revolution, and harbour a monstrous scheme of utilising the madness of men the better to establish one's power over them. All republics are forms of anarchy, and there can be no more criminal act, one which must for ever shake the principle of authority, order, and religion itself, than that of recognising a republic as legitimate for the sole purpose of indulging a dream of impossible conciliation. And observe how this bears on the question of the temporal power. He continues to claim it, he makes a point of no surrender on that question of the restoration of Rome; but in reality, has he not made the loss irreparable, has he not definitively renounced Rome, by admitting that nations have the right to drive away their kings and live like wild beasts in the depths of the forest?"

All at once the Cardinal stopped short and raised his arms to Heaven in a burst of holy anger. "Ah! that man, ah! that man who by his vanity and craving for success will have proved the ruin of the Church, that man who has never ceased corrupting everything, dissolving everything, crumbling everything in order to reign over the world which he fancies he will reconquer by those means, why, Almighty God, why hast Thou not already called him to Thee?"

So sincere was the accent in which that appeal to Death was raised, to such a point was hatred magnified by a real desire to save the Deity imperilled here below, that a great shudder swept through Pierre also. He now understood that Cardinal Boccanera who religiously and passionately hated Leo XIII; he saw him in the depths of his black palace, waiting and watching for the Pope's death, that death which as *Camerlingo* he must officially certify. How feverishly he must wait, how impatiently he must desire the advent of the hour, when with his little silver hammer he would deal the three symbolic taps on the skull of Leo XIII, while the latter lay cold and rigid on his bed surrounded by his pontifical Court. Ah! to strike that wall of the brain, to make sure that nothing more would answer from within, that nothing beyond night and silence was left there. And the three calls would ring out: "Gioachino! Gioachino! Gioachino!" And, the corpse making no answer, the *Camerlingo* after waiting for a few seconds would turn and say: "The Pope is dead!"

"Conciliation, however, is the weapon of the times," remarked Pierre, wishing to bring the Cardinal back to the present, "and it is in order to make sure of conquering that the Holy Father yields in matters of form."

"He will not conquer, he will be conquered," cried Boccanera. "Never has the Church been victorious save in stubbornly clinging to its integrality, the immutable eternity of its divine essence. And it would for a certainty fall on the day when it should allow a single stone of its edifice to be touched. Remember the terrible period through which it passed at the time of the Council of Trent. The Reformation had just deeply shaken it, laxity of discipline and morals was everywhere increasing, there was a rising tide of novelties, ideas suggested by the spirit of evil, unhealthy projects born of the pride of man, running riot in full license. And at the Council itself many members were disturbed, poisoned, ready to vote for the wildest changes, a fresh schism added to all the others. Well, if Catholicism was saved at that critical period, under the threat of such great danger, it was because the majority, enlightened by God, maintained the old edifice intact, it was because with divinely inspired obstinacy it kept itself within the narrow limits of dogma, it was because it made no concession, none, whether in substance or in form! Nowadays the situation is certainly not worse than it was at the time of the Council of Trent. Let us suppose it to be much the same, and tell me if it is not nobler, braver, and safer for the Church to show the courage which she showed before and declare aloud what she is, what she has been, and what she will be. There is no salvation for her otherwise than in her complete, indisputable sovereignty; and since she has always conquered by non-surrender, all attempts to conciliate her with the century are tantamount to killing her!"

The Cardinal had again begun to walk to and fro with thoughtful step. "No, no," said he, "no compounding, no surrender, no weakness! Rather the wall of steel which bars the road, the block of granite which marks the limit of a world! As I told you, my dear son, on the day of your arrival, to try to accommodate Catholicism to the new times is to hasten its end, if really it be threatened, as atheists pretend. And in that way it would die basely and shamefully instead of dying erect, proud, and dignified in its old glorious royalty! Ah! to die standing, denying nought of the past, braving the future and confessing one's whole faith!"

That old man of seventy seemed to grow yet loftier as he spoke, free from all dread of final annihilation, and making the gesture of a hero who defies futurity. Faith had given him serenity of peace; he believed, he knew, he had neither doubt nor fear of the morrow of death. Still his voice was tinged with haughty sadness as he resumed, "God can do all, even destroy His own work should it seem evil in His eyes. But though all should crumble to-morrow, though the Holy Church should disappear among the ruins, though the most venerated sanctuaries should be crushed by the falling stars, it would still be necessary for us to bow and adore God, who after creating the world might thus annihilate it for His own glory. And I wait, submissive to His will, for nothing happens unless He wills it. If really the temples be shaken, if Catholicism be fated to fall to-morrow into dust, I shall be here to act as the minister of death, even as I have been the minister of life! It is certain, I confess it, that there are hours when terrible signs appear to me. Perhaps, indeed, the end of time is nigh, and we shall witness that fall of the old world with which others threaten us. The worthiest, the loftiest are struck down as if Heaven erred, and in them punished the crimes of the world. Have I not myself felt the blast from the abyss into which all must sink, since my house, for transgressions that I am ignorant of, has been stricken with that frightful bereavement which precipitates it into the gulf which casts it back into night everlasting!"

He again evoked those two dear dead ones who were always present in his mind. Sobs were once more rising in his throat, his hands trembled, his lofty figure quivered with the last revolt of grief. Yes, if God had stricken him so severely by suppressing his race, if the greatest and most faithful were thus punished, it must be that the world was definitively condemned. Did not the end of his house mean the approaching end of all? And in his sovereign pride as priest and as prince, he found a cry of supreme resignation, once more raising his hands on high: "Almighty God, Thy will be done! May all die, all fall, all return to the night of chaos! I shall remain standing in this ruined palace, waiting to be buried beneath its fragments. And if Thy will should summon me to bury Thy holy religion, be without fear, I shall do nothing unworthy to prolong its life for a few days! I will maintain it erect, like myself, as proud, as uncompromising as in the days of all its power. I will yield nothing, whether in discipline, or in rite, or in dogma. And when the day shall come I will bury it with myself, carrying it whole into the grave rather than yielding aught of it, encompassing it with my cold arms to restore it to Thee, even as Thou didst commit it to the keeping of Thy Church. O mighty God and sovereign Master, dispose of me, make me if such be Thy good pleasure the pontiff of destruction, the pontiff of the death of the world."

Pierre, who was thunderstruck, quivered with fear and admiration at the extraordinary vision this evoked: the last of the popes interring Catholicism. He understood that Boccanera must at times have made that dream; he could see him in the Vatican, in St. Peter's which the thunderbolts had riven asunder, he could see him erect and alone in the spacious halls whence his terrified, cowardly pontifical Court had fled. Clad in his white cassock, thus wearing white mourning for the Church, he once more descended to the sanctuary, there to wait for heaven to fall on the evening of Time's accomplishment and annihilate the earth. Thrice he raised the large crucifix, overthrown by the supreme convulsions of the soil. Then, when the final crack rent the steps apart, he caught it in his arms and was annihilated with it beneath the falling vaults. And nothing could be more instinct with fierce and kingly grandeur.

Voiceless, but without weakness, his lofty stature invincible and erect in spite of all, Cardinal Boccanera made a gesture dismissing Pierre, who yielding to his passion for truth and beauty found that he alone was great and right, and respectfully kissed his hand.

It was in the throne-room, with closed doors, at nightfall, after the visits had ceased, that the two bodies were laid in their coffin. The religious services had come to an end, and in the close silent atmosphere there only lingered the dying perfume of the roses and the warm odour of the candles. As the latter's pale stars scarcely lighted the spacious room, some lamps had been brought, and servants held them in their hands like torches. According to custom, all the servants of the house were present to bid a last farewell to the departed.

There was a little delay. Morano, who had been giving himself no end of trouble ever since morning, was forced to run off again as the triple coffin did not arrive. At last it came, some servants brought it up, and then they were able to begin. The Cardinal and Donna Serafina stood side by side near the bed. Pierre also was present, as well as Don Vigilio. It was Victorine who sewed the lovers up in the white silk shroud, which seemed like a bridal robe, the gay pure robe of their union. Then two servants came forward and helped Pierre and Don Vigilio to lay the bodies in the first coffin, of pine wood lined with pink satin. It was scarcely broader than an ordinary coffin, so young and slim were the lovers and so tightly were they clasped in their last embrace. When they were stretched inside they there continued their eternal slumber, their heads half hidden by their odorous, mingling hair. And when this first coffin had been placed in the second one, a leaden shell, and the second had been enclosed in the third, of stout oak, and when the three lids had been soldered and screwed down, the lovers' faces could still be seen through the circular opening, covered with thick glass, which in accordance with the Roman custom had been left in each of the coffins. And then, for ever parted from the living, alone together, they still gazed at one another with their eyes obstinately open, having all eternity before them wherein to exhaust their infinite love.

XVI.

ON the following day, on his return from the funeral Pierre lunched alone in his room, having decided to take leave of the Cardinal and Donna Serafina during the afternoon. He was quitting Rome that evening by the train which started at seventeen minutes past ten. There was nothing to detain him any longer; there was only one visit which he desired to make, a visit to old Orlando, with whom he had promised to have a long chat prior to his departure. And so a little before two o'clock he sent for a cab which took him to the Via Venti Settembre. A fine rain had fallen all night, its moisture steeping the city in grey vapour; and though this rain had now ceased the sky remained very dark, and the huge new mansions of the Via Venti Settembre were quite livid, interminably mournful with their balconies ever of the same pattern and their regular and endless rows of windows. The Ministry of Finances, that colossal pile of masonry and sculpture, looked in particular like a dead town, a huge bloodless body whence all life had withdrawn. On the other hand, although all was so gloomy the rain had made the atmosphere milder, in fact it was almost warm, damply and feverishly warm.

In the hall of Prada's little palazzo Pierre was surprised to find four or five gentlemen taking off their overcoats; however he learnt from a servant that Count Luigi had a meeting that day with some contractors. As he, Pierre, wished to see the Count's father he had only to ascend to the third floor, added the servant. He must knock at the little door on the right-hand side of the landing there.

On the very first landing, however, the priest found himself face to face with the young Count who was there receiving the contractors, and who on recognising him became frightfully pale. They had not met since the tragedy at the Boccanera mansion, and Pierre well realised how greatly his glance disturbed that man, what a troublesome recollection of moral complicity it evoked, and what mortal dread lest he should have guessed the truth.

"Have you come to see me, have you something to tell me?" the Count inquired.

"No, I am leaving Rome, I have come to wish your father good-bye."

Prada's pallor increased at this, and his whole face quivered: "Ah! it is to see my father. He is not very well, be gentle with him," he replied, and as he spoke, his look of anguish clearly proclaimed what he feared from Pierre, some imprudent word, perhaps even a final mission, the malediction of that man and woman whom he had killed. And surely if his father knew, he would die as well. "Ah! how annoying it is," he resumed, "I can't go up with you! There are gentlemen waiting for me. Yes, how annoyed I am. As soon as possible, however, I will join you, yes, as soon as possible."

He knew not how to stop the young priest, whom he must evidently allow to remain with his father, whilst he himself stayed down below, kept there by his pecuniary worries. But how distressful were the eyes with which he watched Pierre climb the stairs, how he seemed to supplicate him with his whole quivering form. His father, good Lord, the only true love, the one great, pure, faithful passion of his life!

"Don't make him talk too much, brighten him, won't you?" were his parting words.

Up above it was not Batista, the devoted ex-soldier, who opened the door, but a very young fellow to whom Pierre did not at first pay any attention. The little room was bare and light as on previous occasions, and from the broad curtainless window there was the superb view of Rome, Rome crushed that day beneath a leaden sky and steeped in shade of infinite mournfulness. Old Orlando, however, had in no wise changed, but still displayed the superb head of an old blanched lion, a powerful muzzle and youthful eyes, which yet sparkled with the passions which had growled in a soul of fire. Pierre found the stricken hero in the same arm-chair as previously, near the same table littered with newspapers, and with his legs buried in the same black wrapper, as if he were there immobilised in a sheath of stone, to such a point that after months and years one was sure to perceive him quite unchanged, with living bust, and face glowing with strength and intelligence.

That grey day, however, he seemed gloomy, low in spirits. "Ah! so here you are, my dear Monsieur Froment," he exclaimed, "I have been thinking of you these three days past, living the awful days which you must have lived in that tragic Palazzo Boccanera. Ah, God! What a frightful bereavement! My heart is quite overwhelmed, these newspapers have again just upset me with the fresh details they give!" He pointed as he spoke to the papers scattered over the table. Then with a gesture he strove to brush aside the gloomy story, and banish that vision of Benedetta dead, which had been haunting him. "Well, and yourself?" he inquired.

"I am leaving this evening," replied Pierre, "but I did not wish to quit Rome without pressing your brave hands."

"You are leaving? But your book?"

"My book—I have been received by the Holy Father, I have made my submission and reprobated my book."

Orlando looked fixedly at the priest. There was a short interval of silence, during which their eyes told one another all that they had to tell respecting the affair. Neither felt the necessity of any longer explanation. The old man merely spoke these concluding words: "You have done well, your book was a chimera."

"Yes, a chimera, a piece of childishness, and I have condemned it myself in the name of truth and reason."

A smile appeared on the dolorous lips of the impotent hero. "Then you have seen things, you understand and know them now?"

"Yes, I know them; and that is why I did not wish to go off without having that frank conversation with you which we agreed upon."

Orlando was delighted, but all at once he seemed to remember the young fellow who had opened the door to Pierre, and who had afterwards modestly resumed his seat on a chair near the window. This young fellow was a youth of twenty, still beardless, of a blonde handsomeness such as occasionally flowers at Naples, with long curly hair, a lily-like complexion, a rosy mouth, and soft eyes full of a dreamy languor. The old man presented him in fatherly fashion, Angiolo Mascara his name was, and he was the grandson of an old comrade in arms, the epic Mascara of the Thousand, who had died like a hero, his body pierced by a hundred wounds.

"I sent for him to scold him," continued Orlando with a smile. "Do you know that this fine fellow with his girlish airs goes in for the new ideas? He is an Anarchist, one of the three or four dozen Anarchists that we have in Italy. He's a good little lad at bottom, he has only his mother left him, and supports her, thanks to the little berth which he holds, but which he'll lose one of these fine days if he is not careful. Come, come, my child, you must promise me to be reasonable."

Thereupon Angiolo, whose clean but well-worn garments bespoke decent poverty, made answer in a grave and musical voice: "I am reasonable, it is the others, all the others who are not. When all men are reasonable and desire truth and justice, the world will be happy."

"Ah! if you fancy that he'll give way!" cried Orlando. "But, my poor child, just ask Monsieur l'Abbe if one ever knows where truth and justice are. Well, well, one must leave you the time to live, and see, and understand things."

Then, paying no more attention to the young man, he returned to Pierre, while Angiolo, remaining very quiet in his corner, kept his eyes ardently fixed on them, and with open, quivering ears lost not a word they said.

"I told you, my dear Monsieur Froment," resumed Orlando, "that your ideas would change, and that acquaintance with Rome would bring you to accurate views far more readily than any fine speeches I could make to you. So I never doubted but what you would of your own free will withdraw your book as soon as men and things should have enlightened you respecting the Vatican at the present day. But let us leave the Vatican on one side, there is nothing to be done but to let it continue falling slowly and inevitably into ruin. What interests me is our Italian Rome, which you treated as an element to be neglected, but which you have now seen and studied, so that we can both speak of it with the necessary knowledge!"

He thereupon at once granted a great many things, acknowledged that blunders had been committed, that the finances were in a deplorable state, and that there were serious difficulties of all kinds. They, the Italians, had sinned by excess of legitimate pride, they had proceeded too hastily with their attempt to improvise a great nation, to change ancient Rome into a great modern capital as by the mere touch of a wand. And thence had come that mania for erecting new districts, that mad speculation in land and shares, which had brought the country within a hair's breadth of bankruptcy.

At this Pierre gently interrupted him to tell him of the view which he himself had arrived at after his peregrinations and studies through Rome. "That fever of the first hour, that financial *debacle*," said he, "is after all nothing. All pecuniary sores can be healed. But the grave point is that your Italy still remains to be created. There is no aristocracy left, and as yet there is no people, nothing but a devouring middle class, dating from yesterday, which preys on the rich harvest of the future before it is ripe."

Silence fell. Orlando sadly wagged his old leonine head. The cutting harshness of Pierre's formula struck him in the heart. "Yes, yes," he said at last, "that is so, you have seen things plainly; and why say no when facts are there, patent to everybody? I myself had already spoken to you of that middle class which hungers so ravenously for place and office, distinctions and plumes, and which at the same time is so avaricious, so suspicious with regard to its money which it invests in banks, never risking it in agriculture or manufactures or commerce, having indeed the one desire to enjoy life without doing anything, and so unintelligent that it cannot see it is killing its country by its loathing for labour, its contempt for the poor, its one ambition to live in a petty way with the barren glory of belonging to some official administration. And, as you say, the aristocracy is dying, discrowned, ruined, sunk into the degeneracy which overtakes races towards their close, most of its members reduced to beggary, the others, the few who have clung to their money, crushed by heavy imposts, possessing nought but dead fortunes which constant sharing diminishes and which must soon disappear with the princes themselves. And then there is the people, which has suffered so much and suffers still, but is so used to suffering that it can seemingly conceive no idea of emerging from it, blind and deaf as it is, almost regretting its ancient bondage, and so ignorant, so abominably ignorant, which is the one cause of its hopeless, morrowless misery, for it has not even the consolation of understanding that if we have conquered and are trying to resuscitate Rome and Italy in their ancient glory, it is for itself, the people, alone. Yes, yes, no aristocracy left, no people as yet, and a middle class which really alarms one. How can one therefore help yielding at times to the terrors of the pessimists, who pretend that our misfortunes are as yet nothing, that we are going forward to yet more awful catastrophes, as though, indeed, what we now behold were but the first symptoms of our race's end, the premonitory signs of final annihilation!"

As he spoke he raised his long quivering arms towards the window, towards the light, and Pierre, deeply moved, remembered how Cardinal Boccanera on the previous day had made a similar gesture of supplicant distress when appealing to the divine power. And both men, Cardinal and patriot, so hostile in their beliefs, were instinct with the same fierce and despairing grandeur.

"As I told you, however, on the first day," continued Orlando, "we only sought to accomplish logical and inevitable things. As for Rome, with her past history of splendour and domination which weighs so heavily upon us, we could not do otherwise than take her for capital, for she alone was the bond, the living symbol of our unity at the same time as the promise of eternity, the renewal offered to our great dream of resurrection and glory."

He went on, recognising the disastrous conditions under which Rome laboured as a capital. She was a purely decorative city with exhausted soil, she had remained apart from modern life, she was unhealthy, she offered no possibility of commerce or industry, she was invincibly preyed upon by death, standing as she did amidst that sterile desert of the Campagna. Then he compared her with the other cities which are jealous of her; first Florence, which, however, has become so indifferent and so sceptical, impregnated with a happy heedlessness which seems inexplicable when one remembers the frantic passions, and the torrents of blood rolling through her history; next Naples, which yet remains content with her bright sun, and whose childish people enjoy their ignorance and wretchedness so indolently that one knows not whether one ought to pity them; next Venice, which has resigned herself to remaining a marvel of ancient art, which one ought to put under glass so as to preserve her intact, slumbering amid the sovereign pomp of her annals; next Genoa, which is absorbed in trade, still active and bustling, one of the last queens of that Mediterranean, that insignificant lake which was once the opulent central sea, whose waters carried the wealth of the world; and then particularly Turin and Milan, those industrial and commercial centres, which are so full of life and so modernised that tourists disdain them as not being "Italian" cities, both of them having saved themselves from ruin by entering into that Western evolution which is preparing the next century. Ah! that old land of Italy, ought one to leave it all as a dusty museum for the pleasure of artistic souls, leave it to crumble away, even as its little towns of Magna Graecia, Umbria, and Tuscany are already crumbling, like exquisite *bibelots* which one dares not repair for fear that one might spoil their character. At all events, there must either be death, death soon and inevitable, or else the pick of the demolisher, the tottering walls thrown to the ground, and cities of labour, science, and health created on all sides; in one word, a new Italy really rising from the ashes of the old one, and adapted to the new civilisation into which humanity is entering.

"However, why despair?" Orlando continued energetically. "Rome may weigh heavily on our shoulders, but she is none the less the summit we coveted. We are here, and we shall stay here awaiting events. Even if the population does not increase it at least remains stationary at a figure of some 400,000 souls, and the movement of increase may set in again when the causes which stopped it shall have ceased. Our blunder was to think that Rome would become a Paris or Berlin; but, so far, all sorts of social, historical, even ethnical considerations seem opposed to it; yet who can tell what may be the surprises of to-morrow? Are we forbidden to hope, to put faith in the blood which courses in our veins, the blood of the old conquerors of the world? I, who no longer stir from this room, impotent as I am, even I at times feel my madness come back, believe in the invincibility and immortality of Rome, and wait for the two millions of people who must come to populate those dolorous new districts which you have seen so empty and already falling into ruins! And certainly they will come! Why not? You will see, you will see, everything will be populated, and even more houses will have to be built. Moreover, can you call a nation poor, when it possesses Lombardy? Is there not also inexhaustible wealth in our southern provinces? Let peace settle down, let the South and the North mingle together, and a new generation of workers grow up. Since we have the soil, such a fertile soil, the great harvest which is awaited will surely some day sprout and ripen under the burning sun!"

Enthusiasm was upbuoying him, all the *furia* of youth inflamed his eyes. Pierre smiled, won over; and as soon as he was able to speak, he said: "The problem must be tackled down below, among the people. You must make men!"

"Exactly!" cried Orlando. "I don't cease repeating it, one must make Italy. It is as if a wind from the East had blown the seed of humanity, the seed which makes vigorous and powerful nations, elsewhere. Our people is not like yours in France, a reservoir of men and money from which one can draw as plentifully as one pleases. It is such another inexhaustible reservoir that I wish to see created among us. And one must begin at the bottom. There must be schools everywhere, ignorance must be stamped out, brutishness and idleness must be fought with books, intellectual and moral instruction must give us the industrious people which we need if we are not to disappear from among the great nations. And once again for whom, if not for the democracy of to-morrow, have we worked in taking possession of Rome? And how easily one can understand that all should collapse here, and nothing grow up vigorously since such a democracy is absolutely absent. Yes, yes, the solution of the problem does not lie elsewhere; we must make a people, make an Italian democracy."

XVI.

Pierre had grown calm again, feeling somewhat anxious yet not daring to say that it is by no means easy to modify a nation, that Italy is such as soil, history, and race have made her, and that to seek to transform her so radically and all at once might be a dangerous enterprise. Do not nations like beings have an active youth, a resplendent prime, and a more or less prolonged old age ending in death? A modern democratic Rome, good heavens! The modern Romes are named Paris, London, Chicago. So he contented himself with saying: "But pending this great renovation of the people, don't you think that you ought to be prudent? Your finances are in such a bad condition, you are passing through such great social and economic difficulties, that you run the risk of the worst catastrophes before you secure either men or money. Ah! how prudent would that minister be who should say in your Chamber: 'Our pride has made a mistake, it was wrong of us to try to make ourselves a great nation in one day; more time, labour, and patience are needed; and we consent to remain for the present a young nation, which will quietly reflect and labour at self-formation, without, for a long time yet, seeking to play a dominant part. So we intend to disarm, to strike out the war and naval estimates, all the estimates intended for display abroad, in order to devote ourselves to our internal prosperity, and to build up by education, physically and morally, the great nation which we swear we will be fifty years hence!' Yes, yes, strike out all needless expenditure, your salvation lies in that!"

But Orlando, while listening, had become gloomy again, and with a vague, weary gesture he replied in an undertone: "No, no, the minister who should use such language would be hooted. It would be too hard a confession, such as one cannot ask a nation to make. Every heart would bound, leap forth at the idea. And, besides, would not the danger perhaps be even greater if all that has been done were allowed to crumble? How many wrecked hopes, how much discarded, useless material there would be! No, we can now only save ourselves by patience and courage—and forward, ever forward! We are a very young nation, and in fifty years we desired to effect the unity which others have required two hundred years to arrive at. Well, we must pay for our haste, we must wait for the harvest to ripen, and fill our barns." Then, with another and more sweeping wave of the arm, he stubbornly strengthened himself in his hopes. "You know," said he, "that I was always against the alliance with Germany. As I predicted, it has ruined us. We were not big enough to march side by side with such a wealthy and powerful person, and it is in view of a war, always near at hand and inevitable, that we now suffer so cruelly from having to support the budgets of a great nation. Ah! that war which has never come, it is that which has exhausted the best part of our blood and sap and money without the slightest profit. To-day we have nothing before us but the necessity of breaking with our ally, who speculated on our pride, who has never helped us in any way, who has never given us anything but bad advice, and treated us otherwise than with suspicion. But it was all inevitable, and that's what people won't admit in France. I can speak freely of it all, for I am a declared friend of France, and people even feel some spite against me on that account. However, explain to your compatriots, that on the morrow of our conquest of Rome, in our frantic desire to resume our ancient rank, it was absolutely necessary that we should play our part in Europe and show that we were a power with whom the others must henceforth count. And hesitation was not allowable, all our interests impelled us toward Germany, the evidence was so binding as to impose itself. The stern law of the struggle for life weighs as heavily on nations as on individuals, and this it is which explains and justifies the rupture between the two sisters, France and Italy, the forgetting of so many ties, race, commercial intercourse, and, if you like, services also. The two sisters, ah! they now pursue each other with so much hatred that all common sense even seems at an end. My poor old heart bleeds when I read the articles which your newspapers and ours exchange like poisoned darts. When will this fratricidal massacre cease, which of the two will first realise the necessity of peace, the necessity of the alliance of the Latin races, if they are to remain alive amidst those torrents of other races which more and more invade the world?" Then gaily, with the *bonhomie* of a hero disarmed by old age, and seeking a refuge in his dreams, Orlando added: "Come, you must promise to help me as soon as you are in Paris. However small your field of action may be, promise me you will do all you can to promote peace between France and Italy; there can be no more holy task. Relate all you have seen here, all you have heard, oh! as frankly as possible. If we have faults, you certainly have faults as well. And, come, family quarrels can't last for ever!"

"No doubt," Pierre answered in some embarrassment. "Unfortunately they are the most tenacious. In families, when blood becomes exasperated with blood, hate goes as far as poison and the knife. And pardon becomes impossible."

He dared not fully express his thoughts. Since he had been in Rome, listening, and considering things, the quarrel between Italy and France had resumed itself in his mind in a fine tragic story. Once upon a time there were two princesses, daughters of a powerful queen, the mistress of the world. The elder one, who had inherited her mother's kingdom, was secretly grieved to see her sister, who had established herself in a neighbouring land, gradually increase in wealth, strength, and brilliancy, whilst she herself declined as if weakened by age, dismembered, so exhausted, and so sore, that she already felt defeated on the day when she attempted a supreme effort to regain universal power. And so how bitter were her feelings, how hurt she always felt on seeing her sister recover from the most frightful shocks, resume her dazzling *gala*, and continue to reign over the world by dint of strength and grace and wit. Never would she forgive it, however well that envied and detested sister might act towards her. Therein lay an incurable wound, the life of one poisoned by that of the other, the hatred of old blood for young blood, which could only be quieted by death. And even if peace, as was possible, should soon be restored between them in presence of the younger sister's evident triumph, the other would always harbour deep within her heart an endless grief at being the elder yet the vassal.

"However, you may rely on me," Pierre affectionately resumed. "This quarrel between the two countries is certainly a great source of grief and a great peril. And assuredly I will only say what I think to be the truth about you. At the same time I fear that you hardly like the truth, for temperament and custom have hardly prepared you for it. The poets of every nation who at various times have written on Rome have intoxicated you with so much praise that you are scarcely fitted to hear the real truth about your Rome of to-day. No matter how superb a share of praise one may accord you, one must all the same look at the reality of things, and this reality is just what you won't admit, lovers of the beautiful as you ever are, susceptible too like women, whom the slightest hint of a wrinkle sends into despair."

Orlando began to laugh. "Well, certainly, one must always beautify things a little," said he. "Why speak of ugly faces at all? We in our theatres only care for pretty music, pretty dancing, pretty pieces which please one. As for the rest, whatever is disagreeable let us hide it, for mercy's sake!"

"On the other hand," the priest continued, "I will cheerfully confess the great error of my book. The Italian Rome which I neglected and sacrificed to papal Rome not only exists but is already so powerful and triumphant that it is surely the other one which is bound to disappear in course of time. However much the Pope may strive to remain immutable within his Vatican, a steady evolution goes on around him, and the black world, by mingling with the white, has already become a grey world. I never realised that more acutely than at the *fete* given by Prince Buongiovanni for the betrothal of his daughter to your grand-nephew. I came away quite enchanted, won over to the cause of your resurrection."

The old man's eyes sparkled. "Ah! you were present?" said he, "and you witnessed a never-to-be-forgotten scene, did you not, and you no longer doubt our vitality, our growth into a great people when the difficulties of to-day are overcome? What does a quarter of a century, what does even a century matter! Italy will again rise to her old glory, as soon as the great people of to-morrow shall have sprung from the soil. And if I detest that man Sacco it is because to my mind he is the incarnation of all the enjoyers and intriguers whose appetite for the spoils of our conquest has retarded everything. But I live again in my dear grand-nephew Attilio, who represents the future, the generation of brave and worthy men who will purify and educate the country. Ah! may some of the great ones of to-morrow spring from him and that adorable little Princess Celia, whom my niece Stefana, a sensible woman at bottom, brought to see me the other day. If you had seen that child fling her arms about me, call me endearing names, and tell me that I should be godfather to her first son, so that he might bear my name and once again save Italy! Yes, yes, may peace be concluded around that coming cradle; may the union of those dear children be the indissoluble marriage of Rome and the whole nation, and may all be repaired, and all blossom anew in their love!"

Tears came to his eyes, and Pierre, touched by his inextinguishable patriotism, sought to please him. "I myself," said he, "expressed to your son much the same wish on the evening of the betrothal *fete*, when I told him I trusted that their nuptials might be definitive and fruitful, and that from them and all the others there might arise the great nation which, now that I begin to know you, I hope you will soon become!"

"You said that!" exclaimed Orlando. "Well, I forgive your book, for you have understood at last; and new Rome, there she is, the Rome which is ours, which we wish to make worthy of her glorious past, and for the third time the queen of the world."

With one of those broad gestures into which he put all his remaining life, he pointed to the curtainless window where Rome spread out in solemn majesty from one horizon to the other. But, suddenly he turned his head and in a fit of paternal indignation began to apostrophise young Angiolo Mascara. "You young rascal!" said he, "it's our Rome which you dream of destroying with your bombs, which you talk of razing like a rotten, tottering house, so as to rid the world of it for ever!"

Angiolo had hitherto remained silent, passionately listening to the others. His pretty, girlish, beardless face reflected the slightest emotion in sudden flashes; and his big blue eyes also had glowed on hearing what had been said of the people, the new people which it was necessary to create. "Yes!" he slowly replied in his pure and musical voice, "we mean to raze it and not leave a stone of it, but raze it in order to build it up again."

Orlando interrupted him with a soft, bantering laugh: "Oh! you would build it up again; that's fortunate!" he said.

"I would build it up again," the young man replied, in the trembling voice of an inspired prophet. "I would build it up again oh, so vast, so beautiful, and so noble! Will not the universal democracy of to-morrow, humanity when it is at last freed, need an unique city, which shall be the ark of alliance, the very centre of the world? And is not Rome designated, Rome which the prophecies have marked as eternal and immortal, where the destinies of the nations are to be accomplished? But in order that it may become the final definitive sanctuary, the capital of the destroyed kingdoms, where the wise men of all countries shall meet once every year, one must first of all purify it by fire, leave nothing of its old stains remaining. Then, when the sun shall have absorbed all the pestilence of the old soil, we will rebuild the city ten times more beautiful and ten times larger than it has ever been. And what a city of truth and justice it will at last be, the Rome that has been announced and awaited for three thousand years, all in gold and all in marble, filling the Campagna from the sea to the Sabine and the Alban mountains, and so prosperous and so sensible that its twenty millions of inhabitants after regulating the law of labour will live with the unique joy of being. Yes, yes, Rome the Mother, Rome the Queen, alone on the face of the earth and for all eternity!"

Pierre listened to him, aghast. What! did the blood of Augustus go to such a point as this? The popes had not become masters of Rome without feeling impelled to rebuild it in their passion to rule over the world; young Italy, likewise yielding to the hereditary madness of universal domination, had in its turn sought to make the city larger than any other, erecting whole districts for people who had never come, and now even the Anarchists were possessed by the same stubborn dream of the race, a dream beyond all measure this time, a fourth and monstrous Rome, whose suburbs would invade continents in order that liberated humanity, united in one family, might find sufficient lodging! This was the climax. Never could more extravagant proof be given of the blood of pride and sovereignty which had scorched the veins of that race ever since Augustus had bequeathed it the inheritance of his absolute empire, with the furious instinct that the world legally belonged to it, and that its mission was to conquer it again. This idea had intoxicated all the children of that historic soil, impelling all of them to make their city The City, the one which had reigned and which would reign again in splendour when the days predicted by the oracles should arrive. And Pierre remembered the four fatidical letters, the S.P.Q.R. of old and glorious Rome, which like an order of final triumph given to Destiny he had everywhere found in present-day Rome, on all the walls, on all the insignia, even on the municipal dust-carts! And he understood the prodigious vanity of these people, haunted by the glory of their ancestors, spellbound by the past of their city, declaring that she contains everything, that they themselves cannot know her thoroughly, that she is the sphinx who will some day explain the riddle of the universe, that she is so great and noble that all within her acquires increase of greatness and nobility, in such wise that they demand for her the idolatrous respect of the entire world, so vivacious in their minds is the illusive legend which clings to her, so incapable are they of realising that what was once great may be so no longer.

"But I know your fourth Rome," resumed Orlando, again enlivened. "It's the Rome of the people, the capital of the Universal Republic, which Mazzini dreamt of. Only he left the pope in it. Do you know, my lad, that if we old Republicans rallied to the monarchy, it was because we feared that in the event of revolution the country might fall into the hands of dangerous madmen such as those who have upset your brain? Yes, that was why we resigned ourselves to our monarchy, which is not much different from a parliamentary republic. And now, goodbye and be sensible, remember that your poor mother would die of it if any misfortune should befall you. Come, let me embrace you all the same."

On receiving the hero's affectionate kiss Angiolo coloured like a girl. Then he went off with his gentle, dreamy air, never adding a word but politely inclining his head to the priest. Silence continued till Orlando's eyes encountered the newspapers scattered on the table, when he once more spoke of the terrible bereavement of the Boccaneras. He had loved Benedetta like a dear daughter during the sad days when she had dwelt near him; and finding the newspaper accounts of her death somewhat singular, worried in fact by the obscure points which he could divine in the tragedy, he was asking Pierre for particulars, when his son Luigi suddenly entered the room, breathless from having climbed the stairs so quickly and with his face full of anxious fear. He had just dismissed his contractors with impatient roughness, giving no thought to his serious financial position, the jeopardy in which his fortune was now placed, so anxious was he to be up above beside his father. And when he was there his first uneasy glance was for the old man, to make sure whether the priest by some imprudent word had not dealt him his death blow.

He shuddered on noticing how Orlando quivered, moved to tears by the terrible affair of which he was speaking; and for a moment he thought he had arrived too late, that the harm was done. "Good heavens, father!" he exclaimed, "what is the matter with you, why are you crying?" And as he spoke he knelt at the old man's feet, taking hold of his hands and giving him such a passionate, loving glance that he seemed to be offering all the blood of his heart to spare him the slightest grief.

"It is about the death of that poor woman," Orlando sadly answered. "I was telling Monsieur Froment how it grieved me, and I added that I could not yet understand it all. The papers talk of a sudden death which is always so extraordinary."

The young Count rose again looking very pale. The priest had not yet spoken. But what a frightful moment was this! What if he should reply, what if he should speak out?

"You were present, were you not?" continued the old man addressing Pierre. "You saw everything. Tell me then how the thing happened."

Luigi Prada looked at Pierre. Their eyes met fixedly, plunging into one another's souls. All began afresh in their minds, Destiny on the march, Santobono encountered with his little basket, the drive across the melancholy Campagna, the conversation about poison while the little basket was gently rocked on the priest's knees; then, in particular, the sleepy *osteria*, and the little black hen, so suddenly killed, lying on the ground with a tiny streamlet of violet blood trickling from her beak. And next there was that splendid ball at the Buongiovanni mansion, with all its *odore di femina* and its triumph of love: and finally, before the Palazzo Boccanera, so black under the silvery moon, there was the man who lighted a cigar and went off without once turning his head, allowing dim Destiny to accomplish its work of death. Both of them, Pierre and Prada, knew that story and lived it over again, having no need to recall it aloud in order to make certain that they had fully penetrated one another's soul.

Pierre did not immediately answer the old man. "Oh!" he murmured at last, "there were frightful things, yes, frightful things."

"No doubt—that is what I suspected," resumed Orlando. "You can tell us all. In presence of death my son has freely forgiven."

The young Count's gaze again sought that of Pierre with such weight, such ardent entreaty that the priest felt deeply stirred. He had just remembered that man's anguish during the ball, the atrocious torture of jealousy which he had undergone before allowing Destiny to avenge him. And he pictured also what must have been his feelings after the terrible outcome of it all: at first stupefaction at Destiny's harshness, at this full vengeance which he had never desired so ferocious; then icy calmness like that of the cool gambler who awaits events, reading the newspapers, and feeling no other remorse than that of the general whose victory has cost him too many men. He must have immediately realised that the Cardinal would stifle the affair for the sake of the Church's honour; and only retained one weight on his heart, regret possibly for that woman whom he had never won, with perhaps a last horrible jealousy which he did not confess to himself but from which he would always suffer, jealousy at knowing that she lay in another's arms in the grave, for all eternity. But behold, after that victorious effort to remain calm, after that cold and remorseless waiting, Punishment arose, the fear that Destiny, travelling on with its poisoned figs, might have not yet ceased its march, and might by a rebound strike down his own father. Yet another thunderbolt, yet another victim, the most unexpected, the being he most adored! At that thought all his strength of resistance had in one moment collapsed, and he was there, in terror of Destiny, more at a loss, more trembling than a child.

"The newspapers, however," slowly said Pierre as if he were seeking his words, "the newspapers must have told you that the Prince succumbed first, and that the Contessina died of grief whilst embracing him for the last time.... As for the cause of death, *mon Dieu*, you know that doctors themselves in sudden cases scarcely dare to pronounce an exact opinion—"

He stopped short, for within him he had suddenly heard the voice of Benedetta giving him just before she died that terrible order: "You, who will see his father, I charge you to tell him that I cursed his son. I wish that he should know, it is necessary that he should know, for the sake of truth and justice." And was he, oh! Lord, about to obey that order, was it one of those divine commands which must be executed even if the result be a torrent of blood and tears? For a few seconds Pierre suffered from a heart-rending combat within him, hesitating between the act of truth and justice which the dead woman had called for and his own personal desire for forgiveness, and the horror he would feel should he kill that poor old man by fulfilling his implacable mission which could benefit nobody. And certainly the other one, the son, must have understood what a supreme struggle was going on in the priest's mind, a struggle which would decide his own father's fate, for his glance became yet more suppliant than ever.

"One first thought that it was merely indigestion," continued Pierre, "but the Prince became so much worse, that one was alarmed, and the doctor was sent for—"

Ah! Prada's eyes, they had become so despairing, so full of the most touching and weightiest things, that the priest could read in them all the decisive reasons which were about to stay his tongue. No, no, he would not strike an innocent old man, he had promised nothing, and to obey the last expression of the dead woman's hatred would have seemed to him like charging her memory with a crime. The young Count, too, during those few minutes of anguish, had suffered a whole life of such abominable torture, that after all some little justice was done.

"And then," Pierre concluded, "when the doctor arrived he at once recognised that it was a case of infectious fever. There can be no doubt of it. This morning I attended the funeral, it was very splendid and very touching."

Orlando did not insist, but contented himself with saying that he also had felt much emotion all the morning on thinking of that funeral. Then, as he turned to set the papers on the table in order with his trembling hands, his son, icy cold with perspiration, staggering and clinging to the back of a chair in order that he might not fall, again gave Pierre a long glance, but a very soft one, full of distracted gratitude.

"I am leaving this evening," resumed Pierre, who felt exhausted and wished to break off the conversation, "and I must now bid you farewell. Have you any commission to give me for Paris?"

"No, none," replied Orlando; and then, with sudden recollection, he added, "Yes, I have, though! You remember that book written by my old comrade in arms, Theophile Morin, one of Garibaldi's Thousand, that manual for the bachelor's degree which he desired to see translated and adopted here. Well, I am pleased to say that I have a promise that it shall be used in our schools, but on condition that he makes some alterations in it. Luigi, give me the book, it is there on that shelf."

Then, when his son had handed him the volume, he showed Pierre some notes which he had pencilled on the margins, and explained to him the modifications which were desired in the general scheme of the work. "Will you be kind enough," he continued, "to take this copy to Morin himself? His address is written inside the cover. If you can do so you will spare me the trouble of writing him a very long letter; in ten minutes you can explain matters to him more clearly and completely than I could do in ten pages.... And you must embrace Morin for me, and tell him that I still love him, oh! with all my heart of the bygone days, when I could still use my legs and we two fought like devils side by side under a hail of bullets."

A short silence followed, that pause, that embarrassment tinged with emotion which precedes the moment of farewell. "Come, good-bye," said Orlando, "embrace me for him and for yourself, embrace me affectionately like that lad did just now. I am so old and so near my end, my dear Monsieur Froment, that you will allow me to call you my child and to kiss you like a grandfather, wishing you all courage and peace, and that faith in life which alone helps one to live."

Pierre was so touched that tears rose to his eyes, and when with all his soul he kissed the stricken hero on either cheek, he felt that he likewise was weeping. With a hand yet as vigorous as a vice, Orlando detained him for a moment beside his armchair, whilst with his other hand waving in a supreme gesture, he for the last time showed him Rome, so immense and mournful under the ashen sky. And his voice came low, quivering and suppliant. "For mercy's sake swear to me that you will love her all the same, in spite of all, for she is the cradle, the mother! Love her for all that she no longer is, love her for all that she desires to be! Do not say that her end has come, love her, love her so that she may live again, that she may live for ever!"

Pierre again embraced him, unable to find any other response, upset as he was by all the passion displayed by that old warrior, who spoke of his city as a man of thirty might speak of the woman he adores. And he found him so handsome and so lofty with his old blanched, leonine mane and his stubborn belief in approaching resurrection, that once more the other old Roman, Cardinal Boccanera, arose before him, equally stubborn in his faith and relinquishing nought of his dream, even though he might be crushed on the spot by the fall of the heavens. These twain ever stood face to face, at either end of their city, alone rearing their lofty figures above the horizon, whilst awaiting the future.

Then, when Pierre had bowed to Count Luigi, and found himself outside again in the Via Venti Settembre he was all eagerness to get back to the Boccanera mansion so as to pack up his things and depart. His farewell visits were made, and he now only had to take leave of Donna Serafina and the Cardinal, and to thank them for all their kind hospitality. For him alone did their doors open, for they had shut themselves up on returning from the funeral, resolved to see nobody. At twilight, therefore, Pierre had no one but Victorine to keep him company in the vast, black mansion, for when he expressed a desire to take supper with Don Vigilio she told him that the latter had also shut himself in his room. Desirous as he was of at least shaking hands with the secretary for the last time, Pierre went to knock at the door, which was so near his own, but could obtain no reply, and divined that the poor fellow, overcome by a fresh attack of fever and suspicion, desired not to see him again, in terror at the idea that he might compromise himself yet more than he had done already. Thereupon, it was settled that as the train only started at seventeen minutes past ten Victorine should serve Pierre his supper on the little table in his sitting-room at eight o'clock. She brought him a lamp and spoke of putting his linen in order, but he absolutely declined her help, and she had to leave him to pack up quietly by himself.

He had purchased a little box, since his valise could not possibly hold all the linen and winter clothing which had been sent to him from Paris as his stay in Rome became more and more protracted. However, the packing was soon accomplished; the wardrobe was emptied, the drawers were visited, the box and valise filled and securely locked by seven o'clock. An hour remained to him before supper and he sat there resting, when his eyes whilst travelling round the walls to make sure that he had forgotten nothing, encountered that old painting by some unknown master, which had so often filled him with emotion. The lamplight now shone full upon it; and this time again as he gazed at it he felt a blow in the heart, a blow which was all the deeper, as now, at his parting hour, he found a symbol of his defeat at Rome in that dolent, tragic, half-naked woman, draped in a shred of linen, and weeping between her clasped hands whilst seated on the threshold of the palace whence she had been driven. Did not that rejected one, that stubborn victim of love, who sobbed so bitterly, and of whom one knew nothing, neither what her face was like, nor whence she had come, nor what her fault had been—did she not personify all man's useless efforts to force the doors of truth, and all the frightful abandonment into which he falls as soon as he collides with the wall which shuts the unknown off from him? For a long while did Pierre look at her, again worried at being obliged to depart without having seen her face behind her streaming golden hair, that face of dolorous beauty which he pictured radiant with youth and delicious in its mystery. And as he gazed he was just fancying that he could see it, that it was becoming his at last, when there was a knock at the door and Narcisse Habert entered.

Pierre was surprised to see the young *attache*, for three days previously he had started for Florence, impelled thither by one of the sudden whims of his artistic fancy. However, he at once apologised for his unceremonious intrusion. "Ah! there is your luggage!" he said; "I heard that you were going away this evening, and I was unwilling to let you leave Rome without coming to shake hands with you. But what frightful things have happened since we met! I only returned this afternoon, so that I could not attend the funeral. However, you may well imagine how thunderstruck I was by the news of those frightful deaths."

Then, suspecting some unacknowledged tragedy, like a man well acquainted with the legendary dark side of Rome, he put some questions to Pierre but did not insist on them, being at bottom far too prudent to burden himself uselessly with redoubtable secrets. And after Pierre had given him such particulars as he thought fit, the conversation changed and they spoke at length of Italy, Rome, Naples, and Florence. "Ah! Florence, Florence!" Narcisse repeated languorously. He had lighted a cigarette and his words fell more slowly, as he glanced round the room. "You were very well lodged here," he said, "it is very quiet. I had never come up to this floor before."

His eyes continued wandering over the walls until they were at last arrested by the old painting which the lamp illumined, and thereupon he remained for a moment blinking as if surprised. And all at once he rose and approached the picture. "Dear me, dear me," said he, "but that's very good, that's very fine."

"Isn't it?" rejoined Pierre. "I know nothing about painting but I was stirred by that picture on the very day of my arrival, and over and over again it has kept me here with my heart beating and full of indescribable feelings."

Narcisse no longer spoke but examined the painting with the care of a connoisseur, an expert, whose keen glance decides the question of authenticity, and appraises commercial value. And the most extraordinary delight appeared upon the young man's fair, rapturous face, whilst his fingers began to quiver. "But it's a Botticelli, it's a Botticelli! There can be no doubt about it," he exclaimed. "Just look at the hands, and look at the folds of the drapery! And the colour of the hair, and the technique, the flow of the whole composition. A Botticelli, ah! *mon Dieu*, a Botticelli."

He became quite faint, overflowing with increasing admiration as he penetrated more and more deeply into the subject, at once so simple and so poignant. Was it not acutely modern? The artist had foreseen our pain-fraught century, our anxiety in presence of the invisible, our distress at being unable to cross the portal of mystery which was for ever closed. And what an eternal symbol of the world's wretchedness was that woman, whose face one could not see, and who sobbed so distractedly without it being possible for one to wipe away her tears. Yes, a Botticelli, unknown, uncatalogued, what a discovery! Then he paused to inquire of Pierre: "Did you know it was a Botticelli?"

"Oh no! I spoke to Don Vigilio about it one day, but he seemed to think it of no account. And Victorine, when I spoke to her, replied that all those old things only served to harbour dust."

Narcisse protested, quite stupefied: "What! they have a Botticelli here and don't know it! Ah! how well I recognise in that the Roman princes who, unless their masterpieces have been labelled, are for the most part utterly at sea among them! No doubt this one has suffered a little, but a simple cleaning would make a marvel, a famous picture of it, for which a museum would at least give—"

He abruptly stopped, completing his sentence with a wave of the hand and not mentioning the figure which was on his lips. And then, as Victorine came in followed by Giacomo to lay the little table for Pierre's supper, he turned his back upon the Botticelli and said no more about it. The young priest's attention was aroused, however, and he could well divine what was passing in the other's mind. Under that make-believe Florentine, all angelicalness, there was an experienced business man, who well knew how to look after his pecuniary interests and was even reported to be somewhat avaricious. Pierre, who was aware of it, could not help smiling therefore when he saw him take his stand before another picture—a frightful Virgin, badly copied from some eighteenth-century canvas—and exclaim: "Dear me! that's not at all bad! I've a friend, I remember, who asked me to buy him some old paintings. I say, Victorine, now that Donna Serafina and the Cardinal are left alone do you think they would like to rid themselves of a few valueless pictures?"

The servant raised her arms as if to say that if it depended on her, everything might be carried away. Then she replied: "Not to a dealer, sir, on account of the nasty rumours which would at once spread about, but I'm sure they would be happy to please a friend. The house costs a lot to keep up, and money would be welcome."

Pierre then vainly endeavoured to persuade Narcisse to stay and sup with him, but the young man gave his word of honour that he was expected elsewhere and was even late. And thereupon he ran off, after pressing the priest's hands and affectionately wishing him a good journey.

Eight o'clock was striking, and Pierre seated himself at the little table, Victorine remaining to serve him after dismissing Giacomo, who had brought the supper things upstairs in a basket. "The people here make me wild," said the worthy woman after the other had gone, "they are so slow. And besides, it's a pleasure for me to serve you your last meal, Monsieur l'Abbe. I've had a little French dinner cooked for you, a *sole au gratin* and a roast fowl."

Pierre was touched by this attention, and pleased to have the company of a compatriot whilst he partook of his final meal amidst the deep silence of the old, black, deserted mansion. The buxom figure of Victorine was still instinct with mourning, with grief for the loss of her dear Contessina, but her daily toil was already setting her erect again, restoring her quick activity; and she spoke almost cheerfully whilst passing plates and dishes to Pierre. "And to think Monsieur l'Abbe," said she, "that you'll be in Paris on the morning of the day after to-morrow! As for me, you know, it seems as if I only left Auneau yesterday. Ah! what fine soil there is there; rich soil yellow like gold, not like their poor stuff here which smells of sulphur! And the pretty fresh willows beside our stream, too, and the little wood so full of moss! They've no moss here, their trees look like tin under that stupid sun of theirs which burns up the grass. *Mon Dieu*! in the early times I would have given I don't know what for a good fall of rain to soak me and wash away all the dust. Ah! I shall never get used to their awful Rome. What a country and what people!"

Pierre was quite enlivened by her stubborn fidelity to her own nook, which after five and twenty years of absence still left her horrified with that city of crude light and black vegetation, true daughter as she was of a smiling and temperate clime which of a morning was steeped in rosy mist. "But now that your young mistress is dead," said he, "what keeps you here? Why don't you take the train with me?"

She looked at him in surprise: "Go off with you, go back to Auneau! Oh! it's impossible, Monsieur l'Abbe. It would be too ungrateful to begin with, for Donna Serafina is accustomed to me, and it would be bad on my part to forsake her and his Eminence now that they are in trouble. And besides, what could I do elsewhere? No, my little hole is here now."

"So you will never see Auneau again?"

"No, never, that's certain."

"And you don't mind being buried here, in their ground which smells of sulphur?"

She burst into a frank laugh. "Oh!" she said, "I don't mind where I am when I'm dead. One sleeps well everywhere. And it's funny that you should be so anxious as to what there may be when one's dead. There's nothing, I'm sure. That's what tranquillises me, to feel that it will be all over and that I shall have a rest. The good God owes us that after we've worked so hard. You know that I'm not devout, oh! dear no. Still that doesn't prevent me from behaving properly, and, true as I stand here, I've never had a lover. It seems foolish to say such a thing at my age, still I say it because it's the sober truth."

She continued laughing like the worthy woman she was, having no belief in priests and yet without a sin upon her conscience. And Pierre once more marvelled at the simple courage and great practical common sense of this laborious and devoted creature, who for him personified the whole unbelieving lowly class of France, those who no longer believe and will believe never more. Ah! to be as she was, to do one's work and lie down for the eternal sleep without any revolt of pride, satisfied with the one joy of having accomplished one's share of toil!

When Pierre had finished his supper Victorine summoned Giacomo to clear the things away. And as it was only half-past eight she advised the priest to spend another quiet hour in his room. Why go and catch a chill by waiting at the station? She could send for a cab at half-past nine, and as soon as it arrived she would send word to him and have his luggage carried down. He might be easy as to that, and need trouble himself about nothing.

When she had gone off Pierre soon sank into a deep reverie. It seemed to him, indeed, as if he had already quitted Rome, as if the city were far away and he could look back on it, and his experiences within it. His book, "New Rome," arose in his mind; and he remembered his first morning on the Janiculum, his view of Rome from the terrace of San Pietro in Montorio, a Rome such as he had dreamt of, so young and ethereal under the pure sky. It was then that he had asked himself the decisive question: Could Catholicism be renewed? Could it revert to the spirit of primitive Christianity, become the religion of the democracy, the faith which the distracted modern world, in danger of death, awaits in order that it may be pacified and live? His heart had then beaten with hope and enthusiasm. After his disaster at Lourdes from which he had scarcely recovered, he had come to attempt another and supreme experiment by asking Rome what her reply to his question would be. And now the experiment had failed, he knew what answer Rome had returned him through her ruins, her monuments, her very soil, her people, her prelates, her cardinals, her pope! No, Catholicism could not be renewed: no, it could not revert to the spirit of primitive Christianity; no, it could not become the religion of the democracy, the new faith which might save the old toppling societies in danger of death. Though it seemed to be of democratic origin, it was henceforth riveted to that Roman soil, it remained kingly in spite of everything, forced to cling to the principle of temporal power under penalty of suicide, bound by tradition, enchained by dogma, its evolutions mere simulations whilst in reality it was reduced to such immobility that, behind the bronze doors of the Vatican, the papacy was the prisoner, the ghost of eighteen centuries of atavism, indulging the ceaseless dream of universal dominion. There, where with priestly faith exalted by love of the suffering and the poor, he had come to seek life and a resurrection of the Christian communion, he had found death, the dust of a destroyed world in which nothing more could germinate, an exhausted soil whence now there could never grow aught but that despotic papacy, the master of bodies as it was of souls. To his distracted cry asking for a new religion, Rome had been content to reply by condemning his book as a work tainted with heresy, and he himself had withdrawn it amidst the bitter grief of his disillusions. He had seen, he had understood, and all had collapsed. And it was himself, his soul and his brain, which lay among the ruins.

Pierre was stifling. He rose, threw the window overlooking the Tiber wide open, and leant out. The rain had begun to fall again at the approach of evening, but now it had once more ceased. The atmosphere was very mild, moist, even oppressive. The moon must have arisen in the ashen grey sky, for her presence could be divined behind the clouds which she illumined with a vague, yellow, mournful light. And under that slumberous glimmer the vast horizon showed blackly and phantom-like: the Janiculum in front with the close-packed houses of the Trastevere; the river flowing away yonder on the left towards the dim height of the Palatine; whilst on the right the dome of St. Peter's showed forth, round and domineering in the pale atmosphere. Pierre could not see the Quirinal but divined it to be behind him, and could picture its long facade shutting off part of the sky. And what a collapsing Rome, half-devoured by the gloom, was this, so different from the Rome all youth and dreamland which he had beheld and passionately loved on the day of his arrival! He remembered the three symbolic summits which had then summed up for him the whole long history of Rome, the ancient, the papal, and the Italian city. But if the Palatine had remained the same discrowned mount on which there only rose the phantom of the ancestor, Augustus, emperor and pontiff, master of the world, he now pictured St. Peter's and the Quirinal as strangely altered. To that royal palace which he had so neglected, and which had seemed to him like a flat, low barrack, to that new Government which had brought him the impression of some attempt at sacrilegious modernity, he now accorded the large, increasing space that they occupied in the panorama, the whole of which they would apparently soon fill; whilst, on the contrary, St. Peter's, that dome which he had found so triumphal, all azure, reigning over the city like a gigantic and unshakable monarch, at present seemed to him full of cracks and already shrinking, as if it were one of those huge old piles, which, through the secret, unsuspected decay of their timbers, at times fall to the ground in one mass.

A murmur, a growling plaint rose from the swollen Tiber, and Pierre shivered at the icy abysmal breath which swept past his face. And his thoughts of the three summits and their symbolic triangle aroused within him the memory of the sufferings of the great silent multitude of poor and lowly for whom pope and king had so long disputed. It all dated from long ago, from the day when, in dividing the inheritance of

Augustus, the emperor had been obliged to content himself with men's bodies, leaving their souls to the pope, whose one idea had henceforth been to gain the temporal power of which God, in his person, was despoiled. All the middle ages had been disturbed and ensanguined by the quarrel, till at last the silent multitude weary of vexations and misery spoke out; threw off the papal yoke at the Reformation, and later on began to overthrow its kings. And then, as Pierre had written in his book, a new fortune had been offered to the pope, that of reverting to the ancient dream, by dissociating himself from the fallen thrones and placing himself on the side of the wretched in the hope that this time he would conquer the people, win it entirely for himself. Was it not prodigious to see that man, Leo XIII, despoiled of his kingdom and allowing himself to be called a socialist, assembling under his banner the great flock of the disinherited, and marching against the kings at the head of that fourth estate to whom the coming century will belong? The eternal struggle for possession of the people continued as bitterly as ever even in Rome itself, where pope and king, who could see each other from their windows, contended together like falcon and hawk for the little birds of the woods. And in this for Pierre lay the reason why Catholicism was fatally condemned; for it was of monarchical essence to such a point that the Apostolic and Roman papacy could not renounce the temporal power under penalty of becoming something else and disappearing. In vain did it feign a return to the people, in vain did it seek to appear all soul; there was no room in the midst of the world's democracies for any such total and universal sovereignty as that which it claimed to hold from God. Pierre ever beheld the Imperator sprouting up afresh in the Pontifex Maximus, and it was this in particular which had killed his dream, destroyed his book, heaped up all those ruins before which he remained distracted without either strength or courage.

The sight of that ashen Rome, whose edifices faded away into the night, at last brought him such a heart-pang that he came back into the room and fell on a chair near his luggage. Never before had he experienced such distress of spirit, it seemed like the death of his soul. After his disaster at Lourdes he had not come to Rome in search of the candid and complete faith of a little child, but the superior faith of an intellectual being, rising above rites and symbols, and seeking to ensure the greatest possible happiness of mankind based on its need of certainty. And if this collapsed, if Catholicism could not be rejuvenated and become the religion and moral law of the new generations, if the Pope at Rome and with Rome could not be the Father, the arch of alliance, the spiritual leader whom all hearkened to and obeyed, why then, in Pierre's eyes, the last hope was wrecked, the supreme rending which must plunge present-day society into the abyss was near at hand. That scaffolding of Catholic socialism which had seemed to him so happily devised for the consolidation of the old Church, now appeared to him lying on the ground; and he judged it severely as a mere passing expedient which might perhaps for some years prop up the ruined edifice, but which was simply based on an intentional misunderstanding, on a skilful lie, on politics and diplomacy. No, no, that the people should once again, as so many times before, be duped and gained over, caressed in order that it might be enthralled—this was repugnant to one's reason, and the whole system appeared degenerate, dangerous, temporary, calculated to end in the worst catastrophes. So this then was the finish, nothing remained erect and stable, the old world was about to disappear amidst the frightful sanguinary crisis whose approach was announced by such indisputable signs.

And he, before that chaos near at hand, had no soul left him, having once more lost his faith in that decisive experiment which, he had felt beforehand, would either strengthen him or strike him down for ever. The thunderbolt had fallen, and now, O God, what should he do?

To shake off his anguish he began to walk across the room. Aye, what should he do now that he was all doubt again, all dolorous negation, and that his cassock weighed more heavily than it had ever weighed upon his shoulders? He remembered having told Monsignor Nani that he would never submit, would never be able to resign himself and kill his hope in salvation by love, but would rather reply by a fresh book, in which he would say in what new soil the new religion would spring up. Yes, a flaming book against Rome, in which he would set down all he had seen, a book which would depict the real Rome, the Rome which knows neither charity nor love, and is dying in the pride of its purple! He had spoken of returning to Paris, leaving the Church and going to the point of schism. Well, his luggage now lay there packed, he was going off and he would write that book, he would be the great schismatic who was awaited! Did not everything foretell approaching schism amidst that great movement of men's minds, weary of old mummified dogmas and yet hungering for the divine? Even Leo XIII must be conscious of it, for his whole policy, his whole effort towards Christian unity, his assumed affection for the democracy had no other object than that of grouping the whole family around the papacy, and consolidating it so as to render the Pope invincible in the approaching struggle. But the times had come, Catholicism would soon find that it could grant no more political concessions without perishing, that at Rome it was reduced to the immobility of an ancient hieratic idol, and that only in the lands of propaganda, where it was fighting against other religions, could further evolution take place. It was, indeed, for this reason that Rome was condemned, the more so as the abolition of the temporal power, by accustoming men's minds to the idea of a purely spiritual papacy, seemed likely to conduce to the rise of some anti-pope, far away, whilst the successor of St. Peter was compelled to cling stubbornly to his Apostolic and Roman fiction. A bishop, a priest would arise—where, who could tell? Perhaps yonder in that free America, where there are priests whom the struggle for life has turned into convinced socialists, into ardent democrats, who are ready to go forward with the coming century. And whilst Rome remains unable to relinquish aught of her past, aught of her mysteries and dogmas, that priest will relinquish all of those things which fall from one in dust. Ah! to be that priest, to be that great reformer, that saviour of modern society, what a vast dream, what a part, akin to that of a Messiah summoned by the nations in distress. For a moment Pierre was transported as by a breeze of hope and triumph. If that great change did not come in France, in Paris, it would come elsewhere, yonder across the ocean, or farther yet, wherever there might be a sufficiently fruitful soil for the new seed to spring from it in overflowing harvests. A new religion! a new religion! even as he had cried on returning from Lourdes, a religion which in particular should not be an appetite for death, a religion which should at last realise here below that Kingdom of God referred to in the Gospel, and which should equitably divide terrestrial wealth, and with the law of labour ensure the rule of truth and justice.

In the fever of this fresh dream Pierre already saw the pages of his new book flaring before him when his eyes fell on an object lying upon a chair, which at first surprised him. This also was a book, that work of Theophile Morin's which Orlando had commissioned him to hand to its author, and he felt annoyed with himself at having left it there, for he might have forgotten it altogether. Before putting it into his valise he retained it for a moment in his hand turning its pages over, his ideas changing as by a sudden mental revolution. The work was, however, a very modest one, one of those manuals for the bachelor's degree containing little beyond the first elements of the sciences; still all the sciences were represented in it, and it gave a fair summary of the present state of human knowledge. And it was indeed Science which thus burst upon Pierre's reverie with the energy of sovereign power. Not only was Catholicism swept away from his mind, but all his religious conceptions, every hypothesis of the divine tottered and fell. Only that little school book, nothing but the universal desire for knowledge, that education which ever extends and penetrates the whole people, and behold the mysteries became absurdities, the dogmas crumbled, and nothing of ancient faith was left. A nation nourished upon Science, no longer believing in mysteries and dogmas, in a compensatory system of reward and punishment, is a nation whose faith is for ever dead: and without faith Catholicism cannot be. Therein is the blade of the knife, the knife which falls and severs. If one century, if two centuries be needed, Science will take them. She alone is eternal. It is pure *naivete* to say that reason is not contrary to faith. The truth is, that now already in order to save mere fragments of the sacred writings, it has been necessary to accommodate them to the new certainties, by taking refuge in the assertion that they are simply symbolical! And what an extraordinary attitude is that of the Catholic Church, expressly forbidding all those who may discover a truth contrary to the sacred writings to pronounce upon it in definitive fashion, and ordering them to await events in the conviction that this truth will some day be proved an error! Only the Pope, says the Church, is infallible; Science is fallible, her constant groping is exploited against her, and divines remain on the watch striving to make it appear that her discoveries of to-day are in contradiction with her discoveries of yesterday. What do her sacrilegious assertions, what do her certainties rending dogma asunder, matter to a Catholic since it is certain that at the end of time, she, Science, will again join Faith, and become the latter's very humble slave! Voluntary blindness and impudent denial of things as evident as the sunlight, can no further go. But all the same the insignificant little book, the manual of truth travels on continuing its work, destroying error and building up the new world, even as the infinitesimal agents of life built up our present continents.

In the sudden great enlightenment which had come on him Pierre at last felt himself upon firm ground. Has Science ever retreated? It is Catholicism which has always retreated before her, and will always be forced to retreat. Never does Science stop, step by step she wrests truth from error, and to say that she is bankrupt because she cannot explain the world in one word and at one effort, is pure and simple nonsense. If she leaves, and no doubt will always leave a smaller and smaller domain to mystery, and if supposition may always strive to explain that mystery, it is none the less certain that she ruins, and with each successive hour will add to the ruin of the ancient hypotheses, those which crumble away before the acquired truths. And Catholicism is in the position of those ancient hypotheses, and will be in it yet more thoroughly to-morrow. Like all religions it is, at the bottom, but an explanation of the world, a superior social and political code, intended to bring about the greatest possible sum of peace and happiness on earth. This code which embraces the universality of things thenceforth becomes human, and mortal like everything that is human. One cannot put it on one side and say that it exists on one side by itself, whilst Science does the same on the other. Science is total and has already shown Catholicism that such is the case, and will show it again and again by compelling it to repair the breaches incessantly effected in its ramparts till the day of victory shall come with the final assault of resplendent truth. Frankly, it makes one laugh to hear people assign a *role* to Science, forbid her to enter such and such a domain, predict to her that she shall go no further, and declare that at this end of the century she is already so weary that she abdicates! Oh! you little men of shallow or distorted brains, you politicians planning expedients, you dogmatics at bay, you authoritarians so obstinately clinging to the ancient dreams, Science will pass on, and sweep you all away like withered leaves!

Pierre continued glancing through the humble little book, listening to all it told him of sovereign Science. She cannot become bankrupt, for she does not promise the absolute, she is simply the progressive conquest of truth. Never has she pretended that she could give the whole truth at one effort, that sort of edifice being precisely the work of metaphysics, of revelation, of faith. The *role* of Science, on the contrary, is only to destroy error as she gradually advances and increases enlightenment. And thus, far from becoming bankrupt, in her march which nothing stops, she remains the only possible truth for well-balanced and healthy minds. As for those whom she does not satisfy, who crave for immediate and universal knowledge, they have the resource of seeking refuge in no matter what religious hypothesis, provided, if they wish to appear in the right, that they build their fancy upon acquired certainties. Everything which is raised on proven error falls. However, although religious feeling persists among mankind, although the need of religion may be eternal, it by no means follows that Catholicism is eternal, for it is, after all, but one form of religion, which other forms preceded and which others will follow. Religions may disappear, but religious feeling will create new ones even with the help of Science. Pierre thought of that alleged repulse of Science by the present-day awakening of mysticism, the causes of which he had indicated in his book: the discredit into which the idea of liberty has fallen among the people, duped in the last social reorganisation, and the uneasiness of the *elite*, in despair at the void in which their liberated minds and enlarged intelligences have left them. It is the anguish of the Unknown springing up again; but it is also only a natural and momentary reaction after so much labour, on finding that Science does not yet calm our thirst for justice, our desire for security, or our ancient idea of an eternal after-life of enjoyment. In order, however, that Catholicism might be born anew, as some seem to think it will be, the social soil would have to change, and it cannot change; it no longer possesses the sap needful for the renewal of a decaying formula which schools and laboratories destroy more and more each day. The ground is other than it once was, a different oak must spring from it. May Science therefore have her religion, for such a religion will soon be the only one possible for the coming democracies, for the nations, whose knowledge ever increases whilst their Catholic faith is already nought but dust.

And all at once, by way of conclusion, Pierre bethought himself of the idiocy of the Congregation of the Index. It had condemned his book, and would surely condemn the other one that he had thought of, should he ever write it. A fine piece of work truly! To fall tooth and nail on the poor books of an enthusiastic dreamer, in which chimera contended with chimera! Yet the Congregation was so foolish as not to interdict that little book which he held in his hands, that humble book which alone was to be feared, which was the ever triumphant enemy that would surely overthrow the Church. Modest it was in its cheap "get up" as a school manual, but that did not matter: danger began with the very alphabet, increased as knowledge was acquired, and burst forth with those *resumes* of the physical, chemical, and natural sciences which bring the very Creation, as described by Holy Writ, into question. However, the Index dared not attempt to suppress those humble volumes, those terrible soldiers of truth, those destroyers of faith. What was the use, then, of all the money which Leo XIII drew from his hidden treasure of the Peter's Pence to subvention Catholic schools, with the thought of forming the believing generations which the papacy needed to enable it to conquer? What was the use of that precious money if it was only to serve for the purchase of similar insignificant yet formidable volumes, which could never be sufficiently "cooked" and expurgated, but would always contain too much Science, that growing Science which one day would blow up both Vatican and St. Peter's? Ah! that idiotic and impotent Index, what wretchedness and what derision!

Then, when Pierre had placed Theophile Morin's book in his valise, he once more returned to the window, and while leaning out, beheld an extraordinary vision. Under the cloudy, coppery sky, in the mild and mournful night, patches of wavy mist had risen, hiding many of the house-roofs with trailing shreds which looked like shrouds. Entire edifices had disappeared, and he imagined that the times were at last accomplished, and that truth had at last destroyed St. Peter's dome. In a hundred or a thousand years, it would be like that, fallen, obliterated from the black sky. One day, already, he had felt it tottering and cracking beneath him, and had foreseen that this temple of Catholicism would fall even as Jove's temple had fallen on the Capitol. And it was over now, the dome had strewn the ground with fragments, and all that remained standing, in addition to a portion of the apse, where five columns of the central nave, still upholding a shred of entablature, and four cyclopean buttress-piers on which the dome had rested—piers which still arose, isolated and superb, looking indestructible among all the surrounding downfall. But a denser mist flowed past, another thousand years no doubt went by, and then nothing whatever remained. The apse, the last pillars, the giant piers themselves were felled! The wind had swept away their dust, and it would have been necessary to search the soil beneath the brambles and the nettles to find a few fragments of broken statues, marbles with mutilated inscriptions, on the sense of which learned men were unable to agree. And, as formerly, on the Capitol, among the buried remnants of Jupiter's temple, goats strayed and climbed through the solitude, browsing upon the bushes, amidst the deep silence of the oppressive summer sunlight, which only the buzzing flies disturbed.

Then, only then, did Pierre feel the supreme collapse within him. It was really all over, Science was victorious, nothing of the old world remained. What use would it be then to become the great schismatic, the reformer who was awaited? Would it not simply mean the building up of a new dream? Only the eternal struggle of Science against the Unknown, the searching, pursuing inquiry which incessantly moderated man's thirst for the divine, now seemed to him of import, leaving him waiting to know if she would ever triumph so completely as to suffice mankind, by satisfying all its wants. And in the disaster which had overcome his apostolic enthusiasm, in presence of all those ruins, having lost his faith, and even his hope of utilising old Catholicism for social and moral salvation, there only remained reason that held him up. She had at one moment given way. If he had dreamt that book, and had just passed through that terrible crisis, it was because sentiment had once again overcome reason within him. It was his mother, so to say, who had wept in his heart, who had filled him with an irresistible desire to relieve the wretched and prevent the massacres which seemed near at hand; and his passion for charity had thus swept aside the scruples of his intelligence. But it was his father's voice that he now heard, lofty and bitter reason which, though it had fled, at present came back in all sovereignty. As he had done already after Lourdes, he protested against the glorification of the absurd and the downfall of common sense. Reason alone enabled him to walk erect and firm among the remnants of the old beliefs, even amidst the obscurities and failures of Science. Ah! Reason, it was through her alone that he suffered, through her alone that he could content himself, and he swore that he would now always seek to satisfy her, even if in doing so he should lose his happiness.

At that moment it would have been vain for him to ask what he ought to do. Everything remained in suspense, the world stretched before him still littered with the ruins of the past, of which, to-morrow, it would perhaps be rid. Yonder, in that dolorous faubourg of Paris, he would find good Abbe Rose, who but a few days previously had written begging him to return and tend, love, and save his poor, since Rome, so dazzling from afar, was dead to charity. And around the good and peaceful old priest he would find the ever growing flock of wretched ones; the little fledglings who had fallen from their nests, and whom he found pale with hunger and shivering with cold; the households of abominable misery in which the father drank and the mother became a prostitute, while the sons and the daughters sank into vice and crime; the dwellings, too, through which famine swept, where all was filth and shameful promiscuity, where there was neither furniture nor linen, nothing but purely animal life. And then there would also come the cold blasts of winter, the disasters of slack times, the hurricanes of consumption carrying off the weak, whilst the strong clenched their fists and dreamt of vengeance. One evening, too, perhaps, he might again enter some room of horror and find that another mother had killed herself and her five little ones, her last-born in her arms clinging to her drained breast, and the others scattered over the bare tiles, at last contented, feeling hunger no more, now that they were dead! But no, no, such awful things were no longer possible: such black misery conducting to suicide in the heart of that great city of Paris, which is brimful of wealth, intoxicated with enjoyment, and flings millions out of window for mere pleasure! The very foundations of the social edifice were rotten; all would soon collapse amidst mire and blood. Never before had Pierre so acutely realised the derisive futility of Charity. And all at once he became conscious that the long-awaited word, the word which was at last springing from the great silent multitude, the crushed and gagged people was *Justice*! Aye, Justice not Charity! Charity had only served to perpetuate misery, Justice perhaps would cure it. It was for Justice that the wretched hungered; an act of Justice alone could sweep away the olden world so that the new one might be reared. After all, the great silent multitude would belong neither to Vatican nor to Quirinal, neither to pope nor to king. If it had covertly growled through the ages in its long, sometimes mysterious, and sometimes open contest; if it had struggled betwixt pontiff and emperor who each had wished to retain it for himself alone, it had only done so in order that it might free itself, proclaim its resolve to belong to none on the day when it should cry Justice! Would to-morrow then at last prove that day of Justice and Truth?

XVI.

For his part, Pierre amidst his anguish—having on one hand that need of the divine which tortures man, and on the other sovereignty of reason which enables man to remain erect—was only sure of one thing, that he would keep his vows, continue a priest, watching over the belief of others though he could not himself believe, and would thus chastely and honestly follow his profession, amidst haughty sadness at having been unable to renounce his intelligence in the same way as he had renounced his flesh and his dream of saving the nations. And again, as after Lourdes, he would wait.

So deeply was he plunged in reflection at that window, face to face with the mist which seemed to be destroying the dark edifices of Rome, that he did not hear himself called. At last, however, he felt a tap on the shoulder: "Monsieur l'Abbe!" And then as he turned he saw Victorine, who said to him: "It is half-past nine; the cab is there. Giacomo has already taken your luggage down. You must come away, Monsieur l'Abbe."

Then seeing him blink, still dazed as it were, she smiled and added: "You were bidding Rome goodbye. What a frightful sky there is."

"Yes, frightful," was his reply.

Then they descended the stairs. He had handed her a hundred-franc note to be shared between herself and the other servants. And she apologised for going down before him with the lamp, explaining that the old palace was so dark that evening one could scarcely see.

Ah! that departure, that last descent through the black and empty mansion, it quite upset Pierre's heart. He gave his room that glance of farewell which always saddened him, even when he was leaving a spot where he had suffered. Then, on passing Don Vigilio's chamber, whence there only came a quivering silence, he pictured the secretary with his head buried in his pillows, holding his breath for fear lest he should speak and attract vengeance. But it was in particular on the second and first floor landings, on passing the closed doors of Donna Serafina and the Cardinal, that Pierre quivered with apprehension at hearing nothing but the silence of the grave. And as he followed Victorine, who, lamp in hand, was still descending, he thought of the brother and sister who were left alone in the ruined palace, last relics of a world which had half passed away. All hope of life had departed with Benedetta and Dario, no resurrection could come from that old maid and that priest who was bound to chastity. Ah! those interminable and lugubrious passages, that frigid and gigantic staircase which seemed to descend into nihility, those huge halls with cracking walls where all was wretchedness and abandonment! And that inner court, looking like a cemetery with its weeds and its damp porticus, where remnants of Apollos and Venuses were rotting! And the little deserted garden, fragrant with ripe oranges, whither nobody now would ever stray, where none would ever meet that adorable Contessina under the laurels near the sarcophagus! All was now annihilated in abominable mourning, in a death-like silence, amidst which the two last Boccaneras must wait, in savage grandeur, till their palace should fall about their heads. Pierre could only just detect a faint sound, the gnawing of a mouse perhaps, unless it were caused by Abbe Paparelli attacking the walls of some out-of-the-way rooms, preying on the old edifice down below, so as to hasten its fall.

The cab stood at the door, already laden with the luggage, the box beside the driver, the valise on the seat; and the priest at once got in.

"Oh! You have plenty of time," said Victorine, who had remained on the foot-pavement. "Nothing has been forgotten. I'm glad to see you go off comfortably."

And indeed at that last moment Pierre was comforted by the presence of that worthy woman, his compatriot, who had greeted him on his arrival and now attended his departure. "I won't say 'till we meet again,' Monsieur l'Abbe," she exclaimed, "for I don't fancy that you'll soon be back in this horrid city. Good-bye, Monsieur l'Abbe."

"Good-bye, Victorine, and thank you with all my heart."

The cab was already going off at a fast trot, turning into the narrow sinuous street which leads to the Corso Vittoria Emanuele. It was not raining and so the hood had not been raised, but although the damp atmosphere was comparatively mild, Pierre at once felt a chill. However, he was unwilling to stop the driver, a silent fellow whose only desire seemingly was to get rid of his fare as soon as possible. When the cab came out into the Corso Vittoria Emanuele, the young man was astonished to find it already quite deserted, the houses shut, the footways bare, and the electric lamps burning all alone in melancholy solitude. In truth, however, the temperature was far from warm and the fog seemed to be increasing, hiding the house-fronts more and more. When Pierre passed the Cancelleria, that stern colossal pile seemed to him to be receding, fading away; and farther on, upon the right, at the end of the Via di Ara Coeli, starred by a few smoky gas lamps, the Capitol had quite vanished in the gloom. Then the thoroughfare narrowed, and the cab went on between the dark heavy masses of the Gesu and the Altieri palace; and there in that contracted passage, where even on fine sunny days one found all the dampness of old times, the quivering priest yielded to a fresh train of thought. It was an idea which had sometimes made him feel anxious, the idea that mankind, starting from over yonder in Asia, had always marched onward with the sun. An east wind had always carried the human seed for future harvest towards the west. And for a long while now the cradle of humanity had been stricken with destruction and death, as if indeed the nations could only advance by stages, leaving exhausted soil, ruined cities, and degenerate populations behind, as they marched from orient to occident, towards their unknown goal. Nineveh and Babylon on the banks of the Euphrates, Thebes and Memphis on the banks of the Nile, had been reduced to dust, sinking from old age and weariness into a deadly numbness beyond possibility of awakening. Then decrepitude had spread to the shores of the great Mediterranean lake, burying both Tyre and Sidon with dust, and afterwards striking Carthage with senility whilst it yet seemed in full splendour. In this wise as mankind marched on, carried by the hidden forces of civilisation from east to west, it marked each day's journey with ruins; and how frightful was the sterility nowadays displayed by the cradle of History, that Asia and that Egypt, which had once more lapsed into childhood, immobilised in ignorance and degeneracy amidst the ruins of ancient cities that once had been queens of the world!

It was thus Pierre reflected as the cab rolled on. Still he was not unconscious of his surroundings. As he passed the Palazzo di Venezia it seemed to him to be crumbling beneath some assault of the invisible, for the mist had already swept away its battlements, and the lofty, bare, fearsome walls looked as if they were staggering from the onslaught of the growing darkness. And after passing the deep gap of the Corso, which was also deserted amidst the pallid radiance of its electric lights, the Palazzo Torlonia appeared on the right-hand, with one wing ripped open by the picks of demolishers, whilst on the left, farther up, the Palazzo Colonna showed its long, mournful facade and closed windows, as if, now that it was deserted by its masters and void of its ancient pomp, it awaited the demolishers in its turn.

Then, as the cab at a slower pace began to climb the ascent of the Via Nazionale, Pierre's reverie continued. Was not Rome also stricken, had not the hour come for her to disappear amidst that destruction which the nations on the march invariably left behind them? Greece, Athens, and Sparta slumbered beneath their glorious memories, and were of no account in the world of to-day. Moreover, the growing paralysis had already invaded the lower portion of the Italic peninsula; and after Naples certainly came the turn of Rome. She was on the very margin of the death spot which ever extends over the old continent, that margin where agony begins, where the impoverished soil will no longer nourish and support cities, where men themselves seem stricken with old age as soon as they are born. For two centuries Rome had been declining, withdrawing little by little from modern life, having neither manufactures nor trade, and being incapable even of science, literature, or art. And in Pierre's thoughts it was no longer St. Peter's only that fell, but all Rome—basilicas, palaces, and entire districts—which collapsed amidst a supreme rending, and covered the seven hills with a chaos of ruins. Like Nineveh and Babylon, and like Thebes and Memphis, Rome became but a plain, bossy with remnants, amidst which one vainly sought to identify the sites of ancient edifices, whilst its sole denizens were coiling serpents and bands of rats.

The cab turned, and on the right, in a huge gap of darkness Pierre recognised Trajan's column, but it was no longer gilded by the sun as when he had first seen it; it now rose up blackly like the dead trunk of a giant tree whose branches have fallen from old age. And farther on, when he raised his eyes while crossing the little triangular piazza, and perceived a real tree against the leaden sky, that parasol pine of the Villa Aldobrandini which rises there like a symbol of Rome's grace and pride, it seemed to him but a smear, a little cloud of soot ascending from the downfall of the whole city.

With the anxious, fraternal turn of his feelings, fear was coming over him as he reached the end of his tragic dream. When the numbness which spreads across the aged world should have passed Rome, when Lombardy should have yielded to it, and Genoa, Turin, and Milan should have fallen asleep as Venice has fallen already, then would come the turn of France. The Alps would be crossed, Marseilles, like Tyre and Sidon, would see its port choked up by sand, Lyons would sink into desolation and slumber, and at last Paris, invaded by the invincible torpor, and transformed into a sterile waste of stones bristling with nettles, would join Rome and Nineveh and Babylon in death, whilst the nations continued their march from orient to occident following the sun. A great cry sped through the gloom, the death cry of the Latin races! History, which seemed to have been born in the basin of the Mediterranean, was being transported elsewhere, and the ocean had now become the centre of the world. How many hours of the human day had gone by? Had mankind, starting from its cradle over yonder at daybreak, strewing its road with ruins from stage to stage, now accomplished one-half of its day and reached the dazzling hour of noon? If so, then the other half of the day allotted to it was beginning, the new world was following the old one, the new world of those American cities where democracy was forming and the religion of to-morrow was sprouting, those sovereign queens of the coming century, with yonder, across another ocean, on the other side of the globe, that motionless

Far East, mysterious China and Japan, and all the threatening swarm of the yellow races.

However, while the cab climbed higher and higher up the Via Nazionale, Pierre felt his nightmare dissipating. There was here a lighter atmosphere, and he came back into a renewal of hope and courage. Yet the Banca d'Italia, with its brand-new ugliness, its chalky hugeness, looked to him like a phantom in a shroud; whilst above a dim expanse of gardens the Quirinal formed but a black streak barring the heavens. However, the street ever ascended and broadened, and on the summit of the Viminal, on the Piazza delle Terme, when he passed the ruins of Diocletian's baths, he could breathe as his lungs listed. No, no, the human day could not finish, it was eternal, and the stages of civilisation would follow and follow without end! What mattered that eastern wind which carried the nations towards the west, as if borne on by the power of the sun! If necessary, they would return across the other side of the globe, they would again and again make the circuit of the earth, until the day should come when they could establish themselves in peace, truth, and justice. After the next civilisation on the shores of the Atlantic, which would become the world's centre, skirted by queenly cities, there would spring up yet another civilisation, having the Pacific for its centre, with seaport capitals that could not be yet foreseen, whose germs yet slumbered on unknown shores. And in like way there would be still other civilisations and still others! And at that last moment, the inspiriting thought came to Pierre that the great movement of the nations was the instinct, the need which impelled them to return to unity. Originating in one sole family, afterwards parted and dispersed in tribes, thrown into collision by fratricidal hatred, their tendency was none the less to become one sole family again. The provinces united in nations, the nations would unite in races, and the races would end by uniting in one immortal mankind—mankind at last without frontiers, or possibility of wars, mankind living by just labour amidst an universal commonwealth. Was not this indeed the evolution, the object of the labour progressing everywhere, the finish reserved to History? Might Italy then become a strong and healthy nation, might concord be established between her and France, and might that fraternity of the Latin races become the beginning of universal fraternity! Ah! that one fatherland, the whole earth pacified and happy, in how many centuries would that come—and what a dream!

Then, on reaching the station the scramble prevented Pierre from thinking any further. He had to take his ticket and register his luggage, and afterwards he at once climbed into the train. At dawn on the next day but one, he would be back in Paris.

PARIS

The Three Cities

Translated By Ernest A. Vizetelly

TRANSLATOR'S PREFACE

WITH the present work M. Zola completes the "Trilogy of the Three Cities," which he began with "Lourdes" and continued with "Rome"; and thus the adventures and experiences of Abbe Pierre Froment, the doubting Catholic priest who failed to find faith at the miraculous grotto by the Cave, and hope amidst the crumbling theocracy of the Vatican, are here brought to what, from M. Zola's point of view, is their logical conclusion. From the first pages of "Lourdes," many readers will have divined that Abbe Froment was bound to finish as he does, for, frankly, no other finish was possible from a writer of M. Zola's opinions.

Taking the Trilogy as a whole, one will find that it is essentially symbolical. Abbe Froment is Man, and his struggles are the struggles between Religion, as personified by the Roman Catholic Church, on the one hand, and Reason and Life on the other. In the Abbe's case the victory ultimately rests with the latter; and we may take it as being M. Zola's opinion that the same will eventually be the case with the great bulk of mankind. English writers are often accused of treating subjects from an insular point of view, and certainly there may be good ground for such a charge. But they are not the only writers guilty of the practice. The purview of French authors is often quite as limited: they regard French opinion as the only good opinion, and judge the rest of the world by their own standard. In the present case, if we leave the world and mankind generally on one side, and apply M. Zola's facts and theories to France alone, it will be found, I think, that he has made out a remarkably good case for himself. For it is certain that Catholicism, I may say Christianity, is fast crumbling in France. There may be revivals in certain limited circles, efforts of the greatest energy to prop up the tottering edifice by a "rallying" of believers to the democratic cause, and by a kindling of the most bitter anti-Semitic warfare; but all these revivals and efforts, although they are extremely well-advertised and create no little stir, produce very little impression on the bulk of the population. So far as France is concerned, the policy of Leo XIII. seems to have come too late. The French masses regard Catholicism or Christianity, whichever one pleases, as a religion of death,—a religion which, taking its stand on the text "There shall always be poor among you," condemns them to toil and moil in poverty and distress their whole life long, with no other consolation than the promise of happiness in heaven. And, on the other hand, they see the ministers of the Deity, "whose kingdom is not of this world," supporting the wealthy and powerful, and striving to secure wealth and power for themselves. Charity exists, of course, but the masses declare that it is no remedy; they do not ask for doles, they ask for Justice.

It is largely by reason of all this that Socialism and Anarchism have made such great strides in France of recent years. Robespierre, as will be remembered, once tried to suppress Christianity altogether, and for a time certainly there was a virtually general cessation of religious observances in France. But no such Reign of Terror prevails there to-day. Men are perfectly free to believe if they are inclined to do so; and yet never were there fewer religious marriages, fewer baptisms or smaller congregations in the French churches. I refer not merely to Paris and other large cities, but to the smaller towns, and even the little hamlets of many parts. Old village priests, men practising what they teach and possessed of the most loving, benevolent hearts, have told me with tears in their eyes of the growing infidelity of their parishioners.

I have been studying this matter for some years, and write without prejudice, merely setting down what I believe to be the truth. Of course we are all aware that the most stupendous efforts are being made by the Catholic clergy and zealous believers to bring about a revival of the faith, and certainly in some circles there has been a measure of success. But the reconversion of a nation is the most formidable of tasks; and, in my own opinion, as in M. Zola's, France as a whole is lost to the Christian religion. On this proposition, combined with a second one, namely, that even as France as a nation will be the first to discard Christianity, so she will be the first to promulgate a new faith based on reason, science and the teachings of life, is founded the whole argument of M. Zola's Trilogy.

Having thus dealt with the Trilogy's religious aspects, I would now speak of "Paris," its concluding volume. This is very different from "Lourdes" and "Rome." Whilst recounting the struggles and fate of Abbe Froment and his brother Guillaume, and entering largely into the problem of Capital and Labour, which problem has done so much to turn the masses away from Christianity, it contains many an interesting and valuable picture of the Parisian world at the close of the nineteenth century. It is no guide-book to Paris; but it paints the city's social life, its rich and poor, its scandals and crimes, its work and its pleasures. Among the households to which the reader is introduced are those of a banker, an aged Countess of the old *noblesse*, a cosmopolitan Princess, of a kind that Paris knows only too well, a scientist, a manufacturer, a working mechanician, a priest, an Anarchist, a petty clerk and an actress of a class that so often dishonours the French stage. Science and art and learning and religion, all have their representatives. Then, too, the political world is well to the front. There are honest and unscrupulous Ministers of State, upright and venal deputies, enthusiastic and cautious candidates for power, together with social theoreticians of various schools. And the *blase*, weak-minded man of fashion is here, as well as the young "symbolist" of perverted, degraded mind. The women are of all types, from the most loathsome to the most lovable. Then, too, the journalists are portrayed in such life-like fashion that I might give each of them his real name. And journalism, Parisian journalism, is flagellated, shown as it really is,—if just a few well-conducted organs be excepted,—that is, venal and impudent, mendacious and even petty.

The actual scenes depicted are quite as kaleidoscopic as are the characters in their variety. We enter the banker's gilded saloon and the hovel of the pauper, the busy factory, the priest's retired home and the laboratory of the scientist. We wait in the lobbies of the Chamber of Deputies, and afterwards witness "a great debate"; we penetrate into the private sanctum of a Minister of the Interior; we attend a fashionable wedding at the Madeleine and a first performance at the Comedie Francaise; we dine at the Cafe Anglais and listen to a notorious vocalist in a low music hall at Montmartre; we pursue an Anarchist through the Bois de Boulogne; we slip into the Assize Court and see that Anarchist tried there; we afterwards gaze upon his execution by the guillotine; we are also on the boulevards when the lamps are lighted for a long night of revelry, and we stroll along the quiet streets in the small hours of the morning, when crime and homeless want are prowling round.

And ever the scene changes; the whole world of Paris passes before one. Yet the book, to my thinking, is far less descriptive than analytical. The souls of the principal characters are probed to their lowest depths. Many of the scenes, too, are intensely dramatic, admirably adapted for the stage; as, for instance, Baroness Duvillard's interview with her daughter in the chapter which I have called "The Rivals." And side by side with baseness there is heroism, while beauty of the flesh finds its counterpart in beauty of the mind. M. Zola has often been reproached for showing us the vileness of human nature; and no doubt such vileness may be found in "Paris," but there are contrasting pictures. If some of M. Zola's characters horrify the reader, there are others that the latter can but admire. Life is compounded of good and evil, and unfortunately it is usually the evil that makes the most noise and attracts the most attention. Moreover, in M. Zola's case, it has always been his purpose to expose the evils from which society suffers in the hope of directing attention to them and thereby hastening a remedy, and thus, in the course of his works, he could not do otherwise than drag the whole frightful mass of human villany and degradation into the full light of day. But if there are, again, black pages in "Paris," others, bright and comforting, will be found near them. And the book ends in no pessimist strain. Whatever may be thought of the writer's views on religion, most readers will, I imagine, agree with his opinion that, despite much social injustice, much crime, vice, cupidity and baseness, we are ever marching on to better things.

In the making of the coming, though still far-away, era of truth and justice, Paris, he thinks, will play the leading part, for whatever the stains upon her, they are but surface-deep; her heart remains good and sound; she has genius and courage and energy and wit and fancy. She can be generous, too, when she chooses, and more than once her ideas have irradiated the world. Thus M. Zola hopes much from her, and who will gainsay him? Not I, who can apply to her the words which Byron addressed to the home of my own and M. Zola's forefathers:—

> "I loved her from my boyhood; she to me
> Was as a fairy city of the heart."

Thus I can but hope that Paris, where I learnt the little I know, where I struggled and found love and happiness, whose every woe and disaster and triumph I have shared for over thirty years, may, however dark the clouds that still pass over her, some day fully justify M. Zola's confidence, and bring to pass his splendid dream of perfect truth and perfect justice.

E. A. V. MERTON, SURREY, ENGLAND,

Feb. 5, 1898.

BOOK I.

I. THE PRIEST AND THE POOR

THAT morning, one towards the end of January, Abbe Pierre Froment, who had a mass to say at the Sacred Heart at Montmartre, was on the height, in front of the basilica, already at eight o'clock. And before going in he gazed for a moment upon the immensity of Paris spread out below him.

After two months of bitter cold, ice and snow, the city was steeped in a mournful, quivering thaw. From the far-spreading, leaden-hued heavens a thick mist fell like a mourning shroud. All the eastern portion of the city, the abodes of misery and toil, seemed submerged beneath ruddy steam, amid which the panting of workshops and factories could be divined; while westwards, towards the districts of wealth and enjoyment, the fog broke and lightened, becoming but a fine and motionless veil of vapour. The curved line of the horizon could scarcely be divined, the expanse of houses, which nothing bounded, appeared like a chaos of stone, studded with stagnant pools, which filled the hollows with pale steam; whilst against them the summits of the edifices, the housetops of the loftier streets, showed black like soot. It was a Paris of mystery, shrouded by clouds, buried as it were beneath the ashes of some disaster, already half-sunken in the suffering and the shame of that which its immensity concealed.

Thin and sombre in his flimsy cassock, Pierre was looking on when Abbe Rose, who seemed to have sheltered himself behind a pillar of the porch on purpose to watch for him, came forward: "Ah! it's you at last, my dear child," said he, "I have something to ask you."

He seemed embarrassed and anxious, and glanced round distrustfully to make sure that nobody was near. Then, as if the solitude thereabouts did not suffice to reassure him, he led Pierre some distance away, through the icy, biting wind, which he himself did not seem to feel. "This is the matter," he resumed, "I have been told that a poor fellow, a former house-painter, an old man of seventy, who naturally can work no more, is dying of hunger in a hovel in the Rue des Saules. So, my dear child, I thought of you. I thought you would consent to take him these three francs from me, so that he may at least have some bread to eat for a few days."

"But why don't you take him your alms yourself?"

At this Abbe Rose again grew anxious, and cast vague, frightened glances about him. "Oh, no, oh, no!" he said, "I can no longer do that after all the worries that have befallen me. You know that I am watched, and should get another scolding if I were caught giving alms like this, scarcely knowing to whom I give them. It is true that I had to sell something to get these three francs. But, my dear child, render me this service, I pray you."

Pierre, with heart oppressed, stood contemplating the old priest, whose locks were quite white, whose full lips spoke of infinite kindliness, and whose eyes shone clear and childlike in his round and smiling face. And he bitterly recalled the story of that lover of the poor, the semi-disgrace into which he had fallen through the sublime candour of his charitable goodness. His little ground-floor of the Rue de Charonne, which he had turned into a refuge where he offered shelter to all the wretchedness of the streets, had ended by giving cause for scandal. His *naivete* and innocence had been abused; and abominable things had gone on under his roof without his knowledge. Vice had turned the asylum into a meeting-place; and at last, one night, the police had descended upon it to arrest a young girl accused of infanticide. Greatly concerned by this scandal, the diocesan authorities had forced Abbe Rose to close his shelter, and had removed him from the church of Ste. Marguerite to that of St. Pierre of Montmartre, where he now again acted as curate. Truth to tell, it was not a disgrace but a removal to another spot. However, he had been scolded and was watched, as he said; and he was much ashamed of it, and very unhappy at being only able to give alms by stealth, much like some harebrained prodigal who blushes for his faults.

Pierre took the three francs. "I promise to execute your commission, my friend, oh! with all my heart," he said.

"You will go after your mass, won't you? His name is Laveuve, he lives in the Rue des Saules in a house with a courtyard, just before reaching the Rue Marcadet. You are sure to find it. And if you want to be very kind you will tell me of your visit this evening at five o'clock, at the Madeleine, where I am going to hear Monseigneur Martha's address. He has been so good to me! Won't you also come to hear him?"

Pierre made an evasive gesture. Monseigneur Martha, Bishop of Persepolis and all powerful at the archiepiscopal palace, since, like the genial propagandist he was, he had been devoting himself to increasing the subscriptions for the basilica of the Sacred Heart, had indeed supported Abbe Rose; in fact, it was by his influence that the abbe had been kept in Paris, and placed once more at St. Pierre de Montmartre.

"I don't know if I shall be able to hear the address," said Pierre, "but in any case I will go there to meet you."

The north wind was blowing, and the gloomy cold penetrated both of them on that deserted summit amidst the fog which changed the vast city into a misty ocean. However, some footsteps were heard, and Abbe Rose, again mistrustful, saw a man go by, a tall and sturdy man, who wore clogs and was bareheaded, showing his thick and closely-cut white hair. "Is not that your brother?" asked the old priest.

Pierre had not stirred. "Yes, it is my brother Guillaume," he quietly responded. "I have found him again since I have been coming occasionally to the Sacred Heart. He owns a house close by, where he has been living for more than twenty years, I think. When we meet we shake hands, but I have never even been to his house. Oh! all is quite dead between us, we have nothing more in common, we are parted by worlds."

Abbe Rose's tender smile again appeared, and he waved his hand as if to say that one must never despair of love. Guillaume Froment, a savant of lofty intelligence, a chemist who lived apart from others, like one who rebelled against the social system, was now a parishioner of the abbe's, and when the latter passed the house where Guillaume lived with his three sons—a house all alive with work—he must often have dreamt of leading him back to God.

"But, my dear child," he resumed, "I am keeping you here in this dark cold, and you are not warm. Go and say your mass. Till this evening, at the Madeleine." Then, in entreating fashion, after again making sure that none could hear them, he added, still with the air of a child at fault: "And not a word to anybody about my little commission—it would again be said that I don't know how to conduct myself."

Pierre watched the old priest as he went off towards the Rue Cartot, where he lived on a damp ground-floor, enlivened by a strip of garden. The veil of disaster, which was submerging Paris, now seemed to grow thicker under the gusts of the icy north wind. And at last Pierre entered the basilica, his heart upset, overflowing with the bitterness stirred up by the recollection of Abbe Rose's story—that bankruptcy of charity, the frightful irony of a holy man punished for bestowing alms, and hiding himself that he might still continue to bestow them. Nothing could calm the smart of the wound reopened in Pierre's heart—neither the warm peacefulness into which he entered, nor the silent solemnity of the broad, deep fabric, whose new stonework was quite bare, without a single painting or any kind of decoration; the nave being still half-barred by the scaffoldings which blocked up the unfinished dome. At that early hour the masses of entreaty had already been said at several altars, under the grey light falling from the high and narrow windows, and the tapers of entreaty were burning in the depths of the apse. So Pierre made haste to go to the sacristy, there to assume his vestments in order that he might say his mass in the chapel of St. Vincent de Paul.

But the floodgates of memory had been opened, and he had no thought but for his distress whilst, in mechanical fashion, he performed the rites and made the customary gestures. Since his return from Rome three years previously, he had been living in the very worst anguish that can fall on man. At the outset, in order to recover his lost faith, he had essayed a first experiment: he had gone to Lourdes, there to seek the innocent belief of the child who kneels and prays, the primitive faith of young nations bending beneath the terror born of ignorance; but he had rebelled yet more than ever in presence of what he had witnessed at Lourdes: that glorification of the absurd, that collapse of common sense; and was convinced that salvation, the peace of men and nations nowadays, could not lie in that puerile relinquishment of reason. And afterwards, again yielding to the need of loving whilst yet allowing reason, so hard to satisfy, her share in his intellect, he had staked his final peace on a second experiment, and had gone to Rome to see if Catholicism could there be renewed, could revert to the spirit of primitive Christianity and become the religion of the democracy, the faith which the modern world, upheaving and in danger of death, was awaiting in order to calm down and live. And he had found there naught but ruins, the rotted trunk of a tree that could never put forth another springtide; and he had heard there naught but the supreme rending of the old social edifice, near to its fall. Then it was, that, relapsing into boundless doubt, total negation, he had been recalled to Paris by Abbe Rose, in the name of their poor, and had returned thither that he might forget and immolate himself and believe in them—the poor—since they and their frightful sufferings alone remained certain. And then it was too, that for three years he came into contact with that collapse, that very bankruptcy of goodness itself: charity a derision, charity useless and flouted.

Those three years had been lived by Pierre amidst ever-growing torments, in which his whole being had ended by sinking. His faith was forever dead; dead, too, even his hope of utilising the faith of the multitudes for the general salvation. He denied everything, he anticipated nothing but the final, inevitable catastrophe: revolt, massacre and conflagration, which would sweep away a guilty and condemned world. Unbelieving priest that he was, yet watching over the faith of others, honestly, chastely discharging his duties, full of haughty sadness at the thought that he had been unable to renounce his mind as he had renounced his flesh and his dream of being a saviour of the nations, he withal remained erect, full of fierce yet solitary grandeur. And this despairing, denying priest, who had dived to the bottom of nothingness, retained such a lofty and grave demeanour, perfumed by such pure kindness, that in his parish of Neuilly he had acquired the reputation of being a young saint, one beloved by Providence, whose prayers wrought miracles. He was but a personification of the rules of the Church; of the priest he retained only the gestures; he was like an empty sepulchre in which not even the ashes of hope remained; yet grief-stricken weeping women worshipped him and kissed his cassock; and it was a tortured mother whose infant was in danger of death, who had implored him to come and ask that infant's cure of Jesus, certain as she felt that Jesus would grant her the boon in that sanctuary of Montmartre where blazed the prodigy of His heart, all burning with love.

Clad in his vestments, Pierre had reached the chapel of St. Vincent de Paul. He there ascended the altar-step and began the mass; and when he turned round with hands spread out to bless the worshippers he showed his hollow cheeks, his gentle mouth contracted by bitterness, his loving eyes darkened by suffering. He was no longer the young priest whose countenance had glowed with tender fever on the road to Lourdes, whose face had been illumined by apostolic fervour when he started for Rome. The two hereditary influences which were ever at strife within him—that of his father to whom he owed his impregnable, towering brow, that of his mother who had given him his love-thirsting lips, were still waging war, the whole human battle of sentiment and reason, in that now ravaged face of his, whither in moments of forgetfulness ascended all the chaos of internal suffering. The lips still confessed that unquenched thirst for love, self-bestowal and life, which he well thought he could nevermore content, whilst the solid brow, the citadel which made him suffer, obstinately refused to capitulate, whatever might be the assaults of error. But he stiffened himself, hid the horror of the void in which he struggled, and showed himself superb, making each gesture, repeating each word in sovereign fashion. And gazing at him through her tears, the mother who was there among the few kneeling women, the mother who awaited a supreme intercession from him, who thought him in communion with Jesus for the salvation of her child, beheld him radiant with angelic beauty like some messenger of the divine grace.

When, after the offertory, Pierre uncovered the chalice he felt contempt for himself. The shock had been too great, and he thought of those things in spite of all. What puerility there had been in his two experiments at Lourdes and Rome, the *naivete* of a poor distracted being, consumed by desire to love and believe. To have imagined that present-day science would in his person accommodate itself to the faith of the year One Thousand, and in particular to have foolishly believed that he, petty priest that he was, would be able to indoctrinate the Pope and prevail on him to become a saint and change the face of the world! It all filled him with shame; how people must have laughed at him! Then, too, his idea of a schism made him blush. He again beheld himself at Rome, dreaming of writing a book by which he would violently sever himself from Catholicism to preach the new religion of the democracies, the purified, human and living Gospel. But what ridiculous folly! A schism? He had known in Paris an abbe of great heart and mind who had attempted to bring about that famous, predicted, awaited schism. Ah! the poor man, the sad, the ludicrous labour in the midst of universal incredulity, the icy indifference of some, the mockery and the reviling of others! If Luther were to come to France in our days he would end, forgotten and dying of hunger, on a Batignolles fifth-floor. A schism cannot succeed among a people that no longer believes, that has ceased to take all interest in the Church, and sets its hope elsewhere. And it was all Catholicism, in fact all Christianity, that would be swept away, for, apart from certain moral maxims, the Gospel no longer supplied a possible code for society. And this conviction increased Pierre's torment on the days when his cassock weighed more heavily on his shoulders, when he ended by feeling contempt for himself at thus celebrating the divine mystery of the mass, which for him had become but the formula of a dead religion.

Having half filled the chalice with wine from the vase, Pierre washed his hands and again perceived the mother with her face of ardent entreaty. Then he thought it was for her that, with the charitable leanings of a vow-bound man, he had remained a priest, a priest without belief, feeding the belief of others with the bread of illusion. But this heroic conduct, the haughty spirit of duty in which he imprisoned himself, was not practised by him without growing anguish. Did not elementary probity require that he should cast aside the cassock and return into the midst of men? At certain times the falsity of his position filled him with disgust for his useless heroism; and he asked himself if it were not cowardly and dangerous to leave the masses in superstition. Certainly the theory of a just and vigilant Providence, of a future paradise where all these sufferings of the world would receive compensation, had long seemed necessary to the wretchedness of mankind; but what a trap lay in it, what a pretext for the tyrannical grinding down of nations; and how far more virile it would be to undeceive the nations, however brutally, and give them courage to live the real life, even if it were in tears. If they were already turning aside from Christianity was not this because they needed a more human ideal, a religion of health and joy which should not be a religion of death? On the day when the idea of charity should crumble, Christianity would crumble also, for it was built upon the idea of divine charity correcting the injustice of fate, and offering future rewards to those who might suffer in this life. And it was crumbling; for the poor no longer believed in it, but grew angry at the thought of that deceptive paradise, with the promise of which their patience had been beguiled so long, and demanded that their share of happiness should not always be put off until the morrow of death. A cry for justice arose from every lip, for justice upon this earth, justice for those who hunger and thirst, whom alms are weary of relieving after eighteen hundred years of Gospel teaching, and who still and ever lack bread to eat.

When Pierre, with his elbows on the altar, had emptied the chalice after breaking the sacred wafer, he felt himself sinking into yet greater distress. And so a third experiment was beginning for him, the supreme battle of justice against charity, in which his heart and his mind would struggle together in that great Paris, so full of terrible, unknown things. The need for the divine still battled within him against domineering intelligence. How among the masses would one ever be able to content the thirst for the mysterious? Leaving the *elite* on one side, would science suffice to pacify desire, lull suffering, and satisfy the dream? And what would become of himself in the bankruptcy of that same charity, which for three years had alone kept him erect by occupying his every hour, and giving him the illusion of self-devotion, of being useful to others? It seemed, all at once, as if the ground sank beneath him, and he heard nothing save the cry of the masses, silent so long, but now demanding justice, growling and threatening to take their share, which was withheld from them by force and ruse. Nothing more, it seemed, could delay the inevitable catastrophe, the fratricidal class warfare that would sweep away the olden world, which was condemned to disappear beneath the mountain of its crimes. Every hour with frightful sadness he expected the collapse, Paris steeped in blood, Paris in flames. And his horror of all violence froze him; he knew not where to seek the new belief which might dissipate the peril. Fully conscious, though he was, that the social and religious problems are but one, and are alone in question in the dreadful daily labour of Paris, he was too deeply troubled himself, too far removed from ordinary things by his position as a priest, and too sorely rent by doubt and powerlessness to tell as yet where might be truth, and health, and life. Ah! to be healthy and to live, to content at last both heart and reason in the peace, the certain, simply honest labour, which man has come to accomplish upon this earth!

The mass was finished, and Pierre descended from the altar, when the weeping mother, near whom he passed, caught hold of a corner of the chasuble with her trembling hands, and kissed it with wild fervour, as one may kiss some relic of a saint from whom one expects salvation. She thanked him for the miracle which he must have accomplished, certain as she felt that she would find her child cured. And he was deeply stirred by that love, that ardent faith of hers, in spite of the sudden and yet keener distress which he felt at being in no wise the sovereign minister that she thought him, the minister able to obtain a respite from Death. But he dismissed her consoled and strengthened, and it was with an ardent prayer that he entreated the unknown but conscious Power to succour the poor creature. Then, when he had divested himself in the sacristy, and found himself again out of doors before the basilica, lashed by the keen wintry wind, a mortal shiver came upon him, and froze him, while through the mist he looked to see if a whirlwind of anger and justice had not swept Paris away: that catastrophe which must some day destroy it, leaving under the leaden heavens only the pestilential quagmire of its ruins.

Pierre wished to fulfil Abbe Rose's commission immediately. He followed the Rue des Norvins, on the crest of Montmartre; and, reaching the Rue des Saules, descended by its steep slope, between mossy walls, to the other side of Paris. The three francs which he was holding in his cassock's pocket, filled him at once with gentle emotion and covert anger against the futility of charity. But as he gradually descended by the sharp declivities and interminable storeys of steps, the mournful nooks of misery which he espied took possession of him, and infinite pity wrung his heart. A whole new district was here being built alongside the broad thoroughfares opened since the great works of the Sacred Heart had begun. Lofty middle-class houses were already rising among ripped-up gardens and plots of vacant land, still edged with palings. And these houses with their substantial frontages, all new and white, lent a yet more sombre and leprous aspect to such of the old shaky buildings as remained, the low pot-houses with blood-coloured walls, the *cites* of workmen's dwellings, those abodes of suffering with black, soiled buildings in which human cattle were piled. Under the low-hanging sky that day, the pavement, dented by heavily-laden carts, was covered with mud; the thaw soaked the walls with an icy dampness, whilst all the filth and destitution brought terrible sadness to the heart.

After going as far as the Rue Marcadet, Pierre retraced his steps; and in the Rue des Saules, certain that he was not mistaken, he entered the courtyard of a kind of barracks or hospital, encompassed by three irregular buildings. This court was a quagmire, where filth must have accumulated during the two months of terrible frost; and now all was melting, and an abominable stench arose. The buildings were half falling, the gaping vestibules looked like cellar holes, strips of paper streaked the cracked and filthy window-panes, and vile rags hung about like flags of death. Inside a shanty which served as the door-keeper's abode Pierre only saw an infirm man rolled up in a tattered strip of what had once been a horse-cloth.

"You have an old workman named Laveuve here," said the priest. "Which staircase is it, which floor?"

The man did not answer, but opened his anxious eyes, like a scared idiot. The door-keeper, no doubt, was in the neighbourhood. For a moment the priest waited; then seeing a little girl on the other side of the courtyard, he risked himself, crossed the quagmire on tip-toe, and asked: "Do you know an old workman named Laveuve in the house, my child?"

The little girl, who only had a ragged gown of pink cotton stuff about her meagre figure, stood there shivering, her hands covered with chilblains. She raised her delicate face, which looked pretty though nipped by the cold: "Laveuve," said she, "no, don't know, don't know." And with the unconscious gesture of a beggar child she put out one of her poor, numbed and disfigured hands. Then, when the priest had given her a little bit of silver, she began to prance through the mud like a joyful goat, singing the while in a shrill voice: "Don't know, don't know."

Pierre decided to follow her. She vanished into one of the gaping vestibules, and, in her rear, he climbed a dark and fetid staircase, whose steps were half-broken and so slippery, on account of the vegetable parings strewn over them, that he had to avail himself of the greasy rope by which the inmates hoisted themselves upwards. But every door was closed; he vainly knocked at several of them, and only elicited, at the last, a stifled growl, as though some despairing animal were confined within. Returning to the yard, he hesitated, then made his way to another staircase, where he was deafened by piercing cries, as of a child who is being butchered. He climbed on hearing this noise and at last found himself in front of an open room where an infant, who had been left alone, tied in his little chair, in order that he might not fall, was howling and howling without drawing breath. Then Pierre went down again, upset, frozen by the sight of so much destitution and abandonment.

But a woman was coming in, carrying three potatoes in her apron, and on being questioned by him she gazed distrustfully at his cassock. "Laveuve, Laveuve? I can't say," she replied. "If the door-keeper were there, she might be able to tell you. There are five staircases, you see, and we don't all know each other. Besides, there are so many changes. Still try over there; at the far end."

The staircase at the back of the yard was yet more abominable than the others, its steps warped, its walls slimy, as if soaked with the sweat of anguish. At each successive floor the drain-sinks exhaled a pestilential stench, whilst from every lodging came moans, or a noise of quarrelling, or some frightful sign of misery. A door swung open, and a man appeared dragging a woman by the hair whilst three youngsters sobbed aloud. On the next floor, Pierre caught a glimpse of a room where a young girl in her teens, racked by coughing, was hastily carrying an infant to and fro to quiet it, in despair that all the milk of her breast should be exhausted. Then, in an adjoining lodging, came the poignant spectacle of three beings, half clad in shreds, apparently sexless and ageless, who, amidst the dire bareness of their room, were gluttonously eating from the same earthen pan some pottage which even dogs would have refused. They barely raised their heads to growl, and did not answer Pierre's questions.

He was about to go down again, when right atop of the stairs, at the entry of a passage, it occurred to him to make a last try by knocking at the door. It was opened by a woman whose uncombed hair was already getting grey, though she could not be more than forty; while her pale lips, and dim eyes set in a yellow countenance, expressed utter lassitude, the shrinking, the constant dread of one whom wretchedness has pitilessly assailed. The sight of Pierre's cassock disturbed her, and she stammered anxiously: "Come in, come in, Monsieur l'Abbe."

However, a man whom Pierre had not at first seen—a workman also of some forty years, tall, thin and bald, with scanty moustache and beard of a washed-out reddish hue—made an angry gesture—a threat as it were—to turn the priest out of doors. But he calmed himself, sat down near a rickety table and pretended to turn his back. And as there was also a child present—a fair-haired girl, eleven or twelve years old, with a long and gentle face and that intelligent and somewhat aged expression which great misery imparts to children—he called her to him, and held her between his knees, doubtless to keep her away from the man in the cassock.

Pierre—whose heart was oppressed by his reception, and who realised the utter destitution of this family by the sight of the bare, fireless room, and the distressed mournfulness of its three inmates—decided all the same to repeat his question: "Madame, do you know an old workman named Laveuve in the house?"

The woman—who now trembled at having admitted him, since it seemed to displease her man—timidly tried to arrange matters. "Laveuve, Laveuve? no, I don't. But Salvat, you hear? Do you know a Laveuve here?"

Salvat merely shrugged his shoulders; but the little girl could not keep her tongue still: "I say, mamma Theodore, it's p'raps the Philosopher."

"A former house-painter," continued Pierre, "an old man who is ill and past work."

Madame Theodore was at once enlightened. "In that case it's him, it's him. We call him the Philosopher, a nickname folks have given him in the neighbourhood. But there's nothing to prevent his real name from being Laveuve."

With one of his fists raised towards the ceiling, Salvat seemed to be protesting against the abomination of a world and a Providence that allowed old toilers to die of hunger just like broken-down beasts. However, he did not speak, but relapsed into the savage, heavy silence, the bitter meditation in which he had been plunged when the priest arrived. He was a journeyman engineer, and gazed obstinately at the table where lay his little leather tool-bag, bulging with something it contained—something, perhaps, which he had to take back to a work-shop. He might have been thinking of a long, enforced spell of idleness, of a vain search for any kind of work during the two previous months of that terrible winter. Or perhaps it was the coming bloody reprisals of the starvelings that occupied the fiery reverie which set his large, strange, vague blue eyes aglow. All at once he noticed that his daughter had taken up the tool-bag and was trying to open it to see what it might contain. At this he quivered and at last spoke, his voice kindly, yet bitter with sudden emotion, which made him turn pale. "Celine, you must leave that alone. I forbade you to touch my tools," said he; then taking the bag, he deposited it with great precaution against the wall behind him.

"And so, madame," asked Pierre, "this man Laveuve lives on this floor?"

Madame Theodore directed a timid, questioning glance at Salvat. She was not in favour of hustling priests when they took the trouble to call, for at times there was a little money to be got from them. And when she realised that Salvat, who had once more relapsed into his black reverie, left her free to act as she pleased, she at once tendered her services. "If Monsieur l'Abbe is agreeable, I will conduct him. It's just at the end of the passage. But one must know the way, for there are still some steps to climb."

Celine, finding a pastime in this visit, escaped from her father's knees and likewise accompanied the priest. And Salvat remained alone in that den of poverty and suffering, injustice and anger, without a fire, without bread, haunted by his burning dream, his eyes again fixed upon his bag, as if there, among his tools, he possessed the wherewithal to heal the ailing world.

It indeed proved necessary to climb a few more steps; and then, following Madame Theodore and Celine, Pierre found himself in a kind of narrow garret under the roof, a loft a few yards square, where one could not stand erect. There was no window, only a skylight, and as the snow still covered it one had to leave the door wide open in order that one might see. And the thaw was entering the place, the melting snow was falling drop by drop, and coming over the tiled floor. After long weeks of intense cold, dark dampness rained quivering over all. And there, lacking even a chair, even a plank, Laveuve lay in a corner on a little pile of filthy rags spread upon the bare tiles; he looked like some animal dying on a dung-heap.

"There!" said Celine in her sing-song voice, "there he is, that's the Philosopher!"

Madame Theodore had bent down to ascertain if he still lived. "Yes, he breathes; he's sleeping I think. Oh! if he only had something to eat every day, he would be well enough. But what would you have? He has nobody left him, and when one gets to seventy the best is to throw oneself into the river. In the house-painting line it often happens that a man has to give up working on ladders and scaffoldings at fifty. He at first found some work to do on the ground level. Then he was lucky enough to get a job as night watchman. But that's over, he's been turned away from everywhere, and, for two months now, he's been lying in this nook waiting to die. The landlord hasn't dared to fling him into the street as yet, though not for want of any inclination that way. We others sometimes bring him a little wine and a crust, of course; but when one has nothing oneself, how can one give to others?"

Pierre, terrified, gazed at that frightful remnant of humanity, that remnant into which fifty years of toil, misery and social injustice had turned a man. And he ended by distinguishing Laveuve's white, worn, sunken, deformed head. Here, on a human face, appeared all the ruin following upon hopeless labour. Laveuve's unkempt beard straggled over his features, suggesting an old horse that is no longer cropped; his toothless jaws were quite askew, his eyes were vitreous, and his nose seemed to plunge into his mouth. But above all else one noticed his resemblance to some beast of burden, deformed by hard toil, lamed, worn to death, and now only good for the knackers.

"Ah! the poor fellow," muttered the shuddering priest. "And he is left to die of hunger, all alone, without any succour? And not a hospital, not an asylum has given him shelter?"

"Well," resumed Madame Theodore in her sad yet resigned voice, "the hospitals are built for the sick, and he isn't sick, he's simply finishing off, with his strength at an end. Besides he isn't always easy to deal with. People came again only lately to put him in an asylum, but he won't be shut up. And he speaks coarsely to those who question him, not to mention that he has the reputation of liking drink and talking badly about the gentle-folks. But, thank Heaven, he will now soon be delivered."

Pierre had leant forward on seeing Laveuve's eyes open, and he spoke to him tenderly, telling him that he had come from a friend with a little money to enable him to buy what he might most pressingly require. At first, on seeing Pierre's cassock, the old man had growled some coarse words; but, despite his extreme feebleness, he still retained the pert chaffing spirit of the Parisian artisan: "Well, then, I'll willingly drink a drop," he said distinctly, "and have a bit of bread with it, if there's the needful; for I've lost taste of both for a couple of days past."

Celine offered her services, and Madame Theodore sent her to fetch a loaf and a quart of wine with Abbe Rose's money. And in the interval she told Pierre how Laveuve was at one moment to have entered the Asylum of the Invalids of Labour, a charitable enterprise whose lady patronesses were presided over by Baroness Duvillard. However, the usual regulation inquiries had doubtless led to such an unfavourable report that matters had gone no further.

"Baroness Duvillard! but I know her, and will go to see her to-day!" exclaimed Pierre, whose heart was bleeding. "It is impossible for a man to be left in such circumstances any longer."

Then, as Celine came back with the loaf and the wine, the three of them tried to make Laveuve more comfortable, raised him on his heap of rags, gave him to eat and to drink, and then left the remainder of the wine and the loaf—a large four-pound loaf—near him, recommending him to wait awhile before he finished the bread, as otherwise he might stifle.

"Monsieur l'Abbe ought to give me his address in case I should have any news to send him," said Madame Theodore when she again found herself at her door.

Pierre had no card with him, and so all three went into the room. But Salvat was no longer alone there. He stood talking in a low voice very quickly, and almost mouth to mouth, with a young fellow of twenty. The latter, who was slim and dark, with a sprouting beard and hair cut in brush fashion, had bright eyes, a straight nose and thin lips set in a pale and slightly freckled face, betokening great intelligence. With stern and stubborn brow, he stood shivering in his well-worn jacket.

"Monsieur l'Abbe wants to leave me his address for the Philosopher's affair," gently explained Madame Theodore, annoyed to find another there with Salvat.

The two men had glanced at the priest and then looked at one another, each with terrible mien. And they suddenly ceased speaking in the bitter cold which fell from the ceiling. Then, again with infinite precaution, Salvat went to take his tool-bag from alongside the wall.

"So you are going down, you are again going to look for work?" asked Madame Theodore.

He did not answer, but merely made an angry gesture, as if to say that he would no longer have anything to do with work since work for so long a time had not cared to have anything to do with him.

"All the same," resumed the woman, "try to bring something back with you, for you know there's nothing. At what time will you be back?"

With another gesture he seemed to answer that he would come back when he could, perhaps never. And tears rising, despite all his efforts, to his vague, blue, glowing eyes he caught hold of his daughter Celine, kissed her violently, distractedly, and then went off, with his bag under his arm, followed by his young companion.

"Celine," resumed Madame Theodore, "give Monsieur l'Abbe your pencil, and, see, monsieur, seat yourself here, it will be better for writing."

Then, when Pierre had installed himself at the table, on the chair previously occupied by Salvat, she went on talking, seeking to excuse her man for his scanty politeness: "He hasn't a bad heart, but he's had so many worries in life that he has become a bit cracked. It's like that young man whom you just saw here, Monsieur Victor Mathis. There's another for you, who isn't happy, a young man who was well brought up, who has a lot of learning, and whose mother, a widow, has only just got the wherewithal to buy bread. So one can understand it, can't one? It all upsets their heads, and they talk of blowing up everybody. For my part those are not my notions, but I forgive them, oh! willingly enough."

Perturbed, yet interested by all the mystery and vague horror which he could divine around him, Pierre made no haste to write his address, but lingered listening, as if inviting confidence.

"If you only knew, Monsieur l'Abbe, that poor Salvat was a forsaken child, without father or mother, and had to scour the roads and try every trade at first to get a living. Then afterwards he became a mechanician, and a very good workman, I assure you, very skilful and very painstaking. But he already had those ideas of his, and quarrelled with people, and tried to bring his mates over to his views; and so he was unable to stay anywhere. At last, when he was thirty, he was stupid enough to go to America with an inventor, who traded on him to such a point that after six years of it he came back ill and penniless. I must tell you that he had married my younger sister Leonie, and that she died before he went to America, leaving him little Celine, who was then only a year old. I was then living with my husband, Theodore Labitte, a mason; and it's not to brag that I say it, but however much I wore out my eyes with needlework he used to beat me till he left me half-dead on the floor. But he ended by deserting me and going off with a young woman of twenty, which, after all, caused me more pleasure than grief. And naturally when Salvat came back he sought me out and found me alone with his little Celine, whom he had left in my charge when he went away, and who called me mamma. And we've all three been living together since then—"

She became somewhat embarrassed, and then, as if to show that she did not altogether lack some respectable family connections, she went on to say: "For my part I've had no luck; but I've another sister, Hortense, who's married to a clerk, Monsieur Chretiennot, and lives in a pretty lodging on the Boulevard Rochechouart. There were three of us born of my father's second marriage,—Hortense, who's the youngest, Leonie, who's dead, and myself, Pauline, the eldest. And of my father's first marriage I've still a brother Eugene Toussaint, who is ten years older than me and is an engineer like Salvat, and has been working ever since the war in the same establishment, the Grandidier factory, only a hundred steps away in the Rue Marcadet. The misfortune is that he had a stroke lately. As for me, my eyes are done for; I ruined them by working ten hours a day at fine needlework. And now I can no longer even try to mend anything without my eyes filling with water till I can't see at all. I've tried to find charwoman's work, but I can't get any; bad luck always follows us. And so we are in need of everything; we've nothing but black misery, two or three days sometimes going by without a bite, so that it's like the chance life of a dog that feeds on what it can find. And with these last two months of bitter cold to freeze us, it's sometimes made us think that one morning we should never wake up again. But what would you have? I've never been happy, I was beaten to begin with, and now I'm done for, left in a corner, living on, I really don't know why."

Her voice had begun to tremble, her red eyes moistened, and Pierre could realise that she thus wept through life, a good enough woman but one who had no will, and was already blotted out, so to say, from existence.

"Oh! I don't complain of Salvat," she went on. "He's a good fellow; he only dreams of everybody's happiness, and he doesn't drink, and he works when he can. Only it's certain that he'd work more if he didn't busy himself with politics. One can't discuss things with comrades, and go to public meetings and be at the workshop at the same time. In that he's at fault, that's evident. But all the same he has good reason to complain, for one can't imagine such misfortunes as have pursued him. Everything has fallen on him, everything has beaten him down. Why, a saint even would have gone mad, so that one can understand that a poor beggar who has never had any luck should get quite wild. For the last two months he has only met one good heart, a learned gentleman who lives up yonder on the height, Monsieur Guillaume Froment, who has given him a little work, just something to enable us to have some soup now and then."

Much surprised by this mention of his brother, Pierre wished to ask certain questions; but a singular feeling of uneasiness, in which fear and discretion mingled, checked his tongue. He looked at Celine, who stood before him, listening in silence with her grave, delicate air; and Madame Theodore, seeing him smile at the child, indulged in a final remark: "It's just the idea of that child," said she, "that throws Salvat out of his wits. He adores her, and he'd kill everybody if he could, when he sees her go supperless to bed. She's such a good girl, she was learning so nicely at the Communal School! But now she hasn't even a shift to go there in."

Pierre, who had at last written his address, slipped a five-franc piece into the little girl's hand, and, desirous as he was of curtailing any thanks, he hastily said: "You will know now where to find me if you need me for Laveuve. But I'm going to busy myself about him this very afternoon, and I really hope that he will be fetched away this evening."

Madame Theodore did not listen, but poured forth all possible blessings; whilst Celine, thunderstruck at seeing five francs in her hand, murmured: "Oh! that poor papa, who has gone to hunt for money! Shall I run after him to tell him that we've got enough for to-day?"

Then the priest, who was already in the passage, heard the woman answer: "Oh! he's far away if he's still walking. He'll p'raps come back right enough."

However, as Pierre, with buzzing head and grief-stricken heart, hastily escaped out of that frightful house of suffering, he perceived to his astonishment Salvat and Victor Mathis standing erect in a corner of the filthy courtyard, where the stench was so pestilential. They had come downstairs, there to continue their interrupted colloquy. And again, they were talking in very low tones, and very quickly, mouth to mouth, absorbed in the violent thoughts which made their eyes flare. But they heard the priest's footsteps, recognised him, and suddenly becoming cold and calm, exchanged an energetic hand-shake without uttering another word. Victor went up towards Montmartre, whilst Salvat hesitated like a man who is consulting destiny. Then, as if trusting himself to stern chance, drawing up his thin figure, the figure of a weary, hungry toiler, he turned into the Rue Marcadet, and walked towards Paris, his tool-bag still under his arm.

For an instant Pierre felt a desire to run and call to him that his little girl wished him to go back again. But the same feeling of uneasiness as before came over the priest—a commingling of discretion and fear, a covert conviction that nothing could stay destiny. And he himself was no longer calm, no longer experienced the icy, despairing distress of the early morning. On finding himself again in the street, amidst the quivering fog, he felt the fever, the glow of charity which the sight of such frightful wretchedness had ignited, once more within him. No, no! such suffering was too much; he wished to struggle still, to save Laveuve and restore a little joy to all those poor folk. The new experiment presented itself with that city of Paris which he had seen shrouded as with ashes, so mysterious and so perturbing beneath the threat of inevitable justice. And he dreamed of a huge sun bringing health and fruitfulness, which would make of the huge city the fertile field where would sprout the better world of to-morrow.

II. WEALTH AND WORLDLINESS

THAT same morning, as was the case nearly every day, some intimates were expected to *dejeuner* at the Duvillards', a few friends who more or less invited themselves. And on that chilly day, all thaw and fog, the regal mansion in the Rue Godot-de-Mauroy near the Boulevard de la Madeleine bloomed with the rarest flowers, for flowers were the greatest passion of the Baroness, who transformed the lofty, sumptuous rooms, littered with marvels, into warm and odoriferous conservatories, whither the gloomy, livid light of Paris penetrated caressingly with infinite softness.

The great reception rooms were on the ground-floor looking on to the spacious courtyard, and preceded by a little winter garden, which served as a vestibule where two footmen in liveries of dark green and gold were invariably on duty. A famous gallery of paintings, valued at millions of francs, occupied the whole of the northern side of the house. And the grand staircase, of a sumptuousness which also was famous, conducted to the apartments usually occupied by the family, a large red drawing-room, a small blue and silver drawing-room, a study whose walls were hung with old stamped leather, and a dining-room in pale green with English furniture, not to mention the various bedchambers and dressing-rooms. Built in the time of Louis XIV. the mansion retained an aspect of noble grandeur, subordinated to the epicurean tastes of the triumphant *bourgeoisie*, which for a century now had reigned by virtue of the omnipotence of money.

Noon had not yet struck, and Baron Duvillard, contrary to custom, found himself the first in the little blue and silver *salon.* He was a man of sixty, tall and sturdy, with a large nose, full cheeks, broad, fleshy lips, and wolfish teeth, which had remained very fine. He had, however, become bald at an early age, and dyed the little hair that was left him. Moreover, since his beard had turned white, he had kept his face clean-shaven. His grey eyes bespoke his audacity, and in his laugh there was a ring of conquest, while the whole of his face expressed the fact that this conquest was his own, that he wielded the sovereignty of an unscrupulous master, who used and abused the power stolen and retained by his caste.

He took a few steps, and then halted in front of a basket of wonderful orchids near the window. On the mantel-piece and table tufts of violets sent forth their perfume, and in the warm, deep silence which seemed to fall from the hangings, the Baron sat down and stretched himself in one of the large armchairs, upholstered in blue satin striped with silver. He had taken a newspaper from his pocket, and began to re-peruse an article it contained, whilst all around him the entire mansion proclaimed his immense fortune, his sovereign power, the whole history of the century which had made him the master. His grandfather, Jerome Duvillard, son of a petty advocate of Poitou, had come to Paris as a notary's clerk in 1788, when he was eighteen; and very keen, intelligent and hungry as he was, he had gained the family's first three millions—at first in trafficking with the *emigres'* estates when they were confiscated and sold as national property, and later, in contracting for supplies to the imperial army. His father, Gregoire Duvillard, born in 1805, and the real great man of the family—he who had first reigned in the Rue Godot-de-Mauroy, after King Louis Philippe had granted him the title of Baron—remained one of the recognized heroes of modern finance by reason of the scandalous profits which he had made in every famous thieving speculation of the July Monarchy and the Second Empire, such as mines, railroads, and the Suez Canal. And he, the present Baron, Henri by name, and born in 1836, had only seriously gone into business on Baron Gregoire's death soon after the Franco-German War. However, he had done so with such a rageful appetite, that in a quarter of a century he had again doubled the family fortune. He rotted and devoured, corrupted, swallowed everything that he touched; and he was also the tempter personified—the man who bought all consciences that were for sale—having fully understood the new times and its tendencies in presence of the democracy, which in its turn had become hungry and impatient. Inferior though he was both to his father and his grandfather, being a man of enjoyment, caring less for the work of conquest than the division of the spoil, he nevertheless remained a terrible fellow, a sleek triumpher, whose operations were all certainties, who amassed millions at each stroke, and treated with governments on a footing of equality, able as he was to place, if not France, at least a ministry in his pocket. In one century and three generations, royalty had become embodied in him: a royalty already threatened, already shaken by the tempest close ahead. And at times his figure grew and expanded till it became, as it were, an incarnation of the whole *bourgeoisie*—that *bourgeoisie* which at the division of the spoils in 1789 appropriated everything, and has since fattened on everything at the expense of the masses, and refuses to restore anything whatever.

The article which the Baron was re-perusing in a halfpenny newspaper interested him. "La Voix du Peuple" was a noisy sheet which, under the pretence of defending outraged justice and morality, set a fresh scandal circulating every morning in the hope of thereby increasing its sales. And that morning, in big type on its front page, this sub-title was displayed: "The Affair of the African Railways. Five Millions spent in Bribes: Two Ministers Bought, Thirty Deputies and Senators Compromised." Then in an article of odious violence the paper's editor, the famous Sagnier, announced that he possessed and intended to publish the list of the thirty-two members of Parliament, whose support Baron Duvillard had purchased at the time when the Chambers had voted the bill for the African Railway Lines. Quite a romantic story was mingled with all this, the adventures of a certain Hunter, whom the Baron had employed as his go-between and who had now fled. The Baron, however, re-perused each sentence and weighed each word of the article very calmly; and although he was alone he shrugged his shoulders and spoke aloud with the tranquil assurance of a man whose responsibility is covered and who is, moreover, too powerful to be molested.

"The idiot," he said, "he knows even less than he pretends."

Just then, however, a first guest arrived, a man of barely four and thirty, elegantly dressed, dark and good looking, with a delicately shaped nose, and curly hair and beard. As a rule, too, he had laughing eyes, and something giddy, flighty, bird-like in his demeanour; but that morning he seemed nervous, anxious even, and smiled in a scared way.

"Ah! it's you, Duthil," said the Baron, rising. "Have you read this?" And he showed the new comer the "Voix du Peuple," which he was folding up to replace it in his pocket.

"Why yes, I've read it. It's amazing. How can Sagnier have got hold of the list of names? Has there been some traitor?"

The Baron looked at his companion quietly, amused by his secret anguish. Duthil, the son of a notary of Angouleme, almost poor and very honest, had been sent to Paris as deputy for that town whilst yet very young, thanks to the high reputation of his father; and he there led a life of pleasure and idleness, even as he had formerly done when a student. However, his pleasant bachelor's quarters in the Rue de Suresnes, and his success as a handsome man in the whirl of women among whom he lived, cost him no little money; and gaily enough, devoid as he was of any moral sense, he had already glided into all sorts of compromising and lowering actions, like a light-headed, superior man, a charming, thoughtless fellow, who attached no importance whatever to such trifles.

"Bah!" said the Baron at last. "Has Sagnier even got a list? I doubt it, for there was none; Hunter wasn't so foolish as to draw one up. And then, too, it was merely an ordinary affair; nothing more was done than is always done in such matters of business."

Duthil, who for the first time in his life had felt anxious, listened like one that needs to be reassured. "Quite so, eh?" he exclaimed. "That's what I thought. There isn't a cat to be whipped in the whole affair."

He tried to laugh as usual, and no longer exactly knew how it was that he had received some ten thousand francs in connection with the matter, whether it were in the shape of a vague loan, or else under some pretext of publicity, puffery, or advertising, for Hunter had acted with extreme adroitness so as to give no offence to the susceptibilities of even the least virginal consciences.

"No, there's not a cat to be whipped," repeated Duvillard, who decidedly seemed amused by the face which Duthil was pulling. "And besides, my dear fellow, it's well known that cats always fall on their feet. But have you seen Silviane?"

"I just left her. I found her in a great rage with you. She learnt this morning that her affair of the Comedie is off."

A rush of anger suddenly reddened the Baron's face. He, who could scoff so calmly at the threat of the African Railways scandal, lost his balance and felt his blood boiling directly there was any question of Silviane, the last, imperious passion of his sixtieth year. "What! off?" said he. "But at the Ministry of Fine Arts they gave me almost a positive promise only the day before yesterday."

He referred to a stubborn caprice of Silviane d'Aulnay, who, although she had hitherto only reaped a success of beauty on the stage, obstinately sought to enter the Comedie Francaise and make her *debut* there in the part of "Pauline" in Corneille's "Polyeucte," which part she had been studying desperately for several months past. Her idea seemed an insane one, and all Paris laughed at it; but the young woman, with superb assurance, kept herself well to the front, and imperiously demanded the *role*, feeling sure that she would conquer.

"It was the minister who wouldn't have it," explained Duthil.

The Baron was choking. "The minister, the minister! Ah! well, I will soon have that minister sent to the rightabout."

However, he had to cease speaking, for at that moment Baroness Duvillard came into the little drawing-room. At forty-six years of age she was still very beautiful. Very fair and tall, having hitherto put on but little superfluous fat, and retaining perfect arms and shoulders, with speckless silky skin, it was only her face that was spoiling, colouring slightly with reddish blotches. And these blemishes were her torment, her hourly thought and worry. Her Jewish origin was revealed by her somewhat long and strangely charming face, with blue and softly voluptuous eyes. As indolent as an Oriental slave, disliking to have to move, walk, or even speak, she seemed intended for a harem life, especially as she was for ever tending her person. That day she was all in white, gowned in a white silk toilette of delicious and lustrous simplicity.

Duthil complimented her, and kissed her hand with an enraptured air. "Ah! madame, you set a little springtide in my heart. Paris is so black and muddy this morning."

However, a second guest entered the room, a tall and handsome man of five or six and thirty; and the Baron, still disturbed by his passion, profited by this opportunity to make his escape. He carried Duthil away into his study, saying, "Come here an instant, my dear fellow. I have a few more words to say to you about the affair in question. Monsieur de Quinsac will keep my wife company for a moment."

The Baroness, as soon as she was alone with the new comer, who, like Duthil, had most respectfully kissed her hand, gave him a long, silent look, while her soft eyes filled with tears. Deep silence, tinged with some slight embarrassment, had fallen, but she ended by saying in a very low voice: "How happy I am, Gerard, to find myself alone with you for a moment. For a month past I have not had that happiness."

The circumstances in which Henri Duvillard had married the younger daughter of Justus Steinberger, the great Jew banker, formed quite a story which was often recalled. The Steinbergers—after the fashion of the Rothschilds—were originally four brothers—Justus, residing in Paris, and the three others at Berlin, Vienna, and London, a circumstance which gave their secret association most formidable power in the financial markets of Europe. Justus, however, was the least wealthy of the four, and in Baron Gregoire Duvillard he had a redoubtable adversary against whom he was compelled to struggle each time that any large prey was in question. And it was after a terrible encounter between the pair, after the eager sharing of the spoils, that the crafty idea had come to Justus of giving his younger daughter Eve in marriage, by way of *douceur*, to the Baron's son, Henri. So far the latter had only been known as an amiable fellow, fond of horses and club life; and no doubt Justus's idea was that, at the death of the redoubtable Baron, who was already condemned by his physicians, he would be able to lay his hands on the rival banking-house, particularly if he only had in front of him a son-in-law whom it was easy to conquer. As it happened, Henri had been mastered by a violent passion for Eve's blond beauty, which was then dazzling. He wished to marry her, and his father, who knew him, consented, in reality greatly amused to think that Justus was making an execrably bad stroke of business. The enterprise became indeed disastrous for Justus when Henri succeeded his father and the man of prey appeared from beneath the man of pleasure and carved himself his own huge share in exploiting the unbridled appetites of the middle-class democracy, which had at last secured possession of power. Not only did Eve fail to devour Henri, who in his turn had become Baron Duvillard, the all-powerful banker, more and more master of the market; but it was the Baron who devoured Eve, and this in less than four years' time. After she had borne him a daughter and a son in turn, he suddenly drew away from her, neglected her, as if she were a mere toy that he no longer cared for. She was at first both surprised and distressed by the change, especially on learning that he was resuming his bachelor's habits, and had set his fickle if ardent affections elsewhere. Then, however, without any kind of recrimination, any display of anger, or even any particular effort to regain her ascendency over him, she, on her side, imitated his example. She could not live without love, and assuredly she had only been born to be beautiful, to fascinate and reap adoration. To the lover whom she chose when she was five and twenty she remained faithful for more than fifteen years, as faithful as she might have been to a husband; and when he died her grief was intense, it was like real widowhood. Six months later, however, having met Count Gerard de Quinsac she had again been unable to resist her imperative need of adoration, and an intrigue had followed.

"Have you been ill, my dear Gerard?" she inquired, noticing the young man's embarrassment. "Are you hiding some worry from me?"

She was ten years older than he was; and she clung desperately to this last passion of hers, revolting at the thought of growing old, and resolved upon every effort to keep the young man beside her.

"No, I am hiding nothing, I assure you," replied the Count. "But my mother has had much need of me recently."

She continued looking at him, however, with anxious passion, finding him so tall and aristocratic of mien, with his regular features and dark hair and moustaches which were always most carefully tended. He belonged to one of the oldest families of France, and resided on a ground-floor in the Rue St. Dominique with his widowed mother, who had been ruined by her adventurously inclined husband, and had at most an income of some fifteen thousand francs[1] to live upon. Gerard for his part had never done anything; contenting himself with his one year of obligatory military service, he had renounced the profession of arms in the same way as he had renounced that of diplomacy, the only one that offered him an opening of any dignity. He spent his days in that busy idleness common to all young men who lead "Paris life." And his mother, haughtily severe though she was, seemed to excuse this, as if in her opinion a man of his birth was bound by way of protest to keep apart from official life under a Republic. However, she no doubt had more intimate, more disturbing reasons for indulgence. She had nearly lost him when he was only seven, through an attack of brain fever. At eighteen he had complained of his heart, and the doctors had recommended that he should be treated gently in all respects. She knew, therefore, what a lie lurked behind his proud demeanour, within his lofty figure, that haughty *facade* of his race. He was but dust, ever threatened with illness and collapse. In the depths of his seeming virility there was merely girlish *abandon*; and he was simply a weak, good-natured fellow, liable to every stumble. It was on the occasion of a visit which he had paid with his mother to the Asylum of the Invalids of Labour that he had first

[1] About 3000 dollars.

seen Eve, whom he continued to meet; his mother, closing her eyes to this culpable connection in a sphere of society which she treated with contempt, in the same way as she had closed them to so many other acts of folly which she had forgiven because she regarded them as the mere lapses of an ailing child. Moreover, Eve had made a conquest of Madame de Quinsac, who was very pious, by an action which had recently amazed society. It had been suddenly learnt that she had allowed Monseigneur Martha to convert her to the Roman Catholic faith. This thing, which she had refused to do when solicited by her lawful husband, she had now done in the hope of ensuring herself a lover's eternal affection. And all Paris was still stirred by the magnificence exhibited at the Madeleine, on the occasion of the baptism of this Jewess of five and forty, whose beauty and whose tears had upset every heart.

Gerard, on his side, was still flattered by the deep and touching tenderness shown to him; but weariness was coming, and he had already sought to break off the connection by avoiding any further assignations. He well understood Eve's glances and her tears, and though he was moved at sight of them he tried to excuse himself. "I assure you," said he, "my mother has kept me so busy that I could not get away." But she, without a word, still turned her tearful glance on him, and weak, like herself, in despair that he should have been left alone with her in this fashion, he yielded, unable to continue refusing. "Well, then," said he, "this afternoon at four o'clock if you are free."

He had lowered his voice in speaking, but a slight rustle made him turn his head and start like one in fault. It was the Baroness's daughter Camille entering the room. She had heard nothing; but by the smile which the others had exchanged, by the very quiver of the air, she understood everything; an assignation for that very day and at the very spot which she suspected. Some slight embarrassment followed, an exchange of anxious and evil glances.

Camille, at three and twenty, was a very dark young woman, short of stature and somewhat deformed, with her left shoulder higher than the right. There seemed to be nothing of her father or mother in her. Her case was one of those unforeseen accidents in family heredity which make people wonder whence they can arise. Her only pride lay in her beautiful black eyes and superb black hair, which, short as she was, would, said she, have sufficed to clothe her. But her nose was long, her face deviated to the left, and her chin was pointed. Her thin, witty, and malicious lips bespoke all the rancour and perverse anger stored in the heart of this uncomely creature, whom the thought of her uncomeliness enraged. However, the one whom she most hated in the whole world was her own mother, that *amorosa* who was so little fitted to be a mother, who had never loved her, never paid attention to her, but had abandoned her to the care of servants from her very infancy. In this wise real hatred had grown up between the two women, mute and frigid on the one side, and active and passionate on the other. The daughter hated her mother because she found her beautiful, because she had not been created in the same image: beautiful with the beauty with which her mother crushed her. Day by day she suffered at being sought by none, at realising that the adoration of one and all still went to her mother. As she was amusing in her maliciousness, people listened to her and laughed; however, the glances of all the men—even and indeed especially the younger ones—soon reverted to her triumphant mother, who seemingly defied old age. In part for this reason Camille, with ferocious determination, had decided that she would dispossess her mother of her last lover

Gerard, and marry him herself, conscious that such a loss would doubtless kill the Baroness. Thanks to her promised dowry of five millions of francs, the young woman did not lack suitors; but, little flattered by their advances, she was accustomed to say, with her malicious laugh: "Oh! of course; why for five millions they would take a wife from a mad-house." However, she, herself, had really begun to love Gerard, who, good-natured as he was, evinced much kindness towards this suffering young woman whom nature had treated so harshly. It worried him to see her forsaken by everyone, and little by little he yielded to the grateful tenderness which she displayed towards him, happy, handsome man that he was, at being regarded as a demi-god and having such a slave. Indeed, in his attempt to quit the mother there was certainly a thought of allowing the daughter to marry him, which would be an agreeable ending to it all, though he did not as yet acknowledge this, ashamed as he felt and embarrassed by his illustrious name and all the complications and tears which he foresaw.

The silence continued. Camille with her piercing glance, as sharp as any knife, had told her mother that she knew the truth; and then with another and pain-fraught glance she had complained to Gerard. He, in order to re-establish equilibrium, could only think of a compliment: "Good morning, Camille. Ah! that havana-brown gown of yours looks nice! It's astonishing how well rather sombre colours suit you."

Camille glanced at her mother's white robe, and then at her own dark gown, which scarcely allowed her neck and wrists to be seen. "Yes," she replied laughing, "I only look passable when I don't dress as a young girl."

Eve, ill at ease, worried by the growth of a rivalry in which she did not as yet wish to believe, changed the conversation. "Isn't your brother there?" she asked.

"Why yes, we came down together."

Hyacinthe, who came in at that moment, shook hands with Gerard in a weary way. He was twenty, and had inherited his mother's pale blond hair, and her long face full of Oriental languor; while from his father he had derived his grey eyes and thick lips, expressive of unscrupulous appetites. A wretched scholar, regarding every profession with the same contempt, he had decided to do nothing. Spoilt by his father, he took some little interest in poetry and music, and lived in an extraordinary circle of artists, low women, madmen and bandits; boasting himself of all sorts of crimes and vices, professing the very worst philosophical and social ideas, invariably going to extremes, becoming in turn a Collectivist, an Individualist, an Anarchist, a Pessimist, a Symbolist, and what not besides; without, however, ceasing to be a Catholic, as this conjunction of Catholicity with something else seemed to him the supreme *bon ton*. In reality he was simply empty and rather a fool. In four generations the vigorous hungry blood of the Duvillards, after producing three magnificent beasts of prey, had, as if exhausted by the contentment of every passion, ended in this sorry emasculated creature, who was incapable alike of great knavery or great debauchery.

Camille, who was too intelligent not to realise her brother's nothingness, was fond of teasing him; and looking at him as he stood there, tightly buttoned in his long frock coat with pleated skirt—a resurrection of the romantic period, which he carried to exaggeration, she resumed: "Mamma has been asking for you, Hyacinthe. Come and show her your gown. You are the one who would look nice dressed as a young girl."

However, he eluded her without replying. He was covertly afraid of her, though they lived together in great intimacy, frankly exchanging confidences respecting their perverse views of life. And he directed a glance of disdain at the wonderful basket of orchids which seemed to him past the fashion, far too common nowadays. For his part he had left the lilies of life behind him, and reached the ranunculus, the flower of blood.

The two last guests who were expected now arrived almost together. The first was the investigating magistrate Amadieu, a little man of five and forty, who was an intimate of the household and had been brought into notoriety by a recent anarchist affair. Between a pair of fair, bushy whiskers he displayed a flat, regular judicial face, to which he tried to impart an expression of keenness by wearing a single eyeglass behind which his glance sparkled. Very worldly, moreover, he belonged to the new judicial school, being a distinguished psychologist and having written a book in reply to the abuses of criminalist physiology. And he was also a man of great, tenacious ambition, fond of notoriety and ever on the lookout for those resounding legal affairs which bring glory. Behind him, at last appeared General de Bozonnet, Gerard's uncle on the maternal side, a tall, lean old man with a nose like an eagle's beak. Chronic rheumatism had recently compelled him to retire from the service. Raised to a colonelcy after the Franco-German War in reward for his gallant conduct at St. Privat, he had, in spite of his extremely monarchical connections, kept his sworn faith to Napoleon III. And he was excused in his own sphere of society for this species of military Bonapartism, on account of the bitterness with which he accused the Republic of having ruined the army. Worthy fellow that he was, extremely fond of his sister, Madame de Quinsac, it seemed as though he acted in accordance with some secret desire of hers in accepting the invitations of Baroness Duvillard by way of rendering Gerard's constant presence in her house more natural and excusable.

However, the Baron and Duthil now returned from the study, laughing loudly in an exaggerated way, doubtless to make the others believe that they were quite easy in mind. And one and all passed into the large dining-room where a big wood fire was burning, its gay flames shining like a ray of springtide amid the fine mahogany furniture of English make laden with silver and crystal. The room, of a soft mossy green, had an unassuming charm in the pale light, and the table which in the centre displayed the richness of its covers and the immaculate whiteness of its linen adorned with Venetian point, seemed to have flowered miraculously with a wealth of large tea roses, most admirable blooms for the season, and of delicious perfume.

The Baroness seated the General on her right, and Amadieu on her left. The Baron on his right placed Duthil, and on his left Gerard. Then the young people installed themselves at either end, Camille between Gerard and the General, and Hyacinthe between Duthil and Amadieu. And forthwith, from the moment of starting on the scrambled eggs and truffles, conversation began, the usual conversation of Parisian *dejeuners*, when every event, great or little, of the morning or the day before is passed in review: the truths and the falsehoods current in every social sphere, the financial scandal, and the political adventure of the hour, the novel that has just appeared, the play that has just been produced, the stories which should only be retailed in whispers, but which are repeated aloud. And beneath all the light wit which circulates, beneath all the laughter, which often has a false ring, each retains his or her particular worry, or distress of mind, at times so acute that it becomes perfect agony.

With his quiet and wonted impudence, the Baron, bravely enough, was the first to speak of the article in the "Voix du Peuple." "I say, have you read Sagnier's article this morning? It's a good one; he has *verve* you know, but what a dangerous lunatic he is!"

This set everybody at ease, for the article would certainly have weighed upon the *dejeuner* had no one mentioned it.

"It's the 'Panama' dodge over again!" cried Duthil. "But no, no, we've had quite enough of it!"

"Why," resumed the Baron, "the affair of the African Railway Lines is as clear as spring water! All those whom Sagnier threatens may sleep in peace. The truth is that it's a scheme to upset Barroux's ministry. Leave to interpellate will certainly be asked for this afternoon. You'll see what a fine uproar there'll be in the Chamber."

"That libellous, scandal-seeking press," said Amadieu gravely, "is a dissolving agent which will bring France to ruin. We ought to have laws against it."

The General made an angry gesture: "Laws, what's the use of them, since nobody has the courage to enforce them."

Silence fell. With a light, discreet step the house-steward presented some grilled mullet. So noiseless was the service amid the cheerful perfumed warmth that not even the faintest clatter of crockery was heard. Without anyone knowing how it had come about, however, the conversation had suddenly changed; and somebody inquired: "So the revival of the piece is postponed?"

"Yes," said Gerard, "I heard this morning that 'Polyeucte' wouldn't get its turn till April at the earliest."

At this Camille, who had hitherto remained silent, watching the young Count and seeking to win him back, turned her glittering eyes upon her father and mother. It was a question of that revival in which Silviane was so stubbornly determined to make her *debut*. However, the Baron and the Baroness evinced perfect serenity, having long been acquainted with all that concerned each other. Moreover Eve was too much occupied with her own passion to think of anything else; and the Baron too busy with the fresh application which he intended to make in tempestuous fashion at the Ministry of Fine Arts, so as to wrest Silviane's engagement from those in office. He contented himself with saying: "How would you have them revive pieces at the Comedie! They have no actresses left there."

"Oh, by the way," the Baroness on her side simply remarked, "yesterday, in that play at the Vaudeville, Delphine Vignot wore such an exquisite gown. She's the only one too who knows how to arrange her hair."

Thereupon Duthil, in somewhat veiled language, began to relate a story about Delphine and a well-known senator. And then came another scandal, the sudden and almost suspicious death of a lady friend of the Duvillards'; whereupon the General, without any transition, broke in to relieve his bitter feelings by denouncing the idiotic manner in which the army was nowadays organised. Meantime the old Bordeaux glittered like ruby blood in the delicate crystal glasses. A truffled fillet of venison had just cast its somewhat sharp scent amidst the dying perfume of the roses, when some asparagus made its appearance, a *primeur* which once had been so rare but which no longer caused any astonishment.

"Nowadays we get it all through the winter," said the Baron with a gesture of disenchantment.

"And so," asked Gerard at the same moment, "the Princess de Harn's *matinee* is for this afternoon?"

Camille quickly intervened. "Yes, this afternoon. Shall you go?"

"No, I don't think so, I shan't be able," replied the young man in embarrassment.

"Ah! that little Princess, she's really deranged you know," exclaimed Duthil. "You are aware that she calls herself a widow? But the truth, it seems, is that her husband, a real Prince, connected with a royal house and very handsome, is travelling about the world in the company of a singer. She with her vicious urchin-like face preferred to come and reign in Paris, in that mansion of the Avenue Hoche, which is certainly the most extraordinary Noah's ark imaginable, with its swarming of cosmopolitan society indulging in every extravagance!"

"Be quiet, you malicious fellow," the Baroness gently interrupted. "We, here, are very fond of Rosemonde, who is a charming woman."

"Oh! certainly," Camille again resumed. "She invited us; and we are going to her place by-and-by, are we not, mamma?"

To avoid replying, the Baroness pretended that she did not hear, whilst Duthil, who seemed to be well-informed concerning the Princess, continued to make merry over her intended *matinee*, at which she meant to produce some Spanish dancing girls, whose performance was so very indecorous that all Paris, forewarned of the circumstance, would certainly swarm to her house. And he added: "You've heard that she has given up painting. Yes, she busies herself with chemistry. Her *salon* is full of Anarchists now—and, by the way, it seemed to me that she had cast her eyes on you, my dear Hyacinthe."

Hyacinthe had hitherto held his tongue, as if he took no interest in anything. "Oh! she bores me to death," he now condescended to reply. "If I'm going to her *matinee* it's simply in the hope of meeting my friend young Lord George Eldrett, who wrote to me from London to give me an appointment at the Princess's. And I admit that hers is the only *salon* where I find somebody to talk to."

"And so," asked Amadieu in an ironical way, "you have now gone over to Anarchism?"

With his air of lofty elegance Hyacinthe imperturbably confessed his creed: "But it seems to me, monsieur, that in these times of universal baseness and ignominy, no man of any distinction can be other than an Anarchist."

A laugh ran round the table. Hyacinthe was very much spoilt, and considered very entertaining. His father in particular was immensely amused by the notion that he of all men should have an Anarchist for a son. However, the General, in his rancorous moments, talked anarchically enough of blowing up a society which was so stupid as to let itself be led by half a dozen disreputable characters. And, indeed, the investigating magistrate, who was gradually making a specialty of Anarchist affairs, proved the only one who opposed the young man, defending threatened civilisation and giving terrifying particulars concerning what he called the army of devastation and massacre. The others, while partaking of some delicious duck's-liver *pate*, which the house-steward handed around, continued smiling. There was so much misery, said they; one must take everything into account: things would surely end by righting themselves. And the Baron himself declared, in a conciliatory manner: "It's certain that one might do something, though nobody knows exactly what. As for all sensible and moderate claims, oh! I agree to them in advance. For instance, the lot of the working classes may be ameliorated, charitable enterprises may be undertaken, such, for instance, as our Asylum for the Invalids of Labour, which we have reason to be proud of. But we must not be asked for impossibilities."

With the dessert came a sudden spell of silence; it was as if, amidst the restless fluttering of the conversation, and the dizziness born of the copious meal, each one's worry or distress was again wringing the heart and setting an expression of perturbation on the countenance. The nervous unconscientiousness of Duthil, threatened with denunciation, was seen to revive; so, too, the anxious anger of the Baron, who was meditating how he might possibly manage to content Silviane. That woman was this sturdy, powerful man's taint, the secret sore which would perhaps end by eating him away and destroying him. But it was the frightful drama in which the Baroness, Camille and Gerard were concerned that flitted by most visibly across the faces of all three of them: that hateful rivalry of mother and daughter, contending for the man they loved. And, meantime, the silver-gilt blades of the dessert-knives were delicately peeling choice fruit. And there were bunches of golden grapes looking beautifully fresh, and a procession of sweetmeats, little cakes, an infinity of dainties, over which the most satiated appetites lingered complacently.

Then, just as the finger-glasses were being served, a footman came and bent over the Baroness, who answered in an undertone, "Well, show him into the *salon*, I will join him there." And aloud to the others she added: "It's Monsieur l'Abbe Froment, who has called and asks most particularly to see me. He won't be in our way; I think that almost all of you know him. Oh! he's a genuine saint, and I have much sympathy for him."

For a few minutes longer they loitered round the table, and then at last quitted the dining-room, which was full of the odours of viands, wines, fruits and roses; quite warm, too, with the heat thrown out by the big logs of firewood, which were falling into embers amidst the somewhat jumbled brightness of all the crystal and silver, and the pale, delicate light which fell upon the disorderly table.

Pierre had remained standing in the centre of the little blue and silver *salon*. Seeing a tray on which the coffee and the liqueurs were in readiness, he regretted that he had insisted upon being received. And his embarrassment increased when the company came in rather noisily, with bright eyes and rosy cheeks. However, his charitable fervour had revived so ardently within him that he overcame this embarrassment, and all that remained to him of it was a slight feeling of discomfort at bringing the whole frightful morning which he had just spent amid such scenes of wretchedness, so much darkness and cold, so much filth and hunger, into this bright, warm, perfumed affluence, where the useless and the superfluous overflowed around those folks who seemed so gay at having made a delightful meal.

However, the Baroness at once came forward with Gerard, for it was through the latter, whose mother he knew, that the priest had been presented to the Duvillards at the time of the famous conversion. And as he apologised for having called at such an inconvenient hour, the Baroness responded: "But you are always welcome, Monsieur l'Abbe. You will allow me just to attend to my guests, won't you? I will be with you in an instant."

She thereupon returned to the table on which the tray had been placed, in order to serve the coffee and the liqueurs, with her daughter's assistance. Gerard, however, remained with Pierre; and, it so chanced, began to speak to him of the Asylum for the Invalids of Labour, where they had met one another at the recent laying of the foundation-stone of a new pavilion which was being erected, thanks to a handsome donation of 100,000 francs made by Baron Duvillard. So far, the enterprise only comprised four pavilions out of the fourteen which it was proposed to erect on the vast site given by the City of Paris on the peninsula of Gennevilliers[1]; and so the subscription fund remained open, and, indeed, no little noise was made over this charitable enterprise, which was regarded as a complete and peremptory reply to the accusations of those evilly disposed persons who charged the satiated *bourgeoisie* with doing nothing for the workers. But the truth was that a magnificent chapel, erected in the centre of the site, had absorbed two-thirds of the funds hitherto collected. Numerous lady patronesses, chosen from all the "worlds" of Paris—the Baroness Duvillard, the Countess de Quinsac, the Princess Rosemonde de Harn, and a score of others—were entrusted with the task of keeping the enterprise alive by dint of collections and fancy bazaars. But success had been chiefly obtained, thanks to the happy idea of ridding the ladies of all the weighty cares of organisation, by choosing as managing director a certain Fonsegue, who, besides being a deputy and editor of the "Globe" newspaper, was a prodigious promoter of all sorts of enterprises. And the "Globe" never paused in its propaganda, but answered the attacks of the revolutionaries by extolling the inexhaustible charity of the governing classes in such wise that, at the last elections, the enterprise had served as a victorious electoral weapon.

However, Camille was walking about with a steaming cup of coffee in her hand: "Will you take some coffee, Monsieur l'Abbe?" she inquired.

"No, thank you, mademoiselle."

"A glass of Chartreuse then?"

"No, thank you."

Then everybody being served, the Baroness came back and said amiably: "Come, Monsieur l'Abbe, what do you desire of me?"

Pierre began to speak almost in an undertone, his throat contracting and his heart beating with emotion. "I have come, madame, to appeal to your great kindness of heart. This morning, in a frightful house, in the Rue des Saules, behind Montmartre, I beheld a sight which utterly upset me. You can have no idea what an abode of misery and suffering it was; its inmates without fire or bread, the men reduced to idleness because there is no work, the mothers having no more milk for their babes, the children barely clad, coughing and shivering. And among all these horrors I saw the worst, the most abominable of all, an old workman, laid on his back by age, dying of hunger, huddled on a heap of rags, in a nook which a dog would not even accept as kennel."

He tried to recount things as discreetly as possible, frightened by the very words he spoke, the horrors he had to relate in that sphere of superlative luxury and enjoyment, before those happy ones who possessed all the gifts of this world; for—to use a slang expression—he fully realised that he sang out of tune, and in most uncourteous fashion. What a strange idea of his to have called at the hour when one has just finished *dejeuner*, when the aroma of hot coffee flatters happy digestion. Nevertheless he went on, and even ended by raising his voice, yielding to the feeling of revolt

---

[1] This so-called peninsula lies to the northwest of Paris, and is formed by the windings of the Seine.—Trans.

which gradually stirred him, going to the end of his terrible narrative, naming Laveuve, insisting on the unjust abandonment in which the old man was left, and asking for succour in the name of human compassion. And the whole company apapproached to listen to him; he could see the Baron and the General, and Duthil and Amadieu, in front of him, sipping their coffee, in silence, without a gesture.

"Well, madame," he concluded, "it seemed to me that one could not leave that old man an hour longer in such a frightful position, and that this very evening you would have the extreme goodness to have him admitted into the Asylum of the Invalids of Labour, which is, I think, the proper and only place for him."

Tears had moistened Eve's beautiful eyes. She was in consternation at so sad a story coming to her to spoil her afternoon when she was looking forward to her assignation with Gerard. Weak and indolent as she was, lacking all initiative, too much occupied moreover with her own person, she had only accepted the presidency of the Committee on the condition that all administrative worries were to fall on Fonsegue. "Ah! Monsieur l'Abbe," she murmured, "you rend my heart. But I can do nothing, nothing at all, I assure you. Moreover, I believe that we have already inquired into the affair of that man Laveuve. With us, you know, there must be the most serious guarantees with regard to every admission. A reporter is chosen who has to give us full information. Wasn't it you, Monsieur Duthil, who was charged with this man Laveuve's affair?"

The deputy was finishing a glass of Chartreuse. "Yes, it was I. That fine fellow played you a comedy, Monsieur l'Abbe. He isn't at all ill, and if you left him any money you may be sure he went down to drink it as soon as you were gone. For he is always drunk; and, besides that, he has the most hateful disposition imaginable, crying out from morning till evening against the *bourgeois*, and saying that if he had any strength left in his arms he would undertake to blow up the whole show. And, moreover, he won't go into the asylum; he says that it's a real prison where one's guarded by Beguins who force one to hear mass, a dirty convent where the gates are shut at nine in the evening! And there are so many of them like that, who rather than be succoured prefer their liberty, with cold and hunger and death. Well then, let the Laveuves die in the street, since they refuse to be with us, and be warm and eat in our asylums!"

The General and Amadieu nodded their heads approvingly. But Duvillard showed himself more generous. "No, no, indeed! A man's a man after all, and should be succoured in spite of himself."

Eve, however, in despair at the idea that she would be robbed of her afternoon, struggled and sought for reasons. "I assure you that my hands are altogether tied. Monsieur l'Abbe does not doubt my heart or my zeal. But how call I possibly assemble the Committee without a few days' delay? And I have particular reasons for coming to no decision, especially in an affair which has already been inquired into and pronounced upon, without the Committee's sanction." Then, all at once she found a solution: "What I advise you to do, Monsieur l'Abbe, is to go at once to see Monsieur Fonsegue, our managing director. He alone can act in an urgent case, for he knows that the ladies have unlimited confidence in him and approve everything he does."

"You will find Fonsegue at the Chamber," added Duthil smiling, "only the sitting will be a warm one, and I doubt whether you will be able to have a comfortable chat with him."

Pierre, whose heart had contracted yet more painfully, insisted on the subject no further; but at once made up his mind to see Fonsegue, and in any event obtain from him a promise that the wretched Laveuve should be admitted to the Asylum that very evening. Then he lingered in the saloon for a few minutes listening to Gerard, who obligingly pointed out to him how he might best convince the deputy, which was by alleging how bad an effect such a story could have, should it be brought to light by the revolutionary newspapers. However, the guests were beginning to take their leave. The General, as he went off, came to ask his nephew if he should see him that afternoon at his mother's, Madame de Quinsac, whose "day" it was: a question which the young man answered with an evasive gesture when he noticed that both Eve and Camille were looking at him. Then came the turn of Amadieu, who hurried off saying that a serious affair required his presence at the Palace of Justice. And Duthil soon followed him in order to repair to the Chamber.

"I'll see you between four and five at Silviane's, eh?" said the Baron as he conducted him to the door. "Come and tell me what occurs at the Chamber in consequence of that odious article of Sagnier's. I must at all events know. For my part I shall go to the Ministry of Fine Arts, to settle that affair of the Comedie; and besides I've some calls to make, some contractors to see, and a big launching and advertisement affair to settle."

"It's understood then, between four and five, at Silviane's," said the deputy, who went off again mastered by his vague uneasiness, his anxiety as to what turn that nasty affair of the African Railway Lines might take.

And all of them had forgotten Laveuve, the miserable wretch who lay at death's door; and all of them were hastening away to their business or their passions, caught in the toils, sinking under the grindstone and whisked away by that rush of all Paris, whose fever bore them along, throwing one against another in an ardent scramble, in which the sole question was who should pass over the others and crush them.

"And so, mamma," said Camille, who continued to scrutinise her mother and Gerard, "you are going to take us to the Princess's *matinee*?"

"By-and-by, yes. Only I shan't be able to stay there with you. I received a telegram from Salmon about my corsage this morning, and I must absolutely go to try it on at four o'clock."

By the slight trembling of her mother's voice, the girl felt certain that she was telling a falsehood. "Oh!" said she, "I thought you were only going to try it on to-morrow? In that case I suppose we are to go and call for you at Salmon's with the carriage on leaving the *matinee*?"

"Oh! no my dear! One never knows when one will be free; and besides, if I have a moment, I shall call at the *modiste's*."

Camille's secret rage brought almost a murderous glare to her dark eyes. The truth was evident. But however passionately she might desire to set some obstacle across her mother's path, she could not, dared not, carry matters any further. In vain had she attempted to implore Gerard with her eyes. He was standing to take his leave, and turned away his eyes. Pierre, who had become acquainted with many things since he had frequented the house, noticed how all three of them quivered, and divined thereby the mute and terrible drama.

At this moment, however, Hyacinthe, stretched in an armchair, and munching an ether capsule, the only liqueur in which he indulged, raised his voice: "For my part, you know, I'm going to the Exposition du Lis. All Paris is swarming there. There's one painting in particular, 'The Rape of a Soul,' which it's absolutely necessary for one to have seen."

"Well, but I don't refuse to drive you there," resumed the Baroness. "Before going to the Princess's we can look in at that exhibition."

"That's it, that's it," hastily exclaimed Camille, who, though she harshly derided the symbolist painters as a rule, now doubtless desired to delay her mother. Then, forcing herself to smile, she asked: "Won't you risk a look-in at the Exposition du Lis with us, Monsieur Gerard?"

"Well, no," replied the Count, "I want to walk. I shall go with Monsieur l'Abbe Froment to the Chamber."

Thereupon he took leave of mother and daughter, kissing the hand of each in turn. It had just occurred to him that to while away his time he also might call for a moment at Silviane's, where, like the others, he had his *entrees*. On reaching the cold and solemn courtyard he said to the priest, "Ah! it does one good to breathe a little cool air. They keep their rooms too hot, and all those flowers, too, give one the headache."

Pierre for his part was going off with his brain in a whirl, his hands feverish, his senses oppressed by all the luxury which he left behind him, like the dream of some glowing, perfumed paradise where only the elect had their abode. At the same time his reviving thirst for charity had become keener than ever, and without listening to the Count, who was speaking very affectionately of his mother, he reflected as to how he might obtain Laveuve's admission to the Asylum from Fonsegue. However, when the door of the mansion had closed behind them and they had taken a few steps along the street, it occurred to Pierre that a moment previously a sudden vision had met his gaze. Had he not seen a workman carrying a tool-bag, standing and waiting on the foot pavement across the road, gazing at that monumental door, closed upon so much fabulous wealth—a workman in whom he fancied he had recognised Salvat, that hungry fellow who had gone off that morning in search of work? At this thought Pierre hastily turned round. Such wretchedness in face of so much affluence and enjoyment made him feel anxious. But the workman, disturbed in his contemplation, and possibly fearing that he had been recognised, was going off with dragging step. And now, getting only a back view of him, Pierre hesitated, and ended by thinking that he must have been mistaken.

III. RANTERS AND RULERS

WHEN Abbe Froment was about to enter the Palais-Bourbon he remembered that he had no card, and he was making up his mind that he would simply ask for Fonsegue, though he was not known to him, when, on reaching the vestibule, he perceived Mege, the Collectivist deputy, with whom he had become acquainted in his days of militant charity in the poverty-stricken Charonne district.

"What, you here? You surely have not come to evangelise us?" said Mege.

"No, I've come to see Monsieur Fonsegue on an urgent matter, about a poor fellow who cannot wait."

"Fonsegue? I don't know if he has arrived. Wait a moment." And stopping a short, dark young fellow with a ferreting, mouse-like air, Mege said to him: "Massot, here's Monsieur l'Abbe Froment, who wants to speak to your governor at once."

"The governor? But he isn't here. I left him at the office of the paper, where he'll be detained for another quarter of an hour. However, if Monsieur l'Abbe likes to wait he will surely see him here."

Thereupon Mege ushered Pierre into the large waiting-hall, the Salle des Pas Perdus, which in other moments looked so vast and cold with its bronze Minerva and Laocoon, and its bare walls on which the pale mournful winter light fell from the glass doors communicating with the garden. Just then, however, it was crowded, and warmed, as it were, by the feverish agitation of the many groups of men that had gathered here and there, and the constant coming and going of those who hastened through the throng. Most of these were deputies, but there were also numerous journalists and inquisitive visitors. And a growing uproar prevailed: colloquies now in undertones, now in loud voices, exclamations and bursts of laughter, amidst a deal of passionate gesticulation, Mege's return into the tumult seemed to fan it. He was tall, apostolically thin, and somewhat neglectful of his person, looking already old and worn for his age, which was but five and forty, though his eyes still glowed with youth behind the glasses which never left his beak-like nose. And he had a warm but grating voice, and had always been known to cough, living on solely because he was bitterly intent on doing so in order to realise the dream of social re-organisation which haunted him. The son of an impoverished medical man of a northern town, he had come to Paris when very young, living there during the Empire on petty newspaper and other unknown work, and first making a reputation as an orator at the public meetings of the time. Then, after the war, having become the chief of the Collectivist party, thanks to his ardent faith and the extraordinary activity of his fighting nature, he had at last managed to enter the Chamber, where, brimful of information, he fought for his ideas with fierce determination and obstinacy, like a *doctrinaire* who has decided in his own mind what the world ought to be, and who regulates in advance, and bit by bit, the whole dogma of Collectivism. However, since he had taken pay as a deputy, the outside Socialists had looked upon him as a mere rhetorician, an aspiring dictator who only tried to cast society in a new mould for the purpose of subordinating it to his personal views and ruling it.

"You know what is going on?" he said to Pierre. "This is another nice affair, is it not? But what would you have? We are in mud to our very ears."

He had formerly conceived genuine sympathy for the priest, whom he had found so gentle with all who suffered, and so desirous of social regeneration. And the priest himself had ended by taking an interest in this authoritarian dreamer, who was resolved to make men happy in spite even of themselves. He knew that he was poor, and led a retired life with his wife and four children, to whom he was devoted.

"You can well understand that I am no ally of Sagnier's," Mege resumed. "But as he chose to speak out this morning and threaten to publish the names of all those who have taken bribes, we can't allow ourselves to pass as accomplices any further. It has long been said that there was some nasty jobbery in that suspicious affair of the African railways. And the worst is that two members of the present Cabinet are in question, for three years ago, when the Chambers dealt with Duvillard's emission, Barroux was at the Home Department, and Monferrand at that of Public Works. Now that they have come back again, Monferrand at the Home Department, and Barroux at that of Finance, with the Presidency of the Council, it isn't possible, is it, for us to do otherwise than compel them to enlighten us, in their own interest even, about their former goings-on? No, no, they can no longer keep silence, and I've announced that I intend to interpellate them this very day."

It was the announcement of Mege's interpellation, following the terrible article of the "Voix du Peuple," which thus set the lobbies in an uproar. And Pierre remained rather scared at this big political affair falling into the midst of his scheme to save a wretched pauper from hunger and death. Thus he listened without fully understanding the explanations which the Socialist deputy was passionately giving him, while all around them the uproar increased, and bursts of laughter rang out, testifying to the astonishment which the others felt at seeing Mege in conversation with a priest.

"How stupid they are!" said Mege disdainfully. "Do they think then that I eat a cassock for *dejeuner* every morning? But I beg your pardon, my dear Monsieur Froment. Come, take a place on that seat and wait for Fonsegue."

Then he himself plunged into all the turmoil, and Pierre realised that his best course was to sit down and wait quietly. His surroundings began to influence and interest him, and he gradually forgot Laveuve for the passion of the Parliamentary crisis amidst which he found himself cast. The frightful Panama adventure was scarcely over; he had followed the progress of that tragedy with the anguish of a man who every night expects to hear the tocsin sound the last hour of olden, agonising society. And now a little Panama was beginning, a fresh cracking of the social edifice, an affair such as had been frequent in all parliaments in connection with big financial questions, but one which acquired mortal gravity from the circumstances in which it came to the front. That story of the African Railway Lines, that little patch of mud, stirred up and exhaling a perturbing odour, and suddenly fomenting all that emotion, fear, and anger in the Chamber, was after all but an opportunity for political strife, a field on which the voracious appetites of the various "groups" would take exercise and sharpen; and, at bottom, the sole question was that of overthrowing the ministry and replacing it by another. Only, behind all that lust of power, that continuous onslaught of ambition, what a distressful prey was stirring—the whole people with all its poverty and its sufferings!

Pierre noticed that Massot, "little Massot," as he was generally called, had just seated himself on the bench beside him. With his lively eye and ready ear listening to everything and noting it, gliding everywhere with his ferret-like air, Massot was not there in the capacity of a gallery man, but had simply scented a stormy debate, and come to see if he could not pick up material for some occasional "copy." And this priest lost in the midst of the throng doubtless interested him.

"Have a little patience, Monsieur l'Abbe," said he, with the amiable gaiety of a young gentleman who makes fun of everything. "The governor will certainly come, for he knows well enough that they are going to heat the oven here. You are not one of his constituents from La Correze, are you?"

"No, no! I belong to Paris; I've come on account of a poor fellow whom I wish to get admitted into the Asylum of the Invalids of Labour."

"Oh! all right. Well, I'm a child of Paris, too."

Then Massot laughed. And indeed he was a child of Paris, son of a chemist of the St. Denis district, and an ex-dunce of the Lycee Charlemagne, where he had not even finished his studies. He had failed entirely, and at eighteen years of age had found himself cast into journalism with barely sufficient knowledge of orthography for that calling. And for twelve years now, as he often said, he had been a rolling stone wandering through all spheres of society, confessing some and guessing at others. He had seen everything, and become disgusted with everything, no longer believing in the existence of great men, or of truth, but living peacefully enough on universal malice and folly. He naturally had no literary ambition, in fact he professed a deliberate contempt for literature. Withal, he was not a fool, but wrote in accordance with no matter what views in no matter what newspaper, having neither conviction nor belief, but quietly claiming the right to say whatever he pleased to the public on condition that he either amused or impassioned it.

"And so," said he, "you know Mege, Monsieur l'Abbe? What a study in character, eh? A big child, a dreamer of dreams in the skin of a terrible sectarian! Oh! I have had a deal of intercourse with him, I know him thoroughly. You are no doubt aware that he lives on with the everlasting conviction that he will attain to power in six months' time, and that between evening and morning he will have established that famous Collectivist community which is to succeed capitalist society, just as day follows night. And, by the way, as regards his interpellation to-day, he is convinced that in overthrowing the Barroux ministry he'll be hastening his own turn. His system is to use up his adversaries. How many times haven't I heard him making his calculations: there's such a one to be used up, then such a one, and then such a one, so that he himself may at last reign. And it's always to come off in six months at the latest. The misfortune is, however, that others are always springing up, and so his turn never comes at all."

Little Massot openly made merry over it. Then, slightly lowering his voice, he asked: "And Sagnier, do you know him? No? Do you see that red-haired man with the bull's neck—the one who looks like a butcher? That one yonder who is talking in a little group of frayed frock-coats."

Pierre at last perceived the man in question. He had broad red ears, a hanging under-lip, a large nose, and big, projecting dull eyes.

"I know that one thoroughly, as well," continued Massot; "I was on the 'Voix du Peuple' under him before I went on the 'Globe.' The one thing that nobody is exactly aware of is whence Sagnier first came. He long dragged out his life in the lower depths of journalism, doing nothing at all brilliant, but wild with ambition and appetite. Perhaps you remember the first hubbub he made, that rather dirty affair of a new Louis XVII. which he tried to launch, and which made him the extraordinary Royalist that he still is. Then it occurred to him to espouse the cause of the masses, and he made a display of vengeful Catholic socialism, attacking the Republic and all the abominations of the times in the name of justice and morality, under the pretext of curing them. He began with a series of sketches of financiers, a mass of dirty, uncontrolled, unproved tittle-tattle, which ought to have led him to the dock, but which met, as you know, with such wonderful success when gathered together in a volume. And he goes on in the same style in the 'Voix du Peuple,' which he himself made a success at the time of the Panama affair by dint of denunciation and scandal, and which to-day is like a sewer-pipe pouring forth all the filth of the times. And whenever the stream slackens, why, he invents things just to satisfy his craving for that hubbub on which both his pride and his pocket subsist."

Little Massot spoke without bitterness; indeed, he had even begun to laugh again. Beneath his thoughtless ferocity he really felt some respect for Sagnier. "Oh! he's a bandit," he continued, "but a clever fellow all the same. You can't imagine how full of vanity he is. Lately it occurred to him to get himself acclaimed by the populace, for he pretends to be a kind of King of the Markets, you know. Perhaps he has ended by taking his fine judge-like airs in earnest, and really believes that he is saving the people and helping the cause of virtue. What astonishes me is his fertility in the arts of denunciation and scandalmongering. Never a morning comes but he discovers some fresh horror, and delivers fresh culprits over to the hatred of the masses. No! the stream of mud never ceases; there is an incessant, unexpected spurt of infamy, an increase of monstrous fancies each time that the disgusted public shows any sign of weariness. And, do you know, there's genius in that, Monsieur l'Abbe; for he is well aware that his circulation goes up as soon as he threatens to speak out and publish a list of traitors and bribe-takers. His sales are certain now for some days to come."

Listening to Massot's gay, bantering voice, Pierre began to understand certain things, the exact meaning of which had hitherto escaped him. He ended by questioning the young journalist, surprised as he was that so many deputies should be in the lobbies when the sitting was in progress. Oh! the sitting indeed. The gravest matters, some bill of national interest, might be under discussion, yet every member fled from it at the sudden threat of an interpellation which might overturn the ministry. And the passion stirring there was the restrained anger, the growing anxiety of the present ministry's clients, who feared that they might have to give place to others; and it was also the sudden hope, the eager hunger of all who were waiting—the clients of the various possible ministries of the morrow.

Massot pointed to Barroux, the head of the Cabinet, who, though he was out of his element in the Department of Finances, had taken it simply because his generally recognised integrity was calculated to reassure public opinion after the Panama crisis. Barroux was chatting in a corner with the Minister of Public Instruction, Senator Taboureau, an old university man with a shrinking, mournful air, who was extremely honest, but totally ignorant of Paris, coming as he did from some far-away provincial faculty. Barroux for his part was of decorative aspect, tall, and with a handsome, clean-shaven face, which would have looked quite noble had not his nose been rather too small. Although he was sixty, he still had a profusion of curly snow-white hair completing the somewhat theatrical majesty of his appearance, which he was wont to turn to account when in the tribune. Coming of an old Parisian family, well-to-do, an advocate by profession, then a Republican journalist under the Empire, he had reached office with Gambetta, showing himself at once honest and romantic, loud of speech, and somewhat stupid, but at the same time very brave and very upright, and still clinging with ardent faith to the principles of the great Revolution. However, his Jacobinism was getting out of fashion, he was becoming an "ancestor," as it were, one of the last props of the middle-class Republic, and the new comers, the young politicians with long teeth, were beginning to smile at him. Moreover, beneath the ostentation of his demeanour, and the pomp of his eloquence, there was a man of hesitating, sentimental nature, a good fellow who shed tears when re-perusing the verses of Lamartine.

However, Monferrand, the minister for the Home Department, passed by and drew Barroux aside to whisper a few words in his ear. He, Monferrand, was fifty, short and fat, with a smiling, fatherly air; nevertheless a look of keen intelligence appeared at times on his round and somewhat common face fringed by a beard which was still dark. In him one divined a man of government, with hands which were fitted for difficult tasks, and which never released a prey. Formerly mayor of the town of Tulle, he came from La Correze, where he owned a large estate. He was certainly a force in motion, one whose constant rise was anxiously watched by keen observers. He spoke in a simple quiet way, but with extraordinary power of conviction. Having apparently no ambition, affecting indeed the greatest disinterestedness, he nevertheless harboured the most ferocious appetites. Sagnier had written that he was a thief and a murderer, having strangled two of his aunts in order to inherit their property. But even if he were a murderer, he was certainly not a vulgar one.

Then, too, came another personage of the drama which was about to be performed—deputy Vignon, whose arrival agitated the various groups. The two ministers looked at him, whilst he, at once surrounded by his friends, smiled at them from a distance. He was not yet thirty-six. Slim, and of average height, very fair, with a fine blond beard of which he took great care, a Parisian by birth, having rapidly made his way in the government service, at one time Prefect at Bordeaux, he now represented youth and the future in the Chamber. He had realised that new men were needed in the direction of affairs in order to accomplish the more urgent, indispensable reforms; and very ambitious and intelligent as he was, knowing many things, he already had a programme, the application of which he was quite capable of attempting, in part at any rate. However, he evinced no haste, but was full of prudence and shrewdness, convinced that his day would dawn, strong in the fact that he was as yet compromised in nothing, but had all space before him. At bottom he was merely a first-class administrator, clear and precise in speech, and his programme only differed from Barroux's by the rejuvenation of its formulas, although the advent of a Vignon ministry in place of a Barroux ministry appeared an event of importance. And it was of Vignon that Sagnier had written that he aimed at the Presidency of the Republic, even should he have to march through blood to reach the Elysee Palace.

"*Mon Dieu*!" Massot was explaining, "it's quite possible that Sagnier isn't lying this time, and that he has really found a list of names in some pocket-book of Hunter's that has fallen into his hands. I myself have long known that Hunter was Duvillard's vote-recruiter in the affair of the African Railways. But to understand matters one must first realise what his mode of proceeding was, the skill and the kind of amiable delicacy which he showed, which were far from the brutal corruption and dirty trafficking that people imagine. One must be such a man as Sagnier to picture a parliament as an open market, where every conscience is for sale and is impudently knocked down to the highest bidder. Oh! things happened in a very different way indeed; and they are explainable, and at times even excusable. Thus the article is levelled in particular against Barroux and Monferrand, who are designated in the clearest possible manner although they are not named. You are no doubt aware that at the time of the vote Barroux was at the Home Department and Monferrand at that of Public Works, and so now they are accused of having betrayed their trusts, the blackest of all social crimes. I don't know into what political combinations Barroux may have entered, but I am ready to swear that he put nothing in his pocket, for he is the most honest of men. As for Monferrand, that's another matter; he's a man to carve himself his share, only I should be much surprised if he had put himself in a bad position. He's incapable of a blunder, particularly of a stupid blunder, like that of taking money and leaving a receipt for it lying about."

Massot paused, and with a jerk of his head called Pierre's attention to Duthil, who, feverish, but nevertheless smiling, stood in a group which had just collected around the two ministers. "There! do you see that young man yonder, that dark handsome fellow whose beard looks so triumphant?"

"I know him," said Pierre.

"Oh! you know Duthil. Well, he's one who most certainly took money. But he's a mere bird. He came to us from Angouleme to lead the pleasantest of lives here, and he has no more conscience, no more scruples, than the pretty finches of his native part, who are ever love-making. Ah! for Duthil, Hunter's money was like manna due to him, and he never even paused to think that he was dirtying his fingers. You may be quite sure he feels astonished that people should attach the slightest importance to the matter."

Then Massot designated another deputy in the same group, a man of fifty or thereabouts, of slovenly aspect and lachrymose mien, lanky, too, like a maypole, and somewhat bent by the weight of his head, which was long and suggestive of a horse's. His scanty, straight, yellowish hair, his drooping moustaches, in fact the whole of his distracted countenance, expressed everlasting distress.

"And Chaigneux, do you know him?" continued Massot, referring to the deputy in question. "No? Well, look at him and ask yourself if it isn't quite as natural that he, too, should have taken money. He came from Arras. He was a solicitor there. When his division elected him he let politics intoxicate him, and sold his practice to make his fortune in Paris, where he installed himself with his wife and his three daughters. And you can picture his bewilderment amidst those four women, terrible women ever busy with finery, receiving and paying visits, and running after marriageable men who flee away. It's ill-luck with a vengeance, the daily defeat of a poor devil of mediocre attainments, who imagined that his position as a deputy would facilitate money-making, and who is drowning himself in it all. And so how can Chaigneux have done otherwise than take money, he who is always hard up for a five-hundred-franc note! I admit that originally he wasn't a dishonest man. But he's become one, that's all."

Massot was now fairly launched, and went on with his portraits, the series which he had, at one moment, dreamt of writing under the title of "Deputies for Sale." There were the simpletons who fell into the furnace, the men whom ambition goaded to exasperation, the low minds that yielded to the temptation of an open drawer, the company-promoters who grew intoxicated and lost ground by dint of dealing with big figures. At the same time, however, Massot admitted that these men were relatively few in number, and that black sheep were to be found in every parliament of the world. Then Sagnier's name cropped up again, and Massot remarked that only Sagnier could regard the French Chambers as mere dens of thieves.

Pierre, meantime, felt most interested in the tempest which the threat of a ministerial crisis was stirring up before him. Not only the men like Duthil and Chaigneux, pale at feeling the ground tremble beneath them, and wondering whether they would not sleep at the Mazas prison that night, were gathered round Barroux and Monferrand; all the latters' clients were there, all who enjoyed influence or office through them, and who would collapse and disappear should they happen to fall. And it was something to see the anxious glances and the pale dread amidst all the whispered chatter, the bits of information and tittle-tattle which were carried hither and thither. Then, in a neighbouring group formed round Vignon, who looked very calm and smiled, were the other clients, those who awaited the moment to climb to the assault of power, in order that they, in their turn, might at last possess influence or office. Eyes glittered with covetousness, hopeful delight could be read in them, pleasant surprise at the sudden opportunity now offered. Vignon avoided replying to the over-direct questions of his friends, and simply announced that he did not intend to intervene. Evidently enough his plan was to let Mege interpellate and overthrow the ministry, for he did not fear him, and in his own estimation would afterwards simply have to stoop to pick up the fallen portfolios.

"Ah! Monferrand now," little Massot was saying, "there's a rascal who trims his sails! I knew him as an anti-clerical, a devourer of priests, Monsieur l'Abbe, if you will allow me so to express myself; however, I don't say this to be agreeable to you, but I think I may tell you for certain that he has become reconciled to religion. At least, I have been told that Monseigneur Martha, who is a great converter, now seldom leaves him. This is calculated to please one in these new times, when science has become bankrupt, and religion blooms afresh with delicious mysticism on all sides, whether in art, literature, or society itself."

Massot was jesting, according to his wont; but he spoke so amiably that the priest could not do otherwise than bow. However, a great stir had set in before them; it was announced that Mege was about to ascend the tribune, and thereupon all the deputies hastened into the assembly hall, leaving only the inquisitive visitors and a few journalists in the Salle des Pas Perdus.

"It's astonishing that Fonsegue hasn't yet arrived," resumed Massot; "he's interested in what's going on. However, he's so cunning, that when he doesn't behave as others do, one may be sure that he has his reasons for it. Do you know him?" And as

Pierre gave a negative answer, Massot went on: "Oh! he's a man of brains and real power—I speak with all freedom, you know, for I don't possess the bump of veneration; and, as for my editors, well, they're the very puppets that I know the best and pick to pieces with the most enjoyment. Fonsegue, also, is clearly designated in Sagnier's article. Moreover, he's one of Duvillard's usual clients. There can be no doubt that he took money, for he takes money in everything. Only he always protects himself, and takes it for reasons which may be acknowledged—as payment or commission on account of advertising, and so forth. And if I left him just now, looking, as it seemed to me, rather disturbed, and if he delays his arrival here to establish, as it were, a moral alibi, the truth must be that he has committed the first imprudent action in his life."

Then Massot rattled on, telling all there was to tell about Fonsegue. He, too, came from the department of La Correze, and had quarrelled for life with Monferrand after some unknown underhand affairs. Formerly an advocate at Tulle, his ambition had been to conquer Paris; and he had really conquered it, thanks to his big morning newspaper, "Le Globe," of which he was both founder and director. He now resided in a luxurious mansion in the Avenue du Bois de Boulogne, and no enterprise was launched but he carved himself a princely share in it. He had a genius for "business," and employed his newspaper as a weapon to enable him to reign over the market. But how very carefully he had behaved, what long and skilful patience he had shown, before attaining to the reputation of a really serious man, who guided authoritatively the most virtuous and respected of the organs of the press! Though in reality he believed neither in God nor in Devil, he had made this newspaper the supporter of order, property, and family ties; and though he had become a Conservative Republican, since it was to his interest to be such, he had remained outwardly religious, affecting a Spiritualism which reassured the *bourgeoisie*. And amidst all his accepted power, to which others bowed, he nevertheless had one hand deep in every available money-bag.

"Ah! Monsieur l'Abbe," said Massot, "see to what journalism may lead a man. There you have Sagnier and Fonsegue: just compare them a bit. In reality they are birds of the same feather: each has a quill and uses it. But how different the systems and the results. Sagnier's print is really a sewer which rolls him along and carries him to the cesspool; while the other's paper is certainly an example of the best journalism one can have, most carefully written, with a real literary flavour, a treat for readers of delicate minds, and an honour to the man who directs it. But at the bottom, good heavens! in both cases the farce is precisely the same!"

Massot burst out laughing, well pleased with this final thrust. Then all at once: "Ah! here's Fonsegue at last!" said he.

Quite at his ease, and still laughing, he forthwith introduced the priest. "This is Monsieur l'Abbe Froment, my dear *patron*, who has been waiting more than twenty minutes for you—I'm just going to see what is happening inside. You know that Mege is interpellating the government."

The new comer started slightly: "An interpellation!" said he. "All right, all right, I'll go to it."

Pierre was looking at him. He was about fifty years of age, short of stature, thin and active, still looking young without a grey hair in his black beard. He had sparkling eyes, too, but his mouth, said to be a terrible one, was hidden by his moustaches. And withal he looked a pleasant companion, full of wit to the tip of his little pointed nose, the nose of a sporting dog that is ever scenting game. "What can I do for you, Monsieur l'Abbe?" he inquired.

Then Pierre briefly presented his request, recounting his visit to Laveuve that morning, giving every heart-rending particular, and asking for the poor wretch's immediate admittance to the Asylum.

"Laveuve!" said the other, "but hasn't his affair been examined? Why, Duthil drew up a report on it, and things appeared to us of such a nature that we could not vote for the man's admittance."

But the priest insisted: "I assure you, monsieur, that your heart would have burst with compassion had you been with me this morning. It is revolting that an old man should be left in such frightful abandonment even for another hour. He must sleep at the Asylum to-night."

Fonsegue began to protest. "To-night! But it's impossible, altogether impossible! There are all sorts of indispensable formalities to be observed. And besides I alone cannot take such responsibility. I haven't the power. I am only the manager; all that I do is to execute the orders of the committee of lady patronesses."

"But it was precisely Baroness Duvillard who sent me to you, monsieur, telling me that you alone had the necessary authority to grant immediate admittance in an exceptional case."

"Oh! it was the Baroness who sent you? Ah! that is just like her, incapable of coming to any decision herself, and far too desirous of her own quietude to accept any responsibility. Why is it that she wants me to have the worries? No, no, Monsieur l'Abbe, I certainly won't go against all our regulations; I won't give an order which would perhaps embroil me with all those ladies. You don't know them, but they become positively terrible directly they attend our meetings."

He was growing lively, defending himself with a jocular air, whilst in secret he was fully determined to do nothing. However, just then Duthil abruptly reappeared, darting along bareheaded, hastening from lobby to lobby to recruit absent members, particularly those who were interested in the grave debate at that moment beginning. "What, Fonsegue!" he cried, "are you still here? Go, go to your seat at once, it's serious!" And thereupon he disappeared.

His colleague evinced no haste, however. It was as if the suspicious affair which was impassioning the Chamber had no concern for him. And he still smiled, although a slight feverish quiver made him blink. "Excuse me, Monsieur l'Abbe," he said at last. "You see that my friends have need of me. I repeat to you that I can do absolutely nothing for your *protege*."

But Pierre would not accept this reply as a final one. "No, no, monsieur," he rejoined, "go to your affairs, I will wait for you here. Don't come to a decision without full reflection. You are wanted, and I feel that your mind is not sufficiently at liberty for you to listen to me properly. By-and-by, when you come back and give me your full attention, I am sure that you will grant me what I ask."

And, although Fonsegue, as he went off, repeated that he could not alter his decision, the priest stubbornly resolved to make him do so, and sat down on the bench again, prepared, if needful, to stay there till the evening. The Salle des Pas Perdus was now almost quite empty, and looked yet more frigid and mournful with its Laocoon and its Minerva, its bare commonplace walls like those of a railway-station waiting-room, between which all the scramble of the century passed, though apparently without even warming the lofty ceiling. Never had paler and more callous light entered by the large glazed doors, behind which one espied the little slumberous garden with its meagre, wintry lawns. And not an echo of the tempest of the sitting near at hand reached the spot; from the whole heavy pile there fell but death-like silence, and a covert quiver of distress that had come from far away, perhaps from the entire country.

It was that which now haunted Pierre's reverie. The whole ancient, envenomed sore spread out before his mind's eye, with its poison and virulence. Parliamentary rottenness had slowly increased till it had begun to attack society itself. Above all the low intrigues and the rush of personal ambition there certainly remained the loftier struggle of the contending principles, with history on the march, clearing the past away and seeking to bring more truth, justice, and happiness in the future. But in practice, if one only considered the horrid daily cuisine of the sphere, what an unbridling of egotistical appetite one beheld, what an absorbing passion to strangle one's neighbour and triumph oneself alone! Among the various groups one found but an incessant battle for power and the satisfactions that it gives. "Left," "Right," "Catholics," "Republicans," "Socialists," the names given to the parties of twenty different shades, were simply labels classifying forms of the one burning thirst to rule and dominate. All questions could be reduced to a single one, that of knowing whether this man, that man, or that other man should hold France in his grasp, to enjoy it, and distribute its favours among his creatures. And the worst was that the outcome of the great parliamentary battles, the days and the weeks lost in setting this man in the place of that man, and that other man in the place of this man, was simply stagnation, for not one of the three men was better than his fellows, and there were but vague points of difference between them; in such wise that the new master bungled the very same work as the previous one had bungled, forgetful, perforce, of programmes and promises as soon as ever he began to reign.

However, Pierre's thoughts invincibly reverted to Laveuve, whom he had momentarily forgotten, but who now seized hold of him again with a quiver as of anger and death. Ah! what could it matter to that poor old wretch, dying of hunger on his bed of rags, whether Mege should overthrow Barroux's ministry, and whether a Vignon ministry should ascend to power or not! At that rate, a century, two centuries, would be needed before there would be bread in the garrets where groan the lamed sons of labour, the old, broken-down beasts of burden. And behind Laveuve there appeared the whole army of misery, the whole multitude of the disinherited and the poor, who agonised and asked for justice whilst the Chamber, sitting in all pomp, grew furiously impassioned over the question as to whom the nation should belong to, as to who should devour it. Mire was flowing on in a broad stream, the hideous, bleeding, devouring sore displayed itself in all impudence, like some cancer which preys upon an organ and spreads to the heart. And what disgust, what nausea must such a spectacle inspire; and what a longing for the vengeful knife that would bring health and joy!

Pierre could not have told for how long he had been plunged in this reverie, when uproar again filled the hall. People were coming back, gesticulating and gathering in groups. And suddenly he heard little Massot exclaim near him: "Well, if it isn't down it's not much better off. I wouldn't give four sous for its chance of surviving."

He referred to the ministry, and began to recount the sitting to a fellow journalist who had just arrived. Mege had spoken very eloquently, with extraordinary fury of indignation against the rotten *bourgeoisie*, which rotted everything it touched; but, as usual, he had gone much too far, alarming the Chamber by his very violence. And so, when Barroux had ascended the tribune to ask for a month's adjournment of the interpellation, he had merely had occasion to wax indignant, in all sincerity be it said, full of lofty anger that such infamous campaigns should be carried on by a certain portion of the press. Were the shameful Panama scandals about to be renewed? Were the national representatives going to let themselves be intimidated by fresh threats of denunciation? It was the Republic itself which its adversaries were seeking to submerge beneath a flood of abominations. No, no, the hour had come for one to collect one's thoughts, and work in quietude without allowing those who hungered for scandal to disturb the public peace. And the Chamber, impressed by these words, fearing, too, lest the electorate should at last grow utterly weary of the continuous overflow of filth, had adjourned the interpellation to that day month. However, although Vignon had not personally intervened in the debate, the whole of his group had voted against the ministry, with the result that the latter had merely secured a majority of two votes—a mockery.

"But in that case they will resign," said somebody to Massot.

"Yes, so it's rumoured. But Barroux is very tenacious. At all events if they show any obstinacy they will be down before a week is over, particularly as Sagnier, who is quite furious, declares that he will publish the list of names to-morrow."

Just then, indeed, Barroux and Monferrand were seen to pass, hastening along with thoughtful, busy mien, and followed by their anxious clients. It was said that the whole Cabinet was about to assemble to consider the position and come to a decision. And then Vignon, in his turn, reappeared amidst a stream of friends. He, for his part, was radiant, with a joy which he sought to conceal, calming his friends in his desire not to cry victory too soon. However, the eyes of the band glittered, like those of a pack of hounds when the moment draws near for the offal of the quarry to be distributed. And even Mege also looked triumphant. He had all but overthrown the ministry. That made another one that was worn out, and by-and-by he would wear out Vignon's, and at last govern in his turn.

"The devil!" muttered little Massot, "Chaigneux and Duthil look like whipped dogs. And see, there's nobody who is worth the governor. Just look at him, how superb he is, that Fonsegue! But good-by, I must now be off!"

Then he shook hands with his brother journalist unwilling as he was to remain any longer, although the sitting still continued, some bill of public importance again being debated before the rows of empty seats.

Chaigneux, with his desolate mien, had gone to lean against the pedestal of the high figure of Minerva; and never before had he been more bowed down by his needy distress, the everlasting anguish of his ill-luck. On the other hand, Duthil, in spite of everything, was perorating in the centre of a group with an affectation of scoffing unconcern; nevertheless nervous twitches made his nose pucker and distorted his mouth, while the whole of his handsome face was becoming moist with fear. And even as Massot had said, there really was only Fonsegue who showed composure and bravery, ever the same with his restless little figure, and his eyes beaming with wit, though at times they were just faintly clouded by a shadow of uneasiness.

Pierre had risen to renew his request; but Fonsegue forestalled him, vivaciously exclaiming: "No, no, Monsieur l'Abbe, I repeat that I cannot take on myself such an infraction of our rules. There was an inquiry, and a decision was arrived at. How would you have me over-rule it?"

"Monsieur," said the priest, in a tone of deep grief, "it is a question of an old man who is hungry and cold, and in danger of death if he be not succoured."

With a despairing gesture, the director of "Le Globe" seemed to take the very walls as witnesses of his powerlessness. No doubt he feared some nasty affair for his newspaper, in which he had abused the Invalids of Labour enterprise as an electoral weapon. Perhaps, too, the secret terror into which the sitting of the Chamber had just thrown him was hardening his heart. "I can do nothing," he repeated. "But naturally I don't ask better than to have my hands forced by the ladies of the Committee. You already have the support of the Baroness Duvillard, secure that of some others."

Pierre, who was determined to fight on to the very end, saw in this suggestion a supreme chance. "I know the Countess de Quinsac," he said, "I can go to see her at once."

"Quite so! an excellent idea, the Countess de Quinsac! Take a cab and go to see the Princess de Harn as well. She bestirs herself a great deal, and is becoming very influential. Secure the approval of these ladies, go back to the Baroness's at seven, get a letter from her to cover me, and then call on me at the office of my paper. That done, your man shall sleep at the Asylum at nine o'clock!"

He evinced in speaking a kind of joyous good nature, as though he no longer doubted of success now that he ran no risk of compromising himself. And great hope again came back to the priest: "Ah! thank you, monsieur," he said; "it is a work of salvation that you will accomplish."

"But you surely know that I ask nothing better. Ah! if we could only cure misery, prevent hunger and thirst by a mere word. However, make haste, you have not a minute to lose."

They shook hands, and Pierre at once tried to get out of the throng. This, however, was no easy task, for the various groups had grown larger as all the anger and anguish, roused by the recent debate, ebbed back there amid a confused tumult. It was as when a stone, cast into a pool, stirs the ooze below, and causes hidden, rotting things to rise once more to the surface. And Pierre had to bring his elbows into play and force a passage athwart the throng, betwixt the shivering cowardice of some, the insolent audacity of others, and the smirchings which sullied the greater number, given the contagion which inevitably prevailed. However, he carried away a fresh hope, and it seemed to him that if he should save a life, make but one man happy that day, it would be like a first instalment of redemption, a sign that a little forgiveness would be extended to the many follies and errors of that egotistical and all-devouring political world.

On reaching the vestibule a final incident detained him for a moment longer. Some commotion prevailed there following upon a quarrel between a man and an usher, the latter of whom had prevented the former from entering on finding that the admission ticket which he tendered was an old one, with its original date scratched out. The man, very rough at the outset, had then refrained from insisting, as if indeed sudden timidity had come upon him. And in this ill-dressed fellow Pierre was astonished to recognise Salvat, the journeyman engineer, whom he had seen going off in search of work that same morning. This time it was certainly he, tall, thin and ravaged, with dreamy yet flaming eyes, which set his pale starveling's face aglow. He no longer carried his tool-bag; his ragged jacket was buttoned up and distended on the left side by something that he carried in a pocket, doubtless some hunk of bread. And on being repulsed by the ushers, he walked away, taking the Concorde bridge, slowly, as if chancewise, like a man who knows not whither he is going.

IV. SOCIAL SIDELIGHTS

IN her old faded drawing-room—a Louis Seize *salon* with grey woodwork—the Countess de Quinsac sat near the chimney-piece in her accustomed place. She was singularly like her son, with a long and noble face, her chin somewhat stern, but her eyes still beautiful beneath her fine snowy hair, which was arranged in the antiquated style of her youth. And whatever her haughty coldness, she knew how to be amiable, with perfect, kindly graciousness.

Slightly waving her hand after a long silence, she resumed, addressing herself to the Marquis de Morigny, who sat on the other side of the chimney, where for long years he had always taken the same armchair. "Ah! you are right, my friend, Providence has left us here forgotten, in a most abominable epoch."

"Yes, we passed by the side of happiness and missed it," the Marquis slowly replied, "and it was your fault, and doubtless mine as well."

Smiling sadly, she stopped him with another wave of her hand. And the silence fell once more; not a sound from the streets reached that gloomy ground floor at the rear of the courtyard of an old mansion in the Rue St. Dominique, almost at the corner of the Rue de Bourgogne.

The Marquis was an old man of seventy-five, nine years older than the Countess. Short and thin though he was, he none the less had a distinguished air, with his clean-shaven face, furrowed by deep, aristocratic wrinkles. He belonged to one of the most ancient families of France, and remained one of the last hopeless Legitimists, of very pure and lofty views, zealously keeping his faith to the dead monarchy amidst the downfall of everything. His fortune, still estimated at several millions of francs, remained, as it were, in a state of stagnation, through his refusal to invest it in any of the enterprises of the century. It was known that in all discretion he had loved the Countess, even when M. de Quinsac was alive, and had, moreover, offered marriage after the latter's death, at the time when the widow had sought a refuge on that damp ground floor with merely an income of some 15,000 francs, saved with great difficulty from the wreck of the family fortune. But she, who adored her son Gerard, then in his tenth year, and of delicate health, had sacrificed everything to the boy from a kind of maternal chasteness and a superstitious fear that she might lose him should she set another affection and another duty in her life. And the Marquis, while bowing to her decision, had continued to worship her with his whole soul, ever paying his court as on the first evening when he had seen her, still gallant and faithful after a quarter of a century had passed. There had never been anything between them, not even the exchange of a kiss.

Seeing how sad she looked, he feared that he might have displeased her, and so he asked: "I should have liked to render you happy, but I didn't know how, and the fault can certainly only rest with me. Is Gerard giving you any cause for anxiety?"

She shook her head, and then replied: "As long as things remain as they are we cannot complain of them, my friend, since we accepted them."

She referred to her son's culpable connection with Baroness Duvillard. She had ever shown much weakness with regard to that son whom she had had so much trouble to rear, for she alone knew what exhaustion, what racial collapse was hidden behind his proud bearing. She tolerated his idleness, the apathetic disgust which, man of pleasure that he was, had turned him from the profession of diplomacy as from that of arms. How many times had she not repaired his acts of folly and paid his petty debts, keeping silent concerning them, and refusing all pecuniary help from the Marquis, who no longer dared offer his millions, so stubbornly intent she was on living upon the remnants of her own fortune. And thus she had ended by closing her eyes to her son's scandalous love intrigue, divining in some measure how things had happened, through self-abandonment and lack of conscience—the man weak, unable to resume possession of himself, and the woman holding and retaining him. The Marquis, however, strangely enough, had only forgiven the intrigue on the day when Eve had allowed herself to be converted.

"You know, my friend, how good-natured Gerard is," the Countess resumed. "In that lie both his strength and weakness. How would you have me scold him when he weeps over it all with me? He will tire of that woman."

M. de Morigny wagged his head. "She is still very beautiful," said he. "And then there's the daughter. It would be graver still if he were to marry her—"

"But the daughter's infirm?"

"Yes, and you know what would be said: A Quinsac marrying a monster for the sake of her millions."

This was their mutual terror. They knew everything that went on at the Duvillards, the affectionate friendship of the uncomely Camille and the handsome Gerard, the seeming idyll beneath which lurked the most awful of dramas. And they protested with all their indignation. "Oh! that, no, no, never!" the Countess declared. "My son in that family, no, I will never consent to it."

Just at that moment General de Bozonnet entered. He was much attached to his sister and came to keep her company on the days when she received, for the old circle had gradually dwindled down till now only a few faithful ones ventured into that grey gloomy *salon*, where one might have fancied oneself at thousands of leagues from present-day Paris. And forthwith, in order to enliven the room, he related that he had been to *dejeuner* at the Duvillards, and named the guests, Gerard among them. He knew that he pleased his sister by going to the banker's house whence he brought her news, a house, too, which he cleansed in some degree by conferring on it the great honour of his presence. And he himself in no wise felt bored there, for he had long been gained over to the century and showed himself of a very accommodating disposition in everything that did not pertain to military art.

"That poor little Camille worships Gerard," said he; "she was devouring him with her eyes at table."

But M. de Morigny gravely intervened: "There lies the danger, a marriage would be absolutely monstrous from every point of view."

The General seemed astonished: "Why, pray? She isn't beautiful, but it's not only the beauties who marry! And there are her millions. However, our dear child would only have to put them to a good use. True, there is also the mother; but, *mon Dieu*! such things are so common nowadays in Paris society."

This revolted the Marquis, who made a gesture of utter disgust. What was the use of discussion when all collapsed? How could one answer a Bozonnet, the last surviving representative of such an illustrious family, when he reached such a point as to excuse the infamous morals that prevailed under the Republic; after denying his king, too, and serving the Empire, faithfully and passionately attaching himself to the fortunes and memory of Caesar? However, the Countess also became indignant: "Oh! what are you saying, brother? I will never authorize such a scandal, I swore so only just now."

"Don't swear, sister," exclaimed the General; "for my part I should like to see our Gerard happy. That's all. And one must admit that he's not good for much. I can understand that he didn't go into the Army, for that profession is done for. But I do not so well understand why he did not enter the diplomatic profession, or accept some other occupation. It is very fine, no doubt, to run down the present times and declare that a man of our sphere cannot possibly do any clean work in them. But, as a matter of fact, it is only idle fellows who still say that. And Gerard has but one excuse, his lack of aptitude, will and strength."

Tears had risen to the mother's eyes. She even trembled, well knowing how deceitful were appearances: a mere chill might carry her son off, however tall and strong he might look. And was he not indeed a symbol of that old-time aristocracy, still so lofty and proud in appearance, though at bottom it is but dust?

"Well," continued the General, "he's thirty-six now; he's constantly hanging on your hands, and he must make an end of it all."

However, the Countess silenced him and turned to the Marquis: "Let us put our confidence in God, my friend," said she. "He cannot but come to my help, for I have never willingly offended Him."

"Never!" replied the Marquis, who in that one word set an expression of all his grief, all his affection and worship for that woman whom he had adored for so many years.

But another faithful friend came in and the conversation changed. M. de Larombiere, Vice-President of the Appeal Court, was an old man of seventy-five, thin, bald and clean shaven but for a pair of little white whiskers. And his grey eyes, compressed mouth and square and obstinate chin lent an expression of great austerity to his long face. The grief of his life was that, being afflicted with a somewhat childish lisp, he had never been able to make his full merits known when a public prosecutor, for he esteemed himself to be a great orator. And this secret worry rendered him morose. In him appeared an incarnation of that old royalist France which sulked and only served the Republic against its heart, that old stern magistracy which closed itself to all evolution, to all new views of things and beings. Of petty "gown" nobility, originally a Legitimist but now supporting Orleanism, he believed himself to be the one man of wisdom and logic in that *salon*, where he was very proud to meet the Marquis.

They talked of the last events; but with them political conversation was soon exhausted, amounting as it did to a mere bitter condemnation of men and occurrences, for all three were of one mind as to the abominations of the Republican *regime*. They themselves, however, were only ruins, the remnants of the old parties now all but utterly powerless. The Marquis for his part soared on high, yielding in nothing, ever faithful to the dead past; he was one of the last representatives of that lofty obstinate *noblesse* which dies when it finds itself without an effort to escape its fate. The judge, who at least had a pretender living, relied on a miracle, and demonstrated the necessity for one if France were not to sink into the depths of misfortune and completely disappear. And as for the General, all that he regretted of the two Empires was their great wars; he left the faint hope of a Bonapartist restoration on one side to declare that by not contenting itself with the Imperial military system, and by substituting thereto obligatory service, the nation in arms, the Republic had killed both warfare and the country.

When the Countess's one man-servant came to ask her if she would consent to receive Abbe Froment she seemed somewhat surprised. "What can he want of me? Show him in," she said.

She was very pious, and having met Pierre in connection with various charitable enterprises, she had been touched by his zeal as well as by the saintly reputation which he owed to his Neuilly parishioners.

He, absorbed by his fever, felt intimidated directly he crossed the threshold. He could at first distinguish nothing, but fancied he was entering some place of mourning, a shadowy spot where human forms seemed to melt away, and voices were never raised above a whisper. Then, on perceiving the persons present, he felt yet more out of his element, for they seemed so sad, so far removed from the world whence he had just come, and whither he was about to return. And when the Countess had made him sit down beside her in front of the chimney-piece, it was in a low voice that he told her the lamentable story of Laveuve, and asked her support to secure the man's admittance to the Asylum for the Invalids of Labour.

"Ah! yes," said she, "that enterprise which my son wished me to belong to. But, Monsieur l'Abbe, I have never once attended the Committee meetings. So how could I intervene, having assuredly no influence whatever?"

Again had the figures of Eve and Gerard arisen before her, for it was at this asylum that the pair had first met. And influenced by her sorrowful maternal love she was already weakening, although it was regretfully that she had lent her name to one of those noisy charitable enterprises, which people abused to further their selfish interests in a manner she condemned.

"But, madame," Pierre insisted, "it is a question of a poor starving old man. I implore you to be compassionate."

Although the priest had spoken in a low voice the General drew near. "It's for your old revolutionary that you are running about, is it not," said he. "Didn't you succeed with the manager, then? The fact is that it's difficult to feel any pity for fellows who, if they were the masters, would, as they themselves say, sweep us all away."

M. de Larombiere jerked his chin approvingly. For some time past he had been haunted by the Anarchist peril. But Pierre, distressed and quivering, again began to plead his cause. He spoke of all the frightful misery, the homes where there was no food, the women and children shivering with cold, and the fathers scouring muddy, wintry Paris in search of a bit of bread. All that he asked for was a line on a visiting card, a kindly word from the Countess, which he would at once carry to Baroness Duvillard to prevail on her to set the regulations aside. And his words fell one by one, tremulous with stifled tears, in that mournful *salon*, like sounds from afar, dying away in a dead world where there was no echo left.

Madame de Quinsac turned towards M. de Morigny, but he seemed to take no interest in it all. He was gazing fixedly at the fire, with the haughty air of a stranger who was indifferent to the things and beings in whose midst an error of time compelled him to live. But feeling that the glance of the woman he worshipped was fixed upon him he raised his head; and then their eyes met for a moment with an expression of infinite gentleness, the mournful gentleness of their heroic love.

"*Mon Dieu*!" said she, "I know your merits, Monsieur l'Abbe, and I won't refuse my help to one of your good works."

Then she went off for a moment, and returned with a card on which she had written that she supported with all her heart Monsieur l'Abbe Froment in the steps he was taking. And he thanked her and went off delighted, as if he carried yet a fresh hope of salvation from that drawing-room where, as he retired, gloom and silence once more seemed to fall on that old lady and her last faithful friends gathered around the fire, last relics of a world that was soon to disappear.

Once outside, Pierre joyfully climbed into his cab again, after giving the Princess de Harn's address in the Avenue Kleber. If he could also obtain her approval he would no longer doubt of success. However, there was such a crush on the Concorde bridge, that the driver had to walk his horse. And, on the foot-pavement, Pierre again saw Duthil, who, with a cigar between his lips, was smiling at the crowd, with his amiable bird-like heedlessness, happy as he felt at finding the pavement dry and the sky blue on leaving that worrying sitting of the Chamber. Seeing how gay and triumphant he looked, a sudden inspiration came to the priest, who said to himself that he ought to win over this young man, whose report had had such a disastrous effect. As it happened, the cab having been compelled to stop altogether, the deputy had just recognized him and was smiling at him.

"Where are you going, Monsieur Duthil?" Pierre asked.

"Close by, in the Champs Elysees."

"I'm going that way, and, as I should much like to speak to you for a moment, it would be very kind of you to take a seat beside me. I will set you down wherever you like."

"Willingly, Monsieur l'Abbe. It won't inconvenience you if I finish my cigar?"

"Oh! not at all."

The cab found its way out of the crush, crossed the Place de la Concorde and began to ascend the Champs Elysees. And Pierre, reflecting that he had very few minutes before him, at once attacked Duthil, quite ready for any effort to convince him. He remembered what a sortie the young deputy had made against Laveuve at the Baron's; and thus he was astonished to hear him interrupt and say quite pleasantly, enlivened as he seemed by the bright sun which was again beginning to shine: "Ah, yes! your old drunkard! So you didn't settle his business with Fonsegue? And what is it you want? To have him admitted to-day? Well, you know I don't oppose it?"

"But there's your report."

"My report, oh, my report! But questions change according to the way one looks at them. And if you are so anxious about your Laveuve I won't refuse to help you."

Pierre looked at him in astonishment, at bottom extremely well pleased. And there was no further necessity even for him to speak.

"You didn't take the matter in hand properly," continued Duthil, leaning forward with a confidential air. "It's the Baron who's the master at home, for reasons which you may divine, which you may very likely know. The Baroness does all that he asks without even discussing the point; and this morning,—instead of starting on a lot of useless visits, you only had to gain his support, particularly as he seemed to be very well disposed. And she would then have given way immediately." Duthil began to laugh. "And so," he continued, "do you know what I'll do? Well, I'll gain the Baron over to your cause. Yes, I am this moment going to a house where he is, where one is certain to find him every day at this time." Then he laughed more loudly. "And perhaps you are not ignorant of it, Monsieur l'Abbe. When he is there you may be certain he never gives a refusal. I promise you I'll make him swear that he will compel his wife to grant your man admission this very evening. Only it will, perhaps, be rather late."

Then all at once, as if struck by a fresh idea, Duthil went on: "But why shouldn't you come with me? You secure a line from the Baron, and thereupon, without losing a minute, you go in search of the Baroness. Ah! yes, the house embarrasses you a little, I understand it. Would you like to see only the Baron there? You can wait for him in a little *salon* downstairs; I will bring him to you."

This proposal made Duthil altogether merry, but Pierre, quite scared, hesitated at the idea of thus going to Silviane d'Aulnay's. It was hardly a place for him. However, to achieve his purpose, he would have descended into the very dwelling of the fiend, and had already done so sometimes with Abbe Rose, when there was hope of assuaging wretchedness. So he turned to Duthil and consented to accompany him.

Silviane d'Aulnay's little mansion, a very luxurious one, displaying, too, so to say, the luxury of a temple, refined but suggestive of gallantry, stood in the Avenue d'Antin, near the Champs Elysees. The inmate of this sanctuary, where the orfrays of old dalmaticas glittered in the mauve reflections from the windows of stained-glass, had just completed her twenty-fifth year. Short and slim she was, of an adorable, dark beauty, and all Paris was acquainted with her delicious, virginal countenance of a gentle oval, her delicate nose, her little mouth, her candid cheeks and artless chin, above all which she wore her black hair in thick, heavy bands, which hid her low brow. Her notoriety was due precisely to her pretty air of astonishment, the infinite purity of her blue eyes, the whole expression of chaste innocence which she assumed when it so pleased her, an expression which contrasted powerfully with her true nature, shameless creature that she really was, of the most monstrous, confessed, and openly-displayed perversity; such as, in fact, often spring up from the rotting soil of great cities. Extraordinary things were related about Silviane's tastes and fancies. Some said that she was a door-keeper's, others a doctor's, daughter. In any case she had managed to acquire instruction and manners, for when occasion required she lacked neither wit, nor style, nor deportment. She had been rolling through the theatres for ten years or so, applauded for her beauty's sake, and she had even ended by obtaining some pretty little successes in such parts as those of very pure young girls or loving and persecuted young women. Since there had been a question, though, of her entering the Comedie Francaise to play the *role* of Pauline in "Polyeucte," some people had waxed indignant and others had roared with laughter, so ridiculous did the idea appear, so outrageous for the majesty of classic tragedy. She, however, quiet and stubborn, wished this thing to be, was resolved that it should be, certain as she was that she would secure it, insolent like a creature to whom men had never yet been able to refuse anything.

That day, at three o'clock, Gerard de Quinsac, not knowing how to kill the time pending the appointment he had given Eve in the Rue Matignon, had thought of calling at Silviane's, which was in the neighbourhood. She was an old caprice of his, and even nowadays he would sometimes linger at the little mansion if its pretty mistress felt bored. But he had this time found her in a fury; and, reclining in one of the deep armchairs of the *salon* where "old gold" formed the predominant colour, he was listening to her complaints. She, standing in a white gown, white indeed from head to foot like Eve herself at the *dejeuner*, was speaking passionately, and fast convincing the young man, who, won over by so much youth and beauty, unconsciously compared her to his other flame, weary already of his coming assignation, and so mastered by supineness, both moral and physical, that he would have preferred to remain all day in the depths of that armchair.

"You hear me, Gerard!" she at last exclaimed, "I'll have nothing whatever to do with him, unless he brings me my nomination."

Just then Baron Duvillard came in, and forthwith she changed to ice and received him like some sorely offended young queen who awaits an explanation; whilst he, who foresaw the storm and brought moreover disastrous tidings, forced a smile, though very ill at ease. She was the stain, the blemish attaching to that man who was yet so sturdy and so powerful amidst the general decline of his race. And she was also the beginning of justice and punishment, taking all his piled-up gold from him by the handful, and by her cruelty avenging those who shivered and who starved. And it was pitiful to see that feared and flattered man, beneath whom states and governments trembled, here turn pale with anxiety, bend low in all humility, and relapse into the senile, lisping infancy of acute passion.

"Ah! my dear friend," said he, "if you only knew how I have been rushing about. I had a lot of worrying business, some contractors to see, a big advertisement affair to settle, and I feared that I should never be able to come and kiss your hand."

He kissed it, but she let her arm fall, coldly, indifferently, contenting herself with looking at him, waiting for what he might have to say to her, and embarrassing him to such a point that he began to perspire and stammer, unable to express himself. "Of course," he began, "I also thought of you, and went to the Fine Arts Office, where I had received a positive promise. Oh! they are still very much in your favour at the Fine Arts Office! Only, just fancy, it's that idiot of a minister, that Taboureau,[1] an old professor from the provinces who knows nothing about our Paris, that has expressly

[1] Taboureau is previously described as Minister of Public Instruction. It should be pointed out, however, that although under the present Republic the Ministries of Public Instruction and Fine Arts have occasionally been distinct departments, at other times they have been united, one minister, as in Taboureau's case, having charge of both.—Trans.

opposed your nomination, saying that as long as he is in office you shall not appear at the Comedie."

Erect and rigid, she spoke but two words: "And then?"

"And then—well, my dear, what would you have me do? One can't after all overthrow a ministry to enable you to play the part of Pauline."

"Why not?"

He pretended to laugh, but his blood rushed to his face, and the whole of his sturdy figure quivered with anguish. "Come, my little Silviane," said he, "don't be obstinate. You can be so nice when you choose. Give up the idea of that *debut*. You, yourself, would risk a great deal in it, for what would be your worries if you were to fail? You would weep all the tears in your body. And besides, you can ask me for so many other things which I should be so happy to give you. Come now, at once, make a wish and I will gratify it immediately."

In a frolicsome way he sought to take her hand again. But she drew back with an air of much dignity. "No, you hear me, my dear fellow, I will have nothing whatever to do with you—nothing, so long as I don't play Pauline."

He understood her fully, and he knew her well enough to realise how rigorously she would treat him. Only a kind of grunt came from his contracted throat, though he still tried to treat the matter in a jesting way. "Isn't she bad-tempered to-day!" he resumed at last, turning towards Gerard. "What have you done to her that I find her in such a state?"

But the young man, who kept very quiet for fear lest he himself might be bespattered in the course of the dispute, continued to stretch himself out in a languid way and gave no answer.

But Silviane's anger burst forth. "What has he done to me? He has pitied me for being at the mercy of such a man as you—so egotistical, so insensible to the insults heaped upon me. Ought you not to be the first to bound with indignation? Ought you not to have exacted my admittance to the Comedie as a reparation for the insult? For, after all, it is a defeat for you; if I'm considered unworthy, you are struck at the same time as I am. And so I'm a drab, eh? Say at once that I'm a creature to be driven away from all respectable houses."

She went on in this style, coming at last to vile words, the abominable words which, in moments of anger, always ended by returning to her innocent-looking lips. The Baron, who well knew that a syllable from him would only increase the foulness of the overflow, vainly turned an imploring glance on the Count to solicit his intervention. Gerard, with his keen desire for peace and quietness, often brought about a reconciliation, but this time he did not stir, feeling too lazy and sleepy to interfere. And Silviane all at once came to a finish, repeating her trenchant, severing words: "Well, manage as you can, secure my *debut*, or I'll have nothing more to do with you, nothing!"

"All right! all right!" Duvillard at last murmured, sneering, but in despair, "we'll arrange it all."

However, at that moment a servant came in to say that M. Duthil was downstairs and wished to speak to the Baron in the smoking-room. Duvillard was astonished at this, for Duthil usually came up as though the house were his own. Then he reflected that the deputy had doubtless brought him some serious news from the Chamber which he wished to impart to him confidentially at once. So he followed the servant, leaving Gerard and Silviane together.

In the smoking-room, an apartment communicating with the hall by a wide bay, the curtain of which was drawn up, Pierre stood with his companion, waiting and glancing curiously around him. What particularly struck him was the almost religious solemnness of the entrance, the heavy hangings, the mystic gleams of the stained-glass, the old furniture steeped in chapel-like gloom amidst scattered perfumes of myrrh and incense. Duthil, who was still very gay, tapped a low divan with his cane and said: "She has a nicely-furnished house, eh? Oh! she knows how to look after her interests."

Then the Baron came in, still quite upset and anxious. And without even perceiving the priest, desirous as he was of tidings, he began: "Well, what did they do? Is there some very bad news, then?"

"Mege interpellated and applied for a declaration of urgency so as to overthrow Barroux. You can imagine what his speech was."

"Yes, yes, against the *bourgeois*, against me, against you. It's always the same thing—And then?"

"Then—well, urgency wasn't voted, but, in spite of a very fine defence, Barroux only secured a majority of two votes."

"Two votes, the devil! Then he's down, and we shall have a Vignon ministry next week."

"That's what everybody said in the lobbies."

The Baron frowned, as if he were estimating what good or evil might result to the world from such a change. Then, with a gesture of displeasure, he said: "A Vignon ministry! The devil! that would hardly be any better. Those young democrats pretend to be virtuous, and a Vignon ministry wouldn't admit Silviane to the Comedie."

This, at first, was his only thought in presence of the crisis which made the political world tremble. And so the deputy could not refrain from referring to his own anxiety. "Well, and we others, what is our position in it all?"

This brought Duvillard back to the situation. With a fresh gesture, this time a superbly proud one, he expressed his full and impudent confidence. "We others, why we remain as we are; we've never been in peril, I imagine. Oh! I am quite at ease. Sagnier can publish his famous list if it amuses him to do so. If we haven't long since bought Sagnier and his list, it's because Barroux is a thoroughly honest man, and for my part I don't care to throw money out of the window—I repeat to you that we fear nothing."

Then, as he at last recognised Abbe Froment, who had remained in the shade, Duthil explained what service the priest desired of him. And Duvillard, in his state of emotion, his heart still rent by Silviane's sternness, must have felt a covert hope that a good action might bring him luck; so he at once consented to intervene in favour of Laveuve's admission. Taking a card and a pencil from his pocket-book he drew near to the window. "Oh! whatever you desire, Monsieur l'Abbe," he said, "I shall be very happy to participate in this good work. Here, this is what I have written: 'My dear, please do what M. l'Abbe Froment solicits in favour of this unfortunate man, since our friend Fonsegue only awaits a word from you to take proper steps.'"

At this moment through the open bay Pierre caught sight of Gerard, whom Silviane, calm once more, and inquisitive no doubt to know why Duthil had called, was escorting into the hall. And the sight of the young woman filled him with astonishment, so simple and gentle did she seem to him, full of the immaculate candour of a virgin. Never had he dreamt of a lily of more unobtrusive yet delicious bloom in the whole garden of innocence.

"Now," continued Duvillard, "if you wish to hand this card to my wife at once, you must go to the Princess de Harn's, where there is a *matinee*—"

"I was going there, Monsieur le Baron."

"Very good. You will certainly find my wife there; she is to take the children there." Then he paused, for he too had just seen Gerard; and he called him: "I say, Gerard, my wife said that she was going to that *matinee*, didn't she? You feel sure—don't you?—that Monsieur l'Abbe will find her there?"

Although the young man was then going to the Rue Matignon, there to wait for Eve, it was in the most natural manner possible that he replied: "If Monsieur l'Abbe makes haste, I think he will find her there, for she was certainly going there before trying on a corsage at Salmon's."

Then he kissed Silviane's hand, and went off with the air of a handsome, indolent man, who knows no malice, and is even weary of pleasure.

Pierre, feeling rather embarrassed, was obliged to let Duvillard introduce him to the mistress of the house. He bowed in silence, whilst she, likewise silent, returned his bow with modest reserve, the tact appropriate to the occasion, such as no *ingenue*, even at the Comedie, was then capable of. And while the Baron accompanied the priest to the door, she returned to the *salon* with Duthil, who was scarcely screened by the door-curtain before he passed his arm round her waist.

When Pierre, who at last felt confident of success, found himself, still in his cab, in front of the Princess de Harn's mansion in the Avenue Kleber, he suddenly relapsed into great embarrassment. The avenue was crowded with carriages brought thither by the musical *matinee*, and such a throng of arriving guests pressed round the entrance, decorated with a kind of tent with scallopings of red velvet, that he deemed the house unapproachable. How could he manage to get in? And how in his cassock could he reach the Princess, and ask for a minute's conversation with Baroness Duvillard? Amidst all his feverishness he had not thought of these difficulties. However, he was approaching the door on foot, asking himself how he might glide unperceived through the throng, when the sound of a merry voice made him turn: "What, Monsieur l'Abbe! Is it possible! So now I find you here!"

It was little Massot who spoke. He went everywhere, witnessed ten sights a day,—a parliamentary sitting, a funeral, a wedding, any festive or mourning scene,—when he wanted a good subject for an article. "What! Monsieur l'Abbe," he resumed, "and so you have come to our amiable Princess's to see the Mauritanians dance!"

He was jesting, for the so-called Mauritanians were simply six Spanish dancing-girls, who by the sensuality of their performance were then making all Paris rush to the Folies-Bergere. For drawing-room entertainments these girls reserved yet more indecorous dances—dances of such a character indeed that they would certainly not have been allowed in a theatre. And the *beau monde* rushed to see them at the houses of the bolder lady-entertainers, the eccentric and foreign ones like the Princess, who in order to draw society recoiled from no "attraction."

But when Pierre had explained to little Massot that he was still running about on the same business, the journalist obligingly offered to pilot him. He knew the house, obtained admittance by a back door, and brought Pierre along a passage into a corner of the hall, near the very entrance of the grand drawing-room. Lofty green plants decorated this hall, and in the spot selected Pierre was virtually hidden. "Don't stir, my dear Abbe," said Massot, "I will try to ferret out the Princess for you. And you shall know if Baroness Duvillard has already arrived."

What surprised Pierre was that every window-shutter of the mansion was closed, every chink stopped up so that daylight might not enter, and that every room flared with electric lamps, an illumination of supernatural intensity. The heat was already very great, the atmosphere heavy with a violent perfume of flowers and *odore di femina*. And to Pierre, who felt both blinded and stifled, it seemed as if he were entering one of those luxurious, unearthly Dens of the Flesh such as the pleasure-world of Paris conjures from dreamland. By rising on tiptoes, as the drawing-room entrance was wide open, he could distinguish the backs of the women who were already seated, rows of necks crowned with fair or dark hair. The Mauritanians were doubtless executing their first dance. He did not see them, but he could divine the lascivious passion of the dance from the quiver of all those women's necks, which swayed as beneath a great gust of wind. Then laughter arose and a tempest of bravos, quite a tumult of enjoyment.

"I can't put my hand on the Princess; you must wait a little," Massot returned to say. "I met Janzen and he promised to bring her to me. Don't you know Janzen?"

Then, in part because his profession willed it, and in part for pleasure's sake, he began to gossip. The Princess was a good friend of his. He had described her first *soiree* during the previous year, when she had made her *debut* at that mansion on her arrival in Paris. He knew the real truth about her so far as it could be known. Rich? yes, perhaps she was, for she spent enormous sums. Married she must have been, and to a real prince, too; no doubt she was still married to him, in spite of her story of widowhood. Indeed, it seemed certain that her husband, who was as handsome as an archangel, was travelling about with a vocalist. As for having a bee in her bonnet that was beyond discussion, as clear as noonday. Whilst showing much intelligence, she constantly and suddenly shifted. Incapable of any prolonged effort, she went from one thing that had awakened her curiosity to another, never attaching herself anywhere. After ardently busying herself with painting, she had lately become impassioned for chemistry, and was now letting poetry master her.

"And so you don't know Janzen," continued Massot. "It was he who threw her into chemistry, into the study of explosives especially, for, as you may imagine, the only interest in chemistry for her is its connection with Anarchism. She, I think, is really an Austrian, though one must always doubt anything she herself says. As for Janzen, he calls himself a Russian, but he's probably German. Oh! he's the most unobtrusive, enigmatical man in the world, without a home, perhaps without a name—a terrible fellow with an unknown past. I myself hold proofs which make me think that he took part in that frightful crime at Barcelona. At all events, for nearly a year now I've been meeting him in Paris, where the police no doubt are watching him. And nothing can rid me of the idea that he merely consented to become our lunatic Princess's lover in order to throw the detectives off the scent. He affects to live in the midst of *fetes*, and he has introduced to the house some extraordinary people, Anarchists of all nationalities and all colours—for instance, one Raphanel, that fat, jovial little man yonder, a Frenchman he is, and his companions would do well to mistrust him. Then there's a Bergaz, a Spaniard, I think, an obscure jobber at the Bourse, whose sensual, blobberlipped mouth is so disquieting. And there are others and others, adventurers and bandits from the four corners of the earth!... Ah! the foreign colonies of our Parisian pleasure-world! There are a few spotless fine names, a few real great fortunes among them, but as for the rest, ah! what a herd!"

Rosemonde's own drawing-room was summed up in those words: resounding titles, real millionaires, then, down below, the most extravagant medley of international imposture and turpitude. And Pierre thought of that internationalism, that cosmopolitanism, that flight of foreigners which, ever denser and denser, swooped down upon Paris. Most certainly it came thither to enjoy it, as to a city of adventure and delight, and it helped to rot it a little more. Was it then a necessary thing, that decomposition of the great cities which have governed the world, that affluxion of every passion, every desire, every gratification, that accumulation of reeking soil from all parts of the world, there where, in beauty and intelligence, blooms the flower of civilisation?

However, Janzen appeared, a tall, thin fellow of about thirty, very fair with grey, pale, harsh eyes, and a pointed beard and flowing curly hair which elongated his livid, cloudy face. He spoke indifferent French in a low voice and without a gesture. And he declared that the Princess could not be found; he had looked for her everywhere. Possibly, if somebody had displeased her, she had shut herself up in her room and gone to bed, leaving her guests to amuse themselves in all freedom in whatever way they might choose.

"Why, but here she is!" suddenly said Massot.

Rosemonde was indeed there, in the vestibule, watching the door as if she expected somebody. Short, slight, and strange rather than pretty, with her delicate face, her sea-green eyes, her small quivering nose, her rather large and over-ruddy mouth, which was parted so that one could see her superb teeth, she that day wore a sky-blue gown spangled with silver; and she had silver bracelets on her arms and a silver circlet in her pale brown hair, which rained down in curls and frizzy, straggling locks as though waving in a perpetual breeze.

"Oh! whatever you desire, Monsieur l'Abbe," she said to Pierre as soon as she knew his business. "If they don't take your old man in at our asylum, send him to me, I'll take him, I will; I will sleep him somewhere here."

Still, she remained disturbed, and continually glanced towards the door. And on the priest asking if Baroness Duvillard had yet arrived, "Why no!" she cried, "and I am much surprised at it. She is to bring her son and daughter. Yesterday, Hyacinthe positively promised me that he would come."

There lay her new caprice. If her passion for chemistry was giving way to a budding taste for decadent, symbolical verse, it was because one evening, whilst discussing Occultism with Hyacinthe, she had discovered an extraordinary beauty in him: the astral beauty of Nero's wandering soul! At least, said she, the signs of it were certain.

And all at once she quitted Pierre: "Ah, at last!" she cried, feeling relieved and happy. Then she darted forward: Hyacinthe was coming in with his sister Camille.

On the very threshold, however, he had just met the friend on whose account he was there, young Lord George Eldrett, a pale and languid stripling with the hair of a girl; and he scarcely condescended to notice the tender greeting of Rosemonde, for he professed to regard woman as an impure and degrading creature. Distressed by such coldness, she followed the two young men, returning in their rear into the reeking, blinding furnace of the drawing-room.

Massot, however, had been obliging enough to stop Camille and bring her to Pierre, who at the first words they exchanged relapsed into despair. "What, mademoiselle, has not madame your mother accompanied you here?"

The girl, clad according to her wont in a dark gown, this time of peacock-blue, was nervous, with wicked eyes and sibilant voice. And as she ragefully drew up her little figure, her deformity, her left shoulder higher than the right one, became more apparent than ever. "No," she rejoined, "she was unable. She had something to try on at her dressmaker's. We stopped too long at the Exposition du Lis, and she requested us to set her down at Salmon's door on our way here."

It was Camille herself who had skilfully prolonged the visit to the art show, still hoping to prevent her mother from meeting Gerard. And her rage arose from the ease with which her mother had got rid of her, thanks to that falsehood of having something to try on.

"But," ingenuously said Pierre, "if I went at once to this person Salmon, I might perhaps be able to send up my card."

Camille gave a shrill laugh, so funny did the idea appear to her. Then she retorted: "Oh! who knows if you would still find her there? She had another pressing appointment, and is no doubt already keeping it!"

"Well, then, I will wait for her here. She will surely come to fetch you, will she not?"

"Fetch us? Oh no! since I tell you that she has other important affairs to attend to. The carriage will take us home alone, my brother and I."

Increasing bitterness was infecting the girl's pain-fraught irony. Did he not understand her then, that priest who asked such naive questions which were like dagger-thrusts in her heart? Yet he must know, since everybody knew the truth.

"Ah! how worried I am," Pierre resumed, so grieved indeed that tears almost came to his eyes. "It's still on account of that poor man about whom I have been busying myself since this morning. I have a line from your father, and Monsieur Gerard told me—" But at this point he paused in confusion, and amidst all his thoughtlessness of the world, absorbed as he was in the one passion of charity, he suddenly divined the truth. "Yes," he added mechanically, "I just now saw your father again with Monsieur de Quinsac."

"I know, I know," replied Camille, with the suffering yet scoffing air of a girl who is ignorant of nothing. "Well, Monsieur l'Abbe, if you have a line from papa for mamma, you must wait till mamma has finished her business. You might come to the house about six o'clock, but I doubt if you'll find her there, as she may well be detained."

While Camille thus spoke, her murderous eyes glistened, and each word she uttered, simple as it seemed, became instinct with ferocity, as if it were a knife, which she would have liked to plunge into her mother's breast. In all certainty she had never before hated her mother to such a point as this in her envy of her beauty and her happiness in being loved. And the irony which poured from the girl's virgin lips, before that simple priest, was like a flood of mire with which she sought to submerge her rival.

Just then, however, Rosemonde came back again, feverish and flurried as usual. And she led Camille away: "Ah, my dear, make haste. They are extraordinary, delightful, intoxicating!"

Janzen and little Massot also followed the Princess. All the men hastened from the adjoining rooms, scrambled and plunged into the *salon* at the news that the Mauritanians had again begun to dance. That time it must have been the frantic, lascivious gallop that Paris whispered about, for Pierre saw the rows of necks and heads, now fair, now dark, wave and quiver as beneath a violent wind. With every window-shutter closed, the conflagration of the electric lamps turned the place into a perfect brazier, reeking with human effluvia. And there came a spell of rapture, fresh laughter and bravos, all the delight of an overflowing orgy.

When Pierre again found himself on the footwalk, he remained for a moment bewildered, blinking, astonished to be in broad daylight once more. Half-past four would soon strike, but he had nearly two hours to wait before calling at the house in the Rue Godot-de-Mauroy. What should he do? He paid his driver; preferring to descend the Champs Elysees on foot, since he had some time to lose. A walk, moreover, might calm the fever which was burning his hands, in the passion of charity which ever since the morning had been mastering him more and more, in proportion as he encountered fresh and fresh obstacles. He now had but one pressing desire, to complete his good work, since success henceforth seemed certain. And he tried to restrain his steps and walk leisurely down the magnificent avenue, which had now been dried by the bright sun, and was enlivened by a concourse of people, while overhead the sky was again blue, lightly blue, as in springtime.

Nearly two hours to lose while, yonder, the wretched Laveuve lay with life ebbing from him on his bed of rags, in his icy den. Sudden feelings of revolt, of well-nigh irresistible impatience ascended from Pierre's heart, making him quiver with desire to run off and at once find Baroness Duvillard so as to obtain from her the all-saving order. He felt sure that she was somewhere near, in one of those quiet neighbouring streets, and great was his perturbation, his grief-fraught anger at having to wait in this wise to save a human life until she should have attended to those affairs of hers, of which her daughter spoke with such murderous glances! He seemed to hear a formidable cracking, the family life of the *bourgeoisie* was collapsing: the father was at a hussy's house, the mother with a lover, the son and daughter knew everything; the former gliding to idiotic perversity, the latter enraged and dreaming of stealing her mother's lover to make a husband of him. And meantime the splendid equipages descended the triumphal avenue, and the crowd with its luxury flowed along the sidewalks, one and all joyous and superb, seemingly with no idea that somewhere at the far end there was a gaping abyss wherein everyone of them would fall and be annihilated!

When Pierre got as far as the Summer Circus he was much surprised at again seeing Salvat, the journeyman engineer, on one of the avenue seats. He must have sunk down there, overcome by weariness and hunger, after many a vain search. However, his jacket was still distended by something he carried in or under it, some bit of bread, no doubt, which he meant to take home with him. And leaning back, with his arms hanging listlessly, he was watching with dreamy eyes the play of some very little children, who, with the help of their wooden spades, were laboriously raising mounds of sand, and then destroying them by dint of kicks. As he looked at them his red eyelids moistened, and a very gentle smile appeared on his poor discoloured lips. This time Pierre, penetrated by disquietude, wished to approach and question him. But Salvat distrustfully rose and went off towards the Circus, where a concert was drawing to a close; and he prowled around the entrance of that festive edifice in which two thousand happy people were heaped up together listening to music.

V. FROM RELIGION TO ANARCHY

AS Pierre was reaching the Place de la Concorde he suddenly remembered the appointment which Abbe Rose had given him for five o'clock at the Madeleine, and which he was forgetting in the feverishness born of his repeated steps to save Laveuve. And at thought of it he hastened on, well pleased at having this appointment to occupy and keep him patient.

When he entered the church he was surprised to find it so dark. There were only a few candles burning, huge shadows were flooding the nave, and amidst the semi-obscurity a very loud, clear voice spoke on with a ceaseless streaming of words. All that one could at first distinguish of the numerous congregation was a pale, vague mass of heads, motionless with extreme attention. In the pulpit stood Monseigneur Martha, finishing his third address on the New Spirit. The two former ones had re-echoed far and wide, and so what is called "all Paris" was there—women of society, politicians, and writers, who were captivated by the speaker's artistic oratory, his warm, skilful language, and his broad, easy gestures, worthy of a great actor.

Pierre did not wish to disturb the solemn attention, the quivering silence above which the prelate's voice alone rang out. Accordingly he resolved to wait before seeking Abbe Rose, and remained standing near a pillar. A parting gleam of daylight fell obliquely on Monseigneur Martha, who looked tall and sturdy in his white surplice, and scarcely showed a grey hair, although he was more than fifty. He had handsome features: black, keen eyes, a commanding nose, a mouth and chin of the greatest firmness of contour. What more particularly struck one, however, what gained the heart of every listener, was the expression of extreme amiability and anxious sympathy which ever softened the imperious haughtiness of the prelate's face.

Pierre had formerly known him as Cure, or parish priest, of Ste. Clotilde. He was doubtless of Italian origin, but he had been born in Paris, and had quitted the seminary of St. Sulpice with the best possible record. Very intelligent and very ambitious, he had evinced an activity which even made his superiors anxious. Then, on being appointed Bishop of Persepolis, he had disappeared, gone to Rome, where he had spent five years engaged in work of which very little was known. However, since his return he had been astonishing Paris by his brilliant propaganda, busying himself with the most varied affairs, and becoming much appreciated and very powerful at the archiepiscopal residence. He devoted himself in particular, and with wonderful results, to the task of increasing the subscriptions for the completion of the basilica of the Sacred Heart. He recoiled from nothing, neither from journeys, nor lectures, nor collections, nor applications to Government, nor even endeavours among Israelites and Freemasons. And at last, again enlarging his sphere of action, he had undertaken to reconcile Science with Catholicism, and to bring all Christian France to the Republic, on all sides expounding the policy of Pope Leo XIII., in order that the Church might finally triumph.

However, in spite of the advances of this influential and amiable man, Pierre scarcely liked him. He only felt grateful to him for one thing, the appointment of good Abbe Rose as curate at St. Pierre de Montmartre, which appointment he had secured for him no doubt in order to prevent such a scandal as the punishment of an old priest for showing himself too charitable. On thus finding and hearing the prelate speak in that renowned pulpit of the Madeleine, still and ever pursuing his work of conquest, Pierre remembered how he had seen him at the Duvillards' during the previous spring, when, with his usual *maestria*, he had achieved his greatest triumph—the conversion of Eve to Catholicism. That church, too, had witnessed her baptism, a wonderfully pompous ceremony, a perfect gala offered to the public which figures in all the great events of Parisian life. Gerard had knelt down, moved to tears, whilst the Baron triumphed like a good-natured husband who was happy to find religion establishing perfect harmony in his household. It was related among the spectators that Eve's family, and particularly old Justus Steinberger, her father, was not in reality much displeased by the affair. The old man sneeringly remarked, indeed, that he knew his daughter well enough to wish her to belong to his worst enemy. In the banking business there is a class of security which one is pleased to see discounted by one's rivals. With the stubborn hope of triumph peculiar to his race, Justus, consoling himself for the failure of his first scheme, doubtless considered that Eve would prove a powerful dissolving agent in the Christian family which she had entered, and thus help to make all wealth and power fall into the hands of the Jews.

However, Pierre's vision faded. Monseigneur Martha's voice was rising with increase of volume, celebrating, amidst the quivering of the congregation, the benefits that would accrue from the New Spirit, which was at last about to pacify France and restore her to her due rank and power. Were there not certain signs of this resurrection on every hand? The New Spirit was the revival of the Ideal, the protest of the soul against degrading materialism, the triumph of spirituality over filthy literature; and it was also Science accepted, but set in its proper place, reconciled with Faith, since it no longer pretended to encroach on the latter's sacred domain; and it was further the Democracy welcomed in fatherly fashion, the Republic legitimated, recognised in her turn as Eldest Daughter of the Church. A breath of poetry passed by. The Church opened her heart to all her children, there would henceforth be but concord and delight if the masses, obedient to the New Spirit, would give themselves to the Master of love as they had given themselves to their kings, recognising that the Divinity was the one unique power, absolute sovereign of both body and soul.

Pierre was now listening attentively, wondering where it was that he had previously heard almost identical words. And suddenly he remembered; and could fancy that he was again at Rome, listening to the last words of Monsignor Nani, the Assessor of the Holy Office. Here, again, he found the dream of a democratic Pope, ceasing to support the compromised monarchies, and seeking to subdue the masses. Since Caesar was down, or nearly so, might not the Pope realise the ancient ambition of his forerunners and become both emperor and pontiff, the sovereign, universal divinity on earth? This, too, was the dream in which Pierre himself, with apostolic naivete, had indulged when writing his book, "New Rome": a dream from which the sight of the real Rome had so roughly roused him. At bottom it was merely a policy of hypocritical falsehood, the priestly policy which relies on time, and is ever tenacious, carrying on the work of conquest with extraordinary suppleness, resolved to profit by everything. And what an evolution it was, the Church of Rome making advances to Science, to the Democracy, to the Republican *regimes*, convinced that it would be able to devour them if only it were allowed the time! Ah! yes, the New Spirit was simply the Old Spirit of Domination, incessantly reviving and hungering to conquer and possess the world.

Pierre thought that he recognised among the congregation certain deputies whom he had seen at the Chamber. Wasn't that tall gentleman with the fair beard, who listened so devoutly, one of Monferrand's creatures? It was said that Monferrand, once a devourer of priests, was now smilingly coquetting with the clergy. Quite an underhand evolution was beginning in the sacristies, orders from Rome flitted hither and thither; it was a question of accepting the new form of government, and absorbing it by dint of invasion. France was still the Eldest Daughter of the Church, the only great nation which had sufficient health and strength to place the Pope in possession of his temporal power once more. So France must be won; it was well worth one's while to espouse her, even if she were Republican. In the eager struggle of ambition the bishop made use of the minister, who thought it to his interest to lean upon the bishop. But which of the two would end by devouring the other? And to what a *role* had religion sunk: an electoral weapon, an element in a parliamentary majority, a decisive, secret reason for obtaining or retaining a ministerial portfolio! Of divine charity, the basis of religion, there was no thought, and Pierre's heart filled with bitterness as he remembered the recent death of Cardinal Bergerot, the last of the great saints and pure minds of the French episcopacy, among which there now seemed to be merely a set of intriguers and fools.

However, the address was drawing to a close. In a glowing peroration, which evoked the basilica of the Sacred Heart dominating Paris with the saving symbol of the Cross from the sacred Mount of the Martyrs,[1] Monseigneur Martha showed that great city of Paris Christian once more and master of the world, thanks to the moral omnipotence conferred upon it by the divine breath of the New Spirit. Unable to applaud, the congregation gave utterance to a murmur of approving rapture, delighted as it was with this miraculous finish which reassured both pocket and conscience. Then Monseigneur Martha quitted the pulpit with a noble step, whilst a loud noise of chairs broke upon the dark peacefulness of the church, where the few lighted candles glittered like the first stars in the evening sky. A long stream of men, vague, whispering shadows, glided away. The women alone remained, praying on their knees.

Pierre, still in the same spot, was rising on tip-toes, looking for Abbe Rose, when a hand touched him. It was that of the old priest, who had seen him from a distance. "I was yonder near the pulpit," said he, "and I saw you plainly, my dear child. Only I preferred to wait so as to disturb nobody. What a beautiful address dear Monseigneur delivered!"

---

[1] Montmartre.

He seemed, indeed, much moved. But there was deep sadness about his kindly mouth and clear childlike eyes, whose smile as a rule illumined his good, round white face. "I was afraid you might go off without seeing me," he resumed, "for I have something to tell you. You know that poor old man to whom I sent you this morning and in whom I asked you to interest yourself? Well, on getting home I found a lady there, who sometimes brings me a little money for my poor. Then I thought to myself that the three francs I gave you were really too small a sum, and as the thought worried me like a kind of remorse, I couldn't resist the impulse, but went this afternoon to the Rue des Saules myself."

He lowered his voice from a feeling of respect, in order not to disturb the deep, sepulchral silence of the church. Covert shame, moreover, impeded his utterance, shame at having again relapsed into the sin of blind, imprudent charity, as his superiors reproachfully said. And, quivering, he concluded in a very low voice indeed: "And so, my child, picture my grief. I had five francs more to give the poor old man, and I found him dead."

Pierre suddenly shuddered. But he was unwilling to understand: "What, dead!" he cried. "That old man dead! Laveuve dead?"

"Yes, I found him dead—ah! amidst what frightful wretchedness, like an old animal that has laid itself down for the finish on a heap of rags in the depths of a hole. No neighbours had assisted him in his last moments; he had simply turned himself towards the wall. And ah! how bare and cold and deserted it was! And what a pang for a poor creature to go off like that without a word, a caress. Ah! my heart bounded within me and it is still bleeding!"

Pierre in his utter amazement at first made but a gesture of revolt against imbecile social cruelty. Had the bread left near the unfortunate wretch, and devoured too eagerly, perhaps, after long days of abstinence, been the cause of his death? Or was not this rather the fatal *denouement* of an ended life, worn away by labour and privation? However, what did the cause signify? Death had come and delivered the poor man. "It isn't he that I pity," Pierre muttered at last; "it is we—we who witness all that, we who are guilty of these abominations."

But good Abbe Rose was already becoming resigned, and would only think of forgiveness and hope. "No, no, my child, rebellion is evil. If we are all guilty we can only implore Providence to forget our faults. I had given you an appointment here hoping for good news; and it's I who come to tell you of that frightful thing. Let us be penitent and pray."

Then he knelt upon the flagstones near the pillar, in the rear of the praying women, who looked black and vague in the gloom. And he inclined his white head, and for a long time remained in a posture of humility.

But Pierre was unable to pray, so powerfully did revolt stir him. He did not even bend his knees, but remained erect and quivering. His heart seemed to have been crushed; not a tear came to his ardent eyes. So Laveuve had died yonder, stretched on his litter of rags, his hands clenched in his obstinate desire to cling to his life of torture, whilst he, Pierre, again glowing with the flame of charity, consumed by apostolic zeal, was scouring Paris to find him for the evening a clean bed on which he might be saved. Ah! the atrocious irony of it all! He must have been at the Duvillards' in the warm *salon*, all blue and silver, whilst the old man was expiring; and it was for a wretched corpse that he had then hastened to the Chamber of Deputies, to the Countess de Quinsac's, to that creature Silviane's, and to that creature Rosemonde's. And it was for that corpse, freed from life, escaped from misery as from prison, that he had worried people, broken in upon their egotism, disturbed the peace of some, threatened the pleasures of others! What was the use of hastening from the parliamentary den to the cold *salon* where the dust of the past was congealing; of going from the sphere of middle-class debauchery to that of cosmopolitan extravagance, since one always arrived too late, and saved people when they were already dead? How ridiculous to have allowed himself to be fired once more by that blaze of charity, that final conflagration, only the ashes of which he now felt within him? This time he thought he was dead himself; he was naught but an empty sepulchre.

And all the frightful void and chaos which he had felt that morning at the basilica of the Sacred Heart after his mass became yet deeper, henceforth unfathomable. If charity were illusory and useless the Gospel crumbled, the end of the Book was nigh. After centuries of stubborn efforts, Redemption through Christianity failed, and another means of salvation was needed by the world in presence of the exasperated thirst for justice which came from the duped and wretched nations. They would have no more of that deceptive paradise, the promise of which had so long served to prop up social iniquity; they demanded that the question of happiness should be decided upon this earth. But how? By means of what new religion, what combination between the sentiment of the Divine and the necessity for honouring life in its sovereignty and its fruitfulness? Therein lay the grievous, torturing problem, into the midst of which Pierre was sinking; he, a priest, severed by vows of chastity and superstition from the rest of mankind.

He had ceased to believe in the efficacy of alms; it was not sufficient that one should be charitable, henceforth one must be just. Given justice, indeed, horrid misery would disappear, and no such thing as charity would be needed. Most certainly there was no lack of compassionate hearts in that grievous city of Paris; charitable foundations sprouted forth there like green leaves at the first warmth of springtide. There were some for every age, every peril, every misfortune. Through the concern shown for mothers, children were succoured even before they were born; then came the infant and orphan asylums lavishly provided for all sorts of classes; and, afterwards, man was followed through his life, help was tendered on all sides, particularly as he grew old, by a multiplicity of asylums, almshouses, and refuges. And there were all the hands stretched out to the forsaken ones, the disinherited ones, even the criminals, all sorts of associations to protect the weak, societies for the prevention of crime, homes that offered hospitality to those who repented. Whether as regards the propagation of good deeds, the support of the young, the saving of life, the bestowal of pecuniary help, or the promotion of guilds, pages and pages would have been needed merely to particularise the extraordinary vegetation of charity that sprouted between the paving-stones of Paris with so fine a vigour, in which goodness of soul was mingled with social vanity. Still that could not matter, since charity redeemed and purified all. But how terrible the proposition that this charity was a useless mockery! What! after so many centuries of Christian charity not a sore had healed. Misery had only grown and spread, irritated even to rage. Incessantly aggravated, the evil was reaching the point when it would be impossible to tolerate it for another day, since social injustice was neither arrested nor even diminished thereby. And besides, if only one single old man died of cold and hunger, did not the social edifice, raised on the theory of charity, collapse? But one victim, and society was condemned, thought Pierre.

He now felt such bitterness of heart that he could remain no longer in that church where the shadows ever slowly fell, blurring the sanctuaries and the large pale images of Christ nailed upon the Cross. All was about to sink into darkness, and he could hear nothing beyond an expiring murmur of prayers, a plaint from the women who were praying on their knees, in the depths of the shrouding gloom.

At the same time he hardly liked to go off without saying a word to Abbe Rose, who in his entreaties born of simple faith left the happiness and peace of mankind to the good pleasure of the Invisible. However, fearing that he might disturb him, Pierre was making up his mind to retire, when the old priest of his own accord raised his head. "Ah, my child," said he, "how difficult it is to be good in a reasonable manner. Monseigneur Martha has scolded me again, and but for the forgiveness of God I should fear for my salvation."

For a moment Pierre paused under the porticus of the Madeleine, on the summit of the great flight of steps which, rising above the railings, dominates the Place. Before him was the Rue Royale dipping down to the expanse of the Place de la Concorde, where rose the obelisk and the pair of plashing fountains. And, farther yet, the paling colonnade of the Chamber of Deputies bounded the horizon. It was a vista of sovereign grandeur under that pale sky over which twilight was slowly stealing, and which seemed to broaden the thoroughfares, throw back the edifices, and lend them the quivering, soaring aspect of the palaces of dreamland. No other capital in the world could boast a scene of such aerial pomp, such grandiose magnificence, at that hour of vagueness, when falling night imparts to cities a dreamy semblance, the infinite of human immensity.

Motionless and hesitating in presence of the opening expanse, Pierre distressfully pondered as to whither he should go now that all which he had so passionately sought to achieve since the morning had suddenly crumbled away. Was he still bound for the Duvillard mansion in the Rue Godot-de-Mauroy? He no longer knew. Then the exasperating remembrance, with its cruel irony, returned to him. Since Laveuve was dead, of what use was it for him to kill time and perambulate the pavements pending the arrival of six o'clock? The idea that he had a home, and that the most simple course would be to return to it, did not even occur to him. He felt as if there were something of importance left for him to do, though he could not possibly tell what it might be. It seemed to him to be everywhere and yet very far away, to be so vague and so difficult of accomplishment that he would certainly never be in time or have sufficient power to do it. However, with heavy feet and tumultuous brain he descended the steps and, yielding to some obstinate impulse, began to walk through the flower-market, a late winter market where the first azaleas were opening with a little shiver. Some women were purchasing Nice roses and violets; and Pierre looked at them as if he were interested in all that soft, delicate, perfumed luxury. But suddenly he felt a horror of it and went off, starting along the Boulevards.

He walked straight before him without knowing why or whither. The falling darkness surprised him as if it were an unexpected phenomenon. Raising his eyes to the sky he felt astonished at seeing its azure gently pale between the slender black streaks of the chimney funnels. And the huge golden letters by which names or trades were advertised on every balcony also seemed to him singular in the last gleams of the daylight. Never before had he paid attention to the motley tints seen on the house-fronts, the painted mirrors, the blinds, the coats of arms, the posters of violent hues, the magnificent shops, like drawing-rooms and boudoirs open to the full light. And then, both in the roadway and along the foot-pavements, between the blue, red or yellow columns and kiosks, what mighty traffic there was, what an extraordinary crowd! The vehicles rolled along in a thundering stream: on all sides billows of cabs were parted by the ponderous tacking of huge omnibuses, which suggested lofty, bright-hued battle-ships. And on either hand, and farther and farther, and even among the wheels, the flood of passengers rushed on incessantly, with the conquering haste of ants in a state of revolution. Whence came all those people, and whither were all those vehicles going? How stupefying and torturing it all was.

Pierre was still walking straight ahead, mechanically, carried on by his gloomy reverie. Night was coming, the first gas-burners were being lighted; it was the dusk of Paris, the hour when real darkness has not yet come, when the electric lights flame in the dying day. Lamps shone forth on all sides, the shop-fronts were being illumined. Soon, moreover, right along the Boulevards the vehicles would carry their vivid starry lights, like a milky way on the march betwixt the foot-pavements all glowing with lanterns and cordons and girandoles, a dazzling profusion of radiance akin to sunlight. And the shouts of the drivers and the jostling of the foot passengers re-echoed the parting haste of the Paris which is all business or passion, which is absorbed in the merciless struggle for love and for money. The hard day was over, and now the Paris of Pleasure was lighting up for its night of *fete*. The cafes, the wine shops, the restaurants, flared and displayed their bright metal bars, and their little white tables behind their clear and lofty windows, whilst near their doors, by way of temptation, were oysters and choice fruits. And the Paris which was thus awaking with the first flashes of the gas was already full of the gaiety of enjoyment, already yielding to an unbridled appetite for whatsoever may be purchased.

However, Pierre had a narrow escape from being knocked down. A flock of newspaper hawkers came out of a side street, and darted through the crowd shouting the titles of the evening journals. A fresh edition of the "Voix du Peuple" gave rise, in particular, to a deafening clamour, which rose above all the rumbling of wheels. At regular intervals hoarse voices raised and repeated the cry: "Ask for the 'Voix du Peuple'—the new scandal of the African Railway Lines, the repulse of the ministry, the thirty-two bribe-takers of the Chamber and the Senate!" And these announcements, set in huge type, could be read on the copies of the paper, which the hawkers flourished like banners. Accustomed as it was to such filth, saturated with infamy, the crowd continued on its way without paying much attention. Still a few men paused and bought the paper, while painted women, who had come down to the Boulevards in search of a dinner, trailed their skirts and waited for some chance lover, glancing interrogatively at the outside customers of the cafes. And meantime the dishonouring shout of the newspaper hawkers, that cry in which there was both smirch and buffet, seemed like the last knell of the day, ringing the nation's funeral at the outset of the night of pleasure which was beginning.

Then Pierre once more remembered his morning and that frightful house in the Rue des Saules, where so much want and suffering were heaped up. He again saw the yard filthy like a quagmire, the evil-smelling staircases, the sordid, bare, icy rooms, the families fighting for messes which even stray dogs would not have eaten; the mothers, with exhausted breasts, carrying screaming children to and fro; the old men who fell in corners like brute beasts, and died of hunger amidst filth. And then came his other hours with the magnificence or the quietude or the gaiety of the *salons* through which he had passed, the whole insolent display of financial Paris, and political Paris, and society Paris. And at last he came to the dusk, and to that Paris-Sodom and Paris-Gomorrah before him, which was lighting itself up for the night, for the abominations of that accomplice night which, like fine dust, was little by little submerging the expanse of roofs. And the hateful monstrosity of it all howled aloud under the pale sky where the first pure, twinkling stars were gleaming.

A great shudder came upon Pierre as he thought of all that mass of iniquity and suffering, of all that went on below amid want and crime, and all that went on above amid wealth and vice. The *bourgeoisie*, wielding power, would relinquish naught of the sovereignty which it had conquered, wholly stolen, while the people, the eternal dupe, silent so long, clenched its fists and growled, claiming its legitimate share. And it was that frightful injustice which filled the growing gloom with anger. From what dark-breasted cloud would the thunderbolt fall? For years he had been waiting for that thunderbolt which low rumbles announced on all points of the horizon. And if he had written a book full of candour and hope, if he had gone in all innocence to Rome, it was to avert that thunderbolt and its frightful consequences. But all hope of the kind was dead within him; he felt that the thunderbolt was inevitable, that nothing henceforth could stay the catastrophe. And never before had he felt it to be so near, amidst the happy impudence of some, and the exasperated distress of others. And it was gathering, and it would surely fall over that Paris, all lust and bravado, which, when evening came, thus stirred up its furnace.

Tired out and distracted, Pierre raised his eyes as he reached the Place de l'Opera. Where was he then? The heart of the great city seemed to beat on this spot, in that vast expanse where met so many thoroughfares, as if from every point the blood of distant districts flowed thither along triumphal avenues. Right away to the horizon stretched the great gaps of the Avenue de l'Opera, the Rue du Quatre-Septembre, and the Rue de la Paix, still showing clearly in a final glimpse of daylight, but already starred with swarming sparks. The torrent of the Boulevard traffic poured across the Place, where clashed, too, all that from the neighbouring streets, with a constant turning and eddying which made the spot the most dangerous of whirlpools. In vain did the police seek to impose some little prudence, the stream of pedestrians still overflowed, wheels became entangled and horses reared amidst all the uproar of the human tide, which was as loud, as incessant, as the tempest voice of an ocean. Then there was the detached mass of the opera-house, slowly steeped in gloom, and rising huge and mysterious like a symbol, its lyre-bearing figure of Apollo, right aloft, showing a last reflection of daylight amidst the livid sky. And all the windows of the house-fronts began to shine, gaiety sprang from those thousands of lamps which coruscated one by one, a universal longing for ease and free gratification of each desire spread with the increasing darkness; whilst, at long intervals, the large globes of the electric lights shone as brightly as the moons of the city's cloudless nights.

But why was he, Pierre, there, he asked himself, irritated and wondering. Since Laveuve was dead he had but to go home, bury himself in his nook, and close up door and windows, like one who was henceforth useless, who had neither belief nor hope, and awaited naught save annihilation. It was a long journey from the Place de l'Opera to his little house at Neuilly. Still, however great his weariness, he would not take a cab, but retraced his steps, turning towards the Madeleine again, and plunging into the scramble of the pavements, amidst the deafening uproar from the roadway, with a bitter desire to aggravate his wound and saturate himself with revolt and anger. Was it not yonder at the corner of that street, at the end of that Boulevard, that he would find the expected abyss into which that rotten world, whose old society he could hear rending at each step, must soon assuredly topple?

However, when Pierre wished to cross the Rue Scribe a block in the traffic made him halt. In front of a luxurious cafe two tall, shabbily-clad and very dirty fellows were alternately offering the "Voix du Peuple" with its account of the scandals and the bribe-takers of the Chamber and the Senate, in voices so suggestive of cracked brass that passers-by clustered around them. And here, in a hesitating, wandering man, who after listening drew near to the large cafe and peered through its windows, Pierre was once again amazed to recognise Salvat. This time the meeting struck him forcibly, filled him with suspicion to such a point that he also stopped and resolved to watch the journeyman engineer. He did not expect that one of such wretched aspect, with what seemed to be a hunk of bread distending his old ragged jacket, would enter and seat himself at one of the cafe's little tables amidst the warm gaiety of the lamps. However, he waited for a moment, and then saw him wander away with slow and broken steps as if the cafe, which was nearly empty, did not suit him. What could he have been seeking, whither had he been going, since the morning, ever on a wild, solitary chase through the Paris of wealth and enjoyment while hunger dogged his steps? It was only with difficulty that he now dragged himself along, his will and energy seemed to be exhausted. As if quite overcome, he drew near to a kiosk, and for a moment leant against it. Then, however, he drew himself up again, and walked on further, still as it were in search of something.

And now came an incident which brought Pierre's emotion to a climax. A tall sturdy man on turning out of the Rue Caumartin caught sight of Salvat, and approached him. And just as the new comer without false pride was shaking the workman's hand, Pierre recognised him as his brother Guillaume. Yes, it was indeed he, with his thick bushy hair already white like snow, though he was but seven and forty. However, his heavy moustaches had remained quite dark without one silver thread, thus lending an expression of vigorous life to his full face with its lofty towering brow. It was from his father that he had inherited that brow of impregnable logic and reason, similar to that which Pierre himself possessed. But the lower part of the elder brother's countenance was fuller than that of his junior; his nose was larger, his chin was square, and his mouth broad and firm of contour. A pale scar, the mark of an old wound, streaked his left temple. And his physiognomy, though it might at first seem very grave, rough, and unexpansive, beamed with masculine kindliness whenever a smile revealed his teeth, which had remained extremely white.

While looking at his brother, Pierre remembered what Madame Theodore had told him that morning. Guillaume, touched by Salvat's dire want, had arranged to give him a few days' employment. And this explained the air of interest with which he now seemed to be questioning him, while the engineer, whom the meeting disturbed, stamped about as if eager to resume his mournful ramble. For a moment Guillaume appeared to notice the other's perturbation, by the embarrassed answers which he obtained from him. Still, they at last parted as if each were going his way. Then, however, almost immediately, Guillaume turned round again and watched the other, as with harassed stubborn mien he went off through the crowd. And the thoughts which had come to Guillaume must have been very serious and very pressing, for he all at once began to retrace his steps and follow the workman from a distance, as if to ascertain for certain what direction he would take.

Pierre had watched the scene with growing disquietude. His nervous apprehension of some great unknown calamity, the suspicions born of his frequent and inexplicable meetings with Salvat, his surprise at now seeing his brother mingled with the affair, all helped to fill him with a pressing desire to know, witness, and perhaps prevent. So he did not hesitate, but began to follow the others in a prudent way.

Fresh perturbation came upon him when first Salvat and then Guillaume suddenly turned into the Rue Godot-de-Mauroy. What destiny was thus bringing him back to that street whither a little time previously he had wished to return in feverish haste, and whence only the death of Laveuve had kept him? And his consternation increased yet further when, after losing sight of Salvat for a moment, he saw him standing in front of the Duvillard mansion, on the same spot where he had fancied he recognised him that morning. As it happened the carriage entrance of the mansion was wide open. Some repairs had been made to the paving of the porch, and although the workmen had now gone off, the doorway remained gaping, full of the falling night. The narrow street, running from the glittering Boulevard, was steeped in bluish gloom, starred at long intervals by a few gas-lamps. Some women went by, compelling Salvat to step off the foot-pavement. But he returned to it again, lighted the stump of a cigar, some remnant which he had found under a table outside a cafe, and then resumed his watch, patient and motionless, in front of the mansion.

Disturbed by his dim conjectures, Pierre gradually grew frightened, and asked himself if he ought not to approach that man. The chief thing that detained him was the presence of his brother, whom he had seen disappear into a neighbouring doorway, whence he also was observing the engineer, ready to intervene. And so Pierre contented himself with not losing sight of Salvat, who was still waiting and watching, merely taking his eyes from the mansion in order to glance towards the Boulevard as though he expected someone or something which would come from that direction. And at last, indeed, the Duvillards' landau appeared, with coachman and footman in livery of green and gold—a closed landau to which a pair of tall horses of superb build were harnessed in stylish fashion.

Contrary to custom, however, the carriage, which at that hour usually brought the father and mother home, was only occupied that evening by the son and daughter, Hyacinthe and Camille. Returning from the Princess de Harn's *matinee*, they were chatting freely, with that calm immodesty by which they sought to astonish one another. Hyacinthe, influenced by his perverted ideas, was attacking women, whilst Camille openly counselled him to respond to the Princess's advances. However, she was visibly irritated and feverish that evening, and, suddenly changing the subject, she began to speak of their mother and Gerard de Quinsac.

"But what can it matter to you?" quietly retorted Hyacinthe; and, seeing that she almost bounded from the seat at this remark, he continued: "Are you still in love with him, then? Do you still want to marry him?"

"Yes, I do, and I will!" she cried with all the jealous rage of an uncomely girl, who suffered so acutely at seeing herself spurned whilst her yet beautiful mother stole from her the man she wanted.

"You will, you will!" resumed Hyacinthe, well pleased to have an opportunity of teasing his sister, whom he somewhat feared. "But you won't unless *he* is willing—And he doesn't care for you."

"He does!" retorted Camille in a fury. "He's kind and pleasant with me, and that's enough."

Her brother felt afraid as he noticed the blackness of her glance, and the clenching of her weak little hands, whose fingers bent like claws. And after a pause he asked: "And papa, what does he say about it?"

"Oh, papa! All that he cares about is the other one."

Then Hyacinthe began to laugh.

But the landau, with its tall horses trotting on sonorously, had turned into the street and was approaching the house, when a slim fair-haired girl of sixteen or seventeen, a modiste's errand girl with a large bandbox on her arm, hastily crossed the road in order to enter the arched doorway before the carriage. She was bringing a bonnet for the Baroness, and had come all along the Boulevard musing, with her soft blue eyes, her pinky nose, and her mouth which ever laughed in the most adorable little face that one could see. And it was at this same moment that Salvat, after another glance at the landau, sprang forward and entered the doorway. An instant afterwards he reappeared, flung his lighted cigar stump into the gutter; and without undue haste went off, slinking into the depths of the vague gloom of the street.

And then what happened? Pierre, later on, remembered that a dray of the Western Railway Company in coming up stopped and delayed the landau for a moment, whilst the young errand girl entered the doorway. And with a heart-pang beyond description he saw his brother Guillaume in his turn spring forward and rush into the mansion as though impelled to do so by some revelation, some sudden certainty. He, Pierre, though he understood nothing clearly, could divine the approach of some frightful horror. But when he would have run, when he would have shouted, he found himself as if nailed to the pavement, and felt his throat clutched as by a hand of lead. Then suddenly came a thunderous roar, a formidable explosion, as if the earth was opening, and the lightning-struck mansion was being annihilated. Every window-pane of the neighbouring houses was shivered, the glass raining down with the loud clatter of hail. For a moment a hellish flame fired the street, and the dust and the smoke were such that the few passers-by were blinded and howled with affright, aghast at toppling, as they thought, into that fiery furnace.

And that dazzling flare brought Pierre enlightenment. He once more saw the bomb distending the tool-bag, which lack of work had emptied and rendered useless. He once more saw it under the ragged jacket, a protuberance caused, he had fancied, by some hunk of bread, picked up in a corner and treasured that it might be carried home to wife and child. After wandering and threatening all happy Paris, it was there that it had flared, there that it had burst with a thunder-clap, there on the threshold of the sovereign *bourgeoisie* to whom all wealth belonged. He, however, at that moment thought only of his brother Guillaume, and flung himself into that porch where a volcanic crater seemed to have opened. And at first he distinguished nothing, the acrid smoke streamed over all. Then he perceived the walls split, the upper floor rent open, the paving broken up, strewn with fragments. Outside, the landau which had been on the point of entering, had escaped all injury; neither of the horses had been touched, nor was there even a scratch on any panel of the vehicle. But the young girl, the pretty, slim, fair-haired errand girl, lay there on her back, her stomach ripped open, whilst her delicate face remained intact, her eyes clear, her smile full of astonishment, so swiftly and lightning-like had come the catastrophe. And near her, from the fallen bandbox, whose lid had merely come unfastened, had rolled the bonnet, a very fragile pink bonnet, which still looked charming in its flowery freshness.

By a prodigy Guillaume was alive and already on his legs again. His left hand alone streamed with blood, a projectile seemed to have broken his wrist. His moustaches moreover had been burnt, and the explosion by throwing him to the ground had so shaken and bruised him that he shivered from head to feet as with intense cold. Nevertheless, he recognised his brother without even feeling astonished to see him there, as indeed often happens after great disasters, when the unexplained becomes providential. That brother, of whom he had so long lost sight, was there, naturally enough, because it was necessary that he should be there. And Guillaume, amidst the wild quivers by which he was shaken, at once cried to him "Take me away! take me away! To your house at Neuilly, oh! take me away!"

Then, for sole explanation, and referring to Salvat, he stammered: "I suspected that he had stolen a cartridge from me; only one, most fortunately, for otherwise the whole district would have been blown to pieces. Ah! the wretched fellow! I wasn't in time to set my foot upon the match."

With perfect lucidity of mind, such as danger sometimes imparts, Pierre, neither speaking nor losing a moment, remembered that the mansion had a back entrance fronting the Rue Vignon. He had just realised in what serious peril his brother would be if he were found mixed up in that affair. And with all speed, when he had led him into the gloom of the Rue Vignon, he tied his handkerchief round his wrist, which he bade him press to his chest, under his coat, as that would conceal it.

But Guillaume, still shivering and haunted by the horror he had witnessed, repeated: "Take me away—to your place at Neuilly—not to my home."

"Of course, of course, be easy. Come, wait here a second, I will stop a cab."

In his eagerness to procure a conveyance, Pierre had brought his brother down to the Boulevard again. But the terrible thunderclap of the explosion had upset the whole neighbourhood, horses were still rearing, and people were running demented, hither and thither. And numerous policemen had hastened up, and a rushing crowd was already blocking the lower part of the Rue Godot-de-Mauroy, which was now as black as a pit, every light in it having been extinguished; whilst on the Boulevard a hawker of the "Voix du Peuple" still stubbornly vociferated: "The new scandal of the African Railway Lines! The thirty-two bribe-takers of the Chamber and the Senate! The approaching fall of the ministry!"

Pierre was at last managing to stop a cab when he heard a person who ran by say to another, "The ministry? Ah, well! that bomb will mend it right enough!"

Then the brothers seated themselves in the cab, which carried them away. And now, over the whole of rumbling Paris black night had gathered, an unforgiving night, in which the stars foundered amidst the mist of crime and anger that had risen from the house-roofs. The great cry of justice swept by amidst the same terrifying flapping of wings which Sodom and Gomorrah once heard bearing down upon them from all the black clouds of the horizon.

BOOK II.

I. REVOLUTIONISTS

IN that out-of-the-way street at Neuilly, along which nobody passed after dusk, Pierre's little house was now steeped in deep slumber under the black sky; each of its shutters closed, and not a ray of light stealing forth from within. And one could divine, too, the profound quietude of the little garden in the rear, a garden empty and lifeless, benumbed by the winter cold.

Pierre had several times feared that his brother would faint away in the cab in which they were journeying. Leaning back, and often sinking down, Guillaume spoke not a word. And terrible was the silence between them—a silence fraught with all the questions and answers which they felt it would be useless and painful to exchange at such a time. However, the priest was anxious about the wound, and wondered to what surgeon he might apply, desirous as he was of admitting only a sure, staunch man into the secret, for he had noticed with how keen a desire to disappear his brother had sought to hide himself.

Until they reached the Arc de Triomphe the silence remained unbroken. It was only there that Guillaume seemed to emerge from the prostration of his reverie. "Mind, Pierre," said he, "no doctor. We will attend to this together."

Pierre was on the point of protesting, but he realised that it would be useless to discuss the subject at such a moment, and so he merely waved his hand to signify that he should act in spite of the prohibition were it necessary. In point of fact, his anxiety had increased, and, when the cab at last drew up before the house, it was with real relief that he saw his brother alight without evincing any marked feebleness. He himself quickly paid the driver, well-pleased, too, at finding that nobody, not even a neighbour, was about. And having opened the door with his latch key, he helped the injured man to ascend the steps.

A little night lamp glimmered faintly in the vestibule. On hearing the door open, Pierre's servant, Sophie, had at once emerged from the kitchen. A short, thin, dark woman of sixty, she had formed part of the household for more than thirty years, having served the mother before serving the son. She knew Guillaume, having seen him when he was a young man, and doubtless she now recognised him, although well-nigh ten years had gone by since he had last crossed that threshold. Instead of evincing any surprise, she seemed to consider his extraordinary return quite natural, and remained as silent and discreet as usual. She led, indeed, the life of a recluse, never speaking unless her work absolutely required it. And thus she now contented herself with saying: "Monsieur l'Abbe, Monsieur Bertheroy is in the study, and has been waiting there for a quarter of an hour."

At this Guillaume intervened, as if the news revived him: "Does Bertheroy still come here, then? I'll see him willingly. His is one of the best, the broadest, minds of these days. He has still remained my master."

A former friend of their father,—the illustrious chemist, Michel Froment,—Bertheroy had now, in his turn, become one of the loftiest glories of France, one to whom chemistry owed much of the extraordinary progress that has made it the mother-science, by which the very face of the earth is being changed. A member of the Institute, laden with offices and honours, he had retained much affection for Pierre, and occasionally visited him in this wise before dinner, by way of relaxation, he would say.

"You showed him into the study? All right, then, we will go there," said the Abbe to the servant. "Light a lamp and take it into my room, and get my bed ready so that my brother may go to bed at once."

While Sophie, without a word or sign of surprise, was obeying these instructions, the brothers went into their father's former laboratory, of which the priest had now made a spacious study. And it was with a cry of joyous astonishment that the *savant* greeted them on seeing them enter the room side by side, the one supporting the other. "What, together!" he exclaimed. "Ah! my dear children, you could not have caused me greater pleasure! I who have so often deplored your painful misunderstanding."

Bertheroy was a tall and lean septuagenarian, with angular features. His yellow skin clung like parchment to the projecting bones of his cheeks and jaw. Moreover, there was nothing imposing about him; he looked like some old shop-keeping herbalist. At the same time he had a fine, broad, smooth brow, and his eyes still glittered brightly beneath his tangled hair.

"What, have you injured yourself, Guillaume?" he continued, as soon as he saw the bandaged hand.

Pierre remained silent, so as to let his brother tell the story as he chose. Guillaume had realised that he must confess the truth, but in simple fashion, without detailing the circumstances. "Yes, in an explosion," he answered, "and I really think that I have my wrist broken."

At this, Bertheroy, whose glance was fixed upon him, noticed that his moustaches were burnt, and that there was an expression of bewildered stupor, such as follows a catastrophe, in his eyes. Forthwith the *savant* became grave and circumspect; and, without seeking to compel confidence by any questions, he simply said: "Indeed! an explosion! Will you let me see the injury? You know that before letting chemistry ensnare me I studied medicine, and am still somewhat of a surgeon."

On hearing these words Pierre could not restrain a heart-cry: "Yes, yes, master! Look at the injury—I was very anxious, and to find you here is unhoped-for good fortune!"

The *savant* glanced at him, and divined that the hidden circumstances of the accident must be serious. And then, as Guillaume, smiling, though paling with weakness, consented to the suggestion, Bertheroy retorted that before anything else he must be put to bed. The servant just then returned to say the bed was ready, and so they all went into the adjoining room, where the injured man was soon undressed and helped between the sheets.

"Light me, Pierre," said Bertheroy, "take the lamp; and let Sophie give me a basin full of water and some cloths." Then, having gently washed the wound, he resumed: "The devil! The wrist isn't broken, but it's a nasty injury. I am afraid there must be a lesion of the bone. Some nails passed through the flesh, did they not?"

Receiving no reply, he relapsed into silence. But his surprise was increasing, and he closely examined the hand, which the flame of the explosion had scorched, and even sniffed the shirt cuff as if seeking to understand the affair better. He evidently recognised the effects of one of those new explosives which he himself had studied, almost created. In the present case, however, he must have been puzzled, for there were characteristic signs and traces the significance of which escaped him.

"And so," he at last made up his mind to ask, carried away by professional curiosity, "and so it was a laboratory explosion which put you in this nice condition? What devilish powder were you concocting then?"

Guillaume, ever since he had seen Bertheroy thus studying his injury, had, in spite of his sufferings, given marked signs of annoyance and agitation. And as if the real secret which he wished to keep lay precisely in the question now put to him, in that powder, the first experiment with which had thus injured him, he replied with an air of restrained ardour, and a straight frank glance: "Pray do not question me, master. I cannot answer you. You have, I know, sufficient nobility of nature to nurse me and care for me without exacting a confession."

"Oh! certainly, my friend," exclaimed Bertheroy; "keep your secret. Your discovery belongs to you if you have made one; and I know that you are capable of putting it to the most generous use. Besides, you must be aware that I have too great a passion for truth to judge the actions of others, whatever their nature, without knowing every circumstance and motive."

So saying, he waved his hand as if to indicate how broadly tolerant and free from error and superstition was that lofty sovereign mind of his, which in spite of all the orders that bedizened him, in spite of all the academical titles that he bore as an official *savant*, made him a man of the boldest and most independent views, one whose only passion was truth, as he himself said.

He lacked the necessary appliances to do more than dress the wound, after making sure that no fragment of any projectile had remained in the flesh. Then he at last went off, promising to return at an early hour on the morrow; and, as the priest escorted him to the street door, he spoke some comforting words: if the bone had not been deeply injured all would be well.

On returning to the bedside, Pierre found his brother still sitting up and seeking fresh energy in his desire to write home and tranquillise his loved ones. So the priest, after providing pen and paper, again had to take up the lamp and light him. Guillaume fortunately retained full use of his right hand, and was thus able to pen a few lines to say that he would not be home that night. He addressed the note to Madame Leroi, the mother of his deceased mistress, who, since the latter's death, had remained with him and had reared his three sons. Pierre was aware also that the household at Montmartre included a young woman of five or six and twenty, the daughter of an old friend, to whom Guillaume had given shelter on her father's death, and whom he was soon to marry, in spite of the great difference in their ages. For the priest, however, all these were vague, disturbing things, condemnable features of disorderly life, and he had invariably pretended to be ignorant of them.

"So you wish this note to be taken to Montmartre at once?" he said to his brother.

"Yes, at once. It is scarcely more than seven o'clock now, and it will be there by eight. And you will choose a reliable man, won't you?"

"The best course will be for Sophie to take a cab. We need have no fear with her. She won't chatter. Wait a moment, and I will settle everything."

Sophie, on being summoned, at once understood what was wanted of her, and promised to say, in reply to any questions, that M. Guillaume had come to spend the night at his brother's, for reasons which she did not know. And without indulging in any reflections herself, she left the house, saying simply: "Monsieur l'Abbe's dinner is ready; he will only have to take the broth and the stew off the stove."

However, when Pierre this time returned to the bedside to sit down there, he found that Guillaume had fallen back with his head resting on both pillows. And he looked very weary and pale, and showed signs of fever. The lamp, standing on a corner of a side table, cast a soft light around, and so deep was the quietude that the big clock in the adjoining dining-room could be heard ticking. For a moment the silence continued around the two brothers, who, after so many years of separation, were at last re-united and alone together. Then the injured man brought his right hand to the edge of the sheet, and the priest grasped it, pressed it tenderly in his own. And the clasp was a long one, those two brotherly hands remaining locked, one in the other.

"My poor little Pierre," Guillaume faintly murmured, "you must forgive me for falling on you in this fashion. I've invaded the house and taken your bed, and I'm preventing you from dining."

"Don't talk, don't tire yourself any more," interrupted Pierre. "Is not this the right place for you when you are in trouble?"

A warmer pressure came from Guillaume's feverish hand, and tears gathered in his eyes. "Thanks, my little Pierre. I've found you again, and you are as gentle and loving as you always were. Ah! you cannot know how delightful it seems to me."

Then the priest's eyes also were dimmed by tears. Amidst the deep quietude, the great sense of comfort which had followed their violent emotion, the brothers found an infinite charm in being together once more in the home of their childhood.[1] It was there that both their father and mother had died—the father tragically, struck down by an explosion in his laboratory; the mother piously, like a very saint. It was there, too, in that same bed, that Guillaume had nursed Pierre, when, after their mother's death, the latter had nearly died; and it was there now that Pierre in his turn was nursing Guillaume. All helped to bow them down and fill them with emotion: the strange circumstances of their meeting, the frightful catastrophe which had caused them such a shock, the mysteriousness of the things which remained unexplained between them. And now that after so long a separation they were tragically brought together again, they both felt their memory awaking. The old house spoke to them of their childhood, of their parents dead and gone, of the far-away days when they had loved and suffered there. Beneath the window lay the garden, now icy cold, which once, under the sunbeams, had re-echoed with their play. On the left was the laboratory, the spacious room where their father had taught them to read. On the right, in the dining-room, they could picture their mother cutting bread and butter for them, and looking so gen-

[1] See M. Zola's "Lourdes," Day I., Chapter II.

tle with her big, despairing eyes—those of a believer mated to an infidel. And the feeling that they were now alone in that home, and the pale, sleepy gleam of the lamp, and the deep silence of the garden and the house, and the very past itself, all filled them with the softest of emotion blended with the keenest bitterness.

They would have liked to talk and unbosom themselves. But what could they say to one another? Although their hands remained so tightly clasped, did not the most impassable of chasms separate them? In any case, they thought so. Guillaume was convinced that Pierre was a saint, a priest of the most robust faith, without a doubt, without aught in common with himself, whether in the sphere of ideas or in that of practical life. A hatchet-stroke had parted them, and each lived in a different world. And in the same way Pierre pictured Guillaume as one who had lost caste, whose conduct was most suspicious, who had never even married the mother of his three children, but was on the point of marrying that girl who was far too young for him, and who had come nobody knew whence. In him, moreover, were blended the passionate ideas of a *savant* and a revolutionist, ideas in which one found negation of everything, acceptance and possibly provocation of the worst forms of violence, with a glimpse of the vague monster of Anarchism underlying all. And so, on what basis could there be any understanding between them, since each retained his prejudices against the other, and saw him on the opposite side of the chasm, without possibility of any plank being thrown across it to enable them to unite? Thus, all alone in that room, their poor hearts bled with distracted brotherly love.

Pierre knew that, on a previous occasion, Guillaume had narrowly escaped being compromised in an Anarchist affair. He asked him no questions, but he could not help reflecting that he would not have hidden himself in this fashion had he not feared arrest for complicity. Complicity with Salvat? Was he really an accomplice? Pierre shuddered, for the only materials on which he could found a contrary opinion were, on one hand, the words that had escaped his brother after the crime, the cry he had raised accusing Salvat of having stolen a cartridge from him; and, on the other hand, his heroic rush into the doorway of the Duvillard mansion in order to extinguish the match. A great deal still remained obscure; but if a cartridge of that frightful explosive had been stolen from Guillaume the fact must be that he manufactured such cartridges and had others at home. Of course, even if he were not an accomplice, the injury to his wrist had made it needful for him to disappear. Given his bleeding hand, and the previous suspicions levelled against him, he would never have convinced anybody of his innocence. And yet, even allowing for these surmises, the affair remained wrapt in darkness: a crime on Guillaume's part seemed a possibility, and to Pierre it was all dreadful to think of.

Guillaume, by the trembling of his brother's moist, yielding hand, must in some degree have realised the prostration of his poor mind, already shattered by doubt and finished off by this calamity. Indeed, the sepulchre was empty now, the very ashes had been swept out of it.

"My poor little Pierre," the elder brother slowly said. "Forgive me if I do not tell you anything. I cannot do so. And besides, what would be the use of it? We should certainly not understand one another.... So let us keep from saying anything, and let us simply enjoy the delight of being together and loving one another in spite of all."

Pierre raised his eyes, and for a long time their glances lingered, one fixed on the other. "Ah!" stammered the priest, "how frightful it all is!"

Guillaume, however, had well understood the mute inquiry of Pierre's eyes. His own did not waver but replied boldly, beaming with purity and loftiness: "I can tell you nothing. Yet, all the same, let us love each other, my little Pierre."

And then Pierre for a moment felt that his brother was above all base anxiety, above the guilty fear of the man who trembles for himself. In lieu thereof he seemed to be carried away by the passion of some great design, the noble thought of concealing some sovereign idea, some secret which it was imperative for him to save. But, alas! this was only the fleeting vision of a vague hope; for all vanished, and again came the doubt, the suspicion, of a mind dealing with one that it knew nothing of.

And all at once a souvenir, a frightful spectacle, arose before Pierre's eyes and distracted him: "Did you see, brother," he stammered, "did you see that fair-haired girl lying under the archway, ripped open, with a smile of astonishment on her face?"

Guillaume in his turn quivered, and in a low and dolorous voice replied: "Yes, I saw her! Ah, poor little thing! Ah! the atrocious necessities, the atrocious errors, of justice!"

Then, amidst the frightful shudder that seemed to sweep by, Pierre, with his horror of all violence, succumbed, and let his face sink upon the counterpane at the edge of the bed. And he sobbed distractedly: a sudden attack of weakness, overflowing in tears, cast him there exhausted, with no more strength than a child. It was as if all his sufferings since the morning, the deep grief with which universal injustice and woe inspired him, were bursting forth in that flood of tears which nothing now could stay. And Guillaume, who, to calm his little brother, had set his hand upon his head, in the same way as he had often caressingly stroked his hair in childhood's days, likewise felt upset and remained silent, unable to find a word of consolation, resigned, as he was, to the eruption which in life is always possible, the cataclysm by which the slow evolution of nature is always liable to be precipitated. But how hard a fate for the wretched ones whom the lava sweeps away in millions! And then his tears also began to flow amidst the profound silence.

"Pierre," he gently exclaimed at last, "you must have some dinner. Go, go and have some. And screen the lamp; leave me by myself, and let me close my eyes. It will do me good."

Pierre had to content him. Still, he left the dining-room door open; and, weak for want of food, though he had not hitherto noticed it, he ate standing, with his ears on the alert, listening lest his brother should complain or call him. And the silence seemed to have become yet more complete, the little house sank, as it were, into annihilation, instinct with all the melancholy charm of the past.

At about half-past eight, when Sophie returned from her errand to Montmartre, Guillaume heard her step, light though it was. And he at once became restless and wanted to know what news she brought. It was Pierre, however, who enlightened him. "Don't be anxious. Sophie was received by an old lady who, after reading your note, merely answered, 'Very well.' She did not even ask Sophie a question, but remained quite composed without sign of curiosity."

Guillaume, realising that this fine serenity perplexed his brother, thereupon replied with similar calmness: "Oh! it was only necessary that grandmother should be warned. She knows well enough that if I don't return home it is because I can't."

However, from that moment it was impossible for the injured man to rest. Although the lamp was hidden away in a corner, he constantly opened his eyes, glanced round him, and seemed to listen, as if for sounds from the direction of Paris. And it at last became necessary for the priest to summon the servant and ask her if she had noticed anything strange on her way to or from Montmartre. She seemed surprised by the question, and answered that she had noticed nothing. Besides, the cab had followed the outer boulevards, which were almost deserted. A slight fog had again begun to fall, and the streets were steeped in icy dampness.

By the time it was nine o'clock Pierre realised that his brother would never be able to sleep if he were thus left without news. Amidst his growing feverishness the injured man experienced keen anxiety, a haunting desire to know if Salvat were arrested and had spoken out. He did not confess this; indeed he sought to convey the impression that he had no personal disquietude, which was doubtless true. But his great secret was stifling him; he shuddered at the thought that his lofty scheme, all his labour and all his hope, should be at the mercy of that unhappy man whom want had filled with delusions and who had sought to set justice upon earth by the aid of a bomb. And in vain did the priest try to make Guillaume understand that nothing certain could yet be known. He perceived that his impatience increased every minute, and at last resolved to make some effort to satisfy him.

But where could he go, of whom could he inquire? Guillaume, while talking and trying to guess with whom Salvat might have sought refuge, had mentioned Janzen, the Princess de Harn's mysterious lover; and for a moment he had even thought of sending to this man for information. But he reflected that if Janzen had heard of the explosion he was not at all the individual to wait for the police at home.

Meantime Pierre repeated: "I will willingly go to buy the evening papers for you—but there will certainly be nothing in them. Although I know almost everyone in Neuilly I can think of nobody who is likely to have any information, unless perhaps it were Bache—"

"You know Bache, the municipal councillor?" interrupted Guillaume.

"Yes, we have both had to busy ourselves with charitable work in the neighbourhood."

"Well, Bache is an old friend of mine, and I know no safer man. Pray go to him and bring him back with you."

A quarter of an hour later Pierre returned with Bache, who resided in a neighbouring street. And it was not only Bache whom he brought with him, for, much to his surprise, he had found Janzen at Bache's house. As Guillaume had suspected, Janzen, while dining at the Princess de Harn's, had heard of the crime, and had consequently refrained from returning to his little lodging in the Rue des Martyrs, where the police might well have set a trap for him. His connections were known, and he was aware that he was watched and was liable at any moment to arrest or expulsion as a foreign Anarchist. And so he had thought it prudent to solicit a few days' hospitality of Bache, a very upright and obliging man, to whom he entrusted himself without fear. He would never have remained with Rosemonde, that adorable lunatic who for a month past had been exhibiting him as her lover, and whose useless and dangerous extravagance of conduct he fully realised.

Guillaume was so delighted on seeing Bache and Janzen that he wished to sit up in bed again. But Pierre bade him remain quiet, rest his head on the pillows, and speak as little as possible. Then, while Janzen stood near, erect and silent, Bache took a chair and sat down by the bedside with many expressions of friendly interest. He was a stout man of sixty, with a broad, full face, a large white beard and long white hair. His little, gentle eyes had a dim, dreamy expression, while a pleasant, hopeful smile played round his thick lips. His father, a fervent St. Simonian, had brought him up in the doctrines of that belief. While retaining due respect for it, however, his personal inclinations towards orderliness and religion had led him to espouse the ideas of Fourier, in such wise that one found in him a succession and an abridgment, so to say, of two doctrines. Moreover, when he was about thirty, he had busied himself with spiritualism. Possessed of a comfortable little fortune, his only adventure in life had been his connection with the Paris Commune of 1871. How or why he had become a member of it he could now scarcely tell. Condemned to death by default, although he had sat among the Moderates, he had resided in Belgium until the amnesty; and since then Neuilly had elected him as its representative on the Paris Municipal Council, less by way of glorifying in him a victim of reaction than as a reward for his worthiness, for he was really esteemed by the whole district.

Guillaume, with his desire for tidings, was obliged to confide in his two visitors, tell them of the explosion and Salvat's flight, and how he himself had been wounded while seeking to extinguish the match. Janzen, with curly beard and hair, and a thin, fair face such as painters often attribute to the Christ, listened coldly, as was his wont, and at last said slowly in a gentle voice: "Ah! so it was Salvat! I thought it might be little Mathis—I'm surprised that it should be Salvat—for he hadn't made up his mind." Then, as Guillaume anxiously inquired if he thought that Salvat would speak out, he began to protest: "Oh! no; oh! no."

However, he corrected himself with a gleam of disdain in his clear, harsh eyes: "After all, there's no telling. Salvat is a man of sentiment."

Then Bache, who was quite upset by the news of the explosion, tried to think how his friend Guillaume, to whom he was much attached, might be extricated from any charge of complicity should he be denounced. And Guillaume, at sight of Janzen's contemptuous coldness, must have suffered keenly, for the other evidently believed him to be trembling, tortured by the one desire to save his own skin. But what could he say, how could he reveal the deep concern which rendered him so feverish without betraying the secret which he had hidden even from his brother?

However, at this moment Sophie came to tell her master that M. Theophile Morin had called with another gentleman. Much astonished by this visit at so late an hour, Pierre hastened into the next room to receive the new comers. He had become acquainted with Morin since his return from Rome, and had helped him to introduce a translation of an excellent scientific manual, prepared according to the official programmes, into the Italian schools.[1] A Franc-Comtois by birth, a compatriot of Proudhon, with whose poor family he had been intimate at Besancon, Morin, himself the son of a journeyman clockmaker, had grown up with Proudhonian ideas, full of affection for the poor and an instinctive hatred of property and wealth. Later on, having come to Paris as a school teacher, impassioned by study, he had given his whole mind to Auguste Comte. Beneath the fervent Positivist, however, one might yet find the old Proudhonian, the pauper who rebelled and detested want. Moreover, it was scientific Positivism that he clung to; in his hatred of all mysticism he would have

---

[1] See M. Zola's "Rome," Chapters IV. and XVI.

naught to do with the fantastic religious leanings of Comte in his last years. And in Morin's brave, consistent, somewhat mournful life, there had been but one page of romance: the sudden feverish impulse which had carried him off to fight in Sicily by Garibaldi's side. Afterwards he had again become a petty professor in Paris, obscurely earning a dismal livelihood.

When Pierre returned to the bedroom he said to his brother in a tone of emotion: "Morin has brought me Barthes, who fancies himself in danger and asks my hospitality."

At this Guillaume forgot himself and became excited: "Nicholas Barthes, a hero with a soul worthy of antiquity. Oh! I know him; I admire and love him. You must set your door open wide for him."

Bache and Janzen, however, had glanced at one another smiling. And the latter, with his cold ironical air, slowly remarked: "Why does Monsieur Barthes hide himself? A great many people think he is dead; he is simply a ghost who no longer frightens anybody."

Four and seventy years of age as he now was, Barthes had spent nearly half a century in prison. He was the eternal prisoner, the hero of liberty whom each successive Government had carried from citadel to fortress. Since his youth he had been marching on amidst his dream of fraternity, fighting for an ideal Republic based on truth and justice, and each and every endeavour had led him to a dungeon; he had invariably finished his humanitarian reverie under bolts and bars. Carbonaro, Republican, evangelical sectarian, he had conspired at all times and in all places, incessantly struggling against the Power of the day, whatever it might be. And when the Republic at last had come, that Republic which had cost him so many years of gaol, it had, in its own turn, imprisoned him, adding fresh years of gloom to those which already had lacked sunlight. And thus he remained the martyr of freedom: freedom which he still desired in spite of everything; freedom, which, strive as he might, never came, never existed.

"But you are mistaken," replied Guillaume, wounded by Janzen's raillery. "There is again a thought of getting rid of Barthes, whose uncompromising rectitude disturbs our politicians; and he does well to take his precautions!"

Nicholas Barthes came in, a tall, slim, withered old man, with a nose like an eagle's beak, and eyes that still burned in their deep sockets, under white and bushy brows. His mouth, toothless but still refined, was lost to sight between his moustaches and snowy beard; and his hair, crowning him whitely like an aureola, fell in curls over his shoulders. Behind him with all modesty came Theophile Morin, with grey whiskers, grey, brush-like hair, spectacles, and yellow, weary mien—that of an old professor exhausted by years of teaching. Neither of them seemed astonished or awaited an explanation on finding that man in bed with an injured wrist. And there were no introductions: those who were acquainted merely smiled at one another.

Barthes, for his part, stooped and kissed Guillaume on both cheeks. "Ah!" said the latter, almost gaily, "it gives me courage to see you."

However, the new comers had brought a little information. The boulevards were in an agitated state, the news of the crime had spread from cafe to cafe, and everybody was anxious to see the late edition which one paper had published giving a very incorrect account of the affair, full of the most extraordinary details. Briefly, nothing positive was as yet known.

On seeing Guillaume turn pale Pierre compelled him to lie down again, and even talked of taking the visitors into the next room. But the injured man gently replied: "No, no, I promise you that I won't stir again, that I won't open my mouth. But stay there and chat together. I assure you that it will do me good to have you near me and hear you."

Then, under the sleepy gleams of the lamp, the others began to talk in undertones. Old Barthes, who considered that bomb to be both idiotic and abominable, spoke of it with the stupefaction of one who, after fighting like a hero through all the legendary struggles for liberty, found himself belated, out of his element, in a new era, which he could not understand. Did not the conquest of freedom suffice for everything? he added. Was there any other problem beyond that of founding the real Republic? Then, referring to Mege and his speech in the Chamber that afternoon, he bitterly arraigned Collectivism, which he declared to be one of the democratic forms of tyranny. Theophile Morin, for his part, also spoke against the Collectivist enrolling of the social forces, but he professed yet greater hatred of the odious violence of the Anarchists; for it was only by evolution that he expected progress, and he felt somewhat indifferent as to what political means might bring about the scientific society of to-morrow. And in like way Bache did not seem particularly fond of the Anarchists, though he was touched by the idyllic dream, the humanitarian hope, whose germs lay beneath their passion for destruction. And, like Barthes, he also flew into a passion with Mege, who since entering the Chamber had become, said he, a mere rhetorician and theorist, dreaming of dictatorship. Meantime Janzen, still erect, his face frigid and his lips curling ironically, listened to all three of them, and vented a few trenchant words to express his own Anarchist faith; the uselessness of drawing distinctions, and the necessity of destroying everything in order that everything might be rebuilt on fresh lines.

Pierre, who had remained near the bed, also listened with passionate attention. Amidst the downfall of his own beliefs, the utter void which he felt within him, here were these four men, who represented the cardinal points of this century's ideas, debating the very same terrible problem which brought him so much suffering, that of the new belief which the democracy of the coming century awaits. And, ah! since the days of the immediate ancestors, since the days of Voltaire and Diderot and Rousseau how incessantly had billows of ideas followed and jostled one another, the older ones giving birth to new ones, and all breaking and bounding in a tempest in which it was becoming so difficult to distinguish anything clearly! Whence came the wind, and whither was the ship of salvation going, for what port ought one to embark? Pierre had already thought that the balance-sheet of the century ought to be drawn up, and that, after accepting the legacies of Rousseau and the other precursors, he ought to study the ideas of St. Simon, Fourier and even Cabet; of Auguste Comte, Proudhon and Karl Marx as well, in order, at any rate, to form some idea of the distance that had been travelled, and of the cross-ways which one had now reached. And was not this an opportunity, since chance had gathered those men together in his house, living exponents of the conflicting doctrines which he wished to examine?

On turning round, however, he perceived that Guillaume was now very pale and had closed his eyes. Had even he, with his faith in science, felt the doubt which is born of contradictory theories, and the despair which comes when one sees the fight for truth resulting in growth of error?

"Are you in pain?" the priest anxiously inquired.

"Yes, a little. But I will try to sleep."

At this they all went off with silent handshakes. Nicholas Barthes alone remained in the house and slept in a room on the first floor which Sophie had got ready for him. Pierre, unwilling to quit his brother, dozed off upon a sofa. And the little house relapsed into its deep quietude, the silence of solitude and winter, through which passed the melancholy quiver of the souvenirs of childhood.

In the morning, as soon as it was seven o'clock, Pierre had to go for the newspapers. Guillaume had passed a bad night and intense fever had set in. Nevertheless, his brother was obliged to read him the articles on the explosion. There was an amazing medley of truths and inventions, of precise information lost amidst the most unexpected extravagance. Sagnier's paper, the "Voix du Peuple," distinguished itself by its sub-titles in huge print and a whole page of particulars jumbled together chance-wise. It had at once decided to postpone the famous list of the thirty-two deputies and senators compromised in the African Railways affair; and there was no end to the details it gave of the aspect of the entrance to the Duvillard mansion after the explosion the pavement broken up, the upper floor rent open, the huge doors torn away from their hinges. Then came the story of the Baron's son and daughter preserved as by a miracle, the landau escaping the slightest injury, while the banker and his wife, it was alleged, owed their preservation to the circumstance that they had lingered at the Madeleine after Monseigneur Martha's remarkable address there. An entire column was given to the one victim, the poor, pretty, fair-haired errand girl, whose identity did not seem to be clearly established, although a flock of reporters had rushed first to the modiste employing her, in the Avenue de l'Opera, and next to the upper part of the Faubourg St. Denis, where it was thought her grandmother resided. Then, in a gravely worded article in "Le Globe," evidently inspired by Fonsegue, an appeal was made to the Chamber's patriotism to avoid giving cause for any ministerial crisis in the painful circumstances through which the country was passing. Thus the ministry might last, and live in comparative quietude, for a few weeks longer.

Guillaume, however, was struck by one point only: the culprit was not known; Salvat, it appeared certain, was neither arrested nor even suspected. It seemed, indeed, as if the police were starting on a false scent—that of a well-dressed gentleman wearing gloves, whom a neighbour swore he had seen entering the mansion at the moment of the explosion. Thus Guillaume became a little calmer. But his brother read to him from another paper some particulars concerning the engine of destruction that had been employed. It was a preserved-meat can, and the fragments of it showed that it had been comparatively small. And Guillaume relapsed into anxiety on learning that people were much astonished at the violent ravages of such a sorry appliance, and that the presence of some new explosive of incalculable power was already suspected.

At eight o'clock Bertheroy put in an appearance. Although he was sixty-eight, he showed as much briskness and sprightliness as any young sawbones calling in a friendly way to perform a little operation. He had brought an instrument case, some linen bands and some lint. However, he became angry on finding the injured man nervous, flushed and hot with fever.

"Ah! I see that you haven't been reasonable, my dear child," said he. "You must have talked too much, and have bestirred and excited yourself." Then, having carefully probed the wound, he added, while dressing it: "The bone is injured, you know, and

I won't answer for anything unless you behave better. Any complications would make amputation necessary."

Pierre shuddered, but Guillaume shrugged his shoulders, as if to say that he might just as well be amputated since all was crumbling around him. Bertheroy, who had sat down, lingering there for another moment, scrutinised both brothers with his keen eyes. He now knew of the explosion, and must have thought it over. "My dear child," he resumed in his brusque way, "I certainly don't think that you committed that abominable act of folly in the Rue Godot-de-Mauroy. But I fancy that you were in the neighbourhood—no, no, don't answer me, don't defend yourself. I know nothing and desire to know nothing, not even the formula of that devilish powder of which your shirt cuff bore traces, and which has wrought such terrible havoc."

And then as the brothers remained surprised, turning cold with anxiety, in spite of his assurances, he added with a sweeping gesture: "Ah! my friends, I regard such an action as even more useless than criminal! I only feel contempt for the vain agitation of politics, whether they be revolutionary or conservative. Does not science suffice? Why hasten the times when one single step of science brings humanity nearer to the goal of truth and justice than do a hundred years of politics and social revolt? Why, it is science alone which sweeps away dogmas, casts down gods, and creates light and happiness. And I, Member of the Institute as I am, decorated and possessed of means, I am the only true Revolutionist."

Then he began to laugh and Guillaume realised all the good-natured irony of his laugh. While admiring him as a great *savant*, he had hitherto suffered at seeing him lead such a *bourgeois* life, accepting whatever appointments and honours were offered him, a Republican under the Republic, but quite ready to serve science under no matter what master. But now, from beneath this opportunist, this hieratical *savant*, this toiler who accepted wealth and glory from all hands, there appeared a quiet yet terrible evolutionist, who certainly expected that his own work would help to ravage and renew the world!

However, Bertheroy rose and took his leave: "I'll come back; behave sensibly, and love one another as well as you can."

When the brothers again found themselves alone, Pierre seated at Guillaume's bedside, their hands once more sought each other and met in a burning clasp instinct with all their anguish. How much threatening mystery and distress there was both around and within them! The grey wintry daylight came into the room, and they could see the black trees in the garden, while the house remained full of quivering silence, save that overhead a faint sound of footsteps was audible. They were the steps of Nicholas Barthes, the heroic lover of freedom, who, rising at daybreak, had, like a caged lion, resumed his wonted promenade, the incessant coming and going of one who had ever been a prisoner. And as the brothers ceased listening to him their eyes fell on a newspaper which had remained open on the bed, a newspaper soiled by a sketch in outline which pretended to portray the poor dead errand girl, lying, ripped open, beside the bandbox and the bonnet it had contained. It was so frightful, so atrociously hideous a scene, that two big tears again fell upon Pierre's cheeks, whilst Guillaume's blurred, despairing eyes gazed wistfully far away, seeking for the Future.

II. A HOME OF INDUSTRY

THE little house in which Guillaume had dwelt for so many years, a home of quietude and hard work, stood in the pale light of winter up yonder at Montmartre, peacefully awaiting his return. He reflected, however, after *dejeuner* that it might not be prudent for him to go back thither for some three weeks, and so he thought of sending Pierre to explain the position of affairs. "Listen, brother," he said. "You must render me this service. Go and tell them the truth—that I am here, slightly injured, and do not wish them to come to see me, for fear lest somebody should follow them and discover my retreat. After the note I wrote them last evening they would end by getting anxious if I did not send them some news." Then, yielding to the one worry which, since the previous night, had disturbed his clear, frank glance, he added: "Just feel in the right-hand pocket of my waistcoat; you will find a little key there. Good! that's it. Now you must give it to Madame Leroi, my mother-in-law, and tell her that if any misfortune should happen to me, she is to do what is understood between us. That will suffice, she will understand you."

At the first moment Pierre had hesitated; but he saw how even the slight effort of speaking exhausted his brother, so he silenced him, saying: "Don't talk, but put your mind at ease. I will go and reassure your people, since you wish that this commission should be undertaken by me."

Truth to tell, the errand was so distasteful to Pierre that he had at first thought of sending Sophie in his place. All his old prejudices were reviving; it was as if he were going to some ogre's den. How many times had he not heard his mother say "that creature!" in referring to the woman with whom her elder son cohabited. Never had she been willing to kiss Guillaume's boys; the whole connection had shocked her, and she was particularly indignant that Madame Leroi, the woman's mother, should have joined the household for the purpose of bringing up the little ones. Pierre retained so strong a recollection of all this that even nowadays, when he went to the basilica of the Sacred Heart and passed the little house on his way, he glanced at it distrustfully, and kept as far from it as he could, as if it were some abode of vice and error. Undoubtedly, for ten years now, the boys' mother had been dead, but did not another scandal-inspiring creature dwell there, that young orphan girl to whom his brother had given shelter, and whom he was going to marry, although a difference of twenty years lay between them? To Pierre all this was contrary to propriety, abnormal and revolting, and he pictured a home given over to social rebellion, where lack of principle led to every kind of disorder.

However, he was leaving the room to start upon his journey, when Guillaume called him back. "Tell Madame Leroi," said he, "that if I should die you will let her know of it, so that she may immediately do what is necessary."

"Yes, yes," answered Pierre. "But calm yourself, and don't move about. I'll say everything. And in my absence Sophie will stop here with you in case you should need her."

Having given full instructions to the servant, Pierre set out to take a tramcar, intending to alight from it on the Boulevard de Rochechouart, and then climb the height on foot. And on the road, lulled by the gliding motion of the heavy vehicle, he began to think of his brother's past life and connections, with which he was but vaguely, imperfectly, acquainted. It was only at a later date that details of everything came to his knowledge. In 1850 a young professor named Leroi, who had come from Paris to the college of Montauban with the most ardent republican ideas, had there married Agathe Dagnan, the youngest of the five girls of an old Protestant family from the Cevennes. Young Madame Leroi was *enceinte* when her husband, threatened with arrest for contributing some violent articles to a local newspaper, immediately after the "Coup d'Etat," found himself obliged to seek refuge at Geneva. It was there that the young couple's daughter, Marguerite, a very delicate child, was born in 1852. For seven years, that is until the Amnesty of 1859, the household struggled with poverty, the husband giving but a few ill-paid lessons, and the wife absorbed in the constant care which the child required. Then, after their return to Paris, their ill-luck became even greater. For a long time the ex-professor vainly sought regular employment; it was denied him on account of his opinions, and he had to run about giving lessons in private houses. When he was at last on the point of being received back into the University a supreme blow, an attack of paralysis, fell upon him. He lost the use of both legs. And then came utter misery, every kind of sordid drudgery, the writing of articles for dictionaries, the copying of manuscripts, and even the addressing of newspaper wrappers, on the fruits of which the household barely contrived to live, in a little lodging in the Rue Monsieur-le-Prince.

It was there that Marguerite grew up. Leroi, embittered by injustice and suffering, predicted the advent of a Republic which would avenge the follies of the Empire, and a reign of science which would sweep away the deceptive and cruel divinity of religious dogmas. On the other hand, Agathe's religious faith had collapsed at Geneva, at sight of the narrow and imbecile practices of Calvinism, and all that she retained of it was the old Protestant leaven of rebellion. She had become at once the head and the arm of the house; she went for her husband's work, took it back when completed, and even did much of it herself, whilst, at the same time, performing her house duties, and rearing and educating her daughter. The latter, who attended no school, was indebted for all she learnt to her father and mother, on whose part there was never any question of religious instruction. Through contact with her husband, Madame Leroi had lost all belief, and her Protestant heredity inclining her to free inquiry and examination, she had arranged for herself a kind of peaceful atheism, based on paramount principles of human duty and justice, which she applied courageously, irrespective of all social conventionalities. The long iniquity of her husband's fate, the undeserved misfortunes which struck her through him and her daughter, ended by endowing her with wonderful fortitude and devotion, which made her, whether as a judge, a manager, or a consoler, a woman of incomparable energy and nobleness of character.

II. A HOME OF INDUSTRY

It was in the Rue Monsieur-le-Prince that Guillaume became acquainted with the Leroi family, after the war of 1870. On the same floor as their little lodging he occupied a large room, where he devoted himself passionately to his studies. At the outset there was only an occasional bow, for Guillaume's neighbours were very proud and very grave, leading their life of poverty in fierce silence and retirement. Then intercourse began with the rendering of little services, such as when the young man procured the ex-professor a commission to write a few articles for a new encyclopaedia. But all at once came the catastrophe: Leroi died in his armchair one evening while his daughter was wheeling him from his table to his bed. The two distracted women had not even the money to bury him. The whole secret of their bitter want flowed forth with their tears, and they were obliged to accept the help of Guillaume, who, from that moment, became the necessary confidant and friend. And the thing which was bound to happen did happen, in the most simple and loving manner, permitted by the mother herself, who, full of contempt for a social system which allowed those of good hearts to die of hunger, refused to admit the necessity of any social tie. Thus there was no question of a regular marriage. One day Guillaume, who was twenty-three years old, found himself mated to Marguerite, who was twenty; both of them handsome, healthy, and strong, adoring one another, loving work, and full of hope in the future.

From that moment a new life began. Since his father's death, Guillaume, who had broken off all intercourse with his mother, had been receiving an allowance of two hundred francs a month. This just represented daily bread; however, he was already doubling the amount by his work as a chemist,—his analyses and researches, which tended to the employment of certain chemical products in industry. So he and Marguerite installed themselves on the very summit of Montmartre, in a little house, at a rental of eight hundred francs a year, the great convenience of the place being a strip of garden, where one might, later on, erect a wooden workshop. In all tranquillity Madame Leroi took up her abode with the young people, helping them, and sparing them the necessity of keeping a second servant. And at successive intervals of two years, her three grandchildren were born, three sturdy boys: first Thomas, then Francois, and then Antoine. And in the same way as she had devoted herself to her husband and daughter, and then to Guillaume, so did she now devote herself to the three children. She became "Mere-Grand"—an emphatic and affectionate way of expressing the term "grandmother"—for all who lived in the house, the older as well as the younger ones. She there personified sense, and wisdom, and courage; it was she who was ever on the watch, who directed everything, who was consulted about everything, and whose opinion was always followed. Indeed, she reigned there like an all-powerful queen-mother.

For fifteen years this life went on, a life of hard work and peaceful affection, while the strictest economy was observed in contenting every need of the modest little household. Then Guillaume lost his mother, took his share of the family inheritance, and was able to satisfy his old desire, which was to buy the house he lived in, and build a spacious workshop in the garden. He was even able to build it of bricks, and add an upper story to it. But the work was scarcely finished, and life seemed to be on the point of expanding and smiling on them all, when misfortune returned, and typhoid fever, with brutal force, carried off Marguerite, after a week's illness. She was then five and thirty, and her eldest boy, Thomas, was fourteen. Thus Guillaume, distracted by his loss, found himself a widower at thirty-eight. The thought of introducing any unknown woman into that retired home, where all hearts beat in tender unison, was so unbearable to him that he determined to take no other mate. His work absorbed him, and he would know how to quiet both his heart and his flesh. Mere-Grand, fortunately, was still there, erect and courageous; the household retained its queen, and in her the children found a manageress and teacher, schooled in adversity and heroism.

Two years passed; and then came an addition to the family. A young woman, Marie Couturier, the daughter of one of Guillaume's friends, suddenly entered it. Couturier had been an inventor, a madman with some measure of genius, and had spent a fairly large fortune in attempting all sorts of fantastic schemes. His wife, a very pious woman, had died of grief at it all; and although on the rare occasions when he saw his daughter, he showed great fondness for her and loaded her with presents, he had first placed her in a boarding college, and afterwards left her in the charge of a poor female relative. Remembering her only on his death-bed, he had begged Guillaume to give her an asylum, and find her a husband. The poor relation, who dealt in ladies' and babies' linen, had just become a bankrupt. So, at nineteen, the girl, Marie, found herself a penniless outcast, possessed of nothing save a good education, health and courage. Guillaume would never allow her to run about giving lessons. He took her, in quite a natural way, to help Mere-Grand, who was no longer so active as formerly. And the latter approved the arrangement, well pleased at the advent of youth and gaiety, which would somewhat brighten the household, whose life had been one of much gravity ever since Marguerite's death. Marie would simply be an elder sister; she was too old for the boys, who were still at college, to be disturbed by her presence. And she would work in that house where everybody worked. She would help the little community pending the time when she might meet and love some worthy fellow who would marry her.

Five more years elapsed without Marie consenting to quit that happy home. The sterling education she had received was lodged in a vigorous brain, which contented itself with the acquirement of knowledge. Yet she had remained very pure and healthy, even very *naive*, maidenly by reason of her natural rectitude. And she was also very much a woman, beautifying and amusing herself with a mere nothing, and ever showing gaiety and contentment. Moreover, she was in no wise of a dreamy nature, but very practical, always intent on some work or other, and only asking of life such things as life could give, without anxiety as to what might lie beyond it. She lovingly remembered her pious mother, who had prepared her for her first Communion in tears, imagining that she was opening heaven's portals to her. But since she had been an orphan she had of her own accord ceased all practice of religion, her good sense revolting and scorning the need of any moral police regulations to make her do her duty. Indeed, she considered such regulations dangerous and destructive of true health. Thus, like Mere-Grand, she had come to a sort of quiet and almost unconscious atheism, not after the fashion of one who reasons, but simply like the brave, healthy girl she was, one who had long endured poverty without suffering from it, and believed in nothing save the necessity of effort. She had been kept erect, indeed, by her conviction that happiness was to be found in the normal joys of life, lived courageously. And her happy equilibrium of mind had ever guided and saved her, in such wise that she willingly listened to her natural instinct, saying, with her pleasant laugh, that this was, after all, her best adviser. She rejected two offers of marriage, and on the second occasion, as Guillaume pressed her to accept, she grew astonished, and inquired if he had had enough of her in the house. She found herself very comfortable, and she rendered service there. So why should she leave and run the risk of being less happy elsewhere, particularly as she was not in love with anybody?

Then, by degrees, the idea of a marriage between Marie and Guillaume presented itself; and indeed what could have been more reasonable and advantageous for all? If Guillaume had not mated again it was for his sons' sake, because he feared that by introducing a stranger to the house he might impair its quietude and gaiety. But now there was a woman among them who already showed herself maternal towards the boys, and whose bright youth had ended by disturbing his own heart. He was still in his prime, and had always held that it was not good for man to live alone, although, personally, thanks to his ardour for work, he had hitherto escaped excessive suffering in his bereavement. However, there was the great difference of ages to be considered; and he would have bravely remained in the background and have sought a younger husband for Marie, if his three big sons and Mere-Grand herself had not conspired to effect his happiness by doing all they could to bring about a marriage which would strengthen every home tie and impart, as it were, a fresh springtide to the house. As for Marie, touched and grateful to Guillaume for the manner in which he had treated her for five years past, she immediately consented with an impulse of sincere affection, in which, she fancied, she could detect love. And at all events, could she act in a more sensible, reasonable way, base her life on more certain prospects of happiness? So the marriage had been resolved upon; and about a month previously it had been decided that it should take place during the ensuing spring, towards the end of April.

When Pierre, after alighting from the tramcar, began to climb the interminable flights of steps leading to the Rue St. Eleuthere, a feeling of uneasiness again came over him at the thought that he was about to enter that suspicious ogre's den where everything would certainly wound and irritate him. Given the letter which Sophie had carried thither on the previous night, announcing that the master would not return, how anxious and upset must all its inmates be! However, as Pierre ascended the final flight and nervously raised his head, the little house appeared to him right atop of the hill, looking very serene and quiet under the bright wintry sun, which had peered forth as if to bestow upon the modest dwelling an affectionate caress.

There was a door in the old garden wall alongside the Rue St. Eleuthere, almost in front of the broad thoroughfare conducting to the basilica of the Sacred Heart; but to reach the house itself one had to skirt the wall and climb to the Place du Tertre, where one found the facade and the entrance. Some children were playing on the Place, which, planted as it was with a few scrubby trees, and edged with humble shops,—a fruiterer's, a grocer's and a baker's,—looked like some square in a small provincial town. In a corner, on the left, Guillaume's dwelling, which had been whitewashed during the previous spring, showed its bright frontage and five lifeless windows, for all its life was on the other, the garden, side, which overlooked Paris and the far horizon.

Pierre mustered his courage and, pulling a brass knob which glittered like gold, rang the bell. There came a gay, distant jingle; but for a moment nobody appeared, and he was about to ring again, when the door was thrown wide open, revealing a passage which ran right through the house, beyond which appeared the ocean of Paris, the endless sea of house roofs bathed in sunlight. And against this spacious, airy background, stood a young woman of twenty-six, clad in a simple gown of black woolen stuff, half covered by a large blue apron. She had her sleeves rolled up above her elbows, and her arms and hands were still moist with water which she had but imperfectly wiped away.

A moment's surprise and embarrassment ensued. The young woman, who had hastened to the door with laughing mien, became grave and covertly hostile at sight of the visitor's cassock. The priest thereupon realised that he must give his name: "I am Abbe Pierre Froment."

At this the young woman's smile of welcome came back to her. "Oh! I beg your pardon, monsieur—I ought to have recognised you, for I saw you wish Guillaume good day one morning as you passed."

She said Guillaume; she, therefore, must be Marie. And Pierre looked at her in astonishment, finding her very different from what he had imagined. She was only of average height, but she was vigorously, admirably built, broad of hip and broad of shoulder, with the small firm bosom of an amazon. By her erect and easy step, instinct with all the adorable grace of woman in her prime, one could divine that she was strong, muscular and healthy. A brunette, but very white of skin, she had a heavy helm of superb black hair, which she fastened in a negligent way, without any show of coquetry. And under her dark locks, her pure, intelligent brow, her delicate nose and gay eyes appeared full of intense life; whilst the somewhat heavier character of her lower features, her fleshy lips and full chin, bespoke her quiet kindliness. She had surely come on earth as a promise of every form of tenderness, every form of devotion. In a word, she was a true mate for man.

However, with her heavy, straying hair and superb arms, so ingenuous in their nudity, she only gave Pierre an impression of superfluous health and extreme self-assurance. She displeased him and even made him feel somewhat anxious, as if she were a creature different from all others.

"It is my brother Guillaume who has sent me," he said.

At this her face again changed; she became grave and hastened to admit him to the passage. And when the door was closed she answered: "You have brought us news of him, then! I must apologise for receiving you in this fashion. The servants have just finished some washing, and I was making sure if the work had been well done. Pray excuse me, and come in here for a moment; it is perhaps best that I should be the first to know the news."

So saying, she led him past the kitchen to a little room which served as scullery and wash-house. A tub full of soapy water stood there, and some dripping linen hung over some wooden bars. "And so, Guillaume?" she asked.

Pierre then told the truth in simple fashion: that his brother's wrist had been injured; that he himself had witnessed the accident, and that his brother had then sought an asylum with him at Neuilly, where he wished to remain and get cured of his injury in peace and quietness, without even receiving a visit from his sons. While speaking in this fashion, the priest watched the effect of his words on Marie's face: first fright and pity, and then an effort to calm herself and judge things reasonably.

"His letter quite froze me last night," she ended by replying. "I felt sure that some misfortune had happened. But one must be brave and hide one's fear from others. His wrist injured, you say; it is not a serious injury, is it?"

"No; but it is necessary that every precaution should be taken with it."

She looked him well in the face with her big frank eyes, which dived into his own as if to reach the very depths of his being, though at the same time she plainly sought to restrain the score of questions which rose to her lips. "And that is all: he was injured in an accident," she resumed; "he didn't ask you to tell us anything further about it?"

"No, he simply desires that you will not be anxious."

Thereupon she insisted no further, but showed herself obedient and respectful of the decision which Guillaume had arrived at. It sufficed that he should have sent a messenger to reassure the household—she did not seek to learn any more. And even as she had returned to her work in spite of the secret anxiety in which the letter of the previous evening had left her, so now, with her air of quiet strength, she recovered an appearance of serenity, a quiet smile and clear brave glance.

"Guillaume only gave me one other commission," resumed Pierre, "that of handing a little key to Madame Leroi."

"Very good," Marie answered, "Mere-Grand is here; and, besides, the children must see you. I will take you to them."

Once more quite tranquil, she examined Pierre without managing to conceal her curiosity, which seemed of rather a kindly nature blended with an element of vague pity. Her fresh white arms had remained bare. In all candour she slowly drew down her sleeves; then took off the large blue apron, and showed herself with her rounded figure, at once robust and elegant, in her modest black gown. He meanwhile looked at her, and most certainly he did not find her to his liking. On seeing her so natural, healthy, and courageous, quite a feeling of revolt arose within him, though he knew not why.

"Will you please follow me, Monsieur l'Abbe?" she said. "We must cross the garden."

On the ground-floor of the house, across the passage, and facing the kitchen and the scullery, there were two other rooms, a library overlooking the Place du Tertre, and a dining-room whose windows opened into the garden. The four rooms on the first floor served as bedchambers for the father and the sons. As for the garden, originally but a small one, it had now been reduced to a kind of gravelled yard by the erection of the large workshop at one end of it. Of the former greenery, however, there still remained two huge plum-trees with old knotted trunks, as well as a big clump of lilac-bushes, which every spring were covered with bloom. And in front of the latter Marie had arranged a broad flower-bed, in which she amused herself with growing a few roses, some wallflowers and some mignonette.

With a wave of her hand as she went past, she called Pierre's attention to the black plum-trees and the lilacs and roses, which showed but a few greenish spots, for winter still held the little nook in sleep. "Tell Guillaume," she said, "that he must make haste to get well and be back for the first shoots."

Then, as Pierre glanced at her, she all at once flushed purple. Much to her distress, sudden and involuntary blushes would in this wise occasionally come upon her, even at the most innocent remarks. She found it ridiculous to feel such childish emotion when she had so brave a heart. But her pure maidenly blood had retained exquisite delicacy, such natural and instinctive modesty that she yielded to it perforce. And doubtless she had merely blushed because she feared that the priest might think she had referred to her marriage in speaking of the spring.

"Please go in, Monsieur l'Abbe. The children are there, all three." And forthwith she ushered him into the workshop.

It was a very spacious place, over sixteen feet high, with a brick flooring and bare walls painted an iron grey. A sheet of light, a stream of sunshine, spread to every corner through a huge window facing the south, where lay the immensity of Paris. The Venetian shutters often had to be lowered in the summer to attenuate the great heat. From morn till night the whole family lived here, closely and affectionately united in work. Each was installed as fancy listed, having a particular chosen place. One half of the building was occupied by the father's chemical laboratory, with its stove, experiment tables, shelves for apparatus, glass cases and cupboards for phials and jars. Near all this Thomas, the eldest son, had installed a little forge, an anvil, a vice bench, in fact everything necessary to a working mechanician, such as he had become since taking his bachelor's degree, from his desire to remain with his father and help him with certain researches and inventions. Then, at the other end, the younger brothers, Francois and Antoine, got on very well together on either side of a broad table which stood amidst a medley of portfolios, nests of drawers and revolving book-stands. Francois, laden with academical laurels, first on the pass list for the Ecole Normale, had entered that college where young men are trained for university professorships, and was there preparing for his Licentiate degree, while Antoine, who on reaching the third class at the Lycee Condorcet had taken a dislike to classical studies, now devoted himself to his calling as a wood-engraver. And, in the full light under the window, Mere-Grand and Marie likewise had their particular table, where needlework, embroidery, all sorts of *chiffons* and delicate things lay about near the somewhat rough jumble of retorts, tools and big books.

Marie, however, on the very threshold called out in her calm voice, to which she strove to impart a gay and cheering accent: "Children! children! here is Monsieur l'Abbe with news of father!"

Children, indeed! Yet what motherliness she already set in the word as she applied it to those big fellows whose elder sister she had long considered herself to be! At three and twenty Thomas was quite a colossus, already bearded and extremely like his father. But although he had a lofty brow and energetic features, he was somewhat slow both in mind and body. And he was also taciturn, almost unsociable, absorbed in filial devotion, delighted with the manual toil which made him a mere workman at his master's orders. Francois, two years younger than Thomas, and nearly as tall, showed a more refined face, though he had the same large brow and firm mouth, a perfect blending of health and strength, in which the man of intellect, the scientific Normalian, could only be detected by the brighter and more subtle sparkle of the eyes. The youngest of the brothers, Antoine, who for his eighteen years was almost as strong as his elders, and promised to become as tall, differed from them by his lighter hair and soft, blue, dreamy eyes, which he had inherited from his mother. It had been difficult, however, to distinguish one from the other when all three were schoolboys at the Lycee Condorcet; and even nowadays people made mistakes unless they saw them side by side, so as to detect the points of difference which were becoming more marked as age progressed.

II. A HOME OF INDUSTRY

On Pierre's arrival the brothers were so absorbed in their work that they did not even hear the door open. And again, as in the case of Marie, the priest was surprised by the discipline and firmness of mind, which amidst the keenest anxiety gave the young fellows strength to take up their daily task. Thomas, who stood at his vice-bench in a blouse, was carefully filing a little piece of copper with rough but skilful hands. Francois, leaning forward, was writing in a bold, firm fashion, whilst on the other side of the table, Antoine, with a slender graver between his fingers, finished a block for an illustrated newspaper.

However, Marie's clear voice made them raise their heads: "Children, father has sent you some news!"

Then all three with the same impulse hurriedly quitted their work and came forward. One could divine that directly there was any question of their father they were drawn together, blended one with the other, so that but one and the same heart beat in their three broad chests. However, a door at the far end of the workroom opened at that moment, and Mere-Grand, coming from the upper floor where she and Marie had their bedrooms, made her appearance. She had just absented herself to fetch a skein of wool; and she gazed fixedly at the priest, unable to understand the reason of his presence.

Marie had to explain matters. "Mere-Grand," said she, "this is Monsieur l'Abbe Froment, Guillaume's brother; he has come from him."

Pierre on his side was examining the old lady, astonished to find her so erect and full of life at seventy. Her former beauty had left a stately charm on her rather long face; youthful fire still lingered in her brown eyes; and very firm was the contour of her pale lips, which in parting showed that she had retained all her teeth. A few white hairs alone silvered her black tresses, which were arranged in old-time fashion. Her cheeks had but slightly withered, and her deep, symmetrical wrinkles gave her countenance an expression of much nobility, a sovereign air as of a queen-mother, which, tall and slight of stature as she was, and invariably gowned in black woollen stuff, she always retained, no matter how humble her occupation.

"So Guillaume sent you, monsieur," she said; "he is injured, is he not?"

Surprised by this proof of intuition, Pierre repeated his story. "Yes, his wrist is injured—but oh! it's not a case of immediate gravity."

On the part of the three sons, he had divined a sudden quiver, an impulse of their whole beings to rush to the help and defence of their father. And for their sakes he sought words of comfort: "He is with me at Neuilly. And with due care it is certain that no serious complications will arise. He sent me to tell you to be in no wise uneasy about him."

Mere-Grand for her part evinced no fears, but preserved great calmness, as if the priest's tidings contained nothing beyond what she had known already. If anything, she seemed rather relieved, freed from anxiety which she had confided to none. "If he is with you, monsieur," she answered, "he is evidently as comfortable as he can be, and sheltered from all risks. We were surprised, however, by his letter last night, as it did not explain why he was detained, and we should have ended by feeling frightened. But now everything is satisfactory."

Mere-Grand and the three sons, following Marie's example, asked no explanations. On a table near at hand Pierre noticed several morning newspapers lying open and displaying column after column of particulars about the crime. The sons had certainly read these papers, and had feared lest their father should be compromised in that frightful affair. How far did their knowledge of the latter go? They must be ignorant of the part played by Salvat. It was surely impossible for them to piece together all the unforeseen circumstances which had brought about their father's meeting with the workman, and then the crime. Mere-Grand, no doubt, was in certain respects better informed than the others. But they, the sons and Marie, neither knew nor sought to know anything. And thus what a wealth of respect and affection there was in their unshakable confidence in the father, in the tranquillity they displayed directly he sent them word that they were not to be anxious about him!

"Madame," Pierre resumed, "Guillaume told me to give you this little key, and to remind you to do what he charged you to do, if any misfortune should befall him."

She started, but so slightly that it was scarcely perceptible; and taking the key she answered as if some ordinary wish on the part of a sick person were alone in question. "Very well. Tell him that his wishes shall be carried out." Then she added, "But pray take a seat, monsieur."

Pierre, indeed, had remained standing. However, he now felt it necessary to accept a chair, desirous as he was of hiding the embarrassment which he still felt in this house, although he was *en famille* there. Marie, who could not live without occupation for her fingers, had just returned to some embroidery, some of the fine needlework which she stubbornly executed for a large establishment dealing in baby-linen and bridal *trousseaux*; for she wished at any rate to earn her own pocket-money, she often said with a laugh. Mere-Grand, too, from habit, which she followed even when visitors were present, had once more started on her perpetual stocking-mending; while Francois and Antoine had again seated themselves at their table; and Thomas alone remained on his legs, leaning against his bench. All the charm of industrious intimacy pervaded the spacious, sun-lit room.

"But we'll all go to see father to-morrow," Thomas suddenly exclaimed.

Before Pierre could answer Marie raised her head. "No, no," said she, "he does not wish any of us to go to him; for if we should be watched and followed we should betray the secret of his retreat. Isn't that so, Monsieur l'Abbe?"

"It would indeed be prudent of you to deprive yourselves of the pleasure of embracing him until he himself can come back here. It will be a matter of some two or three weeks," answered Pierre.

Mere-Grand at once expressed approval of this. "No doubt," said she. "Nothing could be more sensible."

So the three sons did not insist, but bravely accepted the secret anxiety in which they must for a time live, renouncing the visit which would have caused them so much delight, because their father bade them do so and because his safety depended perhaps on their obedience.

However, Thomas resumed: "Then, Monsieur l'Abbe, will you please tell him that as work will be interrupted here, I shall return to the factory during his absence. I shall be more at ease there for the researches on which we are engaged."

"And please tell him from me," put in Francois, "that he mustn't worry about my examination. Things are going very well. I feel almost certain of success."

Pierre promised that he would forget nothing. However, Marie raised her head, smiling and glancing at Antoine, who had remained silent with a faraway look in his eyes. "And you, little one," said she, "don't you send him any message?"

II. A HOME OF INDUSTRY

Emerging from a dream, the young fellow also began to smile. "Yes, yes, a message that you love him dearly, and that he's to make haste back for you to make him happy."

At this they all became merry, even Marie, who in lieu of embarrassment showed a tranquil gaiety born of confidence in the future. Between her and the young men there was naught but happy affection. And a grave smile appeared even on the pale lips of Mere-Grand, who likewise approved of the happiness which life seemed to be promising.

Pierre wished to stay a few minutes longer. They all began to chat, and his astonishment increased. He had gone from surprise to surprise in this house where he had expected to find that equivocal, disorderly life, that rebellion against social laws, which destroy morality. But instead of this he had found loving serenity, and such strong discipline that life there partook of the gravity, almost the austerity, of convent life, tempered by youth and gaiety. The vast room was redolent of industry and quietude, warm with bright sunshine. However, what most particularly struck him was the Spartan training, the bravery of mind and heart among those sons who allowed nothing to be seen of their personal feelings, and did not presume to judge their father, but remained content with his message, ready to await events, stoical and silent, while carrying on their daily tasks. Nothing could be more simple, more dignified, more lofty. And there was also the smiling heroism of Mere-Grand and Marie, those two women who slept over that laboratory where terrible preparations were manipulated, and where an explosion was always possible.

However, such courage, orderliness and dignity merely surprised Pierre, without touching him. He had no cause for complaint, he had received a polite greeting if not an affectionate one; but then he was as yet only a stranger there, a priest. In spite of everything, however, he remained hostile, feeling that he was in a sphere where none of his own torments could be shared or even divined. How did these folks manage to be so calm and happy amidst their religious unbelief, their sole faith in science, and in presence of that terrifying Paris which spread before them the boundless sea, the growling abomination of its injustice and its want? As this thought came to him he turned his head and gazed at the city through the huge window, whence it stretched away, ever present, ever living its giant life. And at that hour, under the oblique sunrays of the winter afternoon, all Paris was speckled with luminous dust, as if some invisible sower, hidden amidst the glory of the planet, were fast scattering seed which fell upon every side in a stream of gold. The whole field was covered with it; for the endless chaos of house roofs and edifices seemed to be land in tilth, furrowed by some gigantic plough. And Pierre in his uneasiness, stirred, despite everything, by an invincible need of hope, asked himself if this was not a good sowing, the furrows of Paris strewn with light by the divine sun for the great future harvest, that harvest of truth and justice of whose advent he had despaired.

At last he rose and took his leave, promising to return at once, if there should be any bad news. It was Marie who showed him to the front door. And there another of those childish blushes which worried her so much suddenly rose to her face, just as she, in her turn, also wished to send her loving message to the injured man. However, with her gay, candid eyes fixed on those of the priest, she bravely spoke the words: "*Au revoir, Monsieur l'Abbe*. Tell Guillaume that I love him and await him."

III. PENURY AND TOIL

THREE days went by, and every morning Guillaume, confined to his bed and consumed by fever and impatience, experienced fresh anxiety directly the newspapers arrived. Pierre had tried to keep them from him, but Guillaume then worried himself the more, and so the priest had to read him column by column all the extraordinary articles that were published respecting the crime.

Never before had so many rumours inundated the press. Even the "Globe," usually so grave and circumspect, yielded to the general *furore*, and printed whatever statements reached it. But the more unscrupulous papers were the ones to read. The "Voix du Peuple" in particular made use of the public feverishness to increase its sales. Each morning it employed some fresh device, and printed some frightful story of a nature to drive people mad with terror. It related that not a day passed without Baron Duvillard receiving threatening letters of the coarsest description, announcing that his wife, his son and his daughter would all be killed, that he himself would be butchered in turn, and that do what he might his house would none the less be blown up. And as a measure of precaution the house was guarded day and night alike by a perfect army of plain-clothes officers. Then another article contained an amazing piece of invention. Some anarchists, after carrying barrels of powder into a sewer near the Madeleine, were said to have undermined the whole district, planning a perfect volcano there, into which one half of Paris would sink. And at another time it was alleged that the police were on the track of a terrible plot which embraced all Europe, from the depths of Russia to the shores of Spain. The signal for putting it into execution was to be given in France, and there would be a three days' massacre, with grape shot sweeping everyone off the Boulevards, and the Seine running red, swollen by a torrent of blood. Thanks to these able and intelligent devices of the Press, terror now reigned in the city; frightened foreigners fled from the hotels *en masse*; and Paris had become a mere mad-house, where the most idiotic delusions at once found credit.

It was not all this, however, that worried Guillaume. He was only anxious about Salvat and the various new "scents" which the newspaper reporters attempted to follow up. The engineer was not yet arrested, and, so far indeed, there had been no statement in print to indicate that the police were on his track. At last, however, Pierre one morning read a paragraph which made the injured man turn pale.

"Dear me! It seems that a tool has been found among the rubbish at the entrance of the Duvillard mansion. It is a bradawl, and its handle bears the name of Grandidier, which is that of a man who keeps some well-known metal works. He is to appear before the investigating magistrate to-day."

Guillaume made a gesture of despair. "Ah!" said he, "they are on the right track at last. That tool must certainly have been dropped by Salvat. He worked at Grandidier's before he came to me for a few days. And from Grandidier they will learn all that they need to know in order to follow the scent."

Pierre then remembered that he had heard the Grandidier factory mentioned at Montmartre. Guillaume's eldest son, Thomas, had served his apprenticeship there, and even worked there occasionally nowadays.

"You told me," resumed Guillaume, "that during my absence Thomas intended to go back to the factory. It's in connection with a new motor which he's planning, and has almost hit upon. If there should be a perquisition there, he may be questioned, and may refuse to answer, in order to guard his secret. So he ought to be warned of this, warned at once!"

Without trying to extract any more precise statement from his brother, Pierre obligingly offered his services. "If you like," said he, "I will go to see Thomas this afternoon. Perhaps I may come across Monsieur Grandidier himself and learn how far the affair has gone, and what was said at the investigating magistrate's."

With a moist glance and an affectionate grasp of the hand, Guillaume at once thanked Pierre: "Yes, yes, brother, go there, it will be good and brave of you."

"Besides," continued the priest, "I really wanted to go to Montmartre to-day. I haven't told you so, but something has been worrying me. If Salvat has fled, he must have left the woman and the child all alone up yonder. On the morning of the day when the explosion took place I saw the poor creatures in such a state of destitution, such misery, that I can't think of them without a heart-pang. Women and children so often die of hunger when the man is no longer there."

At this, Guillaume, who had kept Pierre's hand in his own, pressed it more tightly, and in a trembling voice exclaimed: "Yes, yes, and that will be good and brave too. Go there, brother, go there."

That house of the Rue des Saules, that horrible home of want and agony, had lingered in Pierre's memory. To him it was like an embodiment of the whole filthy *cloaca*, in which the poor of Paris suffer unto death. And on returning thither that afternoon, he found the same slimy mud around it; its yard littered with the same filth, its dark, damp stairways redolent of the same stench of neglect and poverty, as before. In winter time, while the fine central districts of Paris are dried and cleansed, the faraway districts of the poor remain gloomy and miry, beneath the everlasting tramp of the wretched ones who dwell in them.

Remembering the staircase which conducted to Salvat's lodging, Pierre began to climb it amidst a loud screaming of little children, who suddenly became quiet, letting the house sink into death-like silence once more. Then the thought of Laveuve, who had perished up there like a stray dog, came back to Pierre. And he shuddered when, on the top landing, he knocked at Salvat's door, and profound silence alone answered him. Not a breath was to be heard.

However, he knocked again, and as nothing stirred he began to think that nobody could be there. Perhaps Salvat had returned to fetch the woman and the child, and perhaps they had followed him to some humble nook abroad. Still this would have astonished him; for the poor seldom quit their homes, but die where they have suffered. So he gave another gentle knock.

And at last a faint sound, the light tread of little feet, was heard amidst the silence. Then a weak, childish voice ventured to inquire: "Who is there?"

"Monsieur l'Abbe."

The silence fell again, nothing more stirred. There was evidently hesitation on the other side.

"Monsieur l'Abbe who came the other day," said Pierre again.

This evidently put an end to all uncertainty, for the door was set ajar and little Celine admitted the priest. "I beg your pardon, Monsieur l'Abbe," said she, "but Mamma Theodore has gone out, and she told me not to open the door to anyone."

Pierre had, for a moment, imagined that Salvat himself was hiding there. But with a glance he took in the whole of the small bare room, where man, woman and child dwelt together. At the same time, Madame Theodore doubtless feared a visit from the police. Had she seen Salvat since the crime? Did she know where he was hiding? Had he come back there to embrace and tranquillise them both?

"And your papa, my dear," said Pierre to Celine, "isn't he here either?"

"Oh! no, monsieur, he has gone away."

"What, gone away?"

"Yes, he hasn't been home to sleep, and we don't know where he is."

"Perhaps he's working."

"Oh, no! he'd send us some money if he was."

"Then he's gone on a journey, perhaps?"

"I don't know."

"He wrote to Mamma Theodore, no doubt?"

"I don't know."

Pierre asked no further questions. In fact, he felt somewhat ashamed of his attempt to extract information from this child of eleven, whom he thus found alone. It was quite possible that she knew nothing, that Salvat, in a spirit of prudence, had even refrained from sending any tidings of himself. Indeed, there was an expression of truthfulness on the child's fair, gentle and intelligent face, which was grave with the gravity that extreme misery imparts to the young.

"I am sorry that Mamma Theodore isn't here," said Pierre, "I wanted to speak to her."

"But perhaps you would like to wait for her, Monsieur l'Abbe. She has gone to my Uncle Toussaint's in the Rue Marcadet; and she can't stop much longer, for she's been away more than an hour."

Thereupon Celine cleared one of the chairs on which lay a handful of scraps of wood, picked up on some waste ground.

The bare and fireless room was assuredly also a breadless one. Pierre could divine the absence of the bread-winner, the disappearance of the man who represents will and strength in the home, and on whom one still relies even when weeks have gone by without work. He goes out and scours the city, and often ends by bringing back the indispensable crust which keeps death at bay. But with his disappearance comes complete abandonment, the wife and child in danger, destitute of all prop and help.

Pierre, who had sat down and was looking at that poor, little, blue-eyed girl, to whose lips a smile returned in spite of everything, could not keep from questioning her on another point. "So you don't go to school, my child?" said he.

She faintly blushed and answered: "I've no shoes to go in."

He glanced at her feet, and saw that she was wearing a pair of ragged old list-slippers, from which her little toes protruded, red with cold.

"Besides," she continued, "Mamma Theodore says that one doesn't go to school when one's got nothing to eat. Mamma Theodore wanted to work but she couldn't, because her eyes got burning hot and full of water. And so we don't know what to do, for we've had nothing left since yesterday, and if Uncle Toussaint can't lend us twenty sous it'll be all over."

She was still smiling in her unconscious way, but two big tears had gathered in her eyes. And the sight of the child shut up in that bare room, apart from all the happy ones of earth, so upset the priest that he again felt his anger with want and misery awakening. Then, another ten minutes having elapsed, he became impatient, for he had to go to the Grandidier works before returning home.

"I don't know why Mamma Theodore doesn't come back," repeated Celine. "Perhaps she's chatting." Then, an idea occurring to her she continued: "I'll take you to my Uncle Toussaint's, Monsieur l'Abbe, if you like. It's close by, just round the corner."

"But you have no shoes, my child."

"Oh! that don't matter, I walk all the same."

Thereupon he rose from the chair and said simply: "Well, yes, that will be better, take me there. And I'll buy you some shoes."

Celine turned quite pink, and then made haste to follow him after carefully locking the door of the room like a good little housewife, though, truth to tell, there was nothing worth stealing in the place.

In the meantime it had occurred to Madame Theodore that before calling on her brother Toussaint to try to borrow a franc from him, she might first essay her luck with her younger sister, Hortense, who had married little Chretiennot, the clerk, and occupied a flat of four rooms on the Boulevard de Rochechouart. This was quite an affair, however, and the poor woman only made the venture because Celine had been fasting since the previous day.

Eugene Toussaint, the mechanician, a man of fifty, was her stepbrother, by the first marriage contracted by her father. A young dressmaker whom the latter had subsequently wedded, had borne him three daughters, Pauline, Leonie and Hortense. And on his death, his son Eugene, who already had a wife and child of his own, had found himself for a short time with his stepmother and sisters on his hands. The stepmother, fortunately, was an active and intelligent woman, and knew how to get out of difficulties. She returned to her former workroom where her daughter Pauline was already apprenticed, and she next placed Leonie there; so that Hortense, the youngest girl, who was a spoilt child, prettier and more delicate than her sisters, was alone left at school. And, later on,—after Pauline had married Labitte the stonemason, and Leonie, Salvat the journeyman-engineer,—Hortense, while serving as assistant at a confectioner's in the Rue des Martyrs, there became acquainted with Chretiennot, a clerk, who married her. Leonie had died young, only a few weeks after her mother; Pauline, forsaken by her husband, lived with her brother-in-law Salvat, and Hortense alone wore a light silk gown on Sundays, resided in a new house, and ranked as a *bourgeoise*, at the price, however, of interminable worries and great privation.

Madame Theodore knew that her sister was generally short of money towards the month's end, and therefore felt rather ill at ease in thus venturing to apply for a loan. Chretiennot, moreover, embittered by his own mediocrity, had of late years accused his wife of being the cause of their spoilt life, and had ceased all intercourse with her relatives. Toussaint, no doubt, was a decent workman; but that Madame Theodore who lived in misery with her brother-in-law, and that Salvat who wandered from workshop to workshop like an incorrigible ranter whom no employer would keep; those two, with their want and dirt and rebellion, had ended by incensing the vain little clerk, who was not only a great stickler for the proprieties, but was soured by all the difficulties he encountered in his own life. And thus he had forbidden Hortense to receive her sister.

All the same, as Madame Theodore climbed the carpeted staircase of the house on the Boulevard Rochechouart, she experienced a certain feeling of pride at the thought that she had a relation living in such luxury. The Chretiennot's rooms were on the third floor, and overlooked the courtyard. Their *femme-de-menage*—a woman who goes out by the day or hour charring, cleaning and cooking—came back every afternoon about four o'clock to see to the dinner, and that day she was already there. She admitted the visitor, though she could not conceal her anxious surprise at her boldness in calling in such slatternly garb. However, on the very threshold of the little salon, Madame Theodore stopped short in wonderment herself, for her sister Hortense was sobbing and crouching on one of the armchairs, upholstered in blue repp, of which she was so proud.

"What is the matter? What has happened to you?" asked Madame Theodore.

Her sister, though scarcely two and thirty, was no longer "the beautiful Hortense" of former days. She retained a doll-like appearance, with a tall slim figure, pretty eyes and fine, fair hair. But she who had once taken so much care of herself, had now come down to dressing-gowns of doubtful cleanliness. Her eyelids, too, were reddening, and blotches were appearing on her skin. She had begun to fade after giving birth to two daughters, one of whom was now nine and the other seven years of age. Very proud and egotistical, she herself had begun to regret her marriage, for she had formerly considered herself a real beauty, worthy of the palaces and equipages of some Prince Charming. And at this moment she was plunged in such despair, that her sister's sudden appearance on the scene did not even astonish her: "Ah! it's you," she gasped. "Ah! if you only knew what a blow's fallen on me in the middle of all our worries!"

Madame Theodore at once thought of the children, Lucienne and Marcelle. "Are your daughters ill?" she asked.

"No, no, our neighbour has taken them for a walk on the Boulevard. But the fact is, my dear, I'm *enceinte*, and when I told Chretiennot of it after *dejeuner*, he flew into a most fearful passion, saying the most dreadful, the most cruel things!"

Then she again sobbed. Gentle and indolent by nature, desirous of peace and quietness before anything else, she was incapable of deceiving her husband, as he well knew. But the trouble was that an addition to the family would upset the whole economy of the household.

III. PENURY AND TOIL

"*Mon Dieu*!" said Madame Theodore at last, "you brought up the others, and you'll bring up this one too."

At this an explosion of anger dried the other's eyes; and she rose, exclaiming: "You are good, you are! One can see that our purse isn't yours. How are we to bring up another child when we can scarcely make both ends meet as it is?"

And thereupon, forgetting the *bourgeois* pride which usually prompted her to silence or falsehood, she freely explained their embarrassment, the horrid pecuniary worries which made their life a perpetual misery. Their rent amounted to 700 francs,[1] so that out of the 3000 francs[2] which the husband earned at his office, barely a couple of hundred were left them every month. And how were they to manage with that little sum, provide food and clothes, keep up their rank and so forth? There was the indispensable black coat for monsieur, the new dress which madame must have at regular intervals, under penalty of losing caste, the new boots which the children required almost every month, in fact, all sorts of things that could not possibly be dispensed with. One might strike a dish or two out of the daily menu, and even go without wine; but evenings came when it was absolutely necessary to take a cab. And, apart from all this, one had to reckon with the wastefulness of the children, the disorder in which the discouraged wife left the house, and the despair of the husband, who was convinced that he would never extricate himself from his difficulties, even should his salary some day be raised to as high a figure as 4000 francs. Briefly, one here found the unbearable penury of the petty clerk, with consequences as disastrous as the black want of the artisan: the mock facade and lying luxury; all the disorder and suffering which lie behind intellectual pride at not earning one's living at a bench or on a scaffolding.

"Well, well," repeated Madame Theodore, "you can't kill the child."

"No, of course not; but it's the end of everything," answered Hortense, sinking into the armchair again. "What will become of us, *mon Dieu*! What will become of us!" Then she collapsed in her unbuttoned dressing gown, tears once more gushing from her red and swollen eyes.

Much vexed that circumstances should be so unpropitious, Madame Theodore nevertheless ventured to ask for the loan of twenty sons; and this brought her sister's despair and confusion to a climax. "I really haven't a centime in the house," said she, "just now I borrowed ten sous for the children from the servant. I had to get ten francs from the Mont de Piete on a little ring the other day. And it's always the same at the end of the month. However, Chretiennot will be paid to-day, and he's coming back early with the money for dinner. So if I can I will send you something to-morrow."

At this same moment the servant hastened in with a distracted air, being well aware that monsieur was in no wise partial to madame's relatives. "Oh madame, madame!" said she; "here's monsieur coming up the stairs."

"Quick then, quick, go away!" cried Hortense, "I should only have another scene if he met you here. To-morrow, if I can, I promise you."

To avoid Chretiennot who was coming in, Madame Theodore had to hide herself in the kitchen. As he passed, she just caught sight of him, well dressed as usual in a tight-fitting frock-coat. Short and lean, with a thin face and long and carefully tended

---

[1] $140.

[2] $600.

beard, he had the bearing of one who is both vain and quarrelsome. Fourteen years of office life had withered him, and now the long evening hours which he spent at a neighbouring cafe were finishing him off.

When Madame Theodore had quitted the house she turned with dragging steps towards the Rue Marcadet where the Toussaints resided. Here, again, she had no great expectations, for she well knew what ill-luck and worry had fallen upon her brother's home. During the previous autumn Toussaint, though he was but fifty, had experienced an attack of paralysis which had laid him up for nearly five months. Prior to this mishap he had borne himself bravely, working steadily, abstaining from drink, and bringing up his three children in true fatherly fashion. One of them, a girl, was now married to a carpenter, with whom she had gone to Le Havre, while of the others, both boys—one a soldier, had been killed in Tonquin, and the other Charles, after serving his time in the army, had become a working mechanician. Still, Toussaint's long illness had exhausted the little money which he had in the Savings Bank, and now that he had been set on his legs again, he had to begin life once more without a copper before him.

Madame Theodore found her sister-in-law alone in the cleanly kept room which she and her husband occupied. Madame Toussaint was a portly woman, whose corpulence increased in spite of everything, whether it were worry or fasting. She had a round puffy face with bright little eyes; and was a very worthy woman, whose only faults were an inclination for gossiping and a fondness for good cheer. Before Madame Theodore even opened her mouth she understood the object of her visit. "You've come on us at a bad moment, my dear," she said, "we're stumped. Toussaint wasn't able to go back to the works till the day before yesterday, and he'll have to ask for an advance this evening."

As she spoke, she looked at the other with no great sympathy, hurt as she felt by her slovenly appearance. "And Salvat," she added, "is he still doing nothing?"

Madame Theodore doubtless foresaw the question, for she quietly lied: "He isn't in Paris, a friend has taken him off for some work over Belgium way, and I'm waiting for him to send us something."

Madame Toussaint still remained distrustful, however: "Ah!" she said, "it's just as well that he shouldn't be in Paris; for with all these bomb affairs we couldn't help thinking of him, and saying that he was quite mad enough to mix himself up in them."

The other did not even blink. If she knew anything she kept it to herself.

"But you, my dear, can't you find any work?" continued Madame Toussaint.

"Well, what would you have me do with my poor eyes? It's no longer possible for me to sew."

"That's true. A seamstress gets done for. When Toussaint was laid up here I myself wanted to go back to my old calling as a needlewoman. But there! I spoilt everything and did no good. Charring's about the only thing that one can always do. Why don't you get some jobs of that kind?"

"I'm trying, but I can't find any."

Little by little Madame Toussaint was softening at sight of the other's miserable appearance. She made her sit down, and told her that she would give her something if Toussaint should come home with money. Then, yielding to her partiality for gossiping, since there was somebody to listen to her, she started telling stories. The one affair, however, on which she invariably harped was the sorry business of her son

Charles and the servant girl at a wine shop over the way. Before going into the army Charles had been a most hard-working and affectionate son, invariably bringing his pay home to his mother. And certainly he still worked and showed himself good-natured; but military service, while sharpening his wits, had taken away some of his liking for ordinary manual toil. It wasn't that he regretted army life, for he spoke of his barracks as a prison. Only his tools had seemed to him rather heavy when, on quitting the service, he had been obliged to take them in hand once more.

"And so, my dear," continued Madame Toussaint, "it's all very well for Charles to be kind-hearted, he can do no more for us. I knew that he wasn't in a hurry to get married, as it costs money to keep a wife. And he was always very prudent, too, with girls. But what would you have? There was that moment of folly with that Eugenie over the road, a regular baggage who's already gone off with another man, and left her baby behind. Charles has put it out to nurse, and pays for it every month. And a lot of expense it is too, perfect ruination. Yes, indeed, every possible misfortune has fallen on us."

In this wise Madame Toussaint rattled on for a full half hour. Then seeing that waiting and anxiety had made her sister-in-law turn quite pale, she suddenly stopped short. "You're losing patience, eh?" she exclaimed. "The fact is, that Toussaint won't be back for some time. Shall we go to the works together? I'll easily find out if he's likely to bring any money home."

They then decided to go down, but at the bottom of the stairs they lingered for another quarter of an hour chatting with a neighbour who had lately lost a child. And just as they were at last leaving the house they heard a call: "Mamma! mamma!"

It came from little Celine, whose face was beaming with delight. She was wearing a pair of new shoes and devouring a cake. "Mamma," she resumed, "Monsieur l'Abbe who came the other day wants to see you. Just look! he bought me all this!"

On seeing the shoes and the cake, Madame Theodore understood matters. And when Pierre, who was behind the child, accosted her she began to tremble and stammer thanks. Madame Toussaint on her side had quickly drawn near, not indeed to ask for anything herself, but because she was well pleased at such a God-send for her sister-in-law, whose circumstances were worse than her own. And when she saw the priest slip ten francs into Madame Theodore's hand she explained to him that she herself would willingly have lent something had she been able. Then she promptly started on the stories of Toussaint's attack and her son Charles's ill-luck.

But Celine broke in: "I say, mamma, the factory where papa used to work is here in this street, isn't it? Monsieur l'Abbe has some business there."[1]

"The Grandidier factory," resumed Madame Toussaint; "well, we were just going there, and we can show Monsieur l'Abbe the way."

It was only a hundred steps off. Escorted by the two women and the child, Pierre slackened his steps and tried to extract some information about Salvat from Madame Theodore. But she at once became very prudent. She had not seen him again, she declared; he must have gone with a mate to Belgium, where there was a prospect of

---

[1] Although the children of the French peasantry almost invariably address their parents as "father" and "mother," those of the working classes of Paris, and some other large cities, usually employ the terms "papa" and "mamma."—Trans.

some work. From what she said, it appeared to the priest that Salvat had not dared to return to the Rue des Saules since his crime, in which all had collapsed, both his past life of toil and hope, and his recent existence with its duties towards the woman and the child.

"There's the factory, Monsieur l'Abbe," suddenly said Madame Toussaint, "my sister-in-law won't have to wait now, since you've been kind enough to help her. Thank you for her and for us."

Madame Theodore and Celine likewise poured forth their thanks, standing beside Madame Toussaint in the everlasting mud of that populous district, amidst the jostling of the passers-by. And lingering there as if to see Pierre enter, they again chatted together and repeated that, after all, some priests were very kind.

The Grandidier works covered an extensive plot of ground. Facing the street there was only a brick building with narrow windows and a great archway, through which one espied a long courtyard. But, in the rear, came a suite of habitations, workshops, and sheds, above whose never ending roofs arose the two lofty chimneys of the generators. From the very threshold one detected the rumbling and quivering of machinery, all the noise and bustle of work. Black water flowed by at one's feet, and up above white vapour spurted from a slender pipe with a regular strident puff, as if it were the very breath of that huge, toiling hive.

Bicycles were now the principal output of the works. When Grandidier had taken them on leaving the Dijon Arts and Trades School, they were declining under bad management, slowly building some little motive engines by the aid of antiquated machinery. Foreseeing the future, however, he had induced his elder brother, one of the managers of the Bon Marche, to finance him, on the promise that he would supply that great emporium with excellent bicycles at 150 francs apiece. And now quite a big venture was in progress, for the Bon Marche was already bringing out the new popular machine "La Lisette," the "Bicycle for the Multitude," as the advertisements asserted. Nevertheless, Grandidier was still in all the throes of a great struggle, for his new machinery had cast a heavy burden of debt on him. At the same time each month brought its effort, the perfecting or simplifying of some part of the manufacture, which meant a saving in the future. He was ever on the watch; and even now was thinking of reverting to the construction of little motors, for he thought he could divine in the near future the triumph of the motor-car.

On asking if M. Thomas Froment were there, Pierre was led by an old workman to a little shed, where he found the young fellow in the linen jacket of a mechanician, his hands black with filings. He was adjusting some piece of mechanism, and nobody would have suspected him to be a former pupil of the Lycee Condorcet, one of the three clever Froments who had there rendered the name famous. But his only desire had been to act as his father's faithful servant, the arm that forges, the embodiment of the manual toil by which conceptions are realised. And, a giant of three and twenty, ever attentive and courageous, he was likewise a man of patient, silent and sober nature.

On catching sight of Pierre he quivered with anxiety and sprang forward. "Father is no worse?" he asked.

"No, no. But he read in the papers that story of a bradawl found in the Rue Godot-de-Mauroy, and it made him anxious, because the police may make a perquisition here."

Thomas, his own anxiety allayed, began to smile. "Tell him he may sleep quietly," he responded. "To begin with, I've unfortunately not yet hit on our little motor such as I want it to be. In fact, I haven't yet put it together. I'm keeping the pieces at our house, and nobody here knows exactly what I come to do at the factory. So the police may search, it will find nothing. Our secret runs no risk."

Pierre promised to repeat these words to Guillaume, so as to dissipate his fears. However, when he tried to sound Thomas, and ascertain the position of affairs, what the factory people thought of the discovery of the bradawl, and whether there was as yet any suspicion of Salvat, he once more found the young man taciturn, and elicited merely a "yes" or a "no" in answer to his inquiries. The police had not been there as yet? No. But the men must surely have mentioned Salvat? Yes, of course, on account of his Anarchist opinions. But what had Grandidier, the master, said, on returning from the investigating magistrate's? As for that Thomas knew nothing. He had not seen Grandidier that day.

"But here he comes!" the young man added. "Ah! poor fellow, his wife, I fancy, had another attack this morning."

He alluded to a frightful story which Guillaume had already recounted to Pierre. Grandidier, falling in love with a very beautiful girl, had married her; but for five years now she had been insane: the result of puerperal fever and the death of an infant son. Her husband, with his ardent affection for her, had been unwilling to place her in an asylum, and had accordingly kept her with him in a little pavilion, whose windows, overlooking the courtyard of the factory, always remained closed. She was never seen; and never did he speak of her to anybody. It was said that she was usually like a child, very gentle and very sad, and still beautiful, with regal golden hair. At times, however, attacks of frantic madness came upon her, and he then had to struggle with her, and often hold her for hours in his arms to prevent her from splitting her head against the walls. Fearful shrieks would ring out for a time, and then deathlike silence would fall once more.

Grandidier came into the shed where Thomas was working. A handsome man of forty, with an energetic face, he had a dark and heavy moustache, brush-like hair and clear eyes. He was very partial to Thomas, and during the young fellow's apprenticeship there, had treated him like a son. And he now let him return thither whenever it pleased him, and placed his appliances at his disposal. He knew that he was trying to devise a new motor, a question in which he himself was extremely interested; still he evinced the greatest discretion, never questioning Thomas, but awaiting the result of his endeavours.

"This is my uncle, Abbe Froment, who looked in to wish me good day," said the young man, introducing Pierre.

An exchange of polite remarks ensued. Then Grandidier sought to cast off the sadness which made people think him stern and harsh, and in a bantering tone exclaimed: "I didn't tell you, Thomas, of my business with the investigating magistrate. If I hadn't enjoyed a good reputation we should have had all the spies of the Prefecture here. The magistrate wanted me to explain the presence of that bradawl in the Rue Godot-de-Mauroy, and I at once realised that, in his opinion, the culprit must have worked here. For my part I immediately thought of Salvat. But I don't denounce people. The magistrate has my hiring-book, and as for Salvat I simply answered that he worked here for nearly three months last autumn, and then disappeared. They can look for him themselves! Ah! that magistrate! you can picture him a little fellow with fair hair and cat-like eyes, very careful of his appearance, a society man evidently, but quite frisky at being mixed up in this affair."

"Isn't he Monsieur Amadieu?" asked Pierre.

"Yes, that's his name. Ah! he's certainly delighted with the present which those Anarchists have made him, with that crime of theirs."

The priest listened in deep anxiety. As his brother had feared, the true scent, the first conducting wire, had now been found. And he looked at Thomas to see if he also were disturbed. But the young man was either ignorant of the ties which linked Salvat to his father, or else he possessed great power of self-control, for he merely smiled at Grandidier's sketch of the magistrate.

Then, as Grandidier went to look at the piece of mechanism which Thomas was finishing, and they began to speak about it, Pierre drew near to an open doorway which communicated with a long workshop where engine lathes were rumbling, and the beams of press-drills falling quickly and rhythmically. Leather gearing spun along with a continuous gliding, and there was ceaseless bustle and activity amidst the odoriferous dampness of all the steam. Scores of perspiring workmen, grimy with dust and filings, were still toiling. Still this was the final effort of the day. And as three men approached a water-tap near Pierre to wash their hands, he listened to their talk, and became particularly interested in it when he heard one of them, a tall, ginger-haired fellow, call another Toussaint, and the third Charles.

Toussaint, a big, square-shouldered man with knotty arms, only showed his fifty years on his round, scorched face, which besides being roughened and wrinkled by labour, bristled with grey hairs, which nowadays he was content to shave off once a week. It was only his right arm that was affected by paralysis, and moved rather sluggishly. As for Charles, a living portrait of his father, he was now in all the strength of his six and twentieth year, with splendid muscles distending his white skin, and a full face barred by a heavy black moustache. The three men, like their employer, were speaking of the explosion at the Duvillard mansion, of the bradawl found there, and of Salvat, whom they all now suspected.

"Why, only a brigand would do such a thing!" said Toussaint. "That Anarchism disgusts me. I'll have none of it. But all the same it's for the *bourgeois* to settle matters. If the others want to blow them up, it's their concern. It's they who brought it about."

This indifference was undoubtedly the outcome of a life of want and social injustice; it was the indifference of an old toiler, who, weary of struggling and hoping for improvements, was now quite ready to tolerate the crumbling of a social system, which threatened him with hunger in his impotent old age.

"Well, you know," rejoined Charles, "I've heard the Anarchists talking, and they really say some very true and sensible things. And just take yourself, father; you've been working for thirty years, and isn't it abominable that you should have had to pass through all that you did pass through recently, liable to go off like some old horse that's slaughtered at the first sign of illness? And, of course, it makes me think of myself, and I can't help feeling that it won't be at all amusing to end like that. And may the thunder of God kill me if I'm wrong, but one feels half inclined to join in their great flare-up if it's really to make everybody happy!"

He certainly lacked the flame of enthusiasm, and if he had come to these views it was solely from impatience to lead a less toilsome life, for obligatory military service had given him ideas of equality among all men—a desire to struggle, raise himself and obtain his legitimate share of life's enjoyments. It was, in fact, the inevitable step which carries each generation a little more forward. There was the father, who, deceived in his hope of a fraternal republic, had grown sceptical and contemptuous; and there was the son advancing towards a new faith, and gradually yielding to ideas of violence, since political liberty had failed to keep its promises.

Nevertheless, as the big, ginger-haired fellow grew angry, and shouted that if Salvat were guilty, he ought to be caught and guillotined at once, without waiting for judges, Toussaint ended by endorsing his opinion. "Yes, yes, he may have married one of my sisters, but I renounce him.... And yet, you know, it would astonish me to find him guilty, for he isn't wicked at heart. I'm sure he wouldn't kill a fly."

"But what would you have?" put in Charles. "When a man's driven to extremities he goes mad."

They had now washed themselves; but Toussaint, on perceiving his employer, lingered there in order to ask him for an advance. As it happened, Grandidier, after cordially shaking hands with Pierre, approached the old workman of his own accord, for he held him in esteem. And, after listening to him, he gave him a line for the cashier on a card. As a rule, he was altogether against the practice of advancing money, and his men disliked him, and said he was over rigid, though in point of fact he had a good heart. But he had his position as an employer to defend, and to him concessions meant ruin. With such keen competition on all sides, with the capitalist system entailing a terrible and incessant struggle, how could one grant the demands of the workers, even when they were legitimate?

Sudden compassion came upon Pierre when, after quitting Thomas, he saw Grandidier, who had finished his round, crossing the courtyard in the direction of the closed pavilion, where all the grief of his heart-tragedy awaited him. Here was that man waging the battle of life, defending his fortune with the risk that his business might melt away amidst the furious warfare between capital and labour; and at the same time, in lieu of evening repose, finding naught but anguish it his hearth: a mad wife, an adored wife, who had sunk back into infancy, and was for ever dead to love! How incurable was his secret despair! Even on the days when he triumphed in his workshops, disaster awaited him at home. And could any more unhappy man, any man more deserving of pity, be found even among the poor who died of hunger, among those gloomy workers, those vanquished sons of labour who hated and who envied him?

When Pierre found himself in the street again he was astonished to see Madame Toussaint and Madame Theodore still there with little Celine. With their feet in the mud, like bits of wreckage against which beat the ceaseless flow of wayfarers, they had lingered there, still and ever chatting, loquacious and doleful, lulling their wretchedness to rest beneath a deluge of tittle-tattle. And when Toussaint, followed by his son, came out, delighted with the advance he had secured, he also found them on the same spot. Then he told Madame Theodore the story of the bradawl, and the idea which had occurred to him and all his mates that Salvat might well be the culprit. She, however, though turning very pale, began to protest, concealing both what she knew and what she really thought.

"I tell you I haven't seen him for several days," said she. "He must certainly be in Belgium. And as for a bomb, that's humbug. You say yourself that he's very gentle and wouldn't harm a fly!"

A little later as Pierre journeyed back to Neuilly in a tramcar he fell into a deep reverie. All the stir and bustle of that working-class district, the buzzing of the factory, the overflowing activity of that hive of labour, seemed to have lingered within him. And for the first time, amidst his worries, he realised the necessity of work. Yes, it was fatal, but it also gave health and strength. In effort which sustains and saves, he at last found a solid basis on which all might be reared. Was this, then, the first gleam of a new faith? But ah! what mockery! Work an uncertainty, work hopeless, work always ending in injustice! And then want ever on the watch for the toiler, strangling him as soon as slack times came round, and casting him into the streets like a dead dog immediately old age set in.

On reaching Neuilly, Pierre found Bertheroy at Guillaume's bedside. The old *savant* had just dressed the injured wrist, and was not yet certain that no complications would arise. "The fact is," he said to Guillaume, "you don't keep quiet. I always find you in a state of feverish emotion which is the worst possible thing for you. You must calm yourself, my dear fellow, and not allow anything to worry you."

A few minutes later, though, just as he was going away, he said with his pleasant smile: "Do you know that a newspaper writer came to interview me about that explosion? Those reporters imagine that scientific men know everything! I told the one who called on me that it would be very kind of *him* to enlighten *me* as to what powder was employed. And, by the way, I am giving a lesson on explosives at my laboratory to-morrow. There will be just a few persons present. You might come as well, Pierre, so as to give an account of it to Guillaume; it would interest him."

At a glance from his brother, Pierre accepted the invitation. Then, Bertheroy having gone, he recounted all he had learnt during the afternoon, how Salvat was suspected, and how the investigating magistrate had been put on the right scent. And at this news, intense fever again came over Guillaume, who, with his head buried in the pillow, and his eyes closed, stammered as if in a kind of nightmare: "Ah! then, this is the end! Salvat arrested, Salvat interrogated! Ah! that so much toil and so much hope should crumble!"

IV. CULTURE AND HOPE

ON the morrow, punctually at one o'clock, Pierre reached the Rue d'Ulm, where Bertheroy resided in a fairly large house, which the State had placed at his disposal, in order that he might install in it a laboratory for study and research. Thus the whole first floor had been transformed into one spacious apartment, where, from time to time, the illustrious chemist was fond of receiving a limited number of pupils and admirers, before whom he made experiments, and explained his new discoveries and theories.

For these occasions a few chairs were set out before the long and massive table, which was covered with jars and appliances. In the rear one saw the furnace, while all around were glass cases, full of vials and specimens. The persons present were, for the most part, fellow *savants*, with a few young men, and even a lady or two, and, of course, an occasional journalist. The whole made up a kind of family gathering, the visitors chatting with the master in all freedom.

Directly Bertheroy perceived Pierre he came forward, pressed his hand and seated him on a chair beside Guillaume's son Francois, who had been one of the first arrivals. The young man was completing his third year at the Ecole Normale, close by, so he only had a few steps to take to call upon his master Bertheroy, whom he regarded as one of the firmest minds of the age. Pierre was delighted to meet his nephew, for he had been greatly impressed in his favour on the occasion of his visit to Montmartre. Francois, on his side, greeted his uncle with all the cordial expansiveness of youth. He was, moreover, well pleased to obtain some news of his father.

However, Bertheroy began. He spoke in a familiar and sober fashion, but frequently employed some very happy expressions. At first he gave an account of his own extensive labours and investigations with regard to explosive substances, and related with a laugh that he sometimes manipulated powders which would have blown up the entire district. But, said he, in order to reassure his listeners, he was always extremely prudent. At last he turned to the subject of that explosion in the Rue Godot-de-Mauroy, which, for some days, had filled Paris with dismay. The remnants of the bomb had been carefully examined by experts, and one fragment had been brought to him, in order that he might give his opinion on it. The bomb appeared to have been prepared in a very rudimentary fashion; it had been charged with small pieces of iron, and fired by means of a match, such as a child might have devised. The extraordinary part of the affair was the formidable power of the central cartridge, which, although it must have been a small one, had wrought as much havoc as any thunderbolt. And the question was this: What incalculable power of destruction might one not arrive at if the charge were increased ten, twenty or a hundredfold. Embarrassment began, and divergencies of opinion clouded the issue directly one tried to specify what explosive had been employed. Of the three experts who had been consulted, one pronounced himself in favour of dynamite pure and simple; but the two others, although they did not agree together, believed in some combination of explosive matters. He, Bertheroy, had modestly declined to adjudicate, for the fragment submitted to him bore traces of so slight a character, that analysis became impossible. Thus he was unwilling to make any positive pronouncement. But his opinion was that one found oneself in presence of some unknown powder, some new explosive, whose power exceeded anything that had hitherto been dreamt of. He could picture some unknown *savant*, or some ignorant but lucky inventor, discovering the formula of this explosive under mysterious conditions. And this brought him to the point he wished to reach, the question of all the explosives which are so far unknown, and of the coming discoveries which he could foresee. In the course of his investigations he himself had found cause to suspect the existence of several such explosives, though he had lacked time and opportunity to prosecute his studies in that direction. However, he indicated the field which should be explored, and the best way of proceeding. In his opinion it was there that lay the future. And in a broad and eloquent peroration, he declared that explosives had hitherto been degraded by being employed in idiotic schemes of vengeance and destruction; whereas it was in them possibly that lay the liberating force which science was seeking, the lever which would change the face of the world, when they should have been so domesticated and subdued as to be only the obedient servants of man.

Throughout this familiar discourse Pierre could feel that Francois was growing impassioned, quivering at thought of the vast horizon which the master opened up. He himself had become extremely interested, for he could not do otherwise than notice certain allusions, and connect what he heard with what he had guessed of Guillaume's anxiety regarding that secret which he feared to see at the mercy of an investigating magistrate. And so as he, Pierre, before going off with Francois, approached Bertheroy to wish him good day, he pointedly remarked: "Guillaume will be very sorry that he was unable to hear you unfold those admirable ideas."

The old *savant* smiled. "Pooh!" said he; "just give him a summary of what I said. He will understand. He knows more about the matter than I do."

In presence of the illustrious chemist, Francois preserved the silent gravity of a respectful pupil, but when he and Pierre had taken a few steps down the street in silence, he remarked: "What a pity it is that a man of such broad intelligence, free from all superstition, and anxious for the sole triumph of truth, should have allowed himself to be classified, ticketed, bound round with titles and academical functions! How greatly our affection for him would increase if he took less State pay, and freed himself from all the grand cordons which tie his hands."

"What would you have!" rejoined Pierre, in a conciliatory spirit. "A man must live! At the same time I believe that he does not regard himself as tied by anything."

Then, as they had reached the entrance of the Ecole Normale, the priest stopped, thinking that his companion was going back to the college. But Francois, raising his eyes and glancing at the old place, remarked: "No, no, to-day's Thursday, and I'm at liberty! Oh! we have a deal of liberty, perhaps too much. But for my own part I'm well pleased at it, for it often enables me to go to Montmartre and work at my old little table. It's only there that I feel any real strength and clearness of mind."

His preliminary examinations had entitled him to admission at either the Ecole Polytechnique or the Ecole Normale,[1] and he had chosen the latter, entering its scientific section with No. 1 against his name. His father had wished him to make sure of an avocation, that of professor, even if circumstances should allow him to remain independent and follow his own bent on leaving the college. Francois, who was very precocious, was now preparing for his last examination there, and the only rest he took was in walking to and from Montmartre, or in strolling through the Luxembourg gardens.

From force of habit he now turned towards the latter, accompanied by Pierre and chatting with him. One found the mildness of springtime there that February afternoon; for pale sunshine streamed between the trees, which were still leafless. It was indeed one of those first fine days which draw little green gems from the branches of the lilac bushes.

The Ecole Normale was still the subject of conversation and Pierre remarked: "I must own that I hardly like the spirit that prevails there. Excellent work is done, no doubt, and the only way to form professors is to teach men the trade by cramming them with the necessary knowledge. But the worst is that although all the students are trained for the teaching profession, many of them don't remain in it, but go out into the world, take to journalism, or make it their business to control the arts, literature and society. And those who do this are for the most part unbearable. After swearing by Voltaire they have gone back to spirituality and mysticism, the last drawing-room craze. Now that a firm faith in science is regarded as brutish and inelegant, they fancy that they rid themselves of their caste by feigning amiable doubt, and ignorance, and innocence. What they most fear is that they may carry a scent of the schools about with them, so they put on extremely Parisian airs, venture on somersaults and slang, and assume all the grace of dancing bears in their eager desire to please. From that desire spring the sarcastic shafts which they aim at science, they who pretend that they know everything, but who go back to the belief of the humble, the *naive* idealism of Biblical legends, just because they think the latter to be more distinguished."

Francois began to laugh: "The portrait is perhaps a little overdrawn," said he, "still there's truth in it, a great deal of truth."

"I have known several of them," continued Pierre, who was growing animated. "And among them all I have noticed that a fear of being duped leads them to reaction against the entire effort, the whole work of the century. Disgust with liberty, distrust of science, denial of the future, that is what they now profess. And they have such a horror of the commonplace that they would rather believe in nothing or the incredible. It may of course be commonplace to say that two and two make four, yet it's true enough; and it is far less foolish for a man to say and repeat it than to believe, for instance, in the miracles of Lourdes."

---

[1] The purposes of the Ecole Normale have been referred to on p. 197. At the Ecole Polytechnique young men receive much of the preliminary training which they require to become either artillery officers, or military, naval or civil engineers.—Trans.

Francois glanced at the priest in astonishment. The other noticed it and strove to restrain himself. Nevertheless, grief and anger carried him away whenever he spoke of the educated young people of the time, such as, in his despair, he imagined them to be. In the same way as he had pitied the toilers dying of hunger in the districts of misery and want, so here he overflowed with contempt for the young minds that lacked bravery in the presence of knowledge, and harked back to the consolation of deceptive spirituality, the promise of an eternity of happiness in death, which last was longed for and exalted as the very sum of life. Was not the cowardly thought of refusing to live for the sake of living so as to discharge one's simple duty in being and making one's effort, equivalent to absolute assassination of life? However, the *Ego* was always the mainspring; each one sought personal happiness. And Pierre was grieved to think that those young people, instead of discarding the past and marching on to the truths of the future, were relapsing into shadowy metaphysics through sheer weariness and idleness, due in part perhaps to the excessive exertion of the century, which had been overladen with human toil.

However, Francois had begun to smile again. "But you are mistaken," said he; "we are not all like that at the Ecole Normale. You only seem to know the Normalians of the Section of Letters, and your opinions would surely change if you knew those of the Section of Sciences. It is quite true that the reaction against Positivism is making itself felt among our literary fellow-students, and that they, like others, are haunted by the idea of that famous bankruptcy of science. This is perhaps due to their masters, the neo-spiritualists and dogmatical rhetoricians into whose hands they have fallen. And it is still more due to fashion, the whim of the times which, as you have very well put it, regards scientific truth as bad taste, something graceless and altogether too brutal for light and distinguished minds. Consequently, a young fellow of any shrewdness who desires to please is perforce won over to the new spirit."

"The new spirit!" interrupted Pierre, unable to restrain himself. "Oh! that is no mere innocent, passing fashion, it is a tactical device and a terrible one, an offensive return of the powers of darkness against those of light, of servitude against free thought, truth and justice."

Then, as the young man again looked at him with growing astonishment, he relapsed into silence. The figure of Monseigneur Martha had risen before his eyes, and he fancied he could again hear the prelate at the Madeleine, striving to win Paris over to the policy of Rome, to that spurious neo-Catholicism which, with the object of destroying democracy and science, accepted such portions of them as it could adapt to its own views. This was indeed the supreme struggle. Thence came all the poison poured forth to the young. Pierre knew what efforts were being made in religious circles to help on this revival of mysticism, in the mad hope of hastening the rout of science. Monseigneur Martha, who was all-powerful at the Catholic University, said to his intimates, however, that three generations of devout and docile pupils would be needed before the Church would again be absolute sovereign of France.

"Well, as for the Ecole Normale," continued Francois, "I assure you that you are mistaken. There are a few narrow bigots there, no doubt. But even in the Section of Letters the majority of the students are sceptics at bottom—sceptics of discreet and good-natured average views. Of course they are professors before everything else, though they are a trifle ashamed of it; and, as professors, they judge things with no little pedantic irony, devoured by a spirit of criticism, and quite incapable of creating anything themselves. I should certainly be astonished to see the man of genius whom we await come out of their ranks. To my thinking, indeed, it would be preferable that some barbarian genius, neither well read nor endowed with critical faculty, or power of weighing and shading things, should come and open the next century with a hatchet stroke, sending up a fine flare of truth and reality.... But, as for my comrades of the Scientific Section, I assure you that neo-Catholicism and Mysticism and Occultism, and every other branch of the fashionable phantasmagoria trouble them very little indeed. They are not making a religion of science, they remain open to doubt on many points; but they are mostly men of very clear and firm minds, whose passion is the acquirement of certainty, and who are ever absorbed in the investigations which continue throughout the whole vast field of human knowledge. They haven't flinched, they have remained Positivists, or Evolutionists, or Determinists, and have set their faith in observation and experiment to help on the final conquest of the world."

Francois himself was growing excited, as he thus confessed his faith while strolling along the quiet sunlit garden paths. "The young indeed!" he resumed. "Do people know them? It makes us laugh when we see all sorts of apostles fighting for us, trying to attract us, and saying that we are white or black or grey, according to the hue which they require for the triumph of their particular ideas! The young, the real ones, why, they're in the schools, the laboratories and the libraries. It's they who work and who'll bring to-morrow to the world. It's not the young fellows of dinner and supper clubs, manifestoes and all sorts of extravagances. The latter make a great deal of noise, no doubt; in fact, they alone are heard. But if you knew of the ceaseless efforts and passionate striving of the others, those who remain silent, absorbed in their tasks. And I know many of them: they are with their century, they have rejected none of its hopes, but are marching on to the coming century, resolved to pursue the work of their forerunners, ever going towards more light and more equity. And just speak to them of the bankruptcy of science. They'll shrug their shoulders at the mere idea, for they know well enough that science has never before inflamed so many hearts or achieved greater conquests! It is only if the schools, laboratories and libraries were closed, and the social soil radically changed, that one would have cause to fear a fresh growth of error such as weak hearts and narrow minds hold so dear!"

At this point Francois's fine flow of eloquence was interrupted. A tall young fellow stopped to shake hands with him; and Pierre was surprised to recognise Baron Duvillard's son Hyacinthe, who bowed to him in very correct style. "What! you here in our old quarter," exclaimed Francois.

"My dear fellow, I'm going to Jonas's, over yonder, behind the Observatory. Don't you know Jonas? Ah! my dear fellow, he's a delightful sculptor, who has succeeded in doing away with matter almost entirely. He has carved a figure of Woman, no bigger than the finger, and entirely soul, free from all baseness of form, and yet complete. All Woman, indeed, in her essential symbolism! Ah! it's grand, it's overpowering. A perfect scheme of aesthetics, a real religion!"

Francois smiled as he looked at Hyacinthe, buttoned up in his long pleated frock-coat, with his made-up face, and carefully cropped hair and beard. "And yourself?" said he, "I thought you were working, and were going to publish a little poem, shortly?"

"Oh! the task of creating is so distasteful to me, my dear fellow! A single line often takes me weeks.... Still, yes, I have a little poem on hand, 'The End of Woman.'

And you see, I'm not so exclusive as some people pretend, since I admire Jonas, who still believes in Woman. His excuse is sculpture, which, after all, is at best such a gross materialistic art. But in poetry, good heavens, how we've been overwhelmed with Woman, always Woman! It's surely time to drive her out of the temple, and cleanse it a little. Ah! if we were all pure and lofty enough to do without Woman, and renounce all those horrid sexual questions, so that the last of the species might die childless, eh? The world would then at least finish in a clean and proper manner!"

Thereupon, Hyacinthe walked off with his languid air, well pleased with the effect which he had produced on the others.

"So you know him?" said Pierre to Francois.

"He was my school-fellow at Condorcet, we were in the same classes together. Such a funny fellow he was! A perfect dunce! And he was always making a parade of Father Duvillard's millions, while pretending to disdain them, and act the revolutionist, for ever saying that he'd use his cigarette to fire the cartridge which was to blow up the world! He was Schopenhauer, and Nietzsche, and Tolstoi, and Ibsen, rolled into one! And you can see what he has become with it all: a humbug with a diseased mind!"

"It's a terrible symptom," muttered Pierre, "when through *ennui* or lassitude, or the contagion of destructive fury, the sons of the happy and privileged ones start doing the work of the demolishers."

Francois had resumed his walk, going down towards the ornamental water, where some children were sailing their boats. "That fellow is simply grotesque," he replied; "but how would you have sane people give any heed to that mysticism, that awakening of spirituality which is alleged by the same *doctrinaires* who started the bankruptcy of science cry, when after so brief an evolution it produces such insanity, both in art and literature? A few years of influence have sufficed; and now Satanism, Occultism and other absurdities are flourishing; not to mention that, according to some accounts, the Cities of the Plains are reconciled with new Rome. Isn't the tree judged by its fruits? And isn't it evident that, instead of a renascence, a far-spreading social movement bringing back the past, we are simply witnessing a transitory reaction, which many things explain? The old world would rather not die, and is struggling in a final convulsion, reviving for a last hour before it is swept away by the overflowing river of human knowledge, whose waters ever increase. And yonder, in the future, is the new world, which the real young ones will bring into existence, those who work, those who are not known, who are not heard. And yet, just listen! Perhaps you will hear them, for we are among them, in their 'quarter.' This deep silence is that of the labour of all the young fellows who are leaning over their work-tables, and day by day carrying forward the conquest of truth."

So saying Francois waved his hand towards all the day-schools and colleges and high schools beyond the Luxembourg garden, towards the Faculties of Law and Medicine, the Institute and its five Academies, the innumerable libraries and museums which made up the broad domain of intellectual labour. And Pierre, moved by it all, shaken in his theories of negation, thought that he could indeed hear a low but far-spreading murmur of the work of thousands of active minds, rising from laboratories, studies and class, reading and lecture rooms. It was not like the jerky, breathless trepidation, the loud clamour of factories where manual labour toils and chafes. But here, too, there were sighs of weariness, efforts as killing, exertion as fruitful in its results.

Was it indeed true that the cultured young were still and ever in their silent forge, renouncing no hope, relinquishing no conquest, but in full freedom of mind forging the truth and justice of to-morrow with the invincible hammers of observation and experiment?

Francois, however, had raised his eyes to the palace clock to ascertain the time. "I'm going to Montmartre," he said; "will you come part of the way with me?"

Pierre assented, particularly as the young man added that on his way he meant to call for his brother Antoine at the Museum of the Louvre. That bright afternoon the Louvre picture galleries were steeped in warm and dignified quietude, which one particularly noticed on coming from the tumult and scramble of the streets. The majority of the few people one found there were copyists working in deep silence, which only the wandering footsteps of an occasional tourist disturbed. Pierre and Francois found Antoine at the end of the gallery assigned to the Primitive masters. With scrupulous, almost devout care he was making a drawing of a figure by Mantegna. The Primitives did not impassion him by reason of any particular mysticism and ideality, such as fashion pretends to find in them, but on the contrary, and justifiably enough, by reason of the sincerity of their ingenuous realism, their respect and modesty in presence of nature, and the minute fidelity with which they sought to transcribe it. He spent days of hard work in copying and studying them, in order to learn strictness and probity of drawing from them—all that lofty distinction of style which they owe to their candour as honest artists.

Pierre was struck by the pure glow which a sitting of good hard work had set in Antoine's light blue eyes. It imparted warmth and even feverishness to his fair face, which was usually all dreaminess and gentleness. His lofty forehead now truly looked like a citadel armed for the conquest of truth and beauty. He was only eighteen, and his story was simply this: as he had grown disgusted with classical studies and been mastered by a passion for drawing, his father had let him leave the Lycee Condorcet when he was in the third class there. Some little time had then elapsed while he felt his way and the deep originality within him was being evolved. He had tried etching on copper, but had soon come to wood engraving, and had attached himself to it in spite of the discredit into which it had fallen, lowered as it had been to the level of a mere trade. Was there not here an entire art to restore and enlarge? For his own part he dreamt of engraving his own drawings, of being at once the brain which conceives and the hand which executes, in such wise as to obtain new effects of great intensity both as regards perception and touch. To comply with the wishes of his father, who desired each of his sons to have a trade, he earned his bread like other engravers by working for the illustrated newspapers. But, in addition to this current work, he had already engraved several blocks instinct with wonderful power and life. They were simply copies of real things, scenes of everyday existence, but they were accentuated, elevated so to say, by the essential line, with a maestria which on the part of so young a lad fairly astonished one.

"Do you want to engrave that?" Francois asked him, as he placed his copy of Mantegna's figure in his portfolio.

"Oh! no, that's merely a dip into innocence, a good lesson to teach one to be modest and sincere. Life is very different nowadays."

Then, while walking along the streets—for Pierre, who felt growing sympathy for the two young fellows, went with them in the direction of Montmartre, forgetful of all else,—Antoine, who was beside him, spoke expansively of his artistic dreams.

"Colour is certainly a power, a sovereign source of charm, and one may, indeed, say that without colour nothing can be completely represented. Yet, singularly enough, it isn't indispensable to me. It seems to me that I can picture life as intensely and definitely with mere black and white, and I even fancy that I shall be able to do so in a more essential manner, without any of the dupery which lies in colour. But what a task it is! I should like to depict the Paris of to-day in a few scenes, a few typical figures, which would serve as testimony for all time. And I should like to do it with great fidelity and candour, for an artist only lives by reason of his candour, his humility and steadfast belief in Nature, which is ever beautiful. I've already done a few figures, I will show them to you. But ah! if I only dared to tackle my blocks with the graver, at the outset, without drawing my subject beforehand. For that generally takes away one's fire. However, what I do with the pencil is a mere sketch; for with the graver I may come upon a find, some unexpected strength or delicacy of effect. And so I'm draughtsman and engraver all in one, in such a way that my blocks can only be turned out by myself. If the drawings on them were engraved by another, they would be quite lifeless.... Yes, life can spring from the fingers just as well as from the brain, when one really possesses creative power."

They walked on, and when they found themselves just below Montmartre, and Pierre spoke of taking a tramcar to return to Neuilly, Antoine, quite feverish with artistic passion, asked him if he knew Jahan, the sculptor, who was working for the Sacred Heart. And on receiving a negative reply, he added: "Well, come and see him for a moment. He has a great future before him. You'll see an angel of his which has been declined."

Then, as Francois began to praise the angel in question, Pierre agreed to accompany them. On the summit of the height, among all the sheds which the building of the basilica necessitated, Jahan had been able to set up a glazed workshop large enough for the huge angel ordered of him. His three visitors found him there in a blouse, watching a couple of assistants, who were rough-hewing the block of stone whence the angel was to emerge. Jahan was a sturdy man of thirty-six, with dark hair and beard, a large, ruddy mouth and fine bright eyes. Born in Paris, he had studied at the Fine Art School, but his impetuous temperament had constantly landed him in trouble there.

"Ah! yes," said he, "you've come to see my angel, the one which the Archbishop wouldn't take. Well, there it is."

The clay model of the figure, some three feet high, and already drying, looked superb in its soaring posture, with its large, outspread wings expanding as if with passionate desire for the infinite. The body, barely draped, was that of a slim yet robust youth, whose face beamed with the rapture of his heavenly flight.

"They found him too human," said Jahan. "And after all they were right. There's nothing so difficult to conceive as an angel. One even hesitates as to the sex; and when faith is lacking one has to take the first model one finds and copy it and spoil it. For my part, while I was modelling that one, I tried to imagine a beautiful youth suddenly endowed with wings, and carried by the intoxication of his flight into all the joy of the sunshine. But it upset them, they wanted something more religious, they said;

and so then I concocted that wretched thing over there. After all, one has to earn one's living, you know."

So saying, he waved his hand towards another model, the one for which his assistants were preparing the stone. And this model represented an angel of the correct type, with symmetrical wings like those of a goose, a figure of neither sex, and commonplace features, expressing the silly ecstasy that tradition requires.

"What would you have?" continued Jahan. "Religious art has sunk to the most disgusting triteness. People no longer believe; churches are built like barracks, and decorated with saints and virgins fit to make one weep. The fact is that genius is only the fruit of the social soil; and a great artist can only send up a blaze of the faith of the time he lives in. For my part, I'm the grandson of a Beauceron peasant. My father came to Paris to set himself up in business as a marble worker for tombstones and so forth, just at the top of the Rue de la Roquette. It was there I grew up. I began as a workman, and all my childhood was spent among the masses, in the streets, without ever a thought coming to me of setting foot in a church. So few Parisians think of doing so nowadays. And so what's to become of art since there's no belief in the Divinity or even in beauty? We're forced to go forward to the new faith, which is the faith in life and work and fruitfulness, in all that labours and produces."

Then suddenly breaking off he exclaimed: "By the way, I've been doing some more work to my figure of Fecundity, and I'm fairly well pleased with it. Just come with me and I'll show it you."

Thereupon he insisted on taking them to his private studio, which was near by, just below Guillaume's little house. It was entered by way of the Rue du Calvaire, a street which is simply a succession of ladder-like flights of steps. The door opened on to one of the little landings, and one found oneself in a spacious, well-lighted apartment littered with models and casts, fragments and figures, quite an overflow of sturdy, powerful talent. On a stool was the unfinished model of Fecundity swathed in wet cloths. These Jahan removed, and then she stood forth with her rounded figure, her broad hips and her wifely, maternal bosom, full of the milk which nourishes and redeems.

"Well, what do you think of her?" asked Jahan. "Built as she is, I fancy that her children ought to be less puny than the pale, languid, aesthetic fellows of nowadays!"

While Antoine and Francois were admiring the figure, Pierre, for his part, took most interest in a young girl who had opened the door to them, and who had now wearily reseated herself at a little table to continue a book she was reading. This was Jahan's sister, Lise. A score of years younger than himself, she was but sixteen, and had been living alone with him since their father's death. Very slight and delicate looking, she had a most gentle face, with fine light hair which suggested pale gold-dust. She was almost a cripple, with legs so weak that she only walked with difficulty, and her mind also was belated, still full of childish *naivete*. At first this had much saddened her brother, but with time he had grown accustomed to her innocence and languor. Busy as he always was, ever in a transport, overflowing with new plans, he somewhat neglected her by force of circumstances, letting her live beside him much as she listed.

Pierre had noticed, however, the sisterly impulsiveness with which she had greeted Antoine. And the latter, after congratulating Jahan on his statue, came and sat down beside her, questioned her and wished to see the book which she was reading. During the last six months the most pure and affectionate intercourse had sprung up between them. He, from his father's garden, up yonder on the Place du Tertre, could see her through the huge window of that studio where she led so innocent a life. And noticing that she was always alone, as if forsaken, he had begun to take an interest in her. Then had come acquaintance; and, delighted to find her so simple and so charming, he had conceived the design of rousing her to intelligence and life, by loving her, by becoming at once the mind and the heart whose power fructifies. Weak plant that she was, in need of delicate care, sunshine and affection, he became for her all that her brother had, through circumstances, failed to be. He had already taught her to read, a task in which every mistress had previously failed. But him she listened to and understood. And by slow degrees a glow of happiness came to the beautiful clear eyes set in her irregular face. It was love's miracle, the creation of woman beneath the breath of a young lover who gave himself entirely. No doubt she still remained very delicate, with such poor health that one ever feared that she might expire in a faint sigh; and her legs, moreover, were still too weak to admit of her walking any distance. But all the same, she was no longer the little wilding, the little ailing flower of the previous spring.

Jahan, who marvelled at the incipient miracle, drew near to the young people. "Ah!" said he, "your pupil does you honour. She reads quite fluently, you know, and understands the fine books you send her. You read to me of an evening now, don't you, Lise?"

She raised her candid eyes, and gazed at Antoine with a smile of infinite gratitude. "Oh! whatever he'll teach me," she said, "I'll learn it, and do it."

The others laughed gently. Then, as the visitors were going off, Francois paused before a model which had cracked while drying. "Oh! that's a spoilt thing," said the sculptor. "I wanted to model a figure of Charity. It was ordered of me by a philanthropic institution. But try as I might, I could only devise something so commonplace that I let the clay spoil. Still, I must think it over and endeavour to take the matter in hand again."

When they were outside, it occurred to Pierre to go as far as the basilica of the Sacred Heart in the hope of finding Abbe Rose there. So the three of them went round by way of the Rue Gabrielle and climbed the steps of the Rue Chape. And just as they were reaching the summit where the basilica reared its forest of scaffoldings beneath the clear sky, they encountered Thomas, who, on leaving the factory, had gone to give an order to a founder in the Rue Lamarck.

He, who as a rule was so silent and discreet, now happened to be in an expansive mood, which made him look quite radiant. "Ah! I'm so pleased," he said, addressing Pierre; "I fancy that I've found what I want for our little motor. Tell father that things are going on all right, and that he must make haste to get well."

At these words his brothers, Francois and Antoine, drew close to him with a common impulse. And they stood there all three, a valiant little group, their hearts uniting and beating with one and the same delight at the idea that their father would be gladdened, that the good news they were sending him would help him towards recovery. As for Pierre, who, now that he knew them, was beginning to love them and judge them at their worth, he marvelled at the sight of these three young giants, each so strikingly like the other, and drawn together so closely and so promptly, directly their filial affection took fire.

"Tell him that we are waiting for him, and will come to him at the first sign if we are wanted."

Then each in turn shook the priest's hand vigorously. And while he remained watching them as they went off towards the little house, whose garden he perceived over the wall of the Rue Saint Eleuthere, he fancied he could there detect a delicate silhouette, a white, sunlit face under a help of dark hair. It was doubtless the face of Marie, examining the buds on her lilac bushes. At that evening hour, however, the diffuse light was so golden that the vision seemed to fade in it as in a halo. And Pierre, feeling dazzled, turned his head, and on the other side saw naught but the overwhelming, chalky mass of the basilica, whose hugeness shut out all view of the horizon.

For a moment he remained motionless on that spot, so agitated by conflicting thoughts and feelings that he could read neither heart nor mind clearly. Then, as he turned towards the city, all Paris spread itself out at his feet, a limpid, lightsome Paris, beneath the pink glow of that spring-like evening. The endless billows of house-roofs showed forth with wonderful distinctness, and one could have counted the chimney stacks and the little black streaks of the windows by the million. The edifices rising into the calm atmosphere seemed like the anchored vessels of some fleet arrested in its course, with lofty masting which glittered at the sun's farewell. And never before had Pierre so distinctly observed the divisions of that human ocean. Eastward and northward was the city of manual toil, with the rumbling and the smoke of its factories. Southward, beyond the river, was the city of study, of intellectual labour, so calm, so perfectly serene. And on all sides the passion of trade ascended from the central districts, where the crowds rolled and scrambled amidst an everlasting uproar of wheels; while westward, the city of the happy and powerful ones, those who fought for sovereignty and wealth, spread out its piles of palaces amidst the slowly reddening flare of the declining planet.

And then, from the depths of his negation, the chaos into which his loss of faith had plunged him, Pierre felt a delicious freshness pass like the vague advent of a new faith. So vague it was that he could not have expressed even his hope of it in words. But already among the rough factory workers, manual toil had appeared to him necessary and redemptive, in spite of all the misery and abominable injustice to which it led. And now the young men of intellect of whom he had despaired, that generation of the morrow which he had thought spoilt, relapsing into ancient error and rottenness, had appeared to him full of virile promise, resolved to prosecute the work of those who had gone before, and effect, by the aid of Science only, the conquest of absolute truth and absolute justice.

V. PROBLEMS

A FULL month had already gone by since Guillaume had taken refuge at his brother's little house at Neuilly. His wrist was now nearly healed. He had long ceased to keep his bed, and often strolled through the garden. In spite of his impatience to go back to Montmartre, join his loved ones and resume his work there, he was each morning prompted to defer his return by the news he found in the newspapers. The situation was ever the same. Salvat, whom the police now suspected, had been perceived one evening near the central markets, and then again lost sight of. Every day, however, his arrest was said to be imminent. And in that case what would happen? Would he speak out, and would fresh perquisitions be made?

For a whole week the press had been busy with the bradawl found under the entrance of the Duvillard mansion. Nearly every reporter in Paris had called at the Grandidier factory and interviewed both workmen and master. Some had even started on personal investigations, in the hope of capturing the culprit themselves. There was no end of jesting about the incompetence of the police, and the hunt for Salvat was followed all the more passionately by the general public, as the papers overflowed with the most ridiculous concoctions, predicting further explosions, and declaring even that all Paris would some morning be blown into the air. The "Voix du Peuple" set a fresh shudder circulating every day by its announcements of threatening letters, incendiary placards and mysterious, far-reaching plots. And never before had so base and foolish a spirit of contagion wafted insanity through a civilised city.

Guillaume, for his part, no sooner awoke of a morning than he was all impatience to see the newspapers, quivering at the idea that he would at last read of Salvat's arrest. In his state of nervous expectancy, the wild campaign which the press had started, the idiotic and the ferocious things which he found in one or another journal, almost drove him crazy. A number of "suspects" had already been arrested in a kind of chance razzia, which had swept up the usual Anarchist herd, together with sundry honest workmen and bandits, *illumines* and lazy devils, in fact, a most singular, motley crew, which investigating magistrate Amadieu was endeavouring to turn into a gigantic association of evil-doers. One morning, moreover, Guillaume found his own name mentioned in connection with a perquisition at the residence of a revolutionary journalist, who was a friend of his. At this his heart bounded with revolt, but he was forced to the conclusion that it would be prudent for him to remain patient a little longer, in his peaceful retreat at Neuilly, since the police might at any moment break into his home at Montmartre, to arrest him should it find him there.

Amidst all this anxiety the brothers led a most solitary and gentle life. Pierre himself now spent most of his time at home. The first days of March had come, and precocious springtide imparted delightful charm and warmth to the little garden. Guillaume, however, since quitting his bed, had more particularly installed himself in his father's old laboratory, now transformed into a spacious study. All the books and papers left by the illustrious chemist were still there, and among the latter Guillaume found a number of unfinished essays, the perusal of which greatly excited his interest, and often absorbed him from morning till night. It was this which largely enabled him to bear his voluntary seclusion patiently. Seated on the other side of the big table, Pierre also mostly occupied himself with reading; but at times his eyes would quit his book and wander away into gloomy reverie, into all the chaos into which he still and ever sank. For long hours the brothers would in this wise remain side by side, without speaking a word. Yet they knew they were together; and occasionally, when their eyes met, they would exchange a smile. The strong affection of former days was again springing up within them; their childhood, their home, their parents, all seemed to live once more in the quiet atmosphere they breathed. However, the bay window overlooked the garden in the direction of Paris, and often, when they emerged from their reading or their reverie, it was with a sudden feeling of anxiety, and in order to lend ear to the distant rumbling, the increased clamour of the great city.

On other occasions they paused as if in astonishment at hearing a continuous footfall overhead. It was that of Nicholas Barthes, who still lingered in the room above. He seldom came downstairs, and scarcely ever ventured into the garden, for fear, said he, that he might be perceived and recognised from a distant house whose windows were concealed by a clump of trees. One might laugh at the old conspirator's haunting thought of the police. Nevertheless, the caged-lion restlessness, the ceaseless promenade of that perpetual prisoner who had spent two thirds of his life in the dungeons of France in his desire to secure the liberty of others, imparted to the silence of the little house a touching melancholy, the very rhythm as it were of all the great good things which one hoped for, but which would never perhaps come.

Very few visits drew the brothers from their solitude. Bertheroy came less frequently now that Guillaume's wrist was healing. The most assiduous caller was certainly Theophile Morin, whose discreet ring was heard every other day at the same hour. Though he did not share the ideas of Barthes he worshipped him as a martyr; and would always go upstairs to spend an hour with him. However, they must have exchanged few words, for not a sound came from the room. Whenever Morin sat down for a moment in the laboratory with the brothers, Pierre was struck by his seeming weariness, his ashen grey hair and beard and dismal countenance, all the life of which appeared to have been effaced by long years spent in the teaching profession. Indeed, it was only when the priest mentioned Italy that he saw his companion's resigned eyes blaze up like live coals. One day when he spoke of the great patriot Orlando Prada, Morin's companion of victory in Garibaldi's days, he was amazed by the sudden flare of enthusiasm which lighted up the other's lifeless features. However, these were but transient flashes: the old professor soon reappeared, and all that one found in Morin was the friend of Proudhon and the subsequent disciple of Auguste Comte. Of his Proudhonian principles he had retained all a pauper's hatred of wealth, and a desire for a more equitable partition of fortune. But the new times dismayed him, and neither principle nor temperament allowed him to follow Revolutionism to its utmost limits. Comte had imparted unshakable convictions to him in the sphere of intellectual questions, and he contented himself with the clear and decisive logic of Positivism, rejecting all metaphysical hypotheses as useless, persuaded as he was that the whole human question, whether social or religious, would be solved by science alone. This faith, firm as it had remained, was, however, coupled with secret bitterness, for nothing seemed to advance in a sensible manner towards its goal. Comte himself had ended in the most cloudy mysticism; great *savants* recoiled from truth in terror; and now barbarians were threatening the world with fresh night; all of which made Morin almost a reactionist in politics, already resigned to the advent of a dictator, who would set things somewhat in order, so that humanity might be able to complete its education.

Other visitors who occasionally called to see Guillaume were Bache and Janzen, who invariably came together and at night-time. Every now and then they would linger chatting with Guillaume in the spacious study until two o'clock in the morning. Bache, who was fat and had a fatherly air, with his little eyes gently beaming amidst all the snowy whiteness of his hair and beard, would talk on slowly, unctuously and interminably, as soon as he had begun to explain his views. He would address merely a polite bow to Saint-Simon, the initiator, the first to lay down the law that work was a necessity for one and all according to their capacities; but on coming to Fourier his voice softened and he confessed his whole religion. To his thinking, Fourier had been the real messiah of modern times, the saviour of genius, who had sown the good seed of the future world, by regulating society such as it would certainly be organised to-morrow. The law of harmony had been promulgated; human passions, liberated and utilised in healthy fashion, would become the requisite machinery; and work, rendered pleasant and attractive, would prove the very function of life. Nothing could discourage Bache; if merely one parish began by transforming itself into a *phalansterium*, the whole department would soon follow, then the adjacent departments, and finally all France. Moreover, Bache even favoured the schemes of Cabet, whose Icaria, said he, had in no wise been such a foolish idea. Further, he recalled a motion he had made, when member of the Commune in 1871, to apply Fourier's ideas to the French Republic; and he was apparently convinced that the troops of Versailles had delayed the triumph of Communism for half a century. Whenever people nowadays talked of table-turning he pretended to laugh, but at bottom he had remained an impenitent "spiritist." Since he had been a municipal councillor he had been travelling from one socialist sect to another, according as their ideas offered points of resemblance to his old faith. And he was fairly consumed by his need of faith, his perplexity as to the Divine, which he was now occasionally inclined to find in the legs of some piece of furniture, after denying its presence in the churches.

Janzen, for his part, was as taciturn as his friend Bache was garrulous. Such remarks as he made were brief, but they were as galling as lashes, as cutting as sabre-strokes. At the same time his ideas and theories remained somewhat obscure, partly by reason of this brevity of his, and partly on account of the difficulty he experienced in expressing himself in French. He was from over yonder, from some far-away land—Russia, Poland, Austria or Germany, nobody exactly knew; and it mattered little, for he certainly acknowledged no country, but wandered far and wide with his dream of blood-shedding fraternity. Whenever, with his wonted frigidity, he gave utterance to one of those terrible remarks of his which, like a scythe in a meadow, cut away all before him, little less than the necessity of thus mowing down nations, in order to sow the earth afresh with a young and better community, became apparent. At each proposition unfolded by Bache, such as labour rendered agreeable by police regulations, *phalansteria* organised like barracks, religion transformed into pantheist or spiritist deism, he gently shrugged his shoulders. What could be the use of such childishness, such hypocritical repairing, when the house was falling and the only honest course was to throw it to the ground, and build up the substantial edifice of to-morrow with entirely new materials? On the subject of propaganda by deeds, bomb-throwing and so forth, he remained silent, though his gestures were expressive of infinite hope. He evidently approved that course. The legend which made him one of the perpetrators of the crime of Barcelona set a gleam of horrible glory in his mysterious past. One day when Bache, while speaking to him of his friend Bergaz, the shadowy Bourse jobber who had already been compromised in some piece of thieving, plainly declared that the aforesaid Bergaz was a bandit, Janzen contented himself with smiling, and replying quietly that theft was merely forced restitution. Briefly, in this man of culture and refinement, in whose own mysterious life one might perhaps have found various crimes but not a single act of base improbity, one could divine an implacable, obstinate theoretician, who was resolved to set the world ablaze for the triumph of his ideas.

On certain evenings when a visit from Theophile Morin coincided with one from Bache and Janzen, and they and Guillaume lingered chatting until far into the night, Pierre would listen to them in despair from the shadowy corner where he remained motionless, never once joining in the discussions. Distracted, by his own unbelief and thirst for truth, he had at the outset taken a passionate interest in these debates, desirous as he was of drawing up a balance-sheet of the century's ideas, so as to form some notion of the distance that had been travelled, and the profits that had accrued. But he recoiled from all this in fresh despair, on hearing the others argue, each from his own standpoint and without possibility of concession and agreement. After the repulses he had encountered at Lourdes and Rome, he well realised that in this fresh experiment which he was making with Paris, the whole brain of the century was in question, the new truths, the expected gospel which was to change the face of the world. And, burning with inconsiderate zeal, he went from one belief to another, which other he soon rejected in order to adopt a third. If he had first felt himself to be a Positivist with Morin, an Evolutionist and Determinist with Guillaume, he had afterwards been touched by the fraternal dream of a new golden age which he had found in Bache's humanitarian Communism. And indeed even Janzen had momentarily shaken him by his fierce confidence in the theory of liberative Individualism. But afterwards he had found himself out of his depth; and each and every theory had seemed to him but part of the chaotic contradictions and incoherences of humanity on its march. It was all a continuous piling up of dross, amidst which he lost himself. Although Fourier had sprung from Saint-Simon he denied him in part; and if Saint-Simon's doctrine ended in a kind of mystical sensuality, the other's conducted to an unacceptable regimenting of society. Proudhon, for his part, demolished without rebuilding anything. Comte, who created method and declared science to be the one and only sovereign, had not even suspected the advent of the social crisis which now threatened to sweep all away, and had finished personally as a mere worshipper of love, overpowered by woman. Nevertheless, these two, Comte and Proudhon, entered the lists and fought against the others, Fourier and Saint-Simon; the combat between them or their disciples becoming so bitter and so blind that the truths common to them all were obscured and disfigured beyond recognition. Thence came the extraordinary muddle of the present hour; Bache with Saint-Simon and Fourier, and Morin with Proudhon and Comte, utterly failing to understand Mege, the Collectivist deputy, whom they held up to execration, him and his State Collectivism, in the same way, moreover, as they thundered against all the other present-time Socialist sects, without realising that these also, whatever their nature, had more or less sprung from the same masters as themselves. And all this seemingly indicated that Janzen was right when he declared that the house was past repair, fast crumbling amidst rottenness and insanity, and that it ought to be levelled to the ground.

One night, after the three visitors had gone, Pierre, who had remained with Guillaume, saw him grow very gloomy as he slowly walked to and fro. He, in his turn, had doubtless felt that all was crumbling. And though his brother alone was there to hear him, he went on speaking. He expressed all his horror of the Collectivist State as imagined by Mege, a Dictator-State re-establishing ancient servitude on yet closer lines. The error of all the Socialist sects was their arbitrary organisation of Labour, which enslaved the individual for the profit of the community. And, forced to conciliate the two great currents, the rights of society and the rights of the individual, Guillaume had ended by placing his whole faith in free Communism, an anarchical state in which he dreamt of seeing the individual freed, moving and developing without restraint, for the benefit both of himself and of all others. Was not this, said he, the one truly scientific theory, unities creating worlds, atoms producing life by force of attraction, free and ardent love? All oppressive minorities would disappear; and the faculties and energies of one and all would by free play arrive at harmony amidst the equilibrium—which changed according to needs—of the active forces of advancing humanity. In this wise he pictured a nation, saved from State tutelage, without a master, almost without laws, a happy nation, each citizen of which, completely developed by the exercise of liberty, would, of his free will, come to an understanding with his neighbours with regard to the thousand necessities of life. And thence would spring society, free association, hundreds of associations which would regulate social life; though at the same time they would remain variable, in fact often opposed and hostile to one another. For progress is but the fruit of conflict and struggle; the world has only been created by the battle of opposing forces. And that was all; there would be no more oppressors, no more rich, no more poor; the domain of the earth with its natural treasures and its implements of labour would be restored to the people, its legitimate owners, who would know how to enjoy it with justice and logic, when nothing abnormal would impede their expansion. And then only would the law of love make its action felt; then would human solidarity, which, among mankind, is the living form of universal attraction, acquire all its power, bringing men closer and closer together, and uniting them in one sole family. A splendid dream it was—the noble and pure dream of absolute freedom—free man in free society. And thither a *savant's* superior mind was fated to come after passing on the road the many Socialist sects which one and all bore the stigma of tyranny. And, assuredly, as thus indulged, the Anarchist idea is the loftiest, the proudest, of all ideas. And how delightful to yield to the hope of harmony in life—life which restored to the full exercise of its natural powers would of itself create happiness!

When Guillaume ceased speaking, he seemed to be emerging from a dream; and he glanced at Pierre with some dismay, for he feared that he might have said too much and have hurt his feelings. Pierre—moved though he was, for a moment in fact almost won over—had just seen the terrible practical objection, which destroyed all hope, arise before his mind's eye. Why had not harmony asserted itself in the first days of the world's existence, at the time when societies were formed? How was it that tyranny had triumphed, delivering nations over to oppressors? And supposing that the apparently insolvable problem of destroying everything, and beginning everything afresh, should ever be solved, who could promise that mankind, obedient to the same laws, would not again follow the same paths as formerly? After all, mankind, nowadays, is simply what life has made it; and nothing proves that life would again make it other than it is. To begin afresh, ah, yes! but to attain another result! But could that other result really come from man? Was it not rather man himself who should be changed? To start afresh from where one was, to continue the evolution that had begun, undoubtedly meant slow travel and dismal waiting. But how great would be the danger and even the delay, if one went back without knowing by what road across the whole chaos of ruins one might regain all the lost time!

"Let us go to bed," at last said Guillaume, smiling. "It's silly of me to weary you with all these things which don't concern you."

Pierre, in his excitement, was about to reveal his own heart and mind, and the whole torturing battle within him. But a feeling of shame again restrained him. His brother only knew him as a believing priest, faithful to his faith. And so, without answering, he betook himself to his room.

On the following evening, about ten o'clock, while Guillaume and Pierre sat reading in the study, the old servant entered to announce M. Janzen and a friend. The friend was Salvat.

"He wished to see you," Janzen explained to Guillaume. "I met him, and when he heard of your injury and anxiety he implored me to bring him here. And I've done so, though it was perhaps hardly prudent of me."

Guillaume had risen, full of surprise and emotion at such a visit; Pierre, however, though equally upset by Salvat's appearance; did not stir from his chair, but kept his eyes upon the workman.

"Monsieur Froment," Salvat ended by saying, standing there in a timid, embarrassed way, "I was very sorry indeed when I heard of the worry I'd put you in; for I shall never forget that you were very kind to me when everybody else turned me away."

As he spoke he balanced himself alternately on either leg, and transferred his old felt hat from hand to hand.

"And so I wanted to come and tell you myself that if I took a cartridge of your powder one evening when you had your back turned, it's the only thing that I feel any remorse about in the whole business, since it may compromise you. And I also want to take my oath before you that you've nothing to fear from me, that I'll let my head be cut off twenty times if need be, rather than utter your name. That's all that I had in my heart."

He relapsed into silence and embarrassment, but his soft, dreamy eyes, the eyes of a faithful dog, remained fixed upon Guillaume with an expression of respectful worship. And Pierre was still gazing at him athwart the hateful vision which his arrival had conjured up, that of the poor, dead, errand girl, the fair pretty child lying ripped open under the entrance of the Duvillard mansion! Was it possible that he was there, he, that madman, that murderer, and that his eyes were actually moist!

Guillaume, touched by Salvat's words, had drawn near and pressed his hand. "I am well aware, Salvat," said he, "that you are not wicked at heart. But what a foolish and abominable thing you did!"

Salvat showed no sign of anger, but gently smiled. "Oh! if it had to be done again, Monsieur Froment, I'd do it. It's my idea, you know. And, apart from you, all is well; I am content."

He would not sit down, but for another moment continued talking with Guillaume, while Janzen, as if he washed his hands of the business, deeming this visit both useless and dangerous, sat down and turned over the leaves of a picture book. And Guillaume made Salvat tell him what he had done on the day of the crime; how like a stray dog he had wandered in distraction through Paris, carrying his bomb with him, originally in his tool-bag and then under his jacket; how he had gone a first time to the Duvillard mansion and found its carriage entrance closed; then how he had betaken himself first to the Chamber of Deputies which the ushers had prevented him from entering, and afterwards to the Circus, where the thought of making a great sacrifice of *bourgeois* had occurred to him too late. And finally, how he had at last come back to the Duvillard mansion, as if drawn thither by the very power of destiny. His tool-bag was lying in the depths of the Seine, he said; he had thrown it into the water with sudden hatred of work, since it had even failed to give him bread. And he next told the story of his flight; the explosion shaking the whole district behind him, while, with delight and astonishment, he found himself some distance off, in quiet streets where nothing was as yet known. And for a month past he had been living in chance fashion, how or where he could hardly tell, but he had often slept in the open, and gone for a day without food. One evening little Victor Mathis had given him five francs. And other comrades had helped him, taken him in for a night and sent him off at the first sign of peril. A far-spreading, tacit complicity had hitherto saved him from the police. As for going abroad, well, he had, at one moment, thought of doing so; but a description of his person must have been circulated, the gendarmes must be waiting for him at the frontiers, and so would not flight, instead of retarding, rather hasten his arrest? Paris, however, was an ocean; it was there that he incurred the least risk of capture. Moreover, he no longer had sufficient energy to flee. A fatalist as he was after his own fashion, he could not find strength to quit the pavements of Paris, but there awaited arrest, like a social waif carried chancewise through the multitude as in a dream.

"And your daughter, little Celine?" Guillaume inquired. "Have you ventured to go back to see her?"

Salvat waved his hand in a vague way. "No, but what would you have? She's with Mamma Theodore. Women always find some help. And then I'm done for, I can do nothing for anybody. It's as if I were already dead." However, in spite of these words, tears were rising to his eyes. "Ah! the poor little thing!" he added, "I kissed her with all my heart before I went away. If she and the woman hadn't been starving so long the idea of that business would perhaps never have come to me."

Then, in all simplicity, he declared that he was ready to die. If he had ended by depositing his bomb at the entrance of Duvillard's house, it was because he knew the banker well, and was aware that he was the wealthiest of those *bourgeois* whose fathers at the time of the Revolution had duped the people, by taking all power and wealth for themselves,—the power and wealth which the sons were nowadays so obstinately bent in retaining that they would not even bestow the veriest crumbs on others. As for the Revolution, he understood it in his own fashion, like an illiterate fellow who had learnt the little he knew from newspapers and speeches at public meetings. And he struck his chest with his fist as he spoke of his honesty, and was particularly desirous that none should doubt his courage because he had fled.

"I've never robbed anybody," said he, "and if I don't go and hand myself up to the police, it's because they may surely take the trouble to find and arrest me. I'm very well aware that my affair's clear enough as they've found that bradawl and know me. All the same, it would be silly of me to help them in their work. Still, they'd better make haste, for I've almost had enough of being tracked like a wild beast and no longer knowing how I live."

Janzen, yielding to curiosity, had ceased turning over the leaves of the picture book and was looking at Salvat. There was a smile of disdain in the Anarchist leader's cold eyes; and in his usual broken French he remarked: "A man fights and defends himself, kills others and tries to avoid being killed himself. That's warfare."

These words fell from his lips amidst deep silence. Salvat, however, did not seem to have heard them, but stammered forth his faith in a long sentence laden with fulsome expressions, such as the sacrifice of his life in order that want might cease, and the example of a great action, in the certainty that it would inspire other heroes to continue the struggle. And with this certainly sincere faith and illuminism of his there was blended a martyr's pride, delight at being one of the radiant, worshipped saints of the dawning Revolutionary Church.

As he had come so he went off. When Janzen had led him away, it seemed as if the night which had brought him had carried him back into its impenetrable depths. And then only did Pierre rise from his chair. He was stifling, and threw the large window of the room wide open. It was a very mild but moonless night, whose silence was only disturbed by the subsiding clamour of Paris, which stretched away, invisible, on the horizon.

Guillaume, according to his habit, had begun to walk up and down. And at last he spoke, again forgetting that his brother was a priest. "Ah! the poor fellow! How well one can understand that deed of violence and hope! His whole past life of fruitless labour and ever-growing want explains it. Then, too, there has been all the contagion of ideas; the frequentation of public meetings where men intoxicate themselves with words, and of secret meetings among comrades where faith acquires firmness and the mind soars wildly. Ah! I think I know that man well indeed! He's a good workman, sober and courageous. Injustice has always exasperated him. And little by little the desire for universal happiness has cast him out of the realities of life which he has ended by holding in horror. So how can he do otherwise than live in a dream—a dream of redemption, which, from circumstances, has turned to fire and murder as its fitting instruments. As I looked at him standing there, I fancied I could picture one of the first Christian slaves of ancient Rome. All the iniquity of olden pagan society, agonising beneath the rottenness born of debauchery and covetousness, was weighing on his shoulders, bearing him down. He had come from the dark Catacombs where he had whispered words of deliverance and redemption with his wretched brethren. And a thirst for martyrdom consumed him, he spat in the face of Caesar, he insulted the gods, he fired the pagan temples, in order that the reign of Jesus might come and abolish servitude. And he was ready to die, to be torn to pieces by the wild beasts!"

Pierre did not immediately reply. He had already been struck, however, by the fact that there were undoubted points of resemblance between the secret propaganda and militant faith of the Anarchists, and certain practices of the first Christians. Both sects abandon themselves to a new faith in the hope that the humble may thereby at last reap justice. Paganism disappears through weariness of the flesh and the need of a more lofty and pure faith. That dream of a Christian paradise opening up a future life with a system of compensations for the ills endured on earth, was the outcome of young hope dawning at its historic hour. But to-day, when eighteen centuries have exhausted that hope, when the long experiment is over and the toiler finds himself duped and still and ever a slave, he once more dreams of getting happiness upon this earth, particularly as each day Science tends more and more to show him that the happiness of the spheres beyond is a lie. And in all this there is but the eternal struggle of the poor and the rich, the eternal question of bringing more justice and less suffering to the world.

"But surely," Pierre at last replied, "you can't be on the side of those bandits, those murderers whose savage violence horrifies me. I let you talk on yesterday, when you dreamt of a great and happy people, of ideal anarchy in which each would be free amidst the freedom of all. But what abomination, what disgust both for mind and heart, when one passes from theory to propaganda and practice! If yours is the brain that thinks, whose is the hateful hand that acts, that kills children, throws down doors and empties drawers? Do you accept that responsibility? With your education, your culture, the whole social heredity behind you, does not your entire being revolt at the idea of stealing and murdering?"

Guillaume halted before his brother, quivering. "Steal and murder! no! no! I will not. But one must say everything and fully understand the history of the evil hour through which we are passing. It is madness sweeping by; and, to tell the truth, everything necessary to provoke it has been done. At the very dawn of the Anarchist theory, at the very first innocent actions of its partisans, there was such stern repression, the police so grossly ill-treating the poor devils that fell into its hands, that little by little came anger and rage leading to the most horrible reprisals. It is the Terror initiated by the *bourgeois* that has produced Anarchist savagery. And would you know whence Salvat and his crime have come? Why, from all our centuries of impudence and iniquity, from all that the nations have suffered, from all the sores which are now devouring us, the impatience for enjoyment, the contempt of the strong for the weak, the whole monstrous spectacle which is presented by our rotting society!"

Guillaume was again slowly walking to and fro; and as if he were reflecting aloud he continued: "Ah! to reach the point I have attained, through how much thought, through how many battles, have I not passed! I was merely a Positivist, a *savant* devoted to observation and experiment, accepting nothing apart from proven facts. Scientifically and socially, I admitted that simple evolution had slowly brought humanity into being. But both in the history of the globe and that of human society, I found it necessary to make allowance for the volcano, the sudden cataclysm, the sudden eruption, by which each geological phase, each historical period, has been marked. In this wise one ends by ascertaining that no forward step has ever been taken, no progress ever accomplished in the world's history, without the help of horrible catastrophes. Each advance has meant the sacrifice of millions and millions of human lives. This of course revolts us, given our narrow ideas of justice, and we regard nature as a most barbarous mother; but, if we cannot excuse the volcano, we ought to deal with it when it bursts forth, like *savants* forewarned of its possibility.... And then, ah, then! well, perhaps I'm a dreamer like others, but I have my own notions."

With a sweeping gesture he confessed what a social dreamer there was within him beside the methodical and scrupulous *savant*. His constant endeavour was to bring all back to science, and he was deeply grieved at finding in nature no scientific sign of equality or even justice, such as he craved for in the social sphere. His despair indeed came from this inability to reconcile scientific logic with apostolic love, the dream of universal happiness and brotherhood and the end of all iniquity.

Pierre, however, who had remained near the open window, gazing into the night towards Paris, whence ascended the last sounds of the evening of passionate pleasure, felt the whole flood of his own doubt and despair stifling him. It was all too much: that brother of his who had fallen upon him with his scientific and apostolic beliefs, those men who came to discuss contemporary thought from every standpoint, and finally that Salvat who had brought thither the exasperation of his mad deed. And Pierre, who had hitherto listened to them all without a word, without a gesture, who had hidden his secrets from his brother, seeking refuge in his supposed priestly views, suddenly felt such bitterness stirring his heart that he could lie no longer.

"Ah! brother, if you have your dream, I have my sore which has eaten into me and left me void! Your Anarchy, your dream of just happiness, for which Salvat works with bombs, why, it is the final burst of insanity which will sweep everything away! How is it that you can't realise it? The century is ending in ruins. I've been listening to you all for a month past. Fourier destroyed Saint-Simon, Proudhon and Comte demolished Fourier, each in turn piling up incoherences and contradictions, leaving mere chaos behind them, which nobody dares to sort out. And since then, Socialist sects have been swarming and multiplying, the more sensible of them leading simply to dictatorship, while the others indulge in most dangerous reveries. And after such a tempest of ideas there could indeed come nothing but your Anarchy, which undertakes to bring the old world to a finish by reducing it to dust.... Ah! I expected it, I was waiting for it—that final catastrophe, that fratricidal madness, the inevitable class warfare in which our civilisation was destined to collapse! Everything announced it: the want and misery below, the egotism up above, all the cracking of the old human habitation, borne down by too great a weight of crime and grief. When I went to Lourdes it was to see if the divinity of simple minds would work the awaited miracle, and restore the belief of the early ages to the people, which rebelled through excess of suffering. And when I went to Rome it was in the *naive* hope of there finding the new religion required by our democracies, the only one that could pacify the world by bringing back the fraternity of the golden age. But how foolish of me all that was! Both here and there, I simply lighted on nothingness. There where I so ardently dreamt of finding the salvation of others, I only sank myself, going down apeak like a ship not a timber of which is ever found again. One tie still linked me to my fellow-men, that of charity, the dressing, relieving, and perhaps, in the long run, healing, of wounds and sores; but that last cable has now been severed. Charity, to my mind, appears futile and derisive by the side of justice, to whom all supremacy belongs, and whose advent has become a necessity and can be stayed by none. And so it is all over, I am mere ashes, an empty grave as it were. I no longer believe in anything, anything, anything whatever!"

Pierre had risen to his full height, with arms outstretched as if to let all the nothingness within his heart and mind fall from them. And Guillaume, distracted by the sight of such a fierce denier, such a despairing Nihilist as was now revealed to him, drew near, quivering: "What are you saying, brother! I thought you so firm, so calm in your belief! A priest to be admired, a saint worshipped by the whole of this parish! I was unwilling even to discuss your faith, and now it is you who deny all, and believe in nothing whatever!"

Pierre again slowly stretched out his arms. "There is nothing, I tried to learn all, and only found the atrocious grief born of the nothingness that overwhelms me."

"Ah! how you must suffer, Pierre, my little brother! Can religion, then, be even more withering than science, since it has ravaged you like that, while I have yet remained an old madman, still full of fancies?"

Guillaume caught hold of Pierre's hands and pressed them, full of terrified compassion in presence of all the grandeur and horror embodied in that unbelieving priest who watched over the belief of others, and chastely, honestly discharged his duty amidst the haughty sadness born of his falsehood. And how heavily must that falsehood have weighed upon his conscience for him to confess himself in that fashion, amidst an utter collapse of his whole being! A month previously, in the unexpansiveness of his proud solitude, he would never have taken such a course. To speak out it was necessary that he should have been stirred by many things, his reconciliation with his brother, the conversations he had heard of an evening, the terrible drama in which he was mingled, as well as his reflections on labour struggling against want, and the vague hope with which the sight of intellectual youth had inspired him. And, indeed, amid the very excess of his negation was there not already the faint dawn of a new faith?

This Guillaume must have understood, on seeing how he quivered with unsatisfied tenderness as he emerged from the fierce silence which he had preserved so long. He made him sit down near the window, and placed himself beside him without releasing his hands. "But I won't have you suffer, my little brother!" he said; "I won't leave you, I'll nurse you. For I know you much better than you know yourself. You would never have suffered were it not for the battle between your heart and your mind, and you will cease to suffer on the day when they make peace, and you love what you understand." And in a lower voice, with infinite affection, he went on: "You see, it's our poor mother and our poor father continuing their painful struggle in you. You were too young at the time, you couldn't know what went on. But I knew them both very wretched: he, wretched through her, who treated him as if he were one of the damned; and she, suffering through him, tortured by his irreligion. When he died, struck down by an explosion in this very room, she took it to be the punishment of God. Yet, what an honest man he was, with a good, great heart, what a worker, seeking for truth alone, and desirous of the love and happiness of all! Since we have spent our evenings here, I have felt him coming back, reviving as it were both around and within us; and she, too, poor, saintly woman, is ever here, enveloping us with love, weeping, and yet stubbornly refusing to understand. It is they, perhaps, who have kept me here so long, and who at this very moment are present to place your hands in mine."

And, indeed, it seemed to Pierre as if he could feel the breath of vigilant affection which Guillaume evoked passing over them both. There was again a revival of all the past, all their youth, and nothing could have been more delightful.

"You hear me, brother," Guillaume resumed. "You must reconcile them, for it is only in you that they can be reconciled. You have his firm, lofty brow, and her mouth and eyes of unrealisable tenderness. So, try to bring them to agreement, by some day contenting, as your reason shall allow, the everlasting thirst for love, and self-bestowal, and life, which for lack of satisfaction is killing you. Your frightful wretchedness has no other cause. Come back to life, love, bestow yourself, be a man!"

Pierre raised a dolorous cry: "No, no, the death born of doubt has swept through me, withering and shattering everything, and nothing more can live in that cold dust!"

"But, come," resumed Guillaume, "you cannot have reached such absolute negation. No man reaches it. Even in the most disabused of minds there remains a nook of fancy and hope. To deny charity, devotion, the prodigies which love may work, ah! for my part I do not go so far as that. And now that you have shown me your sore, why should I not tell you my dream, the wild hope which keeps me alive! It is strange; but, are *savants* to be the last childish dreamers, and is faith only to spring up nowadays in chemical laboratories?"

Intense emotion was stirring Guillaume; there was battle waging in both his brain and his heart. And at last, yielding to the deep compassion which filled him, vanquished by his ardent affection for his unhappy brother, he spoke out. But he had drawn yet closer to Pierre, even passed one arm around him; and it was thus embracing him that he, in his turn, made his confession, lowering his voice as if he feared that someone might overhear his secret. "Why should you not know it?" he said. "My own sons are ignorant of it. But you are a man and my brother, and since there is nothing of the priest left in you, it is to the brother I will confide it. This will make me love you the more, and perhaps it may do you good."

Then he told him of his invention, a new explosive, a powder of such extraordinary force that its effects were incalculable. And he had found employment for this powder in an engine of warfare, a special cannon, hurling bombs which would assure the most overwhelming victory to the army using them. The enemy's forces would be destroyed in a few hours, and besieged cities would fall into dust at the slightest bombardment. He had long searched and doubted, calculated, recalculated and experimented; but everything was now ready: the precise formula of the powder, the drawings for the cannon and the bombs, a whole packet of precious papers stored in a safe spot. And after months of anxious reflection he had resolved to give his invention to France, so as to ensure her a certainty of victory in her coming, inevitable war with Germany!

At the same time, he was not a man of narrow patriotism; on the contrary he had a very broad, international conception of the future liberative civilisation. Only he believed in the initiatory mission of France, and particularly in that of Paris, which, even as it is to-day, was destined to be the world's brain to-morrow, whence all science and justice would proceed. The great idea of liberty and equality had already soared from it at the prodigious blast of the Revolution; and from its genius and valour the final emancipation of man would also take its flight. Thus it was necessary that Paris should be victorious in the struggle in order that the world might be saved.

Pierre understood his brother, thanks to the lecture on explosives which he had heard at Bertheroy's. And the grandeur of this scheme, this dream, particularly struck him when he thought of the extraordinary future which would open for Paris amidst the effulgent blaze of the bombs. Moreover, he was struck by all the nobility of soul which had lain behind his brother's anxiety for a month past. If Guillaume had trembled it was simply with fear that his invention might be divulged in consequence of Salvat's crime. The slightest indiscretion might compromise everything; and that little stolen cartridge, whose effects had so astonished *savants*, might reveal his secret. He felt it necessary to act in mystery, choosing his own time, awaiting the proper hour, until when the secret would slumber in its hiding-place, confided to the sole care of Mere-Grand, who had her orders and knew what she was to do should he, in any sudden accident, disappear.

"And, now," said Guillaume in conclusion, "you know my hopes and my anguish, and you can help me and even take my place if I am unable to reach the end of my task. Ah! to reach the end! Since I have been shut up here, reflecting, consumed by anxiety and impatience, there have been hours when I have ceased to see my way clearly! There is that Salvat, that wretched fellow for whose crime we are all of us responsible, and who is now being hunted down like a wild beast! There is also that insensate and insatiable *bourgeoisie*, which will let itself be crushed by the fall of the shaky old house, rather than allow the least repair to it! And there is further that avaricious, that abominable Parisian press, so harsh towards the weak and little, so fond of insulting those who have none to defend them, so eager to coin money out of public misfortune, and ready to spread insanity on all sides, simply to increase its sales! Where, therefore, shall one find truth and justice, the hand endowed with logic and health that ought to be armed with the thunderbolt? Would Paris the conqueror, Paris the master of the nations, prove the justiciar, the saviour that men await! Ah! the anguish of believing oneself to be the master of the world's destinies, and to have to choose and decide."

He had risen again quivering, full of anger and fear that human wretchedness and baseness might prevent the realisation of his dream. And amidst the heavy silence which fell in the room, the little house suddenly resounded with a regular, continuous footfall.

"Ah, yes! to save men and love them, and wish them all to be equal and free," murmured Pierre, bitterly. "But just listen! Barthes's footsteps are answering you, as if from the everlasting dungeon into which his love of liberty has thrown him!"

However, Guillaume had already regained possession of himself, and coming back in a transport of his faith, he once more took Pierre in his loving, saving arms, like an elder brother who gives himself without restraint. "No, no, I'm wrong, I'm blaspheming," he exclaimed; "I wish you to be with me, full of hope and full of certainty. You must work, you must love, you must revive to life. Life alone can give you back peace and health."

Tears returned to the eyes of Pierre, who was penetrated to the heart by this ardent affection. "Ah! how I should like to believe you," he faltered, "and try to cure myself. True, I have already felt, as it were, a vague revival within me. And yet to live again, no, I cannot; the priest that I am is dead—a lifeless, an empty tomb."

He was shaken by so frightful a sob, that Guillaume could not restrain his own tears. And clasped in one another's arms the brothers wept on, their hearts full of the softest emotion in that home of their youth, whither the dear shadows of their parents ever returned, hovering around until they should be reconciled and restored to the peace of the earth. And all the darkness and mildness of the garden streamed in through the open window, while yonder, on the horizon, Paris had fallen asleep in the mysterious gloom, beneath a very peaceful sky which was studded with stars.

BOOK III.

I. THE RIVALS

ON the Wednesday preceding the mid-Lent Thursday, a great charity bazaar was held at the Duvillard mansion, for the benefit of the Asylum of the Invalids of Labour. The ground-floor reception rooms, three spacious Louis Seize *salons*, whose windows overlooked the bare and solemn courtyard, were given up to the swarm of purchasers, five thousand admission cards having been distributed among all sections of Parisian society. And the opening of the bombarded mansion in this wise to thousands of visitors was regarded as quite an event, a real manifestation, although some people whispered that the Rue Godot-de-Mauroy and the adjacent streets were guarded by quite an army of police agents.

The idea of the bazaar had come from Duvillard himself, and at his bidding his wife had resigned herself to all this worry for the benefit of the enterprise over which she presided with such distinguished nonchalance. On the previous day the "Globe" newspaper, inspired by its director Fonsegue, who was also the general manager of the asylum, had published a very fine article, announcing the bazaar, and pointing out how noble, and touching, and generous was the initiative of the Baroness, who still gave her time, her money, and even her home to charity, in spite of the abominable crime which had almost reduced that home to ashes. Was not this the magnanimous answer of the spheres above to the hateful passions of the spheres below? And was it not also a peremptory answer to those who accused the capitalists of doing nothing for the wage-earners, the disabled and broken-down sons of toil?

The drawing-room doors were to be opened at two o'clock, and would only close at seven, so that there would be five full hours for the sales. And at noon, when nothing was as yet ready downstairs, when workmen and women were still decorating the stalls, and sorting the goods amidst a final scramble, there was, as usual, a little friendly *dejeuner*, to which a few guests had been invited, in the private rooms on the first floor. However, a scarcely expected incident had given a finishing touch to the general excitement of the house: that very morning Sagnier had resumed his campaign of denunciation in the matter of the African Railway Lines. In a virulent article in the "Voix du Peuple," he had inquired if it were the intention of the authorities to beguile the public much longer with the story of that bomb and that Anarchist whom the police did not arrest. And this time, while undertaking to publish the names of the thirty-two corrupt senators and deputies in a very early issue, he had boldly named Minister Barroux as one who had pocketed a sum of 200,000 francs. Mege would therefore certainly revive his interpellation, which might become dangerous, now that

Paris had been thrown into such a distracted state by terror of the Anarchists. At the same time it was said that Vignon and his party had resolved to turn circumstances to account, with the object of overthrowing the ministry. Thus a redoubtable crisis was inevitably at hand. Fortunately, the Chamber did not meet that Wednesday; in fact, it had adjourned until the Friday, with the view of making mid-Lent a holiday. And so forty-eight hours were left one to prepare for the onslaught.

Eve, that morning, seemed more gentle and languid than ever, rather pale too, with an expression of sorrowful anxiety in the depths of her beautiful eyes. She set it all down to the very great fatigue which the preparations for the bazaar had entailed on her. But the truth was that Gerard de Quinsac, after shunning any further assignation, had for five days past avoided her in an embarrassed way. Still she was convinced that she would see him that morning, and so she had again ventured to wear the white silk gown which made her look so much younger than she really was. At the same time, beautiful as she had remained, with her delicate skin, superb figure and noble and charming countenance, her six and forty years were asserting themselves in her blotchy complexion and the little creases which were appearing about her lips, eyelids and temples.

Camille, for her part, though her position as daughter of the house made it certain that she would attract much custom as a saleswoman, had obstinately persisted in wearing one of her usual dresses, a dark "carmelite" gown, an old woman's frock, as she herself called it with a cutting laugh. However, her long and wicked-looking face beamed with some secret delight; such an expression of wit and intelligence wreathing her thin lips and shining in her big eyes that one lost sight of her deformity and thought her almost pretty.

Eve experienced a first deception in the little blue and silver sitting-room, where, accompanied by her daughter, she awaited the arrival of her guests. General de Bozonnet, whom Gerard was to have brought with him, came in alone, explaining that Madame de Quinsac had felt rather poorly that morning, and that Gerard, like a good and dutiful son, had wished to remain with her. Still he would come to the bazaar directly after *dejeuner*. While the Baroness listened to the General, striving to hide her disappointment and her fear that she would now be unable to obtain any explanation from Gerard that day, Camille looked at her with eager, devouring eyes. And a certain covert instinct of the misfortune threatening her must at that moment have come to Eve, for in her turn she glanced at her daughter and turned pale as if with anxiety.

Then Princess Rosemonde de Harn swept in like a whirlwind. She also was to be one of the saleswomen at the stall chosen by the Baroness, who liked her for her very turbulence, the sudden gaiety which she generally brought with her. Gowned in fire-hued satin (red shot with yellow), looking very eccentric with her curly hair and thin boyish figure, she laughed and talked of an accident by which her carriage had almost been cut in halves. Then, as Baron Duvillard and Hyacinthe came in from their rooms, late as usual, she took possession of the young man and scolded him, for on the previous evening she had vainly waited for him till ten o'clock in the expectation that he would keep his promise to escort her to a tavern at Montmartre, where some horrible things were said to occur. Hyacinthe, looking very bored, quietly replied that he had been detained at a seance given by some adepts in the New Magic, in the course of which the soul of St. Theresa had descended from heaven to recite a love sonnet.

However, Fonsegue was now coming in with his wife, a tall, thin, silent and generally insignificant woman, whom he seldom took about with him. On this occasion he had been obliged to bring her, as she was one of the lady-patronesses of the asylum, and he himself was coming to lunch with the Duvillards in his capacity as general manager. To the superficial observer he looked quite as gay as usual; but he blinked nervously, and his first glance was a questioning one in the direction of Duvillard, as if he wished to know how the latter bore the fresh thrust directed at him by Sagnier. And when he saw the banker looking perfectly composed, as superb, as rubicund as usual, and chatting in a bantering way with Rosemonde, he also put on an easy air, like a gamester who had never lost but had always known how to compel good luck, even in hours of treachery. And by way of showing his unconstraint of mind he at once addressed the Baroness on managerial matters: "Have you now succeeded in seeing M. l'Abbe Froment for the affair of that old man Laveuve, whom he so warmly recommended to us? All the formalities have been gone through, you know, and he can be brought to us at once, as we have had a bed vacant for three days past."

"Yes, I know," replied Eve; "but I can't imagine what has become of Abbe Froment, for he hasn't given us a sign of life for a month past. However, I made up my mind to write to him yesterday, and beg him to come to the bazaar to-day. In this manner I shall be able to acquaint him with the good news myself."

"It was to leave you the pleasure of doing so," said Fonsegue, "that I refrained from sending him any official communication. He's a charming priest, is he not?"

"Oh! charming, we are very fond of him."

However, Duvillard now intervened to say that they need not wait for Duthil, as he had received a telegram from him stating that he was detained by sudden business. At this Fonsegue's anxiety returned, and he once more questioned the Baron with his eyes. Duvillard smiled, however, and reassured him in an undertone: "It's nothing serious. Merely a commission for me, about which he'll only be able to bring me an answer by-and-by." Then, taking Fonsegue on one side, he added: "By the way, don't forget to insert the paragraph I told you of."

"What paragraph? Oh! yes, the one about that *soiree* at which Silviane recited a piece of verse. Well, I wanted to speak to you about it. It worries me a little, on account of the excessive praise it contains."

Duvillard, but a moment before so full of serenity, with his lofty, conquering, disdainful mien, now suddenly became pale and agitated. "But I absolutely want it to be inserted, my dear fellow! You would place me in the greatest embarrassment if it were not to appear, for I promised Silviane that it should."

As he spoke his lips trembled, and a scared look came into his eyes, plainly revealing his dismay.

"All right, all right," said Fonsegue, secretly amused, and well pleased at this complicity. "As it's so serious the paragraph shall go in, I promise you."

The whole company was now present, since neither Gerard nor Duthil was to be expected. So they went into the dining-room amidst a final noise of hammering in the sale-rooms below. The meal proved somewhat of a scramble, and was on three occasions disturbed by female attendants, who came to explain difficulties and ask for orders. Doors were constantly slamming, and the very walls seemed to shake with the unusual bustle which filled the house. And feverish as they all were in the dining-room, they talked in desultory, haphazard fashion on all sorts of subjects, passing from a ball given at the Ministry of the Interior on the previous night, to the popular mid-Lent festival which would take place on the morrow, and ever reverting to the bazaar, the prices that had been given for the goods which would be on sale, the prices at which they might be sold, and the probable figure of the full receipts, all this being interspersed with strange anecdotes, witticisms and bursts of laughter. On the General mentioning magistrate Amadieu, Eve declared that she no longer dared to invite him to *dejeuner*, knowing how busy he was at the Palace of Justice. Still, she certainly hoped that he would come to the bazaar and contribute something. Then Fonsegue amused himself with teasing Princess Rosemonde about her fire-hued gown, in which, said he, she must already feel roasted by the flames of hell; a suggestion which secretly delighted her, as Satanism had now become her momentary passion. Meantime, Duvillard lavished the most gallant politeness on that silent creature, Madame Fonsegue, while Hyacinthe, in order to astonish even the Princess, explained in a few words how the New Magic could transform a chaste young man into a real angel. And Camille, who seemed very happy and very excited, from time to time darted a hot glance at her mother, whose anxiety and sadness increased as she found the other more and more aggressive, and apparently resolved upon open and merciless warfare.

At last, just as the dessert was coming to an end, the Baroness heard her daughter exclaim in a piercing, defiant voice: "Oh! don't talk to me of the old ladies who still seem to be playing with dolls, and paint themselves, and dress as if they were about to be confirmed! All such ogresses ought to retire from the scene! I hold them in horror!"

At this, Eve nervously rose from her seat, and exclaimed apologetically: "You must forgive me for hurrying you like this. But I'm afraid that we shan't have time to drink our coffee in peace."

The coffee was served in the little blue and silver sitting-room, where bloomed some lovely yellow roses, testifying to the Baroness's keen passion for flowers, which made the house an abode of perpetual spring. Duvillard and Fonsegue, however, carrying their cups of steaming coffee with them, at once went into the former's private room to smoke a cigar there and chat in freedom. As the door remained wide open, one could hear their gruff voices more or less distinctly. Meantime, General de Bozonnet, delighted to find in Madame Fonsegue a serious, submissive person, who listened without interrupting, began to tell her a very long story of an officer's wife who had followed her husband through every battle of the war of 1870. Then Hyacinthe, who took no coffee—contemptuously declaring it to be a beverage only fit for door-keepers—managed to rid himself of Rosemonde, who was sipping some kummel, in order to come and whisper to his sister: "I say, it was very stupid of you to taunt mamma in the way you did just now. I don't care a rap about it myself. But it ends by being noticed, and, I warn you candidly, it shows ill breeding."

Camille gazed at him fixedly with her black eyes. "Pray don't *you* meddle with my affairs," said she.

At this he felt frightened, scented a storm, and decided to take Rosemonde into the adjoining red drawing-room in order to show her a picture which his father had just purchased. And the General, on being called by him, likewise conducted Madame Fonsegue thither.

The mother and daughter then suddenly found themselves alone and face to face. Eve was leaning on a pier-table, as if overcome; and indeed, the least sorrow bore her down, so weak at heart she was, ever ready to weep in her naive and perfect egotism. Why was it that her daughter thus hated her, and did her utmost to disturb that last happy spell of love in which her heart lingered? She looked at Camille, grieved rather than irritated; and the unfortunate idea came to her of making a remark about her dress at the very moment when the girl was on the point of following the others into the larger drawing-room.

"It's quite wrong of you, my dear," said she, "to persist in dressing like an old woman. It doesn't improve you a bit."

As Eve spoke, her soft eyes, those of a courted and worshipped handsome woman, clearly expressed the compassion she felt for that ugly, deformed girl, whom she had never been able to regard as a daughter. Was it possible that she, with her sovereign beauty, that beauty which she herself had ever adored and nursed, making it her one care, her one religion—was it possible that she had given birth to such a graceless creature, with a dark, goatish profile, one shoulder higher than the other, and a pair of endless arms such as hunchbacks often have? All her grief and all her shame at having had such a child became apparent in the quivering of her voice.

Camille, however, had stopped short, as if struck in the face with a whip. Then she came back to her mother and the horrible explanation began with these simple words spoken in an undertone: "You consider that I dress badly? Well, you ought to have paid some attention to me, have seen that my gowns suited your taste, and have taught me your secret of looking beautiful!"

Eve, with her dislike of all painful feeling, all quarrelling and bitter words, was already regretting her attack. So she sought to make a retreat, particularly as time was flying and they would soon be expected downstairs: "Come, be quiet, and don't show your bad temper when all those people can hear us. I have loved you—"

But with a quiet yet terrible laugh Camille interrupted her. "You've loved me! Oh! my poor mamma, what a comical thing to say! Have you ever loved *anybody*? You want others to love *you*, but that's another matter. As for your child, any child, do you even know how it ought to be loved? You have always neglected me, thrust me on one side, deeming me so ugly, so unworthy of you! And besides, you have not had days and nights enough to love yourself! Oh! don't deny it, my poor mamma; but even now you're looking at me as if I were some loathsome monster that's in your way."

From that moment the abominable scene was bound to continue to the end. With their teeth set, their faces close together, the two women went on speaking in feverish whispers.

"Be quiet, Camille, I tell you! I will not allow such language!"

"But I won't be quiet when you do all you can to wound me. If it's wrong of me to dress like an old woman, perhaps another is rather ridiculous in dressing like a girl, like a bride."

"Like a bride? I don't understand you."

"Oh! yes, you do. However, I would have you know that everybody doesn't find me so ugly as you try to make them believe."

"If you look amiss, it is because you don't dress properly; that is all I said."

"I dress as I please, and no doubt I do so well enough, since I'm loved as I am."

"What, really! Does someone love you? Well, let him inform us of it and marry you."

"Yes—certainly, certainly! It will be a good riddance, won't it? And you'll have the pleasure of seeing me as a bride!"

Their voices were rising in spite of their efforts to restrain them. However, Camille paused and drew breath before hissing out the words: "Gerard is coming here to ask for my hand in a day or two."

Eve, livid, with wildly staring eyes, did not seem to understand. "Gerard? why do you tell me that?"

"Why, because it's Gerard who loves me and who is going to marry me! You drive me to extremities; you're for ever repeating that I'm ugly; you treat me like a monster whom nobody will ever care for. So I'm forced to defend myself and tell you the truth in order to prove to you that everybody is not of your opinion."

Silence fell; the frightful thing which had risen between them seemed to have arrested the quarrel. But there was neither mother nor daughter left there. They were simply two suffering, defiant rivals. Eve in her turn drew a long breath and glanced anxiously towards the adjoining room to ascertain if anyone were coming in or listening to them. And then in a tone of resolution she made answer:

"You cannot marry Gerard."

"Pray, why not?"

"Because I won't have it; because it's impossible."

"That isn't a reason; give me a reason."

"The reason is that the marriage is impossible that is all."

"No, no, I'll tell you the reason since you force me to it. The reason is that Gerard is your lover! But what does that matter, since I know it and am willing to take him all the same?"

And to this retort Camille's flaming eyes added the words: "And it is particularly on that account that I want him." All the long torture born of her infirmities, all her rage at having always seen her mother beautiful, courted and adored, was now stirring her and seeking vengeance in cruel triumph. At last then she was snatching from her rival the lover of whom she had so long been jealous!

"You wretched girl!" stammered Eve, wounded in the heart and almost sinking to the floor. "You don't know what you say or what you make me suffer."

However, she again had to pause, draw herself erect and smile; for Rosemonde hastened in from the adjoining room with the news that she was wanted downstairs. The doors were about to be opened, and it was necessary she should be at her stall. Yes, Eve answered, she would be down in another moment. Still, even as she spoke she leant more heavily on the pier-table behind her in order that she might not fall.

Hyacinthe had drawn near to his sister: "You know," said he, "it's simply idiotic to quarrel like that. You would do much better to come downstairs."

But Camille harshly dismissed him: "Just *you* go off, and take the others with you. It's quite as well that they shouldn't be about our ears."

Hyacinthe glanced at his mother, like one who knew the truth and considered the whole affair ridiculous. And then, vexed at seeing her so deficient in energy in dealing with that little pest, his sister, he shrugged his shoulders, and leaving them to their folly, conducted the others away. One could hear Rosemonde laughing as she went off below, while the General began to tell Madame Fonsegue another story as they descended the stairs together. However, at the moment when the mother and daughter at last fancied themselves alone once more, other voices reached their ears, those of Duvillard and Fonsegue, who were still near at hand. The Baron from his room might well overhear the dispute.

Eve felt that she ought to have gone off. But she had lacked the strength to do so; it had been a sheer impossibility for her after those words which had smote her like a buffet amidst her distress at the thought of losing her lover.

"Gerard cannot marry you," she said; "he does not love you."

"He does."

"You fancy it because he has good-naturedly shown some kindness to you, on seeing others pay you such little attention. But he does not love you."

"He does. He loves me first because I'm not such a fool as many others are, and particularly because I'm young."

This was a fresh wound for the Baroness; one inflicted with mocking cruelty in which rang out all the daughter's triumphant delight at seeing her mother's beauty at last ripening and waning. "Ah! my poor mamma, you no longer know what it is to be young. If I'm not beautiful, at all events I'm young; my eyes are clear and my lips are fresh. And my hair's so long too, and I've so much of it that it would suffice to gown me if I chose. You see, one's never ugly when one's young. Whereas, my poor mamma, everything is ended when one gets old. It's all very well for a woman to have been beautiful, and to strive to keep so, but in reality there's only ruin left, and shame and disgust."

She spoke these words in such a sharp, ferocious voice that each of them entered her mother's heart like a knife. Tears rose to the eyes of the wretched woman, again stricken in her bleeding wound. Ah! it was true, she remained without weapons against youth. And all her anguish came from the consciousness that she was growing old, from the feeling that love was departing from her now, that like a fruit she had ripened and fallen from the tree.

"But Gerard's mother will never let him marry you," she said.

"He will prevail on her; that's his concern. I've a dowry of two millions, and two millions can settle many things."

"Do you now want to libel him, and say that he's marrying you for your money?"

"No, indeed! Gerard's a very nice and honest fellow. He loves me and he's marrying me for myself. But, after all, he isn't rich; he still has no assured position, although he's thirty-six; and there may well be some advantage in a wife who brings you wealth as well as happiness. For, you hear, mamma, it's happiness I'm bringing him, real happiness, love that's shared and is certain of the future."

Once again their faces drew close together. The hateful scene, interrupted by sounds around them, postponed, and then resumed, was dragging on, becoming a perfect drama full of murderous violence, although they never shouted, but still spoke on in low and gasping voices. Neither gave way to the other, though at every moment they were liable to some surprise; for not only were all the doors open, so that the servants might come in, but the Baron's voice still rang out gaily, close at hand.

"He loves you, he loves you"—continued Eve. "That's what you say. But *he* never told you so."

"He has told me so twenty times; he repeats it every time that we are alone together!"

"Yes, just as one says it to a little girl by way of amusing her. But he has never told you that he meant to marry you."

"He told it me the last time he came. And it's settled. I'm simply waiting for him to get his mother's consent and make his formal offer."

"You lie, you lie, you wretched girl! You simply want to make me suffer, and you lie, you lie!"

Eve's grief at last burst forth in that cry of protest. She no longer knew that she was a mother, and was speaking to her daughter. The woman, the *amorosa*, alone remained in her, outraged and exasperated by a rival. And with a sob she confessed the truth: "It is I he loves! Only the last time I spoke to him, he swore to me—you hear me?—he swore upon his honour that he did not love you, and that he would never marry you!"

A faint, sharp laugh came from Camille. Then, with an air of derisive compassion, she replied: "Ah! my poor mamma, you really make me sorry for you! What a child you are! Yes, really, you are the child, not I. What! you who ought to have so much experience, you still allow yourself to be duped by a man's protests! That one really has no malice; and, indeed, that's why he swears whatever you want him to swear, just to please and quiet you, for at heart he's a bit of a coward."

"You lie, you lie!"

"But just think matters over. If he no longer comes here, if he didn't come to *dejeuner* this morning, it is simply because he's had enough of you. He has left you for good; just have the courage to realise it. Of course he's still polite and amiable, because he's a well-bred man, and doesn't know how to break off. The fact is that he takes pity on you."

"You lie, you lie!"

"Well, question him then. Have a frank explanation with him. Ask him his intentions in a friendly way. And then show some good nature yourself, and realise that if you care for him you ought to give him me at once in his own interest. Give him back his liberty, and you will soon see that I'm the one he loves."

"You lie, you lie! You wretched child, you only want to torture and kill me!"

Then, in her fury and distress, Eve remembered that she was the mother, and that it was for her to chastise that unworthy daughter. There was no stick near her, but from a basket of the yellow roses, whose powerful scent intoxicated both of them, she plucked a handful of blooms, with long and spiny stalks, and smote Camille across the face. A drop of blood appeared on the girl's left temple, near her eyelid.

But she sprang forward, flushed and maddened by this correction, with her hand raised and ready to strike back. "Take care, mother! I swear I'd beat you like a gipsy! And now just put this into your head: I mean to marry Gerard, and I will; and I'll take him from you, even if I have to raise a scandal, should you refuse to give him to me with good grace."

Eve, after her one act of angry vigour, had sunk into an armchair, overcome, distracted. And all the horror of quarrels, which sprang from her egotistical desire to be happy, caressed, flattered and adored, was returning to her. But Camille, still threatening, still unsatiated, showed her heart as it really was, her stern, black, unforgiving heart, intoxicated with cruelty. There came a moment of supreme silence, while Duvillard's gay voice again rang out in the adjoining room.

I. THE RIVALS

The mother was gently weeping, when Hyacinthe, coming upstairs at a run, swept into the little *salon.* He looked at the two women, and made a gesture of indulgent contempt. "Ah! you're no doubt satisfied now! But what did I tell you? It would have been much better for you to have come downstairs at once! Everybody is asking for you. It's all idiotic. I've come to fetch you."

Eve and Camille would not yet have followed him, perhaps, if Duvillard and Fonsegue had not at that moment come out of the former's room. Having finished their cigars they also spoke of going downstairs. And Eve had to rise and smile and show dry eyes, while Camille, standing before a looking-glass, arranged her hair, and stanched the little drop of blood that had gathered on her temple.

There was already quite a number of people below, in the three huge saloons adorned with tapestry and plants. The stalls had been draped with red silk, which set a gay, bright glow around the goods. And no ordinary bazaar could have put forth such a show, for there was something of everything among the articles of a thousand different kinds, from sketches by recognised masters, and the autographs of famous writers, down to socks and slippers and combs. The haphazard way in which things were laid out was in itself an attraction; and, in addition, there was a buffet, where the whitest of beautiful hands poured out champagne, and two lotteries, one for an organ and another for a pony-drawn village cart, the tickets for which were sold by a bevy of charming girls, who had scattered through the throng. As Duvillard had expected, however, the great success of the bazaar lay in the delightful little shiver which the beautiful ladies experienced as they passed through the entrance where the bomb had exploded. The rougher repairing work was finished, the walls and ceilings had been doctored, in part re-constructed. However, the painters had not yet come, and here and there the whiter stone and plaster work showed like fresh scars left by all the terrible gashes. It was with mingled anxiety and rapture that pretty heads emerged from the carriages which, arriving in a continuous stream, made the flagstones of the court re-echo. And in the three saloons, beside the stalls, there was no end to the lively chatter: "Ah! my dear, did you see all those marks? How frightful, how frightful! The whole house was almost blown up. And to think it might begin again while we are here! One really needs some courage to come, but then, that asylum is such a deserving institution, and money is badly wanted to build a new wing. And besides, those monsters will see that we are not frightened, whatever they do."

When the Baroness at last came down to her stall with Camille she found the saleswomen feverishly at work already under the direction of Princess Rosemonde, who on occasions of this kind evinced the greatest cunning and rapacity, robbing the customers in the most impudent fashion. "Ah! here you are," she exclaimed. "Beware of a number of higglers who have come to secure bargains. I know them! They watch for their opportunities, turn everything topsy-turvy and wait for us to lose our heads and forget prices, so as to pay even less than they would in a real shop. But I'll get good prices from them, you shall see!"

At this, Eve, who for her own part was a most incapable saleswoman, had to laugh with the others. And in a gentle voice she made a pretence of addressing certain recommendations to Camille, who listened with a smiling and most submissive air. In point of fact the wretched mother was sinking with emotion, particularly at the thought that she would have to remain there till seven o'clock, and suffer in secret before all those people, without possibility of relief. And thus it was almost like a respite when she suddenly perceived Abbe Froment sitting and waiting for her on a settee, covered with red velvet, near her stall. Her legs were failing her, so she took a place beside him.

"You received my letter then, Monsieur l'Abbe. I am glad that you have come, for I have some good news to give you, and wished to leave you the pleasure of imparting it to your *protege*, that man Laveuve, whom you so warmly recommended to me. Every formality has now been fulfilled, and you can bring him to the asylum to-morrow."

Pierre gazed at her in stupefaction. "Laveuve? Why, he is dead!"

In her turn she became astonished. "What, dead! But you never informed me of it! If I told you of all the trouble that has been taken, of all that had to be undone and done again, and the discussions and the papers and the writing! Are you quite sure that he is dead?"

"Oh! yes, he is dead. He has been dead a month."

"Dead a month! Well, we could not know; you yourself gave us no sign of life. Ah! *mon Dieu*! what a worry that he should be dead. We shall now be obliged to undo everything again!"

"He is dead, madame. It is true that I ought to have informed you of it. But that doesn't alter the fact—he is dead."

Dead! that word which kept on returning, the thought too, that for a month past she had been busying herself for a corpse, quite froze her, brought her to the very depths of despair, like an omen of the cold death into which she herself must soon descend, in the shroud of her last passion. And, meantime, Pierre, despite himself, smiled bitterly at the atrocious irony of it all. Ah! that lame and halting Charity, which proffers help when men are dead!

The priest still lingered on the settee when the Baroness rose. She had seen magistrate Amadieu hurriedly enter like one who just wished to show himself, purchase some trifle, and then return to the Palace of Justice. However, he was also perceived by little Massot, the "Globe" reporter, who was prowling round the stalls, and who at once bore down upon him, eager for information. And he hemmed him in and forthwith interviewed him respecting the affair of that mechanician Salvat, who was accused of having deposited the bomb at the entrance of the house. Was this simply an invention of the police, as some newspapers pretended? Or was it really correct? And if so, would Salvat soon be arrested? In self-defence Amadieu answered correctly enough that the affair did not as yet concern him, and would only come within his attributions, if Salvat should be arrested and the investigation placed in his hands. At the same time, however, the magistrate's pompous and affectedly shrewd manner suggested that he already knew everything to the smallest details, and that, had he chosen, he could have promised some great events for the morrow. A circle of ladies had gathered round him as he spoke, quite a number of pretty women feverish with curiosity, who jostled one another in their eagerness to hear that brigand tale which sent a little shiver coursing under their skins. However, Amadieu managed to slip off after paying Rosemonde twenty francs for a cigarette case, which was perhaps worth thirty sous.

Massot, on recognising Pierre, came up to shake hands with him. "Don't you agree with me, Monsieur l'Abbe, that Salvat must be a long way off by now if he's got good legs? Ah! the police will always make me laugh!"

However, Rosemonde brought Hyacinthe up to the journalist. "Monsieur Massot," said she, "you who go everywhere, I want you to be judge. That Chamber of Horrors at Montmartre, that tavern where Legras sings the 'Flowers of the Streets'—"

"Oh! a delightful spot, madame," interrupted Massot, "I wouldn't take even a gendarme there."

"No, don't jest, Monsieur Massot, I'm talking seriously. Isn't it quite allowable for a respectable woman to go there when she's accompanied by a gentleman?" And, without allowing the journalist time to answer her, she turned towards Hyacinthe: "There! you see that Monsieur Massot doesn't say no! You've got to take me there this evening, it's sworn, it's sworn."

Then she darted away to sell a packet of pins to an old lady, while the young man contented himself with remarking, in the voice of one who has no illusions left: "She's quite idiotic with her Chamber of Horrors!"

Massot philosophically shrugged his shoulders. It was only natural that a woman should want to amuse herself. And when Hyacinthe had gone off, passing with perverse contempt beside the lovely girls who were selling lottery tickets, the journalist ventured to murmur: "All the same, it would do that youngster good if a woman were to take him in hand."

Then, again addressing Pierre, he resumed: "Why, here comes Duthil! What did Sagnier mean this morning by saying that Duthil would sleep at Mazas to-night?"

In a great hurry apparently, and all smiles, Duthil was cutting his way through the crowd in order to join Duvillard and Fonsegue, who still stood talking near the Baroness's stall. And he waved his hand to them in a victorious way, to imply that he had succeeded in the delicate mission entrusted to him. This was nothing less than a bold manoeuvre to hasten Silviane's admission to the Comedie Francaise. The idea had occurred to her of making the Baron give a dinner at the Cafe Anglais in order that she might meet at it an influential critic, who, according to her statements, would compel the authorities to throw the doors wide open for her as soon as he should know her. However, it did not seem easy to secure the critic's presence, as he was noted for his sternness and grumbling disposition. And, indeed, after a first repulse, Duthil had for three days past been obliged to exert all his powers of diplomacy, and bring even the remotest influence into play. But he was radiant now, for he had conquered.

"It's for this evening, my dear Baron, at half-past seven," he exclaimed. "Ah! dash it all, I've had more trouble than I should have had to secure a concession vote!" Then he laughed with the pretty impudence of a man of pleasure, whom political conscientiousness did not trouble. And, indeed, his allusion to the fresh denunciations of the "Voix du Peuple" hugely amused him.

"Don't jest," muttered Fonsegue, who for his part wished to amuse himself by frightening the young deputy. "Things are going very badly!"

Duthil turned pale, and a vision of the police and Mazas rose before his eyes. In this wise sheer funk came over him from time to time. However, with his lack of all moral sense, he soon felt reassured and began to laugh. "Bah!" he retorted gaily, winking towards Duvillard, "the governor's there to pilot the barque!"

The Baron, who was extremely pleased, had pressed his hands, thanked him, and called him an obliging fellow. And now turning towards Fonsegue, he exclaimed: "I say, you must make one of us this evening. Oh! it's necessary. I want something imposing round Silviane. Duthil will represent the Chamber, you journalism, and I finance—" But he suddenly paused on seeing Gerard, who, with a somewhat grave expression, was leisurely picking his way through the sea of skirts. "Gerard, my friend," said the Baron, after beckoning to him, "I want you to do me a service." And forthwith he told him what was in question; how the influential critic had been prevailed upon to attend a dinner which would decide Silviane's future; and how it was the duty of all her friends to rally round her.

"But I can't," the young man answered in embarrassment. "I have to dine at home with my mother, who was rather poorly this morning."

"Oh! a sensible woman like your mother will readily understand that there are matters of exceptional importance. Go home and excuse yourself. Tell her some story, tell her that a friend's happiness is in question." And as Gerard began to weaken, Duvillard added: "The fact is, that I really want you, my dear fellow; I must have a society man. Society, you know, is a great force in theatrical matters; and if Silviane has society with her, her triumph is certain."

Gerard promised, and then chatted for a moment with his uncle, General de Bozonnet, who was quite enlivened by that throng of women, among whom he had been carried hither and thither like an old rudderless ship. After acknowledging the amiability with which Madame Fonsegue had listened to his stories, by purchasing an autograph of Monseigneur Martha from her for a hundred francs, he had quite lost himself amid the bevy of girls who had passed him on, one to another. And now, on his return from them, he had his hands full of lottery tickets: "Ah! my fine fellow," said he, "I don't advise you to venture among all those young persons. You would have to part with your last copper. But, just look! there's Mademoiselle Camille beckoning to you!"

Camille, indeed, from the moment she had perceived Gerard, had been smiling at him and awaiting his approach. And when their glances met he was obliged to go to her, although, at the same moment, he felt that Eve's despairing and entreating eyes were fixed upon him. The girl, who fully realised that her mother was watching her, at once made a marked display of amiability, profiting by the license which charitable fervour authorised, to slip a variety of little articles into the young man's pockets, and then place others in his hands, which she pressed within her own, showing the while all the sparkle of youth, indulging in fresh, merry laughter, which fairly tortured her rival.

So extreme was Eve's suffering, that she wished to intervene and part them. But it so chanced that Pierre barred her way, for he wished to submit an idea to her before leaving the bazaar. "Madame," said he, "since that man Laveuve is dead, and you have taken so much trouble with regard to the bed which you now have vacant, will you be so good as to keep it vacant until I have seen our venerable friend, Abbe Rose? I am to see him this evening, and he knows so many cases of want, and would be so glad to relieve one of them, and bring you some poor *protege* of his."

"Yes, certainly," stammered the Baroness, "I shall be very happy,—I will wait a little, as you desire,—of course, of course, Monsieur l'Abbe."

She was trembling all over; she no longer knew what she was saying; and, unable to conquer her passion, she turned aside from the priest, unaware even that he was still there, when Gerard, yielding to the dolorous entreaty of her eyes, at last managed to escape from Camille and join her.

"What a stranger you are becoming, my friend!" she said aloud, with a forced smile. "One never sees you now."

"Why, I have been poorly," he replied, in his amiable way. "Yes, I assure you I have been ailing a little."

He, ailing! She looked at him with maternal anxiety, quite upset. And, indeed, however proud and lofty his figure, his handsome regular face did seem to her paler than usual. It was as if the nobility of the facade had, in some degree, ceased to hide the irreparable dilapidation within. And given his real good nature, it must be true that he suffered—suffered by reason of his useless, wasted life, by reason of all the money he cost his impoverished mother, and of the needs that were at last driving him to marry that wealthy deformed girl, whom at first he had simply pitied. And so weak did he seem to Eve, so like a piece of wreckage tossed hither and thither by a tempest, that, at the risk of being overheard by the throng, she let her heart flow forth in a low but ardent, entreating murmur: "If you suffer, ah! what sufferings are mine!—Gerard, we must see one another, I will have it so."

"No, I beg you, let us wait," he stammered in embarrassment.

"It must be, Gerard; Camille has told me your plans. You cannot refuse to see me. I insist on it."

He made yet another attempt to escape the cruel explanation. "But it's impossible at the usual place," he answered, quivering. "The address is known."

"Then to-morrow, at four o'clock, at that little restaurant in the Bois where we have met before."

He had to promise, and they parted. Camille had just turned her head and was looking at them. Moreover, quite a number of women had besieged the stall; and the Baroness began to attend to them with the air of a ripe and nonchalant goddess, while Gerard rejoined Duvillard, Fonsegue and Duthil, who were quite excited at the prospect of their dinner that evening.

Pierre had heard a part of the conversation between Gerard and the Baroness. He knew what skeletons the house concealed, what physiological and moral torture and wretchedness lay beneath all the dazzling wealth and power. There was here an envenomed, bleeding sore, ever spreading, a cancer eating into father, mother, daughter and son, who one and all had thrown social bonds aside. However, the priest made his way out of the *salons*, half stifling amidst the throng of lady-purchasers who were making quite a triumph of the bazaar. And yonder, in the depths of the gloom, he could picture Salvat still running and running on; while the corpse of Laveuve seemed to him like a buffet of atrocious irony dealt to noisy and delusive charity.

II. SPIRIT AND FLESH

How delightful was the quietude of the little ground-floor overlooking a strip of garden in the Rue Cortot, where good Abbe Rose resided! Hereabouts there was not even a rumble of wheels, or an echo of the panting breath of Paris, which one heard on the other side of the height of Montmartre. The deep silence and sleepy peacefulness were suggestive of some distant provincial town.

Seven o'clock had struck, the dusk had gathered slowly, and Pierre was in the humble dining-room, waiting for the *femme-de-menage* to place the soup upon the table. Abbe Rose, anxious at having seen so little of him for a month past, had written, asking him to come to dinner, in order that they might have a quiet chat concerning their affairs. From time to time Pierre still gave his friend money for charitable purposes; in fact, ever since the days of the asylum in the Rue de Charonne, they had had accounts together, which they periodically liquidated. So that evening after dinner they were to talk of it all, and see if they could not do even more than they had hitherto done. The good old priest was quite radiant at the thought of the peaceful evening which he was about to spend in attending to the affairs of his beloved poor; for therein lay his only amusement, the sole pleasure to which he persistently and passionately returned, in spite of all the worries that his inconsiderate charity had already so often brought him.

Glad to be able to procure his friend this pleasure, Pierre, on his side, grew calmer, and found relief and momentary repose in sharing the other's simple repast and yielding to all the kindliness around him, far from his usual worries. He remembered the vacant bed at the Asylum, which Baroness Duvillard had promised to keep in reserve until he should have asked Abbe Rose if he knew of any case of destitution particularly worthy of interest; and so before sitting down to table he spoke of the matter.

"Destitution worthy of interest!" replied Abbe Rose, "ah! my dear child, every case is worthy of interest. And when it's a question of old toilers without work the only trouble is that of selection, the anguish of choosing one and leaving so many others in distress." Nevertheless, painful though his scruples were, he strove to think and come to some decision. "I know the case which will suit you," he said at last. "It's certainly one of the greatest suffering and wretchedness; and, so humble a one, too—an old carpenter of seventy-five, who has been living on public charity during the eight or ten years that he has been unable to find work. I don't know his name, everybody calls him 'the big Old'un.' There are times when he does not come to my Saturday distributions for weeks together. We shall have to look for him at once. I think that he sleeps at the Night Refuge in the Rue d'Orsel when lack of room there doesn't force him to spend the night crouching behind some palings. Shall we go down the Rue d'Orsel this evening?"

Abbe Rose's eyes beamed brightly as he spoke, for this proposal of his signified a great debauch, the tasting of forbidden fruit. He had been reproached so often and so roughly with his visits to those who had fallen to the deepest want and misery, that in spite of his overflowing, apostolic compassion, he now scarcely dared to go near them. However, he continued: "Is it agreed, my child? Only this once? Besides, it is our only means of finding the big Old'un. You won't have to stop with me later than eleven. And I should so like to show you all that! You will see what terrible sufferings there are! And perhaps we may be fortunate enough to relieve some poor creature or other."

Pierre smiled at the juvenile ardour displayed by this old man with snowy hair. "It's agreed, my dear Abbe," he responded, "I shall be very pleased to spend my whole evening with you, for I feel it will do me good to follow you once more on one of those rambles which used to fill our hearts with grief and joy."

At this moment the servant brought in the soup; however, just as the two priests were taking their seats a discreet ring was heard, and when Abbe Rose learnt that the visitor was a neighbour, Madame Mathis, who had come for an answer, he gave orders that she should be shown in.

"This poor woman," he explained to Pierre, "needed an advance of ten francs to get a mattress out of pawn; and I didn't have the money by me at the time. But I've since procured it. She lives in the house, you know, in silent poverty, on so small an income that it hardly keeps her in bread."

"But hasn't she a big son of twenty?" asked Pierre, suddenly remembering the young man he had seen at Salvat's.

"Yes, yes. Her parents, I believe, were rich people in the provinces. I've been told that she married a music master, who gave her lessons, at Nantes; and who ran away with her and brought her to Paris, where he died. It was quite a doleful love-story. By selling the furniture and realising every little thing she possessed, she scraped together an income of about two thousand francs a year, with which she was able to send her son to college and live decently herself. But a fresh blow fell on her: she lost the greater part of her little fortune, which was invested in doubtful securities. So now her income amounts at the utmost to eight hundred francs; two hundred of which she has to expend in rent. For all her other wants she has to be content with fifty francs a month. About eighteen months ago her son left her so as not to be a burden on her, and he is trying to earn his living somewhere, but without success, I believe."

Madame Mathis, a short, dark woman, with a sad, gentle, retiring face, came in. Invariably clad in the same black gown, she showed all the anxious timidity of a poor creature whom the storms of life perpetually assailed. When Abbe Rose had handed her the ten francs discreetly wrapped in paper, she blushed and thanked him, promising to pay him back as soon as she received her month's money, for she was not a beggar and did not wish to encroach on the share of those who starved.

"And your son, Victor, has he found any employment?" asked the old priest.

She hesitated, ignorant as she was of what her son might be doing, for now she did not see him for weeks together. And finally, she contented herself with answering: "He has a good heart, he is very fond of me. It is a great misfortune that we should have been ruined before he could enter the Ecole Normale. It was impossible for him to prepare for the examination. But at the Lycee he was such a diligent and intelligent pupil!"

"You lost your husband when your son was ten years old, did you not?" said Abbe Rose.

At this she blushed again, thinking that her husband's story was known to the two priests. "Yes, my poor husband never had any luck," she said. "His difficulties embittered and excited his mind, and he died in prison. He was sent there through a disturbance at a public meeting, when he had the misfortune to wound a police officer. He had also fought at the time of the Commune. And yet he was a very gentle man and extremely fond of me."

Tears had risen to her eyes; and Abbe Rose, much touched, dismissed her: "Well, let us hope that your son will give you satisfaction, and be able to repay you for all you have done for him."

With a gesture of infinite sorrow, Madame Mathis discreetly withdrew. She was quite ignorant of her son's doings, but fate had pursued her so relentlessly that she ever trembled.

"I don't think that the poor woman has much to expect from her son," said Pierre, when she had gone. "I only saw him once, but the gleam in his eyes was as harsh and trenchant as that of a knife."

"Do you think so?" the old priest exclaimed, with his kindly *naivete*. "Well, he seemed to me very polite, perhaps a trifle eager to enjoy life; but then, all the young folks are impatient nowadays. Come, let us sit down to table, for the soup will be cold."

Almost at the same hour, on the other side of Paris, night had in like fashion slowly fallen in the drawing-room of the Countess de Quinsac, on the dismal, silent ground-floor of an old mansion in the Rue St. Dominique. The Countess was there, alone with her faithful friend, the Marquis de Morigny, she on one side, and he on the other side of the chimney-piece, where the last embers of the wood fire were dying out. The servant had not yet brought the lamp, and the Countess refrained from ringing, finding some relief from her anxiety in the falling darkness, which hid from view all the unconfessed thoughts that she was afraid of showing on her weary face. And it was only now, before that dim hearth, and in that black room, where never a sound of wheels disturbed the silence of the slumberous past, that she dared to speak.

"Yes, my friend," she said, "I am not satisfied with Gerard's health. You will see him yourself, for he promised to come home early and dine with me. Oh! I'm well aware that he looks big and strong; but to know him properly one must have nursed and watched him as I have done! What trouble I had to rear him! In reality he is at the mercy of any petty ailment. His slightest complaint becomes serious illness. And the life he leads does not conduce to good health."

She paused and sighed, hesitating to carry her confession further.

"He leads the life he can," slowly responded the Marquis de Morigny, of whose delicate profile, and lofty yet loving bearing, little could be seen in the gloom. "As he was unable to endure military life, and as even the fatigues of diplomacy frighten you, what would you have him do? He can only live apart pending the final collapse, while this abominable Republic is dragging France to the grave."

"No doubt, my friend. And yet it is just that idle life which frightens me. He is losing in it all that was good and healthy in him. I don't refer merely to the *liaisons* which we have had to tolerate. The last one, which I found so much difficulty in countenancing at the outset, so contrary did it seem to all my ideas and beliefs, has since seemed to me to exercise almost a good influence. Only he is now entering his thirty-sixth year, and can he continue living in this fashion without object or duties? If he is ailing it is perhaps precisely because he does nothing, holds no position, and serves no purpose." Her voice again quavered. "And then, my friend, since you force me to tell you everything, I must own that I am not in good health myself. I have had several fainting fits of late, and have consulted a doctor. The truth is, that I may go off at any moment."

With a quiver, Morigny leant forward in the still deepening gloom, and wished to take hold of her hands. "You! what, am I to lose you, my last affection!" he faltered, "I who have seen the old world I belong to crumble away, I who only live in the hope that you at all events will still be here to close my eyes!"

But she begged him not to increase her grief: "No, no, don't take my hands, don't kiss them! Remain there in the shade, where I can scarcely see you.... We have loved one another so long without aught to cause shame or regret; and that will prove our strength—our divine strength—till we reach the grave.... And if you were to touch me, if I were to feel you too near me I could not finish, for I have not done so yet."

As soon as he had relapsed into silence and immobility, she continued: "If I were to die to-morrow, Gerard would not even find here the little fortune which he still fancies is in my hands. The dear child has often cost me large sums of money without apparently being conscious of it. I ought to have been more severe, more prudent. But what would you have? Ruin is at hand. I have always been too weak a mother. And do you now understand in what anguish I live? I ever have the thought that if I die Gerard will not even possess enough to live on, for he is incapable of effecting the miracle which I renew each day, in order to keep the house up on a decent footing.... Ah! I know him, so supine, so sickly, in spite of his proud bearing, unable to do anything, even conduct himself. And so what will become of him; will he not fall into the most dire distress?"

Then her tears flowed freely, her heart opened and bled, for she foresaw what must happen after her death: the collapse of her race and of a whole world in the person of that big child. And the Marquis, still motionless but distracted, feeling that he had no title to offer his own fortune, suddenly understood her, foresaw in what disgrace this fresh disaster would culminate.

"Ah! my poor friend!" he said at last in a voice trembling with revolt and grief. "So you have agreed to that marriage—yes, that abominable marriage with that woman's daughter! Yet you swore it should never be! You would rather witness the collapse of everything, you said. And now you are consenting, I can feel it!"

She still wept on in that black, silent drawing-room before the chimney-piece where the fire had died out. Did not Gerard's marriage to Camille mean a happy ending for herself, a certainty of leaving her son wealthy, loved, and seated at the banquet of life? However, a last feeling of rebellion arose within her.

"No, no," she exclaimed, "I don't consent, I swear to you that I don't consent as yet. I am fighting with my whole strength, waging an incessant battle, the torture of which you cannot imagine."

Then, in all sincerity, she foresaw the likelihood of defeat. "If I should some day give way, my friend, at all events believe that I feel, as fully as you do, how abominable such a marriage must be. It will be the end of our race and our honour!"

This cry profoundly stirred the Marquis, and he was unable to add a word. Haughty and uncompromising Catholic and Royalist that he was, he, on his side also, expected nothing but the supreme collapse. Yet how heartrending was the thought that this noble woman, so dearly and so purely loved, would prove one of the most mournful victims of the catastrophe! And in the shrouding gloom he found courage to kneel before her, take her hand, and kiss it.

Just as the servant was at last bringing a lighted lamp Gerard made his appearance. The past-century charm of the old Louis XVI. drawing-room, with its pale woodwork, again became apparent in the soft light. In order that his mother might not be over-saddened by his failure to dine with her that evening the young man had put on an air of brisk gaiety; and when he had explained that some friends were waiting for him, she at once released him from his promise, happy as she felt at seeing him so merry.

"Go, go, my dear boy," said she, "but mind you do not tire yourself too much.... I am going to keep Morigny; and the General and Larombiere are coming at nine o'clock. So be easy, I shall have someone with me to keep me from fretting and feeling lonely."

In this wise Gerard after sitting down for a moment and chatting with the Marquis was able to slip away, dress, and betake himself to the Cafe Anglais.

When he reached it women in fur cloaks were already climbing the stairs, fashionable and merry parties were filling the private rooms, the electric lights shone brilliantly, and the walls were already vibrating with the stir of pleasure and debauchery. In the room which Baron Duvillard had engaged the young man found an extraordinary display, the most superb flowers, and a profusion of plate and crystal as for a royal gala. The pomp with which the six covers were laid called forth a smile; while the bill of fare and the wine list promised marvels, all the rarest and most expensive things that could be selected.

"It's stylish, isn't it?" exclaimed Silviane, who was already there with Duvillard, Fonsegue and Duthil. "I just wanted to make your influential critic open his eyes a little! When one treats a journalist to such a dinner as this, he has got to be amiable, hasn't he?"

In her desire to conquer, it had occurred to the young woman to array herself in the most amazing fashion. Her gown of yellow satin, covered with old Alencon lace, was cut low at the neck; and she had put on all her diamonds, a necklace, a diadem, shoulder-knots, bracelets and rings. With her candid, girlish face, she looked like some Virgin in a missal, a Queen-Virgin, laden with the offerings of all Christendom.

"Well, well, you look so pretty," said Gerard, who sometimes jested with her, "that I think it will do all the same."

"Ah!" she replied with equanimity. "You consider me a *bourgeoise*, I see. Your opinion is that a simple little dinner and a modest gown would have shown better taste. But ah! my dear fellow, you don't know the way to get round men!"

Duvillard signified his approval, for he was delighted to be able to show her in all her glory, adorned like an idol. Fonsegue, for his part, talked of diamonds, saying that they were now doubtful investments, as the day when they would become articles of current manufacture was fast approaching, thanks to the electrical furnace and other inventions. Meantime Duthil, with an air of ecstasy and the dainty gestures of a lady's maid, hovered around the young woman, either smoothing a rebellious bow or arranging some fold of her lace.

"But I say," resumed Silviane, "your critic seems to be an ill-bred man, for he's keeping us waiting."

Indeed, the critic arrived a quarter of an hour late, and while apologising, he expressed his regret that he should be obliged to leave at half-past nine, for he was absolutely compelled to put in an appearance at a little theatre in the Rue Pigalle. He was a big fellow of fifty with broad shoulders and a full, bearded face. His most disagreeable characteristic was the narrow dogmatic pedantry which he had acquired at the Ecole Normale, and had never since been able to shake off. All his herculean efforts to be sceptical and frivolous, and the twenty years he had spent in Paris mingling with every section of society, had failed to rid him of it. *Magister* he was, and *magister* he remained, even in his most strenuous flights of imagination and audacity. From the moment of his arrival he tried to show himself enraptured with Silviane. Naturally enough, he already knew her by sight, and had even criticised her on one occasion in five or six contemptuous lines. However, the sight of her there, in full beauty, clad like a queen, and presented by four influential protectors, filled him with emotion; and he was struck with the idea that nothing would be more Parisian and less pedantic than to assert she had some talent and give her his support.

They had seated themselves at table, and the repast proved a magnificent one, the service ever prompt and assiduous, an attendant being allotted to each diner. While the flowers scattered their perfumes through the room, and the plate and crystal glittered on the snowy cloth, an abundance of delicious and unexpected dishes were handed round—a sturgeon from Russia, prohibited game, truffles as big as eggs, and hothouse vegetables and fruit as full of flavour as if they had been naturally matured. It was money flung out of window, simply for the pleasure of wasting more than other people, and eating what they could not procure. The influential critic, though he displayed the ease of a man accustomed to every sort of festivity, really felt astonished at it all, and became servile, promising his support, and pledging himself far more than he really wished to. Moreover, he showed himself very gay, found some witty remarks to repeat, and even some rather ribald jests. But when the champagne appeared after the roast and the grand burgundies, his over-excitement brought him back perforce to his real nature. The conversation had now turned on Corneille's "Polyeucte" and the part of "Pauline," in which Silviane wished to make her *debut* at the Comedie Francaise. This extraordinary caprice, which had quite revolted the influential critic a week previously, now seemed to him simply a bold enterprise in which the young woman might even prove victorious if she consented to listen to his advice. And, once started, he delivered quite a lecture on the past, asserting that no actress had ever yet understood it properly, for at the outset Pauline was simply a well-meaning little creature of the middle classes, and the beauty of her conversion at the finish arose from the working of a miracle, a stroke of heavenly grace which endowed her with something divine. This was not the opinion of Silviane, who from the first lines regarded Pauline as the ideal heroine of some symbolical legend. However, as the critic talked on and on, she had to feign approval; and he was delighted at finding her so beautiful and docile beneath his ferule. At last, as ten o'clock was striking, he rose and tore out of the hot and reeking room in order to do his work.

"Ah! my dears," cried Silviane, "he's a nice bore is that critic of yours! What a fool he is with his idea of Pauline being a little *bourgeoise*! I would have given him a fine dressing if it weren't for the fact that I have some need of him. Ah! no, it's too idiotic! Pour me out a glass of champagne. I want something to set me right after all that!"

The *fete* then took quite an intimate turn between the four men who remained and that bare-armed, bare-breasted girl, covered with diamonds; while from the neighbouring passages and rooms came bursts of laughter and sounds of kissing, all the stir and mirth of the debauchery now filling the house. And beneath the windows torrents of vehicles and pedestrians streamed along the Boulevards where reigned the wild fever of pleasure and harlotry.

"No, don't open it, or I shall catch cold!" resumed Silviane, addressing Fonsegue as he stepped towards the window. "Are you so very warm, then? I'm just comfortable.... But, Duvillard, my good fellow, please order some more champagne. It's wonderful what a thirst your critic has given me!"

Amidst the blinding glare of the lamps and the perfume of the flowers and wines, one almost stifled in the room. And Silviane was seized with an irresistible desire for a spree, a desire to tipple and amuse herself in some vulgar fashion, as in her bygone days. A few glasses of champagne brought her to full pitch, and she showed the boldest and giddiest gaiety. The others, who had never before seen her so lively, began on their own side to feel amused. As Fonsegue was obliged to go to his office she embraced him "like a daughter," as she expressed it. However, on remaining alone with the others she indulged in great freedom of speech, which became more and more marked as her intoxication increased. And to the class of men with whom she consorted her great attraction, as she was well aware, lay in the circumstance that with her virginal countenance and her air of ideal purity was coupled the most monstrous perversity ever displayed by any shameless woman. Despite her innocent blue eyes and lily-like candour, she would give rein, particularly when she was drunk, to the most diabolical of fancies.

Duvillard let her drink on, but she guessed his thoughts, like she guessed those of the others, and simply smiled while concocting impossible stories and descanting fantastically in the language of the gutter. And seeing her there in her dazzling gown fit for a queenly virgin, and hearing her pour forth the vilest words, they thought her most wonderfully droll. However, when she had drunk as much champagne as she cared for and was half crazy, a novel idea suddenly occurred to her.

"I say, my children," she exclaimed, "we are surely not going to stop here. It's so precious slow! You shall take me to the Chamber of Horrors—eh? just to finish the evening. I want to hear Legras sing 'La Chemise,' that song which all Paris is running to hear him sing."

But Duvillard indignantly rebelled: "Oh! no," said he; "most certainly not. It's a vile song and I'll never take you to such an abominable place."

But she did not appear to hear him. She had already staggered to her feet and was arranging her hair before a looking-glass. "I used to live at Montmartre," she said, "and it'll amuse me to go back there. And, besides, I want to know if this Legras is a Legras that I knew, oh! ever so long ago! Come, up you get, and let us be off!"

"But, my dear girl," pleaded Duvillard, "we can't take you into that den dressed as you are! Just fancy your entering that place in a low-necked gown and covered with diamonds! Why everyone would jeer at us! Come, Gerard, just tell her to be a little reasonable."

Gerard, equally offended by the idea of such a freak, was quite willing to intervene. But she closed his mouth with her gloved hand and repeated with the gay obstinacy of intoxication: "Pooh, it will be all the more amusing if they do jeer at us! Come, let us be off, let us be off, quick!"

Thereupon Duthil, who had been listening with a smile and the air of a man of pleasure whom nothing astonishes or displeases, gallantly took her part. "But, my dear Baron, everybody goes to the Chamber of Horrors," said he. "Why, I myself have taken the noblest ladies there, and precisely to hear that song of Legras, which is no worse than anything else."

"Ah! you hear what Duthil says!" cried Silviane. "He's a deputy, he is, and he wouldn't go there if he thought it would compromise his honorability!"

Then, as Duvillard still struggled on in despair at the idea of exhibiting himself with her in such a scandalous place, she became all the merrier: "Well, my dear fellow, please yourself. I don't need you. You and Gerard can go home if you like. But I'm going to Montmartre with Duthil. You'll take charge of me, won't you, Duthil, eh?"

Still, the Baron was in no wise disposed to let the evening finish in that fashion. The mere idea of it gave him a shock, and he had to resign himself to the girl's stubborn caprice. The only consolation he could think of was to secure Gerard's presence, for the young man, with some lingering sense of decorum, still obstinately refused to make one of the party. So the Baron took his hands and detained him, repeating in urgent tones that he begged him to come as an essential mark of friendship. And at last the wife's lover and daughter's suitor had to give way to the man who was the former's husband and the latter's father.

Silviane was immensely amused by it all, and, indiscreetly thee-ing and thou-ing Gerard, suggested that he at least owed the Baron some little compliance with his wishes.

Duvillard pretended not to hear her. He was listening to Duthil, who told him that there was a sort of box in a corner of the Chamber of Horrors, in which one could in some measure conceal oneself. And then, as Silviane's carriage—a large closed landau, whose coachman, a sturdy, handsome fellow, sat waiting impassively on his box—was down below, they started off.

The Chamber of Horrors was installed in premises on the Boulevard de Rochechouart, formerly occupied by a cafe whose proprietor had become bankrupt.[1] It was a suffocating place, narrow, irregular, with all sorts of twists, turns, and secluded nooks, and a low and smoky ceiling. And nothing could have been more rudimentary than its decorations. The walls had simply been placarded with posters of

[1] Those who know Paris will identify the site selected by M. Zola as that where 'Colonel' Lisbonne of the Commune installed his den the 'Bagne' some years ago. Nevertheless, such places as the 'Chamber of Horrors' now abound in the neighbourhood of Montmartre, and it must be admitted that whilst they are frequented by certain classes of Frenchmen they owe much of their success in a pecuniary sense to the patronage of foreigners. Among the latter, Englishmen are particularly conspicuous.—Trans.

violent hues, some of the crudest character, showing the barest of female figures. Behind a piano at one end there was a little platform reached by a curtained doorway. For the rest, one simply found a number of bare wooden forms set alongside the veriest pot-house tables, on which the glasses containing various beverages left round and sticky marks. There was no luxury, no artistic feature, no cleanliness even. Globeless gas burners flared freely, heating a dense mist compounded of tobacco smoke and human breath. Perspiring, apoplectical faces could be perceived through this veil, and an acrid odour increased the intoxication of the assembly, which excited itself with louder and louder shouts at each fresh song. It had been sufficient for an enterprising fellow to set up these boards, bring out Legras, accompanied by two or three girls, make him sing his frantic and abominable songs, and in two or three evenings overwhelming success had come, all Paris being enticed and flocking to the place, which for ten years or so had failed to pay as a mere cafe, where by way of amusement petty cits had been simply allowed their daily games at dominoes.

And the change had been caused by the passion for filth, the irresistible attraction exercised by all that brought opprobrium and disgust. The Paris of enjoyment, the *bourgeoisie* which held all wealth and power, which would relinquish naught of either, though it was surfeited and gradually wearying of both, simply hastened to the place in order that obscenity and insult might be flung in its face. Hypnotised, as it were, while staggering to its fall, it felt a need of being spat upon. And what a frightful symptom there lay in it all: those condemned ones rushing upon dirt of their own accord, voluntarily hastening their own decomposition by that unquenchable thirst for the vile, which attracted men, reputed to be grave and upright, and lovely women of the most perfect grace and luxury, to all the beastliness of that low den!

At one of the tables nearest the stage sat little Princess Rosemonde de Harn, with wild eyes and quivering nostrils, delighted as she felt at now being able to satisfy her curiosity regarding the depths of Paris life. Young Hyacinthe had resigned himself to the task of bringing her, and, correctly buttoned up in his long frock-coat, he was indulgent enough to refrain from any marked expression of boredom. At a neighbouring table they had found a shadowy Spaniard of their acquaintance, a so-called Bourse jobber, Bergaz, who had been introduced to the Princess by Janzen, and usually attended her entertainments. They virtually knew nothing about him, not even if he really earned at the Bourse all the money which he sometimes spent so lavishly, and which enabled him to dress with affected elegance. His slim, lofty figure was not without a certain air of distinction, but his red lips spoke of strong passions and his bright eyes were those of a beast of prey. That evening he had two young fellows with him, one Rossi, a short, swarthy Italian, who had come to Paris as a painter's model, and had soon glided into the lazy life of certain disreputable callings, and the other, Sanfaute, a born Parisian blackguard, a pale, beardless, vicious and impudent stripling of La Chapelle, whose long curly hair fell down upon either side of his bony cheeks.

"Oh! pray now!" feverishly said Rosemonde to Bergaz; "as you seem to know all these horrid people, just show me some of the celebrities. Aren't there some thieves and murderers among them?"

He laughed shrilly, and in a bantering way replied: "But you know these people well enough, madame. That pretty, pink, delicate-looking woman over yonder is an American lady, the wife of a consul, whom, I believe, you receive at your house. That other on the right, that tall brunette who shows such queenly dignity, is a Countess, whose carriage passes yours every day in the Bois. And the thin one yonder, whose eyes glitter like those of a she-wolf, is the particular friend of a high official, who is well known for his reputation of austerity."

But she stopped him, in vexation: "I know, I know. But the others, those of the lower classes, those whom one comes to see."

Then she went on asking questions, and seeking for terrifying and mysterious countenances. At last, two men seated in a corner ended by attracting her attention; one of them a very young fellow with a pale, pinched face, and the other an ageless individual who, besides being buttoned up to his neck in an old coat, had pulled his cap so low over his eyes, that one saw little of his face beyond the beard which fringed it. Before these two stood a couple of mugs of beer, which they drank slowly and in silence.

"You are making a great mistake, my dear," said Hyacinthe with a frank laugh, "if you are looking for brigands in disguise. That poor fellow with the pale face, who surely doesn't have food to eat every day, was my schoolfellow at Condorcet!"

Bergaz expressed his amazement. "What! you knew Mathis at Condorcet! After all, though, you're right, he received a college education. Ah! and so you knew him. A very remarkable young man he is, though want is throttling him. But, I say, the other one, his companion, you don't know him?"

Hyacinthe, after looking at the man with the cap-hidden face, was already shaking his head, when Bergaz suddenly gave him a nudge as a signal to keep quiet, and by way of explanation he muttered: "Hush! Here's Raphanel. I've been distrusting him for some time past. Whenever he appears anywhere, the police is not far off."

Raphanel was another of the vague, mysterious Anarchists whom Janzen had presented to the Princess by way of satisfying her momentary passion for revolutionism. This one, though he was a fat, gay, little man, with a doll-like face and childish nose, which almost disappeared between his puffy cheeks, had the reputation of being a thorough desperado; and at public meetings he certainly shouted for fire and murder with all his lungs. Still, although he had already been compromised in various affairs, he had invariably managed to save his own bacon, whilst his companions were kept under lock and key; and this they were now beginning to think somewhat singular.

He at once shook hands with the Princess in a jovial way, took a seat near her without being invited, and forthwith denounced the dirty *bourgeoisie* which came to wallow in places of ill fame. Rosemonde was delighted, and encouraged him, but others near by began to get angry, and Bergaz examined him with his piercing eyes, like a man of energy who acts, and lets others talk. Now and then, too, he exchanged quick glances of intelligence with his silent lieutenants, Sanfaute and Rossi, who plainly belonged to him, both body and soul. They were the ones who found their profit in Anarchy, practising it to its logical conclusions, whether in crime or in vice.

Meantime, pending the arrival of Legras with his "Flowers of the Pavement," two female vocalists had followed one another on the stage, the first fat and the second thin, one chirruping some silly love songs with an under-current of dirt, and the other shouting the coarsest of refrains, in a most violent, fighting voice. She had just finished amidst a storm of bravos, when the assembly, stirred to merriment and eager for a laugh, suddenly exploded once more. Silviane was entering the little box at one end of the hall. When she appeared erect in the full light, with bare arms and shoulders, looking like a planet in her gown of yellow satin and her blazing diamonds, there arose a formidable uproar, shouts, jeers, hisses, laughing and growling, mingled with ferocious applause. And the scandal increased, and the vilest expressions flew about as soon as Duvillard, Gerard and Duthil also showed themselves, looking very serious and dignified with their white ties and spreading shirt fronts.

"We told you so!" muttered Duvillard, who was much annoyed with the affair, while Gerard tried to conceal himself in a dim corner.

She, however, smiling and enchanted, faced the public, accepting the storm with the candid bearing of a foolish virgin, much as one inhales the vivifying air of the open when it bears down upon one in a squall. And, indeed, she herself had sprung from the sphere before her, its atmosphere was her native air.

"Well, what of it?" she said replying to the Baron who wanted her to sit down. "They are merry. It's very nice. Oh! I'm really amusing myself!"

"Why, yes, it's very nice," declared Duthil, who in like fashion set himself at his ease. "Silviane is right, people naturally like a laugh now and then!"

Amidst the uproar, which did not cease, little Princess Rosemonde rose enthusiastically to get a better view. "Why, it's your father who's with that woman Silviane," she said to Hyacinthe. "Just look at them! Well, he certainly has plenty of bounce to show himself here with her!"

Hyacinthe, however, refused to look. It didn't interest him, his father was an idiot, only a child would lose his head over a girl in that fashion. And with his contempt for woman the young man became positively insulting.

"You try my nerves, my dear fellow," said Rosemonde as she sat down. "You are the child with your silly ideas about us. And as for your father, he does quite right to love that girl. I find her very pretty indeed, quite adorable!"

Then all at once the uproar ceased, those who had risen resumed their seats, and the only sound was that of the feverish throb which coursed through the assembly. Legras had just appeared on the platform. He was a pale sturdy fellow with a round and carefully shaven face, stern eyes, and the powerful jaws of a man who compels the adoration of women by terrorising them. He was not deficient in talent, he sang true, and his ringing voice was one of extraordinary penetration and pathetic power. And his *repertoire*, his "Flowers of the Pavement," completed the explanation of his success; for all the foulness and suffering of the lower spheres, the whole abominable sore of the social hell created by the rich, shrieked aloud in these songs in words of filth and fire and blood.

A prelude was played on the piano, and Legras standing there in his velvet jacket sang "La Chemise," the horrible song which brought all Paris to hear him. All the lust and vice that crowd the streets of the great city appeared with their filth and their poison; and amid the picture of Woman stripped, degraded, ill-treated, dragged through the mire and cast into a cesspool, there rang out the crime of the *bourgeoisie*. But the scorching insult of it all was less in the words themselves than in the manner in which Legras cast them in the faces of the rich, the happy, the beautiful ladies who came to listen to him. Under the low ceiling, amidst the smoke from the pipes, in the blinding glare of the gas, he sent his lines flying through the assembly like expectorations, projected by a whirlwind of furious contempt. And when he had finished there came delirium; the beautiful ladies did not even think of wiping away the many affronts they had received, but applauded frantically. The whole assembly stamped and shouted, and wallowed, distracted, in its ignominy.

"Bravo! bravo!" the little Princess repeated in her shrill voice. "It's astonishing, astonishing, prodigious!"

And Silviane, whose intoxication seemed to have increased since she had been there, in the depths of that fiery furnace, made herself particularly conspicuous by the manner in which she clapped her hands and shouted: "It's he, it's my Legras! I really must kiss him, he's pleased me so much!"

Duvillard, now fairly exasperated, wished to take her off by force. But she clung to the hand-rest of the box, and shouted yet more loudly, though without any show of temper. It became necessary to parley with her. Yes, she was willing to go off and let them drive her home; but, first of all, she must embrace Legras, who was an old friend of hers. "Go and wait for me in the carriage!" she said, "I will be with you in a moment."

Just as the assembly was at last becoming calmer, Rosemonde perceived that the box was emptying; and her own curiosity being satisfied, she thought of prevailing on Hyacinthe to see her home. He, who had listened to Legras in a languid way without even applauding, was now talking of Norway with Bergaz, who pretended that he had travelled in the North. Oh! the fiords! oh! the ice-bound lakes! oh! the pure lily-white, chaste coldness of the eternal winter! It was only amid such surroundings, said Hyacinthe, that he could understand woman and love, like a kiss of the very snow itself.

"Shall we go off there to-morrow?" exclaimed the Princess with her vivacious effrontery. "I'll shut up my house and slip the key under the door."

Then she added that she was jesting, of course. But Bergaz knew her to be quite capable of such a freak; and at the idea that she might shut up her little mansion and perhaps leave it unprotected he exchanged a quick glance with Sanfaute and Rossi, who still smiled in silence. Ah! what an opportunity for a fine stroke! What an opportunity to get back some of the wealth of the community appropriated by the blackguard *bourgeoisie*!

Meantime Raphanel, after applauding Legras, was looking all round the place with his little grey, sharp eyes. And at last young Mathis and his companion, the ill-clad individual, of whose face only a scrap of beard could be seen, attracted his attention. They had neither laughed nor applauded; they seemed to be simply a couple of tired fellows who were resting, and in whose opinion one is best hidden in the midst of a crowd.

All at once, though, Raphanel turned towards Bergaz: "That's surely little Mathis over yonder. But who's that with him?"

Bergaz made an evasive gesture; he did not know. Still, he no longer took his eyes from Raphanel. And he saw the other feign indifference at what followed, and finish his beer and take his leave, with the jesting remark that he had an appointment with a lady at a neighbouring omnibus office. No sooner had he gone than Bergaz rose, sprang over some of the forms and jostled people in order to reach little Mathis, into whose ear he whispered a few words. And the young man at once left his table, taking his companion and pushing him outside through an occasional exit. It was all so rapidly accomplished that none of the general public paid attention to the flight.

"What is it?" said the Princess to Bergaz, when he had quietly resumed his seat between Rossi and Sanfaute.

"Oh! nothing, I merely wished to shake hands with Mathis as he was going off."

Thereupon Rosemonde announced that she meant to do the same. Nevertheless, she lingered a moment longer and again spoke of Norway on perceiving that nothing could impassion Hyacinthe except the idea of the eternal snow, the intense, purifying cold of the polar regions. In his poem on the "End of Woman," a composition of some thirty lines, which he hoped he should never finish, he thought of introducing a forest of frozen pines by way of final scene. Now the Princess had risen and was gaily reverting to her jest, declaring that she meant to take him home to drink a cup of tea and arrange their trip to the Pole, when an involuntary exclamation fell from Bergaz, who, while listening, had kept his eyes on the doorway.

"Mondesir! I was sure of it!"

There had appeared at the entrance a short, sinewy, broad-backed little man, about whose round face, bumpy forehead, and snub nose there was considerable military roughness. One might have thought him a non-commissioned officer in civilian attire. He gazed over the whole room, and seemed at once dismayed and disappointed.

Bergaz, however, wishing to account for his exclamation, resumed in an easy way: "Ah! I said there was a smell of the police about the place! You see that fellow—he's a detective, a very clever one, named Mondesir, who had some trouble when he was in the army. Just look at him, sniffing like a dog that has lost scent! Well, well, my brave fellow, if you've been told of any game you may look and look for it, the bird's flown already!"

Once outside, when Rosemonde had prevailed on Hyacinthe to see her home, they hastened to get into the brougham, which was waiting for them, for near at hand they perceived Silviane's landau, with the majestic coachman motionless on his box, while Duvillard, Gerard, and Duthil still stood waiting on the curbstone. They had been there for nearly twenty minutes already, in the semi-darkness of that outer boulevard, where all the vices of the poor districts of Paris were on the prowl. They had been jostled by drunkards; and shadowy women brushed against them as they went by whispering beneath the oaths and blows of bullies. And there were couples seeking the darkness under the trees, and lingering on the benches there; while all around were low taverns and dirty lodging-houses and places of ill-fame. All the human degradation which till break of day swarms in the black mud of this part of Paris, enveloped the three men, giving them the horrors, and yet neither the Baron nor Gerard nor Duthil was willing to go off. Each hoped that he would tire out the others, and take Silviane home when she should at last appear.

But after a time the Baron grew impatient, and said to the coachman: "Jules, go and see why madame doesn't come."

"But the horses, Monsieur le Baron?"

"Oh! they will be all right, we are here."

A fine drizzle had begun to fall; and the wait went on again as if it would never finish. But an unexpected meeting gave them momentary occupation. A shadowy form, something which seemed to be a thin, black-skirted woman, brushed against them. And all of a sudden they were surprised to find it was a priest.

"What, is it you, Monsieur l'Abbe Froment?" exclaimed Gerard. "At this time of night? And in this part of Paris?"

Thereupon Pierre, without venturing either to express his own astonishment at finding them there themselves, or to ask them what they were doing, explained that he had been belated through accompanying Abbe Rose on a visit to a night refuge. Ah!

to think of all the frightful want which at last drifted to those pestilential dormitories where the stench had almost made him faint! To think of all the weariness and despair which there sank into the slumber of utter prostration, like that of beasts falling to the ground to sleep off the abominations of life! No name could be given to the promiscuity; poverty and suffering were there in heaps, children and men, young and old, beggars in sordid rags, beside the shameful poor in threadbare frock-coats, all the waifs and strays of the daily shipwrecks of Paris life, all the laziness and vice, and ill-luck and injustice which the torrent rolls on, and throws off like scum. Some slept on, quite annihilated, with the faces of corpses. Others, lying on their backs with mouths agape, snored loudly as if still venting the plaint of their sorry life. And others tossed restlessly, still struggling in their slumber against fatigue and cold and hunger, which pursued them like nightmares of monstrous shape. And from all those human beings, stretched there like wounded after a battle, from all that ambulance of life reeking with a stench of rottenness and death, there ascended a nausea born of revolt, the vengeance-prompting thought of all the happy chambers where, at that same hour, the wealthy loved or rested in fine linen and costly lace.[1]

In vain had Pierre and Abbe Rose passed all the poor wretches in review while seeking the big Old'un, the former carpenter, so as to rescue him from the cesspool of misery, and send him to the Asylum on the very morrow. He had presented himself at the refuge that evening, but there was no room left, for, horrible to say, even the shelter of that hell could only be granted to early comers. And so he must now be leaning against a wall, or lying behind some palings. This had greatly distressed poor Abbe Rose and Pierre, but it was impossible for them to search every dark, suspicious corner; and so the former had returned to the Rue Cortot, while the latter was seeking a cab to convey him back to Neuilly.

The fine drizzling rain was still falling and becoming almost icy, when Silviane's coachman, Jules, at last reappeared and interrupted the priest, who was telling the Baron and the others how his visit to the refuge still made him shudder.

"Well, Jules—and madame?" asked Duvillard, quite anxious at seeing the coachman return alone.

Impassive and respectful, with no other sign of irony than a slight involuntary twist of the lips, Jules answered: "Madame sends word that she is not going home;

---

[1] Even the oldest Paris night refuges, which are the outcome of private philanthropy— L'Oeuvre de l'Hospitalite de Nuit— have only been in existence some fourteen or fifteen years. Before that time, and from the period of the great Revolution forward, there was absolutely no place, either refuge, asylum, or workhouse, in the whole of that great city of wealth and pleasure, where the houseless poor could crave a night's shelter. The various royalist, imperialist and republican governments and municipalities of modern France have often been described as 'paternal,' but no governments and municipalities in the whole civilised world have done less for the very poor. The official Poor Relief Board— L'Assistance Publique—has for fifty years been a by-word, a mockery and a sham, in spite of its large revenue. And this neglect of the very poor has been an important factor in every French revolution. Each of these—even that of 1870—had its purely economic side, though many superficial historians are content to ascribe economic causes to the one Revolution of 1789, and to pass them by in all other instances.—Trans.

and she places her carriage at the gentlemen's disposal if they will allow me to drive them home."

This was the last straw, and the Baron flew into a passion. To have allowed her to drag him to that vile den, to have waited there hopefully so long, and to be treated in this fashion for the sake of a Legras! No, no, he, the Baron, had had enough of it, and she should pay dearly for her abominable conduct! Then he stopped a passing cab and pushed Gerard inside it saying, "You can set me down at my door."

"But she's left us the carriage!" shouted Duthil, who was already consoled, and inwardly laughed at the termination of it all. "Come here, there's plenty of room for three. No? you prefer the cab? Well, just as you like, you know."

For his part he gaily climbed into the landau and drove off lounging on the cushions, while the Baron, in the jolting old cab, vented his rage without a word of interruption from Gerard, whose face was hidden by the darkness. To think of it! that she, whom he had overwhelmed with gifts, who had already cost him two millions of francs, should in this fashion insult him, the master who could dispose both of fortunes and of men! Well, she had chosen to do it, and he was delivered! Then Duvillard drew a long breath like a man released from the galleys.

For a moment Pierre watched the two vehicles go off; and then took his own way under the trees, so as to shelter himself from the rain until a vacant cab should pass. Full of distress and battling thoughts he had begun to feel icy cold. The whole monstrous night of Paris, all the debauchery and woe that sobbed around him made him shiver. Phantom-like women who, when young, had led lives of infamy in wealth, and who now, old and faded, led lives of infamy in poverty, were still and ever wandering past him in search of bread, when suddenly a shadowy form grazed him, and a voice murmured in his ear: "Warn your brother, the police are on Salvat's track, he may be arrested at any moment."

The shadowy figure was already going its way, and as a gas ray fell upon it, Pierre thought that he recognised the pale, pinched face of Victor Mathis. And at the same time, yonder in Abbe Rose's peaceful dining-room, he fancied he could again see the gentle face of Madame Mathis, so sad and so resigned, living on solely by the force of the last trembling hope which she had unhappily set in her son.

III. PLOT AND COUNTERPLOT

ALREADY at eight o'clock on that holiday-making mid-Lent Thursday, when all the offices of the Home Department were empty, Monferrand, the Minister, sat alone in his private room. A single usher guarded his door, and in the first ante-chamber there were only a couple of messengers.

The Minister had experienced, on awaking, the most unpleasant of emotions. The "Voix du Peuple," which on the previous day had revived the African Railway scandal, by accusing Barroux of having pocketed 20,000 francs, had that morning published its long-promised list of the bribe-taking senators and deputies. And at the head of this list Monferrand had found his own name set down against a sum of 80,000 francs, while Fonsegue was credited with 50,000. Then a fifth of the latter amount was said to have been Duthil's share, and Chaigneux had contented himself with the beggarly sum of 3,000 francs—the lowest price paid for any one vote, the cost of each of the others ranging from 5 to 20,000.

It must be said that there was no anger in Monferrand's emotion. Only he had never thought that Sagnier would carry his passion for uproar and scandal so far as to publish this list—a page which was said to have been torn from a memorandum book belonging to Duvillard's agent, Hunter, and which was covered with incomprehensible hieroglyphics that ought to have been discussed and explained, if, indeed, the real truth was to be arrived at. Personally, Monferrand felt quite at ease, for he had written nothing, signed nothing, and knew that one could always extricate oneself from a mess by showing some audacity, and never confessing. Nevertheless, what a commotion it would all cause in the parliamentary duck-pond. He at once realised the inevitable consequences, the ministry overthrown and swept away by this fresh whirlwind of denunciation and tittle-tattle. Mege would renew his interpellation on the morrow, and Vignon and his friends would at once lay siege to the posts they coveted. And he, Monferrand, could picture himself driven out of that ministerial sanctum where, for eight months past, he had been taking his ease, not with any foolish vainglory, but with the pleasure of feeling that he was in his proper place as a born ruler, who believed he could tame and lead the multitude.

Having thrown the newspapers aside with a disdainful gesture, he rose and stretched himself, growling the while like a plagued lion. And then he began to walk up and down the spacious room, which showed all the faded official luxury of mahogany furniture and green damask hangings. Stepping to and fro, with his hands behind his back, he no longer wore his usual fatherly, good-natured air. He appeared as he really was, a born wrestler, short, but broad shouldered, with sensual mouth, fleshy nose and stern eyes, that all proclaimed him to be unscrupulous, of iron will and fit for the greatest tasks. Still, in this case, in what direction lay his best course? Must he let himself be dragged down with Barroux? Perhaps his personal position was not absolutely compromised? And yet how could he part company from the others, swim ashore, and save himself while they were being drowned? It was a grave problem, and with his frantic desire to retain power, he made desperate endeavours to devise some suitable manoeuvre.

But he could think of nothing, and began to swear at the virtuous fits of that silly Republic, which, in his opinion, rendered all government impossible. To think of such foolish fiddle-faddle stopping a man of his acumen and strength! How on earth can one govern men if one is denied the use of money, that sovereign means of sway? And he laughed bitterly; for the idea of an idyllic country where all great enterprises would be carried out in an absolutely honest manner seemed to him the height of absurdity.

At last, however, unable as he was to come to a determination, it occurred to him to confer with Baron Duvillard, whom he had long known, and whom he regretted not having seen sooner so as to urge him to purchase Sagnier's silence. At first he thought of sending the Baron a brief note by a messenger; but he disliked committing anything to paper, for the veriest scrap of writing may prove dangerous; so he preferred to employ the telephone which had been installed for his private use near his writing-table.

"It is Baron Duvillard who is speaking to me?... Quite so. It's I, the Minister, Monsieur Monferrand. I shall be much obliged if you will come to see me at once.... Quite so, quite so, I will wait for you."

Then again he walked to and fro and meditated. That fellow Duvillard was as clever a man as himself, and might be able to give him an idea. And he was still laboriously trying to devise some scheme, when the usher entered saying that Monsieur Gascogne, the Chief of the Detective Police, particularly wished to speak to him. Monferrand's first thought was that the Prefecture of Police desired to know his views respecting the steps which ought to be taken to ensure public order that day; for two mid-Lent processions—one of the Washerwomen and the other of the Students—were to march through Paris, whose streets would certainly be crowded.

"Show Monsieur Gascogne in," he said.

A tall, slim, dark man, looking like an artisan in his Sunday best, then stepped into the ministerial sanctum. Fully acquainted with the under-currents of Paris life, this Chief of the Detective Force had a cold dispassionate nature and a clear and methodical mind. Professionalism slightly spoilt him, however: he would have possessed more intelligence if he had not credited himself with so much.

He began by apologising for his superior the Prefect, who would certainly have called in person had he not been suffering from indisposition. However, it was perhaps best that he, Gascogne, should acquaint Monsieur le Ministre with the grave affair which brought him, for he knew every detail of it. Then he revealed what the grave affair was.

"I believe, Monsieur le Ministre, that we at last hold the perpetrator of the crime in the Rue Godot-de-Mauroy."

At this, Monferrand, who had been listening impatiently, became quite impassioned. The fruitless searches of the police, the attacks and the jeers of the newspapers, were a source of daily worry to him. "Ah!—Well, so much the better for you Monsieur Gascogne," he replied with brutal frankness. "You would have ended by losing your post. The man is arrested?"

"Not yet, Monsieur le Ministre; but he cannot escape, and it is merely an affair of a few hours."

Then the Chief of the Detective Force told the whole story: how Detective Mondesir, on being warned by a secret agent that the Anarchist Salvat was in a tavern at Montmartre, had reached it just as the bird had flown; then how chance had again set him in presence of Salvat at a hundred paces or so from the tavern, the rascal having foolishly loitered there to watch the establishment; and afterwards how Salvat had been stealthily shadowed in the hope that they might catch him in his hiding-place with his accomplices. And, in this wise, he had been tracked to the Porte-Maillot, where, realising, no doubt, that he was pursued, he had suddenly bolted into the Bois de Boulogne. It was there that he had been hiding since two o'clock in the morning in the drizzle which had not ceased to fall. They had waited for daylight in order to organise a *battue* and hunt him down like some animal, whose weariness must necessarily ensure capture. And so, from one moment to another, he would be caught.

"I know the great interest you take in the arrest, Monsieur le Ministre," added Gascogne, "and it occurred to me to ask your orders. Detective Mondesir is over there, directing the hunt. He regrets that he did not apprehend the man on the Boulevard de Rochechouart; but, all the same, the idea of following him was a capital one, and one can only reproach Mondesir with having forgotten the Bois de Boulogne in his calculations."

Salvat arrested! That fellow Salvat whose name had filled the newspapers for three weeks past. This was a most fortunate stroke which would be talked of far and wide! In the depths of Monferrand's fixed eyes one could divine a world of thoughts and a sudden determination to turn this incident which chance had brought him to his own personal advantage. In his own mind a link was already forming between this arrest and that African Railways interpellation which was likely to overthrow the ministry on the morrow. The first outlines of a scheme already rose before him. Was it not his good star that had sent him what he had been seeking—a means of fishing himself out of the troubled waters of the approaching crisis?

"But tell me, Monsieur Gascogne," said he, "are you quite sure that this man Salvat committed the crime?"

"Oh! perfectly sure, Monsieur le Ministre. He'll confess everything in the cab before he reaches the Prefecture."

Monferrand again walked to and fro with a pensive air, and ideas came to him as he spoke on in a slow, meditative fashion. "My orders! well, my orders, they are, first, that you must act with the very greatest prudence. Yes, don't gather a mob of promenaders together. Try to arrange things so that the arrest may pass unperceived—and if you secure a confession keep it to yourself, don't communicate it to the newspapers. Yes, I particularly recommend that point to you, don't take the newspapers into your confidence at all—and finally, come and tell me everything, and observe secrecy, absolute secrecy, with everybody else."

Gascogne bowed and would have withdrawn, but Monferrand detained him to say that not a day passed without his friend Monsieur Lehmann, the Public Prosecutor, receiving letters from Anarchists who threatened to blow him up with his family; in such wise that, although he was by no means a coward, he wished his house to be guarded by plain-clothes officers. A similar watch was already kept upon the house where investigating magistrate Amadieu resided. And if the latter's life was precious, that of Public Prosecutor Lehmann was equally so, for he was one of those political magistrates, one of those shrewd talented Israelites, who make their way in very honest fashion by invariably taking the part of the Government in office.

Then Gascogne in his turn remarked: "There is also the Barthes affair, Monsieur le Ministre—we are still waiting. Are we to arrest Barthes at that little house at Neuilly?"

One of those chances which sometimes come to the help of detectives and make people think the latter to be men of genius had revealed to him the circumstance that Barthes had found a refuge with Abbe Pierre Froment. Ever since the Anarchist terror had thrown Paris into dismay a warrant had been out against the old man, not for any precise offence, but simply because he was a suspicious character and might, therefore, have had some intercourse with the Revolutionists. However, it had been repugnant to Gascogne to arrest him at the house of a priest whom the whole district venerated as a saint; and the Minister, whom he had consulted on the point, had warmly approved of his reserve, since a member of the clergy was in question, and had undertaken to settle the affair himself.

"No, Monsieur Gascogne," he now replied, "don't move in the matter. You know what my feelings are, that we ought to have the priests with us and not against us—I have had a letter written to Abbe Froment in order that he may call here this morning, as I shall have no other visitors. I will speak to him myself, and you may take it that the affair no longer concerns you."

Then he was about to dismiss him when the usher came back saying that the President of the Council was in the ante-room.[1]

"Barroux!—Ah! dash it, then, Monsieur Gascogne, you had better go out this way. It is as well that nobody should meet you, as I wish you to keep silent respecting Salvat's arrest. It's fully understood, is it not? I alone am to know everything; and you will communicate with me here direct, by the telephone, if any serious incident should arise."

The Chief of the Detective Police had scarcely gone off, by way of an adjoining *salon*, when the usher reopened the door communicating with the ante-room: "Monsieur le President du Conseil."

With a nicely adjusted show of deference and cordiality, Monferrand stepped forward, his hands outstretched: "Ah! my dear President, why did you put yourself out to come here? I would have called on you if I had known that you wished to see me."

But with an impatient gesture Barroux brushed aside all question of etiquette. "No, no! I was taking my usual stroll in the Champs Elysees, and the worries of the situation impressed me so keenly that I preferred to come here at once. You yourself must realise that we can't put up with what is taking place. And pending to-morrow morn-

---

[1] The title of President of the Council is given to the French prime minister.—Trans.

ing's council, when we shall have to arrange a plan of defence, I felt that there was good reason for us to talk things over."

He took an armchair, and Monferrand on his side rolled another forward so as to seat himself with his back to the light. Whilst Barroux, the elder of the pair by ten years, blanched and solemn, with a handsome face, snowy whiskers, clean-shaven chin and upper-lip, retained all the dignity of power, the bearing of a Conventionnel of romantic views, who sought to magnify the simple loyalty of a rather foolish but good-hearted *bourgeois* nature into something great; the other, beneath his heavy common countenance and feigned frankness and simplicity, concealed unknown depths, the unfathomable soul of a shrewd enjoyer and despot who was alike pitiless and unscrupulous in attaining his ends.

For a moment Barroux drew breath, for in reality he was greatly moved, his blood rising to his head, and his heart beating with indignation and anger at the thought of all the vulgar insults which the "Voix du Peuple" had poured upon him again that morning. "Come, my dear colleague," said he, "one must stop that scandalous campaign. Moreover, you can realise what awaits us at the Chamber to-morrow. Now that the famous list has been published we shall have every malcontent up in arms. Vignon is bestirring himself already—"

"Ah! you have news of Vignon?" exclaimed Monferrand, becoming very attentive.

"Well, as I passed his door just now, I saw a string of cabs waiting there. All his creatures have been on the move since yesterday, and at least twenty persons have told me that the band is already dividing the spoils. For, as you must know, the fierce and ingenuous Mege is again going to pull the chestnuts out of the fire for others. Briefly, we are dead, and the others claim that they are going to bury us in mud before they fight over our leavings." With his arm outstretched Barroux made a theatrical gesture, and his voice resounded as if he were in the tribune. Nevertheless, his emotion was real, tears even were coming to his eyes. "To think that I who have given my whole life to the Republic, I who founded it, who saved it, should be covered with insults in this fashion, and obliged to defend myself against abominable charges! To say that I abused my trust! That I sold myself and took 200,000 francs from that man Hunter, simply to slip them into my pocket! Well, certainly there *was* a question of 200,000 francs between us. But how and under what circumstances? They were doubtless the same as in your case, with regard to the 80,000 francs that he is said to have handed you—"

But Monferrand interrupted his colleague in a clear trenchant voice: "He never handed me a centime."

The other looked at him in astonishment, but could only see his big, rough head, whose features were steeped in shadow: "Ah! But I thought you had business relations with him, and knew him particularly well."

"No, I simply knew Hunter as everyone knew him. I was not even aware that he was Baron Duvillard's agent in the African Railways matter; and there was never any question of that affair between us."

This was so improbable, so contrary to everything Barroux knew of the business, that for a moment he felt quite scared. Then he waved his hand as if to say that others might as well look after their own affairs, and reverted to himself. "Oh! as for me," he said, "Hunter called on me more than ten times, and made me quite sick with his talk of the African Railways. It was at the time when the Chamber was asked to authorise the issue of lottery stock.[1] And, by the way, my dear fellow, I was then here at the Home Department, while you had just taken that of Public Works. I can remember sitting at that very writing-table, while Hunter was in the same armchair that I now occupy. That day he wanted to consult me about the employment of the large sum which Duvillard's house proposed to spend in advertising; and on seeing what big amounts were set down against the Royalist journals, I became quite angry, for I realised with perfect accuracy that this money would simply be used to wage war against the Republic. And so, yielding to Hunter's entreaties, I also drew up a list allotting 200,000 francs among the friendly Republican newspapers, which were paid through me, I admit it. And that's the whole story."[2]

Then he sprang to his feet and struck his chest, whilst his voice again rose: "Well, I've had more than enough of all that calumny and falsehood! And I shall simply tell the Chamber my story to-morrow. It will be my only defence. An honest man does not fear the truth!"

But Monferrand, in his turn, had sprung up with a cry which was a complete confession of his principles: "It's ridiculous, one never confesses; you surely won't do such a thing!"

"I shall," retorted Barroux with superb obstinacy. "And we shall see if the Chamber won't absolve me by acclamation."

"No, you will fall beneath an explosion of hisses, and drag all of us down with you."

"What does it matter? We shall fall with dignity, like honest men!"

Monferrand made a gesture of furious anger, and then suddenly became calm. Amidst all the anxious confusion in which he had been struggling since daybreak, a gleam now dawned upon him. The vague ideas suggested by Salvat's approaching arrest took shape, and expanded into an audacious scheme. Why should he prevent the fall of that big ninny Barroux? The only thing of importance was that he, Monferrand, should not fall with him, or at any rate that he should rise again. So he protested no further, but merely mumbled a few words, in which his rebellious feeling seemingly died out. And at last, putting on his good-natured air once more, he said: "Well, after all you are perhaps right. One must be brave. Besides, you are our head, my dear President, and we will follow you."

They had now again sat down face to face, and their conversation continued till they came to a cordial agreement respecting the course which the Government should adopt in view of the inevitable interpellation on the morrow.

---

[1] This kind of stock is common enough in France. A part of it is extinguished annually at a public "drawing," when all such shares or bonds that are drawn become entitled to redemption at "par," a percentage of them also securing prizes of various amounts. City of Paris Bonds issued on this system are very popular among French people with small savings; but, on the other hand, many ventures, whose lottery stock has been authorised by the Legislature, have come to grief and ruined investors.—Trans.

[2] All who are acquainted with recent French history will be aware that Barroux' narrative is simply a passage from the life of the late M. Floquet, slightly modified to suit the requirements of M. Zola's story.—Trans.

III. PLOT AND COUNTERPLOT

Meantime, Baron Duvillard was on his way to the ministry. He had scarcely slept that night. When on the return from Montmartre Gerard had set him down at his door in the Rue Godot-de-Mauroy, he had at once gone to bed, like a man who is determined to compel sleep, so that he may forget his worries and recover self-control. But slumber would not come; for hours and hours he vainly sought it. The manner in which he had been insulted by that creature Silviane was so monstrous! To think that she, whom he had enriched, whose every desire he had contented, should have cast such mud at him, the master, who flattered himself that he held Paris and the Republic in his hands, since he bought up and controlled consciences just as others might make corners in wool or leather for the purposes of Bourse speculation. And the dim consciousness that Silviane was the avenging sore, the cancer preying on him who preyed on others, completed his exasperation. In vain did he try to drive away his haunting thoughts, remember his business affairs, his appointments for the morrow, his millions which were working in every quarter of the world, the financial omnipotence which placed the fate of nations in his grasp. Ever, and in spite of all, Silviane rose up before him, splashing him with mud. In despair he tried to fix his mind on a great enterprise which he had been planning for months past, a Trans-Saharan railway, a colossal venture which would set millions of money at work, and revolutionise the trade of the world. And yet Silviane appeared once more, and smacked him on both cheeks with her dainty little hand, which she had dipped in the gutter. It was only towards daybreak that he at last dozed off, while vowing in a fury that he would never see her again, that he would spurn her, and order her away, even should she come and drag herself at his feet.

However, when he awoke at seven, still tired and aching, his first thought was for her, and he almost yielded to a fit of weakness. The idea came to him to ascertain if she had returned home, and if so make his peace. But he jumped out of bed, and after his ablutions he recovered all his bravery. She was a wretch, and he this time thought himself for ever cured of his passion. To tell the truth, he forgot it as soon as he opened the morning newspapers. The publication of the list of bribe-takers in the "Voix du Peuple" quite upset him, for he had hitherto thought it unlikely that Sagnier held any such list. However, he judged the document at a glance, at once separating the few truths it contained from a mass of foolishness and falsehood. And this time also he did not consider himself personally in danger. There was only one thing that he really feared: the arrest of his intermediary, Hunter, whose trial might have drawn him into the affair. As matters stood, and as he did not cease to repeat with a calm and smiling air, he had merely done what every banking-house does when it issues stock, that is, pay the press for advertisements and puffery, employ brokers, and reward services discreetly rendered to the enterprise. It was all a business matter, and for him that expression summed up everything. Moreover, he played the game of life bravely, and spoke with indignant contempt of a banker who, distracted and driven to extremities by blackmailing, had imagined that he would bring a recent scandal to an end by killing himself: a pitiful tragedy, from all the mire and blood of which the scandal had sprouted afresh with the most luxuriant and indestructible vegetation. No, no! suicide was not the course to follow: a man ought to remain erect, and struggle on to his very last copper, and the very end of his energy.

At about nine o'clock a ringing brought Duvillard to the telephone installed in his private room. And then his folly took possession of him once more: it must be Silviane who wished to speak to him. She often amused herself by thus disturbing him amidst his greatest cares. No doubt she had just returned home, realising that she had carried things too far on the previous evening and desiring to be forgiven. However, when he found that the call was from Monferrand, who wished him to go to the ministry, he shivered slightly, like a man saved from the abyss beside which he is travelling. And forthwith he called for his hat and stick, desirous as he was of walking and reflecting in the open air. And again he became absorbed in the intricacies of the scandalous business which was about to stir all Paris and the legislature. Kill himself! ah, no, that would be foolish and cowardly. A gust of terror might be sweeping past; nevertheless, for his part he felt quite firm, superior to events, and resolved to defend himself without relinquishing aught of his power.

As soon as he entered the ante-rooms of the ministry he realised that the gust of terror was becoming a tempest. The publication of the terrible list in the "Voix du Peuple" had chilled the guilty ones to the heart; and, pale and distracted, feeling the ground give way beneath them, they had come to take counsel of Monferrand, who, they hoped, might save them. The first whom Duvillard perceived was Duthil, looking extremely feverish, biting his moustaches, and constantly making grimaces in his efforts to force a smile. The banker scolded him for coming, saying that it was a great mistake to have done so, particularly with such a scared face. The deputy, however, his spirits already cheered by these rough words, began to defend himself, declaring that he had not even read Sagnier's article, and had simply come to recommend a lady friend to the Minister. Thereupon the Baron undertook this business for him and sent him away with the wish that he might spend a merry mid-Lent. However, the one who most roused Duvillard's pity was Chaigneux, whose figure swayed about as if bent by the weight of his long equine head, and who looked so shabby and untidy that one might have taken him for an old pauper. On recognising the banker he darted forward, and bowed to him with obsequious eagerness.

"Ah! Monsieur le Baron," said he, "how wicked some men must be! They are killing me, I shall die of it all; and what will become of my wife, what will become of my three daughters, who have none but me to help them?"

The whole of his woeful story lay in that lament. A victim of politics, he had been foolish enough to quit Arras and his business there as a solicitor, in order to seek triumph in Paris with his wife and daughters, whose menial he had then become—a menial dismayed by the constant rebuffs and failures which his mediocrity brought upon him. An honest deputy! ah, good heavens! yes, he would have liked to be one; but was he not perpetually "hard-up," ever in search of a hundred-franc note, and thus, perforce, a deputy for sale? And withal he led such a pitiable life, so badgered by the women folk about him, that to satisfy their demands he would have picked up money no matter where or how.

"Just fancy, Monsieur le Baron, I have at last found a husband for my eldest girl. It is the first bit of luck that I have ever had; there will only be three women left on my hands if it comes off. But you can imagine what a disastrous impression such an article as that of this morning must create in the young man's family. So I have come to see the Minister to beg him to give my future son-in-law a prefectoral secretaryship. I have already promised him the post, and if I can secure it things may yet be arranged."

He looked so terribly shabby and spoke in such a doleful voice that it occurred to Duvillard to do one of those good actions on which he ventured at times when they were likely to prove remunerative investments. It is, indeed, an excellent plan to give a crust of bread to some poor devil whom one can turn, if necessary, into a valet or an accomplice. So the banker dismissed Chaigneux, undertaking to do his business for him in the same way as he had undertaken to do Duthil's. And he added that he would be pleased to see him on the morrow, and have a chat with him, as he might be able to help him in the matter of his daughter's marriage.

At this Chaigneux, scenting a loan, collapsed into the most lavish thanks. "Ah! Monsieur le Baron, my life will not be long enough to enable me to repay such a debt of gratitude."

As Duvillard turned round he was surprised to see Abbe Froment waiting in a corner of the ante-room. Surely that one could not belong to the batch of *suspects*, although by the manner in which he was pretending to read a newspaper it seemed as if he were trying to hide some keen anxiety. At last the Baron stepped forward, shook hands, and spoke to him cordially. And Pierre thereupon related that he had received a letter requesting him to call on the Minister that day. Why, he could not tell; in fact, he was greatly surprised, he said, putting on a smile in order to conceal his disquietude. He had been waiting a long time already, and hoped that he would not be forgotten on that bench.

Just then the usher appeared, and hastened up to the banker. "The Minister," said he, "was at that moment engaged with the President of the Council; but he had orders to admit the Baron as soon as the President withdrew." Almost immediately afterwards Barroux came out, and as Duvillard was about to enter he recognised and detained him. And he spoke of the denunciations very bitterly, like one indignant with all the slander. Would not he, Duvillard, should occasion require it, testify that he, Barroux, had never taken a centime for himself? Then, forgetting that he was speaking to a banker, and that he was Minister of Finances, he proceeded to express all his disgust of money. Ah! what poisonous, murky, and defiling waters were those in which money-making went on! However, he repeated that he would chastise his insulters, and that a statement of the truth would suffice for the purpose.

Duvillard listened and looked at him. And all at once the thought of Silviane came back, and took possession of the Baron, without any attempt on his part to drive it away. He reflected that if Barroux had chosen to give him a helping hand when he had asked for it, Silviane would now have been at the Comedie Francaise, in which case the deplorable affair of the previous night would not have occurred; for he was beginning to regard himself as guilty in the matter; if he had only contented Silviane's whim she would never have dismissed him in so vile a fashion.

"You know, I owe you a grudge," he said, interrupting Barroux.

The other looked at him in astonishment. "And why, pray?" he asked.

"Why, because you never helped me in the matter of that friend of mine who wishes to make her *debut* in 'Polyeucte.'"

Barroux smiled, and with amiable condescension replied: "Ah! yes, Silviane d'Aulnay! But, my dear sir, it was Taboureau who put spokes in the wheel. The Fine Arts are his department, and the question was entirely one for him. And I could do nothing; for that very worthy and honest gentleman, who came to us from a provincial faculty, was full of scruples. For my own part I'm an old Parisian, I can understand anything, and I should have been delighted to please you."

At this fresh resistance offered to his passion Duvillard once more became excited, eager to obtain that which was denied him. "Taboureau, Taboureau!" said he, "he's a nice deadweight for you to load yourself with! Honest! isn't everybody honest? Come, my dear Minister, there's still time, get Silviane admitted, it will bring you good luck for to-morrow."

This time Barroux burst into a frank laugh: "No, no, I can't cast Taboureau adrift at this moment—people would make too much sport of it—a ministry wrecked or saved by a Silviane question!"

Then he offered his hand before going off. The Baron pressed it, and for a moment retained it in his own, whilst saying very gravely and with a somewhat pale face: "You do wrong to laugh, my dear Minister. Governments have fallen or set themselves erect again through smaller matters than that. And should you fall to-morrow I trust that you will never have occasion to regret it."

Wounded to the heart by the other's jesting air, exasperated by the idea that there was something he could not achieve, Duvillard watched Barroux as he withdrew. Most certainly the Baron did not desire a reconciliation with Silviane, but he vowed that he would overturn everything if necessary in order to send her a signed engagement for the Comedie, and this simply by way of vengeance, as a slap, so to say,—yes, a slap which would make her tingle! That moment spent with Barroux had been a decisive one.

However, whilst still following Barroux with his eyes, Duvillard was surprised to see Fonsegue arrive and manoeuvre in such a way as to escape the Prime Minister's notice. He succeeded in doing so, and then entered the ante-room with an appearance of dismay about the whole of his little figure, which was, as a rule, so sprightly. It was the gust of terror, still blowing, that had brought him thither.

"Didn't you see your friend Barroux?" the Baron asked him, somewhat puzzled.

"Barroux? No!"

This quiet lie was equivalent to a confession of everything. Fonsegue was so intimate with Barroux that he thee'd and thou'd him, and for ten years had been supporting him in his newspaper, having precisely the same views, the same political religion. But with a smash-up threatening, he doubtless realised, thanks to his wonderfully keen scent, that he must change his friendships if he did not wish to remain under the ruins himself. If he had, for long years, shown so much prudence and diplomatic virtue in order to firmly establish the most dignified and respected of Parisian newspapers, it was not for the purpose of letting that newspaper be compromised by some foolish blunder on the part of an honest man.

"I thought you were on bad terms with Monferrand," resumed Duvillard. "What have you come here for?"

"Oh! my dear Baron, the director of a leading newspaper is never on bad terms with anybody. He's at the country's service."

In spite of his emotion, Duvillard could not help smiling. "You are right," he responded. "Besides, Monferrand is really an able man, whom one can support without fear."

At this Fonsegue began to wonder whether his anguish of mind was visible. He, who usually played the game of life so well, with his own hand under thorough control, had been terrified by the article in the "Voix du Peuple." For the first time in his career he had perpetrated a blunder, and felt that he was at the mercy of some denunciation, for with unpardonable imprudence he had written a very brief but compromising note. He was not anxious concerning the 50,000 francs which Barroux had handed him out of the 200,000 destined for the Republican press. But he trembled lest another affair should be discovered, that of a sum of money which he had received as a present. It was only on feeling the Baron's keen glance upon him that he was able to recover some self-possession. How silly it was to lose the knack of lying and to confess things simply by one's demeanour!

But the usher drew near and repeated that the Minister was now waiting for the Baron; and Fonsegue went to sit down beside Abbe Froment, whom he also was astonished to find there. Pierre repeated that he had received a letter, but had no notion what the Minister might wish to say to him. And the quiver of his hands again revealed how feverishly impatient he was to know what it might be. However, he could only wait, since Monferrand was still busy discussing such grave affairs.

On seeing Duvillard enter, the Minister had stepped forward, offering his hand. However much the blast of terror might shake others, he had retained his calmness and good-natured smile. "What an affair, eh, my dear Baron!" he exclaimed.

"It's idiotic!" plainly declared the other, with a shrug of his shoulders. Then he sat down in the armchair vacated by Barroux, while the Minister installed himself in front of him. These two were made to understand one another, and they indulged in the same despairing gestures and furious complaints, declaring that government, like business, would no longer be possible if men were required to show such virtue as they did not possess. At all times, and under every *regime*, when a decision of the Chambers had been required in connection with some great enterprise, had not the natural and legitimate tactics been for one to do what might be needful to secure that decision? It was absolutely necessary that one should obtain influential and sympathetic support, in a word, make sure of votes. Well, everything had to be paid for, men like other things, some with fine words, others with favours or money, presents made in a more or less disguised manner. And even admitting that, in the present cases, one had gone rather far in the purchasing, that some of the bartering had been conducted in an imprudent way, was it wise to make such an uproar over it? Would not a strong government have begun by stifling the scandal, from motives of patriotism, a mere sense of cleanliness even?

"Why, of course! You are right, a thousand times right!" exclaimed Monferrand. "Ah! if I were the master you would see what a fine first-class funeral I would give it all!" Then, as Duvillard looked at him fixedly, struck by these last words, he added with his expressive smile: "Unfortunately I'm not the master, and it was to talk to you of the situation that I ventured to disturb you. Barroux, who was here just now, seemed to me in a regrettable frame of mind."

"Yes, I saw him, he has such singular ideas at times—" Then, breaking off, the Baron added: "Do you know that Fonsegue is in the ante-room? As he wishes to make his peace with you, why not send for him? He won't be in the way, in fact, he's a man of good counsel, and the support of his newspaper often suffices to give one the victory."

"What, is Fonsegue there!" cried Monferrand. "Why, I don't ask better than to shake hands with him. There were some old affairs between us that don't concern anybody! But, good heavens! if you only knew what little spite I harbour!"

When the usher had admitted Fonsegue the reconciliation took place in the simplest fashion. They had been great friends at college in their native Correze, but had not spoken together for ten years past in consequence of some abominable affair the particulars of which were not exactly known. However, it becomes necessary to clear away all corpses when one wishes to have the arena free for a fresh battle.

"It's very good of you to come back the first," said Monferrand. "So it's all over, you no longer bear me any grudge?"

"No, indeed!" replied Fonsegue. "Why should people devour one another when it would be to their interest to come to an understanding?"

Then, without further explanations, they passed to the great affair, and the conference began. And when Monferrand had announced Barroux' determination to confess and explain his conduct, the others loudly protested. That meant certain downfall, they would prevent him, he surely would not be guilty of such folly. Forthwith they discussed every imaginable plan by which the Ministry might be saved, for that must certainly be Monferrand's sole desire. He himself with all eagerness pretended to seek some means of extricating his colleagues and himself from the mess in which they were. However, a faint smile, still played around his lips, and at last as if vanquished he sought no further. "There's no help for it," said he, "the ministry's down."

The others exchanged glances, full of anxiety at the thought of another Cabinet dealing with the African Railways affair. A Vignon Cabinet would doubtless plume itself on behaving honestly.

"Well, then, what shall we do?"

But just then the telephone rang, and Monferrand rose to respond to the summons: "Allow me."

He listened for a moment and then spoke into the tube, nothing that he said giving the others any inkling of the information which had reached him. This had come from the Chief of the Detective Police, and was to the effect that Salvat's whereabouts in the Bois de Boulogne had been discovered, and that he would be hunted down with all speed. "Very good! And don't forget my orders," replied Monferrand.

Now that Salvat's arrest was certain, the Minister determined to follow the plan which had gradually taken shape in his mind; and returning to the middle of the room he slowly walked to and fro, while saying with his wonted familiarity: "But what would you have, my friends? It would be necessary for me to be the master. Ah! if I were the master! A Commission of Inquiry, yes! that's the proper form for a first-class funeral to take in a big affair like this, so full of nasty things. For my part, I should confess nothing, and I should have a Commission appointed. And then you would see the storm subside."

Duvillard and Fonsegue began to laugh. The latter, however, thanks to his intimate knowledge of Monferrand, almost guessed the truth. "Just listen!" said he; "even if the ministry falls it doesn't necessarily follow that you must be on the ground with it. Besides, a ministry can be mended when there are good pieces of it left."

Somewhat anxious at finding his thoughts guessed, Monferrand protested: "No, no, my dear fellow, I don't play that game. We are jointly responsible, we've got to keep together, dash it all!"

"Keep together! Pooh! Not when simpletons purposely drown themselves! And, besides, if we others have need of you, we have a right to save you in spite of yourself! Isn't that so, my dear Baron?"

Then, as Monferrand sat down, no longer protesting but waiting, Duvillard, who was again thinking of his passion, full of anger at the recollection of Barroux' refusal, rose in his turn, and exclaimed: "Why, certainly! If the ministry's condemned let it fall! What good can you get out of a ministry which includes such a man as Taboureau! There you have an old, worn-out professor without any prestige, who comes to Paris from Grenoble, and has never set foot in a theatre in his life! Yet the control of the theatres is handed over to him, and naturally he's ever doing the most stupid things!"

Monferrand, who was well informed on the Silviane question, remained grave, and for a moment amused himself by trying to excite the Baron. "Taboureau," said he, "is a somewhat dull and old-fashioned University man, but at the department of Public Instruction he's in his proper element."

"Oh! don't talk like that, my dear fellow! You are more intelligent than that, you are not going to defend Taboureau as Barroux did. It's quite true that I should very much like to see Silviane at the Comedie. She's a very good girl at heart, and she has an amazing lot of talent. Would you stand in her way if you were in Taboureau's place?"

"I? Good heavens, no! A pretty girl on the stage, why, it would please everybody, I'm sure. Only it would be necessary to have a man of the same views as were at the department of Instruction and Fine Arts."

His sly smile had returned to his face. The securing of that girl's *debut* was certainly not a high price to pay for all the influence of Duvillard's millions. Monferrand therefore turned towards Fonsegue as if to consult him. The other, who fully understood the importance of the affair, was meditating in all seriousness: "A senator is the proper man for Public Instruction," said he. "But I can think of none, none at all, such as would be wanted. A man of broad mind, a real Parisian, and yet one whose presence at the head of the University wouldn't cause too much astonishment—there's perhaps Dauvergne—"

"Dauvergne! Who's he?" exclaimed Monferrand in surprise. "Ah! yes, Dauvergne the senator for Dijon—but he's altogether ignorant of University matters, he hasn't the slightest qualification."

"Well, as for that," resumed Fonsegue, "I'm trying to think. Dauvergne is certainly a good-looking fellow, tall and fair and decorative. Besides, he's immensely rich, has a most charming young wife—which does no harm, on the contrary—and he gives real *fetes* at his place on the Boulevard St. Germain."

It was only with hesitation that Fonsegue himself had ventured to suggest Dauvergne. But by degrees his selection appeared to him a real "find." "Wait a bit! I recollect now that in his young days Dauvergne wrote a comedy, a one act comedy in verse, and had it performed at Dijon. And Dijon's a literary town, you know, so that piece of his sets a little perfume of 'Belles-Lettres' around him. And then, too, he left Dijon twenty years ago, and is a most determined Parisian, frequenting every sphere of society. Dauvergne will do whatever one desires. He's the man for us, I tell you."

Duvillard thereupon declared that he knew him, and considered him a very decent fellow. Besides, he or another, it mattered nothing!

"Dauvergne, Dauvergne," repeated Monferrand. "*Mon Dieu*, yes! After all, why not? He'll perhaps make a very good minister. Let us say Dauvergne." Then suddenly bursting into a hearty laugh: "And so we are reconstructing the Cabinet in order that that charming young woman may join the Comedie! The Silviane cabinet—well, and what about the other departments?"

He jested, well knowing that gaiety often hastens difficult solutions. And, indeed, they merrily continued settling what should be done if the ministry were defeated on the morrow. Although they had not plainly said so the plan was to let Barroux sink, even help him to do so, and then fish Monferrand out of the troubled waters. The latter engaged himself with the two others, because he had need of them, the Baron on account of his financial sovereignty, and the director of "Le Globe" on account of the press campaign which he could carry on in his favour. And in the same way the others, quite apart from the Silviane business, had need of Monferrand, the strong-handed man of government, who undertook to bury the African Railways scandal by bringing about a Commission of Inquiry, all the strings of which would be pulled by himself. There was soon a perfect understanding between the three men, for nothing draws people more closely together than common interest, fear and need. Accordingly, when Duvillard spoke of Duthil's business, the young lady whom he wished to recommend, the Minister declared that it was settled. A very nice fellow was Duthil, they needed a good many like him. And it was also agreed that Chaigneux' future son-in-law should have his secretaryship. Poor Chaigneux! He was so devoted, always ready to undertake any commission, and his four women folk led him such a hard life!

"Well, then, it's understood." And Monferrand, Duvillard and Fonsegue vigorously shook hands.

However, when the first accompanied the others to the door, he noticed a prelate, in a cassock of fine material, edged with violet, speaking to a priest in the ante-room. Thereupon he, the Minister, hastened forward, looking much distressed. "Ah! you were waiting, Monseigneur Martha! Come in, come in quick!"

But with perfect urbanity the Bishop refused. "No, no, Monsieur l'Abbe Froment was here before me. Pray receive him first."

Monferrand had to give way; he admitted the priest, and speedily dealt with him. He who usually employed the most diplomatic reserve when he was in presence of a member of the clergy plumply unfolded the Barthes business. Pierre had experienced the keenest anguish during the two hours that he had been waiting there, for he could only explain the letter he had received by a surmise that the police had discovered his brother's presence in his house. And so when he heard the Minister simply speak of Barthes, and declare that the government would rather see him go into exile than be obliged to imprison him once more, he remained for a moment quite disconcerted. As the police had been able to discover the old conspirator in the little house at Neuilly, how was it that they seemed altogether ignorant of Guillaume's presence there? It was, however, the usual gap in the genius of great detectives.

"Pray what do you desire of me, Monsieur le Ministre?" said Pierre at last; "I don't quite understand."

"Why, Monsieur l'Abbe, I leave all this to your sense of prudence. If that man were still at your house in forty-eight hours from now, we should be obliged to arrest him there, which would be a source of grief to us, for we are aware that your residence is the abode of every virtue. So advise him to leave France. If he does that we shall not trouble him."

Then Monferrand hastily brought Pierre back to the ante-room; and, smiling and bending low, he said: "Monseigneur, I am entirely at your disposal. Come in, come in, I beg you."

The prelate, who was gaily chatting with Duvillard and Fonsegue, shook hands with them, and then with Pierre. In his desire to win all hearts, he that morning displayed the most perfect graciousness. His bright, black eyes were all smiles, the whole of his handsome face wore a caressing expression, and he entered the ministerial sanctum leisurely and gracefully, with an easy air of conquest.

And now only Monferrand and Monseigneur Martha were left, talking on and on in the deserted building. Some people had thought that the prelate wished to become a deputy. But he played a far more useful and lofty part in governing behind the scenes, in acting as the directing mind of the Vatican's policy in France. Was not France still the Eldest Daughter of the Church, the only great nation which might some day restore omnipotence to the Papacy? For that reason he had accepted the Republic, preached the duty of "rallying" to it, and inspired the new Catholic group in the Chamber. And Monferrand, on his side, struck by the progress of the New Spirit, that reaction of mysticism which flattered itself that it would bury science, showed the prelate much amiability, like a strong-handed man who, to ensure his own victory, utilised every force that was offered him.

IV. THE MAN HUNT

ON the afternoon of that same day such a keen desire for space and the open air came upon Guillaume, that Pierre consented to accompany him on a long walk in the Bois de Boulogne. The priest, upon returning from his interview with Monferrand, had informed his brother that the government once more wished to get rid of Nicholas Barthes. However, they were so perplexed as to how they should impart these tidings to the old man, that they resolved to postpone the matter until the evening. During their walk they might devise some means of breaking the news in a gentle way. As for the walk, this seemed to offer no danger; to all appearance Guillaume was in no wise threatened, so why should he continue hiding? Thus the brothers sallied forth and entered the Bois by the Sablons gate, which was the nearest to them.

The last days of March had now come, and the trees were beginning to show some greenery, so soft and light, however, that one might have thought it was pale moss or delicate lace hanging between the stems and boughs. Although the sky remained of an ashen grey, the rain, after falling throughout the night and morning, had ceased; and exquisite freshness pervaded that wood now awakening to life once more, with its foliage dripping in the mild and peaceful atmosphere. The mid-Lent rejoicings had apparently attracted the populace to the centre of Paris, for in the avenues one found only the fashionable folks of select days, the people of society who come thither when the multitude stops away. There were carriages and gentlemen on horseback; beautiful aristocratic ladies who had alighted from their broughams or landaus; and wet-nurses with streaming ribbons, who carried infants wearing the most costly lace. Of the middle-classes, however, one found only a few matrons living in the neighbourhood, who sat here and there on the benches busy with embroidery or watching their children play.

Pierre and Guillaume followed the Allee de Longchamp as far as the road going from Madrid to the lakes. Then they took their way under the trees, alongside the little Longchamp rivulet. They wished to reach the lakes, pass round them, and return home by way of the Maillot gate. But so charming and peaceful was the deserted plantation through which they passed, that they yielded to a desire to sit down and taste the delight of resting amidst all the budding springtide around them. A fallen tree served them as a bench, and it was possible for them to fancy themselves far away from Paris, in the depths of some real forest. It was, too, of a real forest that Guillaume began to think on thus emerging from his long, voluntary imprisonment. Ah! for the space; and for the health-bringing air which courses between that forest's branches, that forest of the world which by right should be man's inalienable domain! However, the name of Barthes, the perpetual prisoner, came back to Guillaume's lips, and he sighed mournfully. The thought that there should be even a single man whose liberty was thus ever assailed, sufficed to poison the pure atmosphere he breathed.

"What will you say to Barthes?" he asked his brother. "The poor fellow must necessarily be warned. Exile is at any rate preferable to imprisonment."

Pierre sadly waved his hand. "Yes, of course, I must warn him. But what a painful task it is!"

Guillaume made no rejoinder, for at that very moment, in that remote, deserted nook, where they could fancy themselves at the world's end, a most extraordinary spectacle was presented to their view. Something or rather someone leapt out of a thicket and bounded past them. It was assuredly a man, but one who was so unrecognisable, so miry, so woeful and so frightful, that he might have been taken for an animal, a boar that hounds had tracked and forced from his retreat. On seeing the rivulet, he hesitated for a moment, and then followed its course. But, all at once, as a sound of footsteps and panting breath drew nearer, he sprang into the water, which reached his thighs, bounded on to the further bank, and vanished from sight behind a clump of pines. A moment afterwards some keepers and policemen rushed by, skirting the rivulet, and in their turn disappearing. It was a man hunt that had gone past, a fierce, secret hunt with no display of scarlet or blast of horns athwart the soft, sprouting foliage.

"Some rascal or other," muttered Pierre. "Ah! the wretched fellow!"

Guillaume made a gesture of discouragement. "Gendarmes and prison!" said he. "They still constitute society's only schooling system!"

Meantime the man was still running on, farther and farther away.

When, on the previous night, Salvat had suddenly escaped from the detectives by bounding into the Bois de Boulogne, it had occurred to him to slip round to the Dauphine gate and there descend into the deep ditch[1] of the city ramparts. He remembered days of enforced idleness which he had spent there, in nooks where, for his own part, he had never met a living soul. Nowhere, indeed, could one find more secret places of retreat, hedged round by thicker bushes, or concealed from view by loftier herbage. Some corners of the ditch, at certain angles of the massive bastions, are favourite dens or nests for thieves and lovers. Salvat, as he made his way through the thickest of the brambles, nettles and ivy, was lucky enough to find a cavity full of dry leaves, in which he buried himself to the chin. The rain had already drenched him, and after slipping down the muddy slope, he had frequently been obliged to grope his way upon all fours. So those dry leaves proved a boon such as he had not dared to hope for. They dried him somewhat, serving as a blanket in which he coiled himself after his wild race through the dank darkness. The rain still fell, but he now only felt it on his head, and, weary as he was, he gradually sank into deep slumber beneath the continuous drizzle. When he opened his eyes again, the dawn was breaking, and it was probably about six o'clock. During his sleep the rain had ended by soaking the leaves, so that he was now immersed in a kind of chilly bath. Still he remained in it, feeling

[1] This ditch or dry moat is about 30 feet deep and 50 feet wide. The counterscarp by which one may descend into it has an angle of 45 degrees.—Trans.

that he was there sheltered from the police, who must now surely be searching for him. None of those bloodhounds would guess his presence in that hole, for his body was quite buried, and briers almost completely hid his head. So he did not stir, but watched the rise of the dawn.

When at eight o'clock some policemen and keepers came by, searching the ditch, they did not perceive him. As he had anticipated, the hunt had begun at the first glimmer of light. For a time his heart beat violently; however, nobody else passed, nothing whatever stirred the grass. The only sounds that reached him were faint ones from the Bois de Boulogne, the ring of a bicyclist's bell, the thud of a horse's hoofs, the rumble of carriage wheels. And time went by, nine o'clock came, and then ten o'clock. Since the rain had ceased falling, Salvat had not suffered so much from the cold, for he was wearing a thick overcoat which little Mathis had given him. But, on the other hand, hunger was coming back; there was a burning sensation in his stomach, and leaden hoops seemed to be pressing against his ribs. He had eaten nothing for two days; he had been starving already on the previous evening, when he had accepted a glass of beer at that tavern at Montmartre. Nevertheless, his plan was to remain in the ditch until nightfall, and then slip away in the direction of the village of Boulogne, where he knew of a means of egress from the wood. He was not caught yet, he repeated, he might still manage to escape. Then he tried to get to sleep again, but failed, so painful had his sufferings become. By the time it was eleven, everything swam before his eyes. He once nearly fainted, and thought that he was going to die. Then rage gradually mastered him, and, all at once, he sprang out of his leafy hiding-place, desperately hungering for food, unable to remain there any longer, and determined to find something to eat, even should it cost him his liberty and life. It was then noon.

On leaving the ditch he found the spreading lawns of the chateau of La Muette before him. He crossed them at a run, like a madman, instinctively going towards Boulogne, with the one idea that his only means of escape lay in that direction. It seemed miraculous that nobody paid attention to his helter-skelter flight. However, when he had reached the cover of some trees he became conscious of his imprudence, and almost regretted the sudden madness which had borne him along, eager for escape. Trembling nervously, he bent low among some furze bushes, and waited for a few minutes to ascertain if the police were behind him. Then with watchful eye and ready ear, wonderful instinct and scent of danger, he slowly went his way again. He hoped to pass between the upper lake and the Auteuil race-course; but there were few trees in that part, and they formed a broad avenue. He therefore had to exert all his skill in order to avoid observation, availing himself of the slenderest stems, the smallest bushes, as screens, and only venturing onward after a lengthy inspection of his surroundings. Before long the sight of a guard in the distance revived his fears and detained him, stretched on the ground behind some brambles, for a full quarter of an hour. Then the approach first of a cab, whose driver had lost his way, and afterwards of a strolling pedestrian, in turn sufficed to stop him. He breathed once more, however, when, after passing the Mortemart hillock, he was able to enter the thickets lying between the two roads which lead to Boulogne and St. Cloud. The coppices thereabouts were dense, and he merely had to follow them, screened from view, in order to reach the outlet he knew of, which was now near at hand. So he was surely saved.

But all at once, at a distance of some five and thirty yards, he saw a keeper, erect and motionless, barring his way. He turned slightly to the left and there perceived another keeper, who also seemed to be awaiting him. And there were more and more of them; at every fifty paces or so stood a fresh one, the whole forming a *cordon*, the meshes as it were of a huge net. The worst was that he must have been perceived, for a light cry, like the clear call of an owl, rang out, and was repeated farther and farther off. The hunters were at last on the right scent, prudence had become superfluous, and it was only by flight that the quarry might now hope to escape. Salvat understood this so well that he suddenly began to run, leaping over all obstacles and darting between the trees, careless whether he were seen or heard. A few bounds carried him across the Avenue de St. Cloud into the plantations stretching to the Allee de la Reine Marguerite. There the undergrowth was very dense; in the whole Bois there are no more closely set thickets. In summer they become one vast entanglement of verdure, amidst which, had it been the leafy season, Salvat might well have managed to secrete himself. For a moment he did find himself alone, and thereupon he halted to listen. He could neither see nor hear the keepers now. Had they lost his track, then? Profound quietude reigned under the fresh young foliage. But the light, owlish cry arose once more, branches cracked, and he resumed his wild flight, hurrying straight before him. Unluckily he found the Allee de la Reine Marguerite guarded by policemen, so that he could not cross over, but had to skirt it without quitting the thickets. And now his back was turned towards Boulogne; he was retracing his steps towards Paris. However, a last idea came to his bewildered mind: it was to run on in this wise as far as the shady spots around Madrid, and then, by stealing from copse to copse, attempt to reach the Seine. To proceed thither across the bare expanse of the race-course and training ground was not for a moment to be thought of.

So Salvat still ran on and on. But on reaching the Allee de Longchamp he found it guarded like the other roads, and therefore had to relinquish his plan of escaping by way of Madrid and the river-bank. While he was perforce making a bend alongside the Pre Catelan, he became aware that the keepers, led by detectives, were drawing yet nearer to him, confining his movements to a smaller and smaller area. And his race soon acquired all the frenzy of despair. Haggard and breathless he leapt mounds, rushed past multitudinous obstacles. He forced a passage through brambles, broke down palings, thrice caught his feet in wire work which he had not seen, and fell among nettles, yet picked himself up went on again, spurred by the stinging of his hands and face. It was then Guillaume and Pierre saw him pass, unrecognisable and frightful, taking to the muddy water of the rivulet like a stag which seeks to set a last obstacle between itself and the hounds. There came to him a wild idea of getting to the lake, and swimming, unperceived, to the island in the centre of it. That, he madly thought, would be a safe retreat, where he might burrow and hide himself without possibility of discovery. And so he still ran on. But once again the sight of some guards made him retrace his steps, and he was compelled to go back and back in the direction of Paris, chased, forced towards the very fortifications whence he had started that morning. It was now nearly three in the afternoon. For more than two hours and a half he had been running.

At last he saw a soft, sandy ride for horsemen before him. He crossed it, splashing through the mire left by the rain, and reached a little pathway, a delightful lovers' lane, as shady in summer as any arbour. For some time he was able to follow it, concealed from observation, and with his hopes reviving. But it led him to one of those broad, straight avenues where carriages and bicycles, the whole afternoon pageant of society, swept past under the mild and cloudy sky. So he returned to the thickets, fell once more upon the keepers, lost all notion of the direction he took, and even all power of thought, becoming a mere thing carried along and thrown hither and thither by the chances of the pursuit which pressed more and more closely upon him. Star-like crossways followed one upon other, and at last he came to a broad lawn, where the full light dazzled him. And there he suddenly felt the hot, panting breath of his pursuers close in the rear. Eager, hungry breath it was, like that of hounds seeking to devour him. Shouts rang out, one hand almost caught hold of him, there was a rush of heavy feet, a scramble to seize him. But with a supreme effort he leapt upon a bank, crawled to its summit, rose again, and once more found himself alone, still running on amid the fresh and quiet greenery.

Nevertheless, this was the end. He almost fell flat upon the ground. His aching feet could no longer carry him; blood was oozing from his ears, and froth had come to his mouth. His heart beat with such violence that it seemed likely to break his ribs. Water and perspiration streamed from him, he was miry and haggard and tortured by hunger, conquered, in fact, more by hunger than by fatigue. And through the mist which seemed to have gathered before his wild eyes, he suddenly saw an open doorway, the doorway of a coach-house in the rear of a kind of chalet, sequestered among trees. Excepting a big white cat, which took to flight, there was not a living creature in the place. Salvat plunged into it and rolled over on a heap of straw, among some empty casks. He was scarcely hidden there when he heard the chase sweep by, the detectives and the keepers losing scent, passing the chalet and rushing in the direction of the Paris ramparts. The noise of their heavy boots died away, and deep silence fell, while the hunted man, who had carried both hands to his heart to stay its beating, sank into the most complete prostration, with big tears trickling from his closed eyes.

Whilst all this was going on, Pierre and Guillaume, after a brief rest, had resumed their walk, reaching the lake and proceeding towards the crossway of the Cascades, in order to return to Neuilly by the road beyond the water. However, a shower fell, compelling them to take shelter under the big leafless branches of a chestnut-tree. Then, as the rain came down more heavily and they could perceive a kind of chalet, a little cafe-restaurant amid a clump of trees, they hastened thither for better protection. In a side road, which they passed on their way, they saw a cab standing, its driver waiting there in philosophical fashion under the falling shower. Pierre, moreover, noticed a young man stepping out briskly in front of them, a young man resembling Gerard de Quinsac, who, whilst walking in the Bois, had no doubt been overtaken by the rain, and like themselves was seeking shelter in the chalet. However, on entering the latter's public room, the priest saw no sign of the gentleman, and concluded that he must have been mistaken. This public room, which had a kind of glazed verandah overlooking the Bois, contained a few chairs and tables, the latter with marble tops. On the first floor there were four or five private rooms reached by a narrow passage. Though the doors were open the place had as yet scarcely emerged from its winter's rest. There was nobody about, and on all sides one found the dampness common to establishments which, from lack of custom, are compelled to close from November until March. In the rear were some stables, a coach-house, and various mossy, picturesque outbuildings, which painters and gardeners would now soon embellish for the gay pleasure parties which the fine weather would bring.

"I really think that they haven't opened for the season yet," said Guillaume as he entered the silent house.

"At all events they will let us stay here till the rain stops," answered Pierre, seating himself at one of the little tables.

However, a waiter suddenly made his appearance seemingly in a great hurry. He had come down from the first floor, and eagerly rummaged a cupboard for a few dry biscuits, which he laid upon a plate. At last he condescended to serve the brothers two glasses of Chartreuse.

In one of the private rooms upstairs Baroness Duvillard, who had driven to the chalet in a cab, had been awaiting her lover Gerard for nearly half an hour. It was there that, during the charity bazaar, they had given each other an appointment. For them the chalet had precious memories: two years previously, on discovering that secluded nest, which was so deserted in the early, hesitating days of chilly spring, they had met there under circumstances which they could not forget. And the Baroness, in choosing the house for the supreme assignation of their dying passion, had certainly not been influenced merely by a fear that she might be spied upon elsewhere. She had, indeed, thought of the first kisses that had been showered on her there, and would fain have revived them even if they should now prove the last that Gerard would bestow on her.

But she would also have liked to see some sunlight playing over the youthful foliage. The ashen sky and threatening rain saddened her. And when she entered the private room she did not recognise it, so cold and dim it seemed with its faded furniture. Winter had tarried there, with all the dampness and mouldy smell peculiar to rooms which have long remained closed. Then, too, some of the wall paper which had come away from the plaster hung down in shreds, dead flies were scattered over the parquetry flooring; and in order to open the shutters the waiter had to engage in a perfect fight with their fastenings. However, when he had lighted a little gas-stove, which at once flamed up and diffused some warmth, the room became more cosy.

Eve had seated herself on a chair, without raising the thick veil which hid her face. Gowned, gloved, and bonneted in black, as if she were already in mourning for her last passion, she showed naught of her own person save her superb fair hair, which glittered like a helm of tawny gold. She had ordered tea for two, and when the waiter brought it with a little plateful of dry biscuits, left, no doubt, from the previous season, he found her in the same place, still veiled and motionless, absorbed, it seemed, in a gloomy reverie. If she had reached the cafe half an hour before the appointed time it was because she desired some leisure and opportunity to overcome her despair and compose herself. She resolved that of all things she would not weep, that she would remain dignified and speak calmly, like one who, whatever rights she might possess, preferred to appeal to reason only. And she was well pleased with the courage that she found within her. Whilst thinking of what she should say to dissuade Gerard from a marriage which to her mind would prove both a calamity and a blunder, she fancied herself very calm, indeed almost resigned to whatsoever might happen.

But all at once she started and began to tremble. Gerard was entering the room.

"What! are you here the first, my dear?" he exclaimed. "I thought that I myself was ten minutes before the time! And you've ordered some tea and are waiting for me!"

He forced a smile as he spoke, striving to display the same delight at seeing her as he had shown in the early golden days of their passion. But at heart he was much embarrassed, and he shuddered at the thought of the awful scene which he could foresee.

She had at last risen and raised her veil. And looking at him she stammered: "Yes, I found myself at liberty earlier than I expected.... I feared some impediment might arise... and so I came."

Then, seeing how handsome and how affectionate he still looked, she could not restrain her passion. All her skilful arguments, all her fine resolutions, were swept away. Her flesh irresistibly impelled her towards him; she loved him, she would keep him, she would never surrender him to another. And she wildly flung her arms around his neck.

"Oh! Gerard, Gerard! I suffer too cruelly; I cannot, I cannot bear it! Tell me at once that you will not marry her, that you will never marry her!"

Her voice died away in a sob, tears started from her eyes. Ah! those tears which she had sworn she would never shed! They gushed forth without cessation, they streamed from her lovely eyes like a flood of the bitterest grief.

"My daughter, O God! What! you would marry my daughter! She, here, on your neck where I am now! No, no, such torture is past endurance, it must not be, I will not have it!"

He shivered as he heard that cry of frantic jealousy raised by a mother who now was but a woman, maddened by the thought of her rival's youth, those five and twenty summers which she herself had left far behind. For his part, on his way to the assignation, he had come to what he thought the most sensible decision, resolving to break off the intercourse after the fashion of a well-bred man, with all sorts of fine consolatory speeches. But sternness was not in his nature. He was weak and soft-hearted, and had never been able to withstand a woman's tears. Nevertheless, he endeavoured to calm her, and in order to rid himself of her embrace, he made her sit down upon the sofa. And there, beside her, he replied: "Come, be reasonable, my dear. We came here to have a friendly chat, did we not? I assure you that you are greatly exaggerating matters."

But she was determined to obtain a more positive answer from him. "No, no!" she retorted, "I am suffering too dreadfully, I must know the truth at once. Swear to me that you will never, never marry her!"

He again endeavoured to avoid replying as she wished him to do. "Come, come," he said, "you will do yourself harm by giving way to such grief as this; you know that I love you dearly."

"Then swear to me that you will never, never marry her."

"But I tell you that I love you, that you are the only one I love."

Then she again threw her arms around him, and kissed him passionately upon the eyes. "Is it true?" she asked in a transport. "You love me, you love no one else? Oh! tell me so again, and kiss me, and promise me that you will never belong to her."

Weak as he was he could not resist her ardent caresses and pressing entreaties. There came a moment of supreme cowardice and passion; her arms were around him and he forgot all but her, again and again repeating that he loved none other, and would never, never marry her daughter. At last he even sank so low as to pretend that he simply regarded that poor, infirm creature with pity. His words of compassionate disdain for her rival were like nectar to Eve, for they filled her with the blissful idea that it was she herself who would ever remain beautiful in his eyes and whom he would ever love....

At last silence fell between them, like an inevitable reaction after such a tempest of despair and passion. It disturbed Gerard. "Won't you drink some tea?" he asked. "It is almost cold already."

She was not listening, however. To her the reaction had come in a different form; and as though the inevitable explanation were only now commencing, she began to speak in a sad and weary voice. "My dear Gerard, you really cannot marry my daughter. In the first place it would be so wrong, and then there is the question of your name, your position. Forgive my frankness, but the fact is that everybody would say that you had sold yourself—such a marriage would be a scandal for both your family and mine."

As she spoke she took hold of his hands, like a mother seeking to prevent her big son from committing some terrible blunder. And he listened to her, with bowed head and averted eyes. She now evinced no anger, no jealous rage; all such feelings seemed to have departed with the rapture of her passion.

"Just think of what people would say," she continued. "I don't deceive myself, I am fully aware that there is an abyss between your circle of society and ours. It is all very well for us to be rich, but money simply enlarges the gap. And it was all very fine for me to be converted, my daughter is none the less 'the daughter of the Jewess,' as folks so often say. Ah! my Gerard, I am so proud of you, that it would rend my heart to see you lowered, degraded almost, by a marriage for money with a girl who is deformed, who is unworthy of you and whom you could never love."

He raised his eyes and looked at her entreatingly, anxious as he was to be spared such painful talk. "But haven't I sworn to you, that you are the only one I love?" he said. "Haven't I sworn that I would never marry her! It's all over. Don't let us torture ourselves any longer."

Their glances met and lingered on one another, instinct with all the misery which they dared not express in words. Eve's face had suddenly aged; her eyelids were red and swollen, and blotches marbled her quivering cheeks, down which her tears again began to trickle. "My poor, poor Gerard," said she, "how heavily I weigh on you. Oh! do not deny it! I feel that I am an intolerable burden on your shoulders, an impediment in your life, and that I shall bring irreparable disaster on you by my obstinacy in wishing you to be mine alone."

He tried to speak, but she silenced him. "No, no, all is over between us. I am growing ugly, all is ended. And besides, I shut off the future from you. I can be of no help to you, whereas you bestow all on me. And yet the time has come for you to assure yourself a position. At your age you can't continue living without any certainty of the morrow, without a home and hearth of your own; and it would be cowardly and cruel of me to set myself up as an obstacle, and prevent you from ending your life happily, as I should do if I clung to you and dragged you down with me."

Gazing at him through her tears she continued speaking in this fashion. Like his mother she was well aware that he was weak and even sickly; and she therefore dreamt of arranging a quiet life for him, a life of tranquil happiness free from all fear of want. She loved him so fondly; and possessed so much genuine kindness of heart that perhaps it might be possible for her to rise even to renunciation and sacrifice. Moreover, the very egotism born of her beauty suggested that it might be well for her to think of retirement and not allow the autumn of her life to be spoilt by torturing dramas. All this she said to him, treating him like a child whose happiness she wished to ensure even at the price of her own; and he, his eyes again lowered, listened without further protest, pleased indeed to let her arrange a happy life for him.

Examining the situation from every aspect, she at last began to recapitulate the points in favour of that abominable marriage, the thought of which had so intensely distressed her. "It is certain," she said, "that Camille would bring you all that I should like you to have. With her, I need hardly say it, would come plenty, affluence. And as for the rest, well, I do not wish to excuse myself or you, but I could name twenty households in which there have been worse things. Besides, I was wrong when I said that money opened a gap between people. On the contrary, it draws them nearer together, it secures forgiveness for every fault; so nobody would dare to blame you, there would only be jealous ones around you, dazzled by your good fortune."

Gerard rose, apparently rebelling once more. "Surely," said he, "*you* don't insist on my marrying your daughter?"

"Ah! no indeed! But I am sensible, and I tell you what I ought to tell you. You must think it all over."

"I have done so already. It is you that I have loved, and that I love still. What you say is impossible."

She smiled divinely, rose, and again embraced him. "How good and kind you are, my Gerard. Ah! if you only knew how I love you, how I shall always love you, whatever happens."

Then she again began to weep, and even he shed tears. Their good faith was absolute; tender of heart as they were, they sought to delay the painful wrenching and tried to hope for further happiness. But they were conscious that the marriage was virtually an accomplished fact. Only tears and words were left them, while life and destiny were marching on. And if their emotion was so acute it was probably because they felt that this was the last time they would meet as lovers. Still they strove to retain the illusion that they were not exchanging their last farewell, that their lips would some day meet again in a kiss of rapture.

Eve removed her arms from the young man's neck, and they both gazed round the room, at the sofa, the table, the four chairs, and the little hissing gas-stove. The moist, hot atmosphere was becoming quite oppressive.

"And so," said Gerard, "you won't drink a cup of tea?"

"No, it's so horrid here," she answered, while arranging her hair in front of the looking-glass.

At that parting moment the mournfulness of this place, where she had hoped to find such delightful memories, filled her with distress, which was turning to positive anguish, when she suddenly heard an uproar of gruff voices and heavy feet. People were hastening along the passage and knocking at the doors. And, on darting to the window, she perceived a number of policemen surrounding the chalet. At this the wildest ideas assailed her. Had her daughter employed somebody to follow her? Did her husband wish to divorce her so as to marry Silviane? The scandal would be awful, and all her plans must crumble! She waited in dismay, white like a ghost; while

Gerard, also paling and quivering, begged her to be calm. At last, when loud blows were dealt upon the door and a Commissary of Police enjoined them to open it, they were obliged to do so. Ah! what a moment, and what dismay and shame!

Meantime, for more than an hour, Pierre and Guillaume had been waiting for the rain to cease. Seated in a corner of the glazed verandah they talked in undertones of Barthes' painful affair, and ultimately decided to ask Theophile Morin to dine with them on the following evening, and inform his old friend that he must again go into exile.

"That is the best course," repeated Guillaume. "Morin is very fond of him and will know how to break the news. I have no doubt too that he will go with him as far as the frontier."

Pierre sadly looked at the falling rain. "Ah! what a choice," said he, "to be ever driven to a foreign land under penalty of being thrust into prison. Poor fellow! how awful it is to have never known a moment of happiness and gaiety in one's life, to have devoted one's whole existence to the idea of liberty, and to see it scoffed at and expire with oneself!"

Then the priest paused, for he saw several policemen and keepers approach the cafe and prowl round it. Having lost scent of the man they were hunting, they had retraced their steps with the conviction no doubt that he had sought refuge in the chalet. And in order that he might not again escape them, they now took every precaution, exerted all their skill in surrounding the place before venturing on a minute search. Covert fear came upon Pierre and Guillaume when they noticed these proceedings. It seemed to them that it must all be connected with the chase which they had caught a glimpse of some time previously. Still, as they happened to be in the chalet they might be called upon to give their names and addresses. At this thought they glanced at one another, and almost made up their minds to go off under the rain. But they realised that anything like flight might only compromise them the more. So they waited; and all at once there came a diversion, for two fresh customers entered the establishment.

A victoria with its hood and apron raised had just drawn up outside the door. The first to alight from it was a young, well-dressed man with a bored expression of face. He was followed by a young woman who was laughing merrily, as if much amused by the persistence of the downpour. By way of jesting, indeed, she expressed her regret that she had not come to the Bois on her bicycle, whereupon her companion retorted that to drive about in a deluge appeared to him the height of idiocy.

"But we were bound to go somewhere, my dear fellow," she gaily answered. "Why didn't you take me to see the maskers?"

"The maskers, indeed! No, no, my dear. I prefer the Bois, and even the bottom of the lake, to them."

Then, as the couple entered the chalet, Pierre saw that the young woman who made merry over the rain was little Princess Rosemonde, while her companion, who regarded the mid-Lent festivities as horrible, and bicycling as an utterly unaesthetic amusement, was handsome Hyacinthe Duvillard. On the previous evening, while they were taking a cup of tea together on their return from the Chamber of Horrors, the young man had responded to the Princess's blandishments by declaring that the only form of attachment he believed in was a mystic union of intellects and souls. And as such a union could only be fittingly arrived at amidst the cold, chaste snow, they had decided that they would start for Christiania on the following Monday. Their chief regret was that by the time they reached the fiords the worst part of the northern winter would be over.

They sat down in the cafe and ordered some kummel, but there was none, said the waiter, so they had to content themselves with common anisette. Then Hyacinthe, who had been a schoolfellow of Guillaume's sons, recognised both him and Pierre; and leaning towards Rosemonde told her in a whisper who the elder brother was.

Thereupon, with sudden enthusiasm, she sprang to her feet: "Guillaume Froment, indeed! the great chemist!" And stepping forward with arm outstretched, she continued: "Ah! monsieur, you must excuse me, but I really must shake hands with you. I have so much admiration for you! You have done such wonderful work in connection with explosives!" Then, noticing the chemist's astonishment, she again burst into a laugh: "I am the Princess de Harn, your brother Abbe Froment knows me, and I ought to have asked him to introduce me. However, we have mutual friends, you and I; for instance, Monsieur Janzen, a very distinguished man, as you are aware. He was to have taken me to see you, for I am a modest disciple of yours. Yes, I have given some attention to chemistry, oh! from pure zeal for truth and in the hope of helping good causes, not otherwise. So you will let me call on you—won't you?—directly I come back from Christiania, where I am going with my young friend here, just to acquire some experience of unknown emotions."

In this way she rattled on, never allowing the others an opportunity to say a word. And she mingled one thing with another; her cosmopolitan tastes, which had thrown her into Anarchism and the society of shady adventurers; her new passion for mysticism and symbolism; her belief that the ideal must triumph over base materialism; her taste for aesthetic verse; and her dream of some unimagined rapture when Hyacinthe should kiss her with his frigid lips in a realm of eternal snow.

All at once, however, she stopped short and again began to laugh. "Dear me!" she exclaimed. "What are those policemen looking for here? Have they come to arrest us? How amusing it would be!"

Police Commissary Dupot and detective Mondesir had just made up their minds to search the cafe, as their men had hitherto failed to find Salvat in any of the outbuildings. They were convinced that he was here. Dupot, a thin, bald, short-sighted, spectacled little man, wore his usual expression of boredom and weariness; but in reality he was very wide awake and extremely courageous. He himself carried no weapons; but, as he anticipated a most violent resistance, such as might be expected from a trapped wolf, he advised Mondesir to have his revolver ready. From considerations of hierarchical respect, however, the detective, who with his snub nose and massive figure had much the appearance of a bull-dog, was obliged to let his superior enter first.

From behind his spectacles the Commissary of Police quickly scrutinized the four customers whom he found in the cafe: the lady, the priest, and the two other men. And passing them in a disdainful way, he at once made for the stairs, intending to inspect the upper floor. Thereupon the waiter, frightened by the sudden intrusion of the police, lost his head and stammered: "But there's a lady and gentleman upstairs in one of the private rooms."

Dupot quietly pushed him aside. "A lady and gentleman, that's not what we are looking for.... Come, make haste, open all the doors, you mustn't leave a cupboard closed."

Then climbing to the upper floor, he and Mondesir explored in turn every apartment and corner till they at last reached the room where Eve and Gerard were together. Here the waiter was unable to admit them, as the door was bolted inside. "Open the door!" he called through the keyhole, "it isn't you that they want!"

At last the bolt was drawn back, and Dupot, without even venturing to smile, allowed the trembling lady and gentleman to go downstairs, while Mondesir, entering the room, looked under every article of furniture, and even peeped into a little cupboard in order that no neglect might be imputed to him.

Meantime, in the public room which they had to cross after descending the stairs, Eve and Gerard experienced fresh emotion; for people whom they knew were there, brought together by an extraordinary freak of chance. Although Eve's face was hidden by a thick veil, her eyes met her son's glance and she felt sure that he recognised her. What a fatality! He had so long a tongue and told his sister everything! Then, as the Count, in despair at such a scandal, hurried off with the Baroness to conduct her through the pouring rain to her cab, they both distinctly heard little Princess Rosemonde exclaim: "Why, that was Count de Quinsac! Who was the lady, do you know?" And as Hyacinthe, greatly put out, returned no answer, she insisted, saying: "Come, you must surely know her. Who was she, eh?"

"Oh! nobody. Some woman or other," he ended by replying.

Pierre, who had understood the truth, turned his eyes away to hide his embarrassment. But all at once the scene changed. At the very moment when Commissary Dupot and detective Mondesir came downstairs again, after vainly exploring the upper floor, a loud shout was raised outside, followed by a noise of running and scrambling. Then Gascogne, the Chief of the Detective Force, who had remained in the rear of the chalet, continuing the search through the outbuildings, made his appearance, pushing before him a bundle of rags and mud, which two policemen held on either side. And this bundle was the man, the hunted man, who had just been discovered in the coach-house, inside a staved cask, covered with hay.

Ah! what a whoop of victory there was after that run of two hours' duration, that frantic chase which had left them all breathless and footsore! It had been the most exciting, the most savage of all sports—a man hunt! They had caught the man at last, and they pushed him, they dragged him, they belaboured him with blows. And he, the man, what a sorry prey he looked! A wreck, wan and dirty from having spent the night in a hole full of leaves, still soaked to his waist from having rushed through a stream, drenched too by the rain, bespattered with mire, his coat and trousers in tatters, his cap a mere shred, his legs and hands bleeding from his terrible rush through thickets bristling with brambles and nettles. There no longer seemed anything human about his face; his hair stuck to his moist temples, his bloodshot eyes protruded from their sockets; fright, rage, and suffering were all blended on his wasted, contracted face. Still it was he, the man, the quarry, and they gave him another push, and he sank on one of the tables of the little cafe, still held and shaken, however, by the rough hands of the policemen.

Then Guillaume shuddered as if thunderstruck, and caught hold of Pierre's hand. At this the priest, who was looking on, suddenly understood the truth and also quivered. Salvat! the man was Salvat! It was Salvat whom they had seen rushing through the wood like a wild boar forced by the hounds. And it was Salvat who was there, now conquered and simply a filthy bundle. Then once more there came to Pierre, amidst his anguish, a vision of the errand girl lying yonder at the entrance of the Duvillard mansion, the pretty fair-haired girl whom the bomb had ripped and killed!

Dupot and Mondesir made haste to participate in Gascogne's triumph. To tell the truth, however, the man had offered no resistance; it was like a lamb that he had let the police lay hold of him. And since he had been in the cafe, still roughly handled, he had simply cast a weary and mournful glance around him.

At last he spoke, and the first words uttered by his hoarse, gasping voice were these: "I am hungry."

He was sinking with hunger and weariness. This was the third day that he had eaten nothing.

"Give him some bread," said Commissary Dupot to the waiter. "He can eat it while a cab is being fetched."

A policeman went off to find a vehicle. The rain had suddenly ceased falling, the clear ring of a bicyclist's bell was heard in the distance, some carriages drove by, and under the pale sunrays life again came back to the Bois.

Meantime, Salvat had fallen gluttonously upon the hunk of bread which had been given him, and whilst he was devouring it with rapturous animal satisfaction, he perceived the four customers seated around. He seemed irritated by the sight of Hyacinthe and Rosemonde, whose faces expressed the mingled anxiety and delight they felt at thus witnessing the arrest of some bandit or other. But all at once his mournful, bloodshot eyes wavered, for to his intense surprise he had recognised Pierre and Guillaume. When he again looked at the latter it was with the submissive affection of a grateful dog, and as if he were once more promising that he would divulge nothing, whatever might happen.

At last he again spoke, as if addressing himself like a man of courage, both to Guillaume, from whom he had averted his eyes, and to others also, his comrades who were not there: "It was silly of me to run," said he. "I don't know why I did so. It's best that it should be all ended. I'm ready."

V. THE GAME OF POLITICS

ON reading the newspapers on the following morning Pierre and Guillaume were greatly surprised at not finding in them the sensational accounts of Salvat's arrest which they had expected. All they could discover was a brief paragraph in a column of general news, setting forth that some policemen on duty in the Bois de Boulogne had there arrested an Anarchist, who was believed to have played a part in certain recent occurrences. On the other hand, the papers gave a deal of space to the questions raised by Sagnier's fresh denunciations. There were innumerable articles on the African Railways scandal, and the great debate which might be expected at the Chamber of Deputies, should Mege, the Socialist member, really renew his interpellation, as he had announced his intention of doing.

As Guillaume's wrist was now fast healing, and nothing seemed to threaten him, he had already, on the previous evening, decided that he would return to Montmartre. The police had passed him by without apparently suspecting any responsibility on his part; and he was convinced that Salvat would keep silent. Pierre, however, begged him to wait a little longer, at any rate until the prisoner should have been interrogated by the investigating magistrate, by which time they would be able to judge the situation more clearly. Pierre, moreover, during his long stay at the Home Department on the previous morning, had caught a glimpse of certain things and overheard certain words which made him suspect some dim connection between Salvat's crime and the parliamentary crisis; and he therefore desired a settlement of the latter before Guillaume returned to his wonted life.

"Just listen," he said to his brother. "I am going to Morin's to ask him to come and dine here this evening, for it is absolutely necessary that Barthes should be warned of the fresh blow which is falling on him. And then I think I shall go to the Chamber, as I want to know what takes place there. After that, since you desire it, I will let you go back to your own home."

It was not more than half-past one when Pierre reached the Palais-Bourbon. It had occurred to him that Fonsegue would be able to secure him admittance to the meeting-hall, but in the vestibule he met General de Bozonnet, who happened to possess a couple of tickets. A friend of his, who was to have accompanied him, had, at the last moment, been unable to come. So widespread was the curiosity concerning the debate now near at hand, and so general were the predictions that it would prove a most exciting one, that the demand for tickets had been extremely keen during the last twenty-four hours. In fact Pierre would never have been able to obtain admittance if the General had not good-naturedly offered to take him in. As a matter of fact the old warrior was well pleased to have somebody to chat with. He explained that he had simply come there to kill time, just as he might have killed it at a concert or a charity bazaar. However, like the ex-Legitimist and Bonapartist that he was, he had really come for the pleasure of feasting his eyes on the shameful spectacle of parliamentary ignominy.

When the General and Pierre had climbed the stairs, they were able to secure two front seats in one of the public galleries. Little Massot, who was already there, and who knew them both, placed one of them on his right and the other on his left. "I couldn't find a decent seat left in the press gallery," said he, "but I managed to get this place, from which I shall be able to see things properly. It will certainly be a big sitting. Just look at the number of people there are on every side!"

The narrow and badly arranged galleries were packed to overflowing. There were men of every age and a great many women too in the confused, serried mass of spectators, amidst which one only distinguished a multiplicity of pale white faces. The real scene, however, was down below in the meeting-hall, which was as yet empty, and with its rows of seats disposed in semi-circular fashion looked like the auditorium of a theatre. Under the cold light which fell from the glazed roofing appeared the solemn, shiny tribune, whence members address the Chamber, whilst behind it, on a higher level, and running right along the rear wall, was what is called the Bureau, with its various tables and seats, including the presidential armchair. The Bureau, like the tribune, was still unoccupied. The only persons one saw there were a couple of attendants who were laying out new pens and filling inkstands.

"The women," said Massot with a laugh, after another glance at the galleries, "come here just as they might come to a menagerie, that is, in the secret hope of seeing wild beasts devour one another. But, by the way, did you read the article in the 'Voix du Peuple' this morning? What a wonderful fellow that Sagnier is. When nobody else can find any filth left, he manages to discover some. He apparently thinks it necessary to add something new every day, in order to send his sales up. And of course it all disturbs the public, and it's thanks to him that so many people have come here in the hope of witnessing some horrid scene."

Then he laughed again, as he asked Pierre if he had read an unsigned article in the "Globe," which in very dignified but perfidious language had called upon Barroux to give the full and frank explanations which the country had a right to demand in that matter of the African Railways. This paper had hitherto vigorously supported the President of the Council, but in the article in question the coldness which precedes a rupture was very apparent. Pierre replied that the article had much surprised him, for he had imagined that Fonsegue and Barroux were linked together by identity of views and long-standing personal friendship.

Massot was still laughing. "Quite so," said he. "And you may be sure that the governor's heart bled when he wrote that article. It has been much noticed, and it will do the government a deal of harm. But the governor, you see, knows better than anybody else what line he ought to follow to save both his own position and the paper's."

Then he related what extraordinary confusion and emotion reigned among the deputies in the lobbies through which he had strolled before coming upstairs to secure a seat. After an adjournment of a couple of days the Chamber found itself confronted by this terrible scandal, which was like one of those conflagrations which, at the moment when they are supposed to be dying out, suddenly flare up again and devour everything. The various figures given in Sagnier's list, the two hundred thousand francs paid to Barroux, the eighty thousand handed to Monferrand, the fifty thousand allotted to Fonsegue, the ten thousand pocketed by Duthil, and the three thousand secured by Chaigneux, with all the other amounts distributed among So-and-so and So-and-so, formed the general subject of conversation. And at the same time some most extraordinary stories were current; there was no end of tittle-tattle in which fact and falsehood were so inextricably mingled that everybody was at sea as to the real truth. Whilst many deputies turned pale and trembled as beneath a blast of terror, others passed by purple with excitement, bursting with delight, laughing with exultation at the thought of coming victory. For, in point of fact, beneath all the assumed indignation, all the calls for parliamentary cleanliness and morality, there simply lay a question of persons—the question of ascertaining whether the government would be overthrown, and in that event of whom the new administration would consist. Barroux no doubt appeared to be in a bad way; but with things in such a muddle one was bound to allow a margin for the unexpected. From what was generally said it seemed certain that Mege would be extremely violent. Barroux would answer him, and the Minister's friends declared that he was determined to speak out in the most decisive manner. As for Monferrand he would probably address the Chamber after his colleague, but Vignon's intentions were somewhat doubtful, as, in spite of his delight, he made a pretence of remaining in the back, ground. He had been seen going from one to another of his partisans, advising them to keep calm, in order that they might retain the cold, keen *coup d'oeil* which in warfare generally decides the victory. Briefly, such was the plotting and intriguing that never had any witch's cauldron brimful of drugs and nameless abominations been set to boil on a more hellish fire than that of this parliamentary cook-shop.

"Heaven only knows what they will end by serving us," said little Massot by way of conclusion.

General de Bozonnet for his part anticipated nothing but disaster. If France had only possessed an army, said he, one might have swept away that handful of bribe-taking parliamentarians who preyed upon the country and rotted it. But there was no army left, there was merely an armed nation, a very different thing. And thereupon, like a man of a past age whom the present times distracted, he started on what had been his favourite subject of complaint ever since he had been retired from the service.

"Here's an idea for an article if you want one," he said to Massot. "Although France may have a million soldiers she hasn't got an army. I'll give you some notes of mine, and you will be able to tell people the truth."

Warfare, he continued, ought to be purely and simply a caste occupation, with commanders designated by divine right, leading mercenaries or volunteers into action. By democratising warfare people had simply killed it; a circumstance which he deeply regretted, like a born soldier who regarded fighting as the only really noble occupation that life offered. For, as soon as it became every man's duty to fight, none was willing to do so; and thus compulsory military service—what was called "the nation in arms"—would, at a more or less distant date, certainly bring about the end of warfare. If France had not engaged in a European war since 1870 this was precisely due to the fact that everybody in France was ready to fight. But rulers hesitated to throw a whole nation against another nation, for the loss both in life and treasure would be tremendous. And so the thought that all Europe was transformed into a vast camp filled the General with anger and disgust. He sighed for the old times when men fought for the pleasure of the thing, just as they hunted; whereas nowadays people were convinced that they would exterminate one another at the very first engagement.

"But surely it wouldn't be an evil if war should disappear," Pierre gently remarked.

This somewhat angered the General. "Well, you'll have pretty nations if people no longer fight," he answered, and then trying to show a practical spirit, he added: "Never has the art of war cost more money than since war itself has become an impossibility. The present-day defensive peace is purely and simply ruining every country in Europe. One may be spared defeat, but utter bankruptcy is certainly at the end of it all. And in any case the profession of arms is done for. All faith in it is dying out, and it will soon be forsaken, just as men have begun to forsake the priesthood."

Thereupon he made a gesture of mingled grief and anger, almost cursing that parliament, that Republican legislature before him, as if he considered it responsible for the future extinction of warfare. But little Massot was wagging his head dubiously, for he regarded the subject as rather too serious a one for him to write upon. And, all at once, in order to turn the conversation into another channel, he exclaimed: "Ah! there's Monseigneur Martha in the diplomatic gallery beside the Spanish Ambassador. It's denied, you know, that he intends to come forward as a candidate in Morbihan. He's far too shrewd to wish to be a deputy. He already pulls the strings which set most of the Catholic deputies who have 'rallied' to the Republican Government in motion."

Pierre himself had just noticed Monseigneur Martha's smiling face. And, somehow or other, however modest might be the prelate's demeanour, it seemed to him that he really played an important part in what was going on. He could hardly take his eyes from him. It was as if he expected that he would suddenly order men hither and thither, and direct the whole march of events.

"Ah!" said Massot again. "Here comes Mege. It won't be long now before the sitting begins."

The hall, down below, was gradually filling. Deputies entered and descended the narrow passages between the benches. Most of them remained standing and chatting in a more or less excited way; but some seated themselves and raised their grey, weary faces to the glazed roof. It was a cloudy afternoon, and rain was doubtless threatening, for the light became quite livid. If the hall was pompous it was also dismal with its heavy columns, its cold allegorical statues, and its stretches of bare marble and woodwork. The only brightness was that of the red velvet of the benches and the gallery hand-rests.

Every deputy of any consequence who entered was named by Massot to his companions. Mege, on being stopped by another member of the little Socialist group, began to fume and gesticulate. Then Vignon, detaching himself from a group of friends and putting on an air of smiling composure, descended the steps towards his seat. The occupants of the galleries, however, gave most attention to the accused members, those whose names figured in Sagnier's list. And these were interesting studies. Some showed themselves quite sprightly, as if they were entirely at their ease; but others had assumed a most grave and indignant demeanour. Chaigneux staggered and hesitated as if beneath the weight of some frightful act of injustice; whereas Duthil looked perfectly serene save for an occasional twitch of his lips. The most admired, however, was Fonsegue, who showed so candid a face, so open a glance, that his colleagues as well as the spectators might well have declared him innocent. Nobody indeed could have looked more like an honest man.

"Ah! there's none like the governor," muttered Massot with enthusiasm. "But be attentive, for here come the ministers. One mustn't miss Barroux' meeting with Fonsegue, after this morning's article."

Chance willed it that as Barroux came along with his head erect, his face pale, and his whole demeanour aggressive, he was obliged to pass Fonsegue in order to reach the ministerial bench. In doing so he did not speak to him, but he gazed at him fixedly like one who is conscious of defection, of a cowardly stab in the back on the part of a traitor. Fonsegue seemed quite at ease, and went on shaking hands with one and another of his colleagues as if he were altogether unconscious of Barroux' glance. Nor did he even appear to see Monferrand, who walked by in the rear of the Prime Minister, wearing a placid good-natured air, as if he knew nothing of what was impending, but was simply coming to some ordinary humdrum sitting. However, when he reached his seat, he raised his eyes and smiled at Monseigneur Martha, who gently nodded to him. Then well pleased to think that things were going as he wished them to go, he began to rub his hands, as he often did by way of expressing his satisfaction.

"Who is that grey-haired, mournful-looking gentleman on the ministerial bench?" Pierre inquired of Massot.

"Why, that's Taboureau, the Minister of Public Instruction, the excellent gentleman who is said to have no prestige. One's always hearing of him, and one never recognises him; he looks like an old, badly worn coin. Just like Barroux he can't feel very well pleased with the governor this afternoon, for to-day's 'Globe' contained an article pointing out his thorough incapacity in everything concerning the fine arts. It was an article in measured language, but all the more effective for that very reason. It would surprise me if Taboureau should recover from it."

Just then a low roll of drums announced the arrival of the President and other officials of the Chamber. A door opened, and a little procession passed by amidst an uproar of exclamations and hasty footsteps. Then, standing at his table, the President rang his bell and declared the sitting open. But few members remained silent, however, whilst one of the secretaries, a dark, lanky young man with a harsh voice, read the minutes of the previous sitting. When they had been adopted, various letters of apology for non-attendance were read, and a short, unimportant bill was passed without discussion. And then came the big affair, Mege's interpellation, and at once the whole Chamber was in a flutter, while the most passionate curiosity reigned in the galleries above. On the Government consenting to the interpellation, the Chamber decided that the debate should take place at once. And thereupon complete silence fell, save that now and again a brief quiver sped by, in which one could detect the various feelings, passions and appetites swaying the assembly.

Mege began to speak with assumed moderation, carefully setting forth the various points at issue. Tall and thin, gnarled and twisted like a vine-stock, he rested his hands on the tribune as if to support his bent figure, and his speech was often interrupted by the little dry cough which came from the tuberculosis that was burning him. But his eyes sparkled with passion behind his glasses, and little by little his voice rose in piercing accents and he drew his lank figure erect and began to gesticulate vehemently. He reminded the Chamber that some two months previously, at the time of the first denunciations published by the "Voix du Peuple," he had asked leave to interpellate the Government respecting that deplorable affair of the African Railways; and he remarked, truly enough, that if the Chamber had not yielded to certain considerations which he did not wish to discuss, and had not adjourned his proposed inquiries, full light would long since have been thrown on the whole affair, in such wise that there would have been no revival, no increase of the scandal, and no possible pretext for that abominable campaign of denunciation which tortured and disgusted the country. However, it had at last been understood that silence could be maintained no longer. It was necessary that the two ministers who were so loudly accused of having abused their trusts, should prove their innocence, throw full light upon all they had done; apart from which the Chamber itself could not possibly remain beneath the charge of wholesale venality.

Then he recounted the whole history of the affair, beginning with the grant of a concession for the African Lines to Baron Duvillard; and next passing to the proposals for the issue of lottery stock, which proposals, it was now said, had only been sanctioned by the Chamber after the most shameful bargaining and buying of votes. At this point Mege became extremely violent. Speaking of that mysterious individual Hunter, Baron Duvillard's recruiter and go-between, he declared that the police had allowed him to flee from France, much preferring to spend its time in shadowing Socialist deputies. Then, hammering the tribune with his fist, he summoned Barroux to give a categorical denial to the charges brought against him, and to make it absolutely clear that he had never received a single copper of the two hundred thousand francs specified in Hunter's list. Forthwith certain members shouted to Mege that he ought to read the whole list; but when he wished to do so others vociferated that it was abominable, that such a mendacious and slanderous document ought not to be accorded a place in the proceedings of the French legislature. Mege went on still in frantic fashion, figuratively casting Sagnier into the gutter, and protesting that there was nothing in common between himself and such a base insulter. But at the same time he demanded that justice and punishment should be meted out equally to one and all, and that if indeed there were any bribe-takers among his colleagues, they should be sent that very night to the prison of Mazas.

Meantime the President, erect at his table, rang and rang his bell without managing to quell the uproar. He was like a pilot who finds the tempest too strong for him. Among all the men with purple faces and barking mouths who were gathered in front of him, the ushers alone maintained imperturbable gravity. At intervals between the bursts of shouting, Mege's voice could still be heard. By some sudden transition he had come to the question of a Collectivist organisation of society such as he dreamt of, and he contrasted it with the criminal capitalist society of the present day, which alone, said he, could produce such scandals. And yielding more and more to his apostolic fervour, declaring that there could be no salvation apart from Collectivism, he shouted that the day of triumph would soon dawn. He awaited it with a smile of confidence. In his opinion, indeed, he merely had to overthrow that ministry and perhaps another one, and then he himself would at last take the reins of power in hand, like a reformer who would know how to pacify the nation. As outside Socialists often declared, it was evident that the blood of a dictator flowed in that sectarian's veins. His feverish, stubborn rhetoric ended by exhausting his interrupters, who were compelled to listen to him. When he at last decided to leave the tribune, loud applause arose from a few benches on the left.

"Do you know," said Massot to the General, "I met Mege taking a walk with his three little children in the Jardin des Plantes the other day. He looked after them as carefully as an old nurse. I believe he's a very worthy fellow at heart, and lives in a very modest way."

But a quiver had now sped through the assembly. Barroux had quitted his seat to ascend the tribune. He there drew himself erect, throwing his head back after his usual fashion. There was a haughty, majestic, slightly sorrowful expression on his handsome face, which would have been perfect had his nose only been a little larger. He began to express his sorrow and indignation in fine flowery language, which he punctuated with theatrical gestures. His eloquence was that of a tribune of the romantic school, and as one listened to him one could divine that in spite of all his pomposity he was really a worthy, tender-hearted and somewhat foolish man. That afternoon he was stirred by genuine emotion; his heart bled at the thought of his disastrous destiny, he felt that a whole world was crumbling with himself. Ah! what a cry of despair he stifled, the cry of the man who is buffeted and thrown aside by the course of events on the very day when he thinks that his civic devotion entitles him to triumph! To have given himself and all he possessed to the cause of the Republic, even in the dark days of the Second Empire; to have fought and struggled and suffered persecution for that Republic's sake; to have established that Republic amidst the battle of parties, after all the horrors of national and civil war; and then, when the Republic at last triumphed and became a living fact, secure from all attacks and intrigues, to suddenly feel like a survival of some other age, to hear new comers speak a new language, preach a new ideal, and behold the collapse of all he had loved, all he had reverenced, all that had given him strength to fight and conquer! The mighty artisans of the early hours were no more; it had been meet that Gambetta should die. How bitter it all was for the last lingering old ones to find themselves among the men of the new, intelligent and shrewd generation, who gently smiled at them, deeming their romanticism quite out of fashion! All crumbled since the ideal of liberty collapsed, since liberty was no longer the one desideratum, the very basis of the Republic whose existence had been so dearly purchased after so long an effort!

Erect and dignified Barroux made his confession. The Republic to him was like the sacred ark of life; the very worst deeds became saintly if they were employed to save her from peril. And in all simplicity he, told his story, how he had found the great bulk of Baron Duvillard's money going to the opposition newspapers as pretended payment for puffery and advertising, whilst on the other hand the Republican organs received but beggarly, trumpery amounts. He had been Minister of the Interior at the time, and had therefore had charge of the press; so what would have been said of him if he had not endeavoured to reestablish some equilibrium in this distribution of funds in order that the adversaries of the institutions of the country might not acquire a great increase of strength by appropriating all the sinews of war? Hands had been stretched out towards him on all sides, a score of newspapers, the most faithful, the most meritorious, had claimed their legitimate share. And he had ensured them that share by distributing among them the two hundred thousand francs set down in the list against his name. Not a centime of the money had gone into his own pocket, he would allow nobody to impugn his personal honesty, on that point his word must suffice. At that moment Barroux was really grand. All his emphatic pomposity disappeared; he showed himself, as he really was—an honest man, quivering, his heart bared, his conscience bleeding, in his bitter distress at having been among those who had laboured and at now being denied reward.

For, truth to tell, his words fell amidst icy silence. In his childish simplicity he had anticipated an outburst of enthusiasm; a Republican Chamber could but acclaim him for having saved the Republic; and now the frigidity of one and all quite froze him. He suddenly felt that he was all alone, done for, touched by the hand of death. Nevertheless, he continued speaking amidst that terrible silence with the courage of one who is committing suicide, and who, from his love of noble and eloquent attitudes, is determined to die standing. He ended with a final impressive gesture. However, as he came down from the tribune, the general coldness seemed to increase, not a single member applauded. With supreme clumsiness he had alluded to the secret scheming of Rome and the clergy, whose one object, in his opinion, was to recover the predominant position they had lost and restore monarchy in France at a more or less distant date.

"How silly of him! Ought a man ever to confess?" muttered Massot. "He's done for, and the ministry too!"

Then, amidst the general frigidity, Monferrand boldly ascended the tribune stairs. The prevailing uneasiness was compounded of all the secret fear which sincerity always causes, of all the distress of the bribe-taking deputies who felt that they were rolling into an abyss, and also of the embarrassment which the others felt at thought of the more or less justifiable compromises of politics. Something like relief, therefore, came when Monferrand started with the most emphatic denials, protesting in the name of his outraged honour, and dealing blow after blow on the tribune with one hand, while with the other he smote his chest. Short and thick-set, with his face thrust forward, hiding his shrewdness beneath an expression of indignant frankness, he was for a moment really superb. He denied everything. He was not only ignorant of what was meant by that sum of eighty thousand francs set down against his name, but he defied the whole world to prove that he had even touched a single copper of that money. He boiled over with indignation to such a point that he did not simply deny bribe-taking on his own part, he denied it on behalf of the whole assembly, of all present and past French legislatures, as if, indeed, bribe-taking on the part of a representative of the people was altogether too monstrous an idea, a crime that surpassed possibility to such an extent that the mere notion of it was absurd. And thereupon applause rang out; the Chamber, delivered from its fears, thrilled by his words, acclaimed him.

From the little Socialist group, however, some jeers arose, and voices summoned Monferrand to explain himself on the subject of the African Railways, reminding him that he had been at the head of the Public Works Department at the time of the vote, and requiring of him that he should state what he now meant to do, as Minister of the Interior, in order to reassure the country. He juggled with this question, declaring that if there were any guilty parties they would be punished, for he did not require anybody to remind him of his duty. And then, all at once, with incomparable maestria, he had recourse to the diversion which he had been preparing since the previous day. His duty, said he, was a thing which he never forgot; he discharged it like a faithful soldier of the nation hour by hour, and with as much vigilance as prudence. He had been accused of employing the police on he knew not what base spying work in such wise as to allow the man Hunter to escape. Well, as for that much-slandered police force, he would tell the Chamber on what work he had really employed it the day before, and how zealously it had laboured for the cause of law and order. In the Bois de Boulogne, on the previous afternoon, it had arrested that terrible scoundrel, the perpetrator of the crime in the Rue Godot-de-Mauroy, that Anarchist mechanician Salvat, who for six weeks past had so cunningly contrived to elude capture. The scoundrel had made a full confession during the evening, and the law would now take its course with all despatch. Public morality was at last avenged, Paris might now emerge in safety from its long spell of terror, Anarchism would be struck down, annihilated. And that was what he, Monferrand, had done as a Minister for the honour and safety of his country, whilst villains were vainly seeking to dishonour him by inscribing his name on a list of infamy, the outcome of the very basest political intrigues.

The Chamber listened agape and quivering. This story of Salvat's arrest, which none of the morning papers had reported; the present which Monferrand seemed to be making them of that terrible Anarchist whom many had already begun to regard as a myth; the whole *mise-en-scene* of the Minister's speech transported the deputies as if they were suddenly witnessing the finish of a long-interrupted drama. Stirred and flattered, they prolonged their applause, while Monferrand went on celebrating his act of energy, how he had saved society, how crime should be punished, and how he himself would ever prove that he had a strong arm and could answer for public order. He even won favour with the Conservatives and Clericals on the Right by separating himself from Barroux, addressing a few words of sympathy to those Catholics who had "rallied" to the Republic, and appealing for concord among men of different beliefs in order that they might fight the common enemy, that fierce, wild socialism which talked of overthrowing everything!

By the time Monferrand came down from the tribune, the trick was played, he had virtually saved himself. Both the Right and Left of the Chamber[1] applauded, drowning the protests of the few Socialists whose vociferations only added to the triumphal tumult. Members eagerly stretched out their hands to the Minister, who for a moment remained standing there and smiling. But there was some anxiety in that smile of his; his success was beginning to frighten him. Had he spoken too well, and saved the entire Cabinet instead of merely saving himself? That would mean the ruin of his plan. The Chamber ought not to vote under the effect of that speech which had thrilled it so powerfully. Thus Monferrand, though he still continued to smile, spent a few anxious moments in waiting to see if anybody would rise to answer him.

---

[1] Ever since the days of the Bourbon Restoration it has been the practice in the French Chambers for the more conservative members to seat themselves on the President's right, and for the Radical ones to place themselves on his left. The central seats of the semicircle in which the members' seats are arranged in tiers are usually occupied by men of moderate views. Generally speaking, such terms as Right Centre and Left Centre are applied to groups of Moderates inclining in the first place to Conservatism and in the latter to Radicalism. All this is of course known to readers acquainted with French institutions, but I give the explanation because others, after perusing French news in some daily paper, have often asked me what was meant by "a deputy of the Right," and so forth.—Trans.

His success had been as great among the occupants of the galleries as among the deputies themselves. Several ladies had been seen applauding, and Monseigneur Martha had given unmistakable signs of the liveliest satisfaction. "Ah, General!" said Massot to Bozonnet in a sneering way. "Those are our fighting men of the present time. And he's a bold and strong one, is Monferrand. Of course it is all what people style 'saving one's bacon,' but none the less it's very clever work."

Just then, however, Monferrand to his great satisfaction had seen Vignon rise from his seat in response to the urging of his friends. And thereupon all anxiety vanished from the Minister's smile, which became one of malicious placidity.

The very atmosphere of the Chamber seemed to change with Vignon in the tribune. He was slim, with a fair and carefully tended beard, blue eyes and all the suppleness of youth. He spoke, moreover, like a practical man, in simple, straightforward language, which made the emptiness of the other's declamatory style painfully conspicuous. His term of official service as a prefect in the provinces had endowed him with keen insight; and it was in an easy way that he propounded and unravelled the most intricate questions. Active and courageous, confident in his own star, too young and too shrewd to have compromised himself in anything so far, he was steadily marching towards the future. He had already drawn up a rather more advanced political programme than that of Barroux and Monferrand, so that when opportunity offered there might be good reasons for him to take their place. Moreover, he was quite capable of carrying out his programme by attempting some of the long-promised reforms for which the country was waiting. He had guessed that honesty, when it had prudence and shrewdness as its allies, must some day secure an innings. In a clear voice, and in a very quiet, deliberate way, he now said what it was right to say on the subject under discussion, the things that common sense dictated and that the Chamber itself secretly desired should be said. He was certainly the first to rejoice over an arrest which would reassure the country; but he failed to understand what connection there could be between that arrest and the sad business that had been brought before the Chamber. The two affairs were quite distinct and different, and he begged his colleagues not to vote in the state of excitement in which he saw them. Full light must be thrown on the African Railways question, and this, one could not expect from the two incriminated ministers. However, he was opposed to any suggestion of a committee of inquiry. In his opinion the guilty parties, if such there were, ought to be brought immediately before a court of law. And, like Barroux, he wound up with a discreet allusion to the growing influence of the clergy, declaring that he was against all unworthy compromises, and was equally opposed to any state dictatorship and any revival of the ancient theocratic spirit.

Although there was but little applause when Vignon returned to his seat, it was evident that the Chamber was again master of its emotions. And the situation seemed so clear, and the overthrow of the ministry so certain, that Mege, who had meant to reply to the others, wisely abstained from doing so. Meantime people noticed the placid demeanour of Monferrand, who had listened to Vignon with the utmost complacency, as if he were rendering homage to an adversary's talent; whereas Barroux, ever since the cold silence which had greeted his speech, had remained motionless in his seat, bowed down and pale as a corpse.

"Well, it's all over," resumed Massot, amidst the hubbub which arose as the deputies prepared to vote; "the ministry's done for. Little Vignon will go a long way, you know. People say that he dreams of the Elysee. At all events everything points to him as our next prime minister."

Then, as the journalist rose, intending to go off, the General detained him: "Wait a moment, Monsieur Massot," said he. "How disgusting all that parliamentary cooking is! You ought to point it out in an article, and show people how the country is gradually being weakened and rotted to the marrow by all such useless and degrading discussions. Why, a great battle resulting in the loss of 50,000 men would exhaust us less than ten years of this abominable parliamentary system. You must call on me some morning. I will show you a scheme of military reform, in which I point out the necessity of returning to the limited professional armies which we used to have, for this present-day national army, as folks call it, which is a semi-civilian affair and at best a mere herd of men, is like a dead weight on us, and is bound to pull us down!"

Pierre, for his part, had not spoken a word since the beginning of the debate. He had listened to everything, at first influenced by the thought of his brother's interests, and afterwards mastered by the feverishness which gradually took possession of everybody present. He had become convinced that there was nothing more for Guillaume to fear; but how curiously did one event fit into another, and how loudly had Salvat's arrest re-echoed in the Chamber! Looking down into the seething hall below him, he had detected all the clash of rival passions and interests. After watching the great struggle between Barroux, Monferrand and Vignon, he had gazed upon the childish delight of that terrible Socialist Mege, who was so pleased at having been able to stir up the depths of those troubled waters, in which he always unwittingly angled for the benefit of others. Then, too, Pierre had become interested in Fonsegue, who, knowing what had been arranged between Monferrand, Duvillard and himself, evinced perfect calmness and strove to reassure Duthil and Chaigneux, who, on their side, were quite dismayed by the ministry's impending fall. Yet, Pierre's eyes always came back to Monseigneur Martha. He had watched his serene smiling face throughout the sitting, striving to detect his impressions of the various incidents that had occurred, as if in his opinion that dramatic parliamentary comedy had only been played as a step towards the more or less distant triumph for which the prelate laboured. And now, while awaiting the result of the vote, as Pierre turned towards Massot and the General, he found that they were talking of nothing but recruiting and tactics and the necessity of a bath of blood for the whole of Europe. Ah! poor mankind, ever fighting and ever devouring one another in parliaments as well as on battle-fields, when, thought Pierre, would it decide to disarm once and for all, and live at peace according to the laws of justice and reason!

Then he again looked down into the hall, where the greatest confusion was prevailing among the deputies with regard to the coming vote. There was quite a rainfall of suggested "resolutions," from a very violent one proposed by Mege, to another, which was merely severe, emanating from Vignon. The ministry, however, would only accept the "Order of the day pure and simple," a mere decision, that is, to pass to the next business, as if Mege's interpellation had been unworthy of attention. And presently the Government was defeated, Vignon's resolution being adopted by a majority of twenty-five. Some portion of the Left had evidently joined hands with the Right and the Socialist group. A prolonged hubbub followed this result.

"Well, so we are to have a Vignon Cabinet," said Massot, as he went off with Pierre and the General. "All the same, though, Monferrand has saved himself, and if I were in Vignon's place I should distrust him."

That evening there was a very touching farewell scene at the little house at Neuilly. When Pierre returned thither from the Chamber, saddened but reassured with regard to the future, Guillaume at once made up his mind to go home on the morrow. And as Nicholas Barthes was compelled to leave, the little dwelling seemed on the point of relapsing into dreary quietude once more.

Theophile Morin, whom Pierre had informed of the painful alternative in which Barthes was placed, duly came to dinner; but he did not have time to speak to the old man before they all sat down to table at seven o'clock. As usual Barthes had spent his day in marching, like a caged lion, up and down the room in which he had accepted shelter after the fashion of a big fearless child, who never worried with regard either to his present circumstances or the troubles which the future might have in store for him. His life had ever been one of unlimited hope, which reality had ever shattered. Although all that he had loved, all that he had hoped to secure by fifty years of imprisonment or exile,—liberty, equality and a real brotherly republic,—had hitherto failed to come, such as he had dreamt of them, he nevertheless retained the candid faith of his youth, and was ever confident in the near future. He would smile indulgently when new comers, men of violent ideas, derided him and called him a poor old fellow. For his part, he could make neither head nor tail of the many new sects. He simply felt indignant with their lack of human feeling, and stubbornly adhered to his own idea of basing the world's regeneration on the simple proposition that men were naturally good and ought to be free and brotherly.

That evening at dinner, feeling that he was with friends who cared for him, Barthes proved extremely gay, and showed all his ingenuousness in talking of his ideal, which would soon be realised, said he, in spite of everything. He could tell a story well whenever he cared to chat, and on that occasion he related some delightful anecdotes about the prisons through which he had passed. He knew all the dungeons, Ste. Pelagie and Mont St. Michel, Belle-Ile-en-Mer and Clairvaux, to say nothing of temporary gaols and the evil-smelling hulks on board which political prisoners are often confined. And he still laughed at certain recollections, and related how in the direst circumstances he had always been able to seek refuge in his conscience. The others listened to him quite charmed by his conversation, but full of anguish at the thought that this perpetual prisoner or exile must again rise and take his staff to sally forth, driven from his native land once more.

Pierre did not speak out until they were partaking of dessert. Then he related how the Minister had written to him, and how in a brief interview he had stated that Barthes must cross the frontier within forty-eight hours if he did not wish to be arrested. Thereupon the old man gravely rose, with his white fleece, his eagle beak and his bright eyes still sparkling with the fire of youth. And he wished to go off at once. "What!" said he, "you have known all this since yesterday, and have still kept me here at the risk of my compromising you even more than I had done already! You must forgive me, I did not think of the worry I might cause you, I thought that everything would be satisfactorily arranged. I must thank you both—yourself and Guillaume—for the few days of quietude that you have procured to an old vagabond and madman like myself."

Then, as they tried to prevail on him to remain until the following morning, he would not listen to them. There would be a train for Brussels about midnight, and he had ample time to take it. He refused to let Morin accompany him. No, no, said he, Morin was not a rich man, and moreover he had work to attend to. Why should he take him away from his duties, when it was so easy, so simple, for him to go off alone? He was going back into exile as into misery and grief which he had long known, like some Wandering Jew of Liberty, ever driven onward through the world.

When he took leave of the others at ten o'clock, in the little sleepy street just outside the house, tears suddenly dimmed his eyes. "Ah! I'm no longer a young man," he said; "it's all over this time. I shall never come back again. My bones will rest in some corner over yonder." And yet, after he had affectionately embraced Pierre and Guillaume, he drew himself up like one who remained unconquered, and he raised a supreme cry of hope. "But after all, who knows? Triumph may perhaps come tomorrow. The future belongs to those who prepare it and wait for it!"

Then he walked away, and long after he had disappeared his firm, sonorous footsteps could be heard re-echoing in the quiet night.

BOOK IV.

I. PIERRE AND MARIE

ON the mild March morning when Pierre left his little house at Neuilly to accompany Guillaume to Montmartre, he was oppressed by the thought that on returning home he would once more find himself alone with nothing to prevent him from relapsing into negation and despair. The idea of this had kept him from sleeping, and he still found it difficult to hide his distress and force a smile.

The sky was so clear and the atmosphere so mild that the brothers had resolved to go to Montmartre on foot by way of the outer boulevards. Nine o'clock was striking when they set out. Guillaume for his part was very gay at the thought of the surprise he would give his family. It was as if he were suddenly coming back from a long journey. He had not warned them of his intentions; he had merely written to them now and again to tell them that he was recovering, and they certainly had no idea that his return was so near at hand.

When Guillaume and Pierre had climbed the sunlit slopes of Montmartre, and crossed the quiet countrified Place du Tertre, the former, by means of a latch-key, quietly opened the door of his house, which seemed to be asleep, so profound was the stillness both around and within it. Pierre found it the same as on the occasion of his previous and only visit. First came the narrow passage which ran through the ground-floor, affording a view of all Paris at the further end. Next there was the garden, reduced to a couple of plum-trees and a clump of lilac-bushes, the leaves of which had now sprouted. And this time the priest perceived three bicycles leaning against the trees. Beyond them stood the large work-shop, so gay, and yet so peaceful, with its huge window overlooking a sea of roofs.

Guillaume had reached the work-shop without meeting anybody. With an expression of much amusement he raised a finger to his lips. "Attention, Pierre," he whispered; "you'll just see!"

Then having noiselessly opened the door, they remained for a moment on the threshold.

The three sons alone were there. Near his forge stood Thomas working a boring machine, with which he was making some holes in a small brass plate. Then Francois and Antoine were seated on either side of their large table, the former reading, and the latter finishing a block. The bright sunshine streamed in, playing over all the seeming disorder of the room, where so many callings and so many implements found place. A large bunch of wallflowers bloomed on the women's work-table near the window; and absorbed as the young men were in their respective tasks the only sound was the slight hissing of the boring machine each time that the eldest of them drilled another hole.

However, although Guillaume did not stir, there suddenly came a quiver, an awakening. His sons seemed to guess his presence, for they raised their heads, each at the same moment. From each, too, came the same cry, and a common impulse brought them first to their feet and then to his arms.

"Father!"

Guillaume embraced them, feeling very happy. And that was all; there was no long spell of emotion, no useless talk. It was as if he had merely gone out the day before and, delayed by business, had now come back. Still, he looked at them with his kindly smile, and they likewise smiled with their eyes fixed on his. Those glances proclaimed everything, the closest affection and complete self-bestowal for ever.

"Come in, Pierre," called Guillaume; "shake hands with these young men."

The priest had remained near the door, overcome by a singular feeling of discomfort. When his nephews had vigorously shaken hands with him, he sat down near the window apart from them, as if he felt out of his element there.

"Well, youngsters," said Guillaume, "where's Mere-Grand, and where's Marie?"

Their grandmother was upstairs in her room, they said; and Marie had taken it into her head to go marketing. This, by the way, was one of her delights. She asserted that she was the only one who knew how to buy new-laid eggs and butter of a nutty odour. Moreover, she sometimes brought some dainty or some flowers home, in her delight at proving herself to be so good a housewife.

"And so things are going on well?" resumed Guillaume. "You are all satisfied, your work is progressing, eh?"

He addressed brief questions to each of them, like one who, on his return home, at once reverts to his usual habits. Thomas, with his rough face beaming, explained in a couple of sentences that he was now sure of perfecting his little motor; Francois, who was still preparing for his examination, jestingly declared that he yet had to lodge a heap of learning in his brain; and then Antoine produced the block which he was finishing, and which depicted his little friend Lise, Jahan's sister, reading in her garden amidst the sunshine. It was like a florescence of that dear belated creature whose mind had been awakened by his affection.

However, the three brothers speedily went back to their places, reverting to their work with a natural impulse, for discipline had made them regard work as life itself. Then Guillaume, who had glanced at what each was doing, exclaimed: "Ah! youngsters, I schemed and prepared a lot of things myself while I was laid up. I even made a good many notes. We walked here from Neuilly, but my papers and the clothes which Mere-Grand sent me will come in a cab by-and-by.... Ah! how pleased I am to find everything in order here, and to be able to take up my task with you again! Ah! I shall polish off some work now, and no mistake!"

He had already gone to his own corner, the space reserved for him between the window and the forge. He there had a chemical furnace, several glass cases and shelves crowded with appliances, and a long table, one end of which he used for writing purposes. And he once more took possession of that little world. After glancing around with delight at seeing everything in its place, he began to handle one object and another, eager to be at work like his sons.

All at once, however, Mere-Grand appeared, calm, grave and erect in her black gown, at the top of the little staircase which conducted to the bedrooms. "So it's you, Guillaume?" said she. "Will you come up for a moment?"

He immediately did so, understanding that she wished to speak to him alone and tranquillise him. It was a question of the great secret between them, that one thing of which his sons knew nothing, and which, after Salvat's crime, had brought him much anguish, through his fear that it might be divulged. When he reached Mere-Grand's room she at once took him to the hiding-place near her bed, and showed him the cartridges of the new explosive, and the plans of the terrible engine of warfare which he had invented. He found them all as he had left them. Before anyone could have reached them, she would have blown up the whole place at the risk of perishing herself in the explosion. With her wonted air of quiet heroism, she handed Guillaume the key which he had sent her by Pierre.

"You were not anxious, I hope?" she said.

He pressed her hands with a commingling of affection and respect. "My only anxiety," he replied, "was that the police might come here and treat you roughly.... You are the guardian of our secret, and it would be for you to finish my work should I disappear."

While Guillaume and Madame Leroi were thus engaged upstairs, Pierre, still seated near the window below, felt his discomfort increasing. The inmates of the house certainly regarded him with no other feeling than one of affectionate sympathy; and so how came it that he considered them hostile? The truth was that he asked himself what would become of him among those workers, who were upheld by a faith of their own, whereas he believed in nothing, and did not work. The sight of those young men, so gaily and zealously toiling, ended by quite irritating him; and the arrival of Marie brought his distress to a climax.

Joyous and full of life, she came in without seeing him, a basket on her arm. And she seemed to bring all the sunlight of the spring morning with her, so bright was the sparkle of her youth. The whole of her pink face, her delicate nose, her broad intelligent brow, her thick, kindly lips, beamed beneath the heavy coils of her black hair. And her brown eyes ever laughed with the joyousness which comes from health and strength.

"Ah!" she exclaimed, "I have brought such a lot of things, youngsters. Just come and see them; I wouldn't unpack the basket in the kitchen."

It became absolutely necessary for the brothers to draw round the basket which she had laid upon the table. "First there's the butter!" said she; "just smell if it hasn't a nice scent of nuts! It's churned especially for me, you know. Then here are the eggs. They were laid only yesterday, I'll answer for it. And, in fact, that one there is this morning's. And look at the cutlets! They're wonderful, aren't they? The butcher cuts them carefully when he sees me. And then here's a cream cheese, real cream, you know, it will be delicious! Ah! and here's the surprise, something dainty, some radishes, some pretty little pink radishes. Just fancy! radishes in March, what a luxury!"

She triumphed like the good little housewife she was, one who had followed a whole course of cookery and home duties at the Lycee Fenelon. The brothers, as merry as she herself, were obliged to compliment her.

All at once, however, she caught sight of Pierre. "What! you are there, Monsieur l'Abbe?" she exclaimed; "I beg your pardon, but I didn't see you. How is Guillaume? Have you brought us some news of him?"

"But father's come home," said Thomas; "he's upstairs with Mere-Grand."

Quite thunderstruck, she hastily placed her purchases in the basket. "Guillaume's come back, Guillaume's come back!" said she, "and you don't tell me of it, you let me unpack everything! Well, it's nice of me, I must say, to go on praising my butter and eggs when Guillaume's come back."

Guillaume, as it happened, was just coming down with Madame Leroi. Marie gaily hastened to him and offered him her cheeks, on which he planted two resounding kisses. Then she, resting her hands on his shoulders, gave him a long look, while saying in a somewhat tremulous voice: "I am pleased, very pleased to see you, Guillaume. I may confess it now, I thought I had lost you, I was very anxious and very unhappy."

Although she was still smiling, tears had gathered in her eyes, and he, likewise moved, again kissed her, murmuring: "Dear Marie! How happy it makes me to find you as beautiful and as affectionate as ever."

Pierre, who was looking at them, deemed them cold. He had doubtless expected more tears, and a more passionate embrace on the part of an affianced pair, whom so grievous an accident had separated almost on the eve of their wedding. Moreover, his feelings were hurt by the disproportion of their respective ages. No doubt his brother still seemed to him very sturdy and young, and his feeling of repulsion must have come from that young woman whom, most decidedly, he did not like. Ever since her arrival he had experienced increasing discomfort, a keener and keener desire to go off and never return.

So acute became his suffering at feeling like a stranger in his brother's home, that he at last rose and sought to take his leave, under the pretext that he had some urgent matters to attend to in town.

"What! you won't stay to *dejeuner* with us!" exclaimed Guillaume in perfect stupefaction. "Why, it was agreed! You surely won't distress me like that! This house is your own, remember!"

Then, as with genuine affection they all protested and pressed him to stay, he was obliged to do so. However, he soon relapsed into silence and embarrassment, seated on the same chair as before, and listening moodily to those people who, although they were his relatives, seemed to be far removed from him.

As it was barely eleven o'clock they resumed work, but every now and again there was some merry talk. On one of the servants coming for the provisions, Marie told the girl to call her as soon as it should be time to boil the eggs, for she prided herself on boiling them to a nicety, in such wise as to leave the whites like creamy milk. This gave an opportunity for a few jests from Francois, who occasionally teased her about all the fine things she had learnt at the Lycee Fenelon, where her father had placed her when she was twelve years old. However, she was not afraid of him, but gave him tit for tat by chaffing him about all the hours which he lost at the Ecole Normale over a mass of pedagogic trash.

"Ah! you big children!" she exclaimed, while still working at her embroidery. "You are all very intelligent, and you all claim to have broad minds, and yet—confess it now—it worries you a little that a girl like me should have studied at college in the same way as yourselves. It's a sexual quarrel, a question of rivalry and competition, isn't it?"

They protested the contrary, declaring that they were in favour of girls receiving as complete an education as possible. She was well aware of this; however, she liked to tease them in return for the manner in which they themselves plagued her.

"But do you know," said she, "you are a great deal behind the times? I am well aware of the reproaches which are levelled at girls' colleges by so-called right-minded people. To begin, there is no religious element whatever in the education one receives there, and this alarms many families which consider religious education to be absolutely necessary for girls, if only as a moral weapon of defence. Then, too, the education at our Lycees is being democratised—girls of all positions come to them. Thanks to the scholarships which are so liberally offered, the daughter of the lady who rents a first floor flat often finds the daughter of her door-keeper among her school-fellows, and some think this objectionable. It is said also that the pupils free themselves too much from home influence, and that too much opportunity is left for personal initiative. As a matter of fact the extensiveness of the many courses of study, all the learning that is required of pupils at the examinations, certainly does tend to their emancipation, to the coming of the future woman and future society, which you young men are all longing for, are you not?"

"Of course we are!" exclaimed Francois; "we all agree on that point."

She waved her hand in a pretty way, and then quietly continued: "I'm jesting. My views are simple enough, as you well know, and I don't ask for nearly as much as you do. As for woman's claims and rights, well, the question is clear enough; woman is man's equal so far as nature allows it. And the only point is to agree and love one another. At the same time I'm well pleased to know what I do—oh! not from any spirit of pedantry but simply because I think it has all done me good, and given me some moral as well as physical health."

It delighted her to recall the days she had spent at the Lycee Fenelon, which of the five State colleges for girls opened in Paris was the only one counting a large number of pupils. Most of these were the daughters of officials or professors, who purposed entering the teaching profession. In this case, they had to win their last diploma at the Ecole Normale of Sevres, after leaving the Lycee. Marie, for her part, though her studies had been brilliant, had felt no taste whatever for the calling of teacher. Moreover, when Guillaume had taken charge of her after her father's death, he had refused to let her run about giving lessons. To provide herself with a little money, for she would accept none as a gift, she worked at embroidery, an art in which she was most accomplished.

While she was talking to the young men Guillaume had listened to her without interfering. If he had fallen in love with her it was largely on account of her frankness and uprightness, the even balance of her nature, which gave her so forcible a charm. She knew all; but if she lacked the poetry of the shrinking, lamb-like girl who has been brought up in ignorance, she had gained absolute rectitude of heart and mind, exempt from all hypocrisy, all secret perversity such as is stimulated by what may seem mysterious in life. And whatever she might know, she had retained such childlike purity that in spite of her six-and-twenty summers all the blood in her veins would occasionally rush to her cheeks in fiery blushes, which drove her to despair.

"My dear Marie," Guillaume now exclaimed, "you know very well that the youngsters were simply joking. You are in the right, of course.... And your boiled eggs cannot be matched in the whole world."

He said this in so soft and affectionate a tone that the young woman flushed purple. Then, becoming conscious of it, she coloured yet more deeply, and as the three young men glanced at her maliciously she grew angry with herself. "Isn't it ridiculous, Monsieur l'Abbe," she said, turning towards Pierre, "for an old maid like myself to blush in that fashion? People might think that I had committed a crime. It's simply to make me blush, you know, that those children tease me. I do all I can to prevent it, but it's stronger than my will."

At this Mere-Grand raised her eyes from the shirt she was mending, and remarked: "Oh! it's natural enough, my dear. It is your heart rising to your cheeks in order that we may see it."

The *dejeuner* hour was now at hand; and they decided to lay the table in the workshop, as was occasionally done when they had a guest. The simple, cordial meal proved very enjoyable in the bright sunlight. Marie's boiled eggs, which she herself brought from the kitchen covered with a napkin, were found delicious. Due honour was also done to the butter and the radishes. The only dessert that followed the cutlets was the cream cheese, but it was a cheese such as nobody else had ever partaken of. And, meantime, while they ate and chatted all Paris lay below them, stretching away to the horizon with its mighty rumbling.

Pierre had made an effort to become cheerful, but he soon relapsed into silence. Guillaume, however, was very talkative. Having noticed the three bicycles in the garden, he inquired of Marie how far she had gone that morning. She answered that Francois and Antoine had accompanied her in the direction of Orgemont. The worry of their excursions was that each time they returned to Montmartre they had to push their machines up the height. From the general point of view, however, the young woman was delighted with bicycling, which had many virtues, said she. Then, seeing Pierre glance at her in amazement, she promised that she would some day explain her opinions on the subject to him. After this bicycling became the one topic of conversation until the end of the meal. Thomas gave an account of the latest improvements introduced into Grandidier's machines; and the others talked of the excursions they had made or meant to make, with all the exuberant delight of school children eager for the open air.

In the midst of the chatter, Mere-Grand, who presided at table with the serene dignity of a queen-mother, leant towards Guillaume, who sat next to her, and spoke to him in an undertone. Pierre understood that she was referring to his marriage, which was to have taken place in April, but must now necessarily be deferred. This sensible marriage, which seemed likely to ensure the happiness of the entire household, was largely the work of Mere-Grand and the three young men, for Guillaume would never have yielded to his heart if she whom he proposed to make his wife had not already been a well-loved member of the family. At the present time the last week in June seemed, for all sorts of reasons, to be a favourable date for the wedding.

Marie, who heard the suggestion, turned gaily towards Mere-Grand.

"The end of June will suit very well, will it not, my dear?" said the latter.

Pierre expected to see a deep flush rise to the young woman's cheeks, but she remained very calm. She felt deep affection, blended with the most tender gratitude, for

Guillaume, and was convinced that in marrying him she would be acting wisely and well both for herself and the others.

"Certainly, the end of June," she repeated, "that will suit very well indeed."

Then the sons, who likewise had heard the proposal, nodded their heads by way of assenting also.

When they rose from table Pierre was absolutely determined to go off. The cordial and simple meal, the sight of that family, which had been rendered so happy by Guillaume's return, and of that young woman who smiled so placidly at life, had brought him keen suffering, though why he could not tell. However, it all irritated him beyond endurance; and he therefore again pretended that he had a number of things to see to in Paris. He shook hands in turn with the young men, Mere-Grand and Marie; both of the women evincing great friendliness but also some surprise at his haste to leave the house. Guillaume, who seemed saddened and anxious, sought to detain him, and failing in this endeavour followed him into the little garden, where he stopped him in order to have an explanation.

"Come," said he, "what is the matter with you, Pierre? Why are you running off like this?"

"Oh! there's nothing the matter I assure you; but I have to attend to a few urgent affairs."

"Oh, Pierre, pray put all pretence aside. Nobody here has displeased you or hurt your feelings, I hope. They also will soon love you as I do."

"I have no doubt of it, and I complain of nobody excepting perhaps myself."

Guillaume's sorrow was increasing. "Ah! brother, little brother," he resumed, "you distress me, for I can detect that you are hiding something from me. Remember that new ties have linked us together and that we love one another as in the old days when you were in your cradle and I used to come to play with you. I know you well, remember. I know all your tortures, since you have confessed them to me; and I won't have you suffer, I want to cure you, I do!"

Pierre's heart was full, and as he heard those words he could not restrain his tears. "Oh! you must leave me to my sufferings," he responded. "They are incurable. You can do nothing for me, I am beyond the pale of nature, I am a monster."

"What do you say! Can you not return within nature's pale even if you *have* gone beyond it? One thing that I will not allow is that you should go and shut yourself up in that solitary little house of yours, where you madden yourself by brooding over the fall of your faith. Come and spend your time with us, so that we may again give you some taste for life."

Ah! the empty little house which awaited him! Pierre shivered at the thought of it, at the idea that he would now find himself all alone there, bereft of the brother with whom he had lately spent so many happy days. Into what solitude and torment must he not now relapse after that companionship to which he had become accustomed? However, the very thought of the latter increased his grief, and confession suddenly gushed from his lips: "To spend my time here, live with you, oh! no, that is an impossibility. Why do you compel me to speak out, and tell you things that I am ashamed of and do not even understand. Ever since this morning you must have seen that I have been suffering here. No doubt it is because you and your people work, whereas I do nothing, because you love one another and believe in your efforts, whereas I no longer know how to love or believe. I feel out of my element. I'm embarrassed here, and I embarrass you. In fact you all irritate me, and I might end by hating you. There remains nothing healthy in me, all natural feelings have been spoilt and destroyed, and only envy and hatred could sprout up from such ruins. So let me go back to my accursed hole, where death will some day come for me. Farewell, brother!"

But Guillaume, full of affection and compassion, caught hold of his arms and detained him. "You shall not go, I will not allow you to go, without a positive promise that you will come back. I don't wish to lose you again, especially now that I know all you are worth and how dreadfully you suffer. I will save you, if need be, in spite of yourself. I will cure you of your torturing doubts, oh! without catechising you, without imposing any particular faith on you, but simply by allowing life to do its work, for life alone can give you back health and hope. So I beg you, brother, in the name of our affection, come back here, come as often as you can to spend a day with us. You will then see that when folks have allotted themselves a task and work together in unison, they escape excessive unhappiness. A task of any kind—yes, that is what is wanted, together with some great passion and frank acceptance of life, so that it may be lived as it should be and loved."

"But what would be the use of my living here?" Pierre muttered bitterly. "I've no task left me, and I no longer know how to love."

"Well, I will give you a task, and as for love, that will soon be awakened by the breath of life. Come, brother, consent, consent!"

Then, seeing that Pierre still remained gloomy and sorrowful, and persisted in his determination to go away and bury himself, Guillaume added, "Ah! I don't say that the things of this world are such as one might wish them to be. I don't say that only joy and truth and justice exist. For instance, the affair of that unhappy fellow Salvat fills me with anger and revolt. Guilty he is, of course, and yet how many excuses he had, and how I shall pity him if the crimes of all of us are laid at his door, if the various political gangs bandy him from one to another, and use him as a weapon in their sordid fight for power. The thought of it all so exasperates me that at times I am as unreasonable as yourself. But now, brother, just to please me, promise that you will come and spend the day after to-morrow with us."

Then, as Pierre still kept silent, Guillaume went on: "I will have it so. It would grieve me too much to think that you were suffering from martyrdom in your solitary nook. I want to cure and save you."

Tears again rose to Pierre's eyes, and in a tone of infinite distress he answered: "Don't compel me to promise.... All I can say is that I will try to conquer myself."

The week he then spent in his little, dark, empty home proved a terrible one. Shutting himself up he brooded over his despair at having lost the companionship of that elder brother whom he once more loved with his whole soul. He had never before been so keenly conscious of his solitude; and he was a score of times on the point of hastening to Montmartre, for he vaguely felt that affection, truth and life were there. But on each occasion he was held back by a return of the discomfort which he had already experienced, discomfort compounded of shame and fear. Priest that he was, cut off from love and the avocations of other men, he would surely find nothing but hurt and suffering among creatures who were all nature, freedom and health. While he pondered thus, however, there rose before him the shades of his father and mother, those sad spirits that seemed to wander through the deserted rooms lamenting and entreating him to reconcile them in himself, as soon as he should find peace. What was he to do,—deny their prayer, and remain weeping with them, or go yonder in search of the cure which might at last lull them to sleep and bring them happiness in death by the force of his own happiness in life? At last a morning came when it seemed to him that his father enjoined him with a smile to betake himself yonder, while his mother consented with a glance of her big soft eyes, in which her sorrow at having made so bad a priest of him yielded to her desire to restore him to the life of our common humanity.

Pierre did not argue with himself that day: he took a cab and gave Guillaume's address to the driver for fear lest he should be overcome on the way and wish to turn back. And when he again found himself, as in a dream, in the large work-shop, where Guillaume and the young men welcomed him in a delicately affectionate way, he witnessed an unexpected scene which both impressed and relieved him.

Marie, who had scarcely nodded to him as he entered, sat there with a pale and frowning face. And Mere-Grand, who was also grave, said, after glancing at her: "You must excuse her, Monsieur l'Abbe; but she isn't reasonable. She is in a temper with all five of us."

Guillaume began to laugh. "Ah! she's so stubborn!" he exclaimed. "You can have no idea, Pierre, of what goes on in that little head of hers when anybody says or does anything contrary to her ideas of justice. Such absolute and lofty ideas they are, that they can descend to no compromise. For instance, we were talking of that recent affair of a father who was found guilty on his son's evidence; and she maintained that the son had only done what was right in giving evidence against his father, and that one ought invariably to tell the truth, no matter what might happen. What a terrible public prosecutor she would make, eh?"

Thereupon Marie, exasperated by Pierre's smile, which seemingly indicated that he also thought her in the wrong, flew into quite a passion: "You are cruel, Guillaume!" she cried; "I won't be laughed at like this."

"But you are losing your senses, my dear," exclaimed Francois, while Thomas and Antoine again grew merry. "We were only urging a question of humanity, father and I, for we respect and love justice as much as you do."

"There's no question of humanity, but simply one of justice. What is just and right is just and right, and you cannot alter it."

Then, as Guillaume made a further attempt to state his views and win her over to them, she rose trembling, in such a passion that she could scarcely stammer: "No, no, you are all too cruel, you only want to grieve me. I prefer to go up into my own room."

At this Mere-Grand vainly sought to restrain her. "My child, my child!" said she, "reflect a moment; this is very wrong, you will deeply regret it."

"No, no; you are not just, and I suffer too much."

Then she wildly rushed upstairs to her room overhead.

Consternation followed. Scenes of a similar character had occasionally occurred before, but there had never been so serious a one. Guillaume immediately admitted that he had done wrong in laughing at her, for she could not bear irony. Then he told Pierre that in her childhood and youth she had been subject to terrible attacks of passion whenever she witnessed or heard of any act of injustice. As she herself explained, these attacks would come upon her with irresistible force, transporting her to such a point that she would sometimes fall upon the floor and rave. Even nowadays she proved quarrelsome and obstinate whenever certain subjects were touched upon. And she afterwards blushed for it all, fully conscious that others must think her unbearable.

Indeed, a quarter of an hour later, she came downstairs again of her own accord, and bravely acknowledged her fault. "Wasn't it ridiculous of me?" she said. "To think I accuse others of being unkind when I behave like that! Monsieur l'Abbe must have a very bad opinion of me." Then, after kissing Mere-Grand, she added: "You'll forgive me, won't you? Oh! Francois may laugh now, and so may Thomas and Antoine. They are quite right, our differences are merely laughing matters."

"My poor Marie," replied Guillaume, in a tone of deep affection. "You see what it is to surrender oneself to the absolute. If you are so healthy and reasonable it's because you regard almost everything from the relative point of view, and only ask life for such gifts as it can bestow. But when your absolute ideas of justice come upon you, you lose both equilibrium and reason. At the same time, I must say that we are all liable to err in much the same manner."

Marie, who was still very flushed, thereupon answered in a jesting way: "Well, it at least proves that I'm not perfect."

"Oh, certainly! And so much the better," said Guillaume, "for it makes me love you the more."

This was a sentiment which Pierre himself would willingly have re-echoed. The scene had deeply stirred him. Had not his own frightful torments originated with his desire for the absolute both in things and beings? He had sought faith in its entirety, and despair had thrown him into complete negation. Again, was there not some evil desire for the absolute and some affectation of pride and voluntary blindness in the haughty bearing which he had retained amidst the downfall of his belief, the saintly reputation which he had accepted when he possessed no faith at all? On hearing his brother praise Marie, because she only asked life for such things as it could give, it had seemed to him that this was advice for himself. It was as if a refreshing breath of nature had passed before his face. At the same time his feelings in this respect were still vague, and the only well-defined pleasure that he experienced came from the young woman's fit of anger, that error of hers which brought her nearer to him, by lowering her in some degree from her pedestal of serene perfection. It was, perhaps, that seeming perfection which had made him suffer; however, he was as yet unable to analyse his feelings. That day, for the first time, he chatted with her for a little while, and when he went off he thought her very good-hearted and very human.

Two days later he again came to spend the afternoon in the large sunlit work-shop overlooking Paris. Ever since he had become conscious of the idle life he was leading, he had felt very bored when he was alone, and only found relief among that gay, hardworking family. His brother scolded him for not having come to *dejeuner*, and he promised to do so on the morrow. By the time a week had elapsed, none of the discomfort and covert hostility which had prevailed between him and Marie remained: they met and chatted on a footing of good fellowship. Although he was a priest, she was in no wise embarrassed by his presence. With her quiet atheism, indeed, she had never imagined that a priest could be different from other men. Thus her sisterly cordiality both astonished and delighted Pierre. It was as if he wore the same garments and held the same ideas as his big nephews, as if there were nothing whatever to distinguish him from other men. He was still more surprised, however, by Marie's silence on all religious questions. She seemed to live on quietly and happily, without a thought of what might be beyond life, that terrifying realm of mystery, which to him had brought such agony of mind.

Now that he came every two or three days to Montmartre she noticed that he was suffering. What could be the matter with him, she wondered. When she questioned him in a friendly manner and only elicited evasive replies, she guessed that he was ashamed of his sufferings, and that they were aggravated, rendered well-nigh incurable, by the very secrecy in which he buried them. Thereupon womanly compassion awoke within her, and she felt increasing affection for that tall, pale fellow with feverish eyes, who was consumed by grievous torments which he would confess to none. No doubt she questioned Guillaume respecting her brother's sadness, and he must have confided some of the truth to her in order that she might help him to extricate Pierre from his sufferings, and give him back some taste for life. The poor fellow always seemed so happy when she treated him like a friend, a brother!

At last, one evening, on seeing his eyes full of tears as he gazed upon the dismal twilight falling over Paris, she herself pressed him to confide his trouble to her. And thereupon he suddenly spoke out, confessing all his torture and the horrible void which the loss of faith had left within him. Ah! to be unable to believe, to be unable to love, to be nothing but ashes, to know of nothing certain by which he might replace the faith that had fled from him! She listened in stupefaction. Why, he must be mad! And she plainly told him so, such was her astonishment and revolt at hearing such a desperate cry of wretchedness. To despair, indeed, and believe in nothing and love nothing, simply because a religious hypothesis had crumbled! And this, too, when the whole, vast world was spread before one, life with the duty of living it, creatures and things to be loved and succoured, without counting the universal labour, the task which one and all came to accomplish! Assuredly he must be mad, mad with the gloomiest madness; still she vowed she would cure him.

From that time forward she felt the most compassionate affection for this extraordinary young man, who had first embarrassed and afterwards astonished her. She showed herself very gentle and gay with him; she looked after him with the greatest skill and delicacy of heart and mind. There had been certain similar features in their childhood; each had been reared in the strictest religious views by a pious mother. But afterwards how different had been their fates! Whilst he was struggling with his doubts, bound by his priestly vows, she had grown up at the Lycee Fenelon, where her father had placed her as soon as her mother died; and there, far removed from all practice of religion, she had gradually reached total forgetfulness of her early religious views. It was a constant source of surprise for him to find that she had thus escaped all distress of mind at the thought of what might come after death, whereas that same thought had so deeply tortured him. When they chatted together and he expressed his astonishment at it, she frankly laughed, saying that she had never felt any fear of hell, for she was certain that no hell existed. And she added that she lived in all quietude, without hope of going to any heaven, her one thought being to comply in a reasonable way with the requirements and necessities of earthly life. It was, perhaps, in some measure a matter of temperament with her; but it was also a matter of education. Yet, whatever that education had been, whatever knowledge she had acquired, she had remained very womanly and very loving. There was nothing stern or masculine about her.

"Ah, my friend," she said one day to Pierre, "if you only knew how easy it is for me to remain happy so long as I see those I love free from any excessive suffering. For my own part I can always adapt myself to life. I work and content myself no matter what may happen. Sorrow has only come to me from others, for I can't help wishing that everybody should be fairly happy, and there are some who won't.... I was for a long time very poor, but I remained gay. I wish for nothing, except for things that can't be purchased. Still, want is the great abomination which distresses me. I can understand that you should have felt everything crumbling when charity appeared to you so insufficient a remedy as to be contemptible. Yet it does bring relief; and, moreover, it is so sweet to be able to give. Some day, too, by dint of reason and toil, by the good and efficient working of life itself, the reign of justice will surely come. But now it's I that am preaching! Oh! I have little taste for it! It would be ridiculous for me to try to heal you with big phrases. All the same, I should like to cure you of your gloomy sufferings. To do so, all that I ask of you is to spend as much time as you can with us. You know that this is Guillaume's greatest desire. We will all love you so well, you will see us all so affectionately united, and so gay over our common work, that you will come back to truth by joining us in the school of our good mother nature. You must live and work, and love and hope."

Pierre smiled as he listened. He now came to Montmartre nearly every day. She was so nice and affectionate when she preached to him in that way with a pretty assumption of wisdom. As she had said too, life was so delightful in that big workroom; it was so pleasant to be all together, and to labour in common at the same work of health and truth. Ashamed as Pierre was of doing nothing, anxious as he was to occupy his mind and fingers, he had first taken an interest in Antoine's engraving, asking why he should not try something of the kind himself. However, he felt that he lacked the necessary gift for art. Then, too, he recoiled from Francois' purely intellectual labour, for he himself had scarcely emerged from the harrowing study of conflicting texts. Thus he was more inclined for manual toil like that of Thomas. In mechanics he found precision and clearness such as might help to quench his thirst for certainty. So he placed himself at the young man's orders, pulled his bellows and held pieces of mechanism for him. He also sometimes served as assistant to Guillaume, tying a large blue apron over his cassock in order to help in the experiments. From that time he formed part of the work-shop, which simply counted a worker the more.

One afternoon early in April, when they were all busily engaged there, Marie, who sat embroidering at the table in front of Mere-Grand, raised her eyes to the window and suddenly burst into a cry of admiration: "Oh! look at Paris under that rain of sunlight!"

Pierre drew near; the play of light was much the same as that which he had witnessed at his first visit. The sun, sinking behind some slight purple clouds, was throwing down a hail of rays and sparks which on all sides rebounded and leapt over the endless stretch of roofs. It might have been thought that some great sower, hidden amidst the glory of the planet, was scattering handfuls of golden grain from one horizon to the other.

Pierre, at sight of it, put his fancy into words: "It is the sun sowing Paris with grain for a future harvest," said he. "See how the expanse looks like ploughed land; the brownish houses are like soil turned up, and the streets are deep and straight like furrows."

"Yes, yes, that's true," exclaimed Marie gaily. "The sun is sowing Paris with grain. See how it casts the seed of light and health right away to the distant suburbs! And yet, how singular! The rich districts on the west seem steeped in a ruddy mist, whilst the good seed falls in golden dust over the left bank and the populous districts eastward. It is there, is it not, that the crop will spring up?"

They had all drawn near, and were smiling at the symbol. As Marie had said, it seemed indeed that while the sun slowly sank behind the lacework of clouds, the sower of eternal life scattered his flaming seed with a rhythmical swing of the arm, ever selecting the districts of toil and effort. One dazzling handful of grain fell over yonder on the district of the schools; and then yet another rained down to fertilise the district of the factories and work-shops.

"Ah! well," said Guillaume gaily. "May the crop soon sprout from the good ground of our great Paris, which has been turned up by so many revolutions, and enriched by the blood of so many workers! It is the only ground in the world where Ideas can germinate and bloom. Yes, yes, Pierre is quite right, it is the sun sowing Paris with the seed of the future world, which can sprout only up here!"

Then Thomas, Francois and Antoine, who stood behind their father in a row, nodded as if to say that this was also their own conviction; whilst Mere-Grand gazed afar with dreamy eyes as though she could already behold the splendid future.

"Ah! but it is only a dream; centuries must elapse. We shall never see it!" murmured Pierre with a quiver.

"But others will!" cried Marie. "And does not that suffice?"

Those lofty words stirred Pierre to the depths of his being. And all at once there came to him the memory of another Marie[1]—the adorable Marie of his youth, that Marie de Guersaint who had been cured at Lourdes, and the loss of whom had left such a void in his heart. Was that new Marie who stood there smiling at him, so tranquil and so charming in her strength, destined to heal that old-time wound? He felt that he was beginning to live again since she had become his friend.

Meantime, there before them, the glorious sun, with the sweep of its rays, was scattering living golden dust over Paris, still and ever sowing the great future harvest of justice and of truth.

[1] The heroine of M. Zola's "Lourdes."

II. TOWARDS LIFE

ONE evening, at the close of a good day's work, Pierre, who was helping Thomas, suddenly caught his foot in the skirt of his cassock and narrowly escaped falling. At this, Marie, after raising a faint cry of anxiety, exclaimed: "Why don't you take it off?"

There was no malice in her inquiry. She simply looked upon the priestly robe as something too heavy and cumbersome, particularly when one had certain work to perform. Nevertheless, her words deeply impressed Pierre, and he could not forget them. When he was at home in the evening and repeated them to himself they gradually threw him into feverish agitation. Why, indeed, had he not divested himself of that cassock, which weighed so heavily and painfully on his shoulders? Then a frightful struggle began within him, and he spent a terrible, sleepless night, again a prey to all his former torments.

At first sight it seemed a very simple matter that he should cast his priestly gown aside, for had he not ceased to discharge any priestly office? He had not said mass for some time past, and this surely meant renunciation of the priesthood. Nevertheless, so long as he retained his gown it was possible that he might some day say mass again, whereas if he cast it aside he would, as it were, strip himself, quit the priesthood entirely, without possibility of return. It was a terrible step to take, one that would prove irrevocable; and thus he paced his room for hours, in great anguish of mind.

He had formerly indulged in a superb dream. Whilst believing nothing himself he had resolved to watch, in all loyalty, over the belief of others. He would not so lower himself as to forswear his vows, he would be no base renegade, but however great the torments of the void he felt within him he would remain the minister of man's illusions respecting the Divinity. And it was by reason of his conduct in this respect that he had ended by being venerated as a saint—he who denied everything, who had become a mere empty sepulchre. For a long time his falsehood had never disturbed him, but it now brought him acute suffering. It seemed to him that he would be acting in the vilest manner if he delayed placing his life in accord with his opinions. The thought of it all quite rent his heart.

The question was a very clear one. By what right did he remain the minister of a religion in which he no longer believed? Did not elementary honesty require that he should quit a Church in which he denied the presence of the Divinity? He regarded the dogmas of that Church as puerile errors, and yet he persisted in teaching them as if they were eternal truths. Base work it was, that alarmed his conscience. He vainly sought the feverish glow of charity and martyrdom which had led him to offer himself as a sacrifice, willing to suffer all the torture of doubt and to find his own life lost and ravaged, provided that he might yet afford the relief of hope to the lowly. Truth and nature, no doubt, had already regained too much ascendancy over him for those feelings to return. The thought of such a lying apostolate now wounded him; he no longer had the hypocritical courage to call the Divinity down upon the believers kneeling before him, when he was convinced that the Divinity would not descend. Thus all the past was swept away; there remained nothing of the sublime pastoral part he would once have liked to play, that supreme gift of himself which lay in stubborn adherence to the rules of the Church, and such devotion to faith as to endure in silence the torture of having lost it.

What must Marie think of his prolonged falsehood, he wondered, and thereupon he seemed to hear her words again: "Why not take your cassock off?" His conscience bled as if those words were a stab. What contempt must she not feel for him, she who was so upright, so high-minded? Every scattered blame, every covert criticism directed against his conduct, seemed to find embodiment in her. It now sufficed that she should condemn him, and he at once felt guilty. At the same time she had never voiced her disapproval to him, in all probability because she did not think she had any right to intervene in a struggle of conscience. The superb calmness and healthiness which she displayed still astonished him. He himself was ever haunted and tortured by thoughts of the unknown, of what the morrow of death might have in store for one; but although he had studied and watched her for days together, he had never seen her give a sign of doubt or distress. This exemption from such sufferings as his own was due, said she, to the fact that she gave all her gaiety, all her energy, all her sense of duty, to the task of living, in such wise that life itself proved a sufficiency, and no time was left for mere fancies to terrify and stultify her. Well, then, since she with her air of quiet strength had asked him why he did not take off his cassock, he would take it off—yes, he would divest himself of that robe which seemed to burn and weigh him down.

He fancied himself calmed by this decision, and towards morning threw himself upon his bed; but all at once a stifling sensation, a renewal of his abominable anguish, brought him to his feet again. No, no, he could not divest himself of that gown which clung so tightly to his flesh. His skin would come away with his cloth, his whole being would be lacerated! Is not the mark of priesthood an indelible one, does it not brand the priest for ever, and differentiate him from the flock? Even should he tear off his gown with his skin, he would remain a priest, an object of scandal and shame, awkward and impotent, shut off from the life of other men. And so why tear it off, since he would still and ever remain in prison, and a fruitful life of work in the broad sunlight was no longer within his reach? He, indeed, fancied himself irremediably stricken with impotence. Thus he was unable to come to any decision, and when he returned to Montmartre two days later he had again relapsed into a state of torment.

Feverishness, moreover, had come upon the happy home. Guillaume was becoming more and more annoyed about Salvat's affair, not a day elapsing without the newspapers fanning his irritation. He had at first been deeply touched by the dignified and reticent bearing of Salvat, who had declared that he had no accomplices whatever. Of course the inquiry into the crime was what is called a secret one; but magistrate Amadieu, to whom it had been entrusted, conducted it in a very noisy way. The newspapers, which he in some degree took into his confidence, were full of articles and paragraphs about him and his interviews with the prisoner. Thanks to Salvat's quiet admissions, Amadieu had been able to retrace the history of the crime hour by hour, his only remaining doubts having reference to the nature of the powder which had been employed, and the making of the bomb itself. It might after all be true that Salvat had loaded the bomb at a friend's, as he indeed asserted was the case; but he must be lying when he added that the only explosive used was dynamite, derived from some stolen cartridges, for all the experts now declared that dynamite would never have produced such effects as those which had been witnessed. This, then, was the mysterious point which protracted the investigations. And day by day the newspapers profited by it to circulate the wildest stories under sensational headings, which were specially devised for the purpose of sending up their sales.

It was all the nonsense contained in these stories that fanned Guillaume's irritation. In spite of his contempt for Sagnier he could not keep from buying the "Voix du Peuple." Quivering with indignation, growing more and more exasperated, he was somehow attracted by the mire which he found in that scurrilous journal. Moreover, the other newspapers, including even the "Globe," which was usually so dignified, published all sorts of statements for which no proof could be supplied, and drew from them remarks and conclusions which, though couched in milder language than Sagnier's, were none the less abominably unjust. It seemed indeed as if the whole press had set itself the task of covering Salvat with mud, so as to be able to vilify Anarchism generally. According to the journalists the prisoner's life had simply been one long abomination. He had already earned his living by thievery in his childhood at the time when he had roamed the streets, an unhappy, forsaken vagrant; and later on he had proved a bad soldier and a bad worker. He had been punished for insubordination whilst he was in the army, and he had been dismissed from a dozen work-shops because he incessantly disturbed them by his Anarchical propaganda. Later still, he had fled his country and led a suspicious life of adventure in America, where, it was alleged, he must have committed all sorts of unknown crimes. Moreover there was his horrible immorality, his connection with his sister-in-law, that Madame Theodore who had taken charge of his forsaken child in his absence, and with whom he had cohabited since his return to France. In this wise Salvat's failings and transgressions were pitilessly denounced and magnified without any mention of the causes which had induced them, or of the excuses which lay in the unhappy man's degrading environment. And so Guillaume's feelings of humanity and justice revolted, for he knew the real Salvat,—a man of tender heart and dreamy mind, so liable to be impassioned by fancies,—a man cast into life when a child without weapon of defence, ever trodden down or thrust aside, then gradually exasperated by the perpetual onslaughts of want, and at last dreaming of reviving the golden age by destroying the old, corrupt world.

Unfortunately for Salvat, everything had gone against him since he had been shut up in strict confinement, at the mercy of the ambitious and worldly Amadieu. Guillaume had learnt from his son, Thomas, that the prisoner could count on no support whatever among his former mates at the Grandidier works. These works were becoming prosperous once more, thanks to their steady output of bicycles; and it was said that Grandidier was only waiting for Thomas to perfect his little motor, in order to start the manufacture of motor-cars on a large scale. However, the success which he was now for the first time achieving, and which scarcely repaid him for all his years of toil and battle, had in certain respects rendered him prudent and even severe. He did not wish any suspicion to be cast upon his business through the unpleasant affair of his former workman Salvat, and so he had dismissed such of his workmen as held Anarchist views. If he had kept the two Toussaints, one of whom was the prisoner's brother-in-law, while the other was suspected of sympathy with him, this was because they had belonged to the works for a score of years, and he did not like to cast them adrift. Moreover, Toussaint, the father, had declared that if he were called as a witness for the defence, he should simply give such particulars of Salvat's career as related to the prisoner's marriage with his sister.

One evening when Thomas came home from the works, to which he returned every now and then in order to try his little motor, he related that he had that day seen Madame Grandidier, the poor young woman who had become insane through an attack of puerperal fever following upon the death of a child. Although most frightful attacks of madness occasionally came over her, and although life beside her was extremely painful, even during the intervals when she remained downcast and gentle as a child, her husband had never been willing to send her to an asylum. He kept her with him in a pavilion near the works, and as a rule the shutters of the windows overlooking the yard remained closed. Thus Thomas had been greatly surprised to see one of these windows open, and the young woman appear at it amidst the bright sunshine of that early spring. True, she only remained there for a moment, vision-like, fair and pretty, with smiling face; for a servant who suddenly drew near closed the window, and the pavilion then again sank into lifeless silence. At the same time it was reported among the men employed at the works that the poor creature had not experienced an attack for well-nigh a month past, and that this was the reason why the "governor" looked so strong and pleased, and worked so vigorously to help on the increasing prosperity of his business.

"He isn't a bad fellow," added Thomas, "but with the terrible competition that he has to encounter, he is bent on keeping his men under control. Nowadays, says he, when so many capitalists and wage earners seem bent on exterminating one another, the latter—if they don't want to starve—ought to be well pleased when capital falls into the hands of an active, fair-minded man.... If he shows no pity for Salvat, it is because he really believes in the necessity of an example."

That same day Thomas, after leaving the works and while threading his way through the toilsome hive-like Marcadet district, had overtaken Madame Theodore and little Celine, who were wandering on in great distress. It appeared that they had just called upon Toussaint, who had been unable to lend them even such a trifle as ten sous. Since Salvat's arrest, the woman and the child had been forsaken and suspected by one and all. Driven forth from their wretched lodging, they were without food and wandered hither and thither dependent on chance alms. Never had greater want and misery fallen on defenceless creatures.

"I told them to come up here, father," said Thomas, "for I thought that one might pay their landlord a month's rent, so that they might go home again.... Ah! there's somebody coming now—it's they, no doubt."

Guillaume had felt angry with himself whilst listening to his son, for he had not thought of the poor creatures. It was the old story: the man disappears, and the woman and the child find themselves in the streets, starving. Whenever Justice strikes a man her blow travels beyond him, fells innocent beings and kills them.

Madame Theodore came in, humble and timid, scared like a luckless creature whom life never wearies of persecuting. She was becoming almost blind, and little Celine had to lead her. The girl's fair, thin face wore its wonted expression of shrewd intelligence, and even now, however woeful her rags, it was occasionally brightened by a childish smile.

Pierre and Marie, who were both there, felt extremely touched. Near them was Madame Mathis, young Victor's mother, who had come to help Mere-Grand with the mending of some house-linen. She went out by the day in this fashion among a few families, and was thus enabled to give her son an occasional franc or two. Guillaume alone questioned Madame Theodore.

"Ah! monsieur," she stammered, "who could ever have thought Salvat capable of such a thing, he who's so good and so humane? Still it's true, since he himself has admitted it to the magistrate.... For my part I told everybody that he was in Belgium. I wasn't quite sure of it, still I'm glad that he didn't come back to see us; for if he had been arrested at our place I should have lost my senses.... Well, now that they have him, they'll sentence him to death, that's certain."

At this Celine, who had been looking around her with an air of interest, piteously exclaimed: "Oh! no, oh! no, mamma, they won't hurt him!"

Big tears appeared in the child's eyes as she raised this cry. Guillaume kissed her, and then went on questioning Madame Theodore.

"Well, monsieur," she answered, "the child's not old or big enough to work as yet, and my eyes are done for, people won't even take me as a charwoman. And so it's simple enough, we starve.... Oh! of course I'm not without relations; I have a sister who married very well. Her husband is a clerk, Monsieur Chretiennot, perhaps you know him. Unfortunately he's rather proud, and as I don't want any scenes between him and my sister, I no longer go to see her. Besides, she's in despair just now, for she's expecting another baby, which is a terrible blow for a small household, when one already has two girls.... That's why the only person I can apply to is my brother Toussaint. His wife isn't a bad sort by any means, but she's no longer the same since she's been living in fear of her husband having another attack. The first one carried off all her savings, and what would become of her if Toussaint should remain on her hands, paralysed? Besides, she's threatened with another burden, for, as you may know, her son Charles got keeping company with a servant at a wine shop, who of course ran away after she had a baby, which she left him to see to. So one can understand that the Toussaints themselves are hard put. I don't complain of them. They've already lent me a little money, and of course they can't go on lending for ever."

She continued talking in this spiritless, resigned way, complaining only on account of Celine; for, said she, it was enough to make one's heart break to see such an intelligent child obliged to tramp the streets after getting on so well at the Communal School. She could feel too that everybody now kept aloof from them on account of Salvat. The Toussaints didn't want to be compromised in any such business. There was only Charles, who had said that he could well understand a man losing his head and trying to blow up the *bourgeois*, because they really treated the workers in a blackguard way.

"For my part, monsieur," added Madame Theodore, "I say nothing, for I'm only a woman. All the same, though, if you'd like to know what I think, well, I think that it would have been better if Salvat hadn't done what he did, for we two, the girl and I, are the real ones to suffer from it. Ah! I can't get the idea into my head, that the little one should be the daughter of a man condemned to death."

Once more Celine interrupted her, flinging her arms around her neck: "Oh! mamma, oh! mamma, don't say that, I beg you! It can't be true, it grieves me too much!"

At this Pierre and Marie exchanged compassionate glances, while Mere-Grand rose from her chair, in order to go upstairs and search her wardrobes for some articles of clothing which might be of use to the two poor creatures. Guillaume, who, for his part, had been moved to tears, and felt full of revolt against the social system which rendered such distress possible, slipped some alms into the child's little hand, and promised Madame Theodore that he would see her landlord so as to get her back her room.

"Ah! Monsieur Froment!" replied the unfortunate woman. "Salvat was quite right when he said you were a real good man! And as you employed him here for a few days you know too that he isn't a wicked one.... Now that he's been put in prison everybody calls him a brigand, and it breaks my heart to hear them." Then, turning towards Madame Mathis, who had continued sewing in discreet silence, like a respectable woman whom none of these things could concern, she went on: "I know you, madame, but I'm better acquainted with your son, Monsieur Victor, who has often come to chat at our place. Oh! you needn't be afraid, I shan't say it, I shall never compromise anybody; but if Monsieur Victor were free to speak, he'd be the man to explain Salvat's ideas properly."

Madame Mathis looked at her in stupefaction. Ignorant as she was of her son's real life and views, she experienced a vague dread at the idea of any connection between him and Salvat's family. Moreover, she refused to believe it possible. "Oh! you must be mistaken," she said. "Victor told me that he now seldom came to Montmartre, as he was always going about in search of work."

By the anxious quiver of the widow's voice, Madame Theodore understood that she ought not to have mixed her up in her troubles; and so in all humility she at once beat a retreat: "I beg your pardon, madame, I didn't think I should hurt your feelings. Perhaps, too, I'm mistaken, as you say."

Madame Mathis had again turned to her sewing as to the solitude in which she lived, that nook of decent misery where she dwelt without companionship and almost unknown, with scarcely sufficient bread to eat. Ah! that dear son of hers, whom she loved so well; however much he might neglect her, she had placed her only remaining hope in him: he was her last dream, and would some day lavish all kinds of happiness upon her!

At that moment Mere-Grand came downstairs again, laden with a bundle of linen and woollen clothing, and Madame Theodore and little Celine withdrew while pouring forth their thanks. For a long time after they had gone Guillaume, unable to resume work, continued walking to and fro in silence, with a frown upon his face.

When Pierre, still hesitating and still tortured by conflicting feelings, returned to Montmartre on the following day he witnessed with much surprise a visit of a very different kind. There was a sudden gust of wind, a whirl of skirts and a ring of laughter as little Princess Rosemonde swept in, followed by young Hyacinthe Duvillard, who, on his side, retained a very frigid bearing.

"It's I, my dear master," exclaimed the Princess. "I promised you a visit, you remember, for I am such a great admirer of your genius. And our young friend here has been kind enough to bring me. We have only just returned from Norway, and my very first visit is for you."

She turned as she spoke, and bowed in an easy and gracious way to Pierre and Marie, Francois and Antoine, who were also there. Then she resumed: "Oh! my dear master, you have no idea how beautifully virginal Norway is! We all ought to go and drink at that new source of the Ideal, and we should return purified, rejuvenated and capable of great renunciations!"

As a matter of fact she had been well-nigh bored to death there. To make one's honeymoon journey to the land of the ice and snow, instead of to Italy, the hot land of the sun, was doubtless a very refined idea, which showed that no base materialism formed part of one's affections. It was the soul alone that travelled, and naturally it was fit that only kisses of the soul should be exchanged on the journey. Unfortunately, however, Hyacinthe had carried his symbolism so far as to exasperate Rosemonde, and on one occasion they had come to blows over it, and then to tears when this lover's quarrel had ended as many such quarrels do. Briefly, they had no longer deemed themselves pure enough for the companionship of the swans and the lakes of dreamland, and had therefore taken the first steamer that was sailing for France.

As it was altogether unnecessary to confess to everybody what a failure their journey had proved, the Princess abruptly brought her rapturous references to Norway to an end, and then explained: "By the way, do you know what I found awaiting me on my return? Why, I found my house pillaged, oh! completely pillaged! And in such a filthy condition, too! We at once recognised the mark of the beast, and thought of Bergaz's young friends."

Already on the previous day Guillaume had read in the newspapers that a band of young Anarchists had entered the Princess's little house by breaking a basement window. She had left it quite deserted, unprotected even by a caretaker; and the robbers had not merely removed everything from the premises—including even the larger articles of furniture, but had lived there for a couple of days, bringing provisions in from outside, drinking all the wine in the cellars, and leaving every room in a most filthy and disgusting condition. On discovering all this, Rosemonde had immediately remembered the evening she had spent at the Chamber of Horrors in the company of Bergaz and his acolytes, Rossi and Sanfaute, who had heard her speak of her intended trip to Norway. The two young men had therefore been arrested, but Bergaz had so far escaped. The Princess was not greatly astonished by it all, for she had already been warned of the presence of dangerous characters among the mixed cosmopolitan set with which she associated. Janzen had told her in confidence of a number of villanous affairs which were attributed to Bergaz and his band. And now the Anarchist leader openly declared that Bergaz had sold himself to the police like Raphanel; and that the burglary at the Princess's residence had been planned by the police officials, who thereby hoped to cover the Anarchist cause with mire. If proof was wanted of this, added Janzen, it could be found in the fact that the police had allowed Bergaz to escape.

II. TOWARDS LIFE

"I fancied that the newspapers might have exaggerated matters," said Guillaume, when the Princess had finished her story. "They are inventing such abominable things just now, in order to blacken the case of that poor devil Salvat."

"Oh! they've exaggerated nothing!" Rosemonde gaily rejoined. "As a matter of fact they have omitted a number of particulars which were too filthy for publication.... For my part, I've merely had to go to an hotel. I'm very comfortable there; I was beginning to feel bored in that house of mine.... All the same, however, Anarchism is hardly a clean business, and I no longer like to say that I have any connection with it."

She again laughed, and then passed to another subject, asking Guillaume to tell her of his most recent researches, in order, no doubt, that she might show she knew enough chemistry to understand him. He had been rendered thoughtful, however, by the story of Bergaz and the burglary, and would only answer her in a general way.

Meantime, Hyacinthe was renewing his acquaintance with his school-fellows, Francois and Antoine. He had accompanied the Princess to Montmartre against his own inclinations; but since she had taken to whipping him he had become afraid of her. The chemist's little home filled him with disdain, particularly as the chemist was a man of questionable reputation. Moreover, he thought it a duty to insist on his own superiority in the presence of those old school-fellows of his, whom he found toiling away in the common rut, like other people.

"Ah! yes," said he to Francois, who was taking notes from a book spread open before him, "you are at the Ecole Normale, I believe, and are preparing for your licentiate. Well, for my part, you know, the idea of being tied to anything horrifies me. I become quite stupid when there's any question of examination or competition. The only possible road for one to follow is that of the Infinite. And between ourselves what dupery there is in science, how it narrows our horizon! It's just as well to remain a child with eyes gazing into the invisible. A child knows more than all your learned men."

Francois, who occasionally indulged in irony, pretended to share his opinion. "No doubt, no doubt," said he, "but one must have a natural disposition to remain a child. For my part, unhappily, I'm consumed by a desire to learn and know. It's deplorable, as I'm well aware, but I pass my days racking my brain over books.... I shall never know very much, that's certain; and perhaps that's the reason why I'm ever striving to learn a little more. You must at all events grant that work, like idleness, is a means of passing life, though of course it is a less elegant and aesthetic one."

"Less aesthetic, precisely," rejoined Hyacinthe. "Beauty lies solely in the unexpressed, and life is simply degraded when one introduces anything material into it."

Simpleton though he was in spite of the enormity of his pretensions, he doubtless detected that Francois had been speaking ironically. So he turned to Antoine, who had remained seated in front of a block he was engraving. It was the one which represented Lise reading in her garden, for he was ever taking it in hand again and touching it up in his desire to emphasise his indication of the girl's awakening to intelligence and life.

"So you engrave, I see," said Hyacinthe. "Well, since I renounced versification—a little poem I had begun on the End of Woman—because words seemed to me so gross and cumbersome, mere paving-stones as it were, fit for labourers, I myself have had some idea of trying drawing, and perhaps engraving too. But what drawing can portray the mystery which lies beyond life, the only sphere that has any real existence and importance for us? With what pencil and on what kind of plate could one depict it? We should need something impalpable, something unheard of, which would merely suggest the essence of things and beings."

"But it's only by material means," Antoine somewhat roughly replied, "that art can render the essence of things and beings, that is, their full significance as we understand it. To transcribe life is my great passion; and briefly life is the only mystery that there is in things and beings. When it seems to me that an engraving of mine lives, I'm well pleased, for I feel that I have created."

Hyacinthe pouted by way of expressing his contempt of all fruitfulness. Any fool might beget offspring. It was the sexless idea, existing by itself, that was rare and exquisite. He tried to explain this, but became confused, and fell back on the conviction which he had brought back from Norway, that literature and art were done for in France, killed by baseness and excess of production.

"It's evident!" said Francois gaily by way of conclusion. "To do nothing already shows that one has some talent!"

Meantime, Pierre and Marie listened and gazed around them, somewhat embarrassed by this strange visit which had set the usually grave and peaceful workroom topsy-turvy. The little Princess, though, evinced much amiability, and on drawing near to Marie admired the wonderful delicacy of some embroidery she was finishing. Before leaving, moreover, Rosemonde insisted upon Guillaume inscribing his autograph in an album which Hyacinthe had to fetch from her carriage. The young man obeyed her with evident boredom. It could be seen that they were already weary of one another. Pending a fresh caprice, however, it amused Rosemonde to terrorize her sorry victim. When she at length led him away, after declaring to Guillaume that she should always regard that visit as a memorable incident in her life, she made the whole household smile by saying: "Oh! so your sons knew Hyacinthe at college. He's a good-natured little fellow, isn't he? and he would really be quite nice if he would only behave like other people."

That same day Janzen and Bache came to spend the evening with Guillaume. Once a week they now met at Montmartre, as they had formerly done at Neuilly. Pierre, on these occasions, went home very late, for as soon as Mere-Grand, Marie, and Guillaume's sons had retired for the night, there were endless chats in the workroom, whence Paris could be seen spangled with thousands of gas lights. Another visitor at these times was Theophile Morin, but he did not arrive before ten o'clock, as he was detained by the work of correcting his pupils' exercises or some other wearisome labour pertaining to his profession.

As soon as Guillaume had told the others of the Princess's visit that afternoon, Janzen hastily exclaimed: "But she's mad, you know. When I first met her I thought for a moment that I might perhaps utilise her for the cause. She seemed so thoroughly convinced and bold! But I soon found that she was the craziest of women, and simply hungered for new emotions!"

Janzen was at last emerging from his wonted frigidity and mysteriousness. His cheeks were quite flushed. In all probability he had suffered from his rupture with the woman whom he had once called 'the Queen of the Anarchists,' and whose fortune and extensive circle of acquaintance had seemed to him such powerful weapons of propaganda.

"You know," said he, when he had calmed down, "it was the police who had her house pillaged and turned into a pigstye. Yes, in view of Salvat's trial, which is now near at hand, the idea was to damn Anarchism beyond possibility of even the faintest sympathy on the part of the *bourgeois*."

"Yes, she told me so," replied Guillaume, who had become attentive. "But I scarcely credit the story. If Bergaz had merely acted under such influence as you suggest, he would have been arrested with the others, just as Raphanel was taken with those whom he betrayed. Besides, I know something of Bergaz; he's a freebooter." Guillaume made a sorrowful gesture, and then in a saddened voice continued: "Oh, I can understand all claims and all legitimate reprisals. But theft, cynical theft for the purpose of profit and enjoyment, is beyond me! It lowers my hope of a better and more equitable form of society. Yes, that burglary at the Princess's house has greatly distressed me."

An enigmatical smile, sharp like a knife, again played over Janzen's lips. "Oh! it's a matter of heredity with you!" said he. "The centuries of education and belief that lie behind you compel you to protest. All the same, however, when people won't make restoration, things must be taken from them. What worries me is that Bergaz should have sold himself just now. The public prosecutor will use that farcical burglary as a crushing argument when he asks the jury for Salvat's head."

Such was Janzen's hatred of the police that he stubbornly clung to his version of the affair. Perhaps, too, he had quarrelled with Bergaz, with whom he had at one time freely associated.

Guillaume, who understood that all discussion would be useless, contented himself with replying: "Ah! yes, Salvat! Everything is against that unhappy fellow, he is certain to be condemned. But you can't know, my friends, what a passion that affair of his puts me into. All my ideas of truth and justice revolt at the thought of it. He's a madman certainly; but there are so many excuses to be urged for him. At bottom he is simply a martyr who has followed the wrong track. And yet he has become the scapegoat, laden with the crimes of the whole nation, condemned to pay for one and all!"

Bache and Morin nodded without replying. They both professed horror of Anarchism; while Morin, forgetting that the word if not the thing dated from his first master Proudhon, clung to his Comtist doctrines, in the conviction that science alone would ensure the happiness and pacification of the nations. Bache, for his part, old mystical humanitarian that he was, claimed that the only solution would come from Fourier, who by decreeing an alliance of talent, labour and capital, had mapped out the future in a decisive manner. Nevertheless, both Bache and Morin were so discontented with the slow-paced *bourgeoise* Republic of the present day, and so hurt by the thought that everything was going from bad to worse through the flouting of their own particular ideas, that they were quite willing to wax indignant at the manner in which the conflicting parties of the time were striving to make use of Salvat in order to retain or acquire power.

"When one thinks," said Bache, "that this ministerial crisis of theirs has now been lasting for nearly three weeks! Every appetite is openly displayed, it's a most disgusting sight! Did you see in the papers this morning that the President has again been obliged to summon Vignon to the Elysee?"

"Oh! the papers," muttered Morin in his weary way, "I no longer read them! What's the use of doing so? They are so badly written, and they all lie!"

As Bache had said, the ministerial crisis was still dragging on. The President of the Republic, taking as his guide the debate in the Chamber of Deputies, by which the Barroux administration had been overthrown, had very properly sent for Vignon, the victor on that occasion, and entrusted him with the formation of a new ministry. It had seemed that this would be an easy task, susceptible of accomplishment in two or three days at the utmost, for the names of the friends whom the young leader of the Radical party would bring to power with him had been freely mentioned for months past. But all sorts of difficulties had suddenly arisen. For ten days or so Vignon had struggled on amidst inextricable obstacles. Then, disheartened and disgusted, fearing, too, that he might use himself up and shut off the future if he persisted in his endeavours, he had been obliged to tell the President that he renounced the task. Forthwith the President had summoned other deputies, and questioned them until he had found one brave enough to make an attempt on his own account; whereupon incidents similar to those which had marked Vignon's endeavours had once more occurred. At the outset a list was drawn up with every prospect of being ratified within a few hours, but all at once hesitation arose, some pulled one way, some another; every effort was slowly paralysed till absolute failure resulted. It seemed as though the mysterious manoeuvres which had hampered Vignon had begun again; it was as if some band of invisible plotters was, for some unknown purpose, doing its utmost to wreck every combination. A thousand hindrances arose with increasing force from every side—jealousy, dislike, and even betrayal were secretly prompted by expert agents, who employed every form of pressure, whether threats or promises, besides fanning and casting rival passions and interests into collision. Thus the President, greatly embarrassed by this posture of affairs, had again found it necessary to summon Vignon, who, after reflection and negotiation, now had an almost complete list in his pocket, and seemed likely to perfect a new administration within the next forty-eight hours.

"Still it isn't settled," resumed Bache. "Well-informed people assert that Vignon will fail again as he did the first time. For my part I can't get rid of the idea that Duvillard's gang is pulling the strings, though for whose benefit is a mystery. You may be quite sure, however, that its chief purpose is to stifle the African Railways affair. If Monferrand were not so badly compromised I should almost suspect some trick on his part. Have you noticed that the 'Globe,' after throwing Barroux overboard in all haste, now refers to Monferrand every day with the most respectful sympathy? That's a grave sign; for it isn't Fonsegue's habit to show any solicitude for the vanquished. But what can one expect from that wretched Chamber! The only point certain is that something dirty is being plotted there."

"And that big dunderhead Mege who works for every party except his own!" exclaimed Morin; "what a dupe he is with that idea that he need merely overthrow first one cabinet and then another, in order to become the leader of one himself!"

The mention of Mege brought them all to agreement, for they unanimously hated him. Bache, although his views coincided on many points with those of the apostle of State Collectivism, judged each of his speeches, each of his actions, with pitiless severity. Janzen, for his part, treated the Collectivist leader as a mere reactionary *bourgeois*, who ought to be swept away one of the first. This hatred of Mege was indeed the common passion of Guillaume's friends. They could occasionally show some justice for men who in no wise shared their ideas; but in their estimation it was an unpardonable crime for anybody to hold much the same views as themselves, without being absolutely in agreement with them on every possible point.

Their discussion continued, their various theories mingling or clashing till they passed from politics to the press, and grew excited over the denunciations which poured each morning from Sagnier's newspaper, like filth from the mouth of a sewer. Thereupon Guillaume, who had become absorbed in reverie while pacing to and fro according to his habit, suddenly exclaimed: "Ah! what dirty work it is that Sagnier does! Before long there won't be a single person, a single thing left on which he hasn't vomited! You think he's on your side, and suddenly he splashes you with mire!... By the way, he related yesterday that skeleton keys and stolen purses were found on Salvat when he was arrested in the Bois de Boulogne! It's always Salvat! He's the inexhaustible subject for articles. The mere mention of him suffices to send up a paper's sales! The bribe-takers of the African Railways shout 'Salvat!' to create a diversion. And the battles which wreck ministers are waged round his name. One and all set upon him and make use of him and beat him down!"

With that cry of revolt and compassion, the friends separated for the night. Pierre, who sat near the open window, overlooking the sparkling immensity of Paris, had listened to the others without speaking a word. He had once more been mastered by his doubts, the terrible struggle of his heart and mind; and no solution, no appeasement had come to him from all the contradictory views he had heard—the views of men who only united in predicting the disappearance of the old world, and could make no joint brotherly effort to rear the future world of truth and justice. In that vast city of Paris stretching below him, spangled with stars, glittering like the sky of a summer's night, Pierre also found a great enigma. It was like chaos, like a dim expanse of ashes dotted with sparks whence the coming aurora would arise. What future was being forged there, he wondered, what decisive word of salvation and happiness would come with the dawn, and wing its flight to every point of the horizon?

When Pierre, in his turn, was about to retire, Guillaume laid his hands upon his shoulders, and with much emotion gave him a long look. "Ah! my poor fellow," said he, "you've been suffering too for some days past, I have noticed it. But you are the master of your sufferings, for the struggle you have to overcome is simply in yourself, and you can subdue it; whereas one cannot subdue the world, when it is the world, its cruelty and injustice that make one suffer! Good night, be brave, act as your reason tells you, even if it makes you weep, and you will find peace surely enough."

Later on, when Pierre again found himself alone in his little house at Neuilly, where none now visited him save the shades of his father and mother, he was long kept awake by a supreme internal combat. He had never before felt so disgusted with the falsehood of his life, that cassock which he had persisted in wearing, though he was a priest in name only. Perhaps it was all that he had beheld and heard at his brother's, the want and wretchedness of some, the wild, futile agitation of others, the need of improvement among mankind which remained paramount amidst every contradiction and form of weakness, that had made him more deeply conscious of the necessity of living in loyal and normal fashion in the broad daylight. He could no longer think of his former dream of leading the solitary life of a saintly priest when he was nothing of the kind, without a shiver of shame at having lied so long. And now it was quite decided, he would lie no longer, not even from feelings of compassion in order that others might retain their religious illusions. And yet how painful it was to have to divest himself of that gown which seemed to cling to his skin, and how heartrending the thought that if he did remove it he would be skinless, lacerated, infirm, unable, do what he might, to become like other men!

It was this recurring thought which again tortured him throughout that terrible night. Would life yet allow him to enter its fold? Had he not been branded with a mark which for ever condemned him to dwell apart? He thought he could feel his priestly vows burning his very flesh like red-hot iron. What use would it be for him to dress as men dress, if in reality he was never to be a man? He had hitherto lived in such a quivering state, in a sphere of renunciation and dreams! To know manhood never, to be too late for it, that thought filled him with terror. And when at last he made up his mind to fling aside his cassock, he did so from a simple sense of rectitude, for all his anguish remained.

When he returned to Montmartre on the following day, he wore a jacket and trousers of a dark colour. Neither an exclamation nor a glance that might have embarrassed him came from Mere-Grand or the three young men. Was not the change a natural one? They greeted him therefore in the quiet way that was usual with them; perhaps, with some increase of affection, as if to set him the more at his ease. Guillaume, however, ventured to smile good-naturedly. In that change he detected his own work. Cure was coming, as he had hoped it would come, by him and in his own home, amid the full sunlight, the life which ever streamed in through yonder window.

Marie, who on her side raised her eyes and looked at Pierre, knew nothing of the sufferings which he had endured through her simple and logical inquiry: "Why not take your cassock off?" She merely felt that by removing it he would be more at ease for his work.

"Oh, Pierre, just come and look!" she suddenly exclaimed. "I have been amusing myself with watching all the smoke which the wind is laying yonder over Paris. One might take it to be a huge fleet of ships shining in the sunlight. Yes, yes, golden ships, thousands of golden ships, setting forth from the ocean of Paris to enlighten and pacify the world!"

III. THE DAWN OF LOVE

A COUPLE of days afterwards, when Pierre was already growing accustomed to his new attire, and no longer gave it a thought, it so happened that on reaching Montmartre he encountered Abbe Rose outside the basilica of the Sacred Heart. The old priest, who at first was quite thunderstruck and scarcely able to recognise him, ended by taking hold of his hands and giving him a long look. Then with his eyes full of tears he exclaimed: "Oh! my son, so you have fallen into the awful state I feared! I never mentioned it, but I felt that God had withdrawn from you. Ah! nothing could wound my heart so cruelly as this."

Then, still trembling, he began to lead Pierre away as if to hide such a scandal from the few people who passed by; and at last, his strength failing him, he sank upon a heap of bricks lying on the grass of one of the adjoining work-yards.

The sincere grief which his old and affectionate friend displayed upset Pierre far more than any angry reproaches or curses would have done. Tears had come to his own eyes, so acute was the suffering he experienced at this meeting, which he ought, however, to have foreseen. There was yet another wrenching, and one which made the best of their blood flow, in that rupture between Pierre and the saintly man whose charitable dreams and hopes of salvation he had so long shared. There had been so many divine illusions, so many struggles for the relief of the masses, so much renunciation and forgiveness practised in common between them in their desire to hasten the harvest of the future! And now they were parting; he, Pierre, still young in years, was returning to life, leaving his aged companion to his vain waiting and his dreams.

In his turn, taking hold of Abbe Rose's hands, he gave expression to his sorrow. "Ah, my friend, my father," said he, "it is you alone that I regret losing, now that I am leaving my frightful torments behind. I thought that I was cured of them, but it has been sufficient for me to meet you, and my heart is rent again.... Don't weep for me, I pray you, don't reproach me for what I have done. It was necessary that I should do it. If I had consulted you, you would yourself have told me that it was better to renounce the priesthood than to remain a priest without faith or honour."

"Yes, yes," Abbe Rose gently responded, "you no longer had any faith left. I suspected it. And your rigidity and saintliness of life, in which I detected such great despair, made me anxious for you. How many hours did I not spend at times in striving to calm you! And you must listen to me again, you must still let me save you. I am not a sufficiently learned theologian to lead you back by discussing texts and dogmas; but in the name of Charity, my child, yes, in the name of Charity alone, reflect and take up your task of consolation and hope once more."

Pierre had sat down beside Abbe Rose, in that deserted nook, at the very foot of the basilica. "Charity! charity!" he replied in passionate accents; "why, it is its nothingness and bankruptcy that have killed the priest there was in me. How can you believe that benevolence is sufficient, when you have spent your whole life in practising it without any other result than that of seeing want perpetuated and even increased, and without any possibility of naming the day when such abomination shall cease?... You think of the reward after death, do you not? The justice that is to reign in heaven? But that is not justice, it is dupery—dupery that has brought the world nothing but suffering for centuries past."

Then he reminded the old priest of their life in the Charonne district, when they had gone about together succouring children in the streets and parents in their hovels; the whole of those admirable efforts which, so far as Abbe Rose was concerned, had simply ended in blame from his superiors, and removal from proximity to his poor, under penalty of more severe punishment should he persist in compromising religion by the practice of blind benevolence without reason or object. And now, was he not, so to say, submerged beneath the ever-rising tide of want, aware that he would never, never be able to give enough even should he dispose of millions, and that he could only prolong the agony of the poor, who, even should they eat today, would starve again on the morrow? Thus he was powerless. The wound which he tried to dress and heal, immediately reopened and spread, in such wise that all society would at last be stricken and carried off by it.

Quivering as he listened, and slowly shaking his white head, the old priest ended by replying: "that does that matter, my child? what does that matter? One must give, always give, give in spite of everything! There is no other joy on earth.... If dogmas worry you, content yourself with the Gospel, and even of that retain merely the promise of salvation through charity."

But at this Pierre's feelings revolted. He forgot that he was speaking to one of simple mind, who was all love and nothing else, and could therefore not follow him. "The trial has been made," he answered, "human salvation cannot be effected by charity, nothing but justice can accomplish it. That is the gathering cry which is going up from every nation. For nearly two thousand years now the Gospel has proved a failure. There has been no redemption; the sufferings of mankind are every whit as great and unjust as they were when Jesus came. And thus the Gospel is now but an abolished code, from which society can only draw things that are troublous and hurtful. Men must free themselves from it."

This was his final conviction. How strange the idea, thought he, of choosing as the world's social legislator one who lived, as Jesus lived, amidst a social system absolutely different from that of nowadays. The age was different, the very world was different. And if it were merely a question of retaining only such of the moral teaching of Jesus as seemed human and eternal, was there not again a danger in applying immutable principles to the society of every age? No society could live under the strict law of the Gospel. Was not all order, all labour, all life destroyed by the teaching of Jesus? Did He not deny woman, the earth, eternal nature and the eternal fruitfulness of things and beings? Moreover, Catholicism had reared upon His primitive teaching such a frightful edifice of terror and oppression. The theory of original sin, that terrible heredity reviving with each creature born into the world, made no allowance as Science does for the corrective influences of education, circumstances and environment. There could be no more pessimist conception of man than this one which devotes him to the Devil from the instant of his birth, and pictures him as struggling against himself until the instant of his death. An impossible and absurd struggle, for it is a question of changing man in his entirety, killing the flesh, killing reason, destroying some guilty energy in each and every passion, and of pursuing the Devil to the very depths of the waters, mountains and forests, there to annihilate him with the very sap of the world. If this theory is accepted the world is but sin, a mere Hell of temptation and suffering, through which one must pass in order to merit Heaven. Ah! what an admirable instrument for absolute despotism is that religion of death, which the principle of charity alone has enabled men to tolerate, but which the need of justice will perforce sweep away. The poor man, who is the wretched dupe of it all, no longer believes in Paradise, but requires that each and all should be rewarded according to their deserts upon this earth; and thus eternal life becomes the good goddess, and desire and labour the very laws of the world, while the fruitfulness of woman is again honoured, and the idiotic nightmare of Hell is replaced by glorious Nature whose travail knows no end. Leaning upon modern Science, clear Latin reason sweeps away the ancient Semitic conception of the Gospel.

"For eighteen hundred years," concluded Pierre, "Christianity has been hampering the march of mankind towards truth and justice. And mankind will only resume its evolution on the day when it abolishes Christianity, and places the Gospel among the works of the wise, without taking it any longer as its absolute and final law."

But Abbe Rose raised his trembling hands: "Be quiet, be quiet, my child!" he cried; "you are blaspheming! I knew that doubt distracted you; but I thought you so patient, so able to bear suffering, that I relied on your spirit of renunciation and resignation. What can have happened to make you leave the Church in this abrupt and violent fashion? I no longer recognise you. Sudden passion has sprung up in you, an invincible force seems to carry you away. What is it? Who has changed you, tell me?"

Pierre listened in astonishment. "No," said he, "I assure you, I am such as you have known me, and in all this there is but an inevitable result and finish. Who could have influenced me, since nobody has entered my life? What new feeling could transform me, since I find none in me? I am the same as before, the same assuredly."

Still there was a touch of hesitation in his voice. Was it really true that there had been no change within him? He again questioned himself, and there came no clear answer; decidedly, he would find nothing. It was all but a delightful awakening, an overpowering desire for life, a longing to open his arms widely enough to embrace everyone and everything indeed, a breeze of joy seemed to raise him from the ground and carry him along.

Although Abbe Rose was too innocent of heart to understand things clearly, he again shook his head and thought of the snares which the Devil is ever setting for men. He was quite overwhelmed by Pierre's defection. Continuing his efforts to win him back, he made the mistake of advising him to consult Monseigneur Martha, for he hoped that a prelate of such high authority would find the words necessary to restore him to his faith. Pierre, however, boldly replied that if he was leaving the Church it was partly because it comprised such a man as Martha, such an artisan of deception and despotism, one who turned religion into corrupt diplomacy, and dreamt of winning men back to God by dint of ruses. Thereupon Abbe Rose, rising to his feet, could find no other argument in his despair than that of pointing to the basilica which stood beside them, square, huge and massive, and still waiting for its dome.

"That is God's abode, my child," said he, "the edifice of expiation and triumph, of penitence and forgiveness. You have said mass in it, and now you are leaving it sacrilegiously and forswearing yourself!"

But Pierre also had risen; and buoyed up by a sudden rush of health and strength he answered: "No, no! I am leaving it willingly, as one leaves a dark vault, to return into the open air and the broad sunlight. God does not dwell there; the only purpose of that huge edifice is to defy reason, truth and justice; it has been erected on the highest spot that could be found, like a citadel of error that dominates, insults and threatens Paris!"

Then seeing that the old priest's eyes were again filling with tears, and feeling on his own side so pained by their rupture that he began to sob, Pierre wished to go away. "Farewell! farewell!" he stammered.

But Abbe Rose caught him in his arms and kissed him, as if he were a rebellious son who yet had remained the dearest. "No, not farewell, not farewell, my child," he answered; "say rather till we meet again. Promise me that we shall see each other again, at least among those who starve and weep. It is all very well for you to think that charity has become bankrupt, but shall we not always love one another in loving our poor?"

Then they parted.

On becoming the companion of his three big nephews, Pierre had in a few lessons learnt from them how to ride a bicycle, in order that he might occasionally accompany them on their morning excursions. He went twice with them and Marie along the somewhat roughly paved roads in the direction of the Lake of Enghien. Then one morning when the young woman had promised to take him and Antoine as far as the forest of Saint-Germain, it was found at the last moment that Antoine could not come. Marie was already dressed in a chemisette of fawn-coloured silk, and a little jacket and "rationals" of black serge, and it was such a warm, bright April day that she was not inclined to renounce her trip.

"Well, so much the worse!" she gaily said to Pierre, "I shall take you with me, there will only be the pair of us. I really want you to see how delightful it is to bowl over a good road between the beautiful trees."

However, as Pierre was not yet a very expert rider, they decided that they would take the train as far as Maisons-Laffitte, whence they would proceed on their bicycles to the forest, cross it in the direction of Saint-Germain, and afterwards return to Paris by train.

"You will be here for *dejeuner*, won't you?" asked Guillaume, whom this freak amused, and who looked with a smile at his brother. The latter, like Marie, was in black: jacket, breeches and stockings all of the same hue.

"Oh, certainly!" replied Marie. "It's now barely eight o'clock, so we have plenty of time. Still you need not wait for us, you know, we shall always find our way back."

It was a delightful morning. When they started, Pierre could fancy himself with a friend of his own sex, so that this trip together through the warm sunlight seemed quite natural. Doubtless their costumes, which were so much alike, conduced to the gay brotherly feeling he experienced. But beyond all this there was the healthfulness of the open air, the delight which exercise brings, the pleasure of roaming in all freedom through the midst of nature.

On taking the train they found themselves alone in a compartment, and Marie once more began to talk of her college days. "Ah! you've no idea," said she, "what fine games at baseball we used to have at Fenelon! We used to tie up our skirts with string so as to run the better, for we were not allowed to wear rationals like I'm wearing now. And there were shrieks, and rushes, and pushes, till our hair waved about and we were quite red with exercise and excitement. Still that didn't prevent us from working in the class-rooms. On the contrary! Directly we were at study we fought again, each striving to learn the most and reach the top of the class!"

She laughed gaily as she thus recalled her school life, and Pierre glanced at her with candid admiration, so pink and healthy did she look under her little hat of black felt, which a long silver pin kept in position. Her fine dark hair was caught up behind, showing her neck, which looked as fresh and delicate as a child's. And never before had she seemed to him so supple and so strong.

"Ah," she continued in a jesting way, "there is nothing like rationals, you know! To think that some women are foolish and obstinate enough to wear skirts when they go out cycling!"

Then, as he declared—just by way of speaking the truth, and without the faintest idea of gallantry—that she looked very nice indeed in her costume, she responded: "Oh! I don't count. I'm not a beauty. I simply enjoy good health.... But can you understand it? To think that women have an unique opportunity of putting themselves at their ease, and releasing their limbs from prison, and yet they won't do so! If they think that they look the prettier in short skirts like schoolgirls they are vastly mistaken! And as for any question of modesty, well, it seems to me that it is infinitely less objectionable for women to wear rationals than to bare their bosoms at balls and theatres and dinners as society ladies do." Then, with a gesture of girlish impulsiveness, she added: "Besides, does one think of such things when one's rolling along? ... Yes, rationals are the only things, skirts are rank heresy!"

In her turn, she was now looking at him, and was struck by the extraordinary change which had come over him since the day when he had first appeared to her, so sombre in his long cassock, with his face emaciated, livid, almost distorted by anguish. It was like a resurrection, for now his countenance was bright, his lofty brow had all the serenity of hope, while his eyes and lips once more showed some of the confident tenderness which sprang from his everlasting thirst for love, self-bestowal and life. All mark of the priesthood had already left him, save that where he had been tonsured his hair still remained rather short.

"Why are you looking at me?" he asked.

"I was noticing how much good has been done you by work and the open air," she frankly answered; "I much prefer you as you are. You used to look so poorly. I thought you really ill."

"So I was," said he.

The train, however, was now stopping at Maisons-Laffitte. They alighted from it, and at once took the road to the forest. This road rises gently till it reaches the Maisons gate, and on market days it is often crowded with carts.

"I shall go first, eh?" said Marie gaily, "for vehicles still alarm you."

Thereupon she started ahead, but every now and again she turned with a smile to see if he were following her. And every time they overtook and passed a cart she spoke to him of the merits of their machines, which both came from the Grandidier works. They were "Lisettes," examples of those popular bicycles which Thomas had helped to perfect, and which the Bon Marche now sold in large numbers for 250 francs apiece. Perhaps they were rather heavy in appearance, but on the other hand their strength was beyond question. They were just the machines for a long journey, so Marie declared.

"Ah! here's the forest," she at last exclaimed. "We have now reached the end of the rise; and you will see what splendid avenues there are. One can bowl along them as on a velvet carpet."

Pierre had already joined her, and they rode on side by side along the broad straight avenue fringed with magnificent trees.

"I am all right now," said Pierre; "your pupil will end by doing you honour, I hope."

"Oh! I've no doubt of it. You already have a very good seat, and before long you'll leave me behind, for a woman is never a man's equal in a matter like this. At the same time, however, what a capital education cycling is for women!"

In what way?"

"Oh! I've certain ideas of my own on the subject; and if ever I have a daughter I shall put her on a bicycle as soon as she's ten years old, just to teach her how to conduct herself in life."

"Education by experience, eh?"

"Yes, why not? Look at the big girls who are brought up hanging to their mothers' apron strings. Their parents frighten them with everything, they are allowed no initiative, no exercise of judgment or decision, so that at times they hardly know how to cross a street, to such a degree does the traffic alarm them. Well, I say that a girl ought to be set on a bicycle in her childhood, and allowed to follow the roads. She will then learn to open her eyes, to look out for stones and avoid them, and to turn in the right direction at every bend or crossway. If a vehicle comes up at a gallop or any other danger presents itself, she'll have to make up her mind on the instant, and steer her course firmly and properly if she does not wish to lose a limb. Briefly, doesn't all this supply proper apprenticeship for one's will, and teach one how to conduct and defend oneself?"

Pierre had begun to laugh. "You will all be too healthy," he remarked.

"Oh, one must be healthy if one wants to be happy. But what I wish to convey is that those who learn to avoid stones and to turn properly along the highways will know how to overcome difficulties, and take the best decisions in after life. The whole of education lies in knowledge and energy."

"So women are to be emancipated by cycling?"

"Well, why not? It may seem a droll idea; but see what progress has been made already. By wearing rationals women free their limbs from prison; then the facilities which cycling affords people for going out together tend to greater intercourse and equality between the sexes; the wife and the children can follow the husband everywhere, and friends like ourselves are at liberty to roam hither and thither without astonishing anybody. In this lies the greatest advantage of all: one takes a bath of air and sunshine, one goes back to nature, to the earth, our common mother, from whom one derives fresh strength and gaiety of heart! Just look how delightful this forest is. And how healthful the breeze that inflates our lungs! Yes, it all purifies, calms and encourages one."

The forest, which was quite deserted on week days, stretched out in quietude on either hand, with sunlight filtering between its deep bands of trees. At that hour the rays only illumined one side of the avenue, there gilding the lofty drapery of verdure; on the other, the shady side, the greenery seemed almost black. It was truly delightful to skim, swallow-like, over that royal avenue in the fresh atmosphere, amidst the waving of grass and foliage, whose powerful scent swept against one's face. Pierre and Marie scarcely touched the soil: it was as if wings had come to them, and were carrying them on with a regular flight, through alternate patches of shade and sunshine, and all the scattered vitality of the far-reaching, quivering forest, with its mosses, its sources, its animal and its insect life.

Marie would not stop when they reached the crossway of the Croix de Noailles, a spot where people congregate on Sundays, for she was acquainted with secluded nooks which were far more charming resting-places. When they reached the slope going down towards Poissy, she roused Pierre, and they let their machines rush on. Then came all the joyous intoxication of speed, the rapturous feeling of darting along breathlessly while the grey road flees beneath one, and the trees on either hand turn like the opening folds of a fan. The breeze blows tempestuously, and one fancies that one is journeying yonder towards the horizon, the infinite, which ever and ever recedes. It is like boundless hope, delivery from every shackle, absolute freedom of motion through space. And nothing can inspirit one more gloriously—one's heart leaps as if one were in the very heavens.

"We are not going to Poissy, you know!" Marie suddenly cried; "we have to turn to the left."

They took the road from Acheres to the Loges, which ascends and contracts, thus bringing one closer together in the shade. Gradually slowing down, they began to exert themselves in order to make their way up the incline. This road was not so good as the others, it had been gullied by the recent heavy rains, and sand and gravel lay about. But then is there not even a pleasure in effort?

"You will get used to it," said Marie to Pierre; "it's amusing to overcome obstacles. For my part I don't like roads which are invariably smooth. A little ascent which does not try one's limbs too much rouses and inspirits one. And it is so agreeable to find oneself strong, and able to go on and on in spite of rain, or wind, or hills."

Her bright humour and courage quite charmed Pierre. "And so," said he, "we are off for a journey round France?"

"No, no, we've arrived. You won't dislike a little rest, eh? And now, tell me, wasn't it worth our while to come on here and rest in such a nice fresh, quiet spot."

She nimbly sprang off her machine and, bidding him follow her, turned into a path, along which she went some fifty paces. They placed their bicycles against some trees, and then found themselves in a little clearing, the most exquisite, leafy nest that one could dream of. The forest here assumed an aspect of secluded sovereign beauty. The springtide had endowed it with youth, the foliage was light and virginal, like delicate green lace flecked with gold by the sun-rays. And from the herbage and the surrounding thickets arose a breath of life, laden with all the powerful aroma of the earth.

"It's not too warm as yet, fortunately," exclaimed Marie, as she seated herself at the foot of a young oak-tree, against which she leant. "In July ladies get rather red by the time they reach this spot, and all the powder comes off their faces. However, one can't always be beautiful."

"Well, I'm not cold by any means," replied Pierre, as he sat at her feet wiping his forehead.

She laughed, and answered that she had never before seen him with such a colour. Then they began to talk like children, like two young friends, finding a source of gaiety in the most puerile things. She was somewhat anxious about his health, however, and would not allow him to remain in the cool shade, as he felt so very warm. In order to tranquillise her, he had to change his place and seat himself with his back to the sun. Then a little later he saved her from a large black spider, which had caught itself in the wavy hair on the nape of her neck. At this all her womanly nature reappeared, and she shrieked with terror. "How stupid it was to be afraid of a spider!" she exclaimed a moment afterwards; yet, in spite of her efforts to master herself, she remained pale and trembling.

Silence at last fell between them, and they looked at one another with a smile. In the midst of that delicate greenery they felt drawn together by frank affection—the affection of brother and sister, so it seemed to them. It made Marie very happy to think that she had taken an interest in Pierre, and that his return to health was largely her own work. However, their eyes never fell, their hands never met, even as they sat there toying with the grass, for they were as pure, as unconscious of all evil, as were the lofty oaks around them.

At last Marie noticed that time was flying. "You know that they expect us back to lunch," she exclaimed. "We ought to be off."

Thereupon they rose, wheeled their bicycles back to the highway, and starting off again at a good pace passed the Loges and reached Saint-Germain by the fine avenue which conducts to the chateau. It charmed them to take their course again side by side, like birds of equal flight. Their little bells jingled, their chains rustled lightly, and a fresh breeze swept past them as they resumed their talk, quite at ease, and so linked together by friendship that they seemed far removed from all the rest of the world.

They took the train from Saint-Germain to Paris, and on the journey Pierre suddenly noticed that Marie's cheeks were purpling. There were two ladies with them in the compartment.

"Ah!" said he, "so you feel warm in your turn now?"

But she protested the contrary, her face glowing more and more brightly as she spoke, as if some sudden feeling of shame quite upset her. "No, I'm not warm," said she; "just feel my hands.... But how ridiculous it is to blush like this without any reason for it!"

He understood her. This was one of those involuntary blushing fits which so distressed her, and which, as Mere-Grand had remarked, brought her heart to her very cheeks. There was no cause for it, as she herself said. After slumbering in all innocence in the solitude of the forest her heart had begun to beat, despite herself.

Meantime, over yonder at Montmartre, Guillaume had spent his morning in preparing some of that mysterious powder, the cartridges of which he concealed upstairs in Mere-Grand's bedroom. Great danger attended this manufacture. The slightest forgetfulness while he was manipulating the ingredients, any delay, too, in turning off a tap, might lead to a terrible explosion, which would annihilate the building and all who might be in it. For this reason he preferred to work when he was alone, so that on the one hand there might be no danger for others, and on the other less likelihood of his own attention being diverted from his task. That morning, as it happened, his three sons were working in the room, and Mere-Grand sat sewing near the furnace. Truth to tell, she did not count, for she scarcely ever left her place, feeling quite at ease there, however great might be the peril. Indeed, she had become so well acquainted with the various phases of Guillaume's delicate operations, and their terrible possibilities, that she would occasionally give him a helping hand.

That morning, as she sat there mending some house linen,—her eyesight still being so keen that in spite of her seventy years she wore no spectacles,—she now and again glanced at Guillaume as if to make sure that he forgot nothing. Then feeling satisfied, she would once more bend over her work. She remained very strong and active. Her hair was only just turning white, and she had kept all her teeth, while her face still looked refined, though it was slowly withering with age and had acquired an expression of some severity. As a rule she was a woman of few words; her life was one of activity and good management. When she opened her lips it was usually to give advice, to counsel reason, energy and courage. For some time past she had been growing more taciturn than ever, as if all her attention were claimed by the household matters which were in her sole charge; still, her fine eyes would rest thoughtfully on those about her, on the three young men, and on Guillaume, Marie and Pierre, who all obeyed her as if she were their acknowledged queen. If she looked at them in that pensive way, was it that she foresaw certain changes, and noticed certain incidents of which the others remained unconscious? Perhaps so. At all events she became even graver, and more attentive than in the past. It was as if she were waiting for some hour to strike when all her wisdom and authority would be required.

"Be careful, Guillaume," she at last remarked, as she once more looked up from her sewing. "You seem absent-minded this morning. Is anything worrying you?"

He glanced at her with a smile. "No, nothing, I assure you," he replied. "But I was thinking of our dear Marie, who was so glad to go off to the forest in this bright sunshine."

Antoine, who heard the remark, raised his head, while his brothers remained absorbed in their work. "What a pity it is that I had this block to finish," said he; "I would willingly have gone with her."

"Oh, no matter," his father quietly rejoined. "Pierre is with her, and he is very cautious."

For another moment Mere-Grand continued scrutinising Guillaume; then she once more reverted to her sewing.

If she exercised such sway over the home and all its inmates, it was by reason of her long devotion, her intelligence, and the kindliness with which she ruled. Uninfluenced by any religious faith, and disregarding all social conventionalities, her guiding principle in everything was the theory of human justice which she had arrived at after suffering so grievously from the injustice that had killed her husband. She put her views into practice with wonderful courage, knowing nothing of any prejudices, but accomplishing her duty, such as she understood it, to the very end. And in the same way as she had first devoted herself to her husband, and next to her daughter Marguerite, so at present she devoted herself to Guillaume and his sons. Pierre, whom she had first studied with some anxiety, had now, too, become a member of her family, a dweller in the little realm of happiness which she ruled. She had doubtless found him worthy of admission into it, though she did not reveal the reason why. After days and days of silence she had simply said, one evening, to Guillaume, that he had done well in bringing his brother to live among them.

Time flew by as she sat sewing and thinking. Towards noon Guillaume, who was still at work, suddenly remarked to her: "As Marie and Pierre haven't come back, we had better let the lunch wait a little while. Besides, I should like to finish what I'm about."

Another quarter of an hour then elapsed. Finally, the three young men rose from their work, and went to wash their hands at a tap in the garden.

"Marie is very late," now remarked Mere-Grand. "We must hope that nothing has happened to her."

"Oh! she rides so well," replied Guillaume. "I'm more anxious on account of Pierre."

At this the old lady again fixed her eyes on him, and said: "But Marie will have guided Pierre; they already ride very well together."

"No doubt; still I should be better pleased if they were back home."

Then all at once, fancying that he heard the ring of a bicycle bell, he called out: "There they are!" And forgetting everything else in his satisfaction, he quitted his furnace and hastened into the garden in order to meet them.

Mere-Grand, left to herself, quietly continued sewing, without a thought that the manufacture of Guillaume's powder was drawing to an end in an apparatus near her. A couple of minutes later, however, when Guillaume came back, saying that he had made a mistake, his eyes suddenly rested on his furnace, and he turned quite livid. Brief as had been his absence the exact moment when it was necessary to turn off a tap in order that no danger might attend the preparation of his powder had already gone by; and now, unless someone should dare to approach that terrible tap, and boldly turn it, a fearful explosion might take place. Doubtless it was too late already, and whoever might have the bravery to attempt the feat would be blown to pieces.

Guillaume himself had often run a similar risk of death with perfect composure. But on this occasion he remained as if rooted to the floor, unable to take a step, paralysed by the dread of annihilation. He shuddered and stammered in momentary expectation of a catastrophe which would hurl the work-shop to the heavens.

"Mere-Grand, Mere-Grand," he stammered. "The apparatus, the tap... it is all over, all over!"

The old woman had raised her head without as yet understanding him. "Eh, what?" said she; "what is the matter with you?" Then, on seeing how distorted were his features, how he recoiled as if mad with terror, she glanced at the furnace and realised the danger. "Well, but it's simple enough," said she; "it's only necessary to turn off the tap, eh?"

Thereupon, without any semblance of haste, in the most easy and natural manner possible, she deposited her needlework on a little table, rose from her chair, and turned off the tap with a light but firm hand. "There! it's done," said she. "But why didn't you do it yourself, my friend?"

He had watched her in bewilderment, chilled to the bones, as if touched by the hand of death. And when some colour at last returned to his cheeks, and he found himself still alive in front of the apparatus whence no harm could now come, he heaved a deep sigh and again shuddered. "Why did I not turn it off?" he repeated. "It was because I felt afraid."

At that very moment Marie and Pierre came into the work-shop all chatter and laughter, delighted with their excursion, and bringing with them the bright joyousness of the sunlight. The three brothers, Thomas, Francis and Antoine, were jesting with them, and trying to make them confess that Pierre had at least fought a battle with a cow on the high road, and ridden into a cornfield. All at once, however, they became quite anxious, for they noticed that their father looked terribly upset.

"My lads," said he, "I've just been a coward. Ah! it's a curious feeling, I had never experienced it before."

Thereupon he recounted his fears of an accident, and how quietly Mere-Grand had saved them all from certain death. She waved her hand, however, as if to say that there was nothing particularly heroic in turning off a tap. The young men's eyes nevertheless filled with tears, and one after the other they went to kiss her with a fervour instinct with all the gratitude and worship they felt for her. She had been devoting herself to them ever since their infancy, she had now just given them a new lease of life. Marie also threw herself into her arms, kissing her with gratitude and emotion. Mere-Grand herself was the only one who did not shed tears. She strove to calm them, begging them to exaggerate nothing and to remain sensible.

"Well, you must at all events let me kiss you as the others have done," Guillaume said to her, as he recovered his self-possession. "I at least owe you that. And Pierre, too, shall kiss you, for you are now as good for him as you have always been for us."

At table, when it was at last possible for them to lunch, he reverted to that attack of fear which had left him both surprised and ashamed. He who for years had never once thought of death had for some time past found ideas of caution in his mind. On two occasions recently he had shuddered at the possibility of a catastrophe. How was it that a longing for life had come to him in his decline? Why was it that he now wished to live? At last with a touch of tender affection in his gaiety, he remarked: "Do you know, Marie, I think it is my thoughts of you that make me a coward. If I've lost my bravery it's because I risk something precious when any danger arises. Happiness has been entrusted to my charge. Just now when I fancied that we were all going to die, I thought I could see you, and my fear of losing you froze and paralysed me."

Marie indulged in a pretty laugh. Allusions to her coming marriage were seldom made; however, she invariably greeted them with an air of happy affection.

"Another six weeks!" she simply said.

Thereupon Mere-Grand, who had been looking at them, turned her eyes towards Pierre. He, however, like the others was listening with a smile.

"That's true," said the old lady, "you are to be married in six weeks' time. So I did right to prevent the house from being blown up."

At this the young men made merry; and the repast came to an end in very joyous fashion.

During the afternoon, however, Pierre's heart gradually grew heavy. Marie's words constantly returned to him: "Another six weeks!" Yes, it was indeed true, she would then be married. But it seemed to him that he had never previously known it, never for a moment thought of it. And later on, in the evening, when he was alone in his room at Neuilly, his heart-pain became intolerable. Those words tortured him. Why was it that they had not caused him any suffering when they were spoken, why had he greeted them with a smile? And why had such cruel anguish slowly followed? All at once an idea sprang up in his mind, and became an overwhelming certainty. He loved Marie, he loved her as a lover, with a love so intense that he might die from it.

With this sudden consciousness of his passion everything became clear and plain. He had been going perforce towards that love ever since he had first met Marie. The emotion into which the young woman had originally thrown him had seemed to him a feeling of repulsion, but afterwards he had been slowly conquered, all his torments and struggles ending in this love for her. It was indeed through her that he had at last found quietude. And the delightful morning which he had spent with her that day, appeared to him like a betrothal morning, in the depths of the happy forest. Nature had resumed her sway over him, delivered him from his sufferings, made him strong and healthy once more, and given him to the woman he adored. The quiver he had experienced, the happiness he had felt, his communion with the trees, the heavens, and every living creature—all those things which he had been unable to explain, now acquired a clear meaning which transported him. In Marie alone lay his cure, his hope, his conviction that he would be born anew and at last find happiness. In her company he had already forgotten all those distressing problems which had formerly haunted him and bowed him down. For a week past he had not once thought of death, which had so long been the companion of his every hour. All the conflict of faith and doubt, the distress roused by the idea of nihility, the anger he had felt at the unjust sufferings of mankind, had been swept away by her fresh cool hands. She was so healthy herself, so glad to live, that she had imparted a taste for life even to him. Yes, it was simply that: she was making him a man, a worker, a lover once more.

Then he suddenly remembered Abbe Rose and his painful conversation with that saintly man. The old priest, whose heart was so ingenuous, and who knew nothing of love and passion, was nevertheless the only one who had understood the truth. He had told Pierre that he was changed, that there was another man in him. And he, Pierre, had foolishly and stubbornly declared that he was the same as he had always been; whereas Marie had already transformed him, bringing all nature back to his breast—all nature, with its sunlit countrysides, its fructifying breezes, and its vast heavens, whose glow ripens its crops. That indeed was why he had felt so exasperated with Catholicism, that religion of death; that was why he had shouted that the Gospel was useless, and that the world awaited another law—a law of terrestrial happiness, human justice and living love and fruitfulness!

Ah, but Guillaume? Then a vision of his brother rose before Pierre, that brother who loved him so fondly, and who had carried him to his home of toil, quietude and affection, in order to cure him of his sufferings. If he knew Marie it was simply because Guillaume had chosen that he should know her. And again Marie's words recurred to him: "Another six weeks!" Yes, in six weeks his brother would marry the young woman. This thought was like a stab in Pierre's heart. Still, he did not for one moment hesitate: if he must die of his love, he would die of it, but none should ever know it, he would conquer himself, he would flee to the ends of the earth should he ever feel the faintest cowardice. Rather than bring a moment's pain to that brother who had striven to resuscitate him, who was the artisan of the passion now consuming him, who had given him his whole heart and all he had—he would condemn himself to perpetual torture. And indeed, torture was coming back; for in losing Marie he could but sink into the distress born of the consciousness of his nothingness. As he lay in bed, unable to sleep, he already experienced a return of his abominable torments—the negation of everything, the feeling that everything was useless, that the world had no significance, and that life was only worthy of being cursed and denied. And then the shudder born of the thought of death returned to him. Ah! to die, to die without even having lived!

The struggle was a frightful one. Until daybreak he sobbed in martyrdom. Why had he taken off his cassock? He had done so at a word from Marie; and now another word from her gave him the despairing idea of donning it once more. One could not escape from so fast a prison. That black gown still clung to his skin. He fancied that he had divested himself of it, and yet it was still weighing on his shoulders, and his wisest course would be to bury himself in it for ever. By donning it again he would at least wear mourning for his manhood.

All at once, however, a fresh thought upset him. Why should he struggle in that fashion? Marie did not love him. There had been nothing between them to indicate that she cared for him otherwise than as a charming, tender-hearted sister. It was Guillaume that she loved, no doubt. Then he pressed his face to his pillow to stifle his sobs, and once more swore that he would conquer himself and turn a smiling face upon their happiness.

IV. TRIAL AND SENTENCE

HAVING returned to Montmartre on the morrow Pierre suffered so grievously that he did not show himself there on the two following days. He preferred to remain at home where there was nobody to notice his feverishness. On the third morning, however, whilst he was still in bed, strengthless and full of despair, he was both surprised and embarrassed by a visit from Guillaume.

"I must needs come to you," said the latter, "since you forsake us. I've come to fetch you to attend Salvat's trial, which takes place to-day. I had no end of trouble to secure two places. Come, get up, we'll have *dejeuner* in town, so as to reach the court early."

Then, while Pierre was hastily dressing, Guillaume, who on his side seemed thoughtful and worried that morning, began to question him: "Have you anything to reproach us with?" he asked.

"No, nothing. What an idea!" was Pierre's reply.

"Then why have you been staying away? We had got into the habit of seeing you every day, but all at once you disappear."

Pierre vainly sought a falsehood, and all his composure fled. "I had some work to do here," said he, "and then, too, my gloomy ideas cane back to me, and I didn't want to go and sadden you all."

At this Guillaume hastily waved his hand. "If you fancy that your absence enlivens us you're mistaken," he replied. "Marie, who is usually so well and happy, had such a bad headache on the day before yesterday that she was obliged to keep her room. And she was ill at ease and nervous and silent again yesterday. We spent a very unpleasant day."

As he spoke Guillaume looked Pierre well in the face, his frank loyal eyes clearly revealing the suspicions which had come to him, but which he would not express in words.

Pierre, quite dismayed by the news of Marie's indisposition, and frightened by the idea of betraying his secret, thereupon managed to tell a lie. "Yes, she wasn't very well on the day when we went cycling," he quietly responded. "But I assure you that I have had a lot to do here. When you came in just now I was about to get up and go to your house as usual."

Guillaume kept his eyes on him for a moment longer. Then, either believing him or deciding to postpone his search for the truth to some future time, he began speaking affectionately on other subjects. With his keen brotherly love, however, there was blended such a quiver of impending distress, of unconfessed sorrow, which possibly he did not yet realise, that Pierre in his turn began to question him. "And you," said he, "are you ill? You seem to me to have lost your usual serenity."

"I? Oh! I'm not ill. Only I can't very well retain my composure; Salvat's affair distresses me exceedingly, as you must know. They will all end by driving me mad with the monstrous injustice they show towards that unhappy fellow."

Thenceforward Guillaume went on talking of Salvat in a stubborn passionate way, as if he wished to find an explanation of all his pain and unrest in that affair. While he and Pierre were partaking of *dejeuner* at a little restaurant on the Boulevard du Palais he related how deeply touched he was by the silence which Salvat had preserved with regard both to the nature of the explosive employed in the bomb and the few days' work which he had once done at his house. It was, thanks to this silence, that he, Guillaume, had not been worried or even summoned as a witness. Then, in his emotion, he reverted to his invention, that formidable engine which would ensure omnipotence to France, as the great initiatory and liberative power of the world. The results of the researches which had occupied him for ten years past were now out of danger and in all readiness, so that if occasion required they might at once be delivered to the French government. And, apart from certain scruples which came to him at the thought of the unworthiness of French financial and political society; he was simply delaying any further steps in the matter until his marriage with Marie, in order that he might associate her with the gift of universal peace which he imagined he was about to bestow upon the world.

It was through Bertheroy and with great difficulty that Guillaume had managed to secure two seats in court for Salvat's trial. When he and Pierre presented themselves for admission at eleven o'clock, they fancied that they would never be able to enter. The large gates of the Palace of Justice were kept closed, several passages were fenced off, and terror seemed to reign in the deserted building, as if indeed the judges feared some sudden invasion of bomb-laden Anarchists. Each door and barrier, too, was guarded by soldiers, with whom the brothers had to parley. When they at last entered the Assize Court they found it already crowded with people, who were apparently quite willing to suffocate there for an hour before the arrival of the judges, and to remain motionless for some seven or eight hours afterwards, since it was reported that the authorities wished to get the case over in a single sitting. In the small space allotted to the standing public there was a serried mass of sightseers who had come up from the streets, a few companions and friends of Salvat having managed to slip in among them. In the other compartment, where witnesses are generally huddled together on oak benches, were those spectators who had been allowed admittance by favour, and these were so numerous and so closely packed that here and there they almost sat upon one another's knees. Then, in the well of the court and behind the bench, were rows of chairs set out as for some theatrical performance, and occupied by privileged members of society, politicians, leading journalists, and ladies. And meantime a number of gowned advocates sought refuge wherever chance offered, crowding into every vacant spot, every available corner.

Pierre had never before visited the Assize Court, and its appearance surprised him. He had expected much pomp and majesty, whereas this temple of human justice seemed to him small and dismal and of doubtful cleanliness. The bench was so low that he could scarcely see the armchairs of the presiding judge and his two assessors.

Then he was struck by the profusion of old oak panels, balustrades and benches, which helped to darken the apartment, whose wall hangings were of olive green, while a further display of oak panelling appeared on the ceiling above. From the seven narrow and high-set windows with scanty little white curtains there fell a pale light which sharply divided the court. On one hand one saw the dock and the defending counsel's seat steeped in frigid light, while, on the other, was the little, isolated jury box in the shade. This contrast seemed symbolical of justice, impersonal and uncertain, face to face with the accused, whom the light stripped bare, probed as it were to his very soul. Then, through a kind of grey mist above the bench, in the depths of the stern and gloomy scene, one could vaguely distinguish the heavy painting of "Christ Crucified." A white bust of the Republic alone showed forth clearly against the dark wall above the dock where Salvat would presently appear. The only remaining seats that Guillaume and Pierre could find were on the last bench of the witnesses' compartment, against the partition which separated the latter from the space allotted to the standing public. Just as Guillaume was seating himself, he saw among the latter little Victor Mathis, who stood there with his elbows leaning on the partition, while his chin rested on his crossed hands. The young man's eyes were glowing in his pale face with thin, compressed lips. Although they recognised one another, Victor did not move, and Guillaume on his side understood that it was not safe to exchange greetings in such a place. From that moment, however, he remained conscious that Victor was there, just above him, never stirring, but waiting silently, fiercely and with flaming eyes, for what was going to happen.

Pierre, meantime, had recognised that most amiable deputy Duthil, and little Princess Rosemonde, seated just in front of him. Amidst the hubbub of the throng which chatted and laughed to while away the time, their voices were the gayest to be heard, and plainly showed how delighted they were to find themselves at a spectacle to which so many desired admittance. Duthil was explaining all the arrangements to Rosemonde, telling her to whom or to what purpose each bench and wooden box was allotted: there was the jury-box, the prisoner's dock, the seats assigned to counsel for the defence, the public prosecutor, and the clerk of the court, without forgetting the table on which material evidence was deposited and the bar to which witnesses were summoned. There was nobody as yet in any of these places; one merely saw an attendant giving a last look round, and advocates passing rapidly. One might indeed have thought oneself in a theatre, the stage of which remained deserted, while the spectators crowded the auditorium waiting for the play to begin. To fill up the interval the little Princess ended by looking about her for persons of her acquaintance among the close-pressed crowd of sight-seers whose eager faces were already reddening.

"Oh! isn't that Monsieur Fonsegue over there behind the bench, near that stout lady in yellow?" she exclaimed. "Our friend General de Bozonnet is on the other side, I see. But isn't Baron Duvillard here?"

"Oh! no," replied Duthil; "he could hardly come; it would look as if he were here to ask for vengeance." Then, in his turn questioning Rosemonde, the deputy went on: "Do you happen to have quarrelled with your handsome friend Hyacinthe? Is that the reason why you've given me the pleasure of acting as your escort to-day?"

With a slight shrug of her shoulders, the Princess replied that poets were beginning to bore her. A fresh caprice, indeed, was drawing her into politics. For a week past she had found amusement in the surroundings of the ministerial crisis, into which the young deputy for Angouleme had initiated her. "They are all a little bit crazy at the Duvillards', my dear fellow," said she. "It's decided, you know, that Gerard is to marry Camille. The Baroness has resigned herself to it, and I've heard from a most reliable quarter that Madame de Quinsac, the young man's mother, has given her consent."

At this Duthil became quite merry. He also seemed to be well informed on the subject. "Yes, yes, I know," said he. "The wedding is to take place shortly, at the Madeleine. It will be a magnificent affair, no doubt. And after all, what would you have? There couldn't be a better finish to the affair. The Baroness is really kindness personified, and I said all along that she would sacrifice herself in order to ensure the happiness of her daughter and Gerard. In point of fact that marriage will settle everything, put everything in proper order again."

"And what does the Baron say?" asked Rosemonde.

"The Baron? Why, he's delighted," replied Duthil in a bantering way. "You read no doubt this morning that Dauvergne is given the department of Public Instruction in the new Ministry. This means that Silviane's engagement at the Comedic is a certainty. Dauvergne was chosen simply on that account."

At this moment the conversation was interrupted by little Massot, who, after a dispute with one of the ushers some distance away, had perceived a vacant place by the side of the Princess. He thereupon made her a questioning sign, and she beckoned to him to approach.

"Ah!" said he, as he installed himself beside her, "I have not got here without trouble. One's crushed to death on the press bench, and I've an article to write. You are the kindest of women, Princess, to make a little room for your faithful admirer, myself." Then, after shaking hands with Duthil, he continued without any transition: "And so there's a new ministry at last, Monsieur le Depute. You have all taken your time about it, but it's really a very fine ministry, which everybody regards with surprise and admiration."

The decrees appointing the new ministers had appeared in the "Journal Officiel" that very morning. After a long deadlock, after Vignon had for the second time seen his plans fail through ever-recurring obstacles, Monferrand, as a last resource, had suddenly been summoned to the Elysee, and in four-and-twenty hours he had found the colleagues he wanted and secured the acceptance of his list, in such wise that he now triumphantly re-ascended to power after falling from it with Barroux in such wretched fashion. He had also chosen a new post for himself, relinquishing the department of the Interior for that of Finances, with the Presidency of the Council, which had long been his secret ambition. His stealthy labour, the masterly fashion in which he had saved himself while others sank, now appeared in its full beauty. First had come Salvat's arrest, and the use he had made of it, then the wonderful subterranean campaign which he had carried on against Vignon, the thousand obstacles which he had twice set across his path, and finally the sudden *denouement* with that list he held in readiness, that formation of a ministry in a single day as soon as his services were solicited.

"It is fine work, I must compliment you on it," added little Massot by way of a jest.

"But I've had nothing to do with it," Duthil modestly replied.

"Nothing to do with it! Oh! yes you have, my dear sir, everybody says so."

The deputy felt flattered and smiled, while the other rattled on with his insinuations, which were put in such a humorous way that nothing he said could be resented. He talked of Monferrand's followers who had so powerfully helped him on to victory. How heartily had Fonsegue finished off his old friend Barroux in the "Globe"! Every morning for a month past the paper had published an article belabouring Barroux, annihilating Vignon, and preparing the public for the return of a saviour of society who was not named. Then, too, Duvillard's millions had waged a secret warfare, all the Baron's numerous creatures had fought like an army for the good cause. Duthil himself had played the pipe and beaten the drum, while Chaigneux resigned himself to the baser duties which others would not undertake. And so the triumphant Monferrand would certainly begin by stifling that scandalous and embarrassing affair of the African Railways, and appointing a Committee of Inquiry to bury it.

By this time Duthil had assumed an important air. "Well, my dear fellow," said he, "at serious moments when society is in peril, certain strong-handed men, real men of government, become absolutely necessary. Monferrand had no need of our friendship, his presence in office was imperiously required by the situation. His hand is the only one that can save us!"

"I know," replied Massot scoffingly. "I've even been told that if everything was settled straight off so that the decrees might be published this morning, it was in order to instil confidence into the judges and jurymen here, in such wise that knowing Monferrand's fist to be behind them they would have the courage to pronounce sentence of death this evening."

"Well, public safety requires a sentence of death, and those who have to ensure that safety must not be left ignorant of the fact that the government is with them, and will know how to protect them, if need be."

At this moment a merry laugh from the Princess broke in upon the conversation. "Oh! just look over there!" said she; "isn't that Silviane who has just sat down beside Monsieur Fonsegue?"

"The Silviane ministry!" muttered Massot in a jesting way. "Well, there will be no boredom at Dauvergne's if he ingratiates himself with actresses."

Guillaume and Pierre heard this chatter, however little they cared to listen to it. Such a deluge of society tittle-tattle and political indiscretion brought the former a keen heart-pang. So Salvat was sentenced to death even before he had appeared in court. He was to pay for the transgressions of one and all, his crime was simply a favourable opportunity for the triumph of a band of ambitious people bent on power and enjoyment! Ah! what terrible social rottenness there was in it all; money corrupting one and another, families sinking to filth, politics turned into a mere treacherous struggle between individuals, and power becoming the prey of the crafty and the impudent! Must not everything surely crumble? Was not this solemn assize of human justice a derisive parody, since all that one found there was an assembly of happy and privileged people defending the shaky edifice which sheltered them, and making use of all the forces they yet retained, to crush a fly—that unhappy devil of uncertain sanity who had been led to that court by his violent and cloudy dream of another, superior and avenging justice?

Such were Guillaume's thoughts, when all at once everybody around him started. Noon was now striking, and the jurymen trooped into court in straggling fashion and took their seats in their box. Among them one saw fat fellows clad in their Sunday best and with the faces of simpletons, and thin fellows who had bright eyes and sly expressions. Some of them were bearded and some were bald. However, they all remained rather indistinct, as their side of the court was steeped in shade. After them came the judges, headed by M. de Larombiere, one of the Vice-Presidents of the Appeal Court, who in assuming the perilous honour of conducting the trial had sought to increase the majesty of his long, slender, white face, which looked the more austere as both his assessors, one dark and the other fair, had highly coloured countenances. The public prosecutor's seat was already occupied by one of the most skilful of the advocates-general, M. Lehmann, a broad-shouldered Alsatian Israelite, with cunning eyes, whose presence showed that the case was deemed exceptionally important. At last, amidst the heavy tread of gendarmes, Salvat was brought in, at once rousing such ardent curiosity that all the spectators rose to look at him. He still wore the cap and loose overcoat procured for him by Victor Mathis, and everybody was surprised to see his emaciated, sorrowful, gentle face, crowned by scanty reddish hair, which was turning grey. His soft, glowing, dreamy blue eyes glanced around, and he smiled at someone whom he recognised, probably Victor, but perhaps Guillaume. After that he remained quite motionless.

The presiding judge waited for silence to fall, and then came the formalities which attend the opening of a court of law, followed by the perusal of the lengthy indictment, which a subordinate official read in a shrill voice. The scene had now changed, and the spectators listened wearily and somewhat impatiently, as, for weeks past, the newspapers had related all that the indictment set forth. At present not a corner of the court remained unoccupied, there was scarcely space enough for the witnesses to stand in front of the bench. The closely packed throng was one of divers hues, the light gowns of ladies alternating with the black gowns of advocates, while the red robes of the judges disappeared from view, the bench being so low that the presiding judge's long face scarcely rose above the sea of heads. Many of those present became interested in the jurors, and strove to scrutinise their shadowy countenances. Others, who did not take their eyes off the prisoner, marvelled at his apparent weariness and indifference, which were so great that he scarcely answered the whispered questions of his counsel, a young advocate with a wide-awake look, who was nervously awaiting the opportunity to achieve fame. Most curiosity, however, centred in the table set apart for the material evidence. Here were to be seen all sorts of fragments, some of the woodwork torn away from the carriage-door of the Duvillard mansion, some plaster that had fallen from the ceiling, a paving-stone which the violence of the explosion had split in halves, and other blackened remnants. The more moving sights, however, were the milliner's bonnet-box, which had remained uninjured, and a glass jar in which something white and vague was preserved in spirits of wine. This was one of the poor errand girl's little hands, which had been severed at the wrist. The authorities had been unable to place her poor ripped body on the table, and so they had brought that hand!

At last Salvat rose, and the presiding judge began to interrogate him. The contrast in the aspect of the court then acquired tragic force: in the shrouding shade upon one hand were the jurors, their minds already made up beneath the pressure of public terror, while in the full, vivid light on the other side was the prisoner, alone and woeful, charged with all the crimes of his race. Four gendarmes watched over him. He was addressed by M. de Larombiere in a tone of contempt and disgust. The judge was not deficient in rectitude; he was indeed one of the last representatives of the old, scrupulous, upright French magistracy; but he understood nothing of the new times, and he treated prisoners with the severity of a Biblical Jehovah. Moreover, the infirmity which was the worry of his life, the childish lisp which, in his opinion, had alone prevented him from shining as a public prosecutor, made him ferociously ill-tempered, incapable of any intelligent indulgence. There were smiles, which he divined, as soon as he raised his sharp, shrill little voice, to ask his first questions. That droll voice of his took away whatever majesty might have remained attached to these proceedings, in which a man's life was being fought for in a hall full of inquisitive, stifling and perspiring folks, who fanned themselves and jested. Salvat answered the judge's earlier questions with his wonted weariness and politeness. While the judge did everything to vilify him, harshly reproaching him with his wretched childhood and youth, magnifying every stain and every transgression in his career, referring to the promiscuity of his life between Madame Theodore and little Celine as something bestial, he, the prisoner, quietly said yes or no, like a man who has nothing to hide and accepts the full responsibility of his actions. He had already made a complete confession of his crime, and he calmly repeated it without changing a word. He explained that if he had deposited his bomb at the entrance of the Duvillard mansion it was to give his deed its true significance, that of summoning the wealthy, the money-mongers who had so scandalously enriched themselves by dint of theft and falsehood, to restore that part of the common wealth which they had appropriated, to the poor, the working classes, their children and their wives, who perished of starvation. It was only at this moment that he grew excited; all the misery that he had endured or witnessed rose to his clouded, semi-educated brain, in which claims and theories and exasperated ideas of absolute justice and universal happiness had gathered confusedly. And from that moment he appeared such as he really was, a sentimentalist, a dreamer transported by suffering, proud and stubborn, and bent on changing the world in accordance with his sectarian logic.

"But you fled!" cried the judge in a voice such as would have befitted a grasshopper. "You must not say that you gave your life to your cause and were ready for martyrdom!"

Salvat's most poignant regret was that he had yielded in the Bois de Boulogne to the dismay and rage which come upon a tracked and hunted man and impel him to do all he can to escape capture. And on being thus taunted by the judge he became quite angry. "I don't fear death, you'll see that," he replied. "If all had the same courage as I have, your rotten society would be swept away to-morrow, and happiness would at last dawn."

Then the interrogatory dealt at great length with the composition and manufacture of the bomb. The judge, rightly enough, pointed out that this was the only obscure point of the affair. "And so," he remarked, "you persist in saying that dynamite was the explosive you employed? Well, you will presently hear the experts, who, it is true, differ on certain points, but are all of opinion that you employed some other explosive, though they cannot say precisely what it was. Why not speak out on the point, as you glory in saying everything?"

Salvat, however, had suddenly calmed down, giving only cautious monosyllabic replies. "Well, seek for whatever you like if you don't believe me," he now answered. "I made my bomb by myself, and under circumstances which I've already related a score of times. You surely don't expect me to reveal names and compromise comrades?"

From this declaration he would not depart. It was only towards the end of the interrogatory that irresistible emotion overcame him on the judge again referring to the unhappy victim of his crime, the little errand girl, so pretty and fair and gentle, whom ferocious destiny had brought to the spot to meet such an awful death. "It was one of your own class whom you struck," said M. de Larombiere; "your victim was a work girl, a poor child who, with the few pence she earned, helped to support her aged grandmother."

Salvat's voice became very husky as he answered: "That's really the only thing I regret.... My bomb certainly wasn't meant for her; and may all the workers, all the starvelings, remember that she gave her blood as I'm going to give mine!"

In this wise the interrogatory ended amidst profound agitation. Pierre had felt Guillaume shuddering beside him, whilst the prisoner quietly and obstinately refused to say a word respecting the explosive that had been employed, preferring as he did to assume full responsibility for the deed which was about to cost him his life. Moreover, Guillaume, on turning round, in compliance with an irresistible impulse, had perceived Victor Mathis still motionless behind him: his elbows ever leaning on the rail of the partition, and his chin still resting on his hands, whilst he listened with silent, concentrated passion. His face had become yet paler than before, and his eyes glowed as with an avenging fire, whose flames would never more be extinguished.

The interrogatory of the prisoner was followed by a brief commotion in court.

"That Salvat looks quite nice, he has such soft eyes," declared the Princess, whom the proceedings greatly amused. "Oh! don't speak ill of him, my dear deputy. You know that I have Anarchist ideas myself."

"I speak no ill of him," gaily replied Duthil. "Nor has our friend Amadieu any right to speak ill of him. For you know that this affair has set Amadieu on a pinnacle. He was never before talked about to such an extent as he is now; and he delights in being talked about, you know! He has become quite a social celebrity, the most illustrious of our investigating magistrates, and will soon be able to do or become whatever he pleases."

Then Massot, with his sarcastic impudence, summed up the situation. "When Anarchism flourishes, everything flourishes, eh? That bomb has helped on the affairs of a good many fine fellows that I know. Do you think that my governor Fonsegue, who's so attentive to Silviane yonder, complains of it? And doesn't Sagnier, who's spreading himself out behind the presiding judge, and whose proper place would be between the four gendarmes—doesn't he owe a debt to Salvat for all the abominable advertisements he has been able to give his paper by using the wretched fellow's back as a big drum? And I need not mention the politicians or the financiers or all those who fish in troubled waters."

"But I say," interrupted Duthil, "it seems to me that you yourself made good use of the affair. Your interview with the little girl Celine brought you in a pot of money."

Massot, as it happened, had been struck with the idea of ferreting out Madame Theodore and the child, and of relating his visit to them in the "Globe," with an abundance of curious and touching particulars. The article had met with prodigious success, Celine's pretty answers respecting her imprisoned father having such an effect on ladies with sensitive hearts that they had driven to Montmartre in their carriages in order to see the two poor creatures. Thus alms had come to them from all sides; and strangely enough the very people who demanded the father's head were the most eager to sympathise with the child.

"Well, I don't complain of my little profits," said the journalist in answer to Duthil. "We all earn what we can, you know."

At this moment Rosemonde, while glancing round her, recognised Guillaume and Pierre, but she was so amazed to see the latter in ordinary civilian garb that she did not dare to speak to him. Leaning forward she acquainted Duthil and Massot with her surprise, and they both turned round to look. From motives of discretion, however, they pretended that they did not recognise the Froments.

The heat in court was now becoming quite unbearable, and one lady had already fainted. At last the presiding judge again raised his lisping voice, and managed to restore silence. Salvat, who had remained standing, now held a few sheets of paper, and with some difficulty he made the judge understand that he desired to complete his interrogatory by reading a declaration, which he had drawn up in prison, and in which he explained his reasons for his crime. For a moment M. de Larombiere hesitated, all surprise and indignation at such a request; but he was aware that he could not legally impose silence on the prisoner, and so he signified his consent with a gesture of mingled irritation and disdain. Thereupon Salvat began his perusal much after the fashion of a schoolboy, hemming and hawing here and there, occasionally becoming confused, and then bringing out certain words with wonderful emphasis, which evidently pleased him. This declaration of his was the usual cry of suffering and revolt already raised by so many disinherited ones. It referred to all the frightful want of the lower spheres; the toiler unable to find a livelihood in his toil; a whole class, the most numerous and worthy of the classes, dying of starvation; whilst, on the other hand, were the privileged ones, gorged with wealth, and wallowing in satiety, yet refusing to part with even the crumbs from their tables, determined as they were to restore nothing whatever of the wealth which they had stolen. And so it became necessary to take everything away from them, to rouse them from their egotism by terrible warnings, and to proclaim to them even with the crash of bombs that the day of justice had come. The unhappy man spoke that word "justice" in a ringing voice which seemed to fill the whole court. But the emotion of those who heard him reached its highest pitch when, after declaring that he laid down his life for the cause, and expected nothing but a verdict of death from the jury, he added, as if prophetically, that his blood would assuredly give birth to other martyrs. They might send him to the scaffold, said he, but he knew that his example would bear fruit. After him would come another avenger, and yet another, and others still, until the old and rotten social system should have crumbled away so as to make room for the society of justice and happiness of which he was one of the apostles.

The presiding judge, in his impatience and agitation, twice endeavoured to interrupt Salvat. But the other read on and on with the imperturbable conscientiousness of one who fears that he may not give proper utterance to his most important words. He must have been thinking of that perusal ever since he had been in prison. It was the decisive act of his suicide, the act by which he proclaimed that he gave his life for the glory of dying in the cause of mankind. And when he had finished he sat down between the gendarmes with glowing eyes and flushed cheeks, as if he inwardly experienced some deep joy.

To destroy the effect which the declaration had produced—a commingling of fear and compassion—the judge at once wished to proceed with the hearing of the witnesses. Of these there was an interminable procession; though little interest attached to their evidence, for none of them had any revelations to make. Most attention perhaps was paid to the measured statements of Grandidier, who had been obliged to dismiss Salvat from his employ on account of the Anarchist propaganda he had carried on. Then the prisoner's brother-in-law, Toussaint, the mechanician, also seemed a very worthy fellow if one might judge him by the manner in which he strove to put things favourably for Salvat, without in any way departing from the truth. After Toussaint's evidence considerable time was taken up by the discussions between the experts, who disagreed in public as much as they had disagreed in their reports. Although they were all of opinion that dynamite could not have been the explosive employed in the bomb, they indulged in the most extraordinary and contradictory suppositions as to this explosive's real nature. Eventually a written opinion given by the illustrious *savant* Bertheroy was read; and this, after clearly setting forth the known facts, concluded that one found oneself in presence of a new explosive of prodigious power, the formula of which he himself was unable to specify.

Then detective Mondesir and commissary Dupot came in turn to relate the various phases of the man hunt in the Bois de Boulogne. In Mondesir centred all the gaiety of the proceedings, thanks to the guardroom sallies with which he enlivened his narrative. And in like way the greatest grief, a perfect shudder of revolt and compassion, was roused by the errand girl's grandmother, a poor, bent, withered old woman, whom the prosecution had cruelly constrained to attend the court, and who wept and looked quite dismayed, unable as she was to understand what was wanted of her. When she had withdrawn, the only remaining witnesses were those for the defence, a procession of foremen and comrades, who all declared that they had known Salvat as a very worthy fellow, an intelligent and zealous workman, who did not drink, but was extremely fond of his daughter, and incapable of an act of dishonesty or cruelty.

It was already four o'clock when the evidence of the witnesses came to an end. The atmosphere in court was now quite stifling, feverish fatigue flushed every face, and a kind of ruddy dust obscured the waning light which fell from the windows. Women were fanning themselves and men were mopping their foreheads. However, the passion roused by the scene still brought a glow of cruel delight to every eye. And no one stirred.

"Ah!" sighed Rosemonde all at once, "to think that I hoped to drink a cup of tea at a friend's at five o'clock. I shall die of thirst and starvation here."

"We shall certainly be kept till seven," replied Massot. "I can't offer to go and fetch you a roll, for I shouldn't be readmitted."

Then Duthil, who had not ceased shrugging his shoulders while Salvat read his declaration, exclaimed: "What childish things he said, didn't he? And to think that the fool is going to die for all that! Rich and poor, indeed! Why, there will always be rich and poor. And it's equally certain that when a man is poor his one great desire is to become rich. If that fellow is in the dock to-day it's simply because he failed to make money."

While the others were thus conversing, Pierre for his part was feeling extremely anxious about his brother, who sat beside him in silence, pale and utterly upset. Pierre sought his hand and covertly pressed it. Then in a low voice he inquired: "Do you feel ill? Shall we go away?"

Guillaume answered him by discreetly and affectionately returning his handshake. He was all right, he would remain till the end, however much he might be stirred by exasperation.

It was now Monsieur Lehmann, the public prosecutor, who rose to address the court. He had a large, stern mouth, and was squarely built, with a stubborn Jewish face. Nevertheless he was known to be a man of dexterous, supple nature, one who had a foot in every political camp, and invariably contrived to be on good terms with the powers that were. This explained his rapid rise in life, and the constant favour he enjoyed. In the very first words he spoke he alluded to the new ministry gazetted that morning, referring pointedly to the strong-handed man who had undertaken the task of reassuring peaceable citizens and making evil-doers tremble. Then he fell upon the wretched Salvat with extraordinary vehemence, recounting the whole of his life, and exhibiting him as a bandit expressly born for the perpetration of crime, a monster who was bound to end by committing some abominable and cowardly outrage. Next he flagellated Anarchism and its partisans. The Anarchists were a mere herd of vagabonds and thieves, said he. That had been shown by the recent robbery at the Princess de Harn's house. The ignoble gang that had been arrested for that affair had given the apostles of the Anarchist doctrine as their references! And that was what the application of Anarchist theories resulted in—burglary and filth, pending a favourable hour for wholesale pillage and murder! For nearly a couple of hours the public prosecutor continued in this fashion, throwing truth and logic to the winds, and exclusively striving to alarm his hearers. He made all possible use of the terror which had reigned in Paris, and figuratively brandished the corpse of the poor little victim, the pretty errand girl, as if it were a blood-red flag, before pointing to the pale hand, preserved in spirits of wine, with a gesture of compassionate horror which sent a shudder through his audience. And he ended, as he had begun, by inspiriting the jurors, and telling them that they might fearlessly do their duty now that those at the head of the State were firmly resolved to give no heed to threats.

Then the young advocate entrusted with the defence in his turn spoke. And he really said what there was to say with great clearness and precision. He was of a different school from that of the public prosecutor: his eloquence was very simple and smooth, his only passion seemed to be zeal for truth. Moreover, it was sufficient for him to show Salvat's career in its proper light, to depict him pursued by social fatalities since his childhood, and to explain the final action of his career by all that he had suffered and all that had sprung up in his dreamy brain. Was not his crime the crime of one and all? Who was there that did not feel, if only in a small degree, responsible for that bomb which a penniless, starving workman had deposited on the threshold of a wealthy man's abode—a wealthy man whose name bespoke the injustice of the social system: so much enjoyment on the one hand and so much privation on the other! If one of us happened to lose his head, and felt impelled to hasten the advent of happiness by violence in such troublous times, when so many burning problems claimed solution, ought he to be deprived of his life in the name of justice, when none could swear that they had not in some measure contributed to his madness? Following up this question, Salvat's counsel dwelt at length on the period that witnessed the crime, a period of so many scandals and collapses, when the old world was giving birth to a new one amidst the most terrible struggles and pangs. And he concluded by begging the jury to show themselves humane, to resist all passion and terror, and to pacify the rival classes by a wise verdict, instead of prolonging social warfare by giving the starvelings yet another martyr to avenge.

It was past six o'clock when M. de Larombiere began to sum up in a partial and flowery fashion, in which one detected how grieved and angry he was at having such a shrill little voice. Then the judges and the jurors withdrew, and the prisoner was led away, leaving the spectators waiting amidst an uproar of feverish impatience. Some more ladies had fainted, and it had even been necessary to carry out a gentleman who had been overcome by the cruel heat. However, the others stubbornly remained there, not one of them quitting his place.

"Ah! it won't take long now," said Massot. "The jurors brought their verdict all ready in their pockets. I was looking at them while that little advocate was telling them such sensible things. They all looked as if they were comfortably asleep in the gloom."

Then Duthil turned to the Princess and asked her, "Are you still hungry?"

"Oh! I'm starving," she replied. "I shall never be able to wait till I get home. You will have to take me to eat a biscuit somewhere.... All the same, however, it's very exciting to see a man's life staked on a yes or a no."

Meantime Pierre, finding Guillaume still more feverish and grieved, had once again taken hold of his hand. Neither of them spoke, so great was the distress that they experienced for many reasons which they themselves could not have precisely defined. It seemed to them, however, that all human misery—inclusive of their own, the affections, the hopes, the griefs which brought them suffering—was sobbing and quivering in that buzzing hall. Twilight had gradually fallen there, but as the end was now so near it had doubtless been thought unnecessary to light the chandeliers. And thus large vague shadows, dimming and shrouding the serried throng, now hovered about in the last gleams of the day. The ladies in light gowns yonder, behind the bench, looked like pale phantoms with all-devouring eyes, whilst the numerous groups of black-robed advocates formed large sombre patches which gradually spread everywhere. The greyish painting of the Christ had already vanished, and on the walls one only saw the glaring white bust of the Republic, which resembled some frigid death's head starting forth from the darkness.

"Ah!" Massot once more exclaimed, "I knew that it wouldn't take long!"

Indeed, the jurors were returning after less than a quarter of an hour's absence. Then the judges likewise came back and took their seats. Increased emotion stirred the throng, a great gust seemed to sweep through the court, a gust of anxiety, which made every head sway. Some people had risen to their feet, and others gave vent to involuntary exclamations. The foreman of the jury, a gentleman with a broad red face, had to wait a moment before speaking. At last in a sharp but somewhat sputtering voice he declared: "On my honour and my conscience, before God and before man, the verdict of the jury is: on the question of Murder, yes, by a majority of votes."[1]

---

[1] English readers may be reminded that in France the verdict of a majority of the jury suffices for conviction or acquittal. If the jury is evenly divided the prisoner is acquitted.—Trans.

The night had almost completely fallen when Salvat was once more brought in. In front of the jurors, who faded away in the gloom, he stood forth, erect, with a last ray from the windows lighting up his face. The judges themselves almost disappeared from view, their red robes seemed to have turned black. And how phantom-like looked the prisoner's emaciated face as he stood there listening, with dreamy eyes, while the clerk of the court read the verdict to him.

When silence fell and no mention was made of extenuating circumstances, he understood everything. His face, which had retained a childish expression, suddenly brightened. "That means death. Thank you, gentlemen," he said.

Then he turned towards the public, and amidst the growing darkness searched for the friendly faces which he knew were there; and this time Guillaume became fully conscious that he had recognised him, and was again expressing affectionate and grateful thanks for the crust he had received from him on a day of want. He must have also bidden farewell to Victor Mathis, for as Guillaume glanced at the young man, who had not moved, he saw that his eyes were staring wildly, and that a terrible expression rested on his lips.

As for the rest of the proceedings, the last questions addressed to the jury and the counsel, the deliberations of the judges and the delivery of sentence—these were all lost amidst the buzzing and surging of the crowd. A little compassion was unconsciously manifested; and some stupor was mingled with the satisfaction that greeted the sentence of death.

No sooner had Salvat been condemned, however, than he drew himself up to his full height, and as the guards led him away he shouted in a stentorian voice: "Long live Anarchy!"

Nobody seemed angered by the cry. The crowd went off quietly, as if weariness had lulled all its passions. The proceedings had really lasted too long and fatigued one too much. It was quite pleasant to inhale the fresh air on emerging from such a nightmare.

In the large waiting hall, Pierre and Guillaume passed Duthil and the Princess, whom General de Bozonnet had stopped while chatting with Fonsegue. All four of them were talking in very loud voices, complaining of the heat and their hunger, and agreeing that the affair had not been a particularly interesting one. Yet, all was well that ended well. As Fonsegue remarked, the condemnation of Salvat to death was a political and social necessity.

When Pierre and Guillaume reached the Pont Neuf, the latter for a moment rested his elbows on the parapet of the bridge. His brother, standing beside him, also gazed at the grey waters of the Seine, which here and there were fired by the reflections of the gas lamps. A fresh breeze ascended from the river; it was the delightful hour when night steals gently over resting Paris. Then, as the brothers stood there breathing that atmosphere which usually brings relief and comfort, Pierre on his side again became conscious of his heart-wound, and remembered his promise to return to Montmartre, a promise that he must keep in spite of the torture there awaiting him; whilst Guillaume on the other hand experienced a revival of the suspicion and disquietude that had come to him on seeing Marie so feverish, changed as it were by some new feeling, of which she herself was ignorant. Were further sufferings, struggles, and obstacles to happiness yet in store for those brothers who loved one another so dearly? At all events their hearts bled once more with all the sorrow into which they had been cast by the scene they had just witnessed: that assize of justice at which a wretched man had been condemned to pay with his head for the crimes of one and all.

Then, as they turned along the quay, Guillaume recognised young Victor going off alone in the gloom, just in front of them. The chemist stopped him and spoke to him of his mother. But the young man did not hear; his thin lips parted, and in a voice as trenchant as a knife-thrust he exclaimed: "Ah! so it's blood they want. Well, they may cut off his head, but he will be avenged!"

V. SACRIFICE

THE days which followed Salvat's trial seemed gloomy ones up yonder in Guillaume's workroom, which was usually so bright and gay. Sadness and silence filled the place. The three young men were no longer there. Thomas betook himself to the Grandidier works early every morning in order to perfect his little motor; Francois was so busy preparing for his examination that he scarcely left the Ecole Normale; while Antoine was doing some work at Jahan's, where he delighted to linger and watch his little friend Lise awakening to life. Thus Guillaume's sole companion was Mere-Grand, who sat near the window busy with her needlework; for Marie was ever going about the house, and only stayed in the workroom for any length of time when Pierre happened to be there.

Guillaume's gloom was generally attributed to the feelings of anger and revolt into which the condemnation of Salvat had thrown him. He had flown into a passion on his return from the Palace of Justice, declaring that the execution of the unhappy man would simply be social murder, deliberate provocation of class warfare. And the others had bowed on hearing that pain-fraught violent cry, without attempting to discuss the point. Guillaume's sons respectfully left him to the thoughts which kept him silent for hours, with his face pale and a dreamy expression in his eyes. His chemical furnace remained unlighted, and his only occupation from morn till night was to examine the plans and documents connected with his invention, that new explosive and that terrible engine of war, which he had so long dreamt of presenting to France in order that she might impose the reign of truth and justice upon all the nations. However, during the long hours which he spent before the papers scattered over his table, often without seeing them, for his eyes wandered far away, a multitude of vague thoughts came to him—doubts respecting the wisdom of his project, and fears lest his desire to pacify the nations should simply throw them into an endless war of extermination. Although he really believed that great city of Paris to be the world's brain, entrusted with the task of preparing the future, he could not disguise from himself that with all its folly and shame and injustice it still presented a shocking spectacle. Was it really ripe enough for the work of human salvation which he thought of entrusting to it? Then, on trying to re-peruse his notes and verify his formulas, he only recovered his former energetic determination on thinking of his marriage, whereupon the idea came to him that it was now too late for him to upset his life by changing such long-settled plans.

V. SACRIFICE

His marriage! Was it not the thought of this which haunted Guillaume and disturbed him far more powerfully than his scientific work or his humanitarian passion? Beneath all the worries that he acknowledged, there was another which he did not confess even to himself, and which filled him with anguish. He repeated day by day that he would reveal his invention to the Minister of War as soon as he should be married to Marie, whom he wished to associate with his glory. Married to Marie! Each time he thought of it, burning fever and secret disquietude came over him. If he now remained so silent and had lost his quiet cheerfulness, it was because he had felt new life, as it were, emanating from her. She was certainly no longer the same woman as formerly; she was becoming more and more changed and distant. He had watched her and Pierre when the latter happened to be there, which was now but seldom. He, too, appeared embarrassed, and different from what he had been. On the days when he came, however, Marie seemed transformed; it was as if new life animated the house. Certainly the intercourse between her and Pierre was quite innocent, sisterly on the one hand, brotherly on the other. They simply seemed to be a pair of good friends. And yet a radiance, a vibration, emanated from them, something more subtle even than a sun-ray or a perfume. After the lapse of a few days Guillaume found himself unable to doubt the truth any longer. And his heart bled, he was utterly upset by it. He had not found them in fault in any way, but he was convinced that these two children, as he so paternally called them, really adored one another.

One lovely morning when he happened to be alone with Mere-Grand, face to face with sunlit Paris, he fell into a yet more dolorous reverie than usual. He seemed to be gazing fixedly at the old lady, as, seated in her usual place, she continued sewing with an air of queenly serenity. Perhaps, however, he did not see her. For her part she occasionally raised her eyes and glanced at him, as if expecting a confession which did not come. At last, finding such silence unbearable, she made up her mind to address him: "What has been the matter with you, Guillaume, for some time past? Why don't you tell me what you have to tell me?"

He descended from the clouds, as it were, and answered in astonishment: "What I have to tell you?"

"Yes, I know it as well as you do, and I thought you would speak to me of it, since it pleases you to do nothing here without consulting me."

At this he turned very pale and shuddered. So he had not been mistaken in the matter, even Mere-Grand knew all about it. To talk of it, however, was to give shape to his suspicions, to transform what, hitherto, might merely have been a fancy on his part into something real and definite.

"It was inevitable, my dear son," said Mere-Grand. "I foresaw it from the outset. And if I did not warn you of it, it was because I believed in some deep design on your part. Since I have seen you suffering, however, I have realised that I was mistaken." Then, as he still looked at her quivering and distracted, she continued: "Yes, I fancied that you might have wished it, that in bringing your brother here you wished to know if Marie loved you otherwise than as a father. There was good reason for testing her—for instance, the great difference between your ages, for your life is drawing to a close, whilst hers is only beginning. And I need not mention the question of your work, the mission which I have always dreamt of for you."

Thereupon, with his hands raised in prayerful fashion, Guillaume drew near to the old lady and exclaimed: "Oh! speak out clearly, tell me what you think. I don't understand, my poor heart is so lacerated; and yet I should so much like to know everything, so as to be able to act and take a decision. To think that you whom I love, you whom I venerate as much as if you were my real mother, you whose profound good sense I know so well that I have always followed your advice—to think that you should have foreseen this frightful thing and have allowed it to happen at the risk of its killing me!... Why have you done so, tell me, why?"

Mere-Grand was not fond of talking. Absolute mistress of the house as she was, managing everything, accountable to nobody for her actions, she never gave expression to all that she thought or all that she desired. Indeed, there was no occasion for it, as Guillaume, like the children, relied upon her completely, with full confidence in her wisdom. And her somewhat enigmatical ways even helped to raise her in their estimation.

"What is the use of words, when things themselves speak?" she now gently answered, while still plying her needle. "It is quite true that I approved of the plan of a marriage between you and Marie, for I saw that it was necessary that she should be married if she was to stay here. And then, too, there were many other reasons which I needn't speak of. However, Pierre's arrival here has changed everything, and placed things in their natural order. Is not that preferable?"

He still lacked the courage to understand her. "Preferable! When I'm in agony? When my life is wrecked?"

Thereupon she rose and came to him, tall and rigid in her thin black gown, and with an expression of austerity and energy on her pale face. "My son," she said, "you know that I love you, and that I wish you to be very noble and lofty. Only the other morning, you had an attack of fright, the house narrowly escaped being blown up. Then, for some days now you have been sitting over those documents and plans in an absent-minded, distracted state, like a man who feels weak, and doubts, and no longer knows his way. Believe me, you are following a dangerous path; it is better that Pierre should marry Marie, both for their sakes and for your own."

"For my sake? No, no! What will become of me!"

"You will calm yourself and reflect, my son. You have such serious duties before you. You are on the eve of making your invention known. It seems to me that something has bedimmed your sight, and that you will perhaps act wrongly in this respect, through failing to take due account of the problem before you. Perhaps there is something better to be done.... At all events, suffer if it be necessary, but remain faithful to your ideal."

Then, quitting him with a maternal smile, she sought to soften her somewhat stern words by adding: "You have compelled me to speak unnecessarily, for I am quite at ease; with your superior mind, whatever be in question, you can but do the one right thing that none other would do."

On finding himself alone Guillaume fell into feverish uncertainty. What was the meaning of Mere-Grand's enigmatical words? He knew that she was on the side of whatever might be good, natural, and necessary. But she seemed to be urging him to some lofty heroism; and indeed what she had said threw a ray of light upon the unrest which had come to him in connection with his old plan of going to confide his secret to some Minister of War or other, whatever one might happen to be in office at the time. Growing hesitation and repugnance stirred him as he fancied he could again hear her saying that perhaps there might be some better course, that would require search and reflection. But all at once a vision of Marie rose before him, and his heart was rent by the thought that he was asked to renounce her. To lose her, to give her to another! No, no, that was beyond his strength. He would never have the frightful courage that was needed to pass by the last promised raptures of love with disdain!

For a couple of days Guillaume struggled on. He seemed to be again living the six years which the young woman had already spent beside him in that happy little house. She had been at first like an adopted daughter there; and later on, when the idea of their marriage had sprung up, he had viewed it with quiet delight in the hope that it would ensure the happiness of all around him. If he had previously abstained from marrying again it was from the fear of placing a strange mother over his children; and if he yielded to the charm of loving yet once more, and no longer leading a solitary life, it was because he had found at his very hearth one of such sensible views, who, in the flower of youth, was willing to become his wife despite the difference in their ages. Then months had gone by, and serious occurrences had compelled them to postpone the wedding, though without undue suffering on his part. Indeed, the certainty that she was waiting for him had sufficed him, for his life of hard work had rendered him patient. Now, however, all at once, at the threat of losing her, his hitherto tranquil heart ached and bled. He would never have thought the tie so close a one. But he was now almost fifty, and it was as if love and woman were being wrenched away from him, the last woman that he could love and desire, one too who was the more desirable, as she was the incarnation of youth from which he must ever be severed, should he indeed lose her. Passionate desire, mingled with rage, flared up within him at the thought that someone should have come to take her from him.

One night, alone in his room, he suffered perfect martyrdom. In order that he might not rouse the house he buried his face in his pillow so as to stifle his sobs. After all, it was a simple matter; Marie had given him her promise, and he would compel her to keep it. She would be his, and his alone, and none would be able to steal her from him. Then, however, there rose before him a vision of his brother, the long-forgotten one, whom, from feelings of affection, he had compelled to join his family. But his sufferings were now so acute that he would have driven that brother away had he been before him. He was enraged, maddened, by the thought of him. His brother—his little brother! So all their love was over; hatred and violence were about to poison their lives. For hours Guillaume continued complaining deliriously, and seeking how he might so rid himself of Pierre that what had happened should be blotted out. Now and again, when he recovered self-control, he marvelled at the tempest within him; for was he not a *savant* guided by lofty reason, a toiler to whom long experience had brought serenity? But the truth was that this tempest had not sprung up in his mind, it was raging in the child-like soul that he had retained, the nook of affection and dreaminess which remained within him side by side with his principles of pitiless logic and his belief in proven phenomena only. His very genius came from the duality of his nature: behind the chemist was a social dreamer, hungering for justice and capable of the greatest love. And now passion was transporting him, and he was weeping for the loss of Marie as he would have wept over the downfall of that dream of his, the destruction of war *by* war, that scheme for the salvation of mankind at which he had been working for ten years past.

At last, amidst his weariness, a sudden resolution calmed him. He began to feel ashamed of despairing in this wise when he had no certain grounds to go upon. He must know everything, he would question the young woman; she was loyal enough to answer him frankly. Was not this a solution worthy of them both? An explanation in all sincerity, after which they would be able to take a decision. Then he fell asleep; and, tired though he felt when he rose in the morning, he was calmer. It was as if some secret work had gone on in his heart during his few hours of repose after that terrible storm.

As it happened Marie was very gay that morning. On the previous day she had gone with Pierre and Antoine on a cycling excursion over frightful roads in the direction of Montmorency, whence they had returned in a state of mingled anger and delight. When Guillaume stopped her in the little garden, he found her humming a song while returning bare-armed from the scullery, where some washing was going on.

"Do you want to speak to me?" she asked.

"Yes, my dear child, it's necessary for us to talk of some serious matters."

She at once understood that their marriage was in question, and became grave. She had formerly consented to that marriage because she regarded it as the only sensible course she could take, and this with full knowledge of the duties which she would assume. No doubt her husband would be some twenty years older than herself, but this circumstance was one of somewhat frequent occurrence, and as a rule such marriages turned out well, rather than otherwise. Moreover, she was in love with nobody, and was free to consent. And she had consented with an impulse of gratitude and affection which seemed so sweet that she thought it the sweetness of love itself. Everybody around her, too, appeared so pleased at the prospect of this marriage, which would draw the family yet more closely together. And, on her side, she had been as it were intoxicated by the idea of making others happy.

"What is the matter?" she now asked Guillaume in a somewhat anxious voice. "No bad news, I hope?"

"No, no," he answered. "I've simply something to say to you."

Then he led her under the plum-trees to the only green nook left in the garden. An old worm-eaten bench still stood there against the lilac-bushes. And in front of them Paris spread out its sea of roofs, looking light and fresh in the morning sunlight.

They both sat down. But at the moment of speaking and questioning Marie, Guillaume experienced sudden embarrassment, while his heart beat violently at seeing her beside him, so young and adorable with her bare arms.

"Our wedding-day is drawing near," he ended by saying. And then as she turned somewhat pale, perhaps unconsciously, he himself suddenly felt cold. Had not her lips twitched as if with pain? Had not a shadow passed over her fresh, clear eyes?

"Oh! we still have some time before us," she replied.

Then, slowly and very affectionately, he resumed: "No doubt; still it is necessary to attend to the formalities. And it is as well, perhaps, that I should speak of those worries to-day, so that I may not have to bother you about them again."

Then he gently went on telling her all that would have to be done, keeping his eyes on her whilst he spoke, watching for such signs of emotion as the thought of her promise's early fulfilment might bring to her face. She sat there in silence, with her hands on her lap, and her features quite still, thus giving no certain sign of any regret or trouble. Still she seemed rather dejected, compliant, as it were, but in no wise joyous.

"You say nothing, my dear Marie," Guillaume at last exclaimed. "Does anything of all this displease you?"

"Displease me? Oh, no!"

"You must speak out frankly, if it does, you know. We will wait a little longer if you have any personal reasons for wishing to postpone the date again."

"But I've no reasons, my friend. What reasons could I have? I leave you quite free to settle everything as you yourself may desire."

Silence fell. While answering, she had looked him frankly in the face; but a little quiver stirred her lips, and gloom, for which she could not account, seemed to rise and darken her face, usually as bright and gay as spring water. In former times would she not have laughed and sung at the mere announcement of that coming wedding?

Then Guillaume, with an effort which made his voice tremble, dared to speak out: "You must forgive me for asking you a question, my dear Marie. There is still time for you to cancel your promise. Are you quite certain that you love me?"

At this she looked at him in genuine stupefaction, utterly failing to understand what he could be aiming at. And—as she seemed to be deferring her reply, he added: "Consult your heart. Is it really your old friend or is it another that you love?"

"I? I, Guillaume? Why do you say that to me? What can I have done to give you occasion to say such a thing!"

All her frank nature revolted as she spoke, and her beautiful eyes, glowing with sincerity, gazed fixedly on his.

"I love Pierre! I do, I?... Well, yes, I love him, as I love you all; I love him because he has become one of us, because he shares our life and our joys! I'm happy when he's here, certainly; and I should like him to be always here. I'm always pleased to see him and hear him and go out with him. I was very much grieved recently when he seemed to be relapsing into his gloomy ideas. But all that is natural, is it not? And I think that I have only done what you desired I should do, and I cannot understand how my affection for Pierre can in any way exercise an influence respecting our marriage."

These words, in her estimation, ought to have convinced Guillaume that she was not in love with his brother; but in lieu thereof they brought him painful enlightenment by the very ardour with which she denied the love imputed to her.

"But you unfortunate girl!" he cried. "You are betraying yourself without knowing it.... It is quite certain you do not love me, you love my brother!"

He had caught hold of her wrists and was pressing them with despairing affection as if to compel her to read her heart. And she continued struggling. A most loving and tragic contest went on between them, he seeking to convince her by the evidence of facts, and she resisting him, stubbornly refusing to open her eyes. In vain did he recount what had happened since the first day, explaining the feelings which had followed one upon another in her heart and mind: first covert hostility, next curiosity regarding that extraordinary young priest, and then sympathy and affection when she had found him so wretched and had gradually cured him of his sufferings. They were both young and mother Nature had done the rest. However, at each fresh proof and certainty which he put before her, Marie only experienced growing emotion, trembling at last from head to foot, but still unwilling to question herself.

"No, no," said she, "I do not love him. If I loved him I should know it and would acknowledge it to you; for you are well aware that I cannot tell an untruth."

Guillaume, however, had the cruelty to insist on the point, like some heroic surgeon cutting into his own flesh even more than into that of others, in order that the truth might appear and everyone be saved. "Marie," said he, "it is not I whom you love. All that you feel for me is respect and gratitude and daughterly affection. Remember what your feelings were at the time when our marriage was decided upon. You were then in love with nobody, and you accepted the offer like a sensible girl, feeling certain that I should render you happy, and that the union was a right and satisfactory one.... But since then my brother has come here; love has sprung up in your heart in quite a natural way; and it is Pierre, Pierre alone, whom you love as a lover and a husband should be loved."

Exhausted though she was, utterly distracted, too, by the light which, despite herself, was dawning within her, Marie still stubbornly and desperately protested.

"But why do you struggle like this against the truth, my child?" said Guillaume; "I do not reproach you. It was I who chose that this should happen, like the old madman I am. What was bound to come has come, and doubtless it is for the best. I only wanted to learn the truth from you in order that I might take a decision and act uprightly."

These words vanquished her, and her tears gushed forth. It seemed as though something had been rent asunder within her; and she felt quite overcome, as if by the weight of a new truth of which she had hitherto been ignorant. "Ah! it was cruel of you," she said, "to do me such violence so as to make me read my heart. I swear to you again that I did not know I loved Pierre in the way you say. But you have opened my heart, and roused what was quietly slumbering in it.... And it is true, I do love Pierre, I love him now as you have said. And so here we are, all three of us supremely wretched through your doing!"

She sobbed, and with a sudden feeling of modesty freed her wrists from his grasp. He noticed, however, that no blush rose to her face. Truth to tell, her virginal loyalty was not in question; she had no cause to reproach herself with any betrayal; it was he alone, perforce, who had awakened her to love. For a moment they looked at one another through their tears: she so strong and healthy, her bosom heaving at each heartbeat, and her white arms—arms that could both charm and sustain—bare almost to her shoulders; and he still vigorous, with his thick fleece of white hair and his black moustaches, which gave his countenance such an expression of energetic youth. But it was all over, the irreparable had swept by, and utterly changed their lives.

"Marie," he nobly said, "you do not love me, I give you back your promise."

But with equal nobility she refused to take it back. "Never will I do so," she replied. "I gave it to you frankly, freely and joyfully, and my affection and admiration for you have never changed."

Nevertheless, with more firmness in his hitherto broken voice, Guillaume retorted: "You love Pierre, and it is Pierre whom you ought to marry."

"No," she again insisted, "I belong to you. A tie which years have tightened cannot be undone in an hour. Once again, if I love Pierre I swear to you that I was ignorant of it this morning. And let us leave the matter as it is; do not torture me any more, it would be too cruel of you."

Then, quivering like a woman who suddenly perceives that she is bare, in a stranger's presence, she hastily pulled down her sleeves, and even drew them over her hands as if to leave naught of her person visible. And afterwards she rose and walked away without adding a single word.

V. SACRIFICE

Guillaume remained alone on the bench in that leafy corner, in front of Paris, to which the light morning sunshine lent the aspect of some quivering, soaring city of dreamland. A great weight oppressed him, and it seemed to him as if he would never be able to rise from the seat. That which brought him most suffering was Marie's assurance that she had till that morning been ignorant of the fact that she was in love with Pierre. She had been ignorant of it, and it was he, Guillaume, who had brought it to her knowledge, compelled her to confess it! He had now firmly planted it in her heart, and perhaps increased it by revealing it to her. Ah! how cruel the thought—to be the artisan of one's own torment! Of one thing he was now quite certain: there would be no more love in his life. At the idea of this, his poor, loving heart sank and bled. And yet amidst the disaster, amidst his grief at realising that he was an old man, and that renunciation was imperative, he experienced a bitter joy at having brought the truth to light. This was very harsh consolation, fit only for one of heroic soul, yet he found lofty satisfaction in it, and from that moment the thought of sacrifice imposed itself upon him with extraordinary force. He must marry his children; there lay the path of duty, the only wise and just course, the only certain means of ensuring the happiness of the household. And when his revolting heart yet leapt and shrieked with anguish, he carried his vigorous hands to his chest in order to still it.

On the morrow came the supreme explanation between Guillaume and Pierre, not in the little garden, however, but in the spacious workroom. And here again one beheld the vast panorama of Paris, a nation as it were at work, a huge vat in which the wine of the future was fermenting. Guillaume had arranged things so that he might be alone with his brother; and no sooner had the latter entered than he attacked him, going straight to the point without any of the precautions which he had previously taken with Marie.

"Haven't you something to say to me, Pierre?" he inquired. "Why won't you confide in me?"

The other immediately understood him, and began to tremble, unable to find a word, but confessing everything by the distracted, entreating expression of his face.

"You love Marie," continued Guillaume, "why did you not loyally come and tell me of your love?"

At this Pierre recovered self-possession and defended himself vehemently: "I love Marie, it's true, and I felt that I could not conceal it, that you yourself would notice it at last. But there was no occasion for me to tell you of it, for I was sure of myself, and would have fled rather than have allowed a single word to cross my lips. I suffered in silence and alone, and you cannot know how great my torture was! It is even cruel on your part to speak to me of it; for now I am absolutely compelled to leave you.... I have already, on several occasions, thought of doing so. If I have come back here, it was doubtless through weakness, but also on account of my affection for you all. And what mattered my presence here? Marie ran no risk. She does not love me."

"She does love you!" Guillaume answered. "I questioned her yesterday, and she had to confess that she loved you."

At this Pierre, utterly distracted, caught Guillaume by the shoulders and gazed into his eyes. "Oh! brother, brother! what is this you say? Why say a thing which would mean terrible misfortune for us all? Even if it were true, my grief would far exceed my joy, for I will not have you suffer. Marie belongs to you. To me she is as sacred as a sister. And if there be only my madness to part you, it will pass by, I shall know how to conquer it."

"Marie loves you," repeated Guillaume in his gentle, obstinate way. "I don't reproach you with anything. I well know that you have struggled, and have never betrayed yourself to her either by word or glance. Yesterday she herself was still ignorant that she loved you, and I had to open her eyes.... What would you have? I simply state a fact: she loves you."

This time Pierre, still quivering, made a gesture of mingled rapture and terror, as if some divine and long-desired blessing were falling upon him from heaven and crushing him beneath its weight.

"Well, then," he said, after a brief pause, "it is all over.... Let us kiss one another for the last time, and then I'll go."

"Go? Why? You must stay with us. Nothing could be more simple: you love Marie and she loves you. I give her to you."

A loud cry came from Pierre, who wildly raised his hands again with a gesture of fright and rapture. "You give me Marie?" he replied. "You, who adore her, who have been waiting for her for months? No, no, it would overcome me, it would terrify me, as if you gave me your very heart after tearing it from your breast. No, no! I will not accept your sacrifice!"

"But as it is only gratitude and affection that Marie feels for me," said Guillaume, "as it is you whom she really loves, am I to take a mean advantage of the engagements which she entered into unconsciously, and force her to a marriage when I know that she would never be wholly mine? Besides, I have made a mistake, it isn't I who give her to you, she has already given herself, and I do not consider that I have any right to prevent her from doing so."

"No, no! I will never accept, I will never bring such grief upon you... Kiss me, brother, and let me go."

Thereupon Guillaume caught hold of Pierre and compelled him to sit down by his side on an old sofa near the window. And he began to scold him almost angrily while still retaining a smile, in which suffering and kindliness were blended. "Come," said he, "we are surely not going to fight over it. You won't force me to tie you up so as to keep you here? I know what I'm about. I thought it all over before I spoke to you. No doubt, I can't tell you that it gladdens me. I thought at first that I was going to die; I should have liked to hide myself in the very depths of the earth. And then, well, it was necessary to be reasonable, and I understood that things had arranged themselves for the best, in their natural order."

Pierre, unable to resist any further, had begun to weep with both hands raised to his face.

"Don't grieve, brother, either for yourself or for me," said Guillaume. "Do you remember the happy days we lately spent together at Neuilly after we had found one another again? All our old affection revived within us, and we remained for hours, hand in hand, recalling the past and loving one another. And what a terrible confession you made to me one night, the confession of your loss of faith, your torture, the void in which you were rolling! When I heard of it my one great wish was to cure you. I advised you to work, love, and believe in life, convinced as I was that life alone could restore you to peace and health.... And for that reason I afterwards brought you here. You fought against it, and it was I who forced you to come. I was so happy when I found that you again took an interest in life, and had once more become a man and a worker! I would have given some of my blood if necessary to complete your cure.... Well, it's done now, I have given you all I had, since Marie herself has become necessary to you, and she alone can save you."

Then as Pierre again attempted to protest, he resumed: "Don't deny it. It is so true indeed, that if she does not complete the work I have begun, all my efforts will have been vain, you will fall back into your misery and negation, into all the torments of a spoilt life. She is necessary to you, I say. And do you think that I no longer know how to love you? Would you have me refuse you the very breath of life that will truly make you a man, after all my fervent wishes for your return to life? I have enough affection for you both to consent to your loving one another.... Besides, I repeat it, nature knows what she does. Instinct is a sure guide, it always tends to what is useful and trite. I should have been a sorry husband, and it is best that I should keep to my work as an old *savant*; whereas you are young and represent the future, all fruitful and happy life."

Pierre shuddered as he heard this, for his old fears returned to him. Had not the priesthood for ever cut him off from life, had not his long years of chaste celibacy robbed him of his manhood? "Fruitful and happy life!" he muttered, "ah! if you only knew how distressed I feel at the idea that I do not perhaps deserve the gift you so lovingly offer me! You are worth more than I am; you would have given her a larger heart, a firmer brain, and perhaps, too, you are really a younger man than myself.... There is still time, brother, keep her, if with you she is likely to be happier and more truly and completely loved. For my part I am full of doubts. Her happiness is the only thing of consequence. Let her belong to the one who will love her best!"

Indescribable emotion had now come over both men. As Guillaume heard his brother's broken words, the cry of a love that trembled at the thought of possible weakness, he did for a moment waver. With a dreadful heart-pang he stammered despairingly: "Ah! Marie, whom I love so much! Marie, whom I would have rendered so happy!"

At this Pierre could not restrain himself; he rose and cried: "Ah! you see that you love her still and cannot renounce her.... So let me go! let me go!"

But Guillaume had already caught him around the body, clasping him with an intensity of brotherly love which was increased by the renunciation he was resolved upon: "Stay!" said he. "It wasn't I that spoke, it was the other man that was in me, he who is about to die, who is already dead! By the memory of our mother and our father I swear to you that the sacrifice is consummated, and that if you two refuse to accept happiness from me you will but make me suffer."

For a moment the weeping men remained in one another's arms. They had often embraced before, but never had their hearts met and mingled as they did now. It was a delightful moment, which seemed an eternity. All the grief and misery of the world had disappeared from before them; there remained naught save their glowing love, whence sprang an eternity of love even as light comes from the sun. And that moment was compensation for all their past and future tears, whilst yonder, on the horizon before them, Paris still spread and rumbled, ever preparing the unknown future.

Just then Marie herself came in. And the rest proved very simple. Guillaume freed himself from his brother's clasp, led him forward and compelled him and Marie to take each other by the hand. At first she made yet another gesture of refusal in her stubborn resolve that she would not take her promise back. But what could she say face to face with those two tearful men, whom she had found in one another's arms, mingling together in such close brotherliness? Did not those tears and that embrace sweep away all ordinary reasons, all such arguments as she held in reserve? Even the embarrassment of the situation disappeared, it seemed as if she had already had a long explanation with Pierre, and that he and she were of one mind to accept that gift of love which Guillaume offered them with so much heroism. A gust of the sublime passed through the room, and nothing could have appeared more natural to them than this extraordinary scene. Nevertheless, Marie remained silent, she dared not give her answer, but looked at them both with her big soft eyes, which, like their own, were full of tears.

And it was Guillaume who, with sudden inspiration, ran to the little staircase conducting to the rooms overhead, and called: "Mere-Grand! Mere-Grand! Come down at once, you are wanted."

Then, as soon as she was there, looking slim and pale in her black gown, and showing the wise air of a queen-mother whom all obeyed, he said: "Tell these two children that they can do nothing better than marry one another. Tell them that we have talked it over, you and I, and that it is your desire, your will that they should do so."

She quietly nodded her assent, and then said: "That is true, it will be by far the most sensible course."

Thereupon Marie flung herself into her arms, consenting, yielding to the superior forces, the powers of life, that had thus changed the course of her existence. Guillaume immediately desired that the date of the wedding should be fixed, and accommodation provided for the young couple in the rooms overhead. And as Pierre glanced at him with some remaining anxiety and spoke of travelling, for he feared that his wound was not yet healed, and that their presence might bring him suffering, Guillaume responded: "No, no, I mean to keep you. If I'm marrying you, it is to have you both here. Don't worry about me. I have so much work to do, I shall work."

In the evening when Thomas and Francois came home and learnt the news, they did not seem particularly surprised by it. They had doubtless felt that things would end like this. And they bowed to the *denouement*, not venturing to say a word, since it was their father himself who announced the decision which had been taken, with his usual air of composure. As for Antoine, who on his own side quivered with love for Lise, he gazed with doubting, anxious eyes at his father, who had thus had the courage to pluck out his heart. Could he really survive such a sacrifice, must it not kill him? Then Antoine kissed his father passionately, and the elder brothers in their turn embraced him with all their hearts. Guillaume smiled and his eyes became moist. After his victory over his horrible torments nothing could have been sweeter to him than the embraces of his three big sons.

There was, however, further emotion in store for him that evening. Just as the daylight was departing, and he was sitting at his large table near the window, again checking and classifying the documents and plans connected with his invention, he was surprised to see his old master and friend Bertheroy enter the workroom. The illustrious chemist called on him in this fashion at long intervals, and Guillaume felt the honour thus conferred on him by this old man to whom eminence and fame had brought so many titles, offices and decorations. Moreover, Bertheroy, with his position as an official *savant* and member of the Institute, showed some courage in thus venturing to call on one whom so-called respectable folks regarded with contumely. And on this occasion, Guillaume at once understood that it was some feeling of curiosity that had brought him. And so he was greatly embarrassed, for he hardly dared to remove the papers and plans which were lying on the table.

"Oh, don't be frightened," gaily exclaimed Bertheroy, who, despite his careless and abrupt ways, was really very shrewd. "I haven't come to pry into your secrets.... Leave your papers there, I promise you that I won't read anything."

Then, in all frankness, he turned the conversation on the subject of explosives, which he was still studying, he said, with passionate interest. He had made some new discoveries which he did not conceal. Incidentally, too, he spoke of the opinion he had given in Salvat's affair. His dream was to discover some explosive of great power, which one might attempt to domesticate and reduce to complete obedience. And with a smile he pointedly concluded: "I don't know where that madman found the formula of his powder. But if you should ever discover it, remember that the future perhaps lies in the employment of explosives as motive power."

Then, all at once, he added: "By the way, that fellow Salvat will be executed on the day after to-morrow. A friend of mine at the Ministry of Justice has just told me so."

Guillaume had hitherto listened to him with an air of mingled distrust and amusement. But this announcement of Salvat's execution stirred him to anger and revolt, though for some days past he had known it to be inevitable, in spite of the sympathy which the condemned man was now rousing in many quarters.

"It will be a murder!" he cried vehemently.

Bertheroy waved his hand: "What would you have?" he answered: "there's a social system and it defends itself when it is attacked. Besides, those Anarchists are really too foolish in imagining that they will transform the world with their squibs and crackers! In my opinion, you know, science is the only revolutionist. Science will not only bring us truth but justice also, if indeed justice ever be possible on this earth. And that is why I lead so calm a life and am so tolerant."

Once again Bertheroy appeared to Guillaume as a revolutionist, one who was convinced that he helped on the ruin of the ancient abominable society of today, with its dogmas and laws, even whilst he was working in the depths of his laboratory. He was, however, too desirous of repose, and had too great a contempt for futilities to mingle with the events of the day, and he preferred to live in quietude, liberally paid and rewarded, and at peace with the government whatever it might be, whilst at the same time foreseeing and preparing for the formidable parturition of the future.

He waved his hand towards Paris, over which a sun of victory was setting, and then again spoke: "Do you hear the rumble? It is we who are the stokers, we who are ever flinging fresh fuel under the boiler. Science does not pause in her work for a single hour, and she is the artisan of Paris, which—let us hope it—will be the artisan of the future. All the rest is of no account."

But Guillaume was no longer listening to him. He was thinking of Salvat and the terrible engine of war he had invented, that engine which before long would shatter cities. And a new idea was dawning and growing in his mind. He had just freed himself of his last tie, he had created all the happiness he could create around him. Ah! to recover his courage, to be master of himself once more, and, at any rate, derive from the sacrifice of his heart the lofty delight of being free, of being able to lay down even his life, should he some day deem it necessary!

BOOK V.

I. THE GUILLOTINE

FOR some reason of his own Guillaume was bent upon witnessing the execution of Salvat. Pierre tried to dissuade him from doing so; and finding his efforts vain, became somewhat anxious. He accordingly resolved to spend the night at Montmartre, accompany his brother and watch over him. In former times, when engaged with Abbe Rose in charitable work in the Charonne district, he had learnt that the guillotine could be seen from the house where Mege, the Socialist deputy, resided at the corner of the Rue Merlin. He therefore offered himself as a guide. As the execution was to take place as soon as it should legally be daybreak, that is, about half-past four o'clock, the brothers did not go to bed but sat up in the workroom, feeling somewhat drowsy, and exchanging few words. Then as soon as two o'clock struck, they started off.

The night was beautifully serene and clear. The full moon, shining like a silver lamp in the cloudless, far-stretching heavens, threw a calm, dreamy light over the vague immensity of Paris, which was like some spell-bound city of sleep, so overcome by fatigue that not a murmur arose from it. It was as if beneath the soft radiance which spread over its roofs, its panting labour and its cries of suffering were lulled to repose until the dawn. Yet, in a far, out of the way district, dark work was even now progressing, a knife was being raised on high in order that a man might be killed.

Pierre and Guillaume paused in the Rue St. Eleuthere, and gazed at the vaporous, tremulous city spread out below then. And as they turned they perceived the basilica of the Sacred Heart, still domeless but already looking huge indeed in the moonbeams, whose clear white light accentuated its outlines and brought them into sharp relief against a mass of shadows. Under the pale nocturnal sky, the edifice showed like a colossal monster, symbolical of provocation and sovereign dominion. Never before had Guillaume found it so huge, never had it appeared to him to dominate Paris, even in the latter's hours of slumber, with such stubborn and overwhelming might.

This wounded him so keenly in the state of mind in which he found himself, that he could not help exclaiming: "Ah! they chose a good site for it, and how stupid it was to let them do so! I know of nothing more nonsensical; Paris crowned and dominated by that temple of idolatry! How impudent it is, what a buffet for the cause of reason after so many centuries of science, labour, and battle! And to think of it being reared over Paris, the one city in the world which ought never to have been soiled in this fashion! One can understand it at Lourdes and Rome; but not in Paris, in the very field of intelligence which has been so deeply ploughed, and whence the future is sprouting. It is a declaration of war, an insolent proclamation that they hope to conquer Paris also!"

Guillaume usually evinced all the tolerance of a *savant*, for whom religions are simply social phenomena. He even willingly admitted the grandeur or grace of certain Catholic legends. But Marie Alacoque's famous vision, which has given rise to the cult of the Sacred Heart, filled him with irritation and something like physical disgust. He suffered at the mere idea of Christ's open, bleeding breast, and the gigantic heart which the saint asserted she had seen beating in the depths of the wound—the huge heart in which Jesus placed the woman's little heart to restore it to her inflated and glowing with love. What base and loathsome materialism there was in all this! What a display of viscera, muscles and blood suggestive of a butcher's shop! And Guillaume was particularly disgusted with the engraving which depicted this horror, and which he found everywhere, crudely coloured with red and yellow and blue, like some badly executed anatomical plate.

Pierre on his side was also looking at the basilica as, white with moonlight, it rose out of the darkness like a gigantic fortress raised to crush and conquer the city slumbering beneath it. It had already brought him suffering during the last days when he had said mass in it and was struggling with his torments. "They call it the national votive offering," he now exclaimed. "But the nation's longing is for health and strength and restoration to its old position by work. That is a thing the Church does not understand. It argues that if France was stricken with defeat, it was because she deserved punishment. She was guilty, and so to-day she ought to repent. Repent of what? Of the Revolution, of a century of free examination and science, of the emancipation of her mind, of her initiatory and liberative labour in all parts of the world? That indeed is her real transgression; and it is as a punishment for all our labour, search for truth, increase of knowledge and march towards justice that they have reared that huge pile which Paris will see from all her streets, and will never be able to see without feeling derided and insulted in her labour and glory."

With a wave of his hand he pointed to the city, slumbering in the moonlight as beneath a sheet of silver, and then set off again with his brother, down the slopes, towards the black and deserted streets.

They did not meet a living soul until they reached the outer boulevard. Here, however, no matter what the hour may be, life continues with scarcely a pause. No sooner are the wine shops, music and dancing halls closed, than vice and want, cast into the street, there resume their nocturnal existence. Thus the brothers came upon all the homeless ones: low prostitutes seeking a pallet, vagabonds stretched on the benches under the trees, rogues who prowled hither and thither on the lookout for a good stroke. Encouraged by their accomplice—night, all the mire and woe of Paris had returned to the surface. The empty roadway now belonged to the breadless, homeless starvelings, those for whom there was no place in the sunlight, the vague, swarming, despairing herd which is only espied at night-time. Ah! what spectres of destitution, what apparitions of grief and fright there were! What a sob of agony passed by in Paris that morning, when as soon as the dawn should rise, a man—a pauper, a sufferer like the others—was to be guillotined!

As Guillaume and Pierre were about to descend the Rue des Martyrs, the former perceived an old man lying on a bench with his bare feet protruding from his gaping, filthy shoes. Guillaume pointed to him in silence. Then, a few steps farther on, Pierre in his turn pointed to a ragged girl, crouching, asleep with open month, in the corner of a doorway. There was no need for the brothers to express in words all the compassion and anger which stirred their hearts. At long intervals policemen, walking slowly two by two, shook the poor wretches and compelled them to rise and walk on and on. Occasionally, if they found them suspicious or refractory, they marched them off to the police-station. And then rancour and the contagion of imprisonment often transformed a mere vagabond into a thief or a murderer.

In the Rue des Martyrs and the Rue du Faubourg-Montmartre, the brothers found night-birds of another kind, women who slunk past them, close to the house-fronts, and men and hussies who belaboured one another with blows. Then, upon the grand boulevards, on the thresholds of lofty black houses, only one row of whose windows flared in the night, pale-faced individuals, who had just come down from their clubs, stood lighting cigars before going home. A lady with a ball wrap over her evening gown went by accompanied by a servant. A few cabs, moreover, still jogged up and down the roadway, while others, which had been waiting for hours, stood on their ranks in rows, with drivers and horses alike asleep. And as one boulevard after another was reached, the Boulevard Poissonniere, the Boulevard Bonne Nouvelle, the Boulevard St. Denis, and so forth, as far as the Place de la Republique, there came fresh want and misery, more forsaken and hungry ones, more and more of the human "waste" that is cast into the streets and the darkness. And on the other hand, an army of street-sweepers was now appearing to remove all the filth of the past four and twenty hours, in order that Paris, spruce already at sunrise, might not blush for having thrown up such a mass of dirt and loathsomeness in the course of a single day.

It was, however, more particularly after following the Boulevard Voltaire, and drawing near to the districts of La Roquette and Charonne, that the brothers felt they were returning to a sphere of labour where there was often lack of food, and where life was but so much pain. Pierre found himself at home here. In former days, accompanied by good Abbe Rose, visiting despairing ones, distributing alms, picking up children who had sunk to the gutter, he had a hundred times perambulated every one of those long, densely populated streets. And thus a frightful vision arose before his mind's eye; he recalled all the tragedies he had witnessed, all the shrieks he had heard, all the tears and bloodshed he had seen, all the fathers, mothers and children huddled together and dying of want, dirt and abandonment: that social hell in which he had ended by losing his last hopes, fleeing from it with a sob in the conviction that charity was a mere amusement for the rich, and absolutely futile as a remedy. It was this conviction which now returned to him as he again cast eyes upon that want and grief stricken district which seemed fated to everlasting destitution. That poor old man whom Abbe Rose had revived one night in yonder hovel, had he not since died of starvation? That little girl whom he had one morning brought in his arms to the refuge after her parents' death, was it not she whom he had just met, grown but fallen to the streets, and shrieking beneath the fist of a bully? Ah! how great was the number of the wretched! Their name was legion! There were those whom one could not save, those who were hourly born to a life of woe and want, even as one may be born infirm, and those, too, who from every side sank in the sea of human injustice, that ocean which has ever been the same for centuries past, and which though one may strive to drain it, still and for ever spreads. How heavy was the silence, how dense the darkness in those working-class streets where sleep seems to be the comrade of death! Yet hunger prowls, and misfortune sobs; vague spectral forms slink by, and then are lost to view in the depths of the night.

As Pierre and Guillaume went along they became mixed with dark groups of people, a whole flock of inquisitive folk, a promiscuous, passionate tramp, tramp towards the guillotine. It came from all Paris, urged on by brutish fever, a hankering for death and blood. In spite, however, of the dull noise which came from this dim crowd, the mean streets that were passed remained quite dark, not a light appeared at any of their windows; nor could one hear the breathing of the weary toilers stretched on their wretched pallets from which they would not rise before the morning twilight.

On seeing the jostling crowd which was already assembled on the Place Voltaire, Pierre understood that it would be impossible for him and his brother to ascend the Rue de la Roquette. Barriers, moreover, must certainly have been thrown across that street. In order therefore to reach the corner of the Rue Merlin, it occurred to him to take the Rue de la Folie Regnault, which winds round in the rear of the prison, farther on.

Here indeed they found solitude and darkness again.

The huge, massive prison with its great bare walls on which a moonray fell, looked like some pile of cold stones, dead for centuries past. At the end of the street they once more fell in with the crowd, a dim restless mass of beings, whose pale faces alone could be distinguished. The brothers had great difficulty in reaching the house in which Mege resided at the corner of the Rue Merlin. All the shutters of the fourth-floor flat occupied by the Socialist deputy were closed, though every other window was wide open and crowded with surging sightseers. Moreover, the wine shop down below and the first-floor room connected with it flared with gas, and were already crowded with noisy customers, waiting for the performance to begin.

"I hardly like to go and knock at Mege's door," said Pierre.

"No, no, you must not do so!" replied Guillaume.

"Let us go into the wine shop. We may perhaps be able to see something from the balcony."

The first-floor room was provided with a very large balcony, which women and gentlemen were already filling. The brothers nevertheless managed to reach it, and for a few minutes remained there, peering into the darkness before them. The sloping street grew broader between the two prisons, the "great" and the "little" Roquette, in such wise as to form a sort of square, which was shaded by four clumps of plane-trees, rising from the footways. The low buildings and scrubby trees, all poor and ugly of aspect, seemed almost to lie on a level with the ground, under a vast sky in which stars were appearing, as the moon gradually declined. And the square was quite empty save that on one spot yonder there seemed to be some little stir. Two rows of guards prevented the crowd from advancing, and even threw it back into the neighbouring streets. On the one hand, the only lofty houses were far away, at the point where the Rue St. Maur intersects the Rue de la Roquette; while, on the other, they stood at the corners of the Rue Merlin and the Rue de la Folie Regnault, so that it was almost impossible to distinguish anything of the execution even from the best placed windows. As for the inquisitive folk on the pavement they only saw the backs of the guards. Still this did not prevent a crush. The human tide flowed on from all sides with increasing clamour.

I. THE GUILLOTINE

Guided by the remarks of some women who, leaning forward on the balcony, had been watching the square for a long time already, the brothers were at last able to perceive something. It was now half-past three, and the guillotine was nearly ready. The little stir which one vaguely espied yonder under the trees, was that of the headsman's assistants fixing the knife in position. A lantern slowly came and went, and five or six shadows danced over the ground. But nothing else could be distinguished, the square was like a large black pit, around which ever broke the waves of the noisy crowd which one could not see. And beyond the square one could only identify the flaring wine shops, which showed forth like lighthouses in the night. All the surrounding district of poverty and toil was still asleep, not a gleam as yet came from workrooms or yards, not a puff of smoke from the lofty factory chimneys.

"We shall see nothing," Guillaume remarked.

But Pierre silenced him, for he has just discovered that an elegantly attired gentleman leaning over the balcony near him was none other than the amiable deputy Duthil. He had at first fancied that a woman muffled in wraps who stood close beside the deputy was the little Princess de Harn, whom he had very likely brought to see the execution since he had taken her to see the trial. On closer inspection, however, he had found that this woman was Silviane, the perverse creature with the virginal face. Truth to tell, she made no concealment of her presence, but talked on in an extremely loud voice, as if intoxicated; and the brothers soon learnt how it was that she happened to be there. Duvillard, Duthil, and other friends had been supping with her at one o'clock in the morning, when on learning that Salvat was about to be guillotined, the fancy of seeing the execution had suddenly come upon her. Duvillard, after vainly entreating her to do nothing of the kind, had gone off in a fury, for he felt that it would be most unseemly on his part to attend the execution of a man who had endeavoured to blow up his house. And thereupon Silviane had turned to Duthil, whom her caprice greatly worried, for he held all such loathsome spectacles in horror, and had already refused to act as escort to the Princess. However, he was so infatuated with Silviane's beauty, and she made him so many promises, that he had at last consented to take her.

"He can't understand people caring for amusement," she said, speaking of the Baron. "And yet this is really a thing to see.... But no matter, you'll find him at my feet again to-morrow."

Duthil smiled and responded: "I suppose that peace has been signed and ratified now that you have secured your engagement at the Comedie."

"Peace? No!" she protested. "No, no. There will be no peace between us until I have made my *debut*. After that, we'll see."

They both laughed; and then Duthil, by way of paying his court, told her how good-naturedly Dauvergne, the new Minister of Public Instruction and Fine Arts, had adjusted the difficulties which had hitherto kept the doors of the Comedie closed upon her. A really charming man was Dauvergne, the embodiment of graciousness, the very flower of the Monferrand ministry. His was the velvet hand in that administration whose leader had a hand of iron.

"He told me, my beauty," said Duthil, "that a pretty girl was in place everywhere." And then as Silviane, as if flattered, pressed closely beside him, the deputy added: "So that wonderful revival of 'Polyeucte,' in which you are going to have such a triumph, is to take place on the day after to-morrow. We shall all go to applaud you, remember."

"Yes, on the evening of the day after to-morrow," said Silviane, "the very same day when the wedding of the Baron's daughter will take place. There'll be plenty of emotion that day!"

"Ah! yes, of course!" retorted Duthil, "there'll be the wedding of our friend Gerard with Mademoiselle Camille to begin with. We shall have a crush at the Madeleine in the morning and another at the Comedie in the evening. You are quite right, too; there will be several hearts throbbing in the Rue Godot-de-Mauroy."

Thereupon they again became merry, and jested about the Duvillard family—father, mother, lover and daughter—with the greatest possible ferocity and crudity of language. Then, all at once Silviane exclaimed: "Do you know, I'm feeling awfully bored here, my little Duthil. I can't distinguish anything, and I should like to be quite near so as to see it all plainly. You must take me over yonder, close to that machine of theirs."

This request threw Duthil into consternation, particularly as at that same moment Silviane perceived Massot outside the wine shop, and began calling and beckoning to him imperiously. A brief conversation then ensued between the young woman and the journalist: "I say, Massot!" she called, "hasn't a deputy the right to pass the guards and take a lady wherever he likes?"

"Not at all!" exclaimed Duthil. "Massot knows very well that a deputy ought to be the very first to bow to the laws."

This exclamation warned Massot that Duthil did not wish to leave the balcony. "You ought to have secured a card of invitation, madame," said he, in reply to Silviane. "They would then have found you room at one of the windows of La Petite Roquette. Women are not allowed elsewhere.... But you mustn't complain, you have a very good place up there."

"But I can see nothing at all, my dear Massot."

"Well, you will in any case see more than Princess de Harn will. Just now I came upon her carriage in the Rue du Chemin Vert. The police would not allow it to come any nearer."

This news made Silviane merry again, whilst Duthil shuddered at the idea of the danger he incurred, for Rosemonde would assuredly treat him to a terrible scene should she see him with another woman. Then, an idea occurring to him, he ordered a bottle of champagne and some little cakes for his "beautiful friend," as he called Silviane. She had been complaining of thirst, and was delighted with the opportunity of perfecting her intoxication. When a waiter had managed to place a little table near her, on the balcony itself, she found things very pleasant, and indeed considered it quite brave to tipple and sup afresh, while waiting for that man to be guillotined close by.

It was impossible for Pierre and Guillaume to remain up there any longer. All that they heard, all that they beheld filled them with disgust. The boredom of waiting had turned all the inquisitive folks of the balcony and the adjoining room into customers. The waiter could hardly manage to serve the many glasses of beer, bottles of expensive wine, biscuits, and plates of cold meat which were ordered of him. And yet the spectators here were all *bourgeois*, rich gentlemen, people of society! On the other hand, time has to be killed somehow when it hangs heavily on one's hands; and thus there were bursts of laughter and paltry and horrible jests, quite a feverish uproar arising amidst the clouds of smoke from the men's cigars. When Pierre and Guillaume passed through the wine shop on the ground-floor they there found a similar crush and similar tumult, aggravated by the disorderly behaviour of the big fellows in blouses who were drinking draught wine at the pewter bar which shone like silver. There were people, too, at all the little tables, besides an incessant coming and going of folks who entered the place for a "wet," by way of calming their impatience. And what folks they were! All the scum, all the vagabonds who had been dragging themselves about since daybreak on the lookout for whatever chance might offer them, provided it were not work!

On the pavement outside, Pierre and Guillaume felt yet a greater heart-pang. In the throng which the guards kept back, one simply found so much mire stirred up from the very depths of Paris life: prostitutes and criminals, the murderers of to-morrow, who came to see how a man ought to die. Loathsome, bareheaded harlots mingled with bands of prowlers or ran through the crowd, howling obscene refrains. Bandits stood in groups chatting and quarrelling about the more or less glorious manner in which certain famous *guillotines* had died. Among these was one with respect to whom they all agreed, and of whom they spoke as of a great captain, a hero whose marvellous courage was deserving of immortality. Then, as one passed along, one caught snatches of horrible phrases, particulars about the instrument of death, ignoble boasts, and filthy jests reeking with blood. And over and above all else there was bestial fever, a lust for death which made this multitude delirious, an eagerness to see life flow forth fresh and ruddy beneath the knife, so that as it coursed over the soil they might dip their feet in it. As this execution was not an ordinary one, however, there were yet spectators of another kind; silent men with glowing eyes who came and went all alone, and who were plainly thrilled by their faith, intoxicated with the contagious madness which incites one to vengeance or martyrdom.

Guillaume was just thinking of Victor Mathis, when he fancied that he saw him standing in the front row of sightseers whom the guards held in check. It was indeed he, with his thin, beardless, pale, drawn face. Short as he was, he had to raise himself on tiptoes in order to see anything. Near him was a big, red-haired girl who gesticulated; but for his part he never stirred or spoke. He was waiting motionless, gazing yonder with the round, ardent, fixed eyes of a night-bird, seeking to penetrate the darkness. At last a guard pushed him back in a somewhat brutal way; but he soon returned to his previous position, ever patient though full of hatred against the executioners, wishing indeed to see all he could in order to increase his hate.

Then Massot approached the brothers. This time, on seeing Pierre without his cassock, he did not even make a sign of astonishment, but gaily remarked: "So you felt curious to see this affair, Monsieur Froment?"

"Yes, I came with my brother," Pierre replied. "But I very much fear that we shan't see much."

"You certainly won't if you stay here," rejoined Massot. And thereupon in his usual good-natured way—glad, moreover, to show what power a well-known journalist could wield—he inquired: "Would you like me to pass you through? The inspector here happens to be a friend of mine."

Then, without waiting for an answer, he stopped the inspector and hastily whispered to him that he had brought a couple of colleagues, who wanted to report the proceedings. At first the inspector hesitated, and seemed inclined to refuse Massot's request; but after a moment, influenced by the covert fear which the police always has of the press, he made a weary gesture of consent.

"Come, quick, then," said Massot, turning to the brothers, and taking them along with him.

A moment later, to the intense surprise of Pierre and Guillaume, the guards opened their ranks to let them pass. They then found themselves in the large open space which was kept clear. And on thus emerging from the tumultuous throng they were quite impressed by the death-like silence and solitude which reigned under the little plane-trees. The night was now paling. A faint gleam of dawn was already falling from the sky.

After leading his companions slantwise across the square, Massot stopped them near the prison and resumed: "I'm going inside; I want to see the prisoner roused and got ready. In the meantime, walk about here; nobody will say anything to you. Besides, I'll come back to you in a moment."

A hundred people or so, journalists and other privileged spectators, were scattered about the dark square. Movable wooden barriers—such as are set up at the doors of theatres when there is a press of people waiting for admission—had been placed on either side of the pavement running from the prison gate to the guillotine; and some sightseers were already leaning over these barriers, in order to secure a close view of the condemned man as he passed by. Others were walking slowly to and fro, and conversing in undertones. The brothers, for their part, approached the guillotine.

It stood there under the branches of the trees, amidst the delicate greenery of the fresh leaves of spring. A neighbouring gas-lamp, whose light was turning yellow in the rising dawn, cast vague gleams upon it. The work of fixing it in position—work performed as quietly as could be, so that the only sound was the occasional thud of a mallet—had just been finished; and the headsman's "valets" or assistants, in frock-coats and tall silk hats, were waiting and strolling about in a patient way. But the instrument itself, how base and shameful it looked, squatting on the ground like some filthy beast, disgusted with the work it had to accomplish! What! those few beams lying on the ground, and those others barely nine feet high which rose from it, keeping the knife in position, constituted the machine which avenged Society, the instrument which gave a warning to evil-doers! Where was the big scaffold painted a bright red and reached by a stairway of ten steps, the scaffold which raised high bloody arms over the eager multitude, so that everybody might behold the punishment of the law in all its horror! The beast had now been felled to the ground, where it simply looked ignoble, crafty and cowardly. If on the one hand there was no majesty in the manner in which human justice condemned a man to death at its assizes: on the other, there was merely horrid butchery with the help of the most barbarous and repulsive of mechanical contrivances, on the terrible day when that man was executed.

As Pierre and Guillaume gazed at the guillotine, a feeling of nausea came over them. Daylight was now slowly breaking, and the surroundings were appearing to view: first the square itself with its two low, grey prisons, facing one another; then the distant houses, the taverns, the marble workers' establishments, and the shops selling flowers and wreaths, which are numerous hereabouts, as the cemetery of Pere-Lachaise is so near. Before long one could plainly distinguish the black lines of the spectators standing around in a circle, the heads leaning forward from windows and balconies, and the people who had climbed to the very house roofs. The prison of La Petite Roquette over the way had been turned into a kind of tribune for guests; and mounted Gardes de Paris went slowly to and fro across the intervening expanse. Then, as the sky brightened, labour awoke throughout the district beyond the crowd, a district of broad, endless streets lined with factories, work-shops and work-yards. Engines began to snort, machinery and appliances were got ready to start once more on their usual tasks, and smoke already curled away from the forest of lofty brick chimneys which, on all sides, sprang out of the gloom.

It then seemed to Guillaume that the guillotine was really in its right place in that district of want and toil. It stood in its own realm, like a *terminus* and a threat. Did not ignorance, poverty and woe lead to it? And each time that it was set up amidst those toilsome streets, was it not charged to overawe the disinherited ones, the starvelings, who, exasperated by everlasting injustice, were always ready for revolt? It was not seen in the districts where wealth and enjoyment reigned. It would there have seemed purposeless, degrading and truly monstrous. And it was a tragical and terrible coincidence that the bomb-thrower, driven mad by want, should be guillotined there, in the very centre of want's dominion.

But daylight had come at last, for it was nearly half-past four. The distant noisy crowd could feel that the expected moment was drawing nigh. A shudder suddenly sped through the atmosphere.

"He's coming," exclaimed little Massot, as he came back to Pierre and Guillaume. "Ah! that Salvat is a brave fellow after all."

Then he related how the prisoner had been awakened; how the governor of the prison, magistrate Amadieu, the chaplain, and a few other persons had entered the cell where Salvat lay fast asleep; and then how the condemned man had understood the truth immediately upon opening his eyes. He had risen, looking pale but quite composed. And he had dressed himself without assistance, and had declined the nip of brandy and the cigarette proffered by the good-hearted chaplain, in the same way as with a gentle but stubborn gesture he had brushed the crucifix aside. Then had come the "toilette" for death. With all rapidity and without a word being exchanged, Salvat's hands had been tied behind his back, his legs had been loosely secured with a cord, and the neckband of his shirt had been cut away. He had smiled when the others exhorted him to be brave. He only feared some nervous weakness, and had but one desire, to die like a hero, to remain the martyr of the ardent faith in truth and justice for which he was about to perish.

"They are now drawing up the death certificate in the register," continued Massot in his chattering way. "Come along, come along to the barriers if you wish a good view.... I turned paler, you know, and trembled far more than he did. I don't care a rap for anything as a rule; but, all the same, an execution isn't a pleasant business.... You can't imagine how many attempts were made to save Salvat's life. Even some of the papers asked that he might be reprieved. But nothing succeeded, the execution was regarded as inevitable, it seems, even by those who consider it a blunder. Still, they had such a touching opportunity to reprieve him, when his daughter, little Celine, wrote that fine letter to the President of the Republic, which I was the first to publish in the 'Globe.' Ah! that letter, it cost me a lot of running about!"

Pierre, who was already quite upset by this long wait for the horrible scene, felt moved to tears by Massot's reference to Celine. He could again see the child standing beside Madame Theodore in that bare, cold room whither her father would never more return. It was thence that he had set out on a day of desperation with his stomach empty and his brain on fire, and it was here that he would end, between yonder beams, beneath yonder knife.

Massot, however, was still giving particulars. The doctors, said he, were furious because they feared that the body would not be delivered to them immediately after the execution. To this Guillaume did not listen. He stood there with his elbows resting on the wooden barrier and his eyes fixed on the prison gate, which still remained shut. His hands were quivering, and there was an expression of anguish on his face as if it were he himself who was about to be executed. The headsman had again just left the prison. He was a little, insignificant-looking man, and seemed annoyed, anxious to have done with it all. Then, among a group of frock-coated gentlemen, some of the spectators pointed out Gascogne, the Chief of the Detective Police, who wore a cold, official air, and Amadieu, the investigating magistrate, who smiled and looked very spruce, early though the hour was. He had come partly because it was his duty, and partly because he wished to show himself now that the curtain was about to fall on a wonderful tragedy of which he considered himself the author. Guillaume glanced at him, and then as a growing uproar rose from the distant crowd, he looked up for an instant, and again beheld the two grey prisons, the plane-trees with their fresh young leaves, and the houses swarming with people beneath the pale blue sky, in which the triumphant sun was about to appear.

"Look out, here he comes!"

Who had spoken? A slight noise, that of the opening gate, made every heart throb. Necks were outstretched, eyes gazed fixedly, there was laboured breathing on all sides. Salvat stood on the threshold of the prison. The chaplain, stepping backwards, had come out in advance of him, in order to conceal the guillotine from his sight, but he had stopped short, for he wished to see that instrument of death, make acquaintance with it, as it were, before he walked towards it. And as he stood there, his long, aged sunken face, on which life's hardships had left their mark, seemed transformed by the wondrous brilliancy of his flaring, dreamy eyes. Enthusiasm bore him up—he was going to his death in all the splendour of his dream. When the executioner's assistants drew near to support him he once more refused their help, and again set himself in motion, advancing with short steps, but as quickly and as straightly as the rope hampering his legs permitted.

All at once Guillaume felt that Salvat's eyes were fixed upon him. Drawing nearer and nearer the condemned man had perceived and recognised his friend; and as he passed by, at a distance of no more than six or seven feet, he smiled faintly and darted such a deep penetrating glance at Guillaume, that ever afterwards the latter felt its smart. But what last thought, what supreme legacy had Salvat left him to meditate upon, perhaps to put into execution? It was all so poignant that Pierre feared some involuntary call on his brother's part; and so he laid his hand upon his arm to quiet him.

"Long live Anarchy!"

It was Salvat who had raised this cry. But in the deep silence his husky, altered voice seemed to break. The few who were near at hand had turned very pale; the distant crowd seemed bereft of life. The horse of one of the Gardes de Paris was alone heard snorting in the centre of the space which had been kept clear.

Then came a loathsome scramble, a scene of nameless brutality and ignominy. The headsman's helps rushed upon Salvat as he came up slowly with brow erect. Two of them seized him by the head, but finding little hair there, could only lower it by tugging at his neck. Next two others grasped him by the legs and flung him violently upon a plank which tilted over and rolled forward. Then, by dint of pushing and tugging, the head was got into the "lunette," the upper part of which fell in such wise that the neck was fixed as in a ship's port-hole—and all this was accomplished amidst such confusion and with such savagery that one might have thought that head some cumbrous thing which it was necessary to get rid of with the greatest speed. But the knife fell with a dull, heavy, forcible thud, and two long jets of blood spurted from the severed arteries, while the dead man's feet moved convulsively. Nothing else could be seen. The executioner rubbed his hands in a mechanical way, and an assistant took the severed blood-streaming head from the little basket into which it had fallen and placed it in the large basket into which the body had already been turned.

Ah! that dull, that heavy thud of the knife! It seemed to Guillaume that he had heard it echoing far away all over that district of want and toil, even in the squalid rooms where thousands of workmen were at that moment rising to perform their day's hard task! And there the echo of that thud acquired formidable significance; it spoke of man's exasperation with injustice, of zeal for martyrdom, and of the dolorous hope that the blood then spilt might hasten the victory of the disinherited.

Pierre, for his part, at the sight of that loathsome butchery, the abject cutthroat work of that killing machine, had suddenly felt his chilling shudder become more violent; for before him arose a vision of another corpse, that of the fair, pretty child ripped open by a bomb and stretched yonder, at the entrance of the Duvillard mansion. Blood streamed from her delicate flesh, just as it had streamed from that decapitated neck. It was blood paying for blood; it was like payment for mankind's debt of wretchedness, for which payment is everlastingly being made, without man ever being able to free himself from suffering.

Above the square and the crowd all was still silent in the clear sky. How long had the abomination lasted? An eternity, perhaps, compressed into two or three minutes. And now came an awakening: the spectators emerged from their nightmare with quivering hands, livid faces, and eyes expressive of compassion, disgust and fear.

"That makes another one. I've now seen four executions," said Massot, who felt ill at ease. "After all, I prefer to report weddings. Let us go off, I have all I want for my article."

Guillaume and Pierre followed him mechanically across the square, and again reached the corner of the Rue Merlin. And here they saw little Victor Mathis, with flaming eyes and white face, still standing in silence on the spot where they had left him. He could have seen nothing distinctly; but the thud of the knife was still echoing in his brain. A policeman at last gave him a push, and told him to move on. At this he looked the policeman in the face, stirred by sudden rage and ready to strangle him. Then, however, he quietly walked away, ascending the Rue de la Roquette, atop of which the lofty foliage of Pere-Lachaise could be seen, beneath the rising sun.

The brothers meantime fell upon a scene of explanations, which they heard without wishing to do so. Now that the sight was over, the Princess de Harn arrived, and she was the more furious as at the door of the wine shop she could see her new friend Duthil accompanying a woman.

"I say!" she exclaimed, "you are nice, you are, to have left me in the lurch like this! It was impossible for my carriage to get near, so I've had to come on foot through all those horrid people who have been jostling and insulting me."

Thereupon Duthil, with all promptitude, introduced Silviane to her, adding, in an aside, that he had taken a friend's place as the actress's escort. And then Rosemonde, who greatly wished to know Silviane, calmed down as if by enchantment, and put on her most engaging ways. "It would have delighted me, madame," said she, "to have seen this sight in the company of an *artiste* of your merit, one whom I admire so much, though I have never before had an opportunity of telling her so."

"Well, dear me, madame," replied Silviane, "you haven't lost much by arriving late. We were on that balcony there, and all that I could see were a few men pushing another one about.... It really isn't worth the trouble of coming."

"Well, now that we have become acquainted, madame," said the Princess, "I really hope that you will allow me to be your friend."

"Certainly, madame, my friend; and I shall be flattered and delighted to be yours."

Standing there, hand in hand, they smiled at one another. Silviane was very drunk, but her virginal expression had returned to her face; whilst Rosemonde seemed feverish with vicious curiosity. Duthil, whom the scene amused, now had but one thought, that of seeing Silviane home; so calling to Massot, who was approaching, he asked him where he should find a cab-rank. Rosemonde, however, at once offered her carriage, which was waiting in an adjacent street.

She would set the actress down at her door, said she, and the deputy at his; and such was her persistence in the matter that Duthil, greatly vexed, was obliged to accept her offer.

"Well, then, till to-morrow at the Madeleine," said Massot, again quite sprightly, as he shook hands with the Princess.

"Yes, till to-morrow, at the Madeleine and the Comedie."

"Ah! yes, of course!" he repeated, taking Silviane's hand, which he kissed. "The Madeleine in the morning and the Comedie in the evening... . We shall all be there to applaud you."

"Yes, I expect you to do so," said Silviane. "Till to-morrow, then!"

"Till to-morrow!"

The crowd was now wearily dispersing, to all appearance disappointed and ill at ease. A few enthusiasts alone lingered in order to witness the departure of the van in which Salvat's corpse would soon be removed; while bands of prowlers and harlots, looking very wan in the daylight, whistled or called to one another with some last filthy expression before returning to their dens. The headsman's assistants were hastily taking down the guillotine, and the square would soon be quite clear.

Pierre for his part wished to lead his brother away. Since the fall of the knife, Guillaume had remained as if stunned, without once opening his lips. In vain had Pierre tried to rouse him by pointing to the shutters of Mege's flat, which still remained closed, whereas every other window of the lofty house was wide open. Although the Socialist deputy hated the Anarchists, those shutters were doubtless closed as a protest against capital punishment. Whilst the multitude had been rushing to that frightful spectacle, Mege, still in bed, with his face turned to the wall, had probably been dreaming of how he would some day compel mankind to be happy beneath the rigid laws of Collectivism. Affectionate father as he was, the recent death of one of his children had quite upset his private life. His cough, too, had become a very bad one; but he ardently wished to live, for as soon as that new Monferrand ministry should have fallen beneath the interpellation which he already contemplated, his own turn would surely come: he would take the reins of power in hand, abolish the guillotine and decree justice and perfect felicity.

"Do you see, Guillaume?" Pierre gently repeated. "Mege hasn't opened his windows. He's a good fellow, after all; although our friends Bache and Morin dislike him." Then, as his brother still refrained from answering, Pierre added, "Come, let us go, we must get back home."

They both turned into the Rue de la Folie Regnault, and reached the outer Boulevards by way of the Rue du Chemin Vert. All the toilers of the district were now at work. In the long streets edged with low buildings, work-shops and factories, one heard engines snorting and machinery rumbling, while up above, the smoke from the lofty chimneys was assuming a rosy hue in the sunrise. Afterwards, when the brothers reached the Boulevard de Menilmontant and the Boulevard de Belleville, which they followed in turn at a leisurely pace, they witnessed the great rush of the working classes into central Paris. The stream poured forth from every side; from all the wretched streets of the faubourgs there was an endless exodus of toilers, who, having risen at dawn, were now hurrying, in the sharp morning air, to their daily labour. Some wore short jackets and others blouses; some were in velveteen trousers, others in linen overalls. Their thick shoes made their tramp a heavy one; their hanging hands were often deformed by work. And they seemed half asleep, not a smile was to be seen on any of those wan, weary faces turned yonder towards the everlasting task—the task which was begun afresh each day, and which—'twas their only chance—they hoped to be able to take up for ever and ever. There was no end to that drove of toilers, that army of various callings, that human flesh fated to manual labour, upon which Paris preys in order that she may live in luxury and enjoyment.

Then the procession continued across the Boulevard de la Villette, the Boulevard de la Chapelle, and the Boulevard de Rochechouart, where one reached the height of Montmartre. More and more workmen were ever coming down from their bare cold rooms and plunging into the huge city, whence, tired out, they would that evening merely bring back the bread of rancour. And now, too, came a stream of work-girls, some of them in bright skirts, some glancing at the passers-by; girls whose wages were so paltry, so insufficient, that now and again pretty ones among them never more turned their faces homewards, whilst the ugly ones wasted away, condemned to mere bread and water. A little later, moreover, came the *employes*, the clerks, the counter-jumpers, the whole world of frock-coated penury—"gentlemen" who devoured a roll as they hastened onward, worried the while by the dread of being unable to pay their rent, or by the problem of providing food for wife and children until the end of the month should come.[1] And now the sun was fast ascending on the horizon, the whole army of ants was out and about, and the toilsome day had begun with its ceaseless display of courage, energy and suffering.

---

[1] In Paris nearly all clerks and shop-assistants receive monthly salaries, while most workmen are paid once a fortnight.—Trans.

Never before had it been so plainly manifest to Pierre that work was a necessity, that it healed and saved. On the occasion of his visit to the Grandidier works, and later still, when he himself had felt the need of occupation, there had cone to him the thought that work was really the world's law. And after that hateful night, after that spilling of blood, after the slaughter of that toiler maddened by his dreams, there was consolation and hope in seeing the sun rise once more, and everlasting labour take up its wonted task. However hard it might prove, however unjustly it might be lotted out, was it not work which would some day bring both justice and happiness to the world?

All at once, as the brothers were climbing the steep hillside towards Guillaume's house, they perceived before and above them the basilica of the Sacred Heart rising majestically and triumphantly to the sky. This was no sublunar apparition, no dreamy vision of Domination standing face to face with nocturnal Paris. The sun now clothed the edifice with splendour, it looked golden and proud and victorious, flaring with immortal glory.

Then Guillaume, still silent, still feeling Salvat's last glance upon him, seemed to come to some sudden and final decision. He looked at the basilica with glowing eyes, and pronounced sentence upon it.

II. IN VANITY FAIR

THE wedding was to take place at noon, and for half an hour already guests had been pouring into the magnificently decorated church, which was leafy with evergreens and balmy with the scent of flowers. The high altar in the rear glowed with countless candles, and through the great doorway, which was wide open, one could see the peristyle decked with shrubs, the steps covered with a broad carpet, and the inquisitive crowd assembled on the square and even along the Rue Royale, under the bright sun.

After finding three more chairs for some ladies who had arrived rather late, Duthil remarked to Massot, who was jotting down names in his note-book: "Well, if any more come, they will have to remain standing."

"Who were those three?" the journalist inquired.

"The Duchess de Boisemont and her two daughters."

"Indeed! All the titled people of France, as well as all the financiers and politicians, are here! It's something more even than a swell Parisian wedding."

As a matter of fact all the spheres of "society" were gathered together there, and some at first seemed rather embarrassed at finding themselves beside others. Whilst Duvillard's name attracted all the princes of finance and politicians in power, Madame de Quinsac and her son were supported by the highest of the French aristocracy. The mere names of the witnesses sufficed to indicate what an extraordinary medley there was. On Gerard's side these witnesses were his uncle, General de Bozonnet, and the Marquis de Morigny; whilst on Camille's they were the great banker Louvard, and Monferrand, the President of the Council and Minister of Finances. The quiet bravado which the latter displayed in thus supporting the bride after being compromised in her father's financial intrigues imparted a piquant touch of impudence to his triumph. And public curiosity was further stimulated by the circumstance that the nuptial blessing was to be given by Monseigneur Martha, Bishop of Persepolis, the Pope's political agent in France, and the apostle of the endeavours to win the Republic over to the Church by pretending to "rally" to it.

"But, I was mistaken," now resumed Massot with a sneer. "I said a really Parisian wedding, did I not? But in point of fact this wedding is a symbol. It's the apotheosis of the *bourgeoisie*, my dear fellow—the old nobility sacrificing one of its sons on the altar of the golden calf in order that the Divinity and the gendarmes, being the masters of France once more, may rid us of those scoundrelly Socialists!"

Then, again correcting himself, he added: "But I was forgetting. There are no more Socialists. Their head was cut off the other morning."

Duthil found this very funny. Then in a confidential way he remarked: "You know that the marriage wasn't settled without a good deal of difficulty.... Have you read Sagnier's ignoble article this morning?"

"Yes, yes; but I knew it all before, everybody knew it."

Then in an undertone, understanding one another's slightest allusion, they went on chatting. It was only amidst a flood of tears and after a despairing struggle that Baroness Duvillard had consented to let her lover marry her daughter. And in doing so she had yielded to the sole desire of seeing Gerard rich and happy. She still regarded Camille with all the hatred of a defeated rival. Then, an equally painful contest had taken place at Madame de Quinsac's. The Countess had only overcome her revolt and consented to the marriage in order to save her son from the dangers which had threatened him since childhood; and the Marquis de Morigny had been so affected by her maternal abnegation, that in spite of all his anger he had resignedly agreed to be a witness, thus making a supreme sacrifice, that of his conscience, to the woman whom he had ever loved. And it was this frightful story that Sagnier—using transparent nicknames—had related in the "Voix du Peuple" that morning. He had even contrived to make it more horrid than it really was; for, as usual, he was badly informed, and he was naturally inclined to falsehood and invention, as by sending an ever thicker and more poisonous torrent from his sewer, he might, day by day, increase his paper's sales. Since Monferrand's victory had compelled him to leave the African Railways scandal on one side, he had fallen back on scandals in private life, stripping whole families bare and pelting them with mud.

All at once Duthil and Massot were approached by Chaigneux, who, with his shabby frock coat badly buttoned, wore both a melancholy and busy air. "Well, Monsieur Massot," said he, "what about your article on Silviane? Is it settled? Will it go in?"

As Chaigneux was always for sale, always ready to serve as a valet, it had occurred to Duvillard to make use of him to ensure Silviane's success at the Comedie. He had handed this sorry deputy over to the young woman, who entrusted him with all manner of dirty work, and sent him scouring Paris in search of applauders and advertisements. His eldest daughter was not yet married, and never had his four women folk weighed more heavily on his hands. His life had become a perfect hell; they had ended by beating him, if he did not bring a thousand-franc note home on the first day of every month.

"My article!" Massot replied; "no, it surely won't go in, my dear deputy. Fonsegue says that it's written in too laudatory a style for the 'Globe.' He asked me if I were having a joke with the paper."

Chaigneux became livid. The article in question was one written in advance, from the society point of view, on the success which Silviane would achieve in "Polyeucte," that evening, at the Comedie. The journalist, in the hope of pleasing her, had even shown her his "copy"; and she, quite delighted, now relied upon finding the article in print in the most sober and solemn organ of the Parisian press.

"Good heavens! what will become of us?" murmured the wretched Chaigneux. "It's absolutely necessary that the article should go in."

"Well, I'm quite agreeable. But speak to the governor yourself. He's standing yonder between Vignon and Dauvergne, the Minister of Public Instruction."

"Yes, I certainly will speak to him—but not here. By-and-by in the sacristy, during the procession. And I must also try to speak to Dauvergne, for our Silviane particularly wants him to be in the ministerial box this evening. Monferrand will be there; he promised Duvillard so."

Massot began to laugh, repeating the expression which had circulated through Paris directly after the actress's engagement: "The Silviane ministry.... Well, Dauvergne certainly owes that much to his godmother!" said he.

Just then the little Princess de Harn, coming up like a gust of wind, broke in upon the three men. "I've no seat, you know!" she cried.

Duthil fancied that it was a question of finding her a well-placed chair in the church. "You mustn't count on me," he answered. "I've just had no end of trouble in stowing the Duchess de Boisemont away with her two daughters."

"Oh, but I'm talking of this evening's performance. Come, my dear Duthil, you really must find me a little corner in somebody's box. I shall die, I know I shall, if I can't applaud our delicious, our incomparable friend!"

Ever since setting Silviane down at her door on the previous day, Rosemonde had been overflowing with admiration for her.

"Oh! you won't find a single remaining seat, madame," declared Chaigneux, putting on an air of importance. "We have distributed everything. I have just been offered three hundred francs for a stall."

"That's true, there has been a fight even for the bracket seats, however badly they might be placed," Duthil resumed. "I am very sorry, but you must not count on me.... Duvillard is the only person who might take you in his box. He told me that he would reserve me a seat there. And so far, I think, there are only three of us, including his son.... Ask Hyacinthe by-and-by to procure you an invitation."

Rosemonde, whom Hyacinthe had so greatly bored that she had given him his dismissal, felt the irony of Duthil's suggestion. Nevertheless, she exclaimed with an air of delight: "Ah, yes! Hyacinthe can't refuse me that. Thanks for your information, my dear Duthil. You are very nice, you are; for you settle things gaily even when they are rather sad.... And don't forget, mind, that you have promised to teach me politics. Ah! politics, my dear fellow, I feel that nothing will ever impassion me as politics do!"

Then she left them, hustled several people, and in spite of the crush ended by installing herself in the front row.

"Ah! what a crank she is!" muttered Massot with an air of amusement.

Then, as Chaigneux darted towards magistrate Amadieu to ask him in the most obsequious way if he had received his ticket, the journalist said to Duthil in a whisper: "By the way, my dear friend, is it true that Duvillard is going to launch his famous scheme for a Trans-Saharan railway? It would be a gigantic enterprise, a question of hundreds and hundreds of millions this time.... At the 'Globe' office yesterday evening, Fonsegue shrugged his shoulders and said it was madness, and would never come off!"

Duthil winked, and in a jesting way replied: "It's as good as done, my dear boy. Fonsegue will be kissing the governor's feet before another forty-eight hours are over."

Then he gaily gave the other to understand that golden manna would presently be raining down on the press and all faithful friends and willing helpers. Birds shake their feathers when the storm is over, and he, Duthil, was as spruce and lively, as joyous at the prospect of the presents he now expected, as if there had never been any African Railways scandal to upset him and make him turn pale with fright.

"The deuce!" muttered Massot, who had become serious. "So this affair here is more than a triumph: it's the promise of yet another harvest. Well, I'm no longer surprised at the crush of people."

At this moment the organs suddenly burst into a glorious hymn of greeting. The marriage procession was entering the church. A loud clamour had gone up from the crowd, which spread over the roadway of the Rue Royale and impeded the traffic there, while the *cortege* pompously ascended the steps in the bright sunshine. And it was now entering the edifice and advancing beneath the lofty, re-echoing vaults towards the high altar which flared with candles, whilst on either hand crowded the congregation, the men on the right and the women on the left. They had all risen and stood there smiling, with necks outstretched and eyes glowing with curiosity.

First, in the rear of the magnificent beadle, came Camille, leaning on the arm of her father, Baron Duvillard, who wore a proud expression befitting a day of victory. Veiled with superb *point d'Alencon* falling from her diadem of orange blossom, gowned in pleated silk muslin over an underskirt of white satin, the bride looked so extremely happy, so radiant at having conquered, that she seemed almost pretty. Moreover, she held herself so upright that one could scarcely detect that her left shoulder was higher than her right.

Next came Gerard, giving his arm to his mother, the Countess de Quinsac,—he looking very handsome and courtly, as was proper, and she displaying impassive dignity in her gown of peacock-blue silk embroidered with gold and steel beads. But it was particularly Eve whom people wished to see, and every neck was craned forward when she appeared on the arm of General Bozonnet, the bridegroom's first witness and nearest male relative. She was gowned in "old rose" taffetas trimmed with Valenciennes of priceless value, and never had she looked younger, more deliciously fair. Yet her eyes betrayed her emotion, though she strove to smile; and her languid grace bespoke her widowhood, her compassionate surrender of the man she loved. Monferrand, the Marquis de Morigny, and banker Louvard, the three other witnesses, followed the Baroness and General Bozonnet, each giving his arm to some lady of the family. A considerable sensation was caused by the appearance of Monferrand, who seemed on first-rate terms with himself, and jested familiarly with the lady he accompanied, a little brunette with a giddy air. Another who was noticed in the solemn, interminable procession was the bride's eccentric brother Hyacinthe, whose dress coat was of a cut never previously seen, with its tails broadly and symmetrically pleated.

When the affianced pair had taken their places before the prayer-stools awaiting them, and the members of both families and the witnesses had installed themselves in the rear in large armchairs, all gilding and red velvet, the ceremony was performed with extraordinary pomp. The cure of the Madeleine officiated in person; and vocalists from the Grand Opera reinforced the choir, which chanted the high mass to the accompaniment of the organs, whence came a continuous hymn of glory. All possible luxury and magnificence were displayed, as if to turn this wedding into some public festivity, a great victory, an event marking the apogee of a class. Even the impudent bravado attaching to the loathsome private drama which lay behind it all, and which was known to everybody, added a touch of abominable grandeur to the ceremony. But the truculent spirit of superiority and domination which characterised the proceedings became most manifest when Monseigneur Martha appeared in surplice and stole to pronounce the blessing. Tall of stature, fresh of face, and faintly smiling, he had his wonted air of amiable sovereignty, and it was with august unction that he pronounced the sacramental words, like some pontiff well pleased at reconciling the two great empires whose heirs he united. His address to the newly married couple was awaited with curiosity. It proved really marvellous, he himself triumphed in it. Was it not in that same church that he had baptised the bride's mother, that blond Eve, who was still so beautiful, that Jewess whom he himself had converted to the Catholic faith amidst the tears of emotion shed by all Paris society? Was it not there also that he had delivered his three famous addresses on the New Spirit, whence dated, to his thinking, the rout of science, the awakening of Christian spirituality, and that policy of rallying to the Republic which was to lead to its conquest?

So it was assuredly allowable for him to indulge in some delicate allusions, by way of congratulating himself on his work, now that he was marrying a poor scion of the old aristocracy to the five millions of that *bourgeoise* heiress, in whose person triumphed the class which had won the victory in 1789, and was now master of the land. The fourth estate, the duped, robbed people, alone had no place in those festivities. But by uniting the affianced pair before him in the bonds of wedlock, Monseigneur Martha sealed the new alliance, gave effect to the Pope's own policy, that stealthy effort of Jesuitical Opportunism which would take democracy, power and wealth to wife, in order to subdue and control them. When the prelate reached his peroration he turned towards Monferrand, who sat there smiling; and it was he, the Minister, whom he seemed to be addressing while he expressed the hope that the newly married pair would ever lead a truly Christian life of humility and obedience in all fear of God, of whose iron hand he spoke as if it were that of some gendarme charged with maintaining the peace of the world. Everybody was aware that there was some diplomatic understanding between the Bishop and the Minister, some secret pact or other whereby both satisfied their passion for authority, their craving to insinuate themselves into everything and reign supreme; and thus when the spectators saw Monferrand smiling in his somewhat sly, jovial way, they also exchanged smiles.

"Ah!" muttered Massot, who had remained near Duthil, "how amused old Justus Steinberger would be, if he were here to see his granddaughter marrying the last of the Quinsacs!"

"But these marriages are quite the thing, quite the fashion, my dear fellow," the deputy replied. "The Jews and the Christians, the *bourgeois* and the nobles, do quite right to come to an understanding, so as to found a new aristocracy. An aristocracy is needed, you know, for otherwise we should be swept away by the masses."

None the less Massot continued sneering at the idea of what a grimace Justus Steinberger would have made if he had heard Monseigneur Martha. It was rumoured in Paris that although the old Jew banker had ceased all intercourse with his daughter Eve since her conversion, he took a keen interest in everything she was reported to do or say, as if he were more than ever convinced that she would prove an avenging and dissolving agent among those Christians, whose destruction was asserted to be the dream of his race. If he had failed in his hope of overcoming Duvillard by giving her to him as a wife, he doubtless now consoled himself with thinking of the extraordinary fortune to which his blood had attained, by mingling with that of the harsh, old-time masters of his race, to whose corruption it gave a finishing touch. Therein perhaps lay that final Jewish conquest of the world of which people sometimes talked.

A last triumphal strain from the organ brought the ceremony to an end; whereupon the two families and the witnesses passed into the sacristy, where the acts were signed. And forthwith the great congratulatory procession commenced.

The bride and bridegroom at last stood side by side in the lofty but rather dim room, panelled with oak. How radiant with delight was Camille at the thought that it was all over, that she had triumphed and married that handsome man of high lineage, after wresting him with so much difficulty from one and all, her mother especially! She seemed to have grown taller. Deformed, swarthy, and ugly though she was, she drew herself up exultingly, whilst scores and scores of women, friends or acquaintances, scrambled and rushed upon her, pressing her hands or kissing her, and addressing her in words of ecstasy. Gerard, who rose both head and shoulders above his bride, and looked all the nobler and stronger beside one of such puny figure, shook hands and smiled like some Prince Charming, who good-naturedly allowed himself to be loved. Meanwhile, the relatives of the newly wedded pair, though they were drawn up in one line, formed two distinct groups past which the crowd pushed and surged with arms outstretched. Duvillard received the congratulations offered him as if he were some king well pleased with his people; whilst Eve, with a supreme effort, put on an enchanting mien, and answered one and all with scarcely a sign of the sobs which she was forcing back. Then, on the other side of the bridal pair, Madame de Quinsac stood between General de Bozonnet and the Marquis de Morigny. Very dignified, in fact almost haughty, she acknowledged most of the salutations addressed to her with a mere nod, giving her little withered hand only to those people with whom she was well acquainted. A sea of strange countenances encompassed her, and now and again when some particularly murky wave rolled by, a wave of men whose faces bespoke all the crimes of money-mongering, she and the Marquis exchanged glances of deep sadness. This tide continued sweeping by for nearly half an hour; and such was the number of those who wanted to shake hands with the bridal pair and their relatives, that the latter soon felt their arms ache.

Meantime, some folks lingered in the sacristy; little groups collected, and gay chatter rang out. Monferrand was immediately surrounded. Massot pointed out to Duthil how eagerly Public Prosecutor Lehmann rushed upon the Minister to pay him court. They were immediately joined by investigating magistrate Amadieu. And even M. de Larombiere, the judge, approached Monferrand, although he hated the Republic, and was an intimate friend of the Quinsacs. But then obedience and obsequiousness were necessary on the part of the magistracy, for it was dependent on those in power, who alone could give advancement, and appoint even as they dismissed. As for Lehmann, it was alleged that he had rendered assistance to Monferrand by spiriting away certain documents connected with the African Railways affair, whilst with regard to the smiling and extremely Parisian Amadieu, was it not to him that the government was indebted for Salvat's head?

"You know," muttered Massot, "they've all come to be thanked for guillotining that man yesterday. Monferrand owes that wretched fellow a fine taper; for in the first place his bomb prolonged the life of the Barroux ministry, and later on it made Monferrand prime minister, as a strong-handed man was particularly needed to strangle Anarchism. What a contest, eh? Monferrand on one side and Salvat on the other. It was all bound to end in a head being cut off; one was wanted.... Ah! just listen, they are talking of it."

This was true. As the three functionaries of the law drew near to pay their respects to the all-powerful Minister, they were questioned by lady friends whose curiosity had been roused by what they had read in the newspapers. Thereupon Amadieu, whom duty had taken to the execution, and who was proud of his own importance, and determined to destroy what he called "the legend of Salvat's heroic death," declared that the scoundrel had shown no true courage at all. His pride alone had kept him on his feet. Fright had so shaken and choked him that he had virtually been dead before the fall of the knife.

"Ah! that's true!" cried Duthil. "I was there myself."

Massot, however, pulled him by the arm, quite indignant at such an assertion, although as a rule he cared a rap for nothing. "You couldn't see anything, my dear fellow," said he; "Salvat died very bravely. It's really stupid to continue throwing mud at that poor devil even when he's dead."

However, the idea that Salvat had died like a coward was too pleasing a one to be rejected. It was, so to say, a last sacrifice deposited at Monferrand's feet with the object of propitiating him. He still smiled in his peaceful way, like a good-natured man who is stern only when necessity requires it. And he showed great amiability towards the three judicial functionaries, and thanked them for the bravery with which they had accomplished their painful duty to the very end. On the previous day, after the execution, he had obtained a formidable majority in the Chamber on a somewhat delicate matter of policy. Order reigned, said he, and all was for the very best in France. Then, on seeing Vignon—who like a cool gamester had made a point of attending the wedding in order to show people that he was superior to fortune—the Minister detained him, and made much of him, partly as a matter of tactics, for in spite of everything he could not help fearing that the future might belong to that young fellow, who showed himself so intelligent and cautious. When a mutual friend informed them that Barroux' health was now so bad that the doctors had given him up as lost, they both began to express their compassion. Poor Barroux! He had never recovered from that vote of the Chamber which had overthrown him. He had been sinking from day to day, stricken to the heart by his country's ingratitude, dying of that abominable charge of money-mongering and thieving; he who was so upright and so loyal, who had devoted his whole life to the Republic! But then, as Monferrand repeated, one should never confess. The public can't understand such a thing.

At this moment Duvillard, in some degree relinquishing his paternal duties, came to join the others, and the Minister then had to share the honours of triumph with him. For was not this banker the master? Was he not money personified—money, which is the only stable, everlasting force, far above all ephemeral tenure of power, such as attaches to those ministerial portfolios which pass so rapidly from hand to hand? Monferrand reigned, but he would pass away, and a like fate would some day fall on Vignon, who had already had a warning that one could not govern unless the millions of the financial world were on one's side. So was not the only real triumpher himself, the Baron—he who laid out five millions of francs on buying a scion of the aristocracy for his daughter, he who was the personification of the sovereign *bourgeoisie*, who controlled public fortune, and was determined to part with nothing, even were he attacked with bombs? All these festivities really centred in himself, he alone sat down to the banquet, leaving merely the crumbs from his table to the lowly, those wretched toilers who had been so cleverly duped at the time of the Revolution.

That African Railways affair was already but so much ancient history, buried, spirited away by a parliamentary commission. All who had been compromised in it, the Duthils, the Chaigneux, the Fonsegues and others, could now laugh merrily. They had been delivered from their nightmare by Monferrand's strong fist, and raised by Duvillard's triumph. Even Sagnier's ignoble article and miry revelations in the "Voix du Peuple" were of no real account, and could be treated with a shrug of the shoulders, for the public had been so saturated with denunciation and slander that it was now utterly weary of all noisy scandal. The only thing which aroused interest was the rumour that Duvillard's big affair of the Trans-Saharan Railway was soon to be launched, that millions of money would be handled, and that some of them would rain down upon faithful friends.

Whilst Duvillard was conversing in a friendly way with Monferrand and Dauvergne, the Minister of Public Instruction, who had joined them, Massot encountered Fonsegue, his editor, and said to him in an undertone: "Duthil has just assured me that the Trans-Saharan business is ready, and that they mean to chance it with the Chamber. They declare that they are certain of success."

Fonsegue, however, was sceptical on the point. "It's impossible," said he; "they won't dare to begin again so soon."

Although he spoke in this fashion, the news had made him grave. He had lately had such a terrible fright through his imprudence in the African Railways affair, that he had vowed he would take every precaution in future. Still, this did not mean that he would refuse to participate in matters of business. The best course was to wait and study them, and then secure a share in all that seemed profitable. In the present instance he felt somewhat worried. However, whilst he stood there watching the group around Duvillard and the two ministers, he suddenly perceived Chaigneux, who, flitting hither and thither, was still beating up applauders for that evening's performance. He sang Silviane's praises in every key, predicted a most tremendous success, and did his very best to stimulate curiosity. At last he approached Dauvergne, and with his long figure bent double exclaimed: "My dear Minister, I have a particular request to make to you on the part of a very charming person, whose victory will not be complete this evening if you do not condescend to favour her with your vote."

Dauvergne, a tall, fair, good-looking man, whose blue eyes smiled behind his glasses, listened to Chaigneux with an affable air. He was proving a great success at the Ministry of Public Instruction, although he knew nothing of University matters. However, like a real Parisian of Dijon, as people called him, he was possessed of some tact and skill, gave entertainments at which his young and charming wife outshone all others, and passed as being quite an enlightened friend of writers and artists. Silviane's engagement at the Comedie, which so far was his most notable achievement, and which would have shaken the position of any other minister, had by a curious chance rendered him popular. It was regarded as something original and amusing.

On understanding that Chaigneux simply wished to make sure of his presence at the Comedie that evening, he became yet more affable. "Why, certainly, I shall be there, my dear deputy," he replied. "When one has such a charming god-daughter one mustn't forsake her in a moment of danger."

At this Monferrand, who had been lending ear, turned round. "And tell her," said he, "that I shall be there, too. She may therefore rely on having two more friends in the house."

Thereupon Duvillard, quite enraptured, his eyes glistening with emotion and gratitude, bowed to the two ministers as if they had granted him some never-to-be-forgotten favour.

When Chaigneux, on his side also, had returned thanks with a low bow, he happened to perceive Fonsegue, and forthwith he darted towards him and led him aside. "Ah! my dear colleague," he declared, "it is absolutely necessary that this matter should be settled. I regard it as of supreme importance."

"What are you speaking of?" inquired Fonsegue, much surprised.

"Why, of Massot's article, which you won't insert."

Thereupon, the director of the "Globe" plumply declared that he could not insert the article. He talked of his paper's dignity and gravity; and declared that the lavishing of such fulsome praise upon a hussy—yes, a mere hussy, in a journal whose exemplary morality and austerity had cost him so much labour, would seem monstrous and degrading. Personally, he did not care a fig about it if Silviane chose to make an exhibition of herself, well, he would be there to see; but the "Globe" was sacred.

Disconcerted and almost tearful, Chaigneux nevertheless renewed his attempt. "Come, my dear colleague," said he, "pray make a little effort for my sake. If the article isn't inserted, Duvillard will think that it is my fault. And you know that I really need his help. My eldest daughter's marriage has again been postponed, and I hardly know where to turn." Then perceiving that his own misfortunes in no wise touched Fonsegue, he added: "And do it for your own sake, my dear colleague, your own sake. For when all is said Duvillard knows what is in the article, and it is precisely because it is so favourable a one that he wishes to see it in the 'Globe.' Think it over; if the article isn't published, he will certainly turn his back on you."

For a moment Fonsegue remained silent. Was he thinking of the colossal Trans-Saharan enterprise? Was he reflecting that it would be hard to quarrel at such a moment and miss his own share in the coming distribution of millions among faithful friends? Perhaps so; however, the idea that it would be more prudent to await developments gained the day with him. "No, no," he said, "I can't, it's a matter of conscience."

In the mean time congratulations were still being tendered to the newly wedded couple. It seemed as if all Paris were passing through the sacristy; there were ever the same smiles and the same hand shakes. Gerard, Camille and their relatives, however weary they might feel, were forced to retain an air of delight while they stood there against the wall, pent up by the crowd. The heat was now becoming unbearable, and a cloud of dust arose as when some big flock goes by.

All at once little Princess de Harn, who had hitherto lingered nobody knew where, sprang out of the throng, flung her arms around Camille, kissed even Eve, and then kept Gerard's hand in her own while paying him extraordinary compliments. Then, on perceiving Hyacinthe, she took possession of him and carried him off into a corner. "I say," she exclaimed, "I have a favour to ask you."

The young man was wonderfully silent that day. His sister's wedding seemed to him a contemptible ceremony, the most vulgar that one could imagine. So here, thought he, was another pair accepting the horrid sexual law by which the absurdity of the world was perpetuated! For his part, he had decided that he would witness the proceedings in rigid silence, with a haughty air of disapproval. When Rosemonde spoke to him, he looked at her rather nervously, for he was glad that she had forsaken him for Duthil, and feared some fresh caprice on her part. At last, opening his mouth for the first time that day, he replied: "Oh, as a friend, you know, I will grant you whatever favour you like."

Forthwith the Princess explained that she would surely die if she did not witness the *debut* of her dear friend Silviane, of whom she had become such a passionate admirer. So she begged the young man to prevail on his father to give her a seat in his box, as she knew that one was left there.

Hyacinthe smiled. "Oh, willingly, my dear," said he; "I'll warn papa, there will be a seat for you."

Then, as the procession of guests at last drew to an end and the vestry began to empty, the bridal pair and their relatives were able to go off through the chattering throng, which still lingered about to bow to them and scrutinise them once more.

Gerard and Camille were to leave for an estate which Duvillard possessed in Normandy, directly after lunch. This repast, served at the princely mansion of the Rue Godot-de-Mauroy, provided an opportunity for fresh display. The dining-room on the first floor had been transformed into a buffet, where reigned the greatest abundance and the most wonderful sumptuousness. Quite a reception too was held in the drawing-rooms, the large red *salon*, the little blue and silver *salon* and all the others, whose doors stood wide open. Although it had been arranged that only family friends should be invited, there were quite three hundred people present. The ministers had excused themselves, alleging that the weighty cares of public business required their presence elsewhere. But the magistrates, the deputies and the leading journalists who had attended the wedding were again assembled together. And in that throng of hungry folks, longing for some of the spoils of Duvillard's new venture, the people who felt most out of their element were Madame de Quinsac's few guests, whom General de Bozonnet and the Marquis de Morigny had seated on a sofa in the large red *salon*, which they did not quit.

Eve, who for her part felt quite overcome, both her moral and physical strength being exhausted, had seated herself in the little blue and silver drawing-room, which, with her passion for flowers, she had transformed into an arbour of roses. She would have fallen had she remained standing, the very floor had seemed to sink beneath her feet. Nevertheless, whenever a guest approached her she managed to force a smile, and appear beautiful and charming. Unlooked-for help at last came to her in the person of Monseigneur Martha, who had graciously honoured the lunch with his presence. He took an armchair near her, and began to talk to her in his amiable, caressing way. He was doubtless well aware of the frightful anguish which wrung the poor woman's heart, for he showed himself quite fatherly, eager to comfort her. She, however, talked on like some inconsolable widow bent on renouncing the world for God, who alone could bring her peace. Then, as the conversation turned on the Asylum for the Invalids of Labour, she declared that she was resolved to take her presidency very seriously, and, in fact, would exclusively devote herself to it, in the future.

"And as we are speaking of this, Monseigneur," said she, "I would even ask you to give me some advice.... I shall need somebody to help me, and I thought of securing the services of a priest whom I much admire, Monsieur l'Abbe Pierre Froment."

At this the Bishop became grave and embarrassed; but Princess Rosemonde, who was passing by with Duthil, had overheard the Baroness, and drawing near with her wonted impetuosity, she exclaimed: "Abbe Pierre Froment! Oh! I forgot to tell you, my dear, that I met him going about in jacket and trousers! And I've been told too that he cycles in the Bois with some creature or other. Isn't it true, Duthil, that we met him?"

The deputy bowed and smiled, whilst Eve clasped her hands in amazement. "Is it possible! A priest who was all charitable fervour, who had the faith and passion of an apostle!"

Thereupon Monseigneur intervened: "Yes, yes, great sorrows occasionally fall upon the Church. I heard of the madness of the unhappy man you speak of. I even thought it my duty to write to him, but he left my letter unanswered. I should so much have liked to stifle such a scandal! But there are abominable forces which we cannot always overcome; and so a day or two ago the archbishop was obliged to put him under interdict.... You must choose somebody else, madame."

It was quite a disaster. Eve gazed at Rosemonde and Duthil, without daring to ask them for particulars, but wondering what creature could have been so audacious as to turn a priest from the path of duty. She must assuredly be some shameless demented woman! And it seemed to Eve as if this crime gave a finishing touch to her own misfortune. With a wave of the arm, which took in all the luxury around her, the roses steeping her in perfume, and the crush of guests around the buffet, she murmured: "Ah! decidedly there's nothing but corruption left; one can no longer rely on anybody!"

Whilst this was going on, Camille happened to be alone in her own room getting ready to leave the house with Gerard. And all at once her brother Hyacinthe joined her there. "Ah! it's you, youngster!" she exclaimed. "Well, make haste if you want to kiss me, for I'm off now, thank goodness!"

He kissed her as she suggested, and then in a doctoral way replied: "I thought you had more self-command. The delight you have been showing all this morning quite disgusts me."

A quiet glance of contempt was her only answer. However, he continued: "You know very well that she'll take your Gerard from you again, directly you come back to Paris."

At this Camille's cheeks turned white and her eyes flared. She stepped towards her brother with clenched fists: "She! you say that she will take him from me!"

The "she" they referred to was their own mother.

"Listen, my boy! I'll kill her first!" continued Camille. "Ah, no! she needn't hope for that. I shall know how to keep the man that belongs to me.... And as for you, keep your spite to yourself, for I know you, remember; you are a mere child and a fool!"

He recoiled as if a viper were rearing its sharp, slender black head before him; and having always feared her, he thought it best to beat a retreat.

While the last guests were rushing upon the buffet and finishing the pillage there, the bridal pair took their leave, before driving off to the railway station. General de Bozonnet had joined a group in order to vent his usual complaints about compulsory military service, and the Marquis de Morigny was obliged to fetch him at the moment when the Countess de Quinsac was kissing her son and daughter-in-law. The old lady trembled with so much emotion that the Marquis respectfully ventured to sustain her. Meantime, Hyacinthe had started in search of his father, and at last found him near a window with the tottering Chaigneux, whom he was violently upbraiding, for Fonsegue's conscientious scruples had put him in a fury. Indeed, if Massot's article should not be inserted in the "Globe," Silviane might lay all the blame upon him, the Baron, and wreak further punishment upon him. However, upon being summoned by his son he had to don his triumphal air once more, kiss his daughter on the forehead, shake hands with his son-in-law, jest and wish them both a pleasant journey. Then Eve, near whom Monseigneur Martha had remained, smiling, in her turn had to say farewell. In this she evinced touching bravery; her determination to remain beautiful and charming until the very end lent her sufficient strength to show herself both gay and motherly.

She took hold of the slightly quivering hand which Gerard proffered with some embarrassment, and ventured to retain it for a moment in her own, in a good-hearted, affectionate way, instinct with all the heroism of renunciation. "Good by, Gerard," she said, "keep in good health, be happy." Then turning to Camille she kissed her on both cheeks, while Monseigneur Martha sat looking at them with an air of indulgent sympathy. They wished each other "Au revoir," but their voices trembled, and their eyes in meeting gleamed like swords; in the same way as beneath the kisses they had exchanged they had felt each other's teeth. Ah! how it enraged Camille to see her mother still so beautiful and fascinating in spite of age and grief! And for Eve how great the torture of beholding her daughter's youth, that youth which had overcome her, and was for ever wresting love from within her reach! No forgiveness was possible between them; they would still hate one another even in the family tomb, where some day they would sleep side by side.

All the same, that evening Baroness Duvillard excused herself from attending the performance of "Polyeucte" at the Comedie Francaise. She felt very tired and wished to go to bed early, said she. As a matter of fact she wept on her pillow all night long. Thus the Baron's stage-box on the first balcony tier contained only himself, Hyacinthe, Duthil, and little Princess de Harn.

At nine o'clock there was a full house, one of the brilliant chattering houses peculiar to great dramatic solemnities. All the society people who had marched through the sacristy of the Madeleine that morning were now assembled at the theatre, again feverish with curiosity, and on the lookout for the unexpected. One recognised the same faces and the sane smiles; the women acknowledged one another's presence with little signs of intelligence, the men understood each other at a word, a gesture. One and all had kept the appointment, the ladies with bared shoulders, the gentlemen with flowers in their button-holes. Fonsegue occupied the "Globe's" box, with two friendly families. Little Massot had his customary seat in the stalls. Amadieu, who was a faithful patron of the Comedie, was also to be seen there, as well as General de Bozonnet and Public Prosecutor Lehmann. The man who was most looked at, however, on account of his scandalous article that morning, was Sagnier, the terrible

Sagnier, looking bloated and apoplectical. Then there was Chaigneux, who had kept merely a modest bracket-seat for himself, and who scoured the passages, and climbed to every tier, for the last time preaching enthusiasm. Finally, the two ministers Monferrand and Dauvergne appeared in the box facing Duvillard's; whereupon many knowing smiles were exchanged, for everybody was aware that these personages had come to help on the success of the *debutante*.

On the latter point there had still been unfavourable rumours only the previous day. Sagnier had declared that the *debut* of such a notorious harlot as Silviane at the Comedie Francaise, in such a part too as that of "Pauline," which was one of so much moral loftiness, could only be regarded as an impudent insult to public decency. The whole press, moreover, had long been up in arms against the young woman's extraordinary caprice. But then the affair had been talked of for six months past, so that Paris had grown used to the idea of seeing Silviane at the Comedie. And now it flocked thither with the one idea of being entertained. Before the curtain rose one could tell by the very atmosphere of the house that the audience was a jovial, good-humoured one, bent on enjoying itself, and ready to applaud should it find itself at all pleased.

The performance really proved extraordinary. When Silviane, chastely robed, made her appearance in the first act, the house was quite astonished by her virginal face, her innocent-looking mouth, and her eyes beaming with immaculate candour. Then, although the manner in which she had understood her part at first amazed people, it ended by charming them. From the moment of confiding in "Stratonice," from the moment of relating her dream, she turned "Pauline" into a soaring mystical creature, some saint, as it were, such as one sees in stained-glass windows, carried along by a Wagnerian Brunhilda riding the clouds. It was a thoroughly ridiculous conception of the part, contrary to reason and truth alike. Still, it only seemed to interest people the more, partly on account of mysticism being the fashion, and partly on account of the contrast between Silviane's assumed candour and real depravity. Her success increased from act to act, and some slight hissing which was attributed to Sagnier only helped to make the victory more complete. Monferrand and Dauvergne, as the newspapers afterwards related, gave the signal for applause; and the whole house joined in it, partly from amusement and partly perhaps in a spirit of irony.

During the interval between the fourth and fifth acts there was quite a procession of visitors to Duvillard's box, where the greatest excitement prevailed. Duthil, however, after absenting himself for a moment, came back to say: "You remember our influential critic, the one whom I brought to dinner at the Cafe Anglais? Well, he's repeating to everybody that 'Pauline' is merely a little *bourgeoise*, and is not transformed by the heavenly grace until the very finish of the piece. To turn her into a holy virgin from the outset simply kills the part, says he."

"Pooh!" repeated Duvillard, "let him argue if he likes, it will be all the more advertisement.... The important point is to get Massot's article inserted in the 'Globe' tomorrow morning."

On this point, unfortunately, the news was by no means good. Chaigneux, who had gone in search of Fonsegue, declared that the latter still hesitated in the matter in spite of Silviane's success, which he declared to be ridiculous. Thereupon, the Baron became quite angry. "Go and tell Fonsegue," he exclaimed, "that I insist on it, and that I shall remember what he does."

Meantime Princess Rosemonde was becoming quite delirious with enthusiasm. "My dear Hyacinthe," she pleaded, "please take me to Silviane's dressing-room; I can't wait, I really must go and kiss her."

"But we'll all go!" cried Duvillard, who heard her entreaty.

The passages were crowded, and there were people even on the stage. Moreover, when the party reached the door of Silviane's dressing-room, they found it shut. When the Baron knocked at it, a dresser replied that madame begged the gentlemen to wait a moment.

"Oh! a woman may surely go in," replied Rosemonde, hastily slipping through the doorway. "And you may come, Hyacinthe," she added; "there can be no objection to you."

Silviane was very hot, and a dresser was wiping her perspiring shoulders when Rosemonde darted forward and kissed her. Then they chatted together amidst the heat and glare from the gas and the intoxicating perfumes of all the flowers which were heaped up in the little room. Finally, Hyacinthe heard them promise to see one another after the performance, Silviane even inviting Rosemonde to drink a cup of tea with her at her house. At this the young man smiled complacently, and said to the actress: "Your carriage is waiting for you at the corner of the Rue Montpensier, is it not? Well, I'll take the Princess to it. That will be the simpler plan, you can both go off together!"

"Oh! how good of you," cried Rosemonde; "it's agreed."

Just then the door was opened, and the men, being admitted, began to pour forth their congratulations. However, they had to regain their seats in all haste so as to witness the fifth act. This proved quite a triumph, the whole house bursting into applause when Silviane spoke the famous line, "I see, I know, I believe, I am undeceived," with the rapturous enthusiasm of a holy martyr ascending to heaven. Nothing could have been more soul-like, it was said. And so when the performers were called before the curtain, Paris bestowed an ovation on that virgin of the stage, who, as Sagnier put it, knew so well how to act depravity at home.

Accompanied by Duthil, Duvillard at once went behind the scenes in order to fetch Silviane, while Hyacinthe escorted Rosemonde to the brougham waiting at the corner of the Rue Montpensier. Having helped her into it, the young man stood by, waiting. And he seemed to grow quite merry when his father came up with Silviane, and was stopped by her, just as, in his turn, he wished to get into the carriage.

"There's no room for you, my dear fellow," said she. "I've a friend with me."

Rosemonde's little smiling face then peered forth from the depths of the brougham. And the Baron remained there open-mouthed while the vehicle swiftly carried the two women away!

"Well, what would you have, my dear fellow?" said Hyacinthe, by way of explanation to Duthil, who also seemed somewhat amazed by what had happened. "Rosemonde was worrying my life out, and so I got rid of her by packing her off with Silviane."

Duvillard was still standing on the pavement and still looking dazed when Chaigneux, who was going home quite tired out, recognised him, and came up to say that Fonsegue had thought the matter over, and that Massot's article would be duly inserted. In the passages, too, there had been a deal of talk about the famous Trans-Saharan project.

Then Hyacinthe led his father away, trying to comfort him like a sensible friend, who regarded woman as a base and impure creature. "Let's go home to bed," said he. "As that article is to appear, you can take it to her to-morrow. She will see you, sure enough."

Thereupon they lighted cigars, and now and again exchanging a few words, took their way up the Avenue de l'Opera, which at that hour was deserted and dismal. Meantime, above the slumbering houses of Paris the breeze wafted a prolonged sigh, the plaint, as it were, of an expiring world.

III. THE GOAL OF LABOUR

EVER since the execution of Salvat, Guillaume had become extremely taciturn. He seemed worried and absent-minded. He would work for hours at the manufacture of that dangerous powder of which he alone knew the formula, and the preparation of which was such a delicate matter that he would allow none to assist him. Then, at other times he would go off, and return tired out by some long solitary ramble. He remained very gentle at home, and strove to smile there. But whenever anybody spoke to him he started as if suddenly called back from dreamland.

Pierre imagined his brother had relied too much upon his powers of renunciation, and found the loss of Marie unbearable. Was it not some thought of her that haunted him now that the date fixed for the marriage drew nearer and nearer? One evening, therefore, Pierre ventured to speak out, again offering to leave the house and disappear.

But at the first words he uttered Guillaume stopped him, and affectionately replied: "Marie? Oh! I love her, I love her too well to regret what I have done. No, no! you only bring me happiness, I derive all my strength and courage from you now that I know you are both happy. ... And I assure you that you are mistaken, there is nothing at all the matter with me; my work absorbs me, perhaps, but that is all."

That same evening he managed to cast his gloom aside, and displayed delightful gaiety. During dinner he inquired if the upholsterer would soon call to arrange the two little rooms which Marie was to occupy with her husband over the workroom. The young woman, who since her marriage with Pierre had been decided had remained waiting with smiling patience, thereupon told Guillaume what it was she desired—first some hangings of red cotton stuff, then some polished pine furniture which would enable her to imagine she was in the country, and finally a carpet on the floor, because a carpet seemed to her the height of luxury. She laughed as she spoke, and Guillaume laughed with her in a gay and fatherly way. His good spirits brought much relief to Pierre, who concluded that he must have been mistaken in his surmises.

On the very morrow, however, Guillaume relapsed into a dreamy state. And so disquietude again came upon Pierre, particularly when he noticed that Mere-Grand also seemed to be unusually grave and silent. Not daring to address her, he tried to extract some information from his nephews, but neither Thomas nor Francois nor Antoine knew anything. Each of them quietly devoted his time to his work, respecting and worshipping his father, but never questioning him about his plans or enterprises. Whatever he might choose to do could only be right and good; and they, his sons, were ready to do the same and help him at the very first call, without pausing to inquire into his purpose. It was plain, however, that he kept them apart from anything at all perilous, that he retained all responsibility for himself, and that Mere-Grand alone was his *confidante*, the one whom he consulted and to whom he perhaps listened. Pierre therefore renounced his hope of learning anything from the sons, and directed his attention to the old lady, whose rigid gravity worried him the more as she and Guillaume frequently had private chats in the room she occupied upstairs. They shut themselves up there all alone, and remained together for hours without the faintest sound coming from the seemingly lifeless chamber.

One day, however, Pierre caught sight of Guillaume as he came out of it, carrying a little valise which appeared to be very heavy. And Pierre thereupon remembered both his brother's powder, one pound weight of which would have sufficed to destroy a cathedral, and the destructive engine which he had purposed bestowing upon France in order that she might be victorious over all other nations, and become the one great initiatory and liberative power. Pierre remembered too that the only person besides himself who knew his brother's secret was Mere-Grand, who, at the time when Guillaume was fearing some perquisition on the part of the police, had long slept upon the cartridges of the terrible explosive. But now why was Guillaume removing all the powder which he had been preparing for some time past? As this question occurred to Pierre, a sudden suspicion, a vague dread, came upon him, and gave him strength to ask his brother: "Have you reason to fear anything, since you won't keep things here? If they embarrass you, they can all be deposited at my house, nobody will make a search there."

Guillaume, whom these words astonished, gazed at Pierre fixedly, and then replied: "Yes, I have learnt that the arrests and perquisitions have begun afresh since that poor devil was guillotined; for they are in terror at the thought that some despairing fellow may avenge him. Moreover, it is hardly prudent to keep destructive agents of such great power here. I prefer to deposit them in a safe place. But not at Neuilly—oh! no indeed! they are not a present for you, brother." Guillaume spoke with outward calmness; and if he had started with surprise at the first moment, it had been scarcely perceptible.

"So everything is ready?" Pierre resumed. "You will soon be handing your engine of destruction over to the Minister of War, I presume?"

A gleam of hesitation appeared in the depths of Guillaume's eyes, and he was for a moment about to tell a falsehood. However, he ended by replying "No, I have renounced that intention. I have another idea."

He spoke these last words with so much energy and decision that Pierre did not dare to question him further, to ask him, for instance, what that other idea might be. From that moment, however, he quivered with anxious expectancy. From hour to hour Mere-Grand's lofty silence and Guillaume's rapt, energetic face seemed to tell him that some huge and terrifying scheme had come into being, and was growing and threatening the whole of Paris.

One afternoon, just as Thomas was about to repair to the Grandidier works, some one came to Guillaume's with the news that old Toussaint, the workman, had been stricken with a fresh attack of paralysis. Thomas thereupon decided that he would call upon the poor fellow on his way, for he held him in esteem and wished to ascertain if he could render him any help. Pierre expressed a desire to accompany his nephew, and they started off together about four o'clock.

On entering the one room which the Toussaints occupied, the room where they ate and slept, the visitors found the mechanician seated on a low chair near the table. He looked half dead, as if struck by lightning. It was a case of hemiplegia, which had paralysed the whole of his right side, his right leg and right arm, and had also spread to his face in such wise that he could no longer speak. The only sound he could raise was an incomprehensible guttural grunt. His mouth was drawn to the right, and his once round, good-natured-looking face, with tanned skin and bright eyes, had been twisted into a frightful mask of anguish. At fifty years of age, the unhappy man was utterly done for. His unkempt beard was as white as that of an octogenarian, and his knotty limbs, preyed upon by toil, were henceforth dead. Only his eyes remained alive, and they travelled around the room, going from one to another. By his side, eager to do what she could for him, was his wife, who remained stout even when she had little to eat, and still showed herself active and clear-headed, however great her misfortunes.

"It's a friendly visit, Toussaint," said she. "It's Monsieur Thomas who has come to see you with Monsieur l'Abbe." Then quietly correcting herself she added: "With Monsieur Pierre, his uncle. You see that you are not yet forsaken."

Toussaint wished to speak, but his fruitless efforts only brought two big tears to his eyes. Then he gazed at his visitors with an expression of indescribable woe, his jaws trembling convulsively.

"Don't put yourself out," repeated his wife. "The doctor told you that it would do you no good."

At the moment of entering the room, Pierre had already noticed two persons who had risen from their chairs and drawn somewhat on one side. And now to his great surprise he recognised that they were Madame Theodore and Celine, who were both decently clad, and looked as if they led a life of comfort. On hearing of Toussaint's misfortune they had come to see him, like good-hearted creatures, who, on their own side, had experienced the most cruel suffering. Pierre, on noticing that they now seemed to be beyond dire want, remembered what he had heard of the wonderful sympathy lavished on the child after her father's execution, the many presents and donations offered her, and the generous proposals that had been made to adopt her. These last had ended in her being adopted by a former friend of Salvat, who had sent her to school again, pending the time when she might be apprenticed to some trade, while, on the other hand, Madame Theodore had been placed as a nurse in a convalescent home. In such wise both had been saved.

When Pierre drew near to little Celine in order to kiss her, Madame Theodore told her to thank Monsieur l'Abbe—for so she still respectfully called him—for all that he had previously done for her. "It was you who brought us happiness, Monsieur l'Abbe," said she. "And that's a thing one can never forget. I'm always telling Celine to remember you in her prayers."

"And so, my child, you are now going to school again," said Pierre.

"Oh yes, Monsieur l'Abbe, and I'm well pleased at it. Besides, we no longer lack anything." Then, however, sudden emotion came over the girl, and she stammered with a sob: "Ah! if poor papa could only see us!"

Madame Theodore, meanwhile, had begun to take leave of Madame Toussaint. "Well, good by, we must go," said she. "What has happened to you is very sad, and we wanted to tell you how much it grieved us. The worry is that when misfortune falls on one, courage isn't enough to set things right.. .. Celine, come and kiss your uncle.... My poor brother, I hope you'll get back the use of your legs as soon as possible."

They kissed the paralysed man on the cheeks, and then went off. Toussaint had looked at them with his keen and still intelligent eyes, as if he longed to participate in the life and activity into which they were returning. And a jealous thought came to his wife, who usually was so placid and good-natured. "Ah! my poor old man!" said she, after propping him up with a pillow, "those two are luckier than we are. Everything succeeds with them since that madman, Salvat, had his head cut off. They're provided for. They've plenty of bread on the shelf."

Then, turning towards Pierre and Thomas, she continued: "We others are done for, you know, we're down in the mud, with no hope of getting out of it. But what would you have? My poor husband hasn't been guillotined, he's done nothing but work his whole life long; and now, you see, that's the end of him, he's like some old animal, no longer good for anything."

Having made her visitors sit down she next answered their compassionate questions. The doctor had called twice already, and had promised to restore the unhappy man's power of speech, and perhaps enable him to crawl round the room with the help of a stick. But as for ever being able to resume real work that must not be expected. And so what was the use of living on? Toussaint's eyes plainly declared that he would much rather die at once. When a workman can no longer work and no longer provide for his wife he is ripe for the grave.

"Savings indeed!" Madame Toussaint resumed. "There are folks who ask if we have any savings.... Well, we had nearly a thousand francs in the Savings Bank when Toussaint had his first attack. And some people don't know what a lot of prudence one needs to put by such a sum; for, after all, we're not savages, we have to allow ourselves a little enjoyment now and then, a good dish and a good bottle of wine.... Well, what with five months of enforced idleness, and the medicines, and the underdone meat that was ordered, we got to the end of our thousand francs; and now that it's all begun again we're not likely to taste any more bottled wine or roast mutton."

Fond of good cheer as she had always been, this cry, far more than the tears she was forcing back, revealed how much the future terrified her. She was there erect and brave in spite of everything; but what a downfall if she were no longer able to keep her room tidy, stew a piece of veal on Sundays, and gossip with the neighbours while awaiting her husband's return from work! Why, they might just as well be thrown into the gutter and carried off in the scavenger's cart.

However, Thomas intervened: "Isn't there an Asylum for the Invalids of Labour, and couldn't your husband get admitted to it?" he asked. "It seems to me that is just the place for him."

"Oh dear, no," the woman answered. "People spoke to me of that place before, and I got particulars of it. They don't take sick people there. When you call they tell you that there are hospitals for those who are ill."

With a wave of his hand Pierre confirmed her statement: it was useless to apply in that direction. He could again see himself scouring Paris, hurrying from the Lady

President, Baroness Duvillard, to Fonsegue, the General Manager, and only securing a bed for Laveuve when the unhappy man was dead.

However, at that moment an infant was heard wailing, and to the amazement of both visitors Madame Toussaint entered the little closet where her son Charles had so long slept, and came out of it carrying a child, who looked scarcely twenty months old. "Well, yes," she explained, "this is Charles's boy. He was sleeping there in his father's old bed, and now you hear him, he's woke up.... You see, only last Wednesday, the day before Toussaint had his stroke, I went to fetch the little one at the nurse's at St. Denis, because she had threatened to cast him adrift since Charles had got into bad habits, and no longer paid her. I said to myself at the time that work was looking up, and that my husband and I would always be able to provide for a little mouth like that.... But just afterwards everything collapsed! At the same time, as the child's here now I can't go and leave him in the street."

While speaking in this fashion she walked to and fro, rocking the baby in her arms. And naturally enough she reverted to Charles's folly with the girl, who had run away, leaving that infant behind her. Things might not have been so very bad if Charles had still worked as steadily as he had done before he went soldiering. In those days he had never lost an hour, and had always brought all his pay home! But he had come back from the army with much less taste for work. He argued, and had ideas of his own. He certainly hadn't yet come to bomb-throwing like that madman Salvat, but he spent half his time with Socialists and Anarchists, who put his brain in a muddle. It was a real pity to see such a strong, good-hearted young fellow turning out badly like that. But it was said in the neighbourhood that many another was inclined the same way; that the best and most intelligent of the younger men felt tired of want and unremunerative labour, and would end by knocking everything to pieces rather than go on toiling with no certainty of food in their old age.

"Ah! yes," continued Madame Toussaint, "the sons are not like the fathers were. These fine fellows won't be as patient as my poor husband has been, letting hard work wear him away till he's become the sorry thing you see there.... Do you know what Charles said the other evening when he found his father on that chair, crippled like that, and unable to speak? Why, he shouted to him that he'd been a stupid jackass all his life, working himself to death for those *bourgeois*, who now wouldn't bring him so much as a glass of water. Then, as he none the less has a good heart, he began to cry his eyes out."

The baby was no longer wailing, still the good woman continued walking to and fro, rocking it in her arms and pressing it to her affectionate heart. Her son Charles could do no more for them, she said; perhaps he might be able to give them a five-franc piece now and again, but even that wasn't certain. It was of no use for her to go back to her old calling as a seamstress, she had lost all practice of it. And it would even be difficult for her to earn anything as charwoman, for she had that infant on her hands as well as her infirm husband—a big child, whom she would have to wash and feed. And so what would become of the three of them? She couldn't tell; but it made her shudder, however brave and motherly she tried to be.

For their part, Pierre and Thomas quivered with compassion, particularly when they saw big tears coursing down the cheeks of the wretched, stricken Toussaint, as he sat quite motionless in that little and still cleanly home of toil and want. The poor man had listened to his wife, and he looked at her and at the infant now sleeping in her arms. Voiceless, unable to cry his woe aloud, he experienced the most awful anguish. What dupery his long life of labour had been! how frightfully unjust it was that all his efforts should end in such sufferings! how exasperating it was to feel himself powerless, and to see those whom he loved and who were as innocent as himself suffer and die by reason of his own suffering and death! Ah! poor old man, cripple that he was, ending like some beast of burden that has foundered by the roadside—that goal of labour! And it was all so revolting and so monstrous that he tried to put it into words, and his desperate grief ended in a frightful, raucous grunt.

"Be quiet, don't do yourself harm!" concluded Madame Toussaint. "Things are like that, and there's no mending them."

Then she went to put the child to bed again, and on her return, just as Thomas and Pierre were about to speak to her of Toussaint's employer, M. Grandidier, a fresh visitor arrived. Thereupon the others decided to wait.

The new comer was Madame Chretiennot, Toussaint's other sister, eighteen years younger than himself. Her husband, the little clerk, had compelled her to break off almost all intercourse with her relatives, as he felt ashamed of them; nevertheless, having heard of her brother's misfortune, she had very properly come to condole with him. She wore a gown of cheap flimsy silk, and a hat trimmed with red poppies, which she had freshened up three times already; but in spite of this display her appearance bespoke penury, and she did her best to hide her feet on account of the shabbiness of her boots. Moreover, she was no longer the beautiful Hortense. Since a recent miscarriage, all trace of her good looks had disappeared.

The lamentable appearance of her brother and the bareness of that home of suffering chilled her directly she crossed the threshold. And as soon as she had kissed Toussaint, and said how sorry she was to find him in such a condition, she began to lament her own fate, and recount her troubles, for fear lest she should be asked for any help.

"Ah! my dear," she said to her sister-in-law, "you are certainly much to be pitied! But if you only knew! We all have our troubles. Thus in my case, obliged as I am to dress fairly well on account of my husband's position, I have more trouble than you can imagine in making both ends meet. One can't go far on a salary of three thousand francs a year, when one has to pay seven hundred francs' rent out of it. You will perhaps say that we might lodge ourselves in a more modest way; but we can't, my dear, I must have a *salon* on account of the visits I receive. So just count!... Then there are my two girls. I've had to send them to school; Lucienne has begun to learn the piano and Marcelle has some taste for drawing.... By the way, I would have brought them with me, but I feared it would upset them too much. You will excuse me, won't you?"

Then she spoke of all the worries which she had had with her husband on account of Salvat's ignominious death. Chretiennot, vain, quarrelsome little fellow that he was, felt exasperated at now having a *guillotine* in his wife's family. And he had lately begun to treat the unfortunate woman most harshly, charging her with having brought about all their troubles, and even rendering her responsible for his own mediocrity, embittered as he was more and more each day by a confined life of office work. On some evenings they had downright quarrels; she stood up for herself, and related that when she was at the confectionery shop in the Rue des Martyrs she could have married a doctor had she only chosen, for the doctor found her quite pretty enough. Now, however, she was becoming plainer and plainer, and her husband felt that he was condemned to everlasting penury; so that their life was becoming more and more dismal and quarrelsome, and as unbearable—despite the pride of being "gentleman" and "lady"—as was the destitution of the working classes.

"All the same, my dear," at last said Madame Toussaint, weary of her sister-in-law's endless narrative of worries, "you have had one piece of luck. You won't have the trouble of bringing up a third child, now."

"That's true," replied Hortense, with a sigh of relief. "How we should have managed, I don't know.... Still, I was very ill, and I'm far from being in good health now. The doctor says that I don't eat enough, and that I ought to have good food."

Then she rose for the purpose of giving her brother another kiss and taking her departure; for she feared a scene on her husband's part should he happen to come home and find her absent. Once on her feet, however, she lingered there a moment longer, saying that she also had just seen her sister, Madame Theodore, and little Celine, both of them comfortably clad and looking happy. And with a touch of jealousy she added: "Well, my husband contents himself with slaving away at his office every day. He'll never do anything to get his head cut off; and it's quite certain that nobody will think of leaving an income to Marcelle and Lucienne.... Well, good by, my dear, you must be brave, one must always hope that things will turn out for the best."

When she had gone off, Pierre and Thomas inquired if M. Grandidier had heard of Toussaint's misfortune and agreed to do anything for him. Madame Toussaint answered that he had so far made only a vague promise; and on learning this they resolved to speak to him as warmly as they could on behalf of the old mechanician, who had spent as many as five and twenty years at the works. The misfortune was that a scheme for establishing a friendly society, and even a pension fund, which had been launched before the crisis from which the works were now recovering, had collapsed through a number of obstacles and complications. Had things turned out otherwise, Thomas might have had a pittance assured him, even though he was unable to work. But under the circumstances the only hope for the poor stricken fellow lay in his employer's compassion, if not his sense of justice.

As the baby again began to cry, Madame Toussaint went to fetch it, and she was once more carrying it to and fro, when Thomas pressed her husband's sound hand between both his own. "We will come back," said the young man; "we won't forsake you, Toussaint. You know very well that people like you, for you've always been a good and steady workman. So rely on us, we will do all we can."

Then they left him tearful and overpowered, in that dismal room, while, up and down beside him, his wife rocked the squealing infant—that other luckless creature, who was now so heavy on the old folks' hands, and like them was fated to die of want and unjust toil.

Toil, manual toil, panting at every effort, this was what Pierre and Thomas once more found at the works. From the slender pipes above the roofs spurted rhythmical puffs of steam, which seemed like the very breath of all that labour. And in the workshops one found a continuous rumbling, a whole army of men in motion, forging, filing, and piercing, amidst the spinning of leather gearing and the trembling of machinery. The day was ending with a final feverish effort to complete some task or other before the bell should ring for departure.

On inquiring for the master Thomas learnt that he had not been seen since *dejeuner*, which was such an unusual occurrence that the young man at once feared some terrible scene in the silent pavilion, whose shutters were ever closed upon Grandidier's unhappy wife—that mad but beautiful creature, whom he loved so passionate-passionately that he had never been willing to part from her. The pavilion could be seen from the little glazed work-shop which Thomas usually occupied, and as he and Pierre stood waiting there, it looked very peaceful and pleasant amidst the big lilac-bushes planted round about it. Surely, they thought, it ought to have been brightened by the gay gown of a young woman and the laughter of playful children. But all at once a loud, piercing shriek reached their ears, followed by howls and moans, like those of an animal that is being beaten or possibly slaughtered. Ah! those howls ringing out amidst all the stir of the toiling works, punctuated it seemed by the rhythmical puffing of the steam, accompanied too by the dull rumbling of the machinery! The receipts of the business had been doubling and doubling since the last stock-taking; there was increase of prosperity every month, the bad times were over, far behind. Grandidier was realising a large fortune with his famous bicycle for the million, the "Lisette"; and the approaching vogue of motor-cars also promised huge gains, should he again start making little motor-engines, as he meant to do, as soon as Thomas's long-projected motor should be perfected. But what was wealth when in that dismal pavilion, whose shutters were ever closed, those frightful shrieks continued, proclaiming some terrible drama, which all the stir and bustle of the prosperous works were unable to stifle?

Pierre and Thomas looked at one another, pale and quivering. And all at once, as the cries ceased and the pavilion sank into death-like silence once more, the latter said in an undertone: "She is usually very gentle, she will sometimes spend whole days sitting on a carpet like a little child. He is fond of her when she is like that; he lays her down and picks her up, caresses her and makes her laugh as if she were a baby. Ah! how dreadfully sad it is! When an attack comes upon her she gets frantic, tries to bite herself, and kill herself by throwing herself against the walls. And then he has to struggle with her, for no one else is allowed to touch her. He tries to restrain her, and holds her in his arms to calm her.... But how terrible it was just now! Did you hear? I do not think she has ever had such a frightful attack before."

For a quarter of an hour longer profound silence prevailed. Then Grandidier came out of the pavilion, bareheaded and still ghastly pale. Passing the little glazed work-shop on his way, he perceived Thomas and Pierre there, and at once came in. But he was obliged to lean against a bench like a man who is dazed, haunted by a nightmare. His good-natured, energetic face retained an expression of acute anguish; and his left ear was scratched and bleeding. However, he at once wished to talk, overcome his feelings, and return to his life of activity. "I am very pleased to see you, my dear Thomas," said he, "I have been thinking over what you told me about our little motor. We must go into the matter again."

Seeing how distracted he was, it occurred to the young man that some sudden diversion, such as the story of another's misfortunes, might perhaps draw him from his haunting thoughts. "Of course I am at your disposal," he replied; "but before talking of that matter I should like to tell you that we have just seen Toussaint, that poor old fellow who has been stricken with paralysis. His awful fate has quite distressed us. He is in the greatest destitution, forsaken as it were by the roadside, after all his years of labour."

Thomas dwelt upon the quarter of a century which the old workman had spent at the factory, and suggested that it would be only just to take some account of his long efforts, the years of his life which he had devoted to the establishment. And he asked that he might be assisted in the name both of equity and compassion.

"Ah! monsieur," Pierre in his turn ventured to say. "I should like to take you for an instant into that bare room, and show you that poor, aged, worn-out, stricken man, who no longer has even the power of speech left him to tell people his sufferings. There can be no greater wretchedness than to die in this fashion, despairing of all kindliness and justice."

Grandidier had listened to them in silence. But big tears had irresistibly filled his eyes, and when he spoke it was in a very low and tremulous voice: "The greatest wretchedness, who can tell what it is? Who can speak of it if he has not known the wretchedness of others? Yes, yes, it's sad undoubtedly that poor Toussaint should be reduced to that state at his age, not knowing even if he will have food to eat on the morrow. But I know sorrows that are just as crushing, abominations which poison one's life in a still greater degree.... Ah! yes, food indeed! To think that happiness will reign in the world when everybody has food to eat! What an idiotic hope!"

The whole grievous tragedy of his life was in the shudder which had come over him. To be the employer, the master, the man who is making money, who disposes of capital and is envied by his workmen, to own an establishment to which prosperity has returned, whose machinery coins gold, apparently leaving one no other trouble than that of pocketing one's profits; and yet at the same time to be the most wretched of men, to know no day exempt from anguish, to find each evening at one's hearth no other reward or prop than the most atrocious torture of the heart! Everything, even success, has to be paid for. And thus that triumpher, that money-maker, whose pile was growing larger at each successive inventory, was sobbing with bitter grief.

However, he showed himself kindly disposed towards Toussaint, and promised to assist him. As for a pension that was an idea which he could not entertain, as it was the negation of the wage-system such as it existed. He energetically defended his rights as an employer, repeating that the strain of competition would compel him to avail himself of them so long as the present system should endure. His part in it was to do good business in an honest way. However, he regretted that his men had never carried out the scheme of establishing a relief fund, and he said that he would do his best to induce them to take it in hand again.

Some colour had now come back to his checks; for on returning to the interests of his life of battle he felt his energy restored. He again reverted to the question of the little motor, and spoke of it for some time with Thomas, while Pierre waited, feeling quite upset. Ah! he thought, how universal was the thirst for happiness! Then, in spite of the many technical terms that were used he caught a little of what the others were saying. Small steam motors had been made at the works in former times; but they had not proved successes. In point of fact a new propelling force was needed. Electricity, though everyone foresaw its future triumph, was so far out of the question on account of the weight of the apparatus which its employment necessitated. So only petroleum remained, and the inconvenience attaching to its use was so great that victory and fortune would certainly rest with the manufacturer who should be able to replace it by some other hitherto unknown agent. In the discovery and adaptation of the latter lay the whole problem.

"Yes, I am eager about it now," at last exclaimed Grandidier in an animated way. "I allowed you to prosecute your experiments without troubling you with any inquisitive questions. But a solution is becoming imperative."

Thomas smiled: "Well, you must remain patient just a little longer," said he; "I believe that I am on the right road."

Then Grandidier shook hands with him and Pierre, and went off to make his usual round through his busy, bustling works, whilst near at hand, awaiting his return, stood the closed pavilion, where every evening he was fated to relapse into endless, incurable anguish.

The daylight was already waning when Pierre and Thomas, after re-ascending the height of Montmartre, walked towards the large work-shop which Jahan, the sculptor, had set up among the many sheds whose erection had been necessitated by the building of the Sacred Heart. There was here a stretch of ground littered with materials, an extraordinary chaos of building stone, beams and machinery; and pending the time when an army of navvies would come to set the whole place in order, one could see gaping trenches, rough flights of descending steps and fences, imperfectly closing doorways which conducted to the substructures of the basilica.

Halting in front of Jahan's work-shop, Thomas pointed to one of these doorways by which one could reach the foundation works. "Have you never had an idea of visiting the foundations?" he inquired of Pierre. "There's quite a city down there on which millions of money have been spent. They could only find firm soil at the very base of the height, and they had to excavate more than eighty shafts, fill them with concrete, and then rear their church on all those subterranean columns.... Yes, that is so. Of course the columns cannot be seen, but it is they who hold that insulting edifice aloft, right over Paris!"

Having drawn near to the fence, Pierre was looking at an open doorway beyond it, a sort of dark landing whence steps descended as if into the bowels of the earth. And he thought of those invisible columns of concrete, and of all the stubborn energy and desire for domination which had set and kept the edifice erect.

Thomas was at last obliged to call him. "Let us make haste," said he, "the twilight will soon be here. We shan't be able to see much."

They had arranged to meet Antoine at Jahan's, as the sculptor wished to show them a new model he had prepared. When they entered the work-shop they found the two assistants still working at the colossal angel which had been ordered for the basilica. Standing on a scaffolding they were rough-hewing its symmetrical wings, whilst Jahan, seated on a low chair, with his sleeves rolled up to his elbows, and his hands soiled with clay, was contemplating a figure some three feet high on which he had just been working.

"Ah! it's you," he exclaimed. "Antoine has been waiting more than half an hour for you. He's gone outside with Lise to see the sun set over Paris, I think. But they will soon be back."

Then he relapsed into silence, with his eyes fixed on his work.

This was a bare, erect, lofty female figure, of such august majesty, so simple were its lines, that it suggested something gigantic. The figure's abundant, outspread hair suggested rays around its face, which beamed with sovereign beauty like the sun. And its only gesture was one of offer and of greeting; its arms were thrown slightly forward, and its hands were open for the grasp of all mankind.

Still lingering in his dream Jahan began to speak slowly: "You remember that I wanted a pendant for my figure of Fecundity. I had modelled a Charity, but it pleased me so little and seemed so commonplace that I let the clay dry and spoil.... And then the idea of a figure of Justice came to me. But not a gowned figure with the sword and the scales! That wasn't the Justice that inspired me. What haunted my mind was the other Justice, the one that the lowly and the sufferers await, the one who alone can some day set a little order and happiness among us. And I pictured her like that, quite bare, quite simple, and very lofty. She is the sun as it were, a sun all beauty, harmony and strength; for justice is only to be found in the sun which shines in the heavens for one and all, and bestows on poor and rich alike its magnificence and light and warmth, which are the source of all life. And so my figure, you see, has her hands outstretched as if she were offering herself to all mankind, greeting it and granting it the gift of eternal life in eternal beauty. Ah! to be beautiful and strong and just, one's whole dream lies in that."

Jahan relighted his pipe and burst into a merry laugh. "Well, I think the good woman carries herself upright.... What do you fellows say?"

His visitors highly praised his work. Pierre for his part was much affected at finding in this artistic conception the very idea that he had so long been revolving in his mind—the idea of an era of Justice rising from the ruins of the world, which Charity after centuries of trial had failed to save.

Then the sculptor gaily explained that he had prepared his model there instead of at home, in order to console himself a little for his big dummy of an angel, the prescribed triteness of which disgusted him. Some fresh objections had been raised with respect to the folds of the robe, which gave some prominence to the thighs, and in the end he had been compelled to modify all of the drapery.

"Oh! it's just as they like!" he cried; "it's no work of mine, you know; it's simply an order which I'm executing just as a mason builds a wall. There's no religious art left, it has been killed by stupidity and disbelief. Ah! if social or human art could only revive, how glorious to be one of the first to bear the tidings!"

Then he paused. Where could the youngsters, Antoine and Lise, have got to, he wondered. He threw the door wide open, and, a little distance away, among the materials littering the waste ground, one could see Antoine's tall figure and Lise's short slender form standing out against the immensity of Paris, which was all golden amidst the sun's farewell. The young man's strong arm supported Lise, who with this help walked beside him without feeling any fatigue. Slender and graceful, like a girl blossoming into womanhood, she raised her eyes to his with a smile of infinite gratitude, which proclaimed that she belonged to him for evermore.

"Ah! they are coming back," said Jahan. "The miracle is now complete, you know. I'm delighted at it. I did not know what to do with her; I had even renounced all attempts to teach her to read; I left her for days together in a corner, infirm and tongue-tied like a lack-wit.... But your brother came and took her in hand somehow or other. She listened to him and understood him, and began to read and write with him, and grow intelligent and gay. Then, as her limbs still gained no suppleness, and she remained infirm, ailing and puny, he began by carrying her here, and then helped her to walk in such wise that she can now do so by herself. In a few weeks' time she has positively grown and become quite charming. Yes, I assure you, it is second birth, real creation. Just look at them!"

Antoine and Lise were still slowly approaching. The evening breeze which rose from the great city, where all was yet heat and sunshine, brought them a bath of life. If the young man had chosen that spot, with its splendid horizon, open to the full air which wafted all the germs of life, it was doubtless because he felt that nowhere else could he instil more vitality, more soul, more strength into her. And love had been created by love. He had found her asleep, benumbed, without power of motion or intellect, and he had awakened her, kindled life in her, loved her, that he might be loved by her in return. She was his work, she was part of himself.

"So you no longer feel tired, little one?" said Jahan.

She smiled divinely. "Oh! no, it's so pleasant, so beautiful, to walk straight on like this.... All I desire is to go on for ever and ever with Antoine."

The others laughed, and Jahan exclaimed in his good-natured way: "Let us hope that he won't take you so far. You've reached your destination now, and I shan't be the one to prevent you from being happy."

Antoine was already standing before the figure of Justice, to which the falling twilight seemed to impart a quiver of life. "Oh! how divinely simple, how divinely beautiful!" said he.

For his own part he had lately finished a new wood engraving, which depicted Lise holding a book in her hand, an engraving instinct with truth and emotion, showing her awakened to intelligence and love. And this time he had achieved his desire, making no preliminary drawing, but tackling the block with his graver, straight away, in presence of his model. And infinite hopefulness had come upon him, he was dreaming of great original works in which the whole period that he belonged to would live anew and for ever.

Thomas now wished to return home. So they shook hands with Jahan, who, as his day's work was over, put on his coat to take his sister back to the Rue du Calvaire.

"Till to-morrow, Lise," said Antoine, inclining his head to kiss her.

She raised herself on tip-toes, and offered him her eyes, which he had opened to life. "Till to-morrow, Antoine," said she.

Outside, the twilight was falling. Pierre was the first to cross the threshold, and as he did so, he saw so extraordinary a sight that for an instant he felt stupefied. But it was certain enough: he could plainly distinguish his brother Guillaume emerging from the gaping doorway which conducted to the foundations of the basilica. And he saw him hastily climb over the palings, and then pretend to be there by pure chance, as though he had come up from the Rue Lamarck. When he accosted his two sons, as if he were delighted to meet them, and began to say that he had just come from Paris, Pierre asked himself if he had been dreaming. However, an anxious glance which his brother cast at him convinced him that he had been right. And then he not only felt ill at ease in presence of that man whom he had never previously known to lie, but it seemed to him that he was at last on the track of all he had feared, the formidable mystery that he had for some time past felt brewing around him in the little peaceful house.

When Guillaume, his sons and his brother reached home and entered the large workroom overlooking Paris, it was so dark that they fancied nobody was there.

"What! nobody in?" said Guillaume.

But in a somewhat low, quiet voice Francois answered out of the gloom: "Why, yes, I'm here."

He had remained at his table, where he had worked the whole afternoon, and as he could no longer read, he now sat in a dreamy mood with his head resting on his hands, his eyes wandering over Paris, where night was gradually falling. As his examination was now near at hand, he was living in a state of severe mental strain.

"What, you are still working there!" said his father. "Why didn't you ask for a lamp?"

"No, I wasn't working, I was looking at Paris," Francois slowly answered. "It's singular how the night falls over it by degrees. The last district that remained visible was the Montague Ste. Genevieve, the plateau of the Pantheon, where all our knowledge and science have grown up. A sun-ray still gilds the schools and libraries and laboratories, when the low-lying districts of trade are already steeped in darkness. I won't say that the planet has a particular partiality for us at the Ecole Normale, but it's certain that its beams still linger on our roofs, when they are to be seen nowhere else."

He began to laugh at his jest. Still one could see how ardent was his faith in mental effort, how entirely he gave himself to mental labour, which, in his opinion, could alone bring truth, establish justice and create happiness.

Then came a short spell of silence. Paris sank more and more deeply into the night, growing black and mysterious, till all at once sparks of light began to appear.

"The lamps are being lighted," resumed Francois; "work is being resumed on all sides."

Then Guillaume, who likewise had been dreaming, immersed in his fixed idea, exclaimed: "Work, yes, no doubt! But for work to give a full harvest it must be fertilised by will. There is something which is superior to work."

Thomas and Antoine had drawn near. And Francois, as much for them as for himself, inquired: "What is that, father?"

"Action."

For a moment the three young men remained silent, impressed by the solemnity of the hour, quivering too beneath the great waves of darkness which rose from the vague ocean of the city. Then a young voice remarked, though whose it was one could not tell: "Action is but work."

And Pierre, who lacked the respectful quietude, the silent faith, of his nephews, now felt his nervousness increasing. That huge and terrifying mystery of which he was dimly conscious rose before him, while a great quiver sped by in the darkness, over that black city where the lamps were now being lighted for a whole passionate night of work.

IV. THE CRISIS

A GREAT ceremony was to take place that day at the basilica of the Sacred Heart. Ten thousand pilgrims were to be present there, at a solemn consecration of the Holy Sacrament; and pending the arrival of four o'clock, the hour fixed for the service, Montmartre would be invaded by people. Its slopes would be black with swarming devotees, the shops where religious emblems and pictures were sold would be besieged, the cafes and taverns would be crowded to overflowing. It would all be like some huge fair, and meantime the big bell of the basilica, "La Savoyarde," would be ringing peal on peal over the holiday-making multitude.

When Pierre entered the workroom in the morning he perceived Guillaume and Mere-Grand alone there; and a remark which he heard the former make caused him to stop short and listen from behind a tall-revolving bookstand. Mere-Grand sat sewing in her usual place near the big window, while Guillaume stood before her, speaking in a low voice.

"Mother," said he, "everything is ready, it is for to-day."

She let her work fall, and raised her eyes, looking very pale. "Ah!" she said, "so you have made up your mind."

"Yes, irrevocably. At four o'clock I shall be yonder, and it will all be over."

"'Tis well—you are the master."

Silence fell, terrible silence. Guillaume's voice seemed to come from far away, from somewhere beyond the world. It was evident that his resolution was unshakable, that his tragic dream, his fixed idea of martyrdom, wholly absorbed him. Mere-Grand looked at him with her pale eyes, like an heroic woman who had grown old in relieving the sufferings of others, and had ever shown all the abnegation and devotion of an intrepid heart, which nothing but the idea of duty could influence. She knew Guillaume's terrible scheme, and had helped him to regulate the pettiest details of it; but if on the one hand, after all the iniquity she had seen and endured, she admitted that fierce and exemplary punishment might seem necessary, and that even the idea of purifying the world by the fire of a volcano might be entertained, on the other hand, she believed too strongly in the necessity of living one's life bravely to the very end, to be able, under any circumstances, to regard death as either good or profitable.

"My son," she gently resumed, "I witnessed the growth of your scheme, and it neither surprised nor angered me. I accepted it as one accepts lightning, the very fire of the skies, something of sovereign purity and power. And I have helped you through it all, and have taken upon myself to act as the mouthpiece of your conscience.... But let me tell you once more, one ought never to desert the cause of life."

"It is useless to speak, mother," Guillaume replied: "I have resolved to give my life and cannot take it back.... Are you now unwilling to carry out my desires, remain here, and act as we have decided, when all is over?"

She did not answer this inquiry, but in her turn, speaking slowly and gravely, put a question to him: "So it is useless for me to speak to you of the children, myself and the house?" said she. "You have thought it all over, you are quite determined?" And as he simply answered "Yes," she added: "'Tis well, you are the master.... I will be the one who is to remain behind and act. And you may be without fear, your bequest is in good hands. All that we have decided together shall be done."

Once more they became silent. Then she again inquired: "At four o'clock, you say, at the moment of that consecration?"

"Yes, at four o'clock."

She was still looking at him with her pale eyes, and there seemed to be something superhuman in her simplicity and grandeur as she sat there in her thin black gown. Her glance, in which the greatest bravery and the deepest sadness mingled, filled Guillaume with acute emotion. His hands began to tremble, and he asked: "Will you let me kiss you, mother?"

"Oh! right willingly, my son," she responded. "Your path of duty may not be mine, but you see I respect your views and love you."

They kissed one another, and when Pierre, whom the scene had chilled to his heart, presented himself as if he were just arriving, Mere-Grand had quietly taken up her needlework once more, while Guillaume was going to and fro, setting one of his laboratory shelves in order with all his wonted activity.

At noon when lunch was ready, they found it necessary to wait for Thomas, who had not yet come home. His brothers Francois and Antoine complained in a jesting way, saying that they were dying of hunger, while for her part Marie, who had made a *creme*, and was very proud of it, declared that they would eat it all, and that those who came late would have to go without tasting it. When Thomas eventually put in an appearance he was greeted with jeers.

"But it wasn't my fault," said he; "I stupidly came up the hill by way of the Rue de la Barre, and you can have no notion what a crowd I fell upon. Quite ten thousand pilgrims must have camped there last night. I am told that as many as possible were huddled together in the St. Joseph Refuge. The others no doubt had to sleep in the open air. And now they are busy eating, here, there and everywhere, all over the patches of waste ground and even on the pavements. One can scarcely set one foot before the other without risk of treading on somebody."

The meal proved a very gay one, though Pierre found the gaiety forced and excessive. Yet the young people could surely know nothing of the frightful, invisible thing which to Pierre ever seemed to be hovering around in the bright sunlight of that splendid June day. Was it that the dim presentiment which comes to loving hearts when mourning threatens them, swept by during the short intervals of silence that followed the joyous outbursts? Although Guillaume looked somewhat pale, and spoke with unusual caressing softness, he retained his customary bright smile. But, on the other hand, never had Mere-Grand been more silent or more grave.

IV. THE CRISIS

Marie's *creme* proved a great success, and the others congratulated her on it so fulsomely that they made her blush. Then, all at once, heavy silence fell once more, a deathly chill seemed to sweep by, making every face turn pale—even while they were still cleaning their plates with their little spoons.

"Ah! that bell," exclaimed Francois; "it is really intolerable. I can feel my head splitting."

He referred to "La Savoyarde," the big bell of the basilica, which had now begun to toll, sending forth deep sonorous volumes of sound, which ever and ever winged their flight over the immensity of Paris. In the workroom they were all listening to the clang.

"Will it keep on like that till four o'clock?" asked Marie.

"Oh! at four o'clock," replied Thomas, "at the moment of the consecration you will hear something much louder than that. The great peals of joy, the song of triumph will then ring out."

Guillaume was still smiling. "Yes, yes," said he, "those who don't want to be deafened for life had better keep their windows closed. The worst is, that Paris has to hear it whether it will or no, and even as far away as the Pantheon, so I'm told."

Meantime Mere-Grand remained silent and impassive. Antoine for his part expressed his disgust with the horrible religious pictures for which the pilgrims fought—pictures which in some respects suggested those on the lids of sweetmeat boxes, although they depicted the Christ with His breast ripped open and displaying His bleeding heart. There could be no more repulsive materialism, no grosser or baser art, said Antoine. Then they rose from table, talking at the top of their voices so as to make themselves heard above the incessant din which came from the big bell.

Immediately afterwards they all set to work again. Mere-Grand took her everlasting needlework in hand once more, while Marie, sitting near her, continued some embroidery. The young men also attended to their respective tasks, and now and again raised their heads and exchanged a few words. Guillaume, for his part, likewise seemed very busy; Pierre alone coming and going in a state of anguish, beholding them all as in a nightmare, and attributing some terrible meaning to the most innocent remarks. During *dejeuner*, in order to explain the frightful discomfort into which he was thrown by the gaiety of the meal, he had been obliged to say that he felt poorly. And now he was looking and listening and waiting with ever-growing anxiety.

Shortly before three o'clock, Guillaume glanced at his watch and then quietly took up his hat. "Well," said he, "I'm going out."

His sons, Mere-Grand and Marie raised their heads.

"I'm going out," he repeated, "*au revoir*."

Still he did not go off. Pierre could divine that he was struggling, stiffening himself against the frightful tempest which was raging within him, striving to prevent either shudder or pallor from betraying his awful secret. Ah! he must have suffered keenly; he dared not give his sons a last kiss, for fear lest he might rouse some suspicion in their minds, which would impel them to oppose him and prevent his death! At last with supreme heroism he managed to overcome himself.

"*Au revoir*, boys."

"*Au revoir*, father. Will you be home early?"

"Yes, yes.... Don't worry about me, do plenty of work."

Mere-Grand, still majestically silent, kept her eyes fixed upon him. Her he had ventured to kiss, and their glances met and mingled, instinct with all that he had decided and that she had promised: their common dream of truth and justice.

"I say, Guillaume," exclaimed Marie gaily, "will you undertake a commission for me if you are going down by way of the Rue des Martyrs?"

"Why, certainly," he replied.

"Well, then, please look in at my dressmaker's, and tell her that I shan't go to try my gown on till to-morrow morning."

It was a question of her wedding dress, a gown of light grey silk, the stylishness of which she considered very amusing. Whenever she spoke of it, both she and the others began to laugh.

"It's understood, my dear," said Guillaume, likewise making merry over it. "We know it's Cinderella's court robe, eh? The fairy brocade and lace that are to make you very beautiful and for ever happy."

However, the laughter ceased, and in the sudden silence which fell, it again seemed as if death were passing by with a great flapping of wings and an icy gust which chilled the hearts of everyone remaining there.

"It's understood; so now I'm really off," resumed Guillaume. "*Au revoir*, children."

Then he sallied forth, without even turning round, and for a moment they could hear the firm tread of his feet over the garden gravel.

Pierre having invented a pretext was able to follow him a couple of minutes afterwards. As a matter of fact there was no need for him to dog Guillaume's heels, for he knew where his brother was going. He was thoroughly convinced that he would find him at that doorway, conducting to the foundations of the basilica, whence he had seen him emerge two days before. And so he wasted no time in looking for him among the crowd of pilgrims going to the church. His only thought was to hurry on and reach Jahan's workshop. And in accordance with his expectation, just as he arrived there, he perceived Guillaume slipping between the broken palings. The crush and the confusion prevailing among the concourse of believers favored Pierre as it had his brother, in such wise that he was able to follow the latter and enter the doorway without being noticed. Once there he had to pause and draw breath for a moment, so greatly did the beating of his heart oppress him.

A precipitous flight of steps, where all was steeped in darkness, descended from the narrow entry. It was with infinite precaution that Pierre ventured into the gloom, which ever grew denser and denser. He lowered his feet gently so as to make no noise, and feeling the walls with his hands, turned round and round as he went lower and lower into a kind of well. However, the descent was not a very long one. As soon as he found beaten ground beneath his feet he paused, no longer daring to stir for fear of betraying his presence. The darkness was like ink, and there was not a sound, a breath; the silence was complete.

How should he find his way? he wondered. Which direction ought he to take? He was still hesitating when some twenty paces away he suddenly saw a bright spark, the gleam of a lucifer. Guillaume was lighting a candle. Pierre recognised his broad shoulders, and from that moment he simply had to follow the flickering light along a walled and vaulted subterranean gallery. It seemed to be interminable and to run in a northerly direction, towards the nave of the basilica.

IV. THE CRISIS

All at once the little light at last stopped, while Pierre, anxious to see what would happen, continued to advance, treading as softly as he could and remaining in the gloom. He found that Guillaume had stood his candle upon the ground in the middle of a kind of low rotunda under the crypt, and that he had knelt down and moved aside a long flagstone which seemed to cover a cavity. They were here among the foundations of the basilica; and one of the columns or piles of concrete poured into shafts in order to support the building could be seen. The gap, which the stone slab removed by Guillaume had covered, was by the very side of the pillar; it was either some natural surface flaw, or a deep fissure caused by some subsidence or settling of the soil. The heads of other pillars could be descried around, and these the cleft seemed to be reaching, for little slits branched out in all directions. Then, on seeing his brother leaning forward, like one who is for the last time examining a mine he has laid before applying a match to the fuse, Pierre suddenly understood the whole terrifying business. Considerable quantities of the new explosive had been brought to that spot. Guillaume had made the journey a score of times at carefully selected hours, and all his powder had been poured into the gap beside the pillar, spreading to the slightest rifts below, saturating the soil at a great depth, and in this wise forming a natural mine of incalculable force. And now the powder was flush with the flagstone which Guillaume has just moved aside. It was only necessary to throw a match there, and everything would be blown into the air!

For a moment an acute chill of horror rooted Pierre to the spot. He could neither have taken a step nor raised a cry. He pictured the swarming throng above him, the ten thousand pilgrims crowding the lofty naves of the basilica to witness the solemn consecration of the Host. Peal upon peal flew from "La Savoyarde," incense smoked, and ten thousand voices raised a hymn of magnificence and praise. And all at once came thunder and earthquake, and a volcano opening and belching forth fire and smoke, and swallowing up the whole church and its multitude of worshippers. Breaking the concrete piles and rending the unsound soil, the explosion, which was certain to be one of extraordinary violence, would doubtless split the edifice atwain, and hurl one-half down the slopes descending towards Paris, whilst the other on the side of the apse would crumble and collapse upon the spot where it stood. And how fearful would be the avalanche; a broken forest of scaffoldings, a hail of stonework, rushing and bounding through the dust and smoke on to the roofs below; whilst the violence of the shock would threaten the whole of Montmartre, which, it seemed likely, must stagger and sink in one huge mass of ruins!

However, Guillaume had again risen. The candle standing on the ground, its flame shooting up, erect and slender, threw his huge shadow all over the subterranean vault. Amidst the dense blackness the light looked like some dismal stationary star. Guillaume drew near to it in order to see what time it was by his watch. It proved to be five minutes past three. So he had nearly another hour to wait. He was in no hurry, he wished to carry out his design punctually, at the precise moment he had selected; and he therefore sat down on a block of stone, and remained there without moving, quiet and patient. The candle now cast its light upon his pale face, upon his towering brow crowned with white hair, upon the whole of his energetic countenance, which still looked handsome and young, thanks to his bright eyes and dark moustaches. And not a muscle of his face stirred; he simply gazed into the void. What thoughts could be passing through his mind at that supreme moment? Who could tell? There was not a quiver; heavy night, the deep eternal silence of the earth reigned all around.

Then Pierre, having quieted his palpitating heart, drew near. At the sound of his footsteps Guillaume rose menacingly, but he immediately recognised his brother, and did not seem astonished to see him.

"Ah! it's you," he said, "you followed me.... I felt that you possessed my secret. And it grieves me that you should have abused your knowledge to join me here. You might have spared me this last sorrow."

Pierre clasped his trembling hands, and at once tried to entreat him. "Brother, brother," he began.

"No, don't speak yet," said Guillaume, "if you absolutely wish it I will listen to you by-and-by. We have nearly an hour before us, so we can chat. But I want you to understand the futility of all you may think needful to tell me. My resolution is unshakable; I was a long time coming to it, and in carrying it out I shall simply be acting in accordance with my reason and my conscience."

Then he quietly related that having decided upon a great deed he had long hesitated as to which edifice he should destroy. The opera-house had momentarily tempted him, but he had reflected that there would be no great significance in the whirlwind of anger and justice destroying a little set of enjoyers. In fact, such a deed might savour of jealousy and covetousness. Next he had thought of the Bourse, where he might strike a blow at money, the great agent of corruption, and the capitalist society in whose clutches the wage-earners groaned. Only, here again the blow would fall upon a restricted circle. Then an idea of destroying the Palace of Justice, particularly the assize court, had occurred to him. It was a very tempting thought—to wreak justice upon human justice, to sweep away the witnesses, the culprit, the public prosecutor who charges the latter, the counsel who defends him, the judges who sentence him, and the lounging public which comes to the spot as to the unfolding of some sensational serial. And then too what fierce irony there would be in the summary superior justice of the volcano swallowing up everything indiscriminately without pausing to enter into details. However, the plan over which he had most lingered was that of blowing up the Arc de Triomphe. This he regarded as an odious monument which perpetuated warfare, hatred among nations, and the false, dearly purchased, sanguineous glory of conquerors. That colossus raised to the memory of so much frightful slaughter which had uselessly put an end to so many human lives, ought, he considered, to be slaughtered in its turn. Could he so have arranged things that the earth should swallow it up, he might have achieved the glory of causing no other death than his own, of dying alone, struck down, crushed to pieces beneath that giant of stone. What a tomb, and what a memory might he thus have left to the world!

"But there was no means of approaching it," he continued, "no basement, no cellar, so I had to give up the idea.... And then, although I'm perfectly willing to die alone, I thought what a loftier and more terrible lesson there would be in the unjust death of an innocent multitude, of thousands of unknown people, of all those that might happen to be passing. In the same way as human society by dint of injustice, want and harsh regulations causes so many innocent victims, so must punishment fall as the lightning falls, indiscriminately killing and destroying whatever it may encounter in its course. When a man sets his foot on an ant-hill, he gives no heed to all the lives which he stamps out."

Pierre, whom this theory rendered quite indignant, raised a cry of protest: "Oh! brother, brother, is it you who are saying such things?"

Yet, Guillaume did not pause: "If I have ended by choosing this basilica of the Sacred Heart," he continued, "it is because I found it near at hand and easy to destroy. But it is also because it haunts and exasperates me, because I have long since condemned it.... As I have often said to you, one cannot imagine anything more preposterous than Paris, our great Paris, crowned and dominated by this temple raised to the glorification of the absurd. Is it not outrageous that common sense should receive such a smack after so many centuries of science, that Rome should claim the right of triumphing in this insolent fashion, on our loftiest height in the full sunlight? The priests want Paris to repent and do penitence for its liberative work of truth and justice. But its only right course is to sweep away all that hampers and insults it in its march towards deliverance. And so may the temple fall with its deity of falsehood and servitude! And may its ruins crush its worshippers, so that like one of the old geological revolutions of the world, the catastrophe may resound through the very entrails of mankind, and renew and change it!"

"Brother, brother!" again cried Pierre, quite beside himself, "is it you who are talking? What! you, a great scientist, a man of great heart, you have come to this! What madness is stirring you that you should think and say such abominable things? On the evening when we confessed our secrets one to the other, you told me of your proud and lofty dream of ideal Anarchy. There would be free harmony in life, which left to its natural forces would of itself create happiness. But you still rebelled against the idea of theft and murder. You would not accept them as right or necessary; you merely explained and excused them. What has happened then that you, all brain and thought, should now have become the hateful hand that acts?"

"Salvat has been guillotined," said Guillaume simply, "and I read his will and testament in his last glance. I am merely an executor.... And what has happened, you ask? Why, all that has made me suffer for four months past, the whole social evil which surrounds us, and which must be brought to an end."

Silence fell. The brothers looked at one another in the darkness. And Pierre now understood things. He saw that Guillaume was changed, that the terrible gust of revolutionary contagion sweeping over Paris had transformed him. It had all come from the duality of his nature, the presence of contradictory elements within him. On one side one found a scientist whose whole creed lay in observation and experiment, who, in dealing with nature, evinced the most cautious logic; while on the other side was a social dreamer, haunted by ideas of fraternity, equality and justice, and eager for universal happiness. Thence had first come the theoretical anarchist that he had been, one in whom science and chimeras were mingled, who dreamt of human society returning to the harmonious law of the spheres, each man free, in a free association, regulated by love alone. Neither Theophile Morin with the doctrines of Proudhon and Comte, nor Bache with those of St. Simon and Fourier, had been able to satisfy his desire for the absolute. All those systems had seemed to him imperfect and chaotic, destructive of one another, and tending to the same wretchedness of life. Janzen alone had occasionally satisfied him with some of his curt phrases which shot over the horizon, like arrows conquering the whole earth for the human family. And then in Guillaume's big heart, which the idea of want, the unjust sufferings of the lowly and the poor exasperated, Salvat's tragic adventure had suddenly found place, fomenting supreme rebellion. For long weeks he had lived on with trembling hands, with growing anguish clutching at his throat. First had come that bomb and the explosion which still made him quiver, then the vile cupidity of the newspapers howling for the poor wretch's head, then the search for him and the hunt through the Bois de Boulogne, till he fell into the hands of the police, covered with mud and dying of starvation. And afterwards there had been the assize court, the judges, the gendarmes, the witnesses, the whole of France arrayed against one man and bent on making him pay for the universal crime. And finally, there had come the guillotine, the monstrous, the filthy beast consummating irreparable injustice in human justice's name. One sole idea now remained to Guillaume, that idea of justice which maddened him, leaving naught in his mind save the thought of the just, avenging flare by which he would repair the evil and ensure that which was right for all time forward. Salvat had looked at him, and contagion had done its work; he glowed with a desire for death, a desire to give his own blood and set the blood of others flowing, in order that mankind, amidst its fright and horror, should decree the return of the golden age.

Pierre understood the stubborn blindness of such insanity; and he felt utterly upset by the fear that he should be unable to overcome it. "You are mad, brother!" he exclaimed, "they have driven you mad! It is a gust of violence passing; they were treated in a wrong way and too relentlessly at the outset, and now that they are avenging one another, it may be that blood will never cease to flow.... But, listen, brother, throw off that nightmare. You can't be a Salvat who murders or a Bergaz who steals! Remember the pillage of the Princess's house and remember the fair-haired, pretty child whom we saw lying yonder, ripped open.... You do not, you cannot belong to that set, brother—"

With a wave of his hand, Guillaume brushed these vain reasons aside. Of what consequence were a few lives, his own included? No change had ever taken place in the world without millions and millions of existences being stamped out.

"But you had a great scheme in hand," cried Pierre, hoping to save him by reviving his sense of duty. "It isn't allowable for you to go off like this."

Then he fervently strove to awaken his brother's scientific pride. He spoke to him of his secret, of that great engine of warfare, which could destroy armies and reduce cities to dust, and which he had intended to offer to France, so that on emerging victorious from the approaching war, she might afterwards become the deliverer of the world. And it was this grand scheme that he had abandoned, preferring to employ his explosive in killing innocent people and overthrowing a church, which would be built afresh, whatever the cost, and become a sanctuary of martyrs!

Guillaume smiled. "I have not relinquished my scheme," said he, "I have simply modified it. Did I not tell you of my doubts, my anxious perplexity? Ah! to believe that one holds the destiny of the world in one's grasp, and to tremble and hesitate and wonder if the intelligence and wisdom, that are needful for things to take the one wise course, will be forthcoming! At sight of all the stains upon our great Paris, all the errors and transgressions which we lately witnessed, I shuddered. I asked myself if Paris were sufficiently calm and pure for one to entrust her with omnipotence. How terrible would be the disaster if such an invention as mine should fall into the hands of a demented nation, possibly a dictator, some man of conquest, who would simply employ it to terrorize other nations and reduce them to slavery.... Ah! no, I do not wish to perpetuate warfare, I wish to kill it."

Then in a clear firm voice he explained his new plan, in which Pierre was surprised to find some of the ideas which General de Bozonnet had one day laid before him in a very different spirit. Warfare was on the road to extinction, threatened by its very excesses. In the old days of mercenaries, and afterwards with conscripts, the percentage of soldiers designated by chance, war had been a profession and a passion. But nowadays, when everybody is called upon to fight, none care to do so. By the logical force of things, the system of the whole nation in arms means the coming end of armies. How much longer will the nations remain on a footing of deadly peace, bowed down by ever increasing "estimates," spending millions and millions on holding one another in respect? Ah! how great the deliverance, what a cry of relief would go up on the day when some formidable engine, capable of destroying armies and sweeping cities away, should render war an impossibility and constrain every people to disarm! Warfare would be dead, killed in her own turn, she who has killed so many. This was Guillaume's dream, and he grew quite enthusiastic, so strong was his conviction that he would presently bring it to pass.

"Everything is settled," said he; "if I am about to die and disappear, it is in order that my idea may triumph.... You have lately seen me spend whole afternoons alone with Mere-Grand. Well, we were completing the classification of the documents and making our final arrangements. She has my orders, and will execute them even at the risk of her life, for none has a braver, loftier soul.... As soon as I am dead, buried beneath these stones, as soon as she has heard the explosion shake Paris and proclaim the advent of the new era, she will forward a set of all the documents I have confided to her—the formula of my explosive, the drawings of the bomb and gun—to each of the great powers of the world. In this wise I shall bestow on all the nations the terrible gift of destruction and omnipotence which, at first, I wished to bestow on France alone; and I do this in order that the nations, being one and all armed with the thunderbolt, may at once disarm, for fear of being annihilated, when seeking to annihilate others."

Pierre listened to him, gaping, amazed at this extraordinary idea, in which childishness was blended with genius. "Well," said he, "if you give your secret to all the nations, why should you blow up this church, and die yourself?"

"Why! In order that I may be believed!" cried Guillaume with extraordinary force of utterance. Then he added, "The edifice must lie on the ground, and I must be under it. If the experiment is not made, if universal horror does not attest and proclaim the amazing destructive power of my explosive, people will consider me a mere schemer, a visionary!... A lot of dead, a lot of blood, that is what is needed in order that blood may for ever cease to flow!" Then, with a broad sweep of his arm, he again declared that his action was necessary. "Besides," he said, "Salvat left me the legacy of carrying out this deed of justice. If I have given it greater scope and significance, utilising it as a means of hastening the end of war, this is because I happen to be a man of intellect. It would have been better possibly if my mind had been a simple one, and if I had merely acted like some volcano which changes the soil, leaving life the task of renewing humanity."

Much of the candle had now burnt away, and Guillaume at last rose from the block of stone. He had again consulted his watch, and found that he had ten minutes left him. The little current of air created by his gestures made the light flicker, while all around him the darkness seemed to grow denser. And near at hand ever lay the threatening open mine which a spark might at any moment fire.

"It is nearly time," said Guillaume. "Come, brother, kiss me and go away. You know how much I love you, what ardent affection for you has been awakened in my old heart. So love me in like fashion, and find love enough to let me die as I want to die, in carrying out my duty. Kiss me, kiss me, and go away without turning your head."

His deep affection for Pierre made his voice tremble, but he struggled on, forced back his tears, and ended by conquering himself. It was as if he were no longer of the world, no longer one of mankind.

"No, brother, you have not convinced me," said Pierre, who on his side did not seek to hide his tears, "and it is precisely because I love you as you love me, with my whole being, my whole soul, that I cannot go away. It is impossible! You cannot be the madman, the murderer you would try to be."

"Why not? Am I not free. I have rid my life of all responsibilities, all ties.... I have brought up my sons, they have no further need of me. But one heart-link remained—Marie, and I have given her to you."

At this a disturbing argument occurred to Pierre, and he passionately availed himself of it. "So you want to die because you have given me Marie," said he. "You still love her, confess it!"

"No!" cried Guillaume, "I no longer love her, I swear it. I gave her to you. I love her no more."

"So you fancied; but you can see now that you still love her, for here you are, quite upset; whereas none of the terrifying things of which we spoke just now could even move you.... Yes, if you wish to die it is because you have lost Marie!"

Guillaume quivered, shaken by what his brother said, and in low, broken words he tried to question himself. "No, no, that any love pain should have urged me to this terrible deed would be unworthy—unworthy of my great design. No, no, I decided on it in the free exercise of my reason, and I am accomplishing it from no personal motive, but in the name of justice and for the benefit of humanity, in order that war and want may cease."

Then, in sudden anguish, he went on: "Ah! it is cruel of you, brother, cruel of you to poison my delight at dying. I have created all the happiness I could, I was going off well pleased at leaving you all happy, and now you poison my death. No, no! question it how I may, my heart does not ache; if I love Marie, it is simply in the same way as I love you."

Nevertheless, he remained perturbed, as if fearing lest he might be lying to himself; and by degrees gloomy anger came over him: "Listen, that is enough, Pierre," he exclaimed, "time is flying.... For the last time, go away! I order you to do so; I will have it!"

"I will not obey you, Guillaume.... I will stay, and as all my reasoning cannot save you from your insanity, fire your mine, and I will die with you."

"You? Die? But you have no right to do so, you are not free!"

"Free, or not, I swear that I will die with you. And if it merely be a question of flinging this candle into that hole, tell me so, and I will take it and fling it there myself."

He made a gesture at which his brother thought that he was about to carry out his threat. So he caught him by the arm, crying: "Why should you die? It would be absurd. That others should die may be necessary, but you, no! Of what use could be this additional monstrosity? You are endeavouring to soften me, you are torturing my heart!" Then all at once, imagining that Pierre's offer had concealed another design, Guillaume thundered in a fury: "You don't want to take the candle in order to throw it there. What you want to do is to blow it out! And you think I shan't be able then—ah! you bad brother!"

In his turn Pierre exclaimed: "Oh! certainly, I'll use every means to prevent you from accomplishing such a frightful and foolish deed!"

"You'll prevent me!"

"Yes, I'll cling to you, I'll fasten my arms to your shoulders, I'll hold your hands if necessary."

"Ah! you'll prevent me, you bad brother! You think you'll prevent me!"

Choking and trembling with rage, Guillaume had already caught hold of Pierre, pressing his ribs with his powerful muscular arms. They were closely linked together, their eyes fixed upon one another, and their breath mingling in that kind of subterranean dungeon, where their big dancing shadows looked like ghosts. They seemed to be vanishing into the night, the candle now showed merely like a little yellow tear in the midst of the darkness; and at that moment, in those far depths, a quiver sped through the silence of the earth which weighed so heavily upon them. Distant but sonorous peals rang out, as if death itself were somewhere ringing its invisible bell.

"You hear," stammered Guillaume, "it's their bell up there. The time has come. I have vowed to act, and you want to prevent me!"

"Yes, I'll prevent you as long as I'm here alive."

"As long as you are alive, you'll prevent me!"

Guillaume could hear "La Savoyarde" pealing joyfully up yonder; he could see the triumphant basilica, overflowing with its ten thousand pilgrims, and blazing with the splendour of the Host amidst the smoke of incense; and blind frenzy came over him at finding himself unable to act, at finding an obstacle suddenly barring the road to his fixed idea.

"As long as you are alive, as long as you are alive!" he repeated, beside himself. "Well, then, die, you wretched brother!"

A fratricidal gleam had darted from his blurred eyes. He hastily stooped, picked up a large brick forgotten there, and raised it with both hands as if it were a club.

"Ah! I'm willing," cried Pierre. "Kill me, then; kill your own brother before you kill the others!"

The brick was already descending, but Guillaume's arms must have deviated, for the weapon only grazed one of Pierre's shoulders. Nevertheless, he sank upon his knees in the gloom. When Guillaume saw him there he fancied he had dealt him a mortal blow. What was it that had happened between them, what had he done? For a moment he remained standing, haggard, his mouth open, his eyes dilating with terror. He looked at his hands, fancying that blood was streaming from them. Then he pressed them to his brow, which seemed to be bursting with pain, as if his fixed idea had been torn from him, leaving his skull open. And he himself suddenly sank upon the ground with a great sob.

"Oh! brother, little brother, what have I done?" he called. "I am a monster!"

But Pierre had passionately caught him in his arms again. "It is nothing, nothing, brother, I assure you," he replied. "Ah! you are weeping now. How pleased I am! You are saved, I can feel it, since you are weeping. And what a good thing it is that you flew into such a passion, for your anger with me has dispelled your evil dream of violence."

"I am horrified with myself," gasped Guillaume, "to think that I wanted to kill you! Yes, I'm a brute beast that would kill his brother! And the others, too, all the others up yonder.... Oh! I'm cold, I feel so cold."

His teeth were chattering, and he shivered. It was as if he had awakened, half stupefied, from some evil dream. And in the new light which his fratricidal deed cast upon things, the scheme which had haunted him and goaded him to madness appeared like some act of criminal folly, projected by another.

"To kill you!" he repeated almost in a whisper. "I shall never forgive myself. My life is ended, I shall never find courage enough to live."

But Pierre clasped him yet more tightly. "What do you say?" he answered. "Will there not rather be a fresh and stronger tie of affection between us? Ah! yes, brother, let me save you as you saved me, and we shall be yet more closely united! Don't you remember that evening at Neuilly, when you consoled me and held me to your heart as I am holding you to mine? I had confessed my torments to you, and you told me that I must live and love!... And you did far more afterwards: you plucked your own love from your breast and gave it to me. You wished to ensure my happiness at the price of your own! And how delightful it is that, in my turn, I now have an opportunity to console you, save you, and bring you back to life!"

"No, no, the bloodstain is there and it is ineffaceable. I can hope no more!"

"Yes, yes, you can. Hope in life as you bade me do! Hope in love and hope in labour!"

Still weeping and clasping one another, the brothers continued speaking in low voices. The expiring candle suddenly went out unknown to them, and in the inky night and deep silence their tears of redeeming affection flowed freely. On the one hand, there was joy at being able to repay a debt of brotherliness, and on the other, acute emotion at having been led by a fanatical love of justice and mankind to the very verge of crime. And there were yet other things in the depths of those tears which cleansed and purified them; there were protests against suffering in every form, and ardent wishes that the world might some day be relieved of all its dreadful woe.

At last, after pushing the flagstone over the cavity near the pillar, Pierre groped his way out of the vault, leading Guillaume like a child.

Meantime Mere-Grand, still seated near the window of the workroom, had impassively continued sewing. Now and again, pending the arrival of four o'clock, she had looked up at the timepiece hanging on the wall on her left hand, or else had glanced out of the window towards the unfinished pile of the basilica, which a gigantic framework of scaffoldings encompassed. Slowly and steadily plying her needle, the old lady remained very pale and silent, but full of heroic serenity. On the other hand, Marie, who sat near her, embroidering, shifted her position a score of times, broke her thread, and grew impatient, feeling strangely nervous, a prey to unaccountable anxiety, which oppressed her heart. For their part, the three young men could not keep in place at all; it was as if some contagious fever disturbed them. Each had gone to his work: Thomas was filing something at his bench; Francois and Antoine were on either side of their table, the first trying to solve a mathematical problem, and the other copying a bunch of poppies in a vase before him. It was in vain, however, that they strove to be attentive. They quivered at the slightest sound, raised their heads, and darted questioning glances at one another. What could be the matter? What could possess them? What did they fear? Now and again one or the other would rise, stretch himself, and then, resume his place. However, they did not speak; it was as if they dared not say anything, and thus the heavy silence grew more and more terrible.

When it was a few minutes to four o'clock Mere-Grand felt weary, or else desired to collect her thoughts. After another glance at the timepiece, she let her needlework fall on her lap and turned towards the basilica. It seemed to her that she had only enough strength left to wait; and she remained with her eyes fixed on the huge walls and the forest of scaffolding which rose over yonder with such triumphant pride under the blue sky. Then all at once, however brave and firm she might be, she could not restrain a start, for "La Savoyarde" had raised a joyful clang. The consecration of the Host was now at hand, the ten thousand pilgrims filled the church, four o'clock was about to strike. And thereupon an irresistible impulse forced the old lady to her feet; she drew herself up, quivering, her hands clasped, her eyes ever turned yonder, waiting in mute dread.

"What is the matter?" cried Thomas, who noticed her. "Why are you trembling, Mere-Grand?"

Francois and Antoine raised their heads, and in turn sprang forward.

"Are you ill? Why are you turning so pale, you who are so courageous?"

But she did not answer. Ah! might the force of the explosion rend the earth asunder, reach the house and sweep it into the flaming crater of the volcano! Might she and the three young men, might they all die with the father, this was her one ardent wish in order that grief might be spared them. And she remained waiting and waiting, quivering despite herself, but with her brave, clear eyes ever gazing yonder.

"Mere-Grand, Mere-Grand!" cried Marie in dismay; "you frighten us by refusing to answer us, by looking over there as if some misfortune were coming up at a gallop!"

Then, prompted by the same anguish, the same cry suddenly came from Thomas, Francois and Antoine: "Father is in peril—father is going to die!"

What did they know? Nothing precise, certainly. Thomas no doubt had been astonished to see what a large quantity of the explosive his father had recently prepared, and both Francois and Antoine were aware of the ideas of revolt which he harboured in his mind. But, full of filial deference, they never sought to know anything beyond what he might choose to confide to them. They never questioned him; they bowed to whatever he might do. And yet now a foreboding came to them, a conviction that their father was going to die, that some most frightful catastrophe was impending. It must have been that which had already sent such a quiver through the atmosphere ever since the morning, making them shiver with fever, feel ill at ease, and unable to work.

"Father is going to die, father is going to die!"

The three big fellows had drawn close together, distracted by one and the same anguish, and furiously longing to know what the danger was, in order that they might rush upon it and die with their father if they could not save him. And amidst Mere-

Grand's stubborn silence death once more flitted through the room: there came a cold gust such as they had already felt brushing past them during *dejeuner*.

At last four o'clock began to strike, and Mere-Grand raised her white hands with a gesture of supreme entreaty. It was then that she at last spoke: "Father is going to die. Nothing but the duty of living can save him."

At this the three young men again wished to rush yonder, whither they knew not; but they felt that they must throw down all obstacles and conquer. Their powerlessness rent their hearts, they were both so frantic and so woeful that their grandmother strove to calm them. "Father's own wish was to die," said she, "and he is resolved to die alone."

They shuddered as they heard her, and then, on their side, strove to be heroic. But the minutes crept by, and it seemed as if the cold gust had slowly passed away. Sometimes, at the twilight hour, a night-bird will come in by the window like some messenger of misfortune, flit round the darkened room, and then fly off again, carrying its sadness with it. And it was much like that; the gust passed, the basilica remained standing, the earth did not open to swallow it. Little by little the atrocious anguish which wrung their hearts gave place to hope. And when at last Guillaume appeared, followed by Pierre, a great cry of resurrection came from one and all: "Father!"

Their kisses, their tears, deprived him of his little remaining strength. He was obliged to sit down. He had glanced round him as if he were returning to life perforce. Mere-Grand, who understood what bitter feelings must have followed the subjugation of his will, approached him smiling, and took hold of both his hands as if to tell him that she was well pleased at seeing him again, and at finding that he accepted his task and was unwilling to desert the cause of life. For his part he suffered dreadfully, the shock had been so great. The others spared him any narrative of their feelings; and he, himself, related nothing. With a gesture, a loving word, he simply indicated that it was Pierre who had saved him.

Thereupon, in a corner of the room, Marie flung her arms round the young man's neck. "Ah! my good Pierre, I have never yet kissed you," said she; "I want it to be for something serious the first time.... I love you, my good Pierre, I love you with all my heart."

Later that same evening, after night had fallen, Guillaume and Pierre remained for a moment alone in the big workroom. The young men had gone out, and Mere-Grand and Marie were upstairs sorting some house linen, while Madame Mathis, who had brought some work back, sat patiently in a dim corner waiting for another bundle of things which might require mending. The brothers, steeped in the soft melancholy of the twilight hour, and chatting in low tones, had quite forgotten her.

But all at once the arrival of a visitor upset them. It was Janzen with the fair, Christ-like face. He called very seldom nowadays; and one never knew from what gloomy spot he had come or into what darkness he would return when he took his departure. He disappeared, indeed, for months together, and was then suddenly to be seen like some momentary passer-by whose past and present life were alike unknown.

"I am leaving to-night," he said in a voice sharp like a knife.

"Are you going back to your home in Russia?" asked Guillaume.

A faint, disdainful smile appeared on the Anarchist's lips. "Home!" said he, "I am at home everywhere. To begin with, I am not a Russian, and then I recognise no other country than the world."

With a sweeping gesture he gave them to understand what manner of man he was, one who had no fatherland of his own, but carried his gory dream of fraternity hither and thither regardless of frontiers. From some words he spoke the brothers fancied he was returning to Spain, where some fellow-Anarchists awaited him. There was a deal of work to be done there, it appeared. He had quietly seated himself, chatting on in his cold way, when all at once he serenely added: "By the by, a bomb had just been thrown into the Cafe de l'Univers on the Boulevard. Three *bourgeois* were killed."

Pierre and Guillaume shuddered, and asked for particulars. Thereupon Janzen related that he had happened to be there, had heard the explosion, and seen the windows of the cafe shivered to atoms. Three customers were lying on the floor blown to pieces. Two of them were gentlemen, who had entered the place by chance and whose names were not known, while the third was a regular customer, a petty cit of the neighbourhood, who came every day to play a game at dominoes. And the whole place was wrecked; the marble tables were broken, the chandeliers twisted out of shape, the mirrors studded with projectiles. And how great the terror and the indignation, and how frantic the rush of the crowd! The perpetrator of the deed had been arrested immediately—in fact, just as he was turning the corner of the Rue Caumartin.

"I thought I would come and tell you of it," concluded Janzen; "it is well you should know it."

Then as Pierre, shuddering and already suspecting the truth, asked him if he knew who the man was that had been arrested, he slowly replied: "The worry is that you happen to know him—it was little Victor Mathis."

Pierre tried to silence Janzen too late. He had suddenly remembered that Victor's mother had been sitting in a dark corner behind them a short time previously. Was she still there? Then he again pictured Victor, slight and almost beardless, with a straight, stubborn brow, grey eyes glittering with intelligence, a pointed nose and thin lips expressive of stern will and unforgiving hatred. He was no simple and lowly one from the ranks of the disinherited. He was an educated scion of the *bourgeoisie*, and but for circumstances would have entered the Ecole Normale. There was no excuse for his abominable deed, there was no political passion, no humanitarian insanity, in it. He was the destroyer pure and simple, the theoretician of destruction, the cold energetic man of intellect who gave his cultivated mind to arguing the cause of murder, in his desire to make murder an instrument of the social evolution. True, he was also a poet, a visionary, but the most frightful of all visionaries: a monster whose nature could only be explained by mad pride, and who craved for the most awful immortality, dreaming that the coming dawn would rise from the arms of the guillotine. Only one thing could surpass him: the scythe of death which blindly mows the world.

For a few seconds, amidst the growing darkness, cold horror reigned in the workroom. "Ah!" muttered Guillaume, "he had the daring to do it, he had."

Pierre, however, lovingly pressed his arm. And he felt that he was as distracted, as upset, as himself. Perhaps this last abomination had been needed to ravage and cure him.

Janzen no doubt had been an accomplice in the deed. He was relating that Victor's purpose had been to avenge Salvat, when all at once a great sigh of pain was heard in the darkness, followed by a heavy thud upon the floor. It was Madame Mathis falling like a bundle, overwhelmed by the news which chance had brought her. At that moment it so happened that Mere-Grand came down with a lamp, which lighted up the room, and thereupon they hurried to the help of the wretched woman, who lay there as pale as a corpse in her flimsy black gown.

And this again brought Pierre an indescribable heart-pang. Ah! the poor, sad, suffering creature! He remembered her at Abbe Rose's, so discreet, so shamefaced, in her poverty, scarce able to live upon the slender resources which persistent misfortunes had left her. Hers had indeed been a cruel lot: first, a home with wealthy parents in the provinces, a love story and elopement with the man of her choice; next, ill-luck steadily pursuing her, all sorts of home troubles, and at last her husband's death. Then, in the retirement of her widowhood, after losing the best part of the little income which had enabled her to bring up her son, naught but this son had been left to her. He had been her Victor, her sole affection, the only one in whom she had faith. She had ever striven to believe that he was very busy, absorbed in work, and on the eve of attaining to some superb position worthy of his merits. And now, all at once, she had learnt that this fondly loved son was simply the most odious of assassins, that he had flung a bomb into a cafe, and had there killed three men.

When Madame Mathis had recovered her senses, thanks to the careful tending of Mere-Grand, she sobbed on without cessation, raising such a continuous doleful wail, that Pierre's hand again sought Guillaume's, and grasped it, whilst their hearts, distracted but healed, mingled lovingly one with the other.

V. LIFE'S WORK AND PROMISE

FIFTEEN months later, one fine golden day in September, Bache and Theophile Morin were taking *dejeuner* at Guillaume's, in the big workroom overlooking the immensity of Paris.

Near the table was a cradle with its little curtains drawn. Behind them slept Jean, a fine boy four months old, the son of Pierre and Marie. The latter, simply in order to protect the child's social rights, had been married civilly at the town-hall of Montmartre. Then, by way of pleasing Guillaume, who wished to keep them with him, and thus enlarge the family circle, they had continued living in the little lodging over the work-shop, leaving the sleepy house at Neuilly in the charge of Sophie, Pierre's old servant. And life had been flowing on happily for the fourteen months or so that they had now belonged to one another.

There was simply peace, affection and work around the young couple. Francois, who had left the Ecole Normale provided with every degree, every diploma, was now about to start for a college in the west of France, so as to serve his term of probation as a professor, intending to resign his post afterwards and devote himself, if he pleased, to science pure and simple. Then Antoine had lately achieved great success with a series of engravings he had executed—some views and scenes of Paris life; and it was settled that he was to marry Lise Jahan in the ensuing spring, when she would have completed her seventeenth year. Of the three sons, however, Thomas was the most triumphant, for he had at last devised and constructed his little motor, thanks to a happy idea of his father's. One morning, after the downfall of all his huge chimerical schemes, Guillaume, remembering the terrible explosive which he had discovered and hitherto failed to utilise, had suddenly thought of employing it as a motive force, in the place of petroleum, in the motor which his eldest son had so long been trying to construct for the Grandidier works. So he had set to work with Thomas, devising a new mechanism, encountering endless difficulties, and labouring for a whole year before reaching success. But now the father and son had accomplished their task; the marvel was created, and stood there riveted to an oak stand, and ready to work as soon as its final toilet should have been performed.

Amidst all the changes which had occurred, Mere-Grand, in spite of her great age, continued exercising her active, silent sway over the household, which was now again so gay and peaceful. Though she seldom seemed to leave her chair in front of her work-table, she was really here, there and everywhere. Since the birth of Jean, she had talked of rearing the child in the same way as she had formerly reared Thomas, Francois and Antoine. She was indeed full of the bravery of devotion, and seemed to think that she was not at all likely to die so long as she might have others to guide, love and save. Marie marvelled at it all. She herself, though she was always gay and in good health, felt tired at times now that she was suckling her infant. Little Jean indeed had two vigilant mothers near his cradle; whilst his father, Pierre, who had become Thomas's assistant, pulled the bellows, roughened out pieces of metal, and generally completed his apprenticeship as a working mechanician.

On the particular day when Bache and Theophile Morin came to Montmartre, the *dejeuner* proved even gayer than usual, thanks perhaps to their presence. The meal was over, the table had been cleared, and the coffee was being served, when a little boy, the son of a doorkeeper in the Rue Cortot, came to ask for Monsieur Pierre Froment. When they inquired his business, he answered in a hesitating way that Monsieur l'Abbe Rose was very ill, indeed dying, and that he had sent him to fetch Monsieur Pierre Froment at once.

Pierre followed the lad, feeling much affected; and on reaching the Rue Cortot he there found Abbe Rose in a little damp ground-floor room overlooking a strip of garden. The old priest was in bed, dying as the boy had said, but he still retained the use of his faculties, and could speak in his wonted slow and gentle voice. A Sister of Charity was watching beside him, and she seemed so surprised and anxious at the arrival of a visitor whom she did not know, that Pierre understood she was there to guard the dying man and prevent him from having intercourse with others. The old priest must have employed some stratagem in order to send the doorkeeper's boy to fetch him. However, when Abbe Rose in his grave and kindly way begged the Sister to leave them alone for a moment, she dared not refuse this supreme request, but immediately left the room.

"Ah! my dear child," said the old man, "how much I wanted to speak to you! Sit down there, close to the bed, so that you may be able to hear me, for this is the end; I shall no longer be here to-night. And I have such a great service to ask of you."

Quite upset at finding his friend so wasted, with his face white like a sheet, and scarce a sign of life save the sparkle of his innocent, loving eyes, Pierre responded: "But I would have come sooner if I had known you were in need of me! Why did you not send for me before? Are people being kept away from you?"

A faint smile of shame and confession appeared on the old priest's embarrassed face. "Well, my dear child," said he, "you must know that I have again done some foolish things. Yes, I gave money to some people who, it seems, were not deserving of it. In fact, there was quite a scandal; they scolded me at the Archbishop's palace, and accused me of compromising the interests of religion. And when they heard that I was ill, they put that good Sister beside me, because they said that I should die on the floor, and give the very sheets off my bed if I were not prevented."

He paused to draw breath, and then continued: "So you understand, that good Sister—oh! she is a very saintly woman—is here to nurse me and prevent me from still doing foolish things. To overcome her vigilance I had to use a little deceit, for which God, I trust, will forgive me. As it happens, it's precisely my poor who are in question; it was to speak to you about them that I so particularly wished to see you."

Tears had come to Pierre's eyes. "Tell me what you want me to do," he answered; "I am yours, both heart and soul."

"Yes, yes, I know it, my dear child. It was for that reason that I thought of you—you alone. In spite of all that has happened, you are the only one in whom I have any confidence, who can understand me, and give me a promise which will enable me to die in peace."

This was the only allusion he would venture to make to the cruel rupture which had occurred after the young man had thrown off his cassock and rebelled against the Church. He had since heard of Pierre's marriage, and was aware that he had for ever severed all religious ties. But at that supreme moment nothing of this seemed of any account to the old priest. His knowledge of Pierre's loving heart sufficed him, for all that he now desired was simply the help of that heart which he had seen glowing with such passionate charity.

"Well," he resumed, again finding sufficient strength to smile, "it is a very simple matter. I want to make you my heir. Oh! it isn't a fine legacy I am leaving you; it is the legacy of my poor, for I have nothing else to bestow on you; I shall leave nothing behind me but my poor."

Of these unhappy creatures, three in particular quite upset his heart. He recoiled from the prospect of leaving them without chance of succour, without even the crumbs which he had hitherto distributed among them, and which had enabled them to live. One was the big Old'un, the aged carpenter whom he and Pierre had vainly sought one night with the object of sending him to the Asylum for the Invalids of Labour. He had been sent there a little later, but he had fled three days afterwards, unwilling as he was to submit to the regulations. Wild and violent, he had the most detestable disposition. Nevertheless, he could not be left to starve. He came to Abbe Rose's every Saturday, it seemed, and received a franc, which sufficed him for the whole week. Then, too, there was a bedridden old woman in a hovel in the Rue du Mont-Cenis. The baker, who every morning took her the bread she needed, must be paid. And in particular there was a poor young woman residing on the Place du Tertre, one who was unmarried but a mother. She was dying of consumption, unable to work, and tortured by the idea that when she should have gone, her daughter must sink to the pavement like herself. And in this instance the legacy was twofold: there was the mother to relieve until her death, which was near at hand, and then the daughter to provide for until she could be placed in some good household.

"You must forgive me, my dear child, for leaving you all these worries," added Abbe Rose. "I tried to get the good Sister, who is nursing me, to take an interest in these poor people, but when I spoke to her of the big Old'un, she was so alarmed that she made the sign of the cross. And it's the same with my worthy friend Abbe Tavernier. I know nobody of more upright mind. Still I shouldn't be at ease with him, he has ideas of his own.... And so, my dear child, there is only you whom I can rely upon, and you must accept my legacy if you wish me to depart in peace."

Pierre was weeping. "Ah! certainly, with my whole soul," he answered. "I shall regard your desires as sacred."

"Good! I knew you would accept.... So it is agreed: a franc for the big Old'un every Saturday, the bread for the bedridden woman, some help for the poor young mother, and then a home for her little girl. Ah! if you only knew what a weight it is off my heart! The end may come now, it will be welcome to me."

His kind white face had brightened as if with supreme joy. Holding Pierre's hand within his own he detained him beside the bed, exchanging a farewell full of serene affection. And his voice weakening, he expressed his whole mind in faint, impressive accents: "Yes, I shall be pleased to go off. I could do no more, I could do no more! Though I gave and gave, I felt that it was ever necessary to give more and more. And how sad to find charity powerless, to give without hope of ever being able to stamp out want and suffering! I rebelled against that idea of yours, as you will remember. I told you that we should always love one another in our poor, and that was true, since you are here, so good and affectionate to me and those whom I am leaving behind. But, all the same, I can do no more, I can do no more; and I would rather go off, since the woes of others rise higher and higher around me, and I have ended by doing the most foolish things, scandalising the faithful and making my superiors indignant with me, without even saving one single poor person from the ever-growing torrent of want. Farewell, my dear child. My poor old heart goes off aching, my old hands are weary and conquered."

Pierre embraced him with his whole soul, and then departed. His eyes were full of tears and indescribable emotion wrung his heart. Never had he heard a more woeful cry than that confession of the impotence of charity, on the part of that old candid child, whose heart was all simplicity and sublime benevolence. Ah! what a disaster, that human kindness should be futile, that the world should always display so much distress and suffering in spite of all the compassionate tears that had been shed, in spite of all the alms that had fallen from millions and millions of hands for centuries and centuries! No wonder that it should bring desire for death, no wonder that a Christian should feel pleased at escaping from the abominations of this earth!

When Pierre again reached the workroom he found that the table had long since been cleared, and that Bache and Morin were chatting with Guillaume, whilst the latter's sons had returned to their customary occupations. Marie, also, had resumed her usual place at the work-table in front of Mere-Grand; but from time to time she rose and went to look at Jean, so as to make sure that he was sleeping peacefully, with his little clenched fists pressed to his heart. And when Pierre, who kept his emotion to himself, had likewise leant over the cradle beside the young woman, whose hair he discreetly kissed, he went to put on an apron in order that he might assist Thomas, who was now, for the last time, regulating his motor.

Then, as Pierre stood there awaiting an opportunity to help, the room vanished from before his eyes; he ceased to see or hear the persons who were there. The scent of Marie's hair alone lingered on his lips amidst the acute emotion into which he had been thrown by his visit to Abbe Rose. A recollection had come to him, that of the bitterly cold morning when the old priest had stopped him outside the basilica of the Sacred Heart, and had timidly asked him to take some alms to that old man Laveuve, who soon afterwards had died of want, like a dog by the wayside. How sad a morning it had been; what battle and torture had Pierre not felt within him, and what a resurrection had come afterwards! He had that day said one of his last masses, and he recalled with a shudder his abominable anguish, his despairing doubts at the thought of nothingness. Two experiments which he had previously made had failed most miserably. First had come one at Lourdes, where the glorification of the absurd had simply filled him with pity for any such attempt to revert to the primitive faith of young nations, who bend beneath the terror born of ignorance; and, secondly, there had been an experiment at Rome, which he had found incapable of any renewal, and which he had seen staggering to its death amidst its ruins, a mere great shadow, which would soon be of no account, fast sinking, as it was, to the dust of dead religions. And, in his own mind, Charity itself had become bankrupt; he no longer believed that alms could cure the sufferings of mankind, he awaited naught but a frightful catastrophe, fire and massacre, which would sweep away the guilty, condemned world. His cassock, too, stifled him, a lie alone kept it on his shoulders, the idea, unbelieving priest though he was, that he could honestly and chastely watch over the belief of others. The problem of a new religion, a new hope, such as was needful to ensure the peace of the coming democracies tortured him, but between the certainties of science and the need of the Divine, which seemed to consume humanity, he could find no solution. If Christianity crumbled with the principle of Charity, there could remain nothing else but Justice, that cry which came from every breast, that battle of Justice against Charity in which his heart must contend in that great city of Paris. It was there that began his third and decisive experiment, the experiment which was to make truth as plain to him as the sun itself, and give him back health and strength and delight in life.

At this point of his reverie Pierre was roused by Thomas, who asked him to fetch a tool. As he did so he heard Bache remarking: "The ministry resigned this morning. Vignon has had enough of it, he wants to reserve his remaining strength."

"Well, he has lasted more than a twelvemonth," replied Morin. "That's already an achievement."

After the crime of Victor Mathis, who had been tried and executed within three weeks, Monferrand had suddenly fallen from power. What was the use of having a strong-handed man at the head of the Government if bombs still continued to terrify the country? Moreover, he had displeased the Chamber by his voracious appetite, which had prevented him from allowing others more than an infinitesimal share of all the good things. And this time he had been succeeded by Vignon, although the latter's programme of reforms had long made people tremble. He, Vignon, was honest certainly, but of all these reforms he had only been able to carry out a few insignificant ones, for he had found himself hampered by a thousand obstacles. And thus he had resigned himself to ruling the country as others had done; and people had discovered that after all there were but faint shades of difference between him and Monferrand.

"You know that Monferrand is being spoken of again?" said Guillaume.

"Yes, and he has some chance of success. His creatures are bestirring themselves tremendously," replied Bache, adding, in a bitter, jesting way, that Mege, the Collectivist leader, played the part of a dupe in overthrowing ministry after ministry. He simply gratified the ambition of each coterie in turn, without any possible chance of attaining to power himself.

Thereupon Guillaume pronounced judgment. "Oh! well, let them devour one another," said he. "Eager as they all are to reign and dispose of power and wealth, they only fight over questions of persons. And nothing they do can prevent the evolution from continuing. Ideas expand, and events occur, and, over and above everything else, mankind is marching on."

Pierre was greatly struck by these words, and he again recalled the past. His dolorous Parisian experiment had begun, and he was once more roaming through the city. Paris seemed to him to be a huge vat, in which a world fermented, something of the best and something of the worst, a frightful mixture such as sorceresses might have used; precious powders mingled with filth, from all of which was to come the philter of love and eternal youth. And in that vat Pierre first marked the scum of the political world: Monferrand who strangled Barroux, who purchased the support of hungry ones such as Fonsegue, Duthil and Chaigneux, who made use of those who attained to mediocrity, such as Taboureau and Dauvergne; and who employed even the sectarian passions of Mege and the intelligent ambition of Vignon as his weapons. Next came money the poisoner, with that affair of the African Railways, which had rotted the Parliament and turned Duvillard, the triumphant *bourgeois*, into a public perverter, the very cancer as it were of the financial world. Then as a just consequence of all this there was Duvillard's own home infected by himself, that frightful drama of Eve contending with her daughter Camille for the possession of Gerard, then Camille stealing him from her mother, and Hyacinthe, the son, passing his crazy mistress Rosemonde on to that notorious harlot Silviane, with whom his father publicly exhibited himself. Then there was the old expiring aristocracy, with the pale, sad faces of Madame de Quinsac and the Marquis de Morigny; the old military spirit whose funeral was conducted by General de Bozonnet; the magistracy which slavishly served the powers of the day, Amadieu thrusting himself into notoriety by means of sensational cases, Lehmann, the public prosecutor, preparing his speeches in the private room of the Minister whose policy he defended; and, finally, the mendacious and cupid Press which lived upon scandal, the everlasting flood of denunciation and filth which poured from Sagnier, and the gay impudence shown by the unscrupulous and conscienceless Massot, who attacked all and defended all, by profession and to order! And in the same way as insects, on discovering one of their own kind dying, will often finish it off and fatten upon it, so the whole swarm of appetites, interests and passions had fallen upon a wretched madman, that unhappy Salvat, whose idiotic crime had brought them all scrambling together, gluttonously eager to derive some benefit from that starveling's emaciated carcass. And all boiled in the huge vat of Paris; the desires, the deeds of violence, the strivings of one and another man's will, the whole nameless medley of the bitterest ferments, whence, in all purity, the wine of the future would at last flow.

Then Pierre became conscious of the prodigious work which went on in the depths of the vat, beneath all the impurity and waste. As his brother had just said, what mattered the stains, the egotism and greed of politicians, if humanity were still on the march, ever slowly and stubbornly stepping forward! What mattered, too, that corrupt and emasculate *bourgeoisie*, nowadays as moribund as the aristocracy, whose place it took, if behind it there ever came the inexhaustible reserve of men who surged up from the masses of the country-sides and the towns! What mattered the debauchery, the perversion arising from excess of wealth and power, the luxuriousness and dissoluteness of life, since it seemed a proven fact that the capitals that had been queens of the world had never reigned without extreme civilisation, a cult of beauty and of pleasure! And what mattered even the venality, the transgressions and the folly of the press, if at the same time it remained an admirable instrument for the diffusion of knowledge, the open conscience, so to say, of the nation, a river which, though there might be horrors on its surface, none the less flowed on, carrying all nations to the brotherly ocean of the future centuries! The human lees ended by sinking to the bottom of the vat, and it was not possible to expect that what was right would triumph visibly every day; for it was often necessary that years should elapse before the realisation of some hope could emerge from the fermentation. Eternal matter is ever being cast afresh into the crucible and ever coming from it improved. And if in the depths of pestilential workshops and factories the slavery of ancient times subsists in the wage-earning system, if such men as Toussaint still die of want on their pallets like broken-down beasts of burden, it is nevertheless a fact that once already, on a memorable day of tempest, Liberty sprang forth from the vat to wing her flight throughout the world. And why in her turn should not Justice spring from it, proceeding from those troubled elements, freeing herself from all dross, flowing forth with dazzling limpidity and regenerating the nations?

However, the voices of Bache and Morin, rising in the course of their chat with Guillaume, once more drew Pierre from his reverie. They were now speaking of Janzen, who after being compromised in a fresh outrage at Barcelona had fled from Spain. Bache fancied that he had recognised him in the street only the previous day. To think that a man with so clear a mind and such keen energy should waste his natural gifts in such a hateful cause!

"When I remember," said Morin slowly, "that Barthes lives in exile in a shabby little room at Brussels, ever quivering with the hope that the reign of liberty is at hand—he who has never had a drop of blood on his hands and who has spent two-thirds of his life in prison in order that the nations may be freed!"

Bache gently shrugged his shoulders: "Liberty, liberty, of course," said he; "only it is worth nothing if it is not organised."

Thereupon their everlasting discussion began afresh, with Saint-Simon and Fourier on one side and Proudhon and Auguste Comte on the other. Bache gave a long account of the last commemoration which had taken place in honour of Fourier's memory, how faithful disciples had brought wreaths and made speeches, forming quite a meeting of apostles, who all stubbornly clung to their faith, as confident in the future as if they were the messengers of some new gospel. Afterwards Morin emptied his pockets, which were always full of Positivist tracts and pamphlets, manifestos, answers and so forth, in which Comte's doctrines were extolled as furnishing the only possible basis for the new, awaited religion. Pierre, who listened, thereupon remembered the disputes in his little house at Neuilly when he himself, searching for certainty, had endeavoured to draw up the century's balance-sheet. He had lost his depth, in the end, amidst the contradictions and incoherency of the various precursors. Although Fourier had sprung from Saint-Simon, he denied him in part, and if Saint-Simon's doctrine ended in a kind of mystical sensuality, the other's conducted to an inacceptable regimenting of society. Proudhon, for his part, demolished without rebuilding anything. Comte, who created method and declared science to be the one and only sovereign, had not even suspected the advent of the social crisis which now threatened to sweep all away, and had finished personally as a mere worshipper of love, overpowered by woman. Nevertheless, these two, Comte and Proudhon, entered the lists and fought against the others, Fourier and Saint-Simon; the combat between them or their disciples becoming so bitter and so blind that the truths common to them all at first seemed obscured and disfigured beyond recognition. Now, however, that evolution had slowly transformed Pierre, those common truths seemed to him as irrefutable, as clear as the sunlight itself. Amidst the chaos of conflicting assertions which was to be found in the gospels of those social messiahs, there were certain similar phrases and principles which recurred again and again, the defence of the poor, the idea of a new and just division of the riches of the world in accordance with individual labour and merit, and particularly the search for a new law of labour which would enable this fresh distribution to be made equitably. Since all the precursory men of genius agreed so closely upon those points, must they not be the very foundations of to-morrow's new religion, the necessary faith which this century must bequeath to the coming century, in order that the latter may make of it a human religion of peace, solidarity and love?

Then, all at once, there came a leap in Pierre's thoughts. He fancied himself at the Madeleine once more, listening to the address on the New Spirit delivered by Monseigneur Martha, who had predicted that Paris, now reconverted to Christianity, would, thanks to the Sacred Heart, become the ruler of the world. But no, but no! If Paris reigned, it was because it was able to exercise its intelligence freely. To set the cross and the mystic and repulsive symbolism of a bleeding heart above it was simply so much falsehood. Although they might rear edifices of pride and domination as if to crush Paris with their very weight, although they might try to stop science in the name of a dead ideal and in the hope of setting their clutches upon the coming century, these attempts would be of no avail. Science will end by sweeping away all remnants of their ancient sovereignty, their basilica will crumble beneath the breeze of Truth without any necessity of raising a finger against it. The trial has been made, the Gospel as a social code has fallen to pieces, and human wisdom can only retain account of its moral maxims. Ancient Catholicism is on all sides crumbling into dust, Catholic Rome is a mere field of ruins from which the nations turn aside, anxious as they are for a religion that shall not be a religion of death. In olden times the overburdened slave, glowing with a new hope and seeking to escape from his gaol, dreamt of a heaven where in return for his earthly misery he would be rewarded with eternal enjoyment. But now that science has destroyed that false idea of a heaven, and shown what dupery lies in reliance on the morrow of death, the slave, the workman, weary of dying for happiness' sake, demands that justice and happiness shall find place upon this earth. Therein lies the new hope—Justice, after eighteen hundred years of impotent Charity. Ah! in a thousand years from now, when Catholicism will be naught but a very ancient superstition of the past, how amazed men will be to think that their ancestors were able to endure that religion of torture and nihility! How astonished they will feel on finding that God was regarded as an executioner, that manhood was threatened, maimed and chastised, that nature was accounted an enemy, that life was looked upon as something accursed, and that death alone was pronounced sweet and liberating! For well-nigh two thousand years the onward march of mankind has been hampered by the odious idea of tearing all that is human away from man: his desires, his passions, his free intelligence, his will and right of action, his whole strength. And how glorious will be the awakening when such virginity as is now honoured by the Church is held in derision, when fruitfulness is again recognised as a virtue, amidst the hosanna of all the freed forces of nature—man's desires which will be honoured, his passions which will be utilised, his labour which will be exalted, whilst life is loved and ever and ever creates love afresh!

A new religion! a new religion! Pierre remembered the cry which had escaped him at Lourdes, and which he had repeated at Rome in presence of the collapse of old Catholicism. But he no longer displayed the same feverish eagerness as then—a puerile, sickly desire that a new Divinity should at once reveal himself, an ideal come into being, complete in all respects, with dogmas and form of worship. The Divine certainly seemed to be as necessary to man as were bread and water; he had ever fallen back upon it, hungering for the mysterious, seemingly having no other means of consolation than that of annihilating himself in the unknown. But who can say that science will not some day quench the thirst for what lies beyond us? If the domain of science embraces the acquired truths, it also embraces, and will ever do so, the truths that remain to be acquired. And in front of it will there not ever remain a margin for the thirst of knowledge, for the hypotheses which are but so much ideality? Besides, is not the yearning for the divine simply a desire to behold the Divinity? And if science should more and more content the yearning to know all and be able to do all, will not that yearning be quieted and end by mingling with the love of acquired truth? A religion grafted on science is the indicated, certain, inevitable finish of man's long march towards knowledge. He will come to it at last as to a natural haven, as to peace in the midst of certainty, after passing every form of ignorance and terror on his road. And is there not already some indication of such a religion? Has not the idea of the duality of God and the Universe been brushed aside, and is not the principle of unity, *monisme*, becoming more and more evident—unity leading to solidarity, and the sole law of life proceeding by evolution from the first point of the ether that condensed to create the world? But if precursors, scientists and philosophers—Darwin, Fourier and all the others—have sown the seed of to-morrow's religion by casting the good word to the passing breeze, how many centuries will doubtless be required to raise the crop! People always forget that before Catholicism grew up and reigned in the sunlight, it spent four centuries in germinating and sprouting from the soil. Well, then, grant some centuries to this religion of science of whose sprouting there are signs upon all sides, and by-and-by the admirable ideas of some Fourier will be seen expanding and forming a new gospel, with desire serving as the lever to raise the world, work accepted by one and all, honoured and regulated as the very mechanism of natural and social life, and the passions of man excited, contented and utilised for human happiness! The universal cry of Justice, which rises louder and louder, in a growing clamour from the once silent multitude, the people that have so long been duped and preyed upon, is but a cry for this happiness towards which human beings are tending, the happiness that embodies the complete satisfaction of man's needs, and the principle of life loved for its own sake, in the midst of peace and the expansion of every force and every joy. The time will come when this Kingdom of God will be set upon the earth; so why not close that other deceptive paradise, even if the weak-minded must momentarily suffer from the destruction of their illusions; for it is necessary to operate even with cruelty on the blind if they are to be extricated from their misery, from their long and frightful night of ignorance!

All at once a feeling of deep joy came over Pierre. A child's faint cry, the wakening cry of his son Jean had drawn him from his reverie. And he had suddenly remembered that he himself was now saved, freed from falsehood and fright, restored to good and healthy nature. How he quivered as he recalled that he had once fancied himself lost, blotted out of life, and that a prodigy of love had extricated him from his nothingness, still strong and sound, since that dear child of his was there, sturdy and smiling. Life had brought forth life; and truth had burst forth, as dazzling as the sun. He had made his third experiment with Paris, and this had been conclusive; it had been no wretched miscarriage with increase of darkness and grief, like his other experiments at Lourdes and Rome. In the first place, the law of labour had been revealed to him, and he had imposed upon himself a task, as humble a one as it was, that manual calling which he was learning so late in life, but which was, nevertheless, a form of labour, and one in which he would never fail, one too that would lend him the serenity which comes from the accomplishment of duty, for life itself was but labour: it was only by effort that the world existed. And then, moreover, he had loved; and salvation had come to him from woman and from his child. Ah! what a long and circuitous journey he had made to reach this finish at once so natural and so simple! How he had suffered, how much error and anger he had known before doing what all men ought to do! That eager, glowing love which had contended against his reason, which had bled at sight of the arrant absurdities of the miraculous grotto of Lourdes, which had bled again too in presence of the haughty decline of the Vatican, had at last found contentment now that he was husband and father, now that he had confidence in work and believed in the just laws of life. And thence had come the indisputable truth, the one solution—happiness in certainty.

Whilst Pierre was thus plunged in thought, Bache and Morin had already gone off with their customary handshakes and promises to come and chat again some evening. And as Jean was now crying more loudly, Marie took him in her arms and unhooked her dress-body to give him her breast.

"Oh! the darling, it's his time, you know, and he doesn't forget it!" she said. "Just look, Pierre, I believe he has got bigger since yesterday."

She laughed; and Pierre, likewise laughing, drew near to kiss the child. And afterwards he kissed his wife, mastered as he was by emotion at the sight of that pink, gluttonous little creature imbibing life from that lovely breast so full of milk.

"Why! he'll eat you," he gaily said to Marie. "How he's pulling!"

"Oh! he does bite me a little," she replied; "but I like that the better, it shows that he profits by it."

Then Mere-Grand, she who as a rule was so serious and silent, began to talk with a smile lighting up her face: "I weighed him this morning," said she, "he weighs nearly a quarter of a pound more than he did the last time. And if you had only seen how good he was, the darling! He will be a very intelligent and well-behaved little gentleman, such as I like. When he's five years old, I shall teach him his alphabet, and when he's fifteen, if he likes, I'll tell him how to be a man.... Don't you agree with me, Thomas? And you, Antoine, and you, too, Francois?"

Raising their heads, the three sons gaily nodded their approval, grateful as they felt for the lessons in heroism which she had given them, and apparently finding no reason why she might not live another twenty years in order to give similar lessons to Jean.

Pierre still remained in front of Marie, basking in all the rapture of love, when he felt Guillaume lay his hands upon his shoulders from behind. And on turning round he saw that his brother was also radiant, like one who felt well pleased at seeing them so happy. "Ah! brother," said Guillaume softly, "do you remember my telling you that you suffered solely from the battle between your mind and your heart, and that you would find quietude again when you loved what you could understand? It was necessary that our father and mother, whose painful quarrel had continued beyond the grave, should be reconciled in you. And now it's done, they sleep in peace within you, since you yourself are pacified."

These words filled Pierre with emotion. Joy beamed upon his face, which was now so open and energetic. He still had the towering brow, that impregnable fortress of reason, which he had derived from his father, and he still had the gentle chin and affectionate eyes and mouth which his mother had given him, but all was now blended together, instinct with happy harmony and serene strength. Those two experiments of his which had miscarried, were like crises of his maternal heredity, the tearful tenderness which had come to him from his mother, and which for lack of satisfaction had made him desperate; and his third experiment had only ended in happiness because he had contented his ardent thirst for love in accordance with sovereign reason, that paternal heredity which pleaded so loudly within him. Reason remained the queen. And if his sufferings had thus always come from the warfare which his reason had waged against his heart, it was because he was man personified, ever struggling between his intelligence and his passions. And how peaceful all seemed, now that he had reconciled and satisfied them both, now that he felt healthy, perfect and strong, like some lofty oak, which grows in all freedom, and whose branches spread far away over the forest.

"You have done good work in that respect," Guillaume affectionately continued, "for yourself and for all of us, and even for our dear parents whose shades, pacified and reconciled, now abide so peacefully in the little home of our childhood. I often think of our dear house at Neuilly, which old Sophie is taking care of for us; and although, out of egotism, a desire to set happiness around me, I wished to keep you here, your Jean must some day go and live there, so as to bring it fresh youth."

Pierre had taken hold of his brother's hands, and looking into his eyes he asked: "And you—are you happy?"

"Yes, very happy, happier than I have ever been; happy at loving you as I do, and happy at being loved by you as no one else will ever love me."

Their hearts mingled in ardent brotherly affection, the most perfect and heroic affection that can blend men together. And they embraced one another whilst, with her babe on her breast, Marie, so gay, healthful and loyal, looked at them and smiled, with big tears gathering in her eyes.

Thomas, however, having finished his motor's last toilet, had just set it in motion. It was a prodigy of lightness and strength, of no weight whatever in comparison with the power it displayed. And it worked with perfect smoothness, without noise or smell. The whole family was gathered round it in delight, when there came a timely visit, one from the learned and friendly Bertheroy, whom indeed Guillaume had asked to call, in order that he might see the motor working.

The great chemist at once expressed his admiration; and when he had examined the mechanism and understood how the explosive was employed as motive power—an idea which he had long recommended,—he tendered enthusiastic congratulations to Guillaume and Thomas. "You have created a little marvel," said he, "one which may have far-reaching effects both socially and humanly. Yes, yes, pending the invention of the electrical motor which we have not yet arrived at, here is an ideal one, a system of mechanical traction for all sorts of vehicles. Even aerial navigation may now become a possibility, and the problem of force at home is finally solved. And what a grand step! What sudden progress! Distance again diminished, all roads thrown open, and men able to fraternise! This is a great boon, a splendid gift, my good friends, that you are bestowing on the world."

Then he began to jest about the new explosive, whose prodigious power he had divined, and which he now found put to such a beneficent purpose. "And to think, Guillaume," he said, "that I fancied you acted with so much mysteriousness and hid the formula of your powder from me because you had an idea of blowing up Paris!"

At this Guillaume became grave and somewhat pale. And he confessed the truth. "Well, I did for a moment think of it."

However, Bertheroy went on laughing, as if he regarded this answer as mere repartee, though truth to tell he had felt a slight chill sweep through his hair. "Well, my friend," he said, "you have done far better in offering the world this marvel, which by the way must have been both a difficult and dangerous matter. So here is a powder which was intended to exterminate people, and which in lieu thereof will now increase their comfort and welfare. In the long run things always end well, as I'm quite tired of saying."

On beholding such lofty and tolerant good nature, Guillaume felt moved. Bertheroy's words were true. What had been intended for purposes of destruction served the cause of progress; the subjugated, domesticated volcano became labour, peace and civilisation. Guillaume had even relinquished all idea of his engine of battle and victory; he had found sufficient satisfaction in this last invention of his, which would relieve men of some measure of weariness, and help to reduce their labour to just so much effort as there must always be. In this he detected some little advance towards Justice; at all events it was all that he himself could contribute to the cause. And when on turning towards the window he caught sight of the basilica of the Sacred Heart, he could not explain what insanity had at one moment cone over him, and set him dreaming of idiotic and useless destruction. Some miasmal gust must have swept by, something born of want that scattered germs of anger and vengeance. But how blind it was to think that destruction and murder could ever bear good fruit, ever sow the soil with plenty and happiness! Violence cannot last, and all it does is to rouse man's feeling of solidarity even among those on whose behalf one kills. The people, the great multitude, rebel against the isolated individual who seeks to wreak justice. No one man can take upon himself the part of the volcano; this is the whole terrestrial crust, the whole multitude which internal fire impels to rise and throw up either an Alpine chain or a better and freer society. And whatever heroism there may be in their madness, however great and contagious may be their thirst for martyrdom, murderers are never anything but murderers, whose deeds simply sow the seeds of horror. And if on the one hand Victor Mathis had avenged Salvat, he had also slain him, so universal had been the cry of reprobation roused by the second crime, which was yet more monstrous and more useless than the first.

Guillaume, laughing in his turn, replied to Bertheroy in words which showed how completely he was cured: "You are right," he said, "all ends well since all contributes to truth and justice. Unfortunately, thousands of years are sometimes needed for any progress to be accomplished.... However, for my part, I am simply going to put my new explosive on the market, so that those who secure the necessary authorisation may manufacture it and grow rich. Henceforth it belongs to one and all.... And I've renounced all idea of revolutionising the world."

But Bertheroy protested. This great official scientist, this member of the Institute laden with offices and honours, pointed to the little motor, and replied with all the vigour of his seventy years: "But that is revolution, the true, the only revolution. It is with things like that and not with stupid bombs that one revolutionises the world! It is not by destroying, but by creating, that you have just done the work of a revolutionist. And how many times already have I not told you that science alone is the world's revolutionary force, the only force which, far above all paltry political incidents, the vain agitation of despots, priests, sectarians and ambitious people of all kinds, works for the benefit of those who will come after us, and prepares the triumph of truth, justice and peace.... Ah, my dear child, if you wish to overturn the world by striving to set a little more happiness in it, you have only to remain in your laboratory here, for human happiness can spring only from the furnace of the scientist."

He spoke perhaps in a somewhat jesting way, but one could feel that he was convinced of it all, that he held everything excepting science in utter contempt. He had not even shown any surprise when Pierre had cast his cassock aside; and on finding him there with his wife and child he had not scrupled to show him as much affection as in the past.

Meantime, however, the motor was travelling hither and thither, making no more noise than a bluebottle buzzing in the sunshine. The whole happy family was gathered about it, still laughing with delight at such a victorious achievement. And all at once little Jean, Monsieur Jean, having finished sucking, turned round, displaying his milk-smeared lips, and perceived the machine, the pretty plaything which walked about by itself. At sight of it, his eyes sparkled, dimples appeared on his plump cheeks, and, stretching out his quivering chubby hands, he raised a crow of delight.

Marie, who was quietly fastening her dress, smiled at his glee and brought him nearer, in order that he might have a better view of the toy. "Ah! my darling, it's pretty, isn't it? It moves and it turns, and it's strong; it's quite alive, you see."

The others, standing around, were much amused by the amazed, enraptured expression of the child, who would have liked to touch the machine, perhaps in the hope of understanding it.

"Yes," resumed Bertheroy, "it's alive and it's powerful like the sun, like that great sun shining yonder over Paris, and ripening men and things. And Paris too is a motor, a boiler in which the future is boiling, while we scientists keep the eternal flame burning underneath. Guillaume, my good fellow, you are one of the stokers, one of the artisans of the future, with that little marvel of yours, which will still further extend the influence of our great Paris over the whole world."

These words impressed Pierre, and he again thought of a gigantic vat stretching yonder from one horizon to the other, a vat in which the coming century would emerge from an extraordinary mixture of the excellent and the vile. But now, over and above all passions, ambitions, stains and waste, he was conscious of the colossal expenditure of labour which marked the life of Paris, of the heroic manual efforts in work-shops and factories, and the splendid striving of the young men of intellect whom he knew to be hard at work, studying in silence, relinquishing none of the conquests of their elders, but glowing with desire to enlarge their domain. And in all this Paris was exalted, together with the future that was being prepared within it, and which would wing its flight over the world bright like the dawn of day. If Rome, now so near its death, had ruled the ancient world, it was Paris that reigned with sovereign sway over the modern era, and had for the time become the great centre of the nations as they were carried on from civilisation to civilisation, in a sunward course from east to west. Paris was the world's brain. Its past so full of grandeur had prepared it for the part of initiator, civiliser and liberator. Only yesterday it had cast the cry of Liberty among the nations, and to-morrow it would bring them the religion of Science, the new faith awaited by the democracies. And Paris was also gaiety, kindness and gentleness, passion for knowledge and generosity without limit. Among the workmen of its faubourgs and the peasants of its country-sides there were endless reserves of men on whom the future might freely draw. And the century ended with Paris, and the new century would begin and spread with it. All the clamour of its prodigious labour, all the light that came from it as from a beacon overlooking the earth, all the thunder and tempest and triumphant brightness that sprang from its entrails, were pregnant with that final splendour, of which human happiness would be compounded.

Marie raised a light cry of admiration as she pointed towards the city. "Look! just look!" she exclaimed; "Paris is all golden, covered with a harvest of gold!"

They all re-echoed her admiration, for the effect was really one of extraordinary magnificence. The declining sun was once more veiling the immensity of Paris with golden dust. But this was no longer the city of the sower, a chaos of roofs and edifices suggesting brown land turned up by some huge plough, whilst the sun-rays streamed over it like golden seed, falling upon every side. Nor was it the city whose divisions had one day seemed so plain to Pierre: eastward, the districts of toil, misty with the grey smoke of factories; southward, the districts of study, serene and quiet; westward, the districts of wealth, bright and open; and in the centre the districts of trade, with dark and busy streets. It now seemed as if one and the same crop had sprung up on every side, imparting harmony to everything, and making the entire expanse one sole, boundless field, rich with the same fruitfulness. There was corn, corn everywhere, an infinity of corn, whose golden wave rolled from one end of the horizon to the other. Yes, the declining sun steeped all Paris in equal splendour, and it was truly the crop, the harvest, after the sowing!

"Look! just look," repeated Marie, "there is not a nook without its sheaf; the humblest roofs are fruitful, and every blade is full-eared wherever one may look. It is as if there were now but one and the same soil, reconciled and fraternal. Ah! Jean, my little Jean, look! see how beautiful it is!"

Pierre, who was quivering, had drawn close beside her. And Mere-Grand and Bertheroy smiled upon that promise of a future which they would not see, whilst beside Guillaume, whom the sight filled with emotion, were his three big sons, the three young giants, looking quite grave, they who ever laboured and were ever hopeful. Then Marie, with a fine gesture of enthusiasm, stretched out her arms and raised her child aloft, as if offering it in gift to the huge city.

"See, Jean! see, little one," she cried, "it's you who'll reap it all, who'll store the whole crop in the barn!"

And Paris flared—Paris, which the divine sun had sown with light, and where in glory waved the great future harvest of Truth and of Justice.

The Human Comedy, La Comédie humaine, Volume 1
Honore deBalzac
Benediction Classics, 2013
ISBN: 978-1-78139-385-7

Honoré de Balzac (1799 – 1850) was a French novelist and playwright. His great work was a series of short stories and novels collectively entitled La Comédie humaine, which gives a picture of swathes of French society in the years after the 1815 fall of Napoleon Bonaparte. Balzac had plenty of experiences to draw upon, he had been an apprentice in a law office, a publisher, printer, businessman, critic, and politician and failed at all of these pursuits. The novels reveal his difficulties with all these careers.
Many of these books have been adapted for the screen and to this day they are a source of inspiration for writers, filmmakers and critics.
This volume includes the first twenty-one works in La Comédie humaine, in their recommended reading order:

1. Father Goriot
2. The Chouans
3. An Episode Under The Terror
4. Vendetta
5. The Recruit
6. The Red Inn
7. Thought And Act
8. A Double Retribution
9. Juana
10. A Passion In The Desert
11. The Exiles
12. Almae Sorori
13. Christ In Flanders
14. Maitre Cornelius
15. A Second Home
16. An Historical Mystery
17. At The Sign Of The Cat And Racket
18. The Executioner
19. Domestic Peace
20. Louis Lambert
21. The Alkahest

Five Novels by Thomas Hardy - Far From The Madding Crowd, The Return of the Native, The Mayor of Casterbridge, Tess of the d'Urbervilles, Jude the Obscure (complete and unabridged)
Thomas Hardy
Benediction Classics, 2013
1114 pages
ISBN: 978-1-78139-356-7

Available from www.amazon.com, www.amazon.co.uk

Thomas Hardy, (1840 - 1928) was an English novelist and poet. He was highly critical of Victorian society and focussed mainly on the declining rural communities.

E M Forster - Collected Works, including A Room with a View, Howards End, The Longest Journey, Where Angels Fear to Tread and The Celestial Omnibus and other Stories
E M Forster
Oxford City Press, 2013
808 pages
ISBN: 978-1-78139-373-4

Available from www.amazon.com, www.amazon.co.uk

Edward Morgan Forster (1879 - 1970) is best known for his beautiful novels - ironic with delicious plots, highlighting the hypocrisy and discrimination in early 20th-century British society.

Wilkie Collins Collection (complete and unabridged):The Woman in White, The Moonstone, No Name, Armadale
Wilkie Collins
Benediction Classics, 2012
1136 pages
ISBN: 978-1-78139-328-4

Available from www.amazon.com, www.amazon.co.uk

Wilkie Collins (1824-1889) is best known as the innovator of the detective novel. He was a prolific writer, with 30 novels, more than 60 short stories, 14 plays, and more than 100 non-fiction pieces to his name. He was a close friend of Charles Dickens and one of the best known and loved Victorian Fiction writers.

Also from Benediction Books ...

Wandering Between Two Worlds: Essays on Faith and Art
Anita Mathias
Benediction Books, 2007
152 pages
ISBN: 0955373700

Available from www.amazon.com, www.amazon.co.uk

In these wide-ranging lyrical essays, Anita Mathias writes, in lush, lovely prose, of her naughty Catholic childhood in Jamshedpur, India; her large, eccentric family in Mangalore, a sea-coast town converted by the Portuguese in the sixteenth century; her rebellion and atheism as a teenager in her Himalayan boarding school, run by German missionary nuns, St. Mary's Convent, Nainital; and her abrupt religious conversion after which she entered Mother Teresa's convent in Calcutta as a novice. Later rich, elegant essays explore the dualities of her life as a writer, mother, and Christian in the United States-- Domesticity and Art, Writing and Prayer, and the experience of being "an alien and stranger" as an immigrant in America, sensing the need for roots.

About the Author

Anita Mathias is the author of *Wandering Between Two Worlds: Essays on Faith and Art*. She has a B.A. and M.A. in English from Somerville College, Oxford University, and an M.A. in Creative Writing from the Ohio State University, USA. Anita won a National Endowment of the Arts fellowship in Creative Nonfiction in 1997. She lives in Oxford, England with her husband, Roy, and her daughters, Zoe and Irene.

Anita's website:
http://www.anitamathias.com, and
Anita's blog Dreaming Beneath the Spires:
http://dreamingbeneaththespires.blogspot.com

The Church That Had Too Much
Anita Mathias
Benediction Books, 2010
52 pages
ISBN: 9781849026567

Available from www.amazon.com, www.amazon.co.uk

The Church That Had Too Much was very well-intentioned. She wanted to love God, she wanted to love people, but she was both hampered by her muchness and the abundance of her possessions, and beset by ambition, power struggles and snobbery. Read about the surprising way The Church That Had Too Much began to resolve her problems in this deceptively simple and enchanting fable.

About the Author

Anita Mathias is the author of *Wandering Between Two Worlds: Essays on Faith and Art*. She has a B.A. and M.A. in English from Somerville College, Oxford University, and an M.A. in Creative Writing from the Ohio State University, USA. Anita won a National Endowment of the Arts fellowship in Creative Non-fiction in 1997. She lives in Oxford, England with her husband, Roy, and her daughters, Zoe and Irene.

Anita's website:
http://www.anitamathias.com, and
Anita's blog Dreaming Beneath the Spires:
http://dreamingbeneaththespires.blogspot.com

www.ingramcontent.com/pod-product-compliance
Lightning Source LLC
Chambersburg PA
CBHW081130300726
48982CB00005B/910

* 9 7 8 1 7 8 1 3 9 4 3 2 8 *